THE BEET QUEEN

"THE DIALOGUE IS BRILLIANT FROM START TO FINISH. AND MARY, KARL, CELESTINE, SITA AND DOT ARE ALL ORIGINAL AND POWERFUL CHARACTERS WHO, LIKE THEIR RELATIVES IN *LOVE MEDICINE*, LEFT ME EXHILARATED, SOMEWHAT DRAINED, AND VERY GRATEFUL TO THIS IMMENSELY GIFTED NOVELIST FOR *THE BEET QUEEN*."
—*Chicago Sun-Times*

"SHE IS A LUMINOUS WRITER AND HAS PRODUCED A NOVEL RICH IN MOVEMENT, BEAUTY, EVENT. HER PROSE SPINS AND SPARKLES, AND DANCES RIGHT ON THE HEART WHEN IT NEEDS TO."—*Los Angeles Times*

"A WONDERFUL BOOK—ORIGINAL, RICH AND VERY MOVING."—*Vogue*

"WHAT ERDRICH BRINGS TO *THE BEET QUEEN*, AS SHE DID TO *LOVE MEDICINE*, IS A PROSE STYLE OF RINGING CLARITY AND LYRICISM."—*The New Republic*

"*THE BEET QUEEN* IS A SLOWLY GATHERING STORM SHAKING LOOSE EVERY BELIEF YOU HOLD ABOUT THE LIMITS OF YOUR ABILITY TO LOVE."—*The Milwaukee Journal*

"*THE BEET QUEEN* CULMINATES IN AN ENDING OF INCREDIBLE SWEEP, SCOPE AND COMIC POWER... AN ORIGINAL BOOK, A VERY AMERICAN BOOK."
—*Kansas City Star*

"A SEARING NOVEL."

"A STUNNING AND A[...]
—*The Atlanta Journal-Cons[...]*

ALSO BY LOUISE ERDRICH

Jacklight *(poems)*
Love Medicine

THE BEET QUEEN

A NOVEL BY

LOUISE ERDRICH

BANTAM BOOKS
TORONTO · NEW YORK · LONDON · SYDNEY · AUCKLAND

*This low-priced Bantam Book
has been completely reset in a type face
designed for easy reading, and was printed
from new plates. It contains the complete
text of the original hard-cover edition.*
NOT ONE WORD HAS BEEN OMITTED.

THE BEET QUEEN

*A Bantam Book / published by arrangement with
Henry Holt and Company, Inc.*

PRINTING HISTORY
Henry Holt edition first published September 1986
Parts of this book appeared, in slightly altered form, in the following publications: "The
Branch" and "Chapter One: 1932," The Paris Review, as "The Beet Queen." "Chapter
Two: 1932, Sita Kozka, Mary Adare, Celestine James," New Native America, a book by
University of New Mexico Press, as "The Manifestation at Argus." "Chapter Two: 1932, Sita
Kozka," Ms. magazine, August 1986. "Chapter Three: 1932, Karl Adare," The American
Voice, Fall 1986. Part of "Chapter Seven: 1953," Chicago Magazine as "Knives."
"Chapter Six: 1952," Antaeus, as "The Air Seeder." "Chapter Seven: 1953, Celestine
James," as "Chez Sita," Minneapolis-St. Paul Magazine, August 1986. "Chapter Eight:
1953," Formations, as "The Little Book." Parts of Chapters Nine and Fifteen, The
Georgia Review, as "Mister Argus." Part of Chapter Ten, New England Review, Fall
1986. "Chapter Eleven: 1964," The Atlantic Monthly, as "Destiny." "Chapter Thirteen:
1972, Celestine James," The Kenyon Review, as "Pounding the Dog."

The author would like to thank the National Endowment for the Arts and the
Guggenheim Foundation for their support during the years this book was written.

Bantam edition / October 1987

PRINTED IN THE UNITED STATES OF AMERICA

O   0 9 8 7 6 5 4 3 2 1

To Michael

*Complice in every
word, essential
as air.*

ACKNOWLEDGMENTS

Grateful acknowledgments are made, first, to my father Ralph Erdrich, and also to my grandmother Mary Erdrich Korll, to our editor and publisher Richard Seaver, to our Aunt Virginia Burkhardt for her generous enthusiasm and advice, to Charles Rembar, and to Barbara Bonner, friend and passionate reader.

CONTENTS

The Branch

Long before they planted beets in Argus and built the highways, there was a railroad. Along the track, which crossed the Dakota–Minnesota border and stretched on to Minneapolis, everything that made the town arrived. All that diminished the town departed by that route, too. On a cold spring morning in 1932 the train brought both an addition and a subtraction. They came by freight. By the time they reached Argus their lips were violet and their feet were so numb that, when they jumped out of the boxcar, they stumbled and scraped their palms and knees through the cinders.

The boy was a tall fourteen, hunched with his sudden growth and very pale. His mouth was sweetly curved, his skin fine and girlish. His sister was only eleven years old, but already she was so short and ordinary that it was obvious she would be this way all her life. Her name was square and practical as the rest of her. Mary. She brushed her coat off and stood in the watery wind. Between the buildings there was only more bare horizon for her to see, and from time to time men crossing it. Wheat was the big crop then, and the topsoil was so newly tilled that it hadn't all blown off yet, the way it had in Kansas. In fact, times were generally much better in eastern North Dakota than in most places, which is why Karl and Mary Adare had come there on the train. Their mother's sister, Fritzie, lived on the eastern edge of town. She ran a butcher shop with her husband.

The two Adares put their hands up their sleeves and started walking. Once they began to move they felt warmer, although they'd been traveling all night and the chill had reached deep. They walked east, down the dirt and planking of the broad main street, reading the signs on each false-front clapboard store they

1

passed, even reading the gilt letters in the window of the brick bank. None of these places was a butcher shop. Abruptly, the stores stopped, and a string of houses, weathered gray or peeling gray paint, with dogs tied to their porch railings, began.

Small trees were planted in the yards of a few of these houses, and one tree, weak, a scratch of light against the gray of everything else, tossed in a film of blossoms. Mary trudged solidly forward, hardly glancing at it, but Karl stopped. The tree drew him with its delicate perfume. His cheeks went pink, he stretched his arms out like a sleepwalker, and in one long transfixed motion he floated to the tree and buried his face in the white petals.

Turning to look for Karl, Mary was frightened by how far back he had fallen and how still he was, his face pressed in the flowers. She shouted, but he did not seem to hear her and only stood, strange and stock-still among the branches. He did not move even when the dog in the yard lunged against its rope and bawled. He did not notice when the door to the house opened and a woman scrambled out. She shouted at Karl too, but he paid her no mind and so she untied her dog. Large and anxious, it flew forward in great bounds. And then, either to protect himself or to seize the blooms, Karl reached out and tore a branch from the tree.

It was such a large branch, from such a small tree, that blight would attack the scar where it was pulled off. The leaves would fall away later on that summer and the sap would sink into the roots. The next spring, when Mary passed it on some errand, she saw that it bore no blossoms and remembered how, when the dog jumped for Karl, he struck out with the branch and the petals dropped around the dog's fierce outstretched body in a sudden snow. Then he yelled, "Run!" and Mary ran east, toward Aunt Fritzie. But Karl ran back to the boxcar and the train.

PART ONE

MARY ADARE

SO THAT'S HOW I came to Argus. I was the girl in the stiff coat.

After I ran blind and came to a halt, shocked not to find Karl behind me, I looked up to watch for him and heard the train whistle long and shrill. That was when I realized Karl had probably jumped back on the same boxcar and was now hunched in straw, watching out the opened door. The only difference would be the fragrant stick blooming in his hand. I saw the train pulled like a string of black beads over the horizon, as I have seen it so many times since. When it was out of sight, I stared down at my feet. I was afraid. It was not that with Karl gone I had no one to protect me, but just the opposite. With no one to protect and look out for, I was weak. Karl was taller than me but spindly, older of course, but fearful. He suffered from fevers that kept him in a stuporous dream state and was sensitive to loud sounds, harsh lights. My mother called him delicate, but I was the opposite. I was the one who begged spotted apples from the grocery store and stole whey from the back stoop of the creamery in Minneapolis, where we were living the winter after my father died.

This story starts then, because before that and without the year 1929, our family would probably have gone on living comfortably in a lonely and isolated white house on the edge of Prairie Lake.

We rarely saw anyone else. There were just us three: Karl and me and our mother, Adelaide. There was something different about us even then. Our only visitor was Mr. Ober, a tall man

5

with a carefully trimmed black beard. He owned a whole county of Minnesota wheatland. Two or three times a week he appeared, in the late evenings, and parked his automobile in the barn.

Karl hated Mr. Ober's visits, but I looked forward to each one because my mother always brightened. It was like a change of weather in our house. I remember that on the last night Mr. Ober came to visit, she put on the blue silk dress and the necklace of sparkling stones that we knew had come from him. She wound and pinned her dark red braid into a crown, and then brushed my hair one hundred light, even strokes. I closed my eyes and listened to the numbers. "You didn't get this from me," she said at last, letting the hair fall limp and black about my shoulders.

When Mr. Ober arrived, we sat with him in the parlor. Karl posed on the horsehair sofa and pretended a fascination with the red diamonds woven into the carpet. As usual, I was the one whom Mr. Ober singled out for petting. He put me on his lap, called me Schatze. "For your hair, Little Miss," he said, pulling a green satin ribbon from his vest pocket. His voice was deep pitched, but I liked the sound of it in counterpoint to or covering my mother's. Later, after Karl and I were sent to bed, I stayed awake and listened to the grown-up's voices rise and tangle, then fall, first in the downstairs parlor and then, muffled, in the dining room. I heard both of them walk up the stairs. The big door closed at the end of the hall. I kept my eyes open. There was darkness, the creaks and thumps that a house makes at night, wind in the branches, tapping. By morning he was gone.

The next day Karl sulked until our mother hugged and kissed him back into good humor. I was sad, too, but with me she was short of temper.

Karl always read the comics in the Sunday paper first, and so he was the one who found the picture of Mr. Ober and his wife on the front page. There had been a grain-loading accident, and

6

Mr. Ober had smothered. There was a question, too, of suicide. He'd borrowed heavily against his land. Mother and I were cleaning out drawers in the kitchen, cutting white paper out to fit them, when Karl brought the piece in to show us. I remember that Adelaide's hair was plaited in two red crooked braids and that she fell full length across the floor when she read the news. Karl and I huddled close to her, and when she opened her eyes I helped her into a chair.

She threw her head back and forth, would not speak, shuddered like a broken doll. Then she looked at Karl.

"You're glad!" she cried.

Karl turned his head away, sullen.

"He was your father," she blurted.

So it was out.

My mother knew she'd lose everything now. His wife was smiling in the photograph. Our big white house was in Mr. Ober's name, along with everything else except an automobile, which Adelaide sold the next morning. On the day of the funeral, we took the noon train to the Cities with only what we could carry in suitcases. My mother thought that there, with her figure and good looks, she could find work in a fashionable store.

But she didn't know that she was pregnant. She didn't know how much things really cost, or the hard facts of Depression. After six months the money ran out. We were desperate.

I didn't know how badly off we were until my mother stole a dozen heavy silver spoons from our landlady, who was kind, or at least harbored no grudge against us, and whom my mother counted as a friend. Adelaide gave no explanation for the spoons when I discovered them in her pocket. Days later they were gone and Karl and I owned thick overcoats. Also, our shelf was loaded with green bananas. For several weeks we drank quarts of buttermilk and ate buttered toast with thick jam. It was not long after that, I believe, that the baby was ready to be born.

One afternoon my mother sent us downstairs to the landlady.

This woman was stout and so dull that I've forgotten her name, although I recall vivid details of all else that happened at that time. It was a cold late-winter afternoon. We stared into the glass-faced cabinet where the silver stirrup cups and painted plates were locked after the theft. The outlines of our faces stared back at us like ghosts. From time to time Karl and I heard someone cry out. Once something heavy hit the floor directly above our heads. Both of us looked up at the ceiling and threw out our arms, as if to catch it. I don't know what went through Karl's mind, but I thought it was the baby, born heavy as lead, dropping straight through the clouds and my mother's body. I had a confused idea about the process of birth. At any rate, no explanation I could dream up accounted for the long scream that tore through the air, turned Karl's face white, and caused him to slump forward in the chair.

I had given up on reviving Karl each time he fainted. By now I trusted that he'd come to by himself, and he always did, looking soft and dazed and somehow refreshed. The most I ever did was hold his head until his eyes blinked open.

"It's born," he said when he came around.

As if I knew already that our disaster had been accomplished in that cry, I would not budge. Karl argued and made a case for at least going up the stairs, if not through the actual door, but I sat firm until the landlady came down and told us, first, that we now had a baby brother, and second, that she had found one of her grandmother's silver spoons under the mattress and that she wasn't going to ask how it got there, but we had four weeks to move out.

That night I fell asleep sitting in a chair beside Mama's bed, in lamplight, holding the baby in a light wool blanket. Karl was curled in a spidery ball at Mama's feet, and she was sleeping hard, her hair spread wild and bright across the pillows. Her face was white, sunken, but after she spoke I had no pity.

8

"I should let it die," she mumbled. Her lips were pale, frozen in a dream. I would have shaken her awake, but the baby was curved hard against me.

"I could bury it out back in the lot," she whispered, "that weedy place."

"Mama, wake up," I said, but she kept speaking.

"I won't have any milk. I'm too thin."

I looked down at the baby. His face was round, bruised blue, and his eyelids were swollen almost shut. He looked frail, but when he stirred I put my little finger in his mouth, as I had seen women do to quiet their babies, and his suck was eager.

"He's hungry," I told her.

But Adelaide rolled over and turned her face to the wall.

Milk came flooding into Adelaide's breasts, more than the baby could drink at first. She had to feed him. Milk leaked out in dark patches on her light-green plaid shirtwaists. She moved despairingly, burdened by the ache. She did not completely ignore the baby, although she refused to name him. She cut her petticoats up for diapers, sewed a layette from her nightgown, but often left him to howl. Sometimes he cried such a long time that the landlady came puffing upstairs to see what was wrong. She was troubled to see us so desperate and brought up food left by the paying boarders. Still, she did not change her decision. When the month was up, we still had to go.

The spring clouds were high and the air was warm on the day we went out looking for a new place. All of the ordinary clothes Mama owned had been cut up for the baby, so she had nothing but her fine things, lace and silk, good cashmere. She wore a black coat, a black dress trimmed in cream lace, and delicate string gloves. Her hair was in a strict and shining knot. We walked down the brick sidewalks looking for signs in windows, for rooming houses of the cheapest kind, barracks, or hotels. We found nothing and finally sat down to rest on a bench bolted to the side of a store. In those times, the streets of towns were much kindlier. No one minded the destitute gathering strength, taking a load off, discussing their downfall in the world.

"We could go back to Fritzie," Mama said. "She's my sister. She'd have to take us in."

I could tell from her voice that it was the last thing she wanted to do.

"You could sell your jewelry," I told her.

Mama gave me a warning look and put her hand to the brooch at her throat. She was attached to the things that Mr. Ober had given her over the years. When we begged, she showed them off: the complicated garnet necklace, the onyx mourning brooch and drop pearl earrings, the Spanish comb, and the ring with the good yellow diamond. I supposed that she wouldn't sell them even to save us. Our hardship had beaten her and she was weak, but in her weakness she was also stubborn. We sat on the store's bench for perhaps half an hour, then Karl noticed music in the air.

"Mama," he begged, "it's a fair!"

As always with Karl, she began by saying no, but that was just a formality and both of them knew it. In no time, he had wheedled and charmed her into going.

The Orphans' Picnic, a bazaar held to benefit the homeless children of Saint Jerome's, was taking place at the city fairground just a few streets away. We saw the banner blazing cheerful red, stretched across the entrance, bearing bright yellow handmade letters. Plank booths were set up in the long brown grass leftover from winter. Nuns swished between the scapular and holy-medal counters or stood poised behind racks of rosaries, shoe boxes full of holy cards, tiny carved statues of saints, and common toys. We swept into the excitement, looked over the grab bags, games of chance, displays of candy and religious wares. At a booth that

10

sold jingling hardware, Mama stopped and pulled a dollar bill from her purse.

"I'll take that," she said to the vendor, pointing. He lifted a pearl-handled jackknife from his case and gave it to Karl. Then she pointed at a bead necklace, silver and gold.

"I don't want it," I said.

Her face reddened, but after a slight hesitation she bought the necklace anyway. Then she had Karl fasten it around her throat. She put the baby in my arms.

"Here, Miss Damp Blanket," she said.

Karl laughed and took her hand. Wandering from booth to booth, we finally came to the grandstand, and at once Karl began to pull her toward the seats. I had to stumble along behind them. Bills littered the ground. Posters were pasted up the sides of trees and the splintery walls. Mama picked up one of the smaller papers.

THE GREAT OMAR, it said, AERONAUGHT EXTRAORDINAIRE. APPEARING AT NOON. Below the words there was a picture of a man, sleek, moustachioed, his orange scarf whipping in a breeze.

"Please!" Karl said.

And so we joined the gaping crowd.

The plane dipped, rolled, buzzed, glided above us like some kind of insect. I did not crane my neck or gasp, thrilled, like the rest of them. I looked down at the baby and watched his face. He was just emerging from the newborn's endless sleep, and from time to time now he stared at me in deep concentration. I stared back. In his face I found a different arrangement of myself—bolder, quick as light, ill-tempered. He frowned at me, unaware that he was helpless, troubled only at the loud drone of the biplane as it landed and taxied toward the crowd.

Thinking back now, I can't believe that I had no premonition. I hardly glanced when The Great Omar jumped from the plane, and I did not applaud his sweeping bows and pronouncements. I hardly listened when he offered rides to those who dared. I

11

believe he charged a dollar or two for the privilege. I did not notice. I was not prepared for what came next.

"Here!" my mother called, holding her purse up in the sun.

Without a backward look, without a word, with no warning and no hesitation, she elbowed through the people collected at the base of the grandstand and stepped into the cleared space around the pilot. I looked at The Great Omar for the first time. The impression he gave was dashing, like his posters. The orange scarf was knotted at his neck and certainly he had some sort of moustache. I believe he wore a grease-stained white sweater. He was slender and dark, much smaller in relation to his plane than the poster showed, and older. After he helped my mother into the passenger's cockpit and jumped in behind the controls, he pulled a pair of green goggles down over his face. And then there was a startling, endless moment, as they prepared for the takeoff. The aeronaught exchanged signals with two men who had helped him turn the plane.

"Switch on! Switch off! Contact!"

"Clear prop!" Omar shouted, and the men leaped away.

The propeller made a wind. The plane lurched forward, lifted over the low trees, gained height. The Great Omar circled the field in a low swoop, and I saw my mother's long red crinkly hair spring from its tight knot and float free in an arc that seemed to reach out and tangle around his shoulders.

Karl stared in stricken fascination at the sky, and said nothing as The Great Omar began his stunts and droning passes. I could not watch. I studied the face of my little brother and held myself tense, waiting for the plane to smash.

The crowd thinned. People drifted away. The sounds of the engine were harder to hear. By the time I dared look into the sky, The Great Omar was flying steadily away from the fairgrounds with my mother. Soon the plane was only a white dot, then it blended into the pale sky and vanished.

12

I shook Karl's arm, but he pulled away from me and vaulted to the edge of the grandstand. "Take me!" he screamed, leaning over the rail. He stared at the sky, poised as if he'd throw himself into it.

Satisfaction. It surprised me, but that was the first thing I felt after Adelaide flew off. For once she had played no favorites between Karl and me, but left us both. Karl dropped his head in his hands and began to sob into his thick wool sleeves. I looked away.

Below the grandstand, the crowd moved in patternless waves. Over us the clouds spread into a thin sheet that covered the sky like muslin. We watched the dusk collect in the corners of the field. Nuns began to pack away their rosaries and prayer books. Colored lights went on in the little carnival booths. Karl slapped his arms, stamped his feet, blew on his fingers, but I wasn't cold. The baby kept me warm.

The baby woke, very hungry, and I was helpless to comfort him. He sucked so hard that my finger was white and puckered, and then he screamed. People gathered. Women reached out their arms, but I held my brother tighter. I did not trust them. I did not trust the man who sat down beside me, either, and spoke softly. He was a young man with a hard-boned, sad, unshaven face. What I remember most about him was the sadness. He wanted to take the baby back to his wife so she could feed him. She had a newborn of her own, he said, and enough milk for two.

I wouldn't answer.

"When is your mother coming back?" the young man asked.

He waited. Karl sat mute staring into the dark sky. All around, the large interfering people told me what to do.

"Give him the baby, dear."

"Don't be stubborn."

"Let him take the baby home."

13

"No," I said to every order and suggestion. I even kicked hard when a bold woman tried to take my brother from my arms. One by one they grew discouraged and went off. Only the young man remained.

It was the baby himself who finally convinced me. He did not let up screaming. The longer he cried, the longer the sad man sat beside me, the weaker my resistance was, until I could barely hold my own tears in.

"I'm coming with you then," I told the young man. "I'll bring the baby back here when he's fed."

"No," cried Karl, coming out of his stupor suddenly. "You can't leave me alone!"

He grabbed my arm so fervently that the baby slipped, and then the young man caught me, as if to help, but instead he scooped the baby to himself.

"I'll take good care of him," he said, and turned away.

I tried to wrench from Karl's grip, but like my mother he was more stubborn when he was frightened, and I could not break free. The man walked into the shadows. I heard the baby's wail fade. I finally sat down beside Karl and let the cold sink into me.

One hour passed. Another hour. When the colored lights went out and the moon came up, blurred behind the sheets of clouds, I knew for certain the young man lied. He wasn't coming back. And yet, because he looked too sad to do any harm to anyone, I was more afraid for Karl and myself. We were the ones who were thoroughly lost. I stood up. Karl stood with me. Without a word we walked down the empty streets to the rooming house. We had no key, but Karl displayed one unexpected talent. He took the thin-bladed knife Adelaide had given him, and picked the lock.

The cold room was filled with the faint perfume of the dried flowers that our mother scattered in her trunk, the rich scent of the clove-studded orange she hung in the closet, and the lavender

14

oil she rubbed into her skin at night. The sweetness of her breath seemed to linger, the rustle of her silk underskirt, the quick sound of her heels. Our longing buried us. We sank down on her bed and cried, wrapped in her quilt, clutching each other. When that was done, however, I acquired a brain of ice.

I washed my face in the basin, then I woke Karl and told him we were going to Aunt Fritzie's. He nodded without hope. We ate all there was to eat in the room, two cold pancakes, and packed a small cardboard suitcase. Karl carried that. I carried the quilt. The last thing I did was reach far back into my mother's drawer and pull out her small round keepsake box. It was covered in blue velvet and tightly locked.

"We'll have to sell these things," I told Karl. He hesitated but then, with a hard look, he took the box.

We slipped out before sunrise and walked to the train station. In the weedy yards there were men who knew each boxcar's destination. We found the car we wanted and climbed in. We spread the quilt and rolled up together, curled tight, with our heads on the suitcase and Mama's blue velvet box between us in Karl's breast pocket. I clung to the thought of the treasures inside of it, but I had no way of knowing that the comforting rattle I heard once the train started moving that afternoon was not the rich clatter of heirlooms that could save us—the garnet necklace and the good yellow diamond—but pins, buttons, and one silent ticket of retrieval from a Minneapolis pawnshop.

We spent all night on that train while it switched and braked and rumbled toward Argus. We did not dare jump off for a drink of water or to scavenge food. The one time we did try this the train started up so quickly that we were hardly able to catch the side rungs again. We lost our suitcase and the quilt because we took the wrong car, farther back, and for the rest of that night we did not sleep at all because of the cold. Karl was too miserable

15

even to argue with me when I told him it was my turn to hold Mama's box. I put it in the bodice of my jumper. It did not keep me warm, but even so, when I shut my eyes, the sparkle of the diamond, the patterns of garnets that whirled in the dark air, gave me something. My mind hardened, faceted and gleaming like a magic stone, and I saw my mother clearly.

She was still in the plane, flying close to the pulsing stars, when suddenly Omar noticed that the fuel was getting low. He did not love Adelaide at first sight or even care what happened to her. He had to save himself. Somehow he had to lighten his load. So he set his controls. He stood up in his cockpit. Then in one sudden motion he plucked my mother out of her seat and dropped her overboard.

All night she fell through the awful cold. Her coat flapped open and her black dress wrapped tightly around her legs. Her red hair flowed straight upward like a flame. She was a candle that gave no warmth. My heart froze. I had no love for her. That is why, by morning, I allowed her to hit the earth.

When the train stopped at Argus I was a block of sullen cold. It hurt when I jumped, scraping my cold knees and the heels of my hands. The pain sharpened me enough to read signs in windows and to wrack my mind for just where Aunt Fritzie's shop was. It had been years since we visited.

Karl was older, and I probably should not hold myself accountable for losing him too. But I didn't help him. I ran to the end of town. I couldn't stand how his face glowed in the blossoms' reflected light, pink and radiant, so like the way he sat beneath our mother's stroking hand.

When I stopped, hot tears came up suddenly behind my eyes and my ears burned. I ached to cry but I knew that was useless. I turned back, looking carefully at everything around me, and it was lucky I did this, because I'd run past the butcher shop and, suddenly, there it was, set in from the road down a short dirt drive. A white pig was painted on the side, and inside the pig, the lettering KOZKA'S MEATS. I walked toward it between rows of tiny fir trees. The place looked unfinished but prosperous, as though Fritzie and Pete were too busy with customers to care for appearances. I stood on the broad front stoop and noticed everything I could, the way a beggar does. A rack of elk horns was nailed overhead. I passed beneath them.

The entryway was dark, my heart was pounding. I had lost so much and suffered so badly from the grief and cold that I'm sure what I saw was quite natural, understandable, although it was not real.

Again, the dog leapt toward Karl and blossoms fell from his stick. Except that they fell around me in the entrance to the store. I smelled the petals melting on my coat, tasted their thin sweetness in my mouth. I had no time to wonder how this could be happening because they disappeared as suddenly as they'd come when I told my name to the man behind the glass counter.

Uncle Pete was tall and blond and wore an old blue denim cap the same color as his eyes. His smile was slow, sweet for a butcher, and hopeful. "Yes?" he asked. He did not recognize me even after I told him who I was. Finally his eyes rounded and he called out for Fritzie.

"Your sister's girl! She's here!" he shouted down the hall.

I told him I was alone, that I had come in on a boxcar, and he lifted me up in his arms. He carried me back to the kitchen where Aunt Fritzie had been frying a sausage for my cousin, the beautiful Sita, who sat at the table and stared while I tried to tell Fritzie and Pete just how I'd come to walk in their front door out of nowhere.

They watched me with friendly suspicion, thinking that I'd run away. But when I told about The Great Omar, and how Mama held up her purse, and how Omar helped her into the plane, their faces turned grim.

17

"Sita, go polish the glass out front," said Aunt Fritzie. Sita slid unwillingly out of her chair. "Now," Fritzie said. Uncle Pete sat down heavily and pressed his fists together under his chin. "Go on, tell the rest," he said, and so I told all of the rest, and when I had finished I had also drunk a glass of milk and eaten a sausage. By then I was so tired I could hardly sit upright. Uncle Pete lifted me. I remember sagging against him, then nothing. I slept that day and all night and did not wake until the next morning.

I lay still for what seemed like a long while, trying to place the objects in the room, until I remembered they all belonged to Sita.

This was where I would sleep every night for the rest of my life. The paneling was warm stained pine. The curtains were patterned with dancers and musical notes. Most of one wall was taken up by a tall oak dresser with fancy curlicues and many drawers. On it there was a wooden lamp in the shape of a wishing well. A full-length mirror hung on the back of the door. Through that door, as I was taking in my surroundings, walked Sita herself, tall and perfect with a blond braid that reached to her waist.

She sat down on the edge of my trundle bed and folded her arms over her small new breasts. She was a year older than me and one year younger than Karl. Since I'd seen her last, she had grown suddenly, but her growth had not thinned her into an awkward bony creature. Sita grinned. She looked down at me, her strong white teeth shining, and she stroked the blond braid that hung down over one shoulder.

"Where's Auntie Adelaide?" she asked.

I did not answer.

"Where's Auntie Adelaide?" she said, again, in a singsong furious voice. "How come you're here? Where'd she go? Where's Karl?"

"I don't know."

18

I suppose I thought the misery of my answer would quiet Sita, but that was before I knew her.

"How come she left you? Where's Karl? What's this?"

She took the blue velvet box from my pile of clothes and shook it next to her ear.

"What's in it?"

I snatched the box with an angry swiftness she did not expect. Then I rolled from the bed, bundled my clothes into my arms, and walked out of the room. The one door open in the hallway was the bathroom, a large smoky room of many uses that soon became my haven since it was the only door I could bolt against my cousin.

Every day for weeks after I arrived in Argus, I woke slowly, thinking I was back in Prairie Lake and that none of this had happened. Then I saw the dark swirls in the pine and Sita's arm hanging off the bed above me. The day started. I smelled the air, peppery and warm from the sausage makers. I heard the rhythmical whine of meat saws, slicers, the rippling beat of fans. Aunt Fritzie was smoking her sharp Viceroys in the bathroom. Uncle Pete was outside feeding the big white German shepherd that was kept in the shop at night to guard the canvas bags of money.

I got up, put on one of Sita's hand-me-down pink dresses, and went out to the kitchen to wait for Uncle Pete. I cooked breakfast. That I made a good cup of coffee at age eleven and fried eggs was a source of wonder to my aunt and uncle, and an outrage to Sita. That's why I did it every morning until it became a habit to have me there.

I planned to be essential to them all, so depended upon that they could never send me off. I did this on purpose, because I soon found out that I had nothing else to offer. The day after I arrived in Argus and woke up to Sita's accusing questions, I had tried to give them what I thought was my treasure—the blue velvet box that held Mama's jewels.

I did it in as grand a manner as I could, with Sita for a witness and with Pete and Fritzie sitting at the kitchen table. That morning, I walked in with my hair combed wet and laid the box between my uncle and aunt. I looked from Sita to Fritzie as I spoke.

"This should pay my way."

Fritzie had my mother's features sharpened one notch past beauty. Her skin was rough and her short curled hair bleached platinum. Her eyes were a swimming, crazy shade of turquoise that startled customers. She ate heartily, but her constant smoking kept her string-bean thin and sallow.

"You don't have to pay us," said Fritzie. "Pete tell her. She doesn't have to pay us. Sit down, shut up, and eat."

Fritzie spoke like that, joking and blunt. Pete was slower.

"Come. Sit down and forget about the money," he said. "You never know about your mother. . . ." he added in an earnest voice that trailed away. Things had a way of evaporating under Fritzie's eyes, vanishing, getting sucked up into the blue heat of her stare. Even Sita had nothing to say.

"I want to give you this," I said. "I insist."

"She insists," exclaimed Aunt Fritzie. Her smile had a rakish flourish because one tooth was chipped in front. "Don't insist," she said.

But I would not sit down. I picked up a knife from the butter plate and started to pry the lock.

"Here now," said Fritzie. "Pete, help her."

So Pete got up, fetched a screwdriver from the top of the icebox, sat down and jammed the end underneath the lock.

"Let her open it," said Fritzie, when the lock popped up. Pete pushed the little round box across the table.

"I bet it's empty," Sita said. She took a big chance saying that, but it paid off in spades and aces between us growing up because I lifted the lid a moment later and what she said was true. There was nothing of value in the box.

Stickpins. A few thick metal buttons off a coat. And a ticket describing a ring and the necklace set with garnets, pawned for practically nothing in Minneapolis.

There was silence. Even Fritzie was at a loss. Sita nearly buzzed off her chair in triumph but held her tongue until later, when she would crow. Pete put his hand on his head. I stood quietly, my mind working in a circle. If Sita had not been there I might have broken down and let the tears out again, like in the rooming house, but she kept me sharp.

I sat down to eat out of range of Sita's jabbing elbow. Already my mind was working on what revenge I would exact from her, and already I was way ahead where getting even was concerned, because Sita never saw me clearly until it was much too late. And so, as the years went on, I became more essential than any ring or necklace, while Sita flowered into the same frail kind of beauty that could be broken off a tree by any passing boy and discarded, cast away when the fragrance died.

I put the jewel box on the dresser I now shared with Sita, and never looked inside again. I didn't let myself think or remember, but got on with living. Still, I couldn't stop the dreams. At night they appeared, Karl, Mama, my baby brother, and Mr. Ober with his mouth full of grain. They tried to reach through air and earth. They tried to tell me there was rhyme and reason. But I put my hands over my ears.

I'd lost trust in the past. They were part of a fading pattern that was beyond understanding, and brought me no comfort.

Karl's Night

When Karl lay down in the freight again that morning, he decided not to move until he died. But then the train didn't travel on as it was supposed to. Not ten miles out of Argus, Karl's boxcar separated from the rest of the train and stopped. All that day he dozed and woke and saw the same two tall silver grain elevators just down the line. By late afternoon he was so thirsty, cold and hungry, so tired of waiting to die, that when a man swung through the door he was glad for the excuse to put it off.

Karl had buried himself in hay from the broken bales, and the man sat down not more than two feet away without seeing him. Karl watched the man closely. He seemed old to Karl at first. His face was burned a leathery hard brown. His eyes were almost lost in squinting folds; his lips were thin. He looked flint hard under his clothes, the remains of an old army uniform, and when he lit a cigarette stub the match reflected two thin flames in his eyes. He blew the smoke out in a ring. His hair was longish, the color of sand, and his beard was half grown.

Karl watched the man smoke his cigarette carefully down to the paper end, and then he spoke.

"Hello?"

"Huahh!" The man jumped up and floundered backward, then caught himself. "What the . . ."

"My name is Karl."

"Gave me a hell of a scare." The man glared into the shadows around Karl and then laughed abruptly. "You're a kid," he said, "and God don't you look the fool. Come here."

Karl stepped out and stood in the wide shaft of light from the door. The hay he'd slept in had matted to his overcoat and stuck out of his hair. He stared at the man from beneath a headful of grasses, and his look was so mournful that the man softened.

"You're a girl, aren't you?" he said. "S'cuse my language."

"I'm not a girl."

But Karl's voice hadn't finished changing yet and the man was unconvinced.

"I'm not a girl," Karl repeated.

"What'd you say your name was?"

"Karl Adare."

"Karla," the man said.

"I'm a boy."

"Yeah." The man rolled a new cigarette. "I'm Saint Ambrose."

Karl nodded cautiously.

"It's no joke," said the man. "My last name's Saint Ambrose. First name's Giles."

Karl sat down on the bale next to Giles Saint Ambrose. Hunger was making his head swim. He had to blink to keep his vision clear. Still, he noticed that the man was not as old as he had thought at first. In fact, once he was sitting close, Karl saw that his face was marked by sun and wind, not age.

"I'm from Prairie Lake," Karl managed to say. "We had a house."

"And you lost it," said Giles, looking at Karl through plumes of smoke. "When'd you eat last?"

The word *eat* made Karl's jaws lock, his mouth water. He stared speechlessly at Giles.

"Here." Giles took a newspaper-wrapped square from his jacket pocket. He unwrapped the package. "It's good, it's ham," he said.

Karl took it in both hands and ate with such swift ferocity that Giles forgot to draw on his cigarette.

"It was worth it just to watch," he said when Karl had finished. "I was going to ask you to save me a hunk, but I didn't have the heart."

Karl folded the newspaper and gave it back to Giles.

23

"That's all right." Giles waved the paper away. He reached down and picked up the stick Karl had brought into the boxcar. A few wilted gray blossoms still clung to the nodes. "This would make a good mosquito whip," said Giles.

"It's mine," said Karl.

"Oh?" said Giles, thrashing the air. "Not anymore it isn't. Call it a trade."

What happened to Karl next would shame him later on, but he couldn't help it. The branch made him think of the leaping dog, it's snarling muzzle, of Mary standing rooted in the street and himself tearing at the tree with all his strength, managing to twist off the branch and strike. Karl's eyes filled with tears and spilled over.

"It was only a joke," said Giles. He jiggled Karl's arm. "You can have it back." Giles wrapped Karl's fingers around the branch and Karl held tight to it but could not stop crying. He melted inside, overflowed. Sobs burst from his chest.

"Quiet down," said Giles. He put his arm around Karl's shoulders and the boy fell against him, weeping now in long tearing jagged moans. "You're going to have to practice. Boys don't do this," said Giles. But Karl kept crying until the fury of his grief was exhausted.

When Karl woke later it was dusk. He could hardly see, and the air was full of a dull confusing roar that sounded like torrents of rain or hail. Karl reached for Giles, afraid he'd vanished, but the man was there.

"What's that?" Karl asked, running his hands over Giles's rough army jacket. He fell back, reassured, when Giles mumbled, "It's just the grain loading. Go to sleep."

Karl stared up into the dark exciting sound of the avalanche. He planned how he and Giles would travel in the boxcar, occasionally jumping off at a town they liked the look of, stealing food, maybe finding an abandoned house to live in. He pictured them together, in danger from dogs or police, outrunning farmers and store clerks. He saw them roasting chickens and sleeping together, curled tight in a jolting boxcar, like they were now.

"Giles," he whispered.

"What?"

Karl waited. He'd touched other boys before but just in fun, down the alleys behind the boardinghouse. This was different, and he was not sure he'd dare, but then his body filled with the rushing noise. He took the chance, put his hands out, touched Giles's back.

"What do you want?"

Karl put his hand underneath Giles's jacket, and the man turned to him.

"Do you know what you're doing?" Giles whispered.

Karl felt the breath from Giles's lips and tipped his mouth up to kiss him. He put his hands under Giles's clothes again and edged close. Giles rolled on top of him and pinned him deep in the hay. Karl shivered then flushed warm when Giles began.

"You're no girl," Giles mumbled into Karl's hair, then he kissed Karl on the throat and began to touch him in a new way, all over, roughly but also carefully, until Karl's body tightened unbearably and then let loose, abruptly, in a long dark pulse. When Karl came back to himself he wrapped his arms very tightly around Giles, but the moment had passed. Giles loosened his arms gently and rolled over next to him. They lay together, side by side, both looking up into the sound of the grain, and Karl was certain of what he felt.

"I love you," Karl said.

Giles did not answer.

"I love you," Karl said again.

"Oh, Jesus, it wasn't anything," said Giles, not unkindly. "It happens. Don't get all worked up over it, okay?"

Then he turned away from Karl. After a long moment Karl got up on his knees. "Giles, you asleep?" he asked. There was no answer. Karl felt Giles's breathing slow, his body slacken, his legs jump as he fell into a deeper level of sleep.

"Bastard . . ." Karl whispered. Giles didn't waken. Karl said it, a little louder, again. Giles slept. Then Karl went into a black turmoil, a revery where things got mixed up in time and Adelaide's hair flew out of its knot, once again, to snarl around the shoulders of the slender pilot. He saw her fly off into the sky and then remembered the knife she had given him. He took it out, for the first time since Minneapolis, and tested its point with his finger.

"This is sharp," he warned. He stabbed it once or twice through the dark, even brought it down close enough to prick the torn wool of Giles's jacket. But Giles did not wake, and after a while Karl folded the knife and put it back in his pocket.

The roar stopped abruptly. Giles stirred but didn't wake. Through the cracks between the boards, Karl saw lanterns arc and swing and move away. And then there was a sudden jolt, another and another all down the line of cars, until theirs moved too, pounding, slowly gathering speed.

"It happens," Karl said then, repeating Giles's words. "It happens."

When he said that, it felt like his heart ripped open. Even in his storm of weeping he had not touched the depth of his loss. Now it swallowed him. There was the branch, still faintly good to smell. He picked it up and then stood in the blackness. He didn't want to vomit or scream. He didn't want to cry on the lap of anyone again. So he stood frowning keenly at nothing as the train rolled on, and then, light and quick as a deer, he leaped forward and ran straight out the door of the moving boxcar.

SITA KOZKA

MY COUSIN MARY came in on the early freight train one morning, with nothing but an old blue keepsake box full of worthless pins and buttons. My father picked her up in his arms and carried her down the hallway into the kitchen. I was too old to be carried. He sat her down, then my mother said, "Go clean the counters, Sita." So I don't know what lies she told them after that.

Later on that morning, my parents put her to sleep in my bed. When I objected to this, saying that she could sleep on the trundle, my mother said, "Cry sakes, you can sleep there too, you know." And that is how I ended up that night, crammed in the trundle, which is too short for me. I slept with my legs dangling out in the cold air. I didn't feel welcoming toward Mary the next morning, and who can blame me?

Besides, on her first waking day in Argus, there were the clothes.

It is a good thing she opened the blue keepsake box at breakfast and found little bits of trash, like I said, because if I had not felt sorry for my cousin that day, I would not have stood for Mary and my mother ripping through my closet and bureau. "This fits perfectly," my mother said, holding up one of my favorite blouses, "try it on!" And Mary did. Then she put it in her drawer, which was another thing. I had to clear out two of my bureau drawers for her.

"Mother," I said, after this had gone on for some time and I was beginning to think I would have to wear the same three outfits all the next school year, "Mother, this has really gone far enough."

"Crap," said my mother, who talks that way. "Your cousin hasn't got a stitch."

Yet she had half of mine by then, quite a wardrobe, and all the time it was increasing as my mother got more excited about dressing the poor orphan. But Mary wasn't really an orphan, although she played on that for sympathy. Her mother was still alive, even if she had left my cousin, which I doubted. I really thought that Mary just ran away from her mother because she could not appreciate Adelaide's style. It's not everyone who understands how to use their good looks to the best advantage. My Aunt Adelaide did. She was always my favorite, and I just died for her to visit. But she didn't come often because my mother couldn't understand style either.

"Who are you trying to impress?" she'd hoot when Adelaide came out to dinner in a dress with a fur collar. My father would blush red and cut his meat. He didn't say much, but I knew he did not approve of Adelaide any more than her older sister did. My mother said she'd always spoiled Adelaide because she was the baby of the family. She said the same of me. But I don't think that I was ever spoiled, not one iota, because I had to work the same as anyone cleaning gizzards.

I hated Wednesdays because that was the day we killed chickens. The farmer brought them stacked in cages made of thin wooden slats. One by one, Canute, who did most of the slaughtering, killed them by sticking their necks with the blade of his long knife. After the chickens were killed, plucked, and cut open, I got the gizzards. Coffee can after coffee can full of gizzards. I still have dreams. I had to turn each gizzard inside out and wash it in a pan of water. All the gravel and hard seed fell out into the bottom. Sometimes I found bits of metal and broken glass. Once I found a brilliant. "Mother!" I yelled, holding it out in

28

my palm. "I found a diamond!" Everyone was so excited that they clustered around me. And then my mother took the little sparkling stone to the window. It didn't scratch the glass at all, of course, and I had to clean the rest of the gizzards. But for one brief moment I was sure the diamond had made us rich, which brings me to another diamond. A cow's diamond, my inheritance.

It was a joke, really, about the inheritance, at least it was a joke to my papa. A cow's diamond is the hard rounded lens inside a cow's eye that shines when you look through it at the light, almost like an opal. You could never make a ring of it or use it for any kind of jewelry, since it might shatter, and of course it had no worth. My father mainly carried it as a lucky piece. He'd flip it in the air between customers, and sometimes in a game of cribbage I'd see him rub it. I wanted it. One day I asked if he would give it to me.

"I can't," he said. "It's my butcher's luck. It can be your inheritance, how about that?"

I suppose my mouth dropped open in surprise because my father always gave me anything I asked for. For instance, we had a small glass candy case out front, over the sausages, and I could eat candy anytime I wanted. I used to bring root-beer barrels into class for the girls I liked. I never chewed gum balls though, because I heard Auntie Adelaide tell mother once, in anger, that only tramps chewed gum. This was when my mother was trying to quit smoking and she kept a sack of gum balls in the pocket of her apron. I was in the kitchen with them when they had this argument. "Tramps!" my mother said, "That's the pot calling the kettle black!" Then she took the gum from her mouth and rubbed it into Adelaide's long wavy hair. "I'll kill you!" my Auntie raged. It was something to see grown-ups behaving this way, but I don't blame Auntie Adelaide. I'd feel the same if I had to cut out a big knot of gum like she did and have a shorter patch of hair. I never chewed gum. But anything else in the store I wanted, I just took. Or I asked and it was handed right over. So you can see why my father's refusal was a surprise.

I had my pride even as a child, and I never mentioned it again. But here is what happened two days after Mary Adare came.

We were waiting to be tucked in that night. I was in my own bed, and she was in the trundle. She was short enough to fit there without hanging off the edge. The last thing she did before going to sleep was to put Adelaide's old keepsake box up on my bureau. I didn't say anything, but really it was sad. I guess my papa thought so, too. I guess he took pity on her. That night he came in the room, tucked the blankets around me, kissed me on the forehead, and said, "Sleep tight." Then he bent over Mary and kissed her too. But to Mary he said, "Here is a jewel."

It was the cow's diamond that I wanted, the butcher's luck. When I looked over the edge of my bed and saw the pale lens glowing in her hand, I could have spit. I pretended to be asleep when she asked me what it was. Find out for yourself, I thought, and said nothing. A few weeks later, when she knew her way around town, she got some jeweler to drill a hole through one end of the lucky piece. Then she hung the cow's diamond around her neck on a piece of string, as if it were something valuable. Later on she got a gold link chain.

First my room, then my clothing, then the cow's diamond. But the worst was yet to come when she stole Celestine.

My best friend, Celestine, lived three miles out of town with her half brother and much older half sister, who were Chippewas. There weren't all that many who came down from the reservation, but Celestine's mother had been one. Her name was Regina I-don't-know-what, and she worked for Dutch James, keeping his house when he was a bachelor and after, once they married. I overheard how Celestine came just a month past the wedding, and how Regina brought down the three other children

30

Dutch James hadn't known about. Somehow it worked out. They all lived together up until the time of Dutch James's peculiar death. He froze solid in our very meat locker. But that is an event no one in this house will discuss.

Anyway, those others were never court adopted and went by the last name Kashpaw. Celestine was a James. Because her parents died when Celestine was young, it was the influence of her big sister that was more important to Celestine. She knew the French language, and sometimes Celestine spoke French to lord it over us in school, but more often she got teased for her size and the odd flimsy clothes that her sister Isabel picked out of the dime store in Argus.

Celestine was tall, but not clumsy. More what my mother called statuesque. No one told Celestine what to do. We came and went and played anywhere we felt like. My mother would never have let me play in a graveyard, for example, but when visiting Celestine, that's what we did. There was a cemetery right on the land of Dutch James's homestead, a place filled with the graves of children who died in some plague of cough or influenza. They'd been forgotten, except by us. Their little crosses of wood or bent iron were tilted. We straightened them, even recarved the names on the wooden ones with a kitchen knife. We dug up violets from the oxbow and planted them. The graveyard was our place, because of what we did. We liked to sit there on hot afternoons. It was so pleasant. Wind ruffled the long grass, worms sifted the earth below us, swallows from the mudbanks dove through the sky in pairs. It was a nice place, really, not even very sad. But of course Mary had to ruin it.

I underestimated Mary Adare. Or perhaps I was too trusting, since it was I who suggested we go visit Celestine one day in early summer. I started out by giving Mary a ride on the handlebars of my bicycle, but she was so heavy I could hardly steer.

"You pedal," I said, stopping in the road. She fell off, then jumped up and stood the bicycle upright. I suppose I was heavy, too. But her legs were tireless. Celestine's Indian half brother, Russell Kashpaw, approached us on the way to Celestine's. "Who's your slave today?" he said. "She's cuter than you'll ever be!" I knew he said things like that because he meant the opposite, but Mary didn't. I felt her swell proudly in my old sundress. She made it all the way to Celestine's, and when we got there I jumped off and ran straight in the door.

Celestine was baking, just like a grown-up. Her big sister let her make anything she wanted, no matter how sweet. Celestine and Mary mixed up a batch of cookie dough. Mary liked cooking too. I didn't. So they measured and stirred, timed the stove and put out the cooling racks while I sat at the table with a piece of waxed paper, rolled out the dough, and cut it into fancy shapes.

"Where did you come from?" Celestine asked Mary as we worked.

"She came from Hollywood," I said. Celestine laughed at that, but then she saw it wasn't funny to Mary, and she stopped.

"Truly," said Celestine.

"Minnesota," said Mary.

"Are your mother and father still there?" asked Celestine. "Are they still alive?"

"They're dead," said Mary promptly. My mouth fell open, but before I could get a word of the real truth in, Celestine said.

"Mine are dead too."

And then I knew why Celestine had been asking these questions, when she already knew the whole story and its details from me. Mary and Celestine smiled into each other's eyes. I could see that it was like two people meeting in a crowd, who knew each other from a long time before. And what was also odd, they looked suddenly alike. It was only when they were together. You'd never notice it when they weren't. Celestine's hair was a tarnished red brown. Her skin was olive, her eyes burning black. Mary's eyes were light brown and her hair was dark and lank. Together, like I said, they looked similar. It wasn't even their build. Mary was short and stocky, while Celestine was tall. It was something else, either in the way they acted or the way they talked. Maybe it was a common sort of fierceness.

After they went back to their mixing and measuring, I could see that they were friendlier too. They stood close together, touched shoulders, laughed and admired everything the other one did until it made me sick.

"Mary's going to Saint Catherine's next fall," I interrupted. "She'll be downstairs with the little girls."

Celestine and I were in the seventh grade, which meant our room was on the top floor now, and also that we would wear special blue wool berets in choir. I was trying to remind Celestine that Mary was too young for our serious attention, but I made the mistake of not knowing what had happened last week, when Mary went into the school to take tests from Sister Leopolda.

"I'll be in your class," said Mary.

"What do you mean?" I said. "You're only eleven!"

"Sister put me ahead one grade," said Mary, "into yours."

The shock of it made me bend to my cookie cutting, speechless. She was smart. I already knew she was good at getting her way through pity. But smartness I did not expect, or going ahead a grade. I pressed the little tin cutters of hearts, stars, boys, and girls into the cookie dough. The girl shape reminded me of Mary, square and thick.

"Mary," I said, "aren't you going to tell Celestine what was in the little blue box you stole out of your mother's closet?"

Mary looked right at me. "Not a thing," she said.

Celestine stared at me like I was crazy.

"The jewels," I said to Mary, "the rubies and the diamonds."

We looked each other in the eye, and then Mary seemed to

decide something. She blinked at me and reached into the front of the dress. She pulled out the cow's diamond on a string.

"What's that?" Celestine showed her interest at once.

Mary displayed the wonder of how the light glanced through her treasure and fell, fractured and glowing, on the skin of her palm. The two of them stood by the window taking turns with the cow's lens, ignoring me. I sat at the table eating cookies. I ate the feet. I nibbled up the legs. I took the arms off in two snaps and then bit off the head. What was left was a shapeless body. I ate that up too. All the while I was watching Celestine. She wasn't pretty, but her hair was thick and full of red lights. Her dress hung too long behind her knees, but her legs were strong. I liked her tough hands. I liked the way she could stand up to boys. But more than anything else, I liked Celestine because she was mine. She belonged to me, not Mary, who had taken so much already.

"We're going out now," I told Celestine. She always did what I said. She came, although reluctantly, leaving Mary at the window.

"Let's go to our graveyard," I whispered, "I have to show you something."

I was afraid she wouldn't go with me, that she would choose right there to be with Mary. But the habit of following me was too strong to break. She came out the door, leaving Mary to take the last batch of cookies from the oven.

We left the back way and walked out to the graveyard.

"What do you want?" said Celestine when we stepped into the long secret grass. Wild plum shaded us from the house. We were alone.

We stood in the hot silence, breathing air thick with dust and the odor of white violets. She pulled a strand of grass and put the tender end between her lips, then stared at me from under her eyebrows.

Maybe if Celestine had quit staring, I wouldn't have done what I did. But she stood there in her too-long dress, chewing a stem of grass, and let the sun beat down on us until I thought of what to show her. My breasts were tender. They always hurt. But they were something that Mary didn't have.

One by one, I undid the buttons of my blouse. I took it off. My shoulders felt pale and fragile, stiff as wings. I took off my undervest and cupped my breasts in my hands.

My lips were dry. Everything went still.

Celestine broke the stillness by chewing grass, loud, like a rabbit. She hesitated just a moment and then turned on her heel. She left me there, breasts out, never even looking back. I watched her vanish through the bushes, and then a breeze flowed down on me, passing like a light hand. What the breeze made me do next was almost frightening. Something happened, I turned in a slow circle. I tossed my hands out and waved them. I swayed as if I heard music from below. Quicker, and then wilder, I lifted my feet. I began to tap them down, and then I was dancing on their graves.

MARY ADARE

How LONG WAS Sita going to shimmy there, I wondered, with her shirt off and thunderclouds lowering? I heard Celestine walk into the kitchen below and bang the oven door open, so I came down. I stood in the kitchen door watching her lift each cookie off the sheet with a spatula. She never broke one. She never looked up. But she knew I was there, and she knew that I'd been up on the second floor, watching Sita. I know that she knew because she hardly glanced up when I spoke.

"It's dark all of a sudden," I said; "there's a storm."

"Sita's mother'll be mad," said Celestine, dusting flour off her hands.

We went out to get Sita, but before we were halfway across the yard Sita came, walked right past us, jumped on her bicycle, and rode away. That is how I got caught in the rain that afternoon. It swept down in sheets while I still had a mile left to walk. I slogged in the back door of the house and stood dripping on the hemp mat.

Fritzie rushed at me with a thick towel and practically took my head off rubbing it dry.

"Sita! Get out here and apologize to your cousin," she hollered. She had to call Sita twice before she came.

On the first day of school that next fall, we walked out of the door together, both carrying fat creamy tablets and new pencils in identical wooden pencil boxes, both wearing blue. Sita's dress was new with sizing, mine was soft from many washings. It didn't bother me to wear Sita's hand-me-downs because I knew it bothered her so much to see those outgrown dresses, faded and unevenly hemmed by Fritzie, diminished by me and worn to tatters, not enshrined as Sita probably wished.

We walked down the dirt road together and then, hidden from Fritzie's view by the short pines, we separated. Or rather, Sita ran long legged, brightly calling, toward a group of girls also dressed in stiff new material, white stockings, unscuffed shoes. Colored ribbons, plumped in bows, hung down their backs. I lagged far behind. It didn't bother me to walk alone.

And yet, once we stood in the gravel school yard, milling about in clumps, and once we were herded into rows, and once Celestine began to talk to me and once Sita meanly said I'd come in on the freight train, I suddenly became an object of fascination.

Popular. I was new in Argus. Everybody wanted to be my friend. But I had eyes only for Celestine. I found her and took her hand. Her flat black eyes were shaded by thick lashes, soft as paintbrushes. Her hair had grown out into a tail. She was strong. Her arms were thick from wrestling with her brother Russell, and she seemed to have grown even taller than a month ago. She was bigger than the eighth-grade boys, almost as tall as Sister Leopolda, the tallest of all the nuns.

We walked up the pressed-rock stairs following our teacher, a round-faced young Dominican named Sister Hugo. And then, assigned our seats in alphabetical order, I was satisfied to find myself in the first desk, ahead of Sita.

Sita's position soon changed, of course. Sita always got moved up front because she volunteered to smack erasers together, wash blackboards, and copy out poems in colored chalk with her perfect handwriting. Much to her relief, I soon became old hat. The girls no longer clustered around me at recess but sat by her on the merry-go-round and listened while she gossiped, stroked her long braid and rolled her blue eyes to attract the attention of the boys in the upper grade.

Halfway through the school year, however, I recaptured my classmates awe. I didn't plan it or even try to cause the miracle, it simply happened, on a cold frozen day late in winter.

Overnight that March, the rain had gone solid as it fell. Frozen runnels paved the ground and thick cakes of ice formed beneath the eaves where the dripping water solidified midair. We slid down the glossy streets on the way to school, but later that morning, before we got our boots and coats from the closet for the recess hour, Sister Hugo cautioned us that sliding was forbidden. It was dangerous. But once we stood beneath the tall steel slide outdoors, this seemed unfair, for the slide was more a slide than ever, frozen black in one clear sheet. The railings and steps were coated with invisible glare. At the bottom of the slide a pure glass fan opened, inviting the slider to hit it feet first and swoop down the center of the school yard, which was iced to the curbs.

I was the first and only slider.

I climbed the stairs with Celestine behind me, several boys behind her, and Sita hanging toward the rear with her girl friends, who all wore dainty black gum boots and gloves, which were supposed to be more adult, instead of mittens. The railings made a graceful loop on top, and the boys and bolder girls used it to gain extra momentum or even somersault before they slid down. But that day it was treacherous, so slick that I did not dare hoist myself up. Instead, I grabbed the edges of the slide. And then I realized that if I went down at all, it would have to be head first.

From where I crouched the ride looked steeper, slicker, more dangerous than I'd imagined. But I did have on the product of my mother's stolen spoons, the winter coat of such heavy material I imagined I would slide across the school yard on it as if it were a piece of cardboard.

I let go. I went down with terrifying speed. But instead of landing on my padded stomach I hit the ice full force, with my face.

I blacked out for a moment, then sat up, stunned. I saw forms run toward me through a haze of red and glittering spots. Sister Hugo got to me first, grabbed my shoulders, removed my wool scarf, probed the bones of my face with her strong, short fingers. She lifted my eyelids, wacked my knee to see if I was paralyzed, waggled my wrists.

"Can you hear me?" she cried, mopping at my face with her big manly handkerchief, which turned bright red. "If you hear me, blink your eyes!"

I only stared. My own blood was on the cloth. The whole playground was frighteningly silent. Then I understood my head was whole and that no one was even looking at me. They were all crowded at the end of the slide. Even Sister Hugo was standing there now, her back turned. When several of the more pious students sank to their knees, I could not contain myself. I lurched to my feet and tottered over. Somehow I managed to squeeze through their cluster, and then I saw.

The pure gray fan of ice below the slide had splintered, on impact with my face, into a shadowy white likeness of my brother Karl.

He stared straight at me. His cheeks were hollowed out, his eyes dark pits. His mouth was held in a firm line of pain and the hair on his forehead had formed wet spikes, the way it always did when he slept or had a fever.

Gradually, the bodies around me parted and then, very gently, Sister Hugo led me away. She took me up the stairs and helped me onto a cot in the school infirmary.

She looked down at me. Her cheeks were red from the cold, like polished apples, and her brown eyes were sharp with passion.

"Father is coming," she said, then popped quickly out.

As soon as she was gone, I jumped off the cot and went straight to the window. An even larger crowd had collected at the base of the slide, and now Sister Leopolda was setting up a tripod and other photographic equipment. It seemed incredible that Karl's picture should warrant such a stir. But he was always like that. People noticed him. Strangers gave him money while I was ignored, just like now, abandoned with my wounds. I heard the priest's measured creak on the stairs, then Sister Hugo's quick skip, and I jumped back.

Father opened the back door and allowed his magnificence to be framed in it for a moment while he fixed me with his most penetrating stare. Priests were only called in on special cases of discipline or death, and I didn't know which one this was.

He motioned to Sister Hugo, and she ducked from the room.

He drew a chair up beneath his bulk and sat down. I lay flat, as if for his inspection, and there was a long and uncomfortable silence.

"Do you pray to see God?" he asked finally.

"Yes!" I said.

"Your prayers were answered," Father stated. He folded his fingers into the shape of a church and bit harshly on the steeple, increasing the power of his stare.

"Christ's Dying Passion," he said. "Christ's face formed in the ice as surely as on Veronica's veil."

I knew what he meant at last, and so kept silent about Karl. The others at Saint Catherine's did not know about my brother, of course. To them the image on the ice was that of the Son of God.

As long as the ice on the playground lasted, I was special in the class again, sought out by Sita's friends, teachers, even boys who were drawn to the glory of my black eyes and bruises. But I stuck with Celestine. After the sliding, we were even better friends than before. One day the newspaper photographer came to school and I made a great commotion about not having my picture taken unless it was with her. We stood together in the cold wind, at the foot of the slide.

GIRL'S MISHAP SHAPES MIRACLE was the headline in the *Argus Sentinel*.

For two weeks the face was cordoned off and farmers drove for miles to kneel by the cyclone fence outside of Saint Catherine's school. Rosaries were draped on the red slats, paper flowers, little ribbons and even a dollar or two.

And then one day, the sun came out and suddenly warmed the earth. The face of Karl, or Christ, dispersed into little rivulets that ran all through the town. Echoing in gutters, disappearing, swelling through culverts and collecting in basements, he made himself impossibly everywhere and nowhere all at once so that all spring before the town baked hard, before the drought began, I felt his presence in the whispering and sighing of the streams.

CELESTINE JAMES

I HAVE A BACK view of Mary when she shoots down the slide to earth. Her heavy gray wool coat stands out like a bell around the white clapper of her drawers, but the wind never ruffles her blue scarf. She is motionless in her speed, until she hits. Then suddenly things move fast, everywhere, all at once. Mary rolls over twice. Blood drenches her face. Sister Hugo runs toward her and then there are screams. Sita draws attention to herself by staggering to the merry-go-round, dizzy at the sight of her cousin's blood. A tortured saint, maybe even Catherine herself, she drapes her body among the iron spokes at the center of the wheel, and calls out, in a feeble but piercing tone, for help.

Sita is five times as strong as she looks, and can beat me in a fight, so I do not go to her. Sister Hugo is now leading Mary up the stairs with her handkerchief and the blue scarf pressed on Mary's forehead. I have backed down the iced-over slide steps like magic, and now I run after the two of them. But Sister Hugo bars me from the door once they reach the infirmary.

"Go back down," she says in a shaking voice. Her eyes blaze strangely underneath her starched linen brow. "It may not last," she says. "Run to the convent! Tell Leopolda to haul herself right over with the camera!"

I am confused.

"The ice, the face," said Sister Hugo frantically. "Now, *get*!"

And so I run, so amazed and excited at how she has expressed herself, not like a teacher but just like a farmer, that I do not ring the convent bell but leap straight into the entryway and scream up the echoing stairs. By then I know, because it is in the air of the school yard, that some kind of miracle had resulted from Mary's fall.

So I shout, "A MIRACLE" at the top of my lungs. To do that in a convent is like shouting fire in a crowded movie. They all rush down suddenly, an avalanche of black wool. Leopolda springs down last of all, with a fearsome eagerness. A tripod is strapped on one shoulder. Drapes, lights, and a box camera are crammed in her arms. It is like she has been right behind her door, armed with equipment, praying year in and year out for this moment to arrive.

Back on the school ground, all is chaos. A crowd has formed around the end of the slide. Later on, the face they stare at is included in the catechism textbooks throughout the Midwest as The Manifestation At Argus, with one of Sister Leopolda's photographs to illustrate. In the article, Mary is described as "a local foundling," and the iced slide becomes "an innocent trajectory of divine glory." The one thing they never write about is how Sister Leopolda is found several nights after Mary's accident. She is kneeling at the foot of the slide with her arms bare, scourging herself past the elbows with dried thistles, drawing blood. After that she is sent somewhere to recuperate.

But that day, in all of the confusion, I sneak back into the school building. As I walk down the hall Father comes out of the infirmary door. He is lost in a serious thought and never lifts his head, so he does not see me. As soon as he is down the hall I slip straight in, alarmed because a priest near a sick person spells doom.

But Mary is recovered from the blow, I think at first, because she's sitting up.

"Did you see him!" she says immediately, clutching my arm. She looks deranged, either with her sudden importance or with the wound. Her head is taped in gauze now, which would give her a nun-like air except that the pits of her eyes are beginning to show disreputable black and purple bruises.

"They say it's a miracle," I tell her. I expect her to laugh but she grips my hand hard. Her eyes take on a glitter that I start to suspect.

"It was a sign," she says, "but not what they think."

"How do you mean?"

"It was Karl."

She has never mentioned Karl before, but from Sita I know he is her brother who has run off on a boxcar heading west.

"Lay back," I tell Mary. "Your head got knocked."

"He's got to bother me," she says loudly. "He can't leave me alone."

Her face screws up. She is thinking deeply like the priest and has lost all track of me or even of herself. Her eyes glare into the distance, light and still, and I see that she is very annoyed.

After Sister Hugo sends me out of the infirmary, I walk down the stairs, out into the cold overcast weather, and join the throng clustered around the miraculous face. Only to me, it is not so miraculous. I stare hard at the patterns of frozen mud, the cracked ice, the gravel that shows through the ice, the gray snow. Other people looking from the same angle see it. I do not, although I kneel until my knees grow numb.

That night the face is all that Russell and my big sister Isabel can talk about.

"Your girl friend's going to put us on the map," declares Isabel. She's all we have, and she takes care of us by holding down jobs with farmers, cooking, and sometimes even threshing right along with the men. "Girls have been canonized for less," she now says. Isabel carries the banner in Saint Catherine's Procession every year, looking huge and sorrowful, but pure. My mother was big too. It seems like I got all of my father's coloring, but am growing very quickly into my mother's size.

"I bet Sita's about ready to kill that little Mary," Russell says with a sharp laugh. Sita has made fun of him for being an Indian, and he is always glad to see her taken down a notch.

"They are taking a picture of Mary for the papers," I tell him. Isabel is impressed, but not Russell, because he plays football and has been in the papers many times for making touchdowns. People say he is one Indian who won't go downhill in life but have success, and he does, later, depending on how you look at it.

The next morning, before school starts, he comes with me to inspect the ice. During the night, someone has put up a low slat and wire fence around the sacred patch. Russell kneels by the fence and blesses himself. He says some sort of prayer, and then walks his bicycle down the icy road to the high school. He has seen it too. I am left at the bottom of the slide again, kneeling and squinting, even crossing my eyes to try and make the face appear. All the while the nuns are setting up the altar, right there in the school yard, for a special mass. I begin to wish that I had asked Russell to point out the features for me exactly, so that I can see Christ, too. Even now, I consider questioning the nuns, but in the end I don't have the courage, and all through the mass, standing with the seventh grade, watching Mary, Sita, Fritzie and Pete take communion first, I pretend that I am moved by the smashed spot, which is all I can see.

Rescue

In a small frame house in Minneapolis, a young woman sat reading the newspaper, her fingers rustling in and out of the pages. Her husband sat across the room watching her read. Their son was in his arms.

"Here's another ad," said Catherine Miller.

"Why do you look for them anyway?" said her husband, Martin.

She lowered the paper and stared calmly at him. Her brows were plucked into slender bows that made her eyes seem intelligent. Her light brown hair was poked into a swirling topknot.

"You know why," she said, flipping the paper back and forth. "The police, Martin. Kidnapping's a criminal offense."

Having no answer, Martin looked down at the baby. The child's eyes lost focus, his mouth drooped, and Martin held him closer, taking such pleasure in the sleeping baby's trust that he did not notice when his wife tensed, held her breath, scanned an article quickly, and then lowered the paper.

She sat with the paper in her lap, watching Jude, her son, the tiny baby she had named for the patron saint of lost causes, lost hopes, and last-ditch resorts. She remembered that first night after their other son, the one who had only lived three days, was buried.

That night was a small quiet place in her she rarely visited. But now she thought back. How still the world had been, and the sky, such a dark spring blue. Her bound breasts ached unbearably. Her mind was frozen blank with loss, yet every nerve throbbed. She could not sleep.

From time to time such blind agony had swept over her that she thought she would drown, or lose her mind. She had even

45

refused anodynes. She wanted nothing to dull the pain, no laudanum, not even a glass of whiskey. But with Martin gone that night, she decided suddenly she needed something. So she stumbled to the cabinet where the bottle was hidden and poured a quick, large toothglass full of bootleg. Standing alone in the cold dark house, a tall frowzy figure in a nightgown printed with flannel roses, she drank. The liquor burned with a clear fire. She poured another glass and downed it more slowly, allowing the heat to envelop her. To her surprise, the whiskey helped. At least it was a distraction, and as she floated back to bed and straight into sleep, the pain, duller now and heavier, was held at arm's length and not cradled inside of her.

Relaxed in dead exhaustion, she had not heard Martin come through the front door. Once he entered the bedroom and put the baby in the crib, she heard it howl, but she retreated mentally from the sound. Even in her stupor she was certain that it was some sort of terrible hallucination. She felt Martin's hands at her breasts, untying the strips of cloth now soaked with her faintly sweet milk, and she tried to fight him away. Martin calmed her with words and low croons, as if she were a frightened animal, and once she lay still again he put the baby to her breast.

Instantly, although she knew it could not be happening, she let go and fed the child, as if from her own heart. Even in her confusion she realized that the child was different, as small as her first, but older, more adept.

Now, waiting for Martin to look up and see her expression, a tide of feeling that she'd held back without knowing it rolled out. Even looking at the baby warmed her. What a marvel—those dark red curls!

"You look like the cat that ate the bird," said Martin, smiling at her.

"I'm happy."

"I'm happy too," said Martin cautiously. "He's ours."

"I know it."

And then she read the article aloud, the one accompanying the usual ad with the reward offered for information leading to the recovery of a month-old baby boy. The article described the mother, her incredible behavior, and said that she was also sought by the Kozka family of Argus.

After she finished reading the article, Catherine Miller saved the paper away carefully in a drawer, along with the tiny cap of pale blue, the thick blanket pieced from scraps of coat fabric, and the strange little green plaid gown the baby had been wearing on the night he came to her rescue.

KARL ADARE

I HAD LANDED in tall dead grass. It was daylight. The pain in my legs was horrible and the ground under me was cold. As the day wore on the light warmed, grew hotter, and beat through my clothes. The pain spun me long and shrank me into a knot. Any slight movement made it worse, and so I lay still.

I thought Giles would come back when he found out what I had done. I saw him waking up alone in the jerking boxcar. He would wait until the train slowed, then hike back and take me in his arms. I trusted that since I hadn't died I certainly would be saved.

My salvation dragged a cart of scavenged boards down the tracks. Its wheels were shrieking iron. The sound stopped just above me. She was massive. Her shadow fell from above. I opened my cracked throat, but no word came out of it, then a woman stumbled down the low embankment. Her head was bound in a white scarf that blazed against her dark skin. Twin silver mirrors dangled from her earlobes, flashed, dizzied me. She crouched over me, lifted my eyelids with fingers tough and flexible as pliers. Then she opened my jaw and poured raw whiskey down my throat. It went through me like a rope of fire, tangling my guts, lighting a pinpoint of sense in my brain.

"Feet," I said.

She bent closer.

But I couldn't stand to have them touched, and twisted away from her probing fingers.

Blue in the dusk, a formation of scarves and blankets, she

disappeared. There was a clattering and banging beyond my sight, and I slept until she came back and carried me over to the fire. Water was steaming in a pot on a hook. I saw a knife, a few packets of flour, some dried beans and dirty roots. She put me on a mound of reeds.

"What are you going to do!" I struggled in her arms.

Days would pass before I realized that Fleur Pillager almost never spoke, though she had the ability. She told me only her name, but I heard her sing and talk to herself.

She covered me with a horse blanket then dribbled more whiskey between my lips until my coughing stopped her. She cut off my shoes, slicing carefully into the leather, then my socks too. I begged her to use that same knife to cut my feet off, but when she put my feet firmly in her lap I arched into blackness. At the first squeeze of her hand, she told me later, I passed out.

While I was dead to the world, Fleur Pillager proceeded to knead, mold, and tap the floating splinters of my bones back into the shape of ankles, feeling her own from time to time to get the shape right. The packets I thought were flour were really plaster of Paris. Out of it she made my casts and shaped them with carved splinters from the only branch within a mile of the railroad track, the apple branch, torn from an Argus tree, that she found lying next to me.

She bundled me into oilskins and more blankets and got me drunk, but I could not sleep that night. The sky changed gradually, black to gray, red to pink, and then the sun broke out. Fleur had drawn her cart down the railroad embankment onto the margin of a reedy slough almost deep enough to be a lake. The cattails were the tallest things in sight. The world was bare as far as the eye could see. We were the only detail in it. Fleur poked up the fire, mixed bread in a pan, and heated the slough-water coffee. I sipped a rank, sweet cup of it and studied her as best I could.

Her face was young, broad and dark, but fine around the edges, even delicate. Her heavy mouth curved at the corners, her nose arched like the nose of a royal princess. She was an Indian, a Pillager, one of a wandering bunch that never did take hold. She made her living by peddling whatever came her way to sell. Pans hung from her cart, and bundles that held packets of needles, colored string. Calico dress lengths were piled on top. She dealt in mismatched plates, mended cups, and secondhand forks. She bought handmade white lace from the mission school and traded it for berries pounded into jerky, birch-bark picture frames.

I wanted to tell her who I was, to tell her everything. But then, just as I started to speak, the sky rushed down. The earth pressed close, so close I couldn't breath.

"There's something wrong with me," I choked.

Fleur pounded my chest, put her ear on my heart, then got up and started throwing things off her cart. I had pneumonia, a common hazard of sleeping in cold boxcars. Most every longtime hobo walked around with it, died of it or survived. Fleur put rocks in the fire to heat, but the reeds smoked too much. So she split some railroad ties and stoked the blaze until the rocks were red hot.

The sun lowered. The grass rustled in the slight breeze and the noise seemed unnaturally loud, and the ducks too, mumbling in their soft nests, and the muskrats. I seemed to hear them slapping through the water after insects. Even the massing clouds seemed to make a light *whooshing* sound as they puckered and folded and gained color.

Fleur rolled the hot stones, sizzling, onto the mud by the slough, and then she put the wagon box over them. On it she put a chair that had been tied on top of everything. She stripped me naked in a few short jerks and rolled me back up in a dry blanket. She sat me on the chair on top of the box, as on a throne, and then wound a length of rope around me. Over it all, down to the ground, surrounding me like a cape and tied firmly around my shoulders, she draped her blankets.

50

Then I was sealed into a sweltering cone.

I was the highest point in the world. I was out of my mind. I faced west as the sun settled in a fierce glow that lit my face. I shone back like a beacon through my transparent skin and imagined I could be seen as the dark came on, red like a lantern, glowing like a heart in crackling papers. The outlines of my bones were etched black. I was a signal. All through the night I pulsed on and off, calling any of them back to me—Giles or Mary, my mother, even the baby who'd ruined my life by driving her away.

Animals surrounded the edges of my heat. I saw the eyes of skunks, red marbles, heard the chatter of coons, watched the bitterns land, blacker than the black sky, and drowsy hawks. A bear rose between the fire and the reeds. In the deepest part of the night, the biggest animal of all came through in a crash of sparks and wheels.

It was not quite dawn when Fleur took me down. I was limp and sodden but breathing more easily. My fever had broken sometime during the night. She rolled me in the outermost dry blankets and put me on the reeds again. She piled more reeds on top of me. And over all that, she lay herself, a crushing weight, and at first I was cold again and felt my lungs tightening, but then, from above, her warmth pressed down.

When I was better we moved on. Fleur's cart ran on specially grooved wheels, and she pulled it, her head through a horse collar. We traveled slowly, our ears stopped with cattail down to muffle the wheels' shocks and groans. I was lashed on top, in my chair, legs sticking out and an umbrella tied to shade me. Because both of our ears were stopped up, I worried about hearing trains. But Fleur wore hobnail boots with flattened cans nailed upon the toes. Those slats of metal vibrated to signal a train's approach, and Fleur had time to lift the cart off and trundle it to one side.

I didn't know where we were going, didn't care. We passed

farms, some near the tracks, some far, and each time Fleur took the cart off and dragged it overland or down a road until we reached the yard. You would have thought dogs would worry her, farmers would lock their doors. But outside each yard the dogs met us eagerly. Next came the children, clutching nickels, to get the first look. Then the women appeared, hesitating, faces flushed with steam, hands raw from the laundry, feet aching. Fleur showed them buffalo-horn buttons, twinned geese in an agate, a brooch made of claws. At last, the men arrived for ax heads and lengths of twine. Fleur's customers were wary and approached her with a hint of fear, as if she were a witch or maybe a saint cast off to wander.

And they looked at me, Fleur's captive in every way, shamefully dependent on her. I don't know what they saw. A stick boy. A poor fool.

Sometimes we stayed in a tool shed or barn, and once a man with lumps on his neck big as goose eggs invited us to sleep in his dead wife's parlor. We never stayed more than one night anywhere. At dawn Fleur packed the wagon piece by piece, with me on top. She put her head in the collar, and pulled me along the track.

Between farms, I had plenty of time to think, and sometimes the first few days I took out my knife with the mother-of-pearl handle. Holding it tight, I could see my mother sweeping the floor with short, bored strokes or pinning her hair up. When she did that she hardly looked in the mirror. I saw the milky white underside of her arms, the little frown by which she clenched pins in her mouth, her fingers precisely stabbing. I longed for her then and I let myself cry, beneath Fleur's umbrella. It wasn't long, though, before I tired of weeping and began inventing scenes of my mother that gave me more pleasure. For instance, her suffering when we finally met again and I ignored her, turning a marble cheek. Or the shock with which she tried to comprehend my cruelty.

52

"I shall never forgive you," I murmured, out loud sometimes to increase the thrill.

But as my fantasies grew harsher, she began to sob in my pictures, to pound her fists into her mattress, scratch her smooth skin, and even to tear out her hair by the handful, until at length I was frightened by the violence of her shame and sorrow. I began to believe, then, that she hadn't really abandoned me. It came to me quite naturally that the man in the white sweater, leather helmet, orange gold scarf had stolen her off against her will.

I realized this one day when we had stopped to let a train pass by. I thought of the way my mother's lips had grazed mine before she thrust her arm up, to offer her money for a plane ride with the skinny barnstormer. Her lips were cold, in spite of the full sun. Her jaw was clenched. She had never gone up in a plane before and she must have been afraid. Although her gesture was bold, her smile, as she tendered the bill from her purse, was too bright, too hollow. An adventure to break the tedium was all she'd wanted. Her fear and the cool kiss proved it. Naturally, Omar had been taken with her, had fallen in love with her when she offered the bill, had then secretly planned not to bring her back but to keep on flying no matter how she pleaded, how loud her cries rang above the engine.

Even now, as I sat with Fleur in the wind of approaching trains, my mother was captive to that man.

I would save her. Once I could walk I'd hunt him down. One morning I would stand at his door. He'd appear, wiping soap from his chest, and with no warning I'd strike. I killed the pilot many times and in many ways as we traveled. Always, at the end of each episode, my mother rushed to me over his dead body. She held me close, and when she kissed me her lips were lingering and warm.

I suppose it was a week or two before we got to the reservation where Fleur lived. We traveled not more than a mile or two each day, because the farms were spread evenly along the route and

53

required detours. During that time, the wind seared my face. The rain hardened my skin. If it was cold at night or drizzly, Fleur rolled me in a mound of blankets and oilcloths. Sometimes, by morning, I was rolled up tight and warm next to her, close but never quite touching her skin. I think I could have gone on living endlessly under her protection, but then, suddenly, we got where we were going.

One day Fleur left the track and we began down two ox-trail ruts, passing out of farm country and into open prairie. It was a long time before there were any houses. We began to visit low cabins of mud-mortared logs, inhabited by Chippewa or fiercer-looking French-Indians with stringy black beards and long moustaches. There were board houses, too, with wells, barns, and neat screen doors that whined open when we approached. The women who came out of these doors wore housedresses and had their hair cut, curled, and bound in flimsy nets. They were not like Fleur, but all the same they were Indians and spoke a flowing language to each other.

After a few days of walking the paths deeper into the small hills, we came to a settlement. It wasn't much. A few board houses and two larger buildings that looked like schools or offices. We headed up a winding road to a church. Fleur left her cart at the bottom of the hill and carried me in her arms straight up to the back door of a whitewashed house.

"What's this!" cried a nun who opened the door. She was fat and mild and very clean looking. I smelled so bad that she covered her mouth with her hand.

Fleur continued to hold me like an offering. No explanation. And after a while the nun opened the door wider and gestured us in. She rang a small bell near the entryway, and several of her sisters gathered.

"She picked me up," I said. "I fell off the westbound train."

They peered at me with round eyes, then turned and held a conference as to whether I would stay or not, whether they should

54

fetch their Superior or the priests, whether or not I was an Indian, or dangerous. As it happened, their talk was useless, for even while they hissed and murmured Fleur bent over, laid me in a heap on their polished linoleum, and walked back out the door.

I'd been cast off so many times that by then it didn't matter. It occurred to me while I was sitting on the floor that the three things I'd done on my own had caused my life to go from bad to worse. These were, first, hopping the train back out of Argus, then Giles Saint Ambrose and finally jumping off the boxcar. I'd ended up completely helpless. So this time I simply sat still until the next person took charge of me. I did not resist sleeping on a pallet in the broom closet of the priest's house and then drudging in the churchyard when I was finally healed. I went along when the nuns found the money to send me back to Minneapolis, where other members of their order met the train and then walked me back full circle, beneath the red banner of Saint Jerome's, past the trees that had been strung with colored lights for the Orphans' Picnic, around the grandstand, and still farther, to the large brick orphanage with many doors and windows where I spent the next year before I entered the seminary.

I had a great talent for obedience. I was in love with the picture of myself in a slim black cassock, and felt that the green lawns of the seminary and white brick of the chapels set me off to good advantage. While I walked the grounds, reading my daily lessons, I was exposed to many eyes. Between the lines of sacred texts, I rendezvoused with thin hard hoboes who had slept in the bushes. Ghostly, rank in their own sweat and travel dust, they saw me as a pure black flame. They could not resist me. I always knew that if I kept my eyes moving strictly down the page of print, if I paused in the darkest corners of the landscape, if I closed my eyes as if in communion with someone greater, they would come. They would force me to worship them like an animal. I would fall. I would burn and burn until by grace I was consumed.

Aerial View of Argus

One day Aunt Fritzie invited Mary into her office, where the black and gold safe was kept, where ledgers filled six shelves and white tape from the adding machine curled like spindrift across the floor. The long strips tangled around Mary's ankles when she sat down next to the gray steel desk. Fritzie rummaged in the drawers and pulled out clips, paper, more adding tape. A stand-up ashtray was handy at one elbow; a radio hummed in the oak cabinet above her head. The plants that grew in Aunt Fritzie's office had leaves flat as dollar bills and never needed water. The fluorescent lights she turned on at night buzzed and snapped and attracted soft brown moths.

This office was Mary's favorite place. Already she had decided that when she was in high school, she would learn how to keep books like Aunt Fritzie. She wanted to sit among the dry plants on cold nights and work with numbers. On one night at the end of every month, when Fritzie sent the bills out, Mary fell asleep to the soothing *tick*, *tick*, *whirr* of Aunt Fritzie's fingers on the adding machine keys.

"I guesss you're old enough to figure this out for yourself," said Aunt Fritzie now. She had found what she was looking for and handed the card to Mary. It was a postcard. Mary observed the picture carefully before turning it over. On the front, a man in a formal suit was photographed standing in the branches of a tree. *The largest Live-oak in So. Jacksonville, Fla.* was written in ornate green script below him. On the back of the card there was a short message.

> **I am living down here. I think about the children every day. How are they? Adelaide.**

56

Mary glanced up in time to catch the way Aunt Fritzie blew the smoke out, in two thin streams of contempt. Then she looked down at the card again. Fritzie was waiting for a reaction, but Mary didn't feel anything in particular.

"Well," said Aunt Fritzie, "what are you going to do?"

In Aunt Fritzie's loud voice, Mary heard a conspirator. Fritzie was Adelaide's only sister, after all. Adelaide had abandoned her too.

"I don't know yet," said Mary.

"Of course not," said Fritzie. She put out her cigarette with one harsh stab. "I'd like to horsewhip her."

Mary pulled a dead leaf off the plant that crowded the window.

"Write her back if you want, she's your mother. But I washed my hands of Adelaide when you walked in the door."

Mary stole a look at Aunt Fritzie's expression. But Aunt Fritzie caught her eyes and Mary couldn't break free.

"Don't go back to her, is all I ask," said Fritzie.

Something like a tight band in Mary's chest snapped and she laughed, a sudden awkward bray of intense relief that embarrassed her.

"Fat chance," she said. "you're more a mother to me."

Fritzie fumbled another cigarette from her pack. Her yellow skin flushed golden and she squinted at her automatic lighter. "Why don't I quit? These things are killing me."

"They stink too," said Mary.

"That's according to Sita."

Mary laughed.

"After this pack," Aunt Fritzie promised.

"After this pack," Mary agreed.

Aunt Fritzie picked up a green pen labeled KOZKA'S FOR THE FINEST IN MEAT PRODUCTS and started paging through her bound ledger. Mary shook the curls of paper away from her ankles.

"I'll take this," Mary said, holding up the postcard, and then she left.

Mary didn't think specifically about the postcard, but it was there in the back of her mind all the next few weeks, and sometimes she would find herself addressing long imaginary letters, full of hatred and grief, to Adelaide. Then one day she answered her mother's postcard with one that she chose almost unthinkingly from the rack at the corner drugstore. *Aerial View of Argus, North Dakota* it said on the front. Argus's brown dots of buildings, bare streets, and puffs of green trees were surrounded by a patchwork of dull brown fields. What she wrote on the back of the card surprised Mary as much as it would have surprised and gratified Aunt Fritzie, whose name and style of handwriting she carefully copied.

All three of your children starved dead, Mary wrote.

She addressed the card and walked down to the post office with it in her hands. She bought a stamp, licked it, and placed it in the upper right-hand corner. When her fingers released the card into the mail slot she thought that she felt nothing. But that night, the last night of the month, as she was falling asleep to Aunt Fritzie's adding machine, she imagined that she saw the postcard alight in her mother's hands. Adelaide stared down and examined each detail of the picture, but although she searched the fine marks, she could not see her daughter, who was too small to tell of, looking directly through her, not dead but securely hidden in the aerial view.

Mary's postcard, forwarded through two addresses and held for several weeks at the booking agency that handled The Great Omar, came into Omar's hands just after the accident. He put it in his pocket and would have forgotten about it except that, in the hospital watching Adelaide, he had nothing to distract himself. And so he painfully extracted the card with his burnt hands, looked at it several times, and put it back.

Omar tried not to move much and took shallow breaths, his face white from the pain of his bound ribs, his shattered leg splinted from the hip. Only his eyes moved, from the peak of Adelaide's feet under the hospital sheet, to the curve of her wrist, to the stern plane of her left cheekbone and back again. There was a small window over her head, a patch of Florida indigo. The day was sweltering. Just behind the rubbery curtain someone groaned, and farther down the ward water gushed on and on until he wondered if any could be left. He opened his mouth, tried to speak, but he rarely knew what to say to Adelaide when she was alive, and now that she was so near death he felt even less sure of himself.

He couldn't even touch her. His hands were puffy soft clubs, bound in lengths of gauze. During the accident, sparks had jumped from the controls but he had not taken his hands away. He'd screamed while everything was happening, but Adelaide had not, that he could remember, and now he could imagine that she'd sat beside him, ice cold as he tried to arrest their plunge.

He had, remarkably, brought them to earth and avoided a total crack-up, although what happened was bad enough. They had been flying a county fair, so there were plenty of people to run for doctors, ice, splints, bandages, stretchers, and salts. He remembered the commotion and, above it, the roaring of the alligator wrestlers, the tinny twinkling of some Ferris wheel tune. He'd called Adelaide's name, but the eyes of the strangers who held him were wide with excitement and told him nothing.

He still didn't know how badly she was hurt, or whether she'd wake up sound in the mind or whether she'd wake up at all. He didn't know it would turn out that her injuries were far less serious

59

than they seemed, or that she would carry one scar only, at the nape of her neck, while he would live on with pains in his knees and a rolling limp. He thought that any moment could easily be her last and he would never know it.

A nurse strode in, clanged a few pans, and withdrew. On the other side of the curtain the groans changed to a low and monotonous curse. Adelaide's hand trembled. Omar almost called the nurse back, then stopped himself, afraid the shaking might signal some turn for the worse. He kept watch. It was a shock to him when she spoke.

"I've got to send Mary a sewing machine," said Adelaide.

Her voice came from the unseen area beyond her cheekbone, drifted down over Omar, and drew him. He leaned over to her.

"If Mary learns how to sew, she'll always have a skill to fall back on."

Her lips were pursed in the practical frown Omar knew from the evenings when she counted money, the day's take, and decided how much for the room, whether they'd eat high or low, and what they'd put aside for repairs and gas. Adelaide was good at this. Since she had joined him they not only managed to have enough but some left over, which she kept in her winter account and would not let him withdraw.

Omar reached toward Adelaide. He gasped at the stab in his ribs, but she didn't seem to notice him anyway.

"Look at me," he said.

Her gray-blue eyes focused on the wall, her lovely eyebrows drew imperiously together.

"There's enough money saved for a Singer," she said.

Then she shut her eyes. It was real sleep this time. She frowned as if daring anyone to wake her up. Omar moved away, disturbed and jealous. Adelaide almost never talked about her children or her life before him.

Flies threw themselves busily against the screened blue. The

60

air was close. Omar didn't like to think that while Adelaide was sleeping now it might be Mary, or that other one, a boy, that she dreamed of and not him. He'd never had the slightest doubt about her before. He was proud that she'd left her children and her whole life, which he gathered had been comfortable from her fine clothes and jewelry, for a bootlegger with nothing to his name but a yellow scarf and an airplane held together with baling wire.

Now the airplane was painted, in the repair shop even now, and his name was known on the circuit. He didn't drink, either.

Thanks to her, he thought. Her hand was still. He watched it for a sign of weakness that did not come. Her knuckles pinked, as if she had been knocking on a door. She made a fist and began to tighten it over and over. Omar felt his throat shut, even though she was just squeezing air.

He sat with Adelaide until he fully understood that she was out of danger. Then he got to his feet, took the card from Argus out of his pocket, and propped it on the wood nightstand where she would see it.

PART TWO

MARY ADARE

AFTER THE MIRACULOUS sheets of black ice came the floods, stranding boards and snaky knots of debris high in the branches, leaving brown leeches to dry like raisins on the sidewalks when the water receded, and leaving the smell of river mud, a rotten sweetness, in the backyards and gutters. Long into the drought there would be evidence of how far up the river had come: oddities like snails in the wet straw of the stock pens, and the moldy ring halfway up the wall of Pete's garage. The pipes clogged with sewage and backed up all that summer, letting off a sharp ammonia that gave Sita terrible headaches. She spent days lying perfectly still in our darkened bedroom, with her head packed in ice.

For a while I was still the girl who had caused the miracle, an attraction to customers and neighbors who stopped to touch me, holding their fingers out as if my body was filled with divine electricity. I wished it was. I wished something else unusual would happen. But nothing special came of their touching, no luck at cards or last-ditch cures, no sudden grace. There were no spectacular side effects to anything I did. And so the touching stopped. I became an ordinary girl again, and maybe something worse than that, in the town's eye, as years went by.

I was never much for looks, and I saw that right off. My face was broad and pale, not homely, but simply unremarkable, except for the color of my eyes. That was the feature I liked best about myself. My eyes turned a light brown almost yellow, and I had no eyebrows to detract from the effect. They never grew back after the accident with the slide. My hair stayed thin, black as tar. Although I washed it, like Sita, in beer and eggs, it could only be worn lank or tied in two pencil braids. For years I used Sita's hand-me-downs, let out at the seams and shortened. Then I dressed to suit myself. But by that time I couldn't have cared less. So what if I smelled like white pepper from the sausage table? So what if I was plain? At least I had the shop, Pete and Fritzie, and Celestine, although sometimes even she wearied of my blunt ways.

I said things too suddenly. I was pigheaded, bitter, moody, and had fits of unreasonable anger. Things I said came out wrong, even if I thought first. All through school it bothered me when other children turned away, or just looked shocked when I spoke. I don't apologize, and there's really no excuse, but what happened in the Minneapolis grandstand, the boxcar, and on the playground in Argus had affected me, set me above the rest in my differentness. I had perspective. Sometimes before sleep I looked down from my bed and saw Argus as in the postcard view I sent to my mother. It was small, a simple crosshatch of lines on the earth, nothing that an ice age or perhaps even another harsh flood could not erase.

As the town around me ceased to matter, though, Celestine mattered more. And Pete and Fritzie too, even Sita, although I was less important to her. We never actually liked one another, only grew in tolerance and became accustomed to each other's presence in the way only people who sleep in the same room can. Night after night we blended and fought in dreams. Vibrations left our minds and hung trembling about us. By morning, our ghostly selves had made peace.

So maybe I was closer to Sita than I ever was to Celestine, even though by daylight I couldn't stand Sita's careful slenderness and practiced voice, her way of turning with an eyebrow raised and trying to shut me up, her thin mouth that she painted and blotted a dozen times while waiting for customers. I couldn't stand her. I felt relieved when Celestine came by the shop. She had quit school before she was half finished and taken a job with the telephone company. This job made her seem older, but there was still an ease between us.

Celestine looked good in those days, big and lean. She wore tailored suits instead of dresses and carried a leather shoulderbag. Striding into the kitchen, she was handsome like a man. Her voice was low and penetrating and she smoked Viceroys like Fritzie. We sat and complained about her boss and read V-mail. Leaving, she would light a last cigarette and smoke it halfway down before she got into Russell's car. The cigarette dangled from her lips as she pulled out.

I kept hoping I would get some of Celestine's height. But I stopped growing at eighteen, still short. For a while I was depressed to realize that as long as I ran the shop I would have to look through, not over, the lighted case at customers.

The shop was my perfect home. The house was built on one level. The floors were cast of concrete with hot-water pipes running through them for warmth. The thick walls were finished off with stucco, painted a smooth glossy white. Because so many of the doorways were rounded, the place seemed like a cave carved out of a hillside. The light fell green and watery through thick glass window-blocks except in the kitchen where the screen door let through a blast of sun. Customers came back there to talk. Across Fritzie's garden and the wide yard, they could watch cows and sheep moving in the darkness of the stockpens, half visible between the heavy rail ties.

Pete brought links of his sausages in for them to taste, and they ate them with soda crackers or soft white bread, comparing the summer sausage and the beerwurst and the Swedish. They were heavy people, Germans and Poles or Scandinavians, rough handed and full of opinions, delicate biters, because their teeth hurt or plates did not fit well. Grizzled hairs sprouted from surprising places upon them. Their hands were misshapen and calloused. Their light eyes did not shift nor their conversation falter when they happened to look up, on a slaughtering day perhaps, to see a pig penned in the killing chute, having its throat cut.

Sometimes I waited on customers. But more often, Fritzie and I cut meat or ground it or spiced it in the big room. Sita refused to do much more than help out when back orders pressed. On the day everything changed, when I was still eighteen, I was at the steel-plate table cubing stew meat and Fritzie was standing at the big electric saw. I might have heard some sound she made under the saw's shrill whine, or perhaps I just felt it. Anyway I turned as she was falling to her knees. Beet red and choking, she pounded the floor for air while I pounded her, but not enough air came and she slumped, unconscious, dragging only an occasional shuddering breath to let us know she was still alive.

What struck me then, suddenly, as Pete carried her out the door to the ambulance that saved her life, was the frailty of her body once she wasn't there to move it. She was a stick figure, cartoon thin and broken in Pete's arms. Later that night, at the hospital, when she was sealed in a tent of oxygen, and alert, I sat beside her and watched her fingers trace the hem on the sheet. In that gesture I saw everything. Her wonder, her awareness of the texture of the thin material, her surprise that she wasn't dead after all.

When Fritzie came home she stopped smoking for good. She sat at the kitchen table, in the light from the screen door, chewing gum, sucking sourballs, nibbling buttered toast. After a few tobaccoless, idle months, her face bloomed from acid yellow, to peach, to rose. She gained weight and let her hair grow from the peroxide bleach to brown. She had been hard, one track, always someone to reckon with, but now she softened. Overnight she became a stout woman of no particular menace. She began to feel that she'd neglected her girls, and took up crocheting some afghans she had started when she was young. The old blocks were faded, the tint in the yarn was dull, but she surrounded them with blazing colors and then branched off in ever more complicated efforts. Piles of patterned wools collected at her feet.

"You keep these in your hope chest," she told me one afternoon.

"I don't have one," I said.

So Sita got the afghans, but I didn't care. I was going to need a lot more than afghans. Even then I knew that the shape of my life was to be no tunnel of love in darkness, no open field.

I did not choose solitude. Who would? It came on me like a kind of vocation, demanding an effort that married women can't picture. Sometimes, even now, I look on the married girls the way a wild dog might look through the window at tame ones, envying the regularity of their lives but also despising the low pleasure they get from the master's touch. I was only tempted once, but that was to romance. Marriage would not have been a comfort with Russell Kashpaw, or likely even possible. He was not the type to marry, even in the years he was able.

It began the second time he came home from a war, from Korea, on the night Celestine got the news that her brother was wounded in action. She came by the house late, tapping at my window until I woke up. Although Sita didn't make a sound, I sensed her building up an insomniac fury in the dark. So I signaled Celestine to the kitchen door. I let her in, and when she showed me the news about Russell I went straight to the cupboard. I chose the thickest of Pete's little shot glasses and poured us a whiskey. We drank the first one quick, the next slow, and then we went outside to smoke underneath the cold white stars. The shock wore off after some time, and she came back down to earth.

He would recuperate. We got the news of it soon after. I sent a get-well card to his hospital address in Virginia. *We'll see you soon in Argus*, my note said. Nothing personal. Still I expected an answer, even a message through Celestine. But the thing about Russell was he had no manners or consideration. Having gone through high school as a football star, then having hit the big time with the war, he was even more socially backward than I was. Before I knew this, though, I thought he would come by the shop when he first got home. But nothing, not a word, not a hello or kiss my foot, only rumor that he'd taken a good bank-clerk job Argus National had offered him as a returning home-town hero, even though he was an Indian.

The first time I saw Russell after he returned was on the muggy summer day I went over to deposit the week's total. I knew I might run into him but hadn't yet pictured him as changed. I still imagined the same bull-chested boy with the soft voice, teasing eyes, the shaggy hair.

The air was humid, the sky hung low, but the lobby of the bank was cool. A procession of veined green marble, brass, and velvet ropes led to his cage. I paused before I walked it, and let the fans beat down.

He recognized me when I finally stood before him. "I got your card," he said.

"It's about time," I answered.

That was all. He took my canvas money bag, and then I looked straight at him and stood rooted in surprise. The scars stretched up his cheeks like claw marks, angry and long, even running past his temples and parting his hair crooked. I could see that they went downward, too, mapping him below. He counted my money. The sight of him embarrassed me, not because he was ugly, but just the opposite. Scarred, his face took on an unsettling dark grandeur. He was richly carved and compelling in those terrible wounds. I looked down. But even there I was not safe. Russell's hands were thin and muscular, softening from mechanic's into banker's, and on one finger he wore a pink rubber cap.

He used that capped finger to press the bills up so that he could count them swiftly. I couldn't tear my gaze away.

"Here's your receipt," he said, breaking the spell.

I left in a daze at myself. I didn't even say good-bye.

All right, I thought, I am in love with the half brother of my best friend, Celestine. Or at least I am in love with his scars and the rubber cap on his finger.

So I decided to get to know Russell.

One day I told Celestine to bring him by for dinner.

"How come?" she asked.

"He's your brother," I said.

"Well, he won't," she told me.

"He can suit himself." I wouldn't show it meant something. But Celestine caught on.

"I'll try and convince him," she promised.

When Russell came to dinner, he was hardly even civil. He spent the whole time staring out the door, straight past me, at the stockpens and the heavy barred gates. The pens were empty, but he watched them anyway. Several times I turned in spite of myself and glanced across the yard. He seemed to make Pete uncomfortable, too. A heavy silence fell at the table and Pete finally left. He went back to the utility room, where we soon heard him tinkering with and cursing his broken motors.

The rest of us, Celestine, Sita, Fritzie, Russell, and myself went out back to sit in the wood-slat and cedar chairs Pete had built so that Fritzie could lounge in the open with visitors. I made a pitcher of cold whiskey sour. The four of us women talked easily, our glasses cooling our fingers, but our talk was like waves that washed in to break on Russell's silence. He sat there, like a stiff, as the last of the sun burned the weeds beyond the smokehouse.

71

"You're a real ball of fire," I said to him, annoyed.

He looked at me for the first time that night. I'd drawn my eyebrows on for the evening in brown pencil. I'd carefully pinned my braids up and worn a black chiffon scarf to set off my one remarkable feature, yellow cat eyes, which did their best to coax him. But I don't know coaxing from a box lunch.

Russell turned, unaffected by any of my charms, and looked at Sita in a way that I was meant to see. I understood that if he was going to think that way of anyone, it was her. She had been talking more than usual and had a rare color in her cheeks. Her hair washed down her neck in a clean shining sweep. But when she saw that Russell Kashpaw was looking at her, she tipped her head away and her red lips tightened. She pulled a white hankie from her sleeve, turned a cold cheek, and let him know that Sita Kozka was off limits to his type.

I suppose most girls who had set their cap for a man would have despised him for looking at another, but I was different. It was Sita whom I wanted to kill.

"I'm going to tell your fortune," I said, leaning toward her, brushing her pale arm. "I'll get the deck."

Fortune-telling was a pastime that Sita hated herself for loving. It never failed. She always always tried to look disgusted, as if telling the future was the most low-class idea in the world, but then she bent, spellbound, to the cards as they were laid out. She bit her lips but could not refuse a small glimpse into the beyond. So I walked inside and got a deck from the kitchen drawer. Then I laid the cards out one by one on the broad arm of her chair.

"There's the jack of hearts," I said, "and here's a deuce. What's this?" I paused. She had drawn the queen of spades.

"What's it mean?" Sita flushed in helpless shame at her curiosity. I sat straight up in my chair and took a long drink of whiskey sour.

"Well?" asked Sita.

"Well," I said flatly.

"*Come on*," she said.

I hesitated, took another drink, shook my head until she fidgeted.

"I hope you like Buicks," was my only comment.

"For Godsakes!" Now Sita was ready to explode. Celestine hated arguments, so she got up and walked into the shop to get more ice. Russell craned to see the cards. Sita stood and ordered me to tell her. "What's the matter, run out of miracles?"

"Sit back down," I said. "You should be sitting when you hear this." She sat. I told her. "I hope you like Buicks, because I see that you'll be riding in a Buick on the day you croak."

Her mouth opened. She made a hoarse little furious sound and struck all the cards off the end of her chair. "Dry up like a prune," she shouted.

"You girls give each other such a hard time," observed Fritzie. Her face was mildly bored. She was used to us pecking at one another, but Russell wasn't.

"So," he said. "Sita will be riding in a Buick. What about me?"

He picked the cards up off the grass and put them in my hands. He couldn't help but smile when, all business now, I slapped the cards down on the arm of his chair. When they were all laid out he studied them in silence, along with me. Celestine came through the door with a big red plastic bowl of ice in her hands.

"What did I miss?" she asked.

"Tales of doom," Fritzie said.

"You're always telling someone they're going to die or get mangled or divorced." Celestine settled next to Fritzie, lit a Viceroy, and breathed thick blue smoke. "Why don't you ever predict something good? For instance, here's Russell, home safe. Why don't you predict something good like that?"

73

"What's there?" Russell said.

"A woman," I answered, looking straight into his eyes.

"Only one?" Celestine said, then caught herself, remembering how I'd wanted Russell to come out to dinner, I suppose. She moved abruptly, dropping ice in everybody's glass to shut herself up.

"Whoever she is," said Russell, "I know one thing."

"What's that?" I said.

"I'm not going to marry her," he answered.

The bottom fell out for a moment, but then I recovered. I got my wits back.

"That's right," I said, "you're not. But you're going to owe her a lot of money."

"I am?" He looked distressed.

"See what I mean?" Celestine settled back. "Why can't you ever predict something good?"

"This is good," I insisted, raking the cards up. "He'll pay through the shorts."

Russell started to laugh. He was getting loose on the whiskey sours. All of us, even Sita, were beginning to feel disconnected and bumbling. We laughed easily now over nothing and hardly even noticed the mosquitoes that swarmed us as the sun went down.

"Light the citronella candle," Fritzie said at one point. But no one paid any attention until she said it louder. That was why there must have been some light, enough to see by. Maybe it was me who lit the yellow candles in their buckets; I don't remember. But I haven't forgotten what came after, when Russell pulled his shirt up high, on a dare from Sita, and showed us his hidden scars.

I got up and went over to see them closer. I bent until I felt his warmth. The wounds had been so deep that he was ridged like a gullied field. His chest had been plowed like a tractor gone haywire. I reached out. He said nothing, and so I touched him.

And then everyone was silent with drunk surprise.

"God she's fresh!" said Sita, upsetting the quiet in a shrill and disapproving voice.

Russell shifted beneath my hands, and when I still didn't move them he took them off gently and folded them together.

"Bless you, my child," he said, so that we all laughed. I shook my head to clear it, but the shaking only set my teeth on edge. I went to bed soon afterward, and fell into a deadening sleep.

I was exhausted when I woke, thick and swollen with unknown dreams, but I was cured, as though a fever had burned off. One thought was clear. I would never go out of my way for romance again. Romance would have to go out of its way for me.

Pete and Fritzie sent away for brochures from the chamber-of-commerce departments of cities like Phoenix and El Paso. The doctor said that Fritzie's lungs needed dry warmth, a desert climate, and she shouldn't undergo even one more Dakota winter. So all of a sudden Pete was making plans to send her south, but then, once she put her foot down and refused to go alone, he included himself. This all happened without the benefit of any discussion over what would become of the shop, or of Sita, or me.

So I sat down with Fritzie one day. She was making something out of plum-colored bits of yarn. Because of her, I had taken up crocheting now and then myself. But I didn't find it relaxing. I pulled the yarn so hard it broke, and the things I made ended up as tight useless lumps.

"I've got to ask you something," I said, "about the shop. Are you selling it when you go down south?"

She was surprised, enough to pull a stitch. "We thought you'd run it," she told me.

"I will then," I answered. And that was settled, although the complicated part of it was not. "But Sita," I wondered. "What will she do?"

Fritzie frowned into the purple network she was slowly enlarging. "Sita could run the grocery section," she said. "She could help if she wanted to." Both of us knew Sita wasn't interested in the shop. I knew more. She hated it, in fact, and wanted only to move down to Fargo and live by herself in a modern apartment, and model clothes for DeLendrecies. She imagined that she would also work behind the men's hat counter. There she would meet a young rising professional. They would marry. He would buy her a house near the county courthouse, on the street of railroad mansions not far from Island Park. Every winter she would walk down the hill to skate. She would wear powder blue tights and a short dress with puffs of rabbit fur at the sleeves, collar, and all around a flared hem that would lift as she twirled. I knew all of this because, on an evening of friendliness, Sita had told me it was her dream.

"Sita wants to go to Fargo," I told Fritzie, "and work in a department store."

Fritzie nodded and said, "She might as well."

So that was how it happened that fall. Sita made plans to move to Fargo. Fritzie and Pete packed all of the suitcases and trunks that they owned for the trip. I did nothing special. In fact, the only way I can account for Sita's last night is that I did the most customary thing that day. I washed down steel tables in the preparations room with the same strong milky cleaning solvent that we always used. But maybe it was an odd batch that affected my hands.

Whatever it was, Sita was upset by the incident to the point that she never speaks of it. Perhaps she pretends it never happened. I don't know anything about Sita's mental habits anymore, not since she moved to Blue Mound and stopped communicating with us all. But that night we went to sleep in our twin beds as

76

usual. Sita liked the curtains shut tightly. I wanted them open for moonlight. But as always, since it was her room, she got her way. The old furnace at the end of the hall woke me in the middle of the night. It came to life with a wild and throbbing complaint that no one ever noticed in the day. It often woke Sita too. I kept my eyes shut because I knew what the noise was, and tried to let myself drift off again. That wasn't Sita's habit. She awakened and lay with teeth clenched, arms rigid, praying for sleep to take her but at the same time too maddened to let it happen. I usually slept all the better, sensing her alert watch in the dark. But that night I did not drift off again, because she spoke.

"My dear God, my dear God," she said in a pinched little voice. "Mary, I know you're awake."

I heard the tense undertone, but I sighed as if falling to a deeper level in my dreams. She'd probably heard a mouse behind the walls, or thought of some drastic mix-up she'd made in managing her boyfriends during this important move. Or maybe it was her hair. She'd suddenly realized the tight new wave she'd got to impress the manager of DeLendrecies, the curly bangs, the slight yet bold tint job, was wrong for her shape of face.

But it was none of these.

"Mary," she shrilled, "WAKE UP."

So I opened my eyes. The room was half lit. I thought at first that she had left the curtains open, but the light in the room was coming from me, or from my hands, to be entirely exact. They glowed with a dead blue radiance.

I lifted them in wonder. The light began to weaken and fade. I shook them, and for a moment they pulsed brightly, as if there had been a loose connection. Then they dimmed no matter what I did until the room was pitch dark again. Only when their light was put out did Sita dare jump from bed, hop to the end of the room, and throw the switch. He teeth clicked together in fear.

"I'm so goddamn glad I'm getting out of here," she whispered.

She stepped back into the room just long enough to pull the blankets off her bed, and she slept the rest of the night on the living room couch. As for me, for once I caught Sita's insomnia and lay awake.

After a long while, the thickly curtained windows went light gray and I heard Pete get up to switch off the yard light and let the dogs out. Soon, when they'd left for Arizona, I'd be up at Pete's hours, doing just as he did, making the rounds to assure myself that the temperatures were proper in the freezers and the smoke rooms, that the safe was still locked, that the back door was open for Canute, who started work at seven, and that coffee was boiling for the men who came in later.

I imagined myself doing all that Pete did, alone in the early stillness, and again at night when the stillness was blue-black. I'd go around to rattle each door lock, pull down the front blinds, check the thermostat and gauges. When it came to running the shop in the daylight, I'd do a few things differently too, like change the front sign, put an add in the *Sentinel* now and then, plus more pepper in the blood sausage. I'd change this very room, sleep with the curtains open if I wanted, or throw the damn curtains out. To hell with the full-length mirror and the wishing-well lamp. Sita could take them, the way she'd already taken Adelaide's blue velvet box. I'd seen her hide it in her suitcase.

After she left I missed Sita more than I thought I would. For weeks I slept fitfully and woke, disturbed by the absence of her level breathing, often overwhelmed by my own dreams. They became too real now that there was no one to distract my sleeping mind. I passed some nights caught in blizzards, or startling orchards, or cramped in the cages of small animals.

One dream in particular I had for months running. I walked into a rickety wooden house, no place I had ever lived in, but

78

one I knew. Inside, there were many small empty rooms, some hidden deep in the interior. I wandered through the whole place, never lost but never quite certain of where I was until I came to the room I recognized, the room where I would wait for him. It was always the same. I entered this last room carefully. The floor creaked as I stepped over the threshold and edged along the whitewashed and peeling wall. This room was stark and windowless, but full of flimsy doors that opened out in each direction.

Always, when he entered, I was certain that the floor would break beneath him. It gave as he walked toward me, but even when he reached for me, stepping down heavily, nothing snapped. His lips were deep and curved. His eyes were the same burnt-butter brown as his hair, and his horns branched like a young buck's.

I grew impatient for him, for the way he bent toward me, breathing eagerly, for his long smooth thighs and for the sound of the doors that never fitted their frames, tapping back and forth as we moved.

The Orphans' Picnic

Karl walked quickly through the wrought-iron gate onto the fair-grounds, and then stopped at the edge of the crowd. He was waiting to be seen. They were all here. Fathers Mullen and Bonaventure. Sisters Ivalo, Mary Thomas, Ursula, and George. As always, each presided over a game, cakewalk, a table for knitting or white elephants. Each was busy taking tickets or making change from a cigar box. When they failed to recognize him immediately, Karl bought a lemonade and sat down in their plain view.

He lounged for a good half an hour, shifting his feet in the dry spring grass, smoking one heavy cigarette after another and crushing them out on the metal frame of his chair. His black hair gleamed like shoe leather, and his teeth were very white. He made a lot of easy sales to women and had come up in the world. The new clothes, he thought, and the thick wad of dollar bills would throw the priests off. The truth was he'd turned out worse than their wildest dreams.

"Step up! Step up! You there in the gangster suit!"

Someone laughed. Karl turned. It was a chubby redheaded seminarian running the nearest booth, a fishing booth. With one quick glance Karl dismissed him as unattractive. He knew the type: cheerfully pious and self-important, a raffler of door prizes, a shiner of the priests' shoes.

"Help out the orphans," the boy grinned. His creamy white neck bulged in the tight collar of his cassock. He was about sixteen. His eyes were long lashed, like Karl's, but they were a deep, sweet hazel color. His hair, dark red and springy, curled back from his forehead in a way that struck Karl, suddenly, as familiar. It was just like Adelaide's. Karl frowned at the coincidence. There was more too, once he looked. The marble skin. The pointed cheekbones. The arch of the boy's black eyebrows was picture perfect. He was a ringer except for the baby fat. He was almost too much like her.

Karl's face went numb. The memories of this place jolted him. He sat not twenty feet from the spot where Adelaide had flown away, and again he saw the luminous sky into which Omar's plane vanished. He heard his tiny brother's loud relentless cries.

The young man who stole the baby must have lived in the neighborhood. He must have come to the Picnic because he was a Catholic. He would have raised his son a Catholic too, and the boy would probably have been a day student at Saint Jerome's.

Karl took a dollar from his roll and stood up.

The boy's smile sharpened when Karl approached with money in his hand.

"Fish today, sir? Three chances for a quarter."

Karl put the bill down.

"What's your name?" he said.

"Jude Miller," said the boy. "How many chances?"

"How many have you got?"

Jude attached a basket to a hook and dropped it over a wall painted with blue waves.

"Fishy fishy in the brook," he began in a practiced drone, "come and nibble on my hook."

"Cut that," said Karl.

Jude was flustered. "I have to tell Sister what prize to give you, sir, boy's or girl's. It's in the rhyme." He jumped to tug the basket back over the wall. It already held the prize, a small picture of a juicy-looking sacred heart.

"Throw it back, it's too small," said Karl.

The boy gripped the basket stupidly. "But it's a holy card."

"It's a piece of crap," Karl said. "I expect something better for my money."

At the mention of money, Jude closed the lid of his cigar box.

"Aren't you a Catholic?" he asked.

Karl looked down. A creamy white owl guarded the bills and small change. Jude's long-fingered, quick, fat hands rested protectively on either side. Karl decided that he disliked his brother as intensely now as he had long ago.

"You're a piece of crap too," said Karl.

Jude Miller looked wildly around for help. He was penned in the booth. "Step right up!" he called to a woman and child who passed near. He craned around Karl to attract them, but they continued toward the midway with only a smiling glance. The priests and nuns paid him no attention either. He turned and knocked on the waves.

"Sister? Could you come out here?"

"No doubt about it," said Karl.

"About what?"

"You," said Karl.

"What is it, Jude?" said a woman's voice through the wall.

Karl leaned right into the boy's face and said, "Do you know who you are?"

Jude's face was red and straining. He bit his lip, almost in tears. His hands had locked in panic around the cigar box full of money.

"I'm crap," he whispered.

"Jude?" said the voice again.

Karl laughed. "Just like your mother. Now who am I?" He let the light flood his face, and looked expectantly at Jude. The boy didn't hesitate.

"You're the devil," he said.

Karl touched his moustache, and laughed again.

"That's what Father Mullen said. Tell him Karl Adare came back to say hello."

SITA KOZKA

EVEN THOUGH IT was winter and snow blew through the fine black screens of my apartment porch, I liked to sit there and look out on the street. Broadway in Fargo, just above the downtown area, was always full of nurses walking to the hospital, nuns gliding back from the cathedral, and long-term patients tottering between their relatives.

I was doing well enough in spite of a married doctor who strung me on for three years before I knew he would never leave his wife, the old story. I got away from him, then came Jimmy, who stepped in to help me recover from the experience. I was grateful to Jimmy at the time, but then I could not get rid of him. It seemed like he was outside my door, waiting in his plush car, every other night. He drove down from Argus whenever I modeled in a DeLendrecies style show. He clipped out and saved the fuzzy newsprints of me posing in a ballgown, a coat with platter-sized buttons, even matching swimwear. Jimmy was persistent, and always showed me a good time, but he belonged in Argus where he owned a steakhouse. The right man hadn't come along.

I kept my looks up with more care than ever. I was ten years older than some of the girls I modeled with and I was no longer the one most sought after. I had to wonder how much time I had left. The years were showing, the wear and tear. I kept slim, kept my waist the 22 ½ of Vivien Leigh's, kept attending refresher courses at The Dorothy Ludlow Evening School of Charm. The most important thing Dorothy taught me was to sit up straight and never, under any circumstance, to frown. One trick I learned was that dining in the evening alone, or playing cards with girl friends, I should wear a Band-Aid tightly taped across my forehead to keep it smooth. Frown lines aged a woman more quickly than her hands. I bought a little metal grinder to pulverize apricot kernals, which I mixed with cold cream and rubbed on my skin. After bathing I freshened my face with a bit of cotton dipped in white vinegar. I wore kidskin glove liners when I walked outdoors in winter.

Determination, that's what it was. I made good money and bought a television. But I was thirty years old. Something more should have happened. People told me I should have gone to Hollywood, and now I had to agree. Hollywood had been a missed chance I should have taken when I could. The only thing that would save me, now, was to find the ideal husband. So I was looking. I kept an eye out, but Mr. Right refused to show his face and the months ticked by. Maybe if I'd found him, or gone to Hollywood, or even gotten a big promotion at DeLendrecies, the letter would not have mattered when it came and I would have sent it back to Mary instead of using it as an excuse to put off Jimmy.

I was sitting on the little porch I mentioned. It was a sunny winter Saturday and I was waiting for Jimmy to come and pick me up in his coupe. We were going ice skating and I worried that he would make some romantic gesture. Perhaps that evening as we sat around the oil-drum fire, drinking cocoa, he'd pop the question or draw the jewelry store box from his thick plaid jacket. I imagined ways I could discourage him, not completely, but just enough to give me time. As it happened, though, the postman arrived before Jimmy.

I went downstairs when I heard the letter slide into the box. I didn't get much mail. This letter had been forwarded, readdressed in black grease marker and in Mary's peaked script. I always told Mary that her handwriting looked like the writing of a witch. Mine is close to perfect, at least so the nuns said. The letter itself was written in an unfamiliar hand and addressed to the Kozka family. Since Mama and Papa had still not settled in a permanent residence, Mary had sent the letter on to me.

Dear Mrs. Kozka,

I saved the newspaper ads ever since he was a baby. And now I had to come clean about him in confessional, as I asked Father Flo about it. Father Flo says to write you, telling you the circumstance. Well it happened I lost my own and couldn't have any after that. So I kept Jude when my husband brought him over from the fairgrounds. I always might have given him back except I heard about the mother flying off. So I raised him. My husband's heart gave out six years ago. But now that baby's going to have his ordination in one week. He's going to be a deacon, on his way to a priest. February 18, at the Cathedral in Saint Paul is where he'll be ordained. Jude doesn't know he's adopted. Now is the time to tell the whole thing if you want. Father Flo says this letter is the right thing to do, so I wrote. You may reply to me.

His mother,
Mrs. Catherine Miller

I read the letter over like it was gibberish, and then I read it again. I was about to read it a third time when Jimmy pulled up outside and sat on his horn. Try as I might I couldn't get him to ring the bell, or to develop any manners whatsoever when it came to dating. He always said there were no parking spaces big enough to fit his car on my side street, but the avenue was wide and, in places, completely curbless. There was always room. Jimmy was just too lazy to get out, lock his car, walk the half block, and ring my doorbell. He could dance, play cards all night, ice skate in toe loops and waltz steps and figure eights. But he couldn't get out of his car and ring my bell. It was irritating. And so, even more on that day than most, we started off on the wrong foot.

I put down the letter and ran outside to stop his racket. I'd tied my skates over my shoulder and they knocked. The blades could have hurt me if I'd fallen. Jimmy reached across the car seat and flipped the handle. That was another thing. He had no courtesy for opening a girl's door. In restaurants he barged through and let me fend for myself behind him. But I suppose he was better than my married doctor, even so.

"How many times have I told you to park, then ring?" I said this first, then slid into the passenger's side of the car.

"Sita Cakes!" He shouted, then revved the engine above my voice.

"Don't say anything about the parking spaces, Jimmy!" I screamed. "And don't call me Cakes."

Another thing. He called me by his favorite desserts. Sweetpie. Muffin. Sugardonut. No wonder he was getting fat. Being called these names made me feel puffed up too, unpleasantly sweet, and too soft, like risen dough.

"Come on over here," he said, patting the upholstery beside him.

And at once, although I had been so annoyed I wanted to slap his cheek, I slid over and wedged myself against Jimmy's side. This was how he always won me—at the last minute and against my better judgment. Once there, however, I relaxed and got comfortable. I could just be myself with Jimmy, that was for sure. Since he didn't appreciate anything I really stood for, or even acknowledge the improvements as to culture and charm I had made in myself, I went back to being Sita Kozka, daughter of Pete, the butcher. Or just about. I never let Jimmy forget that I was a model and had paid my own way in life.

86

We drove over to the Moorhead side, to try out their rink. Someone had put up a little warming shack there, and inside, after the brilliance of the snow, the air seemed steamy as a lagoon. The benches were scored and gouged by children's blade tips, carved with initials and arrow-pierced hearts. We laced up and stowed our boots in a corner, then clattered down the splintery ramp onto the ice. The rink was frozen a clear deep gray. I could see the cracks running down several feet and the brown oak leaves floating, suspended where they'd fallen. We crossed our arms and held hands, started gliding back and forth. We went around and around the rough oval rink.

"Sita," said Jimmy after some time. He hesitated. Then at last he blurted out, "Let's get married."

I panicked. I didn't want to have to say yes or no. Maybe it was instinct, a flair for self-preservation, that caused me to suddenly realize the sense of the letter that came in the mail that morning. It was strange how the meaning of it popped into my mind just then. But it did, hitting me so unexpectedly that I gasped.

Jimmy stopped and looked at me in amazement.

"That's yes?" he asked.

"I don't know. Wait," I said, "I've figured something out."

Jimmy balanced, holding tight to my shoulders, very still.

"You know that baby brother Mary had? The one they lost? No . . . you don't know." I shrugged off his hands and skated forward. "Don't say anything. I have to think." The snow along the edge of the pond was piled in crisp boulders. It had fallen deep and packed hard. The shadows were a flimsy blue.

"It's that baby," I said out loud. I knew all about it, not from Mary, who never spoke about her life before she came to Argus, but from overhearing Mama's conversations in the kitchen. Her friends came by to sit with her and drink watery coffee. They smoked each other's cigarettes and chewed on tough molasses cake. As they talked I used to stand just outside and listen in. They went on and on about Aunt Adelaide, how the children's father had not married her, and why she had left her children. They speculated on what might have happened to the baby. When the young man took him out of Mary's arms, and walked away, had it been a curse or a blessing? Had he really had a wife?

And now, at last, there were answers to these incompletes. I had the letter that could solve the mystery.

"So, enough thinking?" said Jimmy, behind me. He touched my arm.

"I know what I'll do," I said, turning to face him.

"What?"

"I'll go to Minneapolis. He's getting ordained this week."

Jimmy's face was a study.

"Look," I said, "something real important has come up. I'll have to think about . . ." I waved my hand in the direction of the place we had been skating when he proposed. ". . . all of that. But right now I've got to pack."

Jimmy didn't sulk. He was too upset and too confused. Perhaps I worried him with my sudden conviction and the firm plans about my travel. Perhaps it seemed unusual. At any rate, he dropped me off with only a peck on the cheek. I was impatient to read the letter once more and to make the arrangements necessary in my work schedule. I'd take the train, a small overnight bag, stay at a hotel. I wouldn't call this Catherine Miller long distance or let her know that I'd appear. I'd simply slip into the crowd at the baby's ordination, incognito, and after I had seen Mary's lost brother I'd decide what to do, select the right moment to reveal who I was. I'd make a drama of it.

I packed. I made my arrangements and booked the ticket. The night before I was to leave I lay awake in excitement. What was happening was so interesting, like a plot in the mystery books I read to soothe myself. Of everything that happened, of all the circumstances that had caused my cousin Mary to arrive by freight one early spring, the letter was now the only other clue besides Adelaide's blue velvet box. I'd packed that, for no reason except that it seemed appropriate. I put a photograph of Adelaide inside the box among the old pawn tickets and popped-off buttons. If the boy wanted to know what his mother looked like, I'd have her picture. I shivered, knowing the letter had been in Mary's own hands, the hands that glowed blue in the dark and yet picked up no unusual vibrations as to the envelope's contents.

Minneapolis was a nice town then, built up by Minnesota grain and railroad fortunes. Spanking new sidewalks ran along the wide streets and trees were everywhere, not like in Fargo, which would always have a bare old cowtown look about it even when the big money came in from sugar, beans, and wheat. This was a real metropolis, with a landmark skyscraper called Foshay Tower amid miles of fine residential areas. My hotel room had good thick furniture in it, drapes with big ferns on them, and a smart dresser with a long rectangular mirror.

I hadn't slept the night before, so that night I was out. I woke up at the late-winter dawn, just as the first light filtered through the pattern on the curtains. I knew exactly where I was, knew just what I would do. I'd have black coffee in the hotel café. I would take an elevator to the top of Foshay Tower, then I would visit a department store. After that I'd just have time to get a taxi to the cathedral.

The black coffee came in an elegant cup with a paper doily underneath it, but I never got past the doors of the Foshay elevators. The operator said, "Coming up, ma'am?" But I just shook my head, suddenly dizzy. The latticed metal gates unfolded shut in front of me. The doors were inscribed with shining plaques of the tower. To focus my vision I stared at the replica, rising mighty from crests of gilded brass, radiating beams of light from its heavy peak. The department store visit was even worse. I should have known how it would affect me just from looking in the windows at the pinch-waisted mannequins. Their eyes were deep and black, painted on with a fringed brush. Their mouths shone wetly as if they'd just drunk something from a glass. They wore hats with little poked stitchwork designs and carried purses in shapes I'd never seen. Worse then that, they wore dresses with off-center buttons and a hemline that was lower, strictly lower, than the style our store had ordered.

"How could this have happened?" I said out loud. "Who decreed?"

I marched in the store to check the racks and it was true. Even the shopgirls were wearing this new look. My legs felt long, revealed, clumsy, and outdated. I took off my gloves and touched the dresses. I wanted the black one with inset stripes.

"May I help you?"

It was as if one of the mannequins had come to life, she was so perfect. Her hair was set in the kind of finger wave it was impossible to get in Fargo. And her ensemble! I could have thrown myself down on the carpet.

"I'm just looking."

Her eyes were flat, gorgeously indifferent. She didn't work on commission, I was sure of it. Either that or she was independently rich and only sold clothing for amusement. I held the dress up without a word. She took it and whirled off, expecting me to follow. I did. I tried on the dress. When I stepped out and looked into the three-way mirror, I was thrilled. But then she appeared behind me and I was just an imitation of her.

"Are you visiting here in Minneapolis?"

"No," I said.

Before she could say anything else, I twirled the skirt and said, "I'll take it."

She didn't smile. She didn't offer the slightest compliment. Then, back in the dressing room, I took the dress off and carefully hung it. The tag was beneath the sleeve and I didn't have enough money along with me to meet the price. I could have written a draft on my bank account, but the amount was simply too high. It was way out of line. I stood there in my slip, so unnerved I could hardly think straight. I read the numbers over and over, as if I could change them by force of will. But they stayed the same, written out in a thin black flourish. I dressed slowly and walked out, hoping that the shopgirl had gone off on coffee break. But she was waiting at the counter.

"Shall I wrap that for you, miss?" she asked in a bored, flat voice.

"I've changed my mind," I told her.

"Ah."

"I was looking for something more formal."

"Of course."

She turned to wait on another customer, and I escaped.

The cathedral was lovely in the snow, and already cars had pulled up to the curbs for blocks in advance. I walked up the stone steps with others, family and friends of those who were about to take the Holy Orders. The door closed behind us with a great crash that echoed, and the ceiling sprang upward, higher than high, enormous. Wheels of blue, green, golden light fell through the round stained-glass windows. The church was already filled downstairs, so I climbed the back steps to the organ loft. There were a few seats left, extra folding chairs beside the pews. I genuflected and sat in a wedge of gold light that seemed to warm me although the church itself was not well heated. Soon I heard the whine of bellows as an aged nun flipped switches and set the pipe organ breathing close by.

She began to play. Her small arched feet fled up and down

the low register. The music swelled. I took a missal and opened it, just as those young men to be ordained filed in, dressed in white robes, each carrying a long, lit candle and a stole. I tried to see them but they were too far away. I hadn't pictured this. I'd given no thought to how I'd recognize this Jude Miller. The young men made a half circle around the bishop's faldstool. Then the bishop himself entered and knelt down and prayed. The church was full of white chrysanthemums, white gladiolas, white carnations. The people smelled of mothballs and hair oil and perfume. Fat white satin bows were draped at the saints' feet, and the colored candles in the racks were lit in faltering rows.

The bishop went to his seat and put on his vestments with slow and studied gestures. I observed each young man in turn. The boy would be about eighteen, short perhaps, like Mary, perhaps red haired, perhaps a handsome version of Adelaide. But then again he might be like his father. I'd never seen a picture of the man or even heard him described, except as married.

And then, once the service began and the bishop spoke, I realized that my visit could be more than dramatic anyway. It could be dangerous. I realized that I could spoil Jude Miller's future.

Large and splendid in his robes and mitre, the bishop addressed the whole assembled crowd in Latin. We followed in our dark green missals.

Reverendissimus in Christo Pater, et Dominus, Dominus, Dei.
I read along with him on the opposite side of the page.

THE MOST REVEREND FATHER IN CHRIST, BY THE GRACE OF GOD AND THE FAVOR OF THE APOSTOLIC SEE, ORDERS AND COMMANDS, UNDER PENALTY OF EXCOMMUNICATION, ALL AND EACH HERE PRESENT FOR RECEIVING ORDERS, THAT NONE OF THOSE WHO MAY PERCHANCE BE IRREGULAR OR EXCOMMUNICATED BY THE CANONS OR BY HIS SUPERIOR, OR UNDER INTERDICT, OR SUS-

He went on listing those who shouldn't dare come forward to
receive the Orders. But I kept seeing *illegitimate*. The candidates
stretched out prone on the floor as the Litany of Saints began. I
followed the text out of habit and asked to be delivered from the
spirit of fornication, from lightning and tempest, from the scourge
of earthquakes, plague, famine, war, and everlasting death.

Now those who were to be deacons stood, stepped forward,
and made a kneeling semicircle close to the bishop. Although I
looked closely I still couldn't see them well enough to decide
which was Mary's brother. The bishop laid his hands on their
heads, one by one. But he didn't say their names. He let them
touch the Book of Gospels, then prayed, and it was over. They
filed back to their places. Having come all this way I wished I
could at least solve the mystery for myself, but they all looked
perfectly normal, not special in any detail, and not familiar. So
I edged through the crowd and walked out of the cathedral onto
the wide sunny steps.

The air was fresh, cold, and full of ordinary sounds. Behind
me, the music was muffled and grand. I took the blue box from
my purse and opened it. Perhaps I needed to refresh my memory.
Perhaps I'd see some feature that would point to one of the young
men. But Adelaide looked like no one else. She stared boldly
from her locket-sized photograph, hair coiled, eyebrows arched
like wings. I poked the buttons about. I unfolded the pawn ticket.

It was a crumpled yellow scrap with a simple address, numbers,
and a description carefully written out in tiny script.

*Flawed yellow diamond ring in gold setting. Fair condition.
Victorian garnet filigree necklace with individual settings.*

I imagined the old necklace, the ring, first on Adelaide and then on me. I hadn't much good jewelry to my name beyond a string of cultured pearls.

I walked to the curb and held my hand up when a cab appeared. I wasn't sure of my destination until I got in. As if I'd always meant to, I read the driver the address off the pawn ticket. Then I settled back into the cracked leather.

We drove for miles. The streets turned shabby, and gray snow was piled off to either side in icy walls. I began to wonder if I wasn't crazy to come all this way. But the shop was still there. It was a hole filled with junk up to the windows. I got out without paying the full fare and asked the driver to wait, then I walked into the shop. JOHN's, the sign said.

I stood beyond the door, in the overflowing gloom, and waited for my eyes to adjust. The place was cold and full of sour smells, littered with camera parts and broken musical instruments. An enormous young man in several topcoats walked through a pair of curtains and put his hands on the counter.

"Buying or selling?"

"I'm here for this ring and necklace," I said, handing him the ticket.

He pursed his lips, "Nineteen thirty-two." He laughed, looking at the handwriting. "John Senior took this," he said. "John Senior's dead."

He held the ticket out but I didn't take it.

"Oh please," I said. "I'm sure you could find it if you looked. It would mean so much."

He rubbed his beard. He couldn't say no. "Wait a minute," he sighed. "I still got a boxful of stuff I never sorted through."

He tugged a flat metal case from underneath a pile of newspapers and put it down on the counter. Inside, it was divided into tiny compartments, each holding some scrap. Jewelry, war medals, broken watches, tie clasps.

He sorted the rings from the rest of the stuff. Not one of them was a diamond by any stretch. But then, pawing through the rest of the heap, he nudged aside a blackened tangle of delicate links and spread it on the counter with his fingers.

"This could be it, I guess," he said, scratching at a setting with a dirty fingernail.

"That?" I was disappointed.

"We had this fire and things got covered with oil and soot. It's red stones all right. Maybe you could tell if you shined it up."

It was almost too filthy to touch, so I opened the blue box and let him drop it in. I wrote a bank draft, thanking heaven I hadn't bought the new black dress. I put the box in the bottom of my purse and walked out.

Back in Fargo I brought the necklace to a jeweler. He cleaned it, repaired a few of the settings, and gave it back. When I saw it laid out on a sheet of white cotton, I couldn't believe my eyes. The stones glowed like rubies. It was fit for royalty. I put it on, turned back and forth in front of the bathroom mirror. The jewels distinguished me. A low-cut dress of cream lace would set them off perfectly. I wore the necklace all that night while I made my dinner and watched my television programs. But when I unclasped it to go to bed, and put it in my drawer, there was the letter from Mrs. Miller, still unanswered. I sat down at my table with a sheet of my best stationary, and wrote.

February 19, 1950

Dear Mrs. Miller,

In answer to your letter, which was forwarded to me from Argus, as far as I am concerned what you tell your boy is up to you. He would be my cousin, and there is a sister too. He also had one brother, but no one knows what became of him. I, on the other hand, have become a leading fashion model and clerk for

DeLendrecies here in Fargo. My parents own a successful meat marketing concern on the east side of Argus, North Dakota. There is nothing else to say, so I will sign myself.

Yours truly,
Sita Kozka

I addressed the envelope, sealed the letter inside, even used a stamp. Perhaps I should have marched out there and then, however, even though it was midnight, and mailed it away, because even by the next morning I was starting to hesitate. I had enough to think about already.

For days that letter sat on the dresser. And then one night, as Jimmy was on his way to my apartment for dinner, I was straightening the tops of things, fussing with shades and lamps. I came across the letter and slipped it beneath a crocheted piece of linen. I needed everything just so.

Sita's Wedding

Beneath the loud polka music of The Six Fat Dutchmen, the brother and cousins of Jimmy Bohl huddled close in the Legion Pavilion booth and discussed how they would kidnap the bride from the wedding dance and where they would deposit Sita for Jimmy to find. Because they were loaded on sloe gin and schnapps, they agreed on everything and nothing. All they could do was laugh, their faces dark red, exploding, eyes popping, when they thought of Jimmy yelling, "WHERE'S SITA?" They nearly choked imagining his rage when he jumped into his toilet-paper-and-shaving-cream-decorated Lincoln, revved the motor, raced into the cold March night to find her, and suddenly smelled the terrible odor released from within the heater.

"Limburger cheese," was all one cousin had to say to make the other double up and fall sideways against the wooden panels of the truck.

"There he is now," said Jimmy's brother, nodding at the dance floor.

Jimmy whirled by, a tall, pudgy man barely saved from complete blandness by his short wavy pompadour and precise goatee. He was light on his feet, a practiced ballroom dancer. Sita wore a glazed look of surrender as she was flung back and forth across the floor.

"What about the Kozkas? Think they'll be pissed?" asked Jimmy's brother. The cousins took stock of Pete and Fritzie, but the two looked so placid in their new suntans and added girth, sipping beer and nodding at the dancers, that the possibility of their anger seemed remote. The bride and groom were waltzing now. Red stones glittered at her throat. Rhinestones sparkled in the tiara that held up Sita's veil. Her dress was special, the skirt enormous and layered, the bodice stitched with pearly beads. It seemed to the huddled men that a soft light glowed around Sita's face, a mist of loveliness, but that was only the effect of her wispy veil, and their drunkenness, for in reality Sita's smile was bleak and her stare, over Jimmy's shoulder, was razor sharp with nervous exhaustion.

Watching her, one of the cousins snorted.

"She's a looker, though," he said. His voice was malicious. Jimmy's brother hunched and pursed his lips.

"She used to think she was too good," he said. "Kept Jimmy on a string until she figured nothing better would show up." He winked blearily, at no one. "Tonight, even steven."

When the number was over, Sita fled down a corridor to the ladies' room, her veil wrapped over one arm. Seeing this, the cousins rose together in a common, unconscious agreement. Jimmy's eager brother led them, as one by one they slipped drunkenly through the dancers toward that same corridor where Sita had disappeared and which led, beyond the ladies' room, out into the beaten-dirt parking lot.

And so it happened. No one witnessed Sita's abduction when she stepped from the ladies' room door. By the time Jimmy finished dancing with all of his waitresses and looked for her, his new bride was well on her way up north on Highway 30, wedged in the backseat of Jimmy's brother's car between two of Jimmy's cousins, whose sex jokes and sweated-through rental suit coats threw Sita into a state of such repulsion that she lost her voice.

They did not speak to her anyway. The road was straight, slick looking under the cold stars, and the pint they passed around evaporated quickly. The sweetness of their schnapps breath was more than Sita could bear and she tried, once, to say she was sick and that they had to let her out. But her words came out a hoarse croak and when she lunged over a cousin's hard paunch for the back door handle they all, suddenly, noticed her.

"Oopsy daisy!"

"Catch her!"

"Soon enough!" Their voices knocked her back against the seat cushions, and their clumsy hands pinioned her. She sank into herself, hating them so thoroughly it sent a raw current down the middle of her. She glared at each of them in turn, wishing that her eyes could melt the flesh from their bones.

"Where we taking her?" Jimmy's brother finally wondered. He was driving.

"I don't know!" said a cousin, at which the others let loose in hoots of laughter that left them weak. After that they quieted, momentarily pensive.

"Let's go ice fishing this winter," said one of them. For half an hour they discussed which lake to visit, whose house they'd haul there. Sita drowsed, certain they'd turn and bring her back. But just when it seemed that they'd satisfied their urge to drive in the dark and perhaps even forgotten about her crushed among them, they came onto reservation land, unfenced, fallow, deserted except for one small yard light.

Jimmy's brother drove into the circle of light and stopped in front of a sagging wooden structure, unnamed but recognizable to all of the men.

"Hoo boy!" whooped a cousin, acknowledging Jimmy's brother's genius.

"Let her out now," Jimmy's brother instructed the backseat cousins. "And give her your jacket; goddamn it's cold out there!"

The cousin jumped out, deposited Sita, and fell back into the car. Frightened suddenly, she huddled in the shell of the suit jacket. But the cousin's warmth left it before Jimmy's brother had honked, blinked, and driven off. The wind tore at her veil like teeth. The cold flowed up her skirt, down her arms.

Sita tried to scream.

"Jackass!" she whispered.

The taillights vanished. The wind was harsh, a storm almost, and Sita had to fight it as she stumbled between the cars in the lot and tapped on the plain wood door. No one answered. She stood a moment and then the wind opened her dress suddenly from behind, turned it inside out and over her head like an umbrella, and tumbled her in the door.

What she entered was a small Indian bar, patronized on that cold night by seven quietly drinking old men, two loud women, and Russell Kashpaw, who was with both of the women for the evening. What the ten people and the bartender experienced coming at them through the door was a sudden explosion of white net, a rolling ball of it tossed among them by freezing winds. Two bare spike-heeled legs scissored within the ball, slashing lethal arcs, tearing one old man's jacket before he reared away in fright. And the white ball *was* frightening, for while the wind tumbled it about and the patrons of the bar dodged to avoid danger, it kept up a muffled and inhuman croaking. But then, when the door was finally slammed shut, the gown came to a slow rest, arms emerged and madly smoothed the dress down layer by layer until a face finally stood out within the torn foam.

"It's a fucking queen," said one of the women in the hush of amazement.

"Shut your mouth," said the other woman, clutching Russell's arm. "It's a bride."

And it was a bride, everyone could see that now. She rose to her feet, disheveled but normal in all respects except that her face was loose and raging, distorted, working horribly in silence.

KARL ADARE

GENTLEMEN AND LADIES *of the Crop and Livestock Convention,
I have come to unveil a miracle.*

That's how I begin my spiel.

*Each one of us survived the dust bowl, those clouds of blowing
grit. Precious topsoil on the whim of the wind! Well gentlemen
and ladies, plowing caused that, tilling made it happen, and one
way to stop that infernal process is not to till.*

But. . . .

I pause dramatically.

I have to till to plant, *you tell me. Well no more! Beneath this
tarp I've got the answer to nature's prayers. Gentlemen . . .*

I pull the string and drop the canvas.

THE AIR SEEDER!

And then I proceed to explain the mechanism. I point to the
thin tubes that conduct the seeds from the box down to the
surface. I explain how, assisted by a puff of the motorized bellows,
each seed is blown gently into the earth. The Air Seeder does
not disturb the soil, I tell them, thereby conserving moisture,
reducing your surface loss.

There are the usual questions, then, the usual scepticism. I
caught the man's eye, a yearning guarded glance, while I was
answering those questions, handing out leaflets, and demonstrat-
ing the process as best I could.

We were both at the convention in Minneapolis. He was a
slim man with a lot of thick blond hair, wide gray eyes, and an

easy manner about him. He asked questions relating to process and durability. He liked the concept, he told me. Innovation was his game.

"I'm Wallace Pfef. I speculate over in Argus," he said. "I'd like to do more promotional work, put the town on the map, boost agriculture. That's why I'm interested in your seeder," he went on.

I said this machine was the coming thing, showed him charts and farm news write-ups, but all the while I was thinking Why Argus? It seemed like that two-bit town popped up every time I turned around. Argus citizens were always shaking my hand. Or the newspapers were full of freak accidents, catastrophes, multiple births at Saint Adalbert's Hospital in Argus. I wondered if someday I'd read my sister's name in these accounts, and I knew that it wouldn't matter if I did. I'd never call, visit, even write a letter. It had simply been too long. Yet I had a fascination, a curiosity that drew coincidence, and it was probably this that led me to ask the man, Pfef, to join me for a drink.

And, too, a salesman makes friends where he can. He wasn't my type, but he wasn't as bad as some.

We walked out of the convention room, crossed the lobby, and entered the dim hotel bar.

"I'll stand you one," I said, putting down a five-dollar bill when our drinks arrived. The waitress took the right amount from the five and left the change on the table. I did not touch the change.

He thanked me, took a slow drink, and said nothing else, which at first I found unsettling, but then, when I purposely waited also and didn't fill in the space he'd opened up, it was clear we had allowed our drink to shift the ground between us.

"Are you from Minneapolis?" he asked. Somehow the subject seemed more personal now than when we'd spoken of his being from Argus.

"Here . . . different places," I told him.

"Which places?"

I paused, feeling the old discomfort over questions about my past, yet wanting to reveal just enough to keep him interested.

"Saint Jerome's," I said. "It's a Catholic home for bastards."

He clearly hadn't expected this. "I'm sorry," he said. "That's too bad."

I waved it off.

He didn't have much to say about anything now, but he kept that waiting look on his face, and although I don't usually talk about myself, try to keep my distance, I added what I never told anyone.

"I've got a sister," I said. "She lives in your town."

He looked expectant. Clearly, he knew everyone in Argus, and I realized I'd gone too far. He would tell Mary that he'd met me if I told him her name, which he clearly anticipated. I'd considered giving him a business card, but now I'd have to be more cautious.

"But I don't know who she is," I backpedaled. "It could be just a rumor. That kind of thing always happens in a home. Other kids pretend they've seen your files, or the nuns make up stories. . . ."

"You believe it though," he said, looking straight at me with conviction. At that moment, the ground dwindled considerably between us as it always does when one person admits to observing another that closely and meets your eyes. It was now my turn to say something that would penetrate still farther. I took my chance.

"Let's have dinner in my hotel room," I said.

His stare changed to surprise. We'd downed three quick drinks by then, and the five he'd insisted on putting down also lay broken between us. Three drinks was where I started feeling loose, and as I watched him stand up I knew the same was true of him.

"Oh no," he said, rummaging below his seat. "I dropped my pamphlets."

His hips were fine and thin, I noticed, but he wasn't strong or muscular. There was more to admire about my appearance. I lifted weights, swam laps, or ran an occasional mile even when I was on the road. I took care of myself mentally too. I'd had enough setbacks with other people, and perhaps because of them I never let anything go far enough to cause me trouble.

"Coming?" I asked.

He had recovered his pamphlets. He stood up with a quick nervous smile, and together we walked down the carpeted corridor, up two flights of stairs, and entered my room. It was a single, dominated by a bed with a bright orange bedspread. Pfef managed to avoid looking at the bed by making a beeline for the window and admiring my view. Which was of the parking lot.

There really were menus in the desk-table drawer, and I was honestly hungry. I found that once we were alone in the room I didn't even care much what happened, one way or the other. It wasn't that Pfef was unattractive, it was his sudden nervousness that bored me, the awkward pretense when it was he who put his hand out once, stopping mine, when I'd tried to lay down another bill for drinks.

I sat on the bed and opened the menu. I knew what I was hungry for but it wasn't available.

"Game hens," I compromised, "even though they'll send them dry and tough."

He relaxed, sat down in the little chair beside the bed, and picked up a menu.

"The prime rib. That's my choice."

"We're settled then." I phoned the desk. While we waited for the trolley I poured him a shot from the bottle I kept in my suitcase.

"Is this your only water glass?" he wondered, politely, before raising it to his lips.

"I'm not particular," I said, taking a pull from the bottle; "not like you."

He had been the one with the bold observant statements downstairs, but once I tagged him he flushed and fell silent, swirled the whiskey in his glass, and then got that waiting look on his face again.

So I didn't say anything, just took the glass from his hand.

"The dinner," he said in a faint voice.

But he bent forward anyway, and I held his shoulders, drew him to me. Then we lay back on the startling spread.

By the time the bellhop knocked on the door we were back where we'd started, dressed, the only difference being now we shared the water glass. The truth is I liked drinking from a glass.

The boy just shoved the cart in, put his hand out for the tip, and left us. Maybe he thought we were plotting gangsters, or knew the truth. Pfef ate quickly, avidly, with obvious relief. He cut his meat into small squares and popped them into his mouth. It had not been as bad as he thought, I guessed, or now that it was over he could put it behind him, pretend it never happened, go quietly back to Argus and tell his wife how well the convention had gone and ply her with some Minneapolis souvenir to oil the creaky little hinge of his guilt.

"I've never done this before," he said.

I just turned away and carved the tiny birds, remembering the guarded yearning, his waiting eye. He was married for sure, at least I assumed it. He wore a wedding-type ring and had a cared-for look—pressed, shined, and starched.

"So how's the little woman?" I could not help myself. I said this with a sneer.

He looked up, uncomprehending, wiped his chin. I tapped his hand.

"Oh," he said. "I was engaged once, long ago."

"I bet you were."

Then he turned the tables, or tried to.

"What about you?" he asked.

"What about me?"

"You know."

"You mean women?" He nodded. I told him I'd known plenty and very closely, although the truth is I had always found their touch unbearable, a source of nameless panic.

"But no love and marriage for me," I told him.

He was fascinated.

"Why don't you let me try and find your sister?" he asked. This came out of the blue, unexpected, and when he looked at me with his clear sad eyes, I suddenly had the feeling that had always frightened me, the blackness, the ground I'd stood on giving way, the falling no place. Maybe it was true about him, the awkwardness, no experience, the awful possibility that he wanted to get to know me.

"I'm done," I said, shoving away my plate and, just to do something, just to stop the feeling, wheeling the cart madly out the door too. I came back in the room and leapt onto the bed. I had to stop myself from falling, so I jumped. I felt silly and light, bouncing in the air. I felt like a child who would ruin the bedsprings.

"You'd better stop," Pfef said, shocked, dropping meat from his fork. "The management."

"Screw the management!" I laughed at his maidenly face. "I've got a trick I'm going to show you." I didn't actually have anything in mind, but as I bounced, hitting the ceiling almost, I was suddenly inspired. I'd watched hard-muscled boys so closely on the diving boards downtown. They sprang up, whirled over, threw themselves precisely through the air in a somersault and split the water harshly with their toes. I would do the same. I took a great bounce. Then I tucked, spun, whirled, and I still believe that if it hadn't been for Pfef's sudden yell I would have landed perfectly on my feet. But the cry of alarm threw me off. I kept my body

106

tucked too long and hit the floor at the foot of the bed, in an area so small it seemed impossible I could have landed perfectly within it, but I did, and wrenched my back too.

I knew it was bad the instant I hit. I stayed conscious.

"Pfef," I said, the moment he bent down, "don't touch me."

He had the sense not to, the sense to call the hospital, the sense to sit beside me without talking and keep the orderlies from moving me until the doctor ordered up a plank. The stupid thing I kept thinking all this time, too, was not about my neck or how I could be paralyzed for life. For some reason I had no fear of it. No fear of anything. I looked at Pfef, and by the way he stared back, purely stricken, eyes naked, I knew if I wanted I could have him for life. But I didn't even think about that. It was my sister I remembered.

"Her name's Mary," I said out loud. "Mary Adare."

And then the injection took hold, the black warmth. I realized the place I'd landed on was only a flimsy ledge, and there was nothing else to stop me if I fell.

Wallace's Night

Nighthawks dived through his headlamps, small triangular shadows, their fringed mouths spread for insects. The air off the ditches smelled wet, and sometimes he caught the gleam of water standing mirrorlike between the endless black furrows. Far off the highway between Minneapolis and Argus, lone lights signaled like boats anchored far at sea. The first glimpse that Wallace actually had of Argus was the little tame red beacon that shone on top of the water tower.

He turned his car off the highway onto a small dirt road famous for harboring high school sweethearts. His friend, Officer Ronald Lovchik, was under pressure from certain parents to patrol this stretch on weekend nights. This Saturday night the road was deserted. He caught no reflections; no lovers blinked their headlights farther down the crooked, potholed rut. He let his car bounce softly to a halt and then cut the engine.

All around him a night music opened. Crickets sawed. The new wheat rustled. Dreaming birds that nested in the culverts and low windbreaks let out small sharp cries. Wallace slid low in the seat and breathed the mild sweet wind. The steering wheel curved like a smooth bone where he rested his fingers. Over him, the whole moonless sky was spread with planets and stars.

He didn't want to go back to his half-built empty house yet, but he didn't want to think too closely about what had happened to him in Minneapolis either. He shut his eyes but couldn't doze. He was too alert, too conscious. He tried to occupy his mind with anything but Karl.

There was the problem of the swimming pool that Wallace managed along with his other jobs. The pool had been a WPA project, an elaborate one, much too large and fancy for Argus.

Now the plumbing was rotten and cracks had appeared in the deep end. The filtering system was worthless and the valuable hand-painted friezes that adorned the dressing-room walls were chipping. Vandals had sliced the fence.

The pool was too big a headache. He thought about First National. He sat on the board that put the okay on its investments. He tried to keep his mind on the last stock portfolio he'd seen, but the smell of standing rain was in the breeze. He drifted. He saw Karl's hands, his dark hair, the drawn face in the crisp and disinfected hospital sheets. When the lights went on suddenly behind him, Wallace was dazzled.

A car door slammed. His front seat was full of the glare. Someone bent into his window.

"Wally Pfef!"

"Ron!"

"What are you doing here?"

"I'm . . ." what *was* he doing here anyway? ". . . thinking."

Lovchik straightened. Wallace groped along the front seat and grabbed a pile of pamphlets he'd taken back from the convention. He pressed them to his chest and sprang from the car.

"Look at this," he said, handing one out. Ron Lovchik looked put upon. He unhooked a flashlight from his belt and focused it on the pamphlet.

"It says here 'the Sugarbeet.' "

"That's it!" said Wallace, and swung an arm out toward the empty night, the vast and silent fields.

"These fields, everything you see, well it's beet country Ron."

Wallace grabbed Lovchik's arm, tapped his finger on the glossy paper booklet. "Listen. Table sugar is a staple of the worldwide menu. You like sugar. I like it. Sugar's got to come from somewhere, and it might as well be here. It could mean a face-lift for Argus! Money in the coffers. It could mean a new squad car. A two-way radio!"

Officer Lovchik shifted his weight and peered down at the small writing, at the picture of beets.

"Isn't it a lovely sight?" said Wallace. His voice soared. "A big white fat root just waiting to be made into $C_{12}H_{22}O_{11}$. That's sugar. Imagine it, Ron. All the fields around here planted. A beet refinery. The money flowing in. Your jail gets new windows. Argus builds two new swimming pools. When the wind blows off the piled beets the people hold their noses, but they smile, Ron. They know which side their bread is buttered on."

The ideas began to pour into Wallace's brain.

Officer Lovchik shook his head, looked down at the pamphlet again, flipped it in his hands. He gave Wallace a light whack on the shoulder.

"You never quit, Wally. You've even got plans for Lover's Lane.

Wallace jumped into his car, started the engine, and roared the gas enthusiastically.

"What a twist!" he shouted, driving off into the night. "This road will become a major bypass!" Before him, like Oz, the imaginary floodlit stacks of the beet refinery poured a stinking smoke straight upward in twin white columns.

CELESTINE JAMES

"ALL NIGHT LONG I've been grappling with killer robots," says Mary to herself, although I am working right next to her.

It is one whole decade before the president is shot and the world goes haywire, but Mary is ahead of her time. The idea of robots, which is current in magazines, has taken root in her mind along with other things. Atomic weapons. Space travel. Ginseng. She thinks that the beet sugar this town has gone crazy for is unhealthful. She has started to talk about raising bees. But her favorite is still the subject of mechanical people.

"Robots would have no feelings," she says now, darkly. "You could not appeal to their mercy."

"Since when," I say to her, "could you appeal to the common soldier? They sweat the mercy out of them in boot camp."

That's according to Russell, who should know. He has been discharged from the VA hospital, where he's been ever since he got back from his latest war, Korea. He is home now at last, never again to be a soldier. But he is riddled with even more wounds than before, so that now there is talk of making him North Dakota's most-decorated hero. I think it's stupid, that this getting shot apart is what he's lived for all his life. Now he must wait until some statehouse official scores the other veterans, counting up their wounds on a paper tablet, and figures out who gave away the most flesh.

He has been in the service so long that he's used to waiting. And then we hear the bad news about our sister Isabel, who married into a Sioux family and moved down to South Dakota. We hear she has died of beating, or in a car wreck, some way that's violent. But nothing else. We hear nothing from her husband, and if she had any children we never hear from them. Russell goes down there that weekend, but the funeral is long past. He comes home, telling me it's like she fell off the earth. There is no trace of her, no word.

Russell stays in the bars all night, or mopes around the house with his toolbox, until Mary gets wind of this and hires him to work on the shop's delivery van and motorized cooling system. Now he's in and out all day, limping, creased head to foot with new scars and stripes that almost look like the markings of an animal. He works for such long hours on the freezers that his hands are frostbit and raw, but he seems to improve a bit, mentally, to take an interest in life.

As Russell is getting better, the bottom is falling out of Sita's situation. Not that we hear it directly from her, more from rumors that customers bring through the door, and from things we observe ourselves. She has been heard out back in the kitchen of The Poopdeck Restaurant, criticizing her husband Jimmy for his method of frying food. Everything The Poopdeck makes is first dipped in batter then fried in deep fat. His food is fixed the way people around here like it. But Sita wants to make The Poopdeck into a first-class restaurant, a *four star*, our customers have heard her yell. They have seen Jimmy storm out stamping his small, sharp-toed feet, popping red in the face. He sits down at the edge of the counter, to a whole plate of glazed cinnamon rolls, and snaps them up daintily without losing his pout. He has gained so much weight from sweets eaten in anger that he hardly fits into a booth anymore.

Sita, however, remains toothpick thin and sour. To stay beautiful, she has to work harder than ever on herself. She spends hours at the hairdressers, money on skin treatments, and she ends up looking stuffed and preserved.

So Russell has war depression. Sita's pickled in her own juice. And Mary has a million ideas bouncing off the wall. The killer robot army that I have mentioned was in her dreams the night before.

"They came at me," she says with vigor, "shooting death rays from their fingers." We are sitting in plastic chairs out back of her kitchen on the cement slab floor of her glass porch. It is a rich and tangled garden of steamy vines. I think her whole idea's out of the ball park, and I tell her so.

"Of course," she returns, "it takes a mind that's unusual."

"You are unusual," I tell her. "I'm sure that nothing could make you happier."

Whether she hears this or ignores it, I don't know. She seems to have grown heavier in the past few years, not stouter, just more unshakable in deed and word. What she doesn't like, she doesn't hear. Now she walks among the teeming pots and cold-frames where she practices her ideas on growing plants.

In these flats, the soil is mixed fine with coffee grounds and broken eggshells. Her roses grow dark red and electric on crushed bones. The tiny heads of lettuce tighten in garters. The tomato plants droop on thick stems mulched with dried blood and oak leaves. Asparagus fern and chives blow everyplace like hair. Mary uses anything around her that's available. She bends over, tying her tomatoes up on thin steel rods that I think she has lifted from a construction site.

We have stopped for lunch, but now the boy, Adrian, who helps out anywhere he's needed and is supposed to be a cousin of mine, shouts that there's customers.

"Don't get too caught up," I warn Mary as I walk through the door, "we've got the liver sausage waiting." It is mixed up in a huge steel vat, but now one of us has to wash the beef casings, send the mixture spurting through the nozzle of the sausage machine, then tie the long tube into rings.

"I know, I know," she says, but whether she's answering me

113

or merely soothing her tomatoes I can't tell. I walk down the hall, out to the counter, and the customer I see standing there is our old classmate, Wallace Pfef, now the head of the chamber of commerce and still a bachelor. He is watching our steaks intently through the thick glass, as if they might suddenly shake off their green paper frills. The lights from the case glow up into his face, making purple shadows beneath his eyes and nose.

"What can I get you today?" I ask. Wallace is usually a regular, but has not been in for weeks.

"Good afternoon, Celestine," he says. "I was hoping to see Mary." He looks around me, but she is not visible down the hall or through the window that leads to her office.

"She's out back," I tell him, "tying up her tomato vines."

He looks both relieved and disappointed. "Never mind, I'll talk to her next time," he says. I ask if it's important, but he only smiles his little businessman smile and taps the glass with a fingernail.

"Could I see that one?" he asks.

Pfef must be shown his meat up close, as if it were jewelry from a case. I display the red steak on a piece of waxed paper and he examines it before nodding his acceptance.

"Wrap it up," he says, "and one-quarter pound of the longhorn cheddar."

I cut this, wrap both of his purchases in white paper. And then, because his interest in Mary has made me curious, I ask him if he's sure I shouldn't get her.

"No," he waves away my offer, "no, please don't. It was only this."

He shows me *The Sentinel*. It is an ad. One full page. GRANDE OPENING, it says, CHEZ SITA, HOME OF THE FLAMBÉED SHRIMP. The ad goes on to talk about "your dining pleasure," "subtle ambiance," "food exquisitely displayed." A menu is listed.

114

"Doesn't it look delicious," says Wallace. "You know, Sita's restaurant is a prestigious addition to our town." His voice is raised in such enthusiasm that Mary hears him as she walks down the hallway with the ball of string.

"What's this?" she says.

"Mary!" says Wallace. He smiles at her and offers a small whitish envelope from the inner pocket of his suit jacket. He explains. "All the businesses in town are getting these, but your cousin Sita asked me to make especially sure that you received it."

"I'll bet she did," says Mary. She has opened the envelope and I see that it's an invitation. Engraved. Mary hands it to me. I read how we are cordially invited to the grand opening of Chez Sita, one week from this evening. There is a note on the bottom, in Sita's tight little handwriting, that tells us ties and suitcoats are required wearing for men, and also that ladies must dress in an appropriate fashion. This is Sita's way of telling us she doesn't really want us to come, her low-class former friends and relatives. She is sending us the invitation just to rub our faces in the subtle ambiance of her new and very prosperous life.

While I'm musing on the creamy little card, Mary is reading the newspaper ad.

"Chez Sita." She says Chez to rhyme with Pez. She does not seem impressed by the menu or the ad. And I find, as soon as Wallace has left us, that a customer has already told Mary the story behind Sita's restaurant. As we stand at the counter, Mary relates it to me. Sita and Jimmy have finally divorced, she says. It was all a secret and now it's final. They are living apart. Jimmy took the real estate agency, the scrapyard, the storage and rental warehouse, even The Trampoline, which is a bar he thought up to attract the younger set; and also his miniature golf course. Sita took the house and the restaurant. She closed The Poopdeck, remodeled the interior and hired all new staff including a chef,

Mary says, *all the way from Minneapolis*. This last fact clearly angers Mary, and her face clouds in the telling.

"It is expensive," I say, looking at the menu. "Who do you think will eat at Chez Sita?"

Mary cannot say, cannot imagine. But the customer's story explains to us what I've noticed over the past few weeks about the outer transformation of The Poopdeck.

I've watched workers tear the colorful plastic banners from The Poopdeck's mast, lower the lifeboat, and finally cover all the blue and white nautical trim with a dark wine-red paint. Still, there is no disguising the shape of the building's hull, the portholes, the mast that probably cannot be severed without structural damage to the building below. Now, approaching the restaurant from the edge of town, it is not a boat that you see, beached cheerfully like before, but a ship so dark it's almost frightful. It is Sita's black ship, unmoored in tossing yew shrubs, ready to sail as if gathering souls.

It is an odd thought, but I was traveling with Mary when we first saw the changes and she maintained that the place looked like the ship of the dead.

Now Mary tosses the invitation into the trash and walks out to the liver sausage table. She does not intend to go to Sita's grand opening, that is evident, but I follow behind her and pick the card from the bin.

"Don't you want to know what it's like on the inside?" I ask.

"What what's like." Mary is sorting out the dishpan of casings now, untangling the long opaque strings, preparing them to be filled.

"Sita's place."

"Why waste money?"

I don't answer, to see if she will go on from there.

"That place gives me the creeps," she says.

"Some people feel like that about butcher shops," I say, and

116

I turn from her, annoyed at how she won't understand what she doesn't want to think about. I take the cover off the sausage machine and start packing the liver mixture into its bin with a flat trowel. Mary fits the end of the casing onto the nozzle, and then wipes her hands off on her apron.

"I'm going anyway," I tell her. "With or without you."

One week or so later, on the very day of the grande opening, Mary changes her mind and asks what time I'm leaving.

"Suppertime," I answer.

"Then let's take the shop truck."

I'd rather not show up in Sita's parking lot in the low maroon van lettered boldly on each panel HOUSE OF MEATS, but it's not worth the price of arguing. So we gather that night, dressed in our finest summer clothing. Russell slides into the driver's seat. Mary settles into the passenger's side. I must crawl into the back and crouch behind them, taking care not to ruin the knees of my stockings.

Russell is dressed in the new gray suit, which I bought him because his two dress uniforms were asked for by the county museum. They now hang off a tailor's dummy in a display case along with a list of Russell's medals and a photograph. That picture shows him as he was when he came back from Germany, before Korea, when his scars were more attractive than now. Mary has twisted her salt-and-pepper hair into a French knot, and she is dressed in electric sea-blue. Her dress is made of a shiny taffeta, and fastened on the shoulder with rhinestone bows. The dress is not Mary's color, or her style either with its tight bodice and enormous gathered skirt. It is the kind of mistake that ladies shops sell cheap at their year-end clearance, and that is very likely where Mary acquired it. For my part, I have always been advised, with my height and big bones, to dress in a soft yet tailored style. I wear a ruffled pink shirt, a brown suit jacket

117

and pleated skirt out of summer-weight wool. Except for Mary, I think, we look presentable. She is hunched over, polishing the tops of her shoes with a piece of newsprint, and then she is muttering into the glove compartment. She doesn't like Russell driving, but I've convinced her to let him, I'm not sure why, except that I'm anxious about appearances and it's customary for the man to take the wheel. I still wish we didn't have to use the van. I don't want to stick out in the elegant surroundings.

"Where in the hell are my yarrow sticks!" says Mary, peering up at us, one hand still groping through the maps and sunglasses and delivery orders.

These sticks are supposed to tell what is going to happen in the short run. But I doubt they could have predicted much about that night. Lately, Mary has been sending off for special offers and reading books on mental projection. She claims she had psychic ability when she was young and caused the face of Christ to appear where she hit the ground beneath the school slide. That event is so old no one here remembers it anymore. And for myself, I never saw it no matter how hard I looked so I don't buy it. I tell Mary that she has started to believe her old newspaper clippings, but nothing seems to shake her deep faith.

"Here we are," I say. My eyes are full of the glaring fabric of Mary's dress. Russell gets out of the van. I am used to the way his face looks, all sewn together, but he often startles others. And I do not even feel so sure about myself. I tower. My face is too broad. My teeth look fierce when I grin, a trait from my mother's side. But I know that any concern for how we look to others is absolutely useless on my part, so I resign myself.

Walking into the restaurant I do not shrink or sidle. I take my usual long step and tell the puffy little hostess in her prom gown that I've got reservations.

"James?" she says, simpering into her leather-covered guest book. "I'm afraid not."

"Adare," says Mary, and starts to spell it.

118

"Oh yes," the hostess says. "We have your table waiting, madam. Right this way."

She leads us through doors that have been padded like the walls of a lunatic's cell, and on into the high-class gloom.

"What did I tell you," says Mary. "This is eerie."

I throw my arm out to stop her comment, but hit thin air. I think I see a ghostly flare of light off her dress, but the room is so deceptive, so large and full of shadows. As we walk, we grip each other's sleeves. Russell, up front, has taken the arm of our hostess, who is surefooted in this atmosphere as a guide in a cave. At each table we pass, a candle flickers in a bowl and I see that many of these tables are occupied. People have come, drawn by the novelty like us, or perhaps even the legitimate wish to experience dining pleasure. I think at first they are squinting at huge photograph albums, but once we sit down and are handed our own I see that of course they are menus.

"Our proprietor, Mrs. Sita Bohl, will be by to greet you personally," says the hostess.

"Tell her not to bother," says Mary before I kick her.

The hostess lifts her eyebrows then vanishes into the shade between the tables. A waiter comes. We all order highballs. But it is really too dark in here, and I believe that Sita has covered the portholes, which is too bad, because even a gleam of starlight would help us read our menus. Our candle is especially dim, too, in its bowl. It does not shed enough light to read by. But luckily Russell smokes, or not so luckily, because as chance would have it, while he is holding his lighter close to the pages to see the words, he sets his menu on fire. He doesn't notice it at first. None of us notice, except that the glow at our table gets brighter. I take advantage of the flare to quickly make my selection. Then Russell is slapping the fire out with his napkin, a heavy starched linen that was folded into a crown. The napkin absorbs the fire, puts it out.

"Excitement's over," Russell assures the waiter who stands

behind us, poised with a pitcher of iced water. A small cloud of smoke now drifts in the dark air above our table. We have created a stir that I know will inevitably draw Sita. And sure enough, she soon materializes, with us suddenly, dressed in a black sheath and pearls. She bends over the table, trying not to make a scene, and hisses something indistinguishable. The light from below distorts her face into a Halloween mask, witchlike and gruesome. It is a moment before I register the fact that she is whispering not about the charred paper, the cloud of smoke, the disturbance we have created, but about some dilemma of her own.

"Come out back," she says. "Follow me."

But Mary asks in a loud voice, "What for?"

Sita tries to hush her but Mary is adamant.

"We're not going to budge," she says from deep in her chair.

Sita is forced to plead with her, but nothing she whispers convinces Mary, who fairly shouts, "You in some kind of trouble, or what?"

"Come on." I finally cannot bear the suspense. "Let's go with Sita." I pull Russell to his feet, so then Mary is forced to follow or sit alone. Sita leads us. But she blends into the darkness in her black dress, and we fumble, banging into other people's tables, before we finally locate some door that leads us into the bright kitchen area. There we see, blinking, that Sita has transformed herself. She wears an apron, stands before an open grill, and behind her two long tables are covered with a welter of open cookbooks and empty pots.

A waiter leaps through the door.

"Anything!" he cries out. "They're chewing on their forks!"

"My God," says Sita, stirring a pot of soup with one hand, checking a piece of meat with the other, "hold them off! Give them each a free drink!"

"They're already drunk!"

"My chef," gasps Sita, explaining over her shoulder to us,

"came down with food poisoning. All the helpers too. It was the shrimp stuffed with crab."

I had been going to order that.

"Too bad," Mary says. In her voice there is victory, and I feel somewhat ashamed of her because Sita is driven to her limit. Her face is strained with shock. Her hair is fairly on end. Her movements are jerky and stunned, like the robots in Mary's dream. Even after all that Sita has done to make us feel beneath her, I can't enjoy watching this. But Mary has the most to complain about in Sita's case, and I pause in the feeling that she should decide what to do next.

"All right," she says. "Let's get to work."

Sita sags as if the wire that held her up was severed, and then unties her apron. She hangs it on a hook, smoothes her hair, and moves out the door.

"Put these on," Mary orders, handing white coats and wide aprons down from a shelf to Russell and me. "Now you," she tells the next waiter who pokes his head in through the door, "go out there and tell the customers that their side dishes are on the house and their whole total meal is twenty percent off. That'll shut them up."

The waiter darts out. On the counter there is a tall stack of orders. I start to read them. The renovators, luckily, have left behind one of The Poopdeck's large deep fryers. I turn the controls up to high. Mary finds plastic bags of jumbo breaded shrimp in the freezer. Once the grease bubbles, Mary fries up a batch, then another, and Russell sends a plateload, twelve or fifteen, to every table. "Home of the Flambéed Shrimp," Sita's ad declared. Almost every order included shrimp.

I am trying to read cookbooks, meanwhile, and figure out how to poach frog's legs, ball *Foie Gras*, prepare a *Velouté de Volaille Froid*, not to mention the main courses: *Poulet Sauté d'Artois, Filet de Boeuf Saint-Florentin, Huîtres à la Mornay*, and of course the nearly fatal shrimp-and-crab dish. But that is temporarily not available.

"I can't do this," I say to Russell in despair.

He has grated potatoes next, having finished the shrimp. He is frying an enormous load of golden hashbrowns.

"Relax," he says, grinning beneath his chef's hat. He seems to be enjoying this. "No one out there understood the menu," he explains. "In case you hadn't noticed, the damn thing was in French."

I don't get his drift.

"They won't know what their food is supposed to be," he says; "just cook it up the way you would at home."

He's right, so that's what I do.

We make fried chicken, roast beef, oysters in a pie. Mary tosses together Pete's famous Polish noodle soup. Russell finds several boxes of delicate French wafers and coats them with chocolate, berry glaze, sherbets, and ice cream. We make something out of everything we uncover in the kitchen. Sita pops in occasionally. Her look, as the waiters carry plates of fried chicken past her, is both beaten and full of relief.

It is well past eleven o'clock before we get a breath. The regular employees, sons and daughters of our customers, have been sworn to secrecy concerning the state of the chef's health and our contribution. But of course, I can see it from their eyes, there is no way they will be silent about what has taken place.

The food was good, too. The customers left satisfied, full, ready to come back, and declaring that the French deep-fry method was expensive but delicious, and the quantity was worth it for the price. Almost every one of them goes out with a white, foil-lined bag that says "*pour le chien*." We three sit down at last, in the wreckage of the kitchen.

The hostess has rolled down her stockings and dropped the straps of her gown. She sits with us, feet up on a chair. Slowly, the waiters and waitresses straggle in, exhausted and hungry. The dishwashers are still going. Everyone begins to eat scraps of this, tastes of that, bits of Russell's confections and leftover hash-browns.

"You saved the night," says the same waiter who stood behind us with the pitcher of iced water. "She's still out there totaling up."

She, of course, is Sita, who finally comes through the door.

"Well," she says, massaging her temples, "I suppose I should thank you."

"Don't mention it," says Russell.

"Wait," Mary holds Sita's gaze, "if you want to thank something, go ahead and thank your father's noodle soup."

Sita nods briefly, but that's all she can bring herself to do. After a while she turns around and walks out the door.

After Sita departs, things loosen up. "Have a drink?" the hostess asks us in a friendly voice. We agree. There is plenty of open wine, which we polish off, and even champagne. The hostess slumps lower in her chair, makeup blurred, and lets Russell rub her back.

It is almost dawn before Mary, Russell, and myself are finally let out the door beneath the dark ship's prow. The air is cool and gray. The sky sparkles and the dew makes everything smell fresh, even the gravel in the parking lot. Russell lounges on the side of the truck for a moment, lighting a cigarette between his palms. The cupped glow reflects onto his face. Mary glows too. Her dress is spectral, floating across the flat ground. She is rummaging in her purse for the keys, forgetting Russell has them. Before he can give them back to her, Mary's hand lights on something.

"My sticks," she exclaims, drawing out a thin bundle that looks like broomstraws.

"Throw them here, on the car hood," says Russell. "Let's see the future."

So Mary chants beneath her breath, and tosses her yarrow sticks according to some mail-order instruction. They land every which way, in a jumble, but she looks at them with keen eyes as though their exciting design is plain. No matter how we pester Mary she will say nothing of what she sees, and just leaves them scrambled on the hood when Russell gives her the keys to the truck. We get in and Mary starts driving. As we move along, the sticks slide off the hood one by one and we laugh every time this happens, as though we're throwing caution to the winds.

Not long after the night in which we rescue Sita from the grande opening's certain disaster, more rumors start to fly about her. A customer comes into the shop and says that the state health inspector, who was sent over from Bismarck to investigate Chez Sita after word leaked out on the food poisoning, has been back and forth many times. He does not always wear his badge or carry his briefcase, and no one knows whether he is paying social calls or if there is yet more to fear from the unfamiliar food. The hostess and most of the waiters are laid off, we hear. Chez Sita is usually empty. But this fact does not seem to bother Sita.

One day, picking up some barrels of salt down at the warehouse in Fargo, I see her snapping a green bean, then sniffing the end to determine its freshness. A man is standing with her. He is tall and sober, with gray steel glasses and gray hair. Sita holds the end of the green bean to his nose and he frowns. She smiles and looks almost girlish again. Her hair is tousled. I turn away before she sees me there, watching. The man with Sita looks like the kind of expert you see on television commercials, the type whose low calm voice advises us on pain relief. I feel he must be the state health inspector, and from Sita's smile I think that his visits are probably not so official anymore. This man seems a way out of the restaurant business, a chance for Sita to make a new start in life. I am relieved for her, glad of her good spirits.

But as I am driving back from the big market with the barrels of preserving salt, I think of Sita's face again, and see the crisp bean in her fingers. It makes me wonder about myself. Will I ever smile, flush, offer a tidbit of food? Are these things that Sita feels, these pleasures I have read about in books, the sort of feelings I might experience? It has never happened yet, although I've known men. Perhaps, I think, I'm too much like them, too strong or imposing when I square my shoulders, too eager to take control.

I drive for a distance among the quiet, flat fields, but the long views of crops do not calm me, nor the clouds, just scratches high in the atmosphere, nor the strung poles that endlessly pass and revolve. I'm not calm even when I reach the shop. I find Mary's note saying that she left and I should lock up for the night. Perhaps because I'm in this mood—strange, disturbed, lonely at the core—perhaps because Mary is unexpectedly not there, I'm not at my best when the man comes through the door.

He is fine boned, slick, agreeable, and dressed to kill in his sharp black suit, winy vest, knotted brown tie. His hair is oiled. His lips are fevered and red as two buds. For a long while he stands there, eyeing me, before he opens his mouth.

"You're not pretty," are the first words he speaks.

And I, who have never bit off my words even to a customer, am surprised into a wounded silence although I don't look in the mirror for pleasure, but only to take stock of the night's damage.

I am standing on a stool, changing the prices I chalk above the counter each week on a piece of slate. Blutwurst. Swedish sausage. Center-cut chops. Steak. I keep writing and do not give him the satisfaction of an answer. He stands below me, waiting. He has the patience of a cat with women. When I finish, there is nothing left for me to do but climb down.

"But pretty's not the only thing," the man continues smoothly, as though all my silence has not come between.

125

I cut him off. "Tell me what you want," I say. "I'm closing shop."

"I bet you never thought I'd come back," he says. He steps close to the glass counter full of meats. I can see, through the false, bright glare inside the case, his dumbbell-lifting chest. His sharp, thick hands. Even above the white pepper and sawdust of the shop, I can smell the wildroot, tobacco, penetrating breath mint.

"I never saw you the first time," I tell him. "I'm closing."

"Look here," he says, "Mary . . ."

"I'm not Mary."

"Oh, my God, *Sita*?"

"Sita's gone," I say. "She lives in the biggest house in Blue Mound. That's the next town over."

He goes rigid, puts his hand to the back of his skull, pats the hair in place thoughtfully.

"Who are you then?"

"Celestine," I say, "as if it's any of your business."

I have to ring out the register, secure the doors, set the alarm on the safe before I can walk home. Around that time of early evening the light floods through the thick block-glass windows, a golden light that softens the shelves and barrels. Dusk is always my time, that special air of shifting shapes, and it occurs to me that, even though he says I am not pretty, perhaps in the dusk I am impossible to resist. Perhaps there is something about me, like he says.

"Adare. Karl Adare."

He introduces himself without my asking. He crosses his arms on the counter, leans over, and deliberately smiles at my reaction. His teeth are small, shiny, mother-of-pearl.

"This is something," I say. "Mary's brother."

"She ever talk about me?"

"No," I have to answer, "and she's out on a delivery right now. She won't be back for a couple of hours."

"But you're here."

I guess my mouth drops a little. Me knowing who he is has only slightly diverted what seem like his firm intentions, which are what? I can't read him. I turn away from him and make myself busy with the till, but I am fumbling. I think of Sita testing vegetables. Now it seems as though something is happening to me. I turn around to look at Karl. His eyes are burning holes and he tries to look right through me if he can. This is, indeed, the way men behave in the world of romance. Except that he is slightly smaller than me, and also Mary's brother. And then there is his irritating refrain.

"Pretty's not everything," he says to me again. "You're built . . ." He stops, trying to hide his confusion. But his neck reddens and I think maybe he is no more experienced at this than I.

"If you curled the ends at least," he says, attempting to recover, "if you cut your hair. Or maybe it's the apron."

I always wear a long white butcher's apron, starched and swaddled around my middle with thick straps. Right now I take it off, whip it around me, and toss it on the radiator. I decide I will best him at his game, as I have studied it in private, have thought it out.

"All right," I say, walking around the counter. "Here I am." Because of the market visit I am wearing a navy blue dress edged in white. I have a bow at my waist, black shoes, and a silver necklace. I have always thought I looked impressive in this outfit, not to be taken lightly. Sure enough, his eyes widen. He looks stricken and suddenly uncertain of the next move, which I see is mine to make.

"Follow me," I say. "I'll put a pot of coffee on the stove."

It is Mary's stove, of course, but she will not be back for several hours. He does not follow me directly, but lights a cigarette. He smokes the heavy kind, not my brand anymore. The smoke curls from his lips.

"You married?" he asks.

127

"No," I say. He drops the cigarette on the floor, crushes it out with his foot, and then picks it up and says, "Where shall I put this?"

I point at an ashtray in the hall, and he drops the butt in. Then, as we walk back to Mary's kitchen, I see that he is carrying a black case I have not noticed before. We are at the door of the kitchen. It is dark. I have my hand on the light switch and am going to turn on the fluorescent ring, when he comes up behind me, puts his hands on my shoulders, and kisses the back of my neck.

"Get away from me," I say, not expecting this so soon. First the glances, the adoration, the many conversations must happen.

"How come?" he asks. "This is what you want."

His voice shakes. Neither one of us is in control. I shrug his hands off.

"What I want." I repeat this stupidly. Love stories always end here. I never had a mother to tell me what came next. He steps in front of me and hugs me to himself, draws my face down to his face. I am supposed to taste a burning sweetness on his lips, but his mouth is hard as metal.

I lunge from his grip, but he comes right with me. I lose my balance. He is fighting me for the upper hand, straining down with all his might, but I am more than equal to his weight-lifting arms and thrashing legs. I could throw him to the side, I know, but I grow curious. There is the smell of corn mash, something Mary has dropped that morning. That's what I notice even when it happens and we are together, rolling over, clasped, bumping into the legs of the table. I move by instinct, lurching under him, my mind held up like a glass in which I see my own face, amused, embarrassed, and relieved. It is not so complicated, not even as painful, as I feared and it doesn't last long either. He sighs when it is over, his breath hot and hollow in my ear.

"I don't believe this happened," he says to himself.

That is, oddly, when I lash out against his presence. He is so heavy that I think I might scream in his face. I push his chest, a dead weight, and then I heave him over so he sprawls in the dark, away from me so I can breathe. Then we smooth our clothing and hair back so carefully in the dark, that when we finally turn the light on and blink at the place where we find ourselves, it is as though nothing has happened.

We are standing up, looking anyplace but at each other.

"How about that coffee?" he says.

I turn to the stove.

And then, when I turn around again with the coffeepot, I see that he is unlatching a complicated series of brass fittings that unfold his suitcase into a large stand-up display. He is absorbed, one-minded, not too different from the way he was down on the floor. The case is lined in scarlet velvet. Knives gleam in the plush. Each rests in a fitted compartment, the tips capped so as not to pierce the cloth, the bone handles tied with small strips of pigskin leather.

I sit down. I ask what he is doing but he does not answer, only turns and eyes me significantly. He holds out a knife and a small rectangle of dark wood.

"You can slice," he begins, "through wood, even plaster with our serrated edge. Or . . ." he produces a pale dinner roll from his pocket, "the softest bread." He proceeds to demonstrate, sawing the end of the block of balsa wood with little difficulty, then delicately wiggling the knife through the roll so it falls apart in transparent, perfect ovals.

"You could never butter those," I hear myself say. "They'd fall apart."

"It's just as good with soft-skinned vegetables," he says to the air. "Fruits. Fish fillets."

He is testing the edge of the knife. "Feel," he says, holding the blade toward me. I ignore him. One thing I know is knives

129

and his are cheap-john, not worth half the price of the fancy case. He keeps on with his demonstration, slicing bits of cloth, a very ripe tomato, and a box of ice cream from Mary's freezer. He shows each knife, one after the other, explaining its usefulness. He shows me the knife sharpener and sharpens all Mary's knives on its wheels. The last thing he does is take out a pair of utility shears. He snips the air with them as he speaks.

"Got a penny?" he asks.

Mary keeps her small change in a glass jar on the windowsill. I take out a penny and lay it on the table. And then, in the kitchen glare, Karl takes his scissors and cuts the penny into a spiral.

So, I think, this is what happens after the burning kiss, when the music roars. Imagine. The lovers are trapped together in a deserted mansion. His lips descend. She touches his magnificent thews.

"Cut anything," he says, putting the spiral beside my hand. He begins another. I watch the tension in his fingers, the slow frown of enjoyment. He puts another perfect spiral beside the first. And then, since he looks as though he might keep on going, cutting all the pennies in the jar, I decide that I now have seen what love is about.

"Pack up and go," I tell him.

But he only smiles and bites his lip, concentrating on the penny that uncoils in his hands. He will not budge. I can sit here watching the man and his knives, or call the police. But neither of these seem like a suitable ending.

"I'll take it," I say, pointing at the smallest knife.

In one motion he unlatches a vegetable parer from its velvet niche and sets it between us on the table. I dump a dollar in change from the penny-ante jar. He snaps the case shut. I handle my knife. It is razor sharp, good for cutting the eyes from potatoes. But he is gone by the time I have formed the next thought.

In my stories, they return as a matter of course. So does Karl. There is something about me he has to follow. He doesn't know what it is and I can't tell him either, but not two weeks go by before he breezes back into town, still without ever having seen his sister. Russell looks outside one morning and sees him straddling the chubstone walk to our house.

"It's a noodle," says Russell. I glance out the window over his shoulder and see Karl.

"I've got business with him," I say.

"Answer the door then," Russell says. "I'll get lost."

He walks out the back door with his tools.

The bell rings twice. I open the front door and lean out.

"I can't use any," I say.

The smile falls off his face. He is confused a moment, then shocked. I see that he has come to my house by accident. Maybe he thought that he would never see me again. His face is what decides me that he has another thing coming. I am standing there in layers of flimsy clothing with a hammer in my hand. I can tell it makes him nervous when I ask him in, but he thinks so much of himself that he can't back down. I pull a chair out, still dangling the hammer, and he sits. I go into the kitchen and fetch him a glass of the lemonade I have been smashing the ice for. I half expect him to sneak out, but when I return he is still sitting there, the suitcase humbly at his feet, an oily black fedora on his knees.

"So, so," I say, taking a chair beside him.

He has no answer to my comment. As he sips on the lemonade, however, he glances around and seems slowly to recover his salesman's confidence.

"How's the paring knife holding out?" he asks.

I just laugh. "The blade snapped off the handle," I say. "Your knives are duck-bait."

He keeps his composure somehow, and slowly takes in the

living room with his stare. When my ceramics, books, typewriter, pillows and ashtrays are all added up, he turns to the suitcase with a squint.

"You live here by yourself?" he asks.

"With my brother."

"Oh."

I fill his lemonade glass again from my pitcher. It is time, now, for Karl to break down with his confession that I am a slow-burning fuse in his loins. A hair trigger. I am a name he cannot silence. A dream that never burst.

"Oh well . . ." he says.

"What's that supposed to mean?" I ask.

"Nothing."

We sit there for a while collecting dust until the silence and absence of Russell from the house grows very evident. And then, putting down our glasses, we walk up the stairs. At the door to my room, I take the hat from his hand. I hang it on my doorknob and beckon him in. And this time, I have been there before. I've had two weeks to figure out the missing areas of books. He is shocked by what I've learned. It is like his mind darkens. Where before there was shuffling and silence, now there are cries. Where before we were hidden, now the shocking glare. I pull the blinds up. What we do is well worth a second look, even if there are only the squirrels in the box elders. He falls right off the bed once, shaking the whole house. And when he gets up he is spent, in pain because of an aching back. He just lies there.

"You could stay on for supper," I finally offer, because he doesn't seem likely to go.

"I will." And then he is looking at me with his eyes in a different way, as if he cannot figure the sum of me. As if I am too much for him to compass. I get nervous.

"I'll fix the soup now," I say.

"Don't go." His hand is on my arm, the polished fingernails

clutching. I cannot help but look down and compare it with my own. I have the hands of a woman who has handled too many knives, deep-nicked and marked with lines, toughened from spice and brine, gouged, even missing a tip and nail.

"I'll go if I want," I say. "Don't I live here?"

And I get up, throwing a housecoat and sweater over myself. I go downstairs and start a dinner on the stove. Presently, I hear him come down, feel him behind me in the doorway, those black eyes in a skin white as veal.

"Pull up a chair," I say. He settles himself heavily and drinks down the highball I give him. When I cook, what goes into my soup is what's there. Expect the unexpected, Russell always says. Butter beans and barley. A bowl of fried rice. Frozen oxtails. All this goes into my pot.

"God almighty," says Russell, stepping through the door. "You still here?" There is never any doubt Russell is my brother. We have the same slanting eyes and wide mouth, the same long head and glaring white teeth. We could be twins, but for his scars and except that I am a paler version of him.

"Adare," says the salesman, holding out his perfect hand. "Karl Adare. Representative at Large."

"What's that?" Russell ignores the hand and rummages beneath the sink for a beer. He makes it himself from a recipe that he learned in the army. Whenever he opens that cupboard I stand back, because sometimes the brew explodes on contact with air. Our cellar is also full of beer. In the deepest of summer, on close, hot nights, we sometimes hear the bottles go smashing into the dirt.

"So," says Russell, "you're the one who sold Celestine here the bum knife."

"That's right," Karl says, taking a fast drink.

"You unload many?"

"No."

"I'm not surprised," Russell says.

Karl looks at me, trying to gauge what I've told. But because he doesn't understand the first thing about me, he draws blank. There is nothing to read on my face. I ladle the soup on his plate and sit down across the table. I say to Russell, "He's got a suitcase full."

"Let's see it then."

Russell always likes to look at tools. So again the case comes out, folding into a display. While we eat, Russell keeps up a running examination of every detail a knife could own. He tries them out on bits of paper, on his own pants and fingers. And all the while, whenever Karl can manage to catch my eye, he gives a mournful look of pleading as if I am forcing this performance with the knives. As if the apple in Russell's fingers is his own heart getting peeled. It is uncomfortable. In the love magazines, when passion holds sway, men don't fall down and roll on the floor and lay there like dead. But Karl does that. Right that very evening, in fact, not long after the dinner, when I tell him he must go, he suddenly hits the floor like a toppled statue.

"What's that!" I jump up, clutching Russell's arm. We are still in the kitchen. Having drunk several bottles in the mellow dusk, Russell isn't clear in the head. Karl has drunk more. We look down. He is slumped beneath the table where he's fallen, passed out, so pale and still I fetch a mirror to his pencil-moustache and am not satisfied until his breath leaves a faint silver cloud.

The next morning, the next morning after that, and still the next morning Karl is here in the house. He pretends to take ill at first, creeping close to me that first night in order to avoid deadly chills. The same the night after, and the night after that, until things began to get too predictable for my taste.

Sitting at the table in his underwear is something Karl starts doing once he feels at home. He never makes himself useful.

134

He never sells any knives. Every day when I leave for work the last thing I see is him killing time, talking to himself like the leaves in the trees. Every night when I come home there he is, taking space up like one more piece of furniture. Only now, he's got himself clothed. Right away, when I enter the door, he rises like a sleepwalker and comes forward to embrace me and lead me upstairs.

"I don't like what's going on here," says Russell after two weeks of hanging around on the outskirts of this affair. "I'll take off until you get tired of the Noodle."

So Russell goes. Whenever things heat up at home he stays up on the reservation with Eli, his half brother, in an old house papered with calendars of naked women. They fish for crappies or trap muskrats and spend their Saturday nights half drunk, paging through the long years on their wall. I don't like to have him go up there, but I'm not ready to say good-bye to Karl.

I get into a habit with Karl and don't look up for two months. Mary tells me what I do with her brother is my business, but I catch her eyeing me, her gaze a sharp yellow. I do not blame her. Karl has gone to her only once for dinner. It was supposed to be their grand reunion, but it fell flat. They blamed each other. They argued. Mary hit him with a can of oysters. She threw it from behind and left a goose egg, or so Karl says. Mary never tells me her side, but after that night things change at work. She talks around me, delivers messages through others. I even hear through one of the men that she says I've turned against her.

Meanwhile, love wears on me. Mary or no Mary, I am tired of coming home to Karl's heavy breathing and even his touch has begun to oppress me.

"Maybe we ought to end this while we're still in love," I say to him one morning.

He just looks at me.

"You want me to pop the question."

"No."

"Yes you do," he says, edging around the table.

I leave the house. The next morning, when I tell him to leave again, he proposes marriage. But this time I have a threat to make.

"I'm calling the state asylum," I say. "You're berserk."

He leans over and spins his finger around his ear.

"Commit me then," he says. "I'm crazy with love."

Something in this all has made me realize that Karl has read as many books as I, and that his fantasies have always stopped before the woman came home worn out from cutting beef into steaks with an electric saw.

"It's not just you," I tell him. "I don't want to get married. With you around I get no sleep. I'm tired all the time. All day I'm giving wrong change and I don't have any dreams. I'm the kind of person that likes having dreams. Now I have to see you every morning when I wake up and I forget if I dreamed anything or even slept at all, because right away you're on me with your hot breath."

He stands up and pushes his chest, hard, against mine, and runs his hands down my back and puts his mouth on my mouth. I don't have a damn thing to defend myself with. I push him down hard on the chair and sit, eager, in his lap. But all the while, I am aware that I am living on Karl's borrowed terms.

They might as well cart me off in a wet sheet too, I think.

"I'm like some kind of animal," I say, when it is over.

"What kind?" he asks, lazy. We are laying on the kitchen floor.

"A big stupid heifer."

He doesn't hear what I say though. I get up. I smooth my clothes down and drive off to the shop. But all day, as I wait on customers and tend fire in the smoke room, as I order from suppliers and slice the head cheese and peg up and down the cribbage board, I am setting my mind hard against the situation.

"I'm going home," I say to Mary, when work is done, "and getting rid of him."

We are standing in the back entry alone; all the men are gone. I know she is going to say something strange.

"I had an insight," she says. "If you do, he'll take his life."

I look at the furnace in the corner, not at her, and I think that I hear a false note in her voice.

"He's not going to kill himself," I tell her. "He's not the type. And you . . ."—I am angry now—"you don't know what you want. At the same time you're jealous of Karl and me, you don't want us apart. You're confused."

She takes her apron off and hangs it on a hook. If she wasn't so proud, so good at hardening her heart, she might have said what kind of time this had been for her alone. She might have said how all this hurt because she once made a play for Russell, and he resisted.

But she turns and sets her teeth.

"Call me up when it's over," she says, "and we'll drive out to The Brunch Bar."

This is a restaurant where we like to go on busy nights when there is no time for cooking. I know her saying this has taken effort, so I feel sorry.

"Give me one hour, then I'll call you," I say.

As usual, when I get home, Karl is sitting at the kitchen table. The first thing I do is fetch his sample case from the couch where he parks it, handy for when the customers start pouring in. I carry it into the kitchen, put it down, and kick it across the linoleum. The leather screeches but the knives make no sound inside their velvet.

"What do you think I'm trying to tell you?" I ask.

He is sitting before the day's dirty dishes, half-full ashtrays,

137

and crumbs of bread. He wears his suit pants, the dark red vest, and a shirt that belongs to Russell. If I have any hesitations, the shirt erases them.

"Get out," I say.

But he only shrugs and smiles.

"I can't go yet," he says. "It's time for the matinee."

I step closer, not close enough so he can grab me, just to where there is no chance he can escape my gaze. He bends down. He lights a match off the sole of his shoe and starts blowing harsh smoke into the air. My mind is shaking from the strain, but my expression is still firm. It isn't until he smokes his Lucky to the nub, and speaks, that I falter.

"Don't chuck me. I'm the father," he says.

I hold my eyes trained on his forehead, not having really heard or understood what he said. He laughs. He puts his hands up like a bank clerk in a holdup and then I give him the once over, take him in as if he was a stranger. He is better looking than I am, with the dark eyes, red lips and pale complexion of a movie actor. His drinking has not told on him, not his smoking either. His teeth have stayed pearly and white, although his fingers are stained rubbery orange from the curling smoke.

"I give up! You're the stupidest woman I ever met." He puts his arms down, lights another cigarette from the first. "Here you're knocked up," he says suddenly, "and you don't even know it."

I suppose I do look stupid, knowing at that instant what he says is true.

"You're going to have my baby," he says in a calmer voice, before I can recover my sense.

"You don't know."

I grab his suitcase and heave it past him through the screen door. It tears right through the rotten mesh and thumps hard on the porch. He is silent for a long time, letting this act sink in.

"You don't love me," he says.

"I don't love you," I answer.

"What about my baby?"

"There's not a baby."

And now he starts moving. He backs away from me toward the door, but he cannot go through it.

"Get going," I say.

"Not yet." His voice is desperate.

"What now?"

"A souvenir. I don't have anything to remember you." If he cries, I know I'll break down, so I grab the object closest to my hand, a book I've had sitting on the top of the refrigerator. I won it somewhere and never opened the cover. I hold it out to him.

"Here," I say.

He takes the book, and then there is no other excuse. He edges down the steps and finally off at a slow walk through the grass, down the road. I stand there a long time, watching him from the door, before he shrinks into the distance and is gone. And then, once I feel certain he has walked all the way to Argus, maybe hopped a bus or hitched down Highway 30 south, I lay my head down on the table and let my mind go.

The first thing I do once I am better is to dial Mary's number.

"I got rid of him," I say into the phone.

"Give me ten minutes," she says, "I'll come and get you."

"Just wait," I say. "I have to have some time off."

"What for?"

"I went and got myself into the family way."

She says nothing. I listen to the silence on her end before I finally hear her take the phone from her ear, and put it down.

In the love books a baby never comes of it all, so again I am not prepared. I do not expect the weakness in my legs or the swelling ankles. The tales of burning love never mention how I lie awake, alone in the heat of an August night, and panic. I know the child feels me thinking. It turns over and over, so furiously that I know it must be wound on its cord. I fear that something has gone wrong with it. The mind is not right, just like the father's. Or it will look like the sick sheep I had to club. A million probable, terrible, things will go wrong. And then, as I am lying there worrying into the dark, bottles start going off under the house. Russell's brew is exploding and all night, with the baby turning, I keep dreaming and waking to the sound of glass flying through the earth.

Mary's Night

After Mary hung up the phone on Celestine, she took the crowbar from the top of the refrigerator, where Pete had kept it, too, and went back to her utility room to open the crate that was delivered last month from Florida.

The box had been sitting in one spot so long that drill bits, clothespins, and burned-out light bulbs had collected on top. Mary moved the clutter to a windowsill and began prying nails from the rough pine boards. It was just turning to dusk outside, but she had enough light to see by and didn't stop until she'd pulled off two sides of the wooden box. It contained a cabinet. She switched on the lights in a blaze.

The cabinet was small, elegant, carved of dark-stained wood with ornate cast-iron legs and drawer pulls. Each drawer was decorated with a curving design of amber-colored wood. The top was hinged. Mary opened it, removed the packing, and lifted out the sewing machine. Then she stood back and contemplated. It was like a little black mechanical dragon, with one busy, murderous fang. After a while, she put the machine down and let the hinged top fall over it. Then she switched off the light, went back to the kitchen, and picked up the phone.

It was Sita's number that she dialed, an out-of-town exchange because Sita had just sold the restaurant and moved out to Blue Mound with her scientific husband.

"What do you want?" said Sita, when she heard Mary's voice.

"Nothing from you," said Mary. "I've got something of yours, though."

Sita was silent, trying to think what this thing could be. She finally had to ask.

"A sewing machine," said Mary.

"I've already got one," said Sita.

"I know," Mary answered. "Your aunt sent you another."

Sita had to think for a moment, then she remembered Adelaide and how she had liked to sew. She remembered the fur collars, the turned-out bows, the fashionable adjustments to out-of-date dresses.

"I'll get Louis to pick it up," she said.

"It's in the back room," said Mary.

Then she hung up and put the bar away on the refrigerator. She stood in the brilliance and faint buzzing of the fluorescent ring.

Nothing came back to her from the stillness outside except the faint, restless clinking of the dog's chain, and the acid fragrance of tomato vines he had broken digging bones along the wall. This time of night, Mary usually called her dogs in and fell asleep reading. But tonight was ripe with significance. Tonight was full of hidden signs.

She thought of her tarot pack, kept beneath her mattress to absorb her dream's vibrations as the gypsy instructions advised. She had a Ouija board. A customer had shown her a certain way to crack an egg into a jar of water and read the yolk. But none of these methods came close to duplicating the splendor of the day she had smashed her face in ice and seen her brother as if through a magic mirror. Standing on her clean linoleum, thinking forward, she willed a sign to come.

A steer moaned in the stock pens. A light breeze set up a rustle in the thickets of clenched and ragged roses in the yard. Moths banged the screen door.

Mary turned off the light and went outside. She began to walk. Beyond her fences the backyards were a maze of pens, storage sheds, old boxcars and chicken runs full of rusting equipment. Uncle Pete got his hands on a lot of things in his life. A great iron bathtub, used for scalding the hair off pigs, sat in the weeds collecting ferrous rainwater, breeding midges. Beyond the junk there was Fritzie's shelterbelt of mulberry, evergreen, wild plum and cedar. Around the trees, the grass was cool, layered, densely green. Mary stood breathing the scent of needles and leaves, and thought of Karl.

Again, she saw him gathering the branch, its white blooms and invisible scent to his face so long ago. She saw his eyes close in delicate greed. His lips opened. And then she saw Celestine too, her mouth deep, her arms spread and grasping, her body more solid than the tree Karl had embraced before he vanished.

The yard light cast a faint glow from behind. The evergreens seemed impenetrably dark, even frightening. Mary thought of bums, owls, rabid skunks and mice that the shelterbelt might harbor. Yet, she stepped forward into the overgrown grass. With that first step, she felt gravity collect in her legs. At the next step her eyes itched for sleep. She plunged forward anyway, through the crossed branches.

The earth was damp, cool, and Mary sank into the grass. It seemed, in her trance, that a great deal of time went by. The plums were green and hard when she first lay down, the mulberry pips invisible, the grass green and pliable. Then the moon came up, stars wheeled in sequined patterns, birds took flight. The season waned and Celestine's baby grew large as day.

It was a girl, much larger than Mary's lost baby brother, but just as vigorous, and with a headful of blazing dark red curls.

She peered at Mary, her eyes the gray-blue of newborns, unfocused but willful already, and of a stubborn intensity that Mary recognized as her own. Then the dark deepened and the night grew deliciously soft. From where she lay, Mary heard the wild plums ripen. They grew plump on their thin stems and fell, knocked off by wind. In her sleep she heard them drop through the long brittle grass and collect all around her in a glorious waste.

SITA KOZKA

JUST WEEKS AFTER the food-poisoning fiasco at my restaurant, I quietly married Louis and he resigned as state health inspector to take a county job that would keep us near forever. Louis sold his house in Bismarck and moved all of his scientific equipment to Blue Mound, where we lived in the big split-level house, with colonial details and shutters, that Jimmy had built as a kind of showplace. And there, although we had only been married two months, it was as if Louis and I had been together all our lives. Maybe it was because he had to take care of me. During the excitement of moving and a failing business, my nerves were strained to nothing. Luckily our house has a huge backyard, and while I was recuperating from my troubles, I occupied myself with growing ornamental shrubs, perennials, and climbing vines.

Because of the divorce, I had lapsed from the church. Louis tried to convince me there was nothing to it in the first place, but I was not entirely happy about leaving. For many years Saint Catherine's had been important in my life, and religion itself still had a strict hold. Among other things, the idea of relying only on Louis and myself for answers and assistance was new. I was not sure I liked it. But I tried to be strong, ready for the unexpected, and perhaps for that reason I was not dismayed the morning I found my cousin sleeping, sodden, in my trained clematis. I did not recognize him when I first discovered him. I hadn't seen him in twenty-five years. He had one arm around a suitcase and he held a little book.

He opened his eyes.

"Hello there, Sita," he said from where he lay. He had got into my backyard by rolling beneath the fence. "I suppose you don't recognize me," he said, scrambling to his feet and then carefully untangling himself from the leaves, "I'm your cousin Karl."

A wanderer and a salesman is what I'd heard he'd become. He looked well-trampled by the adventures of life. He was frayed at the neck and cuff. Hatless. His face was handsome in an overly pretty, disturbing way, but his lips were too red, as if he had a hangover. His eyes hung half shut, pouched and weary. His oiled black hair flopped down in strands around his ears.

He looked suspicious, even dangerous in his shabby clothes. Yet I was interested. I knew if he attacked me all I had to do is scream. Louis was in the garage, not ten feet away, feeding his entomological specimens. I gripped my trowel like a weapon while Karl was talking, and decided if he made a fast move I would split his skull. My white canvas gloves would obscure any fingerprints. Louis and I could bury him beneath the dahlias with the murder weapon. In the past weeks I'd consumed boxes of mysteries to soothe my nerves.

"Karl Adare," he repeated. "I'm your cousin, remember? I was on my way to a sales conference. I got here early and didn't want to wake you."

I supposed it was a compliment to have a long-lost cousin visit, even if he crawled in through the flower bed. It certainly would have been news around here, second only to my own divorce and sudden remarriage. With my nerves, and the restaurant, on top of all that, it seemed I had supplied Blue Mound and Argus with gossip all month. The thought gave me a headache. I put down my trowel.

"How nice to see you," I said, remembering my manners, "after all this time. You'll join us for lunch, I hope?"

He nodded yes, and looked around at the yard. "Not bad," he said. The way his voice squeezed shut I knew he was envious of my banks of rich flowers, the tile patio, the house which I'd heard people call a mansion, the largest house in Blue Mound. Louis had inherited good farmland, which he rented out. Even though Louis had closed down the restaurant, we could afford to keep the place up.

"And tell me about yourself," I said, indicating his suitcase and the thick little book in his hands. The book looked familiar, black with reddish diamonds on the cover, and once he cracked the paper glued inside and opened it, I knew why. It was a Bible, a rather typical cheap version of the New Testament.

"There's room to record family events," he said, looking into the cover. "Births, deaths, marriages."

He seemed to be talking to himself, so I made no comment. I didn't want him to try and sell me the book.

"Let's sit down," I said, but he seemed to have read my mind because he didn't snap the book shut or follow me, but continued to look morosely into the cover.

He's preparing a pitch, I thought, and I took his arm.

"You must be tired," I said, "on the road so often."

"I am," he agreed, looking at me steadily and gratefully. "I'm awfully glad to see you, Sita. It's been a long time."

"Too long," I said in a warm voice, although the truth was I'd never missed him, hardly thought about him in all those years, and I was beginning to suspect, just slightly, from nothing I could put my finger on really, that he'd looked me up in the hope of an easy sale.

Just at that moment Louis walked out into the yard. He always looked keenly at people but then never seemed to recall the slightest thing about them once they were gone. Now he stared penetratingly at Karl. Karl smiled back, uncertainly. "I'm Sita's cousin," he called to Louis. "Been a long time!" But Louis ignored him and walked over to the compost pile to gather a few more of his specimens.

"What's he doing?" Karl wondered.

"Digging worms."

"What for?"

"To see how they break down organic matter."

Louis kept me abreast of his every thought. For his new post as extension agent, he was now collecting data about the area pests and local helpers. Earthworms were helpers, and Louis was experimenting with their habitat. What to put in the ground to attract their help.

"They make humus," I informed Karl in a stern voice, for his attention had wandered. He was taking in the details of our home again, my white cast-iron lawn furniture, the clipped and flowering shrubs. He soon included me in his accounts, giving me a slow, bold look. I was not at my slimmest, but according to Louis contentment fit me best, and I knew that my color was good.

"Have I changed?" I said, and then, embarrassed by the coy note in my voice, I answered my own question. "Of course I have. Who wouldn't?"

"Beautiful as ever," said Karl. I turned away. Louis rarely gave me compliments. But then he was often deep in his abstract thoughts. What Karl said meant more to me than it should have, and so I was unable to keep from saying what I said next.

"Gray hairs, a few lines here and there. The years show."

"Oh no," said Karl, "you're prettier now. Maturity becomes you."

"It does?" I was acting foolish as a peacock.

"Yes," he said.

We had a long silent moment between us, almost intimate, and then more words popped out of my mouth.

"All flesh is grass," I said, hardly believing my own voice, and

147

because of the strangeness hearing the phrase as entirely new. We stood uncomfortably, looking at the lawn, and I noticed that the whole yard was covered with the same kind of grass that grew in cemeteries—fine, short-cropped grass of a brilliant green color.

"I'll get lunch," I said, to interrupt myself.

I left my cousin watching Louis pull worms from the mulch, and I went in to make us a plateful of sandwiches for an early lunch. Ham salad. I have a grinder that attaches to my sink. I was mixing the ground ham with capers and mayonnaise when Karl stepped up to the screen door and banged on it lightly.

"Could I use your facilities?"

"Of course," I said.

I let him in. He put the suitcase by the door and laid the book on my kitchen counter as he walked past. He did it so casually that I thought he had done it on purpose, to interest me in it. And so, while he was upstairs, I picked up the book. I examined the dull red diamonds on the cover. Besides being a New Testament, the book still reminded me of something else. It took several moments of concentration for me to place where I had seen it before. Then I knew. Last year at a raffle for the Saint Catherine's Society we had given away a New Testament like this, and Celestine James had won it.

"This may be a coincidence," I said to Karl when he returned from upstairs, "but a book just like this belonged to a former friend of mine."

He picked up the book, weighed it, and pressed it in my hands.

"You can have it," he said. "Fill it up."

Then he hoisted his suitcase and went out to sit on the lawn furniture with Louis. I was puzzled by his words until I remembered about the spaces for family events. I opened the book.

Saint Catherine Society, was stamped inside the cover, and then the date. May 4, 1952, and the name Celestine James.

"Aha!" I said, just like a detective in a poorly written crime

148

drama. Then, obscurely ashamed at my discovery, I snapped the book shut and continued mixing ingredients in the milk glass bowl. Having outgrown my acquaintance with Celestine James, I wasn't sure how to handle the Bible anyway. For years I'd had nothing to do with her. I spread the mixture on pieces of bread and cut the sandwiches in triangles and went out. Karl had evidently told my husband that lunch was coming, for Louis had washed with the garden hose, and now the men were balanced on the little wrought-iron chairs. The table came no higher than their knees. The sight was comical. But I had learned not to laugh at everything that looked absurd. Laughter had been one symptom of my thinning nerves.

"Isn't it lovely," I said, "the sun's so mild."

I put the tray down, with everything on it except the pitcher and glasses, and I went back for those. When I came out again I saw that the men had started eating, which annoyed me.

"What bad manners the two of you have!" I exclaimed.

"You're right," said Louis, putting down his sandwich and passing me the plate. My cousin, however, continued to take his food. I watched him pick up a sandwich and bring it to his lips, then bite it with his white teeth. One, two, and the sandwich was snapped down. I stared, wondering if he'd done something to Celestine, perhaps threatened her, in order to get the book. Or perhaps he knocked her out. And then there was the suitcase. Did he have more of her possessions tucked away inside of that?

Louis cleared his throat and spoke in the humoring tone I knew.

"Sita, you're keeping rather a close eye on our visitor, aren't you?"

I looked down at my plate. I couldn't help myself. I whispered.

"The way my cousin eats is very sinister."

"No it's not," said Louis, and cast around for some other topic of conversation. "Hummingbirds are attracted to Sita's trumpet vines," he said. I smiled at Karl, but he was eating faster than ever. I supposed he had not heard my whispered comment.

"Yes," I went on, "they hover with their beaks reaching down into the . . . what is it . . . ?"

"The ovary."

". . . the ovary of the flower."

Karl gulped down a last bite of sandwich and nodded faintly at both of us. I noticed suddenly, although it must have been happening all along, that the sharp iron legs of his chair were digging into the damp lawn. The ground beneath him was evidently very soft, perhaps from all the earthworm activity, and he was settling by slow degrees. The table fit over his knees quite easily now. He seemed not to notice, however, and gave me a tight smile.

I returned the smile, but as we bit into more sandwiches without speaking, I realized why Karl was here.

He had robbed Celestine and we were next. Why else would he have been hiding in the clematis, spying, learning our habits, if not in order to steal from us with ease? And another thing. He had not gone upstairs to use the facilities, but to loot my jewelry box. It seemed as though I had even seen him do this myself. I saw him snap off the tiny lock, pluck up my silver pin, diamond locket, reclaim my necklace of old garnets. I saw him drop my treasures in his pocket. My brooches, my rings, my amethyst.

"I'm going inside, fellows," I announced lightly, and rose.

Louis seemed to sense something. He frowned at the heavy lace of the table. But I was certain of Karl's guilt, now, and went indoors to use the phone.

"The largest hummingbird," I heard Louis say as I walked off, "is a whopping nine inches. Lives down in South America." I knew that Louis was keeping my cousin entertained with some marvel, and sure enough, when I had made the proper phone call and returned, I saw that he had so entranced Karl that my cousin had sunk noticeably farther. He was now at chest level with the table. His arms were crossed in front of him.

"It's sad," I said, fixing him with a look, "how some people just can't keep their hands off of other people's property."

"That's true," said my husband in an earnest voice. "Remember how the little scissors used to vanish from the dissecting kits?"

"Louis taught," I informed my cousin. "He taught in a high school."

"Know where those scissors went?" asked Louis.

Karl's eyes widened and he lifted his shoulders. His mouth was full of sandwich, so he couldn't answer.

"Girls stole them to manicure their nails!" said my husband.

Just then Sheriff Pausch came down the flagstones. He was a little man with a sharp doggish face and a deep, surprising voice that boomed godlike from his bullhorn during tornado alerts. Before becoming a sheriff he'd taught botany, so he and Louis had much in common. They were members of the Blue Mound Mycological Society, which had already had its first meeting in our basement. It seemed odd to have him here on official business, in his tan uniform, with a paper in his hand instead of bread bags full of dried fungus.

Karl's eyes went still wider when he saw the sheriff. His alarm put the last convincing touches on his guilt. He put his hand out and said, "Please, take my seat."

"No thank you," said Sheriff Pausch firmly, motioning Karl to stay seated. "There's been a complaint."

Karl's face turned childish, tipped upward from his low seat, stricken.

"I'll get the evidence," I muttered, rising to go.

"Stay here," said Louis. "What's all of this about?"

"Your wife called me," said Sheriff Pausch, looking surprised and lowering his voice. "She said something about a theft."

I pointed down at Karl, and gave him a cold glare. "He stole

Celestine James's New Testament," I said, "then he went through my jewelry box. He took necklaces, pins, whatever he could lay his hands on. Stuffed them in his pocket. Search him!" I urged the two men. "See for yourself!"

"Put your hands in the air," said Sheriff Pausch in his deep voice. He stepped behind Karl and quickly patted him up and down.

"Excuse me," he said, moving back to face Karl, who had gone pale as a sheet. "You can put your hands down now," said the sheriff, flushing down to the opening in his shirt. "There seems to have been a mistake."

There was a long moment of tension. I looked at each of the men carefully. They looked carefully at me.

"It's true," I finally said. "Let me fetch the book."

"I think there has been a mistake," Sheriff Pausch repeated, and just that suddenly, because there was a wary gentleness in his voice, I knew that I had done something very wrong. Worse yet, I knew that something even more wrong was going to happen. I looked down at Karl. The legs of his chair had sunk still farther.

"Stop . . . that," I slowly commanded.

"Sita, sit down now, please," said Louis.

But I was locked in an upright position by Karl's dark strained stare. I could not take my eyes away although I had to bend across the table to see him clearly, he'd sunk so far. The air was very still. The tiny birds, light as moths, hovered in the trumpet flowers. One note sounded. I meant to ask Louis if he heard it as well. But then my cousin leaned over sideways and pulled the heavy-looking case, the one he'd dragged through the clematis, onto his lap. He sat there with the case clasped in his arms, perhaps intending to open it, perhaps intending to go. Instead, something happened.

The case was so heavy, resting on his lap and knees, that his feet began to bury themselves in the earth and very swiftly the

152

lawn rose to his knees. I said nothing. I was paralyzed with fear. I had betrayed him and now I could only watch as the man, the chair, continued to sink. The case submerged. The lawn crept up his oxblood shirt. The grass brushed his chin. And still he continued to go down.

It is too late, I thought, watching him, unless he says the healing words.

"*Mea culpa*," I gasped. "*Mea maxima culpa*."

But already his mouth was sealed by earth. His ears were stopped. His mild, sad eyes were covered and then there was only the pale strip of his forehead. The earth paused before swallowing him entirely, and then, quite suddenly, the rest of him went under. The last I saw was the careless white cross in his oiled hair. The ground shook slightly to cover him, and there was nothing where he had been.

I stared at the peaceful grass for a long while and then looked up. Louis and the sheriff were watching me. It seemed as though they were waiting for me to tell them what this meant.

"We wake when we die. We are all judged," I said.

Then I went down to the tree where my silver was hung. Bracelets and rings and old coins of it. I put my hands out. The leaves moved over me, gleaming and sharpened, with tarnished edges. They fell off in mounds. The air was a glittering dry rain. While I was down there I said many things. Louis wrote them all on a pad of paper.

I described the tree in detail. It bore the leaves of my betrayal. The roots reached under everything. Everywhere I walked I had to step on the dead, who lay tangled and cradled, waiting for the trumpet, for the voice on the bullhorn, for the little book to open that held a million names.

"You are not in the book," I told Louis. "You are down there with your specimens."

Russell's Night

Over the summer, Russell slowly built himself a fishing shack, and then, in the fall, he dragged it through two fields and left it on the bank where the river slowed and deepened before it bent away from Argus. When the river froze into an angle of black iron, he pushed the shack out onto the ice, drilled a hole with his auger, and began going there often.

Sliding down the steep bank on a raw December afternoon, he caught his scoop net in a nest of old flood debris and plunged into a spider web of thick dead vines that held him. He thrashed for several moments and then quit. The web was oddly comfortable, a hammock in just his shape once he relaxed. He groped for the flask of Four Roses stowed inside the blanket lining of his long denim jacket, then took a pull.

Russell blew into his fingers and put the bottle back in his pocket. No matter how cold it was he never wore gloves anymore, preferring his hands to harden now that he didn't have to count bills or change. He needed callous to tighten bolts, touch hot radiator caps, work lug nuts free and on the weekends clean fish. He looked up into the low clouds and tilted his pint back. Maybe it would snow. The breeze was warm enough. What he liked about not working at a regular job was exactly this. He could lay here all afternoon if he felt like it and just get drunk. But he wasn't much of a drinker, and after a while he freed himself and made his way down to his shack.

He kept a padlock on the door now that Celestine had found his place. Weeks ago, he'd gone in and found everything was tampered with, not drastically, just enough so he knew she had been there. He was positive that it was her, even though she had left no direct evidence. The place had the skewed feeling of something vaguely wrong, but then he realized it was only that everything had been neatened. That was Celestine's habit around the house when she was restless. His coffee cans of fishing tackle had been pushed into a careful row. One of the sandbags he used to weight the house so it wouldn't blow over was patched with cloth tape where sand had trickled out. He always kept the tape in his tackle box. She had put it back. Russell noticed that a can of Sterno had been punched, burned, then replaced on its shelf with the others. His little wire stove was hung back on its hook, and his water can and coffeepot were clean, like he always left them. Still, he didn't like Celestine to visit. He knew she kept coming back because she wanted to talk to him, but he wanted to avoid her for a while longer.

Now, since the padlock was on the door, he knew she hadn't been inside, though her footprints were scattered in the snow.

He took out his key and snapped the lock open, then stepped into the mild green fish-smelling air. Today it seemed warm inside even with no heater. Warmth was trapped in the tarpaper walls. In the middle of the house, black in the center of the ice floor, the hole he'd cut two days ago was still open. He scooped out the slush with a coffee can and dumped it beside the door. Then he baited a hook and a large dangling lure that was beaten and polished like a woman's silver earring. He unfolded the woven-mesh lawn chair he kept propped against one wall, sat down, and started to fish. His eyes had completely adjusted to the dim interior now, and the gray light, spreading down from the small window, one he'd scavenged from a ruined chicken-house, lit the board walls with a calm and diffuse low radiance.

His leg, the one with the old spiral fracture and shrapnel wounds, the left gimp leg, ached from the fall he'd taken coming down the bank. He rubbed his thigh slowly with one hand and kept the other on the pole he'd stuck through a slat of his chair. He watched the line, the red-white bobber, and thought about nothing. Whenever Celestine came into his mind he put her out of it. He hadn't been home, or spoken to her, except for that one day when he'd noticed the obvious.

Back in July, he'd heard that her boyfriend had left, but Russell had been in no hurry to come down from the reservation. Then one night he'd caught a ride down to Argus, late, and slipped into his room while Celestine was sleeping. He meant to surprise her with breakfast, but she was already awake and up by the time he came out of his door into the narrow hall.

He'd mumbled, looking down, ashamed to be caught in a sagging pair of union long johns. Celestine was wearing nothing but her slip though, and her jutting outline registered.

Before she recognized him, she shouted in alarm, and then she blushed, looked down, and smiled at her news.

"I wasn't going to tell you this way, but you're an uncle."

Russell walked past her without a word and went into the bathroom. He carefully latched the door. Inside, he stared at the brownish speckled linoleum floor until he felt suddenly and strangely dizzy. To clear his thoughts, he shook himself all over like a dog, then washed his face. Celestine banged on the door.

"You don't have to be like that," she said. "I'm married."

"It's your funeral," he answered. Those were the last words they had spoken.

After he was done in the bathroom, he went downstairs and rifled through the refrigerator shelves quickly, hoping Celestine or the salesman would not come into the kitchen before he'd packed himself a lunch and left.

Even when Mary told him that Karl was long gone, he couldn't make himself go back. Something held him.

Now the pole lurched against his hand, pulling down the bobber. He grabbed the line between his fingers, waited seconds, then tugged it gently back, hoping he could secure the hook in the fish's jaw. The line burned off his thumb. He'd done it. The fish must be large, he thought, a half-starved northern maybe, one he'd have to play to land. He reeled in and out, tiring it slowly, until finally he brought it up, not so big as he'd imagined once it broke water, and so exhausted it hardly flopped in the net. It was a long thin many-toothed pike, mottled a dark rich green, beautiful and ferociously cold, and too young. After he'd unfastened his hook and tackle gingerly from its mouth, then wet his hands and slid the fish back beneath the ice, Russell reset his line and settled into his chair again. His body heat and the colorless light had warmed the house. He flexed his hands on his knees to warm the fingers and hoped that he would not catch the same fish twice. As he sat there, waiting, the picture of Celestine in the slip, shadowed in the narrow hall, full and outcurved like the prow of a boat, rose in his mind. This time he let her stay.

She was there when he felt the first tightening in his chest.

Soon it turned into a slow tingling, a nerve throbbing in his arm and a feeling of rich tiredness elsewhere. There was no pain. Only a sharp burst as if the whiskey had expanded, as if it had flooded his brain. He looked around in surprise. As on the day he'd come here weeks ago to find things tampered with, everything looked vaguely distorted. It seemed as though the light itself had now been disturbed. It hung in wavering sheets. Then the pain crashed out. It coiled and uncoiled like a big steel spring, out and in, until it suddenly shrank and collapsed to a black button.

Around five that evening, Celestine came down the banks, falling just where Russell had, but getting out at once and retrieving her flashlight from the snow. When she reached the ice she almost turned back. It was near dusk and he would have needed light. The shack was dark. But then, in the play of her flashlight beam, she saw the unsnapped padlock.

She walked over the hard-packed river snow and opened the door. Her flashlight picked out Russell's slumped form in the lawn chair, and at first she thought, ridiculously, that he'd fallen asleep with the pole wedged in his hands. Then she noticed that the line had snapped. She walked in, touched his back, and spoke his name. When he took a shuddering breath she put her arm around his chest and pulled him out of the chair, dragged him over to the sandbags, and laid him down. After a moment he opened his eyes.

"I'll get help," she whispered. Her voice echoed in the shack, and then everything around her went into slow motion like a nightmare. Things tried to hold her back as she started running. The ice. The snow. The tangled brush. The fields. Even the air. It seemed like hours before she finally reached her car.

WALLACE PFEF

I HAVE NEVER married, but I do have a girl friend referred to by the people of Argus as "Pfef's poor dead sweetheart." She is a long gray face behind glass. Her photograph, in its polished brass frame, keeps discreet watch over my living room. My visitors inquire about the collection of Hummel figures, the souvenir spoons in their rack, the icy bells I collect, crystal bells. But they do not ask about my poor dead sweetheart, although, as they examine my objects, they will pause before her portrait as if to pay their respects.

To tell the truth, I don't know the woman in the picture.

I bought her many years ago at one of those sad Minnesota farm auctions. She was among the empty canning jars, pincushions, butter dishes, and chipped vases in a box I bid out for five dollars. Whoever she is, with her prominent jaw, young worn mouth, and neatly waved hair, she is part of town legend now. I've invented little things about her as they occur to me: her disease was encephalitis. Common at the time, if you lived around horses. She went into a trance from which she never awakened. Her feet were slim and long to match her jaw, and she was tall.

Because of the poor dead sweetheart, I've never had to marry. I've squired women around and made myself available as a sort of one-man dinner-partner service to Argussian widows. Husbands have even hinted jealously of my attentions to their wives. But people have long since stopped believing I would ever desert the picture in my living room.

"She has too strong a hold on him. He can't forget her," they say.

I live in the flat, treeless valley where sugar beets grow. It is intemperate here, a climate of violent extremes. I do like storms, though, and bad weather of all types. For then I have an excuse to stay in bed, reading crime and espionage, dozing occasionally, and listening to the wind, a great hand slapping at my house. *Whap! Whap!* The beams and hidden studs squeak and quiver. I never regret having built so far out of town, on the road out of Argus, heading north, even though it is rarely traveled by any but those who must. It is beautiful here. My view is a stark horizon of grays and browns. I built as an incentive to other home builders, but my only neighbors have been here all along. Celestine and her baby now are my nearest, only the two of them since her brother's unfortunate stroke.

But first, to introduce myself.

I'm Wallace Pfef. Chamber of commerce, Sugar Beet Promoters, Optimists, Knights of Columbus, park board, and other organizations too numerous to mention. In addition to supporting the B♯ Piano Club and managing the town swimming pool, I am the one who is bringing beets to the valley, beets that have yet to fail as a cash crop anywhere, beets that will make refined white sugar every bit as American as corn on the cob.

There has been resistance to my proposition, and why not? Agronomists value cyclical regularities. They are suspicious of innovation, and my business is courting change. To woo them, I've become the friend to agricultural co-ops and visited each area farmer individually. I've drunk sloe gin and schnapps and nameless basement brews. In town I've joined up with a vengeance, for I know that within the fraternal orders lies power. Eagles, Moose, Kiwanis, Elk. I need to belong. I've gained a hundred ears, pumped hands, exchanged secret passwords with my brothers. I've told them how beets are much more than a simple crop. They are the perfect marriage between nature and technology. Like crude oil, the beet needs refining, and that means Refinery. That spells local industry. Everyone benefits.

I got sold on the beet at the 1952 Home, Crop, and Livestock Convention in Minneapolis. Many of those in the audience around me were salesmen, but none as good as Karl Adare.

I never knew it, had probably hidden it deep away, but I found the attraction as easy as breathing in and breathing out. And so it happened. And there I was, member of the Kiwanis, eating prime rib and accepting choice bits of game hen from the fork of another man. Sheer madness. Yet I felt amazed, as if the clouds had blown away, as if the bare bones were finally visible. I was queer.

I don't know why, either, except that the Pfefs have always been dissatisfied. We came over from the great Ruhr Valley, perhaps even then carrying a race memory of the raw white beet. In America, we moved often, complaining that something was not quite right. Maybe in the end it was us, my father's schemes that failed, and my sisters, who have turned into alcoholic, wasting farmwives. Up until Minneapolis, I was the stability, the surprise in the family.

It was a shock when Karl jumped on the bed and began to bounce. I'd looked for some topic of mutual interest, and hit a nerve when I asked about his sister. I didn't blame him once he told me her name. I knew Mary from grade school. She was ruthless. I'd seen her slow work on Sita Kozka. Mary pulled nerves like string in a blanket until the whole loose-woven fabric of Sita's mind came unraveled. There had been one, two, crack-ups by that time. And, too, Mary was shrewd. She had a reputation for getting and keeping, while I already had a partial sense of what slipped past Karl.

But while Karl went up and down, smacking the ceiling with

the palm of his hand, I had no thought of this. I feared some sort of damage, to the bed, not him. I feared he would break the springs in the mattress or the frame would collapse. I can still see it clearly, as in a snapshot: Karl hunched in his tight black pants, tie whirling free, a cutout against the ornate pressed tin of the hotel ceiling.

Then he hit.

I am a good man in someone else's crisis and did not panic. The back was injured. *Immobilize*, I thought. I saw that the right things were done. When he came to in traction, cast in plaster, in what must have been unimaginable pain, he smiled dreamily through grit teeth and rolled his eyes.

"Still here," he observed.

"Of course."

I was not allowed to touch, just look, and I tried to convey everything that way. My mistake. He seemed repelled by my sympathy. Then the drugs sent him back where he'd been, and I was left to sit. I watched for hours. It was midnight before I went back to my room. And even then I racked up a phone bill searching Minneapolis and Saint Paul for a florist who would deliver that time of night.

In the days that followed the accident, Karl hummed tunes or stared at the ceiling all day, living in his own mind, not at all interested in me or the hospital surroundings. He hardly spoke to me; however, I made friends. To this day, I correspond with the morning nurse there. She thought that Karl was mentally unbalanced, he enjoyed his confinement so.

"Good-bye," I said one morning, walking onto the ward. He'd had a private room for one week and not a single visitor except me. I held my hat. My light coat was draped on one arm. "I have to dash," I said. "Everyone in Argus will wonder what's become of me."

He looked well, shaved already, skin freshened, hair combed. It was as though he'd put on the cast for a joke.

"Bon voyage," he said, and turned the page of some magazine.

I walked out, angry at myself for being a fool. I thought I'd never see him again.

I had my half-finished house to complete, and I was living in the basement while the top was constructed. I took my time getting it done right. Things went slow, but when the home was finally livable it was perfect. The walls were real plaster. I had an insulated picture window, built-in shelves, and recessed lights to set off my collections. I moved in before the carpets were laid, before the kitchen appliances were hooked up, before the cabinets were sanded. The first thing I brought in was the photograph of my poor dead sweetheart, younger and more earnest than when I'd bought her. I set her on my living-room shelf. She stared out at the raw white room, the primed walls, the plastic-sheeted easy chair and picture window.

"In theory," I said to her, "all this is yours." I drank a toast to her with vegetable juice and got on with my work.

I am good at hiding facts for my own self-protection, at forgetting. So I forgot Karl most days. Yet there were times, walking into his sister's shop for my chop or stew meat, that I found him uncomfortably on the tip of my tongue. I wanted to tell her about him. I wanted to disrupt her smugness. But I was afraid of her grim manner, her cold eye, and couldn't get past the impersonal patience she felt was due to a customer. I only kept going there because The House of Meats had the freshest steak in town, and I preferred to have Celestine wait on me. In spite of her forbidding height and how she stood, knuckles on her hips, confronting each customer, she remembered names, problems, preferences and purchases from week to week. She'd ask how I liked the last of their homemade sauerbraten, or why I'd stopped buying the herring. I enjoyed our chats. I would never have guessed the outcome of things.

I'd just come home from the shop, in fact, one spring dusk, when the call came.

"How's Argus?" said the voice.

I said it was fine, although as usual the farmers were needing rain. I waited for the voice to identify itself, though from the first word I knew it was Karl.

"I'm in the cutlery line now," he told me. "Superior quality. I'm coming through tomorrow morning and thought I'd stop by. Maybe drop in on you, on Mary. Did you tell her about me?"

"Never," I said. I was so shocked that I stuttered and choked over directions to Argus. And that night I stayed up to all hours cleaning the house.

He showed up the night after, very late. In both relief and disappointment, I'd given up and turned off my porch lamp. I had put on pajamas, a quilted silk smoking jacket, tasseled slippers. When he rang the bell I peered from the upstairs window. I knew it would be better if my caller were anyone else.

The dark shape was indistinguishable. But once I'd flooded him with light, there he stood, blinking.

"Well," he said eventually, "you're a sight for sore eyes. Should I just stand here or are you going to let me in?"

"Come in," I said. And in he came.

I don't know how he got to my house. There was no car. Days went by. He seemed to have no firm intentions, besides his knives, and simply looked at me with his light cool eyes when I asked him what company he worked for. I didn't really care. It was enough for him to be there, wearing my clothes and towels, fixing toast for himself, at last making sense of my bed. I never knew what to ask from life, but now I did.

What I wished for and what I expected, however, were two different futures. So it did not surprise me two weeks later when he left one afternoon without a note, without warning.

I thought he might have finally gone to visit Mary, but when I stopped by her shop to pick up the ingredients for my dinner there was no sign of him. I went ahead with the evening's preparations. He'd seemed to like my meat loaf, an unusual mixture of ground veal, pork, beef, cream, and parsley, crisscrossed with bacon and baked in a slow oven. I mashed potatoes, strained squash, melted a little cheese for the potatoes. The careful stirring and constant checking helped me pass the time. It was a warm dusk, too. The heat gave me discomfort. That helped divert me, but yet the night came on.

At last, I put aluminum foil over everything. I had a big glass door in the kitchen, and beyond that a brick patio with two folding lounge chairs of blocky redwood. I planned an arbor there, of climbing grapes, lilacs, roses. I brought a light crocheted blanket out for comfort, swaddled myself, lay back in the lounge chair, and let the night come over me. My seeded lawn stretched thirty feet west, then the field began. It was sugar beets, of course, a low crop of thick, abrasive leaves. Over it the moon hung, a great bell in emptiness.

What surprised me, what caused me the worst shock, was where he went.

A week passed and only one dry, black corner of the meat loaf remained. I fed it to the dog, a grumpy stray with tattered white hair and a tail kinked and thin as a rat's. It lived around the edges of the yard, fading in and out of the tall brush and sugar beets, hunting cottontails. Sometimes it came directly to the glass door and I'd feel its dull cold stare. I'd turn just in time to see its starved haunches whirl. Then it would vanish, having eaten what I'd set out.

Sometimes I think the dog was a kind of quisling, appearing like that, leading me eventually to the house. I would never have gone there myself, but then around dusk, one evening, I was driving home when my headlights caught her up ahead on the road toward the James place. She trotted just to the side of the road, and I was afraid she'd be hit. I stopped ahead, tried to get her to enter the car, but of course there was no chance of that. So I followed, low gear, straight to Celestine's. The dog went up the dirt drive and disappeared around back. I was anxious. She was so stealthy I thought she'd had a litter. I turned my headlights off, stepped from the car, and followed her into the backyard. I trespassed. Russell had once told me about his gun, filled with bird shot and hung directly over the back door. I felt the hot sting of those imaginary pellets as I crept around the foundation, just under the square of yellow light from the back windows. I heard voices. First there were only mumbles, then rising tones, then Karl.

When I recognized his voice, my brain stopped.

"That's a hell of a good thing," he called from inside. I heard footsteps creak. He came to the back door and tossed a cigarette into the grass. A thin scarf of smoke drifted out, beyond the screen, slow in the humid air. Karl came down the steps and, crouching with his elbows on his knees, lit another cigarette. I could have reached out and touched him. His form was dim, but I could see that he was just in underwear, mine most likely as I'd given him the run of my closet.

The door banged. It was Celestine. She stood on the steps behind him, tall, monumental from my perspective, and clad only in a white bra and half slip. The thin fabric glowed. Her bra was stiff and pointed. She put her hand out. She was holding a small pair of scissors. She sat down by Karl and took his hand. He clenched his cigarette in his teeth when she started snipping his nails.

"Why the manicure?" he asked.

"You scratched me last night," she answered. Karl gave a sudden laugh and nuzzled his face in Celestine's shoulder, beneath her hair.

"Watch out." She drew the scissors from between them and put them down on the steps.

I could not take my eyes from the sharp blades.

"Come back in," she said to Karl after a while, "there's mosquitoes."

"They don't like the smoke," he said, lighting another cigarette from the pack on the steps beside him.

It was true. He was driving them all over to my hiding place, adding insult to my injury. At first I thought I could endure the shrill whining. It filled my ears then swelled abominably as more descended, a cloud in fact. Some lit, more of them, and then the blood feast was on. I did not dare brush them off for fear of rustling the long dry weeds.

"I guess you're right," said Celestine, sitting down beside him on the steps.

"Hold this," said Karl, giving her a lighted cigarette. More mosquitoes veered away from their tobacco cloud and then found me.

"What's that?" Celestine said.

"What's what?" said Karl, blowing rings.

"Shut up."

I worked my face, trying to shrug the insects off. They were everywhere, attached to my eyelids, my temples, thick at my neck, sipping at the small of my back.

"Hah . . . don't . . ." said Celestine, shrugging his hand off. "There's something out there. I hear it."

I squinted miserably, hating them, my teeth grinding. Karl's hand was still hidden. Celestine slapped the place beneath her slip where it must have been.

I slapped my own face, involuntarily, when she did this.

"Hear that?" She stood up. "Like an echo."

"Come on," said Karl. "You'll draw them." He lit still another cigarette and put it in her hand. She sat down. I was in agony, almost unconscious of them, involved with my own distress, when the dog slunk along the brush opposite the yard.

"Hey," said Celestine, "that dog's over here again."

She stepped down from the porch steps and crossed the grass, calling softly, intent on luring the dog to her. In perfect time with Celestine, I rose and stepped through the weeds and out, past Karl, whose face went stark with shock when I appeared.

The land was wide, the sky was a comfort. The view from my window was my only haven. In those first weeks, time passed slowly, or not at all. Days repeated themselves, alike in so many ways, but there were small differences that saved me. The dog came back one day, gaunt as before, and I fed her a can of smoked salmon. She moved with less caution around me, and one day as I banked and mulched a Silver Maple I hoped would take hold, she came near and put her head to my leg. She let me pet her. She had a dry silky coat, surprisingly clean, and when I touched her I felt, quite suddenly, all my sadness breaking out. I put my face to her neck. She smelled of grass, dust, rain, and faintly underneath that, skunk. She had borne far worse than I, most certainly, in her dog's life. Still, she stood quietly and did not move away.

Months after what I'd seen in Celestine's yard, I heard that she was pregnant and no one knew who the father was. Of course, there were speculations, a customer most likely, they said, or someone living near, like me. No one but me seemed to know that Karl had been with her.

Sometimes I saw Celestine from a distance. She was hard to avoid since she drove past my house to go to work. I saw the side of her face only, a harsh profile that sharpened thinner in my mind after she went by. Only once did we come face-to-face. This was in town, not long before Christmas. She was tall, swathed in plaid wool, and so enormous that it looked like her baby was due any day.

After Christmas, the winter turned nasty and the pressure dropped until by January a blizzard was taking shape. I was lying up, dozing and reading, jotting in my almanac. I noticed the wind strengthening, heard sleet strike my house, and pulled the covers tighter around me. The dog slept at the foot of my bed now, which was lucky, for had it not been for her whines and her troubled barking there is no telling what would have happened to Celestine, who had taken advantage of a lull in the growing storm to set out for the hospital.

She was in labor, real labor, but the lull was false. The snow swirled and her Buick smacked into a snowbank. My porch lights were just barely visible through the waves of snow, and she started toward me. The fields around my house were blown nearly clean by the fierce wind, a piece of luck. The baby could have been born in that field, if it had not been so easy for her mother to walk the thin frozen crust. Celestine encountered the deepest drifts when she hit the fence around my yard. She says that she split her lungs yelling for help under my window. But think of it! The noise was so loud I did not hear her, or thought her cries were wind. Ever since that time I have gone to my window periodically during blizzards and I have looked out, to every side, and listened closely. Celestine and the baby could have died beneath my window while I read history. In the morning I would have found mother and baby huddled tight against my red snow fence like the foolish pheasants I sometimes find there, drifted out of snow, their feathers lit with such a warm and iridescent glow it seems impossible for them to be frozen, as though the burning colors should keep them warm.

But the dog roused me, pacing and snapping at the air, and after a time, just to check, I went to the door. Even then I did not see Celestine, just snow. I almost closed my door against the wind but then she floundered forward, I caught her, and we stumbled through the door into my living room, ringing my shelf of glass bells. Newly carpeted and finished, with a blue shag rug and walls the color of dark eggshells, the room was my pride and joy. My navy blue brushed-velvet couch had just arrived and was still encased in plastic. Celestine gained her balance and stood up, huge in her plaid coat and farmer pants. She immediately chose the couch. A padded cotton sleeping bag was tied around her waist. Until she lay back and untied it and opened it like a nest, I did not remember she was pregnant. Then I saw her belly, covered in a flowery housecoat material, rising in a mound.

"Take off my snow pants," she ordered.

Then she closed her eyes and began a soft, quick whooping sound, like bitterns in the park make when they fly up from the pond. It was only after the look of concentration left her face and she opened her eyes, so deeply spent of their color, that I saw she was in pain.

"They're coming fast," she said. "Another." Then she made her sounds again. When she began this time, I took my wet slippers off and ran upstairs to fetch some thick dry woolen socks for both of our feet. I came back down and saw that her eyes were shut. Her face was gray, a mask of absorption. She'd taken off her own snow pants and now lay back in nothing but her housecoat.

"Get sheets," she said, before the next contraction.

I ran from the room and collected fresh towels, an ice pack, a first-aid kit. I removed brand new sheets from their wrappings and brought all of this back to her, dumped everything beside the couch. She nodded briefly. So I continued, encouraged, to collect things. I boiled water, sterilized my best pair of shears. I made a bed for the baby in a laundry basket. I warmed up wash-cloths and wrung out hot towels to wipe Celestine's face. All this time she was working at this, tensing and rocking, sometimes kneeling beside the couch and sometimes on it. The wind was terrible, blowing so hard the timbers rattled. There was electricity, but the phone lines were down.

I was fishing a hot washrag out of a pot when Celestine wailed loudly.

"Gawd! Gawd! Gawd!"

Three times, like someone in the throes of love or giving up their soul. I ran into the living room and steadied myself at Celestine's elbow.

"I felt the head!" she gasped. "Just for a minute. It went back."

There was something in the moment that calmed me then. Perhaps the astonishment in her face, so like the surprise on Karl's in that hotel room when he found himself suddenly on the floor, and yet so much stronger. There was something in her expression that gave me strength too. I knelt at the other end of the couch and held her legs.

She closed her eyes and instead of the whooping sound she made a kind of low whine. It didn't sound to me like pain though, just effort. She roared when the head came. Then she pushed down again and held herself, pushing down, for a long time. The sound she made was a deeper one, of vast relief, and the baby slid into my hands.

Clay blue, dazed, eyes wide open even then, she came out shockingly alive and complete. Fully present. It did not occur to me to slap her because she looked so ready, so formidable. She took breath and turned pink immediately, deepening to red even as I gave her to Celestine, put a clothespin on the cord between them, and cut.

Later that evening, when I'd finally put a call through and we were waiting for the emergency jeep that would not arrive until morning, Celestine held the baby toward me.

"Hold her," she said, "and listen. I've got to name her after you."

Stunned, I drew the baby to me. She'd retreated into a deep hypnotic sleep, but her tiny calm face seemed full of stubborn

171

purpose. I pored over the set of her wide mouth, the pointed and minuscule chin. I was taken with her, completely, and blinded by happiness at the unlikely thought of her having my name.

"What's your second name?" Celestine asked.

I told her, but it was worse than Wallace. Horst.

"Give me her back," said Celestine. "I'll have to think."

When the snowplows came through the next morning, an ambulance was sent out to bring Celestine and the baby back to Saint Adalbert's. I rode along, helped them fill out forms and settle them into their room on the empty maternity ward. Then I drove home, ate a sandwich, and sat down in the living room. The dog curled in the chair across from me, dozing in the complacent way she'd learned. I was unwilling to let the deep significance of all that had happened diminish, and so I didn't turn on the television, pick up a book, or otherwise divert myself.

The phone woke me. I stumbled to the little alcove where I'd had it mounted, and put the receiver to my ear. There was the sound of Celestine's voice on the crackling, ice-laden wire, a dry pause afterward.

"Wallacette," was all she said.

But Wallacette Darlene wasn't destined to be my namesake for long. From the first, Mary had a nickname for her. Dot. By the time we brought the baby into Saint Catherine's for the baptism, Celestine was calling her Dot too. I said nothing. But to me, the child would always be Wallacette. As her male sponsor, I was glad to give her full name for the church records, and her date of birth. But when it came to the names of Wallacette's parents, I paused. I had to gather myself before I said them without a tremble.

Just after Wallacette was born, Celestine had married Karl in Rapid City, South Dakota. I'd pried out the details of her bus schedule and found that she had stayed overnight in some hotel. Honeymoon? I'd never dared to wonder. Nor had I asked if he'd return. Their picture would appear soon in the wedding section of the *Sentinel*, and for the time being that seemed to be the whole extent of their union.

The sacristy was in the rear of the church, next to the doors and uninsulated stained-glass windows, which is to say it was damp and terribly cold.

"We needn't take our coats off," said Father, striding in with his equipment. "Don't unwrap the baby either. We don't want our little girl to catch a chill." He smiled and took the cover off the baptismal font. With a slight tap of his finger he cracked the film of ice that had formed on the surface of the water.

"Say there," said Mary. "You can't pour freezing water on a baby's head!" She stared belligerently into the priest's eyes.

"Of course not." The priest took a small glass jug of water from inside his jacket. "We'll just use a bit of this. It's blessed. Then we'll wipe her head off and cover her back up again."

Mary nodded, satisfied, and the questioning began. The priest held the oblong bundle of our baby and asked what she wanted of the Church of God. Mary and I had memorized the baby's answer.

"Faith," we said.

"What does faith bring to thee?" the priest asked.

"Life everlasting."

Then he prayed and put the stole on the baby. All together we recited the Apostles' Creed and the Our Father. The priest shifted Wallacette slightly in his arms. She woke and stared out at us from under a little green wool beret.

"Wallacette Darlene," the priest asked, "dost thou renounce Satan?"

"I do renounce him," Mary and I replied. Our voices echoed, loud and solemn. Our answers gathered in the cold air and filled the little alcove. I could not help seeing Karl, his thin black moustache, slenderness, his streams of blue smoke.

"And all his works?" the priest asked.

"I do renounce them." My voice was rising. I felt Mary look at me, annoyed.

"And all his pomps?"

"I do renounce them."

Mary outspoke me this time. My voice was barely a whisper, then silence. Celestine reached over and held the wool baby sweater away from the priest's fingers. He dipped them in holy oil and marked crosses on Wallacette's breast and between her shoulder blades. He asked what she believed, and we answered. And then, because Celestine had insisted on this part, the priest gave Wallacette to me to hold. I took her in my arms.

"Wallacette Darlene," he asked, "wilt thou be baptized?"

I answered that she would.

When the priest poured the first small cross of water on her head, Wallacette looked mystified. The next drops came. Outrage screwed her face tight. She opened her mouth as the priest made a pass with the white cloth of purity, and she gathered herself into a long scream as he lighted the candles that Mary held.

He recited another prayer. Mary blew the candles out. Wallacette roared on and on as if she'd never stop.

Celestine's Night

The first summer, Celestine brought her baby to work, and all day the child slept, sucked on her fingers, and woke to watch Celestine from the bottom of an old shopping cart that was padded with blankets. Sometimes Celestine turned around and met the direct gaze of her daughter, a look so penetrating that Celestine's breath caught. She dropped the spice, the string, the knife she was using, and took the girl up in her arms, ready for her to speak as if a spell had suddenly lifted.

When the baby flexed her entire body and struggled to free herself, Celestine put her down. No matter how thorough Celestine's exhaustion, no matter how little sleep she'd had, there was a nerve of excitement running through each hour. Common objects and events seemed slightly strange, as if she were encountering them in the clarity of a strong dream. It was Dot's presence, her heavy sweetness, the milk of Celestine's own body on her breath, the soft odor of her hair, her glorious wealth of pink and lavender skin, that changed the cast of Celestine's daily world.

Sometimes, watching the baby as she slept or reaching for her in the dark, it was passion that Celestine felt, even stronger than with Karl. She stole time to be with Dot as if they were lovers. Days, it was half hours of nursing in the shop's back room, sometimes with the raw smell of blood on her hands. In the evenings, Celestine had the baby all to herself at home. As she read her novels, talked on the telephone, or cooked or sat, Dot slept nearby in a laundry basket, breathing in fits and starts.

In those days and nights, Celestine's mind was flooded, green as jade. Her love for the baby hung around her in clear, blowing sheets.

One night Dot slept past her feeding time and Celestine woke in the half-light of dawn with full breasts. The baby clung like a sloth, heavy with sleep, and latched on in hunger, without waking. She drew milk down silently in one long inhalation. It was then that Celestine noticed, in the fine moonlit floss of her baby's hair, a tiny white spider making its nest.

It was a delicate thing, close to transparent, with long sheer legs. It moved so quickly that it seemed to vibrate, throwing out invisible strings and catching them, weaving its own tensile strand. Celestine watched as it began to happen. A web was forming, a complicated house, that Celestine could not bring herself to destroy.

PART THREE

MARY ADARE

DURING THREE HARD winters after Dot was born, the snow packed so deep that starved deer drifted from the fields to my stock pens, and leapt in. They could not be driven back up the loading ramp. The only other way out was the slaughter chute. But they were useless, full of lung bot, every rib jutting; even their hides were tissue thin. My fruit trees suffered. The snow came so high that rabbits gnawed the trunks and upper limbs, girdling them completely so that even spring, when new buds should have shown, was a time of death. In the shelterbelts, I came across more of the deer's frail hulks and the banks of the river stank of bleached carp. An old man was found, one who for years had lived alone. He was curled in a large drift beneath his clothesline and his arms were full of towels.

As if to repair this sad work, then, the weather turned mild and we had a spate of slow January rains. It was during that time, five years after her winter birth, that I began to wonder how I'd ever kept my distance from Dot.

At first it was the name. If anyone, Celestine should have named her after me. I hated the name Wallacette and I knew it would give the girl trouble for the rest of her life. So I thought up the nickname to Darlene. That was Dot. One round syllable, so much easier to say.

Of course, Celestine never admitted how bad the real name was. When I told her that the name Wallacette was terrible, she only shrugged, looking down at me from all her height, and said

179

that it had distinction. Because having Dot and giving her the name was the first thing Celestine ever did out of the ordinary, she was stingy. She wouldn't really give in to another opinion, not on the name or on other things. Feeding and dressing and burping were her domain. She would be the only one to change the diapers, to give the bath, to cut the soft little nails and even carry the child in and out of the car. I had to sit by watching all of this done. I had to wait and bide my time, and I managed, although it was a struggle because every time I looked at that baby I'd feel a piercing shock. Dot and I had a mental connection, I was sure of it. I understood things about the baby that her mother could not accept.

For instance, she was never meant to be a baby.

Dot was as impatient with babyhood as I. She tried at once to grow out of it. Celestine never saw that, because she, and only she, took pleasure in Dot's helpless softness. Only Celestine was saddened by her daughter's fierce progress. Day by day, Dot grew stronger. In her shopping-cart stroller she exercised to exhaustion, bouncing for hours to develop her leg muscles. She hated lying on her back and when put that way immediately flipped over to assume a wrestler's crouch. Sleep, which she resisted, did not come upon her gently but felled her in odd positions. Draped over the side of the cart or packed in its corner, she seemed to have fallen in battle. But it was only a momentary surrender. She woke, demanding food, and when set free exploded in an astonishing fast creep that took her across a room in seconds.

Celestine moped when her baby stopped nursing, but secretly I was glad. One more independent step. Dot grew teeth. They came in all at once, tiny flat buds with a wide eager gap between the two top front. She grinned, flexed, stood solid, and soon had to be tied up in a neutral corner while we worked, for fear she'd drag down the knives and get into the machinery. She worked her knots free and stumbled desperately toward danger, toward the boiling vats or freezers. The House of Meats, which I'd renamed from Kozka's Meats, was no place for a child. I feared a side of pork would fall and crush her, that she'd crawl into the stock pens or fall beneath the hooves of a dull heifer. But unlike her father, who attracted it, Dot repelled harm. Falling cans bounced past her, and she stepped without looking over open drains.

I think now that maybe she scared off bad luck with the loud volume of her voice. Once she discovered what she had, she became a bully, a demanding child, impossible to satisfy. In our hearts, as time went on, we knew that we were making a selfish girl whose first clear word was MORE. She was greedy, grew fat, because we sympathized too much. We had gone hungry as children and could not deny her a morsel. Celestine tried to discipline her, teach her the word *please*. But she couldn't teach Dot the right way to say it. Dot growled, "PLEEZ MORE," her eyes hard as buttons.

We handed things over. She guzzled milk, screamed, threw her bottle on the floor in a fit, bit Celestine, tore the plastic barrettes from her own head, and the hair too, by the roots. Then she offered us the clump in her hand. It seemed that her hurt was nothing to her, because ours was always worse. We made more fuss than she did over the bald spots, the scraped knees, the purple lumps on her forehead. We were thorough in living through her, in living our childhoods over.

By the time Celestine allowed Dot to enter first grade, she was as big as most children twice her age, strong and spoiled. Her clipped curls were a dark clear red, and her face was square, heavily brooding. I saw my brother in Dot's pout and in the deep-set eyes, and in the eyebrows so straight and fine they seemed traced on with a level and a pale brown crayon. She had my mother's hair. Otherwise, she positively resembled me. Pale, broad, and solid. I don't think I am inventing this, although the one time I pointed this out to Celestine, she puffed large with outrage in her stiff white apron and said, "You're her aunt and that's all. I'm her *mother*," defining for me the sideline role she imagined I would take on. That is, giver of birthday gifts, always a skirt or blouse. Attender of graduations and recitals and school plays. Baby-sitter if a pinch ever came, and, most definitely, not a person to resemble. Not physically, not mentally. Not mentally most of all.

But that was hopeless on Celestine's part. I saw myself in Dot's one-track mind and doubled fists. I indulged the girl royally, I'll be the first to admit.

I went with them on the first day of school. Dot had skipped kindergarten, so the children all knew one another. She walked into the classroom with her mother while I watched, in the aunt's role. I stood outside the classroom of mild-tempered children. I saw the pots of glue, the box of blunt scissors, the stacks of colored paper, the small sturdy chairs. I smelled the dry and sour school smell, the chalk dust and wax, the pink powder that the janitor spread on the bathroom floors. The teacher, Mrs. Shumway, jerked her thin arms, and two boys rose to pass out the red-and-white cartons of milk. Celestine had brought along a box of bakery cookies, a treat she gave to the teacher in order to ensure her daughter's welcome with the other children. But I could see that the cookies didn't matter, not only then, but ever. For Dot was like a wolf ready to descend on the fold. There would be no resisting her. I could tell this from where I stood. Even Mrs. Shumway, a young but wizened, observant woman, would not be able to control her. I knew the teacher was in for a surprise when she put her arm around Dot's shoulders and introduced her as "*our* new girl." Dot swelled at this. Her eyes gleamed. Her chin stuck out. Watching her, the boys went mute and the spines of the little girls stiffened like pulled twine. Children have an extra special sense about each other. They all saw what neither

Celestine and even the tough little Mrs. Shumway could not. They were the sparrows. Dot was the hawk keenly circling. For seven years, until high school, when everything would change, each of these children would be subject to her whims.

And they were, from the very first, for Dot at once set about her business of fiercely pursuing them. She didn't want to hurt them, she just wanted their affection. But this was hard to explain since her means of acquiring their love took such violent turns.

One day, about the time Dot usually clanged through the front door of the shop, Celestine put her knife down and told me this was the day she expected a note from Shumway.

"What for?" I said, intrigued, too much so for Celestine's liking.

"Never mind," she mumbled, "it was just some little tiff Dot had with another girl. The girl's mother called."

Celestine began untying her apron as she walked around the counter. I followed to the door. Looking out, we saw Dot walking slowly up the dust-and-cinder driveway, dragging her thick shoes in a tragic way. She had allowed her hair to droop from its swan-shaped clips and obscure her face. Even through the hair and from a distance, I could tell that her eyes were dull with apprehension. I imagined that her firm mouth trembled.

"I'll go to her," I offered. "Sometimes it's better."

Celestine turned to me. The very flesh of her face seemed to harden when she was annoyed, and her eyes became dark and opaque as if they had been dabbed on.

"What do you mean," she said, " 'sometimes it's better'?"

"For the aunt to go."

" 'For the *aunt* to go,' " she repeated. She put the bundle of her apron in my arms and marched out the front door with an abruptness that was meant to discourage me. But I followed even then, unable to resist, although I stood slightly behind Celestine as she confronted her daughter.

"Give me the note," she firmly ordered. She put her hand out the way a parent must, open and stern. Dot put her hands in her pockets. Her neck reddened and she would not meet her mother's eyes.

"I don't have one yet," she said at last.

"Did you give my note to Mrs. Shumway?" Celestine interrogated.

"Yes."

"No!" Celestine then cried. "You did not! Young lady you have just told me a lie."

Dot looked straight up at her mother in what I saw as miserable appeal. I thought her cheeks blazed in sudden grief, but maybe it was defiance. She was beyond speech, so I stuck up for her. I could not bear it. I reached briskly around Celestine, took her daughter's wrist, and dragged her safely toward me.

"Let's sit down in back," I said. "We'll talk. It can't be that bad."

"Oh yes it *can* be that bad," said Celestine, striding wrathfully beside us up the driveway. "Yesterday your darling knocked a first-grader's tooth out."

"*Pulled* it out," corrected Dot. "It was already loose."

"The little girl's mother called me up last night," Celestine went on. "The tooth wasn't ready to come out."

"Oh yes it was," Dot insisted. "She asked me to get it out. She gets a quarter from the fairy."

"You didn't have to use a rock. A *rock*!" cried Celestine. "And then the note! You were supposed to give the note to Mrs. Shumway to apologize for your behavior."

Celestine suddenly stopped, blocking our paths, having had an arresting thought.

"Did something else happen today, something bad?" she grimly questioned.

"No," Dot replied, with what seemed, even to me, suspicious speed. But Celestine was growing weary and did not pursue the thread.

"It better not have." She took her apron from my arms and retied it around herself. "Now go have your snack, go on; I'll clean up out back and then we're going home and get to the bottom of this."

I went out to the kitchen with Dot, to fix her a sandwich and a cookie and talk in private. That is how I got to hear firsthand about what really did happen that day in the naughty box. That is also how I came to damage Shumway, who probably deserved it, even though Dot was lying through her teeth and even though the naughty box was not exactly the instrument of torture that I pictured. At any rate, I've regretted the episode since and know I should have been more suspicious with Dot when she told me, after I poured her a milk and put some bran cookies down before her, that she'd spent all day in the naughty box where it was dark.

"The naughty box," I said, sitting down with her, upset by the picture of her dim confinement. "Is it a real box?"

But Dot, with her mouth full, let her eyes speak the volumes for her. They glistened with unshed tears of shame. She only cried to get her way, but this afternoon tears coated her hazel eyes in a film that seemed more piteous and noble than sobs. She chewed ravenously, gulped her milk, and went on to describe the box.

"It's a red box in the back of the room, underneath the clock. Mrs. Shumway can fit lots of children inside of it. She pushes you in and slams down the lid. It's big. It's made of wood. It has *splinters*."

Dot stopped in horror, remembering all too well, or so I thought at the time. "And inside the air is very, very black," she whispered. Her gaze was bleak and distant. She put a whole cookie in her mouth for comfort, and while she chewed it she reached for another. But I was never much at correcting Dot's manners. In fact, I employed any ruse to keep from saying no to the girl. That word to her was like an electric shock, inflating her with lightning fury. No sent up the voltage until the current flew out of her and jolted us. I let her cram another cookie in her mouth. I thought of Shumway. The teacher's methods gave me a thrill down my neck, as if I was reading a storybook.

"Shumway . . . that Shumway . . . is a witch!" I rose unsteadily to my feet. "She won't get away with this!"

I looked down at Dot, and she looked up at me. In her eyes I thought I saw adoration, innocent trust. I was her godmother of the fairy tales, her protector.

"Just finish your snack," I said, patting her shoulder with adult authority. "I'll take care of Shumway."

Dot's smile turned on full force, was eager and dazzling. I stamped off in its light, got into the truck, and hit the starter. I did not even take the time to put on my hat or drape a scarf around my throat. I drove pell-mell to the school to catch Shumway before she slunk off, to her duplex or wherever Argus first-grade teachers slunk to when they had emptied their naughty boxes and ground their red pencils sharp as needles.

The school was my school, Saint Catherine's, where long ago I had performed a major miracle. Now it had enlarged for our growing population and become more secular, with lay teachers in many grades and no obligatory mass on weekdays. Still, I banged through the new double insulated glass doors with confidence. I strode the deserted hallway until I reached Shumway's classroom. My mind had blackened with rage by then. I couldn't wait to lay my hands on her. And I was in luck. For she was there, just as I'd been hoping, making ready to go home. She was pinning a bright blue beret on her head, eyeing herself in the face mirror of the teacher's closet as she did so. I watched her for one moment and then looked to the back of the room. What I saw doubled my rage past containing.

186

Beneath the clock, in the precise spot Dot had described, there was a glazed box painted a sinister and shining red. It was long as a coffin and twice as broad. I walked past Mrs. Shumway, who jerked her head around in a startled woodpeckerish way, and I threw open the lid. I half expected to find pale children huddled there. But the box was full of toys.

"Do you fill it up each night?" I turned, accusing Shumway. "What?"

I pointed to the box, then lifted one end and dumped the toys out. Blocks, fire engines, plastic doll furniture and bright rubber rings spilled across the floor. I let it fall with an empty crash.

"Mrs. Shumway, come here," I said.

She walked over to me, not obediently, but with a nervy terrier's menace.

"What is the meaning of this!" she cried. "Who are you?" Her blue hat seemed to lift off her hair in surprise, and her voice shook apprehensively. She stared at me, edged forward. Her face was faceted and sharp, the kind of thin face that wrinkled young. She could not have been more than twenty-six but already her eyes were rimmed in red like a very old woman's. Her hair was cut into a strange elfin shape.

I put my hands on my hips, butcher's hips, used to shifting heavy loads and moving hams down the smoke rails.

"Your little game is up, Mrs. Shumway," I said.

She coughed in surprise. "What are you talking about?" she squeaked. She stepped backward, laughed uncertainly. I suppose, thinking of it now, she merely thought I was harmlessly lunatic, but at the time I took her nervous laugh as an admission of guilt. I reached out and grabbed the shoulders of her camel coat. I dragged her toward the red box.

At first, she was so shocked that her knees buckled and her heels dragged, but when we reached the box, and when I tried to force her in by pushing her and bending her arms and legs up like a doll's, she suddenly regained her poise and stood fast.

187

She was surprisingly agile, and very strong, so that I had a harder time than you would expect shoving her inside the box and crushing all of her limbs in besides. Also, she was proud. For she made no outcry until she was trapped and all was lost. And then, once I'd sat down on top of the red box, breathing heavily, recovering my composure, Mrs. Shumway began to hammer and howl.

"It's no use," I called down to her, satisfied beyond all measure, "you're in the naughty box! You can't get out until you promise to be good."

There was silence, a period of thought for Mrs. Shumway, who, even in her shock, heeded the sense of my words.

"This is not the naughty box," she said, muffled, below me. "It's on the blackboard."

But the chalkboard at the front of the room was wiped clear and not even black, but a dull and soothing green.

"Mrs. Shumway," I said, "I am not a five-year-old that you can fool."

Again, there was silence.

"Let me out," she said after a long while, "or I'll have you arrested."

"You wouldn't do that, Mrs. Shumway," I answered, having given this some thought. "I'll tell them about the naughty box and they'll revoke your teacher's license."

"There's nothing wrong with the naughty box. It's on the blackboard," she replied.

But I wasn't listening to her excuses. I looked around the room for something heavy enough to weight the lid. There were long wooden tables, chairs, fire extinguishers, and gray tin wastebaskets. There was Shumway's own desk, which I thought I could move and even lift if she would only stay put long enough. But I could see that, since there was no way to keep her inside by force, I would have to intimidate her into keeping still. I picked up a rectangular purple block and beat the cover of the box with it.

"I'll hit you with this if you jump out!" I warned, convincingly I hoped, but nevertheless once I'd left the box and started to push Shumway's desk across the room, she popped out. The red cover of the box crashed backward and out she leapt, still neat in her tan coat and pointed black shoes, her blue beret flattened only slightly. She reached down, grabbed a block like mine, and brandished it as she stepped slowly, backward, toward the door. I moved around her desk and picked up the block I'd dropped. Then both of us edged, at the same pace, into the hall where we then continued our unusual and wary progress through the front doors and out onto the playground, which was where I lost Shumway. She took advantage of the few children who had lingered to play after school, by walking in among them and starting up a desperate conversation. I retreated. But I did so in the secure conviction that I'd revenged Dot, that I'd taught Shumway an unforgettable lesson and, in that way, done something for all of the children of Argus, who would be forced to spend one school year of their lives in her hands.

I didn't think about much besides that, and certainly not about Shumway's threat to have me arrested, but then it turned out she went to the police and told the whole story and presented a list of the badly behaved children, any of whose mothers she suspected of being me.

That's why Officer Ronald Lovchik came to the shop next day. He was a tall, sad, soft-shouldered man with a horror of confronting criminals. The years since the beet had come to town were hard on him. Construction workers from the beet refinery roistered in the bars, and the asphalt haulers set up wild camps on the edge of town where the bypass was going in. All Lovchik needed at the time was a grade-school squabble. Besides, he didn't like to come to the back rooms of the shop at all. He'd always had a hopeless crush on Sita, until he lost her to Jimmy. It pained him even to be in rooms she once inhabited. Back then, he wrote Sita letters and sent small yellow boxes of Whitman's chocolates, which Fritzie and I always ate to save Sita's figure. His very presence reminded me of those chocolates, and made me want one. But he was visiting on serious business. Now he described the incident with Shumway, knitting his brow as if he was unable to look at Celestine for fear she might think he was making an accusation.

"And so . . ." he gulped, bringing his story to a close, "the gist of it is I have to know where you were yesterday afternoon."

"Let me think," Celestine commented, with measured consideration. I could tell that she was impressed with the idea of being a suspect in something she hadn't done, that she relished being asked this dramatic question. I knew she was framing a complex answer in her mind, but before she got the pleasure of voicing her alibi I solved Lovchik's case.

"I did it, Ron," I admitted in a loud voice, unashamed. "I did it with good cause."

"Oh?" He was surprised for a moment only, then resigned. "I'm sorry to hear that." He drooped, dismayed by the conviction in my voice. His eyes took on a wet despondence, and he asked if we could sit down somewhere private to discuss the charge.

"Be my guest." I motioned him down the hall to the kitchen. Celestine, all agape, followed us. We all three sat down at the kitchen table, and Lovchik took a spiral notebook from his shirt pocket and unclipped a ballpoint pen from his tie.

"All right," he said, "what's your side?"

"It was my duty as a citizen," I said. "Mrs. Shumway has been cruel to children."

"In what way?" Lovchik asked, scribbling quickly. I proceeded to tell Officer Lovchik about the naughty box, describing it in detail. As I spoke, his eyebrows lifted, his head shook back and forth, and he hummed disapprovingly beneath his breath.

"Just a minute," Celestine said, interrupting my description of the splinters that pricked into the children's clawing hands; "you're talking about the naughty box?"

"You know about it too?" I looked at her, terribly surprised that she had known and never mentioned it.

"Sure I know about it. . . . Mary," she said with a strange look, ". . . its not a real box, it's a corner of the blackboard where children get their names written if they smart off."

I stopped, confused.

"You're sure?"

"I've seen it myself."

Officer Lovchik put his pen down.

"Let me try and get this straight," he said, but then he seemed to despair of that possibility and merely sat, frowning at his knuckles, waiting for one of us to say something.

"All right," he said at last, "it was all some kind of big mistake?"

After putting two and two together in that time, I had to answer that it was.

"Well . . . I'll try and get those charges dropped," he sighed. Then he rose unhappily and walked back down the hallway and out the door.

"Just tell me one thing," said Celestine, after the bell in the front rang behind him. "Did Dot lie to you about this? Did she make the whole thing up?"

I couldn't answer, thinking of the passion in Dot's face, the mute appeal, the unshed tears of her shame—all that had taken me in.

"It sounds like her," Celestine said. "I'm trying to teach her the difference between a lie and the truth."

"That seems simple enough." I busied myself measuring ground coffee into the basket of the percolator. Maybe I didn't know the difference myself, or at least what the episode meant. It's hard to trace these things back, but I do think that the incident over Mrs. Shumway's naughty box was the first time Celestine and I

191

went opposite ways with Dot, and all because I'd been deceived.

"You don't make it any easier," she said, tracing the pattern in Fritzie's crocheted string tablecloth. "In fact you make it worse."

I kept pouring the coffee in, spoonful by spoon, making a strong batch. I didn't want to turn around because I couldn't say anything to defend myself or make much sense, not after stuffing Mrs. Shumway in her toy box. Standing there with the spoon in my hand, I suddenly pictured her telling this story to the police, thin face twitching, her blue beret righteous and flat as a pancake on her elf's hair.

"You should have seen her," I said, then I started laughing, which was the wrong thing to do as far as Celestine was concerned because when I turned around she had gone. All the next day and into the summer she refused to speak to me, and only answered what I said by yes or no, so that it was summer vacation before the whole incident blew over.

That summer, Karl sent Dot a very nice electric wheelchair that he won as a doorprize at some medical-supplies show. The chair was delivered in pieces, which Celestine managed to assemble on the first two days of her week's vacation.

I went over there because she had just started speaking to me on June first, and by then I was as relieved to talk as she was. I knew she'd given herself exactly until that day to maintain strict one-syllable relations. Once June arrived she called me up and babbled all of her pent-up stories of Dot's interesting observations and behaviors. I was the only one in town who'd listen to Celestine and not turn her off. People have long memories in Argus. They still thought Celestine was strange, even disreputable, to have a baby so late in life by a flighty husband who only married her after the baby was born. The postmaster and postmistress, husband and wife, who looked carefully at every piece of mail and were eventually caught steaming open certain bank statements on commission, spread it around about how rarely Karl wrote and what unusual packages he sent to Dot.

Matchbooks. Coaster trays. Hotel towels and washclothes. He sent her samples of whatever he was selling at the time. Fuller brushes. Radio antennas. Cans of hair spray or special wonder-working floor cleaners. These arrived every few months by parcel post. If he wrote, it was on a postcard from the drawer of a cheap hotel. He kept the hotel stationary too, reams of it, and sent it on whenever it piled up.

This wheelchair, though, was something more out of the ordinary. At least the writing paper, brushes, complimentary advertising pens and cans of hair spray could be put to practical use.

"It's got forward and backward controls," said Celestine. "Really, it's very nice."

The three of us were grouped around tne wheelchair in the driveway, watching Celestine put in the last few chrome screws. She was hunched, intent, over the complex directions while Dot and I sat together on the steps. During the ban on me, Celestine had stopped all after-school snacks and friendly outings, and the truth is, at Dot's age, it was out of sight, out of mind. I missed her more than she did me. I felt half there without her, absent, forgetful, and blue. Now I was so happy to get back to the way things were before the naughty-box incident that I bore no grudge. While Celestine muttered over the oddly shaped components, Dot and I discussed Shumway's improved behavior and speculated on Sister Seraphica, her teacher-to-be next year, a tall dreamy nun who played the organ and directed choir. Dot expected there to be a rhythm band, and looked forward to hitting sand blocks together.

"I'll teach you the woodwinds too," I said, blowing on a stalk of crabgrass.

But Celestine was finished and Dot was diverted. She jumped

into the seat of the wheelchair and started maneuvering up and down the dirt-and-cinder drive. Celestine came over to the steps to sit by me.

"Somehow . . ." she began, then quit.

"What?"

"I don't think it's the most thoughtful present he ever sent."

I'd taken to defending my brother, not that he would have cared or ever returned the compliment, but out of the sheer bond of blood. Maybe I was grateful that, however accidentally, he'd given me my one tie of kinship, to Dot.

"I think it's inventive," I said. "Different, yes, but look how she enjoys the chair!"

Indeed, Dot had quickly mastered the controls and now zoomed and bumped in mad circles, half tipping, catching herself at the last moment. She was having a good time, but to Celestine the sight of Dot was an unpleasant reminder, or perhaps a kind of bad omen.

"It makes me . . ." She searched for the word through her romantic-book vocabulary: ". . . shudder. Yes, shudder," she decided. "We're not going to keep the thing."

"What!" shouted Dot. Her ears were sharp.

"We're going to give it to someone who really needs it," said Celestine. "It's much too expensive to treat as a toy."

Dot wheeled up and stuttered the machine to a halt. "It's from my father. It's mine!" She lowered her eyebrows and gave us a startling, evil glare.

But Celestine was in one of her determined moods. "Yes," she said again, "we're going to give it to someone."

"Someone who?" I said. I thought she could have let Dot keep it.

Celestine was silent for a while, pondering. Then she turned and gave me a long reproachful stare, as if I had missed out somewhere, as if I should have known.

"Think," she said. "It's obvious who."

Dot jumped out of the chair and wheeled it to the slope in the backyard. She sat down, took off the brake, and gave herself a wild short ride.

"Don't string me out," I said, irritated.

"Russell," she answered.

She was right. I had to see that. After his paralyzing stroke, the attendants took Russell up to the reservation to live with his half brother, Eli Kashpaw, in a little wooden house that Celestine said was full of stretched furs, traps, fox musk, and calendars of bathing beauties, a place where sugar stayed in a twisted sack and all the forks were bent and splayed from opening cans or prying nails from the rough board walls.

Eli had left the reservation only twice, according to Celestine. The first time was three days after Celestine's mother died, when he had shown up at the church, slipping into the back pew quiet as a marten and slipping out again without a word to anyone. To get to know him, Isabel and Pauline and Russell had to track down Eli almost with the same finesse he used on animals. And they often made the effort, because Eli was only shy at first, and after that he was fine company, as the lonely often are. He took a child in, a girl that he raised to trap and hunt, go hungry in the woods, and hide from game wardens, a girl named June, who turned out even wilder than he'd raised her.

Eli kept so much to himself that half of his relations didn't know about his feelings for Russell, who was famous for his decorations. So when Eli showed up at Saint Adalbert's hospital and signed his brother's release forms with the shape of the Kashpaw name—the only shape Eli had ever learned to scrawl—a cousin living off reservation and working at the hospital desk said she was just as surprised as any of them. That was the second time Eli left—to fetch Russell home. And now Russell was living in Eli's two rooms, sleeping upright, letting his brother bathe him, change him, and in good weather wheel him out into the trampled yard, where he was left to doze guarded by ragged and panther-thin dogs.

Celestine went up to see them a couple times a year. In between their visits, it seemed like she couldn't stay off the subject, and that was one reason that I wanted to come along. I wanted to see for myself whether Russell spoke a word yet or ate with a knife and fork or had the use of his hands. I'd always felt bad about the way things had been left between us the last time I'd seen him in the hospital.

I'd come home shaken from that encounter. It had been his silence, or maybe even worse, his speech. Russell had opened his mouth and huge shattered vowels poured out, urgent sounds that wrenched me. Sounds I tried to understand. I'd picked up his pitcher of juice and offered it, then the newspaper. I'd pointed to the bathroom and wheeled him nearer to the window. And eventually, when I'd tried hard enough and offered every possibility I saw in the room, he'd gone dim and silent once more. He'd stared past me and sunk into a quiet I could not crack.

He had thinned as he recovered, and when he sat absolutely still that way he was hard to look at. The contrast between his ravaged cheeks and forehead and his eyes—slanting, deep black, of a delicate shape—was unbearable. I knew that his mind was active. I took his hand.

"Russell," I said, "believe me that I'm sorry."

He stared down at our two hands, mine so tough, with thick split nails and many scars. His long and dry and brown. He was unable to will his hand out of mine, unable to move his hand the slightest distance. I felt such raw anger shooting from his bones that I dropped his hand and jumped up. I left without even saying that I was going, and all the way home in the truck I was embarrassed at my trespass. I tried to pretend I'd done it with no pleasure, or out of sheer attraction like the time summers past

196

when I'd touched the war scars on his chest, but the truth was I'd captured his hand with a thrill. He went to Eli's soon after that, and now it had been years. Six years.

"Your Uncle Russell would appreciate the chair," Celestine called after her daughter. "You can come when we take it up there. It can be from you."

Dot paused in her game, then zoomed off again, determined to extract every moment of enjoyment from her present. Celestine sighed, slapped her knees hard, and stood.

"She's doing her best to wreck it before we go."

"How are you going to haul it?" I asked after a moment. I already knew the answer. My truck. And Celestine knew I knew as well. She looked thoughtfully across the yard at the wheelchair.

"You want to drive?" she asked.

"I'll drive," I told her. "But I never met this Eli."

"Or my aunt," said Celestine. "She's over there a lot now."

"What aunt?"

"Fleur. The one that came down here, you know, when Mama died."

"What a name. Floor."

Celestine looked down at me with strained indulgence. "Fleur," she said. "It's French for flower."

"Ooo-la-la," I said, getting up to go. "Don't be so superior. I took bookkeeping instead of French in high school."

So the next morning, when I came out to the shop, Celestine was wrapping a headcheese in some newspaper, securing it with rubber bands. I gathered we'd take that along, plus a sausage, and if I'd baked we would have taken a sheet cake too. When we visited I always had to shoulder the burden of the food. I took a few bags of gingersnaps from the grocery-section shelves, went back to my room, tied on my head scarf, and then it seemed easy enough to leave. Adrian was there to watch the trade, and nothing special was going on in the way of preparations. It was late morning and Dot was out back with my dogs. She'd ride behind us. The delivery truck was enclosed like a van and padded nicely behind the front seats with foam-rubber pillows. The wheelchair could be laid on its side next to her. So we started out. Before we were halfway through town, Dot sank down in the rubber cushions, dropped her head into her arms, and fell into a sound sleep.

Getting out of Argus was an obstacle course now, with all the orange-and-white drums, oil pots, reflectors, and flaggers ranging down the new highway that was going in. It took us the better part of half an hour to get past them, but then it was a short pretty drive until we hit the boundary line. I stopped the truck next to the sign that announced the reservation and told Celestine it was her turn, she must take over. So she got out and came around the front and slid behind the steering wheel. The roads turned gravel. Dust rose in a tan plume behind us. We left all trace of town buildings and the houses we passed looked strangely abandoned, except for dogs.

Dot crawled into the front and sat between us on the glove case and helped her mother steer. Celestine had cut Dot's thick hair into the shape of a football helmet. In the summer it had gold highlights along with the rust and tarnished brown. One side of her face was creased and reddened where she'd lain. Now that she was conscious there was no end to her questions and exclamations, for Dot was a born traveler, meant to go places, unlike us. My one real trip in life had been the freight train to Argus. I didn't care much for changes of scenery, but Dot was excited by the emptiness and dust, by the solid bands of trees and the half-hidden houses. She was interested in the pitted road that led up to Eli's.

"Watch that," she called sternly, pulling on the wheel. "Go left! Now right!"

Mrs. Shumway had taught her class the concepts of right and

left at the end of the school year, and applying them to real life was one of Dot's manias. But there were so many ruts and twists on our way that by the time we came to Eli's clearing she finally grew bored with her game.

Eli's house was tiny, covered with dull gray shingles and surrounded by a narrow yard of dust wallows. Before we were completely stopped, fierce-looking dogs bounded toward us and Dot scrambled across my lap, was out the door and among them before Celestine could open her mouth.

Russell was there, farther on a bit, pushed up beside the screened door in a little wedge of shade. He blended so well into the mottled light and dark of the house, the weathered boards and worn-in paint, that Dot didn't even see him at first. She didn't see Eli either when he appeared, passing soundlessly from a dim tangle of bushes at the edge of the clearing. He watched Dot, the dogs, and Celestine as she got out of the truck. He watched Russell watch his sister.

Celestine carried a headcheese and a long hard stick of summer sausage, and she approached Russell with a smile of eagerness. But in her stride there must have been nerves, because the dogs flew past Dot and landed in a circle of teeth around her mother. She stood, trapped. And then suddenly she swung the summer sausage down, hard, on the nose of the largest dog and yelled, "Beat it!"

Eli walked over to Celestine, holding his hand out to shake hers, and then the door to his house opened and out came the aunt. The only thing that Celestine had told me about Fleur was that she used to work for Uncle Pete, and that she was unbalanced. But Fleur struck me as balanced, and then some. She stood right next to Russell and dropped her hand on his shoulder, maybe to calm him, although he didn't seem to notice us. This Fleur was big-boned but lean, very much the build of Celestine, and had a face like Sitting Bull. Her eyes were black and narrow, watchful. Her mouth was broad. She wore a baggy blue flowered housedress that looked like old slipcovers.

Celestine walked over and kissed Russell on the cheek. He tipped his head away, and gazed off into the woods. Celestine took his arm, but he looked at her hand as if it were a leaf that had fallen on him by accident.

"He's glad to see you," said Fleur.

Dot walked up cautiously and stood before Russell, hands hooked in her pockets. She took him in as if he were frozen in a block of ice or enclosed in a cage of wires.

"Don't stare," Fleur said.

Celestine's breath caught. Direct orders displeased Dot, made her stubborn and resentful. Sure enough, without a word, Dot turned and stamped back toward the truck.

"Help me get *my* wheelchair out," she ordered. So I helped her unload the thing. She wheeled it forward, determined that since she had to give it up she would do so herself. The new chrome gleamed, the leather creaked.

"This is for him," Dot said, pushing the chair up to Russell.

No one said a word.

"He's doing all right here," Fleur said at last to Celestine. "You couldn't handle him."

"Hey," Dot called, "I'm *giving* this to Uncle Russell."

"We didn't come to get him," Celestine said to Fleur. "It's just a present."

At that, the aunt seemed friendlier and showed her teeth in something like a smile. "Where did that chair come from?"

I couldn't stop myself from jumping in.

"The wheelchair is from her father."

"Who are you?" said Fleur, with a freezing stare.

"I'm her aunt that owns the sausage plant," I said.

Fleur's eyes caught fire in a flash, then went cold.

"Go on in," she said, gesturing us past her toward the house.

Eli's place was small, mostly the kitchen where we sat. In the next room I could see an old-model radio. On top of two orange crates sat Russell's war mementos, those that weren't in the museum. I recognized the folded cloth flags, small leather cases that held Russell's medals, as well as the shrapnel and bullets that the doctors had carved out of him. A German Luger was pinned up in a web of nails and strings.

Celestine took the headcheese out. "You mind if I put this in your refrigerator?"

Eli had an ancient, fat, yellowing contraption that took up half the wall. On its door an old pencil drawing of a deer was taped and retaped.

"That's well done," I said, touching the picture.

"That's June," he said. "She did that one in high school."

I looked around. There was no evidence of the girl in the room, except what I took to be her photograph, high on a shelf. A little glass jar in front of that picture held a red velvet rose that looked as though it had been snipped off a dress. The girl was dark and pretty, with short black hair and a big serious smile.

"That's her," he said, noticing my glance.

"Your daughter?"

"More or less." Eli shrugged and hefted a coffeepot.

"I just made some fresh," he said, in such a soft voice that I suddenly wanted coffee very much and sat down in the chair near Celestine. He poured three cups.

We heard Dot's voice, subdued but still penetrating.

"I don't have to give my chair away if I don't want to. I could keep it."

"Hush up." It was Fleur's voice, very cold.

We heard a scuffling sound. Some metal clanked.

"I suppose they got Russell set up," Celestine said.

But it was not Russell in the new wheelchair. We heard wheels rip through dirt, a sudden slamming, a wallop as Dot flashed by through a bush.

"Try and get it," she screamed, her voice fading off as she vanished.

"She's showing Russell how to use the thing," I said, making an excuse.

"They hit it off out there," said Eli; "how much you want to bet?"

We listened to the clatter of little rocks in the wheels, to Dot's shout as she reared up and turned in quick short skids, heading back toward the house.

Fleur was just outside the window. "Quit it," she said, when Dot reached her. "That's enough."

Both Celestine and I went tense in our chairs, looked at each other knowingly.

"What?" said Dot as if she hadn't heard Fleur.

"Get off," said Fleur.

During the absence of sound that followed this, I pictured Dot's face burgeoning with rage, her fists becoming rocks. So it surprised me when she tried to wheedle.

"Can't I ride it just a little longer?"

"No," said Fleur in an iron tone.

We pushed our cups aside and stood, ready, silly with apprehension. We were a mystifying sight to Eli.

"Sit down," he urged. "Sit down and have a bun."

Dot's shriek began, low, a growl, gaining in tortured resonances, and we moved toward the door.

"I'd better see what's going on," said Celestine, and then Dot's scream snapped off, suddenly, as if stuffed back into her mouth.

I left my cup on Eli's table and went outside. Fleur was gone. Russell was sitting in his new chair. Dot was sprawled on her rear end in the dirt with an addled look on her face. Celestine stood over them both, her anxiousness changing to satisfaction.

"Let's go," I said abruptly. But she was glad enough. Russell hadn't offered the slightest flicker in her direction. Dot stood, brushed her seat off, and ran to the truck. I bent down and looked at Russell because I had to, at least to say good-bye.

"Remember me?" I asked, then felt ridiculous.

"You look good," I said, although the truth was that Russell's face had sunken to the bone. He was clean. His clothes were ironed. But there was less of him than four years ago, and I turned away as Celestine began talking to him, loud, in a way that struck me as childish.

"It's Celestine. Can you look at me? How you making out?"

Eli came out and, with slow practiced movements, gently pulled Russell to his feet.

"Say good-bye to them," he told his brother. Russell's mouth opened, but no words came out, and his eyes dulled. He leaned against Eli, swaying like a tree half uprooted in a wind. We left them there, braced in the yard, and got back on the road.

We drove twenty miles in silence. I thought that Dot would pester out the details of Russell's case, but she didn't seem interested, put her head down again, and slept. Celestine didn't speak either until around the turnoff to Argus.

"Where did it go?" she said, all of a sudden. She stared out the windshield, her voice rising.

"Where did what go?" I said.

"Everything."

I saw she wasn't really speaking to me, or asking. She didn't look in my direction but to the strips of crops to either side, the neat endless rows that seemed to revolve beside us as we moved.

"Everything that ever happened to him in his life," she said, "all the things we said and did. Where did it go?"

I didn't have an answer, so I just drove. Once I had caused a miracle by smashing my face on ice, but now I was an ordinary person. In the few miles we had left I could not help drawing out Celestine's strange idea in my mind. In my line of work I've seen thousands of brains that belonged to sheep, pork, steers. They were all gray lumps like ours. Where did everything go? What was really inside? The flat fields unfolded, the shallow ditches ran beside the road. I felt the live thoughts hum inside of me, and I pictured tiny bees, insects made of blue electricity, in a colony so fragile that it would scatter at the slightest touch. I imagined a blow, like a mallet to the sheep, or a stroke, and I saw the whole swarm vibrating out.

Who could stop them? Who could catch them in their hands?

Sita's Night

The windows on ward A were regular glass, Louis pointed out, not barred or even locked. They looked out on expansive lawns, just turning from brown to green this early spring. There was even a screened porch. "You can sit out there on warm days," said Louis, "just like home." He put his arm around Sita and watched her face. They stood before a low brick building set off from the rest of the state mental hospital. But Sita wouldn't look at the windows, or at Louis either.

Louis and the psychiatrist had explained to Sita that ward A was a halfway place for patients with a very good chance of returning to society and leading a normal life. She was going there because four months ago she'd pretended to lose her voice, and ever since then Louis and her neighbors had been reading her lips. She grew to like the way they bent close, puzzling out her words, studying her face for clues. She grew to like it so much, in fact, that she lost the ability to speak out loud. Now when she opened her mouth to try and say something in an ordinary tone, nothing happened. But if she came to the state mental hospital, she might be cured. She might speak out loud. The psychiatrist had said as much.

"You've been encouraging her, Mr. Tappe. You've been altogether far too kind."

That's what the psychiatrist said to them both as they sat in his office. They watched him thumb through the dozens of black-bound artist's notebooks that Louis had kept over the years in an attempt to cure her episodes. In those notebooks Sita's dreams were recorded, her conversations with objects and flowers, fantasies she had related to Louis. The notebooks had seemed as private between them as their own embraces. It was a shock to see them stacked on the doctor's desk. And Sita was frightened now. Louis was holding her good brown leather suitcase.

She tried to tell him that she wouldn't stay, that she wanted to go home.

"Wait," said Louis, watching her mouth move slowly, "I didn't get that. Try again."

Sita used her whole face emphatically. She ordered him to take her home.

"I can't," said Louis. He was miserable. "I'm not even supposed to try and understand you unless you verbalize your thoughts."

Sita told him silently that she hated ward A, and him too.

"Come on," Louis sighed, steering her up the sidewalk toward the entrance, "let's go find your room."

Sita let him guide her up the front steps, through a pair of glass doors that looked like they had chicken wire running through them, and down a hallway. The walls of the hallway were a dull leafy color. The floor was green-and-black linoleum tile. They walked up to a very large nurse in a limp white dress and sweater.

"Who have we here?" the nurse said, eyeing Sita, who was obviously the patient since she was being propelled by Louis. "Oh yes," the nurse remembered. "I had a call from Administration. You're Mrs. Tappe."

The nurse walked around the desk and loomed over Sita.

"You'll be getting a private room next week, Mrs. Tappe, but until then we have you in with Mrs. Waldvogel."

Sita pulled away from Louis and moved her lips angrily. The nurse ignored her, striding off.

"Let's bring your bag down the hall, shall we?" she called.

Louis pressed Sita's shoulder gently with his hand and she stumbled after the nurse, down another hallway, also green. All the green made Sita think of an aquarium, of living in a glass tank lined with algae. She wanted to tell this to Louis, to have him write her interesting thought down in his notebook. But then

206

they came to her room and from outside the door Sita saw that the walls were painted mustard yellow.

She tried to make Louis understand that she couldn't sleep in that room. The color made her sick to her stomach. She also hated roommates. Having another woman in her room would remind her of sleeping in the same room as Mary. All night she used to lay awake listening to Mary enjoy her sleep, hating her for each breath of unconsciousness. In the morning Sita would be groggy and tired no matter how much coffee she drank. She tried to say this. But Louis was talking to the nurse, writing down phone numbers and visiting hours on a little pad. Sita's suitcase was already on the bed. Louis kissed her and took her hand off of his arm and led her over to the bed. He sat her down. Once she sat there she couldn't move. The walls paralyzed her with their terrible color.

Sita sat on the bed for a long time, her mouth moving in jammed-up sentences. When she finally was able to tear her eyes from the walls, she realized that Louis was gone and the nurse was putting the last of her things in a steel bureau.

Stop! she tried to call out. Put everything back in my suitcase! I'm leaving!

"You'll have to speak out loud, Mrs. Tappe," said the nurse. "We don't read lips here."

Sita shut her mouth and glared. The nurse smiled into her face.

"Please be ready for supper in one-half hour," she said. "Until then why don't you sit here and get used to your new room?"

As soon as the nurse had left, Sita jumped up to examine the window. It was not locked or barred, but it didn't open very far. Not far enough for her to fit through, anyway. She pushed at the outside screen, to see if it was firmly in place.

"Wanting a little spring breeze, Mrs. Tappe?" It was the nurse again, barging into the room with an elderly lady so docile that

207

she let herself be led in by the wrist. "Mrs. Waldvogel," the nurse said, "here's your new roommate."

Sita looked at the old woman. Mrs. Waldvogel was the perfect grandmother, the type who holds plates of ham in magazine advertisements or sniffs over bouquets of wired flowers on television. Her white hair was held back with a little tortoiseshell comb. She wore an old-fashioned housedress and a ruffled apron.

"I'll leave you two alone to get acquainted," said the nurse.

Mrs. Waldvogel walked up to Sita and took her by the hand. "What a pretty girl you are," she said. "I hope you'll be happy here."

Sita nodded her thank-you. It was calming to be called a girl. She found herself sitting on the bed across from Mrs. Waldvogel, who took some pictures of her family from her drawer and began to show them to Sita one by one.

"This is Markie," she said, "and here's my son. And this baby in the picture is already four years old."

Sita looked at each picture very carefully. There was nothing strange about the people in the pictures or about the old lady. Perhaps, she thought, Louis was telling the truth. Staying in this place would be a restful vacation. And when the vacation was over she would speak out loud again instead of just moving her lips.

"It's nice to have you here," Mrs. Waldvogel said. "I was beginning to think they wouldn't put anyone in here again."

Sita felt a pang of sympathy for the old woman. Although the walls still glared horribly, and although she was exhausted from the long trip and the anxiety, she smiled. Mrs. Waldvogel blushed as she slowly put away her pictures.

"It's terrible to eat human flesh," she said in her sweet, old, cracked voice.

Mrs. Waldvogel patted her bundle of pictures and shut the drawer. "I devoured the last one," she said.

Sita gasped and turned away. Mrs. Waldvogel didn't notice. She twined a stray bit of white hair back into her hairdo and smoothed down her dress.

"It's time for supper. Shall we go?" she asked.

But Sita sat quite still.

After refusing supper and watching the light lengthen to soft gold in the window, Sita got up from her bed, took a pen and a small dime-store notebook from her purse, and wrote. Then she walked down the hallway to the lounge. The big nurse was working a crossword puzzle at her desk. Sita stood before her and displayed the note she had written.

Please call my husband, the note said. *I will not sleep in a room with a woman who believes she is a cannibal.*

But the nurse didn't even look at the note.

"I'm sorry, Mrs. Tappe," she said, "but I'm not supposed to read your lips or your notes. Doctor's orders."

The nurse waited to see if Sita would speak out loud to her. Sita opened her mouth, moved muscles in her throat, but no sound came out. She hated the absurd picture she must have made, standing before the desk gawking silently. She put her notebook back in her purse and walked over to sit before the television with the other patients.

Rowan and Martin's Laugh-In was on, a show she detested. Sitting before the wide screen, watching the slim bikini girls gyrate, was torture. The jokes weren't funny or the skits either, but the patients howled at the man who rammed trees with his tricycle and fell over, at the spinster in her ugly hair net, at anything.

Sita observed the patients because the show was so bad. Like Mrs. Waldvogel, they seemed normal, except perhaps that they laughed too eagerly and, Sita could not help notice, all of them were badly groomed. The men had a one or two day's growth of beard and were not in the least attractive. Their faces seemed slack and old no matter what age they really were. And the women were even worse. They all had bad permanents. Their clothing fit poorly, or the colors of their pants and sweaters clashed. The air was blue around them because they all smoked. The lounge was full of ashtrays, not breakable cut-glass ones like Sita kept for the charred wet tobacco from Louis's pipe, but scratched coffee cans weighted with sand.

Mrs. Waldvogel came into the room. She sat down on a split plastic chair next to Sita.

"Supper was delicious," she said contentedly. "It's a shame you missed it."

Sita did not acknowledge her. Still the old woman went on.

"I'm having my hair done tomorrow dear. We have a patients' beauty school."

Sita looked around again at the women's ugly uncombed sets and ragged ends. Then she controlled her horror, snapped her lips shut, and walked back to her room. She flipped the switch. She hated stark overhead lighting, but there weren't any lamps.

Patients' beauty school! Even at her worst Sita had always kept her weekly hair appointments. She was proud that she'd never let herself go to seed. But in the patients' beauty school there was no telling what could happen. Frizz. Burned scalp. Savagely applied coloring. Sita's head began to hurt, each hair on it.

The light made the sick yellow of the walls blaze and throb. Sita decided that she would lay down in the dark even if Mrs. Waldvogel came in and bit her. She switched off the light and found her bed. She sank backward into the springs, unfolded a frayed white cotton blanket, and tucked it around her legs. The blanket, the pillow, and the spread smelled like someone else had sweat a sharp medicine into their seams. Sita closed her eyes and breathed into her cupped hands. Before she left, she had remembered to perfume her wrist with Muguet.

The faint odor of that flower, so pure and close to the earth, was comforting. She had planted real lilies of the valley because she liked them so much as a perfume.

Just last fall, before the hard freeze, when she was feeling back to normal, the pips had arrived in a little white box. Her order from a nursery company. The ground was stiff with frost but still workable. She'd put on her deerskin gloves and, on her knees, using a hand trowel, dug a shallow trench along the border of her blue Dwarf iris. Then one by one she'd planted the pips. They looked like shelled acorns, only tinier. "To be planted points upward," said a leaflet of directions. They came up early in the spring. The tiny spears of their leaves would be showing soon.

Lying there, sleepless, she imagined their white venous roots, a mass of them fastening together, forming new shoots below the earth, unfurling their stiff leaves. She saw herself touching their tiny bells, waxen white, fluted, and breathing the ravishing fragrance they gave off because Louis had absently walked through her border again, dragging his shovel, crushing them with his big, careless feet.

It seemed as though hours of imaginary gardening passed before Mrs. Waldvogel tiptoed in without turning on the light. Sita was still awake.

"Sleeping?" the old woman whispered.

Sita watched through slitted eyes as Mrs. Waldvogel took off and folded her dress and slip, then pulled a blue cotton nightgown over her head. She groped her way along the end of Sita's bed to her own. The two were right next to each other. Mrs. Waldvogel fluffed her pillow up and sat down on her covers. Enough light came through the transom for Sita to see her clearly. If the old woman was a cannibal, now was her chance.

Here I am, Sita thought, laid out like a human sacrifice.

The old woman grimaced hugely and bared her teeth. They were strong, white, perfect, and gleamed in the hallway light.

Sita's eyes opened in alarm. She sat bolt upright. But then Mrs. Waldvogel calmly and expertly plucked her false teeth out and dropped them into a plastic cup of water.

"You're still awake," she mumbled pleasantly, noticing Sita's stare. But Sita sank down and turned over. For a long time before sleep dragged her under, she stared at the dim wall opposite her bed. Already, she could feel it happening. The knot in her tongue was loosening.

The sun was barely up when she wakened, but even this early she could hear the television's hollow murmur in the lounge. Sita put on her clothing and walked down to the desk. A new nurse and an orderly were there, watching a morning talk show over Styrofoam cups of coffee. Sita had written a note.

I'd like to phone my husband, this note said.

"All right, I guess, although you're supposed to wait till seven," said this nurse. "Take her down there," she told the orderly, a stocky boy with a short black pigtail. He got up laughing at some joke the morning weatherman had made, and, assuming that Sita was mute or deaf, made exaggerated signs that she should follow him down the hall. He unlocked the door to the office that held medications and a phone. He picked up the receiver and held it out to her, then shook his head.

"Wait a sec," he puzzled, "if you can't talk . . ."

Sita snatched the receiver from the boy's hand and held it to her ear. She dialed and waited two rings while Louis groped his way out of sleep. She heard him pick up the phone. Before he even said hello she spoke.

"Get me out!" she cried to him. "I'm cured."

CELESTINE JAMES

ONE NIGHT MARY calls me up to tell me that I shouldn't bother driving in to work tomorrow. Then she waits, holding her breath on the phone, for me to ask her why not. So I ask.

"The shop's burnt," she answers in a satisfied tone.

"What!" I'm horrified.

"Don't worry," she says, "I'm safe. There was mainly smoke damage. The place is crawling with insurance adjusters."

"Should I come over?" I wonder.

"I'm coming over there," she says.

So that is how she ends up living in my house through December.

Mary is not too badly upset about the damage to the shop because, to tell the truth, it isn't doing quite so well as when Pete and Fritzie ran it. This is not Mary's fault. Since the boom with the sugar beet began, supermarkets have been setting up with one-stop-shopping convenience. I can see the attraction, but Mary calls them junk. At any rate, this accident is a chance to renovate. She could not afford to otherwise. She is excited. Workmen start in on the repairs to the butcher shop even before the insurance comes through. A hole burned through the smoke room and spread along the inner electrical connections. Mary is lucky. The only harm to her living quarters is a few gray plumes of smoke blown up the walls. She doesn't want to live with smoke or hammering, with plaster or men tramping through her back rooms, however, and says that she is much more comfortable bedding down in Russell's old room with Dot. If I don't mind, that is.

"I don't mind," I tell her.

But the truth is after three days I'm edgy. I don't know why. Maybe it's that Dot and I have gotten used to our daily ways and Mary disrupts the evenings with her constant reports. She has been to the library for books and has taken her favorite out once more. It is a book by a man named Cheiro and is all about reading the lines in your hands. Mary has been doing this for years, and I'm tired of it. I know what the lines in my hands mean.

"No love, no money, no travel to Hawaii," I tell her when she asks for a look. "No thanks."

"I just want to see if that island in your Head Line has shrunk," she says, consulting her book. "It could mean a tumor of the brain or a nasty blow."

We are sitting in the front room around the gas furnace. I watch its blue ripple in the little crosshatched window. I tell Mary that there's more mystery right there in the jumping flames than in all of Cheiro's books.

"Well then answer me this," she says, leaning off her chair for emphasis, "a child is born with certain lines in its hand. Those lines and no others. How do you explain it?"

The flames reflect across her face, so ordinary yet so fierce. She has taken to wearing a different colored turban each day, covering her hair. She is wearing a white one now. Her slanting eyes are sharp yellow, and the little purple spider veins in her cheeks have darkened like stitches. If you didn't know she was a woman you would never know it. She could be the famous Cheiro himself.

"There's nothing to explain," I tell her stubbornly. "They're just lines."

But Mary isn't listening. She is looking into Dot's palm, which

214

she has already read at least a thousand times before. It's the one thing Dot never tires of, however. Now she wonders if Mary can figure out the initials of the boy she will marry. Dot is almost eleven, but already, more than once, she has been deeply in love. I can hardly stand to see her lose out when it happens and she gets a crush. To attract attention she has developed a loud, booming voice, and like me, she is big and imposing, with a large-jawed grin full of teeth. She frightens off the other children with her hot pursuit. To get boyfriends she knocks them down and grinds their faces in the snowy grit. To get girls, she ties the string waistbands of their dresses to her own dress strings. She drags them around the playground until they promise to write her a note.

The nuns don't know what to do with Dot, and I don't either. So I do the wrong thing and give her everything until there is nothing left. I try to be the mother that I never had, to the daughter I never was. I see too much of myself in Dot. I know how it is. I was too big for all the boys. But I never went so far as to beat them senseless, which Dot has done.

I discourage violence and love-crushes, but Mary eggs her on.

"I see an S," she muses, "then a little j. S.j., S.j."

"It's not him," says Dot, disappointed. She broods into her hand as if her stare could rearrange the lines.

"Take your homework in the kitchen," I say, "and get it done."

I can feel Dot make a face behind my back. A sense develops in a parent.

"I'll help," says Mary, too quickly. So they go in, leaving me alone. For a while then I hear them snicker as they flip through the pages of Dot's books. I have no doubt that they are laughing at me, and I know I will feel this way later on as well. Mary will sleep in Dot's bed and Dot will flop out on a cot. As I am trying to sleep I will hear the two of them whispering, but I won't tell them to be quiet, because I know that Mary will not obey.

That's it, I realize now, looking at the gas glow. That is why I'm so depressed since Mary has been around. It is like having two unruly daughters who won't listen or mind me. I am outnumbered, the only grown-up.

When Mary and Dot come back into the room, I am all set to ask how the work on Mary's house is coming and maybe suggest she could live back there quite soon. But before I can open my mouth Dot announces that she has a secret that she has been keeping for one week. By the way Mary smiles knowingly and by the way she sharply gestures for me to listen, it is obvious that Dot has already told her. This upsets me, but with effort I form my face into an eager mask.

We are quiet. Then Dot speaks in a loud voice.

"I am going to play Joseph, father of the Christ child," she states. "We've been practicing for the Christmas play next week."

I think it's terrible that they picked my little girl to play the father of Christ in their pageant. Then I look at Dot, imagining her in a long grizzled beard and coarse robe. I see the carpenter's maul wielded in her fist. I sigh. I try to smile. It's true that she will be convincing.

Dot hands me a folded-up mimeograph from her teacher, and I read that there will be a Christmas play the second week in December. Parents are invited to attend, and also to bring a pan of hotdish or dessert for a potluck afterward. There is a dotted line on which I'm supposed to write the dish I'll bring. But the dish is already filled in with the word *Jell-O*.

"Jell-O salad," Mary says, noticing my stare. I look at Dot and try to be reasonable.

"I'm proud of you," I tell Dot. "Of course I'll be there."

Then I ask Dot to put her pajamas on and wash her face. She says no. I say yes. Mary acts the coward and stays out of it. One hour later, excited and satisfied at having caused a delay, Dot tramps upstairs, loudly singing her favorite carol, which has a chorus of "Pa-rup-pa-pa-pum." Listening to her footsteps in the upstairs hall my heart fills up. Even though she's difficult, I'm her mother. I'm the one who should sign her Christmas mimeograph. But I can't say this to Mary because it seems small and foolish, so instead I blurt out something more idiotic yet.

"I suppose you're going to put your damn radishes in the Jell-O!"

I say this suddenly, in a grating voice that seems to echo.

Mary's answer is an attempt to act innocent. She says that she thought she'd save me trouble by bringing along the dish. She thought because I was so busy she would make one of her special Jell-O salads. I do not say I am glad she has done this, because it isn't her place. And there is another thing as well: she knows I don't like her Jell-O salads. I've said so before. She puts in walnuts or chopped celery, macaroni, onions, miniature marshmallows, or, worst of all, sliced radishes.

Even thinking about her strange Jell-O makes me furious. Nothing she cooks is normal, not her bran cookies, not her sheet cakes, not her liver casseroles. I don't want her awful cooking to reflect on Dot.

"All right," I say coldly, however, "do as you like."

Dot comes down the stairs in a woolly nightgown, fresh and washed. She is so happy about having stayed up an hour late, about her starring role and our acceptance of the invitation, that I don't have the heart to put a damper on any of her joy. But she puts the damper on herself, for a moment, in a startling way.

"I forgot to tell you what the play is called," she says. "It's *The Donkey of Destiny*."

And then her expression changes suddenly.

"I hate the donkey," she says, almost as if to herself.

"Dot?" I ask.

But already she has turned, surprisingly with no more argument, and run upstairs to climb in bed.

That night, I keep Mary downstairs talking for a long time. I am still annoyed with her, and really, the reason I talk so late is merely to keep her from keeping Dot awake. I don't let Mary go to bed until her eyes droop. She yawns, exhausted, and can hardly drag herself from the chair.

I'm tired too. And I know that by diverting Mary I've left Dot to face her problem with the donkey alone. Whatever that problem is, I should have helped her. I should have gone upstairs after her and got her to admit what was wrong. But I know if I had, Mary would have climbed right after me and tried to take over the situation.

This must stop! I think, getting into bed when the house is quiet. I decide that no matter what, even if it causes a misunderstanding, Mary must go back to her own house after the Christmas play is finished. Until then I will endure her acting girlish with Dot. I will try to stand them whispering late across the hall and telling secrets to each other. But just until the play is over. After that, I decide I will keep my daughter to myself.

But the next day I have to remember all that I intend and bite my lip. For Mary tells me something I do not know about my own daughter, although I would have known if it hadn't been for keeping Mary up the night before.

We are at the shop. It is late morning and after having been closed for a few weeks we're opening for business in a few hours. We've started back into preparing orders for our regular customers, which seems to me a hopeful sign. Repair work is going on around us. I want to urge the men with their aprons full of tools to work quickly. But they are going as fast as they can already. To me, their frenzied hammering and the whine of their drills is a cheerful industrious sound. To Mary, it is irritating.

"It gets on my nerves," she says, wrapping pound after pound of bratwurst.

"The harder they work, the sooner you can move back home,"

I answer. I am unable to keep a note of anticipation from my voice.

"Well," says Mary, with a close glance, "I could always check into the Fox."

"Oh no," I answer in a voice I cannot keep sincere. "Don't go to a hotel. I'm sure that your presence is very beneficial to Dot."

"I'm sure it is too," Mary says, giving me the same narrow-eyed stare she uses often on hard cases who want credit. But I do not want credit. She is the one in that position. She wants to stay with me and weasel her way into Dot's affection, not that I don't understand: Mary is alone, I know. It's her way of doing it that I object to. Wallace Pfef, for instance, likes my daughter very much, but he never butts into our business the way Mary does.

So I return Mary's stare with blank windows she cannot read, and hit the cash button on the register. I am adding up an order. By the time I find the total she has recovered and swung around.

"Do you know what it was about the donkey last night?" She asks this as soon as I slam the drawer shut. I do not want to have to ask her.

But Mary doesn't wait for me to ask.

"Dot *loves* the donkey. One half of it, that is." She fairly crows. "The little boy who plays the front end is her beau."

"That's no surprise to me," I say calmly, but inside I am thinking that I really could be driven past my limit. I really could be forced to do something I'd regret.

I turn from Mary and start thinking. If she has been able to worm her way into my daughter's heart to this extent, where will it leave off? If Dot ever runs away I think she'll hitch into town and live with her aunt. What a victory for Mary! I'll be fired and barred from The House of Meats. I'll have to hire a lawyer to get my daughter back. It isn't fair. I'm the one who has to be strict and tell Dot to do her homework. Mary is the one who keeps her up late, having fun, so that the next day she dozes off in school. I'm the one who tries to make Dot eat lima beans and wash her neck. Mary tells lies looking into the palm of her hand. I ached for a mother because I never had one. I would have been glad for a mother to tell me what to do. But Dot has always had me there no matter what. I've been steady but unexciting. For dinner I make hamburger casserole, while Mary would serve anything that fell into her hands.

A week goes by, and then it is the morning of the Christmas play, bleak and cold and with the usual traveler's warning. Dot is spinning with excitement, nearly out of control. She bolts down her breakfast and in a surge of affection hugs me, then Mary. I can see that Mary is so touched and surprised that she has no words, can't even say good-bye or wish Dot luck. Dot forgets to brush her hair and jumps out the door, looking wild and unruly. Hug or no hug, I run after her with a hairbrush, slipping and sliding. I catch her at the bus stop.

"Dot," I say, "stand still. Calm down or you'll be tired by the time you get on stage."

Her cheeks glow and her eyes are dagger bright. She is carrying an old bathrobe of Wallace's and a pair of my leather sandals in a paper sack. The rest of her costume will be supplied by the nuns. The wind is harsh. My legs are bare. The road is slick and welted with frozen grime. Dot struggles while I brush her hair and pluck lint from her blue plush coat. The bus rescues her. She leaps in the very second its thin door swishes open.

"Next time you see me I'll be *disguised*," she screams.

The gears of the bus groan impatiently, and she runs down the aisle to sit in back with, as I have heard, the other trouble-makers. She waves, though. Her face is a pure blob of light through the caked dust of the window. The bus pulls carefully

220

down the road, and she is gone. I walk back to the house with my plan firm in mind.

The first thing I'm going to do is call Wallace Pfef, because my car has one rotten snow tire and tonight, in this ice, I'm going to need a ride. I can't ask Mary, because I'm bringing along a special secret dish that I don't want her to know about. Not until the play is finished, that is, not until the parents are wandering hungrily toward the back of the auditorium where the long hot-lunch tables are set, full of uncovered dishes. Then she'll find out about it. Soon enough. For I've decided to go more hog-wild than Mary would have the nerve to. I've decided a jealous mother has the right to be unpredictable. And I've also fixed it so all the strange looks will go in Mary's direction and not toward Dot or her mother. We'll be eating off our paper plates, talking to Wallace Pfef, ignoring the scratched heads and titters at the table. Mary, for her part, will be someplace else. I don't care. I don't even plan to sit with her during the play.

When I get back to the house she is already prepared to drive into town. I'm glad she's going early. I'm taking the day off. That way I'll have time to perfect my special dish for this evening.

"Don't bother to wait for me," I say as she is going out; "just find a place in the auditorium tonight, and sit. It will be crowded."

She nods at me and drives off, squinting forward to see through the little antifrost square of plastic fixed onto her windshield. I call Wallace and agree on a time and think that everything will go like clockwork. But of course, as with most things in life, it doesn't.

The gymnasium that night is packed full and noisy. I walk into the confusion with Wallace and my foil-covered pan, but before I can safely deposit it on the table, along with the offerings of the other parents, we are caught by Mary. She is dressed to the hilt, in a black turban with a rhinestone buckle, and a new rayon dress. The material is so unusual I can hardly stop looking at it. The background is blue, covered everywhere with markings that could have been drawn by prehistorics with charcoal sticks. It is writing of a sort, legible yet meaningless. It almost makes you want to lean forward and decipher it.

"I saved us seats," she says, "right up front. Come on, before someone grabs them."

"I'll find you," I say, pushing Pfef to go with her. Luckily, she is so anxious to get back to the seats that she doesn't notice I've brought a dish. So I am able to slip it in among the others. I say hello to the teachers who are standing at the back marshaling the paper cups. Even Mrs. Shumway gives a pleasant smile tonight, although her eyes, darting over the crowd, light a moment on Mary's flashing buckle, and take on a glazed wariness.

At length, I make my way to where Mary has kept the seat open between herself and Wallace. She has nothing to say to Wallace since he has become Dot's friend. She also blames him for sugar beets, which have brought the new franchise supermarkets that have cost her so much business. We look around, caught up in the excitement of it all. The lights blaze in steel-mesh buckets. Dads with rolled sleeves are lifting additional folding chairs from side carts and settling mink-collared grandmothers. In front, by the entries to the stage wings, nuns are huddled together in their black veils. The gym is run-down, a parish all-purpose room used for wedding and funeral dinners, budget meetings, bingo. The purple velveteen curtain is a shabby cast-off from the public school. The wood floor creaks and wavers. But the walls shine, decked in strands of tinsel. The feverish noise mounts and mounts, then, suddenly, it hushes and there is only the sound of programs rustling. In whispers, we find and admire Dot's name. The lights go down. There is complete silence. Then the curtains squeak open. The spotlight shows a boy wearing a knit poncho and a huge sombrero of the kind people who have been to Mexico hang on their walls. This boy makes a long sad speech about his friend the donkey, who he must sell to the glue factory in order to buy food. On a darkened set of bleachers behind him, a chorus of first-graders laments the donkey's fate.

The boy pulls the rope he has been twisting in his hands, and the donkey bumbles out of the wings. It is wearing gray pants and tennis shoes. The body is barrel shaped, lopsided, and the paper mache head lolls like it was drunk. The mouth, painted open in a grin, and the slanted black-rimmed eyes give it a strange expression of cruelty.

Parents *ooh* and *ahh*, but some look startled. The donkey is an unpleasant creature. Its dyed burlap-and-rug hide looks moth-eaten. One ear is long and one is short. Mary must be the only person in the crowd who thinks the donkey is cute. "Oh look at it prance," she whispers into my ear.

Her tartar eyes gleam softly; she bites her lip. Her gloves are in a tight ball like socks. She smiles as the boy and his donkey start out on the long road to the glue factory. Tragedy, her favorite element, is in the air. Her eyes sparkle when the chorus wails.

"Amigos! We are amigos!" the boy shouts from beneath the sombrero. Then they slowly begin to walk across the stage. They are weeping. But before they reach the glue factory, Saint Joseph appears.

My heart jumps. I am so afraid that she will trip or say the wrong thing. But she is just right.

She wears a long beard of spray-painted cotton, an old piece of upholstery fabric tied to her head, and the brown towel-cloth bathrobe that Wallace loaned to her. My summer sandals look biblical on her. As in my vision of her, she is carrying a wooden maul. Mary nods proudly, and I guess that the maul is her old sheep knocker. I don't like that. Saint Joseph should carry a construction tool, I think, not an instrument of death. Perhaps because of the maul, Dot looks grimmer than the mild church statues, and more powerful. I believe in her as Saint Joseph, even though she is my daughter. The donkey sidles up to her with its evil, silly grin. She stands before it with her legs spread wide, balancing on the balls of her feet. All I can see of the boy who, according to Mary, she loves are the gray corduroy knees and frayed black shoes. Dot grabs the donkey around the neck, and the gray legs twitch for a moment in the air. Then she sets the donkey down and says her lines to the donkey's amigo.

"Señor, where are you going with this donkey?"

"I must sell it to the glue factory, for my family is hungry," says the boy sadly.

"Perhaps I can help you out," says Dot. "My wife Mary, myself, and our little boy Baby Jesus want to flee King Herod. My wife could ride this donkey if you would sell it."

"I will sell my donkey to help you," shouts the boy. "He will not be killed!"

"Of course not," says Dot. "We will only ride him across the desert to Egypt."

She takes some large coins made of crushed aluminum foil from her bathrobe pocket and gives them to the boy.

And so it is, the transaction is accomplished. The donkey of destiny now belongs to Dot, who then tries to pat its snarling paper mache muzzle. But here is where the episode occurs which, I later hope, will not scar the mind of my daughter for life. The donkey balks. Is this in the script? I glance at Wallace, then Mary, wondering. But Wallace shrugs and Mary's look narrows to a flashlight focus of premonitions.

"Come along little donkey," says Saint Joseph through grit teeth. She pulls, perhaps a bit roughly, at the rope on its neck. Suddenly, a hand snakes from the front of the donkey's neck flap and rips the rope out of Saint Joseph's surprised knuckles.

My hands fly up, helplessly, as if they could stop everything. But too late.

The audience twitters, a few loud men guffaw, and Saint Joseph hears the audience, laughing at her! She jerks the rope back from the donkey. The hand slips out again, and this time pulls the cotton fluff right off Saint Joseph's chin.

Dot's arm tightens. I can feel it. Her face goes red with fury, purple, white, and she raises the maul, high! I know what will happen. The audience gapes. Then she brings it down clean, like swift judgment, on the cardboard skull of the beast.

The front of the donkey drops. The head flies off, smashed. The last of that scene that we see is Saint Joseph standing in criminal triumph, maul gripped tight, over the motionless body of a tow-haired boy.

The curtain has closed and the audience is in a rumble of consternation. A fat blond hysterical woman flies down the aisle, no doubt the mother of the donkey's felled front end. I sit rooted.

"Come!" Mary hisses, hoisting her handbag on her elbow. "Or the nuns will take it out on her hide!"

We leave the chairs to Wallace and find the side door. We slip behind the curtains into the backstage area. Angels and shepherds are standing in dismayed clumps. The Virgin Mary has torn off her veil and sobs in a corner. The painted wood silhouettes of sheep and cattle look stupidly baffled.

"Where's Dot?" Mary's voice booms. Everybody swivels.

"She escaped out the back door of the gym," says one of the sisters, tight lipped.

"Get out a search party then!" says Mary. "She's barefoot in the snow!"

But no search party forms at her words.

I take Mary's elbow and steer her out the back entrance.

"We'll look for her in your truck," I say, "and don't worry. I'm sure she put on boots."

We drive slowly up and down the streets of Argus. There are so many new streets that sometimes we hardly know where we are. We drive back, stop in at Mary's, and finally make it all the way home where we find Dot bundled in a blanket, sitting on the living-room coffee table with her bare feet by the heat ducts. The pair of red boots she took are drying out on a plastic mat.

"Young lady!" I shout in relief, marching toward her, but Mary gets there first.

"Wait," says Mary, holding me back. "She *is* hurt."

Sure enough, Dot is hiding something. She sits, clutching her play beard, shaking with the cold or maybe holding herself together. Defeated, wrapped in a blanket, she looks, oddly, like an ordinary middle-aged man. Her face is pale, streaked with misery, and her blue eyes are distant, unfamiliar with not even a hint of anger.

"Dot," I say, opening my arms.

She hesitates, wants to come, won't let herself, won't look at my face, but she starts to move toward me. Mary, however, is in the way between us. Mary kneels with a stiff creak and then suddenly, fiercely, lunges and catches my daughter full across the chest and neck with a stranglehold. Right then, I don't even care it is Mary who holds her, because I can only feel Dot's sadness. But Dot charges suddenly into my arms, runs right over Mary like a bull, sends Mary tumbling in a heap of black signs. Then Dot bolts up the stairs. The door to her room slams.

Mary thumped so loudly, falling over, that I pause just a moment to help her. But she is not hurt and even tries to look perversely delighted over what Dot has done. She pushes away my helping hands and lifts herself up.

"That's my girl," she says, adjusting her turban.

I go upstairs.

"Dot," I say, tapping on her door.

After a while I hear her muffled voice and so I enter. I sit down with her in the dark, on the cot where she has thrown herself, and slowly let my arms fall around her, as if by accident. She doesn't move, but she is tense as an animal in fear, ready to snap or go limp beneath its keeper's grasp. I adjust my hands, flattening my palms so that I touch her by inches. When I move them, pressing my fingers in her hair, stroking down the side of her neck, she almost shrugs me off. But she cannot, the fight has left her and she needs me too much to resist when I gather her close. Her heavy head falls against me, salty, smelling of sour wool. Her shoulders rock, but I can't tell she's crying until my skirt sticks to my thighs damp, and she breathes out, harsh and deep.

It is so long before she draws another breath that I almost shake her in alarm. But she is just asleep, and nothing will disturb her now. I don't leave, even though my arms go numb and Mary waits downstairs. I don't leave when she tosses in her first dream, throwing more weight against me. I sit perfectly still.

Then her fingers uncurl, as if sand is trickling out, and she seems lighter. The radiator shudders in the corner. Dot's room smells like the nests of shoes and socks she has made this week. It smells of the mildewed stuffing of her battered and abandoned dolls and of the sawdust where her hamsters hide. It smells of oil that she puts on her softball glove, lilac water that she dumps on her hair. It smells of cold grit between the window and the sill. It smells of Dot, a clean and bitter smell, like new bark, that I'd know anywhere.

I fall asleep sitting in the peace like that, and when I wake up I can't tell how late it is. I go downstairs and see that Mary is sitting by the gas heater. She has a piece of bread and butter in one hand and a mug of weak coffee in the other. The clock says midnight.

"I made a pot." She gestures toward the kitchen. "Get some for yourself."

So I do, and for a while we sit munching and sipping without a word.

"Wallace must have stayed back to talk with the parents," I say at last. "I suppose somehow the nuns salvaged the event."

"That kid deserved it," Mary says. "He was really the donkey's ass."

I agree with her. Mary speculates that he is a new child in the area, one of those who live in the big six-plexes known as cardboard acres. I tell her that children have had their moments of violence since time began, and this will pass. She begins to talk about the supper, about how they'll all mill back and fill their plates and talk about her specially concocted Jell-O. She has found a recipe she never tried before. I am dreamy and half-asleep after sitting with Dot and so, when I tell her about the dish I brought, I don't think.

"Did you notice that I brought in a special pan?" I ask.

"No," she says. She doesn't even ask what it was. I touch her chair and laugh.

"Well listen a minute," I say. "It had your name on it."

"My name?" She is interested.

"I taped it on the bottom of the pan," I tell her, "although I made the dish myself."

She is silent now and curious.

"What was in it?" she asks.

"I made a Jell-O salad."

"Oh," she says, "what kind?"

"The kind full of nuts and bolts," I say, "plus washers of all types. I raided Russell's toolbox for the special ingredients."

Her pupils harden to pinpoints. She trains a long look on my face. Then she turns away and huffs on her coffee, as if to cool it. I expect she will laugh at any moment and see the joke. I expect from her anything but what actually happens. For she never speaks. Her shoulders slump down and her back relents. And then, in the odd print of her dress, I finally read that she is hurt. She won't admit it, I know, but Mary wanted this evening

228

to be successful even more than I did. She wanted to taste here and there among the hotdishes and discuss them. She wanted to boast about her niece's starring role. It was the first time that she was ever included to this extent in the life of Dot, and unless a wind hits and the shop is completely leveled, this will probably be the last. She has no excuse to stay here, even now.

"I'm going," she says. "I left the shop unlocked and the dogs are out."

She puts on her coat and walks out of the door. I am left standing in the entry as her lights swing away into the dark. I hardly ever think about Mary's feelings, but now I do. I think of her alone in the small throbbing cave of her vehicle. She has worn thin, fancy gloves for the play, and now the night is so cold that she can only keep one hand at a time on the wheel. As she drives, she blows on the other hand to warm it. Then she changes hands. It is three miles between my house and Argus, and the road is bad. I watch Mary's car move cautiously down the dangerously frozen gravel ruts. Her red taillights tremble at the far intersection, then wink out.

The Birdorama

For days, Adelaide's silence and the brooding look she turned on the rain-wet leaves outside the tiny window of their bedroom warned Omar that she was building up a fit of anger. Her rage had nothing to do with him. It damned up regularly as water and there was no use in his trying to stop it. When she let loose, Omar stayed out of her way and let her pound on tables and chairs, let her kick and curse and bang screens and break whatever brought her peace.

In blue darkness, awakening to find her gone from their bed, he sneaked downstairs to spy on her mood. She was sitting at her kitchen table with a cup of cocoa. Adelaide's skin had gone paper white with age, and her hair too, a halo that stood out, electric. Her throat and slim waist had stayed supple. Her touch was quick and hard. She snapped when she spoke, and her eyes gave off a cool harsh light that subdued the customers who came to see their birds. Now, her housecoat heaped around her in a white billow, Adelaide poked at a little jade plant in a pot with a sharpened pencil. Omar watched her for a moment then retreated upstairs, dressed himself, and climbed down the flimsy back stairway.

Outside, the steam was rising from the grass and the palms were gray blue, alive and shuddering with breezes that stirred at dawn. The first few waking birds were starting to complain, to throw themselves back and forth across the inside of the wire dome. They hung for a wingbeat and then fell, flapping two or three times depending on their span, to the other side. Every morning they had to test the limits of their quarters and find the shape of it all over before they could calm down to sing and feed. Their brains were tiny, the size of watch mechanisms, accurate but stupid. They couldn't hold one idea in their heads overnight.

When Omar stepped into the great silver gazebo that glittered through the palms and attracted visitors from the local resorts, all the birds wheeled up, threw their claws out, and beat the air in circles, then settled to hone their beaks on the dead tree limbs planted in concrete. The arched ribs of the cage soared, black against the pearl-gray sky. From across the yard, Adelaide began. He did not look back, but her wordless scream caught him in the stomach. Out in the boat sometimes his trawling buddies tied two trash fish together, threw them out for seagulls, and watched the birds snap the fish up and kill themselves, bewildered, bound through the guts. At times like this, he and Adelaide were tied together just as viciously. He felt her pain like it was inside of him, but could do nothing.

He walked through the dome, back to the feed room. The birds knew the routine and collected, their eyes bright as snakes'. They had to eat more than their weight, and their morning frenzy was unpleasant to watch, even though it was the only time they seemed intelligent. Their heads bobbed in greed like pistons and their beaks stabbed up bits of fruit and animal fat. Turning away, Omar heard glass begin to break in long silvery muffled waves inside the house. Adelaide was sweeping ornaments off shelves, or perhaps she had pulled down the kitchen rack of wineglasses. She never hurt herself, and there was really no reason to stop her. Glassware was cheap and the closest neighbor was a quarter mile off. It was the waiting that oppressed Omar.

To pass the time he imagined what they would do once Adelaide came back to herself. He saw them holding hands in the front yard, behind the jacaranda, laughing at some foolish thing a customer had said. He saw her beating him at cards, tossing down the whole deck in a sprawl. She found a flat glittering stone from their driveway and held it against his cheek. She looked into his eyes. Gave him a piece of soap. A section of a ripe

231

orange. A newspaper. He saw them sleeping, curled tight in their sagging bed.

The house went huge with quiet and he got up to go. The birds were talking to each other now, oblivious of him. The sky was low and dense, the heat already close, and the rain an invisible warm spray. He heard the sound of Adelaide's broom and waited outside the door until the dustpan spilled musically, twice. Then he went in. She stood in the middle of the kitchen floor, her feet smeared with blood. Her hair was combed tight into a bent steel clip, and the cumulus puffs of her white gown hung flat. Her lips were pinched pale, and her spent eyes held his, frightened. She picked up a coffee cup, poured it shakily full, and he reached forward to take it from her hands before it spilled.

WALLACE PFEF

THEY LOVED DOT too much, and for that sin she made them miserable. Sometimes it was as if all of her family's worst qualities were crowded into her—Mary's stubborn, abrupt ways, Sita's vanity, Celestine's occasional cruelties, Karl's lack of responsibility. I went through fits, avoiding Celestine and Dot for months, then giving in. Dot had one trait that always drew me back.

She feared nothing. Not darkness, heights, nor any type of reptile. She jumped off high dives, climbed my ladders, walked through night as if she owned it. She showed me jars of loathsome creatures, which she watched tenderly for hours—slugs and caterpillars, even a yellow spider, and black snakes with orange stripes running their full length. She kept other small animals too. In the summer, she gave off the hay smell of the pressed alfalfa pellets she fed her rabbits, and the sewery odor of turtle food. But she was kinder to her dumb animals than to her mother and aunt.

Them, she starved.

I think that Dot's behavior was partly the result of Celestine and Mary's squabbling. Sometimes I thought the friction between the two women would grind Dot to dust, but instead she hardened between them, grew tough. She stood solid in the yard when she was five years old, put her fists on her hips and yelled at cats. When she was ten, she could do a full day's work, if she ever wanted.

Sometimes in the afternoons Dot came over, supposedly to

prune the spirea and flowering crab trees, or rake up the fresh-mowed grass clippings. I had prospered along with the sugar beet. Those acres I had bought up hit the ceiling once beets came in, and I had part share in the new sugar refinery. I could afford time off to putter. She watched me do it, all the while taking chances with my tools. She loved to hammer, and anything was vulnerable to her steel. Floors, pots, tables, walls. I convinced her to build a birdhouse, which turned out enormous, skewed, big enough for a pack of dogs. We put up a drainpipe, and nailed together a dead drunk trellis.

The nicest thing she ever did for me, the one present I remember, was a cardboard egg carton filled with neatly broken eggshells. Each shell held a teaspoon of earth and, she assured me, a surprise seed that would grow if sprinkled diligently. I kept my carton on the windowsill, sprinkled, and a few seeds did germinate. They sent up split fragile shoots that paled and withered before I could tell what they were.

I was proud that when Dot ran away, she ran through me. I came upon her suddenly, once, curled up, spent and drowsing at the top of my cellar steps, and sat down beside her. She was barefoot, in summer shorts. She had wrapped herself in an old gray gardening sweater that I kept on a downstairs hook.

"I'm running away," she said. "I even left a note."

"Why?"

"I'm going to live with my dad."

"Now, now," I said in a soothing voice, "just tell Uncle Wallace and he'll make it all right."

Dot's eyes widened, shooting rays of burning disdain.

"It is all right. He sends me things," she said, "neat things like soap. He sends me bus schedules and doll watches. He wants me and he's not what Aunt Mary says."

"What does Aunt Mary say he is?"

"A bum."

234

I hesitated. Once I would have defended Karl. It took seconds to realize that my loyalties had shifted through the years, that it had happened without a word to myself, without acknowledgment.

"I wouldn't exactly call him that," I got out.

She took that for approval.

"I know," she agreed. "If he's nothing but a bum where'd he get that big wheelchair? A bum couldn't get a wheelchair like that."

"That's right," I said, thinking of the ridiculous gift.

Dot considered this, suspicious.

"You know," she said at last, pointing her chin at me, "all the matchbooks in my collection? They're almost all from far-off places. Sometimes he sends an Iowa or Minnesota, but hardly ever. He's been around the world!"

Her claim didn't stand up, even in her own ears. I knew by the way she turned aside, unable to stare me down.

"Dot," I said, "come on upstairs and let me make a sandwich for you. Toasted cheese and tuna?"

She followed but was not to be distracted from her purpose by any one of her favorite foods, not even the cookie she loved called Mystic Mint. I kept a box of them on ice for her. We both liked them better frozen. She made me tie half a dozen in a plastic bag for her to take on her trip. Not until I asked her where she thought she would find Karl did she stop chattering about the bright future, the things they'd see together. It took a good while longer before she let me phone Celestine.

"Look here," I said to Dot after I hung up. "You should forget him."

She put down her sandwich and looked hostile.

"How come?"

I took a deep breath. My heart was pounding, foolish I suppose, but thinking of Karl just then made it hard to breathe normally.

Something had happened in the long period of time when I had not let myself remember him. Unexamined, unaired, feelings can change, rot to shreds or brew poison. I found myself saying surprising things.

"He's worse than a bum," I told Dot. "He got your mother pregnant and ran away. He stole some money from me and then went to Aunt Sita, took a handout, drove her into an asylum, then disappeared. He tries to sell things, but they don't work. He drinks and lies, can't make a living, cons and fools people. He's a nothing . . . he kicked my dog."

I stopped, out of breath, astonished and sick. But I needn't have worried so, for Dot's whole face gleamed. She was transported by my words, ready to fly off, find him.

"And," I said, mustering a desperate lie, the only one, "he hates children."

"Not me," Dot cried, jumping from the chair, stamping up and down in a dance that became a frenzy. "Not me, not me, not me!"

I had the awful urge to twist her arm, hiss, kill her fantasy. Yes you, I wanted so much to say, especially you.

But of course I didn't go that far. Celestine was at the door. She barged in and went straight through the house like a freight train, almost wailing. I would have been touched if I hadn't been so distressed with myself. But then, as time passed I learned the lesson parents do early on. You fail sometimes. No matter how much you love your children, there are times you slip. There are moments you stutter, can't give, lose your temper, or simply lose face with the world, and you can't explain this to a child.

It was a year so many other things began, things of greater and more terrible import. There was a war building up overseas, and death seemed to stalk our public heroes. The government could not be trusted, either, not even close to home. Here in North Dakota the missiles went in, a series of underground silos that didn't store grain. Right in town, there was an uproar of construction and new plans. Our developers were running out of the usual street names and had started naming cul-de-sacs for their wives and children.

But for all that was going on out there, that year stands out as the one I failed Dot.

Christmas is hard on a man alone. I was always included in someone's family dinner, but then I had to go home. It was the time of year I felt the emptiest, and sorry for myself. Books diverted me only for a short time, television made it worse with all those Christmas specials, movie stars dressed in velvet, singing carols, taking sleigh rides, wrapped in big white furs. The one event I truly looked forward to that year was seeing Dot play Saint Joseph in the Christmas pageant. She'd invited me herself and even borrowed an old bathrobe I kept around. Her starring role of Saint Joseph could have been that of Christ himself, she was so proud. It wasn't only for her size that they gave it to her, but also her voice. She had developed her vocal cords keeping up the outfield chatter for her baseball team all summer, droning like a maddened locust, "Humm baby," and "Hey battah, hey battah, hey battah." I don't remember Saint Joseph ever saying much in Christmas plays, but Dot claimed that she had twenty lines. And so I looked forward to the pageant night, was happy when that night came, and hummed Burl Ives Christmas tunes driving out to fetch Celestine. I wasn't prepared at all for the disaster.

I'm speaking of the private disaster, my secret one, not about the boy who enraged Dot or the punishment she delivered with Mary's old sheep mallet. That was not so surprising, for the fact is Dot was often in trouble for her temper. I don't know why the nuns even let her play such a vital role. The disaster that shocked me, that pierced me through, happened right before the public one, when I saw Karl.

It was the old brown bathrobe that I'd lent Dot for a costume. I'd been a fool to forget its significance. That bathrobe was the kind of thing you lend to a man who comes to visit, but I'd not thought of that for years, or how he looked standing in the doorway.

And then he appeared.

It happened when the boy's hand snaked out of the donkey's coat and pulled Saint Joseph's beard off. I did not think that Dot resembled Karl, but I was wrong. For there he lounged, suddenly, half in shadow, with the light behind him on the white woodwork. His eyes lowered so his lashes brushed down, then lifted to look me full and square so that there was no distance in the room and none between us.

I started up, stood. The gym was a hive of golden insects buzzing, floating, gathering the honey that filled me. I was in tears. My glasses fogged. Nobody noticed, for which thank God. Through a gap in the crowd I saw the front of the donkey fall in a heap. Then its back end pitched forward, and a boy scrambled from the husk of gray carpet samples, shouting.

I turned my head, slapped my hands to my temples, but it was no use. Karl was still there, across from me in the morning, at the table, pouring coffee and stirring in three spoonfuls of sugar, combing his black hair from his eyes with his fingers, licking the drops of milk from his moustache.

The curtains swept shut. One of the sisters emerged to announce that the play would have to end. Applause spattered through the audience, and people began to fill the aisles. "Shouldn't we at least eat?" someone asked. I was forced to answer, forced to mop my brow and clean my glasses off with studious care. Then I walked through the clumps of people who were already finding comfort at the back table.

The Pyrex covers of the dishes had been removed. Cups of

urn coffee were poured and handed out. I went through the line mechanically, collected mysterious dollops, ate in frantic haste. Between mouthfuls I made excuses for Saint Joseph's temper, and soon the topics switched as always to sugar-beet forecasts and mortgage rates, bond levies and pavement costs. Then I almost cracked my tooth on a metal bolt.

"Someone's idea of a joke," said the principal, to whom I'd been talking. "No one knows who did it. Some teenage prank perhaps. Whoever it was filled a whole pan with hardware, but if there was a name attached to that dish it fell off."

"It's very strange," I said, nudging the piece of hardware aside.

The bolt brought me to my senses. It was time I went home, out of harm's path, where I could soak my delusions away in the bathtub. A hot bath was what I wanted desperately. I looked around, but Celestine and Mary were nowhere in sight. I thought after the fiasco they had probably taken Dot home in Mary's truck. I should have thought of Dot then. I should have wondered what drove her to fell the donkey. But I was too far gone, dragged under by memory, by the strain of keeping Karl under too. I left the school gymnasium, got into my car, and drove home. And in that whole drive I did not let Karl come up once, although he struggled beneath my hands, although his body was pale and lean and his cries were soft. I held him down with all my might.

At home, I stumbled over to my couch, too exhausted to weep or thrash about, too bitterly sad to answer the door the first time the bell rang.

Then she rang again. I don't think I would have answered even then if I hadn't schooled myself since the night of Dot's birth to believe I should always be available to a person in distress. Anyway, the dog was barking. It was cold and I'd left her tied in the backyard. I went to answer the door and stood behind it, patting my hair back into place, gathering myself before I'd see what she wanted.

"Uncle Wallace?"

There was no need to wonder. I heard her voice and it was dangerous with need, like his. I opened the door a tiny crack.

"Let me in, it's freezing cold."

"No," I said. "I mean, please go home."

Dot was silent, unbelieving. "I've got something to tell you," she insisted. She put her foot in the space and then barged through, just like her mother, or more like her father perhaps, the salesman.

"No," I said again, catching her by surprise and spinning her back toward the door. "I mean it. Go!" I fairly threw her out, and then tried to salvage something.

"Dear, I'm sorry."

But her face had clenched like a pale wax-paper mask, into a ball of hate. It was strange. She looked transparent with the cold, like a child of glass. The snow's blue light shone through her when she tore off my old robe and stood a moment, facing me. I saw that she was anyone but Karl, and half frozen in nothing but a little girl's sprigged undershirt and cotton panties, which glowed whiter as she jumped down off my steps, across the crumpled brown robe.

"Come back!" I cried, but even then, and most unforgivably of all, I did not mean it enough to rush after her. She headed home. But it was almost one-half mile. I folded the bathrobe into my arms, told myself that I would stand outside on my step the length of time I thought it would take her to get there. That way I'd convince myself she was all right. Within minutes I was shivering from deep inside and my face had numbed.

I ran inside, grabbed my keys, and tore hell for leather out of my garage, following her. I thought of the first time I'd headed for that house through the night, following the stray dog. Even then, Dot had existed, a small collision. She could have curled into the crook of a typed question mark.

I looked hard but couldn't see her, drove slowly, alert to any movement in the ditches to either side. She might be hiding from my headlights, and it was cold out, so cold. I reached the house without having found her, but then a light went on, and suddenly I saw her through the window, a shadow bolting up the stairs.

All my Christmas presents to Dot that year netted nothing but a thank-you note written by Celestine, in a hand that was supposed to resemble her daughter's. I phoned. Celestine forced Dot to speak to me, but all my fond questionings and jokes left her cold. I racked my mind for something that would win her back. I thought of giving her a dog, but I knew that Celestine had refused dogs from Mary. Celestine would hate me if I gave her daughter a pony. An automobile perhaps? Had she been old enough I would have dipped into my savings account to purchase a little runabout. Or I would have bought her a ring of pearls and diamonds. Dot hated jewelry. She liked parties, though. I called Celestine and asked her what she was doing for Dot's eleventh birthday next week.

"Nothing, I mean I don't have plans."

"Then let me plan," I said. "Let me give her the party."

Celestine was easily convinced. Parties were to Celestine an unpleasant task. I knew full well that she only gave them to try and help Dot make school friends, and that so far they'd done the opposite. That was mainly because of Mary, who had to be invited. Children were afraid of Mary's yellow glare, her gravel-bed voice. She organized games with casual but gruesome threats, and the children complied like hostages with a gun trained on them. They played mechanically, with an anxious eye to her approval. Their laughs were false. But Mary didn't notice this and took no hint from Celestine to stop her intimidation tactics. As for Dot, she became Mary's sidekick, second in command, and carried out her aunt's orders with grim and businesslike dispatch. It didn't seem to bother Dot that when the party finished, the other children dashed from her yard in relief.

"Maybe you can get Mary to lay off the children," Celestine said now. "She will be on unfamiliar turf."

If it were up to me I wouldn't have invited Mary at all. But that was the wages of being allowed to give this party. Naturally, I had to have Dot's aunt. But if I had to have Mary, I decided, I would also have Louis and Sita. They'd not been much in circulation lately, although Louis had said it was important for Sita to socialize. I knew Louis from the Lions, from local town government, and of course through his job diagnosing the few pests that threatened sugar beets. He was an important man in our area, always called on in times of crisis. He'd been the perfect man for Sita when she needed care—strong and skillful. But it was obvious how caring for Sita had worn on him. Every time I saw Louis now, he looked thinner and grayer. He had developed angina and had to carry nitroglycerin capsules. Still, I thought that his reasonableness and authority might temper Mary.

"This will be a mixed gathering," I told Louis on the phone. "Family, a few of Dot's school friends, perhaps a fellow Lion or two."

"It's been years since I've been to a birthday party," Louis said. "We've missed out on them with no children of our own. We'd love to come."

"Where?" It was Sita's voice; she had picked up the other phone and was now on the line.

"I've asked you not to do that, dear," said Louis.

"I know," said Sita, "dear."

"I called to ask you both to come to Dot's eleventh birthday." Sita's line clicked.

"We'll be there. She's truly fond of the girl. We'll see you then," said Louis.

When they were all invited, Dot's school friends and Mary too, I sat back and for the first time considered the fact that I

242

was asking Mary and Sita to coexist for several hours when they hadn't sat beneath the same roof at the same time for years. I considered that I was asking Louis to attend also, counting on his stable influence, but that if he couldn't make it at the last minute I'd be lost. Without him, I thought that I would never keep the caldron of elements I had mixed from boiling over. As it turned out, his influence was not enough.

In spite of the potential problems, I took joy in my preparations. I decided that Hawaii would be our birthday theme. We'd have an indoor luau, "South Pacific" playing in the background, Pin the Tail on the Wild Pig. Dot would have a basket of crepe-paper leis to deck each guest with at the door. We'd have a pineapple upside-down cake for the birthday cake. I bought a windup cake stand at the gift shop downtown. I imagined how the cake would revolve as the music box within the stand tinkled out "Happy Birthday to You." We'd sing. There would be lots of exotic drinks made with canned juices, crushed ice and paper umbrellas on top. I'd give Dot a ukulele that I ordered down in Fargo. Most important of all, she would forgive me.

January 18 dawned. Eleven years since I had answered my front door in a blizzard. The day was calm and not terribly cold. In town, the sun gleamed off the street pavement, melting the snow in patches, and the children I picked up seemed eager, if a little nervous. Perhaps they'd been to Dot's other parties. But this one would be different.

There were four children, Dot's only friends, three hefty boys and one small fresh-faced girl with a sweet expression. When we got to my house, however, and Mary's truck nosed up behind us like some big dark red predatory fish, this little girl's face sharpened.

"Don't worry," I began as we scrambled out, but whatever I might have said to reassure her was drowned out by Dot's yodel of delight and Mary's rasp.

"Let's get cracking. We've got a birthday to celebrate!"

Mary's face was ruddy with excitement and she hardly even noticed me, so deeply was she concentrating on the children. She rounded them up behind her and marched them to the door before I could get organized enough to intervene.

"Company halt!" she yelled.

Then she opened the door to my house and they entered. Dot had trooped in behind her but the other children dragged their feet and looked back with imploring eyes.

"Don't worry!" I called again, but the door shut and I had to gather up the last-minute purchases—paper cups, extra clothespins for Drop the Clothespin in the Bottle, and special party straws—before I could rush to protect them.

Inside the door, however, there was little to be done. The children stood in a resigned clump, bending their heads to let Dot or Mary slip the leis on. The exposed backs of their necks were delicate and vulnerable. I tried to liven up the party, dressed in a loud orange Hawaiian shirt, beach-bum trousers, a big straw hat. First thing off, I handed out the favors, little bird whistles that soon had the place chirping like an aviary. Celestine walked in and stood at the living-room entrance, looking expectant, but no one noticed her except for me. Her face darkened as she took in the situation.

"See what I mean about Mary?" she said.

The children stood in a straight line as Mary numbered them off for some team that she was organizing. Each one had the look of being singled out for the firing squad.

I lifted my hands in a gesture of defeat.

"I couldn't stop her," I said.

"I never can either." Celestine shrugged.

As we stood there, Sita and Louis drove up in their big silver car. They walked in. As always, Louis was calm and controlled; he also looked more frail. His eyes were tired and shadowed. Perhaps Sita had had a difficult night. Still, he smiled at the ear-splitting bird whistles that had begun again. Mary had organized whistling teams. Louis gave Dot his coat and he kissed her when she put the lei around his neck. She kissed him back, enthusiastically, and hugged Sita too. I'd been the only one except her mother that Dot had not showered with affection.

I trusted that, minutes from now, her attitude would change. The ukulele rested in its case. The graceful blond-wood instrument came with clear instructions, and a beginners book called *Island Favorites*, from which Dot would be able to learn "Tahitian Lovesong," "Beyond the Reef," and "A Papeete Lullaby."

Sita tapped me on the shoulder. She'd gotten too thin and lost her bloom in the mental hospital, I knew that. But she seemed to have gone downhill even since then. Her face was cavernous and delicately wrinkled like a fine thin notepaper. She looked ill, yet she was still striking with her fine bone structure and her fashionable clothing.

"It's very nice," she said, indicating the green crepe paper strung from the light fixture, the plastic hibiscus, travel poster, the centerpiece of coconuts. "Where is your powder room?"

I directed her up the stairs and she gracefully ascended. That was the last we would see of her until the refreshments were served.

Meanwhile, it was time for the wild pig. And now it was clear that the plan to inhibit Mary had been a failure. There was no advantage in holding the party at my house. She was in charge. I had painted a large brown pig on a piece of cardboard and hung it on the wall. I had cut out a curly paper tail and stuck that on a hatpin. Mary held the tail and the hatpin now. Blindfolded, brandishing the long wicked-looking pin before her, she had every child in the room, save Dot, backed against the wall. Dot fearlessly dodged the pin and gave her aunt a great push forward. The pig was impaled with such force that Mary's arm buckled. She ripped off her blindfold.

"Who's next!" she cried, wiggling the pin and the tail loose.

"I am," said Louis in his low, calm voice. He took the pin and the tail from her hand, let himself be blindfolded and spun. The children hung closer, as if he was safe, King's X. He held the pin within the shelter of his body and suddenly the whole game was comical and fun, the way it should have been. Only Mary, no longer the center of attention, seemed less interested.

She followed me into the kitchen, where I went to baste the luau ham, a fifteen pounder covered with pineapple wedges, scored, and dotted with red maraschino cherries.

"That's a decent-sized ham," she commented. I knew what she was trying to get at, but I held my own.

"On special at Dotzenrud's Super Valu," I said.

She leaned close to the ham, inspecting it, then grabbed a knife from the top of the stove and, before I could move to stop her, cut a wedge right out of the center, ruining my pineapple and cherry design. I stared in shock as she popped the bit of ham into her mouth and chewed, narrowing her eyes critically.

"It's cured with cheap chemicals," she said at last, "not wood. And the water content. I bet you could squeeze two gallons out."

I slammed the oven shut and clenched my teeth. If it hadn't been for Dot I would have asked the aunt to leave right then.

"Why Mary," I crooned instead, acting the good host, "you haven't had the special drink yet, reserved for VIP guests in this house."

"No, I haven't."

So I went to make it. I was merely going to mix her a stiff one. But when I opened my cabinet the first bottle that my eyes lighted on was the one an Elk had left, Everclear, just about pure grain alcohol. If she hadn't cut through my decorated ham I wouldn't have done it. But she had, so a percentage of Everclear went into the drink, disguised by Hawaiian Punch and a can of purple passion Shasta, that would have knocked a prizefighter sideways. I thought of setting the little Chinese umbrella on fire as I served this drink, just to signal its potency. But I did not. It would be better to let Mary discover its effects on her own.

She took a healthy gulp.

"Bottoms up!" I smiled, upending my own glass of punch. To my horror and delight, Mary drained the entire concoction.

Once she'd set her empty glass down on the counter, I asked if I could refill it.

"I wouldn't mind," she said, and then she actually smiled. The effects of the drink were stronger than I'd imagined. Still, I threw an extra shot into the next one. She walked out of the kitchen with the drink in her hand. I followed. She was steady on her feet, but when she reached the entrance to the living room she paused. Her head tipped to the side, and then tipped farther to rest against the woodwork as she surveyed the scene. I edged around to get a side view, and even in profile I could see that her smile was uncharacteristically dreamy. She sipped lightly now, and made no move to join the game of Drop the Clothespin. She merely stood, watching the children take aim from atop a chair, and even nodded approvingly when Celestine handed out the prizes—more leis, plastic watches, rings with glass stones.

When everything was finished, laid out on the carefully set table, when the cake in all of its upside-down splendor was placed on the Happy Birthday cake stand and the tropical punch was poured, I walked out to call the guests. At the last moment I had set three little bears riding motorcycles on top of the cake with the candles. I would light the candles soon. The party had turned warm and joyful with Louis and Celestine in charge. Mary watched from the floor. As I came out of the dining room I saw that she had collapsed where I'd left her, in the doorway. I bent down and touched her arm. The material of her dress was the color of orchids, splattered with dark little marks that looked like accidental stains. As I assisted her into the dining room I saw that they were stains.

"Don't bother," she said, when I offered to fetch a damp sponge. "They'll blend in." She laughed, throwing her head from side to side, and offered the empty glass. I took the glass and mixed her another drink, just strong enough to keep her mood from evaporating. She took a sip as soon as I put the drink in her hand, and then, looking me full in the face, spoke in a voice that was almost tender.

"From now on, you get your ham from me, you get it wholesale."

"I'll hold you to that," I joked, guiding her forward. Before she fumbled into her chair she turned and gave me an even more benign gaze. Her eyes changed color, softened from the harsh yellow of two gold coins to a radiant amber.

"I mean it, you old coot," she whispered affectionately. Her turban had gone awry. It had slipped back off her forehead and barely stuck to her head, so that her hair, which I'd rarely seen, fell out in gray wisps. She leaned across the table and spoke to Louis.

"Where's my crazy cousin?"

Louis gave her a surprised look then glanced involuntarily at the staircase where Sita sat, peering at us through the cast-iron leaves of the banister rail. I'd noticed her from the corner of my eye for some time now, drawn to us warily but helplessly, like a starved deer. She resembled one. Her cheeks were hollow, her eyes were stark, and her ribs were caved in. She melted back from our attention into the shadows of the upper landing.

"Join the party!" hollered Mary, straining in her chair.

"Let her alone," said Celestine, reaching over the heads of two children and tapping Mary's back. "It's about time we toasted the birthday girl."

But Mary shrugged Celestine's hand off and pulled herself

laboriously to her feet. Her eyes had now deepened to the color of caramel, like sugar coming to a boil. She staggered to the bottom of the staircase.

"Ready or not here I come!" she cried. But Louis brushed past her before she could move, and she slammed herself back against the wall just beneath the electrical connection to my doorbell chimes, setting them off in a merry *tink-tonk*. She whirled, her face uncreased in delight. The bell kept playing. She continued to whirl and hop in a strange dance. Evidently the chimes had shorted somewhere in the wires. The children watched Mary with rapt attention. Even to them it was obvious that something was abnormal. I climbed a chair quickly and disconnected the bell, but the damage was already done.

"She's completely plowed," Celestine noticed.

She rushed to Mary's side and dragged her back to the table.

"What was in that drink?" she said, frowning.

Sita saved me.

"Here I am!" she called in a voice so loud and bright it temporarily froze her. She recovered though, gripped Louis tightly, and accompanied him over to the table. They both looked ashen, almost skeletal, and I noticed Louis pat his pocket to make sure of the presence of his nitro capsules. They sat down and then we were all, finally, assembled.

But what an example to the children we had set. They'd go home traumatized as every year before.

The thought spurred my determination. I would rescue this event from what had begun to happen by at least allowing Mary to sober up. As soon as everyone was served and eating happily I went out back to put the coffee in the percolator.

While I was gone, the whole thing blew.

Much later, I was to piece together what happened from conversations with Celestine, and with Mary, who was chagrined at the results. For it was Mary who took a House of Meats matchbook from her pocket while everyone else was eating, and lit the birthday-cake candles. That didn't seem so terribly bad, though a little off the traditional timing. No one stopped her. And what she did next would not have been out of line either, except for the fact that in her mind's disarray she wound the cake stand so tightly that it sprung.

I came back into the room as the cake began to move. The music box tinkled the birthday song, but quickly, so quickly that Mary's mouth could not keep up with it. Speed built. The brown glaze blurred. The candles fused into a single flame, and the toy bears began a mad chase that led nowhere.

"Stop!" I cried, lunging for the controls.

"HappyBirthdayToYou!" Mary cried.

Then the cake stand's spring snapped. It whipped around once, jerked, and flung the entire cake at Sita. She went backward with it, clutching thin air, fending off the bulk as if it were alive and attacking her. She flung bits of it from side to side and slapped her arms, thereby effectively demolishing what survived, mashing the rings of pineapple, beating the cake itself to crumbs.

The little wheels of the bears' motorcycles spun themselves out against the wall. Sita's high laugh rose above the sounds of surprise. Louis leaped up, grabbed Sita, and held her pinned against his chest. The children combusted in a frenzy of pent nerves, and Celestine had her hands full, calming them. As for Mary, she sat quite still. A statue couldn't have been more motionless. A gaunt and Halloweenish grin was plastered to her face. Her eyes had gone a full black, and her hands were pressed together on her heart. Although Louis was the one I should have worried about, for even then he was reaching around Sita and into his pocket for a capsule, my one thought was that Mary's heart had given out. She'd had a stroke. I rushed around the table and checked her pulse. The beat was slow, even. It then seemed very clear that the tall purple drinks had turned her to stone.

Sita began to scream with laughter and point her finger in Mary's direction. Whatever Mary really felt about the cake accident, her face was a mask of devilish glee. And she sat there like that, smiling without moving, as the party broke up. Louis spoke calmly to Sita and convinced her to leave. The children were ushered into Celestine's car with all of Dot's presents to be opened en route. From my front porch, my party in ruins, I saw them out. But as they backed from the drive, the last minute before they were obscured by my decorative hedges, Dot rolled down the window.

"Uncle Wallace!" she cried. "That was the best birthday ever!"

I stood there until the last of the engine's noise had disappeared, and back inside, even as I swept up the crumbs of my lovely cake, even as I plastic wrapped all the remains of my luau, I was pleased.

I looked at Mary, but with guilt now, for thanks to me she had made a complete horse's ass of herself. As far as I knew, she rarely touched spirits. She sat in the same chair. Her grin had not faded. From time to time she rolled her eyes. I sat down beside her.

"If you can hear me," I said, "blink twice."

Blink. Blink. So she was conscious.

"Are you all right? One blink means yes and two means no."

One blink.

"Shall I call the ambulance?"

Two blinks.

"Shall I do anything?"

Two more.

So I just left her sitting at the table as I continued to clean up the litter of paper plates and party favors. After perhaps a half an hour passed she began to speak in a slow drawl.

"Wallace," she called out. A long minute passed. "I had a good time."

I came into the dining room wiping my hands, put the dish towel down, and sat across from her at the table. Mary's face was coming back to life.

"That's nice," I said.

She nodded. Her first sentence had taken an effort. By the way she cocked her head I knew that she was still drunk, but sobering up. It crossed my mind that she'd be hell with a hangover, and I should really try to get her home before the Everclear wore off. I made the suggestion.

"No," she said. "Let's talk."

I wrapped my hands in the dish towel. I wasn't sure that I wanted to talk to her. We had never been friends. She had wounded me when possible, beginning with the first day she gave my namesake, Wallacette, the unremarkable nickname Dot. She had resented me, taken jealous potshots at my friendship with Celestine, been perpetually cunning where she could have been kind, and tried her best to spoil this party. There was no warmth in her, no generous heart. She was a tough case.

"What's there to talk about?" I said. "I'll bring you home."

She leaned across the table and waggled her finger.

"There's lots to talk about," she said. "I don't want to go. I've got your number in the book of numbers. I know what card you played."

"You're making *no* sense," I said, trying to be firm. I was not going to let her get underneath my skin.

"Coward."

"What?"

"You're two yolks in the same damn egg," she said.

"You've lost me."

"You're lonely."

I looked at her. I shook off the dish towel, smoothed back my hair. I touched my eyeglasses, chin, cheekbones, as if I were putting myself together.

"I'm not lonely," I said to her. "I am a member of three fraternal orders and have a social life that's, well, I'm in *demand* Mary."

She blew air through her teeth, then suddenly, so quick I couldn't react, snatched across the table and drew my hands into hers.

"Liar," she said. "When I pass sometimes, late, you're up burning the midnight oil. A couple times I've stopped and looked right in your window."

I was indignant but also fascinated.

"Why?" I said. I tried to pull my hand back but she gripped it tight.

"I've thought about things."

While I was trying to decide whether or not I wanted to know what she thought about, she turned my palm upward in her hand and gazed down into it. Her mouth moved as if an article was written there. She finally said "It's no good," dropped my hand, and looked straight into my eyes. I was too curious to keep quiet.

"What?" I said.

"Say, do you have a cigarette?"

"A few stale ones," I muttered, looking down into my palm now that I had drawn my hand back. I got up and took an old pack from a drawer in the highboy. I gave it to her with some matches, and she lit one, blew the heavy smoke out with great authority.

"You have a big cross on your mount of Venus," she finally revealed, "and no marriage line."

I sat down and kept looking into my hand. There were lines there I'd never noticed. Tiny crisscrossing hatch marks, long swooping lines, braids and ropes.

"I'm not surprised," I said.

"Too bad," she said, rising unsteadily. "But you two could still chance it."

I must have looked confused.

"You and Celestine."

I couldn't believe my ears.

"Oh," I said, "well . . . that's something. Yes."

"What are you trying to say, Wallace?"

"I'm trying . . ." I couldn't go on.

"I read you like a book."

"Yes, well. I'm flattered. But she's already married."

"Karl hasn't been back since Dot was born," she said, and then, after a moment of frowning she lifted her eyebrows. "She deserves better out of life."

She was waiting but I wouldn't say what she wanted me to say. Her figure made a dense patch of jungle-dark shade, and her eyes glared out like the points of two tacks. She was holding herself up by pushing down on the back of the chair. Neither of us moved until the cigarette burned completely down to the filter. Then I reached over the table and drew the end from her fingers. I put it in the blue club-shaped ashtray.

"Time to go," I said, walking around the table. I took her elbow when she swayed.

"My coat's on the front couch," she said. We walked into the living room and I helped fit her into the woolen armholes. She buttoned the thing around her like a shield.

Outside we opened the car doors without speaking and got in. We drove in silence. The early dusk fell and the shadows on the road spread in insubstantial pools. I thought at least the strange afternoon, the conversation, might bring us closer. But by the time we reached the shop, so many stubborn seconds of silence had accumulated between us that we were back where we'd started.

The ox Motel

Karl liked motels with strange or inviting names, so he pulled in when he saw the blinking sign, even though the town was Argus. As he stepped out of his car into the sweet, fresh night, he saw that it was merely the Fox. The *F* had burned out. He checked in anyway.

He found his room, turned on the television, showered, and stretched out naked on the bed. He paged through the telephone book, found their names. He planned to stop with that, but then he dialed Wallace Pfef's number. The phone rang once and Wallace answered.

"Hello? Hello? Hello?" By the third hello, Wallace's voice sounded strained, bewildered. Karl held the phone away from his ear, then lowered it toward the cradle. Wallace's voice turned tinny, comical, and was finally cut off. Karl thought of dialing Mary's number next, but felt embarrassed at talking to her with his clothes off. He could have slipped on a pair of pants, but instead he called Celestine.

"Guess who?" he said when she answered.

He listened to the thin empty hum of the open line. It did not occur to him that she might not recognize his voice, and when she finally said, "Who is this?" in a sharp suspicious tone, he had a sudden blue pang that he covered over with talk.

"You know who it is. I was passing through and stopped for the night, unexpectedly you know, and since I was here I thought maybe I'd just drop by."

When she still did not answer he went on.

"Or you'd come meet me for a drink, maybe. Or I'd take you and Wallacette out for dinner."

"Karl," Celestine said at last. "You promised you'd stay away."

He waited. "It's been fourteen years."

"I'm not going to dredge up old times."

"Fine, just fine."

"All right," said Celestine after a moment. "I guess you have a right to see her. Just give me a minute to think."

She thought.

"I suppose you'll be pushing on tomorrow," Celestine said. "Why not breakfast then, seven-thirty, over at the Flickertail?"

"I'll be waiting there," said Karl. There was an undertone of longing in his voice that surprised him. He pulled himself up against the pillows. "Don't be late!" he said harshly.

But the line was already buzzing.

He woke too early, got ready too soon, and found himself sitting in a booth drinking cup after cup of coffee before they finally arrived. By the time they walked through the door he was jittery and faintly ill from the caffeine on an empty stomach, and all the cigarettes he'd smoked. He stood up but he hardly knew what to say, the sight of Wallacette was so unexpected. She stood in the café entrance with her mother, a short solid girl with light olive skin, brown-red hair, the dangling hoop earrings and tight short skirt of a juvenile delinquent. It surprised him to see the clothes her mother let her wear, so cheap looking, and the eye makeup. She scanned the people in the booths through narrow black slits. Under blue hoods, her look was eager. She passed him over, came back when he raised his hand and smiled at them. He stepped forward and her face fell.

Later on, thinking back, he would brush away her disappointment. He had aged, become shrewd and hard and gray, with frown lines down the side of his mouth and many small marks of strain around his eyes. He was so used to driving, so used to distance and movement, that he sometimes found it hard to focus properly on anything within the reach of his arms.

So he saw his wife and daughter most clearly when they stood in the doorway. When they slid into the booth across from him, their faces smoothed and blurred.

"Sorry to be late," said Celestine. She didn't look sorry. She looked like she wanted to be somewhere else. Her coat was thick and rough, furlike, sewn of light and dark gray patches. She kept it draped over her shoulders and squeezed Dot into the corner of the booth. Their faces stared at him, from fur and hair, fuzzy, almost like animals from a den. Karl could make out Celestine's big, raw features best. Her face was bare of makeup. Her lips were pointed in the middle, brown, and her dark eyes like drops of molasses. Her cheekbones and her nose stood out, and her hair, in lake-brown waves, sprung stiffly around her skull. He wanted to press it down, to get close enough to breathe the pepper that clung to her skin from sausage making.

But her eyes stopped him. He looked at Dot.

Her face was bolder, vivid in its rouge and orange cake. Her hair was cut in a long shag that looked like a flattened mane. Her neck was powerful.

The two watched him closely. He adjusted his tie, straightened his collar, smiled, tried to dazzle. He nudged the menu at Dot's place.

"This is on me," he said. "Order anything you want." He tried not to stare at Wallacette Darlene, but she was staring at him, frowning in unblinking concentration, her lips slightly parted, her breath shallow. Karl's eyes kept darting back to meet hers, his lips kept forming a nervous smile.

He said in a hearty voice, "How old are you now Wallacette?"

"Fourteen," she said, and her expression changed, as if she had decided something. She sat back and lowered her powdered lids. "Didn't you tell him, Mama," she said through one side of her mouth, "that I'm Dot?"

"Dot," she said to Karl, "Dot."

"She goes by Mary's nickname," said Celestine. Then she gave Karl a look of resigned complicity that warmed him a little. It was the kind of look that nuns had exchanged in the halls at Saint Jerome's. It was the kind of look that passes between adults over the heads of their children.

Dot caught the look between them and blew the stiff bangs off her forehead. "I'm out of the ordinary enough," she said. "I don't need a weird name." Her voice was hard and final. Karl found nothing to say to her.

"You're not what I expected," she said coolly, to his face.

Karl looked to Celestine for help, but she was studying the menu.

"You're not," he raised his eyes to Dot's, "what I expected, either."

This stirred her a little, took her by surprise. She held the menu up and mumbled, "I'll have the number two with coffee and tomato juice. Where's that waitress?"

They were all three silent, reading the typewritten sheets behind the plastic, the combinations of eggs and hashbrowns and toast. The waitress seemed to have forgotten them, however, and they sat, suspended among the other customers, farmers and construction workers already on their coffee breaks. Across the street a new building of tan aluminum was rising. Hammering and the muffled whine of electric saws filled the street. The sun shone on the stacks of candy under the counter, on the coffee urns and the spigots of the milk machine. The waitresses had just come on their shifts. The cook, a large blond woman in an orange bib apron, said things that made the men at the counter laugh into their cups. The radio blared livestock futures and farm reports into the bacon-smelling air. But none of this suggested anything that the three in the booth might say to one another.

"Does Dot have some sort of, well, male influence in her life?" Karl surprised himself by asking this, and then realized during Celestine's pause that he wanted very much to know.

"Wallace Pfef is like a father to her," Celestine said.

Dot pretended not to hear at first, but in the silence Karl kept after Celestine's hard answer she spoke. "I go up to Uncle Russell's a lot now. Eli's teaching me to fish."

Karl nodded, remembering Russell as a ravaged-looking Indian with a box of clanking tools, a man who didn't like him.

When the waitress made her way at last, they all ordered. Celestine tried her best to make talk about the shop and Mary, but carefully did not ask whether or not Karl planned on visiting there. Karl tried too. He told Celestine all about his new job, high pay, even though he hadn't known much about stereo components at first. He was working for a budding chain of hi-fi and record stores, in the supply end.

Celestine smiled at him for the first time.

"That explains the record player you sent."

"The latest," he said, pleased even though she hadn't called it a portable stereo system, which it was, and of the best quality.

"Did you like it?" he asked Dot, who looked down at her hands and regarded her chipped pink nails as if they had something to tell her.

"Of course I liked it," she said to her fingers.

Karl decided to take a chance and tried to get her attention. "D.O. Double T.I.E./Dottie is the girl for me," Karl sang. "Do you know that one?"

Dot's face sprang into an ugly mask.

"No," she said. "I listen to hard rock."

"Do you know," said Celestine, embarrassed and a bit flustered, "that Dot tried to run away and find you once?"

The waitress put their steaming plates down, and Dot lowered her head to the food. She ate fast, without looking up. The long dangly loops in her ears hit her chin every time she took a bite. Karl watched her and had the sad thought that he could have influenced her taste in music if he'd been around more. Maybe not living with them, but at least settling down in the area, maybe

259

not seeing her that often, but at least once in a while. He felt reckless and desperate, suddenly, with the loss of this unattractive girl.

"I'll tell you what," he said, "would you listen to some records if I sent them?"

"It depends," said Dot.

Her voice had an edge of knowing. She was conscious of where she stood. She put her fork down and frowned into her plate for such a long time that Celestine finally turned on the bench and put her hand over Dot's.

"Honey," she said, "would it kill you to say yes?"

"Yes," said Dot.

PART FOUR

CELESTINE JAMES

"WE ARE VERY much like the dead," Mary argues, "except that we have the use of our senses."

We are talking about the afterlife, her pet subject, and she is kneading Polish sausage meat with bare hands that have thickened and calloused through the years so they look like tough paws. We're getting old. Mary's hair has grayed to the color of a mouse, and she wears it pinned just over her ears in two pugs. Her back is curved like a shell, and her face is set in deep folds of conviction. She is being mental again, going off to flights of fantasy. She slaps down a ball of meat and sends up a cloud of white pepper. It is always my job to bring her back.

"Sounds like Tol Bayer," I joke. "He had all the symptoms of an alcoholic except that he never drank."

Mary still brings out my worst, and I can't help myself from pulling her leg. This time I've gotten to her. She walks over to the salt barrel and stands there, looking quizzical, before she picks up a handful. She walks back, throws it in the meat, starts kneading while she thinks. And for a while that is enough of her boolah about the dead.

Mary tries to get her imagination to mend the holes in her understanding. I come to see her in the grape arbor the next day. It is Sunday, so the shop is closed down and quiet. We're barely keeping even with our layout of expenses now, but we don't care. We won't open Sundays like the chain store and discount parlors.

263

Mary is sitting in a lawn chair picking stems off the sour blue grapes that she claims make fine jelly. When she sees me she puts her basket down, reaches underneath her chair, and then hands me a common red brick.

"This flew in my window," she says. "Smashed it too."

I know she won't hire a glazer to fix the window. It will be a taped-up eyesore to go with the peeling exterior. Along with us, it seems that everything about the shop, the business, is going to seed. But I don't care. When Mary sells the place, which has become valuable real estate, we both plan to live off the money. I have insisted that Mary give me retirement benefits.

"I hope you caught the kid," I say to her.

"There was no kid."

I tell myself not to argue with Mary, but I can't help arguing like I can't help the man in the moon.

"Someone chucked it and ran off," I say.

"Nobody chucked it."

"So what do you suggest did happen?"

"This brick is a sign," she says.

"Of what?"

"Trouble."

That does not surprise me. Mary has never had a sign announcing something good. She goes in to wash casings, and I finish cleaning grapes in the arbor. I don't give her red brick a second thought. I don't want to hear any more of her mysterious claims.

But then, that night, something happens that is unlike me. I have a dream.

I dream that Sita is standing in her front yard underneath the Mountain Ash. I see the orange berries glowing behind her, the ferny leaves tossing in the air. She is twisting her hands in a fancy hostess apron and looking out on the road. She is watching for someone.

"I call and you don't come," she mutters.

"What?" I say.

Her eyes have retreated in bruised pits and her cheeks are sunken, pale as dough.

"I call and you don't come," she says again.

Maybe it is the brilliance of the berries in the tree, the blue and white lace of the apron, or Sita's long look of sickness. Whatever it is, the dream is more real than life to me. I awaken and the sky is the dim gray of predawn. I cannot sleep again but lay in bed watching the windows gradually lighten.

In full morning I walk into the shop and right away I ask Mary to come sit down before we get to work. I put her percolator on the table between us and then I tell her about my dream.

"She's got an illness," says Mary.

"She looked half dead to me."

"She's asking for you."

I lift my shoulders and say, offhand, "I haven't talked to her in years. I don't know what she'd want to see me for."

Yet I think back to the days when Sita and I were best friends. That was before Mary appeared off the Argus freight. Sita and I grew up together, thick as thieves, fighting and making up. I never got the best of her. She was not as tall as me, but she was stronger than she looked, and she got so hysterical in a fight that I always gave in. Then she would sit on my chest and bat me with her long heavy braid. Her hair is short now, fixed by a beauty operator and curly as a poodle. In the dream, it stuck out in spikes, flattened on one side and gray at the roots. So I know she has not been to the hairdresser in some time.

"I'll go along with you," says Mary. "After all, she's my cousin. I should go."

So we sit there and discuss what we're going to do.

Dot is no problem since she can take care of herself, but I still hate to leave her because she has been so anxious. Since she was nominated as a princess in the contest that Wallace has invented for the Beet Festival, Dot spends half her time trying to lose weight and the other half writing in a secret diary that she keeps locked in a drawer. Sometimes I find her on the back steps, glaring in a morose way at the pages of a book. Other times she mows the grass furiously short. Each night she goes to work at the concessions counter of the Argus theater. She watches the movies from the back of the aisle, smoking cigarettes. I cannot stop her from doing that. Her clothes are stale with the smell, along with the popcorn oil and licorice. It seems to me that the films she watches depress her, give her strange ideas, put bad language in her mouth. I think that perhaps I should not leave her for Sita, but Dot says that's crazy.

We decide to motor thirteen miles to Blue Mound and answer Sita's call. She's close, but very far. In the years since she's been there, she has never called or asked us over for a meal. We don't even know what her house looks like inside, except from hearsay. Yet it seems very natural that in her hour of need we come, and just in case we have to stay there long, we pack our nightgowns, one of Mary's sheet cakes, and two summer sausages in the delivery truck. We leave my cousin Adrian in charge of the shop, but he will not care for Mary's dog, Dickie, so we must visit Wallace Pfef on the way out of town.

Wallace has painted his raised ranch a dull-looking tan color I don't like, but he says it blends in with the fields. Earth colors are his theme. When he shows up at the door, we see that he's even dressing in them. His pants are gray. His shirt is the same color as his skin. Flesh color.

"That shirt is unbecoming," Mary tells him.

He looks down and pinches some of the cloth between his fingers. Meanwhile, I see that we can't leave the dog here. Pfef's nasty female dog glares unblinkingly at us, then snaps. Little Dickie strains and yaps back from the safety of Mary's arms.

"Let's go," says Mary. "I don't care for Little Dickie to get pounded."

"I'm sorry," I tell Wallace. "I didn't mean to disturb you."

He tells us to give his best wishes to Sita and waves us off. We have no choice now but to take the dog along. Dickie yaps at strangers when they come into the shop, but there is no harm in him beyond that. I do remember Sita hates dogs, and I ask Mary if she thinks Sita will mind.

"She'll have to take the bad along with us," says Mary. "After all, it was her that asked you."

"Yes," I say. "But of course she asked in my dream."

"There's no difference," says Mary, and I know there is none to her. She wants to do some knitting, so she tells me to take the wheel. As soon as we are on the road, she pulls out her yarn and needles. She casts on, and begins the sleeve to a sweater she is making for Dot. Her clicking needles start me thinking about Mary's sewing machine and how Sita accepted it even though it was the only thing given to Mary by her mother. Sita was the one who told me about it, proudly, when we met in town by accident. I told her she should not have taken it. If my own mother had lived, I know I would have forgiven her anything and in my middle years accepted that machine. But Mary gave it up. And that machine was a nice cabinet style, antique by now. I think that we could haul it back in our truck, providing that Sita still has it sitting in her garage.

"Maybe we could get the sewing machine, Mary," I say.

"What sewing machine?" She will not admit it was ever hers. She holds the first knitted rows up to admire them, a cream background with dark red lines. She is making the sweater pattern up as she goes along. It is a maze like the kind that scientists train rats to run through. We drive in silence and then, after a few miles, she turns to me and says, "Sita hasn't got long now."

"What makes you think that?"

Mary takes the brick from her pocket and spits on it. The spit will dry in the shape of a calendar date, she says. She stares at the brick like it was suddenly going to talk, and my patience wears through. "Put that thing away," I tell her.

Although her eyes have gotten ever harsher and brighter, she has aged like an ordinary enough person. It's the way she dresses that makes her look like such a fringe element. For the trip she's wound her head in a black silk scarf with tassels. She's hunched over like an old turtle, and her purple dress is all straining seams. I can't help wondering, as usual, what's going through her mind. She's got the dog in her lap and she's eating raisins from a little bag.

Sita lives in the only new house in Blue Mound, a big white ten-room house, landscaped on two levels, that she calls a colonial because it has shutters that do not shut and a tall, heavy, carved oak front door with a brass knocker on it. She is standing on her front lawn when we turn into the drive. Just like in the dream, her hands are twisted in a stiff lace apron. Just like in the dream, the orange berries glow behind her head. She looks sick. We get out of the car. Unlike in the dream, she puts her hands on her hips and yells.

"Get your damn dog out of my roses!"

Then she reaches into her tree, pulls down a hard clod of those berries, and throws them at Little Dickie. The dog scampers away.

"He was just watering them for you," says Mary. "Don't get all set back."

I try to smooth the situation over by complimenting Sita. Admiration usually calms her, but this time it doesn't work.

"You look good," I tell her.

Her eyes pick me apart.

"So do the leaves before they fall," she states.

At that, Mary starts to laugh, which turns Sita's face white.

"I'm sick," says Sita, glaring nowhere, "sick as a sick cat."

Then she turns on her heel, stamps up the columned entry into her house, and slams the door shut behind her. Mary catches Little Dickie and then we tie him to the ash tree with a piece of clothesline. We get our bags and our sheet cake from the delivery truck, and Mary follows me up the walk with the summer sausages.

Looking at her, all in mournful purple and black with those sausages wrapped in white paper, I think she reminds me of something. What is it? I pause at Sita's door and look back at Mary. Then I know. She's like the picture of the grim reaper on the month of January. The hem of her black skirt drags. She looks like she's seen it all. And she carries those sausages like they were symbols of her calling.

Inside of Sita's house everything is neutral. What I mean is, Sita doesn't let things pile up, so you don't get any feeling about anyone who lives there. Sita's tables have nothing on them but an ashtray. They are not like Mary's, for instance. You walk into her back rooms and right away there is a deck of cards on the table, balls of wool, or a *Fate* magazine to tell you who she is.

We hear Sita upstairs in the bathroom, the water flushing. So we walk through the house to the kitchen, hang the sausages in her pantry, and put the sheet cake on her big Formica kitchen table. It is here that we particularly expect to see a few signs of Sita's sickness and neglect. But the kitchen is clean and lighted, the plants watered. Every pot is washed and put away. The steel sink is shined, and even the tile floor is freshly waxed.

"I don't know how she does it," I say in a loud voice, thinking she will hear me. But Sita isn't on the stairs, coming down to greet us. The water is still gushing.

"The answer is she has a cleaning woman," Mary says.

We set our traveling bags on the kitchen floor. Not knowing

what to do with ourselves, we shift aimlessly from foot to foot until at last we grow tired and sit at the modern dinette arrangement in her breakfast nook.

"I suppose she's trying to get fixed up a little," says Mary after several minutes go by. We listen. The water stops flowing through the pipes, but then it slaps and gurgles, as if she is bathing.

"At least she can manage that by herself," I say.

Mary is looking at the pot with a longing expression. "I'll brew some coffee. It'll be nice and hot for her when she gets down here," she says.

"We'll all have a snack," I agree, hungry for the uncut cake.

Mary rifles through the cupboards for the coffee, but of course it's on the counter in the green cannister labeled COFFEE.

"Naturally she'd keep it here," says Mary.

I agree. "Sita does things by the book."

She is taking her bath by the book now, washing every inch of herself. From the early years we spent close, when I slept over some nights, I know she is using exactly one capful of bath powder. Afterward she'll dust herself with talcum. Then she'll sit down on the edge of her bed, wrapped in a towel, and file her nails into perfect ovals.

"As for me," says Mary, reading my thoughts, "I like to rub a lemon on my face."

"That's why your skin's all puckered up," I blurt. I hate for her to read my mind, but now I've hurt her feelings.

"I'll knit," she says after a moment, subdued. She rummages in her strained valise for the sweater sleeve and can't seem to find it. I have gotten touchy. I begin to question whether we should have come. The Sita in my dreams was more desperate and hospitable. Outside, Little Dickie begins to bawl and whine. He's probably wound so tight to that tree trunk he cannot move.

"I use my coffee cannister for trading stamps," I tell Mary. "It fills up exactly the size of two booklets."

Mary brightens and draws her hand out of her bag.

"The flour bins," she says, "they're too small in those sets. That's where I like to keep my screwdriver and my canning tongs. . . ."

She looks over at Sita's cannisters, sharpens her eyes at me, and listens up the stairs to see if Sita is still occupied.

"Go ahead, look," I say. "See if she keeps flour in her cannister."

So Mary opens the green container.

"Wouldn't you know it," she whispers. "Of course she would keep her flour where it belongs." Then, suddenly, she snaps her head down and peers closer. "What's this?" She cups the bin in the crook of her arm and plucks out an orange capsule. "It's crawling with pills." She puts her hand into the flour, digs around, and comes up with more. We don't know what to think.

At last, there is a sign that Sita isn't managing for herself. I feel reckless. I can still hear Sita moving around upstairs.

"Throw it out," I say. "There's no telling how old those are. She must be losing her marbles."

"She could poison herself," says Mary, fascinated. If it were her choice, I think she'd run upstairs and show them to Sita. "All right," she says at last. She opens the cabinet beneath Sita's sink, finds the garbage can, and dumps out the pills and the flour.

She puts the empty cannister back in place. We are just pouring the coffee out in three of Sita's matching cups and cutting the cake, when she walks down the stairs.

"We just brewed up some coffee," I say in a pleasant voice.

"There wasn't any made," says Mary in an accusing tone. Then she remembers some sort of manners. "This cake's fresh," she says.

Her black scarf has slipped down over her forehead in a little visor, and when she stares at Sita she looks like she is placing a bet.

I turn to Sita quickly, meaning to comment on how she's fixed herself up. But Sita looks exactly the same, no fresher than when we first met her in the yard. She hasn't changed her clothes, and her hairdo is still lopsided. I wonder if she still sleeps in a roll of pinned toilet paper all week to save her hairdo, like she did as a model. And she does. Now I find another sign of the strain.

As she turns to the refrigerator to get out the cream, I see a neat pink square of toilet paper has been left pinned to the back of her head. When she turns back I don't say anything. But Mary is smiling at me.

"I hope you enjoy this," she says in a sweet syrupy voice, setting the brown and yellow square of cake before Sita.

Sita opens a drawer and takes out three white paper napkins with scalloped borders. She sets those carefully beside our plates. Then she sits down and takes a bite, and a sip, and another bite. She's about to take a third bite when she looks at her fork.

Mary and I have nearly finished our slices, and I am thinking how empty this kitchen looks, with no sign of cooking. Does Sita eat from a can or box?

Sita is gazing with shocked attention at something on the end of her fork. She puts the cake down, and then, prinking her finger, delicately draws a transparent scrap out of the cake bite and puts it on the edge of her dessert plate.

We see that the scrap on the edge of Sita's plate is a finely baked amber wing, brittle and threaded with fragile veins.

"That's a wing," Mary observes, putting down her fork.

"It is the wing of an Indian meal moth, to be exact," says Sita. Her voice is acid, her mouth pinched and dry. "They usually don't get to be this size."

Mary gazes at the wing for a moment, politely, but not as though it had anything to do with her. She picks up her fork and begins to eat her cake again, relishing it even.

Sita's head slowly turns. The toilet paper on the back of her

272

head flutters like a feather. Her eyes watch the cake moving from plate to fork to mouth of Mary. Sita looks like an outraged hen sitting there, so boney beaked and peckish.

"How do you know the name of it?" I ask, to divert her attention. Then I remember her late husband had something to do with infestations. "Did you learn that from Louis?"

"After he resigned his post as health inspector," she says between her teeth, still intent on the moving bites of cake, "Louis was the county extension entomologist." I try to signal Mary not to take another piece, but already she is lifting the square out of the pan.

"Bugs can't hurt a person when they're cooked," she tells us.

I don't want to look at Sita. I sip my coffee as long as possible. Then I do look at her and see that all the color has left her face, she is fearfully pale. She is so mad that her lips have turned blue. I put the cup down and brace myself, knowing from those early years that her rage must fall.

"You won't bring those filthy insects in my house!" Sita shrieks, jumping up so suddenly that the piece of toilet paper floats off the back of her head.

Mary looks uncertainly at her fork, but it is too late.

Sita picks up the sheet cake, and without a word or glance, takes it out the back door. I hear her walking down the steps, the trash can clanging, and then she slams back in with the empty pan and puts it in the sink. She walks behind Mary, snakes a thin arm around, and plucks the saucer away and the fork from her hand.

Now Sita has gone too far. When she walks toward the door again, meaning to shake the cake off the fork and throw the crumbs in the garbage, Mary leaps up. Her head scarf drops over her eyes, so she has to jut her chin in Sita's face to see beneath it.

"You should talk!" she shouts. Yellow sparks are spinning from her eyes. "Talk about the pills in your flour, Miss High Nose!"

Sita looks stunned, then she rushes to the cannister, rips the cover off, and sure enough it's empty. She stands there so long, peering into the bottom of the metal cannister, that I wonder if the shock has been too much.

"What have you done with them?" she says. "Where are they? Tell me this instant."

When Mary points, Sita falls to her knees before the sink and opens the cabinet. She drags the garbage pail out and starts to paw through the flour. It falls through the air, covers the floor, flies up into her face. Her arms are white with its dust. In her hand she collects a few brilliant capsules, orange and blue, and holds them tight to her chest, guarding them from our sight.

Poor Little Dickie. We have forgotten his food, so in the days that follow we give him scraps or go down to the corner market for expensive emergency cans. A dog living in a butcher shop gets spoiled. Often Little Dickie has to fend for himself. He digs holes in Sita's iris borders, looking for a bone. That first night, he sneaks into the garbage can and gobbles up the sheet cake, bugs and all. We can't keep him on the cord, because he bites through it with his strong little teeth whenever he feels like roaming. He's a house dog. But of course we can't keep him inside.

Sita hates him. You can tell it in her eyes when he begs at the door. I fill the holes up behind him and replant the irises, hoping she will not be too hard on Little Dickie. If she notices the patched ground, she never says so. We can see now that Sita is as sick as my dream said, and yet she won't let us take her to the doctor. Every time I suggest a visit, she says she's already been there and got a five-year dosage of medicine. Sometimes I catch her smashing pills together in a cup, or rolling them about in her hands before she pops them down. They are pain medicine, she tells me. She's been taking pills for many years, so I don't ask questions.

I worry that Mary will make some mean remark about Sita's behavior that first day, but she cleans up the flour without a word and settles in to this visit. It seems to me that she blooms in the presence of illness the way some women perk up around a good-looking man. She removes her black fringed scarf and pins her hair up in a skinny coil. She wears a dress with yellow flowers and hums as she cooks custards and broths to tempt Sita's picky appetite. She shakes her can of brewer's yeast in everything she makes, while Sita grinds and swallows the bitter pills that do nothing but set her on edge and then exhaust her with sleep. Everything we eat is flavored with the stale yeast powder. But Sita hardly notices what she eats anymore.

Indeed, she moves less, says less, as the days go by. In the evenings, when we sit on the porch, she wraps up in her best afghans, the ones that Fritzie crocheted so long ago. It is a bad sign. No woman uses the best afghans on herself. But who else is there to save them for?

The visit lengthens from days into weeks. I go back and forth between Blue Mound and Dot, but Mary stays because Sita is in such a weakened state.

One night Sita is talkative.

"Why did you come here," she asks, "you and my cousin and that damn little dog?"

"Because I dreamed you were sick," I say.

"You dreamed I was sick." She rocks in the falling blue light. Her face is like a carved bone. "Oh yes, you dreamed you might inherit something that I own."

This gets my goat. "We're good to you because your mother was good to us," I tell her. "We're not here because we want anything of yours."

She sits there, creaking in her chair. There is a long silence between us, but then I think how superior she has always been, and I know I won't be able to help myself from asking what I thought of in the truck.

"But you could will Mary the sewing machine her mother sent her," I say.

The rocker stops. Sita's mouth is open, black and wide as an attic. A bat could swoop in there and perch. Her mouth opens even wider when she starts to laugh. I realize I haven't heard her laugh yet, not since we got here, then all of a sudden she chokes to a halt.

"That hoary old thing broke down ten years ago and I gave it to the Grinnes."

I know the Grinne family. They are the disreputed prodigals of Blue Mound who live mainly off their sales of balled aluminum foil. I know that Grinne girl couldn't sew with that machine, wouldn't sew with it, never intended to sew with it in the future, and probably chopped the cabinet up to kindle fires one cold winter.

I have nothing more to say to Sita. I leave her creaking, her wasted bosom shielded in her arms, and I walk upstairs to see what Mary is doing.

We share the upstairs guest room, which is decorated with dull, perfectly blended pinkish colors and pictures of the same tree through different seasons. Some nights in that room I lay awake for hours as Mary rambles in her sleep. She has long threatening conversations with unknown people. "Hand it over," she says. "I've heard that one before."

One night, as I am listening, I realize what she is doing in her sleep. She is collecting outstanding bills. She has her foot in the front door of the dream. She shouts when it closes on her foot. "You signed the note," she hollers. "I'll see you in court!"

Mary has spread out in the room. Her valise unpacked a surprising number of things. The red brick is on the stand beside her bed, wrapped carefully in a washcloth so none of its cosmic powers leak into the air. She is not one to hide her clothes, even underclothes, from view. They are stacked or draped on bureaus or the backs of chairs. Only her great white cotton bloomers are neatly hung, clothespinned to hangers and swung off the closet doorknobs because Sita will not allow her to dry them out on the line. A chipped green statue of the Virgin Mary is set up behind the brick. She has stacked her astrology books and knitting yarns in handy corners. I see now that she has finished Dot's sweater.

She holds it up for me to admire.

The red lines run in zigzags and squares within squares, forming paths that lead to dead ends.

"Where's Start?" I ask.

Mary doesn't understand until I trace the pattern with my finger, trying to find an exit. She begins to search along with me, through the tangle of pathways across the chest, down the undersides of arms, across the shoulders. But we can discover no way out.

I pick up a book that is on her bed, and flip through it.

"The night sky is full of baffling holes," I read.

This is a subject that has been on Mary's mind, and she is happy to explain. She tells me about holes in space that suck everything into them. They even suck space into space. I cannot picture that. In my mind I see other things, though, drawn away at high speed into the blackness. Just this morning I discovered a pocket of junk in Sita's house. In an old cabinet in the basement, behind the recreation room, I found a disorganized clutter, spider nests, real dirt. The shelves of the cabinet held old bottles and cans. Venetian shoe cream. Moroline. Coconut hair oil. KILL-ALL Rat Tablets. And a book called *The Black Rose*, by Thomas B. Costain. There were papers too, a whole scrap pile of Sita's newspaper clippings and rent receipts from the years she spent in Fargo as a single girl. There was a letter. It was stamped, sealed, and ready to mail. I read the envelope carefully, wondering and wondering what to do with it. The address was written out to a Mrs. Catherine Miller, Minneapolis. There was no telling exactly how old this letter was, or when Sita had forgotten to mail it.

I closed the cabinet and walked upstairs. I put the letter in my purse. In the end I decided to retrieve it, and sent it off to this Mrs. Miller with a few cents more postage. But all day today, any time I have thought of the cabinet of junk, a sadness has taken hold of me. Sita is the reason all those things are there, and when she goes they will still be there. They will outlast her as they have already outlasted her husband. They will outlast me. Common things, but with a power we cannot match. It makes me sad to think of them, so humble yet indestructible, while Sita, for all her desperation of a lifetime, must die.

And now, as Mary is talking, I have a strange thought that everything a person ever touched should be buried along with them, because things surviving people does not make sense. As she goes on and on about invisible gravities, I see all of us sucked headlong through space. I see us flying in a great wind of our own rubber mats and hairbrushes until we are swallowed up, with fearful swiftness, and disappear.

Everything is getting confused. Nothing seems to matter. I'm not even angry when Mary reads my thoughts again and says how the Indian burial mounds this town is named for contain the things that each Indian used in their lives. People have found stone grinders, hunting arrows, and jewelry of colored bones.

So I think it's no use. Even buried, our things survive.

The dog is barking under the window. The evening is growing chill, and I realize that Little Dickie has bitten his rope and gone digging in the iris beds again. I hear Sita, yelling from the porch. Her voice is rising and rising until it cracks off. Her chair tips, or something else goes crash. I hear Little Dickie barking and grunting. Or is it Sita? One of them is groaning. We open the window and Mary leans out to see, but it is too dark. Lilac branches shield Little Dickie from our view. We hear panting and pounding.

"He found something," says Mary. "Sita's going to kill him if he digs up her border."

"Get out of there! Scat!" Mary yells.

But the panting and pounding still goes on.

So Mary reaches behind her. Two things are within her grasp. The chipped statue of the Virgin and the special brick. She flings the brick out the window. There is a thud, silence, then Little Dickie whines.

We run downstairs. The moon isn't up yet. I fumble for the porch light but can't find it, and follow Mary down the front steps. I have to grope my way, holding on to lawn chairs and rose stakes. I cross the grass, and then I see their huddled shapes. Mary's flowered dress patches into the bush, but the white shape on the ground—that is Sita. I know her afghan by touch. It is the cream-colored pancake-posy stitch that Fritzie made before she left.

I am kneeling, bending close to her. She does not move for many long seconds, and then her body gives a rippling shudder. It flashes into my mind that it's time. Things are being snatched from our grips. The scattered dirt is dry and cold. She whispers in my face.

"You'll eat shit with the chickens someday too."

That's Pete's phrase. It means that no matter how high and mighty, we all get to ground level someday. Sita's hair is wet where the brick slammed down on her head. I think that she's right. She's right. I'll eat shit with the chickens. We carry her indoors. She is light as toast. We lay her on the long beige couch in the living room. I'm almost afraid to switch on the lamp, but finally Mary does, and then I see how bad Sita looks. Black shadows are in her cheeks.

I sit with her the rest of the night, bathing her forehead and listening to her breath fall and sink. I pack the best afghans around her. The rippling stripes and whirling clouds. The mouse-and-trap stitch. Mary is dozing in the chair with her head on her hand, not moving, so that sometime in the night I forget she's there.

I forget Little Dickie too. That dog got pounded anyway. I forget what we have come here for. At some point Mary begins to mumble, so I know she is asleep.

"Don't argue with me," she says. "I have checked your account."

Sita smiles at those words and opens her eyes. She looks peacefully around, then focuses at me and frowns. I don't know if she's frowning at me or someone else, but I look down into her face.

She takes a deep troubled breath. I don't hear when she lets it out, because I am suddenly remembering how she used to look when we were girls and she got the better of me. She sat above me like I am sitting above her. Her pink lips curved. Her teeth were white and square. She swung her long thick braid over her head. It whipped down, plopped against my cheek, brushed my nose and mouth. I remember, now, that Sita's braid did not hurt. It was only soft and heavy, smelling of Castile soap, but still I yelled as though something terrible was happening. Stop! Get Off! Let Go! Because I could not stand how strong she was, her knees against my chest. I could not stand her holding me down helpless in the dirt.

SITA TAPPE

Ever since they came with their cake full of bugs and their spicy sausages, I've taken to sleeping downstairs on the pool table. It's not just that Mary talks in her sleep so loud that she can be heard from the end of the upstairs hallway, or even that Celestine is up and down all night fetching glasses of water, eating cereal or frying eggs. It isn't just that I never asked for their companionship, don't want it, even wish they would fall sick themselves and leave. I sleep downstairs for many reasons of my own. The pool table itself, for one. I like the feel of green French baize. I like the smooth surface. I like the pockets, useful places for rolled-up magazines, tumblers, my hairbrush. Sleeping, I breathe a grade-school scent of blue chalk dustings, along with the grown-up odors of spilled cocktails and ash. I've explained to Celestine and Mary that the hard flat surface of the pool table is good for my back, but the truth is I like sleeping in the basement.

My first husband used to call this large, windowless area his recreation center. Jimmy had it soundproofed and paneled in expensive oak, but the wall decorations are gifts of junk from his friends in beverage distribution and local taverns. Along one side of the room there are shelves full of stereo equipment, drawers of records, a color television console. When I got married again, Louis added classical to Jimmy's country-western and easy-listening records. Sometimes Louis did experiments in the un-finished areas of the basement or held meetings of his fungus group. He put in a shortwave radio set and called places behind the Iron Curtain. There is so much here of both Louis and Jimmy that the room is a kind of monument to both of them and to neither one.

It is mine now. I've moved all of my favorite things down here.

There is a nest of jewelry in the tape case, photographs of my father on the Mexican end tables, and folded in a pile three of my best cashmere sweaters and a pair of Italian leather sling-back shoes. I even cleaned out the bathroom just behind one wall. I scrubbed it three times with Dutch Cleanser, then with Lysol. I threw away Louis's darkroom chemicals and the pint bottles left underneath the sink by Jimmy's brothers. Now the bathroom cabinet holds my makeup, but not what's left of the pills, the little stockpiled prescriptions that were Louis's legacy. I have a safer, surer, place for them.

At one time I used to have the pills stashed everywhere. But I kept forgetting where I hid them. They'd turn up unexpectedly, and that was undependable. I couldn't stand to lose a one after Louis died because there is no doctor in town anymore who will write out a ticket. "You'll become addicted," they tell me. They want to cut me off. They think I am cut off. They don't know what Louis left.

The room is dark at any time of the day. I do not like being wakened by the sun anymore. This morning, even knowing that I have to get up soon and meet Celestine and Mary, I lay flat on my back, swathed in covers that have absorbed an earthen smell from the basement air.

Lying here, I imagine all that I could do by remote control.

Louis was the one who ran wires beneath the shag carpeting. He liked to sit in his wing-back armchair and push buttons. Jimmy, I know, would have lounged on the fat Mediterranean-style couch and cursed with awe at what Louis had done. From here, I can turn on the television if I want. The face of the Morning Hostess might be flipping in a blur, but I can stabilize her with one twist. Headphones are at my elbow. I can push on the stereo power, the radio. I can listen to 8-track tapes, or, in silence, watch the brightly lit dials and barometers slide and flicker. I can operate the light control to dim or illuminate the imitation Tiffany overhead. I can turn on all of the beer lamps and watch them. One is a long silhouette of a stagecoach pulled by horses that flee silently around and around a lit screen of mountains and desert cacti. Another is of a canoe endlessly revolving in a blue lake. Some are Hamm's, some are Schmidt's, some are simple diamond-shaped Grain Belt. On the far side of the room, Jimmy installed a wet bar shaped like the letter U and padded with thick black vinyl.

Since the night Mary tried to brain me with a thrown brick, there is less pain. It was as if the blow shorted out a series of nerve connections. That was one reason I did not call the police when I finally could—that and the fact of the pills. I had a fear they would make an examination, search the house, find what's left of them floating in the toilet tank, in the waterproof container Louis used to keep his matches in whenever he went out to the field to gather botanical specimens. I almost hate to take the pills anymore, there are so few left. A month, month and a half from now, what will happen? I'm just lucky that the brick jogged the nerve ends out of kilter. That makes the whole prospect easier to bear. I am more comfortable. However, I have lost the use of my left arm and must hold it crimped up at my ribs like the wing of a chicken.

I should rise, before they make their deliveries and come back to get me in that truck that smells of blood and scorched leather. Later on sometime, they want to take me to watch the Beet Parade in Argus, and then the coronation, which will be held in a grandstand of hard backless seats. I refused at first, but they insisted.

"You'll get real enjoyment from seeing Dot crowned," coaxed Celestine.

"You'd be surprised," I answered, "at how much enjoyment I can get from laying down."

Mary, still sullen at having almost killed me prematurely, tries to downplay what she did. She will take no responsibility. She says we're wound up and we don't stop until we wind down.

"So you might as well have a day out," she said, without enthusiasm. Her lack of it was probably what made me agree.

Getting up is no light task, however. It involves the use of too many muscles, and of my legs, which I prefer to pack in warm knits and pillows. The recreation room is chill, not something I mind much in this summer heat, except during that first long walk across the carpet, or the moment I have to step onto the frigid bathroom tiles.

I roll onto my stomach and lower my legs from the table. From the left side pocket I lift a tumbler of water, and drink deeply. I have not removed the colored pool balls from within the table, and now they roll and click in their hidden channels. I find it a friendly sound, soothing and distracting. The table is built so solid that they only move when I get on or off. I begin to walk across the carpet. But this morning I do not even get as far as the heavy couch. There is something changed, a weakness deeper than I've felt since the brick smashed down. I wish that I'd asked for some food before the two went out or that there were even a few stale pretzels left behind Jimmy's bar. But then, I remember, the pretzels would be fifteen or maybe twenty years old by now. I do not mean to do this, but I find that I am laying very suddenly upon the floor. I do not think I've fallen, but I am unmistakably stretched out, flat on my stomach, my face pressed into the shag strands that are like a thick wool grass. I have to lay there. I can't call out for help. I don't know how long it takes before I gather back my strength, crouch up on all fours, and crawl. I have my pride, but I must save it for even harder moments and for times when Mary and Celestine are around to watch.

Death is a weekly chore to them, I think, no more than that, no more than the sound that causes it. The rifle report. The dull blow. The fork in the chicken's neck. I'm sure that they never hear the sounds the animals make. But as a girl, before I left the butcher shop, I always heard the cries and bellows. The pigs screamed like it was our neighbors being murdered in their beds. And when the chickens got their heads knocked off, their wings flapped and flapped, beating the lime sand into a brilliant cloud.

I still hear their wings. They sweep the ground in a hopeful frenzy. Even brainless the body continues its puppet dance. When it happens to me, I do not want Celestine or Mary to hear the sound. That's another reason I sleep in the recreation room. I remember Jimmy's truckload of acoustic tiles, his special insulation. I remember Jimmy testing the stereo full blast downstairs while I stood up in the kitchen, sensing the bass drum's vibration, hearing no music but a faint insectlike whining.

Now the bathroom. The door. The switch.

Jimmy had steel handles installed. He said he put them in for the handicapped, but of course he meant his brothers, who could not aim straight even with the handrail, being soused, and left the evidence of their drunken relief on the pale blue tiles. I am glad for the handrails and the no-slip strips now. I bring myself to the toilet. Lifting the glazed ceramic top off the tank is the most demanding event of my day. I always fear that it will crash to the floor as I slide it over. This operation takes every ounce of my control. I pluck the waterproof box out. I put the cover back, not over all the way, just enough so it won't slide. And then I breathe easier. I fill my toothbrush cup with water. I open the little bottle and shake three into my palm. Not three. No. No. I have limited myself to one. I put two back. Then for some reason I empty the whole container. I'm just curious to see how many days I've got left before they're gone. That's when I see how few there are.

I stare down at the bright orange capsules for I don't know how long. It is as though we are held in a beam of comprehension.

Only half a bottle left to go. I want to swallow one now, but the capsules won't let me. I have to listen. I have to know what this means. So we look at each other, up and down, and up and down. It isn't really very long before I understand.

Without us, they say, without Louis, it's the state hospital again. It's the cannibal ward. The needle. It is sights that you won't like seeing in your garden.

There is no question. I know quite suddenly that I've come to this moment over time. I have walked over empty spaces to get here. I have arrived.

And then it's easy. I swallow them all.

Sometime after that, I lower myself onto the toilet with my good arm. I do not think ahead. I get up in a crouch that takes me over to the sink. I would like to bathe. I don't think past the thought of water. That makes it easier to let myself down into the tub. And then, when I am sitting and I have turned on the taps, the pills take hold with the rush of hot white water, and at once I begin to float.

I love plants. For the longest time I thought that they died without pain. But of course after I had argued with Mary she showed me clippings on how plants went into shock when pulled up by their roots, and even uttered something indescribable, like panic, a drawn-out vowel that only registered on special instruments. Still, I love their habit of constant return. I don't like cut flowers. Only the ones that grow in the ground. And these water lilies. Printed in a toxic paint upon my bath curtain, they melt me with their purity. Each white petal is a great tear of milk. Each slender stalk is a green life rope.

Such a sound. Such a cascade of water is coming down. I've never seen a waterfall or even heard a moving stream. It is too flat for the water to make a rushing sound where I have lived. I know the river though, its punishments and torn banks. I know it as a tongue of destruction that dwindles by summer to a foul mud rope. No, the river is not the marvel of clean water from a spout, hot and wild, buoying me up with this strange illusion that I'm well.

Out, dry, the pills blocking nerve pathways, I stand.

There is a mist on the mirror. I wipe it off with a hand towel. I have to wait for my hand to stop trembling before I take off the rose-plastic puff of the bath cap and brush my hair. My color's sea gray now, and really I'm too thin. But I take the garnet necklace from its embroidered case and fasten the old filigree clasp very carefully around my throat. Naked but for the blood-red stones, I think of my aunt. I listened beside the door once as Fritzie told some friend the tale of Aunt Adelaide's coldhearted flight. They thought she was cracked by misery, but how I understood her! I saw her sucked up into a cloud. Her bones hollowed like a bird's. Her wings never made that terrible chicken sound, thrashing earth, but no sound at all. She didn't have to flap, but effortlessly swerved into the streams and the currents that flow, invisible, above us. So she flew off. That's what I should have done instead of transplanting phlox. Their roots were tough, and I could never find the proper place to put them, the proper fence to set them off. White phlox up against a white fence. It never worked. I should have painted the fence blue. I should have brought down a more attractive dress.

This one, with its white pleats gone dull in the shower steam, with its belt of lavender and prickling lace at each pulse point, I don't like. I don't even think it does justice to the necklace, but I'll wear the garnets anyway, for Mary's benefit. She's never seen them on me before, but then, she probably doesn't care. She is hard, not a woman of sentiment. I never got to her, or Celestine, except through the daughter.

On one of those few times I had to go to their shop on business, I encountered the girl. Dot sat at the counter eating a lunch, took large gobbling bites of the spiced-meat sandwich, licked her

287

fingers. She had her father's same bad manners. I told her that. She stopped, seemed interested. I told her that she wasn't like her mother at all and resembled, around the nose and eyes, her grandmother Adelaide. I said this just to spite Mary, who never talked about the woman. I went a step farther, told Dot what Adelaide had done. I made it romantic, almost like a legend. Dot was riveted to me, demanded more. I hushed her when Mary came.

For an instant I had taken Dot away from them both the same way Mary stole Celestine. All these years and I still remember that terrible small moment when I stood in the graveyard with my shirt off.

So many things run together. One odd memory I have from the notes Louis kept, was my vision of those underground children on the Day of Judgment.

The horn sounds, I said. All the sirens go off. The municipal water tower spouts blood. And then, I told him, the tough-rooted sod parts over each small resting place. Out the children walk. They are pure bone skeletons. They are surprisingly tiny, made of ivory, carved with precision tools under a jeweler's glass eye. Magnification would show the symmetry of each small joint. But there is no time to marvel, for as they walk down the streets of Argus, their bones are swathed and enveloped in flesh and wrapped in skin and then, finally, in clothing.

What kind of clothing, though, and of what era?

And what will they do, I asked Louis, about their parents? What if their parents had sinned themselves into hell? Would there be schools, bus lines, orphanages, stepmothers and stepfathers, some kind of organization to care for them all? If not, what terror! Imagine the poor children left to wander, searching through the ranks of the dead for someone or something familiar.

It is too heartbreaking, Louis, I'd said.

Now I'm ready. The necklace gleams, sharp as malice, against the ruin of my throat. It's too late to change the way I am. I do not take the necklace off. My arms creak as I shrug into the dress. There is the makeup, the hair, and all the concentration this requires. The effort of moving each separate finger, of grasping the tiny brushes and tubes, is immense. Who would believe the strict will this demands? I amaze myself with each light stroke. The results are a vast improvement. And necessary. I must do a good job up here to draw attention from my legs, for I cannot bend to pull on my stockings anymore. I cannot wear stockings. So I will not look down except to admire the tips of my white glove-leather pumps.

And now the lights. Out. The bathroom door. They will soon drive that truck into the yard and lean hard on the horn. I will be upstairs for it, out on the front porch. I'll rise to meet them. But before I climb the fourteen deceptively simple, deep-carpeted stairs, I rest. I rest right here. I sink back in the dim, cool room, on the couch of maroon leather that Jimmy loved and where once, long ago, the only time in my life, in fact, I surprised myself by taking no precautions and lay afterward, in Jimmy's arms, awed at the blank window into the future.

Such were the possibilities.

Papa would have loved a grandchild, and Fritzie too. They never dared say anything right to my face about it, but I knew from their small broad hints. When they came up north to visit they always looked into my face for some sign, some softening, a change in my body's weather. Fritzie lingered over children we happened into, and once, in a fit of her old fierceness, asked if I was going against the church with some method.

Papa loved Jimmy's beer lamps. When Jimmy and I first married, Papa would come over and the two would sit and watch them while drinking beer and listening to records. Later on they'd come upstairs glazed over, hoping for sandwiches and pickles. I'd provide, but I never went downstairs with them. I thought the lamps were vulgar. That was then. Not until I moved down here for good did I understand what a comfort they can be, almost hypnotizing, more soothing than any real scenery you might find, and with the added advantage that I can watch in a darkened room.

I wonder how long it will take if the pills do work. I touch a switch by my right hand and a beer lamp comes on. It is the one of sky blue waters, my favorite. Again and again, waiting, I watch the small canoe leave the Minnesota lakeshore and venture through the sleek waves. The pines along the shore stand green black and crisp. The water shimmers, lit within. The boat travels. I can almost see the fish rise, curious, beneath its shadow.

MARY ADARE

AS WE DROVE up to the house we saw Sita, all in white, standing upright in the yew bushes and inspecting us through the curling dry needles. She looked impatient. Her purse was by her feet and her legs were oddly set, propped to support her as if they were made of wood. I steered the truck halfway around the circle of her driveway.

"First she didn't want to go, and now I suppose we're late," I said to Celestine, who was annoyed that Sita had decided to go. She wanted to enjoy the parade and the crowning of Dot with no interference and no judgment from Sita, no worry about the state of her nerves. Turning off the engine, stopping to get out, I could tell Sita was going to be unpleasant.

There was no greeting from her. Not one grudging sound. Celestine sighed loudly and pushed her hair up off her neck. She slammed out of the truck with an angry air of having to make the best of it. Then she stalked across the lawn, calling. I followed, distracted by Little Dickie's barking. He was tied up out back of the house, and I thought that I should give him some water from the hose even though I'd no sooner suggest this than Sita would frown at the delay.

So we stood right up next to Sita and touched her arms, thinking to help her from the tangle of branches.

Celestine and I both noticed her coldness at the same time. Sita's expression never gave her away. Her eyes were open, staring right at the place our truck had stopped. Her lips were set in exasperation, as if she had just been about to say something and found out her voice was snatched in death. Celestine picked Sita's purse up to give it back, but then she held it, dangling from her fingers by the strap. She didn't know what else to do with it. I was no help. I suppose that we were in a state of shock. I don't know how long we stood there, half listening to Little Dickie bark, smelling the dry, hot air and, strange thing, Sita's French perfume, a penetrating scent from the stoppered flasks that she kept in the basement bathroom.

"What should we do?" Celestine finally asked.

I looked at her, but Celestine did not seem to be asking me. Rather, she was asking Sita. I looked at Sita too, then, as if to consider her opinion. That was when I noticed details, like the necklace of red stones, familiar looking and antique, which had snagged on a broken branch and held her head up, and her arms, which she had managed to wedge at even heights in the scrawny, divided trunks. She had dressed very carefully, as usual. Maybe she had gotten tired of waiting and leaned back in the bush. Maybe she had been about to say, To hell with them. They're late. She had taken to using words like *hell* and *damn* around us constantly, something she hadn't done even when she'd quit the church. Sita was never easy to live with. We had to bring her trays down the basement stairs and serve them to her while she lounged on the pool table. Even then, she turned her nose up or picked her casserole suspiciously apart as if she thought I had hidden more insects between the noodles.

"I suppose we should take her down," I said.

"But then what?" wondered Celestine.

Celestine's cheekbones were colored with rouge. Her hair twisted back in waves, gray brown, newly set. But she looked rattled.

"We have to think clearly," I said.

"Have you got an idea?" Celestine asked. She was annoyed that Sita died in a yew bush on the morning of her daughter's glory. I don't think it had entirely struck Celestine yet that Sita's condition was permanent.

"Is there a funeral parlor in Blue Mound?" Celestine asked.

"This town's too small," I said.

What Sita's death meant was sinking into our minds. Langenwalter's. That was the funeral home in Argus, a long place made of pink and orange stucco, with a Spanish tile roof and black-grilled windows. To think of Sita in one of its familiar rooms was impossible. Besides that, there was the Beet Parade. Everyone would be there, even the Langenwalters. "They probably won't be available," she said, "either to fetch Sita or take her in."

"We'll bring her with us in the truck," I said.

Celestine shook her head. "I thought we'd just put her inside the house, lay her out on the couch."

"Celestine," I said, "do you want strangers to haul her off?"

"No," said Celestine.

"We'll take her with us," I said again.

But then we just stood still, drawn back into the circle of Sita's silence. I heard the hum of crickets in the flax field across the road, the drone of some machinery far off.

"Take her other arm," I finally said. I reached out, lifting Sita by the elbow. We unhooked Sita's necklace from the twig and her head fell a fraction to one side so that she seemed, now, more alert and observant than she had been in weeks. She seemed to have fixed on some fascinating scene that she disapproved of and yet could not be diverted from watching.

We supported her between us and walked toward the truck. She was higher on Celestine's side and dragged on mine, and she was heavy. That struck me. She'd been so light and thin before. It was as if death had entered and filled the marrows of her bones with sand. The truck seemed immeasurably far across the lawn. Sita's feet scraped.

"Hold her up more," said Celestine. "You're getting her shoes dirty."

I tried to hoist her higher but her weight was immense. I was panting and my breath came like fire by the time we reached the truck. It had been my intention to lay her full length in the back. Celestine held her propped up and I opened the double doors. Once I looked inside, though, I couldn't see loading Sita in like any common delivery.

"On second thought," I said, "let's put her up in front."

"Are you nuts?" said Celestine.

"No I am not." I felt sharp toward Celestine because I thought she just didn't want to ride behind and run her stockings. I didn't say another word to her, just opened the passenger's side door and helped move Sita toward it. But once we got there we found that Sita was so stiff she didn't want to bend. It was a problem. Celestine put Sita's legs in and I tried to fit the rest of her. But no matter how we did it, legs first or head first, Sita ended up leaning onto the driver's side, looking like she was thrown there. And she was getting more bedraggled as we pushed and shoved. Then, suddenly, in the middle of our exertions, Celestine hit Sita's back in a certain place and it was magical, as if she'd touched a hidden spring. Sita folded into a perfect sitting position right in the seat. There she waited, with her hands in her lap, her head slightly cocked, gazing out the front windshield.

"All right," I said, gaining back my breath, standing away from the truck, feeling a little dizzy. "Let's go."

Celestine didn't answer, and I saw the reason when I looked at her. She was staring at Sita, wordless, running over with tears. Her face was completely drenched with them, and the bosom of her dress too. I shoved my handkerchief at her, but she didn't even take it, or understand. Then she put her hand up and found that her cheeks were wet.

"Oh," she said, in a surprised way, as if she'd hurt herself.

I put the handkerchief into her hands and walked around to the driver's side. Celestine bent over, fastened Sita in with a belt, and put the white leatherette purse in her lap. Then Celestine climbed through the back and sat down just behind me. I started the motor and drove out of Sita's yard.

With the air cooling on and the vents and windows shut, we were enclosed. The fields spread, dry and failed, between Blue Mound and Argus. Dust rode on the horizon in buffeting shapes. The drought had turned the landscape a uniform white-brown. But all of that was outside our vehicle. We almost seemed to float. Ditches skimmed by in a blur. We had the road to ourselves for a long while and drove in silence, our minds distracted. I didn't notice the speedometer.

The siren and the flashing lights gave me such a start that I wrenched the wheel hard, pulling over, still thinking to let the police pass and surprised when the car stopped behind me.

"He's walking over to the truck," said Celestine in an amazed voice, looking out the back window. I could see him from my side mirror now. Officer Lovchik.

"Hello Ronald," I said, rolling down my window when he bent to speak to me. "I thought you'd be directing the parade."

"Or in it yourself," said Celestine.

"I'm on my way there," said Lovchik, "but I clocked you at eighty."

I had no answer.

"Morning, Sita," he said, smiling across me into the passenger's seat. Since Louis had died Ronald Lovchik had renewed his old pursuit of Sita, even sent her boxes of those chocolates. I knew because I'd found a stack of Whitman's in her cupboard, still sealed in cellophane. I'd eaten some and they were fresh. But now he had no chance. Sita looked forward, sternly, into the distance. Lovchik looked down, hurt but unsurprised, and flipped open his pad of tickets. Then he sighed and closed it.

"What the hell," he said bitterly, straightening so I looked at the tight tan buttons in his shirt. "It's your first offense, right?"

I leaned out and said yes.

"I won't ticket you," he decided. "First warning. That's all."

Celestine tapped me. "Thank him," she hissed.

"Thanks," I said.

"I hope I didn't disturb you, Mrs. Tappe." His voice floated over the roof of the car, and then his footsteps retreated. His car door thudded; he veered around us and flashed down the highway.

"Why didn't we let him take over," I asked, restarting the truck.

Celestine did not answer.

My voice rang too loud in my ears. I drove carefully, well under the speed limit, into Argus and followed Eighth Street down as it led into Main. We planned on getting to the fairgrounds by the most direct route. So I cut through an alley and entered a line of cars that was pushing slowly onto the congested corner of Main. It was somewhere in the crowd of cars, misdirected and confused, that we made our mistake. Perhaps the windows shouldn't have been rolled up so tightly or the air on so high. I didn't hear the high school band, is what I'm saying, or the squeak horns of clowns until they were upon us. Until then, I didn't realize that we were in the parade.

By then there was no turning back. I swung in behind a float made of spray-painted sheets and Kleenex, and wire that was shaped into a gigantic sugar beet. It loomed before us, fat and white. Long crepe paper leaves floated off the top. The beet bobbled in the hot wind, drawn lurching behind a high schooler's car. From time to time tissues sheered off, blew into the crowds on either curbside, or settled on our windshield. The pace was slow. Behind us a club of precision marchers displayed themselves in uniforms of gold and blue. Every so often the parade stopped to let them form a scene or letter with their bodies.

"Wave and smile," said Celestine. "Those people are looking at you."

It was true. Although the huge beet and the drill team took up most of the crowd's attention as we passed, there were some curious enough to peer in at us and wave. Perhaps they glimpsed Sita, imperial and stern in her gleaming necklace, and assumed that she was someone important, an alderwoman or the governor's wife. Others in the crowd were customers and waved simply because they were pleased to recognize us.

"There's Langenwalter standing next to Adrian," Celestine whispered.

"You wave," I told Celestine. "I'm keeping both hands on the wheel."

So as we moved along, close to overheating in first gear, Celestine occasionally flapped a hand at the window.

It seemed as though hours passed before we made the turnoff, coasted slowly down the incline into the county fairgrounds, and cut the engine under a tall horseshoe of elms. We parked directly behind the grandstand where it was cool, in the dim shade where we hoped no one would linger or notice Sita.

I left the motor running with the air cooling on and climbed out. We stood under a big tree, looking through the windshield at Sita.

"I guess we have no choice," said Celestine. "We have to leave her."

We waited there a moment longer, hesitating as if to make sure. Under the dappled light that turned through the leaves, Sita's expression had shifted now to a deeper watchfulness. She stared right through us, past us, and then beyond us to the other side, where booths and games were set up in the clearing of trampled grass.

Most-Decorated Hero

The orderly hoisted Russell out of his wheelchair, rolled him onto the bed, and stripped him of his thin cotton pajamas. Eli Kashpaw sat at his kitchen table with a coffee, watching. Fleur was stationed in the shadows of the next room, supervising the orderly with stern attention. She unpacked Russell's uniform from an old cracked valise. The green wool exuded naphthalene. The orderly dressed Russell in it, moving carefully under Fleur's eye. He strained to lift Russell back into his chair. Fleur took Russell's medals from a leather case and pinned the whole bright pattern over his heart. Then she put his rifle, in a long bag of olive drab, across his lap. Russell waited for his hat to be set on at an angle, the way it was in his portrait-studio pictures.

When everything was done, he locked his hands on the armrests. He could use his arms to push. The orderly wheeled Russell into the morning heat, across the yard of tough grass, and up a ramp into the nursing-home van. He slammed the door. The van pulled out and then it was driving the back roads. There were no windows on the sides, but there was a plastic bubble in the ceiling. Tipping his head Russell saw sky, clouds, and after a while some crisscrossing wires. After an hour of driving, they stopped. Outside the van he heard horses blowing and stamping. An amplified voice called out numbers and directions.

Suddenly his chair was yanked from behind and, in one swoop, went down the ramp out of the van backward. Across the street, in a parking lot of armory trucks, he saw lines of antique cars, drivers in goggles, women under old-time parasols. A majorette was stretching her golden legs out on the ground. Legionnaires passed him, not feet away. Nobody looked at him. Finally the son of his old boss at Argus National clapped him lightly on the arm and bent over his chair.

"What a day for it," he said, and that was all.

The air was dry and the sun far away, veiled by clouds of dust. A jeep rumbled up, hauling his float. It was the same one the American Legion always used. The orderly strained to lift Russell onto the float, then strapped him upright between raised wooden bunkers. A field of graves stretched down before him, each covered with plastic grass and red poppies. A plain white cross was planted at his feet.

Very soon, the parade would start to move. The skirted, flimsy high school floats and go-cart clowns were falling into place. The announcer's high-pitched voice had gone ragged. The bands tuned up, hoisted their drums and tubas.

The float moved.

Russell felt the small jolts in his face as they bounced over potholes. With each lurch, the cross above the grave at his feet shook. He sat high, hands clutching his knees, and stared above the crowd as he passed. There were men with children on their shoulders, girls in bright dresses. His float continued past the glass storefronts and banks, past the bars that featured dancing girls and Happy Nites, past the post office. The drums rattled and the plastic horns squawked in the clown's go-cart. The noise was tiring. Russell tried to hold his head high, to keep the fierce gaze smoking, but his chin dropped. His eyes closed, and suddenly the noise and people seemed far off.

He thought of a distant storm. Low thunderheads collided and the air was charged with a vibrant, calm menace. Before him he saw a large hunched woman walking slowly down a dirt road. He started after her, and then he recognized his sister Isabel, dead these many years. Now she was walking this road, wearing a traditional butterfly-sleeved calico dress and quilled moccasins. Her black hair hung loose. She turned and signaled him to follow. Russell hesitated, although he felt it happening. He felt his mind spread out like a lake. His heart slowed and numbed and seemed to grow until it pressed against his ribs.

"He looks stuffed," cried a shrill woman from the curb. Russell heard her clearly. At one time her comment would have shamed him, but now he simply opened his eyes to the blurred scene, then shut them down. His sister was still there, not far in front of him. Isabel looked over her shoulder with her old grin. He saw that she'd had a tooth knocked out.

"Wait for me," he called.

She turned and kept walking. The road was narrow. The grass on either side flowed off forever, and the clouds pressed low. He followed her, thinking that he might see Celestine. She might join them. But then it occurred to him this wouldn't happen, because this was the road that the old-time Chippewas talked about, the four-day road, the road of death. He'd just started out.

I'm dead now, he thought with calm wonder.

At first he was sorry that it had happened in public, instead of some private place. Then he was glad, and he was also glad to see he hadn't lost his sense of humor even now. It struck him as so funny that the town he'd lived in and the members of the American Legion were solemnly saluting a dead Indian, that he started to shake with laughter.

The damn thing was that he laughed too hard, fell off the road, opened up his eyes before he'd gone past the point of no return, and found himself only at the end of the parade. He quickly shut his eyes again. But the road had gone too narrow. He stumbled. No matter how hard he called, his sister continued forward and wouldn't double back to help.

WALLACE PFEF

DOT GREW ANGRIER each year, frightening us, making havoc, causing danger to herself. Some nights she stayed out till two or three and, once, she didn't come back until dawn. She smoked in her room, filling the windowsills with stubs, and kept secret diaries that she locked with small gold keys.

It wasn't hard to guess the sort of things she wrote in the books.

She was persecuted, miserable, plotting her revenge. Instead of her grade-school lack of friends, she now had active enemies. And there was Celestine, me, and Mary. We were the banes of her existence, until she needed us. Then we gave her all we had, which she resented. She filled boxes with papers. Her diaries collected. And she told us these things to our faces too, not sparing us a single word.

More than anything we had in common, Dot's spite drove Celestine, Mary, and me together. Dot had not been an easy child, but before this we'd been able to out-talk her. Now she out-talked us, listed each fault, left us stricken. She ate our hearts to the bone, devoured us, grew robust on our grief and our bewilderment. More than anything, we were shocked by what we had created. Dot wore fishnet stockings and a vinyl skirt to classes, teased her hair into a nest, came home with merchandise she couldn't have purchased on her minimum wage at the Argus Theater. Her friends were hoods, drinkers, smokers, motorcycle riders, and assorted deadbeats who haunted the street of bars that did not donate to the Christmas Lighting Fund.

We tried to interest Dot in hobbies, in school sports, in scholastics. But she only seemed happy when she was riding in a souped-up car, or parked in one. That was not my observation, but Celestine's. Mary observed that if Dot were not all she had in the world, she would have disowned her niece. My reason for sticking by Dot, though, was different. I had faith, fundamental and abiding, in Dot's courage.

True, her lack of fear had become quite tedious and rude. Her utter honesty turned teachers and classmates to stone. But she was what I was not. She was not afraid to be different, and this awed me. Besides, I loved her and wanted to make her happy.

But I couldn't entirely do that alone.

I had a theory, that if those who really loved Dot could hardly stand her, what could she think of herself? One spring, in order to help her, to give her pride in an accomplishment, to allow her self-image to soar, I gave her a twenty-pound shot for the shot put. It was the best investment of my life, or so I thought, because at first Dot took to it and would not be parted from the iron ball.

That was the first spring of the drought. The days were unremittingly fair, the rainfall at a record low. All that month Dot walked past my house, carrying the shot to and from the corner where her bad influences dropped her off. She was trimming down, she said, for the track-and-field tryouts. She was serious about all of this and it seemed like a new start. In the late afternoon, she stopped by if she saw my car parked in the drive. This was also new, and she would be so pale with hunger, having eaten nothing all day long, that she wouldn't have the strength to point out my failings. Besides I would disarm her. I'd sit her down at the table with a quart of milk and a pan of walnut brownies. She'd plow right through them while telling me her plans.

She would live by the ocean like a movie star, or disappear

like her Aunt Mary, who told Dot she'd hitched a boxcar. Dot would own a fried-chicken chain. She would drive trucks, bull-dozers, fly off forever like her grandmother Adelaide. She would travel the world and seek knowledge, or live up north on the reservation with her uncles Russell and Eli. She'd put the shot in the state track, from there to the Olympics. Argus would display her gold medals in the county museum right next to Russell's war mementos and her now-famous diaries.

Dot was either lit up by her imaginary future, or depressed, a dark lump, by what she saw as her life's realities, harsh and awful. She told of parties to which she was not invited, good-looking hoods who ignored her, girls who filled her locker with balled-up paper towels, teachers who asked her questions in class they knew she couldn't answer, even janitors who waxed the halls so she would slip and embarrass herself.

In her worst moods, the world was out to destroy Dot.

"You think I have a bad attitude," she'd say. "You think I'm just feeling sorry for myself, but listen to this!"

And then she'd relate another grievance.

Dot had started to collect things that worked against her, and she took a morose satisfaction in telling them to me.

"Show your bright side," I'd say to her.

"You're out of your head," she'd answer.

I was raking the winter leaves off my lawn the afternoon Dot came around to the back entryway. She was carrying the shot. It made a deep *thump* when she dropped it into the grass.

"I made the team," she announced, but she did not sound very pleased. "They said I'd be a good shot-putter because I'm dense for my height."

"Dense?" I was indignant. "You're perfect. I'll get out my insurance chart and prove it to you."

"Those things lie." She hefted the shot, held the iron ball dreamily within the curve of her neck. "Sometimes I fantasize—

like, you'll think this is completely absurd, Wallace, but—I'm picked out by a magazine to pose on their cover. They discover me living like a nobody here in Argus, and they take me and dress me up, do my hair, and suddenly I'm gorgeous." She spun into a sudden crouch, turned, straightened her arm and lunged forward. The shot arced and fell, directly into my rose bed.

"I didn't think I could throw it that far," she said, satisfied. She retrieved the ball. I didn't have the heart to tell her she had broken my favorite bush, Intrigue. Besides that, her words were percolating deep below the surface of my thoughts. I fed Dot and sent her on. But all that evening I was distracted. I could feel it slowly surfacing. And then it took shape when I was tucked between my sheets.

Wallacette Darlene must think well of herself, have a fantasy come true for once, be perfect, on top. This would change her whole view of the world as against her. Give her confidence. Inspire her. But which fantasy? Which wild plan? Which hope? It was not in my power to do much, and her list was so farfetched. But I was determined. I would be like the godmother in a children's story, grant one wish. But which would it be?

I thought through them all and came up with the last.

There will be four queens in Argus, I imagined, just like in a deck of cards. There was already a Snow Queen, a Pork Queen, and a Homecoming Queen. There would be one more queen, and she would be queen of the beets! Yes! And the Beet Queen would be queen of them all, because in Argus the sugar beet is king!

I could see it so clearly, from the moment it first occurred to me. Dot ascending foil-covered steps, her face bright, the tiara catching spotlights and sunlight. I saw the Beefeater roses, plump and breathing, dark red. I saw Dot's eyes, that light amber color so strangely like Mary's, running over with tears of shock, of pride. And I also saw myself, for we do things for our children so many times for our own benefit. I was among the audience, but I was behind it, the cause and prime mover. Dot's eyes were trained upon me, full of amazed respect. People stopped me, shook my hand, said "Wallace, she's gorgeous," "You've done it again," or "I don't know when I've had such fun." For of course I had already begun to see the crowning as part of something larger. My mind just works like that. It would be one long extravaganza, drawing people from out of state. A five-day festival, a fair, a big show in honor of the sugar beet, and topping it all off—the queen.

I was too excited to sleep that night. Such possibilities ran through my head. I saw the carnival, floats, a long parade that would celebrate the changes that ten years of the beet had brought to Argus. I planned an elegant float from the Farmer's Cooperative, and another from the new Sears outlet. Our franchises could be persuaded to donate refreshments. Fried chicken. Hamburgers. The sugar beet had been bigger than I had ever dreamed, and Argus had become its capital. A celebration was overdue, the more I worked it out.

I sat at my desk and typed up my inspirations while the dog snored on my feet. The night passed and the April dawn came early, a gray suffusing light. I collapsed to sleep the morning out. But I was up in only hours, talking my idea around with the other chamber of commerce members, club presidents, the doers and the shakers of the town. There was uniform acceptance, enthusiasm, excitement. We began to see the festival as something annual, a must-see in travel guides as well as a local attraction. We took donations, started raising money from the local beet cooperatives, town businesses. We'd have a sidewalk sale, a big craft show. Things blossomed beyond my farthest hopes.

Between the night of my vision and the day it dawned, however, the months of preparation were long. For one year, I hardly thought about anything else but the festival, even though I had a committee made up of concerned young Jaycees and Jaycee-ettes. "Wallace," they told me, "leave some of this to us!" But I just couldn't. I was obsessed by every detail, down to the order of the floats in the parade and the young person we must hire to clean up after the horses of the Western Riding Club. There was a city ordinance on horse manure that I had drafted myself.

Most important of all, the thing I never lost sight of, was the crowning of the queen. It had to be more than perfect: it had to be regal. All of Dot's fantasies rolled up in one and come to life. I wanted posters. I wanted flyers with the royal candidates prominently displayed. I hired Tommy B.'s Aviation, just west of town, a fellow Moose Lodger who dusted crops and seeded clouds. He would be sworn to secrecy and then skywrite the queen's name just above the grandstand at the moment she was crowned. Driving into town some days with all the sky stretching out blue and aqua before me, I saw the loop-de-loop of her name:

Queen Wallacette That's how I saw it. Never Dot.

I don't care how much she pouted or insisted, or grew up, I don't care how brief her skirt or thick her makeup and blue her language, she would always be Wallacette in my heart. Sometimes I sat on her couch, the one she was born on, and time collapsed. I saw reels of home movies in my head. Dot taking two steps at a time, always running off the edges of steps or landings because in her eager frenzy she never looked down. Dot older, full of swagger in the outfield, practicing her swing on the dried heads of dandelions, filling the air with downy seeds. And lately, Dot a hard-faced girl, despised by classmates, and feared. But I knew once the crown dazzled and drew attention to her sense of command, her unusual bearing, and, yes, her beauty, the town would see it too. Girls would envy her, boys would flock. I wished her enemies would go further, eat dirt to please her, bow and scrape, but I would settle for seeing her crowned.

I'd rig the vote.

To that end, I worked like a Trojan and broke my health. The exhaustion, the strain, the loss of weight, these were nothing new. I started running myself into the ground long before I'd even thought up the festival. It was my nature to attend to the details of any event, down to designing posters and composing slogans. I typed long into the night, making up my own press releases, preparing committee reports. Besides that I had enlarged my weekly column "About 'n' Around" to include a community-events calendar spiced with interesting commentary, many pertinent asides, and reportage of gatherings I'd attended.

"Don't think twice," began one of my columns, "before putting aside these dates on your calendar: July 8–12, 1972. These five days will be the acme of entertainment. Games, floats, prizes galore, and of course the crowning of a local reigning lovely."

Who would be Dot.

The only thing that wasn't cooperating was the weather, and that was beyond my control.

We needed rain, a soaking rain that began very slow and steady to open up the earth's pores. We needed it to stop, collect, and to start again next day or day after, sinking deeper, longer, never driving down harsh enough to flay off the topsoil or fast enough to gully the fields. We needed a kind rain, a blessing rain, one that lasted a whole week. We needed water. We tried things, cloud seeding, but the chemistry wasn't right once, and another time the clouds blew off. Whole congregations prayed for the drought to cease. But the days were rainless, hot, and everywhere the earth dried and cracked. For the first time in years there were crop failures, land for sale. And as July neared I couldn't ignore the fact that I was drained, pulled tense, my face sagged with the rapid weight loss.

"It's simple nervous exhaustion," my doctor said, and wrote out a prescription for a muscle relaxant, which I never had filled. I never took his advice on a vacation either. Instead of quitting,

I went at it harder. Perhaps I made my condition worse with the guilt as well. I had nomination ballots printed up so that everyone in town could vote in their bank lobbies. Then I collected the votes myself. I spent one whole night filling out a new set of ballots in different colored pens and pencils, changing my style of X. The same thing when they cast their final votes for the queen. I had to rehearse myself in the bathroom before I presented the results to my friends on the festival committee, and still, when I said Dot's name, my smile shook. I had never been dishonest in my life.

Things went from bad to worse. The drought did not relent. There were those who wanted to cancel the festival, but I told them there was no turning back. The governor and his wife had been invited, along with nine high school marching bands and a precision motorcycle-riding team. The contract for the carnival had been signed, and we had also signed with the rock bands, polka bands, a stunt and stock-car show. We had a demolition derby featuring The Battle of the Mammoths, a fight to the scrap heap between two tractor combines. There was a tractor-pulling contest and a guard alert in which we would see the readiness of our local reserve forces. Once you start the ball rolling like this, there's no stopping it. I said so. But there were those who just looked up at the drained white sky and shook their heads and walked off.

I didn't blame them, for desperate times had hit the beet. But desperate times had hit the area before, and we'd survived. I worked harder. I saw all the more reason for the town to have a big bash, take their minds off the daily weather, which had become the one topic on everyone's lips. People quoted Dewey Berquist, the weatherman out of Fargo, and dragged out scraps of folklore, examined tree rings and the depth of sloughs. But when the river dried to a thick narrow trickle, the banks revealed, all lined with dead fish and twisted hulks of cars, I wished I could call it quits, too. The heat shriveled my enthusiasm. And then, almost the last day, something happened even worse, something so improbable I finally cracked.

One morning, I bumped into Celestine at the post office. She had just reached into the box for her mail.

"What do you know," she mused. In her hand she had a flyer. Dot glowered off the front, her eyes dark as two pools of steam. The other sugar-beet princesses were pictured, too. Their smiles were sweet but their faces were forgettable. Celestine also held a long white card.

"What's this," she said, turning over a postcard.

The card was printed with a logo: ELMO'S LANDSCAPE SYSTEMS. Beneath the logo the words *I'm on my way* were printed, and the name *Karl*.

The high cool ceiling of the post office suddenly seemed to stretch upward forever, collecting the echoes of our voices. The brass fronts of the numbered postal boxes held a thousand small glass mirrors that gave me back the face of an old man, lined and ancient. My hair had thinned on the crown and changed from light blond to gray. Even my new square wire-rimmed glasses seemed, now, a sad attempt to grasp at youth. I was in no shape to see him, or be seen.

There was no turning back, no stopping, and the day finally came in a swirl of grit and dead heat. I woke up more exhausted than I'd gone to bed. Nothing helped. I was worn to the bone and knew I'd have to stumble through the day on sheer willpower. I made it through that morning, and then through the parade, by drinking gallons of weak iced tea. The waxed cups thinned and softened in my hands; the paper shredded. After twelve noon no ice was to be had anywhere, and even the stuff in the soft-drink cannisters was expanding, seeping out of the pressured lids. I was on the edge of collapse, and so what could have been fun or easy became an awful challenge, almost life and death. I staggered on, until I reached the first task of my afternoon.

The Lion's Club had constructed a dunk tank as a community fund-raising device. It was simple. A padded stool was placed several feet above a deep wide stock tank full of water. Under a bigwig's dangling feet a small round lever, supporting the chair, would spring away if it was hit by a three-for-a-dollar softball. The seat would slam backward and the VIP would get doused. The mayor, police chief, sheriff, and the members of the town council had a stint at the tank. To be included was a status symbol and the tank was a popular stop on the midway. For my turn, I wore a costume of course, just as all the dunkees did. To acquire the courage I needed to don my outfit—the orange Hawaiian shirt, straw hat, the beachcomber's pants, the same getup I'd worn at Dot's long-ago luau—I'd convinced myself that Karl wouldn't show. I looked all around the booth before I dared to appear. The mere climb winded me. Once I got there the water glittered in my eyes.

I hadn't known it would be so hard to keep my balance on the dunking stool. I gritted my teeth and held on, sick. I tried to joke with my friends, each of whom took three or six or nine tries and left me sitting.

"He's here! He's the one you've been waiting for!" cried the ticket taker, Arnie Dotzenrud, a slow and uncomprehending fellow Lion. I swooned, gripped the edge of the stool. Yellow stars turned.

"Let me down, please," I whispered, and that's when I saw Dot walking toward me from a distance, dressed in a green cloud. She was electric, tense with life. Just the sight of her was a transfusion. I doted on her sturdy form, the way she swung her arms, and her walk, bold with purpose. I didn't understand the menace that was there as well.

She stood in front of me, and everything else faded out and

310

blurred. It was like looking at a stopped tornado. Her face was ready to explode and her stormy green dress stood out like an invert funnel. She walked up to the ticket taker, slammed down a dollar bill, and said, "I'll take three." She locked her teeth and cocked her arm back. The green mesh sleeves strained across her muscles. I had watched her pitch a thousand softballs, and so I knew that when she concentrated she never missed the strike zone.

"Please don't," I said, holding my hands up. "Wallacette?"

The first ball slammed. The seat crashed out from under me and I went down. Even through the water I heard the next two hit home.

The Passenger

After they planted the beets in Argus, and put the new bypass in that connected the town with the interstate, most everything that the town needed came by truck. It was the same way with what the town produced. People came to Argus by way of the interstate too, but not Father Miller, who didn't much like traveling by car, and only drove long-distance as a last resort. He took the train across the border from Minneapolis, into North Dakota, and upward in a long curve that brought him to Argus. The coach was nearly empty, and he was the only passenger to disembark, even though there seemed to be a celebration going on. He stepped off the portable footstool, waved off the conductor's helping hand, and answered the perfunctory "watch your step, Father," with a burst of worried enthusiasm. How, he wondered, would the Empire Builder continue the level of excellent service with no passengers? The conductor made his chin long in rue and said he didn't know. Both men paused a moment beneath the blistering Dakota sky, and then the train made a starting lurch. The conductor threw the footstool aboard, swung himself behind, and soon the priest stood alone on the apron of new cement that skirted the Argus depot.

He rocked on his heels, looked side to side, flapped a large white handkerchief out of his pocket, and touched his forehead. The hot dry air fueled him, set him at a boil.

He was here to find out the truth behind the letter that his mother had put into his hand two days before. At first he had not even been curious. He was reliable, a man of good sense, a satisfied priest admired for his tactful sermons and his warmth with the elderly. His first reaction to the letter had been annoyance, worry for his mother. But she was very weak now and not overly concerned about anything besides her illness. Later on, sitting in his office over some accounts, he began to wonder. He tried to imagine what the town was like, the people, the butcher shop. But he now saw that there had been no need. Nothing about Argus was unusual.

He lifted his black case and stepped purposefully beneath the wide cool eaves of the old depot. His foam-soled shoes were soundless on the octagonal tiles, and when he stopped before the brass-barred ticket booth, he made an important-sounding cough to attract the attention of the young man behind the counter.

"Is there a butcher shop close by?" he asked.

The ticket agent thought so, or maybe it was a grocery.

"How about a family named Kozka?"

The man had no idea, so Father Miller walked over to the telephone booth and began to page through its slim directory. He found no uncle and aunt in its pages, but when he drew Sita Kozka's letter from his suitcoat again, and read it, he decided that he might try to find the butcher shop. From her description, the enterprise that her parents owned was located on the eastern side of town.

Father Miller slipped off his jacket, slung it over one shoulder, and started down the main street of Argus. He was a medium-sized man, trim but not muscular. His main exercise was walking, and his stride was energetic and swift. It took him only a few blocks to find The House of Meats. The town had grown large around the shop, and the property was something of an eyesore among the neat modern buildings on Main Avenue. A cracked blue electric sign on stilts announced it from the street, and an unpaved drive led, between tall grown pines, to a low slate-green shingled building with several chimneys of pointed tin. The place looked run-down but not deserted. Johnny-jump-ups flourished against the front wall and leggy white geraniums bloomed in the dirt. The grass was unevenly mowed. The windows were dim

313

and dirty, but patched with tape. From the end of the drive, he could see the black cardboard in the front and read the bright pink word CLOSED.

There was no telling whether the Mary Adare named on the broken sign was a relation or not. More than twenty years had passed since the letter in his breast pocket had been written, and who knew what had taken place during that time? The name *Sita Kozka* was all he had to go on, and this derelict building.

In the heat his wiry curls were beginning to spring to life. He combed his fingers through his dark red hair and looked down at his hands. He privately thought they revealed a side of his personality. They were oddly unlike the rest of him—sinewy and long, nimble as a monkey's, with delicate oval nails. They were the hands of a safecracker, devious and finely tuned, and so sensitive to cold that he invested in fat goose-down mitts to keep them from getting frostbitten when he made his winter rounds. Now, regarding them on a street in this town, the gnarled knuckles and sharp tips dizzied him. They belonged to someone else.

Down street, the muffled flourishing of drums, waves of clapping, beeping horns and cheers began. Jude Miller put his hands in his pocket and the crowd collected around him, pressing him fast where he stood, mingling their sweat and hair spray and food smells with hot asphalt and the faint alkaline dust he scuffed up beneath the blue glass sign. He closed his eyes and tried to think of his mother. Catherine Miller's long broad serious face was turned away from him. He strained up on his toes like everyone else, or bent toward the street, hoping that the first glimpse of the gold and pink majorettes, the banners, the antique cars and cartwheeling clowns would put everything back into perspective. But his heart quickened as the crowd surged together in a pack. His hands popped free. His face streamed in the heat. His body was shoved and molded, arranged into a new form by the crowd's hips and elbows. He squeezed tight, held his breath, barely fit. All around him the noise of the parade rushed and rolled and the colors spun in a blur so bright he could not contain the picture. He tried to keep his mind in check, but still the thought came. All that held him together now was the crowd, and when the parade was finally over and they drew apart he would disperse, too, in so many pieces that not even the work of his own clever hands could shape him back the way he was.

KARL ADARE

ALL MY LIFE, I traveled light. I made a habit of throwing out worn clothes, books I finished, even Celestine's notes. I only had one piece of furniture, an expensive portable stereo, and once I got tired of a record I simply left it behind in a motel room. But then, in the past few months, I started to miss recordings that I'd ditched ten, twelve, fifteen years before. Even tunes I left behind in the last week would run through my head, only missing a line or a word. I started hearing them at work. I had gone from treating Dutch elm disease, thrips, and leafy spurge, to selling and installing preplanned landscape designs down in booming Texas. It was a living, I scraped by, but there was nothing to the job I liked. So I got careless. Dreamed things. Heard things. Laying out the seepage fields and septic tanks on graph paper for a contractor, suddenly I'd think of a song. Irving Berlin's classics, "All By Myself" and "Happy Talk." Eddie Fisher's smooth deadpan backed up by Hugo Winterhalter and his Orchestra. Patti Page's "Throw Mama from the Train." "Softly, Softly." Jaye P. Morgan's voice would fill my head. I'd hum along. I'd get a strange look from the contractor.

"Never mind," I'd say, "just listen. What comes after this?" I'd sing, " 'Throw Mama from the train a kiss, a kiss. Throw Mama a kiss good-bye. Throw Mama from the train a kiss, a kiss.' Then what? It's something about her old country ways."

The guy would either laugh and shake his head or I would get a stranger look and lose the job. But I'd stopped caring. Where was Joe "Fingers" Carr? Where was "Tequila"? Where were the old hits they never played on the radio anymore?

The Great Ones are gone, I would think, sitting at the edge of the dry motel pool with a margarita sweating in my hand. But it was more than that. I had outlived something careless in myself. Most men get to my age and suddenly they're dissatisfied with all that they've accumulated around them. Not me. I wanted everything I'd left behind.

I wanted the cars repossessed after fifteen payments, the customer's houses into which I never got past the doormat, the ones I did get past, their rooms and rich smells of wax and burned food. I wanted the food itself, burned or not, and the women who had left it in the oven too long. I wanted their husbands. I wanted the men in blind alleys, truck beds, the men who had someone else or, like Wallace Pfef, never anyone before. I wanted the whole world of people who belonged to each other and owned things and cooked food and remembered old songs.

But it didn't hit me until I had lived month after month in dissatisfaction, that what I really wanted was their future. I wanted their children. So when Celestine's note caught up with me in the Plano branch office, I shouted out loud, showed the clipping around. It was a newspaper photograph of the Beet Queen candidates, and Dottie's name was circled. Behind them, with a big square grin on his face and new wire-rimmed glasses, stood Wallace Pfef. I crowed over Dot and altogether made a fool of myself, until one of the managers couldn't take it anymore, sneered, asked me the last time I'd seen her.

I quit the place.

It had been a comedown anyway, and I had no feel for the merchandise.

I went back to my hotel and packed everything I owned in the trunk of my old Plymouth. Then I sat down beside the pool, just a moment, to think what I would do next. There had been plenty of times like this in my life, lulls of indecision. They lasted longer and longer though, and this one lasted longest of all. I sat there drinkless and coatless, my hat on, my keys dangling off a ring, until the sky turned orange and one by one the neon signs around the place flashed in bows and zippers. They made no sense. They were just moving figures. Nothing around me spoke. And as I sat there and the shadows gathered and the lizards scraped along the tiles, I made less and less sense, too, until I made none at all. I was part of the senseless landscape. A pulse, a strip, of light.

I give nothing, take nothing, mean nothing, hold nothing.

This is what I said to myself in that strange false dusk. I shut my eyes against it. I shut my mind against the thought. I held my breath. And in that darkened, bleak, smothering moment, something came back to me. One thing. Not an object, not a plan, not even the nagging words to a song, but a sweetness. That's the most I can describe of it. Just a breath, but so pure.

I opened my eyes, walked down the steps, and got into my car. I started driving north and didn't stop but to gas up, because of the date on the newspaper clipping, because of Dot. I linked her with that moment of sweetness even though I'd wondered, since I last saw her, whether she was still at large or locked in jail. As I drove I began to link other people with that moment too, even people I thought I had left behind forever, like my sister.

The last time I saw her I got a slight concussion for my trouble. This was during dinner, when she hit me with a can of oysters. I picked the can up and rubbed my temple. I said, "You've got no family feelings." And she answered that she had no family. She was a hard one, with no reprieve. Then there was Wallace. As his only experience, I was some sort of God he worshipped by acting like he was my personal maid. He ironed everything I wore, washed my shirts fresh, brought coffee, squeezed oranges because I said I liked real juice, and cooked up big dinners every night. An ash wouldn't drop from my cigarette but that he'd catch it in his bare palm and brush it into a wastebasket. Sleeping with him was no different from that. He'd do anything to please me, but didn't have the nerve to please himself. I like a person to be selfish so I can stop thinking that they're thinking something that I can't understand. He drove me out of my mind with attention, and even though I did feel sorry for him there was no question, ever, of staying.

And yet I was coming back.

I drove into Argus on the day of the parade, just at dawn, with all I owned packed in the trunk and flowing over the backseat. I sailed right through. It was as if my hands had stuck to the wheel. Or maybe I'd been driving in a straight line so long I had forgotten how to turn. Sunup, with the air so full of dust and reflected light, looked ferocious. All the merchandise was burning in the big plate-glass windows on Main Avenue. Even the street signs gave back a red glow. The streets looked glazed and hot. They turned back into highway and far in the distance, on the other side of town, the air folded in glossy continual waves of rising heat. Two silver grain elevators floated above the ground and I started toward them, thinking maybe I could park in some shade, catnap, wake refreshed and then drive back in once the festivities began.

I stopped on the shady western side and parked in tall wild mustard. I got out and stood in the weedy gravel. With day, a wind had come up, so loud it filled my ears and made them ache. I had forgotten the force of a Dakota wind. It was so long ago that I had the territory that included the Badlands, where Celestine and I went for our justice-of-the-peace wedding. We said our vows, and then I took her and the baby out to dinner at the Alex Johnson Hotel, the fanciest place in Rapid City. I tried to bring up the subject of my living with them again because I hoped that Celestine might be having second thoughts. But she only showed her harsh white teeth, forked up her salad, and jiggled the baby curled in her lap.

"Let's not get carried away." She nodded at the table between us, as if it was representative. "This is only a formality."

I could tell that she hated having marriage thrown on her, and that even though she bought our Black Hills Gold wedding bands herself, in the Alex Johnson lobby, she wasn't fond of hers. During dinner, she worked it on and off her finger like it hurt. Once she removed it entirely and set it on her coffee saucer. The busboy nearly ran it through the dishwasher.

That's where we parted company, and where I got back on the road. And that's also where I really became a father for the first time. One thing they never say, one thing I've never heard about, is a man's side of having a baby. Nothing happened in me while Celestine was actually pregnant, because of course I never knew her symptoms, pleasures, and complaints firsthand. It was after seeing baby Dot that I got hit.

I left Rapid City by route of that endless stretch of highway that runs beneath the border between the two Dakotas. During long drives my trick was usually to hit on a catchy tune or talk back to the radio, but after a while I switched it off. I found it pleasant to have the peace of the afternoon around me, to be at the center of unchanging fields of snow and brown branches. The landscape stayed so much the same, in fact, that at one point I seemed suspended, my wheels spinning in thin air. I hung motionless in speed above the earth like a fixed star.

A wind had drawn me along, the same wind blowing now, only sugar beets had taken over, mile after mile, and no one grew grain around Argus anymore. The elevator was a hollow shaft of two-by-four studs and flapping tarpaper. The accountant's office was nailed shut with boards. The tracks of the rail spur looked overgrown, the banks undercut, some of the ties were missing. I was probably trespassing, and from the way I looked I would not have blamed the state police for picking me up.

I was disreputable, unshaven, unwashed, covered with road dust, and I was hungry. I waited until my watch said nine o'clock, then I went to the Flickertail and sat in a booth with coffee and a bismarck roll. I sat there long enough to watch the whole parade, or at least the backs of people in the crowd and the tops of floats, and then I washed up in the restaurant bathroom, combed my hair, and shook out my jacket. I slapped cold water on my eyes. But I still looked like a bleary old bum with my three-day beard and cheap blue suit.

I felt worse than that when I finally got to the fairgrounds. The parade was breaking up, and in the confusion I drove through the wrong entrance and parked on the other side of everything. I started wandering, stumbling in a haze of exhaustion, in a whirl of canned organ music from the merry-go-round, in a big stew of noise and confusion. It was such an awful mess that I was almost glad when I got to the edge of a long row of booths and saw The House of Meats truck. It was parked in unmowed grass, in the slanting shade of elms, and Sita was sitting in the front seat, alone.

Although her face was shadowed and distorted by the dusty windows of the truck, she didn't look as though the years had told her tale. If anything, age had made her more attractive by refining her features to the bare minimum. Her head was tilted in a modest way, but her gaze was sharp and queenly. She was wearing a rich red garnet necklace.

The necklace made me look away.

Sometimes a small thing, a trinket, brings back a whole world of memories. I hadn't thought of my mother since I don't know when, but the necklace was similar to the one she called her treasure. Maybe it was the necklace that made me take the chance and cross the parking space, or maybe it was the wishful thought that if Sita still looked so well and hadn't changed after all these years, maybe I hadn't either.

"Do you mind?" I slipped into the driver's seat, shut the door, and was suddenly overpowered by tiredness. The air conditioner was on high, and the cab was so wonderfully comfortable that I let all the strain of the road, all the anxiousness, the heat and noise, fall away from me. I sank into the seat and simply let go. I thought I heard myself apologize to Sita as I slowly leaned forward. I folded my arms on the steering wheel and rested my head there.

"Just let me close my eyes for a minute," I heard myself saying. "I'm so damn tired." And then I think I even dozed off a second, or hallucinated, because I jerked suddenly back, gripping the wheel, thinking I was driving.

I glanced at Sita but she was still staring straight ahead, ignoring me so intently that I looked too. Across the dry grass, a crowd surrounded a plank booth. I could hear the tiny faraway hoots and jeers they exchanged with a shrunken-looking figure, absurd in clashing colors, who sat high on a wooden board above a pool of dark water. It was Wallace Pfef.

"Well there he is," I said, "making a perfect ass of himself." But the truth is I didn't feel that way. He wasn't acting the fool. Even from where I sat, above the sound of the air conditioner, I could hear Wallace yell down some remark from his perch. I couldn't make out the words, but the customer laughed and pitched his softballs wide, without taking aim. That was Pfef. People liked him so well that they wouldn't even dunk him on a hot day for a joke.

I was just about to remember my manners, to explain myself to Sita and get on with finding my daughter, when I looked down the row of booths past Wallace and saw Dottie round a corner. It was odd. After driving all this way to see her, I hung back, didn't go to her. She trudged along, her head lowered like a bull's, so I got a good view of her hairdo, anyway, swirled in front, flipped in back, with ringlets hanging down and the whole thing sprayed. It looked indestructible.

"How could Celestine have let her do it?" I said aloud. And the dress too. Dot was squeezed into the heart-shaped top and kept tripping on the bell skirt. As she walked, she swung her muscular short arms and flexed her gloves. A long swatch of white material trailed behind her. I could swear she was looking for trouble. Even from that distance I could see the glitter of her eyes. She reminded me of sailors on shore leave, the dangerous numbers, all pent up from months at sea and looking for a place to use their fists.

She lunged toward the booth where Wallace sat, moving with mechanical purpose. She never even hesitated at the counter, but stripped off her long white gloves and bought three softballs. She hefted one. Testing the weight of it, she took her aim. I watched in a kind of wonder as she threw the balls. One, two, three—each went true, but the first was enough. Wallace disappeared in a flash of orange. His hat seemed to float down after him.

I shot from the truck, caught myself, stumbled, went on. I had let myself smoke too much and I was no longer young. My back pinched, but I put every ounce of speed into my legs and sprinted. He was out cold. I had to get there. I was running for my life.

I pushed past the crowd and fell into the tank with Wallace. I went down on my knees, waded forward to where he rested on the shallow plastic bottom, heavy as a sleeping child. It looked like he was taking a nap there. It looked like he was already drowned. When I pulled him up, streaming water, bewildered and thrashing, sick to the bone with amazement, he threw his arms out, struggled. I dragged him close, and the right words came back.

"Screw the management," I said.

323

The Grandstand

Celestine and Mary were torn as to whether they should sit in the upper seats of the grandstand, beneath the wood-and-shingle awning, or down front in the burning glare close to the royal platform. They chose to suffer. They sat together in the first row middle, silent, each enclosed in her thoughts. The sun was terrible, and their rayon dresses held the heat of it close to their bodies.

"This is the same way you cook a turkey," said Mary after half an hour passed. Notice of the coronation had come over the loudspeaker system, and people were now beginning to straggle to the seats. A red-haired priest sat down in the first row near the end. Celestine and Mary could see him clearly because the grandstand curved around home plate.

Both of them thought of Sita.

"Maybe we should get him," said Celestine.

"I don't know about that," said Mary, pressing her lips together. "She left the church."

"That's true," said Celestine. But she wished she had performed some sort of last rites on Sita herself. It seemed as though she should have done something. She continued to watch the priest, as if he offered hope. He looked solid, and she was sure that if they approached him when this was over he would know what to do.

"They're wheeling Russell up," said Mary. "Look over there."

The orderly had driven the long way around town to get to the end of the parade before Russell's float. Now he pushed Russell over the bumpy diamond.

"Russell's probably burning up in that old uniform," Celestine worried. It seemed to her that everyone must be miserable. The

324

priest, sitting opposite, had folded a program of the ceremony and was now fanning himself with it. Celestine and Mary had programs too, but they wanted to keep them perfect to remember the day.

At last the princesses filed up the platform steps, each holding her skirt in a bunch as she walked. Celestine compared them closely. In their frothy confections, they were like magazine models or mannequins in store windows. Sita had always looked perfect in the same way that they did, lips gleaming, hair held in place by spray. Dot was not among the girls at first, but then she came tramping down the left baseline.

Her dress had gone limp in the heat, like a wilted plant. She didn't even bother to hold it away from her ankles as she ascended the steps.

"There's my girl," breathed Mary.

To her, Dot looked ravishing. The sun reflected off Dot's hairdo. Her dress glowed where an uneven iridescence had been woven into the fabric. Mary thought that her niece resembled an ancient pagan goddess. She had been reading about Atlantis in her *Book of the Unfamiliar*, and she could picture Dot touching the waves with an iron scepter.

Celestine thought that Dot looked uncomfortable and maybe desperate. Her shoulders were hunched and her face sweat in gleaming streaks. She sat in the last folding chair, fists in her lap, and squinted off into the hot white sky.

The whole crowd, uncomfortable, sighed and fanned and frowned beneath the sun, waiting for the mayor to begin. Celestine and Mary stared at Dot, willing her to look at them, exchange some form of recognition from her royal spot. But Dot was completely self-absorbed as if she were alone in her room, and they couldn't catch her eye. Then Wallace sprang with nervous vigor up the first-tier walkway, distracting them. Karl followed in his wake. Both men were steaming, sodden.

325

"She knows," Wallace gasped, falling into a seat directly behind Celestine. Karl sat down more slowly and deliberately, in back of Mary. He nodded, his eyes haggard, but did not say a word. He surveyed the platform, the banners, the folding chair disguised with streamers and higher than the others, on a dais, empty until the queen was announced.

"Who knows what?" Mary twisted around and took Karl in with shrewd eyes, hiding everything. "You're sopping wet."

"I know," said Karl.

"You made it," said Celestine.

Wallace leaned forward and put his face between the two women. Water from his hair and ears dripped on their shoulders. "Dot knows," he said desperately, "I concocted this all, changed votes, rigged everything, got her elected."

Celestine's eyes snapped open, her mouth went down. "You couldn't have," she said.

Mary was impassive, as if she'd always expected the worst. "There will be hell to pay," she pronounced, not taking her eyes from Dot, who sat among the preening beet princesses and did not smile or wave or dimple, but continued to stare into the wide sky like she'd been struck a blow.

"She'll collapse from the heat," Celestine muttered. "They should hurry up."

The sudden roar of the airplane, starting up in the outfield, drowned her words. The platform dignitaries swiveled as one to watch it take off. The flimsy home-run fence had been taken down and a long flat burnt field stretched beyond that—a perfect runway. The mayor shouted across the engine's noise.

"Welcome . . . first annual . . . be writing . . . up there for all to see . . . doing double duty since . . . puny little clouds . . . wish luck . . . cloud seeding is a . . . success rate . . . Tommy B.'s Aviation . . . technical expertise . . . and now . . ."

Dot moved then. Throwing up her dress in a bunch, baring

her strong short legs, she stamped across the board platform and jumped, landed on her toes, then ran, leaving tiny black spike marks in the beaten earth of the diamond. She ran toward outfield, toward the small white plane that was perched there alert and graceful as a bird. And when she got to its doors she vaulted in without a hand up, or permission. There was a pause, as perhaps she argued with the pilot. And then the mayor gained his voice and shouted, "Oh, hey . . ." Celestine and Mary, Karl and Wallace were on their feet, poised to do something, but the pilot leaned out the door, tipped his black mesh tractor hat, and taxied forward. The plane moved with startling, swift, lurching hops and gathered speed until the roar was overpowering, and up it rose, over the booths and canopies, over the tall old elms, over the flat river of mud, over the grandstand and over the town.

The mayor was the mayor of Argus because he never completely lost his footing in any crisis, but could always be counted on to respond with dull remarks. Now he droned with the plane's engine, sticking to his written speech, explaining the story of the beet in Argus up to the present. The crowd grew restless. The people trapped upon the platform fixed expressions of interest on their faces, but what they really followed was the progress of the plane, which went so high it vanished once, then sparkled like a sequin and bored straight into a solid-looking cloud and out the other side again. Then through another and another. It wheeled and banked in turns and loops and then began to write.

Down on the ground, Mary had thrown her hands out, clasped them, put them to her face, and finally kept them there as if her expression would crack if she took them down. Celestine was at a loss, numb with fright, unable to be furious with Wallace, who was so appalled and anxious that he trembled. Only Karl's face was thrown back in wonder.

They watched. Their faces were characters that caught the light. The plane tipped, glided, formed **Queen Wallacette** out of smoke and vapor, and when it was done veered away, disappearing over the treeline.

There were a few seconds of silence on the platform, and then the mayor, halting, pronounced Dot queen and handed fresh red roses around the wire backstop to her mother. Then he stepped down with the princesses and Legion post commander. Russell sat still. There was a murmuring, a rumbling of footsteps on wood, as the crowd left the grandstand. Only the four stood rooted, heads tipped back, ears straining for the engine's return. They made a little group, flung out of nowhere, but together. They did not lower their eyes, but kept watching as above them Dot's name slowly spread, broke apart in air currents, and was sucked into the stratosphere, letter by letter.

DOT

"THIS IS SO fucking hideous," I said, staring down at the wet-looking green material of the dress I was supposed to wear. "I think a dinosaur shed this or something."

Aunt Mary sighed with pain, as if a knife had twisted deep inside, then set her mouth firm to endure me. My mother put her fingers to her lips.

"I don't care," I told them. "I'm not going to wear this even if Aunt Mary paid two hundred dollars."

But you can see how far that got me, because of course that's exactly what I've got on.

I'm standing in the armory parking lot with all these floats made of spray-painted Kleenex and chicken wire. Uncle Wallace is handing the drivers red numbers so they know their order in the parade. It's a mess. All the guys driving the cars that pull the floats are dopers from the Autobody Club. They're half buzzed and slumping against the fenders or laughing their heads off once they get behind the wheel. I don't care about that because those guys are friends of mine, not boyfriends or anything. They let me hang around. What I do care about is wearing this dress, which is like Thumbelina's nightmare. But at least I've got this white lace shawl that looks like a curtain I pulled out of someone's front window. I have it wrapped around me because I'm afraid if P.J. or Eddie or Boomer or any of the guys get a good look they'll split a gut and ram each other. Life is funny enough through their eyes.

And then there's the other members of the royal court. When I see them floating toward me all in simple white eyelet or pastel blue, all slim and tanned orange from laying on their garage roofs smeared with iodined baby oil, I'm irritated. I know from the way that Wallace acts that this is my day. He knows the outcome. I don't have any doubt who will get the crown and think that, really, I should have this float to myself alone.

Some National Guardsmen have taken Uncle Wallace's place organizing everyone, and now a slender man in crisply starched olive drab directs us to get in line. The sight of a uniform brings our driver down to earth, and the five of us girls climb onto our float. It's a tractor-trailer bed. Old sheets are stapled onto the splintered wood, and tinsel garlands left over from Christmas hang off it here and there. Five sheet-wrapped hay bales are arranged for us to sit on. Behind us a big white scalloped fan of cardboard spreads, labeled THE QUEEN AND HER COURT. One hay bale is placed a little higher than the others, and I take it. The princesses spread below me in a swirl.

The streets are still damp, because the fire department sprinkled them down with what was left of the river. The dust only settled for a little while. I can feel the drought. It draws on me, tightening my face. As I drove into town this morning with Uncle Wallace I saw the fields lifting. Low in the sky, flaring like smoke, the dirt moved, and I said, "What's the forecast?"

"Dry," he answered. "More sunshine." His face looked tiny and shriveled when he said this, as if the drought was withering him too.

The parade lurches into motion, and about a half block away, I see this beefy orderly from the rest home unload my uncle from a special dome-top van. Russell's strapped into the wheelchair with harnesses that look like they are part of his uniform. All his medals are pinned on, a bright patch that spills down his chest.

The guy is bumping him, dragging him up the side of the float, tipping him so that he sags over once.

I stand up, scream off the edge of the moving float.

"He needs a drink! Can't you see he's thirsty? Give him a drink!"

People turn. I point at Russell and stand up and yell it again until a Legionnaire comes running with a full canteen. It seems like I'm in command, already queen, because the Legionnaire and orderly put Russell gently in place now, in the middle of his fake battlefield, which is planted with those wire-and-plastic poppies veterans sell every year. Russell drinks from the canteen, tilting his head up to swallow. I see the water go down in gulps and then the whole parade is moving off down the street, and Russell is wedged between the bunkers and crossed rifles, staring into the open back of the National Guard jeep that's going to pull him.

P.J. hits the horn and I sit down on my hay bale. I've dropped the lace shawl, and in some part of my mind I'm aware that my fellow candidates are feasting their eyes on my plantlike dress. But I don't give a crap. I begin my windshield-wiper wave, as instructed by our gym teacher, who has been a contestant for Miss North Dakota. Back and forth very slowly. Smile, smile, smile.

Although the street is wide, people have parked it full of cars and are now standing three deep right up to the sides of the floats. As we pass, they wave, hands fluttering inches from our faces, and we wave back without speaking, our palms only inches from theirs. The illusion of our grandeur encloses us like a bubble. It is as if we're isolated, deaf and dumb to our admirers. That is how I hear the conversation about me so clearly that there can be no mistake.

"Which one'll get it, do you think?"

"Oh, that one. The stocky-looking redhead."

"You're kidding."

"No, she's it for sure. I heard. My brother knows that Pfef."

"Yeah?"

"He rigged it. Got her nominated and then counted the votes himself."

"He related to her?"

"She's supposed to be his niece or something."

"Oh."

"Her mother's that big Indian woman. That six-footer."

"She don't take after her."

At first, I think I go a little numb. Everything outside of me is a whirling blur. I keep wiping at the air, but the crowd just smudges. I smile until my cheeks ache. And then little by little things start coming clear. I am facing up to reality, like for instance the fact that all the other girls heard that conversation, too. I turn to sneak a casual glance down, and all four of the princesses swivel greedily to meet my look. I can tell that they're very pissed off, but also glad at the same time. They're crazed with eagerness to get this story out into the open.

I sink far into myself. In some part of my mind I knew that Uncle Wallace set this up. But that's not something a person really likes to admit, so I never did. I thought at least he would keep it a careful secret. But now it's the latest gossip. One of the princesses starts quacking.

"I don't think it's fair, I don't think it's fair." All the while she is saying this she's waving and smiling. Her head bobs on her long neck, and I decide, as queen, that I will chop it off. "Someone should say something. Someone should tell." She won't stop.

"Be my guest," I shout in her ear. "You think I want to be queen?"

She holds her head and looks at me with a pained expression, but the others take over.

"Why not? Why wouldn't you? You get a gift certificate from

every store. You get to keep the crown. You get a big write-up in the *Sentinel*. I'm sure you'll take a cute picture, like, in curtains, and I hope you wear your dress. It looks like, *I mean really, it's mashed lettuce*."

They are making me dangerous.

"It's a goddamn designer original!" I scream. This shuts them up, or at least makes them hiss among themselves, just loud enough for me to hear.

"I bet you got it with trading stamps."

"I know *just* where she got it—on sale in the window of the Big Gals shop in Grand Forks. I even saw it when I was over there. There was this dummy with the dress on and a little sign around the neck that said 'ninety percent off.' "

I realize that what they are saying about the dress is probably true. The Big Gals is where Aunt Mary likes to shop. She's hard to fit, being built like a cement root cellar, and this place always has fantastic sales.

"I'll kill you," I threaten, wishing I could choke them right there. But I cannot shut them up, of course, and even they can hear that there is a lack of conviction in my voice. There is also stark gloom and depression. I have never felt so desperate.

Far ahead I can see each float or band turn off at the fairground entrance. They move so slow and turn so awkwardly that this last part seems to go on forever. We're trapped in the blare of trumpets, the clatter of high school drums, and an endless medley of the theme from *Doctor Zhivago*. Wherever the high school bands pause, the Old Folks Band takes up. The senior citizens are riding in a hay wagon and all, strangely, dressed in vests and hats made from flattened beer cans crocheted together around the edges. They lift their instruments. They nod three times and all begin. Their music is off-key, tuneless as the wind.

Perhaps the unbearable music affects my mind, because as I am sitting there I start to think revenge.

I've only been mad at Uncle Wallace once before, and when that happened I was madder at him than anybody, ever. But the anger I felt long ago was a pinprick, mere spite. This is real. *How could he do this to me?* I wonder, climbing down from the float. We're at the end of the parade. A red haze drops across my eyes.

There are booths set up everywhere full of 4-H calves and very clean pigs. Catholic Daughters has a bingo shed in full swing and a pie concession. There are carnies too, hucking those enormous pink dogs nobody ever wins, and everywhere the salty warmth of fresh-popped corn, the sugary heat of cotton candy, bright blue syrup, the sizzle of foot-long hot dogs. I feel like I'll faint if I don't stop and eat, but I plunge ahead. Already the crowd is drifting toward the grandstand where the emcee is gabbing on the bullhorn. I run along the edge of the booths, past the shaded stand of elms. I know Uncle Wallace will be somewhere among the charity projects, organizing them or working behind a counter. And sure enough. It's too easy. I find him posed as a complete sitting duck, the world's easiest target. I buy three balls for the dunking tank.

I pick up the first. I can hear the emcee inviting people to the grandstand for the crowning of the Beet Queen.

"Wallacette, please don't!" calls Uncle Wallace.

When he says that name the red curtain drops.

"You told!" I scream. "Cheater!"

For a few seconds, just as the last ball is in the air, I feel good. But then at the splash I turn, almost blinded by what I've done, and I walk toward the grandstand, shamed. Uncle Wallace's face looked so old and thin that I can't stand to think of it. I want to run. I want to jump into P.J.'s Classic and get him to drive me to Canada. First Russell, now Wallace, and next the low point of my life. I don't have to go through with this, I think, I really don't. I could duck through a canning booth, hide out in the cattle barn. There is a plane at the edge of the field, warming up its engine. Even as I step onto the platform where the mayor, Uncle Russell, and the princesses are already sitting, I think that I could fake some sort of massive convulsion. The ambulance would arrive in a wail, lights flashing, and the guys in white would dash for me. They'd hoist me like a feedsack and throw me on a stretcher. They'd fumble me at the ambulance door like they did to Russell. But I do none of these things. I am getting a much better idea.

The sun is a fierce white ball, and under it the boards of the platform have scorched. The seats of the aluminum folding chairs are hot as stove tops. I sit down. This dress comes in handy, useful for something. I adjust the leaves of my skirt to make a cushioning layer, and right there, beneath the eyes of my family and the town, the plan in my head commences to take shape, take form as a kind of logical outcome. There is a thread beginning with my grandmother Adelaide and traveling through my father and arriving at me. That thread is flight.

Before me, in the grandstand, I know that my family sits with eyes like set traps. I do not look at them but turn, instead, to Russell. He sits down the row of burning chairs. His lip has curled, a swatch of hair fallen across his forehead. The lines in his face, deep and brown, jagged, running sideways, are like the dry earth.

"It is with great pleasure," the mayor says, adjusting the microphone, "that I welcome you all to the first Sugar Beet Festival."

There is just barely time.

"The Queen is supposed to fly!" I holler at Tom B. Peske, the pilot. "It's a publicity stunt. Come on. Take off!"

He lets me jump in and as we taxi across the field I tell him that I'm old hand, working on my pilot's license. So he is surprised when, about a hundred feet up, I shut my eyes and drop my head in my lap. The plane wiggles, shudders, spins over like a carnival rocket. I feel too light, unconnected. I sit up and open my mouth, shriek at him to take me back down. He refuses. He's got to write my name. My whole long awful name. Ten letters.

I breathe deep and slow until the world comes clear through the windshield of the plane, and I dare to move. I move by inches, adjusting myself, amazed to find that I am too deathly sick, because of motion or shock, to be afraid. The hugeness up here, the flat world tipping, no end to sky and earth, shakes me. Tunnels of hot air flow straight upward from the plowed fields. Every time we bump over one, every time I think of how we look from down below, I make noise. It's the only thing that distracts me from throwing up. I yell so hard, going over the tops of the letters, that the pilot, Tom B. Peske, shouts that I deafen him. The only thing I do right is help seed clouds. We veer due west, where a group of cumulus are massed. I load the silver-iodide cartridges into the flare gun just the way Tom B. says to, and then I hold it out the window while he flies blind. My fingers rust to the gun's smooth side. My throat tastes like iron. I concentrate on Tom B.'s hands, steady on the panel of instruments. I concentrate on shooting the gun. An hour passes before we come back and circle above the grandstand.

I decide, when we finally descend, to die with my eyes wide open. So I see everything, the sudden magnification as we swoop, the rushing earth, the carnival and fairgrounds like a painting that smears and then suddenly focuses as we slow. The semicircle grandstand is where we stop, just in left field.

Tom B. takes down a clipboard and begins to log in this flight. He hardly notices when I let myself out, or maybe he's disgusted and glad to see me go. I'm so happy to touch the ground that I don't care, and I don't care either that the air is dense, humid, and I'm smothered in my own dress again. The cloth is damp with sweat, scratchy, clinging like a burr-filled sheet. But I could run down third baseline. Home. I start walking, wobbling a little, righting myself. The platform is empty, the chairs disordered, the streamers fallen, and the grandstand is dotted with people catching a stray breeze, eating drumsticks, pie. No one points at me or notices, no one rises in their seat to hail the queen. No one screams and points, either, which is something. The mayor is gone. The princesses. Russell is gone, and Wallace. Aunt Mary is gone too and I stop, struck by a wild pitch.

All the time that I was in the plane, I imagined that they gasped, cried out, covered their eyes and prayed. I was sure that they would wait forever, or until the plane came back down, but they have not.

It is a lonely thought, and not entirely true. For as I am standing there I look closer into the grandstand and see that there is someone waiting. It is my mother, and all at once I cannot stop seeing her. Her skin is rough. Her whole face seems magnetized, like ore. Her deep brown eyes are circled with dark skin, but full of eagerness. In her eyes I see the force of her love. It is bulky and hard to carry, like a package that keeps untying. It is like this dress that no excuse accounts for. It is embarrassing. I walk to her, drawn by her, unable to help myself. She comes down the steps, stands beside the dugout, and gives me the tumbled batch of roses. Heavy, half-opened, the heads have wilted on the stalks.

"Let's get going," she says. "I wonder, can you walk in those shoes?"

I take them off. The soles of my feet are tough as canvas, and we start out. My mother tells me I have to brace myself about Aunt Sita, but I don't falter for a step, just keep walking through the crowd that mills sheeplike, dazed by heat, onto the griddles of asphalt streets and sidewalks. The tar sticks, burns through my callous. On the road to our house past Uncle Wallace's she tells me Aunt Mary is at the funeral parlor, half crazy with worry

337

about me. Then she stops. This is not what she finds so hard to tell.

"He's back, isn't he," I say to her. "He's waiting at the house."

But he's not. As we pass Uncle Wallace's closed, cool place my mother points with her chin and says, "That's his car."

It's an old, lean model, with sprung shocks. It is bruised with unpainted weld marks, coated with thick dry dust. The car is backed into its parking place, ready for a smooth exit.

I put my heels on. The stickers beside the road are mowed short and cut like glass. I touch my mother's arm for balance as we walk. The clouds spread over us. We breathe a powder of hot blowing earth. My dress is unbearable, a prickling mess that I strip off once we walk into the house.

I put on an old soft T-shirt and cutoffs and then come into the kitchen. She has rolled her stockings down to the ankles. She has taken off her tight belt. She has lifted a carton of cold juice from the refrigerator and we sit down at the table to drink it, talking about everything that has happened, then trailing off. Night comes, black and moonless, still and very hot. I sit motionless while my mother cooks, eat the toast and eggs that she prepares, drink the milk poured from under her hand.

I want to lean into her the way wheat leans into wind, but instead I walk upstairs and lie down in my bed alone. I watch the ceiling for a long while, letting the night deepen around me, letting all the distant sounds of cars and people cease, letting myself go forward on a piece of whirling bark until I'm almost asleep. And then it begins.

Low at first, ticking faintly against the leaves, then steadier, stronger on the roof, rattling in the gutters, the wind comes. It flows through the screens, slams doors, fills the curtains like sails, floods the dark house with the smell of dirt and water, the smell of rain.

I breathe it in, and I think of her lying in the next room, her covers thrown back too, eyes wide open, waiting.

Algae are ubiquitous. A multitude of species, ranging from microscopic unicells to gigantic kelps, inhabit the world's oceans, freshwater bodies, soils, rocks and trees. To understand the basic role of algae in the global ecosystem, a reliable and modern introduction to their kaleidoscopic diversity, systematics and phylogeny is indispensable. This volume provides such an introduction.

The text represents a completely revised and updated edition of a highly acclaimed German textbook, which was heralded for its clarity as well as its breadth and depth of information. This new edition takes into account recent re-evaluations in algal systematics and phylogeny that have been made necessary by insights provided by the powerful techniques of molecular genetics and electron microscopy, as well as more traditional life history studies.

Each main algal group is considered in turn, its principal characteristics outlined and its ecological peculiarities and phylogenetic relationships discussed, to provide a unique and comprehensive survey of this fascinating group of plants. A final chapter summarizes the phylogeny of algae in relation to other phyla.

This book provides a wealth of information for all those studying or working with algae. A full glossary and comprehensive list of references are two additional features that will make this book an indispensable source of reference for many years to come.

ALGAE

An introduction to phycology

ALGAE

An introduction to phycology

C. van den Hoek

D. G. Mann

H. M. Jahns

CAMBRIDGE
UNIVERSITY PRESS

Published by the Press Syndicate of the University of Cambridge
The Pitt Building, Trumpington Street, Cambridge CB2 1RP
40 West 20th Street, New York, NY 10011-4211, USA
10 Stamford Road, Oakleigh, Melbourne 3166, Australia

© Cambridge University Press 1995

First published 1995

*A catalogue record for this book is available from the British
Library*

Library of Congress cataloguing in publication data

Hoek, C. van den (Christiaan)
[Algen. English]
Algae: an introduction to phycology / C. van den Hoek,
D. G. Mann, and H. M. Jahns
    p.   cm.
Includes bibliographical references and index.
ISBN 0 521 30419 9. – ISBN 0 521 31687 1 (pbk.)
1. Algology.   2. Algae.   I. Mann, D. G.   II. Jahns, Hans Martin.
III. Title.
QK566.H6413   1995
589.3–dc20   93-2078 CIP

ISBN 0 521 30419 9 hardback
ISBN 0 521 31687 1 paperback

Transferred to digital printing 2002

Published in an abridged German edition by George Thieme
Verlag, Stuttgart as *Algen*.
© 1978, 1993 George Thieme Verlag.

Contents

x Contents

Foreword

Something like two-thirds of the earth's surface are covered by oceans and seas. In them live the photosynthetic plants we call 'algae', down to a depth of around 150 m, depending on the transparency of the water. Algae occur on shores and coasts, attached to the bottom (benthic species), or live suspended in the water itself (planktonic species). Freshwaters too are populated by many different species of algae and there are also terrestrial forms, on soils and among bryophytes, although these are for the most part inconspicuous and easily overlooked. Altogether, the algae probably account for more than half the total primary production worldwide; virtually all aquatic organisms are dependent on this production. Algae are extremely important not only ecologically, but also phylogenetically. It is thought that all the major groups (phyla and divisions) of animals and plants originated in the sea, and even today this is where one can find representatives of many ancient evolutionary lineages. Thus, if we are to be able to understand the diversity and the phylogeny of the plant world, it is of fundamental importance, indeed essential, to investigate the algae.

This book had its origins as course notes to accompany lectures on algae, which were given to biology students in their fourth semester at the University of Groningen. The notes seemed necessary because there had been an enormous increase of knowledge about the morphology and cytology of algae, which had not yet found its way into textbooks. Fellow scientists showed interest in the course notes – both within the Netherlands and abroad – and this seemed to show a general need for an up-to-date account of the algae. In the end, thanks to the Georg Thieme Verlag (Stuttgart) and after considerable modification and many additions, the notes were published.

The present edition is a completely revised and updated English version of the original German textbook, published by Thieme in 1978 (a second, unrevised edition appeared in 1984). A thorough revision had been made necessary by the multitude of new papers that have appeared, detailing the results of ultrastructural, molecular and life-history studies. These have led to a complete re-evaluation of the algal system and its phylogenetic interpretation. In particular, there has been an enormous increase in our knowledge of the cytoskeleton, especially in relation to the flagellar apparatus and the processes of mitosis and cytokinesis. As a result, the classification of the green algae (Chlorophyta) has been completely revised, and many advances have also been made in our understanding of other divisions. The classical concept (derived from Pascher), that the different levels of organization – flagellate, coccoid, sarcinoid, filamentous, thalloid, siphonocladous, siphonous – represent natural groups (orders) within each division or class of the algae, has had to be abandoned. The various levels of organization have apparently arisen many times, by convergent or parallel evolution, even within a class, and they have therefore lost their importance as basic criteria for the distinction of major taxonomic groups. In the present edition, therefore, taxa based on organizational level have been maintained only where there is no more satisfactory modern alternative.

Ultrastructural and molecular genetic data, particularly the latter, now allow us to formulate specific phylogenetic hypotheses that are no longer pure speculation. Nucleotide sequences of ribosomal RNAs or their nuclear genes and the structure and sequences of the chloroplast genome are important new sources of data, from which phylogenetic trees can be constructed and compared with trees derived from morphological data. It has been possible, for instance, to test the hypothesis of the endosymbiotic origin of chloroplasts and mitochondria. This was originally thought to be mere speculation, though a fascinating and somewhat elegant concept, but has now gained so much support from molecular and ultrastructural studies that its validity is now scarcely questioned. It is also interesting, and encouraging to us, that Leedale's concept of a fan-shaped phylogenetic tree of all organisms, which was a guiding principle in the first edition, has essentially been supported by molecular evidence. The wealth of new information has encouraged us to put more emphasis on phylogenetic reconstruction in this edition than in the previous two German editions.

This book is meant primarily to provide a clear, modern introduction to the cytology, morphology and systematics of the algae. Each of the main groups of algae is introduced through an enumeration of its principal characteristics, which are subsequently discussed in greater detail. Wherever possible, a number of specific examples are described for each group, within the framework of what is, we hope, a 'natural' classification. By this means we hoped to avoid sweeping generalizations and oversimplification and to convey an idea of the complexity of the biological phenomena being discussed.

It was difficult to decide how to present the results of electron microscopical investigations. In the end it was decided that this is best done through drawings, in which it is possible to summarize the information visible in several electron micrographs. In addition, however, a few electron micrographs have been included. It would have been desirable to have included more such photographs, of course, but this would have increased the cost of the book still further.

This edition is a textbook for advanced undergraduate and postgraduate students but it is also intended as a modern overview of the algae and their classification, which should be of use to all who work with algae, because of either their job or their interests. A list of more than 2000 references has been included, so that readers can easily gain access to the original literature. The glossary of terms and the subject index should also be useful. An abridged German version has been published by Thieme Verlag, Stuttgart (C. van den Hoek, H.M. Jahns & D.G. Mann 1993: *Algen*. Edn. 3), in parallel with this first English edition.

Many colleagues, and also readers of the first and second German editions, have helped to bring the production of this volume to a successful conclusion. In addition to all those who cannot be thanked individually by name, some are due especial mention. The late Prof. Dr H.A. von Stosch (Marburg) generously read the text of the first edition critically and made valuable suggestions, and Prof. Dr W. Nultsch (Marburg) also gave important comments and advice. Prof. Dr F. Round (Bristol) put unpublished electron micrographs at our disposal. Special thanks are also due to Dr A.M. Breeman, Dr W.T. Stam, Dr W.W.C. Gieskes (Groningen) and Prof. Dr K. Kowallik (Düsseldorf) for their critical comments on certain chapters. As in the previous German editions, numerous illustrations, from various publications, have been redrawn or revised; the source of each is given in the text. Others have been taken from the original publications without alteration; this has been done with the agreement of the authors and publishers, to whom we offer our gratitude. Finally, thanks should go to Cambridge University Press and to Thieme Verlag for their patient and sympathetic cooperation.

C. van den Hoek

D.G. Mann

H.M. Jahns

Groningen, Edinburgh and Düsseldorf

Introduction

The daisy; the hierarchy of systematic categories; the concept of relationships in systematics

The botanical entity we call the daisy (scientific name: *Bellis perennis* L.) is an abstract concept, which has been built up from observations of all the separate, individual daisy plants that have been seen. We recognize these plants as daisies because they exhibit certain characteristics; we group them together because of their similarity to each other. The daisy is a systematic category, in this case a **species**. The characteristics of this species, that is to say the features common to all daisy plants, can be listed thus:

> the capitulum bears yellow tube florets at its centre and white ray florets at its edge;
>
> the fruits lack a pappus;
>
> the stalk bears only one capitulum;
>
> the bracts are arranged in two rows and are all of roughly the same length;
>
> the receptacle is conical and does not bear scales;
>
> the leaves are spathulate and obtuse, and are borne on short stalks in a basal rosette; their margins bear several short teeth.

This detailed description of the daisy has clearly been produced by a specialist in plant systematics. But of course, you don't have to be a plant systematist to be able to recognize a daisy. A layman, however, will not use the same characters as a specialist; instead, he will recognize daisies by other features, such as:

> small plant;
>
> weed growing in short turf;
>
> white flower with yellow centre.

In everyday life we use the category 'daisy' in much the same way as we employ words like 'tree', 'shrub' or 'church': each is an abstraction, drawn from a number of similar organisms or entities. Language consists of such abstractions.

Our example can be extended to illustrate other aspects of systematics. We all know that daisies are plants, while churches are buildings. What we are saying, in other words, is that the category 'daisy' belongs to the broader, more inclusive category 'plant', while 'church' belongs to the more inclusive category 'building'. We are constructing hierarchies of concepts, and in such hierarchies the concepts 'building' and 'plant' stand higher than the concepts 'church' and 'daisy'. The 'plant' category belongs in turn to the category 'living thing', which is higher in the hierarchy because it is more inclusive. We can summarize this hierarchy thus:

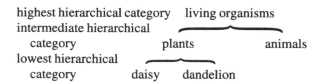

highest hierarchical category   living organisms

intermediate hierarchical

   category   plants   animals

lowest hierarchical

   category   daisy   dandelion

The level of abstraction increases from the lowest category to the highest.

Biologists arrange living organisms in hierarchical systems, which are constructed in essentially the same way as the everyday hierarchies of concepts outlined above. All of us are continually constructing hierarchical systems, to help us deal with and make sense of the world. As we might expect, however, the systems developed by biologists for arranging animals and plants are much more complex than the systems we devise in everyday life; they are much more highly differentiated and the number of characters used in their construction is much greater. To see this, we have only to look again at the lists of characteristics used by botanists and laymen to recognize the daisy!

In plant systematics six main systematic categories are used. From the highest to the lowest these are:

Divisio   (division) e.g. Chlorophyta

Classis   (class)   e.g. Chlorophyceae

Ordo   (order)   e.g. Volvocales

Familia   (family)   e.g. Chlamydomonadaceae

Genus   (genus)   e.g. *Chlamydomonas*

Species   (species) e.g. *Chlamydomonas*
                      eugametos

Often these categories are themselves subdivided, Divisio into Subdivisio, Classis into Subclassis, and so on. In animal systematics the highest category is called **phylum**, rather than division, and this term is often used also in the algae.

Members of a species (e.g. of the species 'daisy') resemble each other more closely than they do the members of any other species. How has this come to be so? Even by the beginning of the nineteenth century the similarities within species were being attributed to the fact that all the individuals in a species belong to a single reproductive unit, an interbreeding community (commiscuum; [31]). But this is not in itself a sufficient explanation. Mixing or re-assortment of the characteristics borne by different individuals can only occur through sexual reproduction, and yet there are many species of algae (and fungi) that do not reproduce sexually, only asexually. How then do individuals of these species come to resemble each other so closely? We must assume that all the living members of a species have descended from a common ancestor, which had a similar appearance to its descendants. This also applies, of course, to all of the species that can reproduce sexually; it must be assumed that all the individuals alive now have descended from one or a few similar ancestors. In other words, whatever the breeding system, individuals belonging to the same species are closely related to each other because of a postulated common ancestry. The great similarity between the members of a single species is explained by their close relationship, although this is generally only presumed, not proven.

Just as the similarity between the members of a species can be accounted for by their close relation-

ship, so too the similarity between the various species within a genus can be taken to reflect their (postulated) close relationship. Species of the same genus are more similar to each other than to species of a different genus because they are more closely related to each other than to the species of any other genus. Correspondingly, genera belonging to one family should be more closely related to each other than to the genera of any other family, and the families within an order should be more closely related to each other than to families belonging to other orders. This train of thought leads us in the end to the idea that all living organisms are at least distantly related: all share a common ancestor, from which they have descended with many modifications. As is well known, this line of argument was pursued with genius by Charles Darwin ([287]) in his theory of evolution.

Evolution and phylogeny: the symbiosis theory

It is now thought that early in the course of evolution, very simply constructed eukaryotic cells captured and ingested prokaryotic cells and then 'tamed' them, so that they became organelles. Prokaryotes (**Prokaryota**) are organisms that have no nucleus, no golgi apparatus, no endoplasmic reticulum, no mitochondria and no plastids (p. 16). The various organisms classed as eukaryotes (**Eukaryota**), on the other hand, have all or most of these organelles. To the Prokaryota belong the bacteria and the blue-green algae (which are also known as the cyanobacteria); all other living organisms belong to the Eukaryota. The idea that the evolution of the eukaryotes has involved the capture and subsequent endosymbiosis of prokaryotic cells is not new. It was formulated in detail by Mereschkowsky ([1195]), long before the nature of the distinction between prokaryotic and eukaryotic cells was fully understood. For a long time Mereschkowsky's ideas were discounted, but in the past 20 years various lines of evidence (from biochemical, electron microscopical and molecular biological studies) have led many people to accept the principles of the symbiosis theory he proposed ([1121, 1122, 1123, 1537]). According to the theory, eukaryotic cell organelles like chloroplasts and mitochondria are supposed to have originally been independent, free-living prokaryotes. Chloroplasts are supposed to have arisen from blue-green algal cells, mitochondria from bacteria. At first the blue-green algae and bacteria lived as symbionts within the host cells; then they were gradually transformed into organelles.

The following arguments have been used to support the symbiosis theory.

1 Even today there are organisms that contain endosymbiotic blue-green algae serving as chloroplasts. An example is *Geosiphon pyriforme*, a filamentous fungus that can be found in the autumn, growing on clay soils together with the liverwort *Anthoceros*. The fungus forms vesicular cells about 1 mm in diameter, which contain filaments of the photosynthetic blue-green alga *Nostoc* (Figs. 1.1*b*, 2.5*b*). Both partners in the symbiosis can be cultured separately ([859]) and indeed, the *Nostoc* species is also to be found free in nature ([1572]).

2 Chloroplasts and mitochondria are to some extent autonomous. Chloroplasts normally divide independently of the nucleus and they possess their own DNA, allowing for a certain degree of genetic independence. The same is true for mitochondria ([16, 93, 1766]). According to the symbiosis theory, these features are a relic from the time when the organelles were free-living prokaryotes. It must be stressed, however, that mitochondria and chloroplasts have undergone profound changes since their origin as endosymbiotic bacteria and blue-green algae. Their genomes are now about a tenth of the size of bacterial genomes, and many of the proteins found within them are imported, having been synthesized elsewhere in the cell under the control of genes in the nucleus ([16]).

3 The chloroplasts of certain algae have retained more of the characteristics of blue-green algae (= cyanobacteria) than 'typical' chloroplasts have, and can therefore be interpreted as being intermediate between chloroplasts and blue-green algae. For instance, the chloroplasts of the freshwater algae *Glaucocystis* and *Cyanophora* (division Glaucophyta: see p. 45) resemble unicellular blue-green algae to such an extent that they have long been considered as symbiotic blue-green algae, living within the cells of a heterotrophic host (Fig. 1.1*a*); they are often referred to as 'cyanelles'. In their ultrastructure,

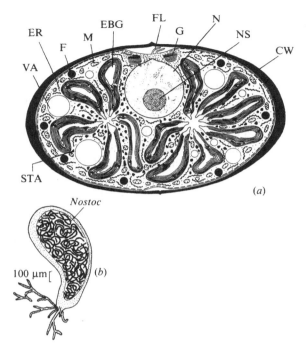

Figure 1.1. (*a*) *Glaucocystis,* cell ultrastructure. (*b*) *Geosiphon pyriforme*, containing filaments of *Nostoc*. CW = cell wall; EBG = hypothetical endosymbiotic blue-green alga (cyanobacterium); ER = endoplasmic reticulum; F = lipid globule; FL = rudimentary flagellum; G = golgi body; M = mitochondrion; N = nucleus; NS = nucleolus; STA = starch; VA = vacuole (*a* from [1579]; *b* after [1555]).

the cyanelles are very similar to blue-green algae, possessing equidistant thylakoids (paired photosynthetic membranes), which are not stacked and bear rows of phycobilisomes (small bodies containing phycobilin pigments). Cyanelles and blue-green algae also resemble each other in the central location of their DNA and the presence around them of a peptidoglycan wall, although this is vestigial in cyanelles (compare Figs. 1.1*a* and 5.1*b* with Fig. 2.1*a*; [356, 840, 841, 842, 843, 844, 845, 1579]). Cyanelles, however, are incapable of living outside their 'host' ([845]) and their genomes are about a tenth the size of blue-green algal genomes ([645]), facts that underline their organellar nature. Recent molecular biological investigations of the evolutionary position of the glaucophyte 'cyanelles', involving studies of genome structure ([960, 1025]), have confirmed their intermediate, bridging position between blue-green algae (cyanobacteria) and chloroplasts; this topic will be treated more fully in chapters 4 (Glaucophyta; p. 45) and 32 (p. 496).

4 Recently, comparisons of nucleotide sequences in the ribosomal RNAs of mitochondria, chloroplasts and prokaryotes have confirmed that there is a close phylogenetic link between mitochondria and certain aerobic, heterotrophic bacteria, and between chloroplasts and the photoautotrophic blue-green algae (= cyanobacteria; [204, 526, 1910, 1914]) (for a fuller treatment, see pp. 39, 503–6).

Fig. 1.2 shows diagrammatically how a eukaryotic, flagellate plant cell might have arisen, through the amalgamation of separate prokaryotic cells with a primitive eukaryotic cell. The main events of this process are outlined below.

1 While the earth's atmosphere was still free of oxygen, a primitive eukaryote arose, which was a phagotrophic, amoeboid anaerobe. This 'Ur-karyote' is only hypothetical, and many changes must have occurred during the evolution of the Ur-karyote from a prokaryotic ancestor. Thus, for instance, cells can form pseudopodia and take up food particles into food vacuoles only if their protoplasm is fluid and can stream rapidly. Eukaryotes have such protoplasm. All extant prokaryotes, on the other hand, have stiff, viscous protoplasm. This cannot form pseudopodia and does not contain vacuoles, so that prokary-

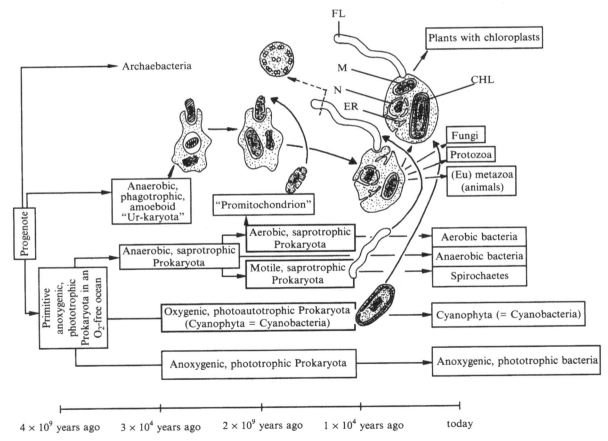

Figure 1.2. Origin of the eukaryotic cell through the association of several different prokaryotic cells with an 'Ur-eukaryote'. CHL = chloroplast; ER = endoplasmic reticulum; FL = flagellum (with '9 + 2' structure); M = mitochondrion; N = nucleus.

otes are unable to feed phagotrophically through the uptake of solid food particles.

2 Around two billion years ago, certain of the phagotrophic Ur-karyotes took up a 'promito-chondrion'. This was an aerobic, saprotrophic prokaryote (an aerobic bacterium), which was not digested by the Ur-karyote, but was instead retained and incorporated into the host cell as the mitochondrion. Henceforth it served as an organelle, carrying out the respiration of the amoeboid, phagotrophic Ur-karyote, which thus became an aerobic organism. It must have been the free-living ancestor of the mitochondrion that was aerobic, rather than the Ur-karyote itself, since today it is the mitochondrion, not the cytoplasm, that is responsible for respiration in eukaryotic cells (this process is absolutely dependent on oxygen).

3 About 1.5 billion years ago, some of the aerobic, heterotrophic Ur-karyotes that had arisen as a result of the first symbiotic union (event 2) took up another motile, saprotrophic prokaryote. This prokaryote (which again is entirely hypothetical) was not amoeboid, but possessed microtubules in a '9 + 2' arrangement, just as in the flagella of eukaryotic cells (where there are two central tubules and nine peripheral doublets). The flagellum was not completely ingested by the amoeboid host Ur-karyote, but remained 'stuck in its throat'; henceforth it acted as a locomotor organelle for the host, becoming the eukaryote flagellum with its typical '9 + 2' internal structure. Meanwhile, the endoplasmic reticulum arose through invagination of the plasma-lemma, and from the endoplasmic reticulum came the nuclear envelope; this surrounded the DNA, which had by now become complexed with histone proteins.

The first authors to suggest this explanation of the origins of eukaryotic flagellates thought that spirochaete-like organisms might have been the ancestors of flagella ([1121, 1122, 1123, 1537]). Spirochaetes are elongate, helical bacteria, which have an axial filament consisting of a bundle of fibrils. This lies beneath the cell surface and by its activities (perhaps through contraction) causes the cell to move. The structure of spirochaetes is quite different from the '9 + 2' structure of flagella, but recently evidence has been presented that indicates that flagella do have a degree of genetic autonomy and this seems to favour the idea of a symbiotic origin. The flagellar basal bodies of the unicellular green alga *Chlamydomonas* (cf. p. 306, Fig. 19.4) appear to contain a linear DNA molecule, with genes coding for proteins in the basal body complex. As in chloroplasts and mitochondria, the organelle genome of the basal body codes for only a portion of the basal body proteins, the others being encoded by nuclear genes ([539, 596]). In spite of the presence of DNA in the basal bodies, however, a symbiotic origin for flagella remains questionable.

The steps outlined so far would have produced the first eukaryotic flagellates, which were heterotrophs. From them various groups of heterotrophic eukaryotes could have arisen, such as unicellular protozoans, and also the multicellular animals and fungi.

4 Finally, the heterotrophic flagellates took up blue-green algal cells (cyanobacteria) and so transformed themselves into the first photoautotrophic eukaryotes. These first photoautotrophic flagellates gave rise to various groups of photoautotrophic algae and ultimately also to the land plants.

Evolution and phylogeny: the fan-shaped phylogenetic tree

The theory explained above assumes a monophyletic origin of the eukaryotes, which is supported by the fundamental similarity between all eukaryote cells ([20]), and also by phylogenetic trees based on nucleotide sequences. Comparisons of ribosomal RNA sequences in a wide variety of prokaryotes and eukaryotes reveal the existence of three major groups or kingdoms of organisms: two kingdoms of prokaryotes, namely the **Archaebacteria** and **Eubacteria**, and the kingdom **Eukaryota**. These three kingdoms are internally coherent and only very distantly related to each other ([526, 589, 735, 1471, 1661]); this topic will be examined in more detail on p. 39.

We will therefore assume the existence of ancestral Ur-karyotes, which later took up and incorporated several prokaryotes to form certain of the cell organelles characteristic of eukaryotes (the symbiosis theory). From the Ur-karyotes came all the eukaryote phyla (= divisions) that exist today, and this can be illustrated in a fan-shaped phylogenetic tree (Fig. 1.3; [982,

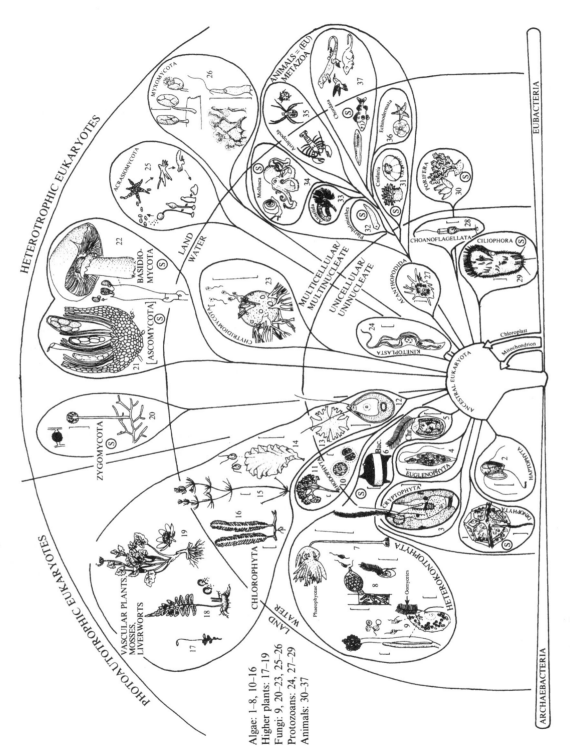

HETEROTROPHIC EUKARYOTES

PHOTOAUTOTROPHIC EUKARYOTES

ANIMALS = (EU) METAZOA

MYXOMYCOTA 26

ACRASIOMYCOTA 25

BASIDIO- MYCOTA (S) 22

[ASCOMYCOTA] (S) 21

CHYTRIDIOMYCOTA 23

LAND
WATER

MULTICELLULAR/ MULTINUCLEATE

UNICELLULAR/ UNINUCLEATE

ACANTHOPODIDA 27

KINETOPLASTA 24

CHOANOFLAGELLATA 28

CILIOPHORA (S) 29

PORIFERA (S) 30

Cnidaria 31

Echinodermata 36

Chordata 37

Arthropoda

Mollusca

Annelida 34

Platyhelminthes 32

Platyhelminthes 33

ANCESTRAL EUKARYOTA

Chloroplast
Mitochondrion

ZYGOMYCOTA (S) 20

VASCULAR PLANTS, MOSSES, LIVERWORTS

CHLOROPHYTA

LAND
WATER

HETEROKONTOPHYTA

HAPTOPHYTA 2

DINOPHYTA (S) 1

CRYPTOPHYTA 3

EUGLENOPHYTA 4

Bac. 6
Chl. 5

Oomycetes
Phaeophyceae 8
9
7

17
18
19
16
15
14
13
12
11
10

EUBACTERIA

ARCHAEBACTERIA

Algae: 1–8, 10–16
Higher plants: 17–19
Fungi: 9, 20–23, 25–26
Protozoans: 24, 27–29
Animals: 30–37

For legend see opposite page.

[1913]). The tree shows the eukaryotes as monophyletic, but with a very early radiation into several major groups. The Archaebacteria and Eubacteria are also shown as monophyletic, sharing a common ancestor with the Eukaryota right at the bottom of the phylogenetic tree; this common ancestor of all living organisms is called the 'Progenote' by Woese ([1913, 1914]; see also Fig. 1.2). The phylogenetic tree also shows the incorporation into the ancestral eukaryotes of the eubacterial ancestors of mitochondria and chloroplasts.

Direct derivation of all the phyla of photoautotrophic and heterotrophic eukaryotes from a single, admittedly hypothetical, group of Ur-karyotes explains two important aspects of eukaryotes. It explains why all eukaryotes have fundamentally the same cell structure and also why great differences exist between the main lineages and divisions. Following the appearance of the ancestral eukaryotes, the first great evolutionary radiation took place at the cellular level. In the course of this many types of unicellular organism arose, differing in the plan and structure of their cells, although all are only variations on a eukaryotic theme. Some of the variants acquired chloroplasts and became photoautotrophic; these are shown on the left-hand side of the phylogenetic tree. Others did not and remained heterotrophic; these are placed on the right-hand side of the tree. Note that this arrangement, of the photoautotrophs on the left and the heterotrophs on the right, has only been made for clarity; we would stress that proximity between different branches in the fan does not in general indicate a close phylogenetic relationship.

A further point worth making is that the fan-shaped tree shows that the fungi, as they have traditionally been circumscribed, are an unnatural group. The fungal class Oomycetes (which includes among others the downy mildews, which are important pathogens of various agricultural crops) belongs in the algal division Heterokontophyta, because its members have typical heterokontophyte zoids (flagellate cells), with mastigonemes (stiff tubular hairs) on the anterior flagellum ([57, 1640, 1862]).

It is somehow a very attractive idea, that chloroplasts might originally have been endosymbionts and perhaps have had different origins, some developing from prokaryotic endosymbionts and others from eukaryotes (as in the endosymbionts of the Cryptophyta and Dinophyta: see pp. 237, 251, 510–12). Unfortunately, until recently only the chloroplasts of red algae seemed to have free-living equivalents, namely the prokaryotic blue-green algae (compare Fig. 2.1a with Fig. 5.11b). Red algal chloroplasts and blue-green algal cells have a similar pigment composition, both containing the accessory photosynthetic pigments phycocyanin, allophycocyanin and phycoerythrin, together with chlorophyll a but not chlorophyll b or c. The three accessory phycobilin pigments are contained in special particles, called phycobilisomes, which lie on the surfaces of the thylakoids (see p. 25), while the thylakoids are single, parallel and more or less equidistant (compare Fig. 2.1a with Fig. 5.11b).

Figure 1.3. Fan-shaped phylogenetic tree. (s = phyla containing heterotrophic species that form photoautotrophic symbioses with algae or higher plants).
1. *Peridinium*, scale = 15 μm. 2. *Chrysochromulina*, scale = 5 μm. 3. *Cryptomonas*, scale = 5 μm.
4. *Euglena*, scale = 40 μm. 5. *Ochromonas* (class Chrysophyceae), scale = 10 μm. 6. *Cerataulus* (class Bacillariophyceae), scale = 10 μm. 7. *Laminaria* (class Phaeophyceae), scale = 1 m. 8. *Ectocarpus* (class Phaeophyceae), scales = 50 μm (thallus) and 10 μm (pleuronematic zoid). 9. *Achlya* (class Oomycetes), scales = 20 μm (thallus) and 2 μm (pleuronematic zoid). 10. *Porphyridium* (class Bangiophyceae), scale = 4 μm. 11. *Chondrus* (class Florideophyceae), scale = 1 cm. 12. *Chlamydomonas* (class Chlorophyceae), scale = 5 μm. 13. *Micrasterias* (class Zygnematophyceae), scale = 50 μm.
14. *Ulva* (class Ulvophyceae), scale = 5 cm.
15. *Chara* (class Charophyceae), scale = 1 cm.
16. *Caulerpa* (class Bryopsidophyceae), scale = 1 cm.
17. A moss (class Bryopsida). 18. *Polypodium*, a fern (class Pteropsida). 19. *Ficaria verna*, a flowering plant (class Magnoliopsida). 20. *Mucor* (bread mould), scale = 50 μm. 21. *Ascobolus* (a tiny ascomycete on dung or plant litter), scale = 50 μm.
22. *Agaricus* (mushroom), scale (for basidium) = 10 μm. 23. *Rhizophlyctis* (a mould on lake mud), scales = 100 μm (cell) and 5 μm (zoid). 24. *Trypanosoma* (protozoan causing human sleeping sickness), scale = 4 μm. 25. *Dictyostelium* (cellular slime mould), cell about 10 μm, sporangium about 0.5 mm. 26. *Physarum* (slime mould), scales = 1 mm (sporangia and plasmodium) and 10 μm (zoid). 27. *Acanthamoeba* (soil amoeba; order Acanthopodida in phylum Rhizopoda), scale = 10 μm. 28. *Codonosiga* (collar flagellate, a freshwater protozoan), scale = 10 μm. 29. *Stylonichia* (a ciliated protozoan), scale = 40 μm. 30. Sponges. 31–37. Examples of the most important phyla of the (Eu)metazoa (multicellular animals).

No prokaryotic algae resembling the chloroplasts of other algal divisions were known until an interesting group of prokaryotes was discovered that are like the chloroplasts of green algae (division Chlorophyta) and could perhaps be regarded as their ancestors. These prokaryotic algae, which are called the Prochlorophyta, contain chlorophylls a and b and have stacked thylakoids, while they lack phycobilin pigments and phycobilisomes. In all these respects they are like the chloroplasts of the Chlorophyta ([167, 998, 999, 1001, 1589]). A direct link between green algal chloroplasts and prochlorophytes, however, is not supported unequivocally by molecular evidence. In fact, rRNA (ribosomal RNA) sequences suggest that the chloroplasts of green algae are more closely related to certain of the blue-green algae than they are to the prochlorophytes (cf. p. 44).

Of the groups of unicellular eukaryotes that evolved from the primitive Ur-karyotes, eight have given rise to multicellular forms: these are three phyla of photoautotrophs – the Heterokontophyta, Rhodophyta and Chlorophyta – together with the Zygomycota, Ascomycota, Basidiomycota, Porifera and Animalia, which are all groups of heterotrophs (Fig. 1.3). The bewildering diversity in these groups reflects the high degree of specialization and division of labour possible in multicellular tissues. Multicellular organisms derived from one of the photoautotrophic lineages (the Chlorophyta), and multicellular representatives of four of the heterotrophic lineages (the Zygomycota, Ascomycota, Basidiomycota and the animals), have successfully invaded terrestrial habitats and now dominate them. The Chlorophyta (green algae) gave rise to the vascular plants, together with the mosses and liverworts, while most terrestrial animals belong to three animal phyla: the Chordata (which includes ourselves), Arthropoda (spiders, insects, etc.), and Mollusca (land snails). The Zygomycota, Ascomycota and Basidiomycota include most of the terrestrial fungi.

The importance of phylogenetic (evolutionary) theories in systematics

Must systematics be deduced from evolution, as is often maintained? In other words, must we first work out the course of evolution, at least in its broad outlines, before we can construct a good system of classification? No, this would be a hopeless undertaking. Most of the evidence we would need has been lost and many organisms have left no trace in the fossil record. Our phylogenetic reconstructions must always remain more or less speculative, to be replaced by other reconstructions as our knowledge improves. They are often only plausible guesses. Furthermore, the example of the daisy (p. 1) shows that an evolutionary basis for classification is not essential. The systematist builds systematic groups and categories on the basis of similarities between organisms; then he arranges the groups in a hierarchical system. The development of a hierarchical system does not depend on evolutionary theory!

On the other hand, it must be admitted that a completely non-phylogenetic system, though it might catalogue organisms in a convenient way, would probably have little biological meaning. It is unlikely that it could be used to generate hypotheses capable of explaining the diversity of life, which is one of the most intriguing aspects of biology. And although we do not know the exact course of evolution and cannot construct an accurate phylogenetic tree, we do now have a good idea about the limits of the main groups of organisms (e.g. the divisions or phyla) that have been produced through evolution. Each of these 'natural' groups or taxa consists of a set of organisms that are more closely related to each other than to organisms of a different group. This interrelationship is inferred from fundamental similarities in their traits (homologies) and is thought to reflect fundamental similarities in their genomes, as a result of common descent. It has recently become possible to check how similar the genomes are within a group of organisms (taxon), by comparing the structures of macromolecules, such as by determining nucleotide sequences within selected genes using molecular biological techniques; this topic will be dealt with in greater detail on pp. 37–40. Let it suffice here to say that studies of macromolecules tend to confirm the internal genetic coherence of the major groups and divisions (= phyla), such as the Cyanophyta (= Cyanobacteria), Hetero-kontophyta, Rhodophyta, Chlorophyta, Tracheophyta (the vascular plants), Ascomycota, Basidiomycota, Ciliophora and Chordata. Molecular biological approaches also allow us to check hypotheses about the phylogeny of taxa. Thus, it has been possible to confirm that the Tracheophyta must have been derived from chlorophyte (green algal) ancestors, and that the various phyla of multicellular animals classified in the (Eu-)-metazoa do indeed all share a common ancestry (Fig. 1.3; [204, 526, 589, 735, 1471]).

What are algae and what is their place in the system?

In 1754 Carl von Linné ([1015]) divided the plant kingdom into 25 classes, of which one, the **Cryptogamia**, contained all plants with 'concealed' reproductive organs, i.e. all plants lacking both seeds and flowers.

Linné referred four groups to the Cryptogamia, namely the **Algae, Fungi, Musci** and **Filices**. His classification is also found, essentially unchanged, in Eichler's system of 1883 ([365]), which is reproduced below:

A   Cryptogamae (spore-producing plants)
  I Division: Thallophyta (lower plants, with a thallus)
    1 Class: Algae (algae, seaweeds)
    2 Class: Fungi (mushrooms, toadstools, moulds)
  II Division: Bryophyta (mosses and liverworts)
  III Division: Pteridophyta (vascular cryptogams)

B   Phanerogamae (seed plants)
  I Division: Gymnospermae (plants with naked seeds)
  II Division: Angiospermae (plants with enclosed seeds)
    1 Class: Monokotyleae (plants with one cotyledon)
    2 Class: Dikotyleae (plants with two cotyledons)

Some other classifications, on the other hand, made a fundamental distinction between the Thallophyta, in which the plant body is not or only slightly differentiated, and the Kormophyta, in which there is differentiation into roots, stems and leaves.

Eichler's system found many adherents. Indeed, it is still used today and therefore must be taught to botanists, but most systematists now consider it to be incorrect. It is doubtful whether any of Eichler's divisions are 'natural', except for the Bryophyta, Gymnospermae and Angiospermae. Eichler's divisions of the plants into two main groups, Cryptogamae and Phanerogamae, implies that ferns (which belong to the Pteridophyta) are to be considered more closely related to the blue-green algae (in the Algae) than they are to flowering plants. This is clearly wrong. Ferns are much closer to flowering plants than to blue-green algae (i.e. they agree with them in many more respects), a fact that can be established without detailed study. Thus, for instance, the leaves, aerial stems and vascular tissues of ferns and flowering plants contrast sharply with the unicellular or simply multicellular organization of blue-green algae, which are also, of course, prokaryotic. The division Thallophyta, and even the classes Algae and Fungi, can also no longer be regarded as satisfactory groupings.

Systematists strive to produce a **natural system**, and their attempts often resemble each other very closely. The classification we use here (Table 1.1) is based on the idea that all the main groups of eukaryotes have evolved independently of each other for a long time, as shown diagrammatically in the fan-shaped phylogenetic tree of Fig. 1.3.

Why, then, have we written a book about algae, when we have just admitted that the algae are an unnatural group of organisms? The answer lies in the history of plant systematics. Even in the last century the study of plant systematics had been split up into a series of separate disciplines, which reflected the classification of the plant kingdom that was then current, i.e. Eichler's system. Thus the discipline called phycology (or algology) is concerned with algae, mycology with fungi, and bryology with mosses and liverworts; workers in these fields call themselves phycologists (algologists), mycologists and bryologists, respectively.

Since this book is about algae, we must attempt to define what algae are, even if the group is unnatural. We might say, perhaps, that algae are very diverse photosynthetic plants that have neither roots nor leafy shoots, and which also lack vascular tissues; certain algae are not able to photosynthesize but are nevertheless classified as algae because of their close resemblance to photosynthetic forms. We could define fungi in a like manner, as systematically very diverse, non-photosynthetic plants without roots, leafy shoots or vascular bundles.

These definitions of 'algae' and 'fungi' shift the problem on one stage further, to the question: what are plants? And in addition, what are animals? How are

Table 1.1. *Summary of the most important kingdoms, divisions (= phyla) and classes of organisms*

All of the divisions and classes of algae are listed (see [1378, 1640, 1862]). The organisms generally regarded as 'plants' are the following.
Cryptogamae: I-XIII, XIV.1–4, XV–XX; Phanerogamae: XIV.5–9; Thallophyta: II–XII, XV–XX; Algae: II–XII; Fungi: XV–XX; Bryophyta: XIII; Pteridophyta: XIV.1–4; Gymnospermae: XIV.5–8; Angiospermae: XIV.9.
The organisms regarded as animals are Protozoa: XXI–XXVI; Parazoa (= Porifera): XXVII; and (Eu)metazoa: XXVIII–XXXIV

Regnum (Kingdom)	Divisio (phylum) (Division)		Classis (Class)		Fig. 1.3
a. ARCHAE-BACTERIA		Phyla of Archaebacteria			
b. EUBACTERIA	I.	Other phyla of the Eubacteria			
	II.	Cyanophyta (= Cyano-bacteria)	1.	Cyanophyceae	
	III.	Prochlorophyta (= Chloroxybacteria)	1.	Prochlorophyceae	
	IV.	Glaucophyta	1.	Glaucophyceae	
	V.	Rhodophyta	1.	Bangiophyceae	10
			2.	Florideophyceae	11
	VI.	Heterokontophyta	1.	Chrysophyceae	5
			2.	Parmophyceae	
			3.	Sarcinochrysidophyceae	
			4.	Xanthophyceae	
			5.	Eustigmatophyceae	
			6.	Bacillariophyceae	6
			7.	Raphidophyceae	
			8.	Dictyochophyceae	
			9.	Phaeophyceae	7,8
			10.	Oömycetes	9
	VII.	Haptophyta	1.	Haptophyceae	2
	VIII.	Cryptophyta	1.	Cryptophyceae	3
	IX.	Dinophyta	1.	Dinophyceae	1
	X.	Euglenophyta	1.	Euglenophyceae	4
	XI.	Chlorarachniophyta	1.	Chlorarachniophyceae	
	XII.	Chlorophyta	1.	Prasinophyceae	
			2.	Chlorophyceae	12
			3.	Ulvophyceae	14
			4.	Cladophorophyceae	
			5.	Bryopsidophyceae	16
			6.	Zygnematophyceae	13
			7.	Trentepohliophyceae	
			8.	Klebsormidiophyceae	
			9.	Charophyceae	15

Prokaryota

c. EUKARYOTA — 'Plants' ('Plantae') — 'Algae'

Table 1.1. (*cont.*)

Regnum (Kingdom)		Divisio (phylum) (Division)		Classis (Class)		Fig. 1.3
c. EUKARYOTA (continued) — Plants (continued) — 'Higher plants'		XIII.	Bryophyta	1.	Hepaticopsida	
				2.	Anthocerotopsida	
				3.	Bryopsida	17
		XIV.	Tracheophyta	1.	Psilotopsida	
				2.	Lycopsida	
				3.	Sphenopsida	
				4.	Pteropsida	18
				5.	Cycadopsida	
				6.	Ginkgopsida	
				7.	Coniferopsida	
				8.	Gnetopsida	
				9.	Magnoliopsida	19
'Fungi'		XV.	Myxomycota	1.	Myxomycetes	26
		XVI.	Acrasiomycota	1.	Acrasiomycetes	25
		XVII.	Chytridiomycota	1.	Chytridiomycetes	23
		XVIII.	Zygomycota	1.	Zygomycetes	20
		XIX.	Ascomycota	1.	Ascomycetes	21
		XX.	Basidiomycota	1.	Basidiomycetes	22
'Protozoa'		XXI.	Kinetoplasta			24
		XXII.	Choanoflagellata			28
		XXIII.	Ciliophora			29
		XXIV.	Rhizopoda	e.g. 1.	Lobosea (contains the order Acanthopodida)	27
				2.	Granuloreticulosea (contains the order Foraminiferida)	
		XXV.	Actinopoda	e.g. 1.	Polycystinea ('Radiolaria')	
		XXVI.	Sporozoa			
'Animals' ('Animalia') — Eumatazoa		XXVII.	Porifera			30
		XXVIII.	Cnidaria			31
		XXXIX.	Platyhelminthes			32
		XXX.	Mollusca			34
		XXXI.	Annelida			33
		XXXII.	Arthropoda			35
		XXXIII.	Echinodermata			36
		XXXIV.	Chordata			37

Table 1.2. *Algal pigments*

⊕ = important pigment; + = pigment is present; ± = pigment occurs rarely, or in small amounts. Dinophyta I: normal Dinophyta. Dinophyta II: Dinophyta with brown endosymbiotic algae.

	Cyanophyta	Prochlorophyta	Glaucophyta	Rhodophyta	Heterokontophyta/Chrysophyceae	Heterokontophyta/Xanthophyceae	Heterokontophyta/Eustigmatophyceae	Heterokontophyta/Bacillariophyceae	Heterokontophyta/Raphidophyceae	Heterokontophyta/Dictyochophyceae	Heterokontophyta/Phaeophyceae	Haptophyta	Cryptophyta	Dinophyta I	Dinophyta II	Euglenophyta	Chlorarachniophyta	Chlorophyta
Chlorophylls																		
chlorophyll a	⊕	⊕	⊕	⊕	⊕	⊕	⊕	⊕	⊕	⊕	⊕	⊕	⊕	⊕	⊕	⊕	⊕	⊕
chlorophyll b		⊕														⊕	⊕	⊕
chlorophyll c_1					⊕	+		⊕	⊕		⊕	⊕			⊕			
chlorophyll c_2					⊕	+		⊕	⊕	⊕[4]	⊕	⊕	⊕	⊕	⊕	⊕		±[8]
chlorophyll c_3					±			⊕			⊕							
Phycobilins																		
phycocyanin	⊕		⊕	⊕									⊕					
allophycocyanin	⊕		⊕	⊕														
phycoerythrin	⊕		⊕										⊕					
phycobilisomes	⊕		⊕	⊕														
Carotenes																		
α-carotene					⊕	+						+	⊕		+			±
β-carotene	⊕	⊕	⊕	⊕	⊕	⊕	⊕	⊕	⊕	⊕	⊕	⊕	⊕	±	⊕	⊕	⊕	⊕
γ-carotene																±		±
ε-carotene						+		+		+		±						
Xanthophylls																		
zeaxanthin	⊕	⊕	⊕	⊕	+			±	+[3]		±		+			±		+
echinenone	⊕	+							+			+			+	±		±
canthaxanthin	⊕							+	+			+			+			
myxoxanthophyll	⊕																	
oscillaxanthin	⊕																	
α-cryptoxanthin					±	+		±					+					
β-cryptoxanthin	+	+	+	±		±	±									±		±
isocryptoxanthin	+	+																
mutachrome	+	+																

Table 1.2. (*cont.*)

	Cyanophyta	Prochlorophyta	Glaucophyta	Rhodophyta	Heterokontophyta/Chrysophyceae	Heterokontophyta/Xanthophyceae	Heterokontophyta/Eustigmatophyceae	Heterokontophyta/Bacillariophyceae	Heterokontophyta/Raphidophyceae	Heterokontophyta/Dictyochophyceae	Heterokontophyta/Phaeophyceae	Haptophyta	Cryptophyta	Dinophyta I	Dinophyta II	Euglenophyta	Chlorarachniophyta	Chlorophyta
lutein				+						+							+	⊕
antheraxanthin				±	+		+				+							+
violaxanthin				±	+		⊕		+[3]		⊕						+	⊕
fucoxanthin					⊕			⊕[3]	⊕	⊕	⊕	⊕			⊕			
neofucoxanthin					+			+							+			
fucoxanthin – der. [1]												⊕[5]			⊕[5]			
fucoxanthin – der. [2]												⊕[5]						
diatoxanthin					+	⊕		⊕		+	+	⊕			⊕		±	
diadinoxanthin					+	⊕		⊕	⊕	+	+	⊕		⊕	⊕	+		
vaucheriaxanthin						⊕	⊕		+									
heteroxanthin						⊕			+									
alloxanthin													⊕					
dinoxanthin									+			+		+				
peridinin														⊕				
neoxanthin					+	+	+	+	+		+					⊕	+	⊕
siphonein																		+[6]
siphonoxanthin																		+[6,7]
crocoxanthin													+					
monadoxanthin													+					
pyrroxanthin														+				

[1] 19'-hexanoyloxyfucoxanthin; [2] 19'-butanoyloxyfucoxanthin; [3] in marine (not in freshwater) species of the division; [4] chlorophyll c of some kind, but not further specified; [5] in some species; [6] in Bryopsidophyceae; [7] scattered in several classes; [8] a chlorophyll c-like pigment is present in 5 green algae of the class Prasinophyceae. (Data from [32, 83, 88, 167, 195, 220, 402, 544, 582, 593, 594, 666, 667, 793, 794, 795, 854, 857, 974, 997a, 1005, 1056, 1128, 1129, 1159, 1284, 1350, 1379, 1442, 1463, 1532a, 1464, 1488, 1525, 1570, 1689, 1885, 1898, 1908]).

Table 1.3. *The main storage products of the algal divisions and classes*

	Cyanophyta	Prochlorophyta	Glaucophyta	Rhodophyta	Heterokontophyta/Chrysophyceae	Heterokontophyta/Xanthophyceae	Heterokontophyta/Eustigmatophyceae	Heterokontophyta/Bacillariophyceae	Heterokontophyta/Raphidophyceae	Heterokontophyta/Dictyochophyceae	Heterokontophyta/Phaeophyceae	Haptophyta	Cryptophyta	Dinophyta	Euglenophyta	Chlorarachniophyta	Chlorophyta
cyanophycin (arginine–asparagine polymer)	⊕																
Starch-like compounds (α-1, 4-glucans)																	
cyanophytan starch	⊕	⊕															
floridean starch				⊕													
starch			⊕										⊕	⊕			⊕
β-1, 3-glucans																	
chrysolaminaran					⊕	⊕	⊕	⊕	?	?	⊕	⊕					
paramylon												⊕[1]			⊕	?	

[1] In *Pavlova*. (Data from [269, 402, 675, 842, 854, 974, 997, 998, 1148, 1395, 1396]).

we to determine which organisms belong to the plant kingdom (Regnum Plantarum) and which to the animal kingdom (Regnum Animalium)? The division of all living organisms into these two kingdoms dates from the time of Linné and two centuries later we still have no difficulty, in everyday life, in distinguishing between rooted green, photosynthetic plants and motile, food-consuming animals. Microscopic organisms too sometimes cause us no problems: unicellular, colourless, motile organisms that 'eat' particles of food can be accommodated without much difficulty in the animal kingdom, as 'Ur-animals' or Protozoa. But what should be done with unicellular organisms (for instance, in the Chrysophyceae and Euglenophyta) that are motile and ingest food particles but are at the same time pigmented and photosynthetic? And what about the phagotrophic, motile slime moulds (myxomycetes)? Such organisms have sometimes been classified in the animal kingdom, sometimes in the plant kingdom, and sometimes in a separate, third kingdom, the 'Protista'. The uncertainties in the classification of these organisms demonstrates that the division of all living things into two kingdoms, plant and animal, is unsatisfactory. Nevertheless, this distinction is still made from time to time ([1378]).

At present it is quite popular to subdivide living organisms into five kingdoms, as given below ([1123, 1124, 1126]):

1 **Monera**. The Eubacteria and Archaebacteria (Table 1.1).
2 **Protoctista**. Eukaryotic algae and protozoa, together with some of the fungi (Table 1.1: IV–XII, XV–XVII, XXI–XXVI).
3 **Fungi** (Table 1.1: XVIII–XX).
4 **Animalia**. Multicellular animals (Table 1.1: XXVII–XXXIV).
5 **Plantae**. Mosses, liverworts and vascular plants (Table 1.1: XIII, XIV).

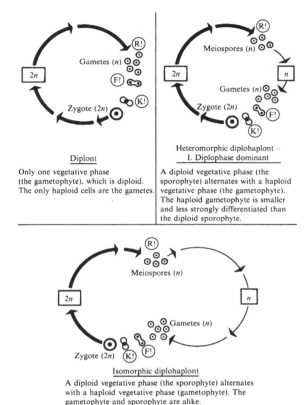

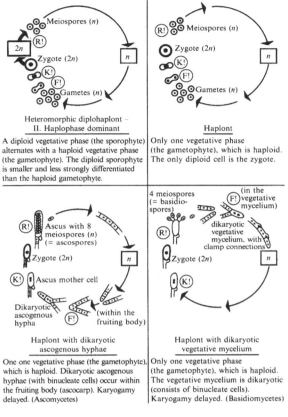

Figure 1.4. The life cycles of eukaryotic plants. Broad arrows = diploid phase; thin arrows = haploid phase;

F! = fertilization; K! = karyogamy; R! = reduction division (meiosis); *n* = haploid; 2*n* = diploid.

These kingdoms are not phylogenetically coherent, however, and are consequently as artificial as the Plant and Animal Kingdoms, as traditionally defined, or as the classes Algae and Fungi. For instance, the kingdom Monera includes both the Archaebacteria and the Eubacteria, even though species of these groups are less closely related to each other than archaebacterial species are to eukaryotes ([1914]). Or again, the phylum Chlorophyta, placed in the kingdom Protoctista, is much more closely related to the phyla in the kingdom Plantae than it is to any of the other phyla in the Protoctista.

Algae and fungi are often called 'lower plants' and the vascular plants, 'higher plants', reflecting the higher level of organization and differentiation in vascular plants. The higher plants are thought to have evolved from the lower plants.

The main groups of algae and their characteristics

The names of the divisions and classes of algae often contain a reference to the colour of the organisms included in them: Cyanophyta, blue-green algae; Rhodophyta, red algae; Chrysophyceae, golden algae; Phaeophyceae, brown algae; Chlorophyta, green algae. The kinds and combinations of photosynthetic pigments present (which are what give the algae their colour) accordingly have an important role in algal classification. Table 1.2 lists these pigments and summarizes their occurrence in different groups of algae. The chemical nature of the storage products (Table 1.3) and cell walls also plays an important part in the definition of the various algal groups.

The biochemical characters we have just mentioned

are correlated with many other characters, drawn especially from the cytology and morphology of the organisms, and these are in general even more important for the delineation of the divisions and classes than the photosynthetic pigments, reserve polysaccharides and cell wall constituents. Important criteria include, for instance, the presence or absence of flagellate cells, the structure of the flagella and flagellar roots, the pattern and course of mitosis (nuclear division) and cytokinesis (cell division), the presence or absence of an envelope of endoplasmic reticulum around the chloroplasts, and the possible existence of a connection between this envelope and the nuclear membrane. These characteristics will be discussed in the chapters on particular classes and divisions. Each chapter is prefaced by a summary, giving the most important features of the group.

The kind of **life cycle** is often important in the delimitation of algal classes. Several major types of life cycle can be distinguished – diplontic, heteromorphic diplohaplontic, isomorphic diplohaplontic, and haplontic – and Fig. 1.4 illustrates these. In most classes there is only one kind of life cycle (e.g. the Bacillariophyceae all have diplontic life cycles), whereas in others there are several (e.g. in the Phaeophyceae, where there are heteromorphic diplohaplontic, isomorphic diplohaplontic and diplontic life cycles).

The same levels of organization of the thallus have arisen in parallel in different, phylogenetically separate groups of algae. They will be dealt with in detail on pp. 117–19, and also in Table 6.1 (p. 120). Table 1.1 gives a synopsis of the classification used in this book.

2

Cyanophyta (= Cyanobacteria)

The division Cyanophyta belongs to the kingdom Eubacteria, which together with the Archaebacteria makes up the Prokaryota. Prokaryotes are organisms whose cells possess no nuclei, no golgi apparatus, no mitochondria, no endoplasmic reticulum and no plastids. The DNA lies free in the centre of the cell and is not enclosed within a nuclear membrane; the thylakoids also lie free in the cytoplasm (in those prokaryotes that are photosynthetic), rather than being contained in chloroplasts. The Prokaryota include the Cyanophyta (the blue-green algae, or cyanobacteria) and other bacteria (Fig. 1.3), while the Cyanophyta in turn contains just one class, the Cyanophyceae.

Relatively recently a new name for the blue-green algae has been proposed ([1681a, 1681b]). This name, 'Cyanobacteria', emphasizes two aspects of the blue-green algae better than the traditional name 'Cyanophyta', namely the prokaryotic nature of the blue-green algal cell, and the fairly close relationship between the blue-green algae and the Eubacteria. On the other hand, the traditional name reflects the algal characteristics of the blue-green algae (see p. 24), such as their ability to perform oxygenic (oxygen-evolving) photosynthesis, and the similarity between their structure and the structure of eukaryote chloroplasts. At present, both names are used alongside each other, and this practice will be followed here (for discussion, see [195, 402, 455, 503b, 1501a, 1681b]).

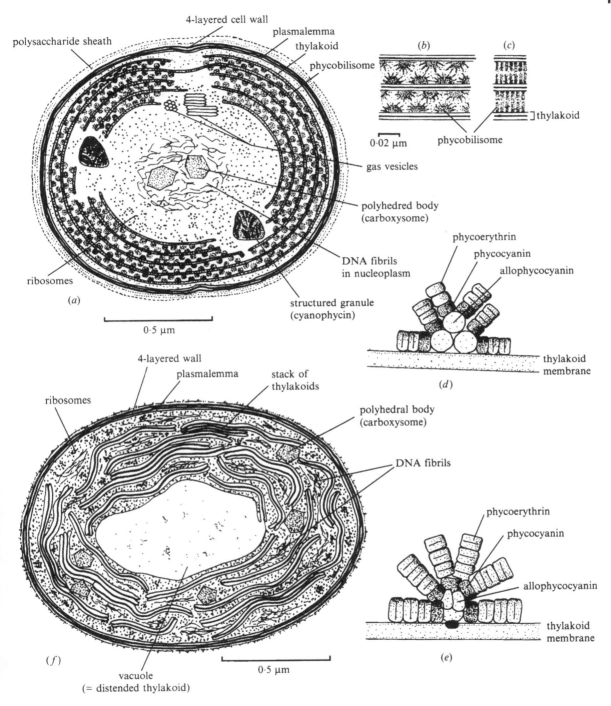

Figure 2.1. The coccoid blue-green alga (cyanobacterium) *Synechocystis* (*a*) and, for comparison, the coccoid prochlorophyte *Prochloron* (*f*). (*b*) Detail of the thylakoids, showing rows of hemidiscoidal phycobilisomes in cross section. (*c*) As (*b*), but showing rows of phycobilisomes in longitudinal section. (*d*) The structure of a hemidiscoidal phycobilisome. (*e*) The structure of a hemispherical phycobilisome. (*b, c* based on [248]; *d, e* on [482].)

The principal characteristics of the Cyanophyta (125, 195, 402, 455)

1 Among the blue-green algae there are unicellular, colonial, and filamentous forms, and there

are even some with a simple parenchymatous organization. Flagellate cells never occur at any stage in the life cycle.

2 Just as in the other bacteria, there are no mitochondria, no nucleus, no golgi apparatus, no

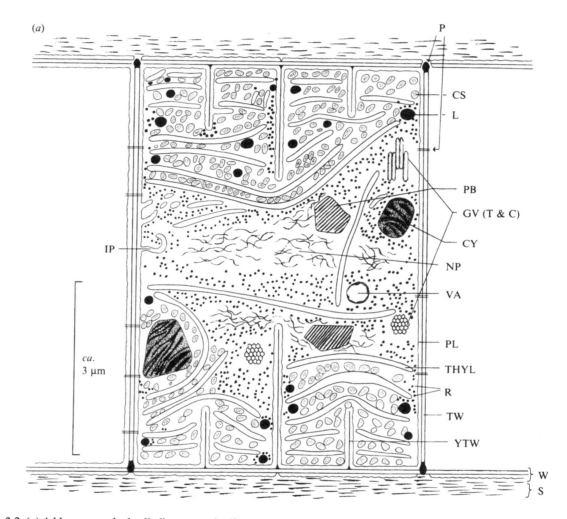

Figure 2.2. (a) A blue-green algal cell, diagrammatic. (b) Electron micrograph of a longitudinal section through *Pseudanabaena* cells. Note the equidistant thylakoids bearing phycobilisomes. Where the rows of phycobilisomes are cut in cross section (C) they can be seen to alternate on opposing thylakoid surfaces; where they are cut tangentially (T) they appear as dark cords running at an angle to the cell's longitudinal axis. C = cross section; CS = cyanophycean starch granule, diameter *ca.* 30 nm; CY = cyanophycin granule, diameter *ca.* 0.5 µm; GV = gas vesicle, 0.1 µm × 1 µm; IP = invagination of the plasmalemma; L = lipid droplet, diameter *ca.* 30–90 nm; NP = nucleoplasm; P = pores; PB = polyhedral body (carboxysome); PL = plasmalemma, 7 nm thick; R = ribosomes, diameter 20–30 nm; S = sheath of mucilaginous material; T = tangential section; THYL = thylakoid, *ca.* 15 nm thick; TW = cross (tranverse) wall; VA = vacuole-like inclusion, not bounded by a tonoplast; W = wall; YTW = young cross-wall, extending inwards like a diaphragm. (*a* after [1356]; *b* from [248], with the permission of the authors and Blackwell Scientific Publications.)

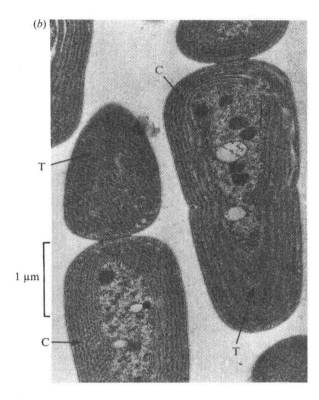

Figure 2.2. (*b*) See caption opposite

endoplasmic reticulum (ER), and no vacuoles bounded by a tonoplast.

3 The photosynthetic pigments are located in thylakoids, which lie free in the cytoplasm, instead of being enclosed in chloroplasts as in photosynthetic eukaryotes. The thylakoids are not stacked, in contrast to the thylakoids of the prokaryotic division Prochlorophyta and most eukaryotic algae, but are single and equidistant (Figs. 2.1, 2.2). The same thylakoid arrangement is found in the chloroplasts of eukaryotic algae belonging to the divisions Rhodophyta (Figs. 5.1*a*, *b*, 5.2*c*, 5.11) and Glaucophyta.

4 The thylakoids contain chlorophyll a, but chlorophylls b and c are absent.

5 The cells are generally blue-green to violet, but sometimes red or green. The green of the chlorophyll is masked by the blue accessory pigments phycocyanin and allophycocyanin, and the red accessory pigment phycoerythrin. These pigments lie in hemidiscoidal or hemispherical bodies, called phycobilisomes, which lie in rows on the outer surfaces of the thylakoids (Fig. 2.1*a*–*c*). Phycobilisomes also occur in eukaryotic algae belonging to the divisions Rhodophyta and Glaucophyta (pp. 48, 45).

6 The reserve polysaccharide is cyanophycean starch. This is formed in tiny granules lying between the thylakoids, which can only be seen by using the electron microscope. In addition, blue-green algal cells often contain cyanophycin granules, which consist of polymers of the amino acids arginine and asparagine; polyphosphate bodies; and carboxysomes (otherwise known as polyhedral bodies), which contain the primary enzyme for photosynthetic CO_2 fixation, ribulose 1,5-bisphosphate carboxylase–oxygenase (RuBisCO) (Figs. 2.1*a*, 2.2).

7 As in other bacteria, the DNA (deoxyribonucleic acid) lies bundled up in the centre of the protoplast. This central part is termed the 'nucleoplasm' (Figs. 2.1*a*, 2.2), although it must be emphasized that there is no nucleus; the nucleoplasm is not surrounded by a double membrane, in contrast to the nucleus of eukaryotes. Many blue-green algae also contain plasmids (small circular DNA molecules), which occur too in other bacteria and in some eukaryotic cells.

8 The structural part of the cell wall consists of murein (= peptidoglycan), as in other Eubacteria, outside which there is a lipopolysaccharide layer. The cells are often embedded in sheaths of mucilage (hydrated polysaccharide; Fig. 2.3*k*–*m*).

9 Blue-green algae can only reproduce asexually; sexual reproduction is absent. The bacterial parasexual processes of transformation and conjugation, however, may bring about genetic recombination.

10 Blue-green algae occur in marine, freshwater and terrestrial habitats.

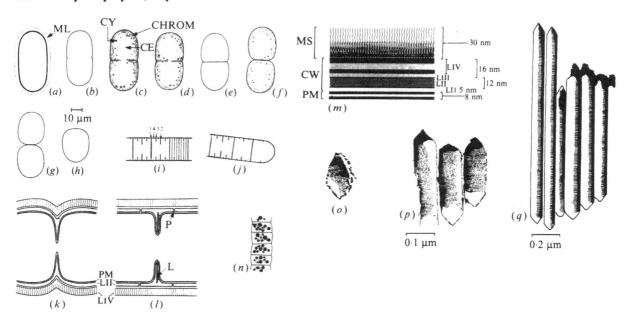

Figure 2.3. (*a–h*) *Cyanothece aeruginosa*, stages in cell division. (*i, j*) *Oscillatoria*, formation of the cross-wall (the numbers indicate the relative ages of the walls). (*k*) Cell division in unicellular blue-green algae and *Nostoc*: all of the wall layers grow inwards. (*l*) Cell division in *Oscillatoria*, diagrammatic: the cross-wall is composed only of a layer of murein. (*m*) Diagram of cell wall structure in blue-green algae. (*n*) Polyphosphate granules ('volutin') in the cells of

Oscillatoria. (*o–q*). Growth and development of gas vacuoles (after 7, 9 and 48 h, respectively.) CE = centroplasm; CHROM = chromatoplasm; CW = cell wall; CY = cyanophycin granule; L I–L IV = the four layers of the cell wall; L II = murein layer; ML = thin layer of mucilage; MS = mucilage sheath; P = pore; PM = plasma membrane (plasmalemma). (*a–j* from [503]; *k–m* from [340]; *o–q* after [1836].)

Size and distribution of the division

The division Cyanophyta contains about 150 genera and 2000 species ([440]). They are found in the most diverse habitats: in freshwater and in the sea, on damp soil, and even in such extreme and inhospitable places as glaciers, deserts and hot springs. Most, however, live in freshwater.

Blue-green algae are frequently to be found in the phytoplankton of still or slowly flowing freshwaters. In temperate lakes they generally form dense populations only after the water column has become stratified at the end of spring, when an upper layer of warm, less dense water (the epilimnion) becomes established above cold, deeper water (the hypolimnion). Late spring and early summer may see the growth of populations of filamentous forms, such as *Anabaena* (Fig. 2.5*j*) or *Aphanizomenon* species (Fig. 2.5*d, e*), while in mid summer the colonial species *Microcystis aerugi-*

nosa (Fig. 2.4*g*) often becomes abundant. Part of the success of these blue-green algae can be ascribed to their ability to use low light intensities effectively, so that they can thrive below the surface, deep in the epilimnion. Indeed, healthy populations of these planktonic blue-green algae can occur at considerable depths, so that it is only under suboptimal conditions that they congregate at the surface; there they may become exposed to direct sunlight, which can bring about photooxidation of the photosynthetic pigments and ultimately the death and disintegration of the algae. Blue-green algae can control their buoyancy, and hence their position in the water column, via gas vacuoles (see p. 26); the role of akinetes (resting stages) in the survival of adverse conditions is discussed on p. 31.

In shallow eutrophic lakes dense blooms of green algae (such as *Scenedesmus* species, p. 370), can reduce the light intensity to such an extent that only very specialized, shade-loving blue-green algae, such as certain *Oscillatoria* species (Fig. 2.4*a, b*), can survive beneath; in time these can themselves give rise to massive populations and out-compete the green algae ([434, 1010]). In lakes that have been polluted with organic sewage or nutrient salts, e.g. phosphates, certain planktonic blue-green algae often form enormous blooms.

Some planktonic blue-green algae possess not only gas vacuoles but also heterocysts: differentiated cells with a colourless interior and thick walls (see p. 30), which can fix atmospheric nitrogen. Blue-green algae with heterocysts can satisfy their nitrogen requirements and grow, even in waters where the nitrate and ammonium levels are relatively low but where the phosphate concentrations are high because of pollution with detergents containing polyphosphates. It has been observed that the growth of blue-green algae is stimulated by organic substances, but the basis of this is as yet unclear ([433]). Perhaps the lowered oxygen concentration in the water, brought about by heterotrophic bacteria breaking down organic material, stimulates blue-green algal photosynthesis and N_2 fixation (see p. 30).

Some species, particularly those that contain gas vacuoles in their cells (Figs. 2.3*o–q*, 2.4*e*, 2.5*j*, p. 26), frequently form thick blue-green algal 'soups' at the surfaces of lakes, which can be driven by the wind into smelly, decaying scums around the lake margins. These phenomena have been known for some time and given various names, such as 'water bloom'. The red cyanophyte *Oscillatoria rubescens* can colour the water blood-red in eutrophic lakes, and even in the nineteenth century red discolourations were being recorded from some Swiss lakes around the edges of the Alps, reflecting pollution of the water by sewage. *Anabaena flos-aquae* (Fig. 2.5*j*) and *Aphanizomenon* species (Fig. 2.5*d, e*), both heterocystous forms, are notorious for producing toxic blooms in freshwaters ([242, 402, 530, 546, 820, 989a, 1603, 1604]), as is the colonial blue-green alga *Microcystis aeruginosa* (Fig. 2.4*g*). In the sea, however, toxic blooms are caused not by blue-green algae but by species of certain groups of eukaryotic algae (of the Dinophyta, Raphidophyceae and Haptophyta). If birds, poultry, or small or large domestic animals drink water containing a toxic bloom, they develop difficulties in breathing and severe diarrhoea, and may die. Fortunately, however, humans scarcely ever drink this poisoned water, because its appearance and smell are so unpleasant.

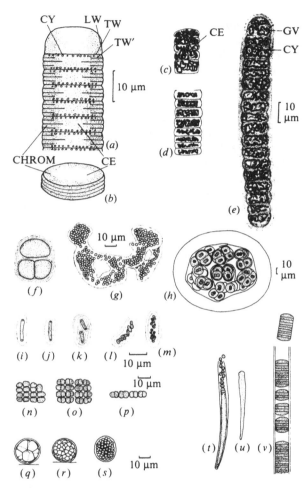

Figure 2.4. (*a, b*) *Oscillatoria* in longitudinal section and in a three-dimensional representation. (*c, d*) *Oscillatoria*: chromosome-like structures revealed using a nuclear stain. (*e*) *Oscillatoria*: gas vacuoles in a hormogonium. (*f*) *Chroococcus turgidus*. (*g*) *Microcystis aeruginosa*. (*h*) *Gloeocapsa alpina*. (*i–m*) *Aphanothece caldariorum*: stages in the formation of nanocytes. (*n–p*) *Merismopedia glauca*. (*q–s*) *Cyanocystis xenococcoides*: formation of endospores. (*t, u*) *Chamaesiphon curvatus*: formation of exospores. (*v*) *Lyngbya*: formation of hormogonia. CE = centroplasm; CHROM = chromatoplasm; CY = cyanophycin granules; GV = gas vesicles; LW = longitudinal wall; TW = cross-wall; TW′ = ingrowing cross-wall. (*c–e, h–u* after [503]; *f, g* after [1657]; *v* after [123].)

Anabaena flos-aquae and *Aphanizomenon flos-aquae* both produce potent neuromuscular poisons (anatoxin and saxitoxin, respectively), which are both alkaloids but chemically quite different. Saxitoxin is also produced by a marine dinoflagellate, *Protogonyaulax tamarensis* (division Dinophyta), and causes paralytic shellfish poisoning (p. 274). Microcystin, the cyclic polypeptide produced by *Microcystis aeruginosa*, causes necrosis and haemorrhage of the liver. Within these three widespread freshwater species only certain strains are toxic, and within *Anabaena flos-aquae* different strains produce different types of toxin (termed anatoxins a, b, c, etc.). If drinking water reservoirs become full of highly eutrophic water, toxic blue-green algae can become a risk to human health, but massive blooms of non-toxic species can also be obnoxious, since they can add an objectionable odour and taste to the water. People swimming off tropical coasts can suffer irritation of the skin and mucous membranes, caused by *Lyngbya* (Fig. 2.4*v*) and *Oscillatoria* species (Fig. 2.4*a, b*).

Until quite recently it was not realized that a considerable proportion of the marine phytoplankton consists of blue-green algae. The reason that they escaped attention is their extremely small size: they belong to the 'picoplankton', i.e. phytoplankton with cells 0.2–2 µm in diameter. Two other size categories of plankton are the nannoplankton (2–20 µm) and the microplankton (20–200 µm). The picoplanktonic blue-green algae, consisting of tiny unicellular, coccoid forms (Fig. 2.1*a*), were discovered by using epifluorescence microscopy to examine fresh, membrane-filtered samples of plankton. Under the microscope the cells exhibit an orange to yellow fluorescence when illuminated with wavelengths shorter than 500 nm, as a result of the presence of the photosynthetic accessory pigment phycoerythrin. Electron microscopical examination confirmed that the organisms were blue-green algae ([432]). In addition, membrane-filtered samples were analysed by HPLC (High Performance Liquid Chromatography) and shown to contain the cyanophyte accessory pigment zeaxanthin ([522]).

Coccoid blue-green algae appear to be ubiquitous in temperate and tropical parts of the ocean. Here they are often important components of the phytoplankton and may even be the main contributors to photosynthetic primary production ([432, 802]). In polar seas blue-green algae are rare or absent ([432, 550, 1115]). They are in general most abundant in nutrient-rich coastal and estuarine waters, where they occur together with microplanktonic algae (mostly diatoms and dinophytes, cf. pp. 134, 246) and nannoplanktonic algae (often cryptophytes and haptophytes, cf. pp. 241, 226). However, in the open ocean, coccoid cyanophytes are often dominant in the rather sparse assemblages of small prokaryotic and eukaryotic algae in the picoplankton and nannoplankton; they are especially important in nutrient-poor (oligotrophic) parts of tropical and subtropical seas. Other groups represented among these tiny algae are the prokaryotic division Prochlorophyta (p. 42; [522, 1337]), and the eukaryotic groups Chrysophyceae (Fig. 6.11*a*), Bacillariophyceae (diminutive species of diatoms), Eustigmatophyceae (Fig. 8.2), Haptophyta, Cryptophyta, Dinophyta and Prasinophyceae (Fig. 20.3*a*). These assemblages often congregate at the thermocline, i.e. the boundary layer between the warm, less dense surface water and the cooler, heavier water beneath, which lies at depths between about 50 and 100 m. The picoplanktonic cyanophytes living here are well adapted to the dim light climate, as are the other members of this 'shade flora'.

One of the most important adaptations of picoplanktonic algae is their small size. The sinking speed of spherical phytoplankton cells is proportional to the square of the radius, and is almost negligible for cells as small as those of the picoplankton. Furthermore, small size means that the surface area/volume ratio is high, so that uptake of nutrients from the oligotrophic water is highly efficient. The cells congregate at the thermocline because the higher density of the colder water compensates for their slight overweight. Larger phytoplankton species (belonging to the microplankton) are generally rare or absent in the open ocean, because they sink too rapidly to be able to maintain a balance between reproduction and losses (to sedimentation, grazing, etc.). In inshore waters the resting cells of larger phytoplankton can be brought back into the water column by resuspension from the sediments and turbulent mixing, but in the open ocean the only large phytoplankton present are those with special buoyancy mechanisms. One example in the Cyanophyta is *Trichodesmium*, a filamentous *Oscillatoria*-like alga (Fig. 2.4*a*), which has gas vacuoles (p. 26). *Trichodesmium* can form extensive blooms in tropical and subtropical oceans, and is often visible as long, orange-brown wind rows at the surface ([402, 431, 432, 434]). *Trichodesmium* is capable of fixing atmospheric N₂ (p. 30) and is probably the most important biological fixer of nitrogen in the open ocean ([432]).

In the shallow water around the edges of polluted lakes and canals the sediments are frequently covered by a thick layer of benthic, filamentous blue-green algae, especially the genus *Oscillatoria* (Fig. 2.4*a*). These algae are frequently dislodged from the bottom by bubbles of oxygen formed through photosynthesis, or by gas escaping from the sediment, and float upwards, forming mats that drift around at the surface. In water that has become badly polluted with organic sewage, blue-green algae are often almost the only algae that can still survive and grow.

In the upper part of the marine intertidal zone and in the spray zone of lakes, there is often a blackish horizontal band on rocks and cliffs, formed by **epilithic** blue-green algae. These include species of *Gloeocapsa* (Fig. 2.4*h*) and *Pleurocapsa* (Fig. 2.5*c*). Where the rocks are of limestone or chalk, however, the blue-green algae live mostly within the rock, because some species can bore into calcium carbonate; these species are called **endolithic** algae. In coral reefs, for instance, the endolithic species *Mastigocoleus testarum* can be found; this alga fixes atmospheric N₂ using its heterocysts and thus enriches the oligotrophic reef ecosystem ([701]) (see the account of heterocysts on p. 30).

Muddy or sandy sediments on salt marshes around North Sea coasts, or seaward of tropical mangroves, are often covered with a gelatinous skin made of interwoven blue-green algal filaments, often of *Lyngbya* (Fig. 2.4*v*) or *Microcoleus chthonoplastes* (Fig. 2.5*i*). These species are well adapted to life just above anoxic sediments (see pp. 25, 30).

Terrestrial blue-green algae live on damp soil, rocks, roofs, or tree trunks. On limestone crags certain blue-green algae, including *Gloeocapsa* (Fig. 2.4*h*) and *Scytonema* species (Fig. 2.5*a*), can produce very striking black stripes, which follow the pattern of water seepage and run-off. These tar- or ink-like patches are subject at times to extreme desiccation.

Some blue-green algae live as symbionts with or even within other plants. They occur, for example, in many lichens, in the roots of *Cycas* (the blue-green alga involved is *Nostoc*, Fig. 2.5*b*), in the leaf cavities of the water fern *Azolla* (*Anabaena*, Fig. 2.5*j*), and in the unicellular fungus *Geosiphon* (Fig. 1.1*b*; as in *Cycas*, the symbiont is *Nostoc*). Lichens are highly integrated associations between fungi (mostly

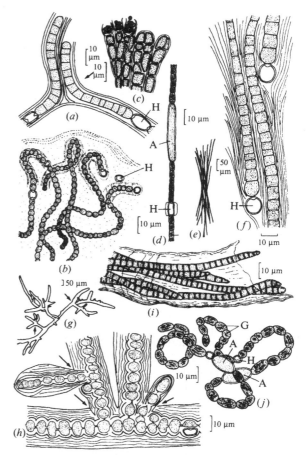

Figure 2.5. (*a*) *Scytonema hofmannii:* false branching (arrow). (*b*) *Nostoc piscinale.* (*c*) *Pleurocapsa minor.* (*d, e*) *Aphanizomenon gracile.* (*f*) *Rivularia haematites.* (*g, h*) *Stigonema ocellatum:* true branching (arrow). (*i*) *Microcoleus vaginatus.* (*j*) *Anabaena flos-aquae.* A = akinete; G = gas vacuole; H = heterocyst. (After [123].)

ascomycetes) and algae. The algae involved are generally green algae (Chlorophyta: see p. 452), but in 8% of lichens the symbiont is a blue-green alga. We can consider a lichen as a fungus, originally heterotrophic, that has become transformed secondarily into a photoautotrophic organism, through the incorporation of an alga. In lichens that contain blue-green algae, the symbiotic alga performs two functions in the association: photosynthesis and nitrogen fixation. It has been demonstrated that photosynthetically fixed carbon and fixed atmospheric nitrogen are both translocated, efficiently, from the alga to the fungus ([402]). Through their ability to fix nitrogen, the symbiotic blue-green algae occurring in some tree-inhabiting lichens may perhaps 'manure' forests that are poor in nutrients, and it is known that the blue-green algae in the roots of *Cycas* and the leaves of *Azolla* do also fix nitrogen. Some blue-green algae live as endosymbionts in the cells of tropical marine sponges.

Mastocladus laminosus and *Phormidium laminosum* are two blue-green algae that are able to live in hot springs, at temperatures of around 50 °C. Indeed they can even tolerate temperatures up to 70 °C.

In tropical countries *Anabaena* species (Fig. 2.5*j*) are important for their contribution to the nitrogen supply of rice plants growing in flooded paddy fields. These algae fix nitrogen in their heterocysts; recently, flooded rice fields have been inoculated with the most efficient nitrogen-fixing strains. It has been estimated that blue-green algae can add about 40 kg bound N to the fields per hectare per year. Even more effective than free-living *Anabaena* for the fertilization of flooded rice fields is the use of the water fern *Azolla*, which harbours symbiotic, nitrogen-fixing *Anabaena* (Fig. 2.5*j*) in cavities in its leaves; growth of *Azolla* in paddy fields can add 120–310 kg N ha^{-1} y^{-1} ([402]). Indeed, in many different terrestrial habitats (e.g rocks, deserts, arctic and antarctic tundra, or in tropical and subtropical regions), soil-dwelling blue-green algae fix atmospheric nitrogen and constitute a source of combined nitrogen for other components of the ecosystem.

During the past 15 years, a considerable amount of research has been carried out on the possibility of growing blue-green algae, especially *Spirulina* species, for human consumption. Dried cakes of *S. platensis* have traditionally been used as food by people living around Lake Chad in N. Africa. This is an alkaline lake, with high concentrations of sodium carbonate and bicarbonate, and the extreme conditions allow massive growth of adapted species such as *Spirulina platensis*, virtually without competition from other algae. Large-scale production in man-made ponds in sunny regions produced 720 tonnes of *S. platensis* in 1984. The protein-rich material (*ca.* 45–60% protein) is used for cattle fodder and 'health foods', but in comparison with animal protein, the amino acid composition is unbalanced and production is as yet very expensive ([989a, 1628]).

This short account shows how very important blue-green algae are ecologically. Two accounts of their biology have been published, in which further details can be found ([192, 403]).

Structure and characteristics of the Cyanophyta ([123, 125, 191, 192, 195, 402, 403, 433, 467, 503, 963])

Pigments and chromatoplasm

The blue-green algae are given their colour by the blue accessory pigments phycocyanin and allophycocyanin (Table 1.2), although red phycoerythrins can also be present. Phycocyanin, allophycocyanin and phycoerythrin are similar types of compound, which are referred to collectively as **phycobiliproteins**; the chromophore of each, i.e. the part of the molecule responsible for producing the colour, is termed a **phycobilin**. In most blue-green algae it is the phycocyanin component that predominates and so the cells are blue or blue-green ([209]). Of the chlorophylls, only chlorophyll a occurs in blue-green algae; chlorophyll b is never found. Various carotenoids are also present. β-carotene has been found in all strains that have been investigated so far, and zeaxanthin, echinenone, canthaxanthin and myxoxanthophyll in the vast majority ([1284]); lutein, on the other hand, is conspicuous by its absence. Myxoxanthophyll occurs in no other group of algae. Phycobiliproteins, on the other hand, are found also in three divisions of eukaryotic algae, the Rhodophyta, Glaucophyta and Cryptophyta, although not in exactly the same forms as in the Cyanophyta.

In all eukaryotic plants the photosynthetic pigments are localized in chloroplasts, which can be seen even using the light microscope. The pigments of the blue-green algae, however, are not contained in chloroplasts though they are for the most part concentrated in the outer part of the protoplast. This coloured, peripheral protoplasm is termed the **chromatoplasm** (Figs. 2.3*c, d, f,* 2.4*a, b*). Electron microscopical studies have shown that the chromatoplasm contains thylakoids, which lie free in the cytoplasm and, in most species, are orientated parallel to the cell surface (Figs. 2.1*a*, 2.2; [964, 1356]). The membranes of the thylakoids contain the lipid-soluble photosynthetic pigments, i.e. chlorophyll a and carotenoids, though a considerable proportion of the carotenoids may be in the plasmalemma and in the lipopolysaccharide layer of the cell wall (see below, 'Cell wall', p. 28).

The phycobiliproteins, which are water-soluble, are contained in small bodies attached to the outer surfaces of the thylakoids (Fig. 2.1*b*, *c*). The bodies are hemidiscoidal or hemispherical (20–70 nm in diameter) and are arranged in rows; they are termed **phycobilisomes**. Close examination reveals each phycobilisome to consist of a triangular core of three double discs (10–12 nm in diameter), from which radiate six rods; each rod is in turn composed of a stack of discs (Fig. 2.1*d*, *e*). The outer ends of the rods form the semicircular outline of the phycobilisome, as seen in profile. The triangular core, which is anchored to the thylakoid by a linking protein, consists of allophycocyanin. The rods, on the other hand, are composed of phycocyanin and phycoerythrin discs, together with the proteins that link them. The relative quantities of phycoerythrin and phycocyanin (and of the corresponding types of disc in the radiating rods within the phycobilisomes) determines the colour of the cell. Some species are bluish-green when grown in red light, and reddish in green light, a phenomenon called 'chromatic adaptation': in the first case phycocyanin predominates, in the second phycoerythrin. Other species do not exhibit chromatic adaptation, and some only have allophycocyanin and phycocyanin, phycoerythrin being quite absent.

Phycobilisomes also occur in the Rhodophyta and Glaucophyta (Fig. 5.1*b*). The chloroplasts of the Rhodophyta and Glaucophyta resemble the cells of blue-green algae in other respects too. Thus, for instance, in all three groups the thylakoids are single and each is more or less equidistant from its neighbours (compare Figs. 2.1*a* and 5.11*b*). The thylakoids of other plants, on the other hand, are usually stacked (Figs. 6.4*d*, 19.3).

The phycobiliproteins function as 'antenna' pigments for photosystem II; light energy harvested by the phycobiliproteins is transferred very efficiently to the chlorophyll a in the photosystem II complex ([248, 528, 1864]). Oxygenic (= oxygen-producing) photosynthesis can be summarized by the equation:

$$h\upsilon\downarrow$$
$$CO_2 + 2H_2O \rightarrow [CH_2O] + H_2O + O_2.$$

A unique property of photosystem II is the use of water as a donor of high-energy electrons and hydrogen (protons), with the concomitant formation of oxygen as a by-product. The light energy captured by the other photosystem (photosystem I) subsequently boosts the electrons to an even higher energy level, sufficient to bring about the reduction of NADP to NADPH, producing chemical reducing power, and also the storage of chemical energy, as ATP. The NADPH and ATP can then be used (in the 'dark reactions' of photosynthesis) for carbon fixation, during the reduction of CO_2 to sugar $[CH_2O]_n$. Within the Eubacteria, only the blue-green algae (cyanobacteria) and the related prochlorophytes (see p. 42) have two photosystems and the capacity for oxygenic photosynthesis; they share this trait with all photosynthetic eukaryotes (algae and higher plants). Other photosynthetic bacteria have only one photosystem and they lack the capacity to use H_2O as an electron donor. Their photosynthesis is thus **anoxygenic** (= without oxygen production) and they need other reduced substrates as electron donors, such as H_2S, H_2 or organic compounds ([16]).

In contrast to photosynthesizing eukaryotes, some cyanophytes can also use H_2S as an electron donor, producing sulphur as a by-product, according to the equation:

$$2H_2S + CO_2 \rightarrow [CH_2O] + 2S + H_2O.$$

The capacity for this type of anoxygenic photosynthesis is shared with certain photosynthetic bacteria ([1352]) and it enables the species involved to thrive in anaerobic, sulphide-rich environments, if there is sufficient light. *Microcoleus chthonoplastes* exhibits another variant type of blue-green algal photosynthesis. This species is a dominant constituent of blue-green algal mats on anoxic, marine intertidal sands (cf. Fig. 2.5*i* and pp. 30, 34). Like the cyanophytes already mentioned, it is capable of using H_2S as an electron donor, but it oxidizes this not to sulphur, but to thiosulphate ($S_2O_3^{2-}$). *Microcoleus chthonoplastes* switches from oxygenic photosynthesis to a mixture of anoxygenic photosynthesis and a limited amount of oxygenic photosynthesis, when conditions become more anaerobic and sulphide concentrations increase. This is an adaptation to living above anaerobic sediments that are rich in sulphide ([1903, 1904, 1905, 1906]).

Some blue-green algae, again including *Microcoleus chthonoplastes*, are also capable of the reverse process: under anaerobic conditions and in the dark they can metabolize stored carbohydrate, bringing about the reduction of elementary sulphur to sulphide

([1677]). In similar conditions (dark anaerobiosis) other species in blue-green algal mats are even capable of fermenting cellular carbohydrate to lactate ([1677]). *Microcoleus* also has a special mode of nitrogen fixation, highly adapted to its life on top of anaerobic sediment; this is treated on p. 30.

In eukaryotic algal cells, photosynthesis and respiration are carried out by two separate types of membrane-bound organelles: chloroplasts and mitochondria. In blue-green algal cells there are no mitochondria, nor are there any equivalent structures. Here the thylakoids are the site not only for photosynthesis, but also for respiration, although this also takes place at the plasmalemma ([1136, 1397, 1887]). However, it has recently been demonstrated that respiration is also performed by the thylakoid membranes of chloroplasts in eukaryotic algae ([63, 1823, 1898]).

Centroplasm

The central part of the blue-green algal cell, the **centroplasm**, is often paler in colour than the peripheral **chromatoplasm** (Figs. 2.3*c, d, f,* 2.4*a, b*). If the cells are treated with nuclear stains and viewed with the light microscope, rod-shaped structures can be seen (Fig. 2.4*c, d*), which are somewhat reminiscent of chromosomes and do indeed contain DNA. They are connected into networks, as can be seen by staining the DNA using the DNA-specific fluorescent dye DAPI (4′, 6-diamidino-2-phenylindole). In some cyanobacteria the DNA occupies the whole of the centroplasm, while in others it is concentrated towards its periphery ([1798a]). The DNA in the centroplasm appears in electron micrographs as a fairly electron-dense, fibrous network, composed of microfibrils about 7 nm in diameter (Figs. 2.1*a*, 2.2). This network consists of one or several circular molecules of DNA, which are highly folded and each represent one genome. The DNA is not associated with nucleohistones, as it is in the chromosomes of Eukaryota ([644, 940]). The part of the centroplasm in which the DNA is located is called the **nucleoplasm** or **nucleoid**. Unlike the nucleus of eukaryotes, it is not surrounded by a fold of endoplasmic reticulum: there is no nuclear envelope (compare Figs. 2.1*a*, 2.2 with Fig. 6.11). Indeed, no endoplasmic reticulum of any kind is ever found in cyanobacteria.

Ribosomes

The protoplasm of cyanobacterial cells is very viscous and so it does not stream like the cytoplasm of most eukaryotic cells. Ribosomes are distributed throughout the protoplasm and are of the prokaryotic type. The ribosomes of prokaryotes and eukaryotes are all quite similar in their overall plan and in their function (protein synthesis). There are differences between them, however, the ribosomes of prokaryotes being somewhat smaller (21 nm × 29 nm) than those in the cytoplasm of eukaryotes (22 nm × 32 nm), and having a slightly different structure ([16]). Prokaryote ribosomes are about the same size as the ribosomes found within the mitochondria and chloroplasts of eukaryotic cells. According to the endosymbiosis theory, these two types of organelle originated as prokaryotic endosymbionts, which were taken up into primaeval eukaryotes; the prokaryotic nature of the ribosomes in plastids and mitochondria may reflect such origins (see pp. 2, 39, 503–6).

Gas vacuoles

In certain conditions **gas vacuoles** are formed within the cells of blue-green algae belonging to quite different systematic groups. Gas vacuoles can be seen with the light microscope as irregular, highly refractile cavities; when viewed with narrow aperture lenses they appear to be edged with black. This is because they are filled with gas and not with liquid, unlike the vacuoles of eukaryotic plants (Figs. 2.4*e*, 2.5*d, j*). Gas vacuoles are also found in bacteria, but not in any eukaryotic plant.

Electron microscopical investigations have shown that each gas vacuole (Fig. 2.4*e*) is made up of many hollow, cylindrical subunits, the **gas vesicles** (Figs. 2.1*a*, 2.2, 2.3*p, q*). By applying just a few atmospheres' pressure (e.g. by pressing down on a microscope preparation of blue-green algae with a dissecting needle), the gas vacuoles can be made to disappear, apparently because the gas vesicles have collapsed following compression. The same process can be demonstrated in another way. A thick suspension of planktonic blue-green algae will appear cloudy, because light is reflected by the many gas vacuoles. If a thick-walled glass tube is filled to the brim with suspension and carefully stoppered with a cork so as to exclude all air, striking the cork with a hammer (thus compressing the fluid and the cells within it) will collapse the gas vesicles, causing the suspension to lose its cloudiness and become clear; subsequently, the blue-green algae sink to the bottom of the tube, having lost their buoyancy.

The wall of a gas vesicle is strong and is composed of protein ([1849]). It is thus quite different from cell membranes like the plasmalemma, or the tonoplast of eukaryotic cells, which consist essentially of a lipid bilayer containing protein on either side. The proteinaceous wall of the gas vesicle is permeable to gases, but not to water, and hence the gas vesicle contains gases in equilibrium with those dissolved in the surrounding protoplasm. The vesicles function as buoyancy organelles, enabling planktonic blue-green algae to have some control over their position in the water column, and allowing them to move up and down. In some cases blue-green algae congregate at depths that are optimal for photosynthesis (the light intensity at the water surface may be too high, depressing the photosynthetic rate). Movement of the algae may also enhance the uptake of nutrients, and this can be brought about in two ways. Firstly, the algae may be able to migrate to depths where nutrients are more readily available, and secondly, movement decreases the thickness of the thin, stagnant (unstirred) layer of water surrounding the cells, thus increasing exchange at the cell surface.

Examples of freshwater blue-green algae exhibiting this kind of buoyancy regulation are *Anabaena flos-aquae* and species of *Aphanizomenon* (Fig. 2.5d, e, j). The mechanism of the upward and downward movement may be as follows. Cells exposed to dim light form more gas vesicles and become positively buoyant, floating upwards to regions of higher light intensity. The resulting increase in photosynthesis is accompanied by an increasing production of low-molecular-mass sugars, and these in turn bring about a higher turgor pressure within the cell. Light-dependent uptake of K^+ ions also contributes to the rise in turgor pressure. As soon as the turgor pressure exceeds a certain critical value, some of the gas vesicles collapse and the blue-green alga starts to sink into regions where the dimmer light promotes the formation of new gas vesicles. The collapse of gas vesicles in itself promotes the formation of new ones, since the proteins of the old vesicle walls can be used for the synthesis of new ones. In other blue-green algae, e.g.

Microcystis species, buoyancy can be lost near the surface of the water through increased production of starch grains; these act as ballast, making the alga sink even without the collapse of the gas vesicles, which here have particularly strong walls ([434]).

In old and very dense blooms of blue-green algae the competition for carbon dioxide can depress photosynthesis to such a degree that the turgor pressure in the cells can no longer rise to the extent that is necessary to bring about vesicle collapse. The bloom then congregates at the water surface and is trapped there (especially in calm weather), and can become moribund, following the destruction of the photosynthetic apparatus by the high light intensities. The algae will then rot, giving rise to unpleasant smells and looking most unattractive. The development of a dense bloom is particularly favoured by the occurrence of calm weather after a period in which the epilimnion (the upper layer of relatively light, warm water in a lake) has been kept mixed by the wind. While the epilimnion is kept well mixed the average light intensity experienced by the blue-green algae is low, and hence the rate of growth and cell division is low. As a result, however, the number (concentration) of gas vesicles per cell remains high, since they are not 'diluted out' by rapid cell division. Hence, when the wind drops and mixing ceases, the algae are overbuoyant and rise rapidly to the surface ([402, 434, 1010, 1850, 1851]).

Reserve substances

Cyanophycean starch

The most important reserve material is an α-1,4-linked glucan – cyanophycean starch – which is similar to glycogen and to the amylopectin fraction of the starch found in higher plants ([468, 1160]). It occurs as small granules (30 nm × 65 nm), invisible in the light microscope, which lie between the thylakoids (Fig. 2.2).

Cyanophycin granules [190, 1632]

The slightly angular granules of cyanophycin (up to 500 nm across), unlike the starch granules, can be seen with the light microscope, even without specific staining. They tend to accumulate near the cross-walls of colonial or filamentous forms (Fig. 2.4a), or at the boundary between the centroplasm and chromatoplasm (Fig. 2.3c, d). Cyanophycin granules, which are also known as 'structured granules' from their appearance in electron micrographs (Figs. 2.1a, 2.2), are clearly composed of protein, since they are decomposed by pepsin. The reserve proteins they contain are polymers of just two amino acids, arginine and asparagine, and constitute an important, easily accessible store of bound nitrogen, in the same way that the polyphosphate granules store easily accessible phosphate (see below). Blue-green algae are capable of rapid capture and storage of mineral N and P, which are then stored in the form of cyanophycin and polyphosphate granules. The reserves make it possible for blue-green algae to maintain active growth even when the water around them has already been depleted of nitrate and phosphate, through the activities of other algae [433].

Polyphosphate granules [1632]

Blue-green algal cells frequently contain granules of highly polymerized polyphosphate (Fig. 2.3n):

$$HO-\underset{\underset{H}{|}}{\overset{\overset{O}{\|}}{P}}-O-\left[\underset{\underset{H}{|}}{\overset{\overset{O}{\|}}{P}}-O\right]_n-\underset{\underset{H}{|}}{\overset{\overset{O}{\|}}{P}}-OH$$

The polyphosphate ('volutin') granules are about 0.5–2 µm in diameter, stain with toluidine blue, and dissolve in slightly acid environments. They serve as a reserve of phosphate for the cell. Bacteria, fungi and eukaryotic algae also possess polyphosphate deposits, but higher plants do not [466, 467, 468, 611, 936].

Polyhedral bodies (= carboxysomes) [16320]

The polyhedral bodies, each 200–300 nm in diameter, are reserves of the enzyme ribulose-1,5-bisphosphate carboxylase–oxygenase (RuBisCO), which catalyses the primary step in the dark reactions of photosynthesis leading to the production of carbohydrate, namely the photosynthetic fixation of CO_2 [402].

Poly-β-hydroxybutyric acid

Vesicles about 200 nm in diameter and containing poly-β-hydroxybutyric acid have been encountered in a few blue-green algae. This storage product is found in many bacteria [241a, 1655].

Cell wall [195, 340, 340a]

Some cyanobacteria are surrounded only by their cell wall (e.g. *Oscillatoria*, Fig. 2.4a), but in others there is also an outer sheath of mucilage (e.g. in *Cyanothece*, Fig. 2.3a, and *Chroococcus*, Fig. 2.4f). In many species the sheaths develop into a large common mass of mucilage, in which the cells or filaments lie embedded (e.g. in *Gloeocapsa*, Fig. 2.4h, *Microcoleus*, Fig. 2.5i, and *Nostoc*, Fig. 2.5b).

Electron microscopical investigations have shown that the cell wall itself consists of four layers (Fig. 2.3m, L I – L IV; [340]). As in other eubacteria, the rigid, load-bearing part of the cell wall (L II in Fig. 2.3m) is composed of murein, a peptidoglycan with peptide side-chains attached to linked, alternating residues of N-acetylglucosamine and N-acetylmuramic acid. The murein layer is often perforated by tiny pores (about 70 nm in diameter), containing extensions of the cytoplasm. As far as is known, no eukaryotic alga ever has murein in its cell walls. The similarity between cyanobacterial cell walls and those of other eubacteria is shown also by their common susceptibility to breakdown by the enzyme lysozyme; furthermore the antibiotic penicillin inhibits the growth of both cyanobacteria and gram-negative bacteria, as it prevents the assembly of the murein layer.

The cell wall layers lying outside the murein layer consist for the most part of lipopolysaccharides. The mucilage sheaths are composed predominantly of complex polysaccharides and exhibit a fibrillar structure when viewed with the electron microscope.

During division of the cell a new cross-wall grows in towards the centre from the periphery, like an iris diaphragm being closed (Figs. 2.3a–g, i, j, 2.4a). In unicellular and colonial species the daughter cells then separate along the newly formed cross-wall, whereas in multicellular forms they remain together. Electron microscopical investigations show that the first stage in cell division is an invagination of the plasmalemma around the whole circumference of the cell (PM in Fig. 2.3k, l). Immediately after this the rigid, structural layer of the cell wall (L II in Fig. 2.3*k, l*) begins to grow inwards, while in unicellular forms (and in *Nostoc* and its allies) there is a final stage, in which the outermost wall layers (L IV in Fig. 2.3*k*) also grow in towards the centre, separating the two daughter cells. Each layer is formed centripetally, as an ingrowing diaphragm. In many multicellular, filamentous blue-green algae, the last phase of cell division is missing and so the cross-walls consist only of the rigid, load-bearing layer (Fig. 2.3*l*). The filaments can break, however, and this is facilitated by rows of pores, which encircle the filaments near the cross-walls (Figs. 2.2, 2.3*l*).

Gliding movement [592]

Many blue-green algae, be they single cells (e.g. *Cyanothece aeruginosa*, Fig. 2.3*a–h*) or filaments, are capable of gliding movements. Single cells tend to make irregular, jerky movements, while *Oscillatoria* filaments and the hormogonia of other filamentous blue-green algae (Fig. 2.4*a, e, v*) glide about in a more orderly, controlled way, the filaments moving backwards and forwards at speeds of 2–11 $\mu m \ s^{-1}$. Movement cannot occur, however, unless the cells are in contact with a solid substratum. As they creep around like tiny slugs, they leave behind them a trail of mucilage, as do motile diatoms (p. 139) and desmids (p. 469). It used to be thought that it was the secretion of this mucilage through pores in the cell wall that generated motion [503]. According to more recent theories, however, mucilage is not directly involved in movement. It is suggested instead that immediately outside the murein layer there are numerous microfibrils in the cell wall which wind spirally around the filament or cell: waves propagated in rapid succession along these fibrils could produce a rotating forward movement of the whole organisms, through friction between microfibrils and substratum [340, 592]. A microfibrillar layer has been discovered with the electron microscope that could be responsible for producing movement in the way described [595]. The microfibrils are packed close together, proteinaceous, and about 5 nm thick. The waves of contraction (length about 70 nm, breadth about 40 nm) have also been observed. Rotatory movement occurs only in the family Oscillatoriaceae; other blue-green algae move

without rotating. The slime secreted by blue-green algae often serves them as a solid substratum over which they can move.

The gliding movements of blue-green algae are influenced in three ways by light; each category of response is mediated by its own set of photoreceptor pigments and has its own physiological mechanism [592]. In **phototaxis** the light source determines the direction of movement. As in many other motile algae (cf. pp. 311–12), blue-green algae exhibit positive phototaxis with respect to dim light (i.e. they move towards the source of the light), and negative phototaxis in bright light (moving away from it). **Photokinesis** involves changes in the *speed* of movement; again, however, the response is dependent on the intensity of the light. The third type of response, the **photophobic response**, entails a rapid *reversal* of movement and is induced by a sudden increase or decrease of light intensity.

The phototactic and photophobic responses enable blue-green algae that live in benthic habitats or in soils to congregate in places with more-or-less optimum conditions for photosynthetic growth, and to avoid places where light intensities are deleteriously high. Blue-green algae, like many other types of algae, are generally adapted to rather low levels of illumination. At low or intermediate light intensities a photophobic response is brought about by a *decrease* in light intensity; at high light intensities it is an *increase* in light intensity that elicits a photophobic response. Hence a population of gliding blue-green algae will be trapped in dimly lit patches. If the filaments pass the border between light and darkness, they will reverse direction and re-enter the dimly lit area; if, on the other hand, they enter a region with very high illumination, deleterious to their health, again they will reverse and return to the dimly lit area.

In the Wadden Sea and elsewhere, intertidal sand-flats can be coloured a striking green, as a result of the presence of the colonial blue-green alga *Merismopedia* (Fig. 2.4*n–p*). *Merismopedia* is motile and can creep into and out of the sediments. At high tide it migrates into the sediments and thus perhaps prevents itself being washed away. When the tide has receded, *Merismopedia* re-emerges from the sediments and the sandflats quickly become green again. Most sandflats and mudflats in the Wadden Sea, however, are coloured brown, because the dominant microalgae are diatoms (p. 136).

Heterocysts and nitrogen fixation [401, 402, 479, 940, 1677, 1678, 1809a]

Heterocysts can be distinguished from vegetative cells by their hyaline protoplasts, which are often yellowish and are characterized by an absence of granular reserve materials and gas vacuoles. Another striking feature of the heterocyst is its thick wall, which is even thicker at one or both ends of the cell, where it projects into the cell interior as a knob, called the **polar nodule** (Fig. 2.5a, b, d). Terminal heterocysts, i.e. heterocysts located at the end of filaments, have only one polar nodule, which lies at the end of the cell nearest the rest of the filament (Fig. 2.5f). The nodule is pierced by several fine canals, which connect the heterocyst with adjacent vegetative cells. Heterocysts occur in many of the multicellular blue-green algae, such as the members of the Nostocales and Stigonematales (see below).

Heterocysts have the function of fixing atmospheric nitrogen, although some non-heterocystous blue-green algae can also fix nitrogen, if the surrounding environment is anaerobic [401, 403, 548, 1137]. Inside the heterocysts the blue-green alga creates an oxygen-free environment, in which N_2 can be fixed: nitrogenase, the enzyme that catalyses the reduction of N_2 to NH_4^+, is very sensitive to oxygen, and poisoned by it. The thick wall of the heterocyst is thought to reduce the diffusion of atmospheric gases into the cell to such an extent that all the oxygen is used up in respiration, although sufficient nitrogen enters to saturate the nitrogenase [402]. A further adaptation of the heterocyst is the loss of the O_2-evolving component of the photosynthetic apparatus, photosystem II (including the phycobiliproteins). Photosystem I is retained and, in the light, generates the energy (in the form of ATP) and reducing power necessary for the reduction of N_2. Additional energy and reducing power are provided by dark respiration, using the O_2 that seeps into the heterocyst. Carbon is probably imported from adjacent, undifferentiated vegetative cells, in the form of low-molecular-mass sugars (disaccharides). In the heterocyst, fixed nitrogen is at first stored in the form of cyanophycin, and later exported to the neighbouring vegetative cells as glutamine. C- and N-export are thought to take place via the fine channels in the polar nodules [548].

The production of heterocysts by blue-green algae is greatly stimulated when there is a deficiency of combined nitrogen (particularly of NH_4^+) in the environment. Where combined nitrogen is plentiful, heterocyst development is either greatly inhibited or stopped altogether. By fixing atmospheric nitrogen, blue-green algae are able to obtain the nitrogen they need for protein synthesis and can continue to grow, even when other algae have exhausted the nitrate and ammonium dissolved in the water. Of course, the water must still possess sufficient phosphate for growth, but often there is no lack of this because modern detergents contain polyphosphate and this enters lakes and rivers in sewage. Thus, in polluted inland waterways and lakes, blue-green algae sometimes give rise to water-blooms, which can be a nuisance or even dangerous, as a result of the production of toxins (see above). Furthermore, when the blue-green algae die they are decomposed by bacteria and this can greatly deplete the water of oxygen.

Initially, only heterocystous blue-green algae were thought to have the capacity to fix atmospheric N_2. Later, however, a variety of other blue-green algae, without heterocysts, were found to be able to fix nitrogen [402, 1677, 1678], examples being the cosmopolitan estuarine species *Microcoleus chthonoplastes* (Fig. 2.5i, p. 34) and *Lyngbya aestuarii* (Fig. 2.4v, p. 33). These two species are the main components of the blue-green algal mats that cover organically enriched sandflats and sandy shores in many sheltered marine and estuarine environments, for instance in the Wadden Sea. These mats may cover large areas of sediment in the upper part of the intertidal zone, and often form an undergrowth beneath salt marsh vegetation, such as below the glasswort, *Salicornia*. In these environments the soil immediately beneath the blue-green algal mat is anoxic and inhabited by layered communities of various anaerobic bacteria. While heterocystous blue-green algae have solved the problem of the oxygen sensitivity of nitrogenase by separating N-fixation and oxygenic photosynthesis **spatially**, *Microcoleus chthonoplastes* and *Lyngbya aestuarii* have solved it by separating these processes **temporally**. They photosynthesize during most of the day and fix nitrogen towards the end of the day and during the night. By the end of the day the phycobiliproteins have become degraded, so that photosystem II ceases to function and O_2 evolution stops. This is followed by a rapid synthesis of nitrogenase, allowing N_2 fixation during the night. As soon as sufficient nitrogen has been fixed and stored in the form of cyanophycin, nitrogenase synthesis stops and then the nitrogenase is degraded by oxygen entering during the rest of the night. The phycobiliproteins are probably resynthesized at the same time, so that photosystem II is functional and oxygenic photosynthesis can start at the beginning of the day.

Akinetes [1886]

Akinetes are large thick-walled cells, full of reserve material, which enable the alga to survive periods when environmental conditions are not favourable to growth (because of drought, cold, nutrient deficiency, etc.). They develop from vegetative cells (Fig. 2.5d, j) and contain large amounts of cyanophycin polypeptide and cyanophycean starch, but not of polyphosphate. Akinetes are often produced in large numbers in senescent populations, as in ageing water-blooms, and ensure survival when the bulk of the population becomes moribund. The precise factors that induce their formation remain obscure: in some species akinete formation seems to be triggered by phosphate deficiency, whereas in others a lack of energy (as light or carbohydrate) seems to be responsible. In yet other species the differentiation of akinetes is induced by particular organic compounds that are themselves secreted by akinetes, so that akinete formation is an autocatalytic process.

Laboratory experiments have shown that akinetes are capable of surviving extreme environmental conditions, which are not tolerated by vegetative cells; thus, for instance, they will endure abnormally high or low temperatures ([1886]). Akinetes may remain viable for years in anoxic lake sediments. *Aphanizomenon flos-aquae* (cf. p. 34) akinetes, for example, have been found in sediments up to 18 years old, while *Anabaena* species (cf. p. 34) may survive for up to 64 years ([1021]). The sediments can therefore provide large inocula for renewed growth upon the return of favourable conditions, as when akinetes are resuspended by turbulence and brought back to the water surface in spring; the increasing light intensity allows germination and, subsequently, growth.

Trichomes and branching

In the blue-green algae a filament of cells, excluding any mucilage sheath that may be present, is called a **trichome**.

Branching is of two kinds. In true branching a cell within the trichome divides, whereupon one of the daughter cells grows out to form a side branch (Fig. 2.5h). In false branching, on the other hand, the trichome breaks within the mucilage sheath and the two new ends (or sometimes only one of them) then grow out laterally, out of the sheath (Fig. 2.5a).

Reproduction

The only known means of reproduction in the blue-green algae are asexual. In many unicellular and colonial forms reproduction is vegetative, occurring as the cells divide (Figs. 2.3a–h, 2.4f, n–p). If cell divisions follow each other quickly, dwarf cells (**nanocytes**) are sometimes produced (Fig. 2.4i–m), because the daughter cells do not have time to grow to their full size before the next division. Other types of asexual reproduction can also occur. In some blue-green algae cells enlarge and each protoplast divides up into a number of daughter cells, within the parent cell wall. Such daughter cells are called **endospores** (Figs. 2.4q–s, 2.5c) and they are motile but not flagellate, as are **exospores**, which are small cells budded off from a larger mother cell (Fig. 2.4t). In multicellular blue-green algae, fragments of the filaments can become detached and glide away (see above). The fragments, called **hormogonia** (Fig. 2.4v), probably break off from the parent filaments at the transverse rings of pores through the peptidoglycan layer of the cell wall; the cells whose walls are broken, then die (Fig. 2.3l, and see p. 29).

Nowhere in the blue-green algae do we find sexual processes in which two haploid cells fuse to give a diploid zygote. Nevertheless, just as in bacteria, genetic recombination can take place, via 'parasexual processes'. It has been possible, for instance, to obtain a strain of a *Synechococcus* species that is resistant to both polymyxin-B and streptomycin, by bringing together two strains of the algae, each resistant to just one of these antibiotics ([53]). Two modes of genetic transfer known in other bacteria have now been discovered to occur also in blue-green algae; these are **transformation** and **conjugation** ([941, 1747]). During transformation, DNA released or derived from donor cells becomes incorporated into recipient cells, in which it may replace homologous sections of DNA. During conjugation, two cells become connected by a narrow conjugation tube, through which DNA moves from one cell into the other; the evidence for conjugation in blue-green algae is as yet rather limited. As in other bacteria (and some eukaryotic cells), many blue-green algae contain plasmids, which are tiny circular molecules of DNA that occur in addition to the normal, large genome molecules. In other bacteria they are often responsible for genetic transfer and the same is probably also true for blue-green algae. The genes responsible for many functions have been assumed to be plasmid-borne, such as those for gas vacuolation, resistance to antibiotics, and toxin production. Molecular genetic research into blue-green algae is growing rapidly ([644, 1747]).

The systematics of the Cyanophyta

At present, two taxonomies exist alongside each other for the blue-green algae. The traditional botanical taxonomy is summarized in Geitler's monumental monograph *Cyanophyceae*, which was published in 1932 ([500]). Geitler's classification was based largely on morphological investigations of samples collected from nature, while the bacteriological taxonomy of Stanier and his collaborators ([1501a, 1681a, 1681b]) that has been developing since 1971 is based for the most part on physiological and morphological investigations of axenic, clonal cultures; these represent only a tiny proportion of the species that have been described, which number more than 2000. A modern revision of the botanical taxonomy of the blue-green algae is under way ([21, 22, 23, 872, 873]), while the bacteriological taxonomy has recently been summarized in *Bergey's Manual of Systematic Bacteriology* ([194, 195, 1858, 1859]). After much initial dispute and controversy, both taxonomies are now in a phase of constructive convergence ([195]).

Here we divide the single class Cyanophyceae of the division Cyanophyta (= Cyanobacteria) into five orders, in accordance with the subdivision given in the recent bacteriological treatment of the blue-green algae ([1858, 1859]). These are:

Chroococcales

Pleurocapsales

Oscillatoriales

Nostocales

Stigonematales.

This is the same as in the modern botanical taxonomy

([21, 22, 23, 872, 873]), except that there the Pleurocapsales and Chroococcales are merged.

A recent comparison of nucleotide sequences in the 16S ribosomal RNAs of 30 strains of blue-green algae, belonging to the five orders listed above, indicates that the orders Pleurocapsales, Nostocales and Stigonematales are probably 'natural', each encompassing a group of related strains. The orders Chroococcales and Oscillatoriales, on the other hand, are heterogeneous and contain phylogenetically unrelated strains ([526]) (see pp. 37, 497 for the use of ribosomal RNA nucleotide sequences for determining phylogenetic relationships).

Order Chroococcales

This order contains unicellular blue-green algae and also species in which the cells form clusters, held together by mucilaginous polysaccharides. Reproduction takes place through cell division, including the formation of nanocytes, and through budding.

Cyanothece (Fig. 2.3*a–h*) [869]
These unicellular algae have broad (≥3 µm) ellipsoidal cells, with an inconspicuous mucilage sheath; cell divisions occur transversely. The genus contains about 10 species, which live in freshwater and in the sea. They have been shown to be able to fix atmospheric nitrogen ([1859]).

Aphanothece (Fig. 2.4*i–m*)
Here the cells are cylindrical and divisions take place transversely; several species produce nanocytes. Gelatinous colonies are formed, each containing great numbers of cells. In contrast to *Gloeocapsa* (see below) the mucilage envelopes of individual cells are almost indistinguishable. Around 20 species are known, living in freshwater and in the sea, on soft mud.

Merismopedia (Fig. 2.4*n–p*)
The rounded cells of *Merismopedia* are often quite strongly flattened against each other. They form plate-like colonies, which are one cell thick and are held together by a homogeneous sheath of mucilage. Cell division is strictly organized, taking place in two

directions only, which lie at right angles to each other. The cells therefore come to lie in regular longitudinal and transverse rows. About 15 species are known; they occur in freshwater and also in the sea, e.g. on the sandflats of the Wadden Sea.

Chroococcus (Fig. 2.4f)
The cells are spherical to hemispherical (if recently divided) and divide in three planes successively, at right angles to each other. Each cell and each group of cells is surrounded by its own envelope of mucilage, but this is usually thin. The 25 or so members of the genus live in fresh or marine habitats, on damp earth, or on damp rocks.

Gloeocapsa (Fig. 2.4h)
In this genus the cells are again spherical or hemispherical, as in *Chroococcus*. Successive divisions take place in three planes at right angles to each other, though not with the same regularity as is found in *Chroococcus*. Each cell is surrounded by a concentrically layered sheath of mucilage; these sheaths unite the cells into extensive gelatinous or crustose colonies. The genus contains about 40 species, which are particularly common on rocks that are usually damp but periodically dry out, as in mountainous areas, streams, lake shores or sea coasts, where *Gloeocapsa* forms black bands on the rocks (p. 23).

Microcystis (Fig. 2.4g)
Here large numbers of spherical cells are held within a common mass of mucilage. The cells divide irregularly, division taking place successively in three planes at right angles to each other. Spherical or irregularly lobed colonies can be built up and these drift around at or near the surface of freshwater ponds and lakes. *Microcystis* species containing gas vacuoles sometimes give rise to toxic blooms (p. 21).

Chamaesiphon (Fig. 2.4t, u)
The cells of *Chamaesiphon* are either oval or more elongate and pear-shaped, and grow attached to solid substrata (rocks or other algae). Exospores are budded off from the upper ends of the cells. The 25 or so species are found for the most part in freshwater, particularly on stones in fast-flowing streams.

Order Pleurocapsales

In this order the algae are unicellular or form colonies of a few cells, or they may consist of irregular aggregates of cells bearing short, branched or unbranched filaments; these are often united into a pseudoparenchyma. Reproduction takes place through cell division and the formation of **endospores**.

Cyanocystis (Fig. 2.4q–s)
The spherical or pear-shaped cells are attached in groups to a solid substratum, which may be rock or another alga. Endospores are produced. About 25 species of *Cyanocystis* are known, occurring for the most part on sea coasts.

Pleurocapsa (Fig. 2.5c)
The short, branched or unbranched filaments of *Pleurocapsa* are united into a crust-like pseudoparenchyma. There are about 10 species, which live in freshwater and in the sea. *Pleurocapsa* forms crusts on rocks in the upper part of the seashore and also on stones in mountain streams.

Order Oscillatoriales

These filamentous blue-green algae reproduce through the formation of **hormogonia**. The only type of branching that occurs is 'false branching', and both heterocysts and akinetes are absent.

Oscillatoria (Fig. 2.4a, b)
In this genus the trichomes are cylindrical and free, never united into colonies; there is no mucilage sheath around them, although a thin, sheath-like trail is left behind as they glide. Individual cells are disc-shaped and always contain ingrowing cross-walls at different stages of development (Fig. 2.3i, j). Heterocysts, akinetes and false branching are absent, and reproduction is effected through the formation of hormogonia. More than 100 species are known and these are widely distributed in the sea, freshwater, hot springs and areas affected by sewage effluents.

Lyngbya (Fig. 2.4v)
The trichomes of *Lyngbya* resemble those of *Oscillatoria*, but each filament is enclosed in a robust mucilage sheath of its own. Over 100 species are

known. They are frequently found in brackish habitats, but they are also found in freshwater and in the sea.

Microcoleus (Fig. 2.5i)

Again, individual trichomes resemble *Oscillatoria*, but here bundles of filaments are held together in colonies by a stiff mucilage sheath. Only a few species have been described. They are especially common in salt water, on silty sand that is regularly exposed at low tide (e.g. in salt marshes), and in lagoons (see pp. 23, 30).

Order Nostocales

The blue-green algae of this order are filamentous and reproduce through the formation of **hormogonia**. False branching occurs but not true branching, and both **heterocysts** and **akinetes** are produced.

Nostoc (Fig. 2.5b)

The curved or bent filaments of *Nostoc* are unbranched and constricted at each cross-wall, so that the trichome looks like a string of beads. Heterocysts and akinetes are both produced. The trichomes grow around and between each other in a disorderly tangle, all being embedded in a single mass of mucilage, which is stiff and homogeneous. The mucilage has a definite shape, so that colonies can be round (in which case they appear like small black grapes or plums), warty, lobed, or leaf-like. There are about 50 species, which occur for the most part in freshwater and on damp soil. Several species live symbiotically with other plants (cf. pp. 3, 23).

Anabaena (Fig. 2.5j)

The trichomes are similar in shape to those of *Nostoc*, but the filaments are not united together in robust mucilaginous colonies. More than 100 species are known. They occur for the most part in freshwater, where some species give rise to water-blooms.

Aphanizomenon (Fig. 2.5d, e)

Individual trichomes resemble those of *Nostoc*, but they lie side by side in bundles, although they are not surrounded by a sheath of stiff mucilage. Four species have been described, all occurring in freshwater. *Aphanizomenon flos-aquae* in particular is well-known as a cause of water-blooms.

Scytonema (Fig. 2.5a)

In *Scytonema* the trichomes are cylindrical or like a string of beads, and possess intercalary heterocysts. Each filament possesses its own thick, robust sheath of mucilage. False branching is frequent, both of the broken ends usually growing out to form new branches. There are about 60 species, which occur mostly in freshwater. *Scytonema myochrous* lives on limestone or dolomite outcrops and here forms inky streaks that mark where water travels as it runs off the rock.

Rivularia (Fig. 2.5f)

Here the trichomes decrease in width from base to tip and often end in long pale hairs. Each filament has at its base a single heterocyst. False branching occurs and the mucilage sheaths around individual trichomes link them together into a solid, hemispherical colony, in which the trichomes are arranged radially. About 20 species are known, occurring in freshwater and on sea coasts.

Order Stigonematales

Here the filaments are often multiseriate, i.e. with several rows of cells. Reproduction occurs through the formation of hormogonia. Genuine branching, heterocysts and akinetes all occur.

Stigonema (Fig. 2.5g, h)

The trichomes often consists of several rows of cells, genuine branching takes place, and young branch tips can be transformed into hormogonia. The cells are linked by pit connections, and both heterocysts and akinetes are present. There are about 25 species, which occur on damp rocks and in freshwater habitats (e.g. mires).

Reflections on the phylogeny of the Cyanophyta (Cyanobacteria)

It has already been mentioned (p. 23) that silty or sandy sediments in salt marshes, or seaward of the mangroves in tropical and subtropical areas, are often covered with a gelatinous skin or crust, held together by the interwoven filaments of blue-green algae (often species of *Lyngbya* and *Microcoleus*). If the muddy sediment dries out for any length of time, cracks appear in the soil, causing the algal mat to be torn into polygonal pieces. When the area is wetted again at the next high tide, the polygonal mats of algae can resume growth and will capture any sediment that falls onto the mat surface. Should this process of fluctuating water levels and intermittent growth continue for some years, columns of finely layered sediment can develop, and in some tropical lagoons these can be petrified to form **stromatolites** (= layered stones): the stromatolites found in sheltered parts of Shark Bay, Western Australia, are a famous example, and stand several decimetres high (Fig. 2.6). Stromatolites are also formed in permanently submerged sites, where upward growing mats of blue-green algae trap sediments and laminations are formed through periodic (e.g. day-night) variations in blue-green algal activity. Calcium carbonate precipitation within the gelatinous sheaths of the blue-green algae can also contribute to the formation of the stromatolite ([1231]).

Stromatolites are widely distributed in sedimentary rocks of Precambrian age (Fig. 2.7) and it is assumed, therefore, that stromatolites, and hence blue-green algae, covered large areas at that time ([148, 1026]). The oldest known stromatolites are about 3.5 billion years old and were discovered in W. Australia (Fig. 2.7; [1585, 1586]). These extremely ancient rocks contain 'organically preserved' microfossils, which means in this case that the organic matter that originally formed their cell walls has been preserved, albeit in a much altered form, embedded within a siliceous matrix. The microfossils resemble present-day microbes, and include both unicellular, coccoid organisms and multicellular, filamentous forms. They are thought to represent *anaerobic* bacteria, some phototrophic, others heterotrophic, because there is good evidence that the earth's atmosphere and oceans were at that time anoxic. The phototrophic bacteria are considered as evolutionary relics of this early period, when photosynthesis first arose. They are incapable of using water

Figure 2.6. Stromatolites in Shark Bay, W Australia. The stromatolites are about 0.5 m high. (From an original colour photograph of C. van den Hoek.)

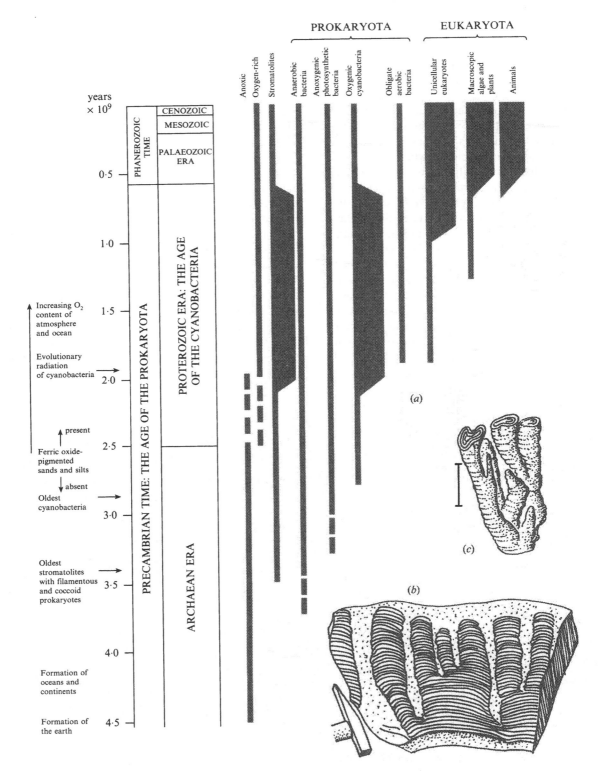

Figure 2.7. (a) The geological occurrence of what are presumed to be blue-green algae (cyanobacteria) and other prokaryotes, compared with eukaryotes.

(b, c) Field sketch and reconstruction of proterozoic stromatolites. (a based on [715, 1585, 1586, 1751, 1827]; b, c on [1197].)

as an electron and hydrogen donor for the light reactions of photosynthesis, and therefore do not give off oxygen. Instead, they use H_2S, H_2, or organic compounds as hydrogen donors. The cyanobacteria (blue-green algae), on the other hand, use water as the electron and hydrogen donor, and therefore generate oxygen during photosynthesis, a property shared with all eukaryotic phototrophs.

Later in the Precambrian, in the early part of the Proterozoic Era (between 2.5 and 2 billion years ago: Fig. 2.7), stromatolites were present in shallow seas almost everywhere, on submerged parts of the continents or around their margins (epicontinental seas), and formed vast reefs of carbonate. They were formed by a variety of microorganisms, the fossil remains of which are morphologically very similar to present-day cyanobacteria. That they were indeed cyanobacteria is suggested by indirect evidence, such as that it is only *after* the beginning of the Proterozoic (2.5 billion years ago) that there is convincing evidence of an increase in the oxygen content of the atmosphere. Thus, for instance, no sediments coloured red by ferric oxide occur in deposits older than 2.5 billion years, while they are abundant in later rocks, indicating that by then the atmosphere was sufficiently oxygen-rich to permit the oxidation of ferrous iron to ferric iron. It is suggested that this change in the atmosphere was brought about by a ubiquitous and richly diversified cyanobacterial flora, because cyanobacteria, unlike other photosynthetic bacteria, perform oxygenic photosynthesis. The Proterozoic Era, a vast tract of time lasting almost two billion years, is sometimes called the 'Age of Cyanobacteria', because it is thought that the earth's biota was dominated by these organisms (Fig. 2.7). During this period, cyanobacteria gradually increased the oxygen content of the atmosphere and thus paved the way for obligately aerobic organisms, in particular the eukaryotes, but also the aerobic bacteria. The first microscopic, unicellular eukaryotes are thought to have arisen around 1.9 billion years ago and to have diversified greatly at around 1 billion years ago. These events are indicated in Fig. 2.7, which also shows the presumed advent and diversification of macroscopic algae and animals. By the end of the Proterozoic Era the cyanobacteria had lost their pre-eminence in the earth's biota, but they still remain important inhabitants of many habitats, especially unusual or extreme ones.

During the Proterozoic radiation of the cyanobacteria, species with heterocysts evolved, showing that atmospheric oxygen concentrations had risen to a level sufficiently high to poison the nitrogenase enzyme, which catalyses the fixation of atmospheric N_2 (see p. 30). The *non*-heterocystous cyanobacteria alive today that are capable of N_2 fixation are apparently relics from the pre-oxygen era [715, 1585, 1586, 1751, 1827].

The account we have given of evolution during the Precambrian is plausible and based on the geological archives, in the form of microfossils of incredible age, preserved in some of the earth's oldest sedimentary rocks. The microfossil record suggests that the present morphological diversity of the blue-green algae had already evolved by around 2 billion years ago, in the Proterozoic Era. The fossil record does not tell us very much, however, about the phylogeny of different groups within the blue-green algae, nor about the relationship between blue-green algae and other major groups of living organisms. For this we must turn to other archives, in particular those stored in the genes of all organisms, as sequences of nucleotides.

Following the evolutionary divergence of two related lineages of organisms, the sequences of nucleotides in their genes, initially identical, become increasingly dissimilar. This is because mutations occur, become fixed, and accumulate, at a more-or-less constant rate. Thus, by comparing gene sequences in the nuclear DNA, the chloroplast DNA, the ribosomal RNA, etc., it is in principle possible to *quantify* the degree of divergence between lineages of closely or distantly related organisms. Recently, nucleotide sequences have been extensively studied in ribosomal RNA (rRNA). Ribosomes have the same function throughout all living organisms (that of translating genetic information into proteins) and are evolutionarily extremely conservative. The sequences of nucleotides in their RNAs can therefore be expected to record the oldest evolutionary divergences.

In the cyanobacteria (and in other bacteria too), the ribosomes consist of three kinds of structural RNA, each associated with protein: these are the 'large' 23S ribosomal RNA, the 'small' 16S ribosomal RNA, and the 'very small' 5S ribosomal RNA ('S' stands for Svedberg Unit, a measure of sedimentation rate in an ultracentrifuge, and thus an indirect measure of size). 23S rRNA is approximately 2900 nucleotides long and 16S rRNA around 1540 nucleotides long, while 5S rRNA contains only about 120 nucleotides. The chloroplasts and mitochondria of eukaryotes have

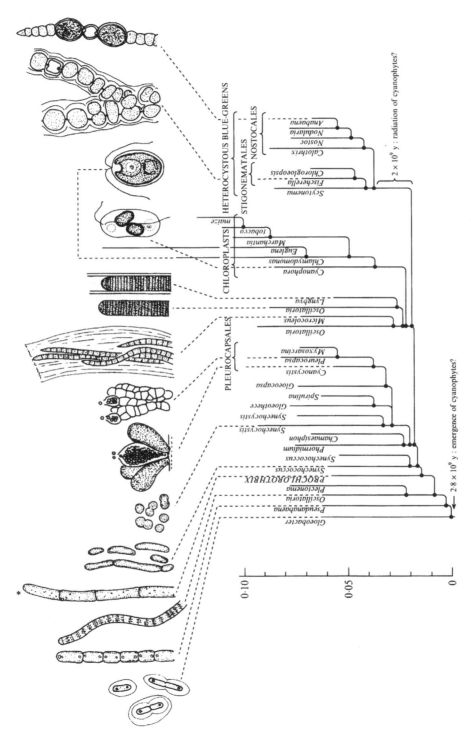

Figure 2.8. Phylogenetic tree of blue-green algae (cyanobacteria), based on similarities in nucleotide sequences in 16S rRNAs (about 670 nucleotides were used for the comparisons). The vertical axis denotes the evolutionary distance between taxa, as the estimated average number of fixed point mutations per sequence position. The horizontal lines are introduced for clarity, to separate the dense knots of branch points, but have no other significance. The times indicated for the divergences are speculative and based upon interpretation of the fossil record (see Fig. 2.7). Note the presence of the prochlorophyte *Prochlorothrix* near the left of the tree (asterisk). (Based on [526, 1806].)

ribosomes like those of prokaryotic organisms, but the cytoplasmic ribosomes of eukaryotes are larger, though again they contain three sizes of rRNA: 25–28S rRNA, 18S rRNA and 5S rRNA.

Nucleotide sequences have been determined for the 5S rRNA in a considerable number of organisms drawn from many different groups, allowing inferences to be made about phylogenetic relationships ([735]). However, because of the small number of nucleotides in 5S rRNA, these results are not very reliable, especially with respect to lineages that diverged either very recently or a very long time ago. Studies of the 'small' 16–18S rRNAs are more satisfactory, since these molecules are sufficiently large to permit statistically accurate measurements of phylogenetic relationships ([1661, 1913, 1914]). As yet, 23S rRNA sequences have been used to measure relationships in a more limited range of organisms ([204]).

Recently, the phylogenetic relationships between the cyanobacteria and the other main lineages of prokaryotes and eukaryotes have been estimated on the basis of 16S rRNA sequences ([1913, 1914]). The results are summarized in Fig. 32.2, which also incorporates the results of studies on 18S rRNA sequences in various eukaryotes ([589, 1471, 1661]). In this phylogenetic tree, the vertical axis indicates the evolutionary distance between taxa, as the estimated average number of point mutations that have occurred, been fixed, and accumulated since the divergence of their lineages. The diagram shows an early separation of the three 'realms' of living organisms, namely the *two* groups of prokaryotic organisms, the **Archaebacteria** and **Eubacteria**, and the **Eukaryota**. [The horizontal lines in Fig. 32.2 are meaningless. They represent the points of divergence between taxa: nodes that have been stretched out horizontally for clarity.] Indeed it was the large-scale survey of 16S rRNA sequences by Woese and his collaborators ([1913, 1914]) that initially led to the realization that there are two unrelated groups (realms) of prokaryotic organisms. The Archaebacteria are unusual organisms adapted to a variety of extreme environments. Among them, for instance, are the methanogens (see Fig. 32.2), which reduce CO_2 and hydrogen, produced as waste products by other bacteria, to methane. They are restricted to strictly anoxic environments, such as the soils of marshes and swamps, rich in decaying organic matter, or the bottom of some marine basins, e.g. the Black Sea. They can be considered as relics from the primaeval anoxic oceans of the Archaean period (Fig. 2.7). Other groups of archaebacteria are the extreme halophiles, which require very high salinities (as in the Dead Sea), and the extreme thermophiles, which need high temperatures and low pH (as in hot sulphur springs).

The **Cyanobacteria** do not belong to the Archaebacteria but constitute a phylogenetically coherent grouping within the realm of the **Eubacteria** (Fig. 32.2). In the 16S rRNA phylogenetic tree, the chloroplasts of eukaryotes also form part of the cyanobacterial lineage, which is of course strong support for the idea that chloroplasts arose as endosymbiotic blue-green algae (cf. pp. 2–4, 7, 504). The analogous explanation of the origin of mitochondria, as endosymbiotic bacteria, is supported by the close phylogenetic relationship between mitochondria and the group containing the purple bacteria and their relatives (cf. Fig. 32.2, p. 500).

It is likely that all Eubacteria stem from a photosynthesizing but non-oxygenic ancestor, which lived in the anoxic Archaean oceans (Fig. 2.7). The main argument in support of this is that the Eubacteria are split into a number of main groups or lineages, several of which contain photosynthetic forms using chlorophyll (in various forms) as the photosynthetic pigment. Certain of the Archaebacteria (the extreme halophiles) are also photosynthetic, but interestingly their photosynthetic mechanism is based on a completely different pigment, namely bacterial rhodopsin ([1913, 1914]). Within the Eubacteria, the capacity for photosynthesis was apparently lost independently in many different lineages: similar loss seems to have occurred in various eukaryote groups that are principally (or were initially) photosynthetic, such as the Dinophyta, Rhodophyta, and Chlorophyta. Within the Eubacteria, the Cyanobacteria acquired photosystem II (together with the phycobiliproteins as antenna pigments) and thereby the capacity for oxygenic photosynthesis, and it was only after this critical evolutionary innovation that the development of an oxygen-rich atmosphere and sea was possible.

rRNA sequences have also been used to estimate relationships within the cyanobacteria, and between cyanobacteria and chloroplasts. Phylogenetic relationships between 29 strains of cyanobacteria (representing the five orders described above), one strain of prochlorophytes (division Prochlorophyta), and the chloroplasts of five strains of eukaryotes have been determined using 16S rRNA sequences ([526, 1806]), and the results are summarized in Fig. 2.8. Looking first at the extreme ends of the phylogenetic tree, we find on the left the lineage that emerges from the lowest, most ancient branching point. This leads to *Gloeobacter*, which seems therefore to be the most primitive type of blue-green alga. In agreement with this, *Gloeobacter* has a very simple and apparently primitive photosynthetic apparatus, since it lacks thylakoids; the plasmalemma functions as the photosynthetic membrane and bears the phycobilisomes ([1859]). On the right-hand side of the tree, forming a relatively recent radiation, are the heterocystous cyanobacteria, and this agrees with other evidence that the heterocystous forms arose relatively late in the evolution of the blue-green algae, almost one billion years after the origin of the group (Fig. 2.7). Within the heterocystous blue-green algae, the Nostocales and Stigonematales both appear as internally coherent groups.

In the centre of the tree are the Pleurocapsales, a group of unicellular and parenchymatous forms producing endospores, and these too seem to be phylogenetically coherent (a 'natural' order). A further interesting feature of the centre of the tree is that various chloroplasts, though drawn from very different eukaryotes, cluster together in another 'cyanobacterial' grouping, suggesting that they all evolved from a group of closely related cyanobacteria, which were in some way predisposed to form endosymbiotic relationships with primitive heterotrophic eukaryotes. This seems reasonable judging by what happens today, since several widespread types of photosynthetic endosymbioses 'use' closely related algal symbionts. For instance, many lichens contain species of the coccoid green alga *Trebouxia* (p. 452), while sea anemones, reef corals and other Cnidaria use species of the dinophyte genus *Symbiodinium* as endosymbionts (p. 277). Other molecular evidence, however, points to endosymbiotic prochlorophytes as the ancestors of green chloroplasts in eukaryotes (see pp. 44, 504).

The rest of the tree shown in Fig. 2.8 consists of several low branchings, and therefore presumably ancient lineages, which contain either coccoid organisms or simple filamentous forms. The orders Chroococcales (containing coccoid blue-green algae) and Oscillatoriales (containing filamentous blue-green algae that lack heterocysts and akinetes) are phylogenetically heterogeneous and hence 'artificial'. One of these lineages leads to *Prochlorothrix*, a filamentous representative of the division Prochlorophyta, which apparently therefore had a cyanophyte ancestor (cf. p. 44).

The early radiation implied by the low branching of lineages containing coccoid and simply filamentous forms accords with the occurrence of similar microfossils in strata of upper Archaean age (2.8 – 2.5 billion years ago). It seems that the simple coccoid or filamentous architecture of the first blue-green algae has been retained virtually unchanged while their genomes have continued to diverge. Comparable conservatism in gross morphology, over long periods of geological time, has probably occurred too in relatively simple unicellular and filamentous forms in the phyla of eukaryotic algae (cf. pp. 489, 491). The fossil record also suggests that the evolutionary radiation that produced the full array of basic cyanophyte forms took place long ago, possibly in the Proterozoic (some 2 billion years ago), and this is shown in Fig. 2.7. The fossil evidence and the RNA data appear at first sight to suggest, therefore, that all extant cyanophyte species are extremely ancient, and that they had all diverged from their common ancestors by the end of the Precambrian. Such evolutionary stagnation seems extremely unlikely, however, in view of the considerable diversity present today in blue-green algal floras, with different species occupying different, and to some extent 'modern' niches. Thus, for instance, the freshwater blue-green algal flora of Cuba includes 330 species, of which 63% are known only from the American tropics, and 45% of these only from Cuba ([870]). It is likely that this flora originated in response to the genesis of the present-day geography and climate of the Caribbean during the Cenozoic era (the past 65 million years).

DNA–DNA hybridization studies have produced evidence that cyanophyte species may in fact have diverged from each other comparatively recently. The DNA–DNA hybridization method is suited to the detection of divergences of intermediate age (taking place several million to around 150 million years ago); it does not yield useful information about earlier or later divergences. DNA–DNA hybridization is based on the property that single strands of DNA, separated from each other by heating, will re-associate into double-stranded DNA when they are cooled. If the single strands are from different species, they too may re-associate into double-stranded DNA, but only if the nucleotide sequences are sufficiently similar. To investigate this, a small quantity of fragmented single-stranded DNA from one species, labelled with a radioactive isotope (tracer DNA), is mixed with a much larger amount of fragmented but unlabelled DNA (driver DNA) from another species, in conditions promoting re-association into double-stranded hybrid DNA (heteroduplex). The tracer DNA is also combined with driver DNA from the *same* species, and again allowed to form double-stranded DNA (homoduplex). The re-association mixtures, including the hybrid DNA, are then loaded onto hydroxyapatite columns, which bind double-stranded DNA, but not single-stranded DNA. The temperature of the column is then raised from 60 °C to 95 °C in steps of 5 °C. With each successive rise in temperature, more double-stranded DNA will dissociate and the resulting single-stranded DNA will be washed out of the column and can be counted. In this way the amount of dissociated hetero- and homoduplex material can be determined. Heteroduplexes should be less stable than homoduplexes, because they are composed of DNA strands whose sequences have diverged to a greater or lesser extent, so that there is more of a mismatch between the base pairs than in homoduplex DNA. Heteroduplexes therefore dissociate at lower temperatures than homoduplexes. A useful measure of this is the temperature at which half of the hybrid DNA has dissociated, referred to as $T_{m(e)}$; the difference between $T_{m(e)}$ for the heteroduplex and that for the homoduplex ($\partial T_{m(e)}$) therefore estimates the extent to which the DNA sequences of the two species have diverged. Another measure of divergence is the 'RB-value' (relative binding, in %), which is 100% when the radioactive and non-radioactive strands are from the same species, and less than 100% when they are from different species.

In one study, of 29 different strains of thin, filamentous *Oscillatoria*-like cyanobacteria ([1679, 1681]), 18 of the strains appeared to be closely related, their DNAs showing RB-values of 95–100% with respect to the DNA of one strain; minute phenotypic differences between the strains showed there had been recent divergence. Three other strains had RB-values in the range 17–22% with respect to the reference strain, which is similar to the 20–53% found among six *Anabaena* species (Fig. 2.5j). Such RB-values correspond to $\partial T_{m(e)}$ values of 9–5 °C ([1728, 1729]) and are comparable to the degree of divergence between species of the flowering plant genus *Atriplex* ([62]), between geographically distant populations of the green algal species *Cladophora albida* ([111]), between certain genera of hominids, or between genera of sea urchins ([144]). All of these divergences are thought to have occurred in the Cenozoic era (between 15 and 60 million years ago), which occupies only a minuscule proportion of the time blue-green algae have been on earth, judging by the geological record (2800 million years; Fig. 2.7). Five of the 29 narrow, *Oscillatoria*-like strains exhibited very low RB-values with respect to the reference strain (6.5–8.5%), which indicate very ancient divergences; the RB value with respect to the bacterium *Bacillus subtilis* was 2.5% ([1681]).

The overall conclusion to be drawn from these studies is perhaps that, in the distant past, the cyanobacteria evolved a limited range of basic morphological types (coccoid, simple filamentous, endosporous, and heterocystous forms), within each of which speciation has continued to occur, over and over again, during the long history of the group ([1729]).

3

Prochlorophyta

The artificial division Prochlorophyta is an assemblage of green Cyanophyta (Cyanobacteria) and consequently belongs to the prokaryotic realm of the Eubacteria. The genus *Prochloron*, which gave its name to the division, was discovered in the early 1970s ([1001, 1589]). The prochlorophytes are interesting because it is possible that they could represent the prokaryotic ancestors of the chloroplasts of green algae and higher plants; the name *Prochloron* expresses this speculation, meaning 'primitive green thing'. The Prochlorophyta contains only one class, the Prochlorophyceae.

The principal characteristics of the Prochlorophyta [167, 576, 998, 999, 1135]

1. Among the prochlorophytes there are unicellular coccoid species and also organisms that produce unbranched filaments (Figs 2.1f, 2.8, 3.1).

2. The cells are prokaryotic and consequently lack a nucleus, mitochondria, golgi bodies, and endoplasmic reticulum (ER).

3. The photosynthetic pigments are bound to thylakoids that lie free in the cytoplasm, not enclosed within chloroplasts. The thylakoids are not single and equidistant (as in the Cyanophyta), but grouped into stacks (lamellae) containing two to several thylakoids, as in the chloroplasts of the green algae (Chlorophyta) and higher plants (compare Fig. 2.1f with 2.1a).

4. The thylakoids contain chlorophylls a **and** b, and thus again resemble the chloroplasts of green algae and higher plants. Chlorophyll c is absent.

5. The cells are bright green, since although accessory pigments are present, they do not mask the chlorophyll. Among the accessory pigments are β-carotene and a variety of xanthophylls, the principal one being zeaxanthin, as in the Cyanophyta. Phycobiliproteins, and consequently also phycobilisomes, are absent ([15]). Phycobilisomes are characteristic of the Cyanophyta (compare Fig. 2.1f with 2.1a) and the chloroplasts of red algae.

6. The reserve polysaccharide is starch-like. Cyanophycin, a nitrogen reserve characteristic of the Cyanophyta and consisting of a polymer of the amino acids arginine and asparagine, is not found in the Prochlorophyta. Polyhedral bodies (carboxysomes), containing RuBisCO (ribulose 1,5-bisphosphate carboxylase–oxygenase, the primary enzyme in photosynthetic CO_2 fixation) are present in both the Cyanophyta and Prochlorophyta (Figs. 2.1a, f, 3.1).

7. The DNA has a diffuse distribution, occurring throughout the cell in regions between the stacks of thylakoids that are rich in ribosomes (Fig. 2.1f). The DNA is not concentrated in the centre of the cell as it usually is in the Cyanophyta.

8. The cell wall is similar to that of the Cyanophyta and contains a peptidoglycan (murein) layer.

9. So far, only three genera are known. Two (*Prochloron* and *Prochlorococcus*) are marine, while the other, containing only one species (*Prochlorothrix hollandica*), occurs in freshwater.

The genus *Prochloron* (Figs. 2.1f, 3.1) contains a number of related coccoid forms, which live as extracellular symbionts within tropical and subtropical colonial ascidians (sea-squirts). Recently, however, coccoid prochlorophytes (*Prochlorococcus*) about 1 μm in diameter have been discovered to be abundant in the picoplankton of the dimly lit deeper waters (at about 50–100 m below the surface) of the open ocean

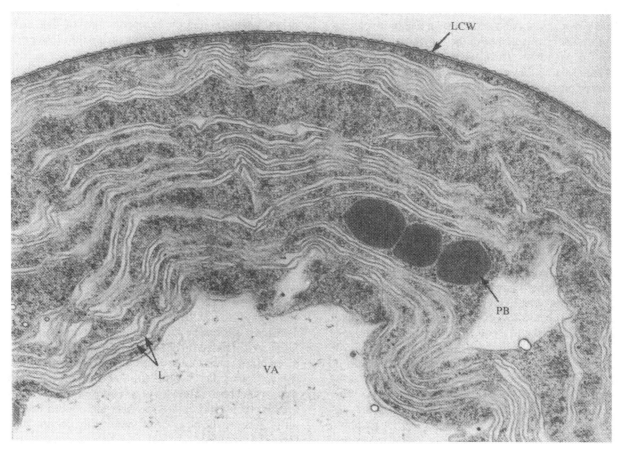

Figure 3.1. Part of a *Prochloron* cell, in thin section. L = lamella (stack) of two appressed thylakoids; LCW = layered cell wall; PB = polyhedral body (= carboxysome); VA = vacuole (distended thylakoid).

(Transmission electron micrograph by courtesy of Dr Kit W. Lee, University of Nebraska; from [997b], with the permission of the author and Springer-Verlag, Berlin.)

([229, 522, 1337, 1822a]). *Prochlorothrix hollandica*, on the other hand, is a filamentous prochlorophyte, which gives rise to massive blooms in the shallow eutrophic lakes of the Netherlands where it was discovered ([168]). The filaments are unbranched and contain gas vesicles (cf. p. 26).

The discovery of *Prochloron* caused much excitement, as it was interpreted as the ancestor of the chloroplasts of green algae and land plants, sharing with them the possession of chlorophylls a *and* b, and a stacked arrangement of the thylakoids. According to the endosymbiosis theory, the chloroplasts of eukaryotic algae originated as prokaryotic algae, which were ingested but not digested by early heterotrophic eukaryotes (cf. pp. 2, 503). The chloroplasts of the

Rhodophyta (red algae) and Glaucophyta can be interpreted as the descendants of ingested cyanophytes, because of the striking resemblances between them and the Cyanophyta in structure and photosynthetic pigments (equidistant thylakoids bearing phycobilisomes, the presence of chlorophyll a but not chlorophyll b, and the presence of phycobiliproteins). The chloroplasts of green algae (division Chlorophyta) and those of the 'brown' algae (mainly the Heterokontophyta) differ considerably from the chloroplasts of the red algae, in ultrastructure and pigment composition, and so in the early development of the endosymbiosis theory, 'green' and 'brown' chloroplasts were often suggested to have been derived independently from two hypothetical photosynthetic prokaryotes: a green one (with chlorophylls a and b, and stacked thylakoids) and a brown one (with chlorophylls a and c, together with the brown accessory pigment fucoxanthin). Thus, when *Prochloron* was discovered, it was thought to represent the missing link between prokaryotic algae and green chloroplasts.

It seems, however, that *Prochloron* and *Prochlorothrix* are closely related to the Cyanophyta (see the list of characters given above). Recently, the phylogenetic relationships have been determined between *Prochlorothrix* and a variety of Cyanophyta (Cyanobacteria), and the results are summarized in the phylogenetic tree shown in Fig. 2.8 ([1806]); a detailed discussion is given on p. 40. The phylogenetic tree seems to establish clearly that *Prochlorothrix* belongs within the lineages of the Cyanophyta: it is a green cyanophyte. The same appears to be true of *Prochloron*, judging by the genetic data available so far, although these are incomplete (see [1676]). In addition, it seems quite likely that, within the Cyanophyta, *Prochloron* and *Prochlorothrix* will not cluster together, since their DNAs differ significantly in gross composition ([167, 1879]). Moreover, comparisons of nucleotide sequences (of 16S ribosomal RNA and of the gene for a subunit of a ribosomal RNA polymerase) in *Prochloron*, *Prochlorococcus* and *Prochlorothrix* indicate that these three genera are unrelated, except that all belong to the Cyanophyta (Cyanobacteria) ([1353a, b, 1808a]). This would mean that the Prochlorophyta are not a phylogenetically coherent group and hence that the division Prochlorophyta is artificial. In the phylogenetic tree of Fig. 2.8, *Prochlorothrix* lies quite far away from the cluster that includes green chloroplasts, which does not accord with the theory that these chloroplasts descended from a prochlorophyte ancestor. However, another molecular comparison that has been made (of amino acid sequences in one of the thylakoid proteins of photosystem II) points to a closer affinity between *Prochlorothrix* and chloroplasts ([1233]). It is interesting to note that chloroplasts form a coherent cluster within the phylogenetic tree of the Cyanophyta, suggesting that all of them have been derived from the same group of cyanophyte ancestors. Within the chloroplasts studied, one (of the glaucophyte *Cyanophora*) resembles the Cyanophyta, having equidistant single thylakoids with phycobilisomes, while the remaining five resemble the prochlorophytes, with stacked thylakoids and chlorophyll b. It seems therefore that within the primaeval cyanophytes the acquisition of chlorophyll b, and the transformation of photosynthesis from a system based on chlorophyll a and phycobilins to one based on chlorophylls a and b, must have taken place at least three times. One of these may have occurred **after** the incorporation of a cyanophyte into a eukaryote host. (The idea of an endosymbiotic origin for eukaryote chloroplasts has been introduced briefly on p. 7, and will be pursued more fully on pp. 211, 504–12.)

4

Glaucophyta

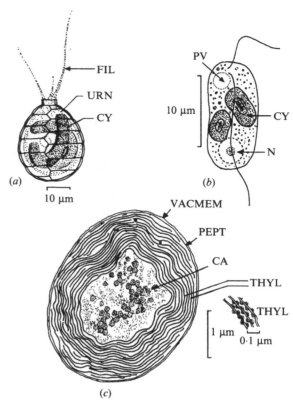

Figure 4.1. (*a*) *Cyanophora paradoxa*. (*b*) *Paulinella chromatophora*, a thecate freshwater amoeba with two cyanelles. (*c*) Transverse section of the cyanelle in *Paulinella*, seen with the electron microscope. CA = carboxysomes (polyhedral bodies); CY = cyanelle; FIL = filopodium; N = nucleus; PEPT = peptidoglycan wall of the cyanelle; PV = pulsating (contractile) vacuole; THYL = thylakoids bearing phycobilisomes; URN = the urn-like envelope, composed of siliceous scales; VACMEM = membrane of the vacuole containing the cyanelle. (*a* based on [125]; *b* based on [840].)

This tiny division belongs to the realm of the Eukaryota and the cells accordingly contain nuclei, golgi bodies, endoplasmic reticulum, mitochondria, and chloroplasts. We place the Glaucophyta immediately after the prokaryotic algae because the chloroplasts of the Glaucophyta are in various respects like unicellular, coccoid cyanophytes (cyanobacteria); they are therefore interpreted as being in some ways intermediate between cyanophytes and the chloroplasts of other algae and higher plants. The division contains one class, the Glaucophyceae.

The principal characteristics of the Glaucophyta [840, 841, 842, 843, 844, 845, 846, 1218, 1570, 1579]

1 The three genera in the class are all basically unicellular flagellates, similar to *Cyanophora* (Fig. 4.1*a*).

2 The flagellate cells are dorsiventral, with a rounded dorsal side and a flat ventral side, and they bear two unequal flagella, which are inserted in a shallow depression just below the apex of the cell. The flagella possess two rows of delicate hairs, which resemble the hairs on the flagella of some green algae (division Chlorophyta: cf. Fig. 19.2*e*); they are quite unlike the stiff tubular hairs (mastigonemes) on

the flagella of the Heterokontophyta (cf. Fig. 6.4*e*).

3 The chloroplasts are very similar to unicellular, coccoid members of the Cyanophyta (Cyanobacteria). Each is surrounded by a thin peptidoglycan wall and lies in a special vacuole (Fig. 4.1*c*).

4 The thylakoids are not stacked (as they are in the prokaryotic division Prochlorophyta and in most eukaryotic algae), but are single and equidistant (Figs. 1.1*a* and 4.1*c*). This thylakoid arrangement is also found in the Cyanophyta (Fig. 2.1*a*)

and in the chloroplasts of the Rhodophyta (Figs. 5.1*a*, *b*, 5.2*c*).

5 The chloroplasts contain chlorophyll a, but *not* chlorophylls b or c, in this respect again resembling the Cyanophyta and the chloroplasts of the Rhodophyta.

6 The colour of the chloroplasts is blue-green, since the green chlorophyll is masked by the blue pigments phycocyanin and allophycocyanin. These accessory photosynthetic pigments are contained in phycobilisomes, which are attached to the thylakoids, as in the Cyanophyta and the chloroplasts of red algae (Figs. 2.1*a*, 4.1*c*). Carotenoid accessory pigments are also present and include β-carotene, zeaxanthin and β-cryptoxanthin ([1570]).

7 The chloroplast DNA is concentrated in the centre of the chloroplast. This arrangement resembles that in the Cyanophyta, where the DNA lies in the centre of each cell ([254]). The centre of the chloroplast also harbours polyhedral bodies (carboxysomes), which again typically occur also in the centres of cyanophyte cells (Figs. 4.1*c*, 2.1*a*). Carboxysomes contain the enzyme ribulose 1,5-bisphosphate carboxylase–oxygenase, which catalyses the photosynthetic fixation of CO_2 into ribulose 1,5-bisphosphate ([844]).

8 The reserve polysaccharide is starch. Grains of this are formed outside the chloroplast (Fig. 1.1*a*), as in the Rhodophyta; in the Chlorophyta, on the other hand, the starch grains are formed within the chloroplast.

9 The flagellate cells of glaucophytes are surrounded by a superficial layer of flat vesicles, subtended by microtubules. The vesicles may be empty, or they may contain scales or fibrillar material. They are very like the thecal vesicles of the Dinophyta (Fig. 16.10*e*).

10 The class contains three rare freshwater genera, each with one species.

General remarks

The flagella of the glaucophytes have the typical '9 + 2' structure found in almost all eukaryote flagella, each one containing an axoneme consisting of 9 peripheral doublet microtubules, together with a central pair of single microtubules (cf. p. 303; Figs. 19.3, 19.4). Within the cell the axoneme ends in a basal body, which consists of a ring of 9 triplet microtubules (cf. Fig. 19.4); this too is typical of eukaryotes of all kinds. The flagella are anchored in the cell by a 'cruciate' (cruciate = in the form of a cross) system of four microtubular 'roots', an arrangement that shows some resemblance to the cruciate microtubular root systems of some green algae (division Chlorophyta: Fig. 19.6). In two of the three genera, the microtubular roots are each subtended by a 'multilayered structure', similar to the multilayered structures found in other green algae (Fig. 19.15). These resemblances are superficial, however, and the Glaucophyta are not closely related to the Chlorophyta; instead, they occupy a separate and rather isolated position within the algae ([842]).

The Glaucophyta are interesting because of the strong resemblance of their chloroplasts to simple, unicellular blue-green algae (cyanophytes, cyanobacteria). Indeed, for a long time the chloroplasts were considered as endosymbiotic blue-green algae (so-called '**cyanelles**'), living in the cells of unicellular heterotrophic eukaryotes ([497]), and this interpretation lent strong support to Mereschkowsky's ([1195]) theory of the endosymbiotic origins of chloroplasts (cf. p. 2). Electron microscopical investigations subsequently confirmed that glaucophyte chloroplasts are very similar to blue-green algae, and also to the chloroplasts of red algae (see the list of glaucophyte characteristics given above). The discovery of a thin peptidoglycan wall around the chloroplast was especially important evidence for a link with the Cyanophyta, since blue-green algae characteristically have a peptidoglycan layer in their cell walls; furthermore, both in the glaucophytes and in the blue-green algae, the peptidoglycan layers are broken down by the enzyme lysozyme, while their assembly is prevented by the antibiotic penicillin ([845]).

The size of the chloroplast genome has been investigated in the Glaucophyta and found to be around ten times smaller than the genomes of free-living blue-green algae; its size, of the order of 125 000 base pairs, is similar to that of other chloroplast genomes ([95, 645]). In its organization too, the chloroplast genome of glaucophytes seems to be more like the chloroplast genomes of other algae and higher plants than the genomes of cyanophytes. Thus, the circular chloroplast genomes of glaucophytes, like those of other plants, contain two 'inverted repeats', which are identical sections, containing the genes for the chloroplast ribosomal RNAs, but which are transcribed in opposite directions (i.e. inverted). The inverted repeats are separated by two sections of DNA present only in single copy ([95, 96, 938]).

These discoveries, together with the fact that the chloroplast cannot be cultured as a 'cyanobacterium' outside its host cytoplasm, the two being incapable of living apart ([845]), have led to the conclusion that the 'cyanelle' is a functional chloroplast and not an endosymbiotic cyanophyte. This does not mean, however, that the glaucophyte chloroplast did not evolve from an endosymbiotic cyanophyte. It remains quite likely that it did, and that the resemblances between the glaucophyte chloroplast and cyanophyte cells are characteristics inherited from the ancestral endosymbiont. This is despite the loss of about 90% of the cyanophyte genome, and consequently also the ability to live independently. In fact, the similarities between the genomes of higher plant chloroplasts and Cyanophyta (Cyanobacteria) are so striking that the cyanobacterial origin of chloroplasts can scarcely be doubted ([16]). Glaucophyte chloroplasts seem to have evolved less from their cyanobacterial ancestors than the chloroplasts of other groups. Not only have they retained a vestigial peptidoglycan wall and single, well-separated thylakoids bearing phycobilisomes, but they also possess gene clusters and sequences that are typical of cyanobacteria ([960, 1025]). A phylogenetic tree calculated for cyanobacteria on the basis of nucleotide sequences of 16S ribosomal RNA also supports the idea that glaucophyte 'cyanelles' are evolutionary links between cyanobacteria and chloroplasts (see *Cyanophora* in Fig. 2.8, and p. 507).

The picture of the Glaucophyta that emerges from this welter of evidence is of an ancient group ([203, 1218]), whose chloroplasts may be ancestral to those of most if not all other photosynthetic eukaryotes. This hypothesis, of the **monophyletic origin** of chloroplasts([938]), contrasts with the hypotheses of **polyphyletic** (multiple) **origin**, which are supported by the existence today of a multitude of different symbiotic associations between various types of heterotroph and a diversity of photosynthetic autotrophs. These associations exhibit different degrees of integration and seem to indicate that the incorporation of photoautotrophic prokaryotes by heterotrophs, and also of photoautotrophic eukaryotes, has occurred many times in the course of evolution. It is relevant here to introduce a further example of an organism that contains cyanelles, namely *Paulinella chromatophora*. This is an amoeba-like organism, which produces an urn-shaped envelope composed of robust siliceous plates (Fig. 4.1*b*). *Paulinella* contains 'cyanelles' that are quite similar to those of the glaucophytes, with vestigial peptidoglycan walls and unstacked thylakoids bearing phycobilisomes; as in the glaucophytes, too, the cyanelles are incapable of living outside the host cell ([840, 843]). *Paulinella* is unrelated to the glaucophytes, so that it must have acquired 'chloroplasts', and hence the capacity to photosynthesize, quite independently, through a different endosymbiotic event. If cyanelles and chloroplasts have had many different origins, evolving over and over again from different cyanobacterial ancestors, then the similarities between them in genome organization and genetic sequences must be ascribed to common descent from a cyanobacterial archetype, coupled with convergent evolution enforced by the functional constraints that apply to chloroplasts. In this view, cyanelles occupy an evolutionarily intermediate position between cyanobacteria and chloroplasts because it is a relatively short time since their incorporation into their heterotrophic host; they therefore retain more cyanobacterial features than chloroplasts. We will return to this topic in Chapter 32 (p. 504).

Two examples

Cyanophora paradoxa (Fig. 4.1*a*)
The cells are ellipsoidal and bear two unequal flagella, which emerge from a shallow depression located just to one side of the cell apex. One flagellum is directed forwards, the other back along the cell. Within the cell there are two rounded 'cyanelles'. *Cyanophora* is often used as a model organism for investigations into the endosymbiotic origins of chloroplasts.

Glaucocystis (Fig. 1.1*a*)
Here the cells are ellipsoidal and non-motile. Each is surrounded by a cellulose wall and possesses two vestigial flagella. The 'cyanelles' form two stellate (star-like) clusters within the cell.

Cyanophora and *Glaucocystis* are only rarely encountered, occurring in shallow freshwaters among floating and attached filamentous algae ([843]).

5

Rhodophyta (red algae)

The principal characteristics of the Rhodophyta

1 The reproductive cells of the Rhodophyta are naked, spherical protoplasts, which never have flagella (contrary to some reports, e.g. [1633, 1634]; see [146, 934]). They are extruded from the sporangia or gametangia as a result of the formation of copious amounts of mucilage (Figs. 5.8, 5.10, 5.11, 5.17, 5.18).

2 Each chloroplast is surrounded only by its own double-membrane envelope, and not by an additional layer of endoplasmic reticulum (Figs. 5.2c, 5.11). This character is shared with the Glaucophyta, Chlorophyta, Bryophyta and Tracheophyta.

3 The thylakoids are not stacked (unlike all other eukaryotic photosynthetic plants except the Glaucophyta) but lie equidistant and singly within the chloroplasts (Figs. 5.1a, 5.2c, 5.11). One or sometimes two thylakoids are usually present around the periphery of the chloroplast, running parallel to the chloroplast envelope (Figs. 5.2c, 5.11).

4 The only chlorophyll is chlorophyll a; chlorophylls b and c are absent.

5 The green of the chlorophyll is masked by the red accessory pigment phycoerythrin; the related blue pigment phycocyanin also occurs in the chloroplasts of Rhodophyta (Table 1.2). These two accessory pigments are phycobiliproteins and are located in hemispherical or hemidiscoidal bodies (phycobilisomes) on the surfaces of the thylakoids (Fig. 5.1b).

6 The chloroplast DNA is organized into numerous small, 1–2 μm diameter blebs (nucleoids), which are scattered throughout the chloroplast ([254]); a ring-shaped nucleoid is not present.

7 The most important storage product is a polysaccharide, floridean starch. Grains of this material are formed in the cytoplasm, next to the chloroplast envelope, unlike the starch grains produced by the green algae (Chlorophyta), which lie within the chloroplasts (Figs. 5.1a, 5.10).

8 Mitosis is closed and the telophase spindle is persistent. The mitotic nucleus is surrounded not only by its own envelope but also by perinuclear endoplasmic reticulum. At each pole of the spindle there is a darkly staining body, which is usually ring-shaped (the polar ring); centrioles are absent (Fig. 5.4a–d). Cytokinesis is brought about by the development of a cleavage furrow (Fig. 5.4e).

9 In the great majority of red algae, cleavage is incomplete. This leads initially to the formation of an open protoplasmic connection (a pit connection) between the daughter cells (Fig. 5.6a), but soon the connection becomes closed by a proteinaceous stopper, the pit plug. The Rhodophyta are the only algae that have pit plugs (Figs. 5.5, 5.6b).

10 Species in which sexual reproduction is known generally have an isomorphic or heteromorphic, diplohaplontic life cycle; only exceptionally is the life cycle haplontic. Gametic fusion is always oogamous. Species that lack sexual reproduction are considered to have lost it secondarily.

11 The red algae are predominantly marine; there are a few exceptions, which live in freshwater ([1620]).

Size and distribution of the division

There are 5000–5500 species of red algae, which are distributed among 500–600 genera. Of these, very few occur in freshwater: only about 150 species from *ca.* 20 genera ([1620]). The number of species shows that the Rhodophyta is really only a small division, especially when one considers that the Compositae, a mere family of dicotyledonous flowering plants, contains about 900 genera and 20 000 species.

Most red algae are marine and live attached to rocks. They can also grow on other solid substrata, such as dykes and sea-walls, or more rarely on shells, eelgrass (*Zostera*, a marine angiosperm) or other algae. Unlike the higher plants that cover the world's land masses, and the phytoplankton drifting in the surface waters of the oceans, the red algae have only a small living space ('Lebensraum'), since they are restricted to the narrow coastal fringes of the sea. Even here their distribution is limited, since in some places the water is turbid and does not transmit enough light for photosynthesis. Along the Dutch coast, for instance, red algae cannot grow below a few metres beneath the low-water mark, whereas in the Mediterranean they can be found at depths of more than 100 m ([408]). Indeed, red algae have been found living at greater depths than any other photosynthetic organisms. On a sea-mount off the Bahamas, red algal crusts have been observed (from a submersible) at a depth of 268 m, where only about 0.001% of the light incident on the surface of the sea remained available for photosynthesis ([1019, 1020, 1056]).

In the lower part of the intertidal zone, exposed only at low water, the rocks are often covered with a thick carpet of red algae, containing many species. Common examples of such intertidal algae on W European and NE American shores, in the temperate zone, are *Chondrus crispus* (Fig. 5.34) and *Mastocarpus stellatus* (Fig. 5.35). In tropical regions lime-encrusted rhodophytes belonging to the order Corallinales (p. 83) are important in the formation of reefs and sediments. Fossil remains of calcified rhodophytes are known from the Cambrian (*ca.* 600 million years ago) and from then onwards the Rhodophyta have been major contributors to marine carbonate sediments and various other types of rock ([1197, 1751]).

A unicellular red alga, belonging to the genus *Porphyridium* (Fig. 5.15*a*), has recently been discovered living as a photosynthetic endosymbiont within large (0.5–1 cm diameter) tropical foraminifera. These foraminifera, which are protozoa, have calcareous shells and live in the benthos in shallow water. Large tropical benthic foraminifera have also been found to harbour endosymbionts belonging to other groups of algae, such as diatoms (p. 136) and unicellular green algae (p. 362); in each case the endosymbionts are used by the protozoan as photosynthetic organelles ([915, 973, 974]). One case is known, too, where the chloroplasts of a red alga are used on their own as photosynthetic organelles; this occurs in a marine gastropod, the chloroplasts being stored in the animal's digestive gland ([913]).

A few rhodophytes are heterotrophic. They are generally non-photosynthetic, obligate parasites of other red algae, and are often reduced and pustular (Fig. 5.7; [391, 534, 535]). Photosynthates are translocated from the host to the parasite ([391, 533, 914, 1022]).

Some red algae are of considerable economic importance. The annual global harvest amounts to almost 1 million tonnes fresh mass, more than half of which comes from 'mariculture', practised mainly in Japan, China and the Philippines; the rest represents collection from natural populations. Red algae are used for two main purposes: for the production of colloid-forming polysaccharides found in the cell walls, such as agar and carrageenan (see the section below on cell wall composition), and for food (for instance, *Porphyra*: cf. p. 63) ([219, 221, 989a, 1056, 1296]).

Structure and properties of red algae

Pigments and chloroplasts

The red colour of these algae is produced by the accessory photosynthetic pigment phycoerythrin, which is located in the chloroplasts (Table 1.2). The blue pigments phycocyanin and allophycocyanin are also present. Phycoerythrin, phycocyanin and allophycocyanin are similar compounds, known as phycobilins. They occur attached to proteins, forming a class of compounds called phycobiliproteins. Phycoerythrin occurs in at least five forms in the red algae (B-phycoerythrin I and II, R-phycoerythrin I, II and III), which differ in their absorption spectra, although all have peaks in the green part of the spectrum (500–570 nm). The five types seem to be almost randomly distributed among the various rhodophyte groups ([529]). Phycocyanin occurs as R-phycocyanin and C-phycocyanin, with absorption peaks at 615 and 620 nm, while allophycocyanin has a peak at 650 nm; these peaks are all in the red part of the spectrum ([343, 1056, 1128, 1464, 1525]). Phycoerythrin is usually the dominant pigment and so the algae are red. In some species however, the colour varies, according to the ratio of phycoerythrin to phycocyanin. Thus, for instance, Irish Moss plants (*Chondrus crispus*; Fig. 5.34) growing in the intertidal zone are often blue-violet whereas plants in deeper water are a dark red; in one phycocyanin predominates, in the other, phycoerythrin. If they grow in direct sunlight *Chondrus* plants take on a yellow-brown or green colour, because the chlorophyll and carotenoids are no longer masked by the phycobilins. When they die, red algae usually become green quickly because the phycobiliproteins, unlike the chlorophyll, are water-soluble. They can therefore be easily washed out of the dying chloroplasts.

Chlorophyll a is an essential component of the photosynthetic apparatus in all plants, and many plants also possess other chlorophylls, such as chlorophyll b. The red algae, however, only have chlorophyll a, chlorophylls b and c being missing. Carotenoids are present, of which the most important are α-carotene, β-carotene, lutein and zeaxanthin (Table 1.2). Antheraxanthin, violaxanthin, α- and β-cryptoxanthin have also been found in some species ([87, 156, 1128, 1464, 1525]).

All these pigments lie in the chloroplasts, which can take a variety of shapes (Figs. 5.1, 5.2, 5.15, 5.17). In most red algae the chloroplasts lie against the cell wall: they are 'parietal'. These parietal plastids can be ribbon-shaped or discoid (Figs. 5.1c, 5.17), and both types sometimes occur together in a single species, e.g. in *Ceramium* (Fig. 5.1c). The thallus of *Ceramium* consists of two main types of cell: large axial cells, and small cortical cells, which cover the surface of each axial cell near the cross wall that separates it from its neighbour. The large axial cells contain straight or band-like chloroplasts, while the small cortical cells have discoid chloroplasts; here and in many other cases, the discoid plastids have lobed margins. A few species, mostly from the class Bangiophyceae, possess fairly irregular, stellate chloroplasts, which lie in the centre of the cell (Figs. 5.1a, 5.2b, 5.15). Only a few red algae have chloroplasts that contain pyrenoids (Figs. 5.1a, 5.2b, d, 5.15), these being visible in the light microscope as round structures lying at the centre of the chloroplast. In the green algae the pyrenoids are the focus for starch production (p. 339), but the function of the red algal pyrenoid is unknown, since while in the green algae starch is formed around the

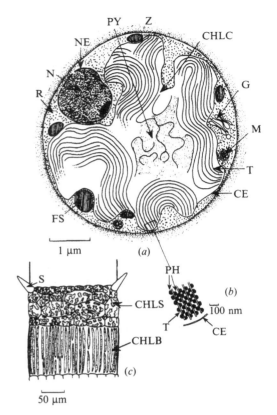

Figure 5.1. (*a*) *Porphyridium purpureum*: ultrastructure. (*b*) Thylakoid ultrastructure. (*c*) *Ceramium* species: part of thallus. CE = chloroplast envelope; CHLB = elongate, band-like chloroplast; CHLC = central stellate chloroplast; CHLS = small discoid chloroplast; FS = floridean starch; G = golgi body; M = mitochondrion; N = nucleus; NE = nuclear envelope; PH = phycobilisomes; PY = pyrenoid; R = ribosomes; S = spine cell; T = thylakoid; Z = fibrous cell wall. (*a* after [483]; *b* after [1006].)

pyrenoids, *within* the chloroplasts, in the red algae the reserve starch is produced in the cytoplasm, although it is formed very close to the chloroplast envelope (Fig. 5.1a).

Red algal chloroplasts have a highly distinctive ultrastructure (Figs. 5.2c, 5.11). Each chloroplast is bounded by two membranes, which lie about 13 nm apart. Inside the chloroplast are thylakoids, which are not stacked but maintain roughly the same distance from each other throughout the organelle. This is unlike any other group of eukaryotic plants (except the Glaucophyta), since everywhere else the thylakoids

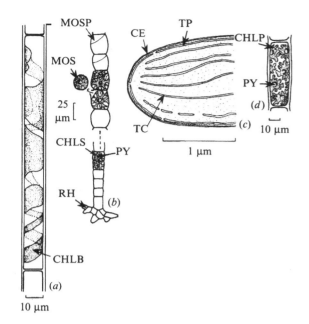

Figure 5.2. (*a*) *Audouinella* species. (*b*) *Erythrotrichia carnea.* (*c*) *Ceramium:* ultrastructure of the chloroplast. (*d*) *Audouinella* species. CE = chloroplast envelope; CHLB = spirally wound, ribbon-like chloroplast; CHLP = lobed parietal chloroplast; CHLS = stellate central chloroplast; MOS = monospore; MOSP = monosporangium; PY = pyrenoid; RH = rhizoid; TC = central thylakoid; TP = peripheral thylakoid. (*a, d* after [948]; *b* after [337]; *c* after [1555].)

are stacked in some way. Each thylakoid is about 18–20 nm thick.

In *Ceramium* (Fig. 5.1*c*) and many other red algae there is a peripheral thylakoid (Fig. 5.2*c*), which runs around the chloroplast, just beneath the chloroplast envelope; in *Porphyridium* this is absent (Fig. 5.1*a*). Apart from this, however, the parietal, plate-like chloroplasts of *Ceramium* and the central, stellate chloroplasts of *Porphyridium* are essentially similar ([605]). In both cases the thylakoids have the structure and arrangement described above.

On the thylakoid surface there are many small granules (about 30–40 nm in diameter), which are closely spaced and often hemispherical. They contain the phycobiliproteins and are therefore called **phycobilisomes**. Fig. 5.1*b* shows a section through part of a chloroplast, with its thylakoids and phycobilisomes ([483]). Phycobilisomes occur in every kind of red alga but are not always hemispherical. Thus in *Porphyridium aerugineum*, for instance, the phycobil-

isomes are hemidiscoidal and lie one behind another on the thylakoids like stacks of coins. In hemispherical phycobilisomes the predominant phycobilin is phycoerythrin, while in hemidiscoidal phycobilisomes it is phycocyanin. Phycobilisomes also occur in the Cyanophyta (p. 17) and here they are usually hemidiscoidal. A more detailed account of phycobilisomes is given on p. 25. They are light-harvesting complexes, which capture light energy and transfer it efficiently to chlorophyll a in the thylakoid membranes ([343, 485, 486]).

The chloroplast DNA is aggregated into numerous small (*ca.* 1–2 μm diameter) nucleoids, which are scattered throughout the chloroplast. This can be demonstrated by staining with the DNA-specific fluorescent dye DAPI (= 4',6-diamidino-2-phenylindole; see also p. 113 and [254]). It is likely that each nucleoid consists of several circular chloroplast DNA molecules, apparently attached to membranous bodies in the chloroplast stroma ([198, 1795]).

Storage products

The food reserve of red algae is the polysaccharide **floridean starch**, an α-1,4 linked glucan. This differs from the starch synthesized by green algae (and higher plants) in that it is devoid of amylose, the unbranched fraction of green algal starch. It resembles instead the branched, amylopectin fraction of chlorophyte and higher plant starch ([1148, 1395, 1396, 1464]). Floridean starch grains are formed in the cytoplasm, not within the chloroplasts as they are in the Chlorophyta (see, however, [1795]).

The low-molecular-mass carbohydrate floridoside has an osmoregulatory function ([1056, 1477]), and occurs not only in the Rhodophyta but also in the Cyanophyta and Cryptophyta ([1464]).

Cell wall composition

The cell wall consists of a fibrillar fraction embedded in an amorphous matrix. The fibrillar fraction gives the cell wall its strength and usually consists predominantly of cellulose ([911, 1064, 1148, 1396, 1464]). In higher plants and some green algae the cellulose forms microfibrils – straight, uniformly wide bundles of glucose chains – and these are arranged parallel to each other. In the red algae, on the other hand, the microfibrils form a more irregular felty network.

In *Porphyra* and *Bangia* (pp. 63, 69) the fibrillar part of the cell wall consists of a polymer of xylose (i.e. a xylan). Mannans (polymers of mannose) are also to be found in these genera ([1022, 1148, 1396, 1464]).

The amorphous part of the red algal cell wall is made of 'slime': mucilaginous material that can be extracted from the wall with hot water. Just as in many other plant groups, the golgi apparatus plays an important role in the deposition of wall material; the slime is synthesized there, transported to the cell surface in golgi vesicles ([1469]) and then incorporated into the wall. It usually consists of galactans (polymers of sulphated galactose residues) and various galactans are to be found, depending on the red alga, of which agar and carrageenan are the most important ([1148, 1149, 1395]).

Agar and **carrageenan** are used on a large scale for the preparation of gels. Agar, for example, is of great importance in microbiological investigations. 1–2% agar gels can be made of aqueous media, containing nutrients suitable for fungi and bacteria; the gel itself, however, is for the most part resistant to degradation by these organisms. Furthermore, because agar is nontoxic, it can also be used extensively in the food industry (e.g. for jams and marmalade, and in the conservation of meat and fish), where it is valued for its colloidal properties ([221, 531, 989a, 1056, 1155]).

Agar is obtained from various red algae (species of *Gelidium, Gracilaria* and *Pterocladia*), which are sometimes called the 'agarophytes'. Agar has been manufactured and processed in Japan since the seventeenth century and Japan is still the most important producer of agar. Together with Korea, it produces about 3500 tonnes annually, but Europe is responsible for *ca.* 2000 tonnes. The total production world-wide amounts to some 7000 tonnes ([1155]).

Carrageenan too is non-toxic and, like agar, is used industrially because of its colloidal properties. It is required in the food, pharmaceutical and textile industries for the stabilization of emulsions and suspensions. Agar and alginate (the colloidal cell wall material of some brown algae) can also be used for this purpose. The use of gel-forming cell wall constituents in industry is considered in more detail on p. 169. Carrageenan is obtained from *Chondrus crispus* (Irish Moss; Fig. 5.34) and *Mastocarpus stellatus* (Fig. 5.35), species that live attached to rocks in the lower part of the intertidal zone, for instance along North Sea coasts. In the Philippines, species of the genus *Eucheuma* are cultivated for carrageenan production.

The most important producer of carrageenan is Europe (about 7900 tonnes annually), followed by North America (4500 tonnes). The total amount produced annually is *ca.* 13 000 tonnes ([421, 989a, 1155, 1396, 1932]).

Calcification of the cell wall

In the order Corallinales the cell walls are encrusted with lime, which occurs as crystals of calcite. Calcareous red algae are particularly abundant in the clear waters of the tropics but do also occur elsewhere, in all the world's seas. Coral reefs consist to a large extent of the remains of calcareous red algae, which cement the coral colonies together into a solid structure. Examples of calcareous red algae include *Lithothamnion, Lithophyllum* (Fig. 5.27a, b) and *Jania* (Fig. 5.27c, d).

Calcification is linked to photosynthetic carbon fixation. Uptake of CO_2 from the cell walls is thought to bring about a rise in pH and hence an increase in the concentration of CO_3^{2-} ions. This in turn can lead to the precipitation of calcium carbonate. Acid polysaccharides, perhaps alginic acid, may act as nucleation sites for the calcite crystals. Alginic acid is known to occur in the cell walls of calcareous red algae ([1321]), although it is much better known as a ubiquitous constituent of the cell walls of brown algae (p. 169). The nucleation of calcite crystals by such polysaccharides is suggested by the fact that the crystals are orientated parallel to the polysaccharide fibrils. Thus, in the middle lamella, both the fibrils and the crystals lie parallel to the cell surface, while in the secondary cell wall, both are orientated perpendicular to the cell surface (Fig. 5.3). Once crystals have been initiated they can act as nuclei for further calcification ([109, 176]).

Mitosis and cytokinesis

The ultrastructure of nuclear division (mitosis) and cell division (cytokinesis) has recently become important in algal systematics, for distinguishing the main evolutionary lineages. Within the division Chlorophyta in particular, so many species have now been investigated with respect to the details of mitosis and cytokinesis, that it is possible to use these characteristics with some confidence to delineate the orders and other major groups (see pp. 323–34).

Mitosis and cytokinesis have been investigated electron microscopically in only a few red algae, but

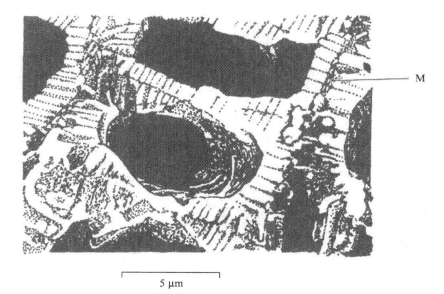

M

5 μm

Figure 5.3. Scanning electron micrograph (redrawn) of a fractured thallus of the crustose coralline alga *Lithothamnion*. Each cell wall is impregnated with calcite crystals, which are orientated predominantly at right angles to the cell within. Only in the middle lamella (M) are the crystals parallel to the cell surface. (Based on [109].)

the data that are available suggest that the basic features are the same throughout the division ([288, 1605, 1606, 1607]), although subtle variation allows the recognition of several subtypes ([140, 738, 1587]).

Polysiphonia (Fig. 5.37, p. 92) will be taken as an example, to demonstrate the characteristics of rhodophyte mitosis and cytokinesis (Fig. 5.4; [1607]). It is probably representative of the majority of red algae.

Mitosis

At early prophase, one of the poles of the future spindle is marked by a darkly staining, ring-shaped structure – one of the two **polar rings** (Fig. 5.4a). Then the other polar ring migrates around the nucleus to establish the other pole of the spindle (Fig. 5.4a). In many other groups of eukaryotes the mitotic spindle is formed between two pairs of centrioles, one pair lying at each spindle pole. Centrioles are similar ultrastructurally to the basal bodies of flagella (Figs. 19.4, 19.6a), each consisting of a short cylinder of nine microtubular triplets, and they are thought in many instances to transmit the capacity to form flagella from one generation to the next ([1218]; see also p. 308); the centriolar pairs (Fig. 19.22, CEP) replicate during cell division. The complete absence of centrioles in red algae, and the presence instead of polar rings, reflects

the absence of flagella and is a fundamental difference between the Rhodophyta and other groups of algae.

New polar rings are formed very close to existing rings, which may well function as templates. The rings are surrounded by an 'empty' zone, lacking ribosomes (Fig. 5.4a), and persist even in cells that do not divide ([1609]). At late prophase there is a ring at each pole of the nucleus, appressed to a small protrusion of the nuclear envelope and surrounded by a ribosome-free zone; this now contains irregular arrays of microtubules (Fig. 5.4b). Perinuclear endoplasmic reticulum (ER) begins to develop around the nucleus (Fig. 5.4b), and the nucleolus disappears.

At metaphase the chromosomes are arranged in a distinct plate (Fig. 5.4c), and are attached to chromosomal spindle microtubules via the distinct, layered kinetochores. The chromosomal and interzonal microtubules do not converge towards the polar rings, so that the spindle poles are very broad. The nuclear envelope remains intact (although perforated by large holes) and mitosis is therefore **closed**. Perinuclear microtubules proliferate between the nucleus and the perinuclear ER. Meanwhile a new polar ring appears next to each old ring.

The interzonal spindle microtubules remain present for some time at late anaphase and early telophase

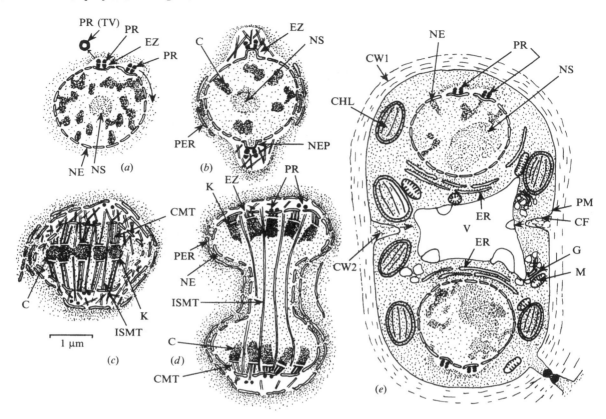

Figure 5.4. Mitosis in *Polysiphonia*, based on EM observations. (*a*) **Early prophase**. One polar ring (PR)
already lies where one of the spindle poles will form,
while the second ring migrates to establish the other
pole. Note that new polar rings are formed very close
to the existing rings, which may perhaps function as
templates. The polar rings are surrounded by an
'empty' zone (EZ), which reflects an absence of ribosomes. (*b*) **Late prophase**. The polar rings are all
appressed to protrusions of the nuclear envelope
(NEP) and are again surrounded by empty zones,
which now contain microtubules. Perinuclear endoplasmic reticulum (PER) develops. (*c*) **Metaphase**.
The chromosomes are arranged in a typical metaphase plate, with chromosome spindle microtubules
attached to distinct kinetochores. The parental polar
rings have now separated from the new daughter rings.
(*d*) **Anaphase**. Note that the nuclear envelope (NE)
and the perinuclear ER (PER) remain more or less
intact. The daughter polar rings are not directly

involved in mitosis but 'kept in reserve' for the next
division. (*e*) **Late telophase**. The daughter nuclei are
held apart by a vacuole. Cytokinesis is brought about
by a cleavage furrow (CF), which is an ingrowing
ring-like invagination of the plasmalemma. This later
impinges upon and constricts the vacuole. The cleavage furrow leaves a connection between the two
daughter cells, as a septal pore, which is stoppered by
a pit plug (cf. Figs. 5.5, 5.6). C = chromosome; CF =
cleavage furrow; CHL = chloroplast; CMT = chromosomal spindle microtubule; CW1 = cell wall of parent
cell; CW2 = young cross-wall between daughter cells;
EZ = 'empty' zone; G = golgi body; ISMT = interzonal spindle microtubule; K = kinetochore; M =
mitochondrion; NE = nuclear envelope; NEP = protrusion of nuclear envelope; NS = nucleolus; PER = perinuclear endoplasmic reticulum; PM = plasma membrane (plasmalemma); PR = polar ring; PR (TV) =
polar ring, viewed from the top; V = vacuole. (Based
on [1607].)

(Fig. 5.4*d*), so that the daughter nuclei are held apart;
in other words, the telophase spindle is persistent and
does not collapse at an early stage, as it does in some
other algae (contrast, for example, the collapsing

spindles of the green algae illustrated in Fig. 19.20 I,
II). Following telophase, the daughter polar rings
remain in reserve for future mitoses.

Cytokinesis

At late telophase, when the spindle has finally been broken down, the daughter nuclei are kept apart by a vacuole (Fig. 5.4*e*). Cytokinesis is brought about by an ingrowing furrow of the plasmalemma, which is filled with cell wall polysaccharides, i.e. an ingrowing septum. The furrow impinges upon the vacuole but leaves open a cytoplasmic connection (the **septal pore** or pit) between the two daughter cells, which is subsequently blocked by a proteinaceous stopper, the so-called **pit plug** (Fig. 5.6*a, b*). Pit plugs are highly characteristic features of the Rhodophyta and various different kinds can be distinguished on the basis of their ultrastructure; these provide important characters for distinguishing between the rhodophyte orders (see below).

Pit plugs

In most red algae, particularly species belonging to the class Florideophyceae, the cells are linked by pit connections, which are conspicuous in the light microscope and appear as dots or lines crossing the walls that separate adjacent cells. The pit connections are often indicated in drawings of red algae (e.g. Fig. 5.9), in order to show which cells form a structural unit. Several electron microscopical investigations have shown that the pits connect one cell to the next, although they are occluded by a bung or plug of electron-dense material (Fig. 5.5; [112, 119, 390, 625]).

Pit plugs are characteristic of the Rhodophyta and are found in no other group of algae, although some red algae too lack them. At least seven different types of plug can be recognized on the basis of ultrastructural features, and their distribution among the Rhodophyta gives valuable taxonomic information ([1067, 1449, 1451, 1452, 1454, 1455, 1456, 1457, 1610]). The characteristics of the seven types are as follows:

Type 1 (Fig. 5.5*a*). The core of the plug is bordered on either side by a darkly staining, two-layered plug cap. The outer layer of the cap is separated from the inner layer by a membrane (the cap membrane), which is continuous with the plasmalemma.

Type 2 (Fig. 5.5*b*). The structure is as in type 1, except that the outer layer of the cap is thick and forms a conspicuous dome.

Type 3 (not illustrated). No cap membrane is present between the outer, dome-shaped layer of the cap

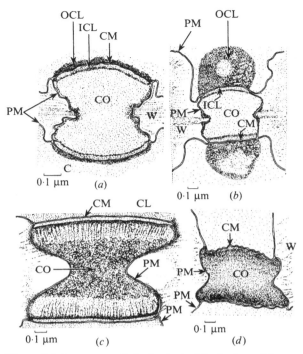

Figure 5.5. Four types of pit plug in the Rhodophyta. (*a*) Type 1, with a cap membrane and a two-layered plug cap (*Palmaria*). (*b*) Type 2, with a cap membrane and a two-layered plug cap, the outer layer being conspicuously domed (*Lemanea*). (*c*) Type 4, with a cap membrane and a one-layered plug cap (*Gelidium*). (*d*) Type 6, with a cap membrane but without a plug cap (*Rhodymenia*). CL = cap layer; CM = cap membrane; CO = core of pit plug; ICL = inner cap layer; OCL = outer cap layer; PM = plasmalemma; W = cell wall. (Based on [1456].)

and the inner, flat layer, but otherwise the structure is as in type 2.

Type 4 (Fig. 5.5*c*). The plug core is bordered on either side by a one-layered plug cap; this in turn is bounded by a cap membrane.

Type 5 (not illustrated). This is like type 4, but without a cap membrane.

Type 6 (Fig. 5.5*d*). Here the plug consists entirely of core, plug caps being absent. The plug is bounded on either side by a cap membrane.

Type 7 (not illustrated). The structure is as in type 6, but without cap membranes; this is the simplest type of pit plug ([1457]).

The plug cores are proteinaceous, whereas the caps are partly composed of polysaccharide ([1452]). During the initial stages in the formation of a pit plug, cister-nae of endoplasmic reticulum (ER) cluster within a young septal pore (e.g. between two recently sepa-rated daughter cells), their long axes orientated per-pendicular to the pore aperture (Fig. 5.6*a*). Darkly staining precursor material then appears both inside and outside the ER cisternae and condenses to produce the plug, although traces of the cisternae often remain visible in the plug core (Fig. 5.6*b*; [1468, 1607]).

Most pit plugs are formed in septal pores left between recently divided, sibling cells (see the account of mitosis and cytokinesis); these are often termed '**primary pit connections**'. Many red algae, however, form '**secondary pit connections**', by local fusion and subsequent pit plug formation between adjacent, non-sibling cells (e.g. Figs. 5.27*b*, 5.34*b*). This process often takes the following course. One of the two adja-cent, fully grown cells divides unequally, so that a small daughter cell is produced (called a conjunctor

cell), containing a nucleus. The conjunctor cell remains connected to its parent by a primary pit connection (containing a pit plug) and subsequently also fuses with the other fully grown cell ([465, 533]), into which it injects its nucleus (Fig. 5.6*c*). Secondary pit connections and plugs can also be formed between red algal parasites and their red algal hosts (Fig. 5.7*c*; [533]).

The function of the pit plugs remains an enigma ([1451, 1878]). At first sight it would seem likely that they would hinder rather than promote translocation of photosyn-thetic assimilates and other organic material. However, the formation of secondary pits and pit plugs between red algal parasites and their hosts (e.g. Fig. 5.7) sug-gests that these connections are involved in the translo-cation of assimilates, which has been demonstrated to occur from host to parasite ([391, 533, 914, 1022]). Perhaps transport takes place along the plasma membranes by which adjacent cells remain connected across the pit plug. Another possible function of secondary pit for-mation between host and parasite may be to allow the parasite to inject nuclei into the host, via conjunctor cells (see above and Fig. 5.6*c*). By such a transfer of parasite genetic information into host cells, the parasite might be able to control and redirect the physiology of the host for its own benefit ([535]). Thus, for instance, the invading parasite may be able to induce the host cells to develop a colourless tumour ([1937]).

Reproductive cells

The reproductive cells of the Rhodophyta, including the male gametes, are non-flagellate spherical proto-plasts, and they are naked. They are extruded from the sporangia or gametangia in which they are produced through the secretion of copious amounts of mucilage. Flagella are never present, nor any vestiges of flagella or related structures, such as basal bodies or centrioles (cf. Figs. 19.4, 19.6), contrary to some previous reports (e.g. [1633, 1634]; see discussion in [146, 934]). The presence of polar rings instead of centrioles at the poles of the mitotic spindle is another reflection of the complete and fundamental absence of flagella and related structures (see also the section on mitosis and cytokinesis, p. 52).

There are several types of sporangia. **Mono-sporangia** produce only one spore per sporangium (Fig. 5.18) and this **monospore** is an asexual structure. **Carposporangia** also produce one spore per spo-rangium, a **carpospore**, except in the Bangiales, where

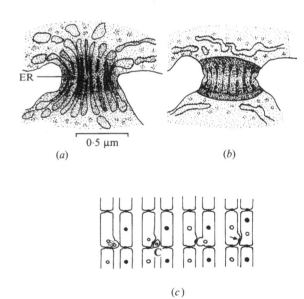

(*c*)

Figure 5.6. (*a*, *b*) Formation of a pit plug (of the type lack-ing plug caps). (*a*) Septal pore completed at the end of cell division and containing cisternae of endoplas-mic reticulum (ER), which stretch across the septal pore. Dark-staining material, representing the pre-cursors of the pit plug, is deposited both within and outside the cisternae. (*b*) The finished pit plug; the positions previously occupied by the ER cisternae can still be detected as darker bands within the core of the pit plug. (*c*) Formation of a secondary pit con-nection (arrow) by a conjunctor cell (C). (*a*, *b* based on [1468, 1607]; *c* based on [412].)

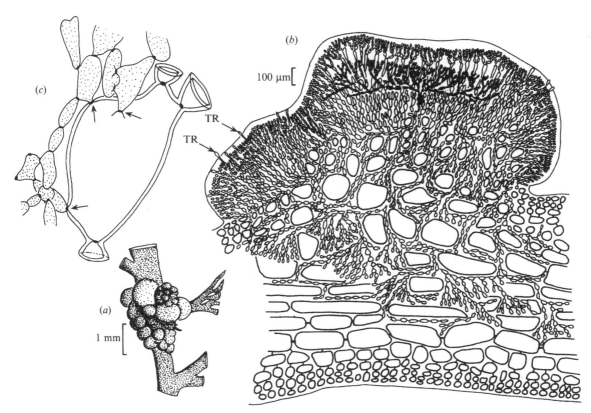

Figure 5.7. (*a, b*) *Harveyella mirabilis*, a parasitic red alga. (*a*) The spherical plants growing on their host, *Odonthalia*. (*b*) A section through host and parasite. Note the filaments of the parasite growing between the host cells. The gonimocarp is shown in black. (*c*) Secondary pit connections (arrows) between a red algal parasite (stippled) and its red algal host. TR = trichogyne. (*a* based on [534]; *b* on [1342]; *c* on [412].)

several are formed. Carpospores are diploid, as an indirect result of gametic fusion (Figs. 5.17*d*, 5.18*k*).

Spermatangia are a kind of diminutive monosporangium. Each spermatangium produces one tiny, naked **spermatium** (Figs. 5.17*a*, *b*, 5.18*d*), except again in the Bangiales, where the spermatangium produces a number of spermatia. Spermatia are reproductive cells, which act as male gametes; their function is to inject a male nucleus into the trichogyne, which is a protruberance borne by the carpogonium (the female gametangium) (Fig. 5.18*i*).

Finally, there are the **tetrasporangia**, which are meiosporangia. Each tetrasporangium produces four naked, haploid meiospores (Figs. 5.18*m*, 5.22*h*).

Other types of sporangia have been distinguished but are of little importance. For instance, 'polysporangia', which produce more than four spores, are only modified tetrasporangia ([1621]).

Monospores, carpospores, spermatia and tetraspores all have a very similar ultrastructure, which will be explained by reference to the production of spermatia and tetrasporangia, in *Polysiphonia* and *Palmaria* respectively ([146, 928, 929, 1450]).

Spermatangium ultrastructure (Figs. 5.8, 5.9c)

The nearly mature spermatium, still enclosed within the spermatangium, contains two large basal vesicles with fibrillar contents; these are sacs of mucilage (Fig. 5.8, MS) and represent specialized, dilated cisternae of endoplasmic reticulum (ER). The base of each vesicle is lined by a characteristic fibrous layer (Fig. 5.8, FTMS), on the inside of the vesicle membrane. This is the remnant of the 'mucilage sac associated organelle' (MSAO in Fig. 5.8*b*), which is interpreted as a modified ER cisterna and initiates the formation of the mucilage sac itself; exactly how this happens is not yet

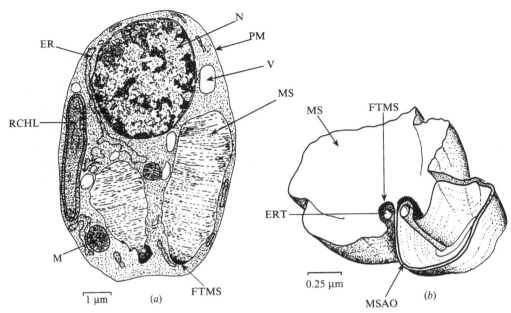

Figure 5.8. (*a*) The ultrastructure of a nearly mature spermatium in a red alga (*Polysiphonia* species). The spermatium characteristically contains two dilated ER cisternae, which in turn contain fibrous mucilage: these
are termed the spermatial mucilage sacs (MS). The
inner face of each mucilage sac membrane bears a
fibrous thickening (FTMS) towards the lower end of
the cell, which represents the remains of the 'mucilage sac associated organelle'; this is represented diagrammatically in (*b*). ER = endoplasmic reticulum; ERT =
a tubule of smooth ER, which forms part of the
MSAO; FTMS = fibrous thickening of the inner face
of the mucilage sac membrane; M = mitochondrion;
MS = mucilage sac; MSAO = mucilage sac associated
organelle; N = nucleus; PM = plasmalemma; RCHL =
rudimentary chloroplast; V = vacuole. (Based on [146].)

clear. Similar organelles, as well as the mucilage sacs
they are supposed to initiate, have also been encountered in tetrasporangia and carposporangia, in various
red algae ([146, 622]).

The contents of the mucilage sacs are carbohydrates
([417]), which swell as they are released and thus bring
about the extrusion of the mature spermatium from the
spermatangium. The carbohydrates are secreted into
the sacs by vesicles from active golgi bodies.

Tetrasporangium ultrastructure (Figs. 5.9–5.11)

The tetrasporangium does not cleave into four
meiospores until both meiotic divisions have been
completed (Fig. 5.9*b*). Mucilage sacs with fibrillar
contents are present in the young tetrasporangia, and
are of the same type as those in young spermatangia
(Figs. 5.10, 5.11*a*: MS). They are lined on one side by
a fibrous layer, lying against the inner face of the sac
membrane (Fig. 5.11*a*, FTMS), as in the mucilage sacs
of young spermatia (Fig. 5.8*a*). The mucilage sacs of
the tetrasporangia are special dilations of the endoplasmic reticulum and receive their polysaccharide
contents, partially at least, from numerous golgi-
derived vesicles (MV in Fig. 5.11*a*). The sacs deposit
their contents around the young tetraspores (Figs.
5.10, 5.11*a*, MU) and when this is complete the golgi
bodies begin to produce large numbers of vesicles
with dark-staining contents. These remain abundant in
the tetraspores after release and are termed 'adhesive
vesicles' (AV in Figs 5.10 and 5.11*b*), because they
probably contain adhesive material used in the attachment of the liberated tetraspores to the solid substrata
on which they settle. When the tetrasporangium is
mature the fibrillar mucilage secreted from the
mucilage sacs absorbs water, swells, and so aids the
extrusion of the naked tetraspores from the tetrasporangium.

Figures 5.10 and 5.11 illustrate another noteworthy
feature: the close association between the chloroplasts, mitochondria and golgi apparatus. This is often
encountered in the Rhodophyta.

Numerous grains of floridean starch are formed in

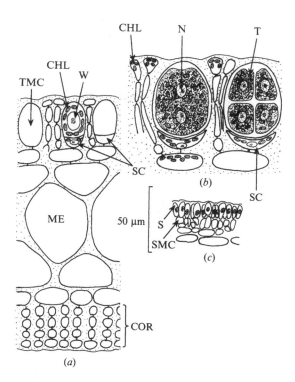

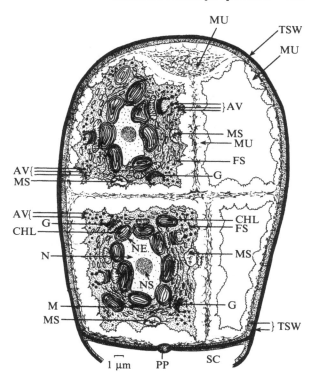

Figure 5.9. Tetrasporangia and spermatangia in *Palmaria palmata*. (*a*) Cross section through a blade with young tetrasporangia within the cortex. (*b*) Two tetrasporangia, immersed in the cortex: one (left) is pictured just after the first meiotic division, while in the other (right) formation of the four tetraspores has just been completed. (*c*) Cross section through part of a spermatangial blade. CHL = chloroplast; COR = cortex; ME = medulla; N = nucleus; S = spermatangium; SC = stem cell of the tetrasporangium; SMC = spermatangium mother cell; T = tetraspore; TMC = tetrasporangium mother cell. (Based on [583, 584].)

Figure 5.10. Ultrastructure of the tetrasporangium of *Palmaria*, redrawn from electron micrographs. AV = vesicles containing adhesive material; CHL = chloroplast; FS = floridean starch; G = golgi body; M = mitochondrion; MS = mucilage sac; MU = mucilage; N = nucleus; NE = nuclear envelope; NS = nucleolus; PP = pit plug; SC = stem cell; TSW = the two-layered tetrasporangial wall. (Based on [1450].)

the tetrasporangia, both during and after the first meiotic division. The sporangium is surrounded by a two-layered wall, which also encases the stalk cell below the sporangium (Fig. 5.10). Both layers contain polysaccharides, and the dark outer layer (the 'cuticle') is rich in protein and remains intact after the tetraspores have been discharged ([1450]; for ultrastructural aspects of carpospore formation, see [1799, 1800, 1801, 1802]).

Meiosis in red algae

There is plenty of light microscopical evidence to show that meiosis occurs in the life cycles of many red

algae (e.g. [1071]). It generally takes place in the tetrasporangia, during the formation of the tetraspores, which are therefore meiospores (Fig. 5.9*b*). Under the light microscope, meiosis can of course be recognized, after suitable staining (for instance, with the DNA-specific Feulgen stain), from particular, characteristic configurations of the chromosomes, which are present during meiosis in all kinds of eukaryotes. One of the most characteristic stages is the pairing (synapsis) of homologous chromosomes during meiotic prophase. This process is complete by the stage known as pachytene, when transmission electron microscopical observations reveal the presence of a special organelle, found only during meiosis: the **synaptonemal complex**. Synaptonemal complexes have been discovered in the young meiosporangia of various rhodophytes ([147, 934, 1450, 1621]) and have the same ultra-

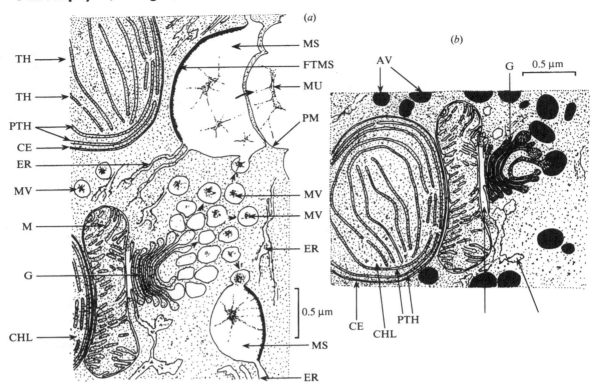

TH

TH

PTH

CE

ER

MV

M

G

CHL

MS

FTMS

MU

PM

MV

MV

ER

0.5 μm

MS

ER

(a)

(b)

AV

G

0.5 μm

CE

PTH

CHL

Figure 5.11. Drawings illustrating the activity of organelles in a tetrasporangium mother cell (*a*) and in a nearly complete tetrasporangium (*b*). (*a*) Massive accumulation of fibrous mucilage in special dilated ER cisternae, the mucilage sacs (MS). The mucilage sacs receive their contents, at least in part, from numerous mucilage vesicles (MV), derived from the golgi apparatus. The mucilage sacs deposit their contents around the young tetraspores (see Fig. 5.10). Note that the inner face of the mucilage sac membrane bears a characteristic fibrous thickening (FTMS) on one side of the sac. (*b*) After mucilage deposition is complete the golgi bodies produce many vesicles with dark-staining contents. These 'adhesive vesicles' (AV) are abundant in the tetraspores after release and probably contain material to attach the tetraspores to solid substrata. Note (in *a* and *b*) the close association between chloroplast, mitochondrion and golgi body. AV = vesicles containing adhesive material; CE = chloroplast envelope; CHL = chloroplast; ER = endoplasmic reticulum; EZ = 'empty' zone (without ribosomes); FTMS = fibrous thickening on the inner face of the mucilage sac membrane; G = golgi body; M = mitochondrion; MS = mucilage sac; MU = mucilage layer outside the cell; MV = mucilage vesicle; PM = plasmalemma; PTH = peripheral, encircling thylakoid; TH = thylakoid. (Based on electron micrographs in [1450].)

structure as in other eukaryotes. They consist of a long ladder-like core, to which two homologous chromosomes are attached, one on each side. The core is proteinaceous and consists of a central element (CE in Fig. 5.12), alongside which are two rows of transverse elements (TE in Fig. 5.12); beyond these are two lateral elements (LE in Fig. 5.12), attached to the looped ohromatin of the chromosomes ([16]). The synaptonemal complex keeps homologous chromosomes together and aligned, and is probably necessary for meiotic crossing over. The ends of the lateral elements are attached to the inner membrane of the nuclear envelope. During pairing they are thought to move within the membrane (through lateral flow of membrane material) and to associate in pairs, bringing the end of one chromosome close to the end of its homologue. Then the homologous chromosomes are apparently zipped together, as the synaptonemal complex assembles.

The synaptonemal complex is a highly conserved feature of eukaryotes; its complicated structure is apparently the same everywhere and this points to a fundamental homology. It seems therefore that the process in which the complex plays a part, meiosis, must also be fundamentally the same throughout the eukaryotes. Meiosis must therefore be extremely ancient, something that evolved in the common ancestors of all eukaryotes. It follows that sexual reproduction must also be an ancestral character, since the necessary obverse to the halving of the chromosome complement during meiosis is the doubling brought about by sexual fusion. Where sexual reproduction and meiosis are absent in eukaryotes, therefore, as they are in a considerable number of red algae, this

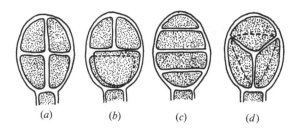

Figure 5.13. Four types of tetrasporangium. (*a*) Cruciate. (*b*) Cruciate-decussate. (*c*) Zonate. (*d*) Tetrahedral. (Based on [412].)

absence must generally (if not always) be secondary: the result of loss. There can be no doubt that sexuality has been lost many times in most phyla of eukaryotes. Nevertheless, some workers have attempted to argue that the absence of sexual reproduction in some red algae is primitive, not derived ([470a]; the opposite view is given in [471]). This is most unlikely and can be rejected. It would mean that sexual reproduction and meiosis (including the intricacies of the synaptonemal complex) have evolved many times in parallel, in quite different lineages of eukaryotes.

Sexually reproducing red algae usually have diplohaplontic life cycles, which can be isomorphic or heteromorphic. Specific examples will be given in the sections devoted to the various classes and orders.

Types of tetrasporangia

In most red algae the meiosporangia are tetrasporangia. By definition, each tetrasporangium contains four meiospores (tetraspores), but the arrangement of the spores varies, allowing four types of tetrasporangia to be recognized (Fig. 5.13). These are:

Cruciate tetrasporangia (Fig. 5.13*a*). The sporangium is divided into four meiospores by a horizontal septum and two vertical septa, which lie in the same plane as each other and therefore appear to intersect the horizontal septum in a cross.

Cruciate decussate tetrasporangia (Fig. 5.13*b*). Here there are horizontal and vertical septa as in the cruciate type, but the two vertical septa are (approximately) at right angles to each other. Thus, depending on how the sporangium is viewed under the microscope, either three or four meiospores are visible.

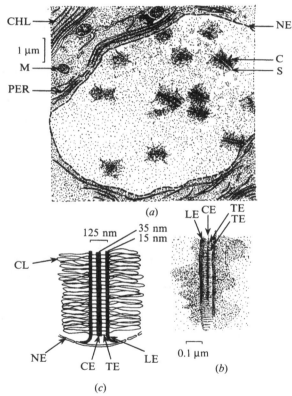

Figure 5.12. Meiosis in a young tetrasporangium. (*a*) A nucleus at pachytene, showing the synaptonemal complexes, one of which is attached to the nuclear envelope. (*b*) Detail of a synaptonemal complex. (*c*) Diagram of the structure of the synaptonemal complex. C = chromosome; CE = central element; CHL = chloroplast; CL = chromatin loops; LE = lateral element; M = mitochondrion; NE = nuclear envelope; PER = perinuclear endoplasmic reticulum (ER); S = synaptonemal complex; TE = transverse element. (*a, b* based on a combination of electron micrographs in [1450] and [935]; *c* based on [16].)

Zonate tetrasporangia (Fig. 5.13*c*). The sporangium is divided into four meiospores by three parallel, horizontal septa.

Tetrahedral tetrasporangia (Fig. 5.13*d*). The four meiospores lie at the apices of a tetrahedron, and are mutually compressed, with flat inner faces.

The type of tetrasporangium present can be used to characterize taxa within the red algae ([585]).

Subdivision of the Rhodophyta into classes and orders

In our account the division Rhodophyta is considered to contain two classes and a number of orders, which will be described in more detail in subsequent sections of this chapter. We have adopted the recent classification of Gabrielson & Garbary ([471, 472]; see also [470a]), with the addition of the Gracilariales ([448, 449]) and Ahnfeltiales ([1067]).

1 **Class Bangiophyceae**
    Orders Porphyridiales
    Rhodochaetales
    Erythropeltidales
    Compsogonales*
    Bangiales

2 **Class Florideophyceae**
    Orders Acrochaetiales
    Palmariales
    Nemaliales
    Batrachospermales
    Corallinales
    Hildenbrandiales*
    Bonnemaisoniales*
    Gelidiales
    Gigartinales
    Gracilariales*
    Ahnfeltiales*
    Rhodymeniales
    Ceramiales
    * These orders will not be considered any further.

The order Cryptonemiales, recognized in many traditional classifications ([100, 412, 440, 703, 948]), does not appear in the above list, since it has been merged with the Gigartinales (for discussion, see [909]).

Rhodophyta: Class 1. Bangiophyceae

The principal characteristics of the Bangiophyceae

1 The thalli are relatively simple: unicellular, filamentous, or blade-like (foliose) (Figs. 5.14, 5.15, 5.17). The cells are uninucleate.
2 Growth is either diffuse (brought about by intercalary cell division) or occurs through division of an apical cell.
3 Pit plugs may or may not be present, but if present they lack cap membranes (pit plug types 5 and 7; p. 55).
4 The chloroplasts are often stellate (star-shaped) and central in the cell (Figs. 5.14, 5.15); some species, however, have parietal chloroplasts or small discoid chloroplasts (Fig. 5.17).
5 The mitochondria and golgi bodies are sometimes closely appressed, sometimes not ([471]).
6 Sexually reproducing species have a diplohaplontic life cycle, which can be isomorphic ([97]) or heteromorphic ([471, 900, 901]).
7 In the sexual forms, the carpogonia (the oogonia of the red algae) scarcely differ morphologically from vegetative cells, lacking the conspicuous trichogynes of the Florideophyceae (compare Figs. 5.14*f* and 5.17*c* with Figs. 5.18*i*, 5.23*a*).
8 The carpogonium does not produce a diploid spore-producing tissue (gonimocarp) after fertilization, as it does in the Florideophyceae (compare Fig. 5.14*f*, *g* with Fig. 5.18*i*–*k*).
9 Tetrasporangia are absent.

This class encompasses a number of red algae with rather simple types of thalli. Most of the characters used to define the Bangiophyceae are either not universally present within the group (characters 2–5), or are negative, referring to the absence of traits present in the Florideophyceae (characters 7–9). This suggests that the Bangiophyceae may be phylogenetically heterogeneous; it represents several rhodophyte lineages, which are presumably primitive and cannot be included in the apparently monophyletic class Florideophyceae [470a, 471, 472, 1608].

An example of a life cycle in the class Bangiophyceae: the heteromorphic, diplohaplontic cycle of *Porphyra* (Fig. 5.14)

The thallus takes the form of an upright sheet or leaf (Fig. 5.14*d*), which is almost always only one layer of cells thick. The sheet is irregularly folded and often torn at its margins, and its base is anchored to the rocky substratum by rhizoids. Growth is intercalary, cell divisions occurring over the whole area of the thallus. Each cell has a central, stellate chloroplast, which contains a pyrenoid.

Porphyra umbilicalis is very common in Europe on rocky coasts, and may occur in great quantities high up in the intertidal zone. It can survive extreme desiccation. At low water, during dry weather, the plants dry out into brittle, papery membranes. Once submerged by the tide, however, or dampened by spray, they regain their normal appearance and look like limp, purple lettuce.

The life cycle of *Porphyra* (Fig. 5.14)

The species whose life cycle will be described below is *Porphyra tenera*, a Japanese alga that has been investigated in greater detail than other *Porphyra* species [943, 944]. Numerous studies of other species (e.g. the North Atlantic species *P. linearis*; [81]) show, however, that their life cycles do not differ significantly from the life cycle of *P. tenera*. *Porphyra tenera* used to be grown in large quantities in Japan as a foodstuff, although *P. yezoensis* has gradually taken its place [1296], and this is why it has been investigated in so much detail.

In Japan, fully grown plants of *Porphyra tenera* (Fig. 5.14*d*) are found in the winter half of the year (September to May). Most are hermaphrodite but some completely 'male' plants do occur. In these, many of the vegetative cells become transformed into **spermatangia**, i.e. the male gametangia (Fig. 5.14*e*). The first stage in this change is the production of a new wall layer, after which the spermatangium divides up, by successive divisions, into many (64 or 128) tiny male gametes, the **spermatia** [621]. Each spermatium has a highly condensed nucleus and a reduced chloroplast, which causes it to be pale, compared with the vegetative cells. The spermatia are liberated from the spermatangia partly by extrusion, through the swelling of the mucilage contained in their mucilage sacs (see p. 57), and partly through the gelatinization of the spermatangial walls (Fig. 5.8*a*; [621]). The nucleus of the mature spermatium loses its envelope.

The female gametangia, or **carpogonia**, are almost indistinguishable from surrounding vegetative cells, except that they bear small papilla-like protrusions (Fig. 5.14*f*). There is no basic difference between carpogonia and oogonia; traditionally, however, the term 'carpogonium' has been used in red algae, in preference to 'oogonium'. Fertilization occurs as follows. Spermatia are transported passively to the carpogonium by water currents and attach themselves to the surface of the thallus. Each spermatium then surrounds itself by a wall and injects its nucleus through a canal into the carpogonium, where fusion takes place between the male and female nuclei (Fig. 5.14*f*). This has been demonstrated in an elegant study, combining light and electron microscopy [621]. After fertilization, the carpogonium, which is now diploid (it is now a zygote), divides into a number of 4, 8, 16 or 32 diploid **carpospores** (Fig. 5.14*g*), apparently through mitosis, and these are liberated from the thallus by the breakdown of the carpogonium wall.

Each carpospore gives rise to a system of branched filaments, which are able to bore into the calcareous shells of molluscs or barnacles (Fig. 5.14*i–k*). This phase of the life cycle of *Porphyra* was discovered while carpospores were being cultured in the laboratory. It quickly became clear, however, that the branched, filamentous plants were identical with a small red alga, known as *Conchocelis rosea*, which had been discovered sometime previously, growing in the wild [336, 337, 338]. As a result, the filamentous phase of the *Porphyra* life cycle is called the '*Conchocelis* phase'. The carpospores and the *Conchocelis* phase are both diploid [527, 621, 1068]. The two multicellular phases differ in the composition of their cell walls. In the foliose *Porphyra* plants, the fibrillar fraction of the wall is composed of a xylan, while in the filamentous *Conchocelis* phase the fibrils are of cellulose. The amorphous fractions differ too: in the *Porphyra* phase the matrix polysaccharide is a mannan, while in the *Conchocelis* phase it is a galactan [1243].

Culture studies have shown that the *Conchocelis* phase produces a special kind of monospore. These spores, called **conchospores**, are formed in sporangia

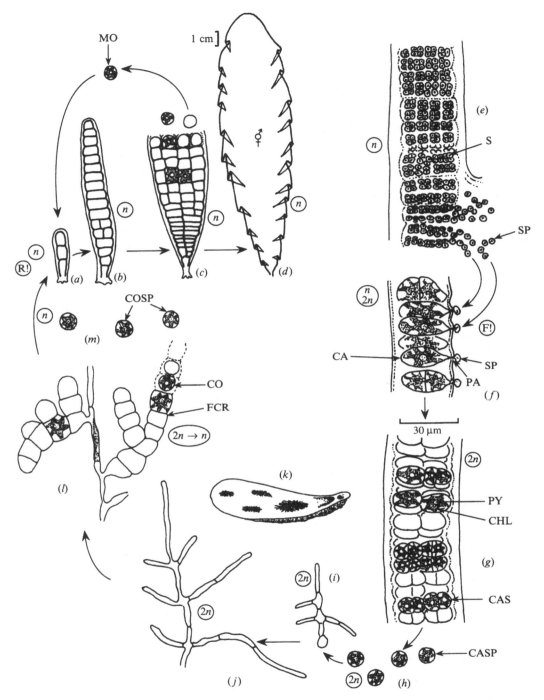

Figure 5.14. The life cycle of *Porphyra tenera*. (*a–c*) Stages in the development of a young blade, including the production of monospores (in *c*), which grow into new blade-like germlings; note the stellate chloroplasts with central pyrenoids. (*d*) A full-grown monoecious blade. (*e*) Cross section through a male portion of a blade: the spermatangium mother cells have divided up into packets of spermatangia and, at the lower end, are releasing spermatia. (*f*) Cross section through a female portion of a blade: the carpogonia are being fertilized by spermatia, while two fertilized carpogonia (top and bottom) have divided into two cells, this division being the first of a series leading to the formation of diploid carpospores. (*g*)

(conchosporangia), which occur in rows along some of the filaments. The conchospores in turn give rise to normal, sheet-like *Porphyra* plants, thus completing the life cycle (Fig. 5.14*l, m*).

Short days are necessary for the differentiation of conchosporangia in *Porphyra tenera*, and probably also in other *Porphyra* species and the closely related genus *Bangia* ([341, 342, 344, 345, 943, 1056, 1485, 1837]). The formation of conchospores is promoted by 8 h illumination per day but inhibited by a light period of 14 h. The critical daylength is 10 h. The induction of conchosporangium formation is apparently mediated by phytochrome, a pigment that is also involved in the daylength responses of many higher plants, for instance, in the induction of flowering.

The production of conchospores is also influenced by temperature, and in *Porphyra tenera* the optimum temperature is 21 °C. On the Japanese coast the *Conchocelis*-phase forms conchospores when the daylength is less than 10 h and the temperature below 22–23 °C. Such conditions occur towards the end of September, and hence it is then that great quantities of conchospores are liberated and grow into new *Porphyra* plants.

Young *Porphyra* plants can reproduce vegetatively, this taking place through the formation of monospores along the upper margins of the blade (Fig. 5.14*c*). These spores, like the spermatia, contain mucilage sacs, which are highly characteristic of the reproductive cells in red algae (pp. 57–8) ([622]).

We can sum up by saying that the *Porphyra* phase is a winter annual whereas the *Conchocelis* phase is a perennial, which lasts several years and ensures the survival (aestivation) of the plant during the summer.

According to Magne ([527, 1068]), who carried out karyological investigations of *Porphyra*, the carpospores and *Conchocelis* phase are diploid, whereas the *Porphyra* plants are haploid. It has been found, however, that meiosis does *not* take place during conchospore formation but during the germination of the conchospores, when typical meiotic figures have been found ([1062]); this was a quite unexpected discovery. The four meiotic products are arranged in a row in the four-celled, uniseriate germling, and this subsequently grows into a single leaf-like thallus. When yellow or green (recessive) colour mutants are crossed with red wild-type thalli, each of the four meiotic products in the germling can be seen to give rise to a differently coloured sector of the same *Porphyra* blade ([1317, 1318]). In the closely related genus *Bangia*, no difference in ploidy could be found between the two phases, so that the life cycle must be wholly asexual ([311, 1487]). In their investigations carpospores and conchospores could both be induced to grow into *Bangia* plants, by subjecting them to short daylengths. Long days, however, caused the carpospores to give rise instead to the *Conchocelis* phase, which was able to propagate itself vegetatively by monospores.

A considerable number of *Porphyra* species are now known in which there is again no change in ploidy between the two phases of the life cycle. These species have secondarily lost their sexuality ([451, 823, 1276a]). The alternation itself, however, is still controlled by temperature and daylength.

Distribution

The *Conchocelis* phase appears to be very widespread on the coasts of Europe, growing not only in sea-shells but also in the calcareous cases of barnacles, which often occur in huge numbers on rocks in the intertidal zone ([691]). Fossil *Conchocelis* has been recorded from the Cambrian and Silurian periods, which suggests that *Porphyra* and its relatives (the Bangiales) are at least 500 million years old ([187, 1751]).

Porphyra as a foodstuff ([221, 944, 989a, 1056, 1296, 1803])

In Japan, *Porphyra* has been grown on a large scale and processed for consumption probably since the seventeenth century. Originally this was done simply by providing additional, artificial substrates to encourage the alga. In 1961, 133 000 tonnes (fresh mass) of

Caption for fig. 5.14 (*cont.*).

Formation of carpospores from the fertilized carpogonia. (*h*) Carpospores. (*i, j*) The *Conchocelis* phase. (*k*) *Conchocelis* phase growing in an oyster shell. (*l*) *Conchocelis* phase with 'fertile cell rows' producing 'conchospores'; one conchospore is produced by each conchosporangium. (*m*) Conchospores. CA = carpogonium; CAS = carposporangium; CASP = carpospore; CHL = chloroplast; CO = conchosporangium; COSP = conchospore; F! = fertilization; FCR = 'fertile cell row'; MO = monospore; PA = papilla on carpogonium; PY = pyrenoid; R! = reduction division (meiosis), during germination of the conchospore; S = spermatangium; SP = spermatium; *n* = haploid; 2*n* = diploid. (Based mainly on [943].)

Porphyra was cultivated by some 68 700 fishermen and farmers. By 1978 the annual crop had risen to 211 500 tonnes, this being worth around 500 million US dollars; in Japan *ca.* 300 000 people were being employed in the industry. The alga is also cultivated on the coasts of China and Korea.

Porphyra (Japanese, 'Nori'; Chinese, 'Zicai') is grown in bays along the coast, where there is a plentiful supply of nutrient salts (phosphate and nitrate) brought in by rivers. At present, around 60 000 ha of the shallow seas along Japanese coasts are occupied by 'Nori-culture'. At first the cultivation of *Porphyra* consisted of nothing more than sticking bamboo canes into the sediment near low water; spores floating around in the water became attached to the canes and grew into *Porphyra* plants. Nowadays wide-meshed nets (mesh size about 15 cm × 15 cm) are used, and are stretched out between posts driven into the sand or mud. The nets hang above the sediments, roughly at mean water level, so that the algae growing on them can be harvested from boats during low tide. Floating rafts bearing nets are also used widely as substrata, especially since they can be used in rather deeper water, where they are anchored to the bottom. Furthermore the colonization of the nets is no longer left to chance. During summer the *Conchocelis* phase is grown in oyster shells contained in concrete basins or ponds. This is done at large fisheries as well as by small, private concerns. The nets are hung out in September or October, but before this each net is submerged in the *Conchocelis* ponds and moved around in the water, so that it becomes colonized by large numbers of conchospores. Sometimes too, oyster shells containing *Conchocelis* plants are hung up beneath the nets in small sacks, so that the conchospores have ready access to the artificial substrate above.

After several weeks the nets have become covered with a dense growth of young *Porphyra* plants, which themselves reproduce vegetatively via monospores (Fig. 5.14c). Fifty to sixty days after the nets are hung out, it is time for the first harvest and between November and March three or four harvests are possible. It has been found that this artificial seeding of the nets increases the yield of *Porphyra* considerably.

In order to increase the fertility of the water around the nets, any sediments exposed at low water are ploughed up, allowing the release of nutrient salts into the water at high tide. Nitrogen is sometimes added in the form of ammonium sulphate $((NH_4)_2SO_4)$ fertilizer ([1803]). Harvesting by hand is very labour intensive and a most unpleasant job in winter, so that semi-automatic harvesting methods have been developed ([989a]).

After the *Porphyra* has been harvested it is washed in freshwater, chopped up finely and dried in the sun on flat screens, or in special drying rooms. It dries into small, thin sheets (19 cm × 21 cm), which are sold in packets of ten, and can be eaten in various ways, described in Japanese recipes ([1296]).

Porphyra is also harvested and eaten in South Wales, where it is known as 'laver', but its importance there is trivial compared with Japan.

Order Porphyridiales

1 Members of the Porphyridiales are unicellular or 'pseudofilamentous' (Fig. 5.15). The unicellular forms often have gelatinous walls or lie embedded in a common gelatinous matrix. The 'pseudofilamentous' types consist of single rows of cells surrounded by wide sheaths of mucilage.

2. Pit connections and pit plugs are never present.

3. Cell structure varies greatly between the genera. Each cell may contain a central stellate chloroplast, or a lobed parietal chloroplast, or many discoid chloroplasts.

4. Sexual reproduction is absent or unknown.

5. Asexual reproduction takes place only through vegetative cell division; special sporangia are absent.

Since the architecture of the cell (including ultrastructural details; see [471, 1608]) varies greatly within the Porphyridiales, this order is considered to be phylogenetically heterogeneous. It may represent a 'bundle' of very ancient lineages that long ago diverged with respect to cell structure, but retained the unicellular organization of the ancestral red algae. Alternatively, the Porphyridiales may be the reduced descendants of more complex, multicellular red algae. *Porphyridium* cells can move by secreting mucilage, and this is similar to the mucilage extrusion carried out by the spores of multicellular rhodophytes (Fig. 5.16, and see below, under *Porphyridium*). Perhaps, therefore, *Porphyridium* evolved from the monospores of multicellular red algae, by losing the capacity to develop into multicellular thalli and hence also the ability to form pit plugs.

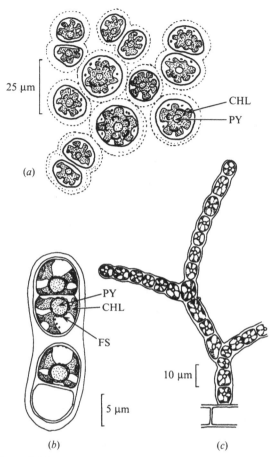

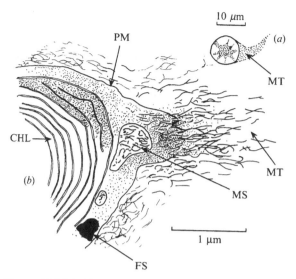

Figure 5.16. Mucilage secretion by *Porphyridium purpureum* during gliding movement, as seen in the light microscope (*a*) and electron microscope (*b*). CHL = chloroplast; FS = floridean starch; MS = mucilage sac; MT = trail of fibrous mucilage; PM = plasmalemma. (Based on [1012].)

Figure 5.15 (*a*) *Porphyridium purpureum*. (*b, c*) *Chroodactylon ramosum*. CHL = chloroplast; FS = floridean starch; PY = pyrenoid. (*a* based on [123]; *b, c* based on [440].)

The simple unicellular and filamentous representatives of other algal divisions are also often phylogenetically heterogeneous. Striking examples of this are found among the unicellular and unbranched filamentous members of the green algae (Chlorophyta). The coccoid genus 'Chlorella' (p. 365) contains strains that are quite unrelated genetically, while the old filamentous genus 'Ulothrix' has now been split into *Ulothrix sensu stricto*, *Uronema* and *Klebsormidium* (pp. 336, 396), which are placed in different classes. In relation to the possible origins of *Porphyridium*, it is interesting that some *Chlorella* species have apparently arisen through simplification of the multicellular green alga *Scenedesmus* (p. 365; [768]).

Members of the Porphyridiales are known from marine, freshwater and moist terrestrial habitats ([100, 123, 125, 452]). Two examples will be given.

Porphyridium purpureum (Fig. 5.15*a*)

The cells of *Porphyridium purpureum* are spherical or flattened against each other. They are usually found growing in groups or mounds, the individual cells being embedded in a common mass of mucilage. Each cell contains a central, irregularly stellate chloroplast and in the middle of this there is a pyrenoid. The nucleus lies to one side of the cell, sandwiched between cell wall and chloroplast (cf. Fig. 5.1*a*). *Porphyridium* reproduces only by vegetative cell division. This alga is often used in the laboratory as an experimental organism, especially for investigations of photosynthesis.

P. purpureum is capable of gliding movement over solid substrata, brought about by extrusion of mucilage from a mucilage sac (Fig. 5.16); this is similar to the means by which the various types of red algal spores become expelled from their sporangia. The gliding cell leaves behind a fibrillar, mucilaginous trail (Fig. 5.16; [1012]) and is positively phototactic ([1662]).

Porphyridium species are known from marine,

brackish, freshwater and terrestrial habitats, where colonies of *P. purpureum* can be found on damp soil or damp walls. The cells of one species occur as photosynthetic endosymbionts in a large (0.5–1 cm) tropical foraminiferan (p. 136).

Chroodactylon ramosum (Fig. 5.15*b, c*)

The spherical ellipsoidal cells of *Chroodactylon* form an unbranched or branched row within a gelatinous sheath (a 'pseudofilament'). Each cell contains a bluish, stellate chloroplast at its centre.

Chroodactylon ramosum grows epiphytically on other algae. It is world-wide in distribution, occurring in fresh and brackish waters ([123, 125]).

Order Rhodochaetales

1 The only known species of this order, *Rhodochaete parvula*, is a minute, delicate epiphyte, which grows attached to other red algae. The thalli consist of simple, branched filaments (Fig. 5.17*a*).

2 Growth is brought about by apical cell divisions.

3 Pit plugs are present. They lack cap membranes and plug caps (type 7 pit plug, p. 55). This is the simplest and perhaps most primitive type of pit plug found in red algae ([1457]).

4 The chloroplasts are parietal and discoid or ribbon-like (Fig. 5.17*b–e*).

5 The life cycle is diplohaplontic and isomorphic. In the monoecious gametophyte, tiny spermatangia are cut off from vegetative cells by curved lateral walls (Fig. 5.17*a, b*). The carpogonia resemble vegetative cells (Fig. 5.17*c*). Following its release from the spermatangium, the spermatium injects its nucleus into a carpogonium (Fig. 5.17*c*) and the fertilized carpogonium then cuts off a single carposporangium by a curved wall (Fig. 5.17*d*). This in turn produces a single carpospore, which is released and grows into a filamentous, diploid sporophyte. The sporophyte is capable of reproducing itself by monospores (Fig. 5.17*e*), and also produces structures at the ends of the sporophyte filaments (Fig. 5.17*f*), which are thought to be meiosporangia. The putative meiospores grow into gametophytes ([97, 1070, 1076]).

6 Asexual reproduction occurs via monospores. Each monosporangium is cut off from a vegeta-

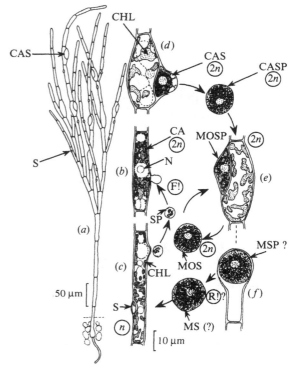

Figure 5.17. The life cycle of *Rhodochaete parvula*. (*a*) Dioecious gametophyte. (*b*) Two spermatangia, one of which has just released a spermatium. (*c*) Carpogonium (which is morphologically indistinguishable from a vegetative cell), after fertilization by a spermatium. Note the large zygote nucleus. (*d*) The swollen, fertilized carpogonium, bearing a single carposporangium, which it has cut off by a curved wall. The carposporangium is just about to release its single carpospore. (*e*) A portion of the sporophyte, with a monosporangium that has been cut off laterally by a curved wall. (*f*) Part of the sporophyte with what appears to be a terminal meiosporangium. CA = carpogonium; CAS = carposporangium; CASP = carpospore; CHL = chloroplast; F! = fertilization; MOS = monospore; MOSP = monosporangium; MS = meiospore; MSP = meiosporangium; N = nucleus; R! = meiosis; S = spermatangium; SP = spermatium; *n* = haploid; *2n* = diploid. (Based on [97, 1070, 1076].)

tive cell by a curved lateral wall, as are the spermatangia, carposporangia and meiosporangia.

7 The mitochondria and golgi bodies are not closely associated (in contrast to the Bangiales and the Florideophyceae; Fig. 5.11).

This rather rare species is known from the Mediterranean and Caribbean seas ([1070, 1765]). It is described here, in spite of its rarity, because it may be the most primitive living red alga ([1457]); this will be discussed further in the section 'Phylogenetic reflections on the Rhodophyta' (p. 95).

Order Erythropeltidales

1 The members of this order are multicellular red algae, forming filaments, blades or discs.

2 Growth is intercalary in the filamentous and foliose types of thallus, and apical in discoid forms.

3 Pit connections and pit plugs are absent (or at least, have not yet been detected!).

4 The chloroplasts are central and stellate.

5 During sexual reproduction one spermatium is cut off from a mother cell, which subsequently functions as a carpogonium. The life cycle is as yet not fully known ([623, 900, 901, 1077]).

6 Asexual reproduction is brought about by monospores. One spore is formed per sporangium, cut off by an oblique curved wall (Fig. 5.2b).

7 The mitochondria and golgi bodies are not closely associated (contrast the Bangiales and Florideophyceae, see Fig. 5.11; [471]).

The species in this order are small epiphytes, living attached to other algae in marine habitats. One example will be given.

Erythrotrichia carnea (Fig. 5.2b)

The thallus of *Erythrotrichia carnea* consists of an upright, unbranched filament of cells, which is anchored to the substratum by a number of short rhizoids. The filament grows by intercalary and apical cell divisions. Each cell is uninucleate and has a central, stellate chloroplast; this in turn contains a central pyrenoid.

The vegetative cells sometimes divide unequally by an oblique wall. The upper cell acts as a monosporangium and produces one spore – the monospore – which escapes through a pore in the monosporangium wall. At first the monospores are naked and they move about for a little while like amoebae. Each monospore then gives rise directly to a new *Erythrotrichia* fila-

ment, thus effecting the asexual reproduction of the plant. During sexual reproduction a monospore grows into a tiny filamentous gametophyte with three cells. The swollen apical cell of the dwarf gametophyte cuts off a spermatium and thereupon becomes a carpogonium. After fertilization, the carpogonium grows into a normal erect filament ([1077]). In two other genera the normal erect plants – multicellular filaments or blades – function as gametophytes ([623, 900, 901]).

Erythrotrichia carnea is a very common epiphyte on larger seaweeds.

Order Bangiales

1 The Bangiales have multicellular thalli, which can take the form of unbranched multiseriate filaments or blades, in the gametophyte phase (Fig. 5.14d), and branched uniseriate filaments, in the sporophyte or 'Conchocelis' phase (Fig. 5.14i–l).

2 Growth is intercalary in the blades and multiseriate filaments, and apical in the uniseriate filaments.

3 Pit connections are absent in the foliose plants and multiseriate filaments, but do occur in the branched filaments of the *Conchocelis* phase. The pit plugs are without cap membranes but have one-layered plug caps (a type 5 pit plug; p. 55).

4 The chloroplasts are central and stellate in the blades and multiseriate filaments, but ribbon-like and parietal in the branched uniseriate filaments.

5 Sexual reproduction is of the type described for *Porphyra* (p. 63; Fig. 5.14). The life cycle is diplohaplontic and heteromorphic, with a *Conchocelis*-like sporophyte stage.

6 Asexual reproduction takes place via monospores (one spore is formed per sporangium; Fig. 5.14c).

7 Mitochondria and golgi bodies are closely associated (as shown in Fig. 5.11; [471]).

This order is almost entirely marine and species of the two genera *Porphyra* and *Bangia* can be found on the coasts of all the seas and oceans. There is one freshwater species of *Bangia* ([123, 125, 1620]).

An example of this order has already been described in detail (*Porphyra*: p. 63).

Rhodophyta: Class 2. Florideophyceae

The principal characteristics of the Florideophyceae

1 The thalli are essentially composed of branched filaments, but these are often united to form pseudoparenchymatous structures, which can be elaborate. The thallus is cylindrical, compressed or foliose. The cells can be uninucleate or multinucleate.

2 Growth is basically apical, through divisions of apical cells; in some derived forms, additional intercalary divisions also occur.

3 Pit plugs are always present, usually with cap membranes (these are absent, however, in the order Corallinales: see below).

4 The chloroplasts are generally parietal and ribbon-like or discoid, lacking pyrenoids (Figs. 5.1*c*, 5.2*a*, 5.38*b, c*), but in a few species they are stellate and have a central pyrenoid, and lie in the middle of the cell.

5 The mitochondria and golgi bodies are tightly appressed to each other (Fig. 5.11; [471]).

6 Species that reproduce sexually have a diplohaplontic, isomorphic or heteromorphic life cycle (rarely a haplontic life cycle).

7 The carpogonia (the oogonia of red algae) of sexually reproducing species are clearly differentiated from the vegetative cells, since each bears a long extension, the trichogyne (Figs. 5.18*b, c, i*, 5.22*d*). The function of this protuberance is to 'catch' a spermatium (male gamete) and to receive its nucleus.

8 The fertilized carpogonium develops into a diploid sporogenous tissue, termed the **gonimocarp** (Figs. 5.18*k*, 5.38*f*). This produces diploid spores, the carpospores, which grow into diploid tetrasporophytes.

9 The diploid tetrasporophytes form meiospores (tetraspores), in tetrasporangia (Figs. 5.9, 5.10, 5.13); the tetraspores grow into haploid gametophytes.

Vegetative structure

There are no unicellular algae in the Florideophyceae. In the simplest members of the group, the thalli are filaments of cells, in which the main axis and side branches are morphologically alike. *Audouinella investiens* is an example of such an alga and will be described in some detail (Fig. 5.18).

Most of the Florideophyceae are much more complicated than *Audouinella investiens*. Even so, their thalli still consist of systems of branched filaments, although there is often marked differentiation between main axes and side branches, or between the side branches themselves. In extreme cases the filaments grow together so closely that the alga appears to be composed of parenchyma. *Acrosymphyton purpuriferum* (Figs. 5.20, 5.21) will be used as an example of complex thallus construction, although compared with some red algae it is quite simple. *Acrosymphyton* has a main axis of large cells, each bearing a whorl of four short shoots in which the cells are much smaller (Fig. 5.21*a*). A comparable structure is found in *Batrachospermum* (Fig. 5.26). The short shoots, which are sometimes called determinate laterals, are side branches that have limited growth and quickly reach their final size. The main axis and the short shoots are embedded together in a common sheath of mucilage.

The thallus of *Ceramium* (Figs. 5.1*c*, 5.39) has the same overall plan as *Acrosymphyton*. The main axis consists of large (axial) cells, and each of these bears a whorl of small-celled side branches, which have limited growth. In *Ceramium*, however, the cells of the short shoots crowd very closely together, forming a thin pseudoparenchymatous cortex, tightly appressed to the main axis.

In highly complex red algae two types of construction can be distinguished. In one, each part of the thallus consists only of a main axis and the short shoots that arise from it (Figs. 5.1*c*, 5.21*a*, 5.31*b*, 5.37, 5.39, 5.41): this is called the **uniaxial** or **central filament** type of construction. In the **multiaxial** type, also known as the **fountain-type**, on the other hand, the thallus consists of several or many main axes, together with the short shoots associated with them (Figs. 5.24*a*, 5.34, 5.36*b*).

The distinction between these two types is not always clear. In *Dumontia contorta* (Figs 5.32, 5.33; p. 87), the tip of each branch of the thallus is uniaxial

(Fig. 5.33*d*), and so this species was originally considered to have a uniaxial construction ([945]). However, the erect parts of the thallus arise from the basal crust (Fig. 5.33*a–c*) as a bundle of embryonic filaments (like a multiaxial bud); these form a fused multiaxial thallus, except at their tips, where they remain uniaxial. The tips later grow and proliferate to give the erect uniaxial branches of the adult ([1495, 1496, 1498, 1893]). Eventually the erect thallus of *Dumontia* dies, after producing reproductive cells (tetraspores, carpospores or spermatia); in this respect the erect part of the thallus resembles the flower of an angiosperm. *Chondrus crispus*, on the other hand, is always distinctly multiaxial, in young plants or old (Fig. 5.34*b*). Here the erect parts of the thallus do not begin as bundles of embryonic filaments but as local outgrowths from the basal crust; crust filaments gradually change into the medullary filaments of the upright parts, and there is increasing meristematic activity in the cortical cells of the outgrowth ([1496]).

These are only a few examples drawn from the many different ways in which the thalli of the Florideophyceae can be constructed and develop (for reviews, see [471, 945, 946, 947, 948, 1893]).

Examples of life cycles in the class Florideophyceae: the isomorphic, diplohaplontic life cycle of Audouinella investiens (order Acrochaetiales) (Fig. 5.18)

It is assumed that the life cycle of this species is the basic type of life cycle for the Florideophyceae, from which others have been derived. *Audouinella investiens* has been selected for description not only because it has relatively simple vegetative organs, but also because it has been possible to follow its whole life cycle in laboratory cultures ([1736]). Unfortunately, during these investigations of the life cycle no observations were made of the nuclei and chromosomes. Hence the position of meiosis in the life cycle is not known with certainty, nor the ploidy of the various stages. Nevertheless, from the many investigations made of red algae, it is very likely that the various phases have the ploidies indicated in Fig. 5.18.

Audouinella investiens is a tiny freshwater alga, which lives epiphytically on the larger red algae *Batrachospermum*. It is not common but related species are widely distributed in the sea.

Full-grown plants of *Audouinella investiens* can be found at any time of the year. They look like small balls of fluff and are made up of branched filaments of cells. These plants can be gametophytes or sporophytes (Fig. 5.18*a, m*). The haploid **gametophytes** are hermaphrodite and therefore bear spermatangia as well as carpogonia. **Spermatangia** (= male gametangia) are produced from the swollen ends of some apical cells (Fig. 5.18*d*). Each spermatangium produces a pale, naked sexual cell, the **spermatium**. The **carpogonia** (= female gametangia; essentially the same as oogonia) are easily recognized by their shape (Fig. 5.18*b, c, i*). Each one consists of two parts. The lower, basal part is somewhat swollen and contains the female gametic nucleus, ready to fuse with the male nucleus from a spermatium. The upper part of the carpogonium consists of a long thin spur, which is colourless and is called the **trichogyne**. Quite a lot of fungi belonging to the Ascomycetes have similar sexual organs, again with trichogynes. This similarity has led to speculation that there may be a phylogenetic link between the red algae and the Ascomycetes.

The carpogonia can be stalked or sessile (Fig. 5.18*b, c*). In most of the Florideophyceae the carpogonium lies at the end of a special, morphologically distinct branch: the carpogonial branch (see for instance Fig. 5.21*b*, which shows the carpogonial branch of *Acrosymphyton*). The spermatia are transported passively to the carpogonium and attach themselves to the trichogyne. The spermatium surrounds itself with a wall and injects its nucleus into the trichogyne, and then the male spermatium nucleus travels down the trichogyne to the carpogonium, where it fuses with the female nucleus (karyogamy, Fig. 5.18*i*).

After fertilization and karyogamy, the carpogonium, which is now diploid, divides and gives rise to a compact system of diploid filaments which produce spores (Fig. 5.18*j, k*). The short, sporogenous (= spore-forming) filaments are termed **gonimoblasts** (Fig. 5.18*k*) and the whole system of gonimoblasts is called the **gonimocarp**. The gonimocarp ensures the production of many diploid carpospores per fertilization, instead of one. In the literature, the term **carposporophyte** is commonly used in place of 'gonimocarp' but this term carries with it certain implications concerning the interpretation of the diploid, sporogenous tissue. According to this interpretation the gonimocarp is a quite separate phase of the life cycle, to be regarded as equivalent to the gametophyte or the

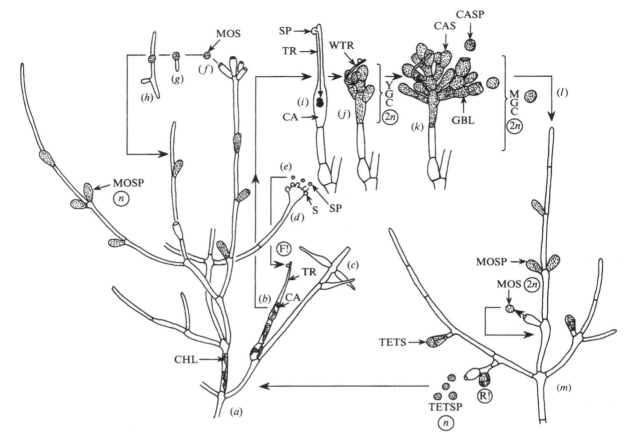

Figure 5.18. The life cycle of *Audouinella investiens*.
(*a*) Gametophyte. (*b*) Stalked carpogonium. (*c*) Un-stalked carpogonia. (*d*) A club-shaped tip, bearing spermatangia. (*e*) Spermatia, which are transported passively to the trichogyne. (*f*) Monospore. (*g, h*) Two stages in the germination of a monospore. (*i*) Fusion of a male nucleus with the female nucleus in the carpogonium. (*j*) Growth of the carpogonium into a young gonimocarp. (*k*) Mature gonimocarp. (*l*) Growth of a carpospore into a tetrasporophyte. (*m*) Tetrasporophyte. CA = carpogonium; CAS = carposporangium; CASP = carpospore; CHL = chloroplast; F! = fertilization; GBL = gonimoblast; MGC = mature gonimocarp; MOS = monospore; MOSP = monosporangium; R! = meiosis; S = spermatangium; SP = spermatium; TR = trichogyne; TETS = tetrasporangium; TETSP = tetraspore; YGC = young gonimocarp; WTR = wilted trichogyne; n = haploid; 2n = diploid. (Based on [1736].)

tetrasporophyte. It has been suggested that the 'carposporophyte' was originally an independent plant but lost its independence in the course of evolution, so that now it lives parasitically on the gametophyte. This, however, is pure speculation, since we know of no red alga with an autonomous 'carposporophyte'. It is best, therefore, to avoid the word 'carposporophyte' and use gonimocarp instead.

In many species of the Florideophyceae, the gonimocarp is surrounded by an urn-shaped sheath and in this case the combination of gonimocarp and envelope is often called the **cystocarp** (Figs. 5.37*f*, 5.40*a, e*).

The **carposporangia** are formed at the ends of the gonimoblasts and each one usually produces a single diploid (2n) carpospore. In many species of Florideophyceae, virtually all the gonimoblast cells function as carposporangia. In *Audouinella*, the diploid carpospores give rise to diploid **tetrasporophytes**, which are morphologically very similar to the haploid gametophytes (Fig. 5.18*m*). The tetrasporophytes in turn bear **tetrasporangia**. Each tetrasporangium undergoes meiosis to produce four haploid tetraspores (Fig. 5.18*m*). The tetraspores grow into new haploid gametophytes and so the life cycle is completed. In several other *Audouinella* species, it has been found that tetraspores are formed only in short-day conditions, but this has not been investigated in *A. investiens* ([3, 4, 5, 136, 344, 345, 347]). Conchospore formation in *Porphyra* is likewise triggered by short days (p. 65).

Both the gametophyte and tetrasporophyte can also propagate themselves vegetatively by asexually produced monospores (Fig. 5.18*f-h, m*).

In summary, *Audouinella investiens* has an isomorphic, diplohaplontic life cycle, in which the zygote initially produces a diploid sporogenous tissue instead of giving rise directly to the independent sporophyte phase (Fig. 5.18). Similar life cycles are known in several marine *Audouinella* species ([2, 1693, 1694, 1911]).

Life cycles in other species of Audouinella

The genus *Audouinella* is large, with more than 300 species; it is widely distributed along the sea coasts of the world and also has a few freshwater representatives. The only type of reproduction known for most species is asexual reproduction via monospores, but in about 20 species it has been possible to investigate the sexual cycle in culture ([1911]). A surprising diversity of life cycles has been found. Even one isolate of a single species can exhibit several different, alternative developmental pathways at certain stages of the cycle.

An example of a variable life cycle is given in Fig. 5.19, which refers to *Audouinella gynandra* ([6]); thick arrows (pathway A) indicate the most usual course for the life cycle. The life cycle is diplohaplontic and slightly heteromorphic, since the gametophytes are slightly smaller and less well developed than the sporophytes. In *A. investiens*, on the other hand, the two generations are equally well developed (Fig. 5.18). During the normal life cycle of *A. gynandra* (Fig. 5.19, pathway A: thick arrows), the fertilized carpogonium develops into a gonimocarp (Fig. 5.19*b–d*), as is usual for most Florideophyceae. However, there are two alternative ways in which the fertilized carpogonium can develop. Firstly, it may develop directly into a tetrasporophyte (Fig. 5.19, pathway B: thin arrow from *c* to *h*), which therefore remains attached to the gametophyte. Secondly, it may

develop directly into a tetrasporangium (Fig. 5.19, pathway C: thin arrows linking *c* and *f*). In this case the life cycle becomes haplontic, with zygotic meiosis.

A third possible mode of development is also indicated in Fig. 5.19 (pathway D, indicated by a dashed line). Here, the fertilized carpogonium develops directly into a single carposporangium, which produces one carpospore. This pattern of development has not been found in *Audouinella gynandra* but in another species, *A. pectinata* ([7]); it has been included in Fig. 5.19 to indicate the full range of possibilities in the genus *Audouinella*.

The different types of life cycle illustrated by Fig. 5.19 are to some extent characteristic of different groups of species in *Audouinella* ([1911]). Pathway B, for instance, is characteristic of *A. purpurea* (= *Rhodochorton purpureum*), a common species forming dark red, velvety coverings on overhanging rocks in the marine intertidal zone of temperate coasts ([1319, 1692, 1871, 1911]). Pathway C is characteristic of at least one *Audouinella* species, in which the zygote develops into a tetrasporangium with a one-celled stalk ([978a]). Pathway D is known from *A. pectinata* but has not yet been found in any other *Audouinella* species, nor in any other red alga. Pathway B is also characteristic of the large blade-forming rhodophyte *Palmaria palmata* (Fig. 5.22, p. 79), while outside *Audouinella*, pathway C is exhibited in the small crustose red alga *Rhodophysema elegans* (Fig. 5.23, p. 80).

The alternative paths of development in *Audouinella gynandra* (Fig. 5.18, pathways B and C) seem to represent simplifications of the basic diplohaplontic life cycle, with its slight heteromorphism and formation of a gonimocarp from the zygote. The simpler, alternative pathways are brought about by the failure of the gonimocarp to develop, so that instead the zygote either grows into a tetrasporophyte (pathway B in Fig. 5.19) or develops as a tetrasporangium; if the latter, the tetraspores then grow directly into new gametophytes. In short, *A. gynandra* can omit from its life cycle either the gonimocarp alone, or the gonimocarp *and* the tetrasporophyte.

In spite of the variation within the genus *Audouinella*, it is clear that the life cycle is basically diplohaplontic and isomorphic, with development of the zygote into a gonimocarp, as in *A. investiens* (Fig. 5.18). All other types of life cycle in the genus can be interpreted as derived: simplifications of the basic plan. *Audouinella* is considered to be phylogenetically

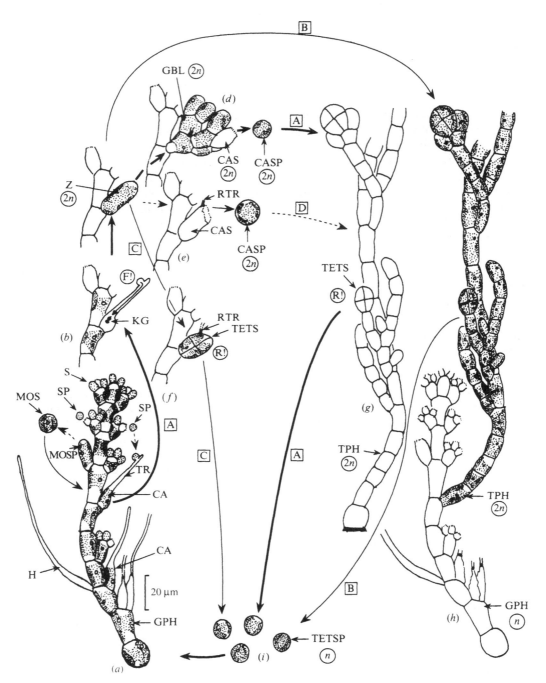

Figure 5.19. The life cycle of *Audouinella gynandra*. Thick arrows (A): the main pathway of the life cycle. Thin arrows (B, C): additional pathways. Dashed arrow (D): an extra pathway present in the related species, *A. pectinata*. (*a*) Monoecious gametophyte. (*b*) Karyogamy in the carpogonium of the gametophyte. (*c*) A diploid (2*n*) zygote, which has developed from the carpogonium. (*d*) Formation from the zygote of a sys-tem of gonimoblasts: branched, diploid, spore-producing filaments, which together form the gonimo-carp. (*e*) Formation from the zygote of a single car-posporangium, producing a single carpospore. (*f*) Formation from the zygote of a single tetraspo-rangium which, after meiosis (R!), produces four haploid tetraspores. (*g*) Tetrasporophyte (diploid), derived from a carpospore. (*h*) Gametophyte (haploid)

the most primitive group of the Florideophyceae ([470a, 471, 472, 586]; cf. p. 98, under Acrochaetiales), and so it is likely that the isomorphic, diplohaplontic type of life cycle, including the development of the zygote into a diploid, spore-producing tissue (the gonimocarp), is also primitive for the Florideophyceae as a whole. Other florideophycean groups have other kinds of life cycle but, as we will see, these can all be interpreted as simplifications from a basic isomorphic, diplohaplontic type, as in *Audouinella* itself.

Next we will consider an example of a strongly heteromorphic life cycle.

Examples of life cycles in the class Florideophyceae: the heteromorphic, diplohaplontic life cycle of Acrosymphyton purpuriferum *(order Gigartinales)*

Most of the Florideophyceae are larger and have more complex thalli than *Audouinella investiens*. The structure and development of the sexual reproductive organs are usually more complicated too; *Acrosymphyton* is a particularly good example to demonstrate this. The development of its gonimocarp has been known for a long time ([1341]) and its whole life cycle has also been followed in laboratory cultures ([264]). The laboratory studies showed that the tetrasporophyte and gametophyte are dissimilar. Furthermore, unlike *Audouinella*, *Acrosymphyton* possesses auxiliary cells: specialized gametophytic cells that play an important part in the development of the gonimocarp. Auxiliary cells are characteristic of many red algae.

Acrosymphyton purpuriferum is a rare species, found in the Mediterranean. Full-grown plants are very slimy and, under water, appear as richly branched, pyramidal structures, 5–15 cm in height. Each of the main 'trunks' at the bottom of the plant can be up to 1 cm thick, whereas at their ends the 'branches' are less than 100 μm wide (Fig. 5.20). Under the microscope it can be seen that each branch – and essentially the whole thallus too – is made up of a

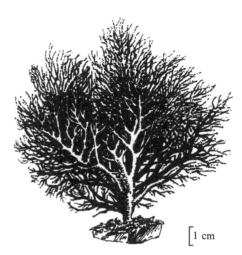

[1 cm

Figure 5.20. *Acrosymphyton purpuriferum*. Habit of gametophyte.

main axis containing large cells, each bearing a whorl of four short shoots (Fig. 5.21a). The main axis and the small-celled laterals are embedded together in a common sheath of mucilage so that, out of water, the plant resembles a mass of frog spawn.

Acrosymphyton is a summer annual and disappears in winter; all the plants are monoecious gametophytes. Initially the tetrasporophyte was unknown, which is not surprising in view of the great difference in morphology between tetrasporophyte and gametophyte. The ploidy of each phase of the life cycle has been determined ([134]) and is indicated in Fig. 5.21. As in most other red algae that have been investigated, the gametophytes are haploid and the tetrasporophytes are diploid, meiosis taking place during the formation of the tetraspores.

The spermatangia are formed at the ends of the short shoots (determinate laterals) and in each spermatangium there develops one pale-coloured, naked male gamete, the spermatium (Fig. 5.21d). The female reproductive structures or carpogonia are easily recognizable by their shape and place of origin (Fig. 5.21b). Each one consists of a somewhat swollen base and a

Caption for fig. 5.19 *(cont.)*.
    bearing a tetrasporophyte (diploid), which has developed directly from a zygote retained on the gametophyte (see (*c*)). CA = carpogonium (*n*); CAS = carposporangium (2*n*); CASP = carpospore (2*n*); F! = fertilization; GBL = gonimoblast (2*n*); GPH = gametophyte (*n*); H = hair; KG = karyogamy; MOS = monospore; MOSP = monosporangium; R! = meiosis; RTR = remnant of trichogyne; S = spermatangium (*n*); SP = spermatium (*n*); TETS = tetrasporangium; TETSP = tetraspore (*n*); TPH = tetrasporophyte (2*n*); TR = trichogyne; Z = zygote (2*n*). (Based on [6, 7].)

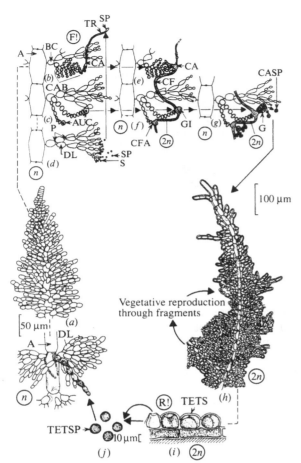

Figure 5.21. Life cycle of *Acrosymphyton purpuriferum*. (*a*) Detail of the gametophyte. (*h*) Tetrasporophyte. For further explanation, see the text. A = monosiphonous axis; AUC = auxiliary cells, borne on auxiliary cell branches; BC = basal, supporting cell of the carpogonial branch; CA = carpogonium; CAB = carpogonial branch; CASP = carpospores; CF = connecting filament; CFA = connecting filament fused to an auxiliary cell; DL = determinate lateral branch (short shoot); F! = fertilization; G = gonimocarp; GI = gonimoblast initials; P = pit connection; R! = meiosis; S = spermatangium; SP = spermatium; TETS = tetrasporangium; TETSP = tetraspore; TR = trichogyne; *n* = haploid; 2*n* = diploid. (After [264, 948, 1341].)

cells, each of which bears a pair of lateral filaments. It arises from the basal cell of a vegetative short shoot, termed the supporting cell. Specialized carpogonial branches occur in most of the Florideophyceae but although their structure is highly diverse, they are always much shorter than in *Acrosymphyton*.

Certain gametophyte cells, the so-called **auxiliary cells**, play an important part in the development of the gonimocarp. Like the carpogonia, they are easily recognized by their shape and position in the *Acrosymphyton* thallus (Fig. 5.21*c*). They are produced on a special branch, the **auxiliary cell branch**, which arises from the basal cell of a vegetative short shoot, just like the carpogonial branch. Unlike the carpogonial branch, however, the small-celled branch bearing the auxiliary cell is simple and not branched. The auxiliary cell is the end cell of the auxiliary branch and is somewhat swollen. Auxiliary cells are found in most of the Florideophyceae and often they are borne on special branches as in *Acrosymphyton*; their shape and position, however, are very variable. The function of the auxiliary cell is not well understood. It receives a diploid nucleus from the fertilized carpogonium and this (and its descendants) may perhaps control and redirect the physiology of the gametophyte, in such a way that the developing gonimocarp becomes a sink for the photoassimilates of the gametophyte; the gonimocarp certainly seems to be nutritionally dependent on the gametophyte ([1805]).

Before fertilization can take place the spermatia must be transported to the carpogonium, and this takes place passively. The spermatia become attached to the trichogyne and subsequently surround themselves with a wall. One injects its nucleus into the trichogyne and this then migrates along the trichogyne to the mouth of the carpogonium, where it fuses with the nucleus.

After fertilization the carpogonium, which of course is now diploid, gives rise to one or two diploid filaments, termed connecting filaments (Fig. 5.21*e*: the diploid parts of the thallus are stippled). These fuse with several of the vegetative cells belonging to the carpogonial branch (Fig. 5.21*e*) and then grow further and fuse with the nearest auxiliary cell or cells (Fig. 5.21*f*). The auxiliary cell receives a diploid nucleus from the connecting filament, following which the nucleus and auxiliary cell divide and cut off a diploid gonimoblast initial cell towards the outside of the thallus. The gonimoblast initial then gives rise to a

thin colourless extension, the trichogyne, which is long and spirally twisted. The carpogonium is the terminal cell of a specialized branch, which is morphologically distinct from normal vegetative filaments and called the carpogonial branch. In *Acrosymphyton* the carpogonial branch consists of a main axis of small compact gonimocarp, in which almost all the cells may subsequently be converted into carposporangia (Fig. 5.21g). Because the connecting filaments can fuse with several auxiliary cells, one fertilized carpogonium can give rise to several gonimocarps.

Studies in the laboratory with cultures ([264]) have shown that the diploid carpospores grow into diploid tetrasporophytes, which differ considerably from the gametophytes (see Figs. 5.20, 5.21a, h).

The tetrasporophyte is a small disc-like plant, which lives appressed to the substratum. It consists of a system of main axes and short shoots, which grow together into a single pseudoparenchymatous structure. Nevertheless, for the most part, the individual filaments of cells remain easy to recognize (Fig. 5.21h). Before the tetrasporophytes had been grown in culture a similar plant had been found in nature and given the name *Hymenoclonium serpens*. As a result the tetrasporophyte of *Acrosymphyton* is sometimes called the 'Hymenoclonium phase', just as the filamentous, shell-borne stage of the *Porphyra* life cycle is called the *Conchocelis* phase (p. 63).

The tetrasporophytes produce tetrasporangia, and each of these in turn produces four haploid tetraspores via meiosis ([134]; Fig. 5.21i, j). In culture, tetrasporangia can be induced only by growing the tetrasporophytes under short-day conditions. With 8 h of light per day tetraspores are formed; with 16 h they are not. The basis of this short-day effect is different from the mechanism underlying the short-day response of *Porphyra tenera*. In *P. tenera* the 'short-day' effect is in fact a response to long nights, since interruption of the long night period by a brief exposure to dim light (for instance, a 1 h interruption of the dark period in an 8 h:16 h day–night cycle) will prevent the formation of conchosporangia. In many 'short-day' higher plants, a 'night break' like that given to *P. tenera* will prevent flowering.

By using monochromatic light sources for the 'night break', it is possible to investigate the action spectrum of the pigments involved in daylength perception, i.e. to determine which wavelengths of light elicit most response. In *Porphyra tenera* red wavelengths are most effective, as in higher plants. Furthermore, the effects of red are reversed by far-red. This suggests that the pigment involved in monitoring daylength is phytochrome, which is widespread in higher plants ([342, 344, 345]). By contrast, in *Acrosymphyton*, night breaks are completely ineffective in inhibiting tetrasporangium formation. However, if the short days (8 h light per 24 h) are supplemented by a period of dim light (e.g. a further 8 h), so dim that effective photosynthesis is impossible, the short-day response is abolished and no tetraspores are formed. The use of monochromatic light during the dim light period indicates that the receptor pigment (a 'cryptochrome') is sensitive principally to blue wavelengths (compare the photoperiodic response of the brown alga *Scytosiphon*, p. 189). Another peculiarity of the photoperiodic response in *Acrosymphyton* is that the photoreceptor is rendered less sensitive by exposure to high light intensities during the day (see [137, 138, 139, 265, 726], for the physiological and ecological implications of this).

It seems, therefore, that there are different types of photoperiodic responses in the red algae, mediated by different pigments, in contrast to the uniformity found in higher plants.

Acrosymphyton produces tetraspores only in short days, and in nature tetraspores arise only in the winter half of the year. Unlike the gametophyte, the tetrasporophyte can propagate itself vegetatively and does so by fragmentation. Short pieces of filament become detached and give rise to new tetrasporophytes. This type of reproduction can take place in short days or long days. The haploid tetraspores germinate and grow into new gametophytes (Fig. 5.21j, a).

To summarize, we can characterize the life cycle of *Acrosymphyton purpuriferum* as being heteromorphic and diplohaplontic, the zygote giving rise to a diploid sporogenous tissue (Fig. 5.21). The gametophyte is a summer annual and will not occur unless there are tetrasporophytes nearby to provide an inoculum of tetraspores. The tetrasporophyte, on the other hand, is independent, since it is a perennial and can propagate itself asexually.

There are other red algae with comparable life cycles. Given that the tetrasporophyte can live independently, it is in theory possible for the gametophyte and tetrasporophyte to have different geographical distributions. This does indeed happen in some species and probably occurs in *Acrosymphyton* too. 'Hymenoclonium serpens', the tetrasporophyte, is known from the English coast, whereas *Acrosymphyton* occurs in the Mediterranean and is absent on the Atlantic coasts of Europe. It is conceivable that the gametophyte could die out altogether, leaving the tetrasporophyte. Alternatively, the gametophyte might in some way become independent (and examples of such gameto-phytes are known) so that, with loss of meiosis in the tetrasporophyte, and loss of functional gametes in the gametophyte, tetrasporophyte and gametophyte could develop into two quite dissimilar species.

Order Acrochaetiales [488]

1 The thalli are simple branched filaments, which are uniseriate and never united in pseudo-parenchymatous tissues (Figs. 5.18, 5.19).

2 The pit plugs have cap membranes and two-layered plug caps (type 1 pit plugs: p. 55, Fig. 5.5a). Some have conspicuous outer domes (type 2 pit plugs: p. 55, Fig. 5.5b; [1455])

3 The tetrasporangia are cruciate or cruciate-decussate (Figs. 5.13a, b, 5.18m, 5.19f–h; [585]).

4 Auxiliary cells are absent.

5 The carpogonia are borne by normal vegetative cells (Fig. 5.18b, c) and not on specialized carpogonial branches (e.g. Fig. 5.21b).

6 The basic life cycle for the order is diplohaplon-tic and isomorphic, with a zygote that grows into a gonimocarp. There are other, derived types of life cycle, which are discussed on p. 73 ('Life cycles in other species of *Audouinella*').

Examples drawn from the genus *Audouinella* have been described in some detail on pp. 71–5, and no further members of the Acrochaetiales will be considered.

It is likely that this order is phylogenetically heterogeneous. It is an assemblage of simple, filamentous red algae, which are often all included in a single genus, *Audouinella* ([75, 979, 1455, 1911])

Order Palmariales [583, 585, 1811]

1 The Palmariales are very diverse in the form of their thalli, varying from deeply lobed, flat blades (Fig. 5.22a, g) to tiny crusts (Fig. 5.23). The blade-like thalli are pseudoparenchymatous (Fig. 5.9a) and multiaxial.

2 The pit plugs have cap membranes and two-layered plug caps (type 1 pit plugs: p. 55, Fig. 5.5a).

3 The tetrasporangia are cruciate. Each one is borne by a stalk cell, which is subsequently capable of regenerating a new tetrasporangium (Figs. 5.9a, b, 5.10, 5.22h); the proliferating stalk cell is a unique feature of the Palmariales.

4 Auxiliary cells are absent.

5 The carpogonia are borne by vegetative cells in the female gametophytes, which are reduced and crustose (Fig. 5.22d). Special carpogonial branches are not produced.

6 The life cycle is either of a special hetero-morphic–diplohaplontic type, or haplontic. This will be discussed further.

This order is characterized primarily by the peculiar way in which the tetrasporangia are formed (characteristic 3 above), and by the reduced, crustose nature of the female gametophytes, which bear the carpogonia on vegetative cells and not on specialized carpogonial branches (characteristics 5 and 6). The Palmariales includes three genera, which live in the temperate to arctic regions of the N Atlantic and N Pacific.

Palmaria palmata (Figs. 5.9, 5.10, 5.22)

Palmaria palmata is a very common species in the lower littoral and upper sublittoral zones of rocky coasts. The foliose thallus takes the form of one to several deeply lobed blades, which can bear marginal proliferations and arise from a disc-like base. It has a multiaxial, pseudoparenchymatous construction and, in section, can be seen to consist of a large-celled medulla bounded on each side by a small-celled cortex (Fig. 5.9a).

The female gametophyte of *Palmaria* is a small crust-like plant, in which the carpogonia are borne directly by the vegetative cells (as in the order Acrochaetiales) (Fig. 5.22c, d). The male gametophyte, on the other hand, is blade-like (Fig. 5.22a), and produces spermatia that can fertilize the carpogonia of the female crusts (Fig. 5.22b). After fertilization, the carpogonium does not develop into a gonimocarp (= a diploid sporogenous tissue for the production of carpospores), but into a blade-like tetrasporophyte. When young, this tetrasporophyte grows attached to the female gametophyte; later its own basal system develops and completely overgrows the tiny female thallus. The adult foliose tetrasporophyte, which is diploid, produces tetraspores meiotically (Fig. 5.22g, h) and

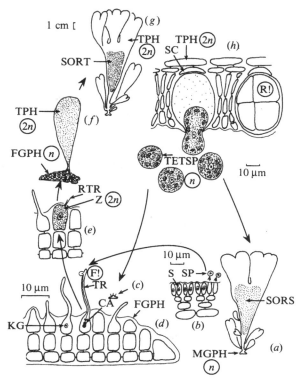

Figure 5.22. Life cycle of *Palmaria palmata*. (*a*) The blade-like male gametophyte (*n*). (*b*) Cross section of the cortex of a male gametophyte, showing the spermatangia. (*c*) The tiny (*ca.* 0.1 mm diameter) crustose female gametophyte (*n*). (*d*) Cross section of female gametophyte and fertilization of a carpogonium by a spermatium (*n*). (*e*) Cross section of female gametophyte, with zygote (2*n*, stippled). (*f*) Young blade-like tetrasporophyte (2*n*). This grows directly from the zygote, which is retained in the gametophyte (*n*). (*g*) Fully grown tetrasporophyte (2*n*). (*h*) Cross section through the cortex of the tetrasporophyte, showing tetrasporangia; one tetrasporangium is releasing its four tetraspores (*n*). CA = carpogonium; F! = fertilization; FGPH = female gametophyte; KG = karyogamy; MGPH = male gametophyte; R! = meiosis; RTR = remnant of the trichogyne; S = spermatangium; SC = stalk cell; SORS = sorus of spermatangia; SORT = sorus of tetrasporangia; SP = spermatium (*n*); TETSP = tetraspore; TPH = tetrasporophyte; TR = trichogyne; Z = zygote; *n* = haploid; 2*n* = diploid. (Based on [1075, 1811].)

these in turn develop into crust-like female gametophytes and foliose male gametophytes.

This very unusual life cycle can be summarized as follows: the life cycle is diplohaplontic and strongly

heteromorphic, with a reduced female gametophyte (= a haploid female microthallus) and a macroscopic male gametophyte (= a haploid male macrothallus) ([1811]). The same type of life cycle has been demonstrated in *Devalerea*, a close relative of *Palmaria* ([1810]; see also [809], as *Halosaccion*).

The life cycle of *Palmaria palmata* is quite similar to one of the alternative life cycles in *Audouinella gynandra* (pathway B in Fig. 5.19; p. 73). Here the fertilized carpogonium develops directly into a tetrasporophyte, which remains attached to the somewhat reduced gametophyte; this course of events is clearly a simplification of the normal *A. gynandra* life cycle, a short-cut in which the gonimocarp stage is omitted. Perhaps, then, the life cycle of *Palmaria* evolved in a similar way, through loss of the gonimocarp in an ancestor of the Palmariales.

Heteromorphic, diplohaplontic life cycles that include macrothallus and crustose microthallus stages are quite common in the Florideophyceae. In general, however, the microthalli are not gametophytes as in *Palmaria*, but tetrasporophytes (e.g. in *Acrosymphyton purpuriferum*, Fig. 5.21; or *Mastocarpus stellatus*, Fig. 5.35).

Rhodophysema elegans (Fig. 5.23)

This species forms smooth, rose-coloured to dark red crusts, which grow up to 45 mm in diameter. *Rhodophysema* crusts are monoecious, producing both spermatangia and carpogonia. The carpogonia are borne by vegetative cells, as in *Palmaria*, and after fertilization develop directly into stalked tetrasporangia. Stalked tetrasporangia are considered to be restricted to the Palmariales ([300]). This life cycle can be summarized as being haplontic, with zygotic meiosis, unless the stalk cell of the tetrasporangium is to be interpreted as a highly reduced vegetative stage.

The life cycle of *Rhodophysema* can also be compared with one of the alternative life cycles of *Audouinella gynandra* (this time with pathway C of Fig. 5.19; p. 73). In this cycle the fertilized carpogonium of the reduced gametophyte is transformed directly into a tetrasporangium, producing tetraspores that give rise to new gametophytes; both the gonimocarp and tetrasporophyte are omitted from the life cycle. In *Audouinella gynandra*, pathway C clearly represents extreme simplification of the normal diplohaplontic life cycle with its usual development of the zygote into a gonimocarp. So, pursuing the same kinds

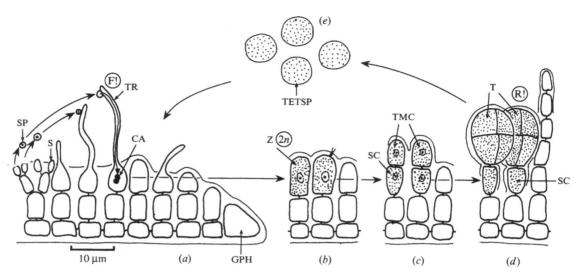

Figure 5.23. Life cycle of *Rhodophysema elegans*. (*a*) Fertile, crustose, monoecious gametophyte (*n*), with fertilization of a carpogonium by a spermatium. (*b*) The same plant, but with formation of zygotes (2*n*, stippled) from the fertilized carpogonia. (*c*) A later stage, in which the zygotes have each divided into a stalk cell (2*n*) and a tetrasporangium mother cell (2*n*). (*d*) Following meiosis, each tetrasporangium mother cell has now devel- oped into a tetrasporangium, containing four tetraspores (meiospores; *n*). (*e*) Tetraspores, which grow into new gametophytes (*n*). CA = carpogonium; F! = fertilization; GPH = gametophyte; R! = meiosis; S = spermatangium; SC = stalk cell of tetrasporangium; SP = spermatium; T = tetrasporangium; TETSP = tetraspores; TMC = tetrasporangium mother cell; TR = trichogyne; Z = zygote. (Based on [300].)

of argument as we have outlined for *Palmaria*, it can be suggested that the life cycle of *Rhodophysema* is highly modified and simplified. The reduction is even more extreme than in *Palmaria* and may have involved complete loss of a tetrasporophytic macrothallus phase.

Order Nemaliales

1 These red algae have cylindrical or slightly flattened, branched thalli, which are often more or less gelatinous and have a multiaxial construction (Fig. 5.24*a*, *b*).

2 The pit plugs have cap membranes and two-layered plug caps (type 1 pit plugs, p. 55; Fig. 5.5*a*).

3 The tetrasporangia are cruciate (Fig. 5.13*a*, *b*; [585]).

4 Auxiliary cells are absent.

5 The carpogonia are borne on specialized carpogonial branches (Fig. 5.24*d*, *e*).

6 The life cycle is in most cases heteromorphic, the tetrasporophyte being reduced and filamentous (see below; for *Nemalion*). This is the same kind of life cycle as in *Acrosymphyton* (p. 75). One genus in this order (*Galaxaura*) has an isomorphic, diplohaplontic life cycle (for an overview, see [100]).

Nemalion helminthoides (Fig. 5.24*a–i*)

This alga is dark red or brown, and shaped like a worm. It is a characteristic species of rocks exposed to breakers in the intertidal zone of temperate coasts world-wide. The thalli have a multiaxial structure: a bundle of axial filaments gives rise to a great number of lateral filaments, which are branched and lie embedded in a stiff sheath of mucilage (Fig. 5.24*a*).

Spermatangia are formed at the tips of the lateral filaments (Fig. 5.24*c*). The three- to five-celled carpogonial branches, on the other hand, arise close to the axis of the plant from cells of the lateral filaments (Fig. 5.24*d*, *e*). After the carpogonium has been fertilized by a spermatium (Fig. 5.24*e*), it divides into an upper and a lower cell (Fig. 5.24*f*). The upper cell, which of course is diploid, gives rise to several densely

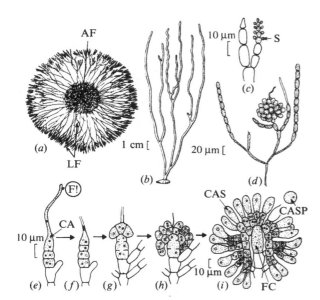

Figure 5.24. *Nemalion helminthoides*. (*a*) Cross section through the thallus, showing the multiaxial construction. (*b*) Habit of plant. (*c*) Lateral filaments with spermatangiophore. (*d*) Lateral filaments with gonimocarp. (*e–i*) Development of a carpogonial branch (stippled) into a ripe gonimocarp. AF = axial filaments; CA = carpogonium; CAS = carposporangium; CASP = carpospore; F! = fertilization; FC = fusion cell; LF = lateral filaments; S = spermatangium. (*a, b* based on [1341]; *c, e–i* on [1658]; *d* on [1283].)

branched gonimoblasts, which grow downwards (Fig. 5.24*g, h*) and ultimately produce carposporangia (Fig. 5.24*i*). The remaining cells of the carpogonial branch fuse with each other, producing a fusion cell which is supposed to 'feed' the gonimocarp as it develops, although how and why is unclear. Ultrastructural investigations do not help to elucidate the role of the fusion cell ([1467]). The fusion cell is sometimes termed an auxiliary cell (auxiliary cells too are supposed to function as food cells) but in this case *Nemalion* could no longer be classified in the Nemaliales, because the Nemaliales are characterized by the absence of auxiliary cells! Such contradictions illustrate how difficult it is to interpret red algal structure and how frail the current classification of the Florideophyceae still is.

The carpospores of *Nemalion* germinate and grow to form a filamentous, *Audouinella*-like, branched tetrasporophyte ([462, 463, 1808]). Tetraspores are formed in short-day conditions (daylengths less than 12 h light per day), and are therefore found in autumn and win-

ter. Like the carpospores, the tetraspores develop initially into filaments, but then they give rise to the multiaxial gametophyte thalli; this takes place at rather low temperatures (7–13 °C) and in long days (greater than or equal to 12 h light per day), in spring. In the summer, when they become fertile, the gametophytes erode away ([274]). The life cycle can be interpreted as having arisen from the basic florideophycean isomorphic–diplohaplontic cycle through the loss of a macroscopic tetrasporophyte phase. This idea gains support from the existence of an isomorphic life cycle in another genus of Nemaliales, *Galaxaura*.

Order Batrachospermales

1 The rhodophytes of this order have cylindrical, branched or unbranched thalli, which are often more or less gelatinous and have a uniaxial or multiaxial structure.

2 The pit plugs probably have cap membranes, while the plug caps are two-layered; the outer layer of the plug cap is conspicuously domed (a type 2 pit plug: p. 55, Fig. 5.5*b*).

3 Tetrasporangia, and hence also tetrasporangial meiosis, are quite absent. Meiosis takes place instead in the apical vegetative cells of the sporophyte (Fig. 5.25*c*).

4 Auxiliary cells are absent.

5 The carpogonia are borne on special carpogonial branches.

6 The Batrachospermales have a unique type of diplohaplontic life cycle, which is heteromorphic and contains a reduced tetrasporophyte (for the basic model of a heteromorphic, diplohaplontic cycle, see *Acrosymphyton*: Fig. 5.21). Meiosis takes place in the apical cells of the diploid sporophyte, which is usually a filamentous, *Audouinella*-like plant. Following meiosis, the haploid apical cells grow into macroscopic gametophytes, which remain attached to the sporophyte (Figs. 5.25*a, c, d*, 5.26; [46, 765, 1072, 1073, 1620, 1768]). In some species meiosis is postponed and takes place in the apical cell of the few-celled gametophyte ([1724]).

7 The Batrachospermales are entirely restricted to freshwater habitats ([1620]).

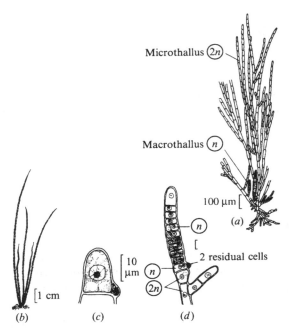

Microthallus (2n)

Macrothallus (n)

100 μm [

(n)

(a)

[

10 μm

(n)   2 residual cells

(n)

(2n)

[1 cm

(b)   (c)   (d)

Figure 5.25. *Lemanea*. (*a*) Microthallus (*Chantransia* phase) with two young macrothalli (*Lemanea* phase). (*b*) Habit. (*c*) The initial cell of the macrothallus, with two residual cells. (*d*) Young macrothallus attached to the microthallus. *n* = Haploid; 2*n* = diploid. (*a–c* after [1341]; *d–e* after [1072, 1073].)

Lemanea (Fig. 5.25)

Lemanea plants look like tufts of stiff, dark brown or black hair. The individual hairs are thickened at regular intervals, forming nodes (Fig. 5.25*b*). The thallus has essentially the same structure as in *Acrosymphyton*, each cell of the main axis (which is a filament of cells) bearing a whorl of four small-celled laterals (short shoots), which are of limited growth. In *Lemanea*, however, the short shoots combine to form a robust pseudoparenchyma. *Lemanea* species are among the few red algae that grow in freshwater and they are to be found attached to stones in swiftly flowing streams.

Just as in *Acrosymphyton*, the carpospores give rise to a diploid phase that differs greatly in shape and structure from the gametophyte. In *Lemanea* this phase consists of small clusters of simple, branched filaments, which are somewhat reminiscent of *Audouinella investiens* (Fig. 5.25*a*). It is referred to as

the microthallus-phase, which is the term applied to simple filamentous stages in the life cycles of structurally complex algae ([231, 700]), the complex stage itself being called the macrothallus phase.

By analogy with the *Hymenoclonium* phase of *Acrosymphyton*, we might expect that the diploid microthallus of *Lemanea* would form tetraspores via meiosis, and that these tetraspores would germinate into new gametophytes (macrothalli). But this does not happen. The young *Lemanea* gametophytes do in fact arise directly from the microthallus, as side branches (Fig. 5.25*a, d*). Meiosis takes place in the apical cell of a young side branch, as a result of which four haploid nuclei are produced ([1072, 1073, 1768]). Only one of these survives, while the others are segregated into small residual cells that have no function (Fig. 5.25*c, d*). The remaining apical cell, now haploid, grows into a new gametophyte (macrothallus). We are dealing here with **vegetative meiosis**, which is a very rare phenomenon. The products of the reduction division are usually either meiospores or gametes; furthermore, meiosis almost always takes place in particular, specialized cells, such as meiosporangia, gametangia, or hypnozygotes.

We can say in summary that *Lemanea* has a heteromorphic, diplohaplontic life cycle, with vegetative meiosis and a zygote that gives rise to a diploid, spore-producing tissue (gonimocarp). The opposite of vegetative meiosis, vegetative diploidization, has never been found in red algae but is known from the brown alga *Elachista stellaris* (p. 198).

Batrachospermum (Fig. 5.26)

The structure of the thallus is similar to that of *Acrosymphyton*. Each cell of the single axial filament of cells bears a whorl of lateral branches, which may themselves be branched and are of limited, determinate growth. These whorls give the gelatinous thalli of *Batrachospermum* their characteristic beaded appearance.

In *Batrachospermum*, vegetative meiosis usually takes place in the apical cells of *Audouinella*-like sporophytes, as in *Lemanea*. The gametophytes produced following vegetative meiosis remain attached to the sporophyte (Fig. 5.26; [46, 765]). In at least one species, however, the sporophyte is crustose, and meiosis takes place in the apical cell of a few-celled gametophyte growing attached to the sporophyte ([1724]).

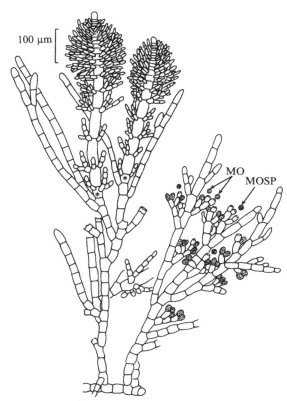

100 μm

MO
MOSP

Figure 5.26. *Batrachospermum ectocarpum*: diploid micro-thallus (= *Audouinella* phase) reproducing asexually by the formation of monospores and bearing two young haploid macrothalli (= *Batrachospermum* phase). * = basal cell of *Batrachospermum* phase; MO = monospores; MOSP = monosporangium. (Based on [1341].)

Order Corallinales [174, 175, 800, 1631, 1912]

1 The thalli are macroscopic and calcareous, tak-ing the form of prostrate crusts (Fig. 5.27a) or erect bushy plants (Fig. 5.27c, d). The thallus structure is multiaxial. The cell walls are impregnated with calcium carbonate, in the form of calcite crystals (Fig. 5.3).

2 The pit plugs lack cap membranes and have two-layered plug caps. The outer layers of the pit plugs are conspicuously domed (type 3 pit plug: p. 55).

3 The tetrasporangia are zonate and are formed in conceptacles (cavities in the thallus; Fig. 5.30).

4 The cells bearing the carpogonial branches (the 'supporting cells') function as auxiliary cells.

After receiving the diploid nucleus from the fer-tilized carpogonium, the auxiliary cell fuses with numerous other auxiliary cells to form a large fusion cell, which then produces gonimo-carps at its margins (Figs. 5.28, 5.29).

5 Each carpogonium is the end cell of a two-celled carpogonial branch (Figs. 5.28a, 5.29) borne by the auxiliary cell. After fertilization, the carpo-gonium transfers the diploid zygotic nucleus to the auxiliary cell, this being facilitated by the fusion of the carpogonium, the single vegetative cell of the carpogonial branch, and the auxiliary cell (Fig. 5.29). The carpogonia, fusion cells, gonimoblasts and carpospores are all formed inside conceptacles (Fig. 5.28); the spermatan-gia too are formed in special conceptacles.

6 The life cycle is diplohaplontic and isomorphic.

Crustose and erect members of the Corallinales are very common along marine coasts, especially in the tropics, and they are important rock builders. Crustose corallines play a primary role in the construction and consolidation of coral reefs, cementing together loose rubble, for example. Erect coralline red algae are among the most important producers of calcium car-bonate sand, which, after lithification in the cavities of reefs, becomes an important matrix component of marine limestones ([10, 1751]; see also p. 52).

Lithophyllum expansum (Figs. 5.27a, b, 5.28 – 5.30; [174, 601])

Lithophyllum expansum is a crustose coralline alga, forming fragile pink crusts, 1–2 mm thick, which can often be quite large, attaining diameters of 15–30 cm. It grows in the Mediterranean sea, at depths of 15–60 m, sometimes deeper (up to 160 m!). On deep sedi-ments *Lithophyllum expansum* is an important con-stituent of the large organic concretions formed by assemblages of various benthic organisms, which themselves also produce calcium carbonate tubes, or other structures ([110, 1056]).

The crust consists of a basal layer (hypothallus), from which there arise upright lines or filaments of cells forming the perithallus (Fig. 5.27b). In a recent paper, the filaments of the hypothallus have been termed 'primigenous filaments' and those of the perithallus, 'postigenous filaments' ([1912]). In *Litho-phyllum expansum*, the hypothallus is one layer of

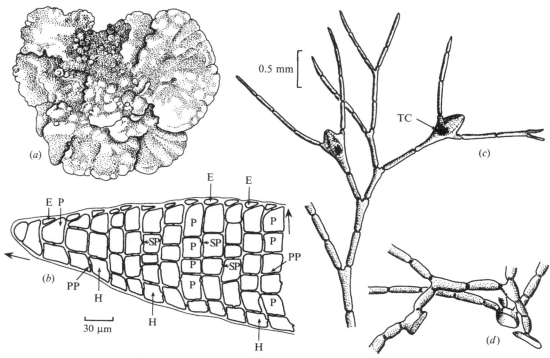

Figure 5.27. (*a, b*) *Lithophyllum expansum,* an example of a crustose coralline red alga. (*a*) Top view of the calcareous thallus. (*b*) Cross section through the growing margin of the thallus. (*c, d*) *Jania adhaerens,* an example of a geniculate coralline red alga. (*c*) Erect portion of the thallus, with tetrasporic conceptacles.

(*d*) Creeping basal parts of thalli, with rounded attachment discs. E = epithallus cells; H = hypothallus cells; P = perithallus cells; PP = primary pit connections; SP = secondary pit connections; TC = tetrasporangial conceptacle. (*a* based on [1341]; *b* on [1733]; *c, d* on [105].)

cells thick but in other *Lithophyllum* species it often contains several layers. The crust expands through division of the apical (i.e. peripheral) cells of the hypothallus (Fig. 5.27*b*, horizontal arrow). It grows in thickness by division of the uppermost perithallus cells (Fig. 5.27*b*, vertical arrow), but these meristematic cells are covered by one to several non-dividing epithallus cells, so that vertical growth (increase in thickness) is in fact brought about by intercalary, not apical cell division. Also noteworthy are the distinct secondary pit connections between cells in different lines of cells in the perithallus (Fig. 5.27, SP).

The reproductive structures have been described briefly in the list of characteristics for the order Corallinales (see above, characters 3–6; Figs. 5.28 – 5.30).

Jania adhaerens (Fig. 5.27c, d)

The bushy plants of *Jania adhaerens* are approxi-

mately 1–3.5 cm high and exhibit repeated dichotomous branching. Each branch consists of a number of calcified segments, which are linked by flexible, non-calcified joints (genicula).

The internal structure is multiaxial. The multiaxial core is like a hypothallus and grows by division of its apical cells. Around this, in the calcified segments, is a perithallus consisting of lines of cells perpendicular to the core, which arise from the hypothallial cells.

Jania adhaerens is very common throughout the tropics, where it is one of the most important producers of calcium carbonate sand.

Order Gelidiales

1 The thalli are macroscopic and cartilaginous, and can be cylindrical or flattened; they are often pinnate (Fig. 5.31*a*). Their internal structure is uniaxial (Fig. 5.31*b*), with determinate

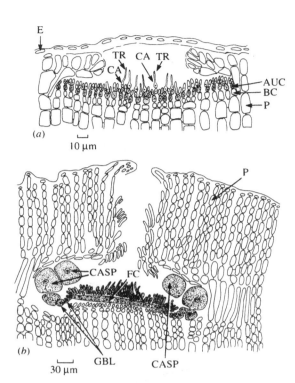

(a)

10 μm

(b)

30 μm GBL CASP

Figure 5.28. Development of carposporic (female) conceptacles in *Lithophyllum expansum*. (*a*) Just before fertilization. (*b*) After fertilization, with mature carpospores. AUC = auxiliary cell; BC = basal cell of
fertile filament; CA = carpogonium; CASP = carpospore; E = epithallus cell; FC = fusion cell; GBL =
gonimoblast filament; P = perithallus cell; TR = trichogyne. (Based on [1733].)

lateral branches that combine to form a compact
pseudoparenchymatous tissue.

2 The pit plugs have cap membranes and one-
layered plug caps (type 4 pit plugs: p. 55, Fig.
5.5*c*).

3 The tetrasporangia are cruciate (Figs. 5.13*a*, *b*,
5.31*d*).

4 Auxiliary cells are present, in the form of
branched 'nutritive' filaments (Fig. 5.31*g*, *i*).

5 The carpogonium is borne at the end of a three-
celled carpogonial branch; the other two cells,
and even the carpogonium itself, bear ordinary
laterals containing vegetative cells (Fig. 5.31*e*;
[465]).

6 In sexually reproducing species, the life cycle is
diplohaplontic and isomorphic.

Gelidium latifolium (Fig. 5.31)

The thallus of this alga is dark red, flat, several times
pinnate, and about 10 cm high (Fig. 5.31*a*); it is cartilaginous and constructed uniaxially (Fig. 5.31*b*).
Gelidium latifolium is widely distributed on rocky
coasts around the Mediterranean and also in the North
Atlantic. It often grows on shady, overhanging rocks
near the low water mark.

Each apical cell has one cutting face and produces a
series of flat segments. Each of these divides into three
in the plane of the thallus. The central cells persist,
forming the axis of the plant, whereas the two pericentral cells grow into tightly branched short shoots
(determinate laterals), which unite to form a pseudoparenchyma.

The carpogonium is the terminal cell of a three-
celled carpogonial branch. The two lower cells bear
ordinary laterals, which form part of the pseudoparenchymatous cortex (Fig. 5.31*e*; [465]). Alternatively,
the carpogonium can be interpreted as being borne
directly upon an intercalary vegetative cell of the cortex: cf. [948]. Often, however, the carpogonium itself can
be interpreted as an intercalary cortex cell (referring to
Fig. 5.31*e*, it then takes the position of the supporting
cell, SC; [724]). The fertilized carpogonium produces a
connecting filament, after fusion with the adjacent cortex cells (Fig. 5.31*f*; [308, 396, 724]). The connecting filaments branch and grow parallel to the axis of the plant
and fuse with branched filaments of 'nutritive cells'
(Fig. 5.31*g*, *i*), produced from nearby vegetative cells.
Following this fusion the carposporangia are formed
(Fig. 5.31*g*). The nutritive filaments resemble the auxiliary cell filaments in *Acrosymphyton* (Fig. 5.21*c*),
which also has carpogonial branches whose cells bear
laterals. Overall, the female reproductive structures of
Gelidium are quite similar to those of *Acrosymphyton*
([396]), with this difference, that in *Acrosymphyton* the
auxiliary cells (after fusion) produce the carposporangia, while in *Gelidium* the nutritive cells do not.
Finally the inner cells of the cortex stretch and so
create a cavity, which contains the mature gonimocarp
(Fig. 5.31*h*) and opens to the exterior by two ostioles.

The complex structure and development of the
female reproductive organs are quite uniform within
the order Gelidiales ([396, 724]). The tetrasporophytes of
Gelidium (Fig. 5.31*d*) are similar to the gametophytes,

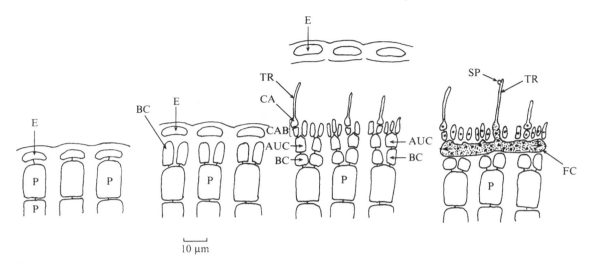

Figure 5.29. Development of female structures in *Lithophyllum expansum*, shown diagrammatically. AUC = auxiliary cell; BC = basal cell of fertile fila-ment; CA = carpogonium; CAB = carpogonial branch; E = epithallus cell; FC = fusion cell; P = perithallus cell; SP = spermatium; TR = trichogyne.

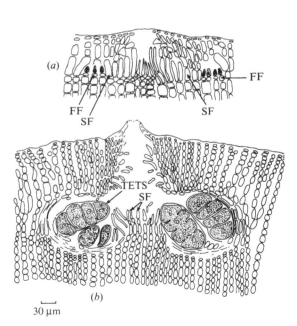

Figure 5.30. Development of a tetrasporangial conceptacle in *Lithophyllum expansum*. (*a*) Young stage. (*b*) Mature stage. FF = fertile filament; SF = sterile fila-ment; TETS = tetrasporangium. (Based on [1733].)

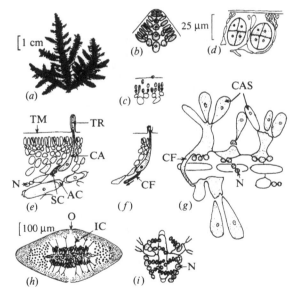

Figure 5.31. *Gelidium latifolium*. (*a*) Habit. (*b*) Apical region. (*c*) Spermatangia. (*d*) Tetrasporangia. (*e–i*) Development of the gonimocarp. AC = axial cell (central cell); CA = carpogonium; CAS = carpospor-angium; CF = connecting filament; IC = cells of inner cortex; N = nutritive cell; O = ostiole; SC = support-ing cell; TM = thallus margin; TR = trichogyne. (*g* after [369]; *b, c, e, f, h, i* after [948].)

so that this genus apparently has an isomorphic, diplohaplontic life cycle.

Species of the genus *Gelidium* and related genera represent the most important source of raw material for the production of agar (cf. p. 52; [14, 531, 989a, 1155]).

Order Gigartinales

1 The thalli of these rhodophytes are very varied. There is a great diversity of frondose forms, and also crustose species. The internal structure of the frondose thalli can be either uniaxial (Fig. 5.21*a*) or multiaxial (Figs. 5.33, 5.34*b*), while the individual filaments can be rather loosely associated (Figs. 5.21*a*, 5.33*e*), or form compact pseudoparenchymatous tissues (Fig. 5.34*b*).

2 The pit plugs have cap membranes but no plug caps (type 6 pit plugs: p. 55, Fig. 5.5*d*).

3 The tetrasporangia are cruciate or zonate (Fig. 5.13*a–c*; [585]).

4 Auxiliary cells are present *before* the carpogonium has been fertilized. They are either borne on special auxiliary cell filaments or on unspecialized filaments of vegetative cells.

5 The carpogonia lie at the ends either of quite distinct, specialized carpogonial branches (Fig. 5.21*b*), or of less differentiated carpogonial branches that take the place of vegetative filaments (Fig. 5.34*d*). The fertilized carpogonium can transfer its diploid nucleus to the auxiliary cell in various ways, but always does so via an external connection; the auxiliary cell subsequently gives rise to a gonimocarp, the form of which varies considerably within the order.

6 The life cycles are diplohaplontic and either isomorphic or heteromorphic; if heteromorphic, the tetrasporophyte is reduced and generally crustose.

The order Gigartinales is clearly heterogeneous phylogenetically, since most of the characters used to define it (characters 1, 3, 4, 5, 6) are themselves variable within the group. It is a residual aggregate of many rhodophyte genera, which have not yet been sorted into more natural groups. The order encompasses the two traditional orders Cryptonemiales and Gigartinales, which have recently been merged because the criteria used to separate them were clearly artificial ([909]). However, the new, expanded Gigartinales certainly includes several different clusters, each containing a number of closely related genera.

Acrosymphyton purpuriferum (Figs. 5.20, 5.21)

This species has been described in detail as an example of a florideophycean red alga with a strongly heteromorphic, diplohaplontic life cycle (p. 75).

Dumontia contorta (Figs. 5.32, 5.33)

Dumontia contorta was used to illustrate various aspects of florideophycean thallus construction (Figs. 5.32, 5.33; p. 70); its structure seems at first sight to be uniaxial but is in fact multiaxial. The erect parts of the *Dumontia* thallus are irregularly branched, compressed and hollow, and arise from a basal crust. The development of the gonimocarp is very similar to that in *Acrosymphyton* ([948]), to which *Dumontia* is closely related. *D. contorta* has an isomorphic diplohaplontic life cycle.

The initiation of the erect fronds from the basal crusts can only take place in short days, with daylengths less than 13 h ([1495, 1496, 1497, 1498]). In nature, therefore, the erect parts are initiated during the winter half of the year, and mature (become fertile) the next spring ([853]). *Dumontia contorta* is commonly found during spring (though present at other times as a crust) along the temperate coasts of the N Atlantic and N Pacific.

It is interesting to note that closely related genera (*Acrosymphyton* and *Dumontia*) can differ with respect to thallus construction (uniaxial or multiaxial) and life cycle (heteromorphic or isomorphic).

Chondrus crispus (Fig. 5.34)

The thalli of *Chondrus* are flat, branched and fan-shaped. Each plant is dark red, cartilaginous and 5–15 cm high (Fig. 5.34*a*). The centre of each branch is composed of many filaments, which lie parallel and anastomose with each other, forming secondary pit connections. The thallus of *Chondrus* therefore has a multiaxial construction (Fig. 5.34*b*). *Chondrus crispus* is widely distributed on temperate N Atlantic coasts in the lower parts of the intertidal zone, and is used in the manufacture of the gelling agent carrageenan (see p. 52).

The three-celled carpogonial branches (Fig. 5.34*d*) lie in the outer part of the cortex. Each arises from a

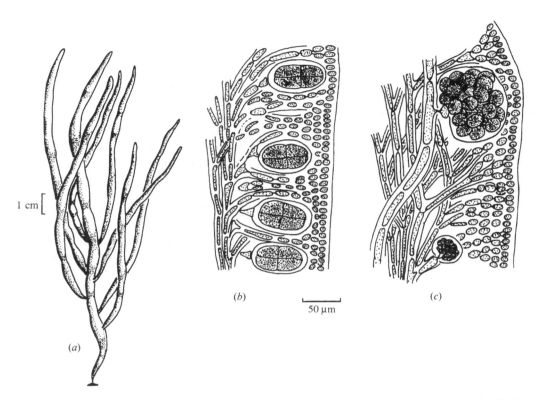

(a)

(b)

50 μm

(c)

Figure 5.32. *Dumontia contorta.* (*a*) Erect plant (macrothallus) growing from a basal crust (microthallus). (*b*) Longitudinal section through part of an erect thallus bearing tetrasporangia. (*c*) Longitudinal section through a part of an erect thallus bearing gonimocarps. (Based on [1283].)

supporting cell, which is a normal intercalary cell of the thallus. The supporting cell also acts as an auxiliary cell and the whole complex of supporting auxiliary cell and carpogonial branch is called the procarp. This term is used when both the auxiliary cells and the carpogonia form part of the same branch system. After fertilization the carpogonium fuses with the auxiliary cell (Fig. 5.34*e*). Then gonimoblast filaments grow out from the fusion cells into the thallus, where they cut off a large number of carposporangia (Fig. 5.34*f*). The ripe gonimocarps bulge out of the thallus on one side (Fig. 5.34*a*). The tetrasporophytes resemble the gametophytes morphologically but produce tetrasporangia in the medullary (pith) tissue, on short side branches borne by the medullary cells (Fig. 5.34*c*). *Chondrus* thus has an isomorphic, diplohaplontic life cycle ([225]).

Mastocarpus stellatus (Fig. 5.35; [587, 588])

The gametophytic thalli are dichotomously branched blades, which arise from a basal crust. They are stiff and cartilaginous, and have a distinctive channelling on one side. The plants are dioecious. The internal structure is multiaxial and resembles that of *Chondrus*. *Mastocarpus stellatus* (previously known as *Gigartina stellata*) and *Chondrus crispus* are also alike in the development of the gonimocarps, which form inside special papillae on the surface of the fronds (Fig. 5.35*a, b*). Furthermore, these two algae live in the same kinds of habitat and both are important raw material for the extraction of carrageenan.

Mastocarpus stellatus (and other *Mastocarpus* species) have a strongly heteromorphic life cycle, in which the gametophytes (described above) are the

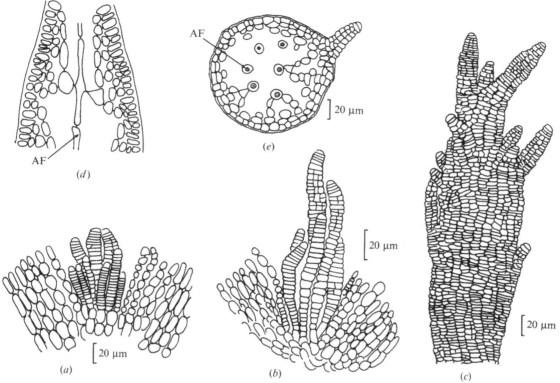

Figure 5.33. *Dumontia contorta*. (*a, b*) Cross sections through parts of basal crusts, showing the young primordium of an erect thallus (*a*) and a slightly older primordium (*b*): note that several uniaxial filaments are present. (*c*) A young erect thallus: the primordial axes have coalesced to form one common, multiaxial thallus, although the primordial axes can still be detected as the uniaxial initials of branches. (*d*) Longitudinal section through a portion of a uniaxial branch, near its tip. (*e*) Cross section through a young erect thallus like that shown in (*c*): note that there are five axial filaments. AF = axial filament. (*a–c, e* based on [1495, 1496]; *d* on [948].)

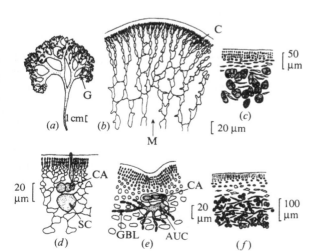

Figure 5.34. *Chondrus crispus*. (*a*) Habit. (*b*) Apical region. (*c*) Tetrasporangia. (*d*) Carpogonium. (*e*) Gonimoblasts. (*f*) Carposporangia. AUC = auxiliary cell; C = cortex; CA = carpogonium; G = gonimocarp; GBL = gonimoblast; M = medulla (pith); SC = supporting cell (= auxiliary cell). (*a* after [1283]; *b–f* after [948].)

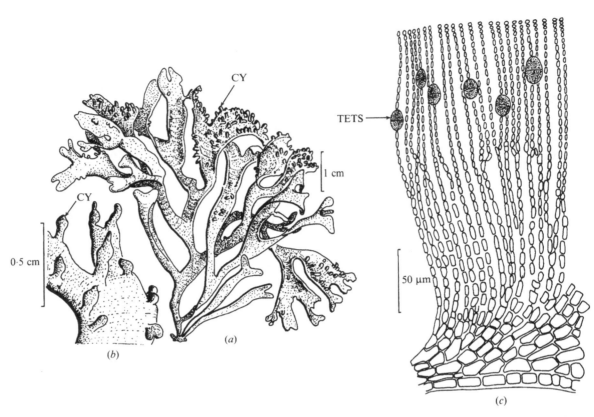

Figure 5.35. *Mastocarpus stellatus*. (*a*) Habit. (*b*) Detail of part of plant, with cystocarps. (*c*) Cross section through crustose tetrasporophyte, showing inter-calary tetrasporangia. CY = cystocarp; TETS = tetrasporangium. (*a, b* based on [310]; *c* on [310, 1695].)

most obvious stage. The tetrasporophytes are rather thick, mucilaginous crusts, formerly known as *Petrocelis* (Fig. 5.35*c*). The tetrasporangia are formed within the crust, intercalated along the upright filaments. *Mastocarpus* also includes a number of entirely asexual strains, in which haploid carpospores are formed without fertilization and grow directly into new gametophytes ([224, 306, 587, 1131, 1435, 1872, 1873, 1874]). Tetraspores are formed only in short days and low temperatures (e.g. with 8 h light per 24 h, but not with 16 h light, and at 10 °C but not 15 °C). This corresponds to winter and spring in nature ([587]).

As with *Acrosymphyton* and *Dumontia* (p. 87), it is interesting that the two genera *Chondrus* and *Mastocarpus*, which seem to be closely related, nevertheless have quite different types of life cycle: isomorphic in *Chondrus* but heteromorphic in *Mastocarpus*. Certain species of *Gymnogongrus*, probably distantly related to *Chondrus* and *Mastocarpus* ([1200]), have a *Petrocelis*-type tetrasporophyte, like *Mastocarpus* ([299]). In this genus there is yet another kind of life cycle: the development of the fertilized carpogonium into a compact, diploid, tetraspore-producing tissue, the so-called tetrasporoblast ([34]). This resembles one of the alternative life cycles in *Audouinella gynandra* (Fig. 5.19, pathway B), where again a zygote gives rise directly to a tetrasporophyte. What this suggests, therefore, is that the different kinds of life cycle in the *Chondrus–Mastocarpus–Gymnogongrus* group are all derived from the isomorphic, diplohaplontic life cycle that we have suggested is primitive for the Florideophyceae; some species have retained an isomorphic cycle, while in others the basic type has been simplified in various ways.

The occurrence of similar simplifications of the basic isomorphic florideophycean life cycle in unrelated groups of the Florideophyceae indicates that these modifications have arisen over and over again during evolution.

Order Rhodymeniales

1 The thalli are erect. Some are blade-like, in which case they are often dichotomously branched; others are cylindrical and often hollow, with constrictions at regular intervals (Fig. 5.36*a*). Internally they have a multiaxial, pseudoparenchymatous structure (Fig. 5.36*b*).

2 The pit plugs have cap membranes but lack plug caps (type 6 pit plugs: p. 55; Fig. 5.5*d*).

3 The tetrasporangia are generally tetrahedral, but sometimes cruciate (Fig. 5.13*d*, *a*; [585]).

4 The auxiliary cell is produced before the carpogonium has been fertilized. It is formed by a daughter cell of the supporting cell (the auxiliary mother cell) and this, together with the supporting cell itself, the auxiliary cell and the carpogonial branch, form the procarp (Fig. 5.36*c*). Procarp structure is remarkably uniform within the whole order.

5 The carpogonium is the terminal cell of a specialized, three- or four-celled carpogonial branch. The fertilized carpogonium transfers its diploid nucleus to the auxiliary cell either directly or via a connecting cell. The mature gonimocarp is surrounded by a distinct pericarp (Fig. 5.36*d*).

6 The life cycle is diplohaplontic and isomorphic.

Chylocladia verticillata (Fig. 5.36)

The thallus is cylindrical, hollow, and constricted at regular intervals along its length (Fig. 5.36*a*). At each constriction there is a whorl of side branches, while the internal cavity is subdivided into sections by transverse partitions. The cystocarps are spherical and are borne on the branches; the tetrasporangia also occur on the branches but lie embedded in the cortex. *Chylocladia verticillata* occurs on the Atlantic and Mediterranean coasts of Europe, from Ireland southwards.

Chylocladia is multiaxially constructed. The 16–20 axial filaments are closely appressed at their apices, but lower down they separate from each other and lie at the edge of the central cavity (Fig. 5.36*b*). Gland

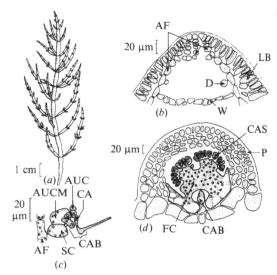

Figure 5.36. *Chylocladia verticillata.* (*a*) Habit. (*b*) Detail of thallus tip. (*c*) Carpogonium. (*d*) Cystocarp. AF = axial filament; AUC = auxiliary cell; AUCM = auxiliary mother cell; CA = carpogonium; CAB = carpogonial branch; CAS = carposporangium; D = gland cell; FC = fusion cell; LB = lateral branch; P = pericarp; SC = supporting cell; W = transverse partition (wall). (*b*–*d* after [948].)

cells project into the cavity. The cross-walls or partitions that subdivide the central cavity develop from the axial filaments, as do great numbers of short shoots (determinate laterals), which grow together to form a pseudoparenchymatous cortex (Fig. 5.36*b*).

The four-celled carpogonial branch grows out from a cortical cell (supporting cell) which is attached to one of the axial filaments. The supporting cell also bears two auxiliary mother cells. (In Fig. 5.36*c* only one of these cells is shown, behind the carpogonial branch; the second cell, which would have hidden the carpogonial branch, has been omitted for clarity.) After fertilization the carpogonium fuses with the auxiliary cells; ultimately the carpogonium, the auxiliary cells, the auxiliary mother cells and several cells from the floor of the cystocarp form a single, large, multinucleate fusion cell. This in turn produces carposporangia from its surface in a fan-shaped array (Fig. 5.36*d*).

Order Ceramiales

1 The thalli of the Ceramiales can be elegant, branched blades (Fig. 5.40), or tufted plants con-

sisting either of delicate, branched uniseriate filaments (Fig. 5.38) or of branched, pluriseriate (= polysiphonous) filaments (Fig. 5.37). The thallus structure is always clearly uniaxial.

2 The pit plugs have cap membranes but lack plug caps (type 6 pit plugs: p. 55; Fig. 5.5*d*).

3 The tetrasporangia are usually tetrahedral but sometimes cruciate (Figs. 5.13*d*, 5.37*j*; [585]).

4 The supporting cell of the carpogonial branch cuts off the auxiliary cell only after the carpogonium has been fertilized. The supporting cell, auxiliary cell and carpogonial branch together form the procarp (Fig. 5.37*c*), which is remarkably uniform in structure throughout the whole order.

5 The carpogonium is the terminal cell of a special four-celled carpogonial branch. The fertilized carpogonium transfers a diploid zygote nucleus to the auxiliary cell either directly or via a connecting cell. The mature gonimocarp is surrounded by a distinct pericarp (Fig. 5.37*b–f*).

6 The life cycle is diplohaplontic and isomorphic.

Polysiphonia (Fig. 5.37)

The thallus consists of finely branched filaments and is up to 25 cm tall. Each cell of the axial filament (i.e. each central cell) cuts off a whorl of 4–25 pericentral cells to the outside, the exact number depending on the species. *Polysiphonia urceolata*, illustrated here, is an example of a species with four pericentral cells. On European coasts there are about 25 species and the genus is found on sea coasts world-wide.

Some of the axial cells cut off cells (trichoblast initials) that grow into special branched lateral filaments called trichoblasts (Fig. 5.37*a*). The trichoblast has no pericentral cells except at the base and is initiated from an axial cell when this has become the third or fourth cell from the apex. Its cells are elongate and colourless. The axial cell giving rise to a trichoblast does not form a whorl of pericentrals until after it has cut off the trichoblast initial. The completion of the whorl (four in Fig. 5.37*a*) produces the 'polysiphonous' (= many-tubed) appearance of the alga. In place of a trichoblast, the axial cells sometimes give rise to long shoots (indeterminate laterals; Fig. 5.37*a*), but long shoots can also develop in two other ways. They may arise from the basal cell of a trichoblast, or may be formed

'endogenously' from one of the central cells; this occurs in the lower part of the thallus, the long shoot growing out between the pericentrals.

Male plants produce spermatangia on special fertile trichoblasts: a branch grows out from the base of the trichoblast and develops into a spermatangiophore (= a bearer of spermatangia; Fig. 5.37*g, h*).

The procarp too is initiated from near the base of a special fertile trichoblast. It develops as a small side branch from the second cell of the trichoblast (counting from the bottom). When ready for fertilization the procarp consists of a supporting cell, which bears a curved, four-celled carpogonial branch (Fig. 5.37*b*), and two sterile initials (of which only one is shown in Fig. 5.37*b*). The procarp lies on the adaxial side of the trichoblast.

After fertilization of the carpogonium, the supporting cell cuts off an auxiliary cell from its upper side (Fig. 5.37*c*) and this fuses with the carpogonium (Fig. 5.37*d*). The diploid nucleus migrates out of the carpogonium into the auxiliary cell, which then gives rise to the first gonimoblast initials (Fig. 5.37*e*). During the subsequent development of the gonimocarp, the supporting cell, auxiliary cell and the cells of the sterile filaments fuse into a large fusion cell (Fig. 5.37*f*). The ripe gonimocarp is enclosed by an urn-shaped pericarp (Fig. 5.37*f*), the gonimocarp and pericarp together forming the 'cystocarp'. The pericarp is initiated before fertilization of the carpogonium, from pericentral trichoblast cells immediately adjacent to the supporting cell (Fig. 5.37*b–e*). For ultrastructural details of the developing gonimocarp, see Broadwater & Scott ([145]).

The tetrasporophyte is morphologically similar to the gametophyte. *Polysiphonia* therefore possesses an isomorphic, diplohaplontic life cycle. The tetrasporangia are produced from normal vegetative axes. One of the cells in a whorl of pericentrals divides into a cover cell, a peripheral cell, a stalk cell and a tetrasporangium (Fig. 5.37*i, j*; [1927]).

Callithamnion (Fig. 5.38)

This alga forms tufts of uniseriate filaments, which exhibit alternate branching. The chloroplasts are parietal and discoid or elongate (Fig. 5.38*b, c*). The tetrahedral tetrasporangia are sessile and borne on the upper (adaxial) sides of the determinate laterals (Fig. 5.38*a*). Clusters of spermatangia are produced in similar positions on the male gametophytes (Fig. 5.38*g*).

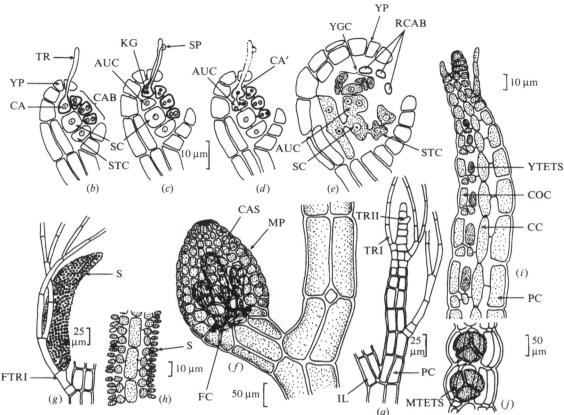

Figure 5.37. *Polysiphonia*. (*a*) Tip of filament. (*b–f*) Development of the cystocarp. (*g*) A fertile trichoblast, bearing an elongate mass of spermatangia on the spermatangiophore. (*h*) Detail of (*g*). (*i*) Longitudinal section through the tip of a tetrasporangium-bearing filament, showing the positions of the young tetrasporangia. (*j*) Two mature tetrahedral tetrasporangia. AUC = auxiliary cell; CA = carpogonium; CA′ = carpogonium fusing with the auxiliary cell after fertilization; CAB = carpogonial branch; CAS = carpospore; CC = central cell; COC = cover cell; FC = fusion cell; FTRI = fertile trichoblast; IL = indeterminate lateral; KG = karyogamy; MP = mature pericarp; MTETS = mature tetrasporangium; PC = pericentral cell; RCAB = remnants of the carpogonial branch; S = spermatangium; SC = supporting cell; SP = spermatium; STC = sterile cell; TR = trichogyne; TRI = trichoblast; TRII = trichoblast initial; YGC = young gonimocarp; YP = young pericarp; YTETS = young tetrasporangium. (Based on [1658].)

The female reproductive structures (procarps) are formed on the female gametophytes as follows. A young axial cell cuts off two opposite cells with dense protoplasmic contents; these are the two auxiliary mother cells (Fig. 5.38*d*). One of them (the right-hand cell in Fig. 5.38*d*) gives rise to the four-celled carpogonial branch. After fertilization, each of the two auxiliary mother cells cuts off an auxiliary cell upwards (adaxially), while at the same time the diploid, fertilized carpogonium divides into two. Each of these two diploid cells then injects a diploid nucleus into one of the two auxiliary cells, via a small conjunctor cell (see

p. 56; Fig. 5.6*c*). After receiving a diploid nucleus, the auxiliary cell develops into a branched gonimocarp, in which all the cells are transformed into carposporangia (Fig. 5.38*f*). The life cycle is diplohaplontic and isomorphic ([364]).

Species of *Callithamnion* are found world-wide along temperate and tropical sea coasts.

Ceramium (Fig. 5.39)

The erect, bushy plants of *Ceramium* appear to be dichotomously branched, although the branches originate as laterals (pseudodichotomy). The filaments

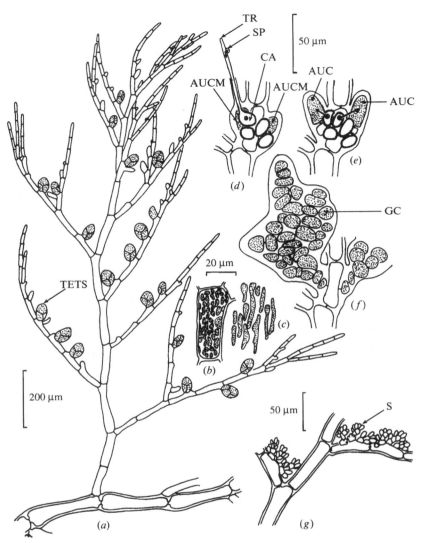

Figure 5.38. *Callithamnion furcellariae.* (*a*) Tetrasporo-phyte. (*b, c*) Chloroplasts in young (*b*) and older (*c*) cells. (*d–f*) Development of the gonimocarp; the car-pogonial branch cells are indicated by thick contour lines. (*g*) Portion of a spermatangial plant, showing groups of spermatangia. AUC = auxiliary cell; AUCM = auxiliary mother cell; CA = carpogonium; GC = gonimocarp; S = spermatangium; SP = sperma-tium; TETS = tetrasporangium; TR = trichogyne; arrows indicate the injection of a diploid nucleus into each of the two auxiliary cells from the divided zygote (by means of a conjunctor cell: see text). (*a, g* based on [1695]; *b, c* on [414]; *d–f* on [948].)

consist of large axial cells, each of which cuts off at its upper end a ring of small primary pericentral cells (Fig. 5.39*a*). The primary pericentral cells then give rise to bands of small cells, which cover the cross walls between the large axial cells (Fig. 5.39*b*). The tetrasporangia are formed in the cortical bands of small cells (Fig. 5.39*c*). The tetrasporophytes and sex-ual plants are similar, and so the life cycle is isomor-phic. *Ceramium* species are common everywhere on sea coasts.

Hypoglossum (Fig. 5.40)

Hypoglossum has narrow, lanceolate blades, which are one layer of cells thick, except at the conspicuous

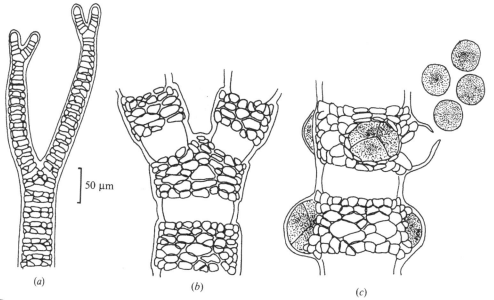

Figure 5.39. *Ceramium deslongschampsii.* (*a*) Tip of thallus. (*b*) Older portion of thallus.

(*c*) Older portion of thallus with tetrasporangia. (Based on [1695].)

midrib; the blades branch from the midrib. Under the microscope, *Hypoglossum* exhibits a very clearly uniaxial construction (Fig. 5.41). Each large axial cell bears two opposite primary laterals, which are of limited growth (determinate laterals) and have very characteristic triangular apical cells. The primary determinate laterals subsequently give rise to a series of secondary determinate laterals, along their lower (abaxial) sides. There are tetrasporangial, spermatangial and carposporangial plants, all morphologically similar. The tetrasporangia and spermatangia are formed in elongate sori along either side of the midrib (Fig. 5.40*b–d*). The cystocarps, on the other hand, are produced on and within the midrib itself (Fig. 5.40*a, e*).

Hypoglossum species are found on sea coasts in warm temperate and tropical regions. The species illustrated is common along the European coasts of the Atlantic and in the Mediterranean.

Phylogenetic reflections on the Rhodophyta

It has been quite widely accepted that the Rhodophyta are one of the most ancient lineages of eukaryotes. The most important argument for this is the absence of flagella, indicating perhaps that the red algae diverged from other primaeval eukaryotes before the evolutionary 'invention' of the typical eukaryotic '9 + 2' flagellum ([200, 201, 231, 232, 440, 1556, 1665, 1751]). This type of flagellum (cf. p. 303; Figs. 19.3, 19.4) occurs in the great majority of eukaryote lineages, and in fact, the Rhodophyta are the only division (= phylum) of algae where '9 + 2' flagella are completely absent (p. 501). In animals '9 + 2' flagella are present in all higher animal phyla and most protozoan phyla. In addition to the red algae three fungal phyla (Zygomycota, Ascomycota and Basidiomycota) lack all traces of '9 + 2' flagella, as do a few amoeboid protozoan phyla. It has often been suggested, therefore, that these fundamentally non-flagellate eukaryote groups arose before the evolution of flagella; the Rhodophyta could have evolved at this early stage from a primaeval heterotrophic eukaryote, through incorporation of a symbiotic cyanophyte.

The supposed primitiveness and great age of the Rhodophyta have been used to support arguments that the oldest Precambrian fossils of unicellular, apparently eukaryotic algae must be red algae. Examples of such fossils are *Eosphaera* and *Huroniospora*, both *ca.* 1.9 billion years old. *Eosphaera*, for instance, is compared with modern *Porphyridium* ([1751]). The same

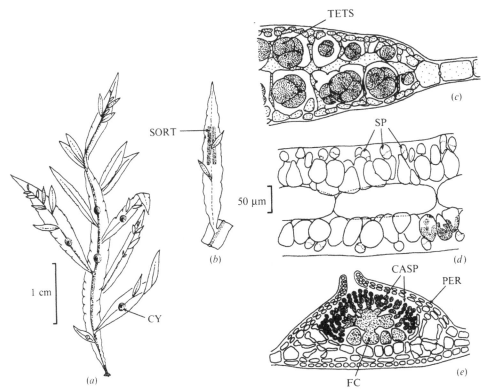

Figure 5.40. *Hypoglossum hypoglossoides.* (*a*) Habit of female thallus with cystocarps. (*b*) Portion of tetrasporic thallus with a sorus of tetrasporangia (stippled area). (*c*) Cross section through part of a tetrasporangial sorus. (*d*) Cross section through part of a spermatangial sorus on a male plant. (*e*) Cross section through a mature cystocarp. CASP = carpospore; CY = cystocarp; FC = fusion cell; PER = pericarp; SORT = sorus of tetrasporangia; SP = spermatangium; TETS = tetrasporangium. (*a–d* based on [1695]; *e* based on [948].)

kind of reasoning has been used to assign very old (1.3–0.7 billion years) fossils of macroscopic, foliose algae to the Rhodophyta ([715, 1751]). But in fact, neither of these types of ancient fossil, microscopic or macroscopic, has any features that are distinctive enough to allow them to be assigned to any known division of algae.

It has recently become possible to test hypotheses regarding the evolution of the main lineages of organisms by consulting the 'historical archives' stored in nucleotide or amino acid sequences. Ribosomal RNA (rRNA) nucleotide sequences in particular are being used extensively in the unravelling of phylogenetic relationships. Ribosomes are organelles that have the same function (protein synthesis) throughout the eukaryotes and prokaryotes, and their structure has been highly conserved during evolution. The cytoplas-

mic ribosomes of eukaryotes contain three kinds of rRNA: 5S, 18S and 28S rRNA; the larger the number, the larger the molecule. Because of the small number of nucleotides (120) contained in 5S rRNA, phylogenetic reconstructions based on analyses of this subunit are statistically unreliable. The 18S and 28S rRNAs, on the other hand, are sufficiently large (containing about 2000 and 5000 nucleotides, respectively) to allow valid measurement of relationships; the approach is discussed further on p. 40.

The first phylogenetic trees based on rRNA sequence analysis employed relatively unreliable 5S rRNA data and in one such tree the Rhodophyta appeared as the first main lineage to diverge from the rest of the eukaryotes ([734, 735]). This seemed to support the hypothesis mentioned above, that the Rhodophyta are an extremely ancient group, which arose before the

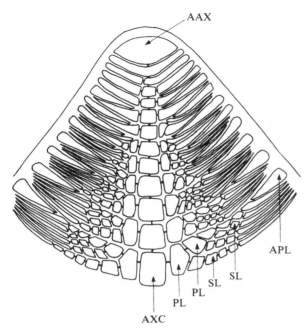

Figure 5.41. *Hypoglossum hypoglossoides:* tip of a blade. AAX = apical cell of the axial row of cells; APL = apical cell of primary determinate lateral; AXC = axial row of cells; PL = primary determinate lateral; SL = secondary determinate lateral. (Based on [948].)

evolution of '9 + 2' flagella. In fact, however, the analysis was not very helpful, since all the main lineages of eukaryotes appeared to diverge from each other at more or less the same time, in a fan-like manner; the resulting phylogenetic tree resembled the fan-like tree discussed in chapter 1 (p. 5, Fig. 1.3). 5S rRNA data do not allow us to resolve the detail of when and how the main groups of eukaryotes evolved.

Recently, a phylogenetic tree (Fig. 32.3) has been constructed, based on comparisons of a section of the 28S rRNA, about 450 nucleotides long, in a wide variety of eukaryotes, including the red alga *Porphyridium* (cf. p. 67; [1393, 1394]). The results do *not* support the hypothesis that the Rhodophyta are an ancient, primitive lineage, and this is confirmed by other rRNA studies ([589]). Instead, the red algae seem to have arisen relatively late, after the evolution of '9 + 2' flagella; they emerged at around the same time, from the same stock, as the Chlorophyta and multicellular animals. This suggests that the ancestral red algae lost their flagella secondarily, since both the Chlorophyta and the Eumetazoa are basically flagellate phyla. The Glauco-

phyta could perhaps be the only living descendants of the primaeval, flagellate ancestors of the red algae, apart from the red algae themselves; they are the only other eukaryotic algae with chloroplasts like those of the Rhodophyta, with equidistant, single thylakoids and phycobilisomes (see p. 507 for further discussion).

Fossils that can be identified with some certainty as rhodophytes begin to appear in the Cambrian (*ca.* 590 million years ago). These fossils are members of the Solenoporaceae, a family of the Corallinales that has been extinct since the Miocene (*ca.* 10 million years ago). The Corallinales (p. 83) fossilize easily, of course, because their cell walls are encrusted with calcium carbonate, in the form of calcite crystals, and several extant genera have long fossil records. For instance, the oldest fossils of the genus *Amphiroa*, an erect, articulated coralline alga, occur in the Upper Devonian (*ca.* 360 m.y. ago; [1066]), while fossils of *Jania* (Fig. 5.27*c, d*) are known from the Upper Cretaceous (*ca.* 80 m.y. ago). Genera of red algae still alive today can thus be very old, with known (and hence minimum) ages of 80–360 million years. Evolutionary change in thallus morphology would appear to be very slow in these genera, and there is no reason to believe that it is any faster in those red algae that do not fossilize so easily. The extreme age of rhodophyte genera agrees with ages determined for various chlorophyte genera (80–300 m.y.), but contrasts markedly with the youth of flowering plant genera (5–60 m.y.; [704]; and see p. 495) or mammal genera (*ca.* 2–5 m.y.; [1682]). The high average age of rhodophyte genera reflects the ancient origin and primitiveness of the red algae and their slow evolutionary advancement.

Although the fossil record supports the general idea that the red algae are an ancient and slowly evolving lineage, it does not yield information about phylogenetic relationships *within* the division. To gain insights into these relationships, we have to make recourse to comparisons between living Rhodophyta, using morphological features and other characteristics; then we have to decide, on the basis of these, which orders are relatively primitive and which are derived. The phylogenetic tree shown in Fig. 5.42 represents the outcome of such an exercise. Hypothetical phylogenetic relationships are presented, which explain and expand upon the subdivision of the Rhodophyta that has been adopted in this text.

In the tree the Rhodochaetales appears as the most

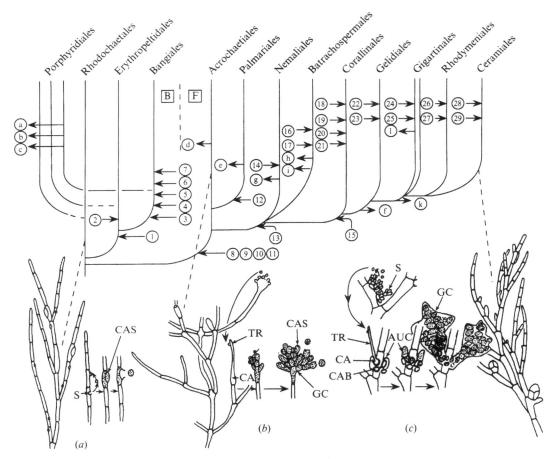

Figure 5.42. A phylogenetic tree of the red algae (Rhodophyta) based on comparative morphology of extant
representatives. In this tree the Rhodochaetales are
considered to be the ancestral group for all red algae
(see the text for the characters of this order). This
means that, of all the red algae, the Rhodochaetales are
considered to have changed least since the origin of the
group. All other red algal orders can be derived from
the Rhodochaetales by the accumulation of phylogenetic 'gains' (arrows pointing in towards the branches
of the tree) or 'losses' (arrows pointing outwards). The
Bangiophyceae (B) are situated to the left of the dashed
vertical line, the Florideophyceae (F) to the right of it.
(a) *Rhodochaete* (representing the ancestral order
Rhodochaetales). (b) *Audouinella* (representing the
most primitive order of the Florideophyceae, the
Acrochaetiales). (c) *Callithamnion* (representing the
most evolved order of the Florideophyceae, the
Ceramiales). AUC = auxiliary cell; CA = carpogonium; CAB = carpogonial branch; CAS = carposporangium; GC = gonimocarp; S = spermatangium;
TR = trichogyne; stippled cells are diploid.

Phylogenetic gains:
1 Erect filaments or parenchymatous fronds in the gametophyte phase, which exhibit intercalary cell division
  but lack pit plugs; these are in addition to the branched
  filaments also produced, with apical cell division and
  pit plugs.
2 Branched filaments with apical growth, arising from
  prostrate discs.
3 Branched filaments with apical growth, which penetrate into calcareous shells (*Conchocelis* phase).
4 Each fertilized carpogonium producing many carpospores (but only one in *Rhodochaete* and Erythropeltidales).
5 Each spermatangium producing many spermatia
  (instead of one, as in all other sexually reproducing red
  algae).
6 Pit plugs with one-layered caps (in *Rhodochaete* the pit
  plugs lack caps).
7 Close association between mitochondria and golgi
  bodies.
8 Pit plugs with cap membranes and two-layered plug
  caps.
9 Trichogynes on the carpogonia.

primitive lineage of all red algae, having retained more ancestral characters than any other order. These characters are (cf. p. 68; Fig. 5.42a): (1) simple branched filaments; (2) growth by division of apical cells; (3) simply constructed pit plugs (lacking cap membranes and plug caps); (4) an isomorphic, diplohaplontic life cycle; (5) a carpogonium that resembles a vegetative cell; (6) the development of the fertilized carpogonium, which cuts off a single carposporangium from the carpogonium by a curved lateral wall, the carposporangium subsequently producing a single carpospore; (7) similar formation of the spermatangium, in which the spermatangium is cut off from a vegetative cell by a curved wall and produces one spermatium; (8) the formation of the meiosporangium, producing only one meiospore; (9) the absence of any close association between the mitochondria and golgi bodies.

The other orders can be derived from the ancestral *Rhodochaete*-like group firstly by the step-wise acquisition of more advanced characters ('phylogenetic gains', indicated in Fig. 5.42 by arrows pointing in towards the branches of the tree), and secondly by the loss of certain characters ('phylogenetic losses', indicated in Fig. 5.42 by arrows pointing away from the branches). The Bangiales appears as a rather specialized, monophyletic order characterized by many 'phylogenetic gains'. The Porphyridiales, on the other hand, are interpreted to be polyphyletic, perhaps derived from the three orders Bangiales, Erythropeltidales and Rhodochaetales, with various 'phylogenetic losses'. Monophyletic means having one common ancestor; polyphyletic, several ancestors (such groups thus being 'unnatural' or 'heterogeneous').

The branch of the tree representing the Florideophyceae is characterized by a distinct set of

Caption for fig. 5.42 *(cont.)*.

10 Development of the fertilized carpogonium into a gonimocarp.
11 Meiosporangia present as tetrasporangia.
12 Association of the branched filaments to form a compact, multiaxial pseudoparenchyma.
13 Carpogonia placed at the tips of specialized carpogonial branches (specialized in both form and position).
14 Association of a bundle of axial filaments to form a loose multiaxial structure.
15 Formation of auxiliary cells.
16 Association of an axial filament and whorls of determinate laterals to form a loose uniaxial structure (rarely several axial filaments are present, when the structure is multiaxial).
17 The ability to grow in freshwater.
18 Multiaxial thalli composed of hypothallus, perithallus and epithallus (Corallinales construction).
19 Inclusion of calcite crystals in the cell wall.
20 Carpogonial branches, auxiliary cells and fusion cell arranged as in the Corallinales.
21 Formation of special reproductive conceptacles, characteristic of the Corallinales.
22 A compact cartilaginous, pseudoparenchymatous thallus, with uniaxial construction.
23 Carpogonial branches, auxiliary cells (= 'nutritive cell rows') and fusion cells arranged as in the Gelidiales.
24 Thallus morphology and structure diverse: uniaxially or multiaxially constructed, loose or compact.
25 Carpogonial branches, auxiliary cells and fusion cells (if present) arranged in various ways.
26 Thalli compact and pseudoparenchymatous, with multiaxial construction; blade-like or hollow and often constricted.

27 Carpogonial branches and auxiliary cells arranged in procarps of the Rhodymeniales type.
28 An increasingly orderly arrangement of the branched filamentous thallus.
29 Carpogonial branches and auxiliary cells arranged in procarps of the Ceramiales type. The auxiliary cell is cut off from the supporting cell of the carpogonial branch after fertilization.

Phylogenetic losses:

a Loss of multicellularity.
b Loss of sexuality.
c Loss of pit plugs.
d Loss of the gonimocarp in some representatives, rarely also of the tetrasporophyte.
e Loss of the gonimocarp in all representatives and, in some representatives, also of the tetrasporophyte.
f Loss of one of the two plug cap layers.
g Loss of the macroscopic tetrasporophyte (except in one genus); the tetrasporophyte is usually reduced and filamentous.
h Loss of the macroscopic tetrasporophyte; the sporophyte is reduced and filamentous.
i Loss of tetrasporangia. Meiosis takes place in a vegetative apical cell of the sporophyte; the resulting haploid cell grows into a macroscopic gametophyte, which remains attached to the sporophyte.
k Loss of the remaining plug cap layer, so that the pit plugs lack cap layers altogether.
l Loss of macroscopic tetrasporophytes in some representatives. The tetrasporophytes become reduced and crustose, or reduced and attached to the gametophyte.

'phylogenetic gains' (8–11 in Fig. 5.42), of which the specializations of the female reproductive structures are the most spectacular advance. The carpogonium acquired a trichogyne, which acts as a 'trap' and receptive surface for spermatia, while the fertilized carpogonium developed into a branched gonimocarp, so that each act of fertilization results in the production of several or many diploid carpospores (instead of the single carpospore produced in *Rhodochaete*: Fig. 5.42*b*). In the tetrasporophyte, the meiosporangia became tetrasporangia. These gains, together with the acquisition of more complex pit plugs (8–11 in Fig. 5.42), accompanied the evolutionary transformation of simple, filamentous, *Rhodochaete*-like algae into the simple, filamentous red algae of the Acrochaetiales. This order is considered to be the ancestral group of the Florideophyceae, or a cluster of ancestral groups, and is exemplified by the genus *Audouinella* (Figs. 5.18, 5.19, 5.42*b*).

Phylogenetic advance apparently continued mainly through further specialization of the female reproductive apparatus, including the acquisition first of carpogonial branches (13 in Fig. 5.42) and then of auxiliary cells (15 in Fig. 5.42). Finally, in the most highly derived order, the Ceramiales, the auxiliary cells came to be produced only after fertilization of the carpogonia (29 in Fig. 5.42). The genus *Callithamnion* (Figs. 5.38, 5.42) serves as an example of a simply filamentous genus in the order Ceramiales, with a very advanced female reproductive apparatus.

In addition to these general trends within the Florideophyceae there are special sets of advanced characters that characterize the individual orders, so that their circumscription is generally uncontroversial (these sets are indicated in Fig. 5.42). Exceptions are the orders Acrochaetiales and Gigartinales, which are apparently heterogeneous.

Various plausible phylogenies can be constructed as alternatives to the tree shown in Fig. 5.42 ([470a, 472]). For instance, the unicellular Porphyridiales have traditionally been considered to be the most primitive group of red algae, while the relative positions of the florideophycean orders can vary, according to how the auxiliary cells and carpogonial branches are defined and interpreted. For example, in the Gelidiales (p. 85, Fig. 5.31*e–g*), the carpogonia are borne on very precisely located rows of cells, which are often not considered as carpogonial branches, and the rows of auxiliary cells are often termed 'nutritive cells'. Furthermore, the auxiliary cells occupy very different positions in the various orders, so that it is difficult to envisage them as homologous.

However, in almost all the phylogenetic schemes that have been put forward, the Bangiophyceae are considered more primitive than the Florideophyceae, while within the Florideophyceae the Acrochaetiales are considered the most primitive order, and the Ceramiales the most advanced. One implication of this is that the diversification of the Florideophyceae into orders took place at the simple, filamentous level of organization, and that the highly derived, pseudo-parenchymatous types of thallus structure found in the florideophycean orders have evolved independently many times, in parallel (Fig. 5.42).

The tree shown in Fig. 5.42 is one of a number of possible evolutionary schemes that can be derived by placing extant red algae in a (hopefully) logical sequence on the basis of morphological characters, a sequence which is then interpreted as a genealogy. It is impossible to test the validity of the tree by reference to the fossil record, since, apart from a few isolated examples, good fossil evidence is available only for one order (the Corallinales). It is now possible, in principle, to test the validity of phylogenetic trees based on morphological evidence, such as the scheme discussed

Table 5.1. *Evolutionary distances between genera in different groups of algae, plants and animals based on 5S ribosomal RNA sequences*

Group of organisms	Evolutionary distances between genera, estimated as the number of base substitutions per nucleotide site ($\times$ 100) (range)
red algae	22.0–56.0
brown algae	1.0–5.0
green algae	<0.2–45
flowering plants	0–5.0
gymnosperms	3.0–5.0
vascular cryptogams	3.0–9.0
mosses	<0.2–9.0
vertebrates	0–6.4
mammals	0

Source: Based on [735].

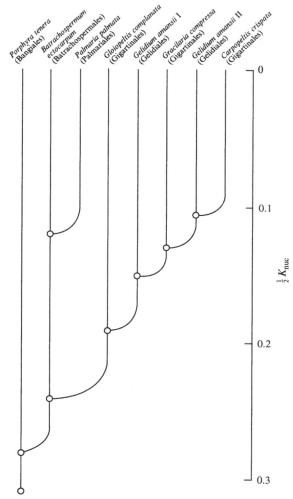

Figure 5.43. Phylogenetic tree of the red algae, based on 5S rRNAs. K_{nuc} = the evolutionary distance between two sequences; it estimates the number of base substitutions per nucleotide site that have occurred since the separation of the sequences. $\frac{1}{2} K_{nuc}$ is the evolutionary distance between the point of divergence and the branch tip. (Modified after [1011].)

above, with trees based on the nucleotide sequences present in the various types of rRNA subunit (see above and p. 37). So far, however, rRNAs have been

investigated in only a limited number of red algae. The results of 5S rRNA studies ([734, 735, 1011]) are summarized in Fig. 5.43, but it should be remembered that 5S rRNA molecules are too small to yield statistically reliable results.

The following points emerge from a comparison of Fig. 5.43 with Fig. 5.42.

1 The primitiveness of the Bangiophyceae relative to the Florideophyceae is confirmed by the 5S rRNA study; *Porphyra* was the most primitive and ancient red alga included in the analysis.

2 Within the Florideophyceae the Batrachospermales and Palmariales occupy primitive positions in both phylogenies, although their relative positions are reversed.

3 The remaining examples of Florideophyceae included in the 5S rRNA study, which all cluster together, are members either of the order Gracilariales (*Gracilaria*), or of the heterogeneous order Gigartinales (*Gloiopeltis, Carpopeltis*) or of the Gelidiales (*Gelidium*). These orders are quite close in the phylogenetic tree of Fig. 5.42. Curiously and incomprehensibly, *Gelidium amansii* appears twice in the rRNA tree.

When 5S rRNA phylogenies for different algal and plant groups are compared (Figs. 5.43, 13.2; [734, 735]), it is striking that the evolutionary distances between red algal genera are higher overall than those between genera in other groups (Table 5.1). Relatively large genetic distances have also been found between genera and species in the rhodophyte order Gracilariales ([81a]), in a phylogenetic analysis of nucleotide sequences in the nuclear gene for 18S rRNA. These distances clearly imply that the red algal genera diverged from each other a very long time ago and this agrees with the limited fossil evidence available, which shows that several genera of the order Corallinales are indeed extremely ancient. In the green algae too, large evolutionary distances have been found separating some genera.

6

Heterokontophyta: Classes (1) Chrysophyceae, (2) Parmophyceae and (3) Sarcino-chrysidophyceae

The principal features of the Heterokontophyta

1 The flagellate cells are heterokont, bearing a long pleuronematic (= flimmer or tinsel) flagellum, which is directed forwards during swimming, and a shorter smooth flagellum, which lacks the stiff hairs of the pleuronematic flagellum and points backwards along the cell. The pleuronematic flagellum bears two rows of special, stiff hairs, called mastigonemes (or flimmers), each one consisting of three subunits: a basal section, a tubular shaft, and one or more terminal hairs (Figs. 6.2a, 6.4e, f, h). The mastigonemes are composed of glycoprotein [115, 1218] and are synthesized in cisternae of the endoplasmic reticulum [319, 1218].

2 The transition region of the flagellum, between the flagellar shaft and the basal body, typically contains a transitional helix (Fig. 6.4a); this is absent in the classes Bacillariophyceae, Raphidophyceae and Phaeophyceae [661, 664, 668, 1218].

3 The chloroplast is enclosed not only by its own double membrane, but also by a fold of endoplasmic reticulum, the so-called chloroplast ER. Where a chloroplast lies up against the nucleus, the chloroplast ER is often continuous with the nuclear envelope (Figs. 6.3, 6.4d, 6.5, 6.6,

7.1b–d), which is itself, of course, a fold of the endoplasmic reticulum [76, 511]. A complex of anastomosing tubules, the periplastidial network, is situated in the narrow space between the chloroplast ER and the chloroplast envelope (Figs. 6.6, 6.11b; [76]).

4 Within the chloroplasts the thylakoids are grouped into stacks of three, the stacks being called lamellae. One lamella usually runs around the whole periphery of the chloroplast, parallel to and just beneath the chloroplast envelope; this is termed the girdle lamella (Figs. 6.4d, 6.5, 6.6, 7.1b). A girdle lamella is lacking in some members of the division, for instance the class Eustigmatophyceae [665, 667].

5 The chloroplasts contain chlorophyll a, c_1 and c_2; chlorophyll b is never present (Table 1.2; [793, 794]).

6 The principal accessory pigment is fucoxanthin (in the Chrysophyceae, Bacillariophyceae, Phaeophyceae and some Raphidophyceae) or vaucheriaxanthin (in the Xanthophyceae, Raphidophyceae and Eustigmatophyceae: Table 1.2).

7 The main reserve polysaccharide is chrysolaminaran, a β-1,3 linked glucan. Chrysolaminaran is formed outside the chloroplasts in special vacuoles (Figs 6.2a, 6.3).

8 The chloroplast DNA is usually arranged in a ring-shaped nucleoid (Figs. 6.4d, 6.5; [83, 84, 254, 384]).

9 The smooth, backwardly directed flagellum bears a swelling near its base, which fits against the concave eyespot. The eyespot lies at the anterior of the cell, enclosed within the chloroplast, and consists of a single layer of globules containing reddish-orange pigment (Figs. 6.3, 6.4a, 7.1c, d). The eyespot and flagellar swelling together form the photoreceptor apparatus, which is the light-perceiving organelle of the cell.

10 One to several golgi bodies (or many, in the Raphidophyceae) lie appressed to the nuclear envelope, often concentrated on the anterior side. Vesicles are pinched off from the nuclear envelope and are added to the side of the golgi body closest to the nucleus: this side is called the forming face of the golgi body. On the opposite

side of the golgi body, facing the cytoplasm, the body pinches off its own vesicles (Figs. 6.3, 6.7b, 7.1c, d).

The Heterokontophyta constitute a natural group and it is amazing in some ways to see how the various classes of the division, though including such diverse organisms as the complex, multicellular brown algae of the order Laminariales (p. 199) and the unicellular silica-walled diatoms, nevertheless agree with respect to the tiny, yet complex ultrastructural features listed above. It should be noted that the division is characterized primarily by similarities in the fine structure of its members and only secondarily by biochemical characters. The division Heterokontophyta contains at least nine algal classes:

1 Chrysophyceae
2 Parmophyceae
3 Sarcinochrysidophyceae
4 Xanthophyceae
5 Eustigmatophyceae
6 Bacillariophyceae
7 Raphidophyceae
8 Dictyochophyceae
9 Phaeophyceae

Two groups of golden-brown algae with special cellular features, namely the **Synurophyceae** (p. 117; [24, 922]) and the **Pedinellophyceae** ([922, 1178]), are sometimes split off from the Chrysophyceae as separate classes; the latter group will not be treated any further here. Classes (1), (4) and (5) are primarily freshwater groups, while classes (2), (3), (8) and (9) are marine; classes (6) and (7) include both freshwater and marine species. Classes (1) to (8) consist only of unicellular or very simple multicellular representatives. Class (9) alone, the Phaeophyceae, includes species that have complex multicellular thalli, with a parenchymatous or pseudoparenchymatous construction and highly specialized structures.

It is now recognized that the phylum (= division) Heterokontophyta contains not only algae but also several classes of colourless (and therefore heterotrophic) unicellular protozoans, and also classes of multicellular or siphonous fungi. This is shown by the presence of pleuronematic flagella in the zoids, with the tripartite mastigonemes typical of the phylum. The main heterotrophic groups are the unicellular protozoans of the class **Bicocoecida** ([354, 1384, 1640]) and the fungal classes **Oomycetes, Hyphochytridiomycetes** and **Labyrinthulomycetes** ([49, 54, 304, 470, 1436, 1640, 1862]). The Bicocoecida includes, for instance, the tiny heterokont flagellates *Pseudobodo* and *Cafeteria*, which are widespread in coastal seas and oceans, where they are often found inhabiting sedimenting detritus ([416, 1384]). They are capable of ingesting bacteria and other microorganisms through phagocytosis. The members of the three fungal classes are mainly freshwater moulds, but the Oomycetes also includes the downy mildews, important pathogens of agricultural crops, such as *Phytophthora infestans,* the cause of late blight of potatoes ([1862]). The evolutionary relationships between the photoautotrophic and heterotrophic members of the Heterokontophyta are discussed further on pp. 210–13 (see also Figs. 1.3, 32.2). The phylum Heterokontophyta illustrates very aptly the taxonomic artificiality of the traditional categories 'algae', 'protozoa' and 'fungi'.

The principal characteristics of the Chrysophyceae

The following characteristics, taken together, distinguish the Chrysophyceae from other classes of the Heterokontophyta.

1 Most of the species are unicellular or colonial organisms, which may or may not be flagellate. A relatively small number of species, however, have a simple multicellular organization (Figs. 6.2a, 6.9a, 6.10b, c, h).

2 The flagella are inserted near the apex of the cell (Figs. 6.1a, d, 6.2a), not laterally as in the Phaeophyceae (Fig. 12.2).

3 A typical heterokontophyte photoreceptor apparatus is present, consisting of a swelling on the short, smooth flagellum, and an eyespot that lies within a chloroplast (Figs. 6.3, 6.4a, b).

4 The transition zone of each flagellum contains a transitional helix (Fig. 6.4a).

5 The chloroplasts are golden-brown, the chlorophyll being masked by the accessory pigment fucoxanthin.

6 The chloroplast DNA is generally arranged in a ring-shaped nucleoid (Figs. 6.4d, 6.5; [254]).

7 Spherical, silica-walled cysts are formed within

the cells, the silica being deposited within a special vesicle, the 'silica deposition vesicle' (SDV); the cyst is closed by a non-siliceous, organic plug (Figs. 6.1*e*, *g*, 6.7; [663]). In several genera, siliceous body scales are present, which are formed in silica deposition vesicles lying against the surfaces of chloroplasts (Fig. 6.9; [967]).

8 Mitosis is open (i.e. the nuclear envelope breaks down during mitosis). The spindle is formed between two rhizoplasts and is long and persistent at telophase (Fig. 6.1*h–l*; [116, 1639, 1824]).

9 The species that reproduce sexually probably have a haplontic life cycle, the zygote being a resting stage (hypnozygote), which takes the form of a siliceous cyst (see character 7). Meiosis is probably zygotic (Figs. 6.2*d*, 6.8; [438, 1545, 1547]).

10 The Chrysophyceae are almost entirely restricted to freshwater habitats.

This class is best known for its many planktonic representatives, both unicellular and colonial, but there are also some filamentous forms and other multicellular types, though these are never very complex in structure. The Chrysophyceae owe their name to the golden yellow to brown colour of their chloroplasts (the Greek *chrysos* means gold). The green colour of the chlorophyll is masked by the principal accessory pigment fucoxanthin. Other xanthophylls are also present, including zeaxanthin, antheraxanthin, violaxanthin, diatoxanthin and diadinoxanthin (Table 1.2; [88]). Fucoxanthin is also found in the Bacillariophyceae and Phaeophyceae, but not, as far as is known, in the Xanthophyceae. Diatoxanthin and diadinoxanthin have been found in almost all the classes of the Heterokontophyta.

The most important storage product is the polysaccharide chrysolaminaran, which is stored in the cell in aqueous solution in special vacuoles (Figs. 6.1*a*, 6.2*a*, 6.3, 6.7, 6.8). In the Chlorophyta, on the other hand, the reserve polysaccharide is starch, which is formed in grains and lies within the chloroplasts (see p. 338). Chrysolaminaran and starch are both glucans (i.e. polymers of glucose), but in chrysolaminaran the glucose residues are β-1,3-linked, whereas in starch they are α-1,4-linked. Chrysolaminaran is also the most important storage product in the Phaeophyceae and Bacillariophyceae. Lipid droplets are to be found in

chrysophycean cells and these too represent reserve material.

Size and distribution of the class

It is estimated that the Chrysophyceae contains about 200 genera and roughly 1000 species ([440]). The class reaches its maximum diversity in freshwater, although a few species are to be found in brackish or salt water.

Freshwater Chrysophyceae tend to be especially dominant in oligotrophic lakes (i.e. those having low productivity) with slightly acid to neutral water (annual mean pH values in the range 5–7.5). Chrysophyceae were formerly thought also to prefer cold water. The reason for this was that they are found throughout the year in arctic, cold-temperate and alpine oligotrophic lakes, and during the cool season in oligotrophic and mesotrophic lakes in temperate regions. Culture experiments with selected species have shown, however, that the optimum temperature for growth (*ca.* 20 °C) can greatly exceed the temperatures at which the species is found in nature; the correlation with low temperatures is therefore likely to be at best indirect. Furthermore, even tropical lakes can have a considerable proportion of chrysophycean species among their phytoplankton.

Lakes with high productivity (eutrophic lakes) and a pH above 7.5 generally harbour a poor chrysophycean flora or none at all. One reason for the predominance of Chrysophyceae in oligotrophic conditions may be their ability to compete successfully for phosphorus under conditions of phosphorus limitation. The absence or scarcity of Chrysophyceae in highly productive lakes (or in moderately productive lakes during the warm season), on the other hand, may be brought about by competition with other phytoplankton and by intense grazing by cladocerans (species of *Daphnia* and *Bosmina*), which can be abundant in summer zooplankton populations. High pH values are probably adverse because carbon dioxide is then available predominantly in the form of bicarbonate, while Chrysophyceae can only use free CO_2; this is present in sufficient quantities only at lower pHs ([1533, 1546]).

It has been appreciated only fairly recently that Chrysophyceae probably play an important role in the primary production of the oceans, as nannoplankton (small planktonic organisms, about 2–20 μm in length) and picoplankton (0.2–2 μm). Tiny *Ochro-*

monas species and picoplanktonic coccoid Chryso-phyceae, for instance, appear to be quite common in the open ocean and also in inshore waters ([375, 725, 1629]).

Ochromonas: a typical member of the Chrysophyceae

The species of this genus are unicellular members of the plankton and live for the most part in freshwater, occupying small ditches, pools (among aquatic macro-phytes), and puddles of rainwater. Only rarely do *Ochromonas* species occur in brackish water or in the sea. About 50 species are known ([122, 124]) and two of them, *Ochromonas danica* and *O. malhamensis*, are frequently used in physiology experiments.

Ochromonas can be taken to represent the most primitive type of organism within the Chrysophyceae, the type from which all the other forms have been derived. This idea is based on the more general hypothesis that colonial and multicellular organisms have arisen over and over again in the various classes and divisions of algae, from simple flagellate ances-tors (except in the Cyanophyta and Rhodophyta, in which flagellate cells are never present). This hypo-thesis was put forward at the beginning of the twen-tieth century, by Pascher (e.g. see [1381]). Electron microscopical observations have since shown that fla-gella have essentially the same internal structure in all eukaryotes, be they animals or plants: in almost all cases the flagellar shaft has a '9 + 2' structure (the **axoneme**), with nine peripheral tubules, which are all double, and two central tubules, which are simple (Figs. 6.4*b*, 19.3, 19.4). The fundamental similarity of all flagella supports the idea that flagellate unicells are the most primitive types of organism in each algal class.

Ochromonas demonstrates the 'Bauplan' not only of the class Chrysophyceae, but also of the whole phy-lum Heterokontophyta. Another example of a typical heterokontophyte cell is the zoospore of the Xanthophyceae (shown in Fig. 7.1*d*, a transmission electron micrograph), which much resembles *Ochro-monas* in its general structure.

Characteristics of Ochromonas *(Figs. 6.1, 6.2a–c, 6.3 – 6.7;* [658]*)*

The cell exterior

The cells are naked and have no cell wall. They are

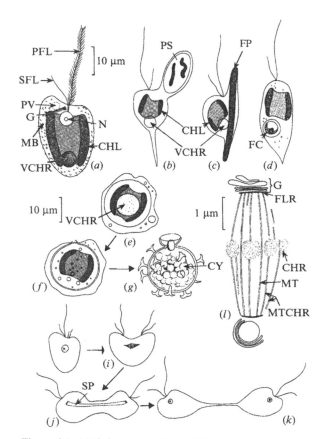

Figure 6.1. (*a*) *Ochromonas.* (*b, c*) *Ochromonas granularis,* phagotrophic nutrition. (*d*) *Ochromonas danica.* (*e–g*) *Ochromonas fragilis:* formation of an endoge-nous cyst. (*h–k*) *Ochromonas:* mitosis and cell divi-sion. (*l*) *Ochromonas:* metaphase of mitosis. CHL = chloroplast; CHR = chromosome; CY = cyst; FC = food vacuole containing a *Chlorella* cell; FLR = fla-gellar rhizoplast; FP = food particle; G = golgi appa-ratus; MB = mucilage bodies; MT = continuous microtubules (interzonal spindle fibres); MTCHR = chromosome microtubules; N = nucleus; PFL = pleu-ronematic flagellum; PS = pseudopodium with food vacuole and two food particles; PV = contractile (pulsing) vacuole; SFL = short flagellum; SP = spin-dle; VCHR = vacuole containing chrysolaminaran. (*l* after [1639].)

capable of amoeboid movements (Figs. 6.1*a–d*, 6.2*a*, 6.3, 6.6).

Flagella

The two flagella, which are dissimilar in size and structure, arise from the anterior of the cell, close to the cell apex. The longer flagellum is directed for-

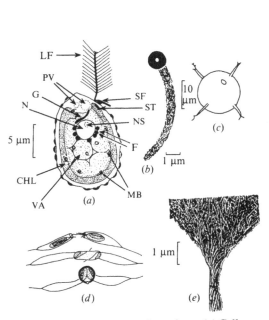

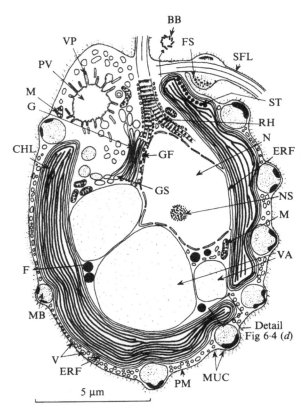

Figure 6.2. (*a–c*) *Ochromonas tuberculatus*. (*a*) Cell, as seen with the light microscope (LM). (*b*) Ultrastructure of an extruded discobolocyst. (*c*) Endogenously produced cyst (LM). (*d*) *Dinobryon borgei*: isogamy. (*e*) *Ochromonas*: portion of the stalk and lorica, composed of cellulose microfibrils (EM observations). CHL = chloroplast; F = lipid globule; G = golgi body; LF = long flagellum; MB = mucilage body; N = nucleus; NS = nucleolus; PV = contractile (pulsing) vacuole; SF = short flagellum; ST = stigma; VA = vacuole containing chrysolaminaran. (*a–c* based on [658]; *e* on [319].)

Figure 6.3. *Ochromonas tuberculatus:* cell ultrastructure. BB = basal body; CHL = chloroplast; ERF = fold of endoplasmic reticulum; F = lipid; FS = flagellar swelling; G = golgi body; GF = forming face of golgi body; GS = secretory face of golgi body; M = mitochondrion; MB = mucilage body; MUC = mucilage; N = nucleus; NS = nucleolus; PM = plasma membrane (plasmalemma); PV = contractile (pulsing) vacuole; RH = rhizoplast; SFL = short flagellum; ST = stigma; V = vesicle; VA = vacuole containing chrysolaminaran; VP = vesicle of the contractile vacuole. (After [658].)

wards during swimming and is **pleuronematic**, being furnished with two rows of short stiff hairs (this type of flagellum is sometimes known as a flimmer or tinsel flagellum). The hairs project out sideways from the flagellum, are about 15 nm thick, and are called **mastigonemes**. By contrast, the backwardly directed flagellum, which is short and blunt, appears smooth and bare (Figs. 6.1*a*, 6.2*a*, 6.4*h*). The mastigonemes of

the pleuronematic flagellum each consist of three parts – a base, a tubular shaft, and three terminal hairs (Fig. 6.4*e*) – which can move relative to one another. In *Ochromonas* the tubular shaft is clad with short fine lateral hairs (Fig. 6.4*f*), which are absent in other genera. The basal parts of the mastigonemes are attached to the peripheral doublets of the flagellar axoneme via densely staining structures ([115, 1218]). The mastigonemes themselves consist of at least four different gly-coproteins ([832]). The bases and shafts of the mastigonemes are assembled in the chloroplast ER, before being transported to the golgi apparatus, where the terminal and lateral hairs are added ([115, 832, 968]); the complete mastigonemes are then exocytosed and added to the surface of the pleuronematic flagellum, although how exactly this is achieved has yet to be established ([986]). Both flagella have the typical '9 + 2' structure of two central microtubules and nine peripheral doublets (Fig. 6.4*b*).

Each flagellum arises from a basal body, which possesses a very characteristic ultrastructure, with nine groups of three tubules ('triplets', in contrast to the doublets of the flagellum itself) arranged in a ring around its periphery. There are no central tubules, since the two central tubules of the flagellum do not extend down this far (Fig. 6.4*a–c*). The basal body ends internally in a structure where the nine tilted triplets are connected to a hub by radial spokes (Fig. 19.4; [1218]); this cart-wheel seems to be present in every group of algae (except, of course, where flagella are absent, as in the Rhodophyta and Cyanophyta).

The transition zone, between the flagellum and its basal body, contains a transitional helix. This is a fibre, which is coiled tightly around the ends of the central pair of axonemal microtubules (Fig. 6.4*a*; [664, 1218]).

The basal body has the same structure in many other eukaryotes, not just in plants but in animals too, and it is interesting that exactly the same arrangement of nine triplet microtubules arranged in a ring occurs also in centrioles, organelles that in many organisms lie at the poles of the spindle during nuclear division. Indeed, in some flagellate cells it has been observed that the basal bodies of the flagella function as centrioles during mitosis. Clearly, then, centrioles, basal bodies and flagella all belong to the same class of cell organelle; collectively, they are termed the **kinetome**.

Other classes or groups of organelles can be distinguished within the cell, such as the **plastidome** (the whole complement of chloroplasts within the cell, together with any other plastids) and the **chondriome** (the whole complement of mitochondria). Genetic continuity of the plastidome and chondriome has been conclusively demonstrated and it is known that both plastids and mitochondria contain their own DNA, which is replicated and ensures genetic continuity ([16, 93, 1354]) (cf. p. 3).

It has sometimes been suggested that the kinetome might also have its own DNA and hence its own genetic continuity, but until recently there was no evidence for this. Molecular probes and genetic analysis have now shown, however, that the basal bodies of *Chlamydomonas reinhardtii* contain DNA. This does not code for all the proteins of the flagellum and so the kinetome can only be partly independent of the nucleus (as indeed are the plastidome and chondriome). Unlike mitochondria and chloroplasts, however, new basal bodies do not arise through division of existing ones; instead they develop in the cytoplasm, close to an older basal body (see also pp. 308, 325).

Only the pleuronematic flagellum seems to be active during swimming in *Ochromonas*. It is directed forwards and executes simultaneous undulatory and helical movements. The shorter flagellum trails backwards passively, lying against the cell; it is capable, however, of acting like a rudder, to steer the cell. The helical movement of the pleuronematic flagellum causes the whole body of the cell to rotate as it moves forwards ([415]).

Tiny cells like *Ochromonas* have such a small mass, and hence so little inertial force, that the viscous drag of the water stops the cell instantaneously when the propulsive force is no longer applied. It is as if the cell is moving in syrup, through which it wriggles by waving the locomotory flagellum. As in many other flagellates, this flagellum undulates in waves that travel from its base to the tip. If the locomotory flagellum were smooth or covered by flaccid hairs, the water would be propelled in the same direction as the waves, thus pushing the cell in the opposite direction, with the flagellum trailing behind the cell. This type of flagellar locomotion is exhibited by many colourless heterotrophic flagellates (and also by the sperm of higher animals). In *Ochromonas,* however, the two rows of stiff mastigonemes cause a reversal of the thrust. Water is therefore propelled along the flagellum from the tip towards the base, so that the cell is towed forward, in the direction of the flagellum ([415, 1640]). The bending of the flagellum, here as elsewhere, is brought about by sliding between the peripheral doublets of the flagellar axoneme (see p. 305).

Flagellar roots (Figs. 6.3, 6.4*g*)

Connected to the basal body of the longer pleuronematic flagellum is a broad band-like root, the rhizoplast, which is transversely striated. This root branches where it approaches the surface of the

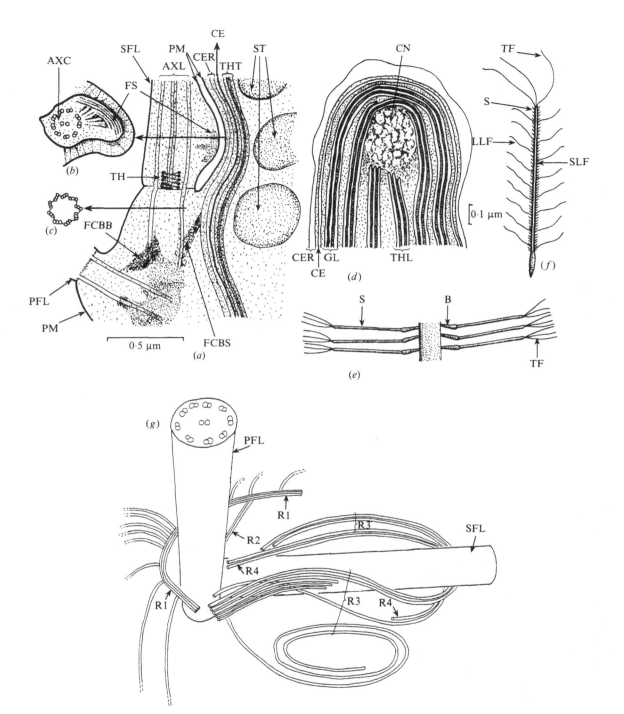

Figure 6.4. Ultrastructural details of flagellate cells in Chrysophyceae. (*a*) Longitudinal section through the basal regions of the two flagella, showing the swelling on the short flagellum and the stigma associated with it, and the transitional helix between basal body and axoneme. (*b*) Transverse section through the flagellar swelling. (*c*) Transverse section through the basal body. (*d*) Section through part of the chloroplast. (*e*) Detail of the long flagellum (see Fig. 6.2 (*a*), LF). (*f*) A mastigoneme. (*g*) Diagram of the microtubular root system in the Chrysophyceae. (*h*) Electron micrograph in which the three main parts of the entire long flagellum of a heterokontophyte (*Synura*), mastigonemes (base, shaft, terminal hairs) can be

nucleus. The rhizoplast of the Prasinophyceae is similarly constructed ([319]) and has been shown to be contractile, a kind of cellular muscle involved in the flagellar beat (pp. 318–19); perhaps the chrysophycean rhizoplast has a similar function.

The two flagella are anchored in the cell by **four highly dissimilar microtubular roots** (Fig. 6.4*g*). Two microtubular roots (roots 1 and 2) originate at the basal body of the long pleuronematic flagellum (Fig. 6.4*g*, R1 and R2), while the other two (roots 3 and 4) originate at the basal body of the short smooth flagellum (Fig. 6.4*g*, R3 and R4). Root 1, consisting of three

microtubules, describes an arc in the anterior part of the cell, just beneath the plasmalemma. Numerous microtubules emanate from root 1 and run below the plasmalemma towards the posterior of the cell, functioning as a cytoskeleton. Root 2, composed of two microtubules, originates at the opposite side of the basal body of the long flagellum and runs close to the plasmalemma. Roots 3 and 4 originate at opposite sides of the short flagellum and form a loop around and under the short flagellum. They consist of various numbers of microtubules, depending on the species (seven and one microtubules, respectively, at their ori-

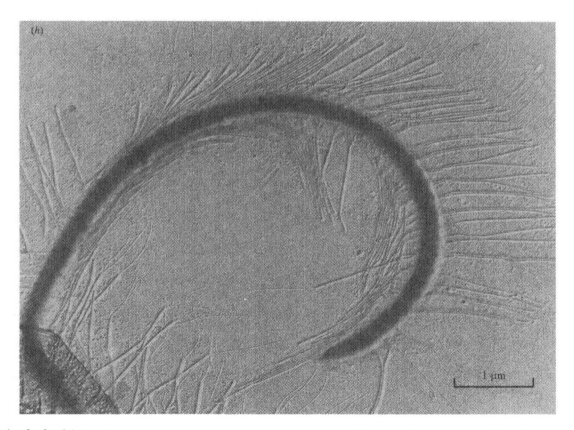

Caption for fig. 6.4 *(cont.).*
　　seen. AXC = axoneme, cross section; AXL = axoneme, longitudinal section; B = base of mastigoneme; CE = chloroplast envelope; CER = chloroplast endoplasmic reticulum; CN = chloroplast nucleoid, containing fibrils of chloroplast DNA; FCBB = fibrillar connection between the basal bodies; FCBS = fibrillar connection between the the basal body of the smooth (short) flagellum and the stigma; FS = flagellar swelling; GL = girdle lamella (= a peripheral stack of three thylakoids); LLF = long lat-

eral filament of mastigoneme; PFL = pleuronematic flagellum (= long flagellum); PM = plasma membrane (plasmalemma); R1 = root 1; R2 = root 2; R3 = root 3; R4 = root 4; S = tubular shaft of mastigoneme; SFL = smooth (short) flagellum; SLF = short lateral filament of mastigoneme; ST = stigma; TF = terminal filament of mastigoneme; TH = transitional helix; THL = stack of thylakoids (lamella); THT = two thylakoids. (*a–c* based on [923]; *d* on [514]; *f* on [115]; *g* on [26]; *h* from [319], with the permission of the author and Academic Press, London.)

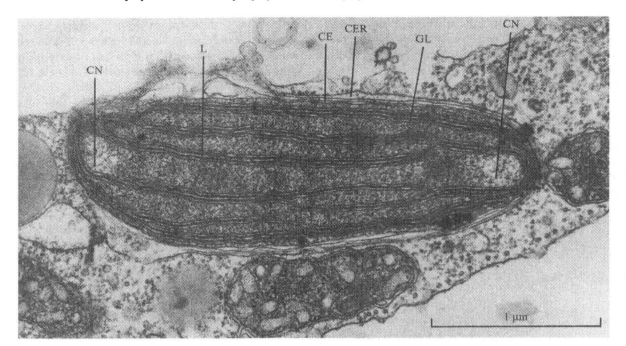

Figure 6.5. *Ochromonas danica:* electron micrograph show-ing a cross section through a chloroplast. Two profiles are visible of the ring-shaped chloroplast nucleoid. CE = chloroplast envelope; CER = chloroplast endo-plasmic reticulum; CN = chloroplast nucleoid; GL = girdle lamella; L = lamella (stack) of three thylakoids. (From [514], with permission.)

gins in the example illustrated in Fig. 6.4*g*; [26, 1347, 1348, 1437]). The microtubular loop encircles the site where the cell takes in prey (e.g. a bacterium) into a food vac-uole during phagocytosis (see p. 116); the short flagel-lum is also involved, pushing the prey into the vacuole ([26]).

The whole complex of flagellar basal bodies, micro-tubular roots and other associated structures is often termed the **flagellar apparatus**. The form of the fla-gellar apparatus seems to be fairly constant within, and hence characteristic of, the major groups of algae. This has been investigated quite extensively in the green algae (division Chlorophyta), but the data avail-able so far indicate that each class of the Hetero-kontophyta also has its own, characteristic type of fla-gellar apparatus ([1437]).

Contractile vacuoles

There may be one or two contractile vacuoles per cell (the number depending on the species), which lie near the bases of the flagella (Figs. 6.2*a*, 6.3). They can be seen in living cells, using light microscopy. Each con-sists of a small vesicle, which contracts at regular intervals, expelling its contents from the cell. Between contractions the vacuole swells, reaching its maxi-mum size just before the next contraction. If two con-tractile vacuoles are present, their activities are out of phase, one contracting while the other is swelling.

Contractile (pulsing) vacuoles occur in various fla-gellate algae, protozoa and fungi, and their primary function is probably to do with the osmoregulation of the cell. Because the cytoplasm contains higher con-centrations of osmotically active compounds than the surrounding water, cells take up water through their plasmalemmas, which are semipermeable. The con-tractile vacuoles remove the superfluous water absorbed by the cell and hence prevent it bursting.

Electron microscopical investigations of *Ochro-monas tuberculatus* have revealed that the contractile vacuole is surrounded by lots of small elongate vesi-cles, which discharge into it (Fig. 6.3). The vesicles are not empty but contain diffuse material, as in other groups of flagellate algae that have been studied. This suggests perhaps that the contractile vacuoles secrete not only water, but also other (superfluous?) substances.

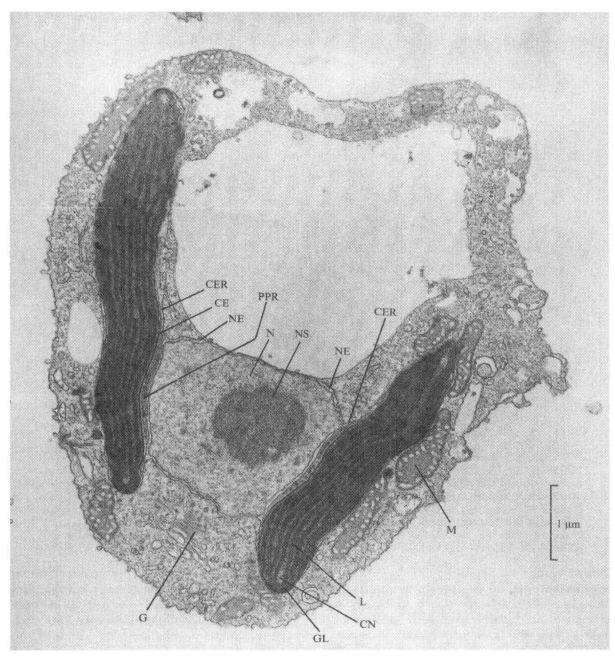

Figure 6.6. *Ochromonas danica:* electron micrograph showing the nucleus and two adjacent chloroplasts. Note that the chloroplast endoplasmic reticulum is continuous with the nuclear envelope. The narrow space between the nuclear envelope and the chloroplast envelope harbours a periplastidial reticulum. CE = the double chloroplast envelope; CER = chloroplast endoplasmic reticulum; CN = chloroplast nucleoid; G = golgi body; GL = girdle lamella; L = lamella (stack), containing three appressed thylakoids; M = mitochondrion; N = nucleus; NE = nuclear envelope; NS = nucleolus; PPR = periplastidial reticulum. (From [509a], with permission.)

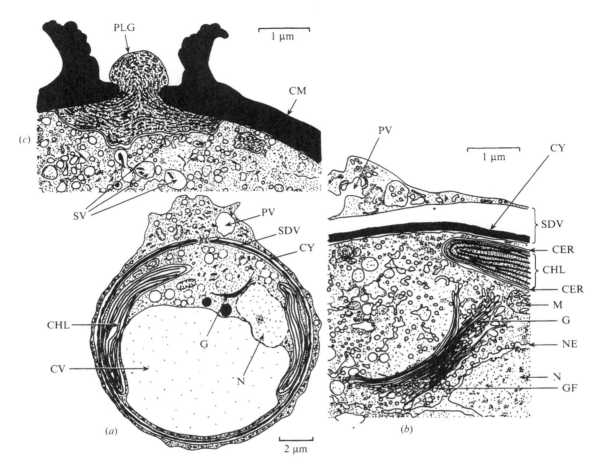

Figure 6.7. Siliceous cyst formation in *Ochromonas,* from EM observations. (*a*) Young cyst, still thin-walled, being deposited inside a cytoplasmic silica deposition vesicle. (*b*) Detail of (*a*), at higher magnification. (*c*) Detail of the collared pore of an almost mature, thick-walled cyst, with a non-siliceous plug; the residual cytoplasm outside the cyst has been sloughed off. CER = chloroplast endoplasmic reticulum; CHL = chloroplast; CM = (almost) mature cyst; CV = chryso-laminaran vacuole; CY = young cyst; G = golgi body; GF = forming face of golgi body; M = mitochondrion; N = nucleus; NE = nuclear envelope; PLG = non-siliceous plug closing the cyst pore; PV = contractile (pulsing) vacuole; SDV = silica deposition vesicle; SV = golgi vesicles containing spicules, which contribute their contents to the plug. (Based on [663].)

Chloroplasts

Ochromonas cells contain one or two plate-like chloroplasts (Figs. 6.1*a–d*, 6.2*a*, 6.3). Within the chloroplasts are thylakoids, which are grouped into stacks of three (Figs. 6.4*d*, 6.5, 6.6), each stack being termed a **lamella**. This arrangement is quite unlike that found in the chloroplasts of higher green plants (the Tracheophyta), where some of the thylakoids are single, while the others are organized into tall stacks, called grana. The arrangement of the thylakoids in *Ochromonas*, however, is quite typical of the Heterokontophyta, Haptophyta and Dinophyta.

One lamella runs around the periphery of the chloroplast, parallel to the chloroplast envelope. This stack of thylakoids therefore encloses all the other lamellae and is called the **girdle lamella**; it is a characteristic feature of most members of the Heterokontophyta.

The chloroplast DNA of *Ochromonas* (and most other Chrysophyceae) is concentrated in a ring-shaped nucleoid, which lies just beneath the girdle lamella (Figs. 6.4*d*, 6.5, 6.6; [254, 514]). It can be made visible in the light microscope by staining with the DNA-specific fluorescent dye DAPI (4′,6-diamidino-2-phenylindole)

([254]). The nucleoid contains many (8–200) copies of the chloroplast genome, which is a circular molecule of DNA ([198, 256]). In two genera of Chrysophyceae, however, *Dinobryon* (Fig. 6.2*d*) and *Synura* (Fig. 6.9*a*), the chloroplast DNA is not organized in distinct rings, but in a three-dimensional network spread throughout the chloroplast ([254]).

A further feature of the *Ochromonas* chloroplast, which again is typical of the Heterokontophyta, is the presence of four membranes around it; two represent the chloroplast envelope itself, while the others (the outer pair) represent a fold of endoplasmic reticulum, which is wrapped tightly around the chloroplast (Figs. 6.4*d*, 6.5, 6.6, 6.7*b*, 7.1). Where the chloroplast abuts onto the nucleus, the membranes of the chloroplast endoplasmic reticulum (ER) and the nuclear envelope are continuous with each other (Figs. 6.3, 6.6, 7.1). A network of interconnected tubules called the periplastidial reticulum is often to be found in the narrow space between the chloroplast envelope and the chloroplast ER (Figs. 6.6, 6.11*b*). Its function may be to transport chloroplast proteins encoded by the nuclear genome, across the space between the chloroplast ER and the chloroplast envelope, into the chloroplast ([510]).

Eyespot (stigma) and flagellar swelling

The eyespot can be seen in the living cell using the light microscope and appears as a small red spot at the anterior of the cell. It lies within one of the chloroplasts and is positioned close to the base of the short flagellum (Fig. 6.2*a*). Eyespots occur in a great many flagellate algae and are generally part of the chloroplast, as in *Ochromonas*, but in some groups (e.g. the Euglenophyta and Eustigmatophyceae, pp. 293, 130) they lie in the cytoplasm.

The term 'eyespot' implies that this organelle is involved in light perception. A light receptor must indeed be present somewhere in the cells of flagellate algae since they usually exhibit phototactic reactions: the direction in which they swim is influenced by the direction of the light incident upon them. Flagellate algae generally swim towards dim light (positive phototaxis) but away from bright light (negative phototaxis) and so the cells must be able to determine where the light is coming from. The eyespot seems to play a part in this (e.g. in *Chlamydomonas*: [1186]) but it is not an essential component of the photoreceptor apparatus, since there are some flagellate algae that lack an

eyespot yet still exhibit phototaxis. For instance, in species that normally have an eyespot, loss of the eyespot (through mutation) does not necessarily bring about the loss of phototactic behaviour.

The eyespot consists of a cluster of lipid globules, each coloured red by carotenoid pigments. In *Ochromonas tuberculatus* the globules form a single layer, which is sandwiched between the girdle lamella and the chloroplast envelope (Fig. 6.3).

Above the eyespot there is a slight invagination of the chloroplast and also of the cell surface; into this depression fits the swollen basal part of the short flagellum (Figs. 6.3, 6.4*a*). Such flagellar swellings, again positioned near the eyespot, seem to be a general feature of the Chrysophyceae and Xanthophyceae (Fig. 7.1*c, d*), and they occur too in some species without eyespots. Flagellar swellings are also to be found in the Euglenophyta (p. 293), although this group is quite unrelated to the Chrysophyceae.

It may well be that it is not the eyespot but the flagellar swelling that is responsible for the perception of light. With unilateral illumination the eyespot of the swimming cell would shade the flagellar swelling at regular intervals, since the cell twists around its longitudinal axis as it swims. The cell could therefore determine the direction of the incident light. This idea was originally put forward not for the Chrysophyceae but for the Euglenophyceae, and as long ago as 1900 ([126, 259, 789]). It was found that individuals of *Euglena* with no chlorophyll, but possessing both an eyespot and a flagellar swelling, exhibited phototaxis, reacting negatively or positively depending on the light intensity. Chlorophyll-free (apochlorotic) cells possessing a flagellar swelling but lacking an eyespot only showed negative phototaxis, while cells lacking both organelles exhibited no phototactic behaviour at all. The flagellar swelling thus appears to be a prerequisite for phototaxis in *Euglena*, whereas the eyespot is necessary only for a *positive* response. Exactly how the flagellar swelling functions as a photoreceptor is unknown. The strongest phototactic responses are induced by blue light (wavelengths of 420–490 nm) and so the swelling must contain a pigment (a flavoprotein) absorbing in this part of the spectrum ([126, 259, 789, 1660]). A similar flavoprotein has recently been demonstrated in the flagellar swelling of various Chrysophyceae and Phaeophyceae: the flagellar swelling, and to a lesser extent the rest of the short flagellum, exhibit a yellow-green autofluorescence when irradiated with blue light (450 nm wavelength), thus indicating the presence of flavoprotein ([831, 831a, 1269]) (see also the perception of light by the green alga *Chlamydomonas*, p. 311).

Mucilage bodies and discobolocysts (Figs. 6.1*a*, 6.2*a, b*, 6.3)

Mucilage bodies are small spheres of mucilage, which lie immediately below the surface of the cell and are shot out when the cell is irritated; not all species of *Ochromonas* have them. A special type of mucilage body, called a discobolocyst, is to be found in *Ochromonas tuberculatus* and some other Chryso-phyceae ([120, 658, 719]). When discharged, the discobolo-cyst can be seen to consist of a dark, ring-shaped disc connected to a threadlike tail, consisting of mucilage (Fig. 6.2*b*); the annular discs can also be seen within the cell, in undischarged discobolocysts (Fig. 6.3). Discobolocysts are probably formed in vesicles derived from the golgi apparatus.

Mucilage bodies are widely distributed in other members of the Chrysophyceae and it is probably via these structures that the mucilage envelopes of colonial forms such as *Hydrurus foetidus* (Fig. 6.10*d, e*) are secreted.

Golgi apparatus (Figs. 6.3, 6.6, 6.7*b*)

The golgi apparatus lies between the nucleus and the contractile vacuole and can just be made out in the light microscope, as a gently curved strip (Figs. 6.1*a*, 6.2*a*). Such organelles are of course typical of eukaryotic cells, in both plants and animals, and each consists of a stack of flat discoid vesicles or sacs (the golgi cisternae), which cut off a series of inflated golgi vesicles from their margins. The vesicles often contain material that is to be secreted from the cell; in plants, cell wall material or structural elements of the cell envelope are frequently secreted via the golgi apparatus.

In the algae of the Haptophyta and Prasinophyceae (pp. 219, 342) the cell envelopes or walls often consist of scales, which have a precise and species-specific structure and ornamentation: these scales are formed within the cell in golgi vesicles and then secreted onto the cell surface. In *Ochromonas tuberculatus* the discobolocysts are probably formed from golgi vesicles (Fig. 6.3), while in *Hydrurus* the first steps in the production of the mucilage sheath probably involve the golgi apparatus ([813]).

Chrysolaminaran vacuoles (Figs. 6.1*a–c*, 6.2*a*, 6.3)

The most important storage product, chrysolaminaran, is to be found in aqueous solution, in special vacuoles located towards the posterior of the cell (Figs. 6.2*a*, 6.3). The cells also store lipid, which occurs as droplets in the cytoplasm.

Nucleus

The nucleus and chloroplast are connected by the fold of chloroplast ER, which is continuous with the nuclear envelope (Figs. 6.3, 6.6; cf. 7.1*d*).

Endogenous cysts (= statospores) (Figs. 6.1*e–g*, 6.2*c*, 6.7)

Ochromonas produces endogenous cysts, i.e. cysts formed within the vegetative cells (Fig. 6.1*e–g*). The cyst walls consist predominantly of silica and so are often preserved as fossils; they are known from sediments dating back to the Upper Cretaceous, 80 million years ago ([1751]), and occur in both freshwater and marine deposits. The cysts are spherical or ellipsoidal, and are often ornamented with spines or other projections. The wall is pierced by a pore, stoppered by an unsilicified 'bung', while within the cyst lie a nucleus, chloroplasts, and an abundance of reserve material (chrysolaminaran and lipid). After a period of dormancy the cyst germinates and liberates its contents in the form of one to several flagellate cells ([273]). This type of cyst, with its bottle-and-cork morphology and endogenous development, is characteristic of the Chrysophyceae.

The cyst wall is formed in a thin vesicle, the 'silica deposition vesicle', which lies around the periphery of the cell, beneath the plasmalemma (Fig. 6.7). The silica deposition vesicle may be produced by the fusion of smaller vesicles derived from the golgi apparatus, but this has not been proved. The vesicle completely encloses the cytoplasm within it, except at one point, where a hole is left, corresponding to the aperture of the mature cyst. This is later closed by a plug composed of polysaccharide, secreted from golgi vesicles (Fig. 6.7*c*; [663]). After the cyst wall has been completed, the cytoplasm outside the wall degenerates and the inner membrane of the silica deposition vesicle becomes the plasmalemma of the cyst. Siliceous cell walls are also found in another class of the Heterokontophyta, the Bacillariophyceae, and here too the silica is deposited within a membrane-bound silica deposition vesicle (p. 141).

The formation of cysts is not induced by environmental factors such as nutrient depletion or critical temperatures, as often occurs in other groups of algae (cf. p. 154), so that the cysts are apparently not a means of direct escape from adverse conditions. Cyst formation seems instead to require a minimum density of vegetative cells. Above this critical level, which in one example was 200 cells ml^{-1}, the number of cysts produced increases with cell density. Cyst formation may be under hormonal control (see the section on sexual reproduction below). Important stocks of viable chrysophycean cysts are present in the bottom sediments of lakes, where they can probably survive for decades.

Cyst germination, like cyst formation, is not controlled by critical environmental factors such as increasing temperatures or nutrient levels (cf. the germination of cysts in the Dinophyta, p. 269). Instead, a small number of cysts germinate at any given time; if these encounter conditions favourable to growth a new population of vegetative cells may be produced. This could explain why lake Chrysophyceae often appear irregularly and unpredictably, with short peaks of growth alternating with long periods of apparent absence ([1546]).

Cell division (Fig. 6.1h–k)

Before the cell divides a pair of new flagella are formed (Fig. 6.1h). It might be expected perhaps that the basal bodies of the flagella would function as centrioles during mitosis, as they do in some other organisms; both organelles have the same structure. This does not occur, however, in *Ochromonas*. The basal bodies replicate during interphase and subsequently give rise to the two new flagella, shortly before the nucleus and cell divide. During early prophase the golgi apparatus divides and a new rhizoplast is formed. Then the two pairs of basal bodies, with their associated flagella, golgi apparatus and rhizoplast, begin to move apart, in preparation for nuclear division (Fig. 6.1i).

As mitosis proceeds, a spindle is formed and the nuclear envelope disperses (Fig. 6.1j, l); this is therefore an example of open mitosis. The pattern of mitosis is very unusual. The poles of the spindle are formed by the two rhizoplasts, and it is to these that the spindle microtubules are attached. Some of the microtubules are continuous from pole to pole (the interzonal microtubules, or central fibres), while others

connect the poles to the chromosomes (the chromosome microtubules, or chromosome fibres). At anaphase the chromosomes become closely associated with part of the chloroplast endoplasmic reticulum and it is from this that the new nuclear membranes are formed; in the light of this, it is easy to see how the characteristic connection arises between the nuclear envelope and the chloroplast ER. At the end of mitosis, in telophase, the spindle is long and persistent, holding the daughter nuclei apart (Fig. 6.1j). This contrasts with what happens in some other flagellates, such as the green alga *Chlamydomonas*, where the spindle collapses during early telophase, allowing the daughter nuclei to collapse back towards each other (Fig. 19.17 II). Following nuclear division the cell divides via a cleavage furrow, which develops from the anterior end of the cell ([116, 1639, 1824]).

Sexual reproduction in the Chrysophyceae

In *Ochromonas* sexual reproduction is unknown, but some members of the Chrysophyceae, such as *Dinobryon*, exhibit isogamy. *Dinobryon* is a genus of flagellates, whose cells resemble those of *Ochromonas* but live within delicate, stalked cups. During sexual reproduction two vegetative cells function as gametes and fuse. In one species the anterior flagella twist around each other, and then the cells leave their cups and fuse fully (hologamy), the zygote going on to form a typical chrysophycean cyst (Fig. 6.2d; [438]). In another species of *Dinobryon*, morphologically similar male and female clones have been distinguished. The female cells produce a female sexual hormone that induces male cells to leave their cups (loricae) and swim towards the female cells, following which hologamous sexual fusion takes place ([1545]). In the colonial chrysophyte *Synura petersenii*, too, the male gametes are attracted by a hormone secreted by the females, and again the male and female cells are morphologically similar and indistinguishable from the vegetative cells. A male gamete leaves its parent colony, swims to a female gamete in a female colony, and fuses with it. After fusion a zygotic cyst is formed, enclosed as usual in a siliceous wall (Fig. 6.8; [1545]). The germination of the cyst may be accompanied by meiosis, in which case the life cycle would be haplontic; unfortunately, no karyological evidence is yet

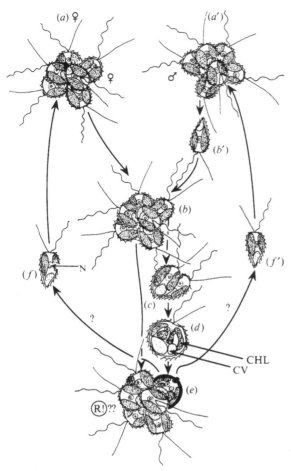

Figure 6.8. The sexual cycle of *Synura petersenii*. (*a*) Female colony. (*a'*) Male colony. (*b*) Female gamete within colony. (*b'*) Solitary male gamete swimming to female gamete. (*c*) Early stage in plasmogamy, which takes place by lateral fusion. (*d*) Biflagellate planozygote with four chloroplasts, two nuclei and two chrysolaminaran vacuoles. (*e*) Fully mature zygotic cyst, which takes the place in the female colony formerly occupied by the female gamete (see (*b*)). CHL = chloroplast; CV = chrysolaminaran vacuole; N = nucleus; R! = the possible position of meiosis. (Based on [1547].)

available to confirm this. Cysts germinate with the formation of one to four flagellate daughter cells [273].

Nutrition

Various types of nutrition occur in the Chrysophyceae: photoautotrophy, saprotrophy and phago-

trophy. *Ochromonas granularis* can live completely heterotrophically if placed in a nutrient solution containing sucrose, and may even lose its photosynthetic pigments. It can also feed phagotrophically. Pseudopodia extend out from the alga and enclose prey such as bacteria or small algae, which are taken up into food vacuoles and there digested (Fig. 6.1*b–d*); undigested material is excreted. The pseudopodia are formed principally at the anterior of the cell and it is here that food particles are taken up into primary food vacuoles; the loop-like flagellar roots and the short flagellum play a role in the formation of the food vacuole and this is treated on p. 110. The primary food vacuoles, together with the food they contain, are then transported to the back of the cell, where the food is digested enzymatically in secondary food vacuoles. The digestive enzymes are derived from lysosomes: small vesicles probably pinched off from the golgi apparatus, which deliver their contents to the food vacuoles by fusing with them. When the cells of *Ochromonas* are growing autotrophically, the secondary food vacuoles serve as containers for the storage product chrysolaminaran. Phagotrophy in these algae may be a primitive character, inherited from the ancestral eukaryotes (Ur-cells), which were unable to photosynthesize ([266]).

Ochromonas malhamensis requires organic substances (proteins, amino acids, sugars, lipids) as sources of nitrogen and carbon. Acetate is used as the carbon source for photosynthesis and this species also requires a number of vitamins. *Ochromonas malhamensis* can take up particles of various kinds (e.g. starch grains, casein or oil droplets, or small organisms such as bacteria, yeasts or unicellular algae) through phagocytosis, and then digest them ([120]).

The quantitative significance of phagotrophy in the nutrition of Chrysophyceae in freshwater lakes has only recently become clear. Thus, in one assemblage of lake phytoplankton dominated by Chrysophyceae, phagotrophy by these algae was responsible for up to 55% of the total consumption of bacteria ([1546]). Chrysophyceae are therefore extremely versatile in their mode of nutrition. During the whole day they can feed on other microorganisms, while during the daylight hours they can also photosynthesize. Their phagotrophy not only provides them with food but also removes other microorganisms (algae, bacteria) that would otherwise compete for the same rare nutrients (e.g. phosphorus, iron).

The various levels of organization present in the Chrysophyceae

It has already been pointed out (p. 105) that flagellates like *Ochromonas* can be considered as the most primitive type of organism within the Chrysophyceae. From monads such as these all the other unicellular and multicellular types of organization are thought to have been derived during evolution ([440]).

The Chrysophyceae exhibit the following levels of organization.

Unicellular flagellate (monadoid) level of organization

One chrysophycean monad, *Ochromonas*, has already been described (Figs. 6.1–6.3). Several other genera also exhibit the same level of organization, among them some that live within urn- or cup-shaped shells, called loricae. Examples of loricate genera are *Pseudokephyrion* (Fig. 6.10*a*) and *Dinobryon* (Fig. 6.2*d*). The lorica of *Dinobryon* and some other Chrysophyceae consists of a felt-like mesh of microfibrils, each 7–15 nm in diameter (Fig. 6.2*e*); these dimensions have led some to suggest that the microfibrils might be composed of cellulose ([824, 910, 1573]).

Colonial flagellate level of organization

In these organisms a number of flagellate cells are linked together to form a colony. One example is *Synura*, in which the spherical or ellipsoidal colonies consist of many pear-shaped cells, attached by their narrow posterior ends (Fig. 6.9*a*). Each cell possesses two chloroplasts and bears two unequal flagella (it is heterokont). Around the cell is a covering of scales (Fig. 6.9*b, c, f*), which are made of silica and overlap each other like the tiles on a roof. The scales are produced in silica deposition vesicles, which lie up against the chloroplast ER (Fig. 6.9*d, e*). The origin of the silica deposition vesicle is unknown and could be formed by the coalescence of golgi vesicles or by elaboration of the chloroplast ER ([967, 1153]). At some stage before scale deposition begins, the vesicle becomes attached to the chloroplast ER by a layer of special, compound filaments. As the scales mature they are transported to the plasmalemma and ultimately extruded onto the cell surface.

A brief description of sexual reproduction in *Synura* has already been given, in the section on 'Sexual reproduction in the Chrysophyceae'. The zygote takes the form of a typical endogenous chrysophycean cyst (Fig. 6.8).

Synura and related genera (for instance, the unicellular scaly flagellate *Mallomonas*) differ from other flagellate Chrysophyceae in several respects: they have chlorophylls a and c_1 (not c_2); they lack the typical chrysophycean photoreceptor apparatus (with a flagellar swelling fitting into a depression above the eyespot, which lies within the chloroplast; [27]); the pleuronematic flagellum is covered by tiny (100 nm) organic scales, which are produced in the golgi apparatus ([660, 1218]); they have their own arrangement of flagellar roots ([26, 59, 1437]); and the chloroplast DNA is not arranged in a ring-shaped nucleoid ([254]). These differences in cellular architecture between the *Synura* group and other Chrysophyceae are believed by some to be so fundamental that *Synura* and its allies should be classified in a separate class, the Synurophyceae ([25, 26]).

About 20 *Synura* species are known, all from freshwaters.

Amoeboid level of organization

Here the cells are naked and bear pseudopodia, which are termed rhizopodia when they are thin and filamentous; the pseudopodia are used to take up solid food particles. An example is the genus *Rhizochrysis* (Fig. 6.10*g*), which includes about ten species, all of them solitary forms. The life cycle includes no flagellate stages. Most of the species are neustonic, i.e. they live at the surface of pools and puddles, kept there by the surface tension of the water; the rhizopodia are spread out for support. In another genus, *Chrysarachnion*, the individual cells are similar to those of *Rhizochrysis*, but are linked by their rhizopodia to form networks (Fig. 6.10*j*). Only one species of *Chrysarachnion* is known and even this is very rare.

Palmelloid (tetrasporal) level of organization

In palmelloid forms the cells lie embedded in a common sheath or envelope of mucilage. They therefore form colonies, which resemble those of the green alga *Tetraspora*. In the chrysophycean alga *Chrysocapsa* (Fig. 6.10*c*) large numbers of round, non-flagellate

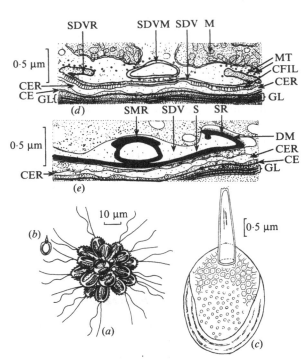

Figure 6.9. *Synura*. (*a*) Colony of scaly flagellate cells. (*b, c*) A scale, seen with LM (*b*) and EM (*c*). (*d*) Transverse section through a silica deposition vesicle, located just above the surface of a chloroplast; synthesis of the siliceous scale has yet to be initiated. Note the overlying microtubules and the underlying layer of compound filaments. (*e*) Late stage in the development of a scale; note the diffuse material on the outer surface of the scale rim. (*f*) Scanning electron micrograph showing a scale-covered cell of *Synura petersenii*. CE = chloroplast envelope; CER = chloroplast endoplasmic reticulum; CFIL = underlayer of compound filaments; DM = diffuse material on the outer side of the scale rim; GL = girdle lamella; M = mitochondrion; MT = microtubule; S = scale; SDV = silica deposition vesicle; SDVM = the part of the silica deposition vesicle in which the hollow median ridge of the scale will be deposited; SDVR = the part of the silica deposition vesicle in which the rim will be deposited; SMR = median ridge of scale; SR = scale rim. (*a, b* based on [122]; *d, e* on [967]; *f* from [968a], with the permission of the author and the British Phycological Society.)

cells are embedded in a spherical mucilage envelope, which can be up to 4 mm in diameter. In *Hydrurus*, on the other hand, the cells, which again lack flagella, are contained in large, highly branched threads of mucilage growing up to 30 cm long (Fig. 6.10*d–f*). The only species of the genus, *Hydrurus foetidus*, is widely distributed in upland or mountain streams.

Coccoid level of organization

These algae have non-motile, non-flagellate cells, each of which is surrounded by a cell wall; sometimes the cells are united into colonies. An example is *Chrysosphaera* (Fig. 6.10*b*), which has round or oval cells that may be single or grouped.

VAN DEN HOEK, MANN AND JAHNS, *Algae*

ISBN 0 521 30419 9 HARDBACK   ISBN 0 521 31687 1 PAPERBACK

ERRATUM p. 119, figure 6.10 is incorrect. The correct figure is given below.

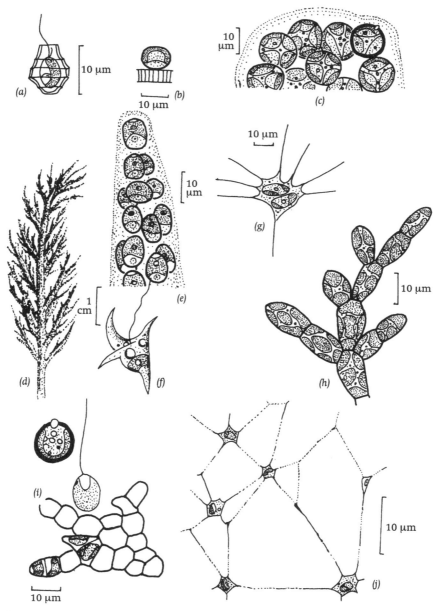

Figure 6.10. *(a) Pseudokephyrion. (b) Chrysosphaera. (c) Chrysocapsa. (d–f) Hydrurus. (g) Rhizochrysis. (h) Phaeothamnion. (i) Thallochrysis. (j) Chrysarachnion. (a, b, f, h–j based on* [122]; *d, e on* [1657,1658].)

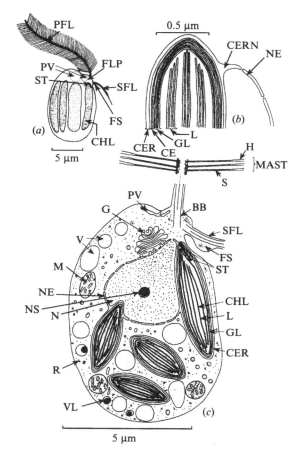

Figure 6.10. (*a*) *Pseudokephyrion*. (*b*) *Chrysosphaera*. (*c*) *Chrysocapsa*. (*d–f*) *Hydrurus*. (*g*) *Rhizochrysis*. (*h*) *Phaeothamnion*. (*i*) *Thallochrysis*. (*j*) *Chrysarachnion*. (*a, b, f, h–j* based on [122]; *d, e* on [1657, 1658].)

Filamentous (trichal) level of organization

At this level of organization the cells are united into branched or unbranched filaments. In the genus *Phaeothamnion* (Fig. 6.10*h*), which contains five species living in freshwater, the thallus consists of small, branched filaments. These reproduce by the formation of zoospores, each resembling an *Ochromonas* cell.

Thalloid level of organization

Here the cells are united into a parenchymatous tissue. *Thallochrysis*, for example, consists of a flat disc one layer of cells thick, which may bear short filaments growing out from the margins (Fig. 6.10*i*). Each cell is

capable of giving rise to a zoospore, which bears a single flagellum (probably a pleuronematic flagellum).

Comparable levels of organization in other classes or divisions of algae

The levels of organization described above for the Chrysophyceae can also be found in other groups of algae. Almost all of them occur in the Xanthophyceae, Dinophyta and Chlorophyta, while in two of these, the Xanthophyceae and Chlorophyta, there is in addition an eighth level of organization, the siphonous level, which is absent in the Chrysophyceae. In siphonous algae the thalli usually consist of branched filaments, but there are no (true) transverse cell walls, so that the alga consists of a single, continuous, multinucleate protoplast within a single, continuous cell wall.

Table 6.1 summarizes the occurrence of different levels of organization within different algal classes and divisions. The existence of similar, analogous levels of organization in quite separate groups of algae suggests that each 'derived' type of organization has evolved many times, from different 'primitive' monads: a good example of parallel evolution.

The eight levels of organization are not distributed equally among the various classes of algae. The table shows, for example, that the Bacillariophyceae are all coccoid, while the Raphidophyceae are all monadoid. In the Chrysophyceae all but one of the eight levels of organization are to be found, but the predominant type of organism is the unicellular flagellate (monadoid level of organization). In the Xanthophyceae, on the other hand, only a few monads are known and it is the coccoid level of organization that is the most frequent. The division Dinophyta consists, with relatively few exceptions, of monads, while the Chlorophyta contains many examples of all the kinds of organization listed, except the amoeboid type, which is absent.

The subdivision of the Chrysophyceae into orders

The current classifications of the Chrysophyceae are based mainly on levels of organization. One recent example ([100, 921]) contains seven orders, namely:

Ochromonadales: unicellular and colonial flagellates;

Table 6.1. *Levels of organization in eukaryotic algae (with examples)*

+ = Present; − = absent; ++ = present in many species.

Division	Class	Level of organization							
		monadoid	monadoid, colonial	amoeboid	palmelloid (tetrasporal)	coccoid	filamentous (trichal)	thalloid	siphonous
Rhodophyta		−	−	−	−	+ *Porphyridium*	++ *Audouinella Acrosymphyton*	+ *Porphyra*	−
Heterokontophyta	Chrysophyceae	++ *Ochromonas*	+ *Synura*	+ *Rhizochrysis*	+ *Chrysocapsa*	+ *Chrysosphaera*	+ *Phaeothamnion*	+ *Thallochrysis*	−
Heterokontophyta	Xanthophyceae	+ *Chloromeson*	−	+ *Rhizochloris*	+ *Gloeochloris*	++ *Chloridella*	++ *Tribonema*	−	+ *Botrydium Vaucheria*
Heterokontophyta	Eustigmatophyceae	−	−	−	+ *Chlorobotrys*	++ *Ellipsoidion*	−	−	−
Heterokontophyta	Bacillariophyceae	−	−	−	−	++ (all species)	−	−	−
Heterokontophyta	Phaeophyceae	−	−	−	−	−	++ *Ectocarpus*	++ *Fucus, Dictyota*	−
Heterokontophyta	Raphidophyceae	+ *Goniostomum*	−	−	−	−	−	−	−
Haptophyta	Haptophyceae	++ *Chrysochromulina*	+ *Corymbellus*	+ amoeboid phase of *Chrysochromulina*	+ palmelloid phase of *Isochrysis*	+ coccoid phase of *Isochrysis*	+ trichal phase of *Pleurochrysis*	−	−
Cryptophyta	Cryptophyceae	++ *Cryptomonas*	−	−	+ palmelloid phase of *Cryptomonas*	−	+ *Bjornbergiella*	−	−
Dinophyta	Dinophyceae	++ *Peridinium*	−	+ *Dinamoebidium*	+ *Gloeodinium*	+ *Dinococcus*	+ *Dinothrix*	−	−
Euglenophyta	Euglenophyceae	++ *Euglena*	−	−	+ palmelloid phase of *Euglena*	−	−	−	−
Chlorophyta		++ *Chlamydomonas*	++ *Volvox*	−	++ *Pseudosphaerocystis*	++ *Chlorococcum*	++ *Ulothrix*	++ *Ulva*	++ *Bryopsis*

Mallomonadales: unicellular and colonial flagellates covered with silica scales (= class Synurophyceae; [24]);

Pedinellales: unicellular flagellates with a peculiar radial symmetry (= class Pedinellophyceae; [922, 1178]);

Chrysamoebidales: amoeboid organisms;

Chrysocapsales: palmelloid (tetrasporal, capsular) organization;

Chrysosphaerales: coccoid organization;

Phaeothamniales: filamentous and thalloid organization.

We have already seen that flagellate Chrysophyceae such as *Synura* and *Ochromonas* differ so much in the architecture of their cells that it may be best to classify them in separate classes; this is probably also true for *Pedinella* and its allies (the Pedinellales, which are not dealt with any further here). Clearly, the flagellate level of organization is phylogenetically heterogeneous and this is probably true too for the other organizational levels, and hence for the other orders mentioned above. Thus the existing classifications of the Chrysophyceae seem to be unsatisfactory, and will probably be superseded as the structure of the cell is studied in a wider variety of chrysophycean algae ([673]).

Some marine relatives of the Chrysophyceae: the genus *Pelagococcus* and the orders Parmales (class Parmophyceae) and Sarcinochrysidales (class Sarcinochrysidophyceae)

Under this heading we describe very briefly three groups of marine Heterokontophyta, which are at present included within the class Chrysophyceae but differ from it in various important respects. They should probably be considered as separate classes within the Heterokontophyta.

Pelagococcus

Pelagococcus is a greenish-golden coccoid alga, which is widespread in the world's oceans as a member of the picoplankton. It has recently become clear that picoplanktonic algae are ubiquitous and very

common, and may be responsible for up to 80 or 90% of the total primary production in some oceanic waters ([613]). Picoplanktonic algae are also very diverse, belonging to groups of organisms as different as the Cyanophyta (cyanobacteria: p. 22, Fig. 2.1a) and the Prasinophyceae (division Chlorophyta: p. 343, Fig. 20.3).

Pelagococcus exhibits several ultrastructural features that are typical of the Heterokontophyta, though it lacks a flagellar apparatus and so does not have the typical tubular mastigonemes of the Heterokontophyta, the helical transition zone, etc. The golgi body lies with its forming face appressed to the nuclear envelope, and the chloroplast contains a girdle lamella (Fig. 6.11); both of these are heterokontophyte features. *Pelagococcus* also has chloroplast ER (Fig. 6.11), though this is also found in the Haptophyta. It differs from the Chrysophyceae in its complement of photosynthetic pigments since, apart from chlorophylls a and c_2, which are present in the Chrysophyceae, it also possesses chlorophyll c_3. The major carotenoid pigments are diadinoxanthin and two fucoxanthin derivatives, whereas the Chrysophyceae have fucoxanthin and violaxanthin ([1825]).

Similar minute coccoid heterokontophytes occur as endosymbionts in planktonic foraminifera growing in tropical and subtropical areas of the Atlantic Ocean ([491]). Foraminifera are protozoa characterized by the presence of a perforate calcareous shell, through which anastomosing pseudopodia extend out into the environment. Many foraminifera can photosynthesize, through the activity of unicellular, endosymbiotic algae drawn from a variety of taxonomic groups ([973]).

The order Parmales

This order was recently established ([104]) for a number of tiny (2–5.5 µm) coccoid species, which have siliceous walls made of round and triradiate plates that abut, edge to edge (Fig. 6.12a). The architecture of the cell resembles that of *Pelagococcus* and is therefore clearly heterokontophyte in nature ([1116]). The Parmales are important components of the nannoplankton (phytoplankton with diameters in the range 2–20 µm) in Antarctic waters and in the subarctic Pacific Ocean. The cells illustrated (Fig. 6.12a) are those of *Pentalamina*, which has walls made of five siliceous plates (three round plates and two triradiate plates).

The Parmales probably represent a second class

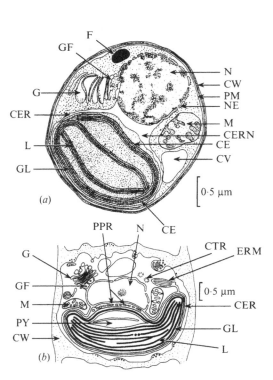

Figure 6.11. (*a*) *Pelagococcus*. (*b*) Cell of a thallose species of the Sarcinochrysidales. CE = chloroplast envelope; CER = chloroplast endoplasmic reticulum; CERN = connection between chloroplast ER and nuclear envelope; CTR = centriole; CV = chrysolaminaran vacuole; CW = cell wall; ERM = endoplasmic reticulum containing mastigonemes; F = lipid globule; G = golgi body; GF = forming face of golgi body; GL = girdle lamella, the peripheral stack of three thylakoids, which encloses all the other lamellae; L = lamella, a stack of three thylakoids; M = mitochondrion; N = nucleus; NE = nuclear envelope; PM = plasma membrane (plasmalemma); PPR = periplastidial reticulum, a network of interconnected tubules found in the narrow space between the chloroplast ER and the chloroplast envelope; PY = pyrenoid. (Based on [1825] and [76].)

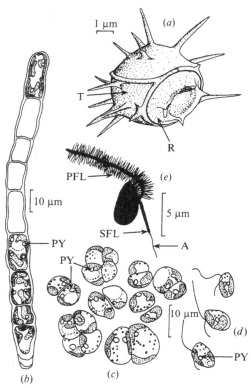

Figure 6.12. (*a*) *Pentalamina corona*, an example of the order Parmales. (*b*) *Nematochrysis*, a uniseriate filamentous representative of the order Sarcinochrysidales. (*c*) *Sarcinochrysis marina*, a palmelloid representative of the order Sarcinochrysidales. (*d*) Flagellate (monadoid) unicells of *Sarcinochrysis*, LM. (*e*) EM detail of a cell as shown in (*d*); note the lateral insertion of the flagella. A = acronema; PFL = pleuronematic flagellum (with mastigonemes); PY = prominent pyrenoid; R = round plate; SFL = smooth (short) flagellum; T = triradiate plate. (*a* based on [104]; *b*–*e* on [493a].)

(Parmophyceae) of non-flagellate Heterokontophyta bearing siliceous walls, the other class being the diatoms (Bacillariophyceae: chapter 9). In the diatoms the siliceous wall is like a box composed of two halves, which overlap centrally (Figs. 9.13, 9.14).

The order Sarcinochrysidales [493, 493a, 1325, 1330]

The algae of this order occur in estuarine and coastal marine waters. Most species are simple multicellular forms, either filamentous (Fig. 6.12*b*) or thalloid, and grow in the upper part of the intertidal zone. Only a few species are planktonic, among them the unicellular flagellate *Ankylochrysis* ([493, 1816]) and the palmelloid alga *Sarcinochrysis* (Fig. 6.12c).

The cells have a typical heterokontophyte architecture (Fig. 6.11b), with chloroplast ER surrounding the chloroplast, golgi bodies that have their forming faces appressed to the nuclear envelope, a girdle lamella within the chloroplast, and mastigonemes that are synthesized within ER cisternae. The zoids (flagellate cells) also exhibit heterokontophyte characteristics, with one long pleuronematic flagellum and one short smooth flagellum (Fig. 6.12e).

The order Sarcinochrysidales shares a number of features with the Phaeophyceae (brown algae), namely:

1 the flagella are laterally inserted on the zoids, arising from the anterior third of the cell (in the Chrysophyceae the flagella are almost apically inserted);
2 the pyrenoids usually protrude out from the chloroplasts in a distinctive way (Fig. 6.12b–d);
3 most of the species are multicellular;
4 the cell walls contain cellulose.

They differ from the Phaeophyceae, however, in that:

5 the flagella contain a transitional helix (this being absent in the Phaeophyceae);
6 the cell walls lack alginate, which is typically a constituent of brown algal cell walls ([493, 493a, 1330]);
7 the multicellular forms lack the characteristic plurilocular and unilocular sporangia found in the Phaeophyceae (Fig. 12.8).

In spite of these differences, the Sarcinochrysidales can reasonably be interpreted as the survivors of the ancestral group that gave rise to the brown algae. The resemblance between the flagellate cells in the two groups is an especially strong argument for this hypothesis, since flagellate cells are generally regarded as repositories of primitive characters (cf. pp. 105, 302). In a natural classification, the Sarcinochrysidales would not be placed within the Chrysophyceae, where they have traditionally been put; it would be better to separate them into a class of their own, the Sarcinochrysidophyceae.

7

Heterokontophyta: Class Xanthophyceae

The principal characteristics of the Xanthophyceae

The following characters distinguish the Xanthophyceae from other classes within the Heterokontophyta ([666, 668a]):

1 Most species are unicellular or colonial, coccoid algae (Fig. 7.2k, m–p, x, y). In addition, there are a considerable number of species in which the thalli are composed of multinucleate siphons (Figs. 7.3k, m, n, 7.4c), and a few that consist of multicellular filaments (Fig. 7.3a, o). Only a tiny minority of the Xanthophyceae are flagellate unicells (monads) or amoeboid organisms (Fig. 7.2a, b, g, h).

2 In the zoids the flagella are inserted close to the apex of the cell and not laterally, as in the Phaeophyceae (compare Figs. 7.1a, c, d with Fig. 12.2).

3 A typical heterokontophyte photoreceptor apparatus is present in the zoids, consisting of a swelling on the short, smooth flagellum and an eyespot lying within a chloroplast (Fig. 7.1a, c, d).

4 The transition zone of each flagellum contains a transitional helix, as in the Chrysophyceae (cf. Fig. 6.4a; [1218]).

5 The chloroplasts are discoid and green or yel-

low-green. In addition to chlorophyll a, there are also very small amounts of chlorophylls c_1 and c_2. The principal accessory pigments are β-carotene, vaucheriaxanthin, diatoxanthin, diadinoxanthin, and heteroxanthin. Fucoxanthin, the brown pigment of the Chrysophyceae, Bacillariophyceae and Phaeophyceae, is absent (Table 1.2).

6   The chloroplast DNA is generally arranged in a ring-shaped nucleoid (cf. Figs. 6.4*d*, 6.5; [254]).

7   Spherical or ellipsoidal cysts are formed by some species. Each cyst is formed within a cell (it is an endogenous cyst). Its wall is impregnated with silica and consists of two unequal halves, which fit tightly together, like a box and its lid (Figs. 7.2*c, j, u,* 7.3*d*).

8   The cell wall too can often be seen to consist of two halves, which overlap to some extent in the middle of the cell. The cell wall, like the cyst wall, is often impregnated with silica, although it seems to consist for the most part of cellulose microfibrils.

9   The Xanthophyceae are widespread in freshwater and terrestrial habitats; only a few species are marine.

Chrysolaminaran is probably the main reserve polysaccharide, as it is in most other heterokontophytes.

So far, the ultrastructural details of mitosis have been investigated only in the siphonous genus *Vaucheria* (Fig. 7.4*a, b*; [1343]): siphonous algae are algae consisting of branched multinucleate filaments that are without cross-walls, these filaments being known as 'siphons' (cf. pp. 128–9). Mitosis in *Vaucheria* is closed, the nuclear envelope remaining intact throughout division. The mitotic spindle is formed between two centrioles. The pole-to-pole spindle microtubules elongate greatly during anaphase, so that at telophase the two daughter nuclei are pushed far apart. Thus, because of the persistence of the nuclear envelope, at telophase the pairs of daughter nuclei take on a dumbbell-like configuration very reminiscent of what is found in siphonous green algae (division Chlorophyta; Fig. 19.22 II), which of course are quite unrelated to the Xanthophyceae. It may be that this special type of mitosis has evolved in connection with the development of the siphonous habit, the extreme elongation of the spindles ensuring that the nuclei are positioned sufficiently far away from each other in the multinucleate siphons. It is unlikely that the mitotic behaviour of *Vaucheria* will prove typical of the Xanthophyceae as a whole.

The Xanthophyceae and Chrysophyceae are distinguished from each other principally by the structure of their cell walls, the morphology of the endogenous cysts, and the kinds and amounts of their photosynthetic pigments. The differences in pigment composition are reflected in the generally brown or yellow-brown colour of the chloroplasts in the Chrysophyceae, and the yellow-green colour of the Xanthophyceae. It is often difficult, however, to decide whether a particular organism belongs to one class or the other.

Size and distribution of the class

There are around 100 genera in the Xanthophyceae and about 600 species ([383, 1381, 1500]). Unicellular and colonial Xanthophyceae occur in the phytoplankton of freshwater ponds and lakes, but are much rarer in the sea. A great many species inhabit soil, growing on damp earth, and species of the branching, filamentous xanthophyte *Heterococcus* have been isolated from terrestrial habitats in the Antarctic ([286]).

Most of the Xanthophyceae are difficult to find, because they rarely grow anywhere in abundance. The main exceptions to this are the species of the filamentous genus *Tribonema* (Fig. 7.3*a*) and the siphonous genus *Vaucheria* (Fig. 7.3*g–n*). *Tribonema* species form bright green growths in freshwaters and are particularly common in the early part of the year, when the water is still cold. They can occur in great quantities in bog pools that have been enriched by bird droppings. Species of *Vaucheria* are widely distributed, growing in damp soils or freshwaters, or in saline habitats, such as the muds of salt marshes; they form thick velvety felts, which sometimes play an important role in the stabilization of sediments.

The zoospore of *Tribonema* (Fig. 7.1): a typical flagellate xanthophycean cell

As has already been mentioned, unicellular flagellates are rare among the Xanthophyceae. One of the few flagellate species is *Chloromeson agile*, which is illus-

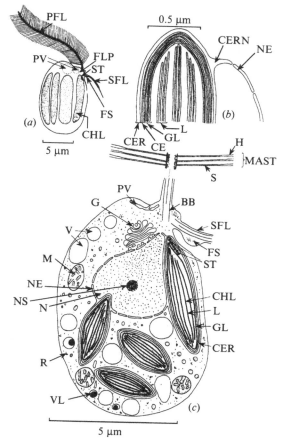

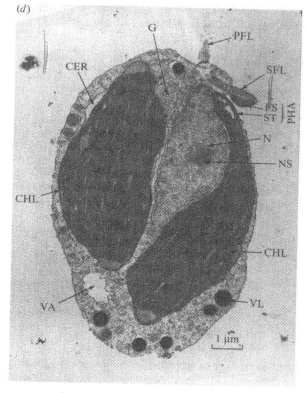

Figure 7.1. (*a–c*) *Tribonema,* zoospore. (*a*) General morphology of cell. (*b*) Detail of chloroplast ultrastructure. (*c*) Ultrastructure of cell. (*d*) *Bumilleria:* electron micrograph, showing a longitudinal section through a zoospore; the structure is typical of the Xanthophyceae. BB = basal body; CE = chloroplast envelope; CER = chloroplast endoplasmic reticulum; CERN = connection between chloroplast ER and nuclear envelope; CHL = chloroplast; FLP = papilla where flagella are inserted; FS = flagellar swelling; G = golgi body; GL = girdle lamella; H = terminal hairs of mastigonemes; L = lamella, composed of a stack of three thylakoids; M = mitochondrion; MAST = mastigonemes; N = nucleus; NE = nuclear envelope; NS = nucleolus; PFL = long pleuronematic flagellum; PHA = photoreceptor apparatus; PV = contractile (pulsing) vacuole; R = ribosomes; S = shaft of mastigoneme; SFL = smooth (acronematic) short flagellum; ST = stigma; V = vesicle; VA = vacuole; VL = vesicle containing lipid. (*a–c* based on [1130]; *d* from [1130], with permission from the authors and the British Phycological Society.)

trated in Fig. 7.2*a–c, e.* Many non-flagellate species, however, produce flagellate cells (zoids) at some stage in their life cycles, and it is the structure of one such zoid, the zoospore of *Tribonema,* that will be dealt with here (Figs. 7.1, 7.3*b*).

In the Xanthophyceae, as elsewhere, the flagellate unicell (monad) is regarded as the most primitive level of organization, and species with other types of organization are thought to have been derived from flagellate ancestors (pp. 105, 483). None of the rare flagellate Xanthophyceae, like *Chloromeson agile* (Fig. 7.2*a–c*), have yet been investigated with the electron microscope; the structure of *Tribonema* zoospores, on the other hand, is known in detail ([1130]). The *Tribonema* zoospore (Figs. 7.1, 7.3*b*) resembles *Ochromonas* (Fig. 6.3) very closely, agreeing with it in the following respects.

1 The chloroplast is surrounded not only by its own envelope, but also by a fold of endoplasmic reticulum (Fig. 7.1*b–d*). As a result each chloro-

plast has four membranes around it: two chloroplast envelope membranes and two chloroplast ER membranes. Where a chloroplast lies appressed to the nucleus, the chloroplast ER can be seen to be continuous with the nuclear envelope.

2 Within each chloroplast the thylakoids are stacked in threes to form lamellae (Fig. 7.1*b*).

3 Directly beneath the chloroplast envelope and running parallel to it, there is a peripheral stack of three thylakoids, the girdle lamella, which encloses all the other lamellae (Fig. 7.1*b*).

4 The long forwardly directed flagellum is a pleuronematic (tinsel) flagellum, bearing mastigonemes. As in *Ochromonas*, the mastigonemes are formed within cisternae of the endoplasmic reticulum, or even in swollen parts of the nuclear envelope ([986]). The short backwardly directed flagellum does not bear hairs (Fig. 7.1*a*, *c*).

5 The short flagellum bears a swelling (photoreceptor?) near to its base, which fits into a depression in the cell surface. Below the depression lies the stigma, which is contained within a chloroplast (Fig. 7.1*a, c, d*).

6 Both flagella arise just below the apex of the cell on one side (they are subapically inserted), and lie at an obtuse angle to each other.

7 The golgi apparatus lies at the anterior end of the cell, between the nucleus and the plasmalemma, with its forming face appressed to the nuclear envelope (Fig. 7.1*c, d*).

8 The flagellar basal bodies are connected to the nucleus by a transversely striated root; this rhizoplast is rather less prominent, however, than in *Ochromonas* ([1218]; the rhizoplast is not shown in Fig. 7.1*c*).

The structure of the *Tribonema* zoospore differs from that of the *Ochromonas* cell (Fig. 6.3) in a number of ways, however, including the following:

1 The two flagella arise from a subapical papilla; this is absent in *Ochromonas*.

2 The smooth, backwardly directed flagellum ends in a thin hair-point (acronema) (Fig. 7.1*a*); in *Ochromonas* the flagellum tip is blunt.

Reproduction

In most of the Xanthophyceae the only known methods of reproduction are asexual and involve vegetative cell division, or the formation of aplanospores or zoospores (Fig. 7.2*m*). Indeed, sexual reproduction has as yet been found only in *Vaucheria*, which exhibits a very characteristic type of oogamy (Fig. 7.3*k–n*; p. 129).

The various levels of organization in the Xanthophyceae

The most primitive type of organization in the Xanthophyceae is represented in flagellates like *Chloromeson* (Fig. 7.2*a–c, e*), which is comparable in its organization with the chrysophycean alga *Ochromonas*. From unicellular flagellates (monads) like this, various other types of unicells have probably evolved, and also a number of multicellular forms (see also pp. 120, 483). The following levels of organization can be found in the Xanthophyceae.

Unicellular flagellate (monadoid) level of organization

Only about seven genera and species of Xanthophyceae are unicellular flagellates and all of them are rare. An example is *Chloromeson* (Fig. 7.2*a–c, e*), which has until now been found only by A. Pascher ([1381]), who discovered it in a brackish pool on the Baltic coast of Germany. The cell is naked and can form pseudopodia (Fig. 7.2*b*).

Amoeboid level of organization

The cells of xanthophycean algae at this level of organization are naked and bear pseudopodia, by which they are able to take up solid particles. *Rhizochloris* (Fig. 7.2*w*) is one such organism and can ingest bacteria or small algae such as diatoms via its broad pseudopodia. The species we illustrate was found in the Adriatic.

A second example is provided by the genus *Myxochloris* (Fig. 7.2*g–j*), whose cells are naked, amoeboid plasmodia containing many chloroplasts. The plasmodia live inside the hyaline water-storing cells of the bog mosses (*Sphagnum* species), which are

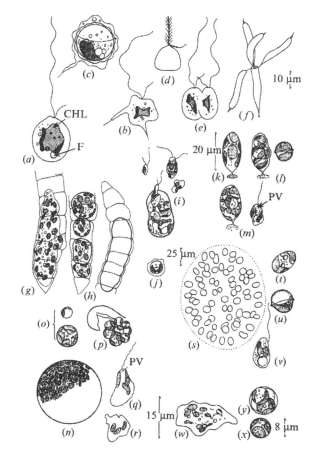

Figure 7.2. (*a–c, e*) *Chloromeson agile* (*a* normal vegetative cell; *b* amoeboid cell; *c* formation of an endogenous cyst; *e* cell division). (*d*) *Botrydiopsis*, zoospore. (*f*) *Ophiocytium*. (*g–j*) *Myxochloris* (*g* vegetative plasmodium within one of the hyaline, water-storing cells of *Sphagnum*; *h* exogenous cyst; *i* zoospores emerging from an exogenous cyst; *j* endogenous cyst). (*k–m*) *Characiopsis* (*k* vegetative cell; *l* aplanosporangium and aplanospore; *m* zoosporangium and zoid). (*n–r*) *Botrydiopsis* (*n* fully grown cell; *o* young cells; *p* autospores; *q* zoospore; *r* a zoospore that has become amoeboid). (*s–v*) *Gloeochloris* (*s* colony; *t* single cell; *u* aplanospore (endogenous cyst); *v* zoospore). (*w*) *Rhizochloris mirabilis*. (*x, y*) *Chloridella neglecta*. CHL = chloroplast; F = lipid or chrysolaminaran; PV = contractile (pulsing) vacuole. (After [1381].)

protoplast (Fig. 7.2*h*). Later, the contents of the cyst can be liberated either in the form of uninucleate zoospores or as multinucleate amoeboid cells (Fig. 7.2*i*). The zoospores and amoebae can then go on to form the bipartite type of endogenous cyst that is characteristic of the Xanthophyceae (Fig. 7.2*j*).

Palmelloid (tetrasporal) level of organization

Here the cells are non-flagellate and lie embedded in a common sheath or envelope of mucilage, thus forming colonies. An example is *Gloeochloris* (Fig. 7.2*s–v*), in which the cells are united in gelatinous colonies, these being spherical or ellipsoidal. This alga reproduces through the formation of zoospores and can also produce endogenous cysts. The species illustrated was found in melt-water.

Coccoid level of organization

At this level of organization the cells are non-motile and lack flagella, being encased in a cell wall. In some cases groups of cells are linked together to form colonies. Most of the Xanthophyceae are coccoid and so we give several examples.

Chloridella (Fig. 7.2*x, y*) is a unicellular form with round cells, which reproduce through the formation of autospores. It superficially resembles the green alga *Chlorella* (division Chlorophyta: p. 365); four species of the genus are known, all of them occurring in freshwater.

Botrydiopsis (Fig. 7.2*n–r*) too is unicellular, producing quite large round cells, which can have diameters of around 50 μm when fully grown. The cells are multinucleate and contain many chloroplasts. Reproduction takes place via aplanospores (Fig. 7.2*p*) and zoospores (Fig. 7.2*q*). Four species are known and these are found in stagnant freshwater (ditches, ponds, etc.) and on soil.

The cells of *Characiopsis* (Fig. 7.2*k–m*) are elongate and stalked and, as in *Botrydiopsis*, reproduction takes place through the formation of aplanospores (Fig. 7.2*l*) and zoospores (Fig. 7.2*m*). About 50 species of this freshwater genus have been described. There is a remarkable resemblance between *Characiopsis* and the green algal genus *Characium*, but they can be distinguished quite easily by staining the cells with iodine. Green algae, such as *Characium*,

dead cells but enable the moss to soak up water like a sponge and retain it. A single *Myxochloris* plasmodium can give rise to one to several cysts, which are exogenous, the cyst walls being laid down outside the

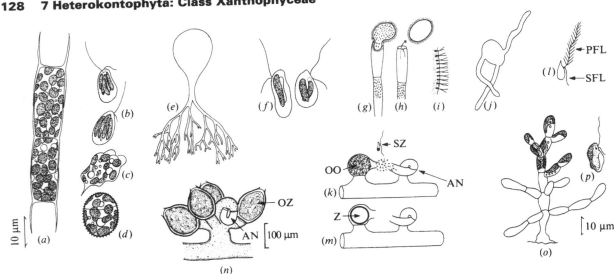

Figure 7.3. (*a–d*) *Tribonema viride* (*a* filaments of vegetative cells; *b* zoids; *c* amoeboid protoplast, which has left the parent cell; *d* aplanospore). (*e, f*) *Botrydium* (*e* habit; *f* two zoids). (*g–m*) *Vaucheria sessilis* (*g, h* release of a synzoospore; *i* detail of the surface of a synzoospore, showing the pairs of flagella: each pair arises just above a nucleus; *j* germinating synzoospore; *k* sexual reproduction; *l* spermatozoid; *m* zygote). (*n*) *Vaucheria verticillata*, sexual stages. (*o, p*) *Heterodendron*. AN = antheridium; OO = oogonium; OZ = oogonium containing a zygote; PFL = pleuronematic flagellum; SFL = smooth (acronematic) short flagellum; SZ = spermatozoid; Z = zygote. (*a–f, o–p* after [1381]; *n* after [1663].)

contain starch as their reserve polysaccharide and this stains purplish-blue with iodine. *Characiopsis*, on the other hand, in common with other Xanthophyceae, does not contain starch, and so of course no blue coloration is produced after addition of iodine.

A further example of coccoid organization is given by *Ophiocytium* (Fig. 7.2*f*). This alga has elongate, cylindrical cells, which are often bent and are attached by a short stalk. During reproduction the uppermost part of the cell wall opens like a lid to liberate the zoospores. The emerging zoospores often settle on the rim of the parent cell wall and there grow up into new *Ophiocytium* cells. As a result colonies may be produced, having the form shown in Fig. 7.2*f*. About 15 species of *Ophiocytium* are known, all of them from freshwater.

Filamentous (trichal) level of organization

In this type of organism the cells are united into branched or unbranched filaments. Among the forms with unbranched filaments is the common freshwater genus *Tribonema* (Fig. 7.3*a–d*). Here the cell walls are composed of H-shaped units, which overlap in the centre of the cell. This structure becomes particularly obvious when the filaments fall apart after death or break. Reproduction takes place through the liberation and dispersal of zoospores or amoeboid protoplasts. There are about 25 species of *Tribonema*, of which several are very widely distributed in cold, fairly nutrient-rich freshwaters.

A further example with filamentous organization is *Heterodendron* (Fig. 7.3*o, p*), which has branched filaments and reproduces by zoospores. Both of the species known are found in spring and autumn on submerged twigs and branches, or on the stems of reeds.

Siphonous organization

These algae have no cross walls and quite often take the form of branching tubes, containing multinucleate protoplasts. *Botrydium*, however, consists of small vesicles the size of a pin-head, which are anchored in the soil by a system of branched rhizoids (Fig. 7.3*e, f*). The protoplast of each vesicle can divide up into a large number of zoids, which are liberated from the vesicle when the environment is flooded with water. If the alga begins to dry out, the protoplast retracts into the rhizoids, where it forms thick-walled resting spores. When dampened again, the spores germinate, with the production of zoids. In this genus there are about five species, which closely resemble those of the green alga *Protosiphon* (division Chlorophyta, order Chlorococcales: see p. 360), which also lives in soil.

The genus *Vaucheria* (Fig. 7.3*g–n*) may be taken as a second example of siphonous organization within the Xanthophyceae. The tube-like, branched filaments of this alga contain a thin parietal layer of cytoplasm, in which there lie many chloroplasts and nuclei; the centre of the tube is occupied by vacuoles (Fig. 7.4*c*). In some species asexual reproduction takes place via **synzoospores** (Fig. 7.3*g–i*), which are interpreted as representing a number of zoospores that remain united in a single, composite structure. The synzoospore bears many pairs of slightly unequal flagella (Fig. 7.3*i*). Both flagella of each pair are smooth and devoid of mastigonemes ([1218, 1345]). Each synzoospore is formed in a club-shaped structure at the tip of a filament, which is cut off from the rest of the algal thallus by a cross wall. Once liberated, the synzoospore can swim around for some time before settling and germinating to form a new system of tube-like filaments (Fig. 7.3*j*).

Sexual reproduction involves a very characteristic type of oogamy, found throughout the genus. The ripe oogonium contains one egg cell ready for fertilization. Each antheridium, on the other hand, produces numerous spermatozoids. Each has a pair of heterokont flagella ([1346]) and contains a compact set of cell organelles – nucleus, mitochondria, golgi apparatus – together with a band of microtubules, which provides stiffening for a projection at the anterior of the spermatozoid, called the proboscis. The structure of the *Vaucheria* spermatozoid resembles that of the sperm produced by the brown alga *Fucus* (Fig. 12.4*d*; [1212]).

The spermatozoids swim to the oogonium and one of them fertilizes the egg cell. After fertilization the zygote surrounds itself with a thick wall (Fig. 7.3*k–n*), thus becoming a hypnozygote. This cannot germinate immediately, but has an obligate dormant phase before it grows into a new *Vaucheria* plant. For a long time, the exact position of meiosis in the life cycle was unknown, but it was assumed that the reduction divisions took place during the germination of the zygote ([1658]). More recently, however, evidence has been presented that meiosis precedes the formation of the gametes, the life cycle therefore being diplontic ([17]).

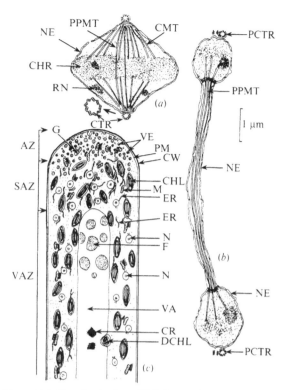

Figure 7.4. *Vaucheria*, from EM observations. (*a*) Metaphase of mitosis. (*b*) Telophase of mitosis. (*c*) Longitudinal section through the growing tip of a siphon. AZ = apical zone where growth takes place, with vesicles containing cell wall material, mitochondria, golgi bodies and ER, but without chloroplasts and nuclei; CHL = chloroplast; CHR = chromosome; CMT = chromosomal spindle microtubule; CR = crystal; CTR = centriole; CW = cell wall; DCHL = degenerating chloroplast; ER = endoplasmic reticulum; F = lipid body; G = golgi body; M = mitochondrion; N = nucleus; NE = nuclear envelope; PCTR = pair of centrioles; PM = plasma membrane (plasmalemma); PPMT = pole-to-pole (interzonal) spindle microtubule; RN = remains of nucleolus; SAZ = subapical zone, with chloroplasts and nuclei but no vacuole; VA = vacuole; VAZ = vacuolar zone; VE = vesicles containing cell wall material, probably produced by the golgi bodies. (*a, b* based on [1343]; *c* on [1344].)

Diplontic life cycles with gametic meiosis also occur in the heterokontophyte class Bacillariophyceae (the diatoms: p. 133).

About 50 species of *Vaucheria* are known ([233, 1500]). Marine species form felty growths on the mud of salt marshes, binding the sediment together. Other species grow on damp soil or in freshwater, and these too often produce dense mats. *Vaucheria* resembles the freshwater green alga *Dichotomosiphon* (division Chlorophyta, class Bryopsidophyceae: p. 425).

The subdivision of the Xanthophyceae into orders

The current classifications reflect the various levels of organization found within the Xanthophyceae. In one recent classification ([383, 668a]), for instance, seven orders are recognized:

1 Chloramoebales: flagellate organisms;
2 Rhizochloridales: amoeboid organisms;
3 Heterogloeales: palmelloid (tetrasporal) organization;
4 Mischococcales: coccoid organisms;
5 Tribonematales: filamentous organization;
6 Botrydiales: siphonous organization; sexual reproduction isogamous or anisogamous ([100]);
7 Vaucheriales: siphonous organization; sexual reproduction oogamous.

This classification is probably unsatisfactory, since it has gradually become evident in other classes of algae that groups based on the level of organization of the thallus are often phylogenetically heterogeneous (cf. pp. 483–5).

8

Heterokontophyta: Class Eustigmatophyceae

The principal characteristics of the Eustigmatophyceae

The following characters distinguish this class from other classes within the Heterokontophyta ([665, 667, 668b, 670]).

1 All species are unicellular and coccoid (Figs. 8.1, 8.2), with polysaccharide walls.

2 In the flagellate cells (zoids), the single flagellum or, where two flagella are present, both flagella, are inserted near the apex of the cell, not laterally, as in the Phaeophyceae and Sarcinochrysidophyceae (compare Fig. 8.1*a*, *f*, *g* with Figs. 12.2 and 6.12*e*).

3 The zoids do not have typical heterokontophyte photoreceptors, with their chloroplast-enclosed eyespots and swellings on the smooth posterior flagella (e.g. see Fig. 7.1*c*). Instead, they possess their own unique type of photoreceptor. At the anterior end of the zoid, there is a conspicuous orange-red eyespot, which lies outside the chloroplast. It consists of a number of carotenoid-containing globules, which are not enclosed by membranes, either individually or as a group (Fig. 8.1*a*). Appressed to the cell just above the eyespot is a wing-like basal expansion of the long pleuronematic flagellum.

4 The transition zone of the flagellum contains a transitional helix, as in the Chrysophyceae, Xanthophyceae and Sarcinochrysidophyceae (Fig. 6.4a; [1218]).

5 Each cell contains one or more yellow-green chloroplasts. The only chlorophyll present is chlorophyll a. The principal accessory pigment is violaxanthin, which is also the main pigment involved in light-harvesting, a role it plays in apparently no other group of photosynthetic organisms. Other accessory pigments present are β-carotene, vaucheriaxanthin, and several minor xanthophylls (Table 1.2; [32, 88, 1129, 1350, 1438, 1882, 1883]).

6 Within the chloroplasts there are no girdle lamellae (peripheral stacks of three thylakoids: Fig. 8.1a).

7 In the coccoid vegetative cells, the chloroplast generally bears a stalked, angular pyrenoid on its inner side (Fig. 8.1c, m).

8 The chloroplast DNA is organized into numerous dot-like aggregates (nucleoids), which may be united to form a reticulum ([254]).

9 The few species known to belong to the class include both freshwater and marine representatives.

The particular combination of photosynthetic pigments found in the Eustigmatophyceae, the unique type of photoreceptor apparatus, and the absence of a girdle lamella in the chloroplasts, serve to differentiate this class from other heterokontophytes and could even justify its classification in a separate division (as done by van den Hoek & Jahns 1978: [703]). Here, however, the Eustigmatophyceae are retained within the Heterokontophyta, since they share the following characters with some or all of the other heterokontophyte classes:

the presence of a pleuronematic anterior flagellum, which is long and bears typical tripartite tubular mastigonemes (Fig. 8.1a);

the possession of chloroplast ER, which, in the coccoid, non-flagellate cells, is continuous with the nuclear envelope (Fig. 8.2);

the grouping of the thylakoids into stacks (lamellae) of three;

the presence of a transitional helix in the zone between the basal body and the flagellar shaft: this feature is not shared by all other heterokontophyte classes.

The vegetative cells possess dictyosomes (golgi apparatus), but the uniflagellate zoids do not. In addition, the vegetative cells have pyrenoids, which are never present in the zoids. The pyrenoid has a characteristic morphology, being polygonal and projecting on a short stalk from the inner side of the chloroplast. It is surrounded by flat plates of an unknown photosynthetic storage product, which is not starch. No thylakoids penetrate into the pyrenoid matrix.

All the methods of reproduction known for the class are asexual, involving zoospores (Fig. 8.1a, f, g) or autospores, the latter being non-flagellate spores that have the same morphology as the parent cell (Fig. 8.1e, j, o, p).

The class Eustigmatophyceae was erected about 20 years ago to include a number of algae previously classified in the Xanthophyceae ([670, 671, 672]). These include species of the genera *Ellipsoidion*, *Eustigmatos* (= *Pleurochloris*), *Polyedriella*, *Vischeria* and *Chlorobotrys*. At present the class contains seven genera and about twelve species. Most of the genera consist of freshwater or soil-dwelling algae. *Nannochloropsis*, however, is marine, containing minute (2–4 μm) forms that live in the picoplankton (planktonic organisms 0.2–2 μm in diameter; Fig. 8.2). The marine picoplankton also includes coccoid representatives of various other algal classes, such as the Cyanophyceae (p. 22, Fig. 2.1a), Chrysophyceae (p. 121, Figs. 6.11a, 6.12a), and Prasinophyceae (p. 343, Fig. 20.3). Picoplanktonic algae are the main primary producers in many pelagic (open ocean) ecosystems ([613]).

Some examples of Eustigmatophyceae
([383, 1381])

Ellipsoidion acuminatum (Fig. 8.1h–k)
This unicellular alga has ellipsoidal cells, which taper to a point at each end; they are about two or three times as long as broad. Each cell contains 3–4(–7) chloroplasts. Reproduction is brought about by the formation of autospores, two or four of these being

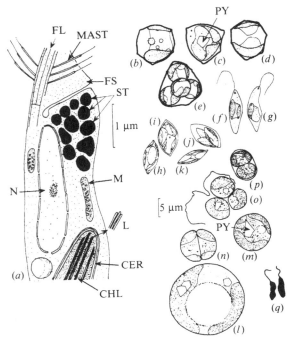

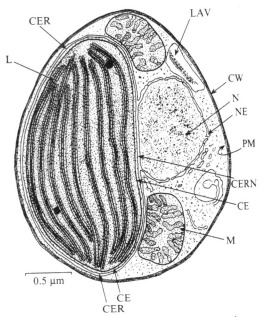

Figure 8.1. (a–g) *Polyedriella helvetica* (a, f, g zoospore; e autospores). (h–k) *Ellipsoidion acuminatum* (h, k vegetative cells; i, j autospore formation). (l–q) *Eustigmatos magnus* (l, m vegetative cells; n–p autospore formation; q zoospores). CER = chloroplast endoplasmic reticulum; CHL = chloroplast; FL = flagellum; FS = flagellar swelling; L = lamella, composed of a stack of three thylakoids; M = mitochondrion; MAST = mastigonemes; N = nucleus; PY = pyrenoid; ST = stigma. (a after [672]; b–q after [1381].)

Figure 8.2. *Nannochloropsis*, a picoplanktonic marine representative of the Eustigmatophyceae. CE = chloroplast envelope; CER = chloroplast endoplasmic reticulum; CERN = connection between the chloroplast ER and the nuclear envelope; CW = cell wall; L = lamella, composed of a stack of three thylakoids; LAV = lamellate vesicles; M = mitochondrion; N = nucleus; NE = nuclear envelope; PM = plasma membrane (plasmalemma). (Based on [1129].)

produced per cell. Autospores are non-motile spores (aplanospores), which adopt the form typical of the parent cell while still enclosed within it. The autospores of *Ellipsoidion acuminatum* possess contractile vacuoles and measure 8–16 μm × 4–6 μm. This species occurs in brackish pools.

Polyedriella helvetica (Fig. 8.1a–g)

This species is unicellular and has polyhedral cells, with a variable number of faces. The cells are 7–11(–20) μm in size and contain one, two or several chloroplasts. They reproduce via autospores, two or four being produced per cell, and through the formation of uniflagellate zoospores, each of which contains an eyespot (stigma) lying free in the cytoplasm. *Polyedriella helvetica* is only known from laboratory cultures.

Eustigmatos magnus (*Pleurochloris magna*) (Fig. 8.1l–q)

Eustigmatos magnus has round cells with thin walls and usually possesses a single parietal chloroplast. Reproduction occurs through autospores and uniflagellate zoids, which measure 7–12(–21) μm. This is a soil alga, which has been isolated three times from soils in Denmark.

Nannochloropsis (Fig. 8.2)

The non-flagellate, spherical to slightly ovoid cells of *Nannochloropsis* measure 2–4 μm in diameter. There is one chloroplast per cell, which does not bear a pyrenoid. The chloroplast ER is continuous with the nuclear envelope. Inside the chloroplast are lamellae, each consisting of three thylakoids, but, as in other eustigmatophytes, there is no girdle lamella. Only one chlorophyll is present, chlorophyll a, and the main accessory pigment is violaxanthin. The cells do not form starch, the reserve polysaccharide of green algae (Chlorophyta), but *Nannochloropsis* was for a long time confused with the coccoid green alga *Chlorella* (Fig. 22.4*a, b*). It is probably widely distributed in the world's oceans ([32, 1129]).

9

Heterokontophyta: Class Bacillariophyceae (= Diatomophyceae; the diatoms)

The principal characteristics of the Bacillariophyceae

The following characters distinguish the Bacillariophyceae from other classes within the Heterokontophyta.

1 All species are unicellular or colonial coccoid algae. Each cell is encased by a unique type of cell wall, which is siliceous and takes the form of a box with an overlapping lid; this is termed the **frustule** (Figs. 9.1*a*, *b*, 9.10, 9.12 – 9.14).

2 The only flagellate cells (zoids) formed in the Bacillariophyceae are the male gametes (spermatozoids) of the centric diatoms (order Centrales). Here there is a single pleuronematic flagellum, which is apically inserted and lacks the central two microtubules of the axoneme (Fig. 9.8; [1114, 1218]).

3 The transition zone of the flagellum lacks a transitional helix (cf. Fig. 6.4*a*).

4 The chloroplasts are usually golden-brown, because the chlorophyll is masked by the accessory pigment fucoxanthin.

5 The chloroplast DNA is organized into a ring-shaped nucleoid (Fig. 9.3*d*, 9.8*c*; [254]).

6 Each element of the siliceous cell wall is formed within the cytoplasm in a silica deposition vesi-

cle (SDV) (Figs. 9.3*a*, *d*, *e*, 9.5; [1427, 1569, 1833]). In the Chrysophyceae too, siliceous structures such as cysts and scales are made in SDVs (Figs. 6.7, 6.9).

7 Mitosis is open, the nuclear envelope breaking down before metaphase, and the telophase spindle is persistent (it does not break down at early telophase as in some organisms). The spindle is formed outside the nucleus, between two darkly staining polar plates, and then sinks down into the nucleus as the nuclear envelope disperses (Fig. 9.6). It consists of two overlapping and interdigitating sets of microtubules (half spindles), each associated with one polar plate. In the region of overlap, the microtubules of the two half spindles slide over each other, thus pushing the poles apart ([1429, 1421]).

8 Species that reproduce sexually have a diplontic life cycle, with gametic meiosis (Figs. 9.9, 9.11).

9 The Bacillariophyceae are widespread in both marine and freshwater habitats.

The Bacillariophyceae also exhibit a number of features that are typical of the Heterokontophyta as a whole, namely:

the presence of typical tripartite mastigonemes (stiff tubular hairs) on the pleuronematic long flagellum of the spermatozoids produced by centric diatoms (Fig. 9.8);

golgi bodies that lie with their forming faces appressed to the nuclear envelope (Figs. 9.3, 9.6*a*);

the presence of chloroplast ER, which can be continuous with the nuclear envelope (Figs. 9.3, 9.8*a*);

the presence of a periplastidial reticulum in the narrow space between the nuclear envelope (where this is continuous with and replaces the chloroplast ER) and the chloroplast. This reticulum is a network of interconnected tubules and occurs in various classes of the Heterokontophyta (Figs. 6.11*b*, 9.3), and also in the Haptophyta ([76]);

chloroplasts that contain girdle lamellae (Figs. 9.3, 9.8);

the presence of chlorophylls a and c_2 (usually together with either chlorophyll c_1 or chlorophyll c_3; [1689]).

Size and distribution of the class

There are well over 250 genera of living diatoms, with around 100 000 species ([1531]). Diatoms occur in the sea, in freshwater, on damp rocks, or on soil. The phytoplankton of the oceans consists to a large extent of diatoms, and in temperate or cold parts of the oceans, particularly in nutrient-rich waters (e.g. in the areas of upwelling off the coasts of southwest Africa, western South America, or California), diatoms are largely responsible for the very high primary productivity that occurs. The annual production of fixed carbon in such areas can amount to 200–400 g m^{-2} (for comparison, the productivity of a cereal or maize crop is of the order of 1000–2500 g m^{-2}; similarly high values are attained by some stands of macroalgae, e.g. *Laminaria*, p. 166). The constant 'rain' of dead diatom frustules to the bottom of these highly productive parts of the oceans results in the accumulation of diatom oozes ([1618]). Large fossil deposits from past geological periods (in the Tertiary) are now mined as 'diatomite' or 'diatomaceous earth', which is used for filters, deodorants and decolouring agents, and as an abrasive, for instance, in toothpaste.

Even though large parts of the sea are less productive than the areas mentioned above, the very extent of the world's oceans makes it easy to see what an enormous role diatoms must play in the production of organic material through photosynthesis. One estimate of the total primary production on earth (both on the continents and in the oceans) is 1.4×10^{14} kg dry mass per year, of which perhaps 20–25% is contributed by marine planktonic diatoms and 15–20% by other marine planktonic algae ([1868]). These figures illustrate the quantitative significance of the diatoms for the functioning of 'ecosystem Earth'. This is underlined still further when one considers that almost all other marine life is directly or indirectly dependent on this primary production for its food. In freshwaters too, diatoms form an important part of the phytoplankton. Here, as in the temperate parts of the oceans, diatoms are particularly abundant at the beginning of spring, when the water tends to contain plenty of nutrients (phosphate, nitrate, silicate), and the increasing light intensities and daylength promote photosynthesis. A second but smaller peak of diatom abundance is often observed in autumn.

Planktonic diatoms, with their rather heavy silica cell walls, are faced with the 'problem' of how to remain in the uppermost layers of lakes or oceans, where there is enough light for photosynthesis. When a mixed sample containing different types of phytoplankton algae is left to settle in the dark, in a measuring cylinder or some other vessel, the diatoms are the first to sink to the bottom ([1528]). In nature, the turbulent mixing of the upper layers by the wind reduces the rate of loss, and several planktonic marine diatoms reduce their density and become more buoyant by excluding heavy ions from their cell sap ([1528, 1653, 1928]). In the marine phytoplankton species *Ditylum brightwellii*, the cells are relatively light during the night and relatively heavy by day. At the end of the night there are relatively high Na^+, low K^+ and low Cl^- concentrations, bringing about a low density, while by the end of the day Na^+ is low, while K^+ and Cl^- are high. It may be that this change in buoyancy promotes vertical movements through the water column, thus facilitating the uptake of nutrients ([30]). In one study, the density of the cell sap of *Ditylum* was calculated to be 1.0202 g cm^{-3}, less than that of the surrounding sea water, which was 1.0227 g cm^{-3} ([578, 1851]).

Many planktonic diatoms bear long spines or other protrusions (Fig. 9.12*g, n–r*). In earlier discussions these bizarre ornamentations were generally regarded as devices that slowed sinking by increasing the surface area : volume ratio of the cell and hence the viscous drag. This hypothesis was supported by experiments conducted using the freshwater planktonic diatom *Thalassiosira fluviatilis* ([1851, 1852]). The cells of this species produce fibres of chitin 70 μm long, which can be removed without damaging the rest of the cell by using the enzyme chitinase (obtained from fungi). In the experiments, cells without chitin fibres sank 1.9 times faster than cells with fibres.

In more recent discussions the siliceous frustule, with its spines and other projections, is interpreted as a sinking device! According to this hypothesis, actively growing populations of planktonic diatoms are kept in the upper layers of lakes or the sea by a combination of active buoyancy control by the cells (see above) and turbulent mixing of the upper layers. During this phase of growth the various projections, etc. are thought to ensure twisting, tumbling and rotation of the cells as they are dragged along by the microscale turbulence of the water. This would enhance exchange of water at the cell surface and hence the capture of rare nutrients ([1851]).

At the end of a diatom bloom, when nutrients (N, P, Si) have become depleted, the diatoms are no longer able to maintain an active buoyancy control mechanism, so their heavy frustules cause them to sink. Furthermore, the spines and other appendages of individual cells can become entangled, producing aggregates of cells that sink much faster than the separate cells (because, all else being equal, larger particles sink faster than small ones). The formation of aggregates is also promoted towards the end of the bloom by the production of sticky mucilage by the cells, often in copious amounts. Thus planktonic blooms in the sea are thought to end rather abruptly, with a shower of 'marine snow' consisting of mucilaginous 'flakes' of diatoms, most of them still alive. The flakes sink at a rate of *ca.* 50–100 m per day, while the actively growing cells sink much more slowly, at perhaps 2 m or less per day. This accelerated sinking rapidly removes the population from the nutrient-depleted, warm surface layers, now inimical to growth, and leads to the formation of a resting population at some depth below the surface or, in shallow seas, on the bottom. The lower temperatures and lower light regime at greater depth ensures better survival, and this is further enhanced by the formation of special resting stages (e.g. resting spores: see p. 156). In the open ocean most of the sinking cells will be lost to the ocean deeps, but a small proportion congregates at the thermocline: the boundary layer between the less dense, warm surface water and the cooler, heavier water below. In the ocean this often lies at depths of 50-100 m (see also p. 22). From this small refuge population seed cells can later be recruited, through vertical mixing of the surface waters, and when conditions are suitable a new diatom bloom will develop ([1654]).

An additional function of the spines may be to discourage grazing by herbivorous zooplankton ([434]).

Besides planktonic diatoms ([581]), there are also many benthic forms, growing on sediments or attached to rocks or other plants ([1154, 1382]). Benthic diatoms belong for the most part to the pennate group (order Pennales). Many of them possess a special organelle, the raphe (see below), by means of which they are able to creep over or through the substratum (which might be other organisms, sand, mud, or rock).

At times intertidal sand or mud flats become noticeably brown, especially towards summer, and this is often as a result of the luxuriant growth of benthic diatoms. The benthic diatom flora of the sandy and muddy sediments of the Wadden Sea, off The Netherlands, is particularly rich, containing hundreds of species ([699]). The productivity of these diatoms is not particularly great, however, amounting only to some 100 g carbon fixed m^{-2} y^{-1} ([183]). Production is less in winter than in summer. In contrast, the annual primary production of the phytoplankton in the Wadden Sea is 150–250 g carbon m^{-2}. The low primary productivity of the benthic diatoms is brought about partly by the high turbidity of the water; at high tide the water covering the sand and mud flats more or less 'switches off' the light! Another important factor is the instability of the substratum, which can be washed away during rough weather ([11, 257, 699]).

Some benthic species living in sand or mud creep into the sediments during high tide, in response to the lower light intensity. It may be that by doing this they are protected from being washed away. When the sediments are exposed again and light intensities increase, the algae re-emerge from the sediment, and this behaviour can be exploited in laboratory experiments to determine primary productivity. The algae are allowed to creep out of the sediment into small pieces of tissue (e.g. lens tissue), which can then be removed, so isolating the algae for experimentation ([1528]). In sandy sediments diatoms can often be found attached to the sand grains, in addition to the motile species that creep on and between the grains.

Many of the benthic diatoms living in sediments are facultative heterotrophs ([12, 635]) and can utilize various organic substrates for growth, at low light intensities or in the dark, as for instance when they are buried by sediment. A few diatoms are quite colourless (apochlorotic) and are obligate heterotrophs, such as *Nitzschia putrida*, which lives on the brown alga *Fucus* ([1003]).

Most diatoms live in water. A few species, however, are soil algae, which grow actively when the soil is damp but can tolerate extreme drought or warmth for some time, surviving as dormant resting stages ([1382]). In damp regions of the tropics, diatoms live together with blue-green algae on the leaves of trees.

All of the larger (0.5–1 cm) benthic foraminifera growing in the shallow waters (within the euphotic zone) of tropical and subtropical seas are hosts for endosymbiotic algae. These foraminifera can be quite abundant and may contribute significantly to the primary production; furthermore, since foraminifera are protozoans that have calcareous shells, they are also important sources of biogenic calcium carbonate. In contrast to the reef-building corals, which all have the same species (a member of the Dinophyta) as an endosymbiont, benthic foraminifera harbour a great variety of endosymbionts, drawn from various algal groups, including the Chlorophyta (p. 362), Dinophyta (p. 275), and Rhodophyta (p. 68). The predominant group among the endosymbionts, however, are diatoms, especially pennate diatoms (order Pennales). In the foraminiferan genus *Amphistegina*, for instance, the endosymbionts are species of the genera *Navicula* (Fig. 9.10e, f) and *Nitzschia* (Fig. 9.12a–e). While within the host, the endosymbiotic diatoms either have vestigial frustules or lack them altogether, but if cultured separately they regain frustules of normal structure. Minute coccoid algae have been found as endosymbionts in some planktonic foraminifera and are clearly heterokontophytes ([491]; cf. p. 121), while several brackish water benthic foraminifera are known to consume diatoms and use their chloroplasts for a while as photosynthetic organelles ([72, 915, 973, 1568]).

In comparison with many other groups of algae, the systematics of diatoms are relatively easy to investigate, because the silica shells bear characteristic patterns of pores and ornamentations, although there is often considerable variation in shell structure within a species. If the shells are to be studied in any detail, the organic contents must first be removed by oxidation. Material treated in this way can then be preserved and subsequently investigated.

Diatom shells can also be preserved as fossils and so, because different diatoms live in the sea, in brackish water or in freshwater, fossil diatom assemblages can be used to determine whether sediments are of marine or non-marine origin. Fossil diatoms can also be used to show how lake characteristics have changed during the Quaternary period, especially in relation to anthropogenic eutrophication and acidification, or to reconstruct past climates or past conditions in the oceans ([1528, 1751]). To achieve this, of course, it must be assumed that species had the same ecological preferences in the past that we can observe today.

The oldest fossil diatoms date from the early Cretaceous (120 million years ago) and were marine; they belong to the centric group ([1197, 1751]). The first marine representatives of the pennate diatom group appear by the end of the Cretaceous (70 million years ago), but the diatoms do not seem to have achieved their present preeminence until the beginning of the Miocene (24 million years ago). The oldest known freshwater diatoms come from the early part of the Tertiary (60 million years ago) and are members of the pennate group ([1751]).

The characteristics of diatoms

The class Bacillariophyceae contains two major groups, the centric diatoms and the pennate diatoms, which are sometimes recognized as two orders (Centrales and Pennales) and are distinguished from each other on the basis of differences in cell wall structure.

The cell wall of pennate diatoms

The silica shell (frustule) of a pennate diatom is elongate and usually bilaterally symmetrical in face (valve) view, with a lanceolate or elliptical outline. Fig. 9.1*a, b* shows an idealized pennate diatom, which corresponds fairly closely to what is found in genera like *Pinnularia* (Figs. 9.1*c–e*, 9.10*a*), *Navicula* (Fig. 9.10*e, f*) or *Mastogloia* (Fig. 9.13*a*). The **frustule** (the whole of the silica shell) consists of two halves: the **hypotheca** (the box in our box-and-lid analogy) and the **epitheca** (the overlapping lid; Fig. 9.1*b*). The epitheca consists in turn of two parts, viz. a flat upper part with down-turned edges, called the **epivalve** (epivalva), and a ring- or hoop-like side wall, the **epicingulum** (upper girdle). Similarly, the hypotheca consists of a **hypovalve** (hypovalva) and a **hypocingulum** (lower girdle). The epicingulum and epivalve are separated by a suture, as are the hypocingulum and hypovalve.

When viewed with the light microscope, diatom shells can present two aspects. When the epivalve or hypovalve is uppermost, the frustule is said to be 'in valve view' (Fig. 9.1*c*); if on the other hand the two parts of the girdle (epicingulum and hypocingulum) are uppermost, the frustule is said to be 'in girdle view' (Fig. 9.1*b, d*). Descriptions of diatoms also often make use of a system of axes and planes, which are explained in Fig. 9.1*a*.

The valves are beautifully structured and orna-mented, and the pattern of markings is to a large extent species-specific. In pennate diatoms the patterns are often bilaterally symmetrical, organized about an axis running from one pole to the other (i.e. symmetrical about the apical plane: Fig. 9.1*a*) (Figs. 9.1*c*, 9.10*a, e*, 9.13*a*). Thus, for example, the relatively coarse ornamentation of *Pinnularia* consists of a series of chambers, which lie roughly parallel to the transapical plane and are bounded by transapical ribs (costae). Each chamber opens externally by a great many small pores and internally by a single large aperture. In many other pennate diatoms the pattern appears at first sight to consist of lines (striae), which are regularly spaced and arranged roughly parallel to the transapical plane. The lines can sometimes be seen to be composed of many separate dots and the electron microscope reveals that the dots are pores (areolae) through the silica; the areolae sometimes have an extremely delicate and complex structure of their own (Fig. 9.3*c*).

The structure of the frustule is further complicated by the fact that each half of the girdle (i.e. each cingulum) is composed of two to many bands (copulae), which are separated by sutures similar to that between cingulum and valve (Fig. 9.1*j, k*). In some species the bands are all alike but elsewhere two or more types of band can present within one cingulum. Thus for instance in *Tabellaria*, the bands nearest the valves bear septa, which project far into the lumen of the cell (Fig. 9.10*h, i*); those nearer the centre of the girdle, away from the valves, are much simpler.

The cell wall of centric diatoms

The structure of the valve, and frequently its outline too, is basically radially symmetrical (Figs. 9.1*h*, 9.12*k*, 9.13*b*), the frustules often resembling a petri dish. There are many exceptions, however, that depart from this simple idealized shape (Fig. 9.12*l, m, q–w*). As in pennate diatoms, the shells are ornamented with species-specific patterns and structures. In many centric diatoms the valves contain radial rows of small, more-or-less hexagonal chambers, called 'loculate areolae'. Each chamber (loculus) has an outer wall and an inner wall, and it is usual that one of these is perforated by a large round hole (foramen) while the other contain a delicate porous plate, sometimes called a 'sieve plate' (cribrum; Figs. 9.1*h*, 9.5*a–e*, 9.12*k*). No centric diatom ever has a raphe system (see below).

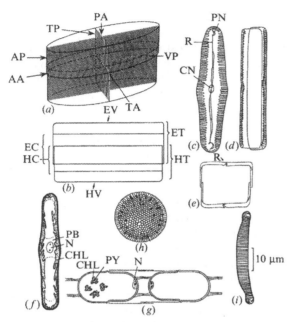

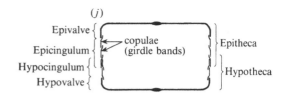

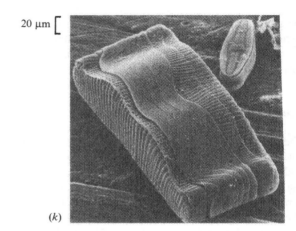

Figure 9.1. (*a, b*) Plan of the cell in a pennate diatom. (*c–e*) *Pinnularia viridis* (*c* valve view; *d* girdle view; *e* cross section, in the transapical plane). (*f*) *Pinnularia.* (*g, h*) *Stephanopyxis turris* (*g* girdle view; *h* valve view). (*i*) *Eunotia arcus.* (*j*) Diagrammatic cross section through the frustule of a diatom, showing how each half of the girdle (cingulum) is composed of several girdle bands (copulae). (*k*) Scanning electron micrograph of *Eunotia*, showing the girdle bands. AA = apical axis;

AP = apical plane; CHL = chloroplast; CN = central nodule; EC = epicingulum; ET = epitheca; EV = epivalve; HC = hypocingulum; HT = hypotheca; HV = hypovalve; N = nucleus; PA = pervalvar axis; PB = protoplasmic bridge; PN = polar nodule; PY = pyrenoid; R = raphe; TA = transapical axis; TP = transapical plane; VP = valvar plane. (*j* based on [1427]; *k* from [1532], with the permission of the authors and Cambridge University Press.)

The raphe and rimoportula (labiate process)

In many pennate diatoms the valve is pierced by a longitudinal slit, usually lying along the apical plane, which is called the raphe (Figs. 9.1*c, e,* 9.10*a, b, e, m*). In cross section, the raphe is sometimes shaped like a V lying on its side (i.e. <) and so, because the raphe slit is particularly narrow at the point of the V, it may be said to consist of an inner and an outer fissure. A raphe of this type is found for instance in *Pinnularia* (Fig. 9.1*e*). At the centre of the valve, the raphe is interrupted by a thickening, called the central nodule; at the

ends of the valve there can be similar thickenings, called polar nodules.

The raphe is somewhat differently constructed in *Nitzschia* and *Surirella*, since here the slits are subtended internally by small siliceous bridges (fibulae), which link the two sides of the valve. As a result, a canal is formed beneath the raphe, which connects with the remainder of the interior of the cell via regularly spaced openings between the fibulae (Fig. 9.12*f*). This type of raphe system is often called a canal raphe and generally lies, not along the apical plane, but near the edge of the valve. The fibulae are usually much more obvious than the raphe slits, so that the canal raphe is most easily detected in the light microscope as a line of bars or dots.

The raphe is involved in locomotion. Diatoms without raphes cannot move actively or, if they can, only sluggishly. Thus, the centric diatoms are largely non-motile, and so are those pennate diatoms that lack a raphe. Raphe-bearing (raphid) diatoms, on the other hand, are capable of rapid, autonomous gliding movements. In the light microscope they sail across the field of view like small ships. *Nitzschia palea*, for example, can achieve speeds of 8–10 μm s^{-1}, and the maximum speed for a diatom is around 20 μm s^{-1} ([791]).

If cells are placed in a dilute solution of Indian ink, ink particles can be seen gliding along the raphe, at speeds not unlike those of the whole cell when it is moving. In large cells, ink particles can sometimes be seen to move along parts of the raphe in the opposite direction from the motion of the cell. Hence it was originally suggested that diatom movement might be brought about by protoplasmic streaming within the raphe slit ([772]). It was thought that protoplasm could stream in one direction in the outer raphe fissure and in the opposite direction in the inner fissure. The two streams were suggested to connect with each other at the central and polar nodules. Friction between the moving protoplasm and the substratum would cause movement of the cell. Electron microscopical observations show, however, that there is no protoplasm in the raphe slits, and so another explanation of motility had to be found.

In another theory, it was suggested that movement involves the secretion of mucilage at the centre and poles ([348, 349]). The mucilage was supposed to stream along in the raphe in the opposite direction to the motion of the cell, and then to be left behind as a trail. The existence of trails can be demonstrated with ink, the ink particles becoming stuck to the slime left behind by the moving cells. It was not explained, however, how the mucilage is moved along the raphe in a particular direction.

Electron microscopical investigations have shown that several cytoplasmic structures are associated with the raphe system, including small vesicles with fibrous material inside, which has been shown to consist of polysaccharide, and bundles of 7 nm diameter microfilaments (Fig. 9.2*a*). According to one of the most recent theories of diatom locomotion, gliding movement is brought about as follows (Fig. 9.2*b–f*; [360]). The vesicles containing fibrous polysaccharide liberate polysaccharide fibrils into the inner raphe fissure by exocytosis, predominantly at the central and polar raphe endings. The polysaccharide fibrils hydrate, swelling and elongating as they do so, and project through the outer raphe fissure to the exterior (Fig. 9.2*b, c*). Here their protruding ends adhere to the substratum or to any other solid objects, such as ink particles. Rows of rod-like mucilaginous strands have been observed in the raphe slits ([360]) and are thought to be attached on the inside of the frustule to a somewhat invaginated part of the plasmalemma, adjacent to the raphe. This section of the plasmalemma is considered to flow along beneath the raphe, dragging along the fibrils of polysaccharide attached to it. Since the fibrils are attached at their distal ends to the substratum, the effect is a gliding motion of the diatom over the substratum, in the opposite direction to the flow of the plasmalemma. Small particles, on the other hand, will be moved along the cell in the same direction as the flow of the plasmalemma (Fig. 9.2*d–f*). The bundles of microfilaments, which consist of the protein actin, are believed to be responsible for generating the plasmalemma flow: actin filaments are involved in various kinds of movements, from muscle contraction to cytoplasmic streaming in the cells of such organisms as the green alga *Chara* (p. 475, Fig. 30.2) ([16]).

Mucilage production by the dense populations of raphid diatoms living on sand or mud flats can result in the formation of a mucilaginous skin or pellicle on the surface of the sediment, protecting it from erosion by waves and tidal scour ([718]).

In some raphid diatoms, the mucilage extruded through the raphe is used for attachment rather than movement. Thus, in the genus *Achnanthes* colonies of a few cells are attached to solid substrata by mucilage stalks (Fig. 9.10*q*). Elsewhere in the centric or pennate diatoms, the pads or stalks of mucilage produced for attachment are secreted through groups of special pores (ocelli), located at the poles of the cell. The mucilage is composed of complex polysaccharides ([284]).

Mucilage secretion has also been shown to occur through a special wall organelle called the rimoportula (labiate process), which is found in most centric and some pennate diatoms. Each rimoportula is a more or less elongate tube through the cell wall, which ends internally in a slit-like opening between two lips (hence the term 'labiate', which means lip-like; Fig. 9.14). Examples of rimoportulae include the paired spines on the valves of *Odontella* (Fig. 9.12*q–s*), the

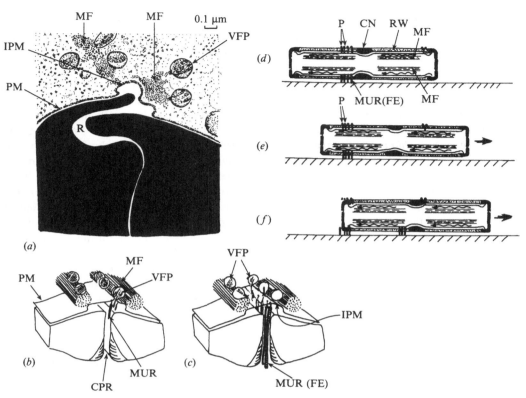

Figure 9.2. Gliding locomotion of pennate diatoms. (*a*) Cross section of the raphe and adjacent cytoplasm in *Navicula,* seen with the EM. (*b, c*) Two stages in the extrusion of polysaccharide fibrils into the raphe near the central pores of the raphe system; the fibrils are secreted from vesicles with fibrous polysaccharide contents. Upon secretion, the polysaccharide fibrils hydrate, swell and elongate, to form mucilaginous rods, which remain attached to the invaginated part of the plasmalemma but also emerge to the exterior through the outer raphe fissure. It is hypothesized that the rods can be moved along the raphe. (*d–f*) Gliding movement of a pennate diatom over a solid substra-tum (hatched), diagrammatic. The wavy arrows indicate the hypothetical flow of the invaginated part of the plasmalemma beneath the raphe; the thick arrows indicate the resulting motion of the cell. CN = central nodule; CPR = central pore of the raphe; IPM = invaginated portion of the plasmalemma beneath the raphe; MF = bundle of microfilaments (actin filaments) (seen in cross section in *a*); MUR = rod of mucilage; MUR(FE) = fully extended, hydrated rod of mucilage, emerging from the raphe; P = particle; PM = plasma membrane (plasmalemma); R = raphe; RW = wall of raphe; VFP = vesicle with fibrous polysaccharide contents. (Based on [360].)

processes that connect the cells of *Stephanopyxis* (Fig. 9.12*g–j*) and the single apical spine of *Rhizosolenia* (Fig. 9.12*n–p*). Recently, slow movements have been demonstrated in two centric diatoms and linked to the secretion of mucilage through rimoportulae. In *Odontella* (Fig. 9.12*q–t*) the cells exhibit irregular shuffling and rocking movements within the mucilaginous matrix produced by the colony ([1426]). The circular cells of *Actinocyclus*, on the other hand, show a slow rotation while moving laterally across the substratum ([1158]). It may be, therefore, that the raphe system evolved from one or more rimoportulae, the raphe representing the greatly extended slit of a rimoportula ([617, 1088b]). The fossil record is consistent with this: the centric diatoms, which have rimoportulae but no raphe, appear earlier (120 million years ago) than the pennate diatoms (70 million years ago).

Gliding locomotion is also to be found in the blue-green algae (division Cyanophyta; p. 29) and in the desmids (division Chlorophyta; p. 469).

Structure and formation of the cell wall
(1427)

The cell wall consists predominantly of polymerized silicic acid, which is amorphous, with no crystalline structure ([285, 996, 1833]). It also contains protein, polysaccharide and lipid ([260, 285, 827]), however, and so if the wall is treated with hydrofluoric acid to dissolve the silica, a thin organic 'ghost' wall is left behind. Each individual siliceous element of the cell wall – valve or girdle band – is formed within its own flattened vesicle (a 'silica deposition vesicle': Fig. 9.3a, d, e).

Directly after a cell has divided, two new valves are produced back-to-back, one in each daughter cell. In Fig. 9.3 the young valves can be seen within flat vesicles, just beneath the plasmalemma. The new elements of the girdle (the various parts of the hypocingulum) are formed later, in their own silica deposition vesicles (SDVs), when valve formation is more or less complete. The formation of SDVs is not well understood; in centric diatoms they appear to develop through the coalescence of vesicles, which may be derived from the golgi apparatus ([1569]).

After each element of the wall has been completed, the inner membrane of the SDV becomes the new plasmalemma. Remnants of cytoplasm external to the element may be left to form thin organic coatings (primary coatings) around the silica, while later a secondary organic wall may be added; this can be thick or thin, depending on the species. The secondary wall consists of complex sulphated polysaccharides, including sulphated glucuronomannan ([270, 1721, 1833]), and apparently functions as a matrix, keeping the various siliceous components of the wall in place ([1721]).

In those pennate diatoms that possess a raphe system, silica deposition begins in the area of the raphe, where a 'primary central band' of silica is deposited in a tubular SDV (Figs. 9.3d, 9.4a, 9.7). The tips of the primary band then curve back and grow towards 'secondary arms' that develop out from the centre (the young central nodule; Fig. 9.4b). The primary and secondary arms fuse, delimiting the two raphe slits (Fig. 9.4c). In the meantime, transapical ribs have begun to develop outwards from the axial ribs bordering the raphe (Fig. 9.4b, c) and these in turn develop rows of small lateral extensions, which fuse with each other to delimit the valve pores (Fig. 9.4d; [127, 360, 1427, 1833]). The

developing raphe system is accompanied by longitudinally aligned microtubules and 'raphe fibres', which are probably proteinaceous but whose function is unknown. The microtubules seem to be important for the proper positioning and integrity of the raphe: if their assembly is inhibited through the use of specific drugs, such as colchicine, the young raphe becomes disorganized ([361]).

The amorphous, non-crystalline silica of the diatom frustule does not assemble itself to form the orderly patterns that are so characteristic of this class of algae; morphogenesis involves cytoplasmic structures and biochemical processes. In some centric diatoms it seems that part at least of the pattern is 'impressed' onto the silica by orderly arrays of vesicles and organelles, kept together and in place through association with the plasmalemma: these act as a mould for the developing SDV. In the genus *Coscinodiscus* (Fig. 9.12k), the formation of the new valve begins with the assembly of small (30–40 nm diameter) vesicles in the central part of the prospective valve, immediately beneath the plasmalemma. The vesicles coalesce to form a centrifugally expanding network of tubular SDVs (Fig. 9.5a), but the course of expansion is constrained by the presence of regularly spaced large vesicles (the areolar vesicles: Fig. 9.5a, f) and seems also to be prefigured by ER cisternae, which lie above where the SDV will develop. The areolar vesicles occupy the positions that will later be occupied by hexagonal chambers ('loculate areolae') in the valve (Fig. 9.5c, h, i). They are bound to the plasmalemma by 'fibrous laminas' and hence the tubular extensions of the SDV cannot push through between the areolar vesicles and the plasmalemma, but can only grow by passing through the interstices between adjacent vesicles. They curve around them to form rings, which mark where the foramina (large holes) of the valve chambers will later be formed (Fig. 9.5a, d, e). Lateral coalescence of the reticulum of tubular SDVs creates the base plate, perforated by large foramina, upon which the system of hexagonal valve chambers (the loculate areolae) will be formed (Fig. 9.5c). At this stage the SDV, containing the base layer, begins to sink down into the cytoplasm and simultaneously vertical walls are built on top of the base plate. The areolar vesicles remain attached to the plasmalemma by their fibrous laminas and, together with ER vesicles that congregate around them, apparently form a mould for the SDV as the vertical walls are deposited, pro-

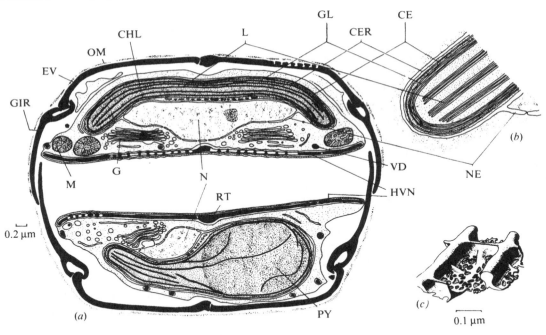

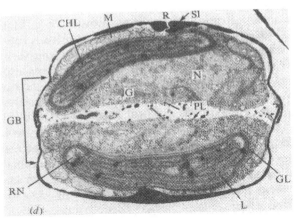

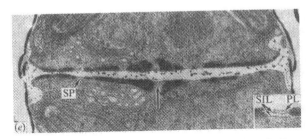

Figure 9.3. (*a, b*) *Amphipleura pellucida,* from EM observations. (*a* cross section through a cell directly after division; *b* part of the chloroplast). (*c*) *Surirella gemma:* one of the pores that make up the transapical striations (striae) of the valve. (*d, e*) Electron micrographs showing cross sections through *Navicula pelliculosa* during valve formation. (*d*) Shortly after cytokinesis: the new valves have been initiated in the two young daughter cells and are present as a primary central band (cf. Fig. 9.4) within a minute silica deposition vesicle (arrows). (*e*) Late stage of valve formation, in which the silica deposition vesicle is almost complete. Note the continuity of the silica deposition vesicle across the raphe (arrow) and the formation of a sieve plate (see also higher magnification inset). CE = chloroplast envelope; CER = chloroplast endoplasmic reticulum;

CHL = chloroplast; EV = epivalve of parent cell; G = golgi body; GB = girdle bands; GIR = girdle; GL = girdle lamella; HVN = hypovalve of daughter cell, developing within a silica deposition vesicle (silica is shown black); L = lamella, composed of a stack of three thylakoids; M = mitochondrion; N = nucleus; NE = nuclear envelope; OM = organic material surrounding the exterior of the silica frustule; PL = plasma membrane (plasmalemma); PY = pyrenoid; R = raphe slit; RN = ring-shaped nucleoid of chloroplast, in cross section; RT = thickening of the valve, containing the raphe slit; SI = silica frustule; SIL = silicalemma (the membrane around the silica deposition vesicle); SP = sieve plate; VD = vesicle with dark contents. (*a, b* after [1707]; *c* after [440]; *d, e* from [226a], with permission from the authors and Springer-Verlag, Vienna.)

ducing a system of open-topped hexagonal chambers (Fig. 9.5c). SDV growth continues to be fed by the addition of small vesicles, perhaps derived from the golgi apparatus. Next the areolar vesicles detach from the plasmalemma and the SDV extends across to form the outer wall of the hexagonal chambers; ER vesicles apparently prefigure the positions where pores are to be left. Finally, the outer pores are themselves filled with a very delicate, fine latticework (a 'sieve plate'), with tiny holes allowing communication between cell and environment (Fig. 9.5e). A new plasmalemma is formed inside the new valve from the inner part of the SDV. Then a delicate organic wall is secreted by the plasmalemma against the inner side of the new valve (Fig. 9.5i) ([1569]).

Cell division and mitosis

Diatom cells always divide in the valvar plane (Figs. 9.1a, 9.3a, 9.10c). Before division the cell contents swell, forcing the epitheca and hypotheca apart, though never so far that the protoplast is exposed. Mitosis then takes place, followed by the division of the protoplast and, immediately after this, the formation of new wall elements in each daughter cell (Fig. 9.10c).

The newly synthesized half of the cell wall in each daughter cell is always a hypotheca; the theca inherited from the parent cell always forms the epitheca, regardless of whether it was previously an epitheca or a hypotheca. The effect of this unique type of division is usually that one daughter cell is the same size as the parent cell, while the other is smaller: it is shorter and narrower by about twice the thickness of the girdle. Thus, because at each division half the daughter cells are smaller than their parents, average cell size in a diatom population decreases with each successive round of cell division. This process is illustrated in Fig. 9.10d.

Not all species get smaller during division. Some have a fairly elastic girdle and these can maintain their size.

The mean size of the cells in a population clearly cannot go on decreasing indefinitely. In the end the cells reach a minimal size and then form **auxospores**, through which the diminution is reversed: the auxospore expands and gives rise to a very much enlarged cell, which then recommences cell division and size diminution. The formation of the auxospore is almost always linked to sexual reproduction and this, together with other facets of the life cycle in pennate and centric diatoms, is discussed further on pp. 148, 152. Auxospores are produced before the cells reach the absolute minimum viable size: the tiniest cells become unable to form auxospores and continue to divide vegetatively until they die.

Mitosis in the diatoms is open, which means that the nuclear envelope breaks down during division (Fig. 9.6c–e); the telophase spindle is persistent. During interphase a small, darkly staining body can often be seen with the electron microscope, embedded in the surface of the nucleus. This is the 'microtubule centre' and numerous microtubules radiate out from it over the nuclear surface (Fig. 9.6a). In early prophase the nucleus and microtubule centre move to one side of the cell and come to lie just beneath the girdle, in the valvar plane (Fig. 9.6a). The spindle begins to be formed near the microtubule centre, outside the nuclear envelope, which is still intact at this stage (Fig. 9.6b). The spindle microtubules are formed between two darkly staining plates, the polar plates, and as the spindle develops the microtubule centre disappears. During late prophase the nuclear envelope disperses and the spindle sinks down into the nucleoplasm, continuing to elongate as it does so. At metaphase the spindle generally takes the form of a dense central cylinder of microtubules, stretched between the two polar plates, together with a few peripheral microtubules radiating out into the nucleoplasm, to which the chromosomes become attached as the spindle enters the nucleus at prometaphase. Closer inspection reveals that the dense 'central spindle' consists of two overlapping, interdigitating half spindles, each one associated with one pole (Fig. 9.6c). During anaphase the spindle elongates, this being brought about partly by the sliding apart of the half spindles, through forces generated in the region of overlap, and partly by growth of the spindle microtubules at the spindle equator (Fig. 9.6d, e). Spindle elongation is thought to occur in a similar way elsewhere, through the sliding apart of two half spindles, and this may be a general feature of eukaryote mitosis ([16]). If so, interzonal spindle microtubules must always form two overlapping half spindles, which are scarcely detectable in many organisms but easily observed in diatoms ([1421, 1429]).

After cytokinesis, which takes place in the valvar plane, each daughter nucleus acquires a new microtubule centre (Fig. 9.7), and the daughter nuclei generally then move from their lateral positions by the

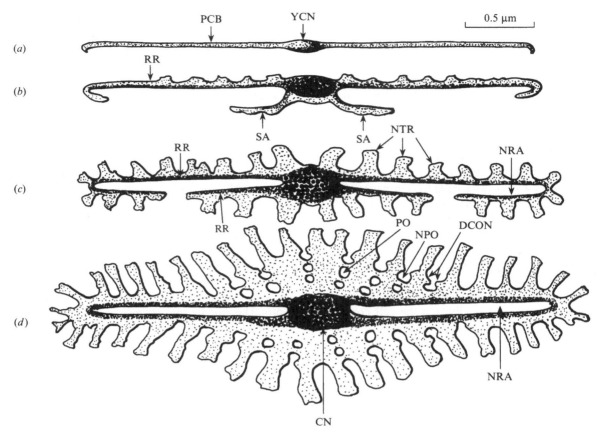

Figure 9.4. Development of the young valve in *Navicula*. (*a*)
First stage: the primary central band and the rudimentary central nodule have been formed. (*b*) Second
stage: extension of secondary arms out from the centre
of the primary band and recurving of the primary band
at the poles. (*c*) Third stage: the extensions of the primary central band are approaching the secondary arms.
Ultimately these fuse to complete the raphe rib and
enclose the raphe slits. Note the nascent transapical
ribs. (*d*) Fourth stage: the young transapical ribs extend
out laterally, forming cross connections that delimit the
pores (areolae) of the valve. Delicate sieve plates are
then formed across the pores. CN = central nodule;
DCON = developing connections between the
transapical ribs; NPO = nascent pore; NRA = nascent
raphe; NTR = nascent transapical rib; PCB = primary
central band; PO = pore (areola); RR = raphe rib; SA =
secondary arm; YCN = young central nodule. (Based
on [1833].)

girdle to the centre of the cell, beneath the cleavage
furrow. Each microtubule centre migrates around its
nucleus and becomes positioned close to the silica
deposition vesicle, which is already present in the centre of the cell, beneath the plasmalemma (Fig. 9.7:
here a tubular SDV is seen in section). In pennate
diatoms microtubules from the microtubule centre
become aligned along the young tubular SDV and are
probably involved in maintaining its position and
integrity (see p. 141): the 'primary central band' is
deposited within the SDV as the first stage in the formation of a new valve (Fig. 9.4*a*; [127]).

Pigments and chloroplasts

Diatoms are brown in colour; this results from the
presence of the accessory pigment fucoxanthin,
located in the chloroplasts. The Chrysophyceae and
Phaeophyceae are also coloured brown by fucoxanthin. Diatoms also possess other xanthophylls (neofucoxanthin, diadinoxanthin and diatoxanthin; see Table
1.2). Of the chlorophylls, chlorophylls a and c_2 seem
to be present throughout and there may also be either
chlorophyll c_1 or chlorophyll c_3 ([793, 1689]); chlorophyll b
is never found in diatoms.

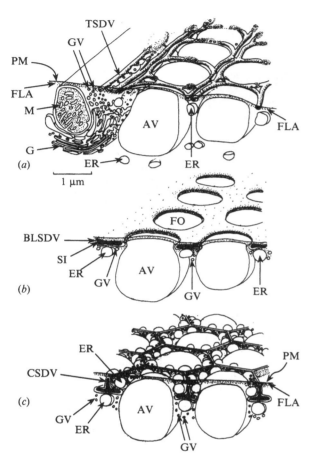

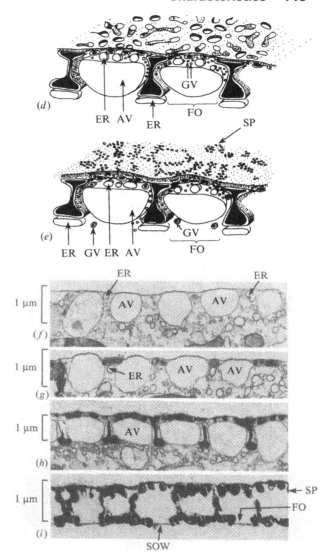

Figure 9.5. Development of the young valve in the centric diatom *Coscinodiscus*. (a) Tubular silica deposition vesicles (TSDVs) forming a net-like system in the interstices between various organelles (areola vesicles, ER vesicles, mitochondria) lying immediately beneath the plasmalemma. (b) The net-like SDV system has coalesced to form the base layer SDV (BLSDV) of the valve. (c) The base layer SDV has sunk into the cytoplasm and the side walls of the chambers begin to form on its upper (outer) side. Note that the areola vesicles ascend through the foramina and that the ER vesicles congregate around them, beneath the plasmalemma, thus apparently forming a mould for the parts of the SDV involved in assembling the side walls of the chambers. (d, e) Formation of the outer layer of the valve, including the sieve plates (cribra). (f–i) Transmission electron micrographs showing sections through valves at various stages of formation. (f) Immediately before the formation of the tubular extensions of the SDV (cf. (a)). (g) See (b). (h) See (d). (i) Completed valve, after the stage illustrated in (e); note the presence of a delicate secondary organic wall outside the plasmalemma, beneath the silica shell. AV = areola vesicle; BLSDV = the part of the SDV involved in the formation of the base layer of the valve; CSDV = parts of the SDV involved in assembling the side walls of the chambers; ER = endoplasmic reticulum; FLA = fibrous lamina; FO = foramen; G = golgi body; GV = golgi vesicles; M = mitochondrion; PM = plasmalemma; SI = silica; SOW = secondary organic wall; SP = sieve plate; TSDV = tubular parts of the SDV. (a–e based on [1984, 1987]; f–i from [1568a], with the permission of the author.)

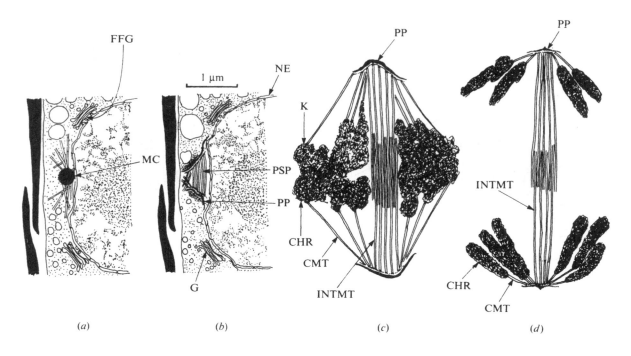

(a)   *(b)*   *(c)*   *(d)*

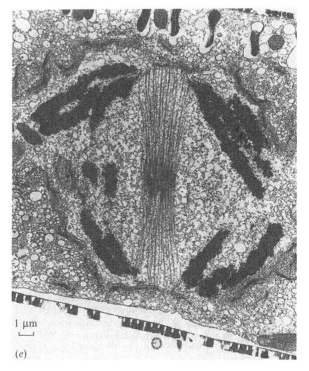

Figure 9.6. (*a–d*) Mitosis in a pennate diatom: drawings made from electron micrographs of sections taken approximately in the transapical plane (see Fig. 9.1*a*). (*a*) Interphase, just before prophase: the nucleus has moved to a position just beneath the girdle. Note the conspicuous microtubule centre, from which numerous microtubules radiate out over the surface of the nucleus. (*b*) Prophase: the early prophase spindle forms between two polar plates. As the spindle develops, the microtubule centre disintegrates and disappears; the nuclear envelope is still intact at this stage. (*c*) The metaphase spindle: note the central region of overlap between the two half spindles of interzonal microtubules. The nuclear envelope has now broken down. (*d*) The anaphase spindle: the chromatids have reached the spindle poles. The overlap between the half spindles has diminished during elongation of the spindle. (*e*) Transmission electron micrograph of a late anaphase spindle. For interpretation, see the legend to (*d*). CHR = chromatid; CMT = chromosomal spindle microtubule; FFG = forming face of golgi body; G = golgi body; INTMT = interzonal spindle microtubule; K = kinetochore; MC = microtubule centre; NE = nuclear envelope; O = overlap between the two half spindles of interzonal microtubules; PP = polar plate; PSP = prophase spindle. (*a–d* based on [127, 1429]; *e* from [1429], with permission from the authors, the editor of *Eur. J. Cell Biol.* and the Wissenschaftliche Verlagsgesellschaft, Stuttgart.)

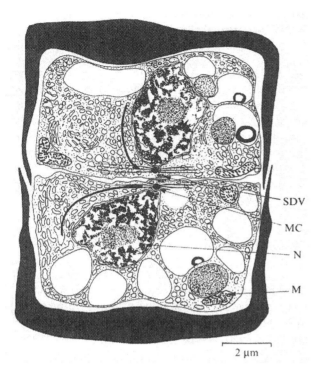

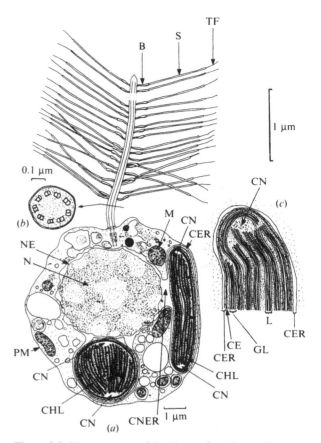

Figure 9.7. Pair of young daughter cells of a pennate diatom, just after cytokinesis: EM section in the transapical plane (see Fig. 9.1a). Each daughter cell has obtained a new interphase microtubule centre (MC), which has become placed close to the new tubular silica deposition vesicle. The two thick arrows indicate the movements of the MCs around the nuclei. M = mitochondrion; MC = microtubule centre; N = nucleus; SDV = silica deposition vesicle. (Based on [127].)

Figure 9.8. Ultrastructure of the diatom flagellate cell: the male gamete of centric diatoms. (a) Longitudinal section through whole cell. (b) Cross section through the flagellum; note the absence of the central pair of microtubules in the axoneme. (c) Detail of the chloroplast. B = base of mastigoneme; CE = chloroplast envelope; CER = chloroplast endoplasmic reticulum; CHL = chloroplast; CN = ring-like chloroplast nucleoid, seen in cross section; CNER = ER forming part of both the chloroplast ER and the nuclear envelope; GL = girdle lamella; L = lamella, composed of a stack of three thylakoids; M = mitochondrion; N = nucleus; NE = nuclear envelope; PM = plasma membrane (plasmalemma); S = tubular shaft of mastigoneme; TF = terminal fibre of mastigoneme. (Based on [1114].)

All the pigments mentioned lie in the chloroplasts. Many pennate diatoms have two large, plate-like chloroplasts, which are parietal and often lobed (Fig. 9.1f). Centric diatoms, on the other hand, generally have large numbers of small discoid chloroplasts (Fig. 9.1g); these too are often lobed. Each chloroplast contains one to several pyrenoids, which can be central within the chloroplast or lie on its inner side, sometimes projecting into the cell lumen (Figs. 9.1g, 9.3a bottom right).

The chloroplasts have the same ultrastructure as in other, typical members of the Heterokontophyta (Figs. 9.3, 9.8; [1707]). Thus, the thylakoids are grouped into stacks (lamellae) of three, and a girdle lamella is present beneath the chloroplast envelope, enclosing all the other lamellae. The chloroplast contains a ring-shaped nucleoid (Figs. 9.3d, 9.8; [254]), and is surrounded by a fold of endoplasmic reticulum as well as its own two membranes. The chloroplasts often lie close to the nucleus and in this case the chloroplast ER is continuous with the nuclear envelope.

A pyrenoid is shown in section in the lower daughter cell of the pair shown in Fig. 9.3*a*. The pyrenoid contents stain rather darker than the rest of the chloroplast. Some lamellae extend into, and indeed run through the pyrenoid, but within the pyrenoid they consist of only two thylakoids, not three as elsewhere.

Other cell organelles

As well as chloroplasts, diatoms cells also contain a nucleus, mitochondria, golgi apparatus, endoplasmic reticulum, ribosomes and vacuoles: all the organelles characteristic of eukaryote cells (Figs. 9.1*f, g,* 9.3). The nucleus often lies in the centre of the cell, in a bridge of cytoplasm (Fig. 9.1*f*), and is surrounded by a number of perinuclear golgi bodies (dictyosomes; Figs. 9.3*a, d, e,* 9.6*a, b*). These may play a part in the formation of the silica deposition vesicle following cell division (see p. 141). The nuclear envelope can be continuous with the chloroplast endoplasmic reticulum (Figs. 9.3*a, d,* 9.8*a*).

Storage products

The most important reserve material is chrysolaminaran, a β-1,3-linked glucan ([1520]), which is stored in solution in special vacuoles. Chrysolaminaran is also the most important storage product in the Chrysophyceae and Phaeophyceae (Table 1.3). Diatom cells often also accumulate lipid.

Zoids

Motile flagellate cells occur in the life cycles of some centric diatoms, but only in the form of the male gametes (spermatozoids). Each spermatozoid is egg-shaped and bears one pleuronematic (tinsel) flagellum (Fig. 9.8*a*). The ultrastructure of the flagellum has been investigated electron microscopically in two species, *Lithodesmium undulatum* and *Pleurosira* (= *Biddulphia*) *laevis,* and in both there are deviations from the normal '9 + 2' pattern of tubules within the axoneme. The two central tubules are absent, leaving only the nine peripheral doublets (Fig. 9.8*b*; [630, 1114]). A further peculiarity is that the basal bodies consist of nine doublets, not nine triplets. As in other members of the Heterokontophyta, however, the mastigonemes of the flagellum are formed within cisternae of the endoplasmic reticulum or in the nuclear envelope ([630]).

Classification within the Bacillariophyceae

The class Bacillariophyceae is subdivided into two groups, which are recognized here as two orders – the Pennales and the Centrales – although a recent account of the diatoms recognizes many more classes and orders ([1531, 1532]): there the diatoms (as the division Bacillariophyta) are subdivided into three classes, the Fragilariophyceae (pennate diatoms without a raphe system), the Bacillariophyceae (pennate diatoms with a raphe system) and the Coscinodiscophyceae (the centric diatoms).

Order Pennales

Here the cells are elongate in valve view. The valves may be linear, lanceolate or oval, and they usually bear a bilaterally symmetrical pattern of ornamentation. The pattern consists of transverse lines, set at right angles to a longitudinal axis. In the light microscope the lines (striae) can often be resolved into rows of dots, each representing a hole through the siliceous framework of the valve. In some of the Pennales there is a raphe along the longitudinal axis, in the plane of symmetry. There are many forms that have straight, bilaterally symmetrical valves (Figs. 9.1*a, c,* 9.10*a, e, g,* 9.13*a*), but there are others in which the valves are bent or curved (e.g. Fig. 9.10*m*). In *Nitzschia* species the raphe is not central but lies to one side of the valve, raised on a keel, and it is subtended by small siliceous bridges (fibulae; Fig. 9.12*a–f*). In still other forms the valves are broader at one pole than at the other.

As far as is known, every sexually reproducing member of the Pennales is a diplont. The diploid vegetative cells undergo meiosis and produce morphologically similar, haploid gametes, which are non-flagellate. These isogametes fuse to produce a zygote, which in turn gives rise to, or rather turns into, an auxospore.

The life cycle of the pennate diatom Eunotia arcus (Fig. 9.9)

In valve view *Eunotia* species are bent, the convex side being referred to as the dorsal side and the concave side as the ventral (Fig. 9.1*i, k*). In girdle view, on the other hand, the cells are rectangular (Figs. 9.1*k,* 9.9). At the poles of the valves there are short, rudi-

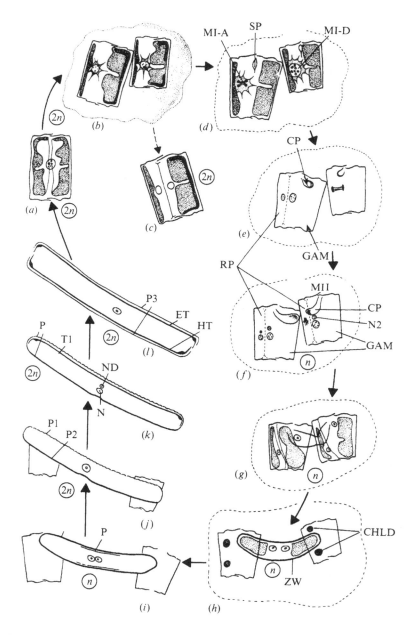

Figure 9.9. The life cycle of *Eunotia arcus* (for explanation, see the text). CHLD = degenerating chloroplast; CP = conjugation papilla; ET = epitheca; GAM = gamete; HT = hypotheca; MI-A = anaphase of meiosis I; MI-D = diakinesis of meiosis I; MII = meiosis II; N = nucleus; ND = degenerating nucleus; N2 = degenerating second gametic nucleus; P = perizonium; P1 = perizonium composed of transverse bands; P2 = strongly silicified section of perizonium; P3 = perizonium being discarded; RP = residual protoplast; SP = split in wall; T1 = first (initial) theca produced within the expanded auxospore; ZW = zygote wall; n = haploid; $2n$ = diploid. (After [501].)

mentary raphes, located on the ventral side and these, together with the shape of the valve and the fact that the transverse striations appear to run unbroken from one side of the valve to the other, are diagnostic of the genus. *Eunotia arcus* has cells that can be anything between 13.5 and 95 µm in length. They live in freshwater, surrounded by a layer of mucilage, and grow attached to rocks or plants; the concave sides of the cells lie pressed against the substratum.

The process of conjugation and auxospore formation is very complex and the different phases follow on directly, one after the other. In Fig. 9.9, the process is represented as if all the stages had been observed in a single pair of copulating cells. In fact, however, the scheme summarizes numerous observations made on many different pairs ([501]). The investigations were carried out on natural populations of *Eunotia arcus*, growing on the transparent leaves of the submerged water plant *Hippuris*. Sexual reproduction is difficult to study in culture because diatoms in these stages of the life cycle are very sensitive to unfavourable environmental conditions. Material from the natural habitat always contains many aborted gametes and zygotes.

The following stages can be distinguished (refer to Fig. 9.9).

a Cells become potentially sexual when they are 15–45 µm long, following a phase of size diminution through repeated vegetative cell division. If they fail to find a partner, they continue to divide vegetatively.

b If two partners encounter each other they move so as to lie as close together as possible, their ventral sides remaining appressed to the substratum. They then surround themselves with a common envelope of mucilage. Changes are also induced in the internal structure of the cells, perhaps stimulated by contact between them. The chloroplast lying in the hypotheca swells, while the chloroplast in the epitheca shrinks. At the same time the nucleus shifts slightly towards the epitheca. Because of the variation in cell size within a natural population, the two partners often differ in size, but even so sexual reproduction is basically isogamous.

c At this stage, one of the partners occasionally divides vegetatively, producing two unequal daughter cells; this, however, is exceptional.

d The first meiotic division now takes place in each partner. The accompanying cell division is unequal, the daughter cell lying towards the parental hypotheca receiving a large nucleus and a large chloroplast in a large protoplast, while the daughter cell lying in the parental epitheca is smaller, with a correspondingly small nucleus and chloroplast. The smaller daughter cell, the so-called residual protoplast, plays no part in subsequent events and aborts. At the same time the hypotheca and epitheca separate a little, both at one pole and also on the ventral side. A crack is thus formed in the siliceous exoskeleton, through which a copulation papilla is extruded.

e In the pair illustrated the left-hand partner has divided into two unequal protoplasts, following meiosis I, and the smaller protoplast (the residual protoplast) is already beginning to degenerate. The right-hand partner is still at telophase of meiosis I. The copulation papillae grow out through the gaps formed in the frustule and grow towards each other; this takes place on the ventral side of the copulating cells.

f Meiosis II is now complete in all cells, so that each of the residual protoplasts and the larger protoplasts contains two haploid nuclei. In each of the larger protoplasts one of the two nuclei degenerates, so that a large, uninucleate, haploid gamete is produced. The copulation papillae continue to grow towards each other.

g The copulation papillae have now fused to form a conjugation canal. The gametes migrate into the canal and fuse. The nucleus of each gamete enters the canal first and the rest of the protoplast, including the chloroplast, follows. During passage through the narrow entrance to the copulation canal, the chloroplasts and nuclei become strongly constricted and distorted. The whole process described in this paragraph takes one to two days.

h The binucleate zygote has been formed and is surrounded by a wall. The residual protoplasts have been left behind in the frustules of the two gametangia and have by now largely degenerated, although two brown spheres, representing the remains of the chloroplast, may remain visible in each gametangium for some time.

i The zygote, still binucleate, swells up into an auxospore. Within the zygote wall, a silicified auxospore wall or **perizonium** is formed centrifugally, new parts being added at each end as the auxospore carries out its bipolar expansion. The perizonium is more heavily silicified on one side (the convex side) and consists of transverse bands or rings of silica ([455, 1722]).

j The auxospore is fully grown. The zygote wall disappears and karyogamy occurs, restoring diploidy.

k The first theca (the initial epitheca) is laid down within the perizonium, on the side opposite the more strongly silicified part of the perizonium. The formation of the initial epitheca is preceded by a mitosis, following which one nucleus degenerates (becoming pyknotic). The formation of the second theca (the initial hypotheca) is also accompanied by a mitosis and again one nucleus survives and the other degenerates. Indeed, it is a common feature of all diatoms that the formation of each theca is preceded by a mitosis.

l The second theca has been formed, producing the first large cell of the new generation. This cell later divides and then, as further divisions take place, the average size of the cells gradually decreases. Eventually, some cells will again reach the size when they become potentially sexual again, and so the life cycle is complete.

The life cycle can therefore be summarized as follows: diploid vegetative cells of a certain size undergo reduction divisions (meiosis), leading to the formation in each of a single haploid gamete. Isogamous copulation takes place between two haploid gametes, producing a diploid zygote. The zygote (the auxospore) swells and then, when it has enlarged fully, a new vegetative cell is formed within it.

The life cycles of other pennate diatoms are essentially similar. In some genera, however, there is no conjugation tube, and sometimes two gametes are formed in each gametangium, not one ([333, 1532]). The reproduction of pennate diatoms was studied for many years by the great Austrian botanist L. Geitler ([499, 502, 503a]).

Examples of pennate diatoms (Pennales)

The following species should illustrate the diversity of form present in the order Pennales.

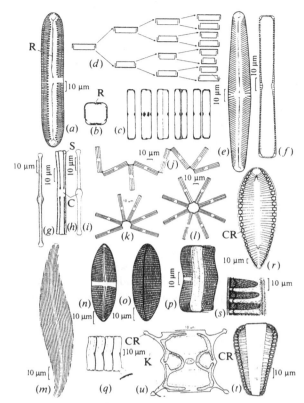

Figure 9.10. (*a–d*) *Pinnularia*: cell structure, cell division and the decrease in cell size during vegetative multiplication. (*e, f*) *Navicula oblonga*: valve view and girdle view. (*g–l*) *Tabellaria fenestrata* (*g* valve view; *h* girdle view; *i* copula (girdle band) with septum; *j–l* various colony forms). (*m*) *Gyrosigma littorale*. (*n–q*) *Achnanthes brevipes* (*n* valve with raphe; *o* valve with pseudoraphe; *p* girdle view; *q* colony attached to the substratum by a mucilage stalk). (*r–u*) *Surirella capronii* (*r* valve view; *s* detail of the valve, in valve view; *t* girdle view; *u* cross section through the cell). C = copula (girdle band); CR = canal raphe; K = keel; R = raphe; S = septum. (*a–d* from [231]; *e–t* from [1867].)

Navicula oblonga (Fig. 9.10*e, f*)

The genus *Navicula* is distinguished from the similar genus *Pinnularia* by its more delicate transverse (transapical) striae, which often appear as lines of small dots when viewed with the light microscope. Both genera have three planes of symmetry, namely the apical, transapical and valvar planes (see Figs. 9.1*a*, 9.10*e, f*), and they have a raphe on both valves. *Navicula*, as it has traditionally been defined, is an enormous genus, with well over 1000 species. It has recently been realized, however, that it is a very unnatural group, and it has therefore been split into several smaller, unrelated genera ([1532]). *Navicula oblonga* is widely distributed in nutrient-rich (eutrophic) fresh and brackish waters.

Gyrosigma litorale (Fig. 9.10m)

In this species the valve is sigmoid (S-shaped), so that the cell is symmetrical only about the valvar plane. The valve is ornamented with longitudinal and transverse striae, which cross each other at right angles. Both valves bear a raphe. *Gyrosigma litorale* is found around the coasts of the North Sea and neighbouring waters.

Pennate diatoms that have a raphe on only one of the valves have traditionally been classified in the suborder Monoraphidineae, species with raphes on both valves in the suborder Biraphidineae. *Pinnularia*, *Navicula* and *Gyrosigma* are therefore classified in the second group.

Achnanthes brevipes (Fig. 9.10n–q)

The elongate elliptical cells of this species have a raphe on one valve but not on the other, and so belong traditionally to the suborder Monoraphidineae. In girdle view the cells are bent, the raphe-bearing valve being slightly concave and the raphe-less valve slightly convex. Several cells may be linked to form a colony, which is attached to a solid substratum by a mucilage stalk. *Achnanthes brevipes* is common on sea coasts.

Tabellaria fenestrata (Fig. 9.10g–l)

Since neither of the valves of *Tabellaria* bears a raphe, this genus is traditionally classified in the suborder Araphidineae. In valve view the cells are linear, with swellings at the centre and both poles, while in girdle view they are rectangular. Some of the girdle bands bear septa. The cells are united into stellate or zigzag colonies by small pads of mucilage secreted from the ends of the valves. *Tabellaria fenestrata* is widely distributed in fairly nutrient-rich freshwaters.

Nitzschia linearis (Fig. 9.12a–e)

In *Nitzschia* each valve bears a canal raphe (Fig. 9.12f), which lies to one side of the apical plane, raised on a ridge or keel (carina). The most obvious structures on the valve are the bar-like fibulae beneath the raphe (Fig. 9.12a), but there are also delicate transapical striae (Fig. 9.12b). *Nitzschia linearis* is a common species of nutrient-rich freshwaters. *Nitzschia* is a large genus, containing hundreds of species.

Surirella capronii (Fig. 9.10r–t)

The valves of *Surirella* also possess a canal raphe, but here the raphe runs around the whole circumference of the valve. It is often raised on a keel (Fig. 9.10u). The cells are egg-shaped in valve view and trapezoidal in girdle view. This species is frequently present in the mud at the bottom of nutrient-rich freshwater pools.

Order Centrales

The cells are circular (Figs. 9.12k, l, 9.13b, 9.14) to elliptical (Fig. 9.12s) in valve view, or even polygonal (Fig. 9.12u, v). The valves never have a raphe and their structure is radially organized about the centre. All the centric diatoms that reproduce sexually are oogamous diplonts. The vegetative cells undergo meiosis and give rise either to haploid egg cells or to haploid spermatozoids (male gametes, each with a single pleuronematic flagellum). The zygote produced by oogamy becomes an auxospore, as in the pennate diatoms.

The life cycle of the centric diatom Stephanopyxis turris (Figs. 9.1g, 9.11, 9.12g–j)

Fig. 9.11 illustrates the life cycle and sexual reproduction of this species. The cells are circular in valve view and are ornamented with an orderly pattern of polygonal markings. Each valve is domed and bears a crown of spines (Figs. 9.1g, 9.12g, h). The interphase cells of *Stephanopyxis* are linked in pairs by their overlapping epicingula; there are no hypocingula at this stage (Fig. 9.1g). The pairs of cells are also connected by the crowns of spines on their valves, and similar connections join them to other pairs, producing chains of cells. Cell shape varies greatly. In large cells the valves are shallow, whereas in small cells they are relatively deep and this compensates to some extent for the decrease in cell volume that would otherwise occur during the life cycle. *Stephanopyxis turris* is very common in the North Sea and in the Wadden Sea.

The life cycle of *Stephanopyxis turris*, as it is

described below, was worked out by von Stosch & Drebes ([1723]), who were able to observe several stages of the cycle in individual living specimens: in most diatoms the course of the life cycle and sexual reproduction has to be reconstructed from isolated observations of many different specimens (e.g. in *Eunotia arcus*). The life cycle of *Stephanopyxis turris* is thus especially well investigated. Von Stosch & Drebes were able to make their observations of living cultures by using a water immersion objective, which could be immersed directly in the culture medium. The stages they distinguished will be described in detail, in order to give an idea of the time course of events in the life cycle.

If we are to understand sexual reproduction properly, it is best to begin by considering the course of vegetative cell division. The nuclear and cell divisions that take place during the formation of the gametes are in many ways only modified vegetative divisions. Figure 9.11 shows the successive steps in the formation of the male gametes (the spermatozoids) (series A); the formation of the female gametes (the eggs) (series B); vegetative cell division (series C); the development of the auxospore (series D); and the formation of the resting spore (series E). Each series is shown in a vertical column, and the duration of the individual stages is indicated. The cultures of *Stephanopyxis turris* were kept in a light regime of 8 h dark (20.00 – 04.00) and 16 h light (04.00 – 20.00), a temperature of 15 °C, and a light intensity of 1600 lux. The numbering of the paragraphs in the following descriptions corresponds to that of the stages drawn in Fig. 9.11.

Vegetative cell division (Fig. 9.11C)

1 At daybreak, following a quiescent interphase period of 15–17 h, the cells begin to elongate.

2. The cells swell through an increase in turgor, the two halves of the silica box sliding apart as the cell grows. Extension growth continues until the cell is twice its initial length. In the meantime the nucleus has entered mitotic prophase and moved from its interphase position against the hypovalve to the middle of the cell (the cell equator). Here metaphase occurs and can be observed in the living cell. The extension growth performed by the cell during prophase is called the prophase extension growth, or prophase expansion.

3. During anaphase the turgor of the cell decreases sharply until finally a ring-shaped plasmolysis appears around the cell equator.

4. As the plasmolytic constriction develops further the cell is cleft in two. By now mitosis has reached telophase. The two daughter nuclei are still connected by the nuclear spindle, but this soon breaks. Stages 3 and 4 are very short and together last only about 7 min.

5. The two daughter protoplasts swell a little, because of a slight increase in turgor. As a result the new valves are inflated and hemispherical. This second swelling is called the post-telophase expansion and is much smaller than the prophase expansion.

6. The new halves of the silica shell (i.e. the hypothecae) now begin to be laid down beneath the new area of plasmalemma. The new valves are formed quickly. The first thin layer of the valve is already complete 5 min or so after cytokinesis, and after 10 min the polygonal mesh is visible. The last parts of the valve to be formed are the spines. One and a half hours after cytokinesis the new hypovalve is complete and the young cell enters a period of apparent inactivity before the next cell division (there are no obvious changes in cell structure).

As soon as a colony consists of 8, 16 or 32 cells, it breaks. When the cells have decreased in size to between 0.4 and 0.2 of their original, maximum diameter, they become potentially sexual, and will produce gametes if environmental conditions are suitable. The very smallest cells of *Stephanopyxis*, however, cannot be induced to form gametes and these tiny cells continue to divide and become smaller still, until they die. All of the potentially sexual cells can form either female or male gametes, but smaller cells usually produce male gametes, and larger cells usually produce female gametes. This size difference is shown in Fig. 9.11.

Formation of the male gametes (spermatozoids) (Fig. 9.11A)

Sexualized male cells perform two or three mitotic divisions in rapid succession. These occupy only as much time as one vegetative division, but the phases of each accelerated mitosis are nevertheless those of a

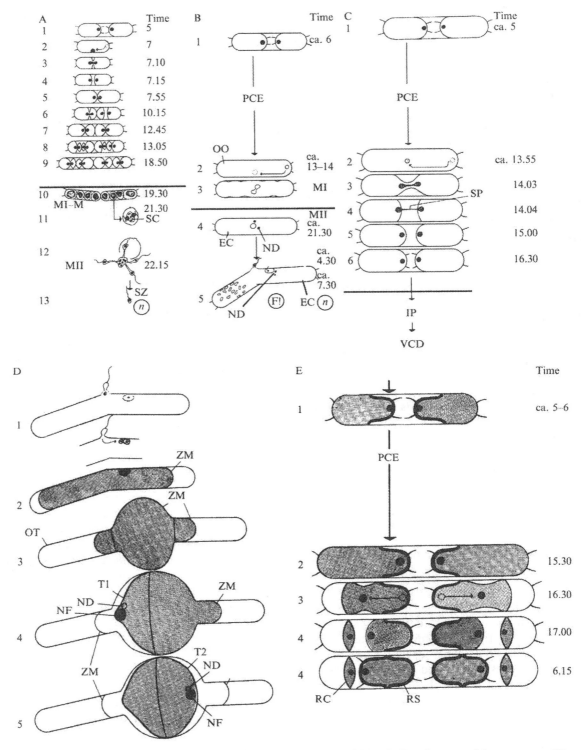

Figure 9.11. Life cycle of *Stephanopyxis turris* (for explanation, see text). (A) Formation of male gametes. (B) Formation of a female gamete. (C) Vegetative cell division. (D) Development of the auxospore. (E) Development of resting spores. EC = egg cell; F! = fertilization; IP = interphase of the following cell

normal mitosis. Male gamete formation is thus as follows:

1. The night-time quiescent period comes to an end.

2. The prophase expansion begins and the nucleus migrates to the equator of the cell.

3. The nucleus divides and at anaphase a ring-shaped plasmolysis begins to cleave the cell in two.

4. Cleavage of the cell is complete.

5. The two daughter cells swell through an increase in turgor (post-telophase expansion). Whereas vegetative cells would now enter interphase, the sexualized cells immediately begin a new round of division. This rapid, successive division of the male cell produces a row of small, short cells, which never develop into normal-sized cells because extension growth is suppressed. Nor do these cells have normal cell walls: the silica shells they form are incomplete and lack the crowns of spines characteristic of the vegetative cells.

6. Mitosis and cell division follow, producing four cells.

7. The post-telophase expansion takes place, as a result of an increase in turgor.

8. Another round of mitosis and cell division is now complete, producing eight cells.

9. Renewed swelling of the cells forces the two thecae of the original vegetative cell (1) apart, creating an opening through which the spermatozoids can later escape.
   Meiosis now begins. During the final post-telophase expansion the nuclei can be seen to be in prophase of meiosis I.

10. In meiosis I, just as in mitosis (compare C3), anaphase is associated with a drop in the turgor of the cell, which begins to plasmolyse. But in contrast to mitosis, the plasmolysis is not ring-shaped. Instead the protoplast becomes detached from the wall, rounds up and loses its vacuole. Each rounded protoplast contains two nuclei.

11. Four pleuronematic flagella are now produced, two for each nucleus.

12. Meiosis II takes place and each of the four haploid nuclei becomes associated with one of the four flagella. Each nucleus, together with its flagellum, is then cut off from the central mass of protoplasm, producing four spermatozoids and a residual protoplast containing the chloroplasts. The residual protoplast degenerates; the colourless spermatozoids, on the other hand, are now ready for fertilization.

Formation of the female gametes (egg cells) (Fig. 9.11B)

1. Following the night-time quiescent phase, the female sexualized cell begins the day by swelling. This extension growth resembles the prophase expansion of vegetative cells and takes roughly the same time. Development is not accelerated as in the male sexualized cells. As the female cell begins to expand its nucleus enters prophase of meiosis I.

2. During meiotic prophase and cell extension, the nucleus migrates from the hypovalve to the equator of the cell.

3. Anaphase of meiosis I can be observed in the living cell. As always, turgor falls during anaphase and becomes negative, so that the cell plasmolyses. Plasmolysis is not restricted to a ring-shaped furrow as in vegetative division (compare C3 and A4) but takes place over the whole surface of the cell, so that the protoplast retracts from the cell wall at various places. One of the two nuclei produced by meiosis I degenerates.

4. The remaining nucleus undergoes meiosis II and again one of the daughter nuclei degenerates.

Caption for fig. 9.11 *(cont.)*.

cycle, lasting a night (until 05.00 h); MI = meiosis I; MI-M = metaphase of meiosis I; MI-P = prophase of meiosis I; MII = following meiosis II; ND = degenerating nucleus; NF = functional nucleus; OO = oogonium; OT = theca of oogonium; PCE = prophase elongation of the cell; RC = degenerating residual cell; RS = resting spore; SC = spermatocyte; SP = spindle; SZ = spermatozoid; T1 = initial epitheca, the first theca formed by the expanded auxospore; T2 = initial hypotheca, the second theca formed by the expanded auxospore; VCD = vegetative cell division; ZM = zygote membrane. (After [1723].)

Thus a single egg cell is produced, containing one functional egg nucleus, which is of course haploid.

5 After a resting period of 5–8 h the egg cell begins to expand. The two halves of the silica wall slide apart and the cell bends in the middle, so that part of the protoplast is exposed as a small papilla. The egg cell is now ready for fertilization by a spermatozoid, which contacts the protoplasmic papilla via its posterior end.

Development of the auxospore from the fertilized egg cell (Fig. 9.11D)

1 Approximately 20 min after the sperm and egg have come into contact the sperm has injected its nucleus into the egg cell, and three minutes later the male and female nuclei lie appressed to each other.

2 After an hour the male and female nuclei have completely fused. This process can be followed in the living cell, something that has been done in very few other plants. Directly after karyogamy the protoplast of the zygote contracts, through loss of turgor, and then it surrounds itself with a polysaccharide wall, which also contains silica scales.

3 As a result of a marked increase in turgor, the zygote swells and this expansion is accommodated by a concomitant growth of the zygote wall. The expanding cell is called the auxospore. The swelling can also be interpreted as a prophase swelling (cf. C2), since at the same time the zygote nucleus enters mitotic prophase.

4 Anaphase of mitosis follows and, as during vegetative cell division (C3), this is accompanied by a decrease in turgor. However, whereas vegetative division is followed by cleavage, taking the form of a ring-shaped plasmolysis, the protoplast of the auxospore does not divide but instead pulls away from the zygote wall on one side. A new siliceous theca (the initial epitheca) is then formed on this side of the expanded auxospore, beneath the free surface of the protoplast. One of the daughter nuclei produced through mitosis degenerates.

5 The remaining, functional daughter nucleus now moves across to the other side of the auxospore and performs a second mitosis, after which the initial hypotheca is produced, in the same way as the initial epitheca. The first frustule of the new generation of vegetative cells is now complete. Just as in pennate diatoms, a mitosis is necessary for the formation of each theca.

The formation of the first much-enlarged cell of the life cycle – the initial cell – is thus the culmination of a very complicated series of events and processes.

Resting spores and their formation (Fig. 9.11E)

Resting spores are produced by relatively large cells, in response to nitrogen deficiency ([610]); they germinate in the light, when nutrient (N, P) concentrations increase ([610]). Resting spores are short cells with particularly thick cell walls, which differ in structure from the walls of vegetative cells. Each spore is produced following two successive mitotic divisions of a vegetative cell, and the various stages of spore formation correspond to the stages of normal cell division. We can take phase C4 (Fig. 9.11) as the starting point for resting spore formation and the next step is shown in E1.

1 After the post-telophase expansion of the protoplast, a special thickened valve is laid down in each daughter cell beneath the new, naked area of the plasmalemma.

2 Following the night-time quiescent phase the cell begins its prophase expansion.

3 The cell begins to retract from the epitheca through a decrease in turgor and at anaphase a ring-shaped plasmolysis occurs.

4 This leads to the division of the cell during telophase.

5 The second thickened valve is now produced beneath the new plasmalemma, thus completing the resting spore. The other cell produced by this division is small and non-functional. It soon degenerates.

The life cycle can be summarized as follows. A diploid vegetative cell, of a particular, characteristic size, produces a large number of haploid male gametes (spermatozoids), following a series of mitoses and finally a meiosis. A second diploid vegetative cell, again of a particular size, undergoes meiosis and produces one haploid egg cell. Through oogamy between

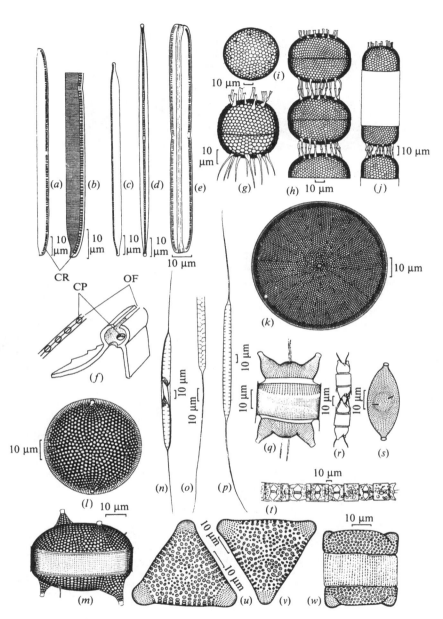

Figure 9.12. (*a–e*) *Nitzschia linearis* (*a* valve, as it normally lies on a slide; *b* detail of the valve; *c* theca viewed along the pervalvar axis; *d* theca seen from the keel; *e* girdle view). (*f*) diagrams showing the structure of a canal raphe. (*g–j*) *Stephanopyxis turris*. (*k*) *Coscinodiscus perforatus*. (*l, m*) *Cerataulus radiatus:* valve and girdle views. (*n–p*) *Rhizosolenia longiseta:* girdle view and cell division. (*q–t*) *Odontella aurita* (*q* broad girdle view; *r* narrow girdle view of two cells; *s* valve view; *t* chain of cells). (*u–w*) *Triceratium reticulatum:* valve and girdle views. CP = pores (carinal dots, 'Kielpunkte') connecting the cell lumen with the canal beneath the raphe; CR = canal raphe; FIB = fibulae (bridges of silica that separate the pores connecting the cell lumen with the canal beneath the raphe); OF = outer fissure of the raphe. (After [1867].)

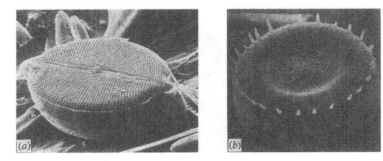

Figure 9.13. (a) *Mastogloia* species. (b) *Stephanodiscus*
astraea. (Scanning electron micrographs, F.E. Round.)

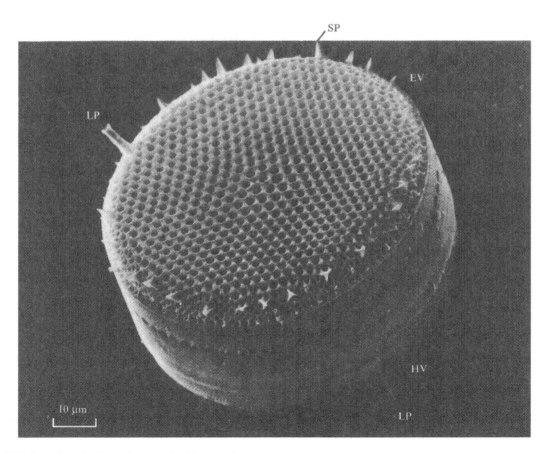

Figure 9.14. Scanning electron micrograph of the centric
diatom *Thalassiosira excentrica*. EV = epivalve;
GB = girdle bands; HV = hypovalve; LP = labiate
process (rimoportula); SP = spines. (From [1568a], with
permission.)

the egg cell and a spermatozoid, a diploid zygote arises, which swells into an auxospore. Later, once the auxospore is fully expanded, a new, enlarged vegetative cell is produced within it.

The other centric diatoms that have been investigated so far have proved to be very similar to *Stephanopyxis* in their sexual reproduction, but there is some variation. For instance, the number of egg cells formed by the female sexualized cell may be one or two; and spermatozoid formation is not always preceded by modified vegetative divisions producing dwarf cells as in *Stephanopyxis* ([333, 450, 1532, 1708, 1709, 1710, 1712, 1714, 1715, 1725]).

In several centric diatoms asexual cell enlargement is much more common than the enlargement of a sexually produced auxospore. In the common planktonic diatom *Skeletonema costatum*, for instance, the frustule splits open and the extruded protoplast swells, subsequently forming a new, enlarged frustule ([477]).

Examples of centric diatoms (Centrales)

The following examples have been chosen to illustrate morphological diversity within the centric diatoms.

Coscinodiscus perforatus (Fig. 9.12k)
The cells of this species have exactly the same shape as a petri dish. The valve bears a fairly regular pattern of areolae, each of these being a small chamber that opens to the outside by several tiny pores and to the inside by one large round hole. *Coscinodiscus perforatus* occurs in the plankton of the North Sea, but is rather uncommon.

Thalassiosira excentrica (Fig. 9.14)
The short cylindrical cells of *Thalassiosira excentrica* have flat circular valves with areolae arranged in arcs. Here the areolae are small chambers, which each open externally by a single large hole (foramen) and internally by several tiny pores; the structure is thus like that in *Coscinodiscus* but reversed. The valves bear a marginal whorl of spines and each has one tube-like

rimoportula (labiate process). This is a cosmopolitan marine species.

Stephanodiscus (Fig. 9.13b)
Here too the cell is shaped like a petri dish. The valve is ornamented with radial lines of dots (= pores) and around the edge it bears a crown of spines. This genus is widely distributed in the plankton of nutrient-rich freshwaters.

Cerataulus radiatus (Fig. 9.12l–m)
The valve is round and arched, and has two small conical horns near its margin. The girdle is short and cylindrical. This species is common in the littoral of the North Sea.

Triceratium reticulatum (Fig. 9.12u–w)
In valve view this alga has an equilateral triangular outline. The valves are ornamented with areolae of various sizes; the centre of the girdle is somewhat arched. *Triceratium reticulatum* occurs in estuaries and in the sea but is uncommon. Other species of the genus are widely distributed.

Odontella aurita (Fig. 9.12q–t)
The valves are elliptical and have an arched centre bearing two spines, which are rimoportulae (labiate processes). There are also two tapering horns, which project out diagonally. The girdle is cylindrical and can be short or long. The valve is ornamented with radial rows of areolae. This alga is very common in coastal regions.

Rhizosolenia longiseta (Fig. 9.12n–p)
Rhizosolenia cells have an extremely long girdle, which consists of a large number of bands or segments. The valve is small and shaped like the calyptra of a moss; it bears a spine. *Rhizosolenia longiseta* is a freshwater species, often found in the plankton of still or slowly flowing, nutrient-rich water. Other members of the genus are important members of the marine phytoplankton.

10

Heterokontophyta: Class Raphidophyceae

The principal characteristics of the Raphidophyceae

The following characters distinguish this class from other classes within the Heterokontophyta ([606, 607, 608, 653, 655, 657, 1298, 1525]).

1 All the species are unicellular flagellates and lack cell walls (Figs. 10.1, 10.2).

2 The two flagella are inserted near the apex of the cell and not laterally, as in the Phaeophyceae and Sarcinochrysidophyceae (compare Fig. 10.1 with Figs. 12.2 and 6.12*e*).

3 The cells are large (50–100 μm) and dorsiventrally constructed, with a curved dorsal side and a flatter ventral side. The ventral side is traversed by a shallow, longitudinal groove.

4 One flagellum points forwards, while the other is directed backwards along the cell and lies in the ventral groove. The anterior flagellum is covered with hairs (mastigonemes), which are of the usual heterokontophyte type; as in other heterokontophytes, the hairs are formed within cisternae of the endoplasmic reticulum ([650, 651]).

5 Both flagella arise from the bottom of a small funnel-shaped invagination (gullet), which lies on the ventral side of the cell, just below the cell apex.

6 The typical heterokontophyte photoreceptor apparatus – composed of a swelling near the base of the smooth posterior flagellum and an eyespot that is enclosed within the chloroplast (see for instance Fig. 7.1*c*) – is not found in members of the Raphidophyceae; nor is any other type of photoreceptor known.

7 The transition zone of the flagellum does not contain a transitional helix, a structure that is present in several other heterokontophyte classes (see for instance Fig. 6.4*a*; [1218]).

8 There are numerous ellipsoidal chloroplasts, which are often somewhat flattened where they press against each other (Figs. 10.1*b*, 10.2). They are green, yellow-green or yellow-brown, and contain chlorophylls a, c_1 and c_2; the main accessory pigments are β-carotene, diadinoxanthin, vaucheriaxanthin and heteroxanthin. In marine representatives of the class, however, the main accessory pigments are β-carotene and fucoxanthin (Table 1.2) ([419, 627, 1525]).

9 Girdle lamellae are usually present within the chloroplasts, but not always ([607]).

10 Beneath the surface of the cell there are rod-shaped trichocysts or spherical mucilage vesicles. Upon stimulation, the trichocysts discharge threads of mucilage (Figs. 10.1*a*, 10.2).

11 On the top of the nucleus there is a cap-like golgi apparatus, which consists of a number of individual golgi bodies (dictyosomes). At regular intervals vesicles from the golgi apparatus fuse with the contractile vacuoles, which discharge their contents to the exterior (Figs. 10.1*a*, 10.2; [1578]).

12 The nucleus lies in a capsule of relatively viscous cytoplasm, surrounded by more fluid cytoplasm. The chloroplasts lie in the outer, fluid layer (Fig. 10.1*a*).

13 The Raphidophyceae includes both freshwater and marine organisms.

The Raphidophyceae also exhibit the following features, which are typical of most Heterokontophyta:

the presence of a pleuronematic, forwardly directed flagellum, bearing characteristic tubular mastigonemes (Fig. 10.2), which are tripartite and are synthesized in ER cisternae;

golgi bodies (dictyosomes) that lie with their forming faces appressed to the nuclear envelope (Fig. 10.2);

a periplastidial reticulum, which lies in the narrow space between the chloroplast envelope and the chloroplast ER (Fig. 10.2b; cf. p. 113);

girdle lamellae within the chloroplasts; these are present in most genera but are lacking in two marine genera, *Chattonella* and *Fibrocapsa* (Fig. 10.2; [607, 655, 657]);

a ring-shaped nucleoid in each chloroplast ([255]);

the presence of chlorophylls a, c_1 and c_2.

Recently, studies of nucleotide sequences in 28S ribosomal RNAs have confirmed that there is a close phylogenetic relationship between the Raphidophyceae and the Chrysophyceae ([1394]).

This class is a small group of easily recognizable, complex flagellates, whose cell structure was known in some detail even before the invention of the electron microscope (see [719]). The chromosome number can be very large: in *Vacuolaria virescens*, for instance, it is 97 ± 2 ([652, 653, 656]). Mitosis takes place within the nuclear envelope (closed mitosis) and during this process the basal bodies may function as centrioles.

The xanthophylls of the freshwater species are similar to those of the Xanthophyceae (see above, character 8), while in the marine species they resemble those of the Chrysophyceae. This difference probably indicates the existence of separate marine and freshwater subgroups within the Raphidophyceae.

Size and distribution of the class

Nine genera are classified in the Raphidophyceae and these occur in both freshwater and marine habitats. The freshwater species tend to occur in rather acid waters, such as small pools on bogs or above barren, sandy substrata. Species of the marine genera, e.g. *Chattonella* and *Fibrocapsa* (Fig. 10.2) sometimes give rise to massive blooms in summer, in bays and enclosed marine waters along the Japanese coast. These 'red tides' cause severe disruption to fish-farming in the bays, especially to cultures of the yellowtail (*Seriola quinqueradiata*). *Chattonella* overwinters in the bottom sediments as dormant cells, which germinate and form active, flagellate cells in early summer ([777]). *Chattonella* species have also been observed in lagoons around the Mediterranean ([653]). Toxic blooms or 'red tides' are well known from many other seas and oceans, but they are generally brought about not by raphidophytes, but by species of Dinophyta (p. 271) ([1320]).

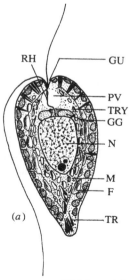

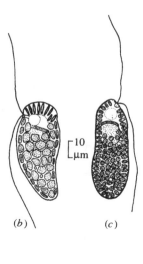

Figure 10.1. (*a*) *Goniostomum semen.* (*b*) *Merotricha bacillata:* side view. (*c*) *Vacuolaria virescens:* side view. F = lipid; GG = numerous golgi bodies; GU = gullet; M = mitochondrion; N = nucleus; PV = contractile (pulsing) vacuole; RH = rhizoplast; TR = rod-shaped trichocyst; TRY = young trichocysts. (*a* after [719]; *b, c* after [439].)

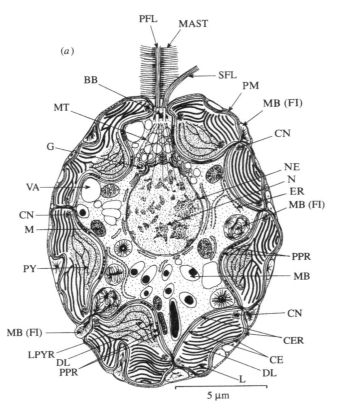

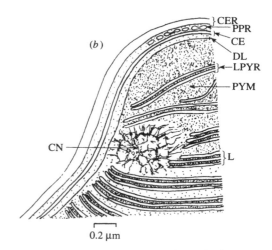

Figure 10.2. *Fibrocapsa japonica.* (*a*) Longitudinal section of a whole cell, based on EM observations. (*b*) Detail of the chloroplast. BB = basal body; CE = chloroplast envelope; CER = chloroplast endoplasmic reticulum; CN = ring-like chloroplast nucleoid; DL = dark-staining layer delimiting the pyrenoid stroma; ER = endoplasmic reticulum; G = golgi body; L = lamella, composed of a stack of three thylakoids; LPYR = lamella within the pyrenoid, consisting of a stack of only two thylakoids; M = mitochondrion; MAST = mastigoneme; MB = muciferous body containing a rounded mass of mucilage; MB(FI) = muciferous body with fibrous contents; MT = microtubules lying between the basal bodies of the flagella and the nucleus; N = nucleus; NE = nuclear envelope; PFL = anterior pleuronematic flagellum; PM = plasma membrane (plasmalemma); PPR = periplastidial reticulum; PY = pyrenoid; PYM = pyrenoid matrix; SFL = smooth posterior flagellum; VA = vacuole. (Based on [607].)

Some examples of Raphidophyceae

Goniostomum semen (Fig. 10.1*a*)

The cells are egg-shaped and measure 60–100 µm × 23–60 µm. At either end of the cell there are clusters of rod-shaped trichocysts. *Gonyostomum semen* occurs in mires and bog pools in Europe and N America.

Merotricha bacillata (Fig. 10.1*b*)

The egg-shaped cells of *Merotricha bacillata* are more elongate than those of *Gonyostomum semen*, measuring 40–50 µm × 18–25 µm. The anterior of the cell is swollen and bears numerous trichocysts. This species is known from four areas: Russia, the former Czechoslovakia, the USA and the Netherlands.

Vacuolaria virescens (Fig. 10.1*c*)

In this alga the cells are elongate to egg-shaped and are only slightly dorsiventral. They attain sizes of 50–85 µm × 20–25 µm and their trichocysts are spherical. Bog pools seem to be the preferred habitat.

Fibrocapsa japonica (Fig. 10.2)

The flattened, yellow-brown or golden brown cells of *Fibrocapsa japonica* are 25–40 µm long and 15–20 µm broad. The chloroplasts are peripheral and packed closely together, each bearing a pyrenoid towards the inside of the cell; there are no girdle lamellae. The pyrenoid is traversed by several thylakoids. Each cell contains numerous muciferous bodies, which can eject threads of mucus up to 300 μm from the cell. The forwardly directed flagellum bears mastigonemes, while the flagellum that points back along the cell is smooth; both emerge from the base of a shallow depression (gullet) at the anterior of the cell. This is one of the Raphidophyceae that cause 'red tides' along the coasts of Japan.

11

Heterokontophyta: Class Dictyochophyceae

The principal characteristics of the Dictyochophyceae

The following characteristics distinguish the Dictyochophyceae from other classes within the Heterokontophyta ([985, 1226, 1812, 1813, 1814, 1815]).

1 The two extant species are unicellular flagellates, which live in the marine phytoplankton (Fig. 11.1).

2 Each cell bears a single flagellum bearing mastigonemes ([1226]).

3 The chloroplasts are golden-brown, the chlorophyll being masked by accessory photosynthetic pigments. Chlorophylls a and c are present, together with the accessory pigments fucoxanthin, diadinoxanthin, diatoxanthin, lutein, and β-carotene.

4 The chloroplast DNA is not organized in a single, ring-shaped nucleoid lying near the periphery of the chloroplast, but is concentrated in a number of nucleoids scattered throughout the chloroplast interior ([254]).

5 The cell has a siliceous skeleton, which lies outside the plasmalemma. The skeleton takes the form of a flat basket, composed of hollow but robust tubes of silica (Fig. 11.1*b*).

6 There is generally a central mass of cytoplasm

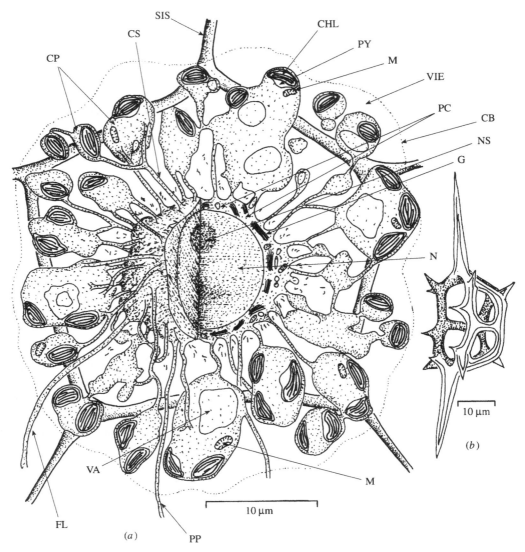

Figure 11.1. *Dictyocha.* (*a*) The radially organized living cell. (*b*) Siliceous skeleton. CB = boundary of cell envelope; CHL = chloroplast; CP = cytoplasmic process; CS = connecting strand; FL = flagellum; G = golgi body; M = mitochondrion; N = nucleus; NS = nucleolus; PC = perinuclear cytoplasm (= perikaryon); PP = pseudopodium; PY = pyrenoid; SIS = siliceous skeleton; VA = vacuole; VIE = the extensive viscous envelope around the cell, without obvious structure. (*a* based on [1812, 1813]; *b* on [300a].)

containing the nucleus and golgi bodies; from this numerous thin strands extend out radially, anastomosing with each other and connecting distally with a peripheral series of lobes and globules of cytoplasm, which contain the chloroplasts. The whole frothy protoplast is contained within a mucilage sheath (Fig. 11.1*a*).

The position of this peculiar group of marine planktonic algae in the Heterokontophyta is supported by the presence of mastigonemes on the flagellum and the structure of the chloroplasts. Each chloroplast is surrounded by chloroplast ER; it contains lamellae composed of three, stacked thylakoids; and it possesses a girdle lamella. During the life cycle naked flagellate cells are produced that are spherical and lack a skeleton. They bear two flagella, which emerge from an apical depression; one is long and pleuronematic, while the other is short and vestigial ([1226]).

Fossil silicoflagellates (the name often used for this group) are known from the early Cretaceous (120 million years ago) onwards. Today they are widely distributed throughout the world's oceans, but are more prevalent in colder waters or, at lower latitudes, colder seasons. Their occurrence in fossil sediments can be used to estimate sea temperatures in past geological epochs ([1751]).

12

Heterokontophyta: Class Phaeophyceae (brown algae)

The principal characteristics of the Phaeophyceae

The following characters, taken together, distinguish the Phaeophyceae from other classes within the Heterokontophyta.

1 All species are multicellular. The morphology and structure of the thalli varies enormously, from microscopic branched filaments to foliose plants many metres long with a complex anatomy. Notwithstanding this variation, the brown algae are a natural group.

2 The flagella are inserted laterally, not apically or subapically as in most other classes of heterokontophytes (compare Fig. 12.2 with Figs. 6.3, 7.1 and 9.8); only in the class Sarcinochrysidophyceae are the flagella inserted laterally, as in the brown algae (Fig. 6.12e). In the Phaeophyceae, flagellate cells are always reproductive; there are no free-living flagellates.

3 The flagellate cells usually have a typical heterokontophyte photoreceptor apparatus, consisting of a flagellar swelling on the posterior flagellum and an eyespot (stigma) contained within a chloroplast (Fig. 12.2). No eyespot apparatus is present in some brown algae, for instance most genera in the order Laminariales ([640, 641]).

4 The transition region of the flagellum lacks a transitional helix (cf. Fig. 6.4a) ([1218]).

5 The chloroplasts are generally discoid (Fig. 12.1b) and are golden-brown in colour, since the chlorophyll is masked by the accessory pigment fucoxanthin. The pyrenoid is stalked, or at least protrudes from the chloroplast (Figs. 12.1, 12.2).

6 The chloroplast DNA is organized in a ring-shaped nucleoid ([83, 84, 254]).

7 Siliceous cysts and siliceous cell walls, such as those formed by various heterokontophytes, including the classes Bacillariophyceae and Chrysophyceae, are never found in the Phaeophyceae.

8 The cell walls are composed of a felt-like network of cellulose microfibrils, which is stiffened by calcium alginate and forms the structural fraction of the wall, together with an amorphous mucilaginous matrix fraction, composed of fucoidan and mucilaginous alginates ([1486]).

9 Mitosis is semi-closed, the nuclear envelope breaking down late in anaphase (Fig. 12.5). The spindle does not persist long at telophase and as it collapses, the daughter nuclei move back towards each other and lie close together. The spindle is formed inside the nucleus, between two polar pairs of centrioles; microtubular asters assemble around the centrioles, radiating out into the cytoplasm ([71, 476, 829, 950, 1241]).

10 In species that reproduce sexually the life cycle is generally diplohaplontic, and can be either isomorphic or heteromorphic. The gametes are produced in plurilocular (= many-chambered) zoidangia, while the meiospores are produced in unilocular (= one-chambered) zoidangia (Fig. 12.8). Plurilocular zoidangia also produce asexual zoospores. The orders Fucales and Durvillaeales are characterized by a diplontic life cycle, with gametic meiosis and oogamy.

11 The Phaeophyceae are almost entirely restricted to marine habitats.

In addition, the Phaeophyceae exhibit a number of characteristics that are typical of the Heterokontophyta as a whole:

the long anterior flagellum of the zoids is pleuro-

nematic, bearing tripartite mastigonemes (tubular hairs; Fig. 12.2), which are formed in ER cisternae ([828]);

the golgi bodies lie with their forming faces appressed to the nuclear envelope (Figs. 12.2, 12.5);

the chloroplasts are surrounded by chloroplast ER, which can be continuous with the nuclear envelope (Figs. 12.1, 12.2);

a periplastidial reticulum – a network of interconnected tubules – is present in the narrow space between the nuclear envelope and the two membranes of the chloroplast envelope itself (Fig. 12.2). Outside the Heterokontophyta, periplastidial reticula occur also in the Haptophyta ([76]);

a girdle lamella (a peripheral stack of three thylakoids) is present beneath the chloroplast envelope in the chloroplast (Figs. 12.1, 12.2);

the chloroplasts contain chlorophylls c_1 and c_2 in addition to chlorophyll a ([793, 794]);

chrysolaminaran is the main reserve polysaccharide.

Size and distribution of the class

The class contains about 265 genera and 1500–2000 species. Most brown algae are marine and live attached to rocks around sea coasts. They therefore occupy the same kinds of habitat as the red algae (p. 49). Brown algae grow attached not only to rocks but also to dykes, quays, unattached molluscs, eelgrass (*Zostera*, a marine angiosperm) or even to other seaweeds. Around N Atlantic and N Pacific coasts large brown algae sometimes grow in great abundance both in the intertidal zone, where there are often belts of *Fucus* (Fig. 12.26), and below low water, where the rocky sea floor is often covered by extensive forests of *Laminaria* (Fig. 12.21a). The primary production of these stands of *Laminaria* is quite high, and amounts to 1–2 kg organic carbon per square metre per year: contrast the much lower primary production of planktonic diatoms (p. 134; [1056]). Even more impressive than the *Laminaria* forests, however, are the beds of the giant brown algae *Macrocystis* and *Nereocystis*, which grow submerged off the Pacific coast of North America, attaining lengths of 30–60 m or more.

Tiny filamentous or disc-shaped brown algae are of course far less obvious than the larger species and are easily overlooked. Nevertheless they are very widely distributed, growing attached to rocks, pebbles, barnacles or molluscs, or living as epiphytes on larger algae. Many small brown algae live within the tissues of other algae, as endophytes.

The brown algae, like the red algae (p. 49), are limited to a relatively small fraction of the earth's surface, since they occur essentially only on rocky coasts and only where sufficient light penetrates the seawater to allow photosynthesis. Terrestrial plants and planktonic plants (phytoplankton) occupy a far larger proportion of the globe. The greatest depth at which brown algae can still grow depends on the turbidity of the water. Around the coasts of the Netherlands the water is very cloudy and few brown algae are found growing below the low water mark; in clear waters, however, they can extend down to depths of around 100 m. Thus, for instance, in the western Mediterranean the lower limits of two *Laminaria* species (*L. rodriguezii* and *L. ochroleuca*) lie at 50–120 m depth. The lower limit for *Laminaria* corresponds to a depth where about 0.6% remains of the light intensity incident upon the surface of the water ([1056]). Certain red algae, particularly some crustose forms, can live at much lower light levels and consequently at much greater depths (see p. 49).

Very few brown algae occur in freshwater; about five genera are known and none contains many species ([122, 124]).

The brown algae, with their soft, unmineralized tissues, are not suited to fossilization, and most fossils that have been suggested to be of Phaeophyceae lack the distinctive features that would allow unambiguous identification. This is especially true for some very ancient, Precambrian (0.7 – 1.3 billion years old) and Devonian (0.35 b.y.) fossils, which show a superficial resemblance to living brown algae ([238, 715, 1197]; see also p. 213). Fossils that are indisputably of brown algae, belonging to the orders Laminariales and Fucales, have been recovered from Miocene deposits in California (*ca.* 7–15 million years old; [1376]); since these fossils belong to the most advanced orders of brown algae, the class as a whole must have a much greater age.

Recently, phylogenetic relationships have been studied among a wide variety of extant organisms by comparing sequences of nucleotides in 5S ribosomal RNA molecules. Among the species investigated have been representatives of several heterokontophyte classes, including the Phaeophyceae ([735, 1011]), and one conclusion that has been drawn is that the Phaeophyceae and Bacillariophyceae (diatoms) diverged from each other comparatively recently, at around 200 m.y. ago. For the Bacillariophyceae there is a rich fossil record, in the form of silica frustules, extending back to the early Cretaceous (120 m.y. ago; p. 136). The brown algae and diatoms have apparently evolved rather recently (much more recently, for instance, than the red algae and green algae: see pp. 97, 489 respectively) and this point will be explored in more detail in Chapter 13, which is devoted to evolution in the Heterokontophyta.

Some brown algae are of considerable economic importance. The annual global harvest of *Laminaria* and related genera is almost two million tonnes fresh mass. Roughly 1.3 million tonnes are produced by mariculture of *Laminaria* along the coasts of China. In Japan too, *Laminaria* and the related genus *Undaria* are cultivated, but in addition the algae are collected from natural stands. *Laminaria* is cultivated attached to floating 'rafts'. Each raft is a single horizontal rope, which is anchored to the bottom but kept afloat by glass floats; from this horizontal rope are suspended vertical ropes, on which the algae grow attached (cf. p. 66). The greater part of the harvest is eaten, while the remainder is used for the production of alginate, a colloidal cell wall polysaccharide (p. 169; [219, 221, 989a, 1056, 1296, 1803, 1835]).

Features of the brown algae

Pigments and chloroplasts

The brown algae owe their colour to the accessory pigment fucoxanthin; the Chrysophyceae and Bacillariophyceae are also coloured brown by this pigment. Other xanthophylls may also be present in brown algae, such as violaxanthin, antheraxanthin, neoxanthin, diadinoxanthin and diatoxanthin (Table 1.2; [88]), and these occur in different combinations in different species. β-carotene too is widely distributed ([1463]). In addition to chlorophyll a, brown algae possess chlorophylls c_1 and c_2, but chlorophyll b is never present ([793, 794]).

All these pigments are contained in the chloroplasts,

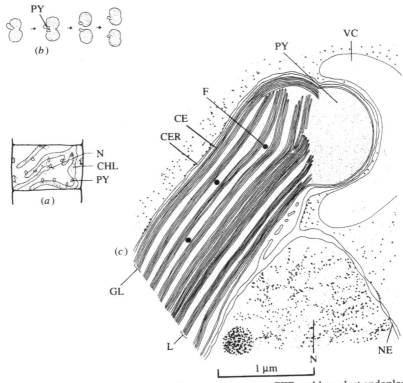

Figure 12.1. (*a*) *Ectocarpus siliculosus:* a single cell with elongate, band-shaped chloroplasts, which bear protruding, pear-shaped pyrenoids. (*b*) *Giffordia* sp.: division of discoid chloroplasts. (*c*) *Pilayella littoralis:* chloroplast ultrastructure. CE = chloroplast envelope; CER = chloroplast endoplasmic reticulum; CHL = chloroplast; F = lipid globule; GL = girdle lamella; L = lamella, composed of a stack of three thylakoids; N = nucleus; NE = nuclear envelope; PY = pyrenoid; VC = vesicle containing chrysolaminaran. (*c* after [389].)

which can be discoid (Fig. 12.1*b*) or ribbon-like (Fig. 12.1*a*). Individual cells may contain one or several chloroplasts, depending on the species. Each chloroplast often bears one or several pyrenoids, which are usually pear-shaped and attached to the inner side of the chloroplast by their narrow ends (Figs. 12.1*b*, 12.2). Vesicles containing reserve material (chrysolaminaran) are formed in the cytoplasm, near the pyrenoid (Fig. 12.1*c*; [113, 389]).

In their ultrastructure the chloroplasts exhibit a series of features that are characteristic of the division Heterokontophyta (Fig. 12.1*c*). Thus, for instance, the thylakoids lie in stacks (lamellae) of three, and one peripheral stack (the girdle lamella) usually encloses all the others. The chloroplast is surrounded not only by its own double membrane, but also by a fold of endoplasmic reticulum, so that altogether there are four membranes around it. Where a chloroplast lies against the nucleus, the nuclear envelope and the chloroplast endoplasmic reticulum are continuous with each other ([113, 389]).

In brown algal cells capable of division (e.g. the apical cells of *Sphacelaria*; Fig. 12.10*a*), it can be seen that the discoid chloroplasts divide autonomously. In this process the chloroplasts elongate and simultaneously become constricted centrally. The constriction deepens and cuts through the chloroplast, producing two daughter chloroplasts (Fig. 12.1*b*).

The chloroplast DNA is organized into a ring-shaped nucleoid, as in most Heterokontophyta ([83, 84, 254]).

Storage products

The most important reserve product of photosynthesis is chrysolaminaran, which is a β-1,3-linked glucan and lies in solution in special vacuoles. The Chrysophyceae and Bacillariophyceae, and probably also the

Xanthophyceae and Haptophyceae, have similar reserve polysaccharides. Mannitol and lipid (in the form of oil droplets) also occur. Mannitol, like chryso-laminaran, can also be found in the Chrysophyceae and Bacillariophyceae. It is a low-molecular-mass sugar alcohol, which in the brown algae has an osmoregulatory role, in addition to its function as a reserve. Its intracellular concentration increases and decreases with increasing and decreasing external salinity ([1478]).

Some other products of metabolism

Around the nucleus lie numerous strongly refractile vesicles, whose contents are formed within the chloro-plast ([392, 393]). The vesicles contain 'phaeophycean tan-nin' or 'phlorotannin' ([1316]). There are many different types of tannins, with different structures, but they mostly contain polyhydroxyphenols or their deriva-tives ([1463]). Phlorotannins are polymers of phloroglucinol and are known only from brown algae ([1465]). When oxidized the tannins of brown algae produce a dark brown dye, and this produces the dark brown discoloration often seen in dead brown algae, washed up by the tide. The main function of phlorotannins is proba-bly to discourage grazing by herbivorous inverte-brates, such as the gastropod *Littorina littorea*. They probably also inhibit colonization by epiphytic algae and animals ([1465]).

Many brown algae concentrate iodine in their cells. Thus, for instance, iodine can make up 0.03–0.3% of the fresh mass of *Laminaria*, whereas the concentra-tion of iodine in seawater is only about 0.000 005% (0.05 mg l^{-1}). Until the 1930s brown algae were used as raw material for the extraction of iodine ([219]).

Marine algae, especially members of the Phaeo-phyceae, release large quantities of volatile bromi-nated methanes into the environment, such as bromo-form, dibromochloromethane and dibromomethane. A recently discovered category of enzymes, the vana-dium bromoperoxidases, are probably involved in their production and are apparently widespread in sea-weeds, but especially in brown algae. The annual global input to the atmosphere of algal organobro-mides has been estimated at *ca.* 10^4 tonnes per year, which is of the same order as the production of such compounds by industry. Some have speculated that ozone (O_3) destruction in the atmosphere above the Arctic during the Arctic spring may be linked to

enhanced seasonal production of volatile brominated methanes by seaweeds. The 'polar hole' in the ozone layer is a matter of public concern because it will allow higher levels of UV radiation through to the earth's surface, which will be deleterious to health. Ozone destruction is often ascribed to the effects of man-made halogenated compounds, such as chloro-fluorocarbons (CFCs) ([1878a, 1878b]).

Cell wall composition

As in the red algae, we can distinguish two fractions within the cell wall: a fibrillar part that gives the wall its strength, and an amorphous part in which the fibrils are embedded. The fibrillar fraction of the brown algal wall consists of cellulose ([392, 911, 1396]), and this struc-tural component is probably stiffened further by insol-uble alginate ([39, 1150, 1151, 1486]). The fibrils form a felt-like network, as in the chrysophycean alga *Ochro-monas* (Fig. 6.2e).

Alginates, which make up the greater part of the cell wall, are salts of alginic acid. This is a polymer of two sugar acids, D-mannuronic acid and L-guluronic acid, which are connected by β-1,4 linkages. The propor-tions of the two acids can vary even within the same species. The acid residues can form salts with various cations, e.g. Ca^{2+}, Mg^{2+} or Na^+. Na-alginate is soluble in water, whereas alginic acid and Ca-alginate are not. By combining cations with alginic acid in different proportions it is possible to produce gels with different viscosities.

It is assumed that insoluble Ca-alginate is the pre-dominant form of alginate in the fibrillar part of the cell wall, whereas the rather slimy, amorphous frac-tion (the matrix or ground substance) consists mainly of water-soluble alginates and/or fucoidan. Fucoidan is a complex sulphated polysaccharide containing, in addition to the monosaccharide fucose, varying pro-portions of the monosaccharides galactose, mannose, xylose and glucuronic acid ([1148, 1149, 1155, 1395]).

Alginates are non-toxic and are used extensively in industry because of their colloidal properties. In the food and pharmaceutical industries, for instance, algi-nates are used to stabilize emulsions and suspensions. Products containing them include ice-cream, jam, whips, blancmange, soups, sauces, mayonnaise, mar-garine, sausage, ointments, lotions, toothpaste, medi-cine capsules (which dissolve in the stomach), and slimming foods (Na-alginate swells in the stomach so that slimmers feel full). Alginates are also processed in the manufacture of dyes, building materials, glue and paper, as well as being used in the petroleum, photographic and textile industries ([219, 221, 531, 989a, 1056, 1396, 1835]).

The use of large brown algae as raw material for the production of alginates began in the 1920s. A recent estimate of the annual global production of alginate is 21 500 tonnes: 1900 tonnes are produced in Japan and Korea, 100 in Latin America, 12 800 in Europe, and 6700 in North America ([1155]). In terms of fresh mass, this corresponds to 575 000 tonnes of brown algae harvested per year. In North America, the raw material for the production of alginate is obtained primarily from the Pacific coast, where there are extensive beds of the giant brown algae *Macrocystis* and *Nereocystis*, which can be harvested mechanically. Around European coasts the algae usually utilized are *Laminaria* species (Fig. 12.21a) and *Ascophyllum*, although these are more difficult to harvest than *Macrocystis* and *Nereocystis*.

Zoids (Figs. 12.2–12.4)

Zoids play a part in the life cycles of almost all brown algae. They are very similar to the zoids of the Chrysophyceae and Xanthophyceae (compare Fig. 12.2 with Figs. 6.2, 6.3 and 7.1), with which they agree in the following respects.

1 The zoid bears two flagella, and the long flagellum is forwardly directed and pleuronematic, bearing two rows of mastigonemes. These are stiff tubular hairs, composed of a basal portion, a shaft, and a terminal fibre (Fig. 12.2). They are formed in ER cisternae, or in the nuclear envelope ([828, 986]).

2 The chloroplast in the zoid is surrounded by chloroplast ER, which is continuous with the nuclear envelope.

3 The chloroplast contains a girdle lamella (a peripheral stack of three thylakoids).

4 A periplastidial reticulum, consisting of a network of interconnected tubules, is present in the narrow space between the chloroplast ER and the two membranes of the chloroplast envelope itself.

5 A golgi body is present, appressed to the nucleus.

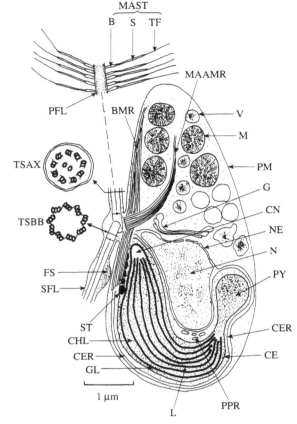

Figure 12.2. Longitudinal section through a phaeophycean zoid (the zoospore of *Scytosiphon*), based on EM observations. B = base of mastigoneme; BMR = bypassing microtubular root; CE = chloroplast envelope; CER = chloroplast endoplasmic reticulum; CHL = chloroplast; CN = ring-shaped chloroplast nucleoid, seen in section; FS = flagellar swelling; G = golgi body; GL = girdle lamella; L = lamella, composed of a stack of three thylakoids; MAAMR = major anterior microtubular root; MAST = mastigoneme; M = mitochondrion; N = nucleus; NE = nuclear envelope; PFL = anterior pleuronematic flagellum; PM = plasma membrane (plasmalemma); PPR = periplastidial reticulum; PY = pyrenoid; S = shaft of mastigoneme; SFL = smooth posterior flagellum; ST = stigma; TF = terminal filament of mastigoneme; TSAX = transverse section of the axoneme of the anterior flagellum; TSBB = transverse section of the basal body of the posterior flagellum; V = vesicle. (Based on [237, 1089, 1327].)

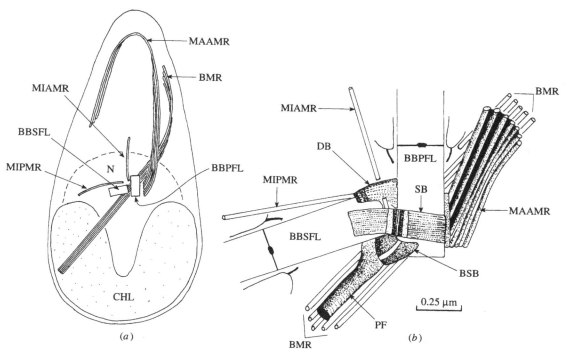

Figure 12.3. The flagellar apparatus of the phaeophycean zoid, based on EM observations. (*a*) Dorsal view of the flagellar apparatus, (seen, therefore, through the zoid, since the apparatus is ventral). (*b*) Dorsal view of the central part of the flagellar apparatus, at high magnification. BBPFL = basal body of anterior, pleuronematic flagellum; BBSFL = basal body of posterior, smooth flagellum; BMR = bypassing microtubular root; BSB = button-shaped striated band; CHL = outline of chloroplast; DB = deltoid striated band; MAAMR = major anterior microtubular root; MIAMR = minor anterior microtubular root; MIPMR = minor posterior microtubular root; N = outline of nucleus; PF = posterior fibrous band; SB = strap-shaped striated band. (Based on [1327].)

6 There is usually a typical heterokontophyte photoreceptor apparatus, which consists of a swelling on the smooth posterior flagellum, together with an eyespot, which lies close to the flagellar swelling but is enclosed within the chloroplast.

Several features differentiate clearly, however, between phaeophycean zoids and the zoids of the Chrysophyceae, Xanthophyceae, and other heterokontophyte classes.

1 The flagella are inserted laterally; in other classes they are apical or subapical (compare Figs. 12.2–12.4 with Figs. 6.2, 6.3, 7.1, 9.8). Lateral insertion is characteristic of only one other heterokontophyte class, the Sarcinochrysidophyceae (Fig. 6.12*e*).

2 Both flagella generally end in thin hair-points (acronemata; Fig. 12.4). An acronema occurs on one of the flagella, the smooth flagellum, in the Xanthophyceae (Fig. 7.1) and Sarcinochrysidophyceae (Fig. 6.12*e*). It consists of the two central microtubules of the flagellar axoneme, surrounded by the flagellar membrane ([641]).

3 The precise positions and configuration of the two basal bodies and their associated microtubular and fibrous roots (Figs. 12.2, 12.3; compare with Fig. 6.4*g*) ([1325, 1437]).

Fig. 12.3 illustrates diagrammatically the configuration of the flagellar apparatus, i.e. the basal bodies and associated structures, in the unizoids (zoids produced in unilocular zoidangia) of the large brown alga *Laminaria* (Figs. 12.21, 12.4*c*). The flagellar appara-

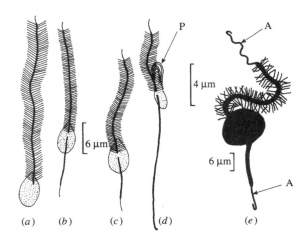

Figure 12.4. (a) *Dictyota*: spermatozoid. (b) *Pilayella*: zoid.
(c) *Laminaria*: zoospore. (d) *Fucus*: spermatozoid.
(e) *Ectocarpus*: male gamete with pleuronematic
anterior flagellum and short posterior flagellum with
acronema. A = acronema; P = proboscis. (a–d based
on [1555]; e on [1261].)

tus is situated on the ventral side of the zoid, which is flat, the dorsal side of the zoid being convex (Fig. 12.2). In Fig. 12.3, the flagellar apparatus is viewed from its dorsal side, as if through the body of the zoid. When seen thus the basal body of the posterior, smooth flagellum always appears to the left of the anterior basal body, and lies at an angle of *ca.* 110° to it. Four microtubular roots anchor the basal bodies in the cell, the most conspicuous of these being the major anterior microtubular root, which consists of about 7 microtubules and extends from the anterior basal body along the ventral surface, towards the apex of the cell; here it curves back (Fig. 12.3a). The next most obvious root is the by-passing microtubular root, which consists of about 5 microtubules and has its origin at the anterior end of the cell. It runs from here roughly parallel to the major anterior microtubular root, past the basal bodies, which it by-passes without contact, and so on to the posterior of the cell. The other two microtubular roots are minor by comparison, each containing only one microtubule; like the larger roots, however, they occupy fixed positions in the cell. The basal bodies are connected to each other by three striated bands: the deltoid striated band, the strap-shaped striated band, and the button-shaped striated band (Fig. 12.3b; [1327]). These fibres resemble the various striated connectives that link the basal bodies in the zoids of green algae

(e.g. Fig. 19.6b), which have been shown to contain the contractile protein centrin (p. 317).

Other Phaeophyceae seem to show only minor variations on the structure we have described for the *Laminaria* unizoid. The particular configuration of the flagellar apparatus, with its two basal bodies and associated microtubular roots and striated bands, seems to characterize the whole class ([237, 640, 641, 1218, 1239, 1325, 1327, 1330]). Within the division Chlorophyta too, the classes have their own characteristic arrangements of basal bodies and microtubular roots (cf. Fig. 19.14 and p. 302). In the Heterokontophyta the flagellar apparatus seems to vary profoundly from one class to another ([1218, 1327, 1330, 1437]). Thus, for instance, in *Ochromonas* (class Chrysophyceae) the basal bodies are connected to the nucleus by a massive rhizoplast (Fig. 6.3), a structure never yet found in any brown alga, while the four microtubular roots of *Ochromonas* are quite differently arranged from the roots in the Phaeophyceae. Only one class, the Sarcinochrysidophyceae, has a flagellar apparatus similar to that of the Phaeophyceae ([1325, 1330]), which correlates with the similarity that we have already noted between the classes in the positioning of the flagella, both having laterally inserted flagella (compare Fig. 12.2 with Fig. 6.12e). The Sarcinochrysidophyceae are therefore thought to be the nearest relatives of the Phaeophyceae and to have retained many of the characteristics of their common ancestors. The zoids of these classes differ in one important respect. In the Sarcinochrysidophyceae there is a transitional helix (a coiled fibril) in the transition zone of the flagellum, between the basal body and the shaft of the flagellum (Fig. 6.4a), while this is absent in the Phaeophyceae, apparently having been lost ([1218, 1330]).

The above account might be taken to imply that all phaeophycean zoids are identical. This is not so. For instance, the male gamete of *Dictyota* lacks a posterior flagellum ([1090]), while the male gametes of *Fucus* have a prominent 'proboscis' (Fig. 12.4; [1097]), which is a flat protuberance at the front end of the cell, supported by the curved major anterior microtubular root. In *Laminaria* and related genera there is no photoreceptor apparatus: neither an eyespot, nor a swelling on the smooth posterior flagellum (cf. Fig. 12.2; [640, 641, 1082]). There can even be minor differences between the different zoids produced by a single species. Thus, for instance, in *Laminaria* the male gametes and unizoids have a slightly different flagellar apparatus and flagellar insertion: in the male gametes they arise from the bottom of a narrow gullet, which is absent in the unizoids ([1239]).

Mitosis and cytokinesis (Fig. 12.5)

Mitosis starts with the duplication of the two centrioles, which lie close to the nuclear envelope (Fig. 12.5a). The new pairs then take up positions at the future poles of the mitotic spindle and become the foci of asters of radiating microtubules. Each centriole consists of a cylindrical array of nine microtubular triplets, as is typical for eukaryote centrioles and basal bodies (cf. Figs. 12.2, 7.4a). During the early stages of mitosis (prophase) the nucleolus disappears and by metaphase, holes (polar fenestrae) have been formed in the nuclear envelope at the poles of the nucleus. At metaphase the chromosomes lie in a plate at the equator of the spindle, which extends across the nucleus, through the polar fenestrae, to end at the pairs of centrioles (Fig. 12.5b). In the course of anaphase the nuclear envelope disintegrates, although remnants of it can remain visible for some time, persisting even until early telophase (Fig. 12.5c). Mitosis can therefore be said to be 'semi-closed': in fully closed mitosis the nuclear envelope remains intact throughout. At early telophase the daughter nuclei are distant from each other, pushed far apart by the elongation of the interzonal spindle microtubules. Soon, however, the interzonal spindle collapses, so that by late telophase the daughter nuclei lie close together (Fig. 12.5d). Mitosis in brown algae resembles that in certain green algae, namely our type IV, 'closed mitosis with a nonpersistent telophase spindle' (p. 328, Fig. 19.20 II). Cytokinesis is brought about by an inward furrowing of the plasmalemma, as in the closure of an iris diaphragm, and takes place after mitosis is complete. A new cell wall, usually pierced by numerous plasmodesmata, is then deposited in the cleavage furrow, thus completing cell division (Fig. 12.5e; [949, 950]).

The Phaeophyceae seem to be remarkably uniform with respect to mitosis and cytokinesis, there being only minor variations on the course of events outlined above ([71, 476, 829, 959, 1241]). Between the various classes of the Heterokontophyta, however, there are enormous differences in mitosis and cytokinesis: compare, for instance, mitosis and cytokinesis in the Phaeophyceae (Fig. 12.5) with the equivalent processes in the classes Bacillariophyceae (Fig. 9.6), Chrysophyceae (*Ochro-monas*: Fig. 6.1l) or Xanthophyceae (*Vaucheria*: Fig. 7.4a, b). In the green algae (division Chlorophyta), on the other hand, it is the orders rather than the classes that have their own, characteristic types of mitosis and cytokinesis.

Sexual reproduction and meiosis

Most brown algae that reproduce sexually exhibit a diplohaplontic life cycle, which may be isomorphic or heteromorphic. In heteromorphic cycles it can be either the haploid gametophyte phase or the diploid sporophyte phase that is reduced (Fig. 1.4).

Gametes are generally produced in **plurilocular gametangia** (= many-chambered gametangia; Figs. 12.8, 12.11f, j, 12.16f, l), each chamber or locule producing one gamete. The gametes may be equal in size (in isogamous species: Figs. 12.8, 12.16) or the female gametes may be larger than the male ones (in anisogamous species: Fig. 12.11). In many brown algae, the female gametes are not only large but non-motile, because they lack flagella; these algae are oogamous (Figs. 12.12, 12.19, 12.24). In many cases, plurilocular reproductive structures produce not gametes but asexual spores; in this case they are **plurilocular sporangia** (Fig. 12.8). The general term for both types of plurilocular structure is **plurilocular zoidangium**, the zoids produced by them being **plurizoids**.

Meiospores are generally produced in **unilocular sporangia** (= one-chambered sporangia; Figs. 12.8, 12.11c, 12.16c), but unilocular sporangia can also produce asexual spores, without any preceding meiosis. Unilocular sporangia can also be referred to as **unilocular zoidangia**, and the flagellate spores they produce are called **unizoids**.

The order Fucales is characterized by a diplontic life cycle, in which meiosis takes place just before the formation of the gametes (gametic meiosis; Fig. 12.26). Here, both the tiny motile male gametes and the large non-motile female gametes (eggs) are produced not in plurilocular but in unilocular structures (Fig. 12.26).

There is an abundance of light microscopical evidence showing that meiosis occurs in unilocular zoidangia and in the gametangia of the Fucales. During pachytene, which is one of the stages of meiotic prophase, a highly characteristic, specialized structure is present in the nucleus, which can be detected with the electron microscope. This structure,

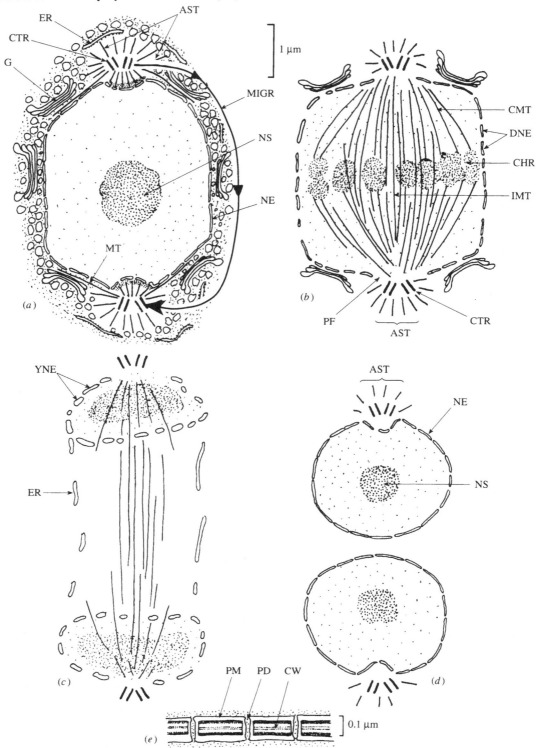

For legend see opposite.

the synaptonemal complex (see Fig. 5.12 and p. 59, where the complex is described) is very similar throughout the eukaryotes, which suggests strongly that meiosis, and consequently also sexual reproduction, has arisen only once during evolution, in the primaeval ancestors of the eukaryotes (cf. p. 61). Typical synaptonemal complexes have been discovered in diverse brown algae ([71, 829, 1779]), indicating that meiosis and sexual reproduction are primitive, ancestral characters in the Phaeophyceae. The many brown algae that only reproduce asexually must therefore have lost their sexuality secondarily, as has happened over and over again in most phyla of eukaryotes.

The subdivision of the class Phaeophyceae

In this account the class Phaeophyceae is considered to contain the following 14 orders ([1554, 1924]):

Ectocarpales

Sphacelariales

Syringodermatales* ([637, 642])

Dictyotales

Scytosiphonales

Cutleriales

Dictyosiphonales

Chordariales

Sporochnales* ([1240, 1259])

Desmarestiales

Laminariales

Fucales

Durvillaeales

Ascoseirales* ([239, 1209, 1274, 1924])

The orders marked with an asterisk will not be treated any further here.

Order Ectocarpales

1 The thalli are simple uniseriate filaments, which are branched but never united into pseudoparenchymatous tissues. The thalli consist of two types of filament, with different modes of growth. There are creeping, prostrate filaments, which grow by the division of apical cells (Fig. 12.7a), and erect filaments, in which growth occurs through the division of intercalary cells (Fig. 12.7b, c). The intercalary growth of the erect filaments may be diffuse, or restricted to distinct meristematic zones (Fig. 12.7b).

2 The basic plan of the life cycle is diplohaplontic and isomorphic (or slightly heteromorphic). The haploid gametophyte produces haploid gametes in plurilocular gametangia. The diploid sporophyte produces haploid meiospores in unilocular meiosporangia and asexual diploid spores in plurilocular sporangia (Fig. 12.8). Physiological anisogamy is probably the rule, but some representatives exhibit morphological anisogamy ([1251]) or even oogamy ([937]). Physiological anisogamy involves gametes that look identical but behave differently: immobilized female gametes are fertilized by motile male gametes of similar size (Fig. 12.8). In morphologically anisogamous forms, the behavioural difference is accompanied by a size distinction, the female gametes being larger than the males.

The Ectocarpales are considered to be the most primitive order of the Phaeophyceae (see Chapter 13).

Phaeostroma bertholdii (Fig. 12.6)

Phaeostroma is one of the most simply constructed brown algae. The thallus consists only of branched, creeping filaments, which exhibit apical growth. The plurilocular zoidangia arise from cells that are scarcely distinguishable from vegetative cells. The creeping filaments bear phaeophycean hairs, which

Figure 12.5. Mitosis in the Phaeophyceae (here in the trichothallic meristem of *Cutleria*, cf. Fig. 12.14). (a) Early prophase. (b) Metaphase. (c) Early telophase. (d) Late telophase. (e) Cross-wall with characteristic plasmodesmata. AST = aster of microtubules radiating from a pair of centrioles at each pole of the spindle; CHR = chromosome; CMT = chromosomal spindle microtubule; CTR = centriole; CW = cell wall; DNE = disintegrating nuclear envelope; ER = endoplasmic reticulum; G = golgi body; IMT = interzonal spindle microtubule; MIGR = migration route of the daughter pair of centrioles around the nucleus to the other spindle pole; MT = microtubule; NE = nuclear envelope; NS = nucleolus; PD = plasmodesma; PF = polar fenestra; PM = plasma membrane (plasmalemma); YNE = young nuclear envelope forming around the telophase nucleus. (Based on [950].)

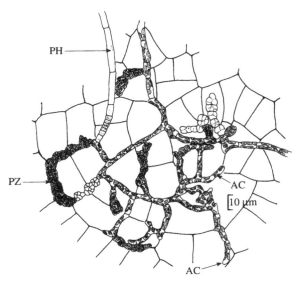

Figure 12.6. *Phaeostroma bertholdii* (Ectocarpales), epiphytic on the brown alga *Scytosiphon* (cf. Fig. 12.13). Note the prostrate system of creeping filaments, which grow through apical cell divisions. AC = apical cell; PH = phaeophycean hair; PZ = plurilocular zoidangium, formed by division of intercalary cells. (Based on [1341].)

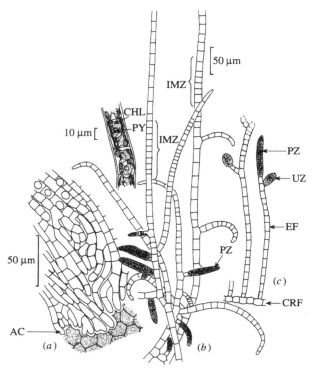

Figure 12.7. *Spongonema tomentosum* (Ectocarpales). (*a*) Creeping filaments, growing through apical cell divisions. (*b*) Erect filaments with intercalary meristematic zones and bearing plurilocular zoidangia. (*c*) Creeping filaments with short erect filaments that bear unilocular and plurilocular zoidangia. AC = apical cell; CHL = chloroplast; CRF = creeping filament; EF = erect filament; IMZ = intercalary meristematic zone; PY = pyrenoid; PZ = plurilocular zoidangium; UZ = unilocular zoidangium. (Based on [926].)

are unbranched, colourless uniseriate filaments with basal meristems; their cells contain vestigial chloroplasts. Phaeophycean hairs occur throughout the class Phaeophyceae. *Phaeostroma* lives epiphytically on other algae. The microthallus (gametophyte) phases in the life cycles of the Chordariales, Dictyosiphonales, Desmarestiales and Laminariales bear an extraordinary resemblance to *Phaeostroma* and other 'primitive' members of the Ectocarpales.

Spongonema tomentosum (Fig. 12.7)

The thalli consist of two types of filament: creeping filaments with apical growth (Fig. 12.7*a*) and erect filaments, which have intercalary meristematic zones (Fig. 12.7*b*). Both types of filament are delicate and about 10 µm wide. In winter and early spring the erect filaments are short and bear both unilocular and plurilocular zoidangia (Fig. 12.7*c*), but during spring the erect filaments grow longer and may attain lengths of 10 cm. These filaments are clad with short hooked branches, which become entangled, linking the filaments into spongy, rope-like strands. The long filaments also bear numerous plurilocular zoidangia (Fig. 12.7*b*).

Spongonema tomentosum is a common epiphyte on larger brown algae, especially *Fucus* species (Fig. 12.26).

Ectocarpus siliculosus (Fig. 12.8)

The plants form hairy brown tufts, which vary in size from several centimetres in height to several decimetres. *Ectocarpus siliculosus* is very common in summer or winter, on the European coasts of the Atlantic and Mediterranean. Intertidal pools in particular often contain good specimens. The species is cosmopolitan.

The branched filaments exhibit diffuse growth,

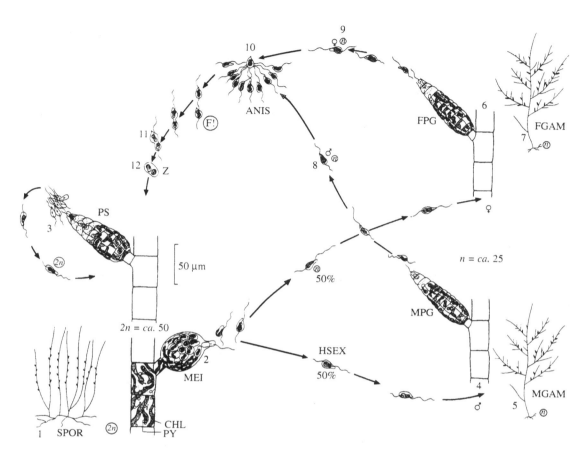

Figure 12.8. *Ectocarpus siliculosus* (Ectocarpales): isomorphic diplohaplontic life cycle. ANIS = 'physiological' anisogamy; CHL = chloroplast; F! = fertilization; FGAM = female gametophyte; FPG = female plurilocular gametangium; HSEX = haplogenotypic sex determination; MEI = meiosis within a unilocular sporangium; this takes place predominantly at low temperatures, e.g. 13 °C; MGAM = male gametophyte; MPG = male plurilocular gametangium; PS = plurilocular sporangium, functioning in the vegetative reproduction of the sporophyte; plurilocular sporangia are formed predominantly at high temperatures, e.g. 20 °C; PY = pyrenoid; SPOR = sporophyte; Z = zygote; n = haploid; $2n$ = diploid. (Based on [1244, 1245].)

through intercalary cell division. Each cell contains several ribbon-like chloroplasts (Figs. 12.1a, 12.8 [2]) and attached to these are many pear-shaped pyrenoids.

Reproduction takes place by the formation and dispersal of zoids, which are produced in two different types of zoidangia: plurilocular (many-chambered) zoidangia (Fig. 12.8 [3, 4]) and unilocular (one-chambered zoidangia) (Fig. 12.8 [2]). These two types are characteristic of the Phaeophyceae and in *Ectocarpus* both are produced at the ends of short side

branches. The plurilocular zoidangia are somewhat elongate, tapering structures, which are divided up by walls into several rows of chambers. Each chamber produces a single zoid, but at maturity the cell walls in the middle and apex of the zoidangium decompose, so that the zoids all escape together, via a hole at the apex (Fig. 12.8 [3]). The unilocular zoidangia, on the other hand, are round to oval and lack cross walls. Their contents divide up into many zoids, which then escape through a pore in the wall of the zoidangium (Fig. 12.8 [2]).

The life cycle of *Ectocarpus siliculosus* (Fig. 12.8) was originally investigated using material collected near Naples ([1244, 1245, 1248]). The sporophyte, which is diploid (chromosome number, $2n = 50$), consists of prostrate, branched filaments of cells, from which there arise almost unbranched, upright filaments (Fig. 12.8 [1–3]). The sporophyte bears both unilocular and plurilocular zoidangia. The plurilocular zoidangia produce diploid zoids which give rise to further sporophytes and are therefore functioning as zoospores. Here, then, the plurilocular zoidangium could also be called a plurilocular sporangium. In general, however, the plurilocular structures of brown algae should be termed 'plurilocular zoidangia', since it is often difficult to establish whether a given structure is a sporangium or a gametangium.

The reduction division takes place in the unilocular zoidangia produced by the sporophyte. As the young unilocular zoidangium develops, meiosis occurs first, followed by many mitoses, so that a large number of haploid zoospores (chromosome number, $n = ca.$ 25) are formed.

This process has also been studied using the electron microscope ([1779]). Unilocular zoidangia play a part in the life cycles of many brown algae. All the meioses that have ever been observed in the Phaeophyceae have been found in unilocular zoidangia, which must therefore be regarded as stages where control is exerted over ploidy. It must be noted, however, that there are also many unilocular zoidangia in which meiosis does not take place.

The formation of different types of zoidangia on the sporophyte is controlled by temperature. At 20 °C (the summer temperature of the sea at Naples) the sporophytes produce only plurilocular zoidangia, while at 13 °C (the winter temperature at Naples) they produce only unilocular zoidangia. Between 13 and 20 °C both types of zoidangia are formed.

The haploid zoospores from the unilocular zoidangia of the sporophyte give rise to haploid gametophytes (Fig. 12.8 [4–7]). About 50% of the zoospores form male gametophytes and 50% female gametophytes, and so a **haplogenotypic sex determination** must have occurred during meiosis. This means that in the diploid nucleus, the genes for 'female' and 'male' occur at the same locus, but are separated on homologous chromosomes. Hence, after meiosis, when the homologues have segregated, two of the daughter nuclei will carry the gene for 'female' and two the

gene for 'male'. Hence 50% of the zoospores are 'male' and 50% are 'female'.

In material collected from around Naples the gametophytes can be distinguished from the sporophytes by their structure and habit. In the gametophytes the prostrate filaments are less well developed while the upright filaments are richly branched (Fig. 12.8: compare [5] with [1]). The female and male gametophytes bear plurilocular zoidangia, in which the gametes are formed. The zoidangia may therefore be termed plurilocular gametangia, although morphologically they are very similar to the plurilocular sporangia of the sporophyte. Furthermore there is no obvious difference between 'male' and 'female' gametangia (Fig. 12.8 [4, 6]). Unlike the sporophyte, however, the gametophyte does not produce unilocular zoidangia.

The male and female gametes are morphologically similar, so that in one sense copulation in *Ectocarpus* can be said to be isogamous. Careful observation, however, reveals a clear distinction in the behaviour of 'male' and 'female' gametes: they exhibit 'physiological anisogamy'. The pairing and fusion of the gametes takes place as follows.

Fairly soon after their liberation (within 24 h), the female gametes come to rest and attach themselves to a substratum. When, subsequently, male gametes are 'let loose' on these female gametes they swim towards them in great numbers, attracted by substances (pheromones) secreted by the females. Each female gamete becomes surrounded by a swarm of males, which contact the female by the tips of their anterior flagella (Fig. 12.8 [10]). Within a few minutes one of the male gametes has usually succeeded in fusing with the female (Fig. 12.8 [11]), and as soon as this happens the crowd of other 'suitors' disperses. Similar phenomena ('**clumping**'), in which groups of gametes are formed during sexual reproduction, occur in several other algae (e.g. *Chlamydomonas*, p. 351).

During his investigations of copulation in *Ectocarpus*, Müller noticed that, during the formation of gametes, cultures of the female plants emitted a strange smell, not dissimilar to that of gin ([1244]). Fertile male plants, on the other hand, did not produce this smell, which suggested that the volatile material might be responsible for the attraction between the male and female gametes. This hypothesis was confirmed by some simple experiments ([1246]).

In one experiment male gametes were placed in hanging-drop culture and exposed to the gas produced by the female gametes; hence there was no contact between male and female gametes, nor between their culture media. Nevertheless, microscopical examination revealed that under the influence of the gas the male gametes behaved just as if female gametes were present: they formed clumps.

In another experiment male gametes were introduced into a glass capillary and observed under the microscope. If the 'female gas' was introduced into the capillary from one side, the male gametes moved towards that side, forming clumps as they did so. Thus the 'female gas' evokes two reactions in the male gametes. Firstly, it causes them to swim towards the gas, or rather, to swim up the concentration gradient of gas. This phenomenon is known as chemotaxis. Secondly it induces the gametes to swim hectically in a clump, a process called chemokinesis. This second reaction is brought about as follows. As soon as a male gamete comes into contact with a solid substratum (e.g. the material to which the female gamete has become attached), it starts to move in loops, clockwise. The posterior flagellum steers this movement by beating from side to side. The frequency of these lateral beats increases the closer the male gamete gets to the source of chemoattractant; thus it inevitably spirals in towards the female gamete ([504, 1083]) and clumps of gametes are produced.

Later Müller and his co-workers succeeded in establishing the chemical formula of the 'female gas' ([1266]). In order to obtain enough gas for analysis they grew and harvested female plants of *Ectocarpus* in culture from June 1968 to August 1970, using 14 900 culture dishes; 1041 g fresh mass (154 g dry mass) of female gametophytes were collected. The 'female gas' was condensed at -80 °C from the stream of air in which it was contained, and 92 mg of the female pheromone (the sex attractant or hormone) extracted. It was subsequently identified as (+)-(S)-6-(1Z-butenyl)-1,4-cycloheptadiene (Fig. 12.9) and originally called *Ectocarpus*-sirenin, because of the analogy with the female gamone of the chytrid *Allomyces*, called sirenin. Later Müller proposed the name ectocarpene ([1249]).

In a series of very elegant studies, carried out between 1971 and 1990, Müller, Jaenicke ([788]) and their collaborators showed that the female gametes of a great variety of Phaeophyceae secrete sexual pheromones, which attract the male gametes (for an overview, see [1083]). All the pheromones were volatile and fragrant, and also related chemically, being low-molecular-mass, highly unsaturated C_{11} and C_8 hydrocarbons, some of which were linear, others cyclic. Related species and genera often produced the same pheromone. Even more surprising was the discovery that the same pheromone could be shared by species in taxonomically widely separated orders. For instance, desmarestene (Fig. 12.9) is produced by two species of *Desmarestia* (order Desmarestiales) and by one species of *Cladostephus* (order Sphacelariales) ([1083, 1260]). Ectocarpene, the pheromone of *Ectocarpus*, is often a by-product during the production of other pheromones, suggesting that ectocarpene is the 'proto-type' phaeophycean pheromone and that other systems of chemoattraction were derived from the ectocarpene system during the phylogenetic diversification of the brown algae ([1260]). Conversely, the bouquet of pheromones of *Ectocarpus siliculosus*, besides ectocarpene, also contains minor amounts of the main pheromones produced by other brown algae ([1271]).

It might be thought that the low species-specificity of the pheromones would result in frequent crosses between species, or even between genera. These are prevented, however, because the initial phases of gamete fusion will usually proceed only between gametes of the same species. Highly species-specific reactions occur during the anchoring of the male gamete's anterior flagellum to the membrane of the female gamete, and these interactions can fail even within a species, between the gametes of incompatible strains ([1253, 1263]). On the other hand, successful crosses between the gametes of different species or in some cases different genera have been reported on quite a number of occasions ([1132]) and so the barriers to hybridization between brown algae cannot be very effective.

The sensitivity of the male gametes to pheromones is amazing. Threshold concentrations for a response range from 10^{-11} to 10^{-9} M, and in one case were 6.1×10^{-13} M! In this last instance, perception of a single molecule by the gamete is enough to elicit a response ([1083]).

After a male gamete has been attracted to a female gamete, the two gametes may fuse, providing that they are compatible. As a result of fusion (Fig. 12.8 [11]) a diploid zygote is formed (Fig. 12.8 [12]), which can germinate immediately, without a period of dormancy, and grow into a new diploid sporophyte.

Structure	Trivial name	Taxa
1	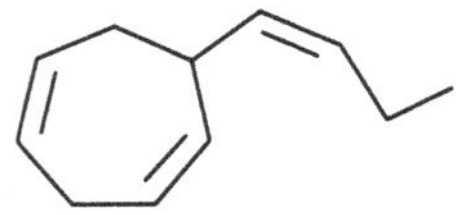 ectocarpene	*Ectocarpus siliculosus* *E. fasciculatus* *Sphacelaria rigidula*
2	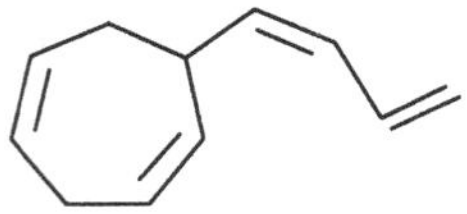 desmarestene	*Desmarestia aculeata* *D. viridis*
3	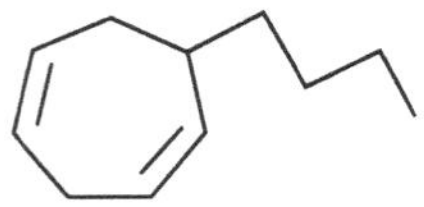 dictyotene	*Dictyota dichotoma*
4	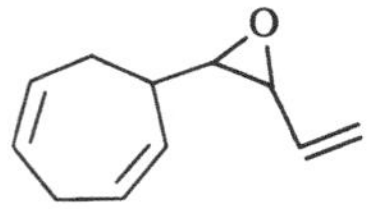 lamoxirene	*Laminaria*
5	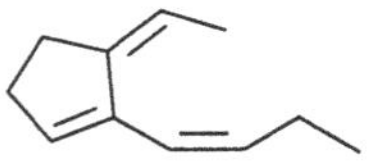 multifidene	*Chorda tomentosa* *Cutleria multifida*
6	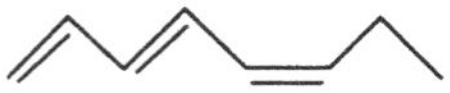 fucoserratene	*Fucus*
7	 finavarrene	*Ascophyllum nodosum* *Dictyosiphon foeniculaceus* *Sphaerotrichia divaricata*
8	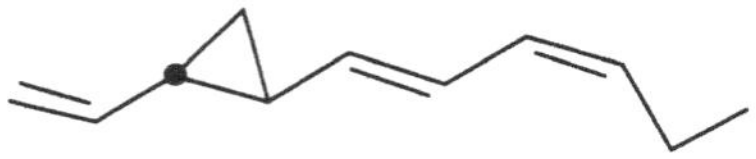 hormosirene	*Hormosira banksii* *Durvillaea* *Scytosiphon lomentaria*

Figure 12.9. Sexual pheromones in several brown algae. (Based on [1083].)

In summary, then, the life cycle of *Ectocarpus*, as determined for material from Naples, can be characterized as being a slightly heteromorphic, diplohaplontic cycle, with physiological anisogamy. Similar life cycles have been demonstrated in strains of *Ectocarpus siliculosus* from elsewhere in its worldwide distribution. Most of the strains are interfertile, but some very distant strains cannot interbreed (for instance, strains from the Mediterranean and Chile). In all cases, however, the female gametes produce the pheromone ectocarpene ([1252, 1253, 1256]).

Fig. 12.8 shows the normal course of the life cycle

in *Ectocarpus* but there can be many complications – detours and short-cuts – and these have been described in some detail by Müller ([1245, 1247]). Here we will mention a few of the alternatives, in order to illustrate how flexible life cycles can be; they are often far more plastic than the standard textbook diagrams imply.

1 Unfertilized male and female gametes can develop vegetatively, giving rise not to new gametophytes but to haploid sporophytes. These plants correspond in every way to normal sporophytes, except of course that they have only one set of chromosomes. Thus, although haploid spores are produced within the unilocular sporangia as usual, spore formation is not accompanied by meiosis. If the haploid sporophyte develops from a male gamete, then the haploid spores produced by the unilocular sporangia are also male and give rise to male gametophytes.

2 A small proportion of the spores formed after meiosis within the unilocular sporangia of normal sporophytes, grow into haploid sporophytes rather than male or female gametophytes.

3 Every kind of zoidangium can produce 'double zoids'. These cells have a double complement of organelles: two chloroplasts, two eyespots, four flagella, and two nuclei. The two nuclei can fuse with each other; 'double zoids' from a male gametangium thus develop into diploid sporophytes, which have the genetic factor for 'maleness' in duplicate. Following meiosis in the unilocular sporangia of these plants, zoids are produced that give rise only to haploid male plants.

There are other possibilities too, such as diploid gametophytes (♂ ♂ as well as ♀ ♀), and tetraploid sporophytes (♂ ♂ ♀ ♀). Their formation will not be discussed here.

So we can conclude that in *Ectocarpus siliculosus* the alternation between morphologically distinct phases (sporophyte and gametophyte) is not rigidly linked to changes in ploidy (between the haploid and diploid levels). In addition, throughout the distribution range of *Ectocarpus siliculosus*, there are populations that reproduce only asexually, through the formation of plurizoids. These plants are incapable of forming unilocular zoidangia and hence also of performing meiosis.

Order Sphacelariales

1 The thalli consist of branched, multiseriate filaments, which are not united into pseudoparenchymatous tissues. Both the creeping and the erect filaments have the same basic structure and also the same mode of growth (Fig. 12.10*a*, *g*). Growth occurs through division of conspicuous, cylindrical apical cells ([829]) and takes place according to a special, characteristic pattern (Fig. 12.10*a*). Each cell cut off by the apical cell – the primary segment – is initially divided into two secondary segments by a transverse wall. Then the secondary segments are divided up into smaller cells by the formation of longitudinal walls, so that the filament becomes pluriseriate ([1447]).

2 The life cycle is basically diplohaplontic, and isomorphic or slightly heteromorphic. Gametic fusion involves isogamy (strictly speaking, physiological anisogamy: [1260]), anisogamy ([702]), or oogamy ([1232]).

As in the order Ectocarpales, the thalli are differentiated into creeping prostrate filaments, which are often united to form discs (Fig. 12.10*g*), and erect filaments (Fig. 12.10*a–e*), which arise from the prostrate ones. In contrast to the Ectocarpales, however, where the erect filaments exhibit intercalary cell division (Fig. 12.7), in the Sphacelariales both the erect and the prostrate filaments grow by the division of apical cells. Perhaps, then, the filaments of the Sphacelariales can be interpreted as an evolutionary elaboration of the prostrate part of the thallus in the Ectocarpales.

Sphacelaria rigidula (Figs. 12.10, 12.11)

The branched filaments of this species form brown tufts 0.5–3 cm high. Vegetative reproduction takes place mainly by the production and dispersal of triradiate propagules (Fig. 12.11). *Sphacelaria rigidula* is a cosmopolitan species, occurring in both temperate and tropical regions. It can grow attached to rock, but also occurs as an epiphyte on larger algae.

Growth is apical, taking place by the division of a large, cylindrical apical cell (Fig. 12.10*a*). The apical cell has a large nucleus containing a nucleolus, and both of these are visible in the living cell; there are also many discoid chloroplasts, which divide actively. The cytoplasm and the organelles (including the

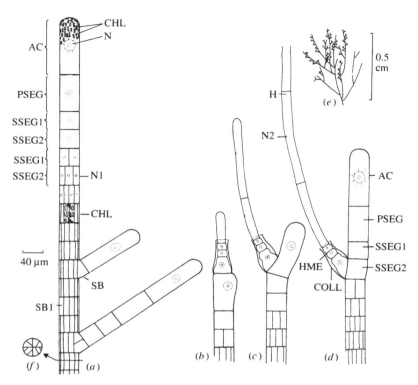

Figure 12.10. *Sphacelaria rigidula*. (*a*) Vegetative structure. (*b*) Apical cell, having formed a hair meristem on its upper side. (*c*) Further growth of the apical cell shown in (*b*) displaces the hair meristem to one side. (*d*) Later stage, in which, as a result of the division of the apical cell, the hair meristem appears to have arisen from the lowermost secondary segment. (*e*) Habit. (*f*) Transverse section through the thallus. (*g*) Creeping system of filaments in *S. radicans*. AC = apical cell; BD = basal disc; CF = creeping filament; CHL = chloroplast; COLL = collar around the base of a hair; EF = erect filament; H = colourless hair cell, with a large vacuole and rudimentary chloroplasts; HME = hair meristem; N = large nucleus; N1 = small nucleus; N2 = tiny nucleus of the hair cell; PSEG = primary segment; SB = side branch, arising from an upper secondary segment; SBI = dormant side branch initial; SSEG1 = upper secondary segment; SSEG2 = lower secondary segment.

chloroplasts) are concentrated in the growing tip of the apical cell and there are many golgi bodies, which produce swarms of golgi vesicles containing polysaccharide. Upon exocytosis the membranes of the vesicles are incorporated into the plasmalemma of the apical cell as it extends, while the vesicles' contents are added to the growing cell wall ([829, 1448]).

At regular intervals the apical cell cuts off a primary segment, which then divides by a transverse wall into two secondary segments: upper and lower. The secondary segments divide up further by vertical walls to form a parenchyma, but the original secondary segments can always be distinguished, even in the oldest parts of the thallus. This is because of the curious fact that the secondary segments achieve their final size while they are being formed from the primary segments; afterwards they grow no further and during the successive divisions of each segment, the nuclei become smaller and smaller (Fig. 12.10*a*). Side branches always arise from cells of the upper secondary segments and develop in the same way as the main axis. In *Sphacelaria rigidula* the side branches can become about as long as the main axis (Fig. 12.10*e*). In other species, however, they remain much shorter and because they then arise in two opposite rows, a pinnate (feather-like) branching pattern is produced.

Active apical cells often cut off small cells at their tips, which develop into phaeophycean hairs (Fig. 12.10*b–d*). At the base of the hair is a meristem, whose

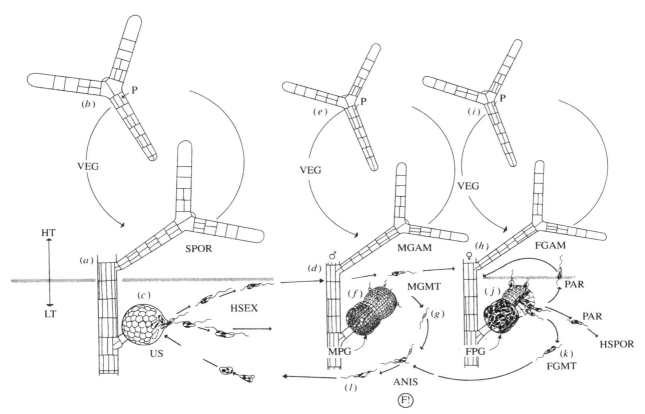

Figure 12.11. *Sphacelaria rigidula*: life cycle. ANIS = anisogamy; F! = fertilization; FGAM = female gametophyte; FGMT = female (macro-) gamete; FPG = female plurilocular gametangium (macrogametangium); HSEX = haplogenotypic sex determination; HSPOR = haploid sporophyte; HT = high temperature, e.g. 12–20 °C; LT = low temperature, e.g. 4–12 °C; MGAM = male gametophyte; MGMT = male (micro-) gamete; MPG = male plurilocular gametangium (microgametangium); P = triradiate propagule; PAR = parthenogenesis; SPOR = sporophyte; US = unilocular sporangium; VEG = vegetative reproduction. (After [702].)

cells divide, cutting off cells towards the hair apex. Hair cells are pale or colourless and can become very long through massive extension growth. The hair meristem is often surrounded by a collar, which represents the remains of the cell from which the hair arose. Phaeophycean hairs are highly characteristic of the Phaeophyceae as a whole, even through they may be absent in particular species or genera. Their function is probably to increase the surface area available for the absorption of nutrients such as phosphate and nitrate ([1022]).

After a hair has been initiated at the upper end of the apical cell in *Sphacelaria rigidula*, the remainder of the apical cell resumes growth, displacing the hair to one side (Fig. 12.10b–d). Thus, once the apical cell

has divided a few times the hair comes to look as though it had arisen laterally, from one of the lower secondary segments.

Sphacelaria rigidula has a very characteristic type of vegetative propagule. These are forked and formed laterally on the thallus (Fig. 12.11). The stem of the propagule usually bears two arms, rarely three, and breaks off at its base at dispersal.

The life cycle of *Sphacelaria* has been followed in the laboratory using material collected from the Hook of Holland ([702]). The sporophyte phase (which is diploid, $2n = ca.$ 50) consists of a system of branched creeping filaments (Fig. 12.11a–c), from which upright branching filaments arise (Fig. 12.10e). The filaments of the diploid sporophyte have diameters of

20–40 μm and are thicker than the filaments of the haploid gametophytes, which attain diameters of only 13–30 μm.

The sporophyte phase can form two types of reproductive organ: triradiate propagules and unilocular zoidangia. In contrast to *Ectocarpus siliculosus*, the sporophyte of *Sphacelaria rigidula* never produces plurilocular zoidangia and vegetative propagation of the sporophyte is brought about through the dispersal and growth of the propagules. Meiosis occurs in the unilocular zoidangia, followed by several rounds of mitosis, producing large numbers of haploid zoospores.

Vegetative propagules are formed only at relatively high temperatures (at 12, 17 and 20 °C in the laboratory) and in long days (16 h light; [258]). Unilocular zoidangia, on the other hand, develop only at low temperatures (4 and 12 °C); whether daylength has any effect on this process has not yet been established conclusively. These experimental results correspond well with observations in nature. On the temperate coasts of the Atlantic *Sphacelaria rigidula* produces copious quantities of propagules in summer, while the unilocular zoidangia are almost always found during the cooler part of the year, from autumn to spring.

The haploid zoospores released by the unilocular zoidangia of the sporophyte grow into haploid gametophytes (Fig. 12.11*d–k*). About 50% of the zoospores give rise to male gametophytes and 50% to female gametophytes. Haplogenotypic sex determination probably occurs therefore during meiosis, as we have already described for *Ectocarpus siliculosus* (p. 178).

The gametophyte is more slender than the sporophyte (see above) but apart from this the two generations are morphologically alike. The female and male gametophytes both bear plurilocular zoidangia, which produce gametes and may therefore be termed plurilocular gametangia. Male plurilocular gametangia can be distinguished from female gametangia by their smaller chambers. Each of these small chambers contains a small, pale chloroplast, so that the male gametangium as a whole is pale yellow in colour. Each chamber of the female gametangium, on the other hand, is large and has a large brown chloroplast, so that the female gametangium is dark brown (Fig. 12.11: compare *f* with *j*).

The plurilocular zoidangia of *Ectocarpus* and *Sphacelaria* differ in two respects (compare Figs. 12.11 and 12.8). Firstly, the plurilocular zoidangium of *Ectocarpus* is elongate and conical, while that of *Sphacelaria* consists of two swollen halves, each of which is more or less spherical. Secondly, in *Ectocarpus* the plurizoids are all liberated through a single opening at the upper end of the zoidangium. In *Sphacelaria*, however, each chamber at the surface of the zoidangium has its own opening, through which its own zoid and the zoids of underlying chambers make their exit. The gametophytes do not produce unilocular zoidangia.

The male gametes are much smaller and paler than the female and so are called microgametes (Fig. 12.11*g, k*). The copulation between these and the female macrogametes is thus an instance of anisogamy or 'heterogamy'. As in *Ectocarpus siliculosus*, the male gametes collect in groups around each female before one of them fuses with it. The female gametes, which become immobile during attraction and copulation, attract the male gametes via the pheromone ectocarpene, as in *Ectocarpus siliculosus* (Fig. 12.9; [1083, 1257]). Female gametes of *Sphacelaria* also produce small amounts of multifidene, the pheromone of *Cutleria multifida* (p. 190; [1257]). Gametophytes of either sex can reproduce vegetatively by triradiate propagules, just like the sporophyte (Fig. 12.11*e, i*).

The formation of propagules is promoted by high temperatures and long days (20 and 17 °C; 16 h light, in the laboratory), just as in the sporophyte. The formation of plurilocular zoidangia, on the other hand, is promoted by a combination of low temperatures (4 and 12 °C) and long days (16 h light). The critical daylength is 14 h light per day: with shorter daylengths no gametangia are formed. However, if the long night is interrupted by a short period (a half hour) of light, the inhibition of gametangium formation brought about by short-day treatment is removed, and gametangia are initiated. The existence of a critical daylength and the effectiveness of a light break in reversing the effects of short days are considered good evidence of the presence of one of several types of true photoperiodic response: that is, the alga is responding to the lengths of the light and dark periods, and not merely to the total amount of light received ([258, 344, 345, 726, 727]; see pp. 65, 77 for other examples of photoperiodic effects in algal life cycles).

On Dutch coasts near where the experimental material was collected, combinations of water temperature and daylength like those shown to induce gametangium formation in the laboratory occur in spring.

Unfortunately there are too few observations of the plurilocular zoidangia in nature for us to be able to say whether they are indeed usually formed in spring, as we might expect.

When a pair of gametes fuses, a diploid zygote is produced, which can develop into a new diploid sporophyte without any intervening period of enforced dormancy.

On the basis of investigations of material collected from the Hook of Holland, we can describe the life cycle of *Sphacelaria rigidula* as being diplohaplontic and slightly heteromorphic, with anisogamous copulation. There can be various deviations from the normal life cycle. Macrogametes, for instance, can develop without fertilization, either into new haploid female gametophytes or into haploid sporophytes. It has already been mentioned several times that the observations described above were made using Dutch material and this was quite deliberate. The possibility exists that other populations of *Sphacelaria rigidula* may have different life cycles and indeed there is some evidence for this. Some populations (or clones), it appears, can only reproduce asexually, by the production of propagules ([1447]).

Order Dictyotales

1 In the Dictyotales the thalli are fan-shaped or like branched ribbons. They are parenchymatous and consist of two, three or more layers of cells; growth is always brought about through division of apical cells (Fig. 12.12*k*), which can be linked to form a marginal meristem. If the thallus has a creeping basal portion, this too exhibits a parenchymatous structure and apical growth.

2 The life cycle is basically diplohaplontic and isomorphic. Sexual fusion is always oogamous (Fig. 12.12), and the male gametes have only one flagellum, which is anterior and pleuronematic (Fig. 12.4*a*). Each unilocular sporangium produces just four, non-flagellate meiospores, sometimes referred to as 'tetraspores' (Fig. 12.12*h–j*).

Dictyota dichotoma (Fig. 12.12)

This alga has strap-like thalli, which branch regularly and dichotomously and can be up to 30 cm high. They are anchored by rhizoids, usually to rocks. *Dictyota*

dichotoma is widely distributed on the temperate and subtropical coasts of Europe and indeed is probably cosmopolitan in all temperate and tropical seas.

Dictyota grows through the division of lens-shaped apical cells, which at regular intervals cut off downwardly arched, disc-like segments (Fig. 12.12*k*). These segments expand and then themselves divide to form a parenchyma, which in the mature thallus consists of three layers. In the two outer layers the cells are small and contain many chloroplasts, while the larger cells of the inner layer are pale and almost devoid of chloroplasts (Fig. 12.12*c, d, h*).

Some time before the branching of the thallus becomes obvious the apical cell divides by a vertical wall into two identical daughter cells, which both function as apical cells. As they in turn divide two similar branches begin to develop, producing equal forking of the thallus. *Dictyota* is the classic example of this type of **dichotomy**, which, because the two branches are alike from their inception, is termed true dichotomy. True dichotomy is rare in the plant kingdom. Much more common is **pseudodichotomy** (= apparent dichotomy), in which a side branch arises close to the growing point but then develops more or less as strongly as the part of the main axis lying above the branching point; as a result the main axis and branch are apparently equal. Pseudodichotomy occurs in branching filamentous algae, and also in higher plants with complex tissues.

The life cycles of *Dictyota dichotoma* (Fig. 12.12) and a series of other Dictyotales are well known and have been investigated by many workers ([465, 1357, 1554]). Apart from small variations characteristic of particular species, the life cycle of *Dictyota* is typical of the whole order. *Dictyota* is an isomorphic diplohaplont, with oogamous sexual reproduction.

The diploid sporophyte phase (Fig. 12.12*g*) bears special unilocular zoidangia, often called tetrasporangia, which are arranged in groups (sori) on the thallus (Fig. 12.12*h*). Meiosis occurs in the tetrasporangia, just as in the tetrasporangia of the Florideophyceae (p. 57), and four haploid, non-motile tetraspores are formed. Two of these grow into male gametophytes and two into female. Haplogenotypic sex determination has therefore taken place.

The haploid gametophyte phase is thus dioecious, with male and female gametophytes (Fig. 12.12*a, b*). The male gametophyte bears pale sori containing plurilocular male gametangia, which are also known

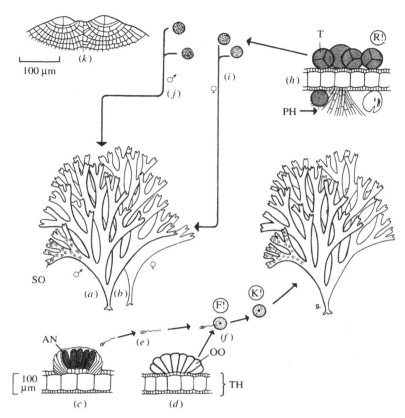

Figure 12.12. *Dictyota dichotoma:* life cycle. (*a, b*) Male and female gametophytes (haploid). (*c*) Transverse section through a gametophyte with a male sorus. (*d*) Transverse section through a gametophyte with a female sorus. (*e, f*) Spermatozoid and egg cell. (*g*) Sporophyte (diploid). (*h*) Transverse section through a sporophyte with tetrasporangia. (*i, j*) Tetraspores. (*k*) Apical cells. AN = antheridium; F! = fertilization; K! = karyogamy; OO = oogonium; PH = phaeophycean hairs; R! = meiosis; SO = sori; T = tetrasporangium; TH = thallus.

as antheridia. The tiny, pale gametes are set free by the dissolution of the walls of the gametangium chambers, and come to lie in a mass of mucilage, which represents the breakdown products of the chamber walls; this is retained for some time by the ensheathing cells of the sorus (Fig. 12.12*c*). The spermatozoids swim out of the mucilage and go in search of egg cells. Each spermatozoid has only one flagellum, which is pleuronematic and directed forwards (Fig. 12.4*a*) and also bears a row of spines, which are thought to be involved in the binding of the spermatozoid to the egg cell.

The female gametophyte bears dark brown sori, each containing 25–50 oogonia. Each oogonium produces a non-motile egg cell (Fig. 12.12*d*) and the life cycle is completed when this fuses with a spermato-zoid, giving a diploid zygote. The eggs attract the male gametes via the pheromone dictyotene (Fig. 12.9; [1083, 1265, 1410]). The zygote grows into a new diploid sporophyte, without any intervening period of dormancy.

The formation and liberation of the gametes is rhythmic, exhibiting a fourteen-day periodicity. The sori are initiated during neap tides, and the gametes are liberated for several days after the highest spring tide. After transfer to the laboratory, where no tidal influence is present, plants of *Dictyota dichotoma* continue to produce gametes periodically for several months, at intervals of approximately two weeks. The persistent rhythm indicates that the production of gametes is regulated internally, by a kind of 'endogenous clock'. In laboratory cultures of *Dictyota* the periodic production of gametes can be induced by replacing the dark phase of every 28th daily light–dark cycle by continuous dim light, which in nature would represent the light of the full moon. This coincides, of course, with the time of a spring tide, so that perception of moonlight during spring tides would trigger off and regulate the periodic production of gametes ([343, 1056, 1250]).

Order Scytosiphonales

1 Two different kinds of thalli are formed during the life cycle: small prostrate microthalli and large erect macrothalli. The microthalli consist of creeping, prostrate filaments, which are uniseriate and grow by division of apical cells. These filaments are usually united to form compact discs (Fig. 12.13c, i, q), which grow into crusts through the production of vertical rows of cells (Fig. 12.13a). The macrothalli are conspicuous parenchymatous structures, which grow erect and can be tubular, blade-like or sac-like; growth is intercalary.

2 The life cycle is basically diplohaplontic and heteromorphic, with a reduced sporophyte phase (Fig. 12.13). The sporophytes are only ever microthalli, whereas the gametophyte consists of a microthallus bearing one or more macrothalli. Sexual reproduction involves slight anisogamy ([234, 235, 236, 1277]).

3 Each cell contains only one chloroplast, which is discoid and contains a pyrenoid ([231, 406]).

The prostrate microthalli, with their apical growth, are quite similar to the systems of prostrate filaments in the order Ectocarpales, where again growth is brought about by divisions of apical cells (compare Fig. 12.13q with Fig. 12.7a). The conspicuous erect thalli of the Scytosiphonales, on the other hand, have intercalary growth and thus may perhaps be evolutionary elaborations of the systems of erect filaments produced by the Ectocarpales, which also have a pronounced intercalary growth pattern.

Scytosiphon lomentaria (Fig. 12.13)

The macrothalli of this species are simple cylindrical structures up to 45 cm high, which are constricted at regular intervals (Fig. 12.13d, j). There is a central medulla of large cells, while outside this there is a small-celled cortex, which bears uniseriate plurilocular zoidangia separated by sterile unicellular paraphyses (Fig. 12.13e, k). Scytosiphon lomentaria occurs world-wide in spring on coasts in the temperate zone.

The macrothallus grows diffusely, by intercalary cell division. The tip of the young macrothallus bears a single apical hair, while lateral hairs are also present (Fig. 12.13c, i). The macrothalli sprout from microthalli, which are prostrate systems of creeping, branched filaments, which grow through the division of apical cells; the filaments coalesce into prostrate discs and these develop and thicken into crusts by the formation of upright rows of cells (Fig. 12.13a).

The macrothalli are gametophytes and their uniseriate plurilocular zoidangia are gametangia. Male gametophytes produce male gametes, and these are somewhat smaller than the female gametes, which are produced on female gametophytes (Fig. 12.13e, f, k, l); sexual fusion is thus anisogamous. The male and female gametophytes are morphologically alike.

After release, the female gametes soon lose their motility and attach themselves to a solid substratum. They attract male gametes via the pheromone hormosirene (Fig. 12.9; [1083, 1257]) and out of the swarm of male gametes that congregates around each female, one succeeds in fusing with it to produce a diploid zygote (Fig. 12.13m–p). The zygote is able to give rise directly to a diploid sporophyte ($2n = ca.$ 44–48), without a period of dormancy. The sporophyte is much smaller and simpler than the gametophyte, and corresponds in its crustose morphology and structure to just one part of the gametophyte, namely the basal microthallus. The microthallus phase was originally described as a separate species, belonging to the crustose genus Ralfsia. The sporophyte never forms plurilocular zoidangia and bears only unilocular zoidangia (Fig. 12.13a), where meiosis takes place, followed by the formation of unizoids; these are therefore meiospores. The haploid meiospores in their turn grow into male and female gametophytes (Fig. 12.13a–c, h, i).

In summary, the life cycle of Scytosiphon lomentaria can be characterized as being diplohaplontic and heteromorphic, with a reduced sporophyte and anisogamous sexual reproduction (Fig. 12.13 A; [234, 235, 236, 1277]).

A common deviation from the basic life cycle pattern is where female or male gametes develop parthenogenetically, i.e. without sexual fusion (Fig. 12.13 B). The unfused gametes develop into haploid

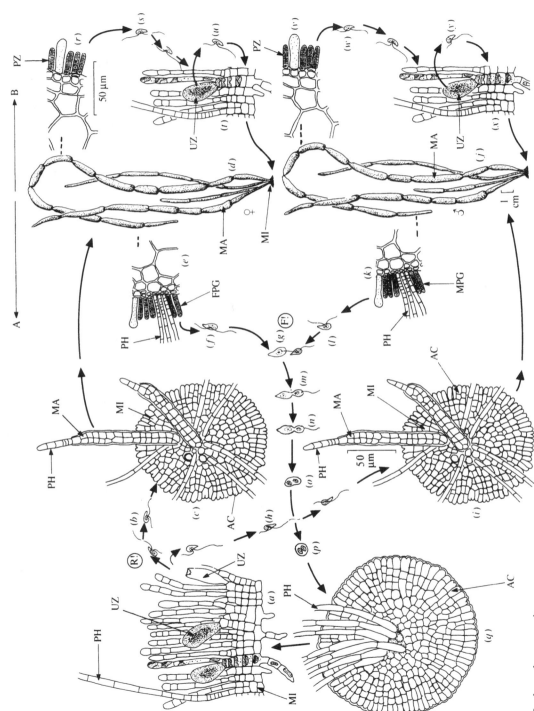

For legend see opposite page.

crusts (microthalli), which may or may not form unilocular zoidangia. New erect macrothalli then develop on the microthalli. This highly simplified, 'deviant' life cycle is in fact far more common than the basic sexual cycle, which has only been observed extremely rarely; it is unclear whether this reflects a true rarity of sexual reproduction, or difficulties in recording the phenomenon. It seems likely that the plurizoids produced by the macrothalli are never sexual in many populations, and are therefore asexual spores. The life cycle of *Scytosiphon lomentaria* has been found to be wholly asexual in numerous populations drawn from sites in temperate waters worldwide, across the whole range of the species ([262, 305, 821, 919, 920, 1922, 1923]). The predominance of asexual reproduction is a general feature of the Phaeophyceae, especially in the orders Ectocarpales, Scytosiphonales, Dictyosiphonales and Chordariales, and highlights the widespread, multiple loss of sexuality that has occurred during evolution in all groups of algae (and in groups of many other kinds of eukaryote).

Switching between one phase of the life cycle and another in *Scytosiphon lomentaria* is influenced by various environmental stimuli and conditions. In many strains, short days and low temperatures induce erect macrothalli to sprout from the crustose microthalli. For instance, the microthalli of a strain from Helgoland (N Germany) form macrothalli if the photoperiod is less than 13 h light per day and temperatures are below 17 °C. The consequence in nature is that macrothalli are initiated in the winter half of the year and mature during spring. After the production

and release of the plurizoids the macrothalli disappear and the species 'oversummers' in the form of the crustose microthalli, which are perennial. The short day response is a genuine photoperiodic response, one of several different types that have been documented from plants, the alga reacting to daylength itself, or rather to the length of the dark period, and not to the total amount of light received per day. The evidence for this is firstly that there is a 'critical daylength' of 13 h, above which macrothalli are not initiated; and secondly that, in 'short-day' conditions, interruption of the long dark period (e.g. 16 h darkness per 24 h) by a short light break inhibits the usual response and prevents the formation of macrothalli. In the latter case, the alga no longer perceives one long night but two short nights. A one-minute exposure to dim blue light is enough in *Scytosiphon lomentaria* to prevent the initiation of macrothalli, indicating that the pigment involved in the perception and measurement of the dark period (a 'cryptochrome') is sensitive to blue light. Other examples of photoperiodic responses in algal life cycles are given on pp. 77 and 184 ([344, 345, 346, 1053, 1055, 1056]).

Scytosiphon lomentaria strains from different latitudes appear to have different critical daylengths and maximum temperatures, above which the initiation of macrothalli is prevented ([1053, 1055]). Other strains lack any photoperiodic response ([262, 305, 919, 920]). The absolute maximum for the temperature at which macrothalli can be initiated seems to be 21 °C, which was determined for a strain from a warm temperate locality. At temperatures higher than this the crusts never form erect fronds;

Figure 12.13. *Scytosiphon lomentaria* (Scytosiphonales): heteromorphic diplohaplontic life cycle, with a reduced sporophyte and anisogamy. (*a*) Crustose diploid sporophyte (microthallus). (*b*) Haploid unispore, which will grow into a female gametophyte. (*c*) Juvenile female gametophyte: the circular, disc-like microthallus bears two erect juvenile macrothalli. (*d*) Adult female gametophyte: four tubular macrothalli grow from the crustose microthallus. (*e*) Detail of the macrothallus in (*d*), showing uniseriate plurilocular female gametangia. (*f*) Female gamete. (*g*) Male gamete beginning to fuse with immobile female gamete. (*h*) Haploid unispore, which will grow into a male gametophyte. (*i*) Young male gametophyte: the disc-like microthallus bears two juvenile erect macrothalli. (*j*) Adult male gametophyte: the crustose microthallus bears four erect tubular macrothalli. (*k*) Detail of the macrothallus in (*j*), showing uniseriate plurilocular male gametangia. (*l*) Male gamete. (*m–p*)

Fusion of gametes. (*q*) Juvenile diploid sporophyte, a disc-like microthallus. (*r*) Plurilocular female zoidangia, producing female 'gametes' that will develop without sexual fusion. (*s*) Parthenogenetic female 'gamete'. (*t*) Haploid crustose microthallus with unilocular zoidangia; this will give rise to female macrothalli. (*u*) Unizoid. (*v*) Plurilocular male zoidangia, producing male 'gametes' that develop without sexual fusion. (*w*) Parthenogenetic male 'gamete'. (*x*) Haploid crustose microthallus bearing unilocular zoidangia; this will give rise to male macrothalli. (*y*) Unizoid. A = sexual life cycle; AC = apical cell; B = asexual life cycle; F! = fertilization; FPG = female plurilocular gametangium; MA = macrothallus; MI = microthallus; MPG = male plurilocular gametangium; PH = phaeophycean hair; PZ = plurilocular zoidangium; R! reduction division (meiosis); UZ = unilocular zoidangium. (Based on [1277, 1283, 1481].)

the absolute maximum for macrothallus initiation is the factor preventing *Scytosiphon lomentaria* from occurring in the tropics ([696]).

Other genera in the order Scytosiphonales have life cycles like that of *Scytosiphon lomentaria* ([236, 1277]). The crustose microthallus phase probably enables *Scytosiphon* and other algae with crustose stages in their life cycles to survive adverse environmental conditions, such as freezing and ice scour in the severe winter conditions encountered towards the poles, or high summer temperatures nearer the equator; throughout the range of *Scytosiphon* the crusts probably offer protection from severe grazing pressure by gastropods and sea urchins ([1018]).

Order Cutleriales

1 There are two different kinds of thallus in the life cycles of the Cutleriales: large erect macrothalli and small prostrate microthalli. The microthalli are small fan-like crusts, which are prostrate and parenchymatous, growing through the activity of a marginal row of apical cells (Fig. 12.14e, f). The erect macrothalli are conspicuous fan-shaped structures, which again are parenchymatous but grow via intercalary meristems located in a fringe of uniseriate filaments at the thallus margin (Fig. 12.14a). This type of meristem, termed a 'trichothallic meristem', will be described in more detail below.

2 The life cycle is basically diplohaplontic and heteromorphic, the sporophyte being reduced relative to the gametophyte (Fig. 12.14), as in the order Scytosiphonales. The macrothalli are gametophytes and the microthalli are sporophytes. Sexual reproduction involves a pronounced anisogamy ('suboogamy'; Fig. 12.14k). The genus *Zanardinia* is exceptional, in that the gametophytes and sporophytes are both macrothalli, with trichothallic meristems ([465]).

The prostrate, crustose microthalli, with their marginal rows of apical cells, resemble those in some genera of the Dictyotales. They can be interpreted, perhaps, as evolutionary developments from the prostrate systems of filaments found in the Ectocarpales, in which growth is again brought about through division of apical cells ([465]). The large erect macrothalli, on the other hand, may have evolved through bundling of the erect filaments in ectocarpalean forms with distinct intercalary meristems (compare Fig. 12.14a with Fig. 12.7b; [465]).

Cutleria multifida (Fig. 12.14)

The cartilaginous, flat thalli of *Cutleria multifida* grow up to 40 cm high and dichotomize repeatedly. They are parenchymatous and exhibit trichothallic growth (Fig. 12.14a), and the thallus margin bears a fringe of hairs. Each of the hairs has a basal meristem (a trichothallic meristem), which cuts off hair cells towards the apex and thallus cells towards the base. The basal cells become fused to each other immediately below the meristem and divide up further by longitudinal and transverse walls, so producing the true parenchyma of the thallus. The full-grown plant consists of large cells inside surrounded by a layer of smaller outer cells (Fig. 12.14h).

The large, dichotomously branched plants (macrothalli) are haploid, dioecious gametophytes (Fig. 12.14b). Male gametophytes bear sori containing small-chambered, plurilocular male gametangia (Fig. 12.14g), while the sori of female gametophytes contain large-chambered female gametangia (Fig. 12.14h). Each chamber (locule) of the gametangium liberates its gamete separately (Fig. 12.14i, j). The very large female gamete, once it has come to rest, attracts the very much smaller male gametes by secreting an attractant, which is called multifiden (Fig. 12.9; [1083, 1249]). At first several male gametes cluster around each female gamete (clumping; Fig. 12.14k), but the group disperses once one of the male gametes has fused with the female ([927]; compare *Ectocarpus*, p. 178).

The zygote develops into a diploid sporophyte, which is membranous and fan-shaped. This microthallus grows appressed to the substratum and can be up to several centimetres in size (Fig. 12.14e, f). Growth is brought about by the activity of a marginal row of apical cells. Before the connection with *Cutleria* was known, the sporophyte had been described and classified in a separate genus, under the name *Aglaozonia reptans*. Sori of unilocular sporangia are produced on the upper surface of the parenchymatous sporophyte, and haploid unizoids are formed via meiosis. The unizoids in turn grow into haploid gametophytes. This is the normal life cycle, but several deviations are known ([925, 927, 1357, 1927]). *Cutleria multifida* occurs in the Mediterranean, on the south European coasts of the Atlantic, and in Southern Australia.

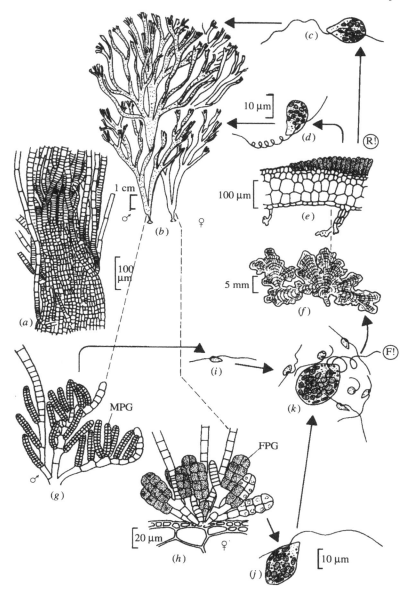

Figure 12.14. *Cutleria multifida:* life cycle. (*a*) Apical region. (*b*) Male and female gametophytes. (*c*, *d*) Unizoids. (*e*, *f*) Crustose sporophyte (= *Aglaozonia*-phase). (*g*, *h*) Male and female sori of the gameto-phyte. (*i*) Male gamete. (*j*) Female gamete. (*k*) Suboogamy. F! = fertilization; FPG = female plurilocular gametangium; MPG = male plurilocular gamet-angium; R! = reduction division (meiosis). (*a* after [232]; *b* after [1283]; *c–e* after [925]; *f* after [395]; *g–h* after [1774]; *i–k* after [925].)

Order Dictyosiphonales

1 Two different types of thallus occur during the life cycles of these algae. The first type is a microthallus and consists of inconspicuous creeping filaments, which are uniseriate and branched, and grow through the division of api-cal cells (Fig. 12.15*f, k*); the filaments are often united into compact discs ([1255]). The second type of thallus, the macrothallus, is a conspicuous erect structure. Macrothalli can be blade-like,

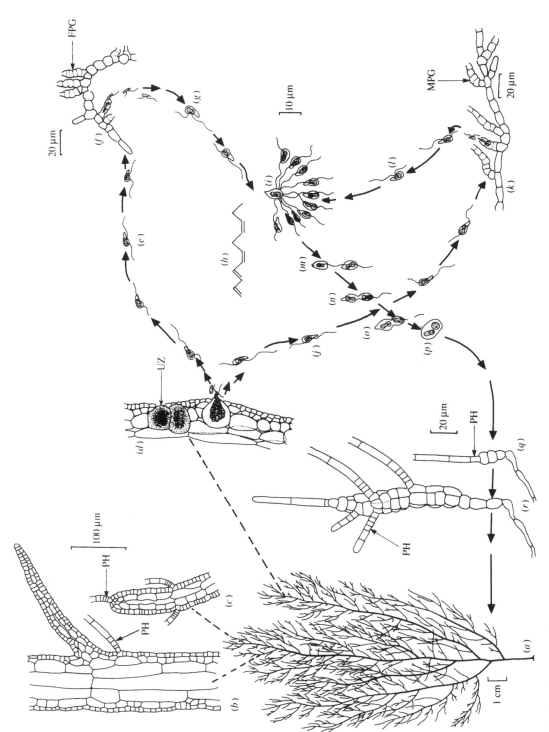

For legend see opposite page.

cylindrical or tubular and are often branched; growth is diffuse and intercalary, and the thalli are parenchymatous (Fig. 12.15a–c).

2 The basic form of the life cycle is diplohaplontic and heteromorphic, with a reduced gametophyte (Fig. 12.15f, k). The gametophyte is only ever a microthallus, whereas the sporophyte phase consists of microthalli bearing one or more macrothalli. Sexual reproduction generally involves physiological anisogamy (as in *Ectocarpus*, p. 178), the gametes resembling each other in size and morphology ([188, 1255, 1401, 1402]); morphological anisogamy, involving gametes of different sizes, is known in one species ([420]).

The microthalli resemble the creeping filaments of the Ectocarpales, with their apical growth (compare Fig. 12.15k, f with Figs. 12.6 and 12.7a). This suggests, perhaps, that during evolution the microthallus phase has been derived from ectocarpalean systems of creeping filaments. The conspicuous macrothalli, on the other hand, should be compared with the erect filament systems of the Ectocarpales and may have evolved from them; both have intercalary growth, though the Dictyosiphonales are much more elaborate.

The microthalli and macrothalli of the Dictyosiphonales show similarities, in structure and mode of growth, to the microthalli and macrothalli of the Scytosiphonales (compare Fig. 12.15 with Fig. 12.13). The difference is that the microthalli of the Dictyosiphonales are gametophytes, while those of the Scytosiphonales are sporophytes.

Dictyosiphon foeniculaceus (Fig. 12.15)

The bushy plants of the macrothallus phase are up to 60 cm high and consist of axes and main branches *ca.*

1 mm thick, which bear numerous more delicate side branches (Fig. 12.15a). The macrothallus is parenchymatous. It has a central medulla of large colourless cells, around which is a small-celled cortex (Fig. 12.15b, c), the cortical cells having numerous discoid chloroplasts with pyrenoids. Older parts of the thallus become hollow. Growth is mainly diffuse, brought about by intercalary cell division (Fig. 12.15q, r; [927]).

The macrothallus is diploid and produces unilocular zoidangia, which lie embedded in the cortex (Fig. 12.15d). Haploid meiospores are formed in the unilocular zoidangia and, once released, grow into microscopic filamentous gametophytes (microthalli); these can be female (Fig. 12.15f) or male (Fig. 12.15k). At low temperatures (1–8 °C) the gametophytes produce gametes in uniseriate plurilocular gametangia. The male and female gametes look alike but behave differently. The female gametes become immobile and attach themselves to a solid substratum, and then they attract male gametes by means of the pheromone finavarrene (Figs. 12.9, 12.15h, i). Fusion of one of the male gametes with the female produces a diploid zygote (Fig. 12.15m–p). This kind of sexual reproduction is termed 'physiological anisogamy', because it involves female and male gametes that differ only in behaviour, not in size (see also the physiological anisogamy of *Ectocarpus*: p. 178, Fig. 12.8). The zygote subsequently grows into a new diploid sporophyte (Fig. 12.15q, r, a).

In one common modification of the basic life cycle, unfused male or female gametes develop directly into haploid sporophytes; the unizoids produced by these macrothalli grow into gametophytes, which have the same sex as the original gamete ([1402]).

Dictyosiphon foeniculaceus is widely distributed along Arctic coasts, and along the cool temperate coasts of both the Pacific and Atlantic Oceans.

Figure 12.15. *Dictyosiphon foeniculaceus* (Dictyosiphonales): a heteromorphic, diplohaplontic life cycle with a reduced gametophyte. (a) The macroscopic sporophyte. (b) Longitudinal section through a portion of the sporophyte. (c) Longitudinal section through an apex of the sporophyte. (d) Longitudinal section through a portion of the sporophyte bearing unilocular zoidangia. (e) Haploid unispore; this will grow into a female gametophyte. (f) Female gametophyte. (g) Female gamete. (h) Finavarrene, the sexual pheromone secreted by the female gamete once it has become immobile. (i) Immobile female gamete, surrounded by male gametes that have been attracted by the female pheromone. (j) Haploid unispore; this will grow into a male gametophyte. (k) Male gametophyte. (l) Male gamete (note that the male and female gametes are morphologically indistinguishable: compare g with l). (m–p) Gametic fusion. (p) Zygote. (q, r) Young stages of the sporophyte that grows from the zygote. FPG = female plurilocular gametangium; MPG = male plurilocular gametangium; PH = phaeophycean hair; UZ = unilocular zoidangium. (Based on [927, 1283, 1402, 1553].)

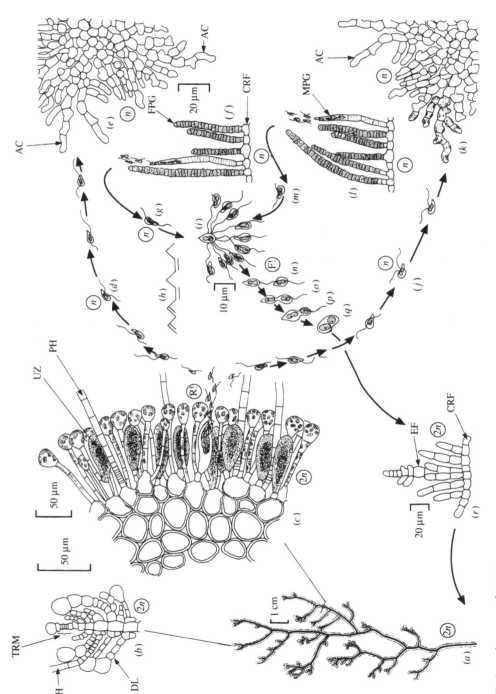

For legend see opposite page.

Order Chordariales

1 Two types of thallus occur during the life cycles of the Chordariales: microthalli and macrothalli. The microthalli are inconspicuous creeping systems of filaments, which are uniseriate and branched, growing by the division of apical cells (Figs. 12.16*e, k*, 12.18*a*); the filaments often cohere to form fairly compact discs (Fig. 12.16*e, k*). The macrothalli consist of erect branched filaments, again uniseriate but with intercalary growth; this takes place in (usually) distinct meristematic zones, termed trichothallic meristems. The erect filaments of the macrothallus are generally united to form gelatinous cushions (Fig. 12.18*g*) or branched, worm-like plants (Fig. 12.16*a–c*).

2 The life cycle is basically diplohaplontic and heteromorphic, with a reduced gametophyte (Fig. 12.16). The gametophytes are always microthalli, whereas the sporophyte phase consists either of microthalli bearing macrothalli, or of macrothalli alone (Figs. 12.16*r, a–c*, 12.17). Sexual reproduction involves physiological anisogamy, as in *Ectocarpus* (p. 178), the gametes being of similar size and morphology (Fig. 12.16*g, i, m*; [1254, 1305, 1307, 1399, 1400, 1403, 1404]).

The microthalli are morphologically similar to the prostrate systems of filaments in the Ectocarpales (compare Fig. 12.16*e, k* with Figs. 12.6 and 12.7*a*), and both exhibit apical growth. Furthermore, the macrothalli of the simpler representatives of the order (e.g. *Elachista*; Fig. 12.18*g*) are very like the erect systems of branched filaments in the Ectocarpales; the pattern of growth is also similar, with distinct intercalary meristems in both (compare Fig. 12.18*g* with Fig. 12.7*b*). In the more complex, worm-like macrothalli of some other Chordariales (e.g. *Liebmannia*, Fig. 12.17*a*; or *Sphaerotrichia*, Fig. 12.16*b*), the intercalary meristematic zone (= trichothallic meristem) lies not far below the apex of each filament and only cuts off cells downwards. The non-growing portion of the filament above the meristem can be short (Fig. 12.16*b*), long (Fig. 12.17*a*), or lacking altogether (as in *Spermatochnus*); in the last case, growth is brought about by an apical cell, which is interpreted to be an anomalous, vestigial trichothallic meristem.

In the worm-like thalli found in some Chordariales there are one to several axial filaments composed of long colourless cells (Fig. 12.17*a*). These bear whorls of branched lateral filaments, whose cells are shorter than in the axial filaments and contain numerous discoid chloroplasts (Fig. 12.16*c*). The axial and lateral filaments are linked by mucilage, which maintains the integrity of the thallus; the structure is often pseudoparenchymatous (Fig. 12.16*c*). Species with one axial filament are like certain red algae with a uniaxial construction, such as *Acrosymphyton* (Fig. 5.21), while species with several axial filaments find a parallel in multiaxial red algae, such as *Nemalion* (Fig. 5.24).

Sphaerotrichia divaricata (Fig. 12.16)

The macrothalli (sporophytes) of *Sphaerotrichia divaricata* are irregularly branched structures growing up to 40 cm high. The axes and branches are worm-like and slippery, and rather cartilaginous, attaining diameters of

Figure 12.16. *Sphaerotrichia divaricata* (Chordariales): a heteromorphic, diplohaplontic life cycle, with a reduced gametophyte. (*a*) The macroscopic sporophyte. (*b*) Longitudinal section through the sporophyte. (*c*) Cross section through an older region of the sporophyte that bears unilocular zoidangia. (*d*) Haploid unispore; this will grow into a haploid female gametophyte. (*e*) Female gametophyte: a creeping, prostrate structure that grows through apical cell divisions. (*f*) Cross section of a female gametophyte, showing a creeping filament bearing female plurilocular gametangia. (*g*) Motile female gamete. (*h*) Finavarrene, the sexual pheromone secreted by the female gametes when they are immobile. (*i*) Immobile female gamete surrounded by motile male gametes attracted by the female pheromone. (*j*) Haploid unispore; this will grow into a haploid male gametophyte. (*k*) Creeping, prostrate male gametophyte, composed of branched filaments that grow apically. (*l*) Cross section of a male gametophyte, showing a creeping filament bearing male plurilocular gametangia. (*m*) Motile male gamete. (*n–q*) Fusion of gametes. (*q*) Zygote. (*r*) The young sporophyte, which grows from the zygote and is composed of creeping filaments bearing an upright whorled axis. AC = apical cell; CRF = creeping filament; DL = determinate lateral; EF = erect filament; F! = fertilization; FPG = female plurilocular gametangium; MPG = male plurilocular gametangium; PH = phaeophycean hair; R! = reduction division (meiosis); TRM = trichothallic intercalary meristem; UZ = unilocular zoidangium; *n* = haploid; 2*n* = diploid. (Based on [615, 1400, 1482].)

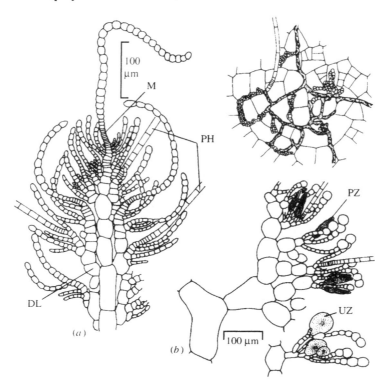

Figure 12.17. *Liebmannia leveillei*. (*a*) Uniaxially constructed thallus, with lateral filaments and trichothallic growth. (*b*) Plurilocular and unilocular zoidangia.

DL = determinate lateral branch (short shoot); M = meristem; PH = phaeophycean hair; PZ = plurilocular zoidangium; UZ = unilocular zoidangium. (After [927].)

0.5–1 mm. The thalli have a uniaxial architecture and grow through the activity of trichothallic meristems, above which are only a few non-dividing cells (Fig. 12.16*b*). In fully grown thalli the axial and lateral filaments coalesce into a hollow pseudoparenchyma, which is covered externally by numerous assimilatory filaments, unilocular zoidangia, and phaeophycean hairs (Fig. 12.16*c*). Each assimilatory filament consists of four to six cells, containing many discoid chloroplasts; the terminal cell of the filament has a characteristic, spherical shape (hence '*Sphaerotrichia*').

Adult macrothalli are to be found in summer. The unilocular zoidangia produce haploid meiospores, which develop into either haploid female (Fig. 12.16*e*) or male (Fig. 12.16*k*) microthalli (gametophytes). The microthalli bear uniseriate plurilocular zoidangia, whose plurizoids are capable of growing into new generations of haploid microthalli. The plurizoids function as gametes only if the plurilocular zoidangia are formed in long day conditions (14–16 h light per day) and at relatively low temperatures (0–15 °C); in

nature, such conditions occur mainly in spring. The male and female gametes are morphologically similar but behave differently; this is therefore another instance of 'physiological anisogamy', as in *Ectocarpus* (p. 178, Fig. 12.8). After it has become immobile and attached itself to a solid substratum, each female gamete attracts male gametes (Fig. 12.16*i*) by means of the pheromone finavarrene (Figs. 12.9, 12.16*h*). One of the male gametes fuses with the female gamete, producing a diploid zygote (Fig. 12.16*n–q*), which develops into a prostrate, diploid microthallus (Fig. 12.16*r*); this in turn gives rise to a new diploid macrothallus, which matures in the course of the summer. The haploid microthalli are capable of surviving the stresses of winter and summer. They can, for instance, tolerate temperatures between −1 and 28 °C, and can continue to reproduce asexually even under adverse conditions ([1307, 1400]).

This species also includes a number of strains that have lost their sexuality. In the cool, long day conditions that induce sexuality in sexual strains, the plurizoids of the asexual thalli develop into new sporophytes; in other circumstances they only multiply the haploid microthallus phase (^{1400}).

Sphaerotrichia divaricata is widespread along the cool temperate coasts of the N Pacific and N Atlantic Oceans.

Liebmannia leveillei (Fig. 12.17)

The slightly cartilaginous thalli of *Liebmannia* are worm-like and branched, and grow up to 20 cm high. The thallus is uniaxially constructed, with a main axis (axial filament) that bears branching lateral filaments; both exhibit trichothallic growth (Fig. 12.17*a*). The growth of the lateral filaments is limited and so they are sometimes called short shoots or determinate laterals. The tapering plurilocular zoidangia and the spherical unilocular zoidangia are formed at the surface of the thallus, at the ends of the determinate laterals (Fig. 12.17*b*). In addition the laterals bear particularly well-developed phaeophycean hairs.

The life cycle of *Liebmannia leveillei* is unknown. The unizoids are probably meiospores that develop into haploid microthalli. The plurizoids may perhaps serve to reproduce the macrothallus phase, which is a spring and summer annual found in southern Europe, along Mediterranean and Atlantic coasts.

Elachista stellaris (Fig. 12.18)

The small hemispherical thalli of this species grow epiphytically on various larger brown algae, where they form gelatinous cushions several millimetres in diameter. They occur on the Atlantic coasts of Europe, from Ireland southwards, and also on Mediterranean coasts.

The compact basal cushion consists of a number of axial filaments, each made up of large colourless cells, which are united into a pseudoparenchymatous tissue. The cushion bears a great many thick filaments, whose cells contain numerous chloroplasts. These filaments grow through the activity of basal meristems, which

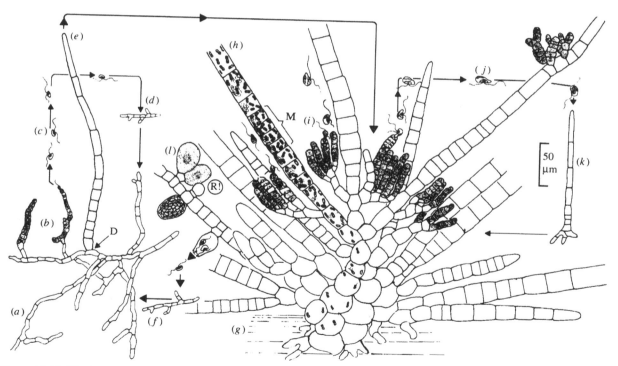

Figure 12.18. *Elachista stellaris:* life cycle. (*a*) Microthallus (*n*). (*b*) A plurilocular sporangium on the microthallus. (*c*) Zoids. (*d*) Young microthallus. (*e*) Young macrothallus (2*n*), borne on the microthallus. (*f*) Young microthallus, which has developed from one of the zoospores produced by a unilocular sporangium. (*g*) Macrothallus (2*n*). (*h*) Assimilator. (*i*) A plurilocular sporangium produced by the macrothallus. (*j*) Zoids. (*k*) Young macrothallus. (*l*) Unilocular sporangia. D = probable site of vegetative diploidization; M = basal meristem; R! = reduction division (meiosis). (After ^{1853}.)

also cut off cells to form part of the cushion; this kind of growth is referred to as trichothallic. Cells added by the meristem to the cushion can subsequently branch. The plurilocular and unilocular zoidangia arise for the most part at the edge of the cushion itself, but they can also occur on the photosynthetic filaments. Plurilocular zoidangia tend to be produced when the days are long (16 h light) and the relatively large plurizoids give rise to new macrothalli (Fig. 12.18*j, k*). Unilocular zoidangia, on the other hand, are usually produced in short days (8 h light) and the small unizoids, whose formation is associated with meiosis, grow into simple, filamentous microthalli (Fig. 12.18*f*). These are haploid, in contrast to the diploid macrothalli, and grow by division of the apical cells.

In short days the microthalli produce plurilocular zoidangia and from these small plurizoids emerge, which grow into new microthalli (Fig. 12.18*b–d*). In long days, however, a new macrothallus is formed. This develops on and indeed from the microthallus, when side branches of microthallus change from apical to intercalary growth. The macrothallus that develops is diploid, yet has arisen vegetatively from a haploid microthallus (Fig. 12.18*e*). This process, which does not involve the formation of gametes, is called vegetative diploidization ([1272, 1853]). Vegetative haploidization (i.e. vegetative meiosis) is known in the red alga *Lemanea* (p. 82).

The life cycle of *Elachista fucicola* is similar to that of *E. stellaris*, described above. Here too the macrothallus arises directly from the microthallus, as a result of vegetative diploidization and a change from apical to intercalary growth. Furthermore, in *E. fucicola* almost all the cells of the microthallus can be transformed into macrothallus tissue by intercalary cell division ([863]). It may well be that vegetative diploidization occurs elsewhere in the Chordariales too, especially since plurizoids from microthalli have only seldomly been seen to copulate, whereas meiosis has often been observed in the unilocular zoidangia.

The macrothallus phase of *Elachista stellaris* is a summer annual, while the microthallus phase probably serves for overwintering.

Order Desmarestiales

1 Two different kinds of thalli, microthalli and macrothalli, occur during the life cycle in species of this order. The microthalli consist of microscopic branched filaments, which are uniseriate and grow through division of apical cells (Fig. 12.19*h, i*). The macrothalli, on the other hand, are bushy or foliose and much larger, attaining lengths of several decimetres (Fig. 12.19*a*) or even several metres (Fig. 12.20*a*).

2 The life cycle is diplohaplontic and strongly heteromorphic, with an alternation between a highly differentiated, diploid macrothallus (sporophyte) and a tiny filamentous microthallus (gametophyte), which is haploid.

The macrothallus is uniaxially constructed. It consists of a branched system of filaments, consisting of an axial filament and determinate lateral filaments or branches, which are all arranged in the same plane (Figs. 12.19*d*, 12.20*b*). The axial filament exhibits trichothallic growth. Determinate laterals are produced both above and below the meristematic zone, but those below the meristem give rise to rhizoid-like filaments, which grow downwards from the basal cells of the laterals and unite to form a pseudoparenchymatous cortex. As this pseudoparenchyma increases in thickness cylindrical thalli several millimetres in diameter can be produced, or flattened structures several centimetres to decimetres wide. These thalli exhibit diffuse intercalary growth, through the meristematic activity of the meristoderm (Fig. 12.19*c*).

The macrothallus, which is the sporophyte generation, bears unilocular zoidangia and it is in these that meiosis takes place (Fig. 12.19*e*). The gametophyte (microthallus) is oogamous. Each oogonium produces one egg (Fig. 12.19*i*), and each antheridium one spermatozoid (Fig. 12.19*h*); plurilocular zoidangia are never present. Release of the spermatozoid from the antheridium and its subsequent attraction to the egg are mediated by a pheromone (desmarestene: Fig. 12.9) secreted by the egg ([1083, 1267]).

In the macrothalli of the Desmarestiales the basic mode of growth is trichothallic, a trichothallic meristem being an intercalary meristematic zone in a uniseriate filament. Trichothallic growth also occurs in the erect filaments of many Ectocarpales (Fig. 12.7*b*, IMZ), in the erect gametophytes of the Cutleriales (Fig. 12.14*a*), and in the erect sporophytes of many Chordariales (Figs. 12.16*b*, 12.17*a*). Most of the cells produced by the trichothallic meristems are cut off downwards. In the Desmarestiales a compact cortex is formed around each axial filament, just below the meristematic zone (Figs. 12.19*d*, 12.20*b*). This develops through the coalescence of rhizoid-like filaments, which grow out from the basal cells of short lateral filaments borne by the axial filament. The lateral filaments (which have determinate growth) are arranged in two opposite rows on the axial filament, and so the whole structure of the thallus is built up around a delicate feather-like central scaffold.

The main body of the thallus, however, is formed through the meristematic activity of the epidermis of the cortex, a meristematic epidermis of this kind generally being referred to as a meristoderm (Fig. 12.19*c*). This pattern of growth can be seen, for instance, in *Himanthothallus grandifolius*, a foliose member of the Desmarestiales, which grows up to 10 m long and is to be found around Antarctic coasts. Here the trichothallic meristems are active only in juvenile plants; by the time the plants are adult, growth is intercalary and diffuse, brought about through the activity of the meristoderm ([1210, 1211]). The life cycle of *Himanthothallus* is similar to that of *Desmarestia* ([1890]).

The life cycles of the orders Laminariales and Sporochnales are identical to those of the Desmarestiales, agreeing even in the details (compare Fig. 12.21 with Fig. 12.19, and see pp. 204–6), and this suggests that these three orders are closely related. The Sporochnales, however, have a very distinct, characteristic type of trichothallic growth (not treated here), while the Laminariales differ from the Desmarestiales by the almost total absence of trichothallic meristems, intercalary growth being brought about entirely by meristoderm activity. Trichothallic meristems are to be found in one genus of the Laminariales, however, namely the bootlace weed *Chorda*, one or more occurring at the apices of the juvenile plantlets (Fig. 12.20*c*, *d*; Fig. 12.25 shows an adult plant of *Chorda*). It seems likely, therefore, that the ancestors of the Laminariales had trichothallic meristems and that these were lost during evolution, being replaced by the meristoderm. Juvenile plants of *Fucus*, in the order Fucales, also have terminal trichothallic meristems (Fig. 12.20*e*, *f*), suggesting that trichothallic growth may be primitive in this order too. Adult plants in the Fucales grow through a combination of apical cell division and meristoderm activity (p. 207, Fig. 12.26; [238, 240]).

Desmarestia aculeata (Fig. 12.19)

The thallus consists of compressed axes, which can attain a thickness of several millimetres. The plants are cartilaginous, 30–180 cm long, and clothed with short side branches, which grow out bilaterally from the main axes and all lie in one plane; they are arranged alternately. Each side branch ends in a tuft of hairs (Fig. 12.19*b*), which fall off in the winter, leaving only the prickle-like side branch itself (Fig. 12.19*a*).

Unilocular zoidangia occur embedded in the outer, cortical part of the thallus (Fig. 12.19*e*). There are no plurilocular zoidangia. In *Desmarestia viridis* it has been observed that meiosis occurs during the formation of the unizoids ([8]), and these subsequently develop into male and female gametophytes (Fig. 12.19*h, i*). Formation of gametangia requires low temperatures (*ca.* 5–12 °C) and blue light. In red light the gametophytes will grow vegetatively but produce no gametangia ([1267]). The antheridia are small cells, borne in clusters at the tips of branched filaments; each antheridium produces a single spermatozoid (Fig. 12.19*h, j*), which lacks an eyespot ([238]). The female gametophytes bear oogonia, each with one egg cell. At maturity the egg cells are extruded but they remain attached to the oogonia, where they are fertilized (Fig. 12.19*i*). Release of the spermatozoids is triggered by the pheromone desmarestene (Fig. 12.9), which is secreted by the eggs, and this chemical also mediates the subsequent attraction of the spermatozoids to the egg cells (Fig. 12.19*i–k*; [1083, 1267, 1270]). The zygote grows into a new *Desmarestia* macrothallus ([8, 885, 1588]).

Desmarestia aculeata occurs along Arctic coasts, and along the cool temperate coasts of the N Atlantic and N Pacific Oceans.

Order Laminariales

1 Two types of thallus occur during the life cycle: microthalli and macrothalli. Each microthallus is microscopic and consists of branched, uniseriate filaments, which grow through the division of apical cells (Fig. 12.21*e, f*); it is often reduced to only a few cells (Fig. 12.24). The macrothallus is generally foliose and can be anything from a few decimetres to several tens of metres long (Figs 12.21*a*, 12.25*a*). The macrothallus has a complex parenchymatous structure and exhibits intercalary growth, through the activity of a meristoderm (Fig. 12.22).

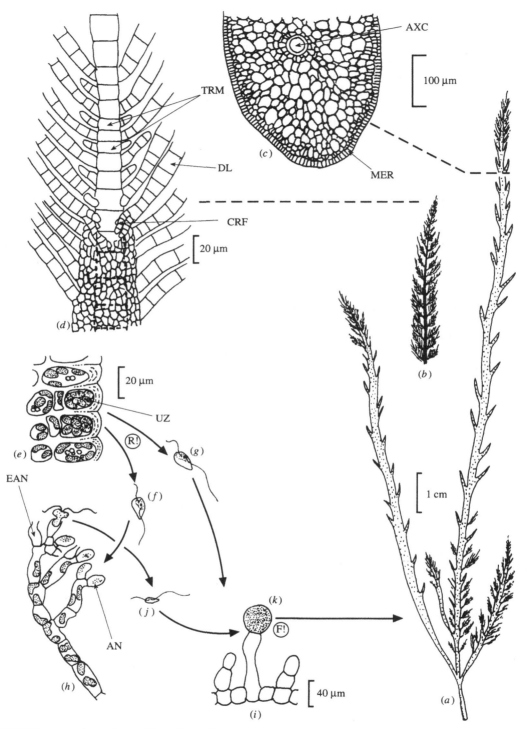

Figure 12.19. *Desmarestia aculeata:* life cycle. (*a*) Sporophyte (macrothallus), as it appears in autumn. (*b*) Sporophyte: tip of branch in spring. (*c*) Cross section through thallus. (*d*) Branched terminal filament of the sporophyte, with trichothallic meristem. (*e*) Uni-locular zoidangia within the surface tissue of the thallus. (*f, g*) Unizoids (meiospores). (*h*) Male gametophyte (microthallus). (*i*) Female gametophyte (microthallus). (*j*) Spermatozoid. (*k*) Egg ready to be fertilized. AN = antheridium; AXC = axial cell;

2 The Laminariales have a strongly hetero-morphic, diplohaplontic life cycle, with an alternation between highly differentiated diploid sporophytes (the macrothalli) and microscopic haploid gametophytes (microthalli) (Fig. 12.21). Meiosis takes place in the unilocular zoidangia of the sporophyte (Figs. 12.21c, 12.25b). The gametophyte phase is oogamous. Each oogonium produces one egg cell (Figs. 12.21f, 12.24), and each antheridium one spermatozoid (Figs. 12.21e, 12.24). Plurilocular zoidangia are completely absent. The triggering of the release of the spermatozoids from the antheridia and the subsequent attraction of the spermatozoids to the eggs are both mediated by pheromones secreted by the eggs ([1060, 1080, 1082, 1083, 1084, 1085, 1086]).

The order Laminariales includes the largest known seaweeds. Species of the genera *Nereocystis* and *Macrocystis*, for instance, can grow up to 50 m long off the northwestern coasts of America. For a discussion of the close relationship between the Laminariales, Desmarestiales and Sporochnales, reference should be made to pp. 199, 216–18.

Laminaria hyperborea (Fig. 12.21)

The sporophyte consists of a stipe and a blade. The stipe can be up to 2 cm thick at the bottom and 1 cm thick at the top, and can attain lengths of 0.5–2 m. It grows attached to rocks by a system of branching, cylindrical haptera, which form a holdfast. The haptera are covered by a meristoderm, whose cells produce innumerable rhizoids; these fill microscopic crevices in the substratum and secrete adhesive mucilage, thus ensuring a strong attachment ([1781]).

The blade is more or less fan-shaped and divided into strips; it is 30 cm to 1 m long. The meristem at the junction between the stalk and blade is active in spring and gives rise to a complete new blade in the period between January and April. New blades are formed only when the days are short (less than 13 h light per day) and temperatures are low (−1.5 to 15 °C), corresponding to the winter half of the year in

nature. The induction of new blades by short days is a true photoperiodic response, which means that the alga is responding to the daylength itself (or rather, to the length of the nights), rather than to the total amount of light incident upon it per day. Thus, if an hour of light is given to the algae in the middle of the long dark period, the effect of the short-day treatment is nullified and no blades are induced. The presence of the light break apparently causes the alga to perceive two short nights instead of one long one ([1057]; see pp. 65, 189 for other examples of true photoperiodic responses in algae).

The growth of the new blade is sustained by reserve materials formed by the plant during the late spring and summer of the previous year (which is when photosynthesis is most active) and stored in the old blade ([1051]). The old blade remains attached to the new blade for some time, the junction between them being marked by a constriction (Fig. 12.21a); if it is cut off the new blade cannot grow to any extent, since the old blade still contains reserves necessary for the new blade's development. Recently, it has been shown that the annual pattern of winter growth in Laminariales is under the direct control of a circa-annual (approximately yearly) endogenous rhythm, which is more finely tuned by the variation in daily photoperiod throughout the year ([1058a, b]). Sporophytes of *Laminaria hyperborea* can live for 10–20 years.

The meristematic zone between stipe and blade (Fig. 12.21a) produces blade tissue on one side and stipe cells on the other. The most actively dividing tissue is the epidermis, which is therefore called the meristoderm (Fig. 12.22). The meristoderm allows for growth upwards, downwards and inwards, since the new walls formed during cell division may be tangential, radial or horizontal. The tangential walls cut off cells towards the inside of the thallus and these therefore become part of the cortex, which lies beneath the meristoderm. The cortical cells compensate for further divisions of the meristoderm cells by stretching. Towards the inside of the cortex the longitudinal walls of the cells become increasingly mucilaginous, so that the cells come to be arranged in separate longitudinal files. From these rows of cells, which look like fila-

Caption for fig. 12.19 *(cont.)*.

CRF = corticating rhizoidal filament; DL = determinate lateral branch; EAN = empty antheridium; F! = fertilization; MER = meristoderm; R! = reduction

division (meiosis); TRM = trichothallic meristem; UZ = unilocular zoidangium. (*a*–*d* based on [1341]; *h, i* on [1588].)

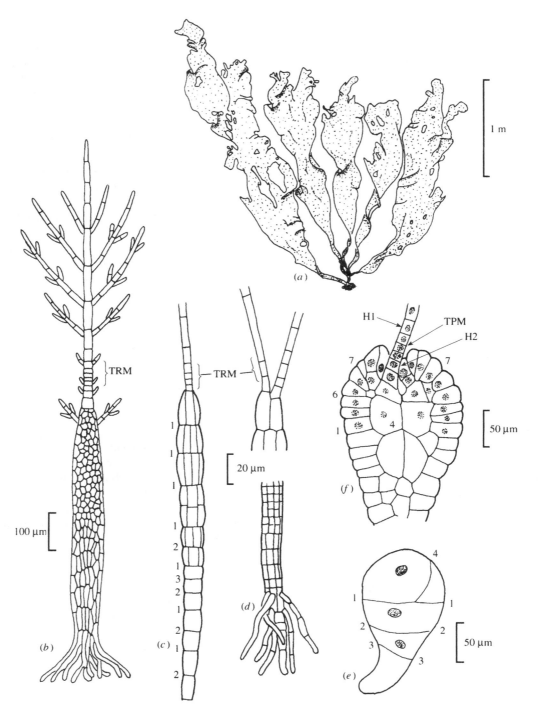

Figure 12.20. (a) *Himanthothallus grandifolius,* an
Antarctic member of the order Desmarestiales. (b)
Development of the young sporophyte in *Desmarestia,* compared with the development of *Chorda
filum* (Laminariales) (c, d) and *Fucus* (Fucales) (e, f).

H1 = first hair; H2 = second hair; TRM = trichothallic
meristem; the numbers indicate the order in which the
walls are formed. (a based on [1056]; b on [1555]; c, d on
[1482]; e, f on [465].)

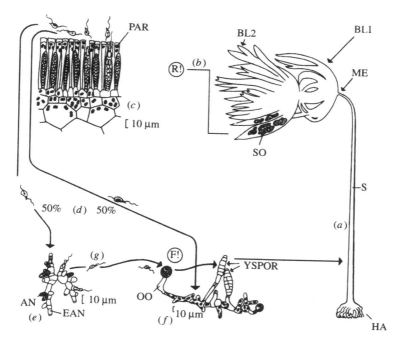

Figure 12.21. *Laminaria hyperborea:* life cycle. (*a*)
Sporophyte (2*n*). (*b*) The reduction division (meiosis)
occurs during the first division within each unilocular
sporangium. (*c*) Cross section through a sorus containing unilocular sporangia. (*d*) Haplogenotypic sex
determination. (*e*) Microscopic male gametophyte
(*n*). (*f*) Microscopic female gametophyte (*n*). (*g*)

Spermatozoid. AN = antheridium; BL1 = blade of the
current year; BL2 = blade formed the previous year;
EAN = empty antheridium; F! = fertilization;
HA = haptera; ME = meristem; OO = oogonium;
PAR = paraphysis; R! = reduction division (meiosis);
S = stipe; SO = sorus; YSPOR = young sporophyte.

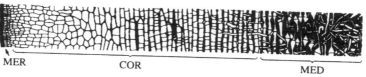

Figure 12.22. *Laminaria.* Longitudinal section through the
meristematic part of the stipe. COR = cortex;

MED = medulla, containing trumpet hyphae; MER =
meristoderm. (After [231].)

ments, lateral outgrowths (hyphae) are produced, which
extend out more or less horizontally and may fuse with
other filaments. The central part of the thallus is called
the medulla (pith) and here the files of cells become
stretched into thin, hypha-like filaments, which are
swollen near their cross-walls like trumpets and are
therefore called trumpet hyphae. The trumpet hyphae
combine with hyphae growing in horizontally from the
cortex to form tangled webs of filaments in the medulla.

The meristoderm is also active in older parts of the
stipe, away from the meristematic zone. Here, however, it is involved for the most part in the thickening
of the stipe. In even older parts of the stipe an inner,
cortical layer takes over the function of the meristoderm and provides for further increase in girth. Older
stipes contain well-marked annual rings which correspond to alternating periods of active growth and qui-
escence.

The same basic types of tissue can be distinguished in the blade. The longitudinal files of cells in the inner cortex and the trumpet hyphae of the medulla, especially those in the related genera *Nereocystis* and *Macrocystis*, bear a remarkable resemblance to the sieve tubes of higher plant phloem. The transverse walls in young filaments are perforated by areas of plasmodesmata, so that they look like sieve plates. The cross walls of older filaments are even more reminiscent of higher plants since they are plugged with callose, like the older sieve plates of higher plant phloem (Fig. 12.23; [1374, 1375]).

The morphological agreement between trumpet hyphae and sieve tubes suggests that their function might be similar, and indeed it was suggested as long ago as 1900 that the trumpet hyphae might transport organic material, produced through photosynthesis ([465]). Transport of photosynthetic assimilates in 'sieve tubes' was demonstrated for the first time in 1965, by supplying *Macrocystis* plants with radioactively labelled carbon, in the form of $NaH^{14}CO_3$ ([1374, 1375, 1377]). At intervals after the supply of the labelled carbon, the whereabouts of the ^{14}C were determined and it was found that photosynthetic assimilates are transported at rates of 65–78 cm h^{-1}. Movement took place towards the top of the plant as well as towards the base. At the apex the photosynthetic products are used to sustain rapid growth. The basal parts of the stipe also require supplies of carbon, since they are shaded by the dense layer of blades growing in the water several metres above; their own photosynthesis is thus inadequate for their needs.

In the blades of *Macrocystis* the photosynthetically active meristoderm is linked to the medulla by a continuous network of protoplasmic connections, in the form of plasmodesmata through the walls of the corti-cal cells. Photo-assimilates produced in the meristoderm are transported across the cortex to the medulla, where long-distance transport occurs to other parts of the plant, via the plasmodesmata of the sieve cells ([163, 164, 165, 1056]). Carbohydrate is translocated mainly in the form of mannitol, the characteristic low-molecular-mass photosynthate of the Phaeophyceae. Nitrogen and phosphorus are also transported, nitrogen as amino acids and phosphorus mainly in the form of hexose monophosphates ([1056]).

In *Laminaria*, too, assimilates are moved through the medulla, material being transported from the flattened blade to areas of active growth. The meristematic zone between stipe and blade is one such area and the growing haptera of the holdfast are another ([1061, 1571]). Transport is much slower than in *Macrocystis*, carbon moving at only 5 cm h^{-1}, and this is correlated with the fact that the transport tissue of *Macrocystis*, with its large plasmodesmata, is far more similar to the phloem of higher plants than the corresponding tissue in *Laminaria*, where the plasmodesmata are much smaller.

The life cycles of *Laminaria hyperborea* (Fig. 12.21) and a series of other Laminariales have been investigated by many workers and are well known ([465, 638, 639, 1357, 1534, 1554]). *Laminaria hyperborea* is a strongly heteromorphic diplohaplont and it is oogamous. The diploid sporophyte phase (Fig. 12.21*a*) bears sori, which appear as large irregular patches on the blade, dark brown in colour. The sori contain unilocular sporangia (Fig. 12.21*c*), between which are club-shaped, sterile paraphyses. In the closely related species *Laminaria saccharina*, the sporangia are formed in short day conditions and relatively high temperatures (10–15 °C; [1058]). In nature, this combina-

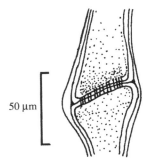
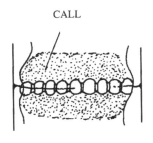

50 μm

CALL

Figure 12.23. *Macrocystis*. Longitudinal section through a young (left) and an old (right) sieve tube. CALL = callose. (After [1341].)

tion of conditions occurs in autumn and this is indeed when the sporangial sori are found. Meiosis takes place in the unilocular sporangia, so that the spores produced are haploid. Half of the unizoids grow into male gametophytes and half into females, and it can therefore be inferred that sex determination is haplogenotypic.

After their release in the autumn, the unizoids grow into unicellular gametophytes, but further development can be arrested for a while, owing to the low light levels in the sublittoral zone during winter; this is certainly the case around the island of Helgoland in NW Germany, where the water is very murky in winter as a result of storms. Here, light levels increase markedly in February and as soon as this occurs the gametophytes resume growth, becoming fertile in one or two weeks ([1052]).

The gametophytes of *Laminaria hyperborea* (which have a chromosome number of $n = 31$) are microscopic and consist of short, branched filaments of cells

(Fig. 12.21*e, f*); gametophytes of either sex can be very small indeed, consisting of only a few cells even at maturity (Fig. 12.24). The formation of gametangia requires low temperatures (below 18 °C) and blue light; at higher temperatures ([101]) or in red light ([1059]), the gametophytes will only develop vegetatively ([1056]). Male gametophytes bear small unicellular antheridia, each producing a single spermatozoid, while female gametophytes bear unicellular oogonia. Each oogonium forms a non-motile egg cell, which comes to lie at the mouth of the empty oogonium and there awaits fertilization. Even though the egg cells are non-motile, in at least one *Laminaria* species the egg initially bears two flagella (both without mastigonemes), which are then abscised during its liberation ([1242]). This shows that oogamy evolved in this group as an extreme form of anisogamy. Following fertilization the zygote develops *in situ* into a young sporophyte (Fig. 12.21*f*).

Mature oogonia release their eggs at night, a few minutes after dusk ([1054, 1080]). The eggs secrete the

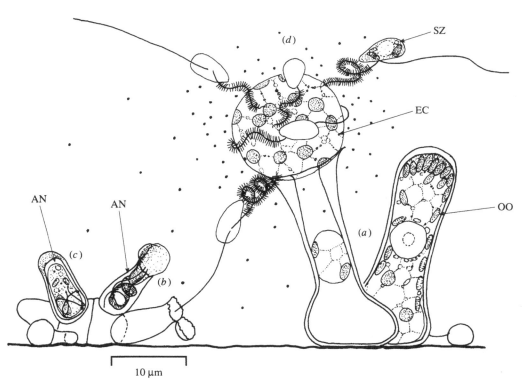

Figure 12.24. *Laminaria* (Laminariales): pheromonal interaction during sexual reproduction. Eggs released from the oogonia (*a*) secrete a pheromone (dots), which causes the release of spermatozoids (*b*) from the antheridia (*c*) and, subsequently, their attraction to the eggs (*d*). AN = antheridium; EC = egg cell; OO = oogonium; SZ = spermatozoid. (After [1080].)

pheromone lamoxirene (Fig. 12.9) and several related by-products, some of which are known to function as pheromones in other brown algae; these include ecto-carpene, desmarestene and multifidene (Fig. 12.9; [1080, 1083, 1085]). Immediately after exposure to the pheromone, the spermatozoids are released from the antheridia ([1060, 1086]), and the pheromone then mediates the attraction of the spermatozoids to the eggs (Fig. 12.24) ([1084]).

The combined effect of all this – the mass matura-tion of gametophytes within a short period in February, the synchronization of egg release at night-fall, the triggering of spermatozoid release by pheromones secreted by the eggs, and the pheromone-guided chemotaxis of the spermatozoids – is to increase greatly the chances of successful fertilization ([1056]). Hence zygotes are produced in great numbers in late winter and early spring, and large crops of young sporophytes begin to appear on submerged substrata a little later.

Laminaria hyperborea is widely distributed on the Atlantic coasts of Europe and forms extensive subma-rine forests. Only the uppermost plants are ever exposed at low tide. *Laminaria hyperborea* is an important raw material for the alginate industry (see p. 169).

Chorda filum (Fig. 12.25)

The sporophytic macrothalli of *Chorda filum* grow up to 5 m long. They are 2–4 mm wide, cylindrical and unbranched, resembling bootlaces. The thalli are hol-low and filled with gas, so that under water they stand erect. Although they are so large, the macrothalli are annuals. They become fertile in summer, when the thallus surface becomes covered with unilocular zoidangia and paraphyses (Fig. 12.25*b*), and then die, the species overwintering as gametophytic micro-thalli. The life cycle is like that of *Laminaria* ([1079, 1306]). The similarity between the juvenile sporophytes of *Chorda* and *Desmarestia* (Fig. 12.20*b–d*) suggests a phylogenetic link between the Laminariales and the Desmarestiales, which is discussed on p. 199.

Chorda filum is distributed along the temperate coasts of the North Atlantic and North Pacific. It is a species of sheltered bays and creeks.

Order Fucales [238]

1 These algae produce only one type of thallus during the life cycle: macrothalli. These grow to

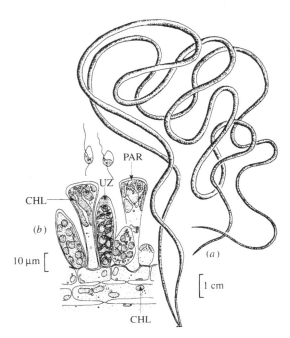

Figure 12.25. *Chorda filum* (Laminariales). (*a*) Sporophyte. (*b*) Portion of thallus bearing unilocular zoidangia and paraphyses. CHL = chloroplast; PAR = para-physis; UZ = unilocular zoidangium. (*a* based on [1283]; *b* on [1482].)

moderate sizes (*ca.* 0.1–2 m), mainly through the activity of apical cells. The shape of the thal-lus varies greatly from genus to genus and even from species to species (Figs. 12.26*b*, 12.27*c*).

2 All Fucales are diplonts (or appear to be: see below) and almost all are oogamous. The antheridia and oogonia develop in cavities in the thallus surface, which are termed conceptacles. One genus has large flagellate female gametes ([515]); otherwise the female gametes are non-motile egg cells. The conceptacles are grouped together on more or less specialized parts of the thallus, at the tips of some of the branches; these differentiated areas are called receptacles (Fig. 12.26*b*).

The diploid macrothallus of the Fucales is generally interpreted to be a sporophyte, the unilocular antheridia and oogonia being considered as modified unilocular meiosporangia; the meiospores, instead of being released, remain within the meiosporangia and develop *in situ* into extremely reduced male and female gametophytes ([238]). This hypothesis is supported by the formation of a few vestigial vegetative cells in the oogonia of some fucalean genera; sometimes, for instance, there are four such cells, together with four eggs. The vestigial cells are considered to be the last remains of the vegetative thallus of the gametophyte. On this interpretation, the life cycle of the Fucales would be analogous to that of flowering plants, where in the female reproductive organs the single functional meiospore is again retained within the meiosporangium and grows into a very much reduced female gametophyte (the embryo sac). If so, then the fucalean life cycle only seems to be diplontic (it is 'pseudodiplontic', like the life cycles of flowering plants), in reality being a very strongly heteromorphic–diplohaplontic cycle, with a highly reduced gametophyte phase. Some species in the two recently established orders Syringodermatales ([637]) and Ascoseirales ([239, 1209, 1274]) apparently also have 'pseudodiplontic' life cycles, with vestigial gametophytes that remain imprisoned within unilocular meiosporangia.

Fucus vesiculosus (bladder wrack) (Fig. 12.26)

The thallus of *Fucus vesiculosus* is strap-like and forks regularly. The thallus has a thick midrib which extends downwards as a stalk and is anchored to the substratum by an attachment disc. At regular intervals the thallus bears pairs of vesicles (bladders), one on each side of the midrib. Where bladders develop at a branching point a third bladder forms directly above the branch, in the angle between the two midribs. As the bladders are full of gas, the thalli stand erect when submerged. The surfaces of the strap-like parts of the thallus are pock-marked with cavities (cryptostomata), which contain tufts of phaeophycean hairs. The fertile tips of the thallus (the receptacles) are swollen and densely studded with conceptacles, which can be regarded as fertile cryptostomata. The floor of the conceptacle bears phaeophycean hairs and also sexual organs: oogonia in female plants, antheridia in male plants (Fig. 12.26c).

The tip of each growing branch is invaginated and at the bottom of the notch is the apical cell (Fig. 12.26m, n). This cuts off cells laterally which become part of the epidermis and remain meristematic for a long time, contributing cells to the cortex and medulla;

this meristematic epidermis is termed the meristoderm, by analogy with *Laminaria*. In the young thallus, the apical cell arises, at the base of a terminal, hair-like filament with a trichothallic meristem (Fig. 12.20e, f). This juvenile feature suggests that the Fucales are related to the orders Laminariales and Desmarestiales, a matter discussed on p. 218 (see also Fig. 12.20b–f).

In the central tissues (medulla) of *Fucus* the longitudinal walls of the cells become mucilaginous, so that the cells come to lie in widely separated files, which resemble filaments. The medulla is especially slimy in the swollen, fertile receptacles.

The life cycle of *Fucus vesiculosus* is well known, as indeed are those of many other Fucales; they are all oogamous diplonts (or 'pseudodiplonts': see above). The life cycle of *Fucus vesiculosus*, then, contains only one vegetative phase, which is diploid. This phase is nevertheless gametophytic, although it is often interpreted as a sporophyte (see p. 206); the reduction of the chromosome number takes place during the formation of the gametes (egg cells and spermatozoids).

The oogonia are formed on female plants in conceptacles (Fig. 12.26c). Each, when ripe, contains 8 haploid egg cells; in other genera the oogonium may contain 1, 2 or 4 egg cells. The oogonium wall consists of three layers and at maturity the outermost layer breaks apart, releasing the cluster of 8 egg cells, still surrounded by the two inner layers of the wall. The clusters are forced out of the conceptacle by secretion of mucilage and then the remaining layers of the wall are shed. First the outer of the two remaining layers degenerates and splits apart (Fig. 12.26d–f) and then the innermost layer swells (Fig. 12.26g), causing the remains of the outer layer to be shed. Finally the innermost layer of the wall itself splits, liberating the 8 egg cells (Fig. 12.26h).

In male plants, branched filaments of colourless cells grow up from the floor of the conceptacle and give rise to elongate antheridia (Fig. 12.26i). The antheridium wall consists of two layers. At maturity the spermatozoids, still contained within the inner wall of the antheridium, are extruded from the conceptacle through secretion of mucilage. Once liberated the 'packet' splits open, releasing the spermatozoids. Fertilization can now take place and the spermatozoids swim in huge numbers to the egg cells, attracted by a chemical released by the eggs. The pheromone

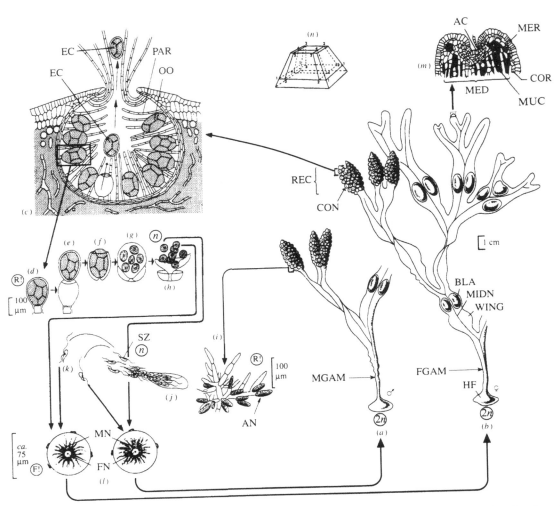

Figure 12.26. *Fucus vesiculosus:* life cycle. (*a*) Male gametophyte. (*b*) Female gametophyte. (*c*) Cross section through a female conceptacle (*ca.* 1 mm across). Note the oogonia, each containing 8 haploid egg cells, which arise following meiosis; the eggs are released, still surrounded by the two inner walls of the oogonium, and ejected from the conceptacle through the secretion of mucilage. (*d–h*) Development of the oogonia and release of the egg cells, which finally takes place through swelling and rupture of the innermost wall layer (*h*). (*i*) Branched colourless filaments bearing antheridia, which develop from the walls of male conceptacles. (*j*) Release of spermatozoids from an antheridium. (*k*) Spermatozoids. (*l*) Fertilization of egg cells. (*m*) Longitudinal section through the apex of the macroscopic gametophyte, showing the apical cell at the base of an apical notch in the thallus. (*n*) Apical cell: the numbers indicate successive division planes. AC = apical cell; AN = antheridium; BLA = bladder; CON = conceptacle; COR = cortex; EC = egg cell; F! = fertilization; FGAM = female gametophyte; FN = female nucleus; HF = holdfast; MED = medulla (pith); MER = meristoderm; MGAM = male gametophyte; MIDN = midrib of thallus; MN = male nucleus; MUC = mucilage; OO = oogonium; PAR = paraphysis; R! = reduction division (meiosis); REC = receptacle; SZ = spermatozoid (*ca.* 7 μm long); WING = flat, wing-like part of the thallus, extending out from the midrib; *n* = haploid; 2*n* = diploid.

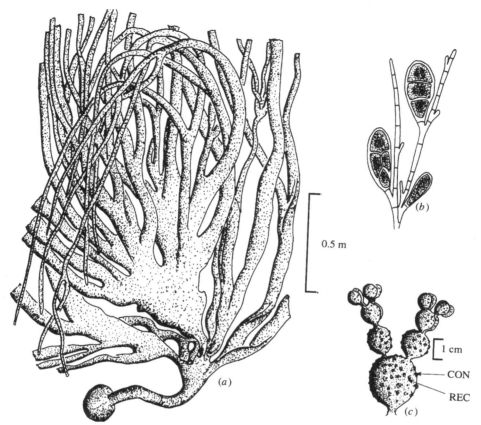

0.5 m

1 cm

CON

REC

Figure 12.27. (a) *Durvillaea antarctica* (Durvillaeales): adult plant. (b) *Durvillaea:* oogonia. (c) *Hormosira* *banksii* (Fucales). CON = conceptacle; REC = receptacle. (Based on [465].)

secreted by *Fucus vesiculosus* eggs (and those of two other *Fucus* species) is fucoserratene (Fig. 12.9; [1083, 1262, 1264, 1265a, 1273]). Many spermatozoids attach themselves to each egg cell and may set the egg in motion, rotating it, as a result of the movement of their flagella. Then, as soon as one spermatozoid penetrates the egg, the other spermatozoids disperse and the fertilized egg cell surrounds itself with a wall. The zygote grows into a new diploid gametophyte.

The spermatozoids of *Fucus* have the characteristics of heterokontophyte zoids, in that for instance they possess two unequal flagella, of which one is pleuronematic and points forwards while the other points backwards (Fig. 12.4d). In one respect, however, the *Fucus* spermatozoid differs from the motile cells of most brown algae, since it has a proboscis ('snout'), i.e. a flat protrusion at the anterior end of the spermatozoid, which is supported by curved microtubules ([1097]).

Fucus vesiculosus is a common intertidal species along the temperate rocky coasts of the North Atlantic, where it often forms a conspicuous belt in the middle of the shore. The thalli are perennial, living up to 5 years.

Hormosira banksii (Fig. 12.27c)

The thalli of this species consist of much inflated, hollow, bead-like vesicles (bladders), which are linked by narrower, solid regions. The plants are dichotomously branched and attain lengths of 40 cm or so. Cryptostomata and fertile conceptacles are scattered over the bladders. The species is dioecious. The eggs secrete a pheromone called hormosirene (Fig. 12.9), which attracts the spermatozoids [1083, 1258].

Hormosira banksii is a common intertidal alga along the temperate shores of Australia and New Zealand. During high water, the plants stand erect, buoyed up by their gas-filled bladders.

Order Durvillaeales (Fig. 12.27a; [241, 628, 1081])

1 Only one type of thallus, a macrothallus, is produced during the life cycle. This consists of a solid disc-like holdfast, a stout cylindrical stipe, also solid, and a broad leathery blade, which is often split deeply into narrow strap-like pieces. Growth is intercalary but concentrated in the apical parts of the fronds; a meristoderm is involved.

2 The Durvillaeales have a diplontic life cycle and are oogamous, like the Fucales. The conceptacles are scattered over the whole thallus, rather than being concentrated on receptacles as in the Fucales. The male conceptacles contain branched filaments, which bear unilocular antheridia. The female conceptacles also contain branched filaments, here bearing oogonia, each of which contains four eggs (Fig. 12.27b). The eggs secrete the pheromone hormosirene (Fig. 12.9), which attracts the spermatozoids [1083, 1258].

In the vegetative habit the Durvillaeales much resemble the Laminariales; their reproduction and life cycle, on the other hand, indicate a close relationship to the Fucales, from which they differ in the absence of apical cells [241]. *Durvillaea* is the only genus in the order.

Durvillaea antarctica (Fig. 12.27a, b)

This species forms extensive stands in the lower littoral and upper sublittoral zones of exposed rocky shores in cool temperate regions of the southern hemisphere (in New Zealand, southern S America, and various subantarctic islands). The other three *Durvillaea* species have a more restricted distribution, again in the cool temperate zone of the southern hemisphere [628].

13

Reflections on the phylogeny of the Heterokontophyta

Heterotrophic Heterokontophyta

The concept of the division (= phylum) Heterokontophyta is based primarily on the architecture of the flagellate cells. These have a forwardly directed pleuronematic flagellum, which bears stiff tripartite mastigonemes, and a smooth hind flagellum. This architecture is considered of such fundamental importance that certain groups of heterotrophic fungi and protists are also now classified in the Heterokontophyta, because they too have an anterior flagellum bearing mastigonemes [49, 54, 304, 354, 470, 1384, 1640, 1862]. Thus, for instance, two fungal classes, the Oomycetes and the Hyphochytriomycetes, are considered as subgroupings within the Heterokontophyta. The Oomycetes include various water moulds and also the downy mildews, which are important pathogens of agricultural crops. The Hyphochytriomycetes are another group of water moulds [1862]. Other heterotrophic heterokontophytes are the Bicosoecida, a group of unicellular flagellates, to which the widely distributed marine flagellate *Cafeteria* belongs; this is like a colourless version of the alga *Ochromonas* [416].

The close phylogenetic link between heterotrophic and photoautotrophic heterokontophytes was recently confirmed by molecular sequencing, which showed similarities between the 18S rRNAs of the autotrophic chrysophycean alga *Ochromonas* and the heterotrophic oomycete *Achlya* (Fig. 32.2, numbers 22 and 23; [34a, 589]) (see p. 37 for a short introduction to the use of rRNA sequences in phylogenetic analysis). A recent phylogenetic analysis of nucleotide sequences in the nuclear gene coding for 18S rRNA in three different oomycetes and five algae, representing five classes of heterokontophytes, firmly supports a common phylogenetic origin for heterotrophic and photoautotrophic heterokontophytes ([34a]; see also [73]). Additional evidence is provided by an analysis of actin sequences in *Achlya* and the brown alga *Costaria* ([73a]).

The origin of the heterokontophyte chloroplast as a eukaryotic endosymbiont

Photoautotrophic heterokontophytes may have arisen through the uptake and retention of a photoautotrophic eukaryote by a primaeval unicellular heterokontophyte; the host would have been a heterotrophic flagellate and the phototrophic eukaryote would initially have been an endosymbiont within it, only later becoming modified into a chloroplast. This hypothesis is suggested by the presence of four membranes around the chloroplast (p. 113, Fig. 6.4*d*). The innermost two membranes can be interpreted as the standard double membrane of the chloroplast envelope, while the inner membrane of the surrounding sheath of chloroplast endoplasmic reticulum may represent the plasmalemma of the endosymbiotic alga. The outer membrane of the chloroplast ER could represent the host's food vacuole. This topic will be pursued further in Chapter 32 (p. 510, step 5; Fig. 32.4).

Evidence from macromolecules for the phylogenetic coherence ('naturalness') of the Heterokontophyta

The phylogenetic coherence of a number of the classes within the Heterokontophyta has recently been confirmed by various macromolecular studies, supporting the idea that the heterokontophytes constitute a 'natural' division. Similarities have been found in the nucleotide sequences of the 28S rRNAs in three representative species of the Chrysophyceae and Raphidophyceae (Fig. 32.3; [1393, 1394]), while a close relationship between the classes Chrysophyceae, Phaeo-

phyceae, Bacillariophyceae, Xanthophyceae and Oomycetes is indicated by 18S rRNA sequences (in this study one species was selected to represent each group; [34a, 73]). In addition, nucleotide sequences in certain chloroplast genes, together with the organization of the chloroplast genome itself, have been shown to be similar in species of the Chrysophyceae, Xanthophyceae, Bacillariophyceae and Phaeophyceae, and this too points to a monophyletic origin for the Heterokontophyta ([331b, 908, 908a, 938]).

As the above studies on 18S and 28S rRNA nucleotide sequences either involved only a few species or did not show sufficient resolution, they do not reveal much about phylogenetic relationships between the various classes within the Heterokontophyta. For instance, they give no indication of whether the Phaeophyceae are more closely related to the Bacillariophyceae or to the Chrysophyceae. The relationships between these particular three classes, however, have been estimated on the basis of 5S rRNA sequences, and the results are summarized in Fig. 13.1 ([735, 1011]). The phylogenetic tree suggests that the Bacillariophyceae and Phaeophyceae have a common ancestor, which diverged from the primaeval Chrysophyceae early in the evolutionary history of the heterokontophytes. It seems that the diatoms (Bacillariophyceae) and brown algae (Phaeophyceae) diverged from each other much more recently, while the evolutionary diversification of the brown algae seems to have taken place quite a short time ago (in geological terms). The relationships indicated in the phylogenetic tree, especially those between the brown algae, should not be trusted, however, since they are statistically unreliable (cf. [1011]); the tree should be interpreted as showing only that the five brown algae investigated are closely related and that they evolved fairly recently (see also the remarks on p. 39 about the statistical limitations of 5S rRNA studies).

The close phylogenetic relationship between the Bacillariophyceae and the Phaeophyceae appears to be confirmed by immunological studies, in which antibodies were raised against the protein of the main photosynthetic pigment–protein complex of a diatom species (containing chlorophylls a and c, and fucoxanthin). These antibodies cross-reacted with similar proteins from other diatoms and also brown algae, but not with those of the Chrysophyceae, Raphidophyceae, Cryptophyta, Dinophyta and Chlorophyta ([454]).

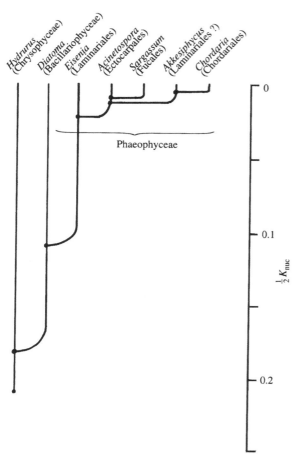

Figure 13.1. A phylogenetic tree of some heterokontophytes, based on comparisons of 5S rRNAs from various representative taxa. K_{nuc} is the evolutionary distance between two sequences; it estimates the number of base substitutions per nucleotide site that have occurred since the separation of the sequences. $\frac{1}{2}K_{nuc}$ is the evolutionary distance between the point of divergence and the branch tip. (Based on [1011]; see also [735].)

The fossil record

The fossil record does not give useful information about evolutionary relationships within the heterokontophytes. Fossils that can be confidently identified as belonging to the Heterokontophyta appear relatively late in geological time, in the early Cretaceous (120 million years ago), when deposits can be found containing the siliceous frustules of marine diatoms (Bacillariophyceae) belonging to the order Centrales;

the remains of the siliceous skeletons of silicoflagellates (Dictyochophyceae) are also present ([1751]). Undeniable fossils of the red and green algae (Rhodophyta and Chlorophyta) appear much earlier, in the late Precambrian (600 million years ago; Fig. 32.1). Since diatoms and silicoflagellates are probably specialized, derived groups within the Heterokontophyta, it seems likely that representatives of other groups were present at an earlier period, but they have left no recognizable traces. If it is true that the diatoms and brown algae diverged relatively recently, as suggested by 5S rRNA sequences (Fig. 13.1), then the appearance of the diatoms in the fossil record (120 million years ago) may not have occurred much later than their origin. On the basis of the 5S rRNA data mentioned above, the age of the Phaeophyceae has been estimated as *ca.* 200 million years ([347a, 1011]). It is quite likely, then, that the brown algae are considerably younger than the red and green algae, and this is reflected in the much smaller evolutionary distances found between brown algal genera, compared with the distances between red and green algal genera (based on 5S rRNA sequences; cf. Table 5.1, p. 100).

It looks as if morphological evolution has taken place much more rapidly within the brown algae than within the red algae, assuming that the rate of RNA evolution has been approximately the same in both groups. The hypothesis of young age coupled with rapid morphological evolution in the brown algae is now supported by several sets of molecular data. Seven morphologically very dissimilar genera of the brown algal order Laminariales have been found to differ very little in their 18S rRNA sequences. The divergence between the most distantly related genera was only 0.66%, which is extremely low compared with differences between genera in the red algal order Gracilariales (4.5%) (see p. 101) or between genera within orders of flowering plants (e.g. 3% between genera of grasses). Assuming a divergence rate of 1% per 25–50 million years in 18S rRNA sequences, the age of the Laminariales can be estimated to be 16–30 million years ([347a, 1551a]), which agrees well with an age of 15–20 million years calculated for the genus *Laminaria*, on the basis of single copy DNA–DNA hybridization ([1680]) (for a brief introduction to the technique of DNA–DNA hybridization, see p. 40). Finally, the sequence divergence between chloroplast genomes within the Laminariales appears to be much lower than among closely related genera of red algae or flowering plants ([347a]). Altogether, then, there is considerable support for the hypothesis that the Phaeophyceae are an evolutionarily young class, which has undergone rapid evolution in thallus morphology.

A speculative phylogenetic tree of the Heterokontophyta, based on comparative morphology

Few heterokontophyte species have been studied using molecular genetic techniques, so that there are few gene sequences from which a phylogenetic tree of the Heterokontophyta can be constructed. Consequently we still have to rely upon the morphology of living species for insights into the relationships between the heterokontophyte classes. The phylogenetic tree given in Fig. 13.2 represents one speculation about relationships within the Heterokontophyta, based on comparative morphology, which attempts to explain the evolution of the various classes of photoautotrophs we have distinguished in this text. The 'core' of the tree, consisting of the groups connected by thick lines, is formed by those heterokontophytes that have **fucoxanthin** as the principal accessory pigment. The classes with other accessory photosynthetic pigments (**vaucheriaxanthin**, **heteroxanthin**), which are connected to the rest of the tree by thin lines, are thought to have emerged during a more fluid phase of evolution, before the evolutionary 'fixation' of the different sets of accessory photosynthetic pigments.

In the 'core' of the tree, a hypothetical marine heterokontophyte, rather like *Ochromonas* but covered with siliceous scales formed within silica deposition vesicles (SDVs), is suggested as the ancestral form (A). All groups of **fucoxanthin-containing heterokontophytes** can be derived from this hypothetical ancestor through a number of phylogenetic 'gains' (arrows pointing in towards the branches of the tree: see the legend to Fig. 13.2) or 'losses' (arrows pointing out from the tree). The **Chrysophyceae** seem to have invaded freshwater habitats after the evolution of stoppered siliceous cysts (B), since although the Chrysophyceae are now predominantly freshwater algae, the great abundance of chrysophycean cysts in marine deposits from the Upper Cretaceous (90 million years ago) onwards, and the presence also of chrysophycean scales, testify that the class

Chrysophyceae has long contained marine forms (C in Fig. 13.2; [1751]).

The **Bacillariophyceae** can perhaps be derived from the ancestral scaly flagellate (A) via a scaly coccoid alga, again marine, with flagellate reproductive cells (D in Fig. 13.2). Again, all the ancestral forms are only hypothetical, but diatom frustules are often thought to have arisen by the fusion of a scaly carapace into the box-and-lid structure present in all diatoms today. The scales present on the auxospores of centric diatoms have been interpreted as relics, an evolutionary 'reminiscence' of the ancestral form, with its scaly covering (cf. p. 156; [1529, 1530]). The same scaly coccoid form (D) that gave rise to the diatoms could also have given rise to the marine **Parmophyceae** via another pathway, involving the evolutionary coalescence and differentiation of the primaeval scale case ([1088c]).

Loss of scales from the hypothetical coccoid alga (D) could have resulted in the origin of simple coccoid and palmelloid algae like those in the **Sarcinochrysidophyceae** (E in Fig. 13.2), which may in turn have given rise to the **Phaeophyceae**.

A recent phylogenetic tree based on nucleotide sequences in the 18S rRNA gene is not incompatible with the hypothesis that the ancestral heterokontophyte was an *Ochromonas*-like alga with the ability to produce silica structures within silica deposition vesicles ([34a]). Rather unexpectedly, however, this tree indicates a close phylogenetic relationship between the Phaeophyceae and Xanthophyceae, which would imply the derivation of the vaucheriaxanthin–heteroxanthin type of pigmentation from the fucoxanthin type.

Speculations about the phylogeny of the Phaeophyceae (brown algae)

The oldest fossils that can be identified indisputably as being brown algae occur in the Miocene deposits of California, which are 7–10 million years old ([238, 1376]). These fossils can be assigned to the orders Laminariales and Fucales, and are therefore derived forms. Clearly, then, brown algae must have existed before the Miocene and the lack of older fossils must be attributed to the softness of the tissues of brown algae, which are unsuited to fossilization. If it is true that the Phaeophyceae are about as old as the

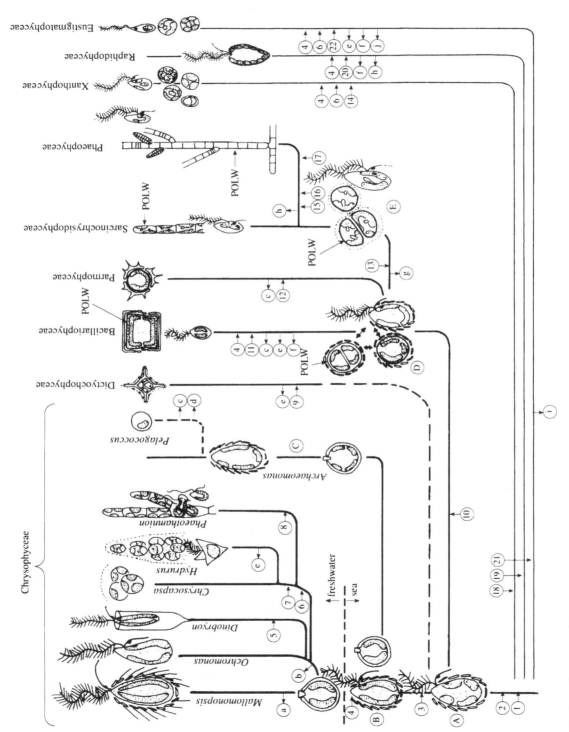

For legend see opposite page.

Bacillariophyceae (see above, 'The fossil record'), then the radiation of the brown algal lineages must presumably have taken place between 150 and 65 million years ago, at the same time as the primary evolutionary radiation of the flowering plants.

A possible phylogeny for the Phaeophyceae is illustrated in the phylogenetic tree of Fig. 13.3, which is based on comparative morphology of living species. In the tree the **Ectocarpales** are considered as the ancestral group for all other brown algae; this means that the Ectocarpales are thought to have changed least since the origin of the Phaeophyceae. The ancestral ectocarpalean brown alga is suggested to have consisted of **creeping filaments with apical growth, together with erect filaments showing intercalary growth**; there was an **isomorphic, diplohaplontic life cycle**. The Ectocarpales probably represent a cluster of separate lineages, which diverged early in the evolution of the brown algae but retained the simple architecture of the ectocarpalean ancestor. All other orders of brown algae can be derived from the ancestral Ectocarpales through various phylogenetic 'gains' (arrows pointing in towards the branches of the phylogenetic tree: see the legend to Fig. 13.3) or 'losses' (arrows pointing away from the branches). Three main lineages (I–III) are thought to have arisen from the ancestral Ectocarpales, through various elaborations of the creeping system of filaments, with their apical growth, and of the erect system, with its intercalary growth.

In lineage I, the erect system and its intercalary meristems were lost and several types of thallus mor-

Figure 13.2. The phylogeny of the Heterokontophyta: a speculative tree based on the comparative morphology of living representatives. For explanation, see the text and the additional information given below. POLW = polysaccharide wall.

Phylogenetic gains:
(1) The xanthophyll fucoxanthin as the main accessory photosynthetic pigment.
(2) Silica deposition vesicles (SDVs), involved in the formation of a scaly carapace.
(3) Two functions for SDVs: first, to form siliceous scales in active, non-dormant cells; second, to secrete a spherical siliceous cyst wall (its pore is closed by an organic stopper).
(4) The capacity to live in freshwater.
(5) A cellulose lorica.
(6) A simple, non-motile, few-celled thallus.
(7) A multicellular mucilaginous thallus ('tetrasporal', 'palmelloid', 'capsal' organization).
(8) Multicellular branched filaments.
(9) The SDV produces siliceous tubes instead of scales, which together form a flat basket.
(10) A life cycle including simple non-motile coccoid cells (with a polysaccharide wall and a scaly carapace), as well as a scaly flagellate stage.
(11) The production of several different SDVs, each for a different element of a multipartite siliceous wall, the frustule (which sometimes betrays its evolutionary origin from a scaly carapace).
(12) The production of several different SDVs, each for one of a small number of closely fitting silica plates, which together form a complete shell around the cell.
(13) A lateral flagellar insertion, instead of subapical insertion.
(14) A simple filamentous habit.
(15) The presence of alginate in the cell walls.
(16) The capacity to form plurilocular and unilocular zoid-angia.
(17) Differentiation of the thallus into systems of creeping filaments that grow apically and systems of erect filaments with intercalary growth.
(18) The xanthophyll vaucheriaxanthin as the main accessory photosynthetic pigment.
(19) Either fucoxanthin (in marine representatives) or heteroxanthin (in freshwater representatives) as the main accessory photosynthetic pigment.
(20) Raphidophycean cell architecture, with many parietal chloroplasts, a flagellar gullet and many golgi bodies.
(21) Violaxanthin and vaucheriaxanthin as the main accessory photosynthetic pigments.
(22) Eustigmatophycean cell architecture, with an eyespot that lies outside the chloroplast and a wing-like swelling at the base of the pleuronematic flagellum.

Phylogenetic losses:
(a) Loss of the eyespot.
(b) Loss of the scaly carapace; SDVs still involved in the formation of spherical stoppered cysts.
(c) Loss of flagellum-based motility (in the Bacillariophyceae, only in the pennate group).
(d) Loss of scales.
(e) Loss of the smooth hind flagellum (this has apparently happened many times in the Chrysophyceae).
(f) Loss of the eyespot lying in the chloroplast.
(g) Loss of silicon deposition vesicles.
(h) Loss of the transitional helix.
(i) Loss of chlorophyll c.
(j) Loss of girdle lamellae.

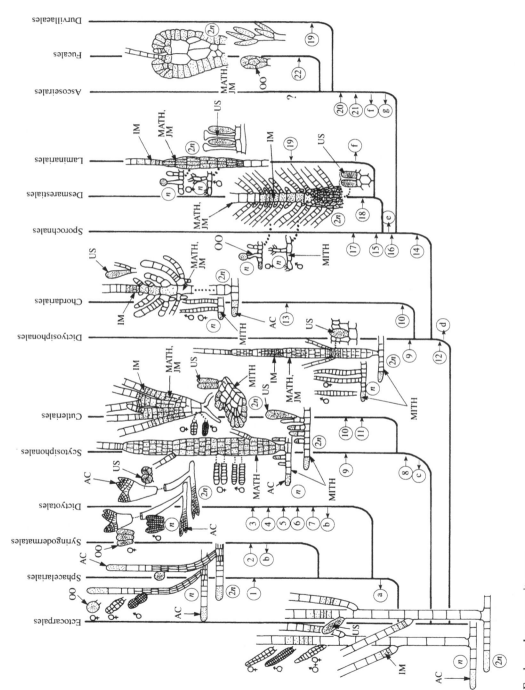

For legend see opposite page.

phology emerged, based on apical growth. This lineage gave rise to the orders **Sphacelariales**, **Dictyotales** and **Syringodermatales**, of which the first two retained an isomorphic, diplohaplontic type of life cycle.

In lineage II, the erect filaments of the haploid (*n*)

gametophyte phase evolved into elaborate thalli with intercalary growth, while the diploid (*2n*) sporophyte phase became reduced to a creeping, prostrate thallus with apical growth. This lineage produced the orders **Scytosiphonales** and **Cutleriales**.

By contrast, in lineage III, it was the erect filaments

Figure 13.3. The phylogeny of the Phaeophyceae: a speculative tree based on the comparative morphology of living representatives. For explanation, see the text and the additional information given below. AC = apical cell; IM = intercalary meristem; JM = juvenile macrothallus; MATH = macrothallus; MITH = microthallus; OO = oogonium; US = unilocular meiosporangium; *n* = haploid gametophyte phase; *2n* = diploid sporophyte phase; ♀ = female gametangium; ♂ = male gametangium.

Phylogenetic gains:

(1) Apical growth according to the pattern characteristic of the Sphacelariales: each cell (primary segment) cut off from the apical cell divides first into two cells (secondary segments) by a cross-wall, and these then divide into smaller cells through the formation of longitudinal walls.

(2) Fan-like fronds, formed through coalescence of the filaments of the sporophyte phase.

(3) Flattened parenchymatous fronds, formed following longitudinal and transverse divisions of the cells cut off from the apical cell.

(4) Strictly oogamous sexual fusion.

(5) Antheridia and oogonia that are arranged in sori.

(6) Unilocular sporangia that produce four non-motile meiospores (tetraspores).

(7) Unilocular sporangia that are arranged in sori.

(8) Elaboration of the erect, gametophytic macrothallus.

(9) A macrothallus that is initially a uniseriate filament but becomes parenchymatous as a result of cell divisions parallel to the longitudinal axis; the macrothallus exhibits diffuse intercalary growth.

(10) A macrothallus that is initially a uniseriate filament but becomes pseudoparenchymatous by the compaction and fusion of branched uniseriate filaments; these grow through the activity of distinct intercalary meristems (trichothallic meristems).

(11) Elaboration of the creeping sporophytic microthallus into a parenchymatous frond, which grows through the activity of a marginal row of apical cells.

(12) Elaboration of the erect sporophytic macrothallus, which grows through the activity of intercalary (trichothallic) meristems.

(13) An erect sporophytic macrothallus that is composed of a compact mass of one to several branched, uniseriate filaments, with trichothallic meristems, held together in a common gelatinous matrix.

(14) A pronounced oogamy.

(15) An erect sporophytic macrothallus that at first consists largely of fused rhizoidal filaments, which grow downwards from below the trichothallic meristem, and which then acquires a meristoderm.

(16) Female pheromones that elicit two responses: the release of spermatozoids from the antheridia and the attraction of the spermatozoids to the egg cells.

(17) Elaboration of the multiaxial type of sporophytic macrothallus characteristic of the Sporochnales (not treated any further here).

(18) Elaboration of the uniaxial type of sporophytic macrothallus characteristic of the Desmarestiales.

(19) Transfer of all meristematic activity (cell division) from the trichothallic meristem to the meristoderm.

(20) Retention of non-motile meiospores in the unilocular meiosporangia, where they develop into extremely reduced gametophytes.

(21) Unilocular meiosporangia that are enclosed in hollows (conceptacles) within the thallus.

(22) Transfer of all meristematic activity from the trichothallic meristems to apical cells and the meristoderm.

Phylogenetic losses:

(a) Loss of the erect macrothallus with its intercalary growth. The microthallus (which exhibits apical growth) develops erect filaments in addition to creeping filaments.

(b) Loss of the smooth hind flagellum in the spermatozoid.

(c) Reduction of the diploid sporophyte phase to a creeping, prostrate microthallus with apical growth (loss of the erect sporophytic macrothallus).

(d) Reduction of the haploid gametophyte phase to a creeping, prostrate microthallus with apical growth (loss of the erect gametophytic macrothallus).

(e) Reduction of the male plurilocular gametangia to a cluster of gametangia, each releasing one spermatozoid.

(f) Loss of the trichothallic meristem, except that in some juvenile microthalli a vestigial trichothallic meristem remains, forming the basal meristem of the terminal hair.

(g) Extreme reduction of the gametophytic microthallus to a few cells, one of which produces a gamete (spermatozoid or egg); a separate, independent gametophyte generation is not present.

of the diploid ($2n$) phase that became elaborated into complex thalli, while the haploid (n) gametophyte phase became reduced to a prostrate thallus. The erect filaments of the diploid sporophyte exhibit intercalary growth, while the prostrate gametophytes grow apically. The two simplest orders in this lineage are the **Dictyosiphonales** and **Chordariales**. The **Desmarestiales** are a more derived group within lineage III, where the sporophyte has lost its microthallus phase; it still has an active intercalary (trichothallic) meristem, but the main meristematic activity has been transferred to the meristoderm. The oogamous gametophyte phase is a reduced microthallus. In the **Laminariales** intercalary (trichothallic) meristems have almost entirely disappeared. The only trichothallic meristems present are vestigial, occurring in the apical hairs of some juvenile sporophytes; all other meristematic activity has been transferred to the meristoderm.

The order **Fucales** represents the most derived and specialized group of brown algae in lineage III. Only a vestigial trichothallic meristem remains, in the form of the basal meristem of the terminal hair in some juvenile macrothalli; the meristematic activities previously carried out by the trichothallic meristems are performed instead by the apical cells and the meristoderm. The meiospores are non-motile and are retained in the unilocular meiosporangia, where they develop into extremely reduced male and female gametophytes ([238, 240]). The reduction is so extreme that the gametophyte phase is virtually suppressed as a separate generation, the life cycle becoming 'pseudodiplontic' (like the life cycles of flowering plants; cf. p. 207).

One important implication of the phylogenetic tree shown in Fig. 13.3 is that the main evolutionary diversification of the brown algae took place at the filamentous level of organization, as in the red algae (cf. p. 100), and that complex parenchymatous and pseudo-parenchymatous types of thallus have evolved independently many times. This also reinforces the idea that the Ectocarpales represent a bundle of parallel evolutionary lineages, rather than a single lineage, which 'failed' to evolve complex, derived structures and 'stagnated', retaining a simple filamentous construction. It is only in three orders, however, that all trace of filamentous stages has been lost from the life cycle (in the Fucales, Ascoseirales and Durvillaeales).

Physiological anisogamy seems to be the basic, 'primitive' type of sexual fusion within the Phaeophyceae. It has evolved into morphological anisogamy and even into oogamy several times, quite independently, in the Ectocarpales, Sphacelariales, Dictyotales, and Cutleriales, and in the lineage leading to the Desmarestiales, Laminariales and Fucales.

14

Haptophyta (= Prymnesiophyta)

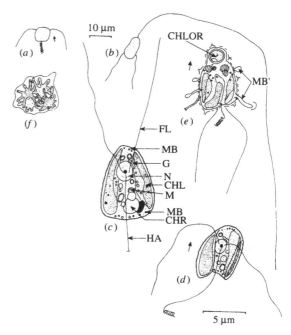

Figure 14.1. (*a–d*) *Chrysochromulina strobilus.* (*a*) Swimming cell with coiled haptonema. (*b*) Immobile cell. (*c*) Immobile cell, showing the internal structure. (*d*) Structure of swimming cell. (*e*) *Chrysochromulina ericina:* phagotrophy. (*f*) *Chrysochromulina brevifilium:* amoeboid cell. CHL = chloroplast; CHLOR = *Chlorella* cell, which has been taken up into a food vacuole; CHR = chrysolaminaran vacuole; FL = flagellum; G = golgi body; HA = haptonema; M = mitochondrion; MB = mucilage bodies; MB' = discharged mucilage bodies; N = nucleus. (After [1369–1372].)

The division Haptophyta contains only one class, the Haptophyceae.

The principal characteristics of the Haptophyta [569, 661, 664a, 674, 1302a, 1751]

1 The great majority of the Haptophyta are unicellular flagellates. Some species, however, also have amoeboid, coccoid, palmelloid, or filamentous stages (Fig. 14.1).

2 The flagellate cells (zoids) bear two flagella, which may be equal or unequal in length (Fig. 14.1). Neither flagellum bears mastigonemes (Figs. 14.2, 14.3*d*), in contrast to the Heterokontophyta, where the forward flagellum is of the tinsel type, with mastigonemes. The anterior flagellum of *Pavlova*, however, bears delicate non-tubular hairs (Fig. 14.13). The flagella are inserted either apically (Fig. 14.2) or laterally (Figs. 14.3*e*, 14.13).

3 As well as the two flagella, each zoid bears a thin, filamentous appendage called a haptonema (Figs. 14.1*c–e*, 14.2, 14.3*d, e*). This may be short or long, and has a structure quite different from that of the flagella. Cross sections of the haptonema reveal six or seven microtubules in a crescent-shaped array, while between these and the plasmalemma is a fold of endoplasmic retic-

ulum. The flagella, on the other hand, have the normal arrangement of two central microtubules and nine peripheral doublets, with no fold of endoplasmic reticulum (see Fig. 14.2).

4 Each chloroplast is enclosed within a fold of endoplasmic reticulum. Where the chloroplast lies up against the nucleus, its own endoplasmic reticulum is continuous with the endoplasmic reticulum around the nucleus (i.e. with the nuclear envelope; Figs. 14.2, 14.3*e*, 14.6*b*, 14.13*b*).

5 As in the Heterokontophyta, there is a periplastidial reticulum (a complex of anastomosing tubules) in the narrow space between the chloroplast ER and the chloroplast envelope [76].

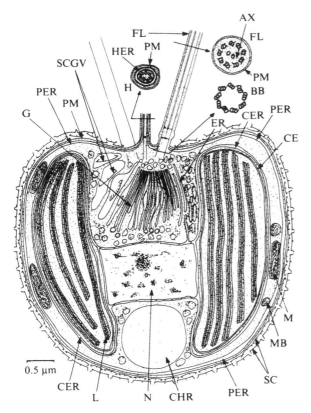

Figure 14.2. Longitudinal section through a *Chysochromulina* cell, based on EM observations. AX = axoneme (the 9 + 2 cylinder of microtubular elements); BB = basal body in cross section, showing a cylinder of nine triplets of microtubules; CE = chloroplast envelope; CER = chloroplast endoplasmic reticulum; CHR = chrysolaminaran vacuole; ER = endoplasmic reticulum; FL = flagellum; G = golgi body; H = haptonema in cross section; HER = extension of the endoplasmic reticulum into the haptonema; L = lamella, composed of a stack of three thylakoids; M = mitochondrion; MB = mucilage body; N = nucleus; PER = peripheral endoplasmic reticulum; PM = plasma membrane (plasmalemma); SC = organic scales; SCGV = scales being transported to the cell surface in golgi vesicles. (Based on [661, 976].)

6 Within the chloroplasts the thylakoids are stacked in threes to form lamellae but, in contrast to the Heterokontophyta, there is no girdle lamella (Figs. 14.2, 14.6*b*, 14.13*b*). Each chloroplast often contains a pyrenoid, which is usually penetrated by lamellae containing two thylakoids (Figs. 14.4, 14.13).

7 The chloroplasts contain chorophylls a, c_1 and/or c_3, and c_2; chlorophyll b is never present (Table 1.2; [400, 794, 797]).

8 The chloroplasts are golden or yellow-brown in colour, because the green of the chlorophylls is masked by accessory pigments, of which the most important is fucoxanthin; in some species the fucoxanthin derivatives 19′-hexanoyloxyfucoxanthin and 19′-butanoyloxyfucoxanthin are also important [88, 1689]. Other important carotenoid pigments present are β-carotene, diadinoxanthin and diatoxanthin (Table 1.2; [36, 66, 88, 418, 626, 1005, 1920]). The photosynthetic pigments possessed by the Haptophyta are similar to those in some Heterokontophyta, particularly the Bacillariophyceae [1689].

9 The chloroplast DNA occurs as numerous nodules (nucleoids) scattered throughout the chloroplast [254].

10 When present (in *Pavlova*), the eyespot lies at the anterior of the cell. It consists of a row or layer of small spherical globules, which lie in the chloroplast just beneath the chloroplast envelope as in *Ochromonas* (Fig. 6.3). Unlike *Ochromonas*, however, there is scarcely ever any flagellar swelling associated with the eyespot [567].

11 The most important storage product is the polysaccharide chrysolaminaran. In addition, paramylon has been found in one species (Table 1.3; [912]). The reserve polysaccharides are formed outside the chloroplast in vacuoles (Figs. 14.1, 14.2, 14.13).

12 The surface of the cell is covered with tiny scales or granules of organic material (cellulose; [158]) (Figs. 14.2, 14.3, 14.7*b*, 14.10*f*, 14.13*b*). In addition there may be calcified scales (coccoliths; Figs. 14.7*a*, 14.8*g–i*), which are easily seen, even with the light microscope. The scales are formed in the golgi apparatus and then secreted from the cell. They usually have a characteristic structure, each scale having radially arranged, spoke-like fibrils on the side that faces the cell, and concentrically arranged fibrils on the outer face (Fig. 14.7*b*).

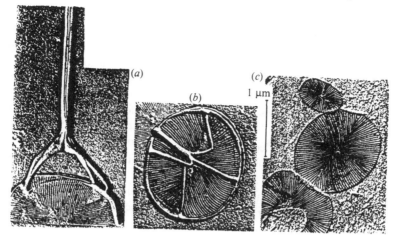

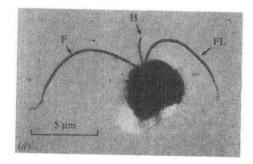

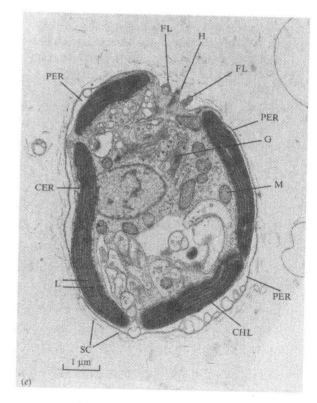

Figure 14.3. (*a–c*) *Chrysochromulina pringsheimii*. (*a*) A large scale with a markedly raised rim and bearing a long spine. (*b*) A large scale with a markedly raised rim and a small spine. (*c*) A large scale (below) and a small one (above), which both lack prominent rims and spines. (*d, e*) *Prymnesium patellifera*. (*d*) Transmission electron micrograph of a whole dried cell, shadowcast preparation. (*e*) Transmission electron micrograph of a longitudinal section, showing the general ultrastructure of the cell. CER = chloroplast endoplasmic reticulum; CHL = chloroplast; FL = flagellum; G = golgi body; H = haptonema; L = lamella, composed of a stack of three thylakoids; M = mitochondrion; N = nucleus; PER = peripheral endoplasmic reticulum; SC = body scales. (*a–c* from [1366]; *d, e* from [563a], with the permission of the authors and the British Phycological Society.)

13 In contrast to the Heterokontophyta, the golgi bodies do not lie with their forming faces appressed to the surface of the nucleus. The cisternae of each golgi body (dictyosome) are inflated centrally and often bunch together just below the flagellar basal bodies, producing a fan-shaped array in longitudinal sections (Figs. 14.2, 14.3*e*).

14 The cytoplasm of each cell is surrounded by a narrow, peripheral cisterna of endoplasmic reticulum (Figs. 14.2, 14.3*e*, 14.13).

15 The Haptophyta have their own characteristic type of mitosis, which is open, the nuclear membrane breaking down during prophase. At metaphase the chromosomes congregate into a massive plate with chromatin-free channels, through which the pole-to-pole microtubules pass. Cisternae of endoplasmic reticulum (ER) assemble on either side of the metaphase plate and are later used in the reconstruction of the nuclear envelope at telophase. Groups of ER vesicles are present at the poles of the spindle, but no centrioles. By telophase the spindle has elongated considerably, through growth of the pole-to-pole microtubules, and then the nuclear envelopes re-form from ER cisternae. Finally the cell cleaves in two by invagination of the plasmalemma (Fig. 14.4; [566, 743, 744, 745, 1675]).

16 A heteromorphic diplohaplontic life cycle has been discovered in some species, in which a diploid flagellate stage alternates with a haploid filamentous stage; the flagellate stage is planktonic, while the filamentous stage is benthic (Fig. 14.11). In other species there is an alternation between flagellate and non-flagellate stages, but the details of the life cycle remain unclear.

17 The great majority of the Haptophyta are marine; only a few species occur in freshwater ([124]).

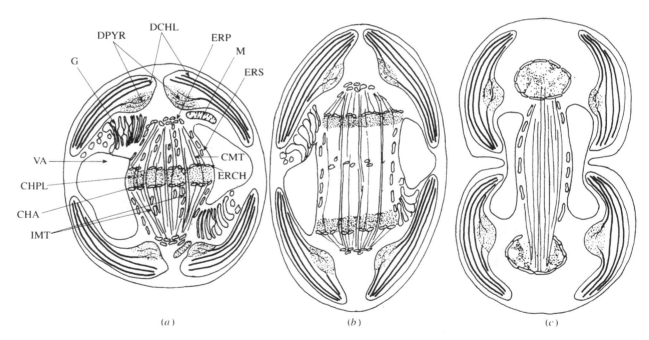

(*a*)   (*b*)   (*c*)

Figure 14.4. Mitosis in *Pleurochrysis carterae,* based on electron microscopical observations. (*a*) Metaphase. (*b*) Anaphase. (*c*) Telophase. CHA = a channel in the massive plate of chromatin, containing a bundle of interzonal (pole-to-pole) microtubules; CHPL = massive plate of chromatin; CMT = chromosomal spindle microtubule; DCHL = daughter chloroplasts, formed by the division of the parental chloroplasts before mitosis; DPYR = daughter pyrenoids, formed by division of the parental pyrenoids before mitosis; ERCH = endoplasmic reticulum lying on the polar sides of the chromatin plate; ERP = endoplasmic reticulum vesicles associated with the spindle pole; ERS = endoplasmic reticulum associated with the spindle; G = golgi body; IMT = interzonal spindle microtubule; M = mitochondrion; VA = vacuole. (Based on [1675].)

General observations

Comparison of the descriptions of the Heterokonto-phyta (p. 102) and Haptophyta (p. 219) shows that the Haptophyta can be distinguished by the following combination of characters:

the lack of pleuronematic flagella bearing mastigonemes:

the presence of a haptonema;

the absence of girdle lamellae in the chloro-plasts;

a different arrangement and structure of the golgi apparatus;

the absence of a flagellar swelling;

the presence of a peripheral ER cisterna imme-diately beneath the plasmalemma;

chloroplast DNA that is organized in numerous small nodules scattered through the chloro-plast;

a characteristic type of mitosis.

It was the discovery of some of these differences that led Christensen ([231, 232]) to erect the new class Haptophyceae for a number of algae that had previously been placed in the Chrysophyceae.

The ultrastructure of the transition zone, between the flagellar shaft and the basal body, is often characteristic of a division or class of algae: many heterokontophytes, for example, have a transitional helix (Fig. 6.4a), while the Chlorophyta are characterized by the presence of a stellate structure (Fig. 19.4; [664, 1218]). In the Haptophyta, on the other hand, the structure of the transition zone is variable and at least three different types can be distinguished ([781, 1218]). One feature exhibited by a number of quite diverse haptophytes is a conspicuous hat-like plug (axosome), lying within the transition zone (Fig. 14.5). Two other features shown in the example illustrated (Fig. 14.5) – a helical band and a stack of rings – are of much more restricted occurrence ([58, 781]); the helical band resembles the transitional helix of the Heterokontophyta but is less compact.

The structure of the flagellar apparatus as a whole, including the root system by which the flagella are anchored in the cell, is another character increasingly used to separate classes or divisions of algae. In the

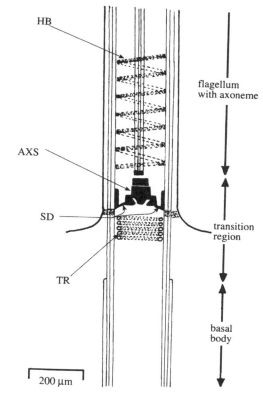

Figure 14.5. Longitudinal section through the basal region of the flagellum of *Pleurochrysis carterae*. AXS = axosome; HB = helical band; SD = septal disc; TR = transitional ring. (After [58].)

Haptophyta there are at least two major types of flagellar root system. The first is found, for example, in *Pleurochrysis*, where the most conspicuous elements are two broad, sheet-like microtubular roots (Fig. 14.6; [58]). The two basal bodies are connected to each other by three transversely striated connectives (Fig. 14.6: USC, ISC, LSC). Such connectives are not restricted to the Haptophyta, being found also, for example, in the Chlorophyta (Fig. 19.6) and Dinophyta (Fig. 16.11); they probably all consist of the contractile protein centrin. Other connectives link the basal bodies to the band of microtubules in the haptonema (Fig. 14.6, H), and to one of the broad microtubular roots (Fig. 14.6, MR1). This root, microtubular root 1, arises near the left basal body (as seen in Fig. 14.6), extends up towards the cell anterior, and then curves backwards, coming to lie in a tongue of cytoplasm between the two chloroplasts (Fig. 14.6b,

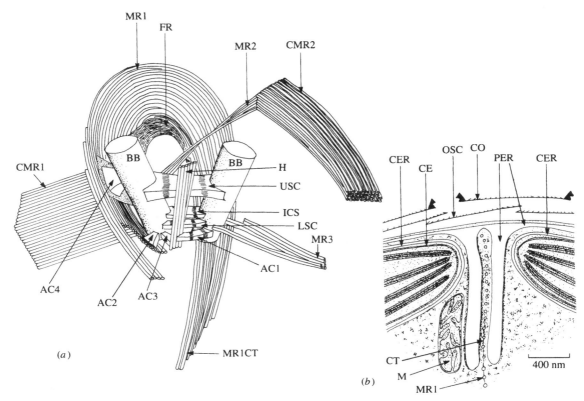

(a)

(b)

Figure 14.6. Flagellar basal bodies and the associated flagellar roots (the flagellar apparatus) in *Pleurochrysis carterae*. (a) Reconstruction based on electron microscopical observations. (b) Cross section of the tongue of cytoplasm containing microtubular root 1. AC1–4 = accessory connectives 1–4; BB = basal body; CE = chloroplast envelope; CER = chloroplast endoplasmic reticulum; CHL = chloroplast; CO = coccolith; CMR1, 2 = crystalline microtubular roots 1, 2; CT = tongue of cytoplasm; FR = fibrous root; H = the basal extensions of the haptonemal microtubules; ISC = intermediate striated basal body connective; LSC = lower striated basal body connective; M = mitochondrion; MR1–3 = microtubular roots 1–3; MR1CT = the portion of microtubular root 1 that runs backwards along one side of the cell within the cytoplasmic tongue (see Fig. 14.6b); OSC = organic body scale; PER = peripheral endoplasmic reticulum; USC = upper striated basal body connective. (Based on [58].)

CT), which runs longitudinally down one side of the cell; here the root is surrounded by extensions of the peripheral endoplasmic reticulum. Closely associated with MR1 is a backwardly curved fibrous root (Fig. 14.6a, FR), which is probably composed of centrin, like the striated connectives between the basal bodies. Crystalline arrays of microtubules are associated with both broad microtubular roots, emerging from them at right angles (Fig. 14.6a, CMR1 and CMR2).

The *Pleurochrysis* type of flagellar root system is found, with various degrees of modification, in a number of different haptophytes [494, 564, 782, 783, 1225]. A second, completely different type of flagellar apparatus is found in *Pavlova* and its allies [563], reflecting their rather isolated taxonomic position within the Haptophyta; the *Pavlova* root system will not be described here.

In the past 25 years the Haptophyta have been studied intensively using the electron microscope. Among the many interesting studies that have been made are some fascinating observations of the formation of the polysaccharide scales. This takes place inside cisternae of the golgi apparatus, each oval scale being formed in its own cisterna, exocytosed, and left on the cell surface. The organic scales usually have a characteristic substructure, with concentrically or spirally arranged cellulose microfibrils on their outer sides and radially orientated microfibrils on their inner sides; the

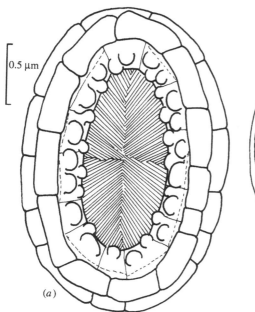

(a)

(b)

Figure 14.7. (a) Coccolith of *Pleurochrysis carterae.* Two layers of calcite crystals are present around the margin of an organic body scale, which has a radial pattern of polysaccharide fibrils arranged in four quadrants. (b) Organic body scale of *Pleurochrysis*

carterae. The outer layer is composed of an irregular coil of polysaccharide fibrils; the inner layer consists of radially orientated polysaccharide fibrils, arranged in four quadrants. (After [1819].)

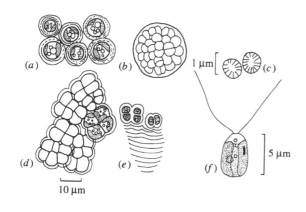

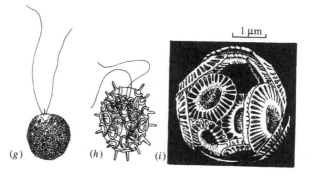

Figure 14.8. (a–f) *Chrysotila lamellosa.* (a) Encapsuled (= tetrasporal, capsal, or palmelloid) phase. (b) Sporangium. (c) Organic body scales. (d) Arrangement of the cells in packets, corresponding to the pattern of cell division. (e) '*Chrysotila*' phase. (f) Zoospore.

(g) *Pleurochrysis (Cricosphaera) carterae:* motile stage. (h) *Syracosphaera subsalsa.* (i) *Emiliania huxleyi:* cell covering, consisting of ornamented coccoliths. (a–f based on [78]; g, h on [301]; i on [851].)

inner fibrils are organized into four distinct quadrants (Fig. 14.7b). The cells are covered by several layers of these scales, which are glued together by a coating of complex acidic polysaccharides. In the coccolitho-phorids the scales in the outer layers are calcified and are termed **coccoliths**. Thus, for instance, the cells of *Pleurochrysis* (= *Cricosphaera*) *carterae* are covered not only by several layers of organic scales but also by an outer layer of coccoliths (Figs. 14.6b, 14.7, 14.8g). These, like the purely organic scales, are stuck together by coatings of acidic polysaccharides. In *Pleurochrysis* the coccolith consists of an organic scale, forming the base plate, with a ring of calcite crystals (a form of calcium carbonate) around its margin (Fig. 14.7a). These crystals do not exhibit the normal angular, rhombohedral structure of calcite because they form within an organic matrix, which afterwards persists as the coating linking the scales together. During the formation of the coccoliths in the golgi apparatus, the first part to appear is the organic base plate (cf. Fig. 14.2). The rim of crystals is added later, after clusters of particles about 25 nm in diameter have been secreted into the flat golgi cisterna containing the base plate from special golgi vesicles. The particles, which are termed coccolithosomes, contain calcium ions and possibly also the precursors of the acidic polysaccharide matrix involved in imprinting the calcitic rim on the scale ([1839, 1840, 1841]).

The coccoid, non-flagellate cells of *Emiliania huxleyi* are surrounded only by a layer of coccoliths, purely organic scales being absent; the life cycle of this organism also includes a flagellate stage, however, which has the usual type of organic scale but lacks coccoliths ([848, 849, 851]). The radially constructed coccoliths of *Emiliania huxleyi* consist of two plates, an inner one and an outer one, connected by a short central cylinder; they therefore resemble collar studs (Fig. 14.8i). Each coccolith is formed on top of a delicate organic base plate, in a coccolith vesicle filled with matrix polysaccharide. The matrix structures the forming coccolith and is composed of a complex acidic polysaccharide, containing Ca^{2+}-binding carboxyl and sulphate-ester groups; the coccolith vesicles (and an associated 'reticular body') are probably formed through the fusion of golgi vesicles ([107, 1834, 1839, 1842]).

In addition, the life cycles of various species have now been studied. Altogether, it is clear that the investigations of the past 25 or more years have confirmed Christensen's conclusion, that the Haptophyta are a distinct and natural group of algae, deserving class or divisional status ([78, 451a, 494, 560, 561, 567, 569, 570, 661, 674, 782, 783, 784, 848, 849, 850, 966, 972, 1092, 1093, 1095, 1104, 1105, 1110, 1112, 1353, 1358, 1361, 1365, 1366, 1369, 1370, 1371, 1372, 1431, 1432, 1476, 1711, 1713, 1718, 1809, 1817, 1818]).

Size and distribution of the division

The division Haptophyta contains around 75 genera of living algae, with about 500 species ([569]). It is becoming increasingly clear that planktonic haptophytes play a prominent role in the world's oceans as primary producers. Almost all of the planktonic haptophytes are small algae, belonging to the nannoplankton (a size category, containing planktonic organisms that measure *ca.* 2–20 µm in length), which, together with the picoplankton (plankton *ca.* 0.2–2 µm in length), are responsible for most of the primary production in the open ocean, away from the neritic and inshore zones ([613]). Haptophytes are also common, however, in nearshore or inshore phytoplankton. The importance of the coccolithophorids (Fig. 14.8g–i), a group of planktonic haptophytes that produce calcareous scales (coccoliths), has long been realized, following many studies by oceanographers and especially by geologists: fossil coccolithophorids are important marker fossils in the stratigraphical correlation and dating of marine sediments ([1751]). Coccolithophorids and dinoflagellates (see p. 247) together make up the phytoplankton communities characteristic of tropical and subtropical regions. Both groups exhibit their greatest diversity here and are often the most important primary producers; the dinoflagellates tend to be more important in neritic waters, while the coccolithophorids are more prominent elsewhere, in the open ocean.

The coccolithophorids and dinoflagellates occur too in temperate and polar seas, but here the number of species is much less than in the tropics ([1751]). Some species, e.g. *Emiliania huxleyi* (Fig. 14.8i), are cosmopolitan and occur right through from the tropics to subpolar regions. Satellite photographs sometimes reveal enormous blooms of this species and we include one, showing a huge 'cloud' of *Emiliania huxleyi* in the Atlantic Ocean south of Iceland (Fig. 14.9). The blooms are visible from space because light is reflected from the coccoliths. *Emiliania huxleyi* is thought to be

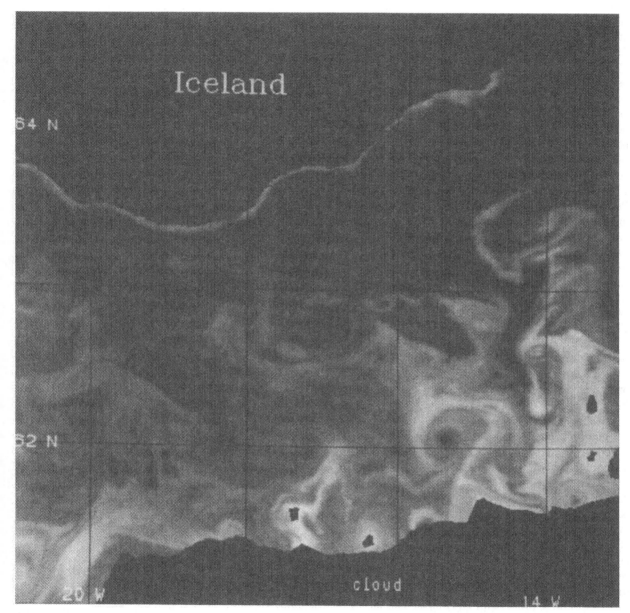

Figure 14.9. A vast bloom of the coccolithophorid *Emiliania huxleyi,* seen from space by a satellite. The bloom is visible because of light being reflected by the coccoliths, produced abundantly and released by ageing cells. The swirling patterns are created by the huge eddies along the Irminger Current, which flows in a westerly direction south of Iceland. (Photograph by courtesy of Dr P. Westbroek, University of Leiden, with the permission of Drs P.M. Holligan and S. Groom, Plymouth Marine Laboratory.)

the world's most important individual producer of biogenic calcium carbonate, and therefore plays an important part in the global CO_2 budget (see pp. 52, 426 for examples of other important algal producers of bio-genic $CaCO_3$). After death, coccolithophorids sink to the bottom of the ocean, where they may form calcareous oozes rich in coccoliths ([1877]).

Recently it has become clear that other haptophytes

besides coccolithophorids can be important constituents of the nannoplankton in tropical ([375]), temperate ([521]) and polar seas ([519]). These non-calcareous forms, such as various species of the genus *Chrysochromulina* (Figs. 14.1 – 14.3), were originally largely overlooked, because they are fragile and easily destroyed by the chemicals often used for the fixation and preservation of plankton samples. Methods have now become available that allow detection of delicate phytoplankton, through identification of their pigments (using their absorption spectra), which are characteristic of classes or divisions of algae (see Table 1.2); this can be done, for instance, by High-Performance Liquid Chromatography (HPLC). Thus, in May 1983, the accessory pigment hexanoyloxyfucoxanthin was detected in the northern part of the North Sea. This pigment is characteristic of haptophytes and its concentration varied in concert with the wax and wane of a bloom of the colonial haptophyte *Corymbellus aureus* (Fig. 14.10*a, b*; [521]), which had only been recorded once previously, from the English Channel ([562]).

Regularly recurring blooms of another non-calcareous haptophyte, *Phaeocystis pouchetii*, have been known for a long time in the southern North Sea and other temperate seas. This species has two phases in its life cycle: a unicellular flagellate phase and a gelatinous colonial phase (Fig. 14.10*c–g*), the latter being the bloom-forming stage. In the North Sea the bloom develops in mid-April or in May, after the spring diatom bloom, which is brought to an end by depletion of silicate (used by the diatoms for the construction of their frustules; see p. 141). The success of *Phaeocystis* is ascribed to the capacity of the colony matrix to accumulate low-molecular-mass photosynthates, thus allowing the alga to continue to grow in the dark and also to accumulate a store of phosphorus-containing compounds, which can be drawn upon when the surrounding water has become depleted of phosphate ([1820], [1821], [1822]). Storms often whip the *Phaeocystis* blooms, with their colony matrix polysaccharides, into soapy foams. These can then be driven ashore onto beaches, annoying or sometimes even amusing tourists, or the colonies may remain at sea and clog fishing nets. There is some evidence that the frequency, duration and intensity of *Phaeocystis* blooms have increased in the southern North Sea over the period 1973–1990, as a result of higher inputs of nutrients (N and P) from increasingly polluted rivers ([182], [961]).

A new and completely unexpected threat from haptophyte algae was posed by the huge bloom of *Chrysochromulina polylepis* that occurred around the western coasts of Sweden and the southern coasts of Norway in May 1988. This bloom was apparently highly toxic to fish, invertebrates, and even to seaweeds attached to rocks in the littoral and sublittoral zones. Much damage was done to fisheries, especially to recently established fish farms where salmon were being grown in netted enclosures positioned out to sea. Quite understandably, the *Chrysochromulina* bloom caused much public concern and was discussed at length, both in daily newspapers and elsewhere. There was much speculation about the cause of the bloom. It was suggested, for instance, that the inputs of nutrients to the sea might have been higher than usual because of the preceding winter, which had been mild and rather wet, and that this might have been compounded by pollution, bringing about a general, background increase in nutrient levels.

Another, or perhaps an additional cause may have been the coincidence of a prolonged period of calm sunny weather in May–June and the accidental presence of a toxic strain of *Chrysochromulina polylepis*. The weather conditions caused the build-up of a relatively warm, less dense, well-illuminated layer of water at the surface, with heavy cold water beneath. Nannoplanktonic algae (2–20 μm in diameter) such as *Chrysochromulina* can flourish at the boundary (the pycnocline) between the two water masses, since there is here sufficient light for photosynthesis but also an ample supply of nutrients from the deeper, nutrient-rich layers. The toxic *Chrysochromulina* strain may then have been able to form a massive bloom, by killing its potential competitors and predators (zooplankton) ([1293], [1522], [1845]).

But in spite of much discussion, the actual cause remains unknown. All that is certain is the identity of the organism involved, which of course is an essential prerequisite if there is to be any further research on the problem ([1845]). *Chrysochromulina polylepis* was discovered and described relatively recently, in one of a series of elegant taxonomic studies made by Manton & Parke ([1110]), and this underlines the importance of careful, detailed taxonomic work to environmental research. Until the appearance of the toxic *Chrysochromulina* bloom, only one other member of the Haptophyta had been reported to cause toxic blooms, namely the brackish-water species *Prymnesium*

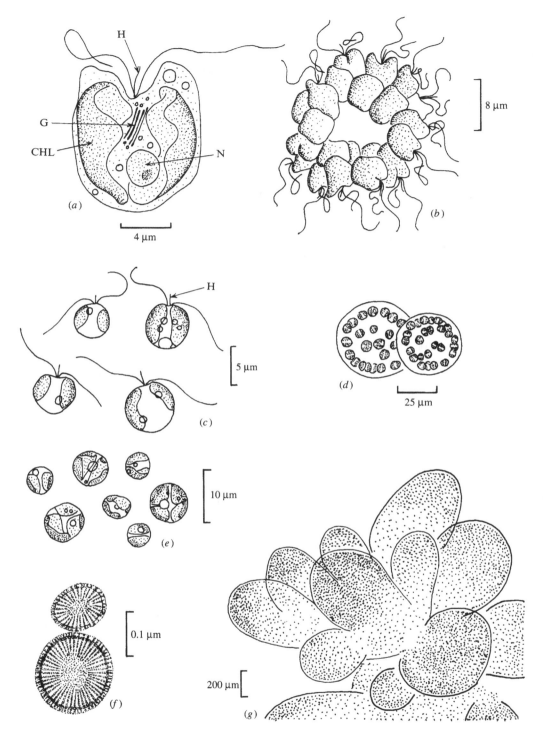

Figure 14.10. (*a, b*) *Corymbellus aureus.* (*a*) Single cell. (*b*) Ring-like colony. (*c–g*) *Phaeocystis pouchetii.* (*c*) Flagellate unicells. (*d*) Young spherical colonies, containing non-flagellate cells embedded in a gelatinous matrix. (*e*) Detail of a colony, showing individual cells. (*f*) Organic scales from the surfaces of cells. (*g*) Old, lobed gelatinous colony. CHL = chloroplast; G = golgi body; H = haptonema; N = nucleus. (*a, b* after [562]; *c–g* based on [674, 880, 1820].)

parvum, which can inflict damage on fish in breeding ponds ([1625]). Most toxic marine phytoplankton are dinoflagellates (p. 271), although a few are members of the heterokontophyte class Raphidophyceae (p. 161).

Planktonic haptophytes such as *Emiliania huxleyi* and *Phaeocystis pouchetii* produce reduced sulphur compounds, among which the most important is dimethylsulphide (DMS). DMS is produced, partly through microbial activity, from intracellular β-dimethylsulphoniopropionate (DMSP), which is involved in the osmoregulation of the cell ([569]). DMS is volatile and is released into the atmosphere, where it is transformed photochemically into tiny drops of sulphuric acid, which may act as nuclei in cloud formation. Thus planktonic haptophytes, growing as they sometimes do in huge blooms, may contribute significantly to the acidity of rainwater and influence climate ([961, 1877]).

The life cycles of some Haptophyta contain benthic stages, which can be filamentous, coccoid or palmelloid. These have sometimes been found in nature, for instance on chalk along the coast of southern England and from low-lying parts of salt marshes, but others are known only from cultures ([76, 569, 966, 1358, 1711, 1713, 1809]). Only a few members of the division live in freshwater.

Fossil coccolithophorids became very diverse and abundant in the Jurassic (*ca.* 180 million years ago), but there are a few rare occurrences in rocks dating back to the Carboniferous (*ca.* 300 million years ago). They seem to have reached their peak, both in terms of diversity and abundance, in the Upper Cretaceous (63–95 million years ago) and the chalk deposits of this period, which occur world-wide, consist largely of coccoliths (as therefore does blackboard chalk!). Indeed, the Cretaceous owes its very name to these coccolith chalks, the Latin 'creta' referring to white earth from the island of Crete. The end of the Cretaceous was marked by a massive extinction of coccolithophorid genera, the great majority of which disappeared. Later, new species evolved, so that diversity increased during the Tertiary to reach a new peak in the Eocene, some 50 million years ago. Coccolithophorids are widely used by geologists as stratigraphical marker fossils, to identify the age of marine strata from the Jurassic onwards. Only a few species and genera survived the late Cretaceous extinction, but one that did is the genus *Braarudosphaera*, still living

today, which can be found as a fossil right back to the Lower Cretaceous, 100 million years ago ([1751]).

Some examples of Haptophyta

Chrysochromulina strobilus (Fig. 14.1a–d; other *Chrysochromulina* species are shown in Fig. 14.1e, f) [1369, 1370, 1371, 1372]

The motile cells of *Chrysochromulina strobilus* are about 6–10 μm long and are able to deform their shape. They are compressed dorsiventrally, the dorsal side being rounded while the ventral side is concave or flat. When they are swimming quickly the cells are horseshoe-shaped, but on coming to rest they become oval.

The cell possesses two flagella, roughly equal in length, which arise from the ventral side of the cell about a third of the way down from the apex. The haptonema is very long (12–18 times as long as the cell itself) and can be extended fully, as when it is attached distally to a solid substratum, or coiled in a tight spiral (Fig. 14.1a, b, d). It contains a fold of endoplasmic reticulum, as well as a ring of six microtubules (H in Fig. 14.2 shows a transverse section through the haptonema of another *Chrysochromulina* species, with seven microtubules).

The cell surface is covered with small polysaccharide scales, 0.15–0.2 μm in diameter, each consisting of a system of radial spokes connected to a raised rim. The scales are packed close together in a coherent outer layer, beneath which is a second layer of spoked scales; these are larger (0.3–0.4 μm) but have a much less well developed rim. Other *Chrysochromulina* species bear different kinds of scale. *Chrysochromulina pringsheimii*, for instance, produces four types of scale: small oval scales (0.8 μm × 0.5 μm: Fig. 14.3c, uppermost scale); larger, more circular scales (1.7 μm × 1.3 μm: Fig. 14.3c, central and lower scales); scales with small spines (Fig. 14.3b); and scales with very long spines, up to 2 μm (Fig. 14.3a). The spines, large or small, are supported by four arms attached to the scale rim (Fig. 14.3a, b) ([1366]).

The cells of *Chrysochromulina strobilus* are uninucleate and contain two or four parietal chloroplasts (Fig. 14.1c, d), which are golden brown in colour. The storage products are chrysolaminaran and lipid, which is present as droplets. Beneath the surface of the cell are mucilage vesicles (Fig. 14.1*c*), whose contents can be expelled, as shown for *Chrysochromulina ericina* in Fig. 14.1*e*. These *Chrysochromulina* species can live either autotrophically or phagotrophically, and Fig. 14.1*e* shows a cell of *C. ericina* that has taken up a *Chlorella* individual into its posterior half. The haptonema can function as a device for capturing prey (bacteria, small algae), which are then ingested through phagocytosis; it acts like a tentacle (M. Kawachi & I. Inouye, personal communication). Sometimes the cells transform themselves into an amoeboid phase, which is illustrated in Fig. 14.1*f* for *Chrysochromulina brevifilium*. Reproduction takes place by longitudinal fission of the flagellate cells, or through the division of an amoeboid cell into four flagellate daughters.

Chrysochromulina strobilus was isolated into culture from seawater collected off England. For information on a recent *Chrysochromulina* bloom off Norway and Sweden, see p. 228.

Prymnesium patellifera (Fig. 14.3*d, e*; [563a])

The cells of this species are nearly spherical to elongate, with a rounded posterior and an obliquely truncate anterior. There are two flagella, which are almost equal, and a short haptonema, which does not coil; this arises subapically from a shallow depression. There are two layers of rather simple organic body scales, which have an ornamentation characteristic of the species. *P. patellifera* is known from the Pacific coasts of N America, from Europe and from S Africa.

Corymbellus aureus (Fig. 14.10*a, b*; [521, 562])

This is a colonial flagellate, in which the cells are linked together in a ring up to 200 μm in diameter. Each cell has two flagella, which are almost equal in length, and one short haptonema; all are inserted close together at the anterior, between two projecting lobes. The cell is covered by two types of organic body scales. *Corymbellus aureus* is known from the English Channel and the northern North Sea, where it can form large blooms (see p. 228).

Phaeocystis pouchetii (Fig. 14.10*c–g*; [674, 880, 1820])

The life cycle of *Phaeocystis pouchetii* includes at least two different stages: free-living flagellate cells, each with two flagella and a small haptonema arising from the base of an apical depression (Fig. 14.10*c*), and gelatinous colonies, which are initially spherical (Fig. 14.10*d*) and later grow into lobed bladders up to 8 mm in diameter (Fig. 14.10*g*). The cells bear two types of organic body scales (Fig. 14.10*f*). The precise details and course of the life cycle are not yet known. *Phaeocystis pouchetii* occurs world-wide in temperate and polar seas, and probably represents a species aggregate. The blooms it forms are described on p. 228.

Chrysotila lamellosa (Fig. 14.8*a–f*; [77, 78, 568])

The flagellate cells of this species are elongate (3 μm × 5 μm) and bear two flagella of approximately equal length at their anterior ends. There is no haptonema. The single chloroplast has an internal pyrenoid and contains an eyespot. Each cell is covered by a layer of scales, which are almost circular (0.16 μm × 0.14 μm) and have a radial structure (Fig. 14.8*c*).

Benthic stages predominate in the life cycle of this species. Young cells are non-motile, hemispherical, and form cuboidal masses (Fig. 14.8*d*), resembling those formed by the genus *Sarcinochrysis* (class Sarcinochrysidophyceae; p. 122). Older cells are spherical and surrounded by concentric layers of mucilage (Fig. 14.8*a*). Sometimes the mucilage is secreted only on one side, in which case branched stalks can be built up, consisting of curved transverse layers (Fig. 14.8*e*). It is this type of colony that was originally named *Chrysotila*, before the rest of the life cycle was known; the flagellate cells were known as *Isochrysis maritima*. The encapsulated and stalked forms of *Chrysotila* belong to the capsular (= tetrasporal or palmelloid) level of organization.

The non-motile cells contain two chloroplasts apiece, each containing its own pyrenoid. During asexual reproduction, a vegetative cell swells and then divides up into zoids (Fig. 14.8*b, f*). A culture of *Chrysotila lamellosa* (= *Isochrysis maritima*) was isolated from chalk rocks on the north coast of France.

Pleurochrysis (= *Hymenomonas*) *carterae* (Figs. 14.8*g*, 14.4–14.7, 14.11; [58, 451a, 494, 966, 1360, 1675, 1711, 1713, 1718, 1840, 1841])

Pleurochrysis carterae is a member of the coccolithophorids (p. 226), which is the group that includes most of the haptophyte species discovered so far. The cells of the coccolithophorids are covered with lime-encrusted scales, the **coccoliths**, which often take bizarre forms (Figs. 14.7a, 14.8g–i, 14.12). Arising at the anterior of their cells are two approximately equal flagella. Only a few coccolithophorid species are known to have haptonemata and these are always short. There are also non-motile coccolithophorids, lacking flagella, such as *Emiliania huxleyi* (Fig. 14.8i). Fossil coccolithophorids play an important role in micropalaeontology as stratigraphical marker fossils ([301, 1751]; see also p. 230).

The cells of *Pleurochrysis carterae* are spherical to ovoid and about 5–10 µm long. The two flagella are roughly equal and near them is a very short haptonema, which ends in a small knob. There are two brown chloroplasts, each with a pyrenoid. The cell surface is covered with oval coccoliths, which in the light microscope have a dark margin and a brighter centre.

Close examination reveals that other types of scale are present besides the coccoliths. Thus, below the layer of coccoliths are two layers of polysaccharide scales, each one with a raised rim, positioned just outside the plasmalemma. The electron microscope reveals that each coccolith also has a polysaccharide component, consisting of a radially structured base plate, on whose margins the lime is deposited (Fig. 14.7a). Both the polysaccharide scales and the coccoliths are formed within cisternae of the golgi apparatus and then secreted ([966, 1839, 1840, 1841, 1842]).

Pleurochrysis carterae has a heteromorphic, diplohaplontic life cycle (Fig. 14.11; [451a, 494, 495, 1711, 1718]). There are two main phases: the '*Hymenomonas*' phase, which is the diploid sporophyte generation, and the '*Apistonema*' phase, which is the haploid gametophyte. The '*Apistonema*' phase consists of branched filaments and was so named because of its resemblance to the chrysophycean genus *Apistonema*.

The diploid '*Hymenomonas*' phase consists of flagellate or non-flagellate unicells, which reproduce vegetatively either by simple division (Fig. 14.11a, b) or through the formation of four spores, which develop within the coccolith casing of the parent cell (Fig. 14.11c, d). In some cases, the formation of the four spores is accompanied by meiosis (Fig. 14.11e), so that the spores are haploid; these then give rise to the filamentous '*Apistonema*' phase (Fig. 14.11f, g). The cells of the '*Apistonema*' plants can divide up to give zoids, which may or may not have haptonemata (Fig. 14.11h). These zoids do not bear coccoliths but

do have polysaccharide scales, which have a typical haptophyte structure, with concentric patterns of fibrils on the outer side of the scale, and radial patterns on the inside, facing the cell (Fig. 14.7b). Some of the zoids grow into new '*Apistonema*' plants (Fig. 14.11h), while others function as gametes (Fig. 14.11j; [494, 1718]). The zygote grows into a new '*Hymenomonas*' phase (Fig. 14.11k–n).

The cells of the filamentous '*Apistonema*' phase possess a thick, laminated cell wall, which consists for the most part of layers of polysaccharide scales packed one on top of another. These scales do not have raised margins but, like the other scales produced during the life cycle, they too are produced from the golgi apparatus. In some haptophytes calcified elements are found within the gelatinous walls of the '*Apistonema*' phase, which resemble the fossil coccoliths known as *Tetralithus*.

Pleurochrysis carterae is a marine alga. The '*Hymenomonas*' stage is to be found in nearshore phytoplankton communities, while the '*Apistonema*' phase is benthic and occurs on chalk cliffs, in the intertidal zone, or on salt marsh soils. The species is widely distributed around the temperate coasts of Europe.

Emiliania huxleyi (Figs. 14.8i, 14.9)

This, like *Pleurochrysis carterae*, is a coccolithophorid. The coccoid (non-flagellate) cells have a diameter of 5–7 µm and are covered by a single layer of coccoliths. Each coccolith consists of two plates, one facing the outside of the cell and the other facing inwards, connected by a short central cylinder; it thus resembles a collar stud. The plates consist of radially arranged I-shaped elements. The life cycle is not known in detail but it includes a biflagellate motile stage, which possesses organic scales but lacks coccoliths and a haptonema. Information about scale formation and the occurrence of blooms is given on p. 226 and Fig. 14.9. This is the commonest and most abundant of all the coccolithophorids and is found world-wide in the marine phytoplankton.

Discosphaera tubifera (Fig. 14.12)

D. tubifera has coccoid cells that are covered by coccoliths bearing trumpet-like protuberances. It is widespread in tropical to warm-temperate seas.

Pavlova helicata (Fig. 14.13; [563, 1818, 1819])

The cells of this alga are compressed dorsiventrally

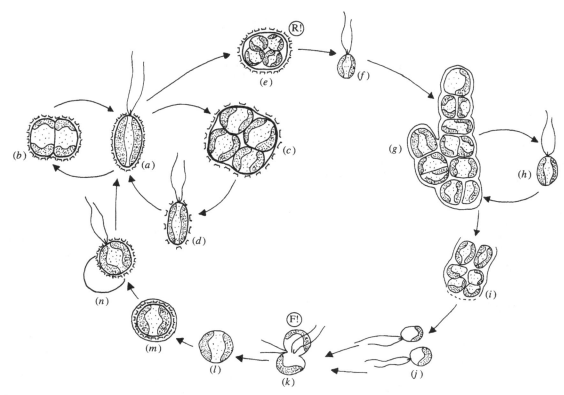

Figure 14.11. The life cycle of *Pleurochrysis*. For explanation, see text. F! = fertilization; R! = reduction division (meiosis). (Based on [494, 1711].)

and shaped like an inverted egg, when seen from the dorsal side. Their shape is fixed, plastic deformation being prevented by a rigid surface layer. Each cell measures 6–9 µm × 5–6 µm × 2 µm.

There are two flagella, which are very differently constructed. One is relatively long and is covered with small tripartite, club-shaped granules (0.02–0.08 µm), together with delicate non-tubular hairs; this flagellum points forwards. The other flagellum usually points back along the cell and is much smaller (Fig. 14.13a). Both flagella, together with a short haptonema, arise from the base of a shallow trough on the ventral side.

Each cell contains two lemon-yellow chloroplasts, which are parietal and sometimes connected to each other by a narrow isthmus; inside the chloroplast is a pyrenoid. The nucleus lies at the anterior end of the cell, while the golgi apparatus is central. A narrow sac several micrometres long, representing an invagination of the plasmalemma, opens to the exterior imme-

diately adjacent to the flagellar bases, rather like the gullet of the Cryptophyta (p. 236). Beneath the plasmalemma is a flat peripheral cisterna of endoplasmic reticulum, a characteristic feature of the Haptophyta, while the cell surface is covered externally by numerous tiny mushroom-like scales or granules. The reserve polysaccharide is paramylon.

Both the tripartite, club-shaped granules of the long flagellum, and the mushroom-shaped granules on the body of the cell are formed in the golgi apparatus, before being secreted to the exterior. They are clearly differentiated from the scales of other Haptophyta, with their characteristic radial structure (Figs. 14.3, 14.7b, 14.10f). Old cultures of *Pavlova* develop palmelloid (= encapsulated) stages, resembling the cells of *Chrysotila* shown in Fig. 14.8a, and in some cultures these benthic (= bottom-inhabiting) stages predominate. *Pavlova helicata* has been isolated from salt marsh pools along the coast of the Wadden Sea.

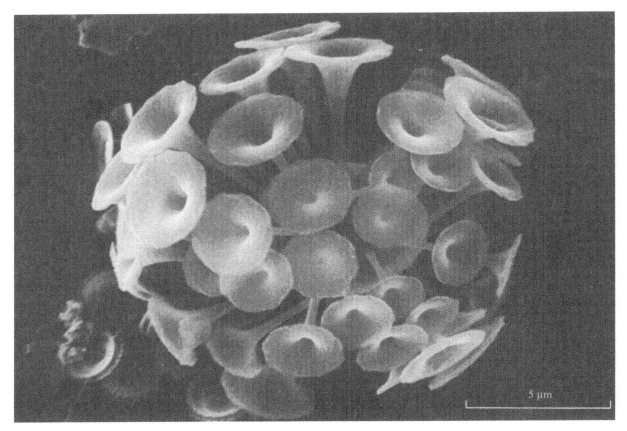

Figure 14.12. Scanning electron micrograph of the tropical coccolithophorid *Discosphaera tubifera,* with trumpet-shaped appendages on its coccoliths. (From [597a], with the permission of the author and CSIRO/ E.J. Brill/ Robert Brown & Associates, Bathurst, Australia.)

Pavlova occupies an isolated position within the Haptophyta, judging by its cell architecture (see above) and the details of mitosis and cytokinesis ([565, 569]).

The subdivision of the Haptophyceae into orders

The current classification of the Haptophyceae is based mainly on characters of the flagella, the haptonema, and the scales (organic scales and coccoliths). The only well-defined order is the Pavlovales. The remaining three orders seem to be artificial, judging by information recently gathered about cell ultrastructure and life cycles; the life cycle of a single species can include stages that would otherwise have been assigned to different orders.

The following four orders are currently recognized ([230a, 569]).

Prymnesiales: cells motile, with two equal or subequal flagella and an obvious haptonema (e.g. *Chrysochromulina, Prymnesium, Corymbellus, Phaeocystis*).

Isochrysidales: cells motile, with two equal or subequal flagella, but with the haptonema reduced or absent (e.g. *Chrysotila, Pleurochrysis*).

Coccolithophorales: cells non-motile (without flagella) or motile with two equal flagella; haptonema reduced or absent; coccoliths present (e.g. *Emiliania, Syracosphaera, Discosphaera*).

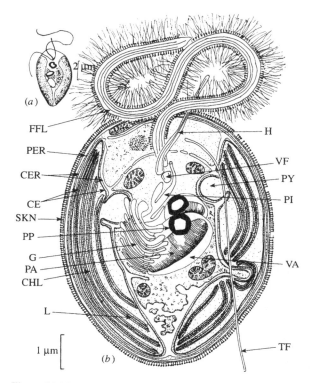

FFL
PER
CER
CE
SKN
PP
G
PA
CHL
L
1 μm
(b)

H
VF
PY
PI
VA
TF

Figure 14.13. *Pavlova helicata*. (*a*) Flagellate cell, as seen in the light microscope. (*b*) Reconstruction based on electron microscopical observations. CE = chloroplast envelope; CER = chloroplast endoplasmic reticulum; CHL = chloroplast; FFL = forwardly directed, anterior flagellum; G = golgi body; H = haptonema; L = lamella, composed of a stack of three thylakoids; PA = paramylon (see VA); PER = peripheral endoplasmic reticulum; PI = pit; PP = polyphosphate (see VA); PY = pyrenoid; SKN = superficial covering of stalked, knob-like particles; TF = trailing filament; VA = vacuole containing paramylon and polyphosphate; VF = vestigial hind flagellum. (Based on [1817, 1819].)

Pavlovales: cells motile, with two unequal flagella, the longer one covered by knob scales and fine hairs; haptonema reduced (*Pavlova*).

15

Cryptophyta

The division Cryptophyta contains only one class, the Cryptophyceae.

The principal characteristics of the Cryptophyta [373, 481, 524, 679, 680, 1045, 1046, 1047, 1461, 1548, 1550]

1 Almost all of the Cryptophyceae are unicellular flagellates (Fig. 15.1*a–c*), although some of them can form sessile, encapsuled (= palmelloid or tetrasporal) stages. One genus, *Bjornbergiella*, possesses a simply constructed, filamentous thallus [74, 125].

2 Each flagellate cell (zoid) bears two flagella, which differ in length. The longer flagellum bears two rows of mastigonemes (stiff lateral hairs, 1.5 μm long, with a tubular shaft and a thinner terminal section; Fig. 15.2*a*), while the shorter flagellum bears a single row of shorter mastigonemes (1 μm long). In some species, however, the flagella have a somewhat different structure [933]. As in the Heterokontophyta, the mastigonemes are formed within the nuclear envelope and endoplasmic reticulum [1218]. The flagella are covered by tiny organic scales (*ca.* 150 nm in diameter), which bear a seven-sided (heptagonal) rosette pattern (Fig. 15.2*d*; [978, 1389]).

3 The transition region of the flagellum shaft con-

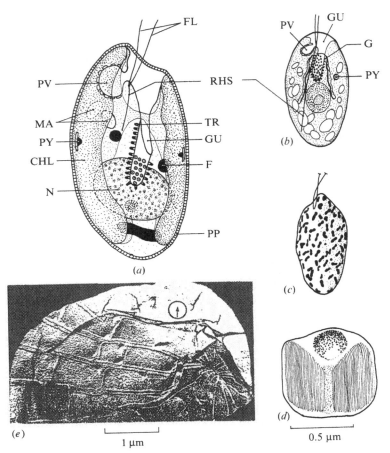

Figure 15.1.(a) *Cryptomonas similis*. (b) *Chilomonas paramecium*, a colourless member of the Cryptophyta. (c) *Chilomonas paramecium*, stained to show the mitochondria. (d) *Cryptomonas reticulata*: a trichocyst, as seen with the electron microscope. (e) *Chroomonas*: an electron micrograph showing the periplast plates.

CHL = chloroplast; F = lipid droplets; FL = flagellum; G = golgi body; GU = gullet; MA = Maupas body; N = nucleus; PP = periplast; PV = contractile (pulsing) vacuole; PY = pyrenoid; RHS = rhizostyle; TR = trichocyst. (a–c after [720a]; d after [1045]; e from [480])

tains two transverse partitions, the lower of which has a central thickening (Fig. 15.5b; [664], [1218]).

4 The cells are dorsiventrally constructed. The dorsal side is convex, while the ventral side is flat, with a shallow longitudinal groove. The upper, anterior end of the cell is obliquely truncate (Fig. 15.1a).

5 On the ventral side, at the anterior end of the groove, there is a deep gullet, whose wall is lined by numerous prominent trichocysts (Figs. 15.1a, d, 15.2a, f).

6 The two flagella emerge from the cell just above and to the right of the gullet (i.e. on the left when the cell is viewed from the flattened ventral side; Figs. 15.1a, b, 15.2a).

7 The chloroplasts are surrounded by a fold of endoplasmic reticulum (ER) and when a chloroplast lies adjacent to the nucleus, the nuclear ER and chloroplast ER are continuous (Fig. 15.2a, f). The narrow space between the chloroplast ER and the chloroplast does not contain a periplastidial reticulum, in contrast to the Heterokontophyta and Haptophyta (see Chapters 6 and 14; [76]).

8 Within the chloroplasts the thylakoids are often arranged in pairs, to form lamellae; lamellae containing larger numbers of thylakoids are also sometimes found. There is no girdle lamella (Fig. 15.2a, c). The thylakoids are thicker than those of most algae and are filled with dark-staining material (as seen with the electron microscope), which represents the phycobilin pigments phycocyanin and phycoerythrin (see character 11; [353, 484, 1666]).

9 The pyrenoid projects out from the inner side of the chloroplast. It may contain lamellae, each with 1–2 thylakoids, or be quite without thylakoids. A characteristic, and indeed unique, feature of the Cryptophyceae is that the starch reserves are accumulated neither in the chloroplast, nor in the cytoplasm, but in the periplastidial compartment between the chloroplast ER and the chloroplast envelope (Fig. 15.2a, f).

10 The chloroplasts contain chlorophylls a and c_2, but not chlorophyll b (Table 1.2) ([793, 794]).

11 The chloroplasts, of which there are one or two per cell, can be blue, blue-green, reddish, red-brown, olive green, brown, or yellow-brown. These colours arise because the chlorophyll is masked by a variety of accessory photosynthetic pigments, which can occur in different proportions. The pigments that can be present include (cryptophyte-) phycocyanin, (cryptophyte-) phycoerythrin, α-carotene and the xanthophylls alloxanthin, crocoxanthin, zeaxanthin and monadoxanthin (Table 1.2; [88, 520, 678]). The phycocyanin and phycoerythrin do not lie in phycobilisomes on the outside of each thylakoid, as they do in the Rhodophyta, Glaucophyta and Cyanophyta, but instead fill the thylakoid lumen (compare Fig. 15.2c with Fig. 4.1b).

12 The chloroplast DNA is concentrated into numerous small bodies (nucleoids), which are scattered through the chloroplast ([254]).

13 There is often no eyespot, but where one is present it consists of a series of spherical globules, as in the Heterokontophyta ([319, 481, 1047]). The eyespot lies in the middle of the cell, just within the chloroplast, and is not associated with a flagellum, in contrast to the eyespots of the Heterokontophyta.

14 The most important storage material is starch ([33]). Grains of this are formed outside the chloroplast but nevertheless close to the pyrenoid (in the Chlorophyta, starch is formed within the chloroplast). In addition there are droplets of lipid (Fig. 15.2a).

15 The cell is enclosed by a stiff, proteinaceous periplast, which is usually made up of rectangular or polygonal plates (Figs. 15.1e, 15.2a, b, e, 15.3). These are anchored to the overlying plasmalemma by roundish or polygonal arrays of intra-membrane particles (Fig. 15.3; [930, 932]). The outer face of the plasmalemma is often covered by additional external plates, which have the same outline as the internal plates and have a crystalline substructure; furthermore, in addition to the external plates or instead of them, rosette scales (Fig. 15.2d) and fibrillar material may be present ([141, 142, 679, 680, 1549]).

16 A peculiar organelle, the nucleomorph, is present in the space between the chloroplast and the chloroplast endoplasmic reticulum, often lying in a depression in the surface of pyrenoid (Fig. 15.2a, f). The nucleomorph has a double membrane around it, which is pierced by pores, and it contains both DNA and a nucleolus-like structure. The nucleomorph is often interpreted as the vestigial nucleus of a photosynthetic, eukaryotic endosymbiont, which is suggested to have been incorporated into the heterotrophic ancestor of the cryptophytes. The compartment of the cell surrounded by the chloroplast ER is interpreted as representing the vestigial endosymbiont ([513, 524, 524a, 1049]). Support for this idea has recently been obtained from a phylogenetic analysis of the sequences coding for 18S ribosomal RNAs in the nucleus and nucleomorph (cf. p. 511).

17 Trichocysts are present. They lie immediately beneath the plasmalemma, large ones in the gullet region, smaller ones scattered around the remainder of the cell's periphery (Figs 15.1a, 15.2a, e, f).

18 At the anterior end of the cell there is a contractile vacuole ([1383, 1385]).

19 Immediately adjacent to the gullet are two structures, the so-called Maupas bodies (Figs 15.1, 15.2a), whose function is unknown. They may, perhaps, be involved in the removal and digestion of superfluous membrane.

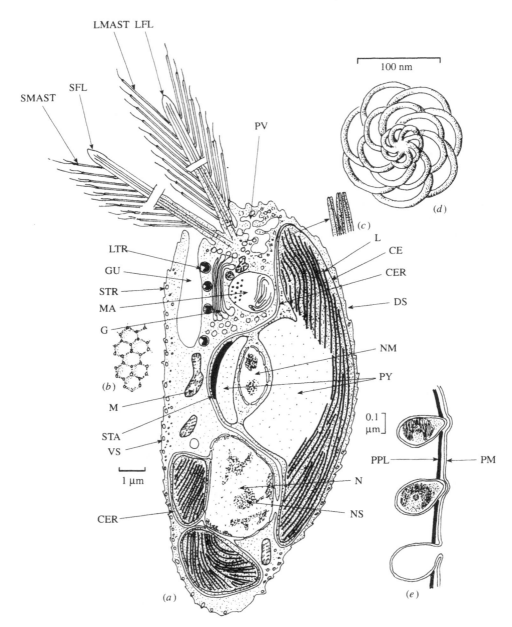

Figure 15.2. (*a–e*) *Cryptomonas*. (*a*) Longitudinal section, based on EM observations. (*b*) Surface view of the periplast, with small trichocysts located at the angles of the hexagonal plates. (*c*) Three chloroplast lamellae, each containing two closely appressed thylakoids. (*d*) One of the rosette scales that cover the flagella. (*e*) Section through the cell surface, showing three small trichocysts, one of which has discharged its contents. (*f*) *Chroomonas*: transmission electron micrograph of a longitudinal section, showing the general ultrastructure of the cell (compare with Fig. 15.2*a*). CE = chloroplast envelope, consisting of two membranes; CER = chloroplast endoplasmic reticulum; CHL = chloroplast; DS = dorsal side of cell; G = golgi body; GU = gullet; L = lamella, composed of a stack of two thylakoids; LFL = long flagellum; LMAST = long mastigoneme on long flagellum, bearing one terminal hair; LTR = large trichocyst; M = mitochondrion; MA = Maupas body; N = nucleus; NM = nucleomorph; NS = nucleolus; PM =

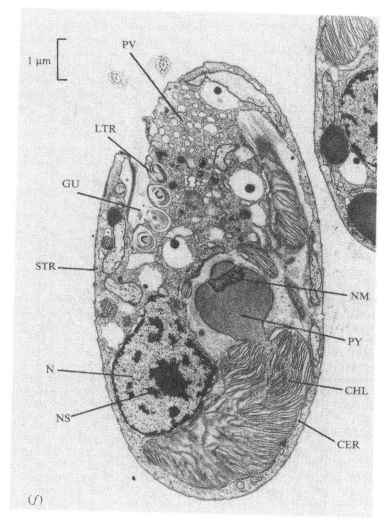

1 μm

PV

LTR

GU

STR

N

NS

NM

PY

CHL

CER

(f)

Caption for fig. 15.2 *(cont.)*.

plasma membrane (plasmalemma); PPL = periplast plate; PV = contractile (pulsing) vacuole; PY = pyrenoid; SFL = short flagellum; SMAST = short mastigoneme on short flagellum, bearing two termi-nal hairs; STA = starch; STR = small trichocyst; VS = ventral side. (*a–c* based on [1045, 1550]; *d* on [978]; *e* on [619]; *f* from [373], with the permission of the authors and the editor of the Botanical Magazine of Tokyo.)

20 The nucleus is large and lies in the posterior half of the cell. The number of chromosomes is very high (between 40 and 210 have been counted at metaphase; [1767]) (Figs. 15.1*a*, *b*, 15.2*a*, *f*). Crypto-phytes have a very characteristic type of mitosis. Mitosis is open (i.e. the nuclear enve-lope disintegrates) and at metaphase the chro-mosomes congregate to form a massive plate. Within this there are chromatin-free channels, containing bundles of pole-to-pole micro-tubules. The spindle poles are flat and delimited by cisternae of rough endoplasmic reticulum; centrioles are absent. Cell division is brought about by a cleavage furrow, which is a ring-like invagination of the plasmalemma (Fig. 15.4*a*; [481, 1310, 1311, 1312]).

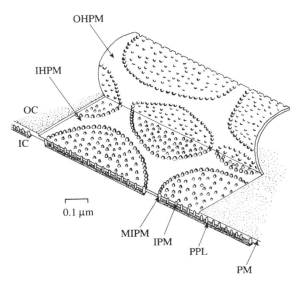

Figure 15.3. Diagram showing the periplast structure of *Cryptomonas*. The periplast plates are anchored to the plasmalemma by arrays of intramembrane particles. The arrays are polygonal or rounded in outline and are revealed by removing the outer half of the plasmalemma (e.g. using freeze–fracture techniques). IC = interior of cell; IHPM = inner half of plasmalemma; IPM = intramembrane particle; MIPM = marginal intramembrane particle of array; OC = outside the cell; OHPM = outer half of the plasmalemma; PM = plasma membrane (plasmalemma); PPL = periplast plate. (After [930].)

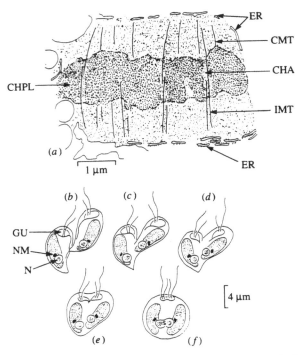

Figure 15.4. (*a*) Metaphase of mitosis in *Chroomonas*. (*b–f*) Isogamous sexual fusion in *Chroomonas acuta*. CHA = channel in the massive plate of chromatin, containing a bundle of interzonal microtubules; CHPL = massive plate of chromatin; CMT = chromosomal spindle microtubule; ER = endoplasmic reticulum; GU = gullet; IMT = interzonal spindle microtubules; N = nucleus; NM = nucleomorph. (*a* based on [1310, 1312]; *b–f* on [931].)

21 Isogamous sexual fusion and karyogamy have recently been observed in one species ([931]), but other aspects of its life cycle remain unknown (Fig. 15.4*b–f*). In another species the life cycle appears to include a haploid flagellate stage and a larger, morphologically dissimilar diploid stage, also flagellate. Each stage can reproduce vegetatively, but can also give rise to the other, suggesting a slightly heteromorphic, diplohaplontic sexual cycle ([679]). This would be the first example of a life cycle in which two flagellate stages alternate, one haploid and the other diploid.

22 The Cryptophyceae are found in both marine and fresh waters, and there are about as many species in each.

General observations

This is a small and easily recognized division. It contains flagellates with a complex but highly characteristic structure, which has been investigated in considerable detail, first using light microscopy ([720a]) and later with the electron microscope ([316, 399, 480, 481, 524, 669, 680, 1045, 1046, 1199, 1548, 1550]). The Cryptophyta are the only major group of algae, apart from the Cyanophyta, Glaucophyta and Rhodophyta, to have phycobilins (phycoerythrin and phycocyanin) as accessory photosynthetic pigments.

The function of the Maupas bodies remains unclear. They contain many membranes and fibrils, and it has been suggested that they are involved in the destruction of particular cell organelles, especially superfluous trichocysts. If so they could perhaps be termed lysosomes ([1045, 1046, 1863]).

The trichocysts each contain a cylindrical structure, which consists of a tightly coiled strip or band of material. The band becomes progressively narrower towards the inside of the coil, so that in median section (Fig. 15.1*d*) the coil has a butterfly-like outline. The trichocysts discharge explosively, the 300–400 nm thick band suddenly unrolling itself. As a result the cell makes an abrupt backward movement and this may perhaps be an avoidance reaction. The trichocysts are formed in golgi vesicles ([619, 1045, 1046, 1863]) and are clearly quite different from the trichocysts of the Dinophyta (p. 263) and Raphidophyceae (p. 160).

The cryptophytes also stand apart from other groups of algae in the structure of the flagellar apparatus, particularly in the arrangement of the roots that anchor the flagella in the cell (Fig. 15.5*a*; [1218, 1505, 1514]). The most striking feature is the rhizostyle, a longitudinal microtubular root containing 6–10 microtubules and running from near the basal body of the longer, dorsal flagellum to the posterior of the cell. A conspicuous, transversely striated fibrous root is present, again associated with the basal body of the dorsal flagellum but lying in a plane roughly perpendicular to the rhizostyle. In the same plane there are also three microtubular roots, one of them closely associated with the transversely striated fibrous root. There are some differences in the arrangement of the roots between the various genera of cryptophytes ([1505]). The transversely striated root and material closely associated with the rhizostyle have been shown to contain the contractile protein centrin ([1590, 1591, 1592]).

Besides autotrophic species, the Cryptophyta also includes colourless, heterotrophic representatives, such as *Chilomonas paramecium*, which lacks chloroplasts but contains leucoplasts (Fig. 15.1*b, c*; [720a, 1461]). Another colourless form, *Cyathomonas*, lacks both chloroplasts and leucoplasts, and may be the nearest modern analogue to the ancestral heterotrophic cryptophyte, which incorporated a photosynthetic endosymbiont (whose vestigial nucleus is still present in photosynthetic species as the nucleomorph) and so became photoautotrophic.

Size and distribution of the class

The class consists of around 12 genera, containing almost 100 freshwater species and 100 marine species.

The freshwater forms occur in lakes and also sporadically in small pools and puddles, especially if these are slightly enriched. The marine species are sometimes to be found in tidal pools or puddles of brackish water, but several species also occur in the phytoplankton of the open ocean ([173, 434, 613, 759, 852]).

In both freshwater and marine environments, cryptophytes can at times constitute a significant fraction of the nannoplankton (phytoplankton 2–20 µm in diameter). Thus, cryptophytes sometimes dominate the spring bloom of phytoplankton in the central North Sea, where they have been detected by increased concentrations of the characteristic accessory pigment alloxanthin ([520]). Cryptophytes also occur in the freshwaters of Antarctica. Certain species inhabit the interstitial water in sandy beaches, providing these are not exposed to heavy surf ([1528]). This special environment is also occupied by cyanophytes (p. 23), pennate diatoms (p. 135) and dinoflagellates.

Some planktonic cryptophytes are capable of vertical migration within the water column, like many planktonic dinoflagellates (p. 271) During calm weather they use their flagella to adjust their vertical position, different species to different optimum positions on the underwater light gradient ([434]).

One highly reduced cryptophyte lives as an endosymbiont in the euryhaline ciliate *Mesodinium rubrum* (Fig. 15.6; [1756, 1761]). The ciliate lacks a cytostome (a 'cell mouth') and is dependent on the endosymbiont's photosynthesis for its nutrition. In contrast, non-photosynthetic species of *Mesodinium* do possess a cytostome, which lies at the apex of the cell. The endosymbiont cytoplasm is surrounded by two membranes, the inner of which is interpreted as the plasmalemma of the endosymbiont, the outer as the food vacuole membrane of the host. The endosymbiont contains several chloroplasts with pyrenoids and nucleomorphs, a nucleus, golgi apparatus, mitochondria and endoplasmic reticulum. The chloroplasts are as usual surrounded by chloroplast ER and have typical cryptophyte thylakoids and pigments. There are no vestiges of the original cell morphology, and periplast, flagellar apparatus and trichocysts are all absent ([662, 1013, 1014]). Endosymbionts showing the same degree of reduction, but belonging to the Heterokontophyta, have been discovered in some species of the Dinophyta, e.g. *Peridinium balticum* (cf. p. 251). Other dinoflagellates contain reduced cryptophyte endosymbionts (p. 253).

Mesodinium rubrum illustrates very nicely the

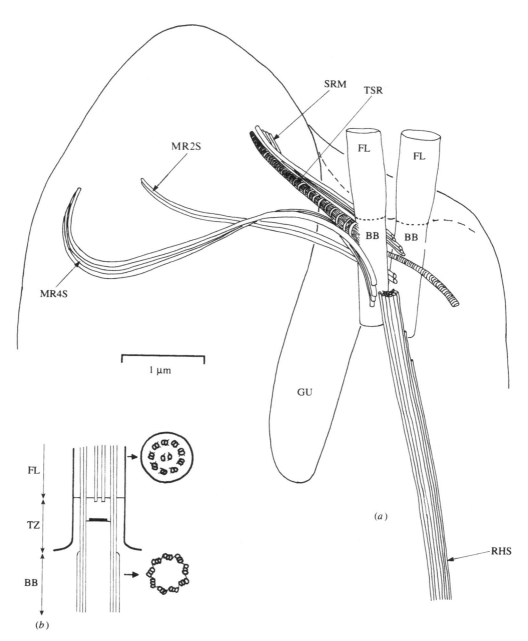

Figure 15.5. (*a*) The flagellar basal bodies and associated roots (i.e. the flagellar apparatus) in *Cryptomonas*. (*b*) Longitudinal section through the basal region of the flagellum, with cross sections through the flagellar axoneme (top), showing the characteristic '9 + 2' pattern, and through the basal body (bottom), showing the ring of nine triplets. BB = basal body; FL = flagellum; GU = gullet; MR4S = four-stranded microtubular root; MR2S = two-stranded microtubular root; RHS = rhizostyle, a conspicuous longitudinal root, composed of 6–10 microtubules; SRM = microtubules running along the transversely striated root; TSR = transversely striated root; TZ = transition zone. (*a* based on [1505]; *b* on [1218].)

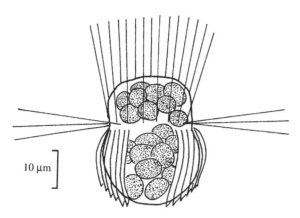

Figure 15.6. A light microscopical picture of the ciliate protozoan *Mesodinium rubrum* (phylum Ciliophora).
The cell consists of two more or less hemispherical
halves, separated by an equatorial girdle of stiff cirri
(each cirrus is a compound flagellum, containing
eight axonemes). The posterior half of the cell is covered by a 'skirt' of locomotory cilia (= flagella).
Inside the cell are many chloroplasts, all belonging to
one endosymbiotic cell. (Based on [43].)

isms, by incorporating the photosynthesizing cells of
the dinophyte *Symbiodinium microadriaticum* (p.
277). *Mesodinium rubrum* can occur in fresh, brackish
or marine waters. In the brackish waters of the southwest of the Netherlands, *Mesodinium* sometimes
blooms in May and June, colouring the water red just
as in 'red tides', although red tides are usually caused
by dense populations of certain species of dinophyte
(p. 271). Massive blooms of *Mesodinium rubrum* also
develop regularly in areas of upwelling, such as those
along the costs of Peru and Baja California, where
nutrient-rich deep oceanic water comes to the surface,
stimulating phytoplankton growth ([1013, 1351, 1659, 1706]).

process of 'serial endosymbiosis'. This ciliate, originally heterotrophic, became a photoautotroph by
incorporating a photosynthetic, unicellular eukaryote
(a cryptophyte), which itself originated through
another symbiosis, involving the acquisition of a unicellular, eukaryotic alga by a heterotrophic flagellate;
the vestigial nucleus of the primary endosymbiont is
still visible in the secondary, cryptophyte endosymbiont of *Mesodinium*, in the form of a nucleomorph.
At each of the two stages of endosymbiosis a non-
photosynthetic 'animal' cell (here a ciliate) has
acquired the ability to photosynthesize, by taking up
an alga into its cytoplasm. In the same way, reef-building corals have also become photosynthetic organ-

Cryptomonas similis (Fig. 15.1*a*)

The cells are elliptical in ventral view, only slightly
compressed, and have an obliquely truncate anterior
end. They possess a ventral groove and a deep gullet,
which is lined with conspicuous trichocysts. The
periplast bears hexagonal plates, arranged in many
spiral rows (Fig. 15.2*b*). Inside the cell there is a parietal chloroplast, which consists of two lobes connected by a narrow isthmus. The cells are olive-green
to yellow-green in colour and measure 20–80 µm ×
6–20 µm.

Cryptomonas similis lives in freshwater plankton of
ponds, ditches and lakes, often where the water is
somewhat enriched or polluted.

Chilomonas paramecium (Fig. 15.1*b, c*)

This species closely resembles *Cryptomonas similis*,
but it is colourless and possesses no chloroplasts; it
does, however, contain leucoplasts. *Chilomonas* is
consequently heterotrophic, and is to be found in
highly polluted freshwater pools. The cells attain
lengths of 20–40 µm.

16

Dinophyta

The division Dinophyta contains only one class, the Dinophyceae.

The principal characteristics of the Dinophyta

1 The vast majority of Dinophyta are unicellular flagellates (Figs. 16.1, 16.2) and only a few are coccoid or filamentous. In addition, there are some curious and highly specialized heterotrophic forms.

2 The flagellate cells possess two dissimilar flagella. Typically, the transverse flagellum moves in a plane at right angles to the longitudinal axis, while the longitudinal flagellum points backwards. Both flagella bear fine lateral hairs, which are much thinner than the mastigonemes of the Heterokontophyta and Cryptophyta; the transverse flagellum bears one row of hairs, the longitudinal flagellum two. The transverse flagellum contains a spiral axoneme. Both flagella arise on the ventral side of the cell (Figs. 16.1, 16.2, 16.10, 16.19a).

3 A transverse furrow is usually present, girdling the cell; in it lies the transverse flagellum. On the ventral side there is a longitudinal groove, along which the longitudinal flagellum runs (Figs. 16.1, 16.2, 16.10).

4 The flagella emerge at the intersection of the transverse and longitudinal grooves (Figs. 16.1, 16.2, 16.10).

5 The transition zone of each flagellum contains two parallel discs at the base of the two central axonemal microtubules, together with one or two further rings which lie below, closer to the basal body (Fig. 16.10h; [664, 1218]).

6 The chloroplasts, where present, are surrounded by three membranes, none of which is connected to the endoplasmic reticulum (Figs. 16.6, 16.8a). A few dinophytes have aberrant chloroplasts, which represent eukaryotic endosymbionts, reduced to a greater or lesser extent (p. 251). Many dinophytes are heterotrophic and lack chloroplasts.

7 Within the chloroplasts the thylakoids are for the most part united in stacks (lamellae) of three (Figs. 16.6, 16.8a). Girdle lamellae are generally absent; girdle lamellae are characteristic of the division Heterokontophyta (p. 102) and are peripheral stacks of three thylakoids, which lie just beneath the chloroplast envelope. Where girdle lamellae are present in chloroplasts within dinophyte cells, the chloroplasts belong in fact, not to the dinophytes themselves, but to more or less reduced eukaryotic algae living endosymbiotically within the dinophyte cell (p. 253).

8 The most important chlorophyll is chlorophyll a, with chlorophyll c_2 also present. Again, there are some interesting exceptions to this among the species with endosymbionts (p. 253). Chlorophyll b is absent (Table 1.2).

9 The chloroplasts are usually brown, since the green chlorophylls are masked by yellow and brown accessory pigments (β-carotene and several xanthophylls, of which the most important is peridinin). Certain species with endosymbiotic algae possess other accessory pigments (p. 253; Table 1.2).

10 The chloroplast DNA is localized in small nodules scattered throughout the chloroplast. Within the endosymbiotic algae of dinophytes, however, other kinds of nucleoid can be present (see p. 253 and [254]).

11 Pyrenoids of various kinds occur in dinophyte chloroplasts. For instance, they can be stalked

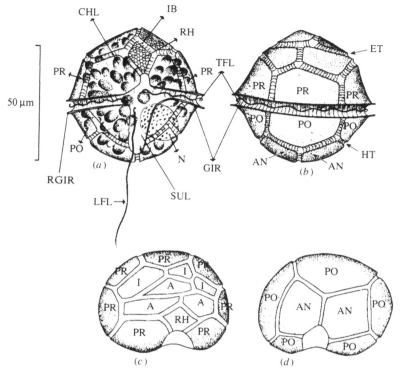

Figure 16.1. *Peridinium cinctum.* (*a*) Ventral side. (*b*) Dorsal side. (*c*) Apical view. (*d*) Antapical view. A = apical plate; AN = antapical plate; CHL = chloroplast; ET = epitheca (apical half, epicone); GIR = girdle (transverse furrow); HT = hypotheca (antapical half, hypocone); I = intercalary plate; IB = intercalary band; LFL = longitudinal flagellum; N = nucleus; PO = postcingular plate; PR = precingular plate; RGIR = raised rim of girdle; RH = rhomboidal area or closing plate; SUL = sulcus (longitudinal furrow); TFL = transverse flagellum.

(Fig. 16.6), or embedded within the chloroplast (Figs. 16.4, 16.10). They may be partly penetrated by thylakoids.

12 There are several different types of eyespot:
  (a) small spherical globules lying free within the cytoplasm (as in the Eustigmatophyta);
  (b) a row of small globules located within the chloroplast (as in the Heterokontophyta; Fig. 16.4);
  (c) layers of globules surrounded by a triple membrane (Fig. 16.7);
  (d) a complex 'eye' composed of a lens and a retinoid (in the family Warnowiaceae; [319], [1667]).

13 The principal reserve polysaccharide is starch, which is synthesized outside the chloroplasts, in the form of grains. Lipid is also found as reserve material (Table 1.3; Figs. 16.4, 16.6, 16.7, 16.19*a*).

14 The interphase nucleus has a unique structure, the chromosomes almost always being highly contracted and condensed, with a characteristic helicoidal, garland-like structure (Figs. 16.4, 16.7, 16.10, 16.12, 16.13*f*, 16.19*a*). This type of nucleus is called a 'dinokaryon', from the class in which it occurs.

15 During mitosis the nuclear envelope remains intact, bundles of the spindle microtubules passing through the mitotic nucleus in tunnels lined by nuclear membrane (Fig. 16.13).

16 The cell usually contains a rather complex system of tubes that opens to the exterior near the

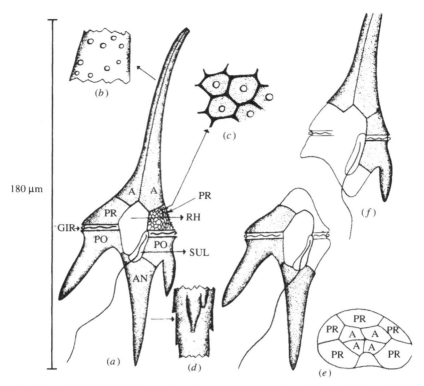

Figure 16.2. *Ceratium hirundinella* (for further explanation, see text). (*a*) Cell, seen from the ventral side. (*b*) Detail of apical horn. (*c*) Detail of one of the precingular plates. (*d*) Detail of antapical horn. (*e*) Apical view. (*f*) Two daughter cells shortly after cell division. The new halves of the theca have yet to be formed. A = apical plate; AN = antapical plate; GIR = girdle; PR = precingular plate; PO = postcingular plate; RH = rhomboidal area; SUL = sulcus.

bases of the flagella. This is called the pusule (Figs. 16.10*a*, *h*, 16.19*a*).

17 At the surface of the cell there are trichocysts, which discharge explosively when stimulated, throwing out transversely striated, four-sided threads (Figs. 16.4, 16.10*a*, *f*, *g*).

18 Around the periphery of the dinophyte cell is a superficial layer of flat, polygonal vesicles (thecal vesicles), which can be empty or almost empty (Figs. 16.6*c*, 16.10, 16.19*a*) but often contain cellulose plates (thecal plates) of varying thickness (Figs. 16.1, 16.2, 16.4, 16.5). The thecal plates generally form a bipartite armour, consisting of an upper half (epicone) and a lower half (hypocone), separated by a girdle.

19 The Dinophyta have a haplontic life cycle, only the zygote nucleus being diploid (Figs. 16.14, 16.15). A thick-walled resting zygote (hypnozygote) is usually produced.

20 Most Dinophyta (about 90% of the species) are marine, the remainder living in freshwater.

Size and distribution of the division

More than 2000 living and 2000 fossil species of Dinophyta are known, belonging to about 130 genera ([1759]). Most dinophytes are unicellular flagellates ('dinoflagellates'), which live in the surface waters either of the sea, or of fresh or brackish waters; roughly 90% of species are marine. Many planktonic species bear horns, ridges or wings (Figs. 16.2, 16.14, 16.17*e–g*, *q–t*, *v*, 16.19*b*), which often have bizarre forms. As a result the cells have a high surface area :

volume ratio. Planktonic diatoms tend to have similar projections and surface elaborations (Fig. 9.12). These peculiar shapes are often interpreted as a way of increasing the friction between cell and water, to slow sinking. However, dinophytes can counteract sinking by swimming, via their flagella, and in their case it seems more likely that the function of the surface elaborations is to permit a more efficient uptake of scarce nutrients from the surrounding water. An additional function of the horns might be to discourage herbivores; cf. thistle spines! ([434]).

Many members of the Dinophyta (about 50%) do not have chloroplasts and are therefore obligately heterotrophic (p. 257). Furthermore, many of the photosynthetic forms are facultatively heterotrophic and indeed are able to feed phagotrophically. They ingest bacteria and small planktonic algae.

Dinophyte species are known from polar, temperate and tropical waters, but tend on the whole to be more predominant in warm water communities. Thus, in the tropics they are present throughout the year, while in temperate regions they reach their maximum abundance in late spring and summer; here, both in the sea and in freshwater, a spring bloom of diatoms is often followed by rich growths of dinophytes (see also p. 134, where the overall preference of diatoms for cold and nutrient-rich waters is discussed). The greatest diversity and maximum abundance of dinophytes are encountered in neritic (= near-shore) parts of the oceans, where nutrients from the land are more abundant and where nutrient enrichment may be brought about by upwelling. Nevertheless, dinophytes can occur also in the open ocean, being common constituents of the 'deep chlorophyll maximum' at 75–150 m below the surface in nutrient-poor tropical and subtropical areas. The deep maximum represents a concentration of tiny planktonic algae belonging to various groups (predominantly Cyanophyta, Heterokontophyta and Haptophyta; see pp. 22, 121, 226). These algae, living in the lower, dim regions of the euphotic zone (the layer where sufficient light penetrates to allow photosynthesis), are probably able to scavenge nutrients from the cold, dark water beneath the euphotic zone. Other dinophyte inhabitants of the open ocean in the tropics are the heterotrophic members of the order Dinophysiales, which often have bizarre shapes.

Although the great majority of Dinophyta are planktonic, some species are benthic. Some live in the uppermost layers of marine sands ([1762]), but of all the benthic dinophytes the most important ecologically must surely be the species that lives endosymbiotically in the tissues of invertebrate animals (Fig. 16.3g–l): all reef-building corals, for instance, depend on the cells of their endosymbiotic dinophyte (called 'zooxanthellae') and could not grow without them.

In favourable conditions, the cells of some species can proliferate rapidly and produce dense blooms. As a result the surface waters of seas or lakes can be turned red; such events are sometimes called 'red tides'. Blooms of certain Dinophyta are poisonous to many different types of animal, and so red tides can be accompanied by the mass death of marine organisms (p. 273). Water blooms can light up the sea at night, through bioluminescence (p. 274). Within the Dinophyta there are also some curious parasitic forms, which infect copepods, fish, tunicates and algae (p. 279, Fig. 16.3a–f). Fossil dinophyte cysts are common in Triassic sediments (230 m.y. ago) and in younger rocks, but the oldest cysts date from the Silurian (410 m.y. ago), or perhaps even from the late Precambrian (600 m.y. ago) (p. 270).

General features of the Dinophyta

In the account that follows, the general characteristics of the Dinophyta will be discussed with particular reference to well-known, representative genera, such as *Peridinium* (Figs. 16.1, 16.4), *Ceratium* (Fig. 16.2) and *Gymnodinium* (Fig. 16.10). For a transmission electron micrograph showing the general organization of the dinophyte cell, see Fig. 16.19a.

Structure of the cell envelope

Like the diatoms (p. 133), most Dinophyta are covered with a species-specific 'armour', which is often strange and beautiful in its shape and ornamentation (Figs. 16.2, 16.17e–g, q–t, 16.19b). The resemblance to the diatoms is only superficial, however, since the armour of the two groups differs in both structure and chemical composition. The dinophyte armour is divided into an upper (**apical**) and a lower (**antapical**) half, and consists of polygonal plates, which fit tightly against each other. The important constituent of the armour is a polysaccharide, apparently cellulose, whereas in the diatoms the wall elements are made of

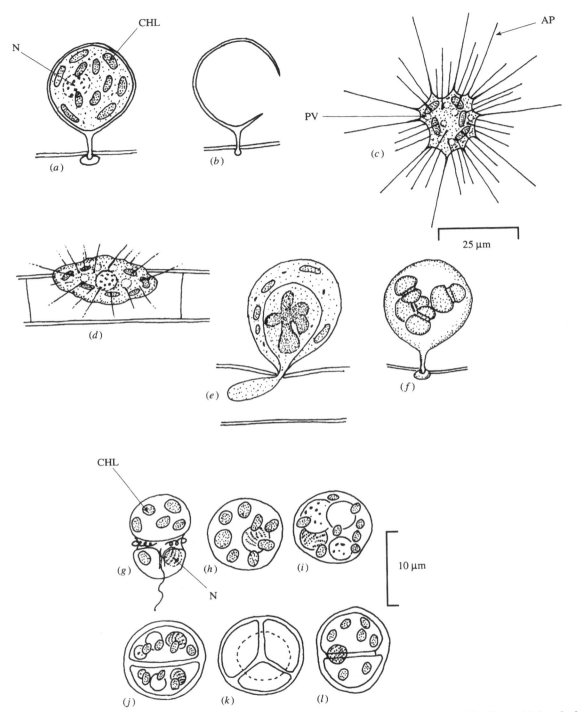

Figure 16.3. (a–f) The parasitic amoeboid dinophyte *Stylodinium sphaera*. (a) Spherical stalked cell epiphytic on the filament of a freshwater *Oedogonium* species (Chlorophyta). (b) Empty cell just after the emergence of two amoebae. (c) Amoeboid cell just after release. (d) Amoeboid cell after settling on *Oedogonium*. (e) Amoeboid cell parasitizing *Oedogonium:* the contents of the host cell are sucked into the amoeba, which begins to develop the typical *Stylodinium* form. (f) Formation of *Gymnodinium*-like zoospores. (g–l) *Symbiodinium microadriaticum,* the endosymbiont of reef corals and other coelenter-

silica. The cellulose sometimes occurs in the form of microfibrils, as for instance in the thick plates of *Ceratium* ([325, 326]).

One very widespread dinophyte species, found in freshwaters all over the world, is *Peridinium cinctum* (Figs 16.1, 16.4). The cells of this alga are more or less circular and measure 40–60 μm in length. Each cell is surrounded by a robust envelope, the **theca**, with two grooves in its surface: a transverse groove, the **girdle**, and a longitudinal groove, the **sulcus**. The transverse groove winds right around the cell, describing a flat spiral. The part of the cell above the transverse furrow is called the apical half of the cell or **epicone**, while the part below is called the antapical half of the cell or **hypocone**; 'above' and 'below' are defined here in relation to the predominant direction of swimming.

Seen from above, the cell has a reniform outline (Fig. 16.1c), the more rounded side being designated the dorsal side and the flattened one, the ventral side. The cell is thus dorsiventral in construction. The longitudinal furrow (sulcus) lies on the ventral side, mostly in the antapical half of the cell; in other genera the sulcus is often much more feebly developed.

The theca of *Peridinium* consists of a number of polygonal plates, with different shapes and sizes, arranged in a characteristic pattern. Plate arrangements are important for distinguishing dinophyte genera and species, and the names used for the different plates are indicated in Fig. 16.1c, d. The plates are themselves decorated with still smaller polygonal areas. These are separated from each other by ridges (Fig. 16.1a, 16.5b) and perforated by several pores, through which the trichocysts discharge (cf. p. 263; Fig. 16.5b). In other species the plates bear grooves or spines. The sulcus is covered by a cluster of tiny platelets ([1759]; these are not shown in Fig. 16.1a).

The plates are connected by transversely striated intercalary bands (Fig. 16.1a). These are in fact the margins of the thecal plates, which grow, permitting the theca and hence the cell inside it to increase in size. The margins of the transverse furrow, which are also striated, are enlarged into wing-like ridges, making the girdle well-defined and obvious in the light microscope.

Species of the genus *Ceratium* are characterized by the presence of several horns. The apical half of the cell extends up into a single horn, while the antapical half bears one to three horns (Fig. 16.2a); for instance, *Ceratium hirundinella*, a widely distributed freshwater species, has two or three antapical horns. Like the *Peridinium* plates described above, the armour plates of *Ceratium* are ornamented with polygonal areas bounded by ridges (Fig. 16.2a, c). Each area is pierced by a hole, through which the underlying trichocyst can discharge its contents ([325, 442]).

Electron microscopical investigations have shown that the structure of the theca is basically the same in all flagellate members of the Dinophyta. It consists of a single layer of thin, flat vesicles, which lie just beneath the plasmalemma. The vesicles may be virtually empty, apart from some amorphous material (e.g. in *Amphidinium*, Figs. 16.6c, 16.19a, or *Gymnodinium*, Fig. 16.10c, d), or each may be filled with a plate, which may be thick or thin (Figs. 16.4, 16.5a). In species without thecal plates, strengthening of the cell periphery seems to be brought about by the superficial layer of tightly fitting, polygonal vesicles together with the microtubules that subtend them (Figs. 16.6c, 16.10c, d, 16.19a; [1759]). In *Ceratium* and *Peridinium* thick plates are present, which overlap each other at the edges and are set with polygonal systems of ridges (Figs. 16.4, 16.5a, b; [319, 325, 326, 351, 969, 1759]).

Many dinophytes (including *Peridinium cinctum*) are surrounded by a thin additional layer, the **pellicle**, which lies beneath the thecal plates. In addition to cellulose the pellicle contains a sporopollenin-like substance, which is resistant to strong acids and bases; a similar substance is also present in many dinophytes as a constituent of the walls of the resting zygotes (hypnozygotes; p. 270). The pellicle probably forms in the thecal vesicles beneath the thecal plates, the initially separate elements (Fig. 16.5a) later fusing to form a coherent layer. The precise origin of the pellicle, however, remains somewhat controversial ([1234, 1235, 1759]).

A layer of delicate organic scales has been discovered in a few dinophytes, lying on the body of the cell

Caption for fig. 16.3 (*cont.*).

ates. (g) *Gymnodinium*-phase. (h, i) Young and old endosymbiotic cells. (j) Cyst containing two aplanospores. (k) Cyst containing four aplanospores.

(l) Cyst containing a single zoospore (*Gymnodinium*-phase). AP = axopod; CHL = chloroplast; N = nucleus; PV = contractile (pulsing) vacuole. (a–f based on [1409]; g–l on [1157].)

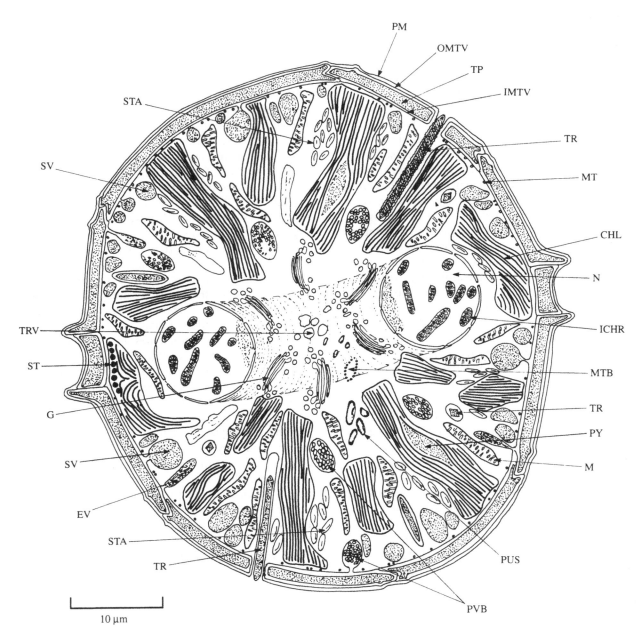

Figure 16.4. Longitudinal section through *Peridinium cinctum*, based on EM observations. CHL = chloroplast; EV = elongate vesicle; G = golgi body; ICHR = interphase chromosome; IMTV = inner membrane of thecal vesicle; M = mitochondrion; MT = microtubule; MTB = microtubular basket; N = nucleus; OMTV = outer membrane of thecal vesicle; PM = plasma membrane (plasmalemma); PUS = branches of the pusular system; PVB = polyvesicular bodies; PY = pyrenoid; ST = stigma (eyespot); STA = starch grains; SV = spherical vesicle; TP = thecal plate; TR = trichocyst; TRV = trichocyst vesicle, the precursor of a trichocyst. (Based on [351].)

outside the theca and plasmalemma (Fig. 16.5c). These scales are very similar to the body scales of some members of the green algal class Prasinophyceae (compare Fig. 16.5c with Fig. 19.10b, c; [324, 603, 1234, 1392]). As in the Prasinophyceae, the scales are manufactured in golgi vesicles ([603]).

The plates of the dinophyte armour resemble the silica elements of the diatom wall in being formed in flat vesicles just beneath the plasmalemma. One difference, however, is that in the Dinophyta the membrane outside the armour remains intact, while in the diatoms the silica elements are exocytosed and thus come to lie outside the cell. In plants, cell coverings made of elements that lie within the cytoplasm are rare, since usually a cell wall is formed, consisting of material deposited outside the plasmalemma. The Dinophyta are exceptions, as are the Euglenophyta (p. 290); here there is a 'pellicle' beneath the plasmalemma, consisting of strips of proteinaceous material. The periplast of the Cryptophyta also consists of proteinaceous material, this time in the form of plates but again lying just under (but also above) the plasmalemma (p. 237).

Pigments and chloroplasts

About half of the Dinophyta are obligate heterotrophs, the other half being capable of photosynthesis ([321]). Most photosynthetic dinophytes are golden-brown, as a result of the presence of accessory photosynthetic pigments, which mask the green of the chlorophylls. The principal accessory pigments are xanthophylls, especially peridinin, which is restricted to the Dinophyta; diadinoxanthin and dinoxanthin are also present (Table 1.2). Peridinin is the main light-harvesting pigment in most photosynthetic dinophytes and is closely associated with chlorophyll a in a water-soluble peridinin – chlorophyll a protein complex. It transfers energy with high efficiency to the reaction centre of photosystem II ([1442]). Some species, however, have the brown pigment fucoxanthin instead of peridinin (p. 253; [795, 1087, 1442]), while a few dinophytes have green, blue or red chloroplasts. The chloroplasts contain chlorophyll c_2 as well as chlorophyll a, but chlorophyll b is absent. β-carotene has also been identified as present.

In the smaller Dinophyta the chloroplasts are plate-like and lie against the cell envelope (they are parietal; Figs. 16.10a, 16.18f–j), while larger species often con-

tain elongate, radially arranged chloroplasts (Figs. 16.1a, 16.4, 16.17c, 16.19a). The ultrastructure of the chloroplast exhibits a series of features which, taken together, are characteristic of the Dinophyta (Figs. 16.6, 16.8a; [314, 317, 319, 321, 324]). The thylakoids are stacked in threes to form lamellae, other groupings (in twos or fours) being exceptional. A peripheral girdle lamella is absent. The chloroplast is surrounded by an envelope consisting of three parallel membranes; these are not connected with the endoplasmic reticulum or nuclear envelope, nor with any other cell organelle.

In two genera (*Aureodinium* and *Glenodinium*) there are stalked, pear-shaped pyrenoids (Fig. 16.6a), which closely resemble the pyrenoids of brown algae (Fig. 12.2). Starch is deposited against the pyrenoid, in the cytoplasm. This type of pyrenoid is not present in all Dinophyta; some, for instance, have pyrenoids that are embedded within the chloroplasts (Figs. 16.7, 16.10).

In dinophytes with typical, peridinin-containing chloroplasts, the chloroplast DNA is concentrated into small nodules, which are scattered through the chloroplast and seem to be connected to each other by fine fibrils. Ring-shaped nucleoids are present, however, in those species where the chloroplasts contain fucoxanthin rather than peridinin (see p. 253). The nucleoids can be made visible in the light microscope by staining them with the DNA-specific fluorescent dye DAPI (4′, 6-diamidino-2-phenylindole; [254]).

Storage products

The most important reserve material is starch, which is formed outside the chloroplasts ([1832]). In this the Dinophyta resemble the Rhodophyta, while in the Chlorophyta starch is produced and stored inside the chloroplasts. Lipid is another important storage product and this is present in the form of globules and droplets.

The nature of the chloroplasts in the Dinophyta: an endosymbiotic origin?

Some time ago a fascinating discovery was made. It was found that the chloroplasts of the fresh- and brackish-water species *Peridinium balticum* belong in fact to an endosymbiotic alga, which lives within the *P. balticum* cells ([1776]). The endosymbiont has its own

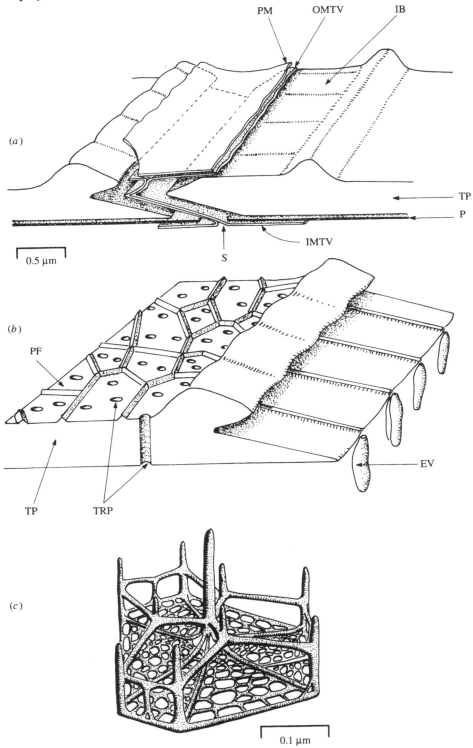

For legend see facing page.

plasmalemma and still contains a nucleus, several chloroplasts, a mitochondrion and a golgi apparatus (Fig. 16.7). Furthermore, the nucleus of the endosymbiont is not a dinokaryon with condensed interphase chromosomes (see below), but a normal nucleus, whose chromosomes are extended and diffuse. Each chloroplast of the endosymbiont is surrounded by a fold of endoplasmic reticulum, which links it to the nucleus; it contains lamellae that are composed of three thylakoids and also a girdle lamella; and it has a ring-shaped nucleoid (Fig. 16.8*b*; [254, 847]), instead of the dispersed nucleoid found in the typical dinophyte chloroplast (see above). The endosymbiont must therefore be a highly reduced member of the Heterokontophyta. Outside the endosymbiont, in the cytoplasm of the host, there are golgi bodies, a dinokaryon, and other organelles.

At least three other species of Dinophyta also have chloroplasts that exhibit structural features characteristic of the Heterokontophyta, and it is interesting that all of them have fucoxanthin as the principal accessory pigment, since fucoxanthin is found in many Heterokontophyta; peridinin, the principal accessory pigment of most photosynthetic Dinophyta, is absent. Further evidence for the heterokontophyte affinities of the chloroplasts in these species is provided by the presence in them of chlorophyll c_1, chlorophyll c_2, neofucoxanthin, diadinoxanthin and diatoxanthin. Of these, only chlorophyll c_2 and diadinoxanthin occur in 'typical' Dinophyta, together with the xanthophyll dinoxanthin ([88, 320, 795, 796, 1907]; Table 1.2).

Dinophytes with unusually coloured chloroplasts (green, blue or red) have been known for a long time (see [475]) and so, after the discovery of brown endosymbionts in *Peridinium balticum* and a few other dinophytes, it was not long before the idea was put forward that these odd colours might reflect a diversity of endosymbionts, derived from several different algal divisions. Support for this has recently come from studies of a marine dinophyte, which is green and

appears to harbour a vestigial green alga (division Chlorophyta), containing chlorophylls a and b ([1855]); chlorophyll b occurs only in the Chlorophyta and Euglenophyta, and in the prokaryotic Prochlorophyta (Table 1.2). The green endosymbiont possesses chloroplasts and these are bounded by two membranes, as in the Chlorophyta (Fig. 16.8*c*), unlike the triple-membrane envelopes of the chloroplasts in the Euglenophyta or indeed of typical dinophyte chloroplasts (Fig. 16.8*a*).

The green endosymbiont seems to be more highly reduced than the brown endosymbiont of *Peridinium balticum*, with its heterokontophyte chloroplasts (see above). Both the green and brown endosymbionts have their own cytoplasm, which fills the narrow spaces between the endosymbiont organelles and differs from the dinophyte cytoplasm by its pronounced granularity, caused by high densities of ribosomes. But while the brown endosymbiont still has a complete nucleus, mitochondria and golgi bodies (Fig. 16.7), the green endosymbiont contains only a spherical structure, which may represent a vestigial nucleus (Fig. 16.8*c*). The green endosymbiont is surrounded by two membranes. The inner one may be interpreted as the endosymbiont's plasmalemma, while the outer probably represents the membrane of the food vacuole into which the ancestral endosymbiont alga was taken by the dinophyte. Surprisingly, however, the brown endosymbiont is surrounded by only one membrane, which probably represents the food vacuole membrane of the host dinophyte (see below). Neither endosymbiont contains reserve polysaccharide; in both cases starch grains are synthesized in the dinophyte cytoplasm.

A blue-green freshwater dinophyte, *Gymnodinium acidotum*, has also been investigated recently and appears to contain an endophytic cryptophyte ([397, 1895]; further examples are described in [1581, 1896]). Like the brown endosymbionts of *Peridinium balticum*, each blue-green endosymbiont is surrounded by only a sin-

Figure 16.5. (*a, b*) Structure of the thecal plates in *Peridinium cinctum*. (*a*) The junction (suture) between two adjacent plates; parts of the thecal vesicles are also shown close to the suture. Below each plate is a thin sporopollenin-containing layer, the pellicle. (*b*) Part of the thecal plate itself, showing the ornamentation of small polygonal fields, each perfo-

rated by several trichocyst pores. (*c*) Body scale of *Heterocapsa*. EV = elongate vesicle; IB = intercalary band; IMTV = inner membrane of thecal vesicle; OMTV = outer membrane of thecal vesicle; P = pellicle; PF = polygonal field; PM = plasma membrane (plasmalemma); S = suture; TP = thecal plate; TRP = trichocyst pore. (*a, b* based on [351, 1234]; *c* based on [1392].)

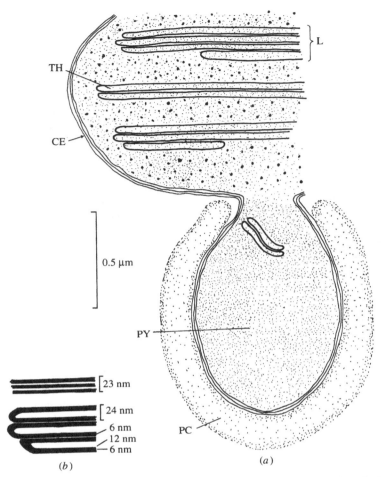

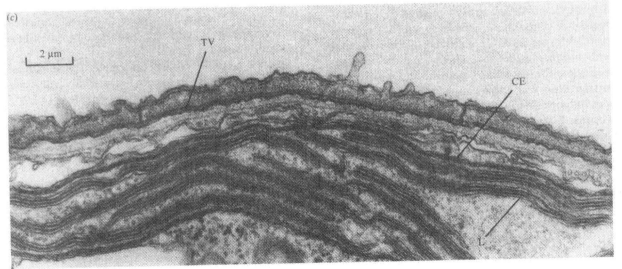

For legend see facing page.

gle membrane, and again it is likely that this was originally the food vacuole membrane of the dinophyte. The evidence for this interpretation comes from studies on feeding in *Amphidinium poecilochroum* and other heterotrophic dinoflagellates. This phagotrophic species, which is found for instance in the Danish section of the Wadden Sea, feeds on small cryptophytes. After puncturing the cryptophyte's periplast with its peduncle, the dinophyte sucks out the cryptophyte cytoplasm, together with the organelles in it (but without its plasmalemma), into a food vacuole, so that the ingested prey cell is surrounded only by the host's food vacuole membrane ([965, 1575, 1576]). This can perhaps be taken as showing what must have happened during the early stages in the evolution of stable endosymbioses like that of *Peridinium balticum*, as the endosymbiont cells were first captured.

The genus *Dinophysis* (Fig. 16.17*e*, *g*) includes colourless heterotrophic species as well as photosynthetic species ([599, 1577]). The photosynthetic forms often have a reddish colour, which reflects the presence of chloroplasts with the same characteristics as the chloroplasts of cryptophytes (cf. p. 235). The *Dinophysis* chloroplasts, however, are surrounded by only two membranes, as in the chloroplast envelopes of green and red algae; there are no vestiges of other cryptophyte organelles or membranes ([496, 1048, 1577]). So, if these chloroplasts have indeed been derived from endosymbiotic cryptophytes, these must in the course of evolution have lost the chloroplast endoplasmic reticulum, the nucleomorph, the nucleus, the plasmalemma and all other organelles. To complicate the matter still further, there are also indications that *Dinophysis* chloroplasts may contain peridinin, the typical dinophyte xanthophyll ([599]).

In SE Asia, cells of the large heterotrophic dinoflagellate *Noctiluca scintillans* (p. 279; Fig. 16.17*i*, *j*) have been found containing cells of the prasinophycean green alga *Pedinomonas*, which swim around in the large vacuole of the host ([1738, 1739]). Elsewhere, however, *Noctiluca* lacks endosymbionts.

This fascinating series of discoveries has led to the hypothesis that the Dinophyta are fundamentally a group of heterotrophic Protozoa, which have acquired photosynthesis again and again, through the incorporation of various photoautotrophic eukaryotic algae ([320, 321]). According to the endosymbiotic theory of chloroplast origins, the first autotrophic photosynthetic eukaryotes evolved by the incorporation of photoautotrophic prokaryotes (e.g. blue-green algae) into heterotrophic eukaryotes (see p. 2). Later, however, other types of eukaryotic photoautotrophs may have arisen, this time through incorporation of various kinds of endosymbiotic eukaryotes (see chapter 32). Thus, the typical dinophyte chloroplast, with a three-membrane chloroplast envelope and containing peridinin, can perhaps be interpreted as representing a highly reduced eukaryotic endosymbiont, the most reduced and evolutionarily most advanced of all the eukaryotic endosymbionts of the Dinophyta. The inner two membranes might be homologous with the double chloroplast envelope of most other chloroplasts, while the outermost membrane could be a vestige of the host's food vacuole; apart from the chloroplast, all the other organelles of the endosymbiont have disappeared in the course of evolution, together with its cytoplasm.

An alternative hypothesis, which is simpler and at first sight seems more elegant, is that the primaeval phagotrophic dinophyte took up a *chloroplast* from a prey alga into a food vacuole and simply retained it as its own photosynthetic organelle ([977]). However, this is extremely unlikely, since chloroplasts retain only a small proportion (*ca.* 10%) of the DNA that must have been present in their cyanobacterial ancestors, while most of the molecules from which they are constructed are synthesized under the control of nuclear genes; they are then imported into the organelle. Hence an ingested chloroplast cannot survive for long within a foreign host cell and is incapable of replication without the presence of its own nucleus. Thus, the prey nucleus can only have been lost gradually during evo-

Figure 16.6. (*a, b*) *Glenodinium.* (*a*) Part of the chloroplast, bearing a stalked pyrenoid. (*b*) Diagram of part of the chloroplast envelope (A) and a lamella (B), composed of a stack of three thylakoids. (*c*) *Amphidinium herdmanae:* transmission electron micrograph of the periphery of the cell, showing the three membranes of the chloroplast envelope, the lamellae of three appressed thylakoids, and the thecal vesicles (containing granules but no thecal plates). CE = chloroplast envelope, consisting of three membranes; L = lamella, composed of 3 or 4 thylakoids; PC = cap of reserve polysaccharide material; PY = pyrenoid; TH = thylakoid; TV = thecal vesicle. (*a, b* based on [314]; *c* from [322], with permission.)

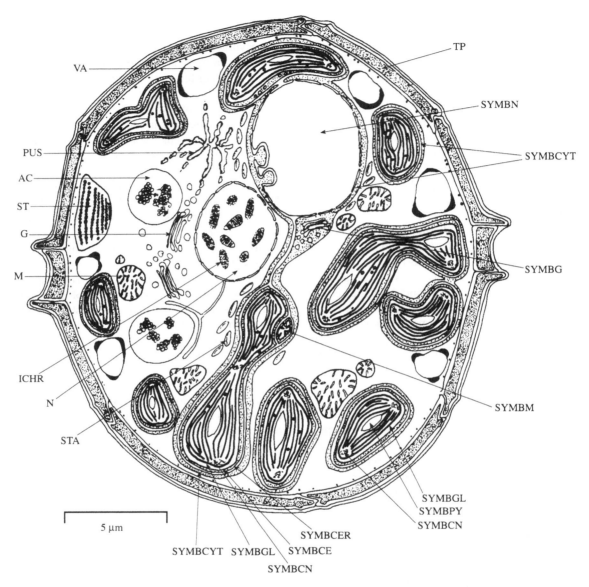

Figure 16.7. Longitudinal section through a cell of
Peridinium balticum and its reduced heterokontophyte endosymbiont, based on EM observations. The
thecal plates of the host cell and the cytoplasm of the
endosymbiont are shown stippled. AC = accumulation body; G = golgi body of host dinophyte; ICHR =
condensed interphase chromosome of the host dinophyte; M = mitochondrion of the host dinophyte; N =
nucleus of host dinophyte; PUS = branches of the
pusule of the host dinophyte; ST = stigma of host
dinophyte; STA = starch grains in host cytoplasm;
SYMBCE = chloroplast envelope of endosymbiont;

SYMBCER = chloroplast endoplasmic reticulum of
endosymbiont; SYMBCN = ring-shaped nucleoid of
chloroplast in endosymbiont; SYMBCYT = cytoplasm of endosymbiont; SYMBG = golgi body of
endosymbiont; SYMBGL = girdle lamella of
endosymbiont chloroplast; SYMBM = mitochondrion of endosymbiont, contained within an envelope
of ER; SYMBN = nucleus of endosymbiont;
SYMBPY = pyrenoid of endosymbiont chloroplast;
TP = thecal plate; VA = vacuole of host dinophyte.
(Based on [1776].)

lution, as nuclear chloroplast genes were transferred from the prey nucleus to the host nucleus.

The dinophyte chloroplast has a *combination* of characters (peridinin and a three-membrane chloroplast envelope) found in no other group of photosynthetic eukaryotes; furthermore, within the Dinophyta, typical dinophyte chloroplasts are found in phylogenetically distant groups. These two observations indicate that the dinophyte chloroplast originated early in the evolution of the Dinophyta, possibly as a eukaryotic endosymbiont as described above, and was retained in many of the dinophyte lineages as they diverged from one another. Other dinophytes lost their chloroplasts and became entirely dependent on phagotrophy, a mode of nutrition now common in the Dinophyta, even among species with chloroplasts. More recently, however, some of these secondary heterotrophs have *regained* the capacity to photosynthesize, by capturing and retaining various prey algae as photosynthetic endosymbionts.

Heterotrophic Dinophyta

Many Dinophyta (about 50% of all species) lack chloroplasts and are thus obligately heterotrophic ([321, 475]). Although saprotrophy has been demonstrated in a variety of dinophytes in the laboratory ([475]), it is unlikely that this mode of nutrition is of much significance in nature. Saprotrophy is particularly effective in small, bacterium-sized organisms with a large surface area : volume ratio. The larger heterotrophic dinophytes, like *Protoperidinium* (Fig. 16.9) or *Noctiluca* (Fig. 16.17*i*, *j*), would be very ineffective as saprotrophs.

The usual method of feeding in heterotrophic dinophytes is phagotrophy, the ingestion of food into food vacuoles. The ingestion of prey by 'naked' dinophytes, with or without chloroplasts, has often been observed. The prey, including large diatoms and ciliate Protozoa, are often bigger than the dinophytes grazing upon them, so that the dinophyte cell is greatly distended while engulfing its victim. Until recently, however, feeding in the larger heterotrophic dinophytes with rigid thecae (such as species of *Protoperidinium* and *Dinophysis*, Figs. 16.9, 16.17*e*) was an enigma, since it seemed impossible that they could accommodate large prey cells. The large thecate forms were therefore thought to be saprotrophic ([321]), which is unlikely for the reasons given above. Recent

investigations show, however, that many dinophytes possess a special organelle for the capture and ingestion of prey, the so-called **peduncle**. This is an extensible pseudopod, which arises in the region of the sulcus. It contains a rod of closely packed microtubules, the **microtubular basket**, which also extends far into the interior of the cell ([975, 1667, 1670]). The peduncle is used in different ways, depending on the species. The small (9–15 µm) estuarine heterotroph *Gymnodinium fungiforme* punctures its prey with the peduncle (probably through enzymatic breakdown), which can be extended up to 12 µm away from the cell; subsequently the prey's cytoplasm or body fluid is ingested through the peduncle into a food vacuole. *Gymnodinium fungiforme* can feed on organisms much bigger than itself, such as the ciliate protozoan *Condylostoma magnum* (600–1000 µm) or even injured individuals of the smaller Metazoa, including nematodes and polychaete larvae. Typically, hundreds of *G. fungiforme* cells collect on the prey and attach to it via their peduncles. They are guided by chemotaxis, attracted by a variety of amino acids and other organic compounds ([1670, 1671, 1673]). Several other dinophytes have been observed to use their peduncles in a similar way ([334, 475, 1575, 1576, 1580]).

Species of the marine heterotrophic genus *Protoperidinium* feed on diatoms, which they capture in a trailing filament. The capture filament is subsequently retracted and the peduncle extends along it, expanding into a broad pseudopod, which is often sheet-like and reticulate. This engulfs the prey, which again is often much larger than the dinophyte itself, and encloses it in a food vacuole. The process of capture and engulfment takes several minutes, while the subsequent enzymatic digestion of the diatom cell contents is completed in 6–30 min. Following this, the empty diatom frustules are jettisoned (Fig. 16.9*a–d*; [787]).

One of the best known phagotrophic dinophytes is the marine planktonic species *Noctiluca scintillans* (Fig. 16.17*i*, *j*). This large dinophyte, up to 1.2 mm across, feeds on such things as phytoplankton, zooplankton, fish eggs, and copepods, and catches its prey with a tentacle, which may be a special modified type of peduncle ([475]).

A final example of feeding is given by the spherical freshwater dinophyte *Stylodinium sphaera*, which attaches itself by a small stipe to the filamentous green alga *Oedogonium* (p. 383) and releases its contents in the form of two amoeboid cells (Fig. 16.3*a–c*). The

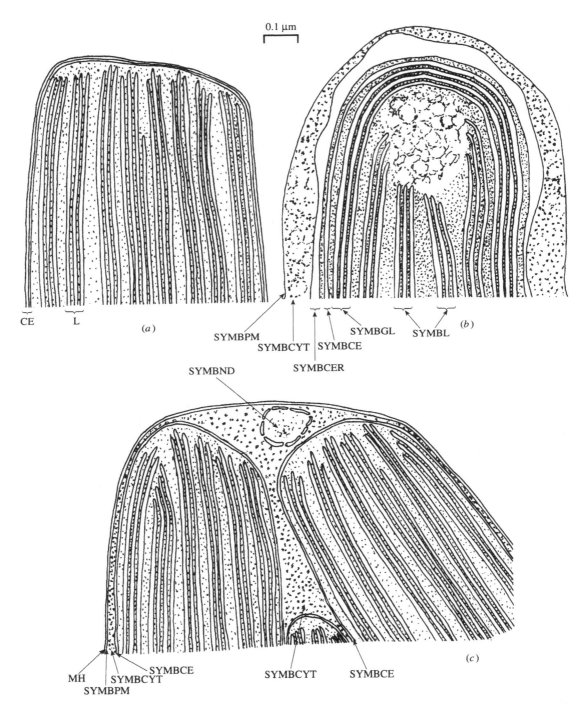

Figure 16.8. Three types of chloroplast found in dinophytes. (a) Type 1. This is the 'true' dinophyte chloroplast, which contains thylakoids grouped in stacks (lamellae) of three (sometimes two or four) and is surrounded by a three-membrane envelope. Peridinin is the most important accessory photosynthetic pigment. This is the commonest type of chloroplast in dinophytes and occurs, for instance, in *Peridinium*

amoebae settle on intact *Oedogonium* cells (Fig. 16.3*d*) and a few seconds later an amoeba punctures the *Oedogonium* cell wall and ingests its contents, swelling very quickly as it does so (Fig. 16.3*d, e*). Subsequently it develops into a spherical stage and may divide up its contents, to form *Gymnodinium*-like swarmers (Fig. 16.3*f*). The cells of *Stylodinium* contain one or two dinophyte chloroplasts, as well as several other chloroplasts, which are the partly digested chloroplasts of prey ([1409]).

These are just a few examples of feeding mechanisms in heterotrophic dinoflagellates; there is a growing realization that such organisms play an important role in aquatic ecosystems, as primary (and secondary) consumers. Heterotrophic dinoflagellates are ubiquitous, especially in marine environments. The wholly heterotrophic genus *Protoperidinium*, for instance, is widespread in marine phytoplankton, as is the partly heterotrophic genus *Dinophysis* ([599]).

Ingestion of organisms by photosynthetic dinophytes (e.g. *Ceratium*) has been observed several times, the dinophytes capturing their prey with pseudopods ([475]). In *Peridinium cinctum* the ability to form a peduncle is inferred from the presence within the cell of a microtubular basket, which forms the cytoskeleton of the peduncle in other species (Fig. 16.4). The occurrence of photosynthetic capacity and phagotrophy in the same organism is also known in several other classes of algae, including the Chrysophyceae, Haptophyceae and Chlorarachniophyceae.

Flagella and flagellar apparatus ([317, 319, 324, 970, 1507, 1508, 1509, 1510, 1511])

The two flagella emerge at the intersection of the girdle (transverse furrow) and sulcus (longitudinal furrow). Both contain an axoneme with a typical '9 + 2' structure (9 peripheral doublets and 2 single central microtubules; Fig. 16.10*c*). Each flagellum arises from the base of a small invagination of the cell surface, called the flagellar canal, which opens to outside by the so-called flagellar pore (Fig. 16.10*h*). Each flagellum has its own flagellar canal ([970]), although in *Ceratium* both flagellar pores open into a single larger invagination of the cell surface, called the ventral chamber ([325]). Within the cell, each flagellum ends in a basal body. This consists of a cylindrical array of 9 triplet microtubules (Fig. 16.10*h*), which is the arrangement generally found in eukaryote basal bodies. A system of connections is present, which link the triplets in a cartwheel-like pattern; this kind of structure is found in a great diversity of organisms but often seems to be absent.

In the flagellar transition region, between the axoneme and the basal body, two parallel discs are present at the base of the two central axonemal microtubules, at least in some species, while further below there are one or two rings of material (Fig. 16.10*h*; [664, 1218]). One species, however, has been found to have a transitional helix, which is generally considered characteristic of the heterokontophyte class Chrysophyceae ([324]).

Caption for fig. 16.8 *(cont.)*.

cinctum (see Fig. 16.4). (*b*) Type 2. Here the chloroplast is contained in a reduced heterokontophyte endosymbiont. The chloroplast is surrounded by a plasma membrane, a layer of endosymbiont cytoplasm, chloroplast ER of the endosymbiont, and a two-membrane chloroplast envelope; within the chloroplast there is a girdle lamella (an encircling stack of three thylakoids). Fucoxanthin is the most important accessory pigment. Type 2 chloroplasts occur, for example, in *Peridinium balticum* (see Fig. 16.7). (*c*) Type 3. The chloroplast is contained in a reduced chlorophyte endosymbiont. The chloroplast is surrounded by a membrane of the dinophyte host cell (perhaps originally the membrane of a food vacuole), the plasmalemma of the endosymbiont, a layer of endosymbiont cytoplasm, and the two membranes of the chloroplast envelope of the endosymbiont. The chloroplast contains chlorophylls a and b, but not chlorophyll c, which is present in types 1 and 2. CE = chloroplast envelope; L = lamella; MH = membrane of the host dinophyte, perhaps originally a food vacuole membrane; SYMBCE = chloroplast envelope of endosymbiont; SYMBCER = chloroplast ER of endosymbiont; SYMBCYT = cytoplasm of endosymbiont; SYMBGL = girdle lamella of endosymbiont chloroplast; SYMBL = lamella of endosymbiont chloroplast; SYMBND = what is presumed to be the vestigial nucleus of the endosymbiont; SYMBPM = plasma membrane surrounding endosymbiont. (*a* based on [351]; *b* on [1776]; *c* on [1855].)

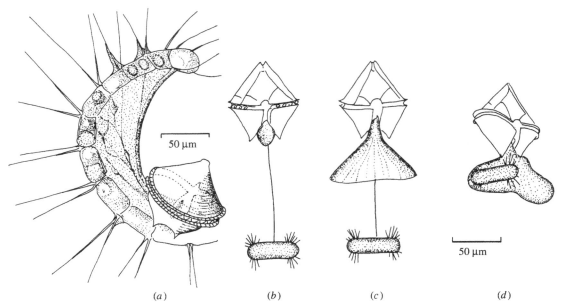

(a)   (b)   (c)   (d)

Figure 16.9. Feeding by some heterotrophic, non-photosynthetic dinophytes. (a) *Protoperidinium spinulosum* feeding on a chain-like colony of the centric diatom *Chaetoceros curvatus*. The diatom colony is engulfed by a sheet-like pseudopodium with a radial, fibrillar structure. (b–d) *Protoperidinium conicum* feeding on the centric diatom *Corethron hystrix*. The whole process of capture and engulfment takes several minutes. (b) Capture of prey via a primary attachment filament. (c) Deployment of a pseudopodium from the sulcal pore. (d) Retraction of the pseudopodium containing the prey diatom. (Based on [787].)

Over the bottom two-thirds of its length, the longitudinal flagellum is relatively thick and also flattened, containing a strand of material with a complex spiral structure, in addition of course to the axoneme itself ([324]). The longitudinal flagellum bears fine hairs (*ca.* 0.5 µm long, 10 nm thick), which seem to be arranged in two rows (Fig. 16.10a). The hairs differ greatly in structure and thickness from the tubular mastigonemes on the flagella of the Heterokontophyta, which are about 25 nm thick (Fig. 6.4e, f). The longitudinal flagellum of the Dinophyta runs along the antapical (lower) section of the sulcus (Figs. 16.1, 16.10a).

The transverse flagellum runs around the cell in the girdle (transverse furrow), and has a very peculiar structure. It consists of a helical axoneme, which is kept in place in the transverse furrow by a tightly drawn thread positioned on the side closest to the cell; the axoneme and thread are enveloped by a flagellar sheath, loosely wrapped around them. The thread is referred to as the 'striated strand' (Fig. 16.10a–c; [65, 324, 1479]) and contains the contractile protein centrin.

This has also been found in the transversely striated fibrous roots and connectives of the flagellar root systems in various algae (see, for example, the rhizoplast of the green alga *Tetraselmis*, p. 319), including the dinophytes themselves ([1541, 1590, 1591, 1592]). On the plasmalemma above the axoneme there is a row of thin but long hairs (diameter *ca.* 10 nm, length *ca.* 2 µm). Each hair has at its base a short stiff section, which can lie at an angle to the rest of the hair. As in the Heterokontophyta, the hairs are formed in cisternae of the endoplasmic reticulum (Fig. 16.10a; [319, 324]).

The basal bodies of the flagella are anchored in the cell by a system of roots. The three most prominent elements of this have been found in various Dinophyta and comprise a posteriorly (backwardly) directed microtubular root (PMR), a transversely striated fibrous root (TSR), and a striated fibrous root connective (SRC), which links the other two ([166, 324, 398, 1507, 1508, 1509, 1510, 1511]). Other features of the root system vary between different species, but *Gymnodinium* can be taken as an example for detailed description (Fig. 16.11; [1508]).

In *Gymnodinium* the basal bodies of the transverse and longitudinal flagella (BBT and BBL, respectively, in Fig. 16.11) lie at almost 180° to each other and overlap slightly; both are parallel to the longitudinal axis of the cell (compare Fig. 16.11 with Fig. 16.10*a*). The broad downwardly directed (posterior) microtubular root (PMR) arises by the basal body of the longitudinal flagellum (BBL), while the transversely striated root (TSR) is associated with the basal body of the transverse flagellum (BBT). This latter root extends into the cell obliquely, upwards (towards the cell apex) and to the left (to the right in Fig. 16.11*a*, where the cell is seen from the ventral side). The fibrous striated connective (SRC) connects the PMR and TSR in the region where the two basal bodies overlap. Other prominent features of the root system in *Gymnodinium* are the two striated collars (SC) that encircle the flagella just above where they emerge into their flagellar canals, and the fibrous connective (NFC), which runs between the posterior microtubular root (PMR) and a lobe of the nucleus. In addition, several small connectives are present, linking the basal bodies to the various components of the root system. It is likely that the fibrous elements contain the contractile protein centrin ([1590], [1591]).

The orientation of the basal bodies, in relation to each other and to the cell, differs greatly from one group of dinophytes to another. In *Gymnodinium* species, the basal bodies are approximately opposite in orientation (antiparallel; Fig. 16.11), whereas in *Ceratium* they are almost at right angles to each other; still other genera, such as *Prorocentrum*, have nearly parallel basal bodies (Fig. 16.17*a*; [166]). The differences in basal body orientation are accompanied by variation in the detail of how the flagellar root system is constructed.

The transverse flagellum is thought to be responsible for driving the cell forward and it also brings about rotation. The longitudinal flagellum seems to be involved in steering the cell, though it too may contribute to propulsion. The two flagella beat in different ways. The longitudinal flagellum beats with a planar waveform, which probably contributes to forward movement, while changes in the direction of swimming are brought about when the flagellum bends, acting as a rudder. In the transverse flagellum a spiral wave is propagated along the axoneme, apparently bringing about backward thrust and rotation at the same time. The mechanism of swimming in the Dinophyta is not yet fully understood ([992]).

Pusules

These organelles, highly characteristic of the Dinophyta, are invaginations of the plasmalemma, which lie near the flagellar bases (Fig. 16.10*a, h*), one opening into each flagellar canal. Pusules do not contract, unlike the contractile vacuoles of *Ochromonas* (p. 110) and many other flagellate algae (e.g. *Chlamydomonas*, p. 312). In certain *Gymnodinium* species the pusules are relatively simple, consisting of a flask-shaped portion bearing several cylindrical side branches. Elsewhere they can be more complicated, with systems of branching tubes that ramify through the whole cell (Figs. 16.7, 16.19*a*; [318]). Parts of the vacuolar network are pressed closely against the pusules (Fig. 16.10*h*; [324]).

The function of the pusule is a matter for speculation. Osmoregulation, excretion, or the uptake of dissolved nutrients from the surrounding water are all possibilities. It has also been suggested that pusules could function in the uptake of solid food (phagotrophy) but this is unlikely. Solid material is taken up via pseudopodia and the peduncle, and digested not in pusules but in special food vacuoles ([325]; see also the section above on heterotrophic Dinophyta).

Miscellaneous vesicles

The cytoplasm of dinophytes is usually highly vesiculate (Fig. 16.19*a*). Many dinophytes contain 'accumulation bodies' (Figs. 16.7, 16.19*a*) or 'polyvesicular bodies (Fig. 16.4), whose function is probably the breakdown of superfluous organelles and membranes ([1667]). In some species 'elongate vesicles' secrete thecal material into the sutures between thecal plates, and this is probably used in the growth of the intercalary bands (Figs. 16.4, 16.5*b*; [351]).

Eyespot (stigma)

Some Dinophyta possess a discrete red eyespot, positioned close to where the flagella arise. In most cases the eyespot lies free in the cytoplasm and is not part of the chloroplast; similar free eyespots occur in the Euglenophyta and Eustigmatophyceae. Other Dinophyta have eyespots that consist of a series of spherical globules lying within the chloroplast, as in the Heterokontophyta (Fig. 16.4).

Electron microscopical investigations have shown

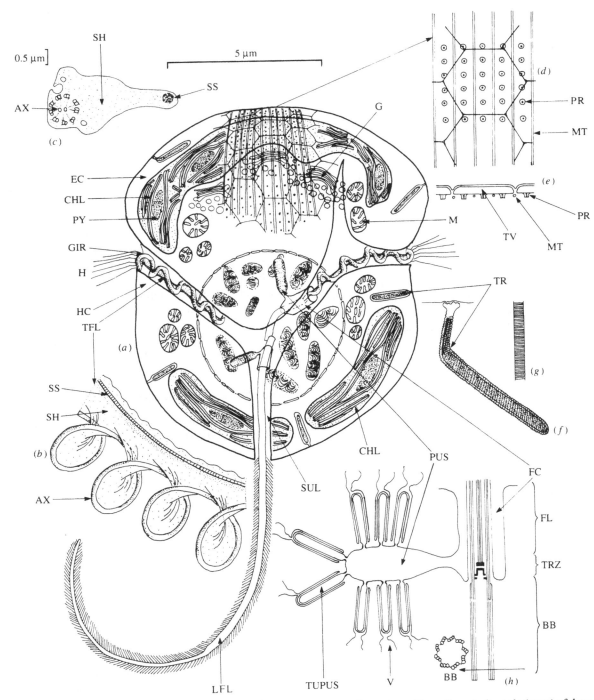

Figure 16.10. Schematic diagram of *Gymnodinium micrum,* based on EM observations. (*a*) Whole cell, seen from the ventral side. (*b*) Portion of the transverse flagellum, viewed from the anterior pole (apex) of the cell, looking towards the equator (girdle). Note the spiral axoneme, enclosed within a flexible flagellar sheath.

that in *Peridinium balticum*, the eyespot consists of several layers of lipid globules containing carotene, surrounded by a triple membrane (Fig. 16.7; [315, 1776]). This structure would therefore appear to be a reduced chloroplast. Elsewhere, it is quite clear that the eyespot globules are completely free in the cytoplasm, with no membrane envelope ([319]).

The family Warnowiaceae (e.g. *Nematodinium*) have a complex eyespot. This remarkable structure contains a retinoid and a layer of eyespot globules ([315, 574]).

Flagellate dinophyte cells (zoids) exhibit positive phototaxis and thus resemble the zoids in many other groups of algae. The eyespot almost certainly plays a direct or indirect part in phototaxis, possibly reflecting light of a particular wavelength onto a light-sensitive area (photoreceptor) located in the overlying plasmalemma. The most effective wavelength for eliciting a phototactic response in *Peridinium* is 475 nm (blue light). However, eyespots are clearly not essential for phototaxis, since the great majority of dinophytes lack them ([992]).

Trichocysts (Figs. 16.10f, g, 16.4)

Each trichocyst consists of an elongate sac, containing a long proteinaceous rod, square or rhombic in cross section. The trichocysts lie at the periphery of the cell, each one beneath a hole in the theca. When stimulated (e.g. by a change in temperature) the trichocyst discharges, hurling forth a transversely striated thread of proteinaceous material. This type of trichocyst is restricted to the Dinophyta. The trichocysts probably develop in vesicles derived from the golgi apparatus ([324, 969, 970]). Their function may be to allow escape from predators through rapid movement in a direction opposite to that of trichocyst discharge.

The dinokaryon: nuclear structure and mitosis in the Dinophyta

In most eukaryotes the chromosomes are only visible in the light microscope during nuclear division, particularly at metaphase and the stages immediately before and after this. In the resting nucleus (interphase) the individual chromosomes cannot be distinguished. They are present, of course, but are long and thin, forming a mass of intertwined filaments within the nucleus. Nuclear stains reveal many small granules, which correspond to locally condensed regions of chromatin along the chromosomes, but the chromosomes themselves cannot be identified. During prophase the chromosomes progressively contract, becoming visible in the light microscope and reaching maximum contraction at metaphase.

The chromosomes of the Dinophyta are unusual, in that they are usually strongly condensed and easily recognizable even during interphase (Figs. 16.4, 16.7, 16.12, 16.19a). Another group with clearly discernible interphase chromosomes is the Euglenophyta (p. 287). In electron micrographs the chromosomes of Dinophyta are particularly noticeable for their unique 'garland structure' (Figs. 16.10, 16.13f). Close inspection shows the patterns of arcs in the garlands to consist of very fine fibrils with a diameter of about 2.5 nm, which is the thickness of a DNA double helix. The chromosomes of other eukaryotes are also made up of submicroscopic fibrils, but here the fibrils have a diameter of *ca.* 25 nm, about ten times as thick as in the Dinophyta. This reflects the presence in most

Caption for fig. 16.10 (cont.).

(c) Cross section through the transverse flagellum. (d) Surface view of the hexagonal thecal vesicles, subtended by regularly spaced microtubules. (e) Cross section through a thecal vesicle, which appears empty. (f) Trichocyst. (g) The transversely striated rod discharged from a trichocyst. (h) Section through the flagellar canal, showing the pusule system that opens into the canal. AX = axoneme; BB = basal body; CHL = chloroplast; EC = epicone; FC = flagellar canal; FL = flagellum proper (with 9 + 2 axoneme);

G = golgi body; GIR = girdle; H = hairs on transverse flagellum; HC = hypocone; LFL = long flagellum; M = mitochondrion; MT = microtubule; PR = plug; PUS = pusule; PY = pyrenoid; SH = sheath of the transverse flagellum; SS = striated strand of the transverse flagellum; SUL = sulcus; TFL = transverse flagellum; TR = trichocyst; TRZ = flagellar transition zone; TUPUS = tubular branch of the pusule system; TV = thecal vesicle, which appears empty in *Gymnodinium*; V = vacuole. (a, d–h based on [969, 970]; b on [65]; c on [1479].)

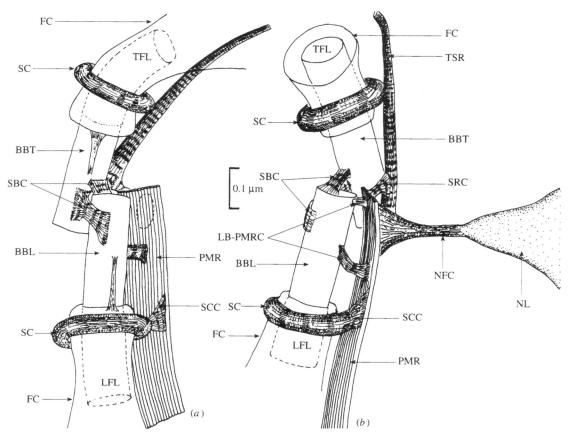

Figure 16.11. Flagellar basal bodies and the associated flagellar roots (the flagellar apparatus) in *Gymnodinium:*
reconstructions based on EM observations. (*a*)
Ventral view (compare with Fig. 16.10). (*b*) Lateral
view, from the cell's left (the dorsal side is to the
right). BBL = basal body of the longitudinal flagellum; BBT = basal body of the transverse flagellum;
FC = flagellar canal; LB-PMRC = connective linking
the basal body of the longitudinal flagellum to the
posteriorly directed microtubular root; LFL = longitudinal flagellum; NFC = fibrous connective linking
the nucleus to the posteriorly directed microtubular
root; NL = lobe of the nucleus; PMR = posteriorly
directed microtubular root; SBC = striated basal body
connective; SC = striated collar; SCC = connective
linking the striated collar to the posteriorly directed
microtubular root; SRC = striated fibrous root connective; TFL = transverse flagellum; TSR = transversely striated root. (After [1508].)

eukaryotes of proteins called 'nucleohistones', which
surround the DNA double helix; dinophyte chromosomes contain very little nucleohistone. In prokaryotes too (bacteria, blue-green algae), the DNA is
always contracted (p. 26) and the electron microscope
reveals fibrils 2.5 nm in diameter, as in the Dinophyta.

The peculiar structure of dinophyte chromosomes
has greatly intrigued scientists and various models
have been proposed to account for their EM appearance ([1668]). It now seems that the dinophyte chromo-

some consists of a single bundle of DNA strands,
which is itself tightly coiled into a double helix (Fig.
16.12; [324, 1314, 1668]). The bundle of DNA strands may in
turn represent a huge, supercoiled circle of DNA ([1668]).
Only during a short period of the cell cycle (S-phase)
do the chromosomes uncoil to allow replication ([1793]).

The Dinophyta not only have atypical chromosomes but also possess a very unusual type of mitosis
(Fig. 16.13). During prophase, bundles of microtubules sink into the nucleus and come to occupy cyto-

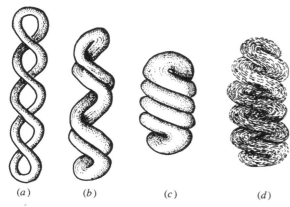

(a)   *(b)*   *(c)*   *(d)*

Figure 16.12. Interpretation of the structure of the dinophyte chromosome during interphase. Each chromosome is a tightly coiled double helix. (*a, b*) Less tightly coiled states. (*c, d*) Tightly coiled states. In (*d*) the DNA strands are shown; it is these that give the typical appearance of the chromosomes when observed using transmission electron microscopy, with curving arcs of fibrils. (Based on [1314].)

plasmic channels traversing the nucleus; the nuclear envelope remains intact throughout mitosis. At metaphase a distinct plate of chromosomes is absent and hence the dividing nucleus has no distinct equator. No centrioles are present at the spindle poles. Each chromosome attaches via a kinetochore to the nuclear envelope lining one of the cytoplasmic channels; corresponding to the kinetochore on the cytoplasmic face of the nuclear envelope is the end of a chromosomal spindle microtubule (Fig. 16.13*f*). The nuclear channels also contain microtubules that are not attached to chromosomes, these being the 'interzonal' microtubules. At anaphase the kinetochores attached to the daughter chromatids of each chromosome move towards opposite poles of the spindle (Fig. 16.13*f*). At the end of anaphase, the envelope of the parent nucleus constricts into two equal halves, creating the envelopes around the daughter nuclei (Fig. 16.13*c, d*). The sets of daughter chromosomes are then pushed further apart by the extension of the interzonal spindle microtubules. Several dinoflagellates exhibit variations on this basic pattern ([324, 1793]).

Cell division

Cell division occurs through cleavage, as in *Ochromonas* (Fig. 6.1*h–k*). The plane of division is oblique to the longitudinal axis of the cell (Fig. 16.2), as indeed is mitosis. In *Ceratium* the armour of the parent cell is partitioned between the daughter cells, each receiving half of the thecal plates (Fig. 16.2*f*), and the daughter cells then construct the missing parts of the armour. In other genera (e.g. *Peridinium*) the whole of the armour is sloughed off before or after cell division, so that each daughter cell must form a complete new set of thecal elements ([351, 1407]).

Sexual reproduction in Dinophyta

Sexual reproduction has been observed in more than 20 species of Dinophyta ([487, 1407]). We will describe the life cycles of the marine species *Ceratium horridum* and the freshwater *Ceratium cornutum* ([604, 1716, 1717, 1719]).

The life cycle of *Ceratium horridum* (Fig. 16.14)

In fairly old cultures of *Ceratium horridum* kept at 21 °C, special depauperizing cell divisions occur, which lead to the formation of ever smaller cells. These function as microgametes, which can copulate with cells of normal size functioning as macrogametes (Fig. 16.14*c, d*). Fusion of the gametes takes place slowly, compared with fusion in other groups, and has been followed in the laboratory. Thus, in one case a male and a female gamete were found at 18.30 h with their ventral sides adjacent. At 21.00 h only an ovoid globule remained of the male gamete. Thirty minutes later, the pair was fixed and the nuclei stained with acetocarmine, revealing the male nucleus lying right next to the female nucleus (Fig. 16.14*f*). The female protoplast could be seen to contain the remnants of the microgamete's armour. Nuclear fusion was observed in other pairs, at later stages of copulation. The zygote of *Ceratium horridum* remains motile and it is in this planozygote that meiosis takes place. We can therefore characterize this marine species as an anisogamous haplont. Anisogamous copulation was first observed as long ago as 1910, but was wrongly interpreted, the microgametes being taken for small 'accessory' cells ('Nebenformen') budded off from the larger cells.

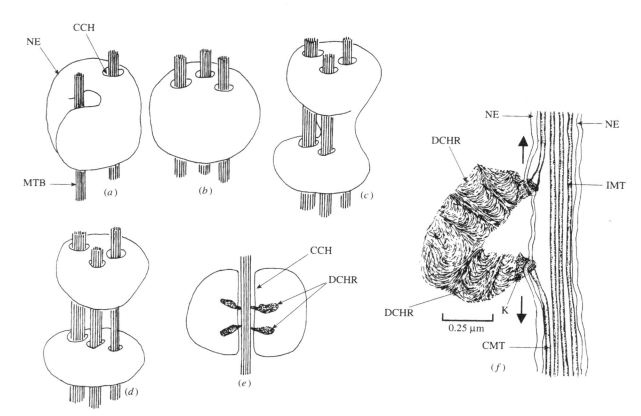

Figure 16.13. Mitosis in Dinophyta, shown diagrammatically (except *f*). (*a, b*) Early mitosis: bundles of microtubules sink into the nucleus and become situated in cytoplasmic channels that traverse it from one side to the other. (*c, d*) Late mitosis (anaphase): daughter nuclei are formed by constriction of the original nuclear envelope. (*e*) Longitudinal section through one lobe of an anaphase nucleus, showing two pairs of daughter chromosomes within the nucleus, which are attached through the nuclear envelope to spindle microtubules lying in a cytoplasmic channel; the daughter chromosomes move to opposite poles of the spindle. (*f*) Detail of a cytoplasmic channel and a pair of daughter chromosomes, which have yet to separate. Interzonal and chromosomal spindle microtubules are present within the channel; kinetochores attach the daughter chromatids to chromosomal spindle microtubules and move towards opposite poles of the spindle, separating the chromatids. CCH = cytoplasmic channel; CMT = chromosomal spindle microtubule; DCHR = daughter chromosome; IMT = interzonal spindle microtubule; K = kinetochore; MTB = bundle of microtubules; NE = nuclear envelope. (*a–e* based on [738]; *f* on [1313, 1669].)

The life cycle of *Ceratium cornutum* (Fig. 16.15)

This species also produces microgametes, while the macrogametes do not differ visibly from vegetative cells. The gametes are formed when an actively growing culture is transferred from 21 °C to 12 °C. Copulation takes place between the ventral sides of the gametes via a bridge of protoplasm. For copulation, the female gamete forms a hole in its theca by swinging open thecal plates in its sulcal region. The male gamete is then completely absorbed into the female gamete through the copulation aperture and, once within, its theca is digested enzymatically. Karyogamy takes place during the next three days and the zygote remains motile for about four weeks. The motile zygote (planozygote) has two longitudinal flagella and one transverse flagellum, and increases greatly in size, the theca accommodating this by extreme widening of the intercalary bands.

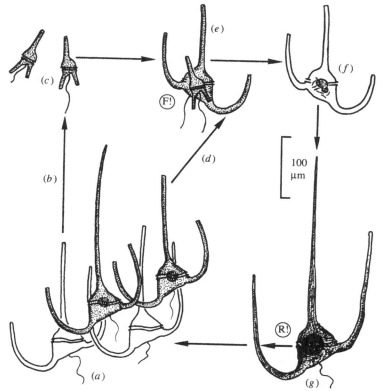

Figure 16.14. *Ceratium horridum:* life cycle. (*a*) Four vegetative cells (*n*). (*b*) Production of small, depauperate cells (microgametes). (*c*) Microgametes (*n*). (*d*) Normal cell division. (*e*) Fusion of macro- and microgametes. (*f*) Karyogamy. (*g*) Planozygote (2*n*), which exhibits nuclear cyclosis and in which meiosis takes place. F! = fertilization; R! = reduction division (meiosis). (After [1716, 1719].)

Only after a considerable time does the planozygote come to rest and form a thick-walled resting stage within the theca: the hypnozygote. The hypnozygote wall consists of three layers and in many dinophytes it contains sporopollenin, which is extremely resistant to strong acids and bases ([1234, 1235]).

A particular combination of culture conditions (low temperature, short days, deficiencies of N and P) has been found to induce the formation of microgametes in all clones that have been investigated. For copulation, however, two compatible clones (A and a) are necessary, since microgametes and macrogametes from the same clone do not, or only rarely, copulate. There is apparently some factor causing self-sterility (Fig. 16.15). After remaining dormant for several weeks at 3 °C, the hypnozygotes can be germinated by incubating them at 21 °C in long days (12 h light). Curiously, there is no reduction division during the germination of the hypnozygote. Instead, the cell that emerges is a naked diploid cell, which makes its exit through a split in the zygote wall. The naked cell, which resembles a *Gymnodinium* cell (Fig. 16.15*b*) afterwards develops an incomplete armour, when it is known as the 'pre-*Ceratium* phase' (Fig. 16.15*c*). It is only now that meiosis occurs, producing four haploid *Ceratium* cells. *Ceratium cornutum* is nevertheless still an anisogamous haplont, since neither the *Gymnodinium*-like cell nor the pre-*Ceratium* phase divides vegetatively by mitosis. Some other dinoflagellates have a similar life cycle, although these species are mostly isogamous and homothallic; in addition, meiosis takes place during the germination of the zygote ([307, 1406, 1407, 1720]). In *Noctiluca scintillans* isogamy occurs between gametes whose form departs considerably from the morphology of the vegetative cells (Fig. 16.17*i, j, n-p*; [1935]). Nutrient depletion, espe-

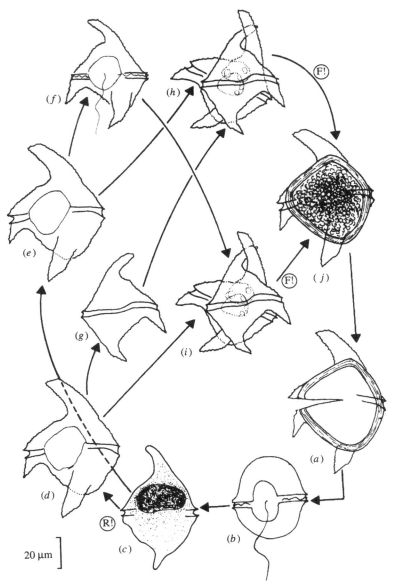

20 μm

Figure 16.15. *Ceratium cornutum:* life cycle. (*a*)
Germination of the hypnozygote (with Aa genotype).
(*b*) *Gymnodinium*-like cell. (*c*) Pre-*Ceratium* phase.
(*d*) Two (a) cells. (*e*) Two (A) cells. (*f*) (A)-micro-
gamete. (*g*) (a)-microgamete. (*h*) (A)-macrogamete

copulating with an (a)-microgamete. (*i*) (a)-macroga-
mete copulating with an (A)-microgamete. (*j*)
Hypnozygote (Aa). F! = fertilization; R! = reduction
division (meiosis). (After [1717].)

cially of nitrogen, induces sexuality in most species
that have been investigated ([1407]).

During meiotic prophase (zygotene to pachytene)
the nucleus of *Ceratium cornutum* swells enormously

and its contents rotate (a circuit would be completed in
about 30 seconds). This phenomenon, referred to as
nuclear cyclosis, was first observed in 1883, but its
true nature and significance was only established in

1972, by von Stosch ([1719]). Von Stosch showed that cyclosis takes place during the meiotic pairing of the chromosomes, which in the Dinophyta can be observed in living nuclei; in most other organisms pairing can only be detected following fixation and nuclear staining. It is possible that cyclosis facilitates pairing between the numerous large chromosomes.

Peridinium balticum, a dinophyte with a brown heterokontophyte endosymbiont (see p. 251; Fig. 16.7), contains two nuclei: one belongs to the dinophyte host, the other to the endosymbiont. During the copulation of a pair of gametes, the dinophytes and their nuclei fuse first and then the endosymbionts and their nuclei. The life cycles of host and endosymbiont are apparently very closely integrated ([226]). Several dinophytes are capable of forming asexual resting spores (hypnospores), which are very similar to hypnozygotes. Indeed, for the great majority of dinophyte resting spores, which are very diverse in form, we do not know whether they are sexual or asexual. Both types, hypnospores and hypnozygotes, are often referred to simply as '**cysts**'.

The main function of hypnozygotes and hypnospores is apparently survival during periods of adverse conditions, especially winter temperatures that are too low for vegetative growth, or summer temperatures that are too high. For a species living at temperate latitudes, the hypnozygotes or hypnospores might be overwintering stages towards the poles and oversummering stages nearer the equator. Thus, for instance, in the common freshwater species *Peridinium cinctum* (Fig. 16.1) and *Ceratium hirundinella*, the cysts are winter stages in temperate Europe, but serve to maintain the alga through the summer in one lake in Israel, where surface temperatures can be up to 30 °C ([1762]). Where they have been investigated, the hypnozygotes have proved to have an obligate period of dormancy, which lasts several weeks to six months. During this time germination is not possible or occurs only rarely, even in conditions that would be optimal for vegetative growth. When hypnozygotes are stored for longer than the refractory period at temperatures too low for vegetative growth, dormancy continues until the temperature is raised. Unfavourably high temperatures have also been shown to prolong dormancy in one species ([1407]).

Hypnozygotes (or hypnospores) are capable of surviving the anoxic conditions found in the muddy sediments onto which the hypnozygotes settle after their formation ([279]). They occur during the life cycles of both freshwater and marine Dinophyta, which contrasts with the situation in the green algae, where hypnozygotes seem to be restricted to freshwater species in the classes Chlorophyceae, Charophyceae and Zygnematophyceae. The evidence suggests that hypnozygotes enable at least some of these green algae to survive temporary drying out of small water bodies, and also allow aerial transport from one water body to another, for instance via waterfowl ([253]). It is likely that dinophyte cysts have a similar function, especially in view of the cosmopolitan nature of freshwater dinoflagellates and their occurrence in many isolated lakes and ponds ([1762]).

The precise conditions necessary for germination of the hypnozygotes have recently been investigated in the laboratory for *Scrippsiella trochoidea*, a marine dinophyte of the temperate zone ([79, 80]). Before germination can occur there is an obligatory period of dormancy, lasting about 25 days, during which temperature has no effect. Germination requires light, is greatly retarded by low temperatures, and is enhanced by temperatures above 12 °C. Enrichment with nutrients (N and P) also promotes germination. From these characteristics it is likely that *Scrippsiella* cysts would function efficiently as an overwintering stage but could also have a role at other times of the year, allowing the survival of shorter periods of adverse conditions (e.g. times of nutrient depletion). High temperatures, even if nearly lethal (24 °C), do not retard germination and so it is improbable that the hypnozygotes could function as an oversummering stage, either in the more equatorial regions of the species' range or in inshore waters at higher latitudes, where these warm up considerably in the summer months.

Important stocks of viable hypnozygotes and hypnospores are present in the sediments of inshore (neritic) parts of the oceans, especially in fjords, bays and lagoons ([278, 279, 280]). These stocks can serve as inocula for planktonic dinophyte blooms, which develop when increasing water temperatures in spring promote the mass germination of hypnospores. Along the Massachusetts coast of the northeastern United States, for instance, hypnozygotes of the toxic dinophyte *Protogonyaulax tamarensis* are present during the winter in the sediments of small estuaries. Mass germination of the cysts occurs by April, as temperatures rise from 5 to about 15 °C, and toxic blooms follow in late spring (see the section on red tides). Flushing of the estuarine growths into adjacent coastal waters, by storms and tides, can bring about spread of the blooms to much larger areas ([28]). In freshwaters, too, overwintering stocks of dinophyte hypnozygotes can 'seed' the water column in spring. For instance, in a small lake in the English Lake District, a rise in temperature from 3 to 5 °C in February or March was accompanied by a rapid increase in *Ceratium hirundinella* numbers, as large numbers of hypnozygotes germinated in the sediments. The hypnozygotes can survive for many years and there may be a large reservoir of cells left even in years when conditions are adverse ([629]).

Fossil dinophyte cysts

Dinophyte cysts are found as fossils, when they are often known as hystrichospheres ([1551, 1751]). These microfossils generally take the form of spherical or ellipsoidal membranes bearing a number of spiny protrusions (Fig. 16.16a).

Hystrichospheres have been found in rocks and sediments from the Precambrian, or at least the Silurian (see below), to the Holocene, and so have occurred on the earth for more than 600 million years. They have been particularly common and diverse since the late Triassic (220 m.y. ago). Hystrichospheres can be separated from the rock matrix using standard micropalaeontological techniques (digestion with strong acids, including hydrofluoric acid if necessary, and with strong alkalis). They survive such treatments presumably because their walls contain sporopollenin or some similar material, like the walls of pollen grains and higher plant spores, which are also resistant to digestion. Hystrichospheres, again like pollen grains and spores, are important marker fossils for stratigraphical correlation and are especially useful in oil exploration.

For a long time micropalaeontologists were frustrated by the fact that no-one knew what group of organisms produced hystrichospheres, but since 1960 it has become clear that most if not all of these microfossils are the cysts (hypnospores) of Dinophyta. The arrangement of the spines on a cyst often bears a definite relation to the structure of the armour in the cell that produced the cyst, the end of each spine corresponding to one of the thecal plates (Fig. 16.16b, c). Other fossil dinophyte cysts, however, are not like hystrichospheres and have a form that closely resembles the morphology of vegetative cells (Fig. 16.16d, e).

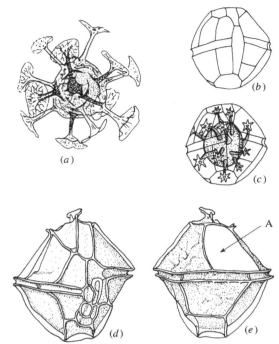

Figure 16.16. Fossil dinophyte cysts. (a) *Areosphaeridium diktyoplokus* from the Middle Eocene (ca. 45 million years old). (b, c) *Hystrichosphaeridium vasiforme*: reconstruction of the theca on the basis of the positions of the spines on the cyst (the hystrichosphere). The spines indicate the former positions of the thecal plates, but the cyst is about the same size as the flagellate cell from which it developed. This organism comes from the Upper Cretaceous (ca. 70 million years old). (d, e) *Gonyaulacysta wetzelii*, an example of a cyst that has the form of a vegetative dinophyte cell, from the early Cenozoic (about 60 million years old). (d) Ventral side. (e) Dorsal side. A = archaeopyle. (a based on [1024]; b, c on [1551]; d, e on [1751].)

In 1950 hystrichospheres were found for the first time in recent sediments, at the bottom of a Swedish fjord, and since then they have been discovered alive in various places. In the winter of 1967, living hystrichospheres were isolated from detritus on the flat sea floor off Woods Hole (on the NE coast of the USA), at water temperatures of 0–3 °C. Germination was brought about by transfer to 16–25 °C, at a light intensity of 5000–8000 lux and with a daylength of 14 h. From three different hystrichospheres, all of them already known and described as fossils, three different species of *Gonyaulax* emerged ([1844]). The hystrichosphere '*Hemicystodinium zoharyii*', which is known as a fossil as far back as the Eocene, was collected alive near the Bahamas and shown to be the encysted stage of the tropical marine dinophyte *Pyrodinium bahamense* ([1843]). Similarly, in culture the cyst '*Ligulodinium machaerophorum*' produced the common marine dinoflagellate *Gonyaulax polyedra* (Fig. 16.17*d*), while the cyst '*Spiniferites elongatus*' gave rise to another marine *Gonyaulax* species, *G. spinifera*. Dinophyte cysts of the *Ligulodinium* and *Spiniferites* type can be found in late Jurassic or early Cretaceous sediments (*ca.* 150 million years ago), which suggests that the genus *Gonyaulax* is very old ([279, 1751]). Extant species can themselves sometimes be traced right back to the late Jurassic ([1760]).

The oldest undoubted dinophyte cysts date from the Silurian and are about 400 m.y. old. Still older, cyst-like microfossils with organic walls may be the cysts of dinophytes, but certain characteristic features are missing, such as the **archaeopyle**, which is the exit hole for the germinating cyst. These ancient microfossils, some of which may be dinophyte cysts, are classed together informally as 'acritarchs' ([279, 543]).

Not all living Dinophyta produce resistant cysts suited to fossilization, with acid-resistant sporopollenin in their walls. Most of those that do belong to the order Peridiniales (p. 280), as do the majority of fossil dinophyte cyst types. Thus the fossil record of the Dinophyta will not be representative of the group as a whole ([279, 543, 1751]).

Daily vertical migration

Many planktonic dinoflagellates make daily migrations up and down in the water column. The organisms involved include species of *Ceratium, Peridinium* and *Prorocentrum*. By day they migrate towards the surface of the water, while at night they move down to a depth of several metres. The vertical migrations probably depend on an underlying endogenous rhythm, the natural alternation of day and night playing only a subsidiary, modifying role. In the absence of a light–dark cycle, daily vertical migrations can go on for some time, and one *Ceratium* species has been shown to continue moving up and down in the water column for six days in complete darkness ([992, 1865]). If the endogenous rhythm is likened to the pendulum of a clock, the alternation of day and night can be imagined as acting

to regulate the pendulum movement, nudging it forward or retarding it slightly ([597, 616, 1740, 1742]).

At first, the upward migration in the morning was thought to be brought about by positive phototaxis and the evening downward migration by passive sinking. However, when upwardly migrating cells of *Ceratium* are illuminated laterally in experimental tanks, instead of from above, they continue to move upwards, though they congregate on the side nearest the light ([992, 1865]). The lateral drift of the cells can be ascribed to positive phototaxis, but the continuing upward movement must be attributed to something else, probably negative geotaxis. Furthermore, the downward migration in the evening is much faster than could occur through passive sinking and is therefore thought to be caused by active downward swimming, guided by positive geotaxis. The underlying, driving rhythm of the vertical migrations would thus be an alternation between negative and positive geotaxis ([992]).

Red tides [1320]

Red tides owe their name to the reddish or brown hue of surface waters sometimes brought about by dense growths of planktonic algae: an accumulation of carotenoid pigments is generally responsible for the colour. In the sea red tides are usually caused by dinoflagellates, particularly photoautotrophic members of the genera *Gymnodinium* (Fig. 16.17*c*), *Gonyaulax* (Fig. 16.17*d*), *Glenodinium, Dinophysis* (Fig. 16.17*e, g*) and *Prorocentrum* (Fig. 16.17*a, b*), but also the heterotrophic genus *Noctiluca* (Fig. 16.17*i, j*). In the coastal waters of Japan, however, toxic red tides are sometimes brought about by members of the heterokontophyte class Raphidophyceae, e.g. species of *Chattonella* and *Fibrocapsa* (p. 161).

Red tides are primarily a phenomenon of tropical and subtropical areas, but they also occur in the temperate zone in late spring and summer. They are particularly frequent close to coasts, which is understandable given that many dinophytes, especially those with cyst stages (hypnozygotes or hypnospores), are restricted to neritic areas (above the continental shelves, where the sea floor is at depths not greater than 200 m); in the deeper, offshore regions of the oceans, the cysts would be lost in the abyss.

In temperate latitudes, red tides generally develop in late spring or early summer, after the decline of the spring diatom bloom. Calm weather favours the devel-

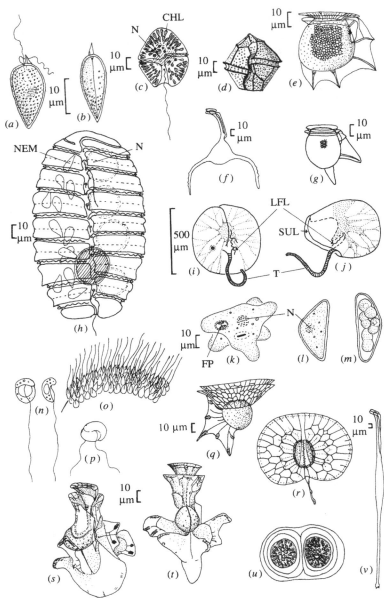

Figure 16.17. (*a, b*) *Prorocentrum micans.*
(*c*) *Gymnodinium splendens.* (*d*) *Gonyaulax polyedra.* (*e*) *Dinophysis joergensenii.* (*f*) *Triposolenia
intermedia.* (*g*) *Dinophysis hastata.* (*h*) *Polykrikos
schwarzii.* (*i, j*) *Noctiluca scintillans.* (*k–m*)
Dinamoebidium varians (*k* amoeboid phase; *l* cyst; *m*
cyst with zoids). (*n–p*) *Noctiluca scintillans* (*n* zoids;
o formation of zoids through budding; *p* copulation
between two zoids). (*q, r*) *Ornithocercus splendidus*:
side view and top view. (*s, t*) *Histioneis josephinae*:
side view and dorsal view. (*u*) *Gloeodinium montanum.* (*v*) *Amphisolenia globifera.* CHL = chloroplast; FP = food particle; LFL = longitudinal flagellum; N = nucleus; NEM = nematocyst; SUL = sulcus
(longitudinal furrow); T = tentacle. (After [1560, 1561].)

opment of blooms by allowing the formation of a stable upper layer of warm, less dense water, which is separated from the dense cold water beneath by a thermocline. The upper layer can form only at some distance from the coast, beyond the zone of strong tidal currents, although protected bays and lagoons can also be suitable for stratification to develop (providing tidal currents are only moderate), especially if there is freshwater run-off from the land, which can significantly lower the density of the upper layers. The spring growth of diatoms can greatly deplete the warm surface layers of nutrients, but dinophytes are often able to grow here nevertheless, possibly because they are able to make daily migrations up and down in the water column (see above). During the night they move down and probably scavenge nutrients from the upper reaches of the nutrient-rich deep water, while during the day they move nearer the surface for photosynthesis; such migrations can only be effective in fairly still water. By day the dinophytes often congregate at some distance below the surface (10 m in some cases), in a thin layer perhaps a metre deep. Their avoidance of the uppermost part of the water column is thought to reflect unfavourable conditions such as high light intensities, high temperature, or the absence of an essential nutrient.

For the build-up of a bloom that is dense enough to be seen as a red tide (cell densities of 10–20 million per litre), dinophyte populations must be concentrated by the action of wind or other physical factors. Thus, if a moderate onshore wind drives surface water containing *Noctiluca* into a bay, the surface water is forced downwards at the head of the bay (forming a return current nearer the sea floor) but the buoyant *Noctiluca* cells accumulate at the surface, forming an inshore bloom. Similar concentrations of cells can develop where oceanic water is driven by the wind against lighter estuarine water. At the boundary (front) between the water masses, the denser oceanic water sinks below the wedge of estuarine water, but the dinophyte cells remain at the surface and accumulate at the front, because of their buoyancy or ability to swim. Yet another type of front is the boundary between an offshore zone of stratified water and a coastal zone where the water is strongly mixed by tidal currents; moderate wind-drift can concentrate dinoflagellate cells from the low density upper layers offshore against the front. Here the high densities of flagellate dinophytes at the surface, along the boundary

between the two water masses, are mirrored by high concentrations of cysts in the sediments immediately below ([1762]).

Red tides occur regularly in some areas, for instance off the SW coasts of Africa, where upwelling water brings an abundance of nutrients to the surface. Here red tides sometimes extend along the coast for hundreds of kilometres. From an aeroplane it can be seen that the tides consist of parallel bands of discoloured water. The red tides last for 15–20 days and can cause the death of enormous numbers of fish and other marine animals. In some cases this is brought about by oxygen depletion and toxic levels of hydrogen sulphide, as great quantities of phytoplankton die and decay, but where dinophytes are responsible for the red tides, the primary cause of death is often the production of poisons by the algae themselves.

The correlation between mass mortality of marine life and the occurrence of red tides has been known for a long time, but no-one knew how the two were linked: deprivation of oxygen, physical interference (through clogging of gills), and toxins were all suggested. Finally it was shown that *Ptichodiscus brevis* cells secrete a poison that can kill fish ([1475]). This dinophyte occurs in the Gulf of Mexico (red tides are in general rarer here than they are off southwest Africa) and is often present there in large numbers when fish die *en masse*. In the laboratory it was shown that bacteria-free cultures of *Ptichodiscus brevis* are just as toxic as unialgal cultures where bacteria are still present; bacteria therefore play no part in the production of the toxin. Laboratory cultures containing $0.6 - 2.1 \times 10^6$ cells l^{-1} were shown to be poisonous to fish, while in nature much higher concentrations of cells can occur during blooms. The toxin is secreted by living cells, and so the filtered medium in which *Ptichodiscus brevis* has been growing is as toxic as the cultures themselves; the toxicity of cultures is not increased if the *Ptichodiscus* cells are killed by gentle heating.

To confirm that it was the toxin that brought about fish losses in nature, other possible causes of death were also investigated. Deaths of fish in the laboratory cultures of *Ptichodiscus brevis* cannot have been caused by oxygen starvation, since the medium was strongly aerated at all times. Furthermore, the gills of the fish were not clogged by *Ptichodiscus* cells, so this possibility too could be eliminated.

The toxin of *Ptichodiscus brevis* (brevetoxin) is

only mildly poisonous to man ([1626, 1696]). Other dinoflagellates pose a greater risk, though usually indirectly, via oysters, mussels and some other shellfish. These molluscs feed on plankton, which they filter from the water. If the plankton consists mainly of Dinophyta, as during a red tide, the oysters and mussels take up the dinophyte toxins and concentrate them in their livers. The shellfish may not themselves be affected by the toxins (though this depends on which dinophytes are involved), but they can be very dangerous to anyone eating them. The red tides of the species *Protogonyaulax catenella* and *P. tamarensis* are particularly notorious in this respect and cause an illness called **'paralytic shellfish poisoning'** (PSP). The toxins produced by *Protogonyaulax catenella* (saxitoxin and neosaxitoxin) and *P. tamarensis* (various gonyautoxins) are similar to each other chemically, but differ from the brevetoxin produced by *Ptichodiscus brevis* ([1626, 1696]). The *Protogonyaulax* toxins cause paralysis, which leads to death by suffocation ([1603, 1604]). In areas affected by red tides, the harvesting of molluscs is forbidden for several months after a tide.

In the North Sea too, red tides can occur and cause poisoning. One occurred in May 1968 off the coast of Northumberland in the UK, involving the dinoflagellate *Protogonyaulax tamarensis* ([9, 267, 778, 1518, 1916]). At the high point of the bloom the water contained 72 000 cells l^{-1}. At night the sea glowed (see below: bioluminescence) and a short time later sea birds began to die from the effects of the dinophyte toxins. By the end of May more than 80 people had become ill with 'paralytic shellfish poisoning'. The collection of edible molluscs (especially mussels) was then forbidden along certain parts of the coast and only resumed towards the end of August, when the concentrations of poison in the shellfish had fallen to an acceptable level. It is interesting that mussels could tolerate high concentrations of the toxin, whereas several other lamellibranchs were killed, e.g. *Cerastoderma edule* (the cockle), *Macoma baltica* and *Venus striatula*. Certain fish (*Ammodytes* species) also died in large numbers, having fed on zooplankton (including copepods), which, like the shellfish, probably concentrate the poison. It was never discovered why *Protogonyaulax tamarensis* built up in such large numbers during the 1968 incident. Generally speaking, water blooms are correlated with particularly rich supplies of nutrient salts, high temperatures and calm weather. It seems not improbable that with increasing eutrophication of the North Sea and similar areas, through pollution with excess phosphate and nitrate, toxic blooms of algae will become progressively more common.

Blooms of dinoflagellates have also been recorded in the North Sea off the Dutch coast and are becoming more regular in their appearance. In summer 1971 one occurred involving the dinophyte *Prorocentrum micans* (Fig. 16.17a, b), and again the toxin produced by the alga was concentrated by the livers of mussels. The *Prorocentrum* toxin is less potent than the poisons produced by *Protogonyaulax* but it still causes stomach upsets and intestinal disorders. The harvesting of mussels therefore had to be discontinued for several weeks in the summer of 1971 ([826]).

Red tides can also have direct effects on humans. Strong winds can produce a fine spray containing *Gymnodinium* cells, which may be blown inland and inhaled by holiday-makers and local residents, causing irritation of the windpipe and bronchioles. People who swim in the discoloured water may develop a skin rash ([1603, 1604]).

As if these problems weren't enough, it has recently been found that a dinophyte is indirectly responsible for ciguatera, a widespread type of poisoning in the tropics, which develops after people have eaten fish. The dinophyte involved is *Gambierdiscus toxicus*, itself a recent discovery, which grows epiphytically on tropical seaweeds and is thus ingested by herbivorous fish grazing on the seaweeds. The herbivores are in turn consumed by carnivorous fish such as barracudas, by which time the dinophyte toxin can have reached dangerously high concentrations ([1626, 1696, 1778]).

Bioluminescence in Dinophyta

During the day blooms of dinophytes are noticeable by their red colour, but they can be no less impressive at night, making the sea glow (phosphorescence, bioluminescence) through their activities. Near north European coasts, phosphorescence is generally caused by the colourless, heterotrophic dinoflagellate *Noctiluca scintillans* (Fig. 16.17i, j, n–p), although various other species, such as *Gonyaulax polyedra* (Fig. 16.17d), are also capable of bioluminescence.

A wide variety of marine animals from several different phyla are bioluminescent, and there are also many bioluminescent marine bacteria. The pitch-black, intermediate depths of the oceans harbour fishes, cephalopods and crustaceans that have light-emitting organs, often with bizarre forms, whose function is to lure prey or frighten predators. The light organs often contain symbiotic bacteria, which are responsible for the bioluminescence ([1562, 1743]). There are also many animals living at the bottom of the ocean that emit light.

Among photosynthetic organisms, bioluminescence occurs only in the Dinophyta, and then only in some species ([1741]). The function of bioluminescence in dinophytes must be to frighten away the small crustaceans (copepods) that graze on the phytoplankton. In experiments with luminescent and non-luminescent strains of the same dinophyte species, predation by copepods was found to be less in the presence of bioluminescence ([1741, 1743, 1881]).

For the cells to emit light they must be stimulated, which can be brought about mechanically (by swimming fish, waves breaking, people walking on the damp sand near the water line, etc.), or by electrical, chemical or osmotic stimuli ([357, 1619, 1741, 1742]). Upon stimulation each cell emits a short flash of light, lasting about 0.1 s, from tiny point sources (probably small membrane-bound particles) scattered throughout the cell. During the production of light an enzyme called luciferase catalyses the oxidation of a substrate, luciferin. The various groups of bioluminescent organisms have different luciferins and luciferases, but within the dinophytes they are probably fairly uniform, since the luciferase from one species can react with the luciferin from another. Dinophyte luciferin seems to be chemically similar to chlorophyll ([1741]). Light inhibits the bioluminescence of some dinoflagellates, but this is not the only reason why bioluminescence is low during the day. Bioluminescence in photosynthetic dinoflagellates is subject to an endogenous circadian rhythm, which persists for some time after the cells have been transferred to continuous light or continuous darkness: during the 'night' phase much more light is emitted than during the 'day', as during a normal daily cycle. Photosynthesis, cell division and vertical migration (see p. 271) also show circadian rhythms ([1740, 1741]).

Endosymbiotic Dinophyta

Many aquatic invertebrates and protozoans harbour photosynthetic algae within their cells and tissues. In freshwater habitats unicellular green algae generally function as the endosymbionts (e.g. in the tissues of

the coelenterate *Chlorohydra* or in some freshwater sponges), but in the sea this role is generally taken by Dinophyta, although unicellular algae from other divisions (Rhodophyta, the heterokontophyte class Bacillariophyceae, Haptophyta, Cryptophyta) also act as endosymbionts in some cases. As a result of these symbiotic relationships, a variety of Protozoa and invertebrate Metazoa are transformed from being purely heterotrophic into partly photoautotrophic organisms (see pp. 47, 365, 512).

In the tissues of their hosts, such as in reef-building corals, the dinophytes occur as small round cells (Fig. 16.3*h, i*), which betray their true affinities only through the presence of a dinokaryon. These small yellow-brown endosymbionts have long been known as **zooxanthellae**, while the green endosymbionts of various freshwater animals are referred to as **zoochlorellae**.

It has been possible in some cases to isolate zooxanthellae from their hosts and culture them separately ([1157]), when they produce flagellate cells resembling *Gymnodinium* (Fig. 16.3*g, l*). Dinophytes occur as endosymbionts in protozoans, such as species of Foraminifera and Polycystinea (= Radiolaria), in cnidarians (various jellyfish, sea anemones, and corals), and in molluscs (some sea slugs, and shells such as *Tridacna*, a large tropical lamellibranch). At first it appeared that the same *Gymnodinium*-like dinophyte, *Symbiodinium microadriaticum* (Fig. 16.3*g–l*), was involved in all of these symbioses, and that it could also live free in the sea, since it has been isolated from seawater. Later, however, it was found that this 'species' is a complex of different entities or races, each one being genetically distinct and occurring in a different host. The different types resemble each other morphologically but differ subtly in features such as chromosome number, the arrangement of the thylakoids in the chloroplasts, and the number of chloroplasts per cell ([90, 1789]).

All the larger benthic foraminifera contain endosymbiotic algae, primarily diatoms (p. 136) but sometimes unicellular red algae, green algae or dinophytes. These photoautotrophic protozoans are some of the most important primary producers in shallow tropical seas. With their perforated calcareous tests (which often superficially resemble tiny snail shells), they are also significant sources of biogenic calcium carbonate. Thus, in tropical lagoons, foraminifera can fix and deposit 150–500 g of carbon per square metre per year. They are therefore comparable in importance to the calcareous nannoplankton of the open ocean (coccolithophorids, division Haptophyta: p. 226) and the various calcareous seaweeds (both red and green algae: pp. 83, 426) found on coral reefs and in other shallow tropical habitats. As calcium carbonate deposition in the skeletons of reef corals is also driven by dinophyte photosynthesis, taking place in the zooxanthellae of the coral polyps, the importance of dinophytes in shallow-water tropical ecosystems can scarcely be overestimated.

Some planktonic foraminifera also possess endosymbiotic dinophytes and photosynthesize [973, 1672]. Another important group of marine planktonic Protozoa are the Polycystinea, traditionally referred to as the Radiolaria [179]. Each individual consists of a central 'body', contained within a perforated organic capsule and surrounded by a radiating network of cytoplasmic strands, which is supported by stiff radial axopods and an elegant, radially organized siliceous skeleton. Some radiolarians of shallow seas contain dinophyte endosymbionts and are photosynthetic. The radiating strands of cytoplasm contain numerous endosymbiont cells, each in its own vacuole, and photosynthates are translocated directly from dinophyte to host [29]. Photosynthetic foraminifera and radiolarians are also capable of phagotrophy, feeding on small prey such as small algae and protozoans. Foraminifera and radiolarians are important constituents of oceanic plankton, and about half of the total area of deep sea sediments is occupied by foraminiferan oozes; radiolarian oozes are also widespread and important [1618].

Reef-building corals contain zooxanthellae, which give many living corals their brown colour. The corals occur in the tropics down to water-depths where there is still sufficient light for the photosynthesis of their zooxanthellae (about 100 m maximum, depending on the transparency of the water). The dinophyte cells are located within the cells of the host and low-molecular-mass metabolites, such as glycerol, glucose, alanine and some organic acids (e.g. glycolate and fumarate), are translocated from alga to host. The traffic is not all one-way, however, and 'waste' nitrogen from the host is transferred to the algal cells, probably in the form of ammonia and urea; phosphorus from the host is thought to become available to the alga in the form of low-molecular-mass organic compounds (phosphoglycerate, nucleic acids; [1656, 1788]).

In some cases the endosymbionts are transmitted from one generation to another via the eggs of the coral polyps. Elsewhere, the young stages of the new generation have to be re-infected by motile cells of the dinoflagellate, which are attracted by ammonium excreted by the host [422]. They are ingested phagotrophically by the cells in the endoderm lining the host's gastric cavity [1788] and then multiply within the host (Fig. 16.3j, k).

The coral–alga symbiosis is often viewed as a highly efficient adaptation to the oligotrophic (nutrient-poor) environments of tropical seas. The alga is thought to assimilate waste nitrogen (urea, ammonia) from the host and rapidly cycles photosynthate back to the coral polyp in the form of amino acids. Scarce supplies of nitrogen are therefore conserved for both partners. In addition, the coral polyps provide a much enlarged surface for photosynthesis and nutrient assimilation (of ammonia and nitrate) from the surrounding water [1754, 1755]. There is no solid evidence, however, for this hypothesis of highly efficient nutrient uptake and internal cycling, attractive though it is. Other animals and plants occur on reefs but are not in intimate symbiotic relationships, and it is not obvious that they are in any way less well adapted than the coral–alga symbiosis.

Besides carbon fixation and nutrient cycling, another important function of the coral–dinophyte symbiosis is calcification, which is directly related to the photosynthesis of the endosymbiont [205, 545, 1755].

Most reef corals capture prey (such as small crustaceans) with their whorls of tentacles, and they can therefore be regarded as 'photosynthetic carnivores'. Some corals have lost the capacity to do this, however, and are therefore entirely dependent on photosynthesis [1276b].

Interpreted in the light of the 'endosymbiotic theory' (p. 2), the examples we have described of highly integrated symbioses between dinophytes and other, initially heterotrophic organisms could perhaps be viewed as the first stages in the evolution of quite new lineages of photosynthetic organisms. They also illustrate that the traditional boundary between 'plants' and 'animals' is quite arbitrary, as, therefore, is the collection of organisms treated in this book.

Levels of organization in the Dinophyta

It has already been mentioned (p. 246) that the Dinophyta are predominantly unicellular, flagellate organisms, although most of the other levels of organization found in the algae are represented by at least one dinophyte genus. Pascher considered that the flagellate unicell is also the most primitive level of organization in the Dinophyta, and that all other types of thallus were derived from it. Comparable developments have occurred in parallel in the Chrysophyceae and Xanthophyceae (Heterokontophyta), and in the Chlorophyta (see pp. 119, 483).

The list below summarizes the various types of organization found in the Dinophyta, and gives a few examples of each (see also Table 6.1).

1 Flagellate unicells.
   Examples: *Peridinium*, *Ceratium* (Figs. 16.1, 16.2), *Gymnodinium* (Figs. 16.10, 16.17*c*), *Prorocentrum* (Figs. 16.17*a*, *b*), *Gonyaulax* (Fig. 16.17*d*), *Polykrikos* (Fig. 16.17*h*), *Dinophysis* (Fig. 16.17*e*, *g*), *Triposolenia* (Fig. 16.17*f*), *Amphisolenia* (Fig. 16.17*v*), *Ornithocercus* (Figs. 16.17*q*, *r*, 16.19*b*), *Histioneis* (Fig. 16.17*s*, *t*).

2 Amoeboid unicells.
   Examples: *Dinamoebidium* (Fig. 16.17*k–m*), *Stylodinium* (Fig. 16.3*c*, *d*).

3 Palmelloid (tetrasporal) colonies.
   Example: *Gloeodinium* (Fig. 16.17*u*).

4 Coccoid unicells.
   Examples: *Dinococcus*, *Phytodinium* (Fig. 16.18*g–i*).

5 Filamentous organization.
   Examples: *Dinothrix*, *Dinoclonium* (Fig. 16.18*f*, *j*).

Subdivision of the class Dinophyceae

We follow Dodge [322, 323] in dividing the Dinophyceae, which is the only class within the Dinophyta, into 12 orders:

Gymnodiniales
Gloeodiniales
Thoracosphaerales
Phytodiniales
Dinotrichales
Dinamoebidales
Noctilucales
Blastodiniales
Syndiniales
Peridiniales
Dinophysiales
Prorocentrales.

A somewhat different classification is given by Taylor ([1759]; see also [327, 1023, 1664a, 1751]).

The Syndiniales will not be treated any further here. They are highly specialized parasites living intracellularly in dinophytes, tintinnids (a group of ciliate protozoans) and metazoans, e.g. crustacea and fish [180].

Order Gymnodiniales

The Gymnodiniales are free-living, motile flagellates with well-developed transverse and sulcal grooves. The cells are more or less compressed dorsiventrally. The order differs from the Peridiniales by the absence of thecal plates, although a layer of numerous empty thecal vesicles, each polygonal in outline, is present around the periphery of the cell (Fig. 16.10*a*, *d*, *e*, 16.19*a*). Both photosynthetic and non-photosynthetic species are included.

Gymnodinium micrum (Fig. 16.10)
A tiny species, isolated from a sample of seawater taken from the English Channel.

Gymnodinium splendens (Fig. 16.17*c*)
As in other *Gymnodinium* species, the cells appear naked in the light microscope since they possess no armour. The transverse furrow spirals slightly towards the base (antapical end) of the cell. Chloroplasts are present. *Gymnodinium splendens* occurs around the British Isles and along the east and west coasts of the USA.

Symbiodinium microadriaticum (Fig. 16.3*g–l*)
This is the widespread endosymbiont of reef-building corals, various other marine invertebrates, and Protozoa (p. 275). It is often classified in the Gymnodiniales because of its *Gymnodinium*-like zoospores; however, its predominantly coccoid mode of growth when inside the host could justify a place in the Phytodiniales.

Polykrikos schwarzii (Fig. 16.17*h*)

In many ways *Polykrikos* resembles *Gymnodinium*, except that two, four or eight 'cells' remain united in a composite, coenocytic individual. The transverse furrows of the component 'cells' spiral slightly towards the antapical pole of the coenocyte, while the longitudinal furrows fuse into a common longitudinal groove. This species is heterotrophic and does not possess chloroplasts. The cells possess nematocysts: organelles that discharge tiny 'harpoons' on stimulation. *Polykrikos schwarzii* occurs in the Atlantic, North Sea, Baltic and Mediterranean, and also on the southwestern coasts of the USA.

Order Gloeodiniales

In this order the species are palmelloid (tetrasporal, encapsuled: see p. 117).

Gloeodinium montanum (Fig. 16.17*u*)

The non-motile cells of *Gloeodinium montanum* are bilaterally flattened or almost spherical, and are united into colonies by thick, stratified sheaths of mucilage. The zoids resemble *Hemidinium* cells ([1408]). This alga occurs on bogs, among *Sphagnum* mosses.

Order Thoracosphaerales

This is an interesting little group, in which the free-living, coccoid cells have calcareous shells. Reproduction takes place by the formation of *Gymnodinium*-like zoids ([1748]).

Thoracosphaera heimii

Each small spherical cell (10–25 μm in diameter) is enclosed within a fairly massive calcareous shell. This is a photosynthetic species found in the plankton of the open ocean, unlike most planktonic dinophytes, which are neritic. The shell confused early investigators, who considered *Thoracosphaera* to be a coccolithophorid (see [280, 1559]).

Order Phytodiniales (= Dinococcales)

The Phytodiniales contains dinophytes with a coccoid organization. They reproduce via non-motile spores (aplanospores, autospores) or by zoids that resemble *Gymnodinium* or *Gonyaulax* cells.

Phytodinium globosum (Fig. 16.18*g–i*)

The cells are spherical, have no trace of a furrow, and propagate themselves by forming aplanospores (each cell produces two aplanospores). It is only the presence of a dinokaryon that makes it obvious that this alga belongs to the Dinophyta. *Phytodinium globosum* was first found in (the former) Czechoslovakia, growing in pools in boggy mires. The order Phytodiniales contains five other genera.

Order Dinotrichales

These dinophytes are filamentous.

Dinoclonium conradii (Fig. 16.18*f, j*)

Dinoclonium conradii consists of branched filaments, which grow epiphytically on other algae. There is a prostrate system of filaments together with erect branches, which become thinner towards their tips. The chloroplasts are brown. During reproduction the contents of the vegetative cells divide up into zoids, which resemble *Gymnodinium* cells. *Dinoclonium conradii* has been found once, on the northwest coast of France.

Order Dinamoebidales

In this group a free-living amoeboid stage alternates with a non-motile coccoid stage, which may produce *Gymnodinium*-like zoids. Some species have vestigial chloroplasts.

Stylodinium sphaera (Fig. 16.3*a–f*)

The coccoid stage of *Stylodinium sphaera* lives on filaments of the freshwater chlorophyte *Oedogonium*, attached by a tiny stipe. It produces amoeboid cells, which ingest the contents of an *Oedogonium* cell after puncturing its cell wall (see p. 257). The cells contain two vestigial chloroplasts.

Dinamoebidium varians (Fig. 16.17*k–m*)

This organism is amoeboid during the vegetative phase and possesses blunt pseudopodia; it has no chloroplasts and feeds phagotrophically. *Dinamoebidium varians* can form elongate cysts, whose contents sometimes divide into *Gymnodinium*-like zoids. It is the only species in the genus *Dinamoebidium* and was found in a marine aquarium.

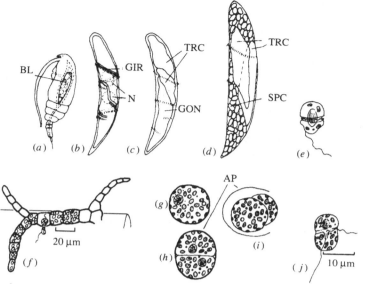

Figure 16.18. (*a–e*) *Blastodinium spinulosum* (*a* cell within the gut of *Paracalanus*; *b* as yet undivided cell; *c, d* division to form zoids; *e* zoid = dinospore). (*f*) *Dinoclonium conradii*. (*g–i*) *Phytodinium globosum*: formation of aplanospores. (*j*) *Dinoclonium conradii*: *Gymnodinium*-like zoid. AP = aplanospores; BL = *Blastodinium*-cell; GIR = girdle (transverse furrow); GON = gonocyte; N = nucleus; SPC = sporocyte; TRC = trophocyte. (After [1560, 1561].)

Order Noctilucales

The Noctilucales are very large dinophytes, which lack chloroplasts (except in one species, where vestigial chloroplasts are present). The cells are vacuolate, with strands of protoplasm traversing the vacuoles. Thecal plates are absent, but the cells are surrounded by a layer of almost empty thecal vesicles [1181]. Prey organisms are captured via a tentacle and ingested through a cytostome (cell mouth).

Noctiluca scintillans (Fig. 16.17*i, j, n–p*)

The cells of *Noctiluca scintillans* are reniform to spherical and distended, reaching diameters of 0.2 – 1.2 mm. They contain large vacuoles. Full-grown, mature cells have no transverse furrow and the cell envelope is not differentiated into epicone and hypocone. The longitudinal furrow (sulcus) takes the form of a large oral (mouth) cavity, from which there projects a transversely striated tentacle; at the bottom of the cavity is the cytostome ('cell mouth'). Zoids can be formed at the surface of the cell by budding, and are fairly similar to *Gymnodinium* cells. They are probably capable of isogamous fusion [1935]. *Noctiluca scin-*

tillans does not possess chloroplasts, although some populations have symbiotic chlorophytes in their vacuoles (p. 255), and it lives phagotrophically.

The large vacuoles contain an acid solution, in which the Na^+, K^+ and other cations of seawater have been replaced by H^+ ions. As a result, the density of the cell sap in the vacuoles is less than that of seawater, and the cells can therefore be positively buoyant and float [1299]. *Noctiluca scintillans* is a member of the plankton in coastal waters world-wide, and frequently brings about phosphorescence of the sea at night and red tides during the day.

Order Blastodiniales

This is a group of parasites, which affect a wide variety of organisms: protozoa, algae, invertebrates, and fish. Each cell is covered by a layer of thecal vesicles, which may or may not contain thecal plates. Reproduction involves the formation of motile, *Gymnodinium*-like cells [180].

Blastodinium spinulosum (Fig. 16.18*a–e*)

Blastodinium spinulosum lives as a parasite in the gut

of copepods, which are small, planktonic crustaceans (Fig. 16.18a). The young cells are banana-shaped and binucleate (Fig. 16.18b). In each of them, one or two 'trophocytes' arise, and a 'gonocyte' (Fig. 16.18c). The trophocytes do not reproduce but the gonocyte divides up into 'dinospores', which are *Gymnodinium*-like zoids (Fig. 16.18d, e). The dinospores leave the host through its anus and infection of a new host occurs when a copepod takes up encysted zoids with its food. Interestingly, eight species of *Blastodinium*, although parasites, nevertheless contain chloroplasts and are still partly autotrophic; only one of the known species is fully heterotrophic.

The Blastodiniales are not the only parasitic dinophytes: members of the order Syndiniales infect algae and various other aquatic organisms.

Order Peridiniales

Here the cells possess an armour of polygonal cellulose plates (p. 247). They are spherical, ovoid or pyramidal, and are usually compressed dorsiventrally. In contrast to the Prorocentrales and Dinophysiales, there is no longitudinal suture in the armour. Each cell has a transverse furrow, which contains the transverse flagellum, and a longitudinal furrow, for the longitudinal flagellum. In several recent classifications, the Gonyaulacales has been split off from the Peridiniales, on the basis of differences in the thecal plate pattern ([1759]).

Peridinium cinctum (Figs. 16.1, 16.4; p. 249)
This alga is a cosmopolitan species of freshwaters in tropical and temperate regions.

Peridinium balticum (Fig. 16.7)
Inside the cells are endosymbiotic algae belonging to the Heterokontophyta (p. 251) and it is these that carry out photosynthesis for the organism. *Peridinium balticum* is a freshwater and brackish species, and is particularly common in the Baltic.

Protoperidinium (Fig. 16.9)
Protoperidinium is an entirely marine genus and differs from the principally freshwater genus *Peridinium* in being non-photosynthetic. It lives phagotrophically, and can capture and ingest prey much bigger than itself via its sheet-like pseudopodia (Fig. 16.9a–d; p. 257).

Ceratium hirundinella (Fig. 16.2; p. 249)
This freshwater species is widely distributed in the temperate parts of North America, northern Asia, and Europe. Other examples of *Ceratium* species are *C. cornutum* (p. 266; Fig. 16.15), another freshwater species, and *C. horridum* (Fig. 16.14), which is a marine species of the North Atlantic. *Ceratium* species contain chloroplasts.

Gonyaulax polyedra (Fig. 16.17d)
Gonyaulax species have a characteristic arrangement of the thecal plates; in addition, the longitudinal furrow extends across the whole cell, from tip to base (apex to antapex). Species of the closely related genus *Protogonyaulax* are known to be toxic, forming poisonous red tides in nature (p. 274). *Gonyaulax polyedra* is a cosmopolitan planktonic species in warm and temperate seas.

Order Dinophysiales

All species are armoured, the armour being divided into a right and left half by a longitudinal suture, as in the Prorocentrales. There is in addition a differentiation into epitheca and hypotheca, which are separated by a transverse furrow. The epitheca is usually small and the cells are compressed laterally, to a lesser or greater extent. Besides the longitudinal suture, there is also a longitudinal furrow. The theca consists of plates, which are always perforated by holes (pores) and ornamented with small indentations or dimples (poroids), while alongside the transverse and longitudinal furrows there are often prominent membranous ridges. As in the Prorocentrales, cell division takes place along the longitudinal suture. Some extremely bizarre dinophytes belong to this order (Figs. 16.17e–g, q–t, 16.19b), which includes both photosynthetic and non-photosynthetic members.

Dinophysis (Fig. 16.17e, g)
The cells are circular to oval in side view. The epitheca is very small. The upper girdle ridge (the moulding on the apical side of the transverse furrow) is generally broader than the lower ridge. Along the longitudinal furrow, the right-hand ridge is feebly developed while the left-hand ridge is large and more or less trapezoidal (as seen from the side); this is stiffened by a number of ribs. About 50 species are known, all marine. Some species have chloroplasts, others do not. *Dinophysis joergensenii* (Fig. 16.17e) is a rare but

widely distributed species found in tropical, subtropical and temperate seas. *Dinophysis hastata* (Fig. 16.17*g*) is even more widespread, extending into arctic and antarctic waters.

Triposolenia intermedia (Fig. 16.17 f)

The hypotheca consists of a central body bearing three thin extensions, one above and two below. The upper protrusion bears the transverse furrow (girdle) and the two girdle ridges, together with a very small epitheca. *Triposolenia intermedia* occurs in tropical, subtropical and warm temperate regions of the eastern Pacific Ocean.

Amphisolenia globifera (Fig. 16.17 v)

This species is characterized by its elongate, needle-like hypotheca and tiny epitheca. It is probably cosmopolitan, occurring in tropical, subtropical and warm temperate seas.

Ornithocercus splendidus (Fig. 16.17 q, r; for a second species see 16.19 b)

The body of this alga is generally more or less circular. The most striking features are the two very wide, funnel-shaped girdle ridges, which are reinforced by networks of ribs. *Ornithocercus splendidus* is widely distributed in tropical, subtropical and warm temperate seas. Chloroplasts are absent.

Histioneis josephinae (Fig. 16.17 s, t)

Histioneis josephinae has a rather small cell body, but projecting out from this are extensive ridges and wings producing a particularly bizarre morphology. The upper girdle ridge forms a narrow, stalked funnel at the top of the cell, while below this is an almost cylindrical lower girdle ridge. The margins of the longitudinal furrow are also extended outwards, especially the left-hand ridge. This species occurs in the tropical part of the eastern Pacific Ocean.

Order Prorocentrales

All species are armoured. The armour is divided by a longitudinal suture into two halves, each shaped more or less like a watch-glass. Transverse and longitudinal furrows are absent. The two flagella arise at the anterior end, one of them being directed forwards during swimming, the other moving more or less spirally and thus perhaps comparable with the transverse flagellum of *Peridinium*. All species contain chloroplasts.

Prorocentrum micans (Fig. 16.17 a, b)

The cell of this species is ovoid to heart-shaped and bears a toothlike projection at the insertion of the flagella. *Prorocentrum micans* occurs in the marine phytoplankton world-wide and is often found in estuaries; it can cause toxic red tides (p. 274).

Phylogeny

Fossil evidence (of cysts) indicates that the Dinophyta are a very ancient group, with a minimum age of 400 million years (perhaps 600 m.y. old or more; see p. 270). The diversity of the fossil dinophyte flora increased markedly in the late Jurassic (150 m.y. ago) to reach a maximum in the middle to late Cretaceous (110–80 m.y. ago) [543].

The fossil evidence also suggests that some extant genera and even some species may be very old. Thus, for instance, cysts like those formed today by *Gonyaulax* can be found as far back as the late Jurassic (*ca.* 150 m.y. ago; [1751, 1760]). Similar ages can be ascribed to some extant genera of other algal divisions, such as the Rhodophyta (p. 48) and Chlorophyta (p. 300).

In spite of their great diversity and age, fossil cysts belong for the most part to only one lineage within the Dinophyta, namely the order Peridiniales. The reason is apparently that this is the only order in which the organisms commonly produce resistant, sporopollenin-containing cysts. The fossil record is therefore biased, containing only a limited amount of information about the relationships between most of the main lineages. We have to rely, therefore, upon comparisons between living dinophytes, if we are to study dinophyte evolution. The phylogenetic tree shown in Fig. 16.20 summarizes how the Dinophyta may have evolved, based on comparative morphology; it is, of course, hypothetical.

In Fig. 16.20 photosynthetic organisms with dinophyte chloroplasts and a gymnodinialean morphology are placed at the bottom of the tree, representing what is thought to be the most primitive lineage of Dinophyta. The Gymnodiniales appear to have retained more ancestral characters than any other order. These are: (1) the presence of a distinct equatorial girdle separating an epicone from a hypocone; (2) the possession of a transverse flagellum and a backwardly directed longitudinal flagellum; (3) the presence of numerous thecal vesicles, which are either empty or contain thin thecal plates (Figs. 16.20, 16.10*a*); (4) the

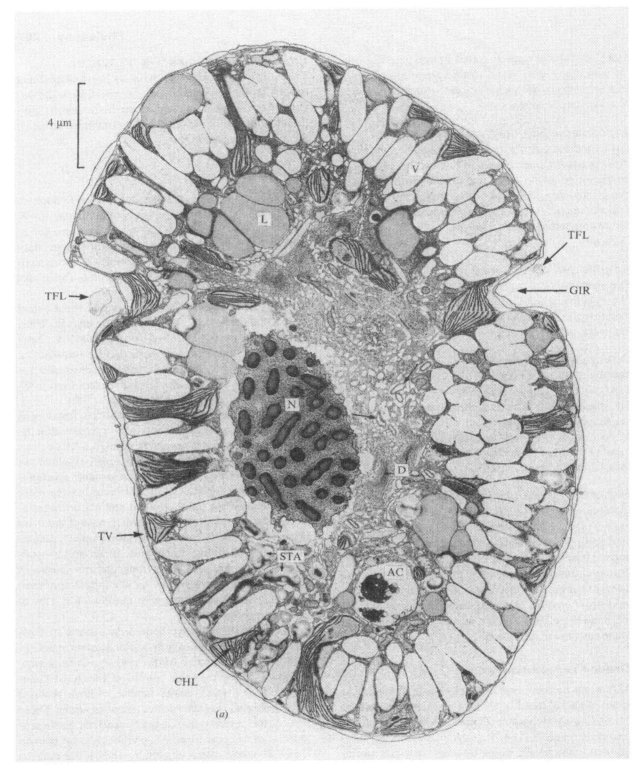

Figure 16.19. (a) *Amphidinium cryophilum:* transmission electron micrograph of a longitudinal section, showing the general organization of the dinophyte cell. (b)

Scanning electron micrograph of *Ornithocercus magnificus.* AC = accumulation body, containing the remains of digested organelles; CHL = chloroplast;

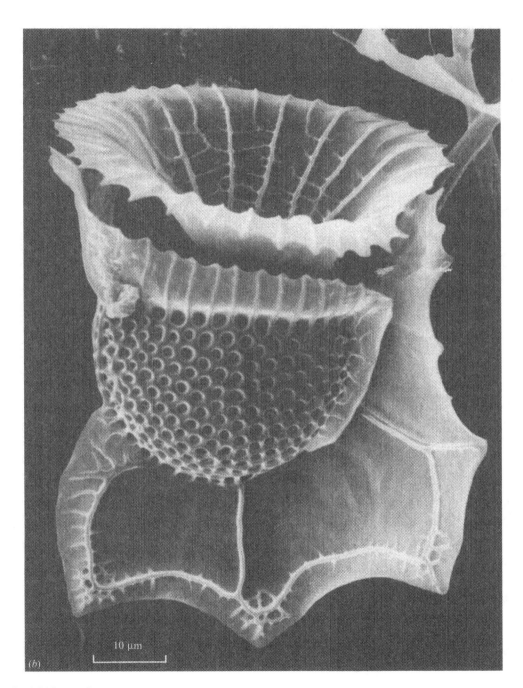

Caption for fig. 16.19 *(cont.)*.

    D = golgi body; GIR = girdle (transverse furrow); L =
lipid globule; N = nucleus; STA = starch grain; TFL =
transverse flagellum; TV = thecal vesicle; V = vesicle;
arrows = tubules of the pusule system, in section.

(a from [1869a], with the permission of the authors and the
editor of the *Journal of Phycology*; *b* from [597a], with the
permission of the author and CSIRO/ E.J. Brill/ Robert
Brown & Associates, Bathurst, Australia.)

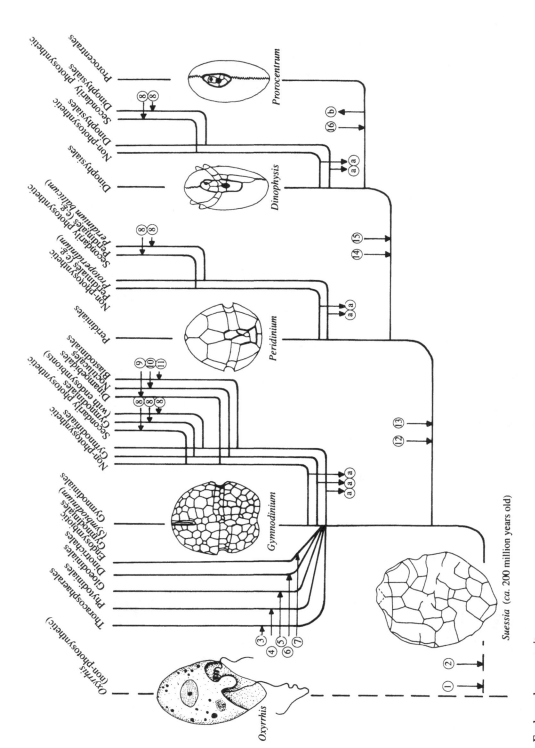

For legend see opposite page.

presence of dinophyte chloroplasts, with peridinin, chlorophyll c_2 and a triple membrane envelope; (5) phagotrophy involving use of a peduncle; (6) a free-living, planktonic mode of existence.

The other orders can be derived from the ancestral *Gymnodinium*-type, either by the step-wise acquisition of more advanced characters (these phylogenetic 'gains' are indicated in Fig. 16.20 by arrows pointing in towards the branches of the phylogenetic tree), or by the loss of characters (indicated by arrows pointing out, away from the branches). The phylogenetic tree illustrates the idea that the various specialized groups of dinophytes with *Gymnodinium*-like reproductive cells (spores, gametes) have been derived from the Gymnodiniales. The Thoracosphaerales and Phytodiniales, for instance, are thought to have arisen by the intercalation of a non-motile, coccoid vegetative stage into the life history; in the Thoracosphaerales this stage is encased in a calcareous test. The Gloeodiniales and Dinotrichales may have arisen from the Gymnodiniales by the acquisition of non-motile palmelloid and filamentous vegetative stages, respectively.

The tree also expresses the hypothesis that non-photosynthetic, phagotrophic dinophytes (again with *Gymnodinium*-like motile stages) have evolved many times, through the loss of dinophyte chloroplasts. In the simplest case of this, colourless, phagotrophic species arose within the ancestral Gymnodinialean lineage itself, even within the genus *Gymnodinium*. More elaborate morphologies and specialized life histories have accompanied the loss or reduction of the chloroplasts during the evolution of the heterotrophic orders Dinamoebidales (with amoeboid cells; Figs. 16.3, 16.17*k–m*), Noctilucales (Fig. 16.17*i, j, n–p*), and Blastodiniales (Fig. 16.18*a–e*).

The evolution of colourless, heterotrophic organisms from photosynthetic ancestors has occurred over and over again, in a variety of different algal divisions, not just in the Dinophyta. Thus, for instance, in the class Chrysophyceae (division Heterokontophyta), the genera *Paraphysomonas* and *Anthophysa* are phagotrophic, while the photosynthetic species of other genera (e.g. *Ochromonas*; Fig. 6.1*b–d*) can also be capable of phagotrophy, as in many photosynthetic Dinophyta. Within the Chlorophyceae (division Chlorophyta), the photoautotrophic genus *Chlamydomonas* has a colourless, heterotrophic equivalent: the genus *Polytoma* (Figs. 21.1*a*, 21.3*q*). The red algae

Figure 16.20. A hypothetical phylogenetic tree of the Dinophyta, based principally on comparative morphology of living species. In the tree the Gymnodiniales are considered to be the ancestral group for all other Dinophyta (except the genus *Oxyrrhis*, which may be the closest relative among living dinophytes of the heterotrophic ancestors of the whole group). All other dinophyte orders can be derived from the Gymnodiniales through various phylogenetic gains (arrows pointing towards the branches of the tree) and losses (arrows pointing away from the branches).

Phylogenetic gains:

1 The dinokaryon and dinophyte mitosis.
2 Incorporation of a eukaryote endosymbiont and evolution of this into the dinophyte chloroplast (with peridinin and a 3-membrane envelope).
3 A coccoid level of organization and a calcareous cell envelope.
4 A coccoid level of organization; acquisition of this character may have happened more than once.
5 A capsal (tetrasporal, palmelloid) level of organization.
6 A filamentous level of organization.
7 Incorporation of the dinophyte cell as a photosynthetic endosymbiont within a heterotrophic host; this has

happened many times.
8 Capture by dinophytes of other unicellular, eukaryotic algae as endosymbionts; the dinophytes thus become secondarily photosynthetic. This has occurred several times.
9 An amoeboid mode of existence. This has probably occurred more than once.
10 A specialized type of heterotrophy, as exhibited by *Noctiluca*.
11 A highly specialized parasitic habit. This has probably occurred more than once.
12 Fusion of thecal vesicles.
13 Thick thecal plates.
14 Further fusion of thecal vesicles and the plates contained within them.
15 Bilateral compression of the cell.
16 Progressive fusion of thecal vesicles and the plates contained within them, resulting in two large lateral plates and a number of tiny platelets near the bases of the flagella, on the ventral side of the cell.

Phylogenetic losses:

a Loss of typical dinophyte chloroplasts (and hence also of peridinin and 3-membrane envelopes). This has occurred many times.
b Loss of the girdle.

(Rhodophyta) too include a number of parasitic heterotrophs, which are often closely related to photosynthetic organisms (p. 49; Fig. 5.7). In no other algal division (except the Euglenophyta, p. 289), however, is the proportion of heterotrophic species so high (50%) as it is in the Dinophyta. This has led some researchers to conclude that heterotrophy is 'normal' and primitive in the Dinophyta and that photoautotrophy is the condition that has evolved over and over again, through repeated incorporation of endosymbiotic eukaryotic algae. This idea became particularly attractive after the discovery of a number of photosynthetic dinophytes containing endosymbiotic algae belonging to various algal divisions ([321]; see p. 251). However, the majority of photosynthetic Dinophyta have typical dinophyte chloroplasts (with peridinin, chlorophyll c_2, and a triple membrane envelope; see p. 251). This kind of chloroplast is found in no other group of algae but is widespread within the Dinophyta, occurring in species of such diverse orders as the Gymnodiniales, Phytodiniales, Peridiniales and Prorocentrales, and possibly also in the Dinophysiales ([599, 795, 1788]). It must surely be concluded, therefore, that dinophyte chloroplasts were present in the ancestors of all these lineages, which we have suggested were Gymnodinium-like organisms. Within most of the principal lineages of dinophytes, some of the species have lost their dinophyte chloroplasts. Subsequently, these dinophytes have either remained exclusively phagotrophic, or have become secondarily photoautotrophic, by incorporating various unicellular algae as endosymbionts. The alternative explanation, that all the features of the typical dinophyte chloroplast have evolved many times independently in the different lineages of the Dinophyta, is very unlikely.

There is indirect evidence that Gymnodinium-like dinophytes existed in the Triassic (ca. 200 million years ago), before the great evolutionary radiation of the group in the Jurassic (ca. 150 m.y. ago). The Triassic witnessed a rapid expansion of the reef-building corals (p. 276), and this ecological success is generally attributed to the acquisition of dinophyte endosymbionts, which today are indispensable to coral growth ([1788]). This in turn suggests that the coral endosymbiont Symbiodinium already existed in the Triassic. Hence we can surmise that certain features possessed by Symbiodinium also existed by the Triassic, namely the Gymnodinium-like morphology of its flagellate cells, and the typical dinophyte chloro-

plasts, with peridinin and a triple membrane envelope ([1788]). In addition, there are Triassic fossils of a group of dinoflagellates (the Suessia group), whose cells were surrounded by numerous thecal plates (Fig. 16.20); extant Gymnodinium-like dinophytes are characteristically surrounded by many thecal vesicles and so again would appear to be primitive.

The presence of typical dinophyte chloroplasts in the common ancestor of the principal lineages of the Dinophyta does not, of course, mean that the dinophyte chloroplast could not have arisen endosymbiotically. It is still quite possible that the chloroplast represents a photoautotrophic alga, which was ingested by a primaeval heterotrophic ancestor of the dinophytes. The colourless marine dinophyte Oxyrrhis marina (Fig. 16.20), which is phagotrophic, has recently been suggested to be a little-changed descendant of such a primaeval heterotroph ([1024]). It has a more 'normal' mitosis than most dinophytes, with an intranuclear spindle instead of the curious nuclear channels of most dinophytes, and its chromosomes contain higher levels of nucleohistone. These features are considered to be primitive, and hence the phylogenetic tree of Fig. 16.20 incorporates the idea that the ancestral Gymnodinium-like photoautotroph evolved through the incorporation of a photosynthetic endosymbiont into an Oxyrrhis-like heterotroph ([1024]).

The Peridiniales (Fig. 16.20) are suggested to have been derived from a Gymnodinium-like ancestor (possessing typical dinophyte chloroplasts) by marked reduction in the number of thecal vesicles (possibly through fusion during evolution), and by the development of strongly thickened thecal plates. In addition, the plates became more fixed in their arrangements, taking one of a limited number of patterns, such as the Peridinium-pattern or the Gonyaulax-pattern. The delicate polygonal patterns on the thecal plates of the Peridiniales may be vestiges of the numerous polygonal thecal vesicles present in the Gymnodiniales ([321]). The Peridiniales exhibit in miniature the various evolutionary trends we have noted for the Dinophyta as a whole (Fig. 16.20). Loss of dinophyte chloroplasts occurred during the evolution of Protoperidinium (Fig. 16.9), while incorporation of endosymbiotic eukaryotes into some heterotrophic Peridiniales has produced secondary photoautotrophs (Fig. 16.7).

In our hypothetical phylogeny, the Dinophysiales are proposed to have evolved from the Peridiniales by further reduction in the number of thecal plates, together with a lateral compression of the cell (so that the theca consists of two lateral halves) and strong reduction of the epicone (Fig. 16.20). As in the Peridiniales, some species may perhaps have retained dinophyte chloroplasts with peridinin, while others have become heterotrophic ([599]). Secondary photo-autotrophy has been acquired by some heterotrophic Dinophysiales, through the incorporation of endosymbiotic cryptophytes (p. 255) or through close associations with unicellular blue-green algae (cyanobacteria) ([598, 599, 1048, 1300, 1577]).

Finally, the phylogenetic tree pictures the idea that the Prorocentrales have arisen from the Dinophysiales. This evolutionary transformation would require still further reduction in the number of thecal plates through fusion, resulting in a theca composed of two large plates covering by far the greater part of the laterally compressed, lens-like cell, and a cluster of small platelets around the insertion of the flagella (Fig. 16.20). The platelets would presumably then be the last vestiges of the small thecal vesicles of the *Gymnodinium*-like ancestor; comparable clusters of small platelets are present around the bases of the flagella in the Dinophysiales and Peridiniales (Fig. 16.20). Epicone and girdle have both been lost in the Prorocentrales, and the longitudinal flagellum has changed its orientation, becoming directed forwards. All the species of this group seem to have retained dinophyte-type chloroplasts.

Thus, according to the hypothesis put forward above, there has been a progressive reduction in the number of thecal plates during the evolution of the Dinophyta; it has therefore been termed the 'plate reduction model'. This idea gains support from the fossil record, which indicates an overall decrease in the number of plates of fossil cysts from the late Triassic to the present. The opposing hypothesis is the 'plate increase model', which sees the Prorocentrales as the most primitive group, from which the Dinophysiales, Peridiniales and Gymnodiniales have evolved, by progressive fragmentation of the armour ([1758]). This model is supported neither by the fossil evidence ([543]), nor by comparative morphology, which points to a *Gymnodinium*-like ancestor as the focus of evolutionary radiation in the Dinophyta.

17

Euglenophyta

This division contains only one class, the Euglenophyceae.

The principal characteristics of the Euglenophyta [162, 319, 657, 976, 981, 983, 1461, 1640, 1846]

1 The great majority of the Euglenophyta are unicellular flagellates (Figs. 17.1*a*, 17.2*a*): they are monads. A few, however, have stages during which the cells are enclosed within a mucilage capsule (= palmelloid stages; see p. 120, Table 6.1).

2 The flagella arise from the bottom of a flask-shaped invagination or **ampulla**, consisting of a canal and a reservoir, which is located at the anterior end of the cell. There are almost always two flagella, but one of these is often so short that it lies entirely within the ampulla (Figs. 17.1*a, b*, 17.2*a*). Locomotion is brought about by the one or two emergent flagella, which bear a unilateral array of delicate hairs (2-3 μm long), together with a felt-like covering of shorter hairs (Figs. 17.2*c*, 17.3).

3 As in the Dinophyta, the chloroplast envelope consists of three membranes (Fig. 17.1*b*). The chloroplasts are never connected to the nucleus by endoplasmic reticulum.

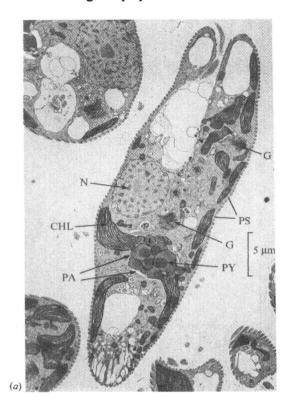

(a)

Figure 17.1. *Eutreptiella eupharyngea* ultrastructure. (*a*) Longitudinal section, showing the characteristic cellular organization of the Euglenophyta. (*b*) Cross section through the ampulla. AMP = ampulla; AX = axoneme; CE = chloroplast envelope (composed of three membranes); CHL = chloroplast; ER = endoplasmic reticulum; FS = flagellar swelling (on short flagellum); G = golgi body; L = lamella, composed of a stack of two or three thylakoids; LFL = long flagellum; M = mitochondrion; MB = mucilage body; MC = mucilage canal; MT = microtubules around the ampulla; N = nucleus; PA = paramylon plates around the pyrenoid; PFR = paraflagellar rod; PS = pellicular strips; PY = cluster of pyrenoids; SFL = short flagellum; ST = stigma (eyespot) globules. (From [1848a], with the permission of the authors and the editor of *Phycologia*.)

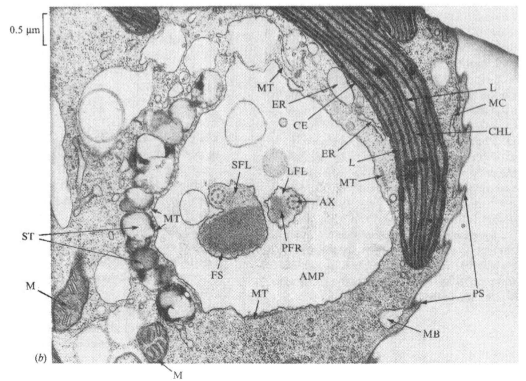

(b)

4   Within the chloroplasts, the thylakoids are usually grouped into threes, forming lamellae (Fig. 17.1b), the same arrangement as is found in the Heterokontophyta and Dinophyta. The Heterokontophyta generally also possess a lamella that encircles and encloses all the others, the girdle lamella, but this is never found in the Euglenophyta. Many Euglenophyta lack chloroplasts and are heterotrophs, living either phagotrophically or saprotrophically (Fig. 17.6d).

5   The chloroplasts contain chlorophylls a and b, and so in this respect the Euglenophyta resemble the green algae (division Chlorophyta). Chlorophyll c is absent (Table 1.2).

6   Since the chlorophylls are not masked by the accessory photosynthetic pigments, the chloroplasts are green. Of the accessory pigments that are present, the most important are β-carotene, neoxanthin and diadinoxanthin, although echinenone, diatoxanthin and zeaxanthin are also found (Table 1.2).

7   The chloroplast DNA occurs as a fine skein of tiny granules, which extends through the whole chloroplast ([254]).

8   The orange-red eyespot is free in the cytoplasm (not contained within the chloroplast) and consists of a number of droplets containing carotenoids (Fig. 17.1b). Similar eyespots are found in the Eustigmatophyceae and some Dinophyta. The eyespot lies under the plasmalemma by the reservoir; near it the long flagellum bears a swelling (Fig. 17.2a).

9   The reserve polysaccharide is paramylon, a β-1,3-linked glucan. This lies in the cytoplasm in the form of granules (Fig. 17.2a), which are often ring-like. If pyrenoids are present that project out from the chloroplasts, the paramylon can be seen to be formed up against them (Fig. 17.1a).

10   The cells have a spiral construction and are surrounded by a pellicle, which lies within the cytoplasm. This is composed of abutting strips of protein (Fig. 17.1a, b), which wind helically around the cell from one end to the other (Fig. 17.2a, b, h). In addition, the cells are often surrounded by a thin layer of mucilage, which is secreted by muciferous bodies situated beneath the pellicle (Figs. 17.1b, 17.2b). Elsewhere, copious mucilage production by the golgi bodies can result in the formation of palmelloid (encapsuled) stages ([1790]).

11   The interphase nucleus contains contracted chromosomes, which can be seen even in the living cell (Fig. 17.2a). Mitosis is closed (the nuclear membrane remains intact) and the nucleolus persists throughout nuclear division (Fig. 17.5).

12   At the anterior end of the cell there lies a large contractile vacuole, which discharges its contents into the reservoir (Figs. 17.2a, 17.6d).

13   Most of the Euglenophyta are freshwater organisms, but some are marine.

Size and distribution of the division

The number of genera in the Euglenophyta is around 40, with more than 800 species. Although most members of the group have green chloroplasts and depend for their nutrition on photosynthesis, there is nevertheless a strong tendency within the Euglenophyta towards heterotrophy. Photosynthetic species (e.g. in the genus *Euglena*, Fig. 17.2) can supplement photosynthesis by taking up organic compounds, but there are also many colourless euglenophytes (e.g. *Astasia*, Fig. 17.6d), which are completely dependent on heterotrophic nutrition. Most of the heterotrophic forms are saprotrophic. Others, however, are phagotrophic, and *Peranema* and *Entosiphon* (and also some other genera) even possess a special apparatus for capturing prey, such as algae, bacteria, or yeasts, and a cytostome ('cell mouth') for ingesting them. Freshwater copepods (a group of small crustaceans) can harbour a variety of parasitic euglenophytes ([1198]).

In nature, members of this division tend to grow in small pools or ditches that have been enriched with organic compounds, such as after pollution with manure. Euglenophytes can also often be found in other polluted waters, and can give rise to very dense populations, causing water blooms. Palmelloid stages, that is, cells that have lost their flagella and have surrounded themselves in a thick envelope of mucilage, sometimes cover the surface of the water with a floating skin. Elsewhere, euglenophytes can form green films on the mud- and sandflats of estuaries. Soon after these areas become exposed by the tide in the daytime, they acquire an intense green colour, as myriads of *Euglena* cells move up to the surface. Shortly before submergence by the incoming tide, the cells move back into the sediments. These movements seem to be steered by variations in phototactic behaviour, under the control of an endogenous, clock-like daily rhythm ([1528]); see Edmunds ([362, 363]) for evidence of other daily rhythms in *Euglena*.

Although euglenophytes seem to be found predominantly in freshwater habitats, their importance in marine inshore environments may have been underestimated. Thus, in Norwegian coastal waters, for instance, euglenophytes may form large populations after the spring diatom bloom and also in summer. The availability of certain organic compounds may explain their occurrence ([1652]).

Species of the genera *Euglena* and *Astasia* have been used for many years as experimental organisms in biochemical and physiological investigations ([131, 182, 363, 981]).

Euglena: the 'archetype' of the Euglenophyta

Some of the light and electron microscopical characteristics of this alga are described below.

The cell exterior and pellicle [980, 983]

The cylindrical body of *Euglena spirogyra* tapers to a point at its posterior and is surrounded by a pellicle (periplast) composed of flat strips, which are wound helically around the cell (Fig. 17.2*a*). The strips lie within the cell, in the cytoplasm immediately beneath the plasmalemma (Fig. 17.2*b*). They overlap one another and in the region of overlap the inner strip bears a longitudinal rib, which fits into a groove in the outer strip, forming a joint (Fig. 17.2*b, h*). The pellicular strips are composed mainly of protein (80%), with some lipid and carbohydrate. Below them are arrays of microtubules (diameter 20–25 nm).

A number of the Euglenophyta exhibit curious squirming movements when they are not using their flagella to swim. This is termed euglenoid movement, and it is particularly often seen in forms with rather thin pellicles, such as *Astasia* species. The pellicular strips can apparently not only flex around the rib-and-groove joint, but also slide relative to each other ([1734]);

they seem too to be elastic. During euglenoid movement, a cytoplasmic bulge moves from the tail of the cell to its apex, thus bringing about backward motion (Fig. 17.6*e*). During the subsequent recovery phase there is cytoplasmic streaming in the reverse direction, from tip to tail. Sliding between the pellicular strips, perhaps involving the underlying systems of microtubules, may cause the formation of the bulge. Restoration of cell shape probably results from the elastic nature of the strips, which spring back to their original positions ([126, 478, 1734]). This would then be an example of movement generated by structures sliding over the surfaces of microtubules, another example being the bending of flagella, brought about as the axoneme microtubules slide past each other (see p. 305). Euglenophyte species with thick pellicles (some *Euglena* species, for instance) do not exhibit euglenoid movement.

Beneath the pellicular strips are helical rows of mucilage bodies, which are peripheral compartments of the endoplasmic reticulum. They discharge their contents to the exterior via canals, which open into the grooves between the pellicular strips (Fig. 17.2*b*). The mucilage thus secreted covers the cell in a thin layer and is composed of glycoproteins and complex polysaccharides ([247]).

Palmelloid stages and cysts can be produced, when thick, concentrically layered sheaths of mucilage are laid down around cells that have stopped moving. The mucilage secreted in such palmelloid phases is secreted by the golgi bodies primarily into the ampulla, from where it is redistributed over the whole cell ([1790]). As already noted, palmelloid stages sometimes form a scum on the surface of nutrient-rich pools.

In *Euglena spirogyra* the pellicular strips can be decorated with rows of small warts (Fig. 17.2*a*), which consist for the most part of iron or manganese hydroxides. Their formation depends, therefore, on whether iron and manganese ions are available. The warts lie outside the plasmalemma and may perhaps be derived in some way from the blobs of mucilage that are discharged from the mucilage bodies.

The ampulla

The flask-shaped ampulla (Latin for flask or bottle) at the anterior end of the cell is differentiated into a reservoir and a canal, which forms the neck of the 'flask'

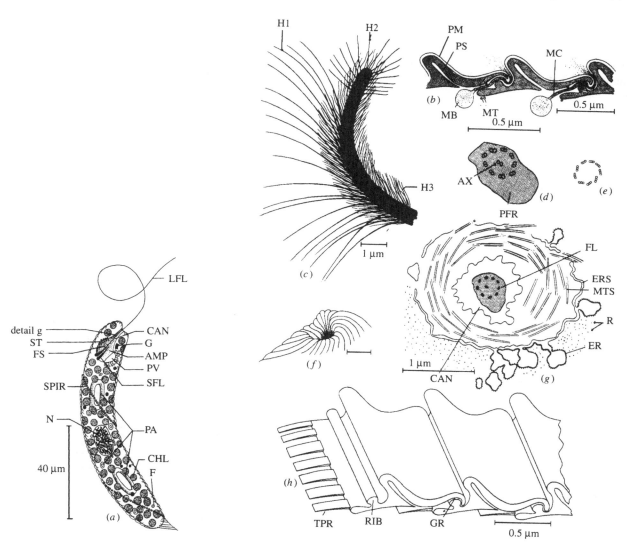

Figure 17.2. *Euglena spirogyra.* (a) Whole cell. (b) Pellicle and mucilage bodies. (c) Detail of flagellum, showing three types of hair. (d) Cross section through flagellum. (e) Cross section through basal body, showing nine triplet microtubules. (f) Apex of cell, showing the pellicular strips spiralling into the flagellar canal. (g) Cross section through the flagellar canal. (h) Three-dimensional reconstruction of three pellicular strips. AMP = ampulla (reservoir); AX = axoneme, of two central microtubules and nine peripheral doublets; CAN = flagellar canal; CHL = chloroplast; ER = endoplasmic reticulum with ribosomes; ERS = sheath of endoplasmic reticulum around the flagellar canal; F = lipid vesicle; FL = flagellum; FS = flagellar swelling (the probable location of the photoreceptor); G = golgi body; GR = groove on the inner side of a pellicular strip (see RIB); H1 = bundle of 3–4 long hairs, attached to one side of the flagellum; H2 = stiff hairs at the apex of the flagellum; H3 = fine hairs, which form a felty covering over the whole flagellum; LFL = long flagellum; MB = mucilage body; MC = mucilage canal; MT = microtubules; MTS = spirally arranged microtubules; N = nucleus; PA = paramylon; PFR = paraflagellar rod; PM = plasma membrane (plasmalemma); PS = pellicular strip; PV = contractile (pulsing) vacuole; R = ribosomes; RIB = rib running along a pellicular strip, which fits into a groove on the adjacent strip; SFL = short flagellum, which does not emerge from the reservoir; SPIR = spiral line of warts on the pellicle; ST = stigma (eyespot); TPR = tooth-like projections on the inner sides of the pellicular strips. (After [981].)

(Fig. 17.2a; [981, 983]). The canal has a rigid, invariable shape, because its wall is reinforced by inward extensions of the pellicular strips (Fig. 17.2f) and also by a layer of microtubules (each 20–25 nm thick), which run around it in a slight spiral. Here the microtubules are clearly playing a skeletal function. The cytoplasm around them is devoid of ribosomes and is surrounded by a cylindrical sheath of endoplasmic reticulum (Fig. 17.2g).

Unlike the canal, the reservoir has a variable shape, correlated with the fact that it is into the reservoir that the contractile vacuole discharges, at regular intervals. The wall of the reservoir consists only of plasmalemma.

The contractile vacuole

As elsewhere, the contractile vacuole is probably concerned with the osmoregulation of the cell (see p. 312 for an account of contractile vacuole function in *Chlamydomonas*). When full, the contractile vacuole is spherical. It is surrounded by a number of small accessory vacuoles (Figs. 17.2a, 17.6d), which take up liquid and swell as the contractile vacuole itself is discharging its contents into the reservoir. Shortly afterwards they discharge their contents into the contractile vacuole, which therefore begins to grow again.

The flagella

Euglena possesses two flagella. One is short and does not emerge from the ampulla, while the other is long and serves to propel the cell (Fig. 17.2a). This emergent flagellum looks unusually thick in the light microscope and this is because, on one side of the axoneme, the flagellum contains a rod of amorphous material termed the **paraflagellar rod**; this is revealed in thin sections prepared for the electron microscope (Fig. 17.2d; [981, 983]). The electron microscope also reveals that the long, emergent flagellum bears long (2–3 µm) fine hairs, though these are quite different in construction from, and thinner than, the mastigonemes of the Heterokontophyta (Fig. 6.4e, f). The long hairs are arranged in tufts of three to four and form a single row that runs along the flagellum, spiralling slowly around it ([676, 1218]). The emergent flagellum is also covered on all sides by a felt of finer hairs, tufts of which are attached to the tips of intricately ornamented rods lying in helical rows on the surface of the flagellum (Fig. 17.3; [117, 118, 676, 1218]).

During swimming the long flagellum trails beside the body of the cell and performs helical undulations, which pass from the flagellar base to the tip; the helical shape of the flagellar waves probably results from the helical insertion of the long hairs. The movements of the long flagellum cause the cell to swim in a spiral path, wobbling on its axis to a lesser or greater extent as it does so. The flagellar hairs probably increase the thrust of the flagellum against the surrounding water ([126]; see pp. 107, 303 for general remarks on the swimming of flagellate cells).

Both flagella contain two central tubules and nine peripheral doublets (the '9 + 2' structure), as is usual for eukaryote flagella (Figs. 17.2d, 17.4a). Within the cell each flagellum ends in a basal body which, like the flagellum itself, has a typical eukaryote structure, with nine triplets of microtubules (Figs. 17.2e, 17.4a, b). The euglenophytes have a characteristic system of

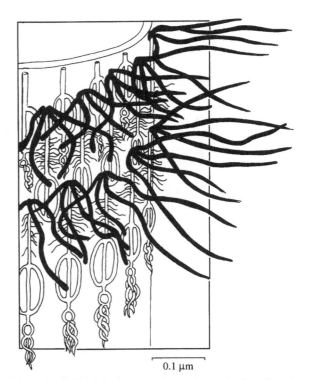

0.1 µm

Figure 17.3. The felty layer of short hairs on the long flagellum of *Euglena*. Bundles of felt hairs are attached to the tips of intricately ornamented rods lying on the surface of the flagellum. These rods are arranged in spiral rows and have their longitudinal axes parallel to the long axis of the flagellum. (Based on [117, 118, 1218].)

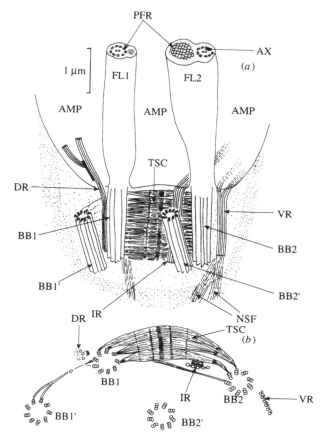

Figure 17.4. The flagellar basal bodies and associated flagellar roots (the flagellar apparatus) in *Entosiphon*, based on electron microscopical observations. (*a*) Three-dimensional reconstruction. (*b*) Cross section of cell, as seen from the cell apex. AMP = ampulla; AX = axoneme; BB1 = basal body of the anterior flagellum; BB1′ = accessory basal body of the anterior flagellum; BB2 = basal body of the posterior, trailing flagellum; BB2′ = accessory basal body of the posterior flagellum; DR = dorsal microtubular root; FL1 = anterior, forwardly directed flagellum; FL2 = posterior, trailing flagellum; IR = intermediate microtubular root; NSF = non-striated fibre; PFR = paraflagellar rod; TSC = transversely striated connective between the basal bodies; VR = ventral microtubular root. (Based on [1661a].)

roots anchoring the flagella in the cell (Fig. 17.4). There are three microtubular roots, composed of various numbers of microtubules (2–8). Two of these are closely associated with the two flagellar basal bodies, while the third lies in between. The three roots extend up towards the tip of the cell along the ampulla. In the example we illustrate (Fig. 17.4), the two flagellar basal bodies are connected by a conspicuous 'transversely striated connective', which is absent in other euglenophytes and therefore not a general feature ([677, 1218, 1349, 1661a, 1899]). In our example, there are also two accessory basal bodies, which are ready for use as flagellar basal bodies after the next cell division.

Eyespot (stigma) and flagellar swelling (Fig. 17.2a)

In *Euglena* and other members of the Euglenophyta the eyespot is not part of the chloroplast, in contrast to the situation in most other classes of algae; it is only in some of the Dinophyta and in the Eustigmatophyceae that the eyespot lies free in the cytoplasm, as in *Euglena* (p. 261). The structure of the eyespot, however, corresponds to what is found elsewhere, consisting of a number of lipid droplets containing red carotenoids (Fig. 17.1*b*). Each droplet is surrounded by its own membrane.

Next to the eyespot, the long flagellum bears a swelling, at around the level where the reservoir narrows into the canal. The flagellar swelling and eyespot (Fig. 17.1*b*) probably act together during the perception of light by the organism, and the swelling has been shown to contain a pigment (a flavoprotein) sensitive to blue light ([1660]). The mechanism by which the cell detects light has already been discussed, in connection with the similarly constructed light receptor organelles of the Chrysophyceae (p. 113).

Chloroplasts

The shape of the chloroplast varies greatly from species to species. In *Euglena spirogyra* (Fig. 17.2*a*) the chloroplasts are small and discoid. Other *Euglena* species, on the other hand, have plate-like chloroplasts with a 'naked' pyrenoid, around which no paramylon accumulates. In still other species paramylon does accumulate near the pyrenoids and indeed forms watch-glass-like plates around them. Euglenophytes can also be found in which the pyrenoids project from the inner sides of the chloroplasts, like the characteristic stalked pyrenoids of the brown algae (Fig. 12.2) and some of the Dinophyta (Fig. 16.6*a*). Extending into the pyrenoids are lamellae composed of two thylakoids .

The chloroplasts have a 35–45 nm wide envelope, which consists of three membranes ([350, 981, 983]); in this they resemble the Dinophyta. It is attractive to interpret the triple membrane as vestigial, having arisen as a result of the endosymbiotic union of a chlorophyte alga (a eukaryotic endosymbiont) with an initially colourless euglenophyte. The innermost two membranes could be interpreted perhaps as homologous with the double membrane envelope around the chlorophyte chloroplast, while the third, outermost membrane could be seen as representing either the membrane of the host's food vacuole, or the plasmalemma of the green algal endosymbiont [350, 511]. A comparable explanation can be applied to the triple membrane present around the chloroplasts of the Dinophyta (cf. p. 255).

If *Euglena gracilis* is grown heterotrophically in the dark, the chloroplasts lose all their chlorophyll and thylakoids in about eight generations (*ca.* 145 h at 21 °C). All that is left after this time are bodies resembling the proplastids found in the meristematic cells of higher plants. These 'proplastids' divide in the dark and so ensure the genetic continuity of the plastidome. When such etiolated (bleached) cultures are returned to the light, even if they have been living in the dark for several years, all the cells become green again, because the colourless proplastids develop back into chloroplasts with thylakoids. Around 6 h after transfer into the light, photosynthesis begins, at about the same time that the first stacks of thylakoids are formed: photosynthesis evidently depends on the presence of thylakoids. Subsequently, over the next 6 h, more stacks of thylakoids are formed, the rate of photosynthesis increasing linearly over this period.

Certain variants of *Euglena gracilis* are interesting in that they lack chloroplasts altogether. The formation of such variants can be induced by growing green cells at sublethal temperatures (32–35 °C); under these conditions the cells themselves continue to divide but the chloroplasts do not. Thus, after several generations cells can be isolated that lack chloroplasts. This is irreversible; the cells are incapable of producing new chloroplasts, showing that in *Euglena* new chloroplasts can be produced only from existing chloroplasts. Chloroplast-free variants of *Euglena gracilis* can also be produced by treating the cells with ultraviolet light, streptomycin, aureomycin, and other antibiotics.

It is now well known that chloroplasts possess their own DNA (and therefore their own genome), which is quite distinct from that of the nucleus; indeed, *Euglena* was one of the first organisms in which chloroplast DNA was demonstrated. The partial genetic autonomy and continuity of chloroplasts is one of the most important arguments for the theory that chloroplasts arose through the endosymbiosis of photosynthetic prokaryotes (p. 2).

The features and possibilities for experimentation that we have outlined explain why *Euglena* species are often used as test organisms in investigations of the biogenesis of chloroplasts, and of the structure and functions of chloroplast genomes [130, 131, 350, 981, 1354, 1558, 1730, 1846].

Reserve polysaccharide

The polysaccharide stored by euglenophyte cells is the glucan paramylon, which is β-1,3 linked, like the chrysolaminaran formed by the Heterokontophyta. Paramylon is produced in the form of granules, which lie in the cytoplasm rather than in the chloroplasts and often have a hollow centre (Fig. 17.2a; [657, 981, 983]). The paramylon granules have a spiral structure. It was originally thought that paramylon occurred only in the Euglenophyta but the haptophyte alga *Pavlova mesolychnon* has since been found also to contain paramylon grains [912].

Nucleus

The chromosomes remain contracted even during interphase, and can be made visible by staining. In this respect, the nuclei of the Euglenophyta resemble those of the Dinophyta (p. 263).

The combination of features exhibited during mitosis (Fig. 17.5) is characteristic of the Euglenophyta. Before mitosis the nucleus migrates forward to the bottom of the reservoir, where the flagella and their basal bodies have already replicated in anticipation of cell division. The two pairs of basal bodies then become associated with the two poles of the spindle. The nuclear envelope remains intact throughout mitosis (which is therefore 'closed') and the nucleolus is also persistent, becoming greatly elongated at metaphase; this is a feature peculiar to the euglenophytes. The spindle consists of pole-to-pole (= interzonal) spindle microtubules and chromosome microtubules, which are attached to the chromosomes by three-layered kinetochores. The chromosomes form an irregular metaphase plate. The nucleus becomes

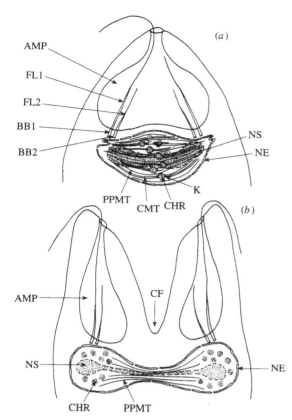

Figure 17.5. Mitosis in *Euglena*. (*a*) Metaphase. (*b*) Telophase. The chromosomes are shown in section, when they appear circular; in reality each is greatly elongate and aligned more or less parallel to the spindle axis. AMP = ampulla; BB1 = basal body of the long flagellum; BB2 = basal body of the short flagellum; CF = cleavage furrow; CHR = chromosome; CMT = chromosomal spindle microtubule; FL1 = long flagellum; FL2 = short flagellum; K = kinetochore; NE = nuclear envelope; NS = nucleolus; PPMT = pole-to-pole (interzonal) spindle microtubule. (Based on [525, 720].)

dumbbell-shaped at telophase, following a great elongation during anaphase, and then a median constriction develops, separating the two daughter nuclei ([525, 981, 1794]).

Cell division and reproduction

During mitosis the ampulla expands laterally and from its floor a new set of flagella arises (Fig. 17.5). Once mitosis is complete the cell cleaves longitudinally, beginning at the anterior end, the division plane spi-

ralling around the cell as division progresses. Sexual reproduction has not been observed.

Mitochondria

Under the light microscope the mitochondria of the Euglenophyta appear for the most part as elongate structures, 0.5–10 µm long, which are sometimes united into networks (Fig. 17.6*a, b*; [983]). In specimens of *Euglena* grown in the light there is a much less well developed system of mitochondria ('chondriome') than in fully heterotrophic, dark-grown organisms (compare Figs. 17.6*a* and 17.6*b*). Chloroplast-free variants also possess a strongly developed 'chondriome'. Mitochondria, of course, are organelles that have an important role in the processes by which cells obtain energy from the oxidative breakdown of organic matter.

The mitochondria of euglenophytes show some features that appear to be unique to the group. Particularly noteworthy are the undulations of the outer membrane and the disc-shaped invaginations ('cristae') of the inner membrane (Figs. 17.1*b*, 17.6*c*; [981, 983]).

Golgi apparatus

The cells of euglenophytes contain one to several golgi bodies, which are distributed throughout the cell, except that there is always a greater concentration of them near the ampulla (Figs. 17.1*a*, 17.2*a*, 17.6*d*; [983]).

Astasia: a colourless member of the Euglenophyta (Fig. 17.6*d*)

Astasia is like a colourless *Euglena*. There are no chloroplasts and no eyespot but each cell contains a great number of mitochondria and many paramylon granules. *Astasia klebsii* is found in polluted freshwaters.

The subdivision of the Euglenophyceae into orders

The current classification of the Euglenophyceae is based on fundamental variation in cell architecture. The following six orders are distinguished ([981, 1848]):

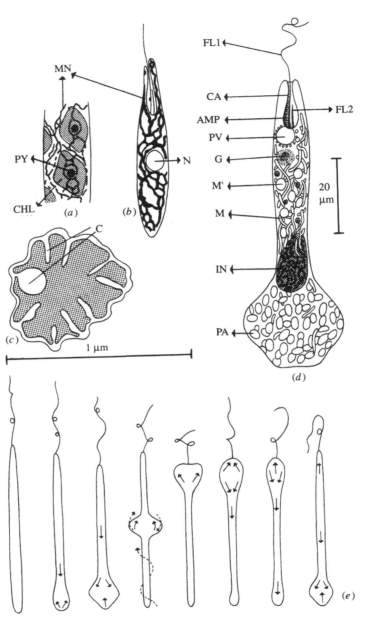

Figure 17.6. (a–c) *Euglena gracilis*. (a) Part of a cell that has been grown in the light. (b) Cell from a dark-grown culture. (c) Cross section through a mitochondrion. (d, e) *Astasia klebsii*, a colourless, heterotrophic species. (d) Structure of the cell. (e) 'Metaboly' (euglenoid movement), involving deformation and spiral movements (dashed arrows) of the pellicle and protoplasmic streaming (solid arrows); these bring about backward movement of the cell (i.e. downwards in the figure). AMP = ampulla; C = cristae; CA = flagellar canal; CHL = chloroplast; FL1 = long flagellum; FL2 = short flagellum; G = golgi body; IN = interphase nucleus; M = elongate mitochondrion; M' = ?round mitochondrion; MN = network of linked mitochondria; N = nucleus; PA = paramylon; PV = contractile (pulsing) vacuole; PY = pyrenoid. (After [981].)

Euglenales*
Eutreptiales*
Euglenamorphales*
Rhabdomonadales
Sphenomonadales
Heteronematales.

Only the orders marked with an asterisk contain both green and colourless species; the remaining orders consist entirely of heterotrophic organisms. The two examples described above – *Euglena* and *Astasia* – both belong to the Euglenales.

18

Chlorarachniophyta

The division Chlorarachniophyta contains only one class, the Chlorarachniophyceae.

The principal characteristics of the Chlorarachniophyta [498, 675, 1381]

1 The cells are naked, amoeboid and uninucleate, and are united via filopodia into net-like plasmodia (Fig. 18.1*a, b*). The cells can transform themselves into coccoid resting stages (Fig. 18.1*c*) or produce uniflagellate reproductive cells (zoospores) (Fig. 18.1*d*).

2 The zoospores are ovoid. Each bears a single flagellum, which is inserted a little below the cell apex. During swimming the flagellum wraps back around the cell in a downward spiral (Fig. 18.1*d*), lying in a groove along the body of the cell. The flagellum bears very delicate hairs, which differ markedly from the stiff, tubular mastigonemes found in the Heterokontophyta (cf. Fig. 6.4*e, f*).

3 There is no photoreceptor apparatus in the zoospore (contrast for instance the Heterokontophyta, Euglenophyta and Chlorophyta, where the photoreceptor apparatus includes an eyespot, and sometimes also a swelling on one flagellum: Figs. 6.3, 17.2 and 19.7*c*).

4 The chloroplasts are bilobed, discoid structures

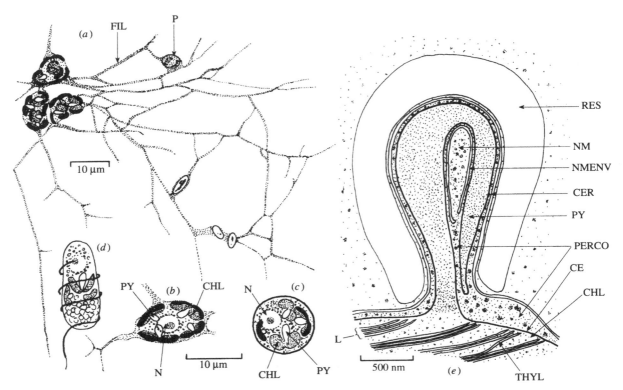

Figure 18.1. *Chlorarachnion.* (*a*) Part of a plasmodium with three individual cells and reticulate filopodia; some of the filopodia have engulfed unicellular prey organisms. (*b*) An individual, naked amoeboid cell. (*c*) A coccoid, walled cell. (*d*) Flagellate zoospore (zoid), with the trailing flagellum wrapped in a spiral around the body of the cell. (*e*) The pyrenoid and the adjacent periplastidial compartment, which is thought to represent the cytoplasm of an endosymbiont; a lobe of the perinuclear compartment extends into the pyrenoid and this contains the nucleomorph, thought to represent the vestigial nucleus of the endosymbiont. Based on electron micrographs. CE = chloroplast envelope, consisting of two membranes; CER = chloroplast endoplasmic reticulum, also consisting of two membranes; CHL = chloroplast; FIL = filopodium; L = lamella, composed of a stack of three thylakoids; N = nucleus; NM = nucleomorph; NMENV = nucleomorph envelope; P = prey organism; PERCO = periplastidial compartment (presumed to represent the endosymbiont cytoplasm); PY = pyrenoid; RES = vesicle containing reserve polysaccharide; THYL = thylakoid. (Based on [498, 675, 1381].)

(Fig. 18.1*b*), which are usually surrounded by four membranes. The inner two are interpreted as the double membrane envelope of the chloroplast itself and the outer two as chloroplast endoplasmic reticulum (Fig. 18.1*e*). The envelope is therefore similar to that of the Heterokontophyta (Fig. 6.4*d*), except that the central pair of membranes in the chlorarachniophyte chloroplast sometimes fuse to form flattened vesicles; on occasions they can apparently even combine into a single membrane (Fig. 18.1*e*).

5 Within the chloroplast the thylakoids are usually grouped into stacks (lamellae) of one to three (Fig. 18.1*e*). No girdle lamella is present (girdle lamellae are lamellae that encircle and enclose all the other lamellae; they are characteristic of most groups within the Heterokontophyta: Fig. 6.4*d*).

6 There is a conspicuous, pear-shaped pyrenoid, which protrudes from the inner side of the chloroplast (Fig. 18.1*b, e*). Around it is a vesicle containing reserve polysaccharide, probably

paramylon, situated outside the four-membrane chloroplast envelope. The pyrenoid is not penetrated by thylakoids.

7 The chloroplasts contain chlorophylls a and b, as in the Euglenophyta and Chlorophyta; chlorophyll c is absent.

8 As the chlorophyll is not masked by accessory photosynthetic pigments, the chloroplasts are bright green. The nature of the carotenoids present is not yet known ([675]).

9 A peculiar organelle, the nucleomorph, is present in a pocket of cytoplasm lying in a depression in the surface of the pyrenoid, between the chloroplast envelope (the two innermost membranes around the chloroplast) and the chloroplast endoplasmic reticulum. The nucleomorph contains DNA and a nucleolus-like body, and is surrounded by a double membrane penetrated by pores ([1050]). It can be interpreted perhaps as the vestigial nucleus of a photosynthetic, eukaryotic endosymbiont (probably a chlorophyte), which became incorporated into the heterotrophic amoeboid ancestor of the Chlorarachniophyta. The compartment of the cell surrounded by the chloroplast ER would then be interpreted as the vestigial cytoplasm of the endosymbiont. Support for this idea is given by the fact that *Chlorarachnion* has a capacity for phagotrophic feeding: it engulfs and digests cells of various unicellular algae in its food vacuoles ([498, 675]).

Similar nucleomorphs occur in the Cryptophyta (cf. p. 237).

10 A scatter of trichocysts is present below the plasmalemma.

So far, the only known representatives of the division Chlorarachniophyta are two species, belonging to two different genera ([184, 675]). Both have been found associated with cultures of tropical or subtropical siphonous green algae.

This group is especially interesting to phylogeneticists, since it provides important additional evidence for the hypothesis that many groups of eukaryotic algae have arisen through the incorporation of other eukaryotic algae as endosymbionts within colourless, heterotrophic protozoa (see character 9 above). This seems to have happened again and again in the course of evolution. Other persuasive examples include some of the Cryptophyta (which, like the Chlorarachniophyta, have nucleomorphs; p. 237) and certain Dinophyta (p. 251).

19

Chlorophyta (green algae)

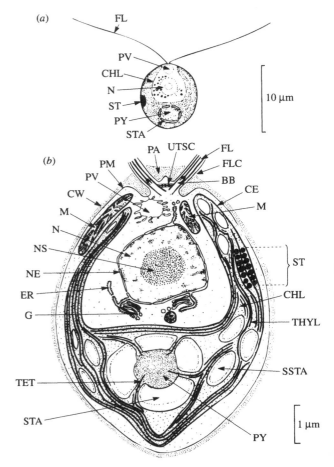

Figure 19.1. *Chlamydomonas reinhardtii:* a zoid with a cruciate 1 o'clock – 7 o'clock type of architecture. (*a*) Light microscopical image. (*b*) Longitudinal section, based on EM observations. BB = basal body; CE = chloroplast envelope; CHL = chloroplast; CW = cell wall; ER = endoplasmic reticulum; FL = flagellum; FLC = flagellar channel or canal; G = golgi body; M = mitochondrion; N = nucleus; NE = nuclear envelope; NS = nucleolus; PA = apical papilla; PM = plasma membrane (plasmalemma); PV = contractile (pulsing) vacuole; PY = pyrenoid; SSTA = stroma starch; ST = stigma (eyespot); STA = starch grains around the pyrenoid; TET = tubular extension of a thylakoid into the pyrenoid; THYL = thylakoid; UTSC = upper transversely striated connective, linking the basal bodies. (*a* based on [382]; *b* on [1501].)

The principal characteristics of the Chlorophyta

1 The zoids (flagellate cells) are isokont, which means that the flagella are similar in structure, though they may differ in length. There are usually two flagella per cell but there can also be four or many (Figs. 19.1*a*, 19.4, 19.15).

2 The flagella lack the tubular hairs of the Heterokontophyta but they may bear various kinds of very delicate hairs and scales (Figs. 19.2*e*, 19.9*c*, 19.15).

3 Between the flagellar axoneme and the basal body there is a stellate transition zone (Fig. 19.4).

4 The chloroplast is enclosed only by the double membrane of the chloroplast envelope; there is no additional envelope of endoplasmic reticulum (Figs. 19.1*b*, 19.7*c*, 19.8, 19.15*b*). In this respect they resemble the Rhodophyta, Glaucophyta, Bryophyta and Tracheophyta.

5 Within the chloroplasts the thylakoids are grouped to form lamellae (stacks formed by apposition of thylakoids over much of their surface area) containing anything from two to six or more thylakoids, pseudograna (stacks formed by the partial overlap of thylakoids), or grana (discrete, almost columnar stacks of thylakoids

with few connections to each other) (Figs. 19.7*c*, *e*, 19.8). Girdle lamellae (peripheral lamellae encircling all the other thylakoids, as in the Heterokontophyta) are absent.

6 The chloroplasts are green, because the chlorophyll is not masked by accessory pigments. Chlorophylls a and b are present. This character is shared by the Prochlorophyta, Euglenophyta, Chlorarachniophyta, Bryophyta and Tracheophyta. In addition, a chlorophyll resembling chlorophyll c is present in a few species of the class Prasinophyceae (p. 337).

7 The Chlorophyta have a characteristic set of accessory pigments, including the xanthophylls lutein, zeaxanthin, violaxanthin, antheraxanthin and neoxanthin. Siphonein and siphonoxanthin occur in the class Bryopsidophyceae, although siphonoxanthin is also to be found in scattered representatives of other classes ([544, 776, 815, 1861, 1931]).

8 Pyrenoids, where present, are embedded within the chloroplast and are often penetrated by thylakoids. Each is surrounded by a shell of starch grains (Figs. 19.1, 19.7e, 19.9c, 19.13c).

9 The most important reserve polysaccharide is starch, which occurs as grains. These can be clustered around the pyrenoids (if present) but are also to be found scattered through the chloroplast stroma (Fig. 19.1).

10 The circular molecules of chloroplast DNA are concentrated in numerous small (1–2 μm diameter) blobs (nucleoids), which are distributed throughout the chloroplast. The DNA is never organized in a single ring-like nucleoid ([254]).

On the basis of the characteristics they share with each other (see above), the green algae appear to form a natural division, well differentiated from all other groups of algae. It is much more difficult, however, to separate the green algae from the bryophytes and vascular plants. All the characters we have listed are also shared by higher plants, or at least by those higher plants with flagellate stages in their life cycles. Hence in a natural classification both the vascular plants (Tracheophyta) and the mosses and liverworts (Bryophyta) could be included within the Chlorophyta ([440, 703]). Here, however, we treat the two enormous groups of terrestrial plants as belonging to two separate divisions, although it must be remembered that they have a very close evolutionary relationship to the Chlorophyta (see Chapter 31; Figs. 31.2, 31.3).

Size and distribution of the division

The division (= phylum) Chlorophyta contains around 500 genera and approximately 8000 species. A lot of these live in freshwater but there are also many marine and terrestrial species. In three classes all of the species (in the Zygnematophyceae and Charophyceae) or most of them (in the Chlorophyceae) are restricted to freshwater. Four other classes (the Ulvophyceae, Cladophorophyceae, Bryopsidophyceae and Dasycladophyceae), on the other hand, are almost exclusively marine.

The division includes many unicellular and colonial planktonic algae but there are also many unicellular or multicellular forms that live in the benthos, growing attached to rocks (epilithically) or other plants (as epiphytes); some of these are macroscopic. Many filamentous green algae are attached to a substratum during the early stages of their development but later become free-floating, forming mats or balls composed of many intertwined filaments. Particularly striking are the green growths and mats of chlorophytes that sometimes cover the surfaces of ditches and ponds, especially in the early part of the year in temperate regions.

On rocky sea coasts green algae are particularly abundant and dominant in the upper part of the intertidal zone. Here rocks are often completely covered with green algae, including species of the genera *Ulva* (sea lettuce; p. 403, Fig. 22.10), *Enteromorpha* (p. 405, Fig. 22.11) and *Ulothrix* (only in spring; p. 394, Fig. 22.2). Species of *Ulva* and *Enteromorpha* can also form dense growths on sandy shores and mudflats in protected, still environments, forming a green carpet over the sediment at low tide. In Japan *Ulva* and *Enteromorpha* species are grown for food. They are cultivated in nutrient-rich bays or estuaries, where they are grown attached to racks or nets, using methods similar to those described already for the cultivation of *Porphyra* (p. 66).

The sandy or muddy bottoms of tropical lagoons often bear impressive growths, one to several centimetres high, composed of species belonging to the genera *Caulerpa*, *Udotea*, *Penicillus* and *Halimeda* (Figs. 24.11, 24.12, 24.15). The *Caulerpa* species are anchored in the sediment by creeping 'stolons', while the basal parts of *Udotea*, *Penicillus* and *Halimeda* are swollen and bulbous.

Some other green algae are aerophytic, living on

tree trunks, soil and rocks. These include species of *Trebouxia* (p. 449, Fig. 27.1*a-c*), which are unicellular coccoid algae, and the filamentous alga *Trentepohlia* (p. 448, Fig. 26.1). Species of these genera are often also found as the symbiotic algae ('phycobionts' or 'photobionts') within lichens. In this symbiosis the photosynthetic products of the alga are used principally by the fungal partner.

Even snow and ice can be covered with green algae ([716]). Thus, for instance, *Chlamydomonas nivalis* can be found high in the mountains on permanent snow, colouring it red. In this species the chlorophyll is masked by 'haematochrome', which is a mixture of carotenoid pigments.

The structure and characteristics of the Chlorophyta: their use for the separation of classes

Electron microscopical investigations carried out in the past 20 years have gradually led to a thorough re-evaluation of evolutionary relationships both within the Chlorophyta and between the Chlorophyta and the higher plants (vascular plants and bryophytes).

According to recent thinking it is the architecture of the flagellate cell (the zoid) that provides the most important characters for distinguishing the main evolutionary lineages (the classes) within the green algae. This is based on the idea that the flagellate cell is a repository for 'primitive' (i.e. evolutionarily old) characters: its architecture tends to be highly conservative. Thus, for instance, the same '9 + 2' flagellar structure is found in a wide variety of eukaryotic organisms (e.g. most algae, some fungi, mosses, ferns, cycads and animals) and has clearly been strongly conserved during evolution. In addition the complexity of the flagellar apparatus means that comparisons between zoids are possible over a great many characters.

Traditionally the unicellular flagellate *Chlamydomonas* (Fig. 19.1) has been considered to represent the ancestral type of green alga, the 'Ur-chlorophyte', from which all other chlorophytes developed in the course of evolution (e.g. [440, 703]). At present, however, we believe that there are at least four fundamentally different types of flagellate cell within the Chlorophyta ([704]) and these are described in the next section; other types of zoid may well await discovery.

The processes of nuclear division (mitosis) and cell division (cytokinesis) also provide important characters for distinguishing the main evolutionary lineages in the Chlorophyta. Mitosis is a very precise mechanism, which ensures that the two daughter nuclei of dividing eukaryote cells receive identical genomes. Likewise, cytokinesis ensures that each daughter cell receives an equal (or at least adequate) complement of cell organelles, including one daughter nucleus. Mitosis and cytokinesis are essential processes in eukaryotes and they are therefore thought to be evolutionarily conservative, retaining old characteristics while other morphological and physiological features undergo selection and change. In the Chlorophyta at least eight groups can be distinguished on the basis of differences in mitosis and cytokinesis ([704]). These will be described in a separate section (pp. 323–34).

Other kinds of characters can also be used for the subdivision of the Chlorophyta and these include the following: the level of organization and morphology of the thallus; the structure of the chloroplasts; the composition of the photosynthetic pigments; storage products; the structure and composition of the cell wall or envelope; and the type of life history.

Types of flagellate cell architecture in the Chlorophyta I. The cruciate 1 o'clock – 7 o'clock type: *Chlamydomonas*, a free-living unicellular flagellate chlorophyte (Figs. 19.1 – 19.8, 19.18; [1784])

The unicellular algae classified in the genus *Chlamydomonas* are egg-shaped or ellipsoidal or spherical. They have two equal flagella, which arise one on each side of an apical papilla at the anterior end of the cell. The cells are surrounded by a wall-like envelope, except where the flagella emerge.

The architecture of the flagellate *Chlamydomonas* cell will be discussed more extensively than the architecture of other types of green algal flagellate. It will be used to illustrate the features generally present in the flagellate cells of algae, and in particular those present in green algae. The structure, physiology, biochemistry and genetics of *Chlamydomonas*, which is a famous 'laboratory organism', have been reviewed in a recent monograph ([612]).

Cell envelope (Fig. 19.7)

The envelope or 'wall' around the cells of *Chlamydomonas* and related genera is unusual in that it consists only of fibrous glycoproteins (proteins with carbohydrates as prosthetic groups). It does not contain polysaccharides, unlike the cell walls of most other algae. The protein fraction is rich in hydroxyproline, to which oligosaccharides are attached, while the carbohydrate fraction consists mainly of galactose, arabinose, mannose and glucose. The envelope is three-layered, containing a central granular layer sandwiched between highly ordered, crystalline lattices of glycoprotein subunits (Fig. 19.7d; [196, 197, 540, 687, 751, 989, 1133, 1502, 1503, 1504]).

The envelope of *Chlamydomonas* is formed outside the cell, against the outer side of the plasmalemma. This is in sharp contrast to the walls of the Dinophyceae and Bacillariophyceae, where the cell wall elements are formed in flat vesicles beneath the plasmalemma. It is also unlike the envelopes of the Haptophyta and Prasinophyceae, which are composed of scales secreted from the golgi apparatus. The apical papilla is a nodular thickening of the envelope at the anterior end of the cell. On either side of it the envelope is pierced by two canals, through which the flagella project (Fig. 19.1).

Flagellar apparatus (Figs. 19.1, 19.3 – 19.6)

Chlamydomonas is **isokont**, which means that its two flagella are similar in structure. The flagella are of equal length and arise at the anterior end of the cell, on either side of the apical papilla; they are about 0.3 μm thick. They can be seen with the light microscope in living cells, but observation is made difficult by their rapid beat. Although the flagellar beat of *Chlamydomonas* is often said to be similar to breast stroke, this is only partly correct. The backward stroke of a swimmer produces a forward momentum that enables him to coast while he moves his arms forward for the next stroke. As water is a viscous, syrupy fluid for tiny cells like *Chlamydomonas* (Fig. 19.1), coasting is not possible. During the effective stroke the flagella push more syrupy water backwards than adheres to them during the forward recovery stroke, thus bringing about net forward movement ([415, 1640]) (Fig. 19.2c). During forward swimming, when the cells perform ciliary beat-

ing (Fig. 19.2c), the cells can reach speeds of *ca.* 100–400 μm s^{-1}. Sometimes the cells swim backwards, during which the flagella perform undulatory movements (Fig. 19.2d).

In many ways the flagella are autonomous organelles, since if detached from the cell they can still execute undulatory movements, provided that they are supplied with ATP ([16, 149, 230, 1308, 1691]).

Both flagella have a short blunt tip. They are covered with very fine hairs, around 0.9 μm long ([1501]; Fig. 19.2e), each one consisting of a chain of ellipsoidal glycoprotein units ([1218, 1784, 1909]).

The flagella have the '9 + 2' structure characteristic of the flagella of almost all eukaryotic cells. This '9 + 2' structure constitutes the flagellar **axoneme**. In the centre of the axoneme there are two single microtubules (the central pair) and these are surrounded by a cylinder containing nine doublet microtubules. The two central microtubules are similar to the countless microtubules found in the cytoplasm of all kinds of eukaryotic cells, whatever their structure or function. Each one is a hollow tube of protein with a diameter of 25 nm (Fig. 19.3d). In cross section the microtubule can be seen to consist of a ring of 13 globular subunits. These correspond to 13 longitudinal rows or 'protofilaments', which are tightly associated laterally to form the tube (Fig. 19.3d). Each protofilament is itself composed of a line of dimers and each dimer consists of a molecule of α-tubulin and a molecule of β-tubulin. The two types of tubulin are both polypeptides and they have very similar amino acid sequences. A pool of depolymerized tubulins is generally present in the cytoplasm and microtubules are assembled from this whenever and wherever necessary. Thus, at mitosis, for example, tubulin is assembled into the microtubules of the spindle (Fig. 19.18a). First, microtubules become attached to the chromosomes and group them at the equator of the spindle; then the daughter chromatids are pulled apart as the microtubules shorten, owing to depolymerization at one or both ends ([16]).

Microtubules often have a skeletal function. Thus, where naked (or at least wall-less) cells have shapes that deviate strongly from the spherical, microtubules are usually to be found supporting the ridges, projections or depressions. For instance, microtubules line the cleavage furrow of *Chlamydomonas* (Fig. 19.2a) and occur around the flagellar canal of *Euglena* (Fig. 17.1b, 17.2g), while, as will be described in detail

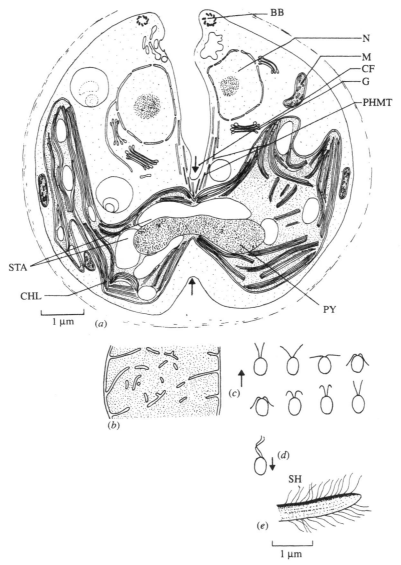

Figure 19.2. (*a*) *Chlamydomonas:* division of the cell, chloroplast and pyrenoid. (*b*) Section through part of the plastid of *Polytoma*. (*c–e*) *Chlamydomonas*. (*c*) Forward swimming, involving breaststroke motion of flagella. (*d*) Backward swimming, as a result of undulatory motion of flagella. (*e*) Detail of the flagellar tip. BB = basal body; CF = cleavage furrow; CHL = chloroplast, shortly before it divides; G = golgi body; M = mitochondrion; N = nucleus; PHMT = phycoplast microtubules (= cleavage microtubules); PY = elongate, bilobate pyrenoid, shortly before division; SH = short, fine, flexible hairs borne laterally by the flagellum; STA = starch grains. (*a* after [538]; *b* after [962]; *c–e* after [1501].)

later, the flagellar apparatus itself is anchored in the cell by sets of microtubular 'roots' (Figs. 19.6, 19.13*c*).

Microtubules are apparently highly conservative organelles, which occur throughout the eukaryotes, performing a variety of roles. They form the principal structural component of the flagellar axoneme, which, like the microtubule itself, is basically similar and

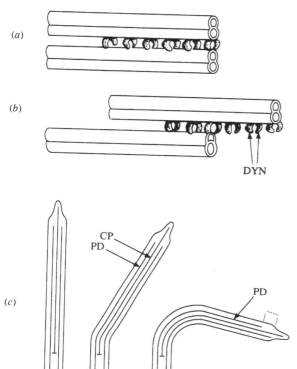

(a)

(b)

DYN

(c)

CP
PD

PD

Figure 19.3. (*a, b*) Diagrams showing how the peripheral doublets of the flagellar axoneme slide over each other. After the addition of ATP, the upper doublet slides over the lower one, as the dynein arms 'walk' along it (like a millipede). (*c*) In the intact flagellum, the sliding of adjacent doublets is restricted by various structures that ensure the cohesion of the axoneme (e.g. nexin linkages and radial spokes), so that the sliding movement is transformed into a bending of the flagellum. (*d*) Cross section of microtubule. (*e*) Side view of a microtubule. (*f*) Cross section of a flagellum, as seen from the cell, showing the fine structure of the axoneme. Some of the features are not widely distributed in eukaryotes, such as the beak-like internal projection of one B microtubule, and the bipartite bridge replacing one dynein arm. A = A microtubule of a peripheral doublet; B = B microtubule of peripheral doublet; B* = B microtubule with beak-like internal projection; BR = bipartite bridge where outer dynein arm is missing; CP = central pair of microtubules of the axoneme; CPMT = one of the two central axoneme microtubules; DYN = dynein arms; IS = inner sheath; NL = nexin link; PD = peripheral doublet; PFIL = protofilaments; PM = plasma membrane (plasmalemma); RS = radial spoke; TUB = tubulin heterodimer, composed of α and β subunits. (Based on [16, 731, 1691].)

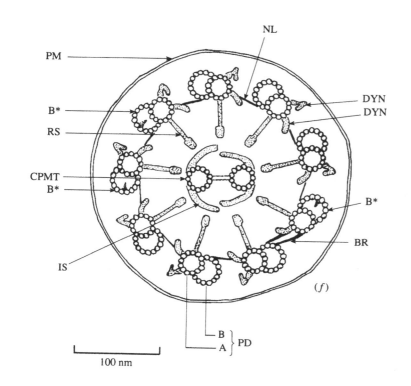

(f)

NL

PM

B*

RS

CPMT
B*

IS

DYN
DYN

B*

BR

B ⎱
A ⎰ PD

100 nm

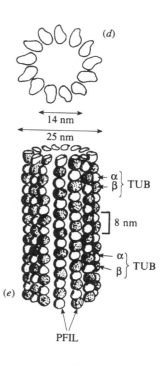

(d)

14 nm

25 nm

α ⎱
β ⎰ TUB

8 nm

α ⎱
β ⎰ TUB

(e)

PFIL

evolutionarily conservative within the Eukaryota. Fig. 19.3f shows a transverse section through a flagellum with its axoneme. The central pair has already been described. Each of the nine outer doublets contains one complete microtubule of 13 protofilaments, called the A-tubule. Connected to it is an incomplete microtubule made of 10 protofilaments, termed the B-tubule; this is C-shaped in section. The doublets and the central pair are interconnected by several different kinds of proteinaceous linkages (see Fig. 19.3f). Between the doublets and the central pair there are radial spokes, while the doublets themselves are interconnected by nexin. In addition, each A-tubule bears two rows of arms made of the protein dynein. These project out towards the B-tubule of the next doublet and are involved in generating the movements of the flagella; the doublets are made to slide past each other as the dynein arms of one doublet 'walk' along the B-tubule of the next doublet (Fig. 19.3a, b). This has been demonstrated very elegantly in isolated axonemes, in which the radial spokes and nexin linkages have been digested enzymatically, using trypsin. When ATP is added to such preparations the doublets slide over each other through the activity of the dynein arms. In the intact axoneme the shear resistance offered by the radial spokes and the nexin links between the doublets converts the sliding movements of the doublets into a bending of the whole flagellum, or part of it (Fig. 19.3c; [16, 352, 1691]). In *Chlamydomonas* pairs of flagella can be detached from cells by osmotic shock. Upon addition of ATP the flagella perform the characteristic 'breast stroke' exhibited by intact cells as they swim forwards (Fig. 19.2c). If calcium is supplied (to a concentration above 10^{-6} M Ca^{2+}) the flagella change to an undulatory movement, which causes intact cells to swim backwards ([773]; for a review see [1186]).

In each experimentally isolated pair, the two flagella form a V and microscopical examination reveals that they remain connected at their bases by a robust, transversely striated fibre (the upper connective in Figs. 19.4, 19.6). This structure is a characteristic feature of *Chlamydomonas* and related genera. In isolated flagellar pairs, the flagella beat in a highly coordinated way, which suggests that the transversely striated connection between them may exchange signals between the flagella, so that their activity is linked ([154, 988, 1174, 1218, 1501]). There are also two other transversely striated

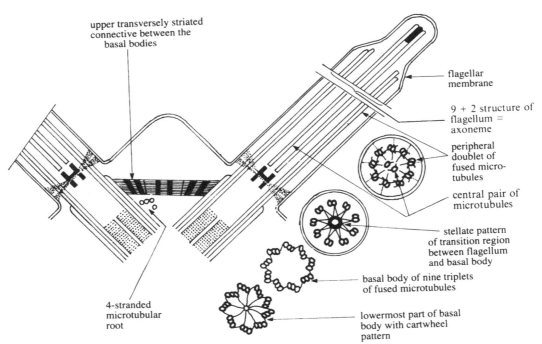

upper transversely striated connective between the basal bodies

flagellar membrane

9 + 2 structure of flagellum = axoneme

peripheral doublet of fused microtubules

central pair of microtubules

stellate pattern of transition region between flagellum and basal body

basal body of nine triplets of fused microtubules

lowermost part of basal body with cartwheel pattern

4-stranded microtubular root

Figure 19.4. *Chlamydomonas reinhardtii*. Longitudinal section through the flagellar apparatus, shown diagrammatically.

structures, which connect the lower parts of the basal bodies, and these too may perhaps be involved in the coordination of flagellar activity (Fig. 19.6). In their transverse striation and fibrous appearance, the upper and lower connectives resemble the rhizoplasts found, for example, in *Pyramimonas* and *Tetraselmis* (Figs. 19.9c, 19.11, 19.12). These are massive, elongate structures, which extend down into the cell from the flagellar basal bodies, often connecting them to the nucleus and plasmalemma. Rhizoplasts have been shown, quite indisputably, to be contractile organelles (a kind of cellular muscle; see p. 318), and this suggests that the connecting fibres in *Chlamydomonas* may also be contractile ([1174]). An alternative or additional function may be to act like elastic bands, stretching during the downward effector stroke of the flagella and then springing back at the beginning of the recovery stroke (Fig. 19.2c).

Chlamydomonas has two rhizoplasts, which connect the basal bodies with the nucleus (Fig. 19.6c). They are much more delicate than the rhizoplasts of *Pyramimonas* and *Tetraselmis* and lack their prominent transverse striations ([394, 774, 830, 987, 1183, 1541]). All rhizoplasts consist predominantly of bundles of filaments of the contractile protein **centrin**. Contraction is brought about by supercoiling of the centrin filaments (cf. contraction in *Tetraselmis*, Fig. 19.2) and results in an upward displacement and deformation of the nucleus (Fig. 19.6c); this is accompanied by shedding of the flagella. Contraction is induced by environmental stress, such as pH shock or mechanical shear, but its biological significance is unclear. The transversely striated connectives we have described, which link the basal bodies of *Chlamydomonas*, also contain centrin ([1541]). Indeed, centrin is found widely, not only in green algae, but in many other algal phyla, usually in the form of rhizoplasts. This has been demonstrated by raising antibodies against *Tetraselmis*-centrin, marking them with fluorescent dyes or gold particles, and using the antibodies to screen for centrin in other organisms; the dyes and gold are detected by fluorescence microscopy and electron microscopy, respectively (i.e. indirect immunofluorescence and immunogold electron microscopy). Centrin-based contractile organelles may well be as ubiquitous in eukaryotic cells as microtubules and axonemes, and consequently just as ancient evolutionarily ([1177, 1590, 1591, 1592]).

So far, in our account of the flagella, we have confined our attention to the structure of the axoneme,

with its '9 + 2' arrangement of microtubules. Nearer the base of the flagellum, however, just above where it emerges from the cell, the axoneme passes into the so-called **transition region**, between the flagellum proper and the basal body. In *Chlamydomonas* the transition region contains structures which appear stellate in cross section; this **stellate pattern** is characteristic of the Chlorophyta, Bryophyta and Tracheophyta ([193, 1217, 1218]) and differs from the structures found in the transition region in other algal divisions. The central pair of microtubules terminates just above the transition region (Fig. 19.4) and immediately below this, within the axonemal cylinder of nine doublets, there is a beaker-like body, consisting of the upper part of the stellate structure and a transition septum. Under this is the ring-like lower part of the stellate structure. In longitudinal section the beaker and the ring together make an 'H', while in transverse section the structure appears as a central cylinder surrounded by a 9-pointed star, which forms links between the cylinder and the axonemal doublets. The star, like the basal body connectives and the rhizoplasts, appears to contain the contractile protein centrin ([1541]).

Immediately above the transition zone with its stellate pattern is an abscission zone, where the flagellum is shed upon irritation of the cell. Abscission can take less than a second to occur and entails loosening of the flagellar membrane from the axoneme, constriction of the membrane, local digestion or disassembly of material in the core of the flagellum, and rupture of the nine doublets, as a result of an inward contraction of the star structure. The plasmalemma then closes over the stump (Fig. 19.5; [1000, 1541]).

Inside the cell each axoneme ends in a basal body (Fig. 19.4). This is composed of nine interconnected triplets of microtubules, the inner two of which are continuous with the doublet microtubules of the flagellar axoneme. The third microtubule is like the 'B' microtubule of the axoneme (to which it is partly fused) in that it is incomplete, containing only 10 protofilaments. In the lowermost part of the basal body the triplets are connected to a central cylinder by delicate spokes, the whole presenting a cart-wheel pattern when sectioned transversely (Fig. 19.4); this pattern, in contrast to the stellate structure of the flagellar transition region, is not restricted to the Chlorophyta.

One important function of the basal body is to act as a template for the assembly of the flagellar axoneme. Tubulin can assemble spontaneously *in vitro* into micro-

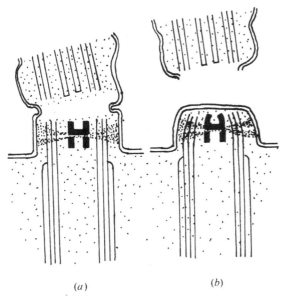

(a)   (b)

Figure 19.5. (a, b) Two stages in the abscission of a flagellum, which occurs just above the transition zone:
compare with Fig. 19.4. (Based on [1000].)

tubules, but formation of the axoneme is only possible
if basal bodies or partly formed axonemes are already
present ([16]). Flagellar axonemes grow by addition of
tubulin subunits to the distal (upper) ends of the
peripheral doublets but to the proximal (lower) ends of
the central pair of microtubules ([303]). Growth occurs
naturally after shedding of the flagella following
shock (see above), or after withdrawal of the flagella
prior to cell division. During withdrawal the doublet
microtubules are disassembled from the flagellum tip
downwards and the tubulin subunits are returned to a
cellular pool, from which they can subsequently be
withdrawn again during flagellar growth; deflagella-
tion also stimulates the synthesis of new tubulin ([16, 155,
159, 1462]).

In many eukaryotic organisms a pair of centrioles is
present at each pole of the mitotic spindle. Centrioles
are ultrastructurally similar to basal bodies, consisting
of a short cylinder of nine microtubular triplets, and it
would therefore seem likely for them to be involved in
the assembly and arrangement of the microtubules
making up the spindle. In some eukaryotes, however,
the spindle poles lack centrioles and yet the spindle
can form and function normally. This fact is used as an
argument against the centrioles themselves being the

microtubule organizing centres (MTOCs or centro-
somes) for the spindle, this function being ascribed
instead to amorphous masses of darkly staining material present at the mitotic poles ([1218, 1419]); the true
MTOCs may or may not have a pair of centrioles
embedded within them. The significance of the centriolar pairs, which replicate during cell division, is now
thought to be that they transmit the capacity to form
flagella from one cell generation to another ([1218]).
Labelled antibodies raised against one of the protein
components of the amorphous material surrounding
the centrioles have been used to stain, and hence
detect, MTOCs in animal and plant cells using fluorescence microscopy ([16]). Recently this method has per-
mitted the detection of MTOC protein at the poles of
the mitotic spindle in a green alga belonging to the
class Cladophorophyceae ([958]). The occurrence of very
similar MTOC proteins in evolutionarily distantly
related organisms suggests that MTOCs appeared
early in the evolution of the eukaryotes and that they
are as ancient and primaeval as microtubules, axonemes and centrin-based organelles (e.g. rhizoplasts).

The two basal bodies of Chlamydomonas lie at
angles of about 90° to each other (Figs. 19.1, 19.4), in
a V configuration. At mitosis they, or more likely the
material surrounding them, act as microtubule organizing centres (see p. 326, Fig. 19.17 II; [1791]).

The flagella are anchored in the cell by four microtubular roots, which can be seen to be arranged in a
cross if the cell is viewed from the anterior end (Fig.
19.6). Two of these four **cruciately arranged microtubular roots** contain two microtubules, while the
other two contain four; the two-stranded roots lie
opposite each other ([542, 1165, 1217, 1501]). The roots
diverge from the basal bodies and run beneath the
plasmalemma towards the posterior of the cell. It is
likely that one function of the microtubular roots is to
anchor the flagellar apparatus in the cell; in addition
they may function as a cellular skeleton.

Cruciate arrangements of microtubular roots are
widespread among green algae ([1217]). In many cases
two of the roots (lying opposite each other) are two-
membered, as in Chlamydomonas, and indeed they
occupy the same positions as the two-membered roots
of Chlamydomonas. The other two roots always contain the same number of microtubules as each other,
but the number varies from taxon to taxon (from 3 to 8
microtubules). The general arrangement of microtubular roots is therefore 'x–2–x–2' ([1217]).

Viewed from the top of the cell (Fig. 19.6a) the whole complex of basal bodies and microtubular roots exhibits neither radial nor bilateral symmetry.

However, if one of the basal bodies, with its associated roots, were to be rotated through 180° it would almost exactly mirror the other basal body with its associated

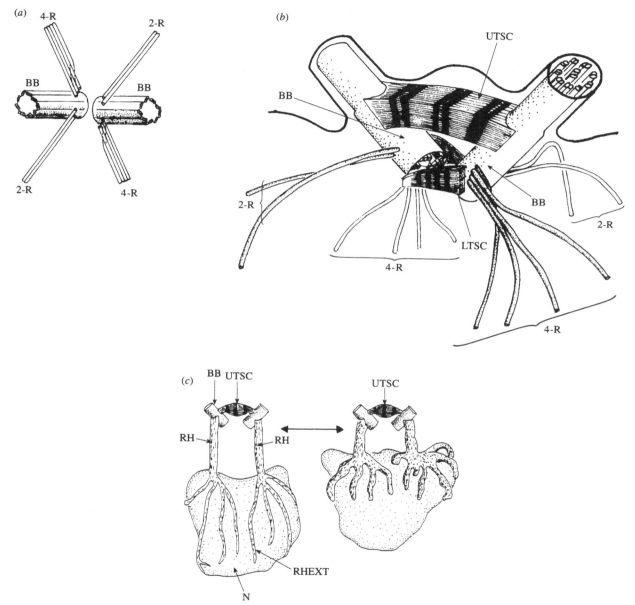

Figure 19.6. The flagellar apparatus of *Chlamydomonas reinhardtii*, a zoid of the cruciate 1 o'clock – 7 o'clock type. (*a*) Top view, showing the arrangement of the basal bodies and the four microtubular roots. (*b*) Three-dimensional view of the flagellar apparatus, as seen from the side. (*c*) The two rhizoplasts connecting the basal bodies to the nucleus, relaxed (left)

and contracted (right). BB = basal body; LTSC = lower transversely striated connective; N = nucleus; RH = rhizoplast; RHEXT = extension or branch of rhizoplast; UTSC = upper transversely striated connective; 2-R = two-stranded microtubular root; 4-R = four-stranded microtubular root. (*a* based on [1140]; *b* original; *c* based on [1541].)

two microtubular roots; some investigators therefore describe the x–2–x–2 pattern as having '**180° rotational symmetry**' [423].

The top, plan view of the two basal bodies and their attached microtubular roots shown in Fig. 19.6a illustrates a feature which, although subtle, is apparently of great significance, since it characterizes a whole evolutionary lineage within the green algae, namely the class Chlorophyceae. The basal bodies are not exactly aligned, but slightly displaced with respect to each other; this is also shown in Fig. 19.14 c-1 (except that here the whole flagellar apparatus has been rotated through 90°). Some other green algae, for instance those belonging to the class Ulvophyceae, also have a cruciate arrangement of the flagellar roots, but with an opposite displacement of the basal bodies. Fig. 19.14 (p. 324) illustrates the configuration of the basal bodies and microtubular roots in *Chlamydomonas*, as a representative of the Chlorophyceae (Fig. 19.14 c-1), and the configuration in a member of the Ulvophyceae (Fig. 19.14 b-1). In order to facilitate comparison we have also included a hypothetical 'ancestral' configuration (Fig. 19.14 a-1), from which both the chlorophycean and the ulvophycean arrangements might have been derived; recently this 'ancestral' type of arrangement has been discovered in several representatives of the Chlorophyceae [1857, 1894]. In the ancestral type the basal bodies, seen from above, are in line with each other. In the chlorophycean configuration, however, there has been a slight **clockwise rotation** with respect to the ancestral arrangement (Fig. 19.14 a-1), while in the ulvophycean configuration there has been an opposite, **anti-clockwise rotation**. Or, to express this in a different way, if in the ancestral configuration the basal bodies are said to be at 12 and 6 o'clock, in the Chlorophyceae they are at 1 and 7 o'clock, and in the Ulvophyceae at 11 and 5 o'clock. To summarize: **the basal bodies of *Chlamydomonas* show a 1 o'clock – 7 o'clock configuration**, i.e. a **clockwise rotation** [1140, 1326, 1328, 1643]. A similar configuration of the basal bodies occurs in the zoids of other Chlorophyceae (e.g. Fig. 21.17h).

Chloroplast (Figs. 19.1, 19.8)

In most *Chlamydomonas* species the chloroplast is cup-shaped and lies against the cell envelope (i.e. it is parietal) but many species have chloroplasts of other types (e.g. in Fig. 21.3g; [381, 382]). The base of the cup is thickened and it is here that the pyrenoid is located.

The chloroplast is surrounded by a double chloroplast membrane. Each membrane is about 5 nm thick, while the distance between them is *ca.* 6–10 nm. Within the chloroplast are the thylakoids, which are grouped into stacks of various sizes (2–6, sometimes up to 20).

The circular chloroplast DNA molecules are organized in several small (*ca.* 1–2 µm diameter) aggregates, the **nucleoids**, which lie scattered throughout the chloroplast; this arrangement is characteristic of the divisions Chlorophyta, Bryophyta and Tracheophyta. The distribution of the chloroplast DNA can be demonstrated by staining, using the DNA-specific fluorescent dye DAPI (= 4′, 6-diamidino-2-phenylindole) [254, 1784]. The structure and function of the chloroplast genome of *Chlamydomonas* have been the subject of many recent studies (e.g. [537, 612, 1354, 1519, 1730, 1804a]).

Pyrenoid (Figs. 19.1, 19.7e, f)

The pyrenoid is easily observed in living cells using the light microscope and appears as a round or oval structure within the chloroplast. It is clearly the centre for intensive starch production. Several or many plates of starch lie against the pyrenoid and these stain violet with potassium iodide.

Studies with the electron microscope show that the pyrenoid does not have a definite boundary separating it from the rest of the chloroplast, although it is enclosed by the plates of starch (Figs 19.1, 19.7e). It has a granular structure which stains rather more darkly than the chloroplast stroma, and it is penetrated by several thylakoids or by tube-like extensions of the thylakoids.

The formation of starch always occurs within the chloroplast but is not restricted to the pyrenoid, since starch grains are also found elsewhere in the chloroplast stroma. Starch deposition is particularly heavy in cells growing in nutrient-poor environments where nitrate and phosphate supplies have been exhausted; in the absence of N and P, photosynthetic activity can no longer find an outlet in protein synthesis and so only carbohydrate can be produced.

Pyrenoid structure varies in detail between species of *Chlamydomonas* [381]. The pyrenoid is proteinaceous and capable of fixing carbon dioxide, since it

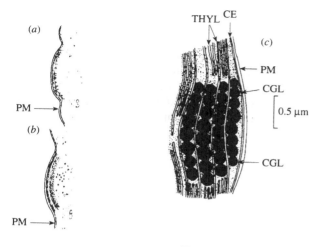

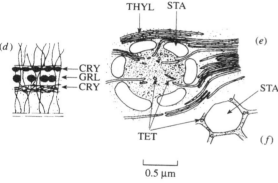

Eyespot (stigma) (Figs. 19.1, 19.7c, 19.8)

In the light microscope the stigma appears as a red spot, which is usually somewhat elongate and frequently lies about halfway along the cell, within the chloroplast. Electron microscopy reveals that the eyespot consists of one to eight rows of closely spaced globules sandwiched between thylakoids. The globules contain carotenoid pigments (hence the red colour) and are polygonal in section, as a result of being flattened against each other.

The term 'eyespot' suggests that this cell organelle has been ascribed some function in light perception. *Chlamydomonas* is phototactic, that is, it swims in a definite direction with respect to the light incident

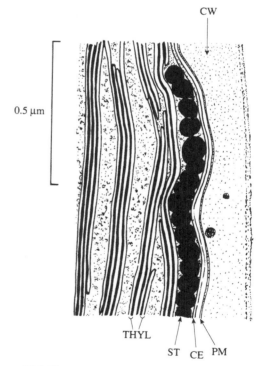

Figure 19.7. *Chlamydomonas reinhardtii.* (*a*) Mating structure of a (–) gamete. (*b*) Mating structure of a (+) gamete. (*c*) Stigma (eyespot), seen in section. (*d*) Cell envelope, in cross section. (*e*) Cross section of pyrenoid. (*f*) Tangential section of the pyrenoid and its starch sheath. CE = chloroplast envelope; CGL = globule containing carotenoids; CRY = crystalline lattice layer; GRL = granular layer; PM = plasma membrane (plasmalemma); STA = starch grain at the surface of the pyrenoid; such grains make a shell around the pyrenoid, within the chloroplast; TET = tubular extension of a thylakoid into the pyrenoid stroma; THYL = thylakoid. (*a, b* based on [541]; *d* on [540].)

Figure 19.8. The stigma in *Chlamydomonas eugametos.* The stigma lies within the chloroplast and is composed of a single layer of globules containing carotenoids, lying immediately below the chloroplast envelope, which in turn is closely appressed to the plasmalemma. Note also the stacking of the thylakoids. CE = chloroplast envelope; CW = cell wall; PM = plasma membrane (plasmalemma); ST = stigma; THYL = thylakoid. (Based on [1847].)

contains the enzyme RuBisCO (= ribulose 1,5-bisphosphate carboxylase–oxygenase), which catalyses the initial reaction in the photosynthetic carbon reduction cycle ([717, 1543]).

upon it. Generally speaking the cells swim towards dim light (positive phototaxis) and away from bright light (negative phototaxis). The phototactic mechanism present in *Chlamydomonas* appears to be similar to those of *Ochromonas* (Chrysophyceae; p. 113) and *Euglena* (Euglenophyceae; p. 293), but there are several differences. In *Ochromonas* and *Euglena*, the photoreceptor (the light-perceiving organelle) is situated not in the eyespot itself but on one of the flagella, in a swelling appressed to the eyespot (Figs. 6.3, 6.4*a*, 17.1*b*, 17.2*a*). In *Chlamydomonas*, on the other hand, the photoreceptor is located in a special area of the plasmalemma overlying the eyespot ([1185, 1186]). The photoreceptor pigment in *Ochromonas* and *Euglena* is probably a flavoprotein, while in *Chlamydomonas* and probably also in other green algae it is, rather surprisingly, rhodopsin, the universal visual pigment of animals ([1660]). Flavoproteins have an absorption maximum at around 450 nm, while rhodopsins have peaks that range over the whole visible and near UV spectrum.

The cells of the three algae mentioned above rotate as they swim. Hence the eyespot (and also part of the body of the cell) periodically shades the photoreceptor when the eyespot lies between it and the light source. The eyespot also periodically enhances the illumination of the photoreceptor when the cell is illuminated from the side, by acting as a tiny mirror, reflecting light back to the region of the plasmalemma where the photoreceptor molecules are located. Thus, when the cell is swimming at right angles to the light path, the photoreceptor of the rotating cell is subjected to maximal fluctuations in illumination; when swimming towards or away from the light source, the fluctuations are minimal (remember that the photoreceptor is orientated at right angles to the longitudinal axis of the cell: Fig. 19.1). In this way the cell is able to detect the direction of the light incident upon it, and indeed it can respond to very low levels of illumination, 1000 times lower than the compensation point for photosynthesis ([1660]).

Mating structures (Fig. 19.7a, b)

Given appropriate inductive conditions (see p. 353), vegetative cells of *Chlamydomonas* can become transformed into (+) or (–) gametes. Both of these mating types develop their own **mating structures**, which lie close to the apex of the cell and are oval areas of the plasmalemma, *ca.* 2–3 µm long. They bulge outwards slightly and overlie one of the two-membered microtubular roots. In the (+) mating structure there are two darkly staining layers beneath the plasmalemma, whereas in the (–) mating structure there is only one ([541, 542]). During fertilization, fusion of the gametes is initiated between the two mating structures. In *Chlamydomonas reinhardtii* a fertilization tube is produced which develops outwards from the (+) mating structure towards the (–) structure (cf. p. 353). Similar mating structures have been found in a few other species in the classes Chlorophyceae ([1118]) and Ulvophyceae ([1169, 1205]).

Contractile (pulsing) vacuoles (Fig. 19.1)

In most species there are two contractile vacuoles at the anterior end of the cell, lying just beneath the two basal bodies. Some species, however, have four or more contractile vacuoles, while others (marine species) lack any ([377, 381]). Where two are present they contract alternately, expelling their contents (water or an aqueous solution) through the flagellar canals. Electron microscopical investigations have shown that the vacuoles are surrounded by branched vesicles, which open into the vacuole itself. It is thought that excess water, drawn into the cell as a result of the higher osmotic pressure (hypertonicity) of the cytoplasm and cell sap, compared with that of the surrounding water, is actively taken up into the branched vesicles. From here it is transported into the contractile vacuoles, which then expel the water from the cell (see also *Ochromonas*, p. 110). The smaller vesicles are formed, at least partly, through fragmentation of the contractile vacuole's membrane during the expulsion of water; the membrane seems therefore to be involved in a process of continuous recycling ([620, 1383]).

Other cell organelles (Fig. 19.1)

Chlamydomonas cells contain the usual organelles of eukaryotic cells: nucleus, golgi apparatus, mitochondria, small vacuoles, lipid droplets, endoplasmic reticulum, and ribosomes. The golgi apparatus often lies around the nucleus and is then often surrounded by a fold of endoplasmic reticulum, which connects with the nuclear envelope ([989]). In the species illustrated the mitochondria lie between chloroplast and plasmalemma, and also in the central part of the cytoplasm.

Types of flagellate cell architecture in the Chlorophyta II. The cruciate prasinophycean type: *Pyramimonas,* another free-living unicellular flagellate (Figs. 19.9 – 19.11)

Pyramimonas cells are obovoid in shape and bear four flagella of equal length, which arise from the base of a conspicuous apical pit. At its anterior the cell bears four prominent lobes, each of which contains a lobe of the single large chloroplast. There is no cell wall or envelope like that of *Chlamydomonas*. Instead, each cell is surrounded by several layers of tiny scales, which can be seen by phase contrast light microscopy, when they appear as small granules.

More than 60 species are known ([1228]) and for their identification electron microscopy is indispensable (for reviews, see [780, 1391]), since the micromorphology of the scales is an important character ([1223, 1304]). *Pyramimonas* occurs in freshwater and in the sea, and some species produce phytoplankton blooms in bays around Japan and probably elsewhere ([779]).

Scales (Figs. 19.9c, 19.10a–f, i, k)

Six kinds of scales coat the body of the cell and the flagella of the species we illustrate ([779]). The scales are organic. The body of the cell bears three types of scales. Small square or diamond-shaped scales (*ca.* 50 nm across) form the inner layer of the scale case, immediately adjacent to the plasmalemma (Figs. 19.9c, 19.10d). The middle layer is composed of much larger box-like scales (*ca.* 290 nm across; Figs. 19.9c, 19.10b), each made of a framework of thin ribs. The outer layer consists of large crown-like scales (680 nm across; Figs. 19.9c, 19.10c, i). In another prasinophycean flagellate, *Tetraselmis*, it has recently been shown that the organic scales coalesce to form a theca. This has a most unusual carbohydrate composition, since the main constituent is 3-deoxy-manno-2-octulosonic acid. The much more widespread compound D-galacturonic acid is also present, but only in small quantities. The composition of the *Tetraselmis* theca is therefore completely different from that of the *Chlamydomonas* envelope (p. 303; [56, 1107]).

Another three types of scale are found on the flagella. Here there is an inner layer of small pentagonal scales (50 nm diameter; Figs. 19.9c, 19.10e, k) while beyond this is a layer of large (300 nm) horseshoe-shaped scales, each of which bears a spine on its back (Figs. 19.9c, 19.10f, k). Finally, on the outside, there are two rows of stiff tubular hairs (hair scales), each 1200 nm long and 15 nm thick (Figs. 19.9c, 19.10a; [1218]).

The flagellar scales and body scales are all produced within the cisternae of the two golgi bodies (Figs. 19.9b, 19.10g), and one cisterna can simultaneously form several different scale types (Fig. 19.10g; [1228]). The scales are transported by golgi vesicles to a series of cylindrical vesicles and from there they are moved to a scale reservoir (Fig. 19.9c). The reservoir has an orifice near the flagellar bases and the scales are finally distributed from it over the body of the cell and the flagella, though how this is done is not yet known.

Flagellar apparatus (Figs. 19.9a–d, 19.10h, j, 19.11)

Four identical flagella, each with a typical '9 + 2' axoneme, arise from the bottom of the flagellar pit. The transition region between the flagellum and the basal body contains a **stellate structure**, which is characteristic of the Chlorophyta ([1218, 1301]; see p. 307, Fig. 19.4). Inside the cell each axoneme ends in a typical eukaryote basal body, containing 9 interconnected triplets of microtubules (Fig. 19.11). In contrast to *Chlamydomonas*, where the basal bodies lie at angles of *ca.* 80° to each other (Fig. 19.6), in *Pyramimonas* the four basal bodies are almost parallel (Fig. 19.11). They are interconnected by an elaborate asymmetrical system of non-striated connecting fibres, whose precise configuration varies from species to species within the genus. Amidst these connections and attached to them is the slightly curved, rectangular **synistosome**, a fibrous bar *ca.* 500 nm long which is longitudinally striated ([1303]). The synistosome appears to be restricted to *Pyramimonas*, as is the lateral fibrous band (Figs. 19.9c, 19.11), a structure that lies to one side of the four basal bodies and appears curved like an arc in transverse sections of the cell; the lateral fibrous band is absent in some *Pyramimonas* species ([1171]). None of these features – the complex of connecting fibres, the synistosome, or the lateral fibrous band – is present in *Chlamydomonas* and related green algae (cf. p. 309, Fig. 19.6). Nevertheless, *Pyramimonas* does resemble *Chlamydomonas* and its allies in one important respect: the arrangement of the flagellar roots. There are **four cruciately arranged micro-**

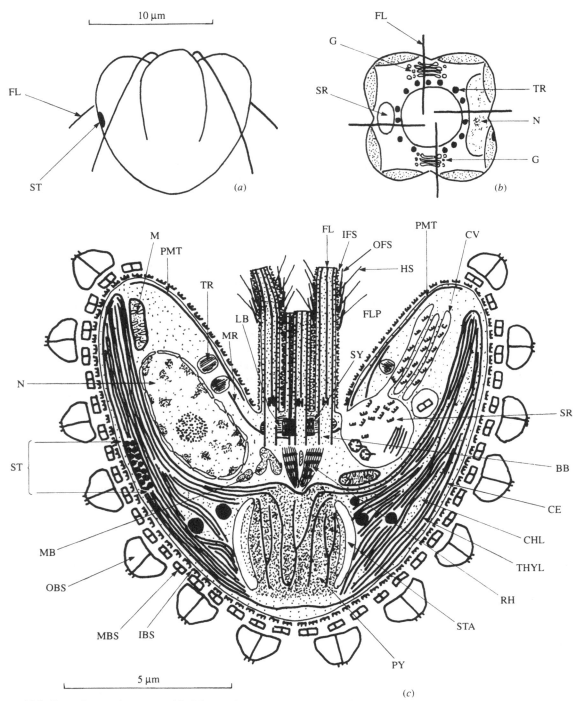

Figure 19.9. *Pyramimonas lunata,* a zoid of the cruciate prasinophycean type. (*a*) Gross features of the cell, showing the four flagella and the anterior lobes. (*b*) Diagram of the cell, as seen from the apex. (*c*) Longitudinal section, based on EM observations.

(*d*) Transmission electron micrograph of a median longitudinal section. BB = basal body; CE = chloroplast envelope; CHL = chloroplast; CV = cylindrical vesicle; FL = flagellum; FLP = flagellar pit; G = golgi body; HS = hair scale; IBS = inner layer of body

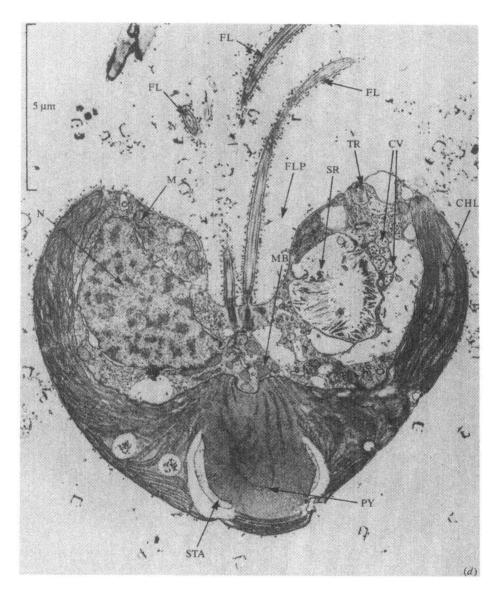

scales; IFS = inner layer of flagellar scales; LB = lateral fibrous band; M = mitochondrion; MB = microbody; MBS = middle layer of body scales; MR = microtubular root of flagellar apparatus; N = nucleus; OBS = outer layer of body scales; OFS = outer layer of flagellar scales; PMT = pit microtubules; PY = pyrenoid; RH = rhizoplast; SR = scale reservoir; ST = stigma (eyespot); STA = starch grain appressed to the pyrenoid; SY = synistosome; THYL = thylakoid; TR = trichocyst. (*a–c* based on [779]; *d* from [779], with the permission of the authors and the editor of the *Japanese Journal of Phycology*.)

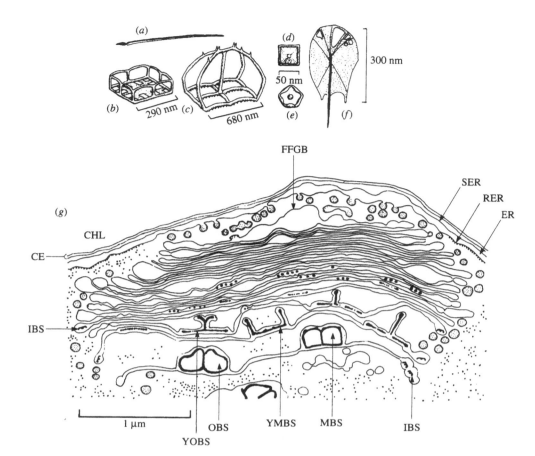

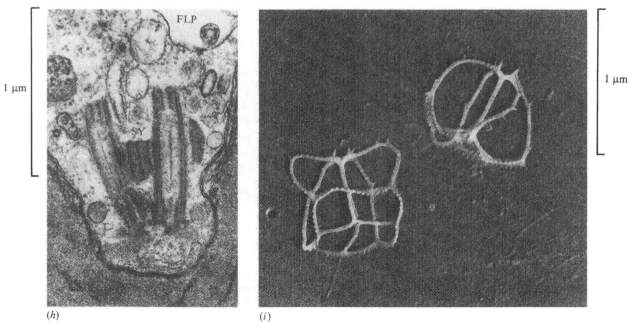

For legend see facing page.

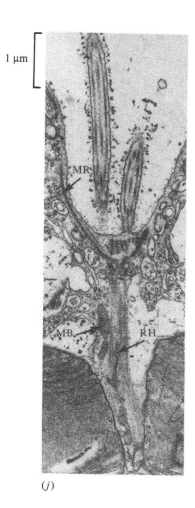

(*j*)

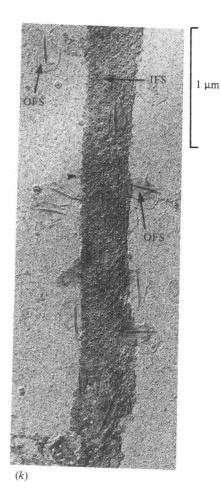

(*k*)

Figure 19.10. *Pyramimonas lunata:* the different types of scale present on the zoids (*a–f*) and scale formation (*g*). (*a*) Hair scale from flagellum. (*b*) Box-like scale from the middle body layer. (*c*) Crown-like scale from the outer body layer. (*d*) Square or diamond scale from the inner body layer. (*e*) Scale from the inner layer on the flagellum. (*f*) Horse-shoe scale from the outer layer on the flagellum. (*g*) Scale formation in the golgi apparatus of *Pyramimonas*. On the forming face of the golgi body (top) vesicles bleb off from the endoplasmic reticulum and coalesce to form golgi cisternae. Scales are formed in the central and lower parts of the golgi body and different types of scales can be formed within a single cisterna. The small inner layer (underlayer) scales are always formed at the periphery of the cisternae, while the remaining types are formed towards the centre. The process of scale formation can be traced within a golgi body; in the illustration the scales become more mature towards the bottom. (*h–k*) Electron micro-

graphs. (*h*) Basal bodies in longitudinal section, connected by the synistosome. (*i*) Outermost body scales. (*j*) Longitudinal section through the flagellar apparatus, showing the rhizoplast and associated microbody, as well as two microtubular roots. (*k*) Flagellum covered by a complete layer of inner flagellar scales; a few detached outer layer scales are also visible. CE = chloroplast envelope; CHL = chloroplast (no details are shown of the interior); ER = endoplasmic reticulum; FFGB = forming face of the golgi body; FLP = flagellar pit; IBS = inner body scale (always formed at the periphery of the golgi body); IFS = inner flagellar scales; MB = microbody; MBS = middle body scale; MR = microtubular root; OBS = outer body scale; OFS = outer flagellar scale; RER = rough endoplasmic reticulum; RH = rhizoplast; SER = smooth endoplasmic reticulum; SY = synistosome; YMBS = young middle body scale; YOBS = young outer body scale. (*a–f* based on [779, 1390]; *g* on [1228]; *h–k* from [779], with permission.)

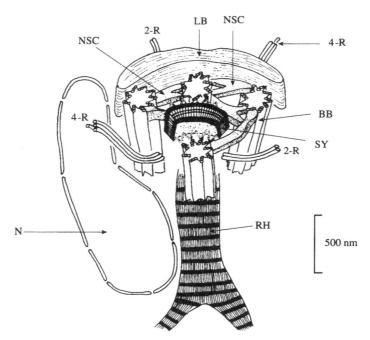

Figure 19.11. The flagellar apparatus of *Pyramimonas,* a zoid of the cruciate prasinophycean type. BB = basal body; LB = lateral fibrous band; N = nucleus; NSC = non-striated connective; RH = rhizoplast; SY = synistosome; 2-R = two-stranded microtubular root; 4-R = four-stranded microtubular root. (After [1433].)

tubular roots, which have the x–2–x–2 pattern described earlier; here the arrangement is 4–2–4–2 (compare Fig. 19.11 with Fig. 19.6a, b). *Pyramimonas* is especially similar to Chlorophyceae with four flagella (compare Fig. 19.14, lower row, with Fig. 19.11). In all of them the microtubular roots are attached to the central pair of basal bodies, in such a way that, if these two basal bodies were pointing in a N–S orientation, the x- (here 4-) membered roots would point NE and SW, while the 2-membered roots would point NW and SE. This uniformity in the spatial arrangement of basal bodies and roots is thought to indicate a common evolutionary origin for the three types of cruciate zoid found in the Chlorophyta ([1171, 1544]).

In *Pyramimonas* the four microtubular roots extend up the sides of the flagellar pit, ascending towards the anterior of the cell. Here they join *ca.* 250–300 microtubules, which radiate out below the plasmalemma from the flagellar region (Fig. 19.9c) and apparently have a skeletal function.

The basal bodies are also associated with one (Fig. 19.11) or several (Fig. 19.9c, 19.10j) **rhizoplasts**.

These are attached to the lower ends of the basal bodies and extend from here down to the chloroplast, where they branch and spread over the chloroplast surface, to which they are attached. The rhizoplasts are fibrillar and have a distinct transverse striation. In *Tetraselmis*, presumed to be a close relative of *Pyramimonas*, the rhizoplasts have been demonstrated to be contractile and to be composed of the contractile protein centrin (p. 307). In this genus two massive rhizoplasts are present and pass from the basal bodies over the surface of the nucleus to attachment sites on the plasmalemma, where the cell is often indented during rhizoplast contraction (Fig. 19.12a). The distance between the transverse striations of the rhizoplast varies from 200–250 nm to 90–120 nm, depending on whether the rhizoplast is relaxed or contracted (Fig. 19.12b–d). The rhizoplast is composed of microfilaments 3–6 nm thick, and the pale-staining transverse striations correspond to positions where the microfilaments anastomose with each other permanently and play little or no part in contraction. Contraction is brought about by spiralling of the microfilaments, which begins close to the pale trans-

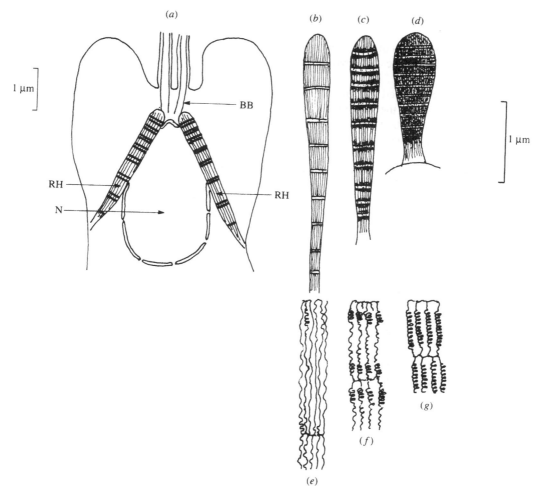

Figure 19.12. *Tetraselmis.* (a) Anterior of the cell, showing the two rhizoplasts, which run from the basal bodies over the surface of the nucleus to the plasmalemma. (b) Relaxed rhizoplast. (c) Partly contracted rhizoplast. (d) Fully contracted rhizoplast. (e–g) Diagrams showing the conformation of the coiling protein filaments in the rhizoplast during contraction, from the relaxed state (e) to fully contracted (g): these correspond to the stages shown in b–d. BB = basal body; N = nucleus; RH = rhizoplast. (Based on [98].)

verse bands and then extends out (Fig. 19.12e–g). As a result, in electron micrographs of the rhizoplasts, densely staining bands appear first on either side of the pale bands (Fig. 19.12c) and then spread throughout the regions between the anastomoses (Fig. 19.12d; [98]). Cyclic contraction and extension of the rhizoplast can be induced by placing the organisms in artificial seawater containing 2 mM $CaCl_2$ and 5 mM ATP. Contraction requires calcium, but not ATP. Binding of Ca^{2+} to the centrin probably brings about profound conformational changes, resulting in the twisting and supercoiling of the centrin filaments and hence in the contraction of the rhizoplast. Re-extension (relaxation) of the rhizoplast can only occur with the removal of the Ca^{2+}, which requires the energy provided by the ATP ([1177, 1541]).

Contraction of the rhizoplasts pulls the basal bodies deeper into the cell and may help to initiate the bend-propagated recovery stroke of the flagella after the completion of each 'breast stroke' (Fig. 19.2c); as elsewhere, flagellar bending is brought about by the axonemal doublets sliding over each another (see p. 305; [1542]). Another function of the contracting rhizoplast may be to alter the orientation of the basal bodies and hence the direction in which the cells swim, i.e. to act as a rudder ([1544]).

Typically a large, well-developed microbody (peroxisome) is present, appressed to the rhizoplasts (Fig. 19.9c, d; in Fig. 19.11 the microbody has been omitted, since it would completely cover the rhizoplast!).

Chloroplast and pyrenoid (Fig. 19.9b–d)

There is a single, cup-shaped chloroplast. It is deeply lobed with two of the eight lobes extending into each of the four anterior lobes of the cell. The oval pyrenoid is situated in the base of the chloroplast and is penetrated by a number of thylakoids.

Stigma (eyespot) (Fig. 19.9a, c)

The stigma lies about halfway along the cell in one of the chloroplast lobes. It consists of one or two layers of carotenoid-containing globules and lies adjacent to the nucleus, which is laterally placed within the cell. Thylakoids do not penetrate into the stigma, in contrast to the situation in *Chlamydomonas* (Fig. 19.7c).

Trichocysts (Fig. 19.9b, c)

Trichocysts are present around the flagellar pit. Under the light microscope they appear as highly refractile granules, about 1 μm in diameter (Fig. 19.9b), while in the electron microscope it can be seen that each is a vesicle containing a highly coiled band, which unrolls when the trichocyst is discharged (Fig. 19.9c). These ejectile organelles are very similar to the trichocysts of the Cryptophyta (p. 241, Fig. 15.1d).

Types of flagellate cell architecture in the Chlorophyta III. The cruciate 11 o'clock – 5 o'clock type: the biflagellate gamete of the multicellular chlorophyte *Acrosiphonia* (Fig. 19.13)

Flagellate cells (zoids) function as reproductive cells in the life histories of most multicellular or multinucleate green algae. The gametes are often biflagellate, while the zoospores (which are often meiospores) are often quadriflagellate. In the class Chlorophyceae the zoids produced by multicellular or multinucleate forms resemble *Chlamydomonas* in their structure. In the remaining classes of the Chlorophyta, however, the architecture of the flagellate reproductive cells does not resemble that of any free-living flagellate green alga, and so the biflagellate gamete of *Acrosiphonia* (cf. p. 398) will be used here as an example of a cruciate 11 o'clock – 5 o'clock zoid (Fig. 19.13, which is based on the account of [1205]).

The *Acrosiphonia* gamete is obovate with a conspicuous 'tail', which is strengthened by numerous skeletal microtubules running below the plasmalemma. At the anterior end of the cell there is a papilla, which contains a number of vesicles (Fig. 19.13e). These probably contain sticky material that promotes adhesion; such vesicles commonly occur in the apical papillae of reproductive zoids. The zoid contains the usual complement of organelles: a single cup-shaped chloroplast in the posterior part of the cell, which contains a pyrenoid with radiating plates of starch and a stigma composed of two layers of carotenoid-containing globules; a nucleus; ER; a golgi body; and a mitochondrion, which lies towards the anterior of the cell. The cell anterior also bears what is probably a mating structure (i.e. the place where the plasmalemmas of the gametes fuse): a bulging oval part of the plasmalemma subtended by a dark-staining layer (compare with Fig. 19.7a, b, which illustrate the mating structures of *Chlamydomonas*).

Flagellar apparatus

The architecture of the flagellar apparatus of the *Acrosiphonia* gamete provides very important taxonomic and phylogenetic characters. As in other Chlorophyta, the flagellar axonemes have the usual '9 + 2' structure; the transition region between each flagellum and its basal body exhibits a **stellate pattern** when seen in transverse section (Fig. 19.4); and the basal bodies have the normal eukaryotic structure of nine triplets arranged in a cylinder (Fig. 19.13d, e). The two flagella emerge from the sides of the apical papilla, their bases forming an angle of almost 180° with each other. Their shafts extend out almost perpendicular to the longitudinal axis of the cell.

The flagella are anchored in the cell by **four microtubular roots**, which can be seen to be **cruciately arranged**, when the cell is viewed from the anterior end (Fig. 19.13*a*, *b*). The roots show the *x*–2–*x*–2 pattern found, for example, in *Chlamydomonas* (p. 308), and in this case the '*x*' roots contain three microtubules. The 2- and 3-membered roots are attached to the two basal bodies and occupy the same positions with respect to them as in *Chlamydomonas* (Fig. 19.6*a*) and *Pyramimonas* (Fig. 19.11); when viewed from the anterior the basal bodies and their associated microtubular roots exhibit '180° rotational symmetry' (see p. 310).

The two basal bodies are not exactly aligned with each other (Figs 19.13*a*, *b*, 19.14*b-1*). In Fig. 19.14*b-1*, the configuration of the basal bodies and microtubule roots in *Acrosiphonia* and related algae (in the class Ulvophyceae) is compared with the configuration in a hypothetical 'ancestral' zoid (Fig. 19.14 *a-1*) and with that of *Chlamydomonas* and related genera (class Chlorophyceae; Fig. 19.14 *c-1*). In the ulvophycean configuration the basal bodies have performed a distinct **anti-clockwise rotation** relative to their arrangement in the hypothetical 'ancestor' (compare Fig. 19.14 *b-1* and *a-1*), so that they occupy **11 o'clock and 5 o'clock** positions. Moreover, in the ulvophycean arrangement the basal bodies show a slight but distinct **overlap**. In the Chlorophyceae, on the other hand, as has already been pointed out, the basal bodies exhibit a clockwise displacement and there is scarcely ever any overlap between them (see p. 324: Fig. 19.14 *c-1*). The anti-clockwise rotation of the basal bodies and the overlap between them are considered to be important features of the Ulvophyceae ([1205, 1326, 1515, 1644, 1645]), but they are not enough on their own to distinguish the Ulvophyceae from all other green algae, since four other classes of green algae (the Cladophorophyceae, Bryopsidophyceae, Dasycladophyceae and Pleurastrophyceae) also have a cruciate 11 o'clock – 5 o'clock configuration of the flagellar apparatus; the Trentepohliophyceae too have a cruciate 11 o'clock – 5 o'clock configuration, but this is of a very special type. Fig. 24.1*e–g* shows an electron micrograph of an 11 o'clock – 5 o'clock type of zoid. The other important characteristics of the Ulvophyceae are discussed in Chapter 22.

In **quadriflagellate zoids** the spatial configurations of the basal bodies and roots are similar to those in biflagellate zoids (Fig. 19.14, bottom row), although it is often difficult to work out the exact arrangement. The microtubular roots are attached to two of the basal bodies, lying opposite each other, and these show anti-

clockwise rotation in the Ulvophyceae and Cladophorophyceae (Fig. 19.14 *b-2*) and clockwise rotation in the Chlorophyceae (Fig. 19.14 *c-2*). The rotation of the second pair of basal bodies, which are not associated with microtubular roots, does not always agree with that of the primary pair ([689]).

The flagellar apparatus of the *Acrosiphonia* gamete exhibits some other features that are more or less characteristic of the Ulvophyceae. For instance, the basal bodies are connected anteriorly by an upper connective (Fig. 19.13*a*, *c*, *d*), which in *Acrosiphonia* is non-striated, although in relatives of *Acrosiphonia* it may bear a more or less distinct median striation ([424]). In *Chlamydomonas* the upper connective is always transversely striated (Figs. 19.4, 19.6*b*). Below the upper connective in *Acrosiphonia* is a second, faintly striated fibre, which forms an additional connection between the basal bodies (Fig. 19.13*e*). Closely appressed to the lower (proximal) sides of the basal bodies are **proximal sheaths** of amorphous, darkly staining material (Fig. 19.13*b*, *e*), which are connected to each other by a finely fibrillar band (Fig. 19.13*e*). The end of each basal body is covered by a **terminal cap** (Fig. 19.13*a*, *b*, *d*), again composed of amorphous, darkly staining material. There are also **two transversely striated fibres**, each linking one of the proximal sheaths to a three-membered microtubular root (Fig. 19.13*d*), and a single '**striated microtubule-associated component**' (SMAC) beneath each two-membered microtubular root (Fig. 19.13*b*).

Types of flagellate cell architecture in the Chlorophyta IV. The unilateral type: the biflagellate zoospore of the unicellular chlorophyte *Chaetosphaeridium* (Figs. 19.15, 19.16; cf. Fig. 28.4)

Chaetosphaeridium is a small unicellular chlorophyte, which lives in freshwater. Several cells usually occur together, forming cushion-like colonies on larger freshwater algae (p. 460, Fig. 28.2*a*). Each cell produces a hair with a basal sheath.

The biflagellate zoospores of *Chaetosphaeridium* (Fig. 19.15) are more or less obovoid and are slightly flattened. The two flagella are equal in length and emerge on one side of the cell, slightly below the apex; during swimming they are directed backwards. The cell contains a single parietal chloroplast with a

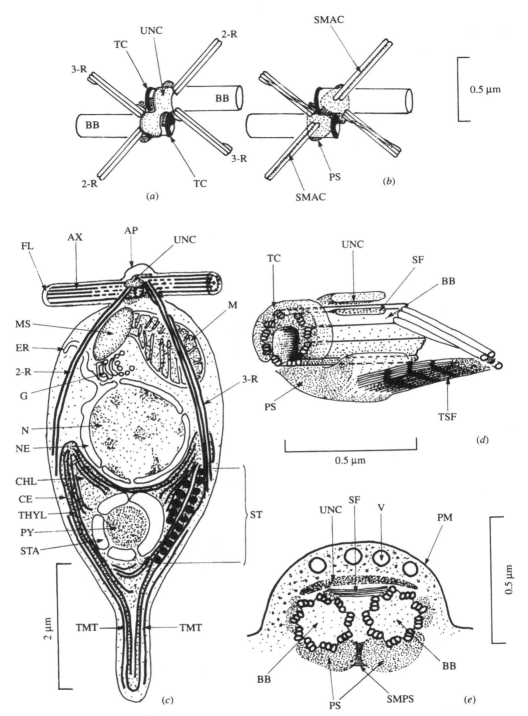

Figure 19.13. *Acrosiphonia* gamete, a zoid of the cruciate 11 o'clock – 5 o'clock type. (*a*) Top view of the flagellar apparatus; the basal bodies are shown as cylinders. (*b*) As (*a*), but with the upper non-striated connective removed and other structures made transparent, to show the positions of the lower parts of the flagellar apparatus. (*c*) Longitudinal section of the zoid, based on EM observations. (*d*) Oblique view of basal body, showing one of the two transversely striated fibres; this links a three-stranded microtubular root to the

pyrenoid, and a golgi body and a mitochondrion are also present. Between the chloroplast and the nucleus there is a conspicuous microbody (peroxisome). The cells are covered by a layer of tiny **quadrangular body scales**, which are organic and are like the innermost scales in the body covering of *Pyramimonas* (compare Fig. 19.15*b* with Figs. 19.10*d* and 19.9*c*). A **stigma** is characteristically **absent**. The biflagellate zoid of *Coleochaete* has a similar, unilateral type of construction and is shown in the electron micrograph of Fig. 28.4.

Flagellar apparatus

The flagella are anchored in the cell by **one broad unilateral band of many (*ca.* 60) microtubules**, which runs from the flagellar bases along the side of the cell towards the posterior. Near the flagellar bases the microtubular band forms part of a **multilayered structure (MLS**; Figs. 19.15, 19.16, 28.4*b*, *c*). In addition to the microtubules the MLS contains two laminate plates, each composed of a stack of differently orientated platelets. The two basal bodies are linked by a transversely striated connective (Figs. 19.16, 28.4*c*; [1215, 1218, 1614]).

Types of mitosis and cytokinesis in the Chlorophyta I. *Pyramimonas,* a unicellular flagellate: open mitosis with a persistent telophase spindle; cytokinesis effected by a cleavage furrow (Fig. 19.17 la–d; 1318, 1919)

Mitosis

In early prophase the basal bodies replicate; in the *Pyramimonas* species illustrated in Fig. 19.17, this results in the presence of eight basal bodies. The cell retains the four flagella that were already present but the new basal bodies do not form flagella until much later (Fig. 19.17 I*a*). The **basal bodies** separate into two sets of four and move towards the future poles of the spindle, where they **function as centrioles**. The spindle is formed between the sets of basal bodies, the spindle microtubules radiating from the basal bodies themselves and from the rhizoplasts associated with them (Fig. 19.17 I*b*).

In the course of prophase the nuclear envelope breaks down and disappears, so that **mitosis is open**. The fully condensed chromosomes have distinct kinetochores, which are plate-like and layered. At metaphase the chromosomes become aligned at the centre of the spindle, forming a compact metaphase plate (Fig. 19.17 I*b*). During the period from metaphase to telophase the distance between the spindle poles remains roughly constant while the pole-to-chromosome distance diminishes, probably through shortening of the chromosome microtubules. By early telophase (Fig. 19.17 I*c*) the nuclear envelopes have reformed but the spindle remains, as a **persistent telophase spindle**.

Cytokinesis

Cytokinesis is accomplished by an **ingrowing cleavage furrow**: an invagination of the plasmalemma, which is initiated during metaphase. Cleavage is completed following the eventual breakdown of the telophase spindle (Fig. 19.17 I*d*).

Caption for fig. 19.13 *(cont.)*.

proximal sheath of the basal body. (*e*) Longitudinal section through the apical papilla, taken at right angles to the plane of the section in (*c*). AP = apical papilla; AX = axoneme; BB = basal body; CE = chloroplast envelope; CHL = chloroplast; ER = endoplasmic reticulum; FL = flagellum; G = golgi body; M = mitochondrion; MS = mating structure; N = nucleus; NE = nuclear envelope; PM = plasma membrane (plasmalemma); PS = proximal sheath; PY = pyrenoid; SF = tiny second (striated) fibre connecting the basal bodies; SMAC = striated microtubule-associated component; SMPS = striated material connecting the two proximal (= lower) sheaths; ST = stigma; STA = starch grain appressed to pyrenoid surface; TC = terminal cap, which closes the lower end of the basal body; THYL = thylakoid ; TMT = tail microtubule; TSF = one of two transversely striated fibres connecting one of the two three-stranded microtubular roots with one of the two proximal sheaths; UNC = upper non-striated connective, which links the basal bodies; V = vesicle, probably containing sticky material for attachment of the zoid; 2-R = two-stranded microtubular root; 3-R = three-stranded microtubular root. (Based on [1205].)

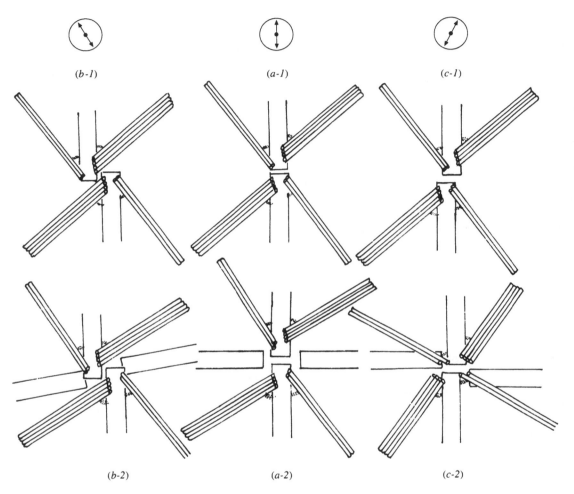

Figure 19.14. Cruciate arrangements of microtubular roots in the flagellar apparatuses of green algae. The basal bodies and flagellar roots are shown from the top (from the anterior of the cell) and the pictures need to be rotated through 90° in order to achieve the same orientation as is shown in Figs. 19.6a and 19.13a. (*a-1*), (*b-1*) and (*c-1*) show biflagellate zoids; (*a-2*), (*b-2*) and (*c-2*) show quadriflagellate zoids. (*a-1*) **Hypothetical ancestral type of flagellar apparatus**, in which the two basal bodies are in line with each other: the basal bodies have a 12 o'clock – 6 o'clock arrangement. (*b-1*) **The flagellar apparatus of a biflagellate zoid of the cruciate 11 o'clock – 5 o'clock type**. The basal bodies have undergone an anti-clockwise rotation relative to the configuration in the ancestral type, so that they have an 11 o'clock – 5 o'clock arrange-ment (they also overlap slightly). (*c-1*) **The flagellar apparatus of a biflagellate zoid of the cruciate 1 o'clock – 7 o'clock type.** The basal bodies have undergone a clockwise rotation relative to the configu-ration in the ancestral type, so that they have a 1 o'clock – 7 o'clock (non-overlapping) arrangement. (*a-2*) Hypothetical ancestral type of quadriflagellate zoid, in which the basal bodies of each pair are exactly aligned across the centre. (*b-2*) The flagellar apparatus of a quadriflagellate zoid of the cruciate 11 o'clock – 5 o'clock type; note the anti-clockwise rotation rela-tive to the ancestral type. (*c-2*) The flagellar apparatus of a quadriflagellate zoid of the cruciate 1 o'clock – 7 o'clock type; note the clockwise rotation relative to the ancestral type. (Based on [1140, 1326].)

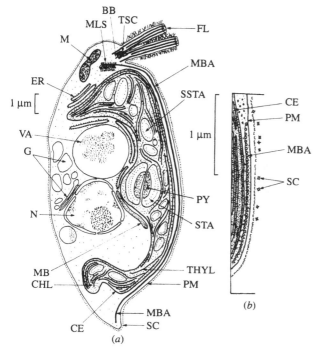

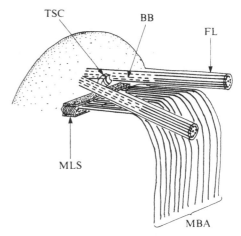

Figure 19.16. *Chaetosphaeridium* zoospore: a zoid of the unilateral type. Three-dimensional side view of the cell apex, showing the flagellar apparatus. BB = basal body; FL = flagellum; MBA = microtubular band (only 12 instead of the full *ca.* 60 microtubules are shown); MLS = multilayered structure; TSC = transversely striated fibre connecting the basal bodies. (Based on [1218].)

Figure 19.15. *Chaetosphaeridium* zoospore: a zoid of the unilateral type. (*a*) Longitudinal section, based on EM observations. (*b*) Transverse section through the cell, showing the microtubular band. BB = basal body; CE = chloroplast envelope; CHL = chloroplast; ER = endoplasmic reticulum; FL = flagellum; G = golgi body; M = mitochondrion; MB = microbody; MBA = microtubular band of the flagellar apparatus; MLS = multilayered structure; N = nucleus; PM = plasma membrane (plasmalemma); PY = pyrenoid; SC = layer of diamond-shaped scales; SSTA = stroma starch; STA = starch grain appressed to the pyrenoid; THYL = thylakoid; TSC = transversely striated fibre connecting the basal bodies; VA = vacuole. (Based on [694, 1215].)

Types of mitosis and cytokinesis in the Chlorophyta II. *Chlamydomonas,* another unicellular flagellate: closed mitosis with a non-persistent telophase spindle; cytokinesis effected by a cleavage furrow operating within a phycoplast (Fig. 19.17 IIa–d; 988, 1791)

Mitosis

Before mitosis the cell sheds its flagella, which detach from the basal bodies at the transition zone (Fig. 19.5).

The dividing protoplast then rotates through 90° within the parent cell wall (arrows in Fig. 19.17 IIa).

During early prophase the basal bodies replicate. The two new sets separate and move toward the poles of the future spindle, where they function as centrioles; the spindle then forms between them. At metaphase the elongate nuclear envelope remains almost intact, so **mitosis is closed** (Figs. 19.17 IIb, 19.18a). At the poles, however, there are **polar fenestrae**, which are *ca.* 300–500 nm wide openings in the nuclear envelope, through which the spindle microtubules penetrate into the nucleus. The fully condensed chromosomes have plate-like, three-layered kinetochores, and at metaphase they become aligned in a distinct metaphase plate. At telophase the spindle soon degenerates (a **non-persistent telophase spindle**) and the nuclear envelope quickly reforms around the daughter nuclei, which remain connected for some time by anastomosing cisternae of endoplasmic reticulum (Fig. 19.18b).

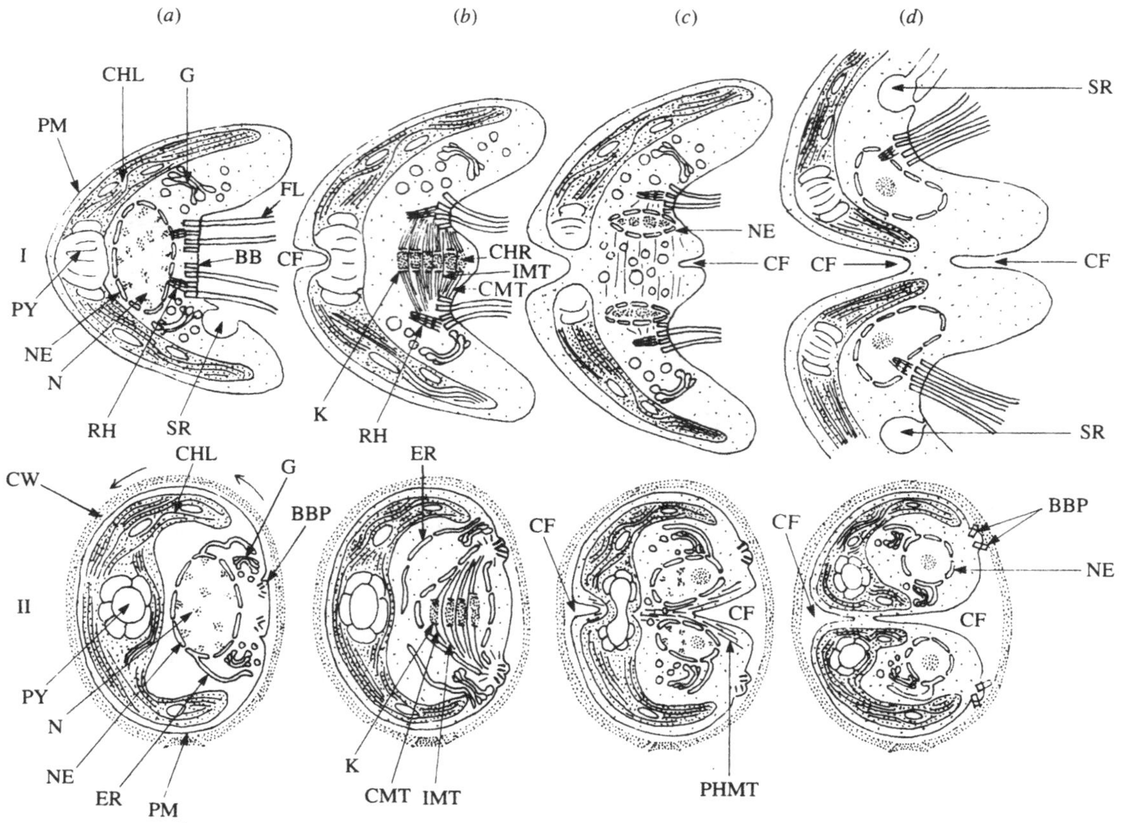

Figure 19.17. Mitosis and cytokinesis in two flagellate green algae. I. *Pyramimonas:* open mitosis with a persistent telophase spindle, cytokinesis brought about via a cleavage furrow. II. *Chlamydomonas:* closed mitosis with a collapsing (= non-persistent) telophase spindle, cytokinesis brought about by a cleavage furrow that develops within a phycoplast. See text for further explanation. Arrows indicate 90° rotation of the dividing cell within the parental cell wall.

(a) Early prophase. (b) Metaphase. (c) Late telophase. (d) Early interphase. BB = basal body; BBP = basal body pair; CF = cleavage furrow; CHL = chloroplast; CHR = chromosome; CMT = chromosomal spindle microtubule; CW = wall-like envelope around cell; ER = endoplasmic reticulum; FL = flagellum; G = golgi body; IMT = interzonal spindle microtubule; K = kinetochore; N = nucleus; NE = nuclear envelope; PY = pyrenoid; PHMT = phycoplast microtubule; PM = plasma membrane (plasmalemma); RH = rhizoplast; SR = scale reservoir. (I based on [1919]; II on [1791].)

Cytokinesis

Cytokinesis is preceded by the development of a **phycoplast**, which then persists during the division of the cell. The phycoplast is a plate of microtubules lying in the plane of division and may steer division, since cytokinesis is accomplished by a diaphragm-like ingrowing furrow, which lies 'within' the phycoplast (Figs. 19.2a, 19.17 IIc). The cleavage furrow passes between the newly divided chloroplasts and their pyrenoids (Fig. 19.17 IIc, d). During the formation of

the phycoplast its microtubules arise from the four-stranded microtubular roots (Fig. 19.6) of both daughter sets of flagellar basal bodies (Fig. 19.19). Indeed, the phycoplast is the initial phase of development of the new cytoskeleton of each daughter cell, which consists of microtubules that run from the tip of the cell to its tail, just beneath the plasmalemma ([1614, 1615, 1616]).

After completion of cell division the daughter cells are liberated from the parent cell through enzymatic digestion of the parental wall by a special 'vegetative autolysin'. Similarly, the gametes are released from

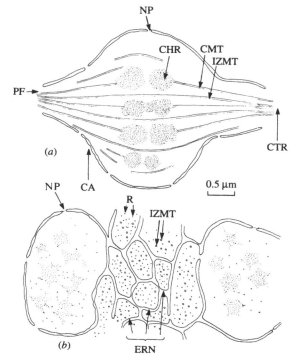

Figure 19.18. *Chlamydomonas*: mitosis. (*a*) Early anaphase, showing that mitosis is intranuclear. (*b*) Telophase. The spindle has disappeared (it is non-persistent). CA = cell axis; CHR = chromosome; CMT = chromosomal spindle microtubule; CTR = position of centriole (not in the plane of section); ERN = network of endoplasmic reticulum cisternae; IZMT = interzonal spindle microtubule (central filament); IMT = internuclear microtubule; NP = nuclear pore; PF = polar fenestra (window) in nuclear envelope; R = ribosomes. (After [804].)

their mother cell wall by a 'gametic autolysin' ([612, 1838]).

Types of mitosis and cytokinesis in the Chlorophyta III. *Cylindrocapsa*, an example of the order Chlorococcales: closed mitosis with a non-persistent telophase spindle; cytokinesis effected by a cell plate of smooth endoplasmic reticulum (ER) vesicles within a phycoplast (Fig. 19.20 I; [1642, 1643, 1644])

Most Chlorococcales are unicellular non-flagellate algae. They often reproduce by **autospores**, which are non-flagellate juvenile cells formed within the wall of the parent cell; each autospore is entirely surrounded by its own young cell wall (e.g. *Chlorella*, Fig. 21.10*a–c*). In some Chlorococcales these young cells are kept together within the parental cell walls, as in the filamentous alga *Cylindrocapsa* (Fig. 21.18).

Mitosis

The parietal chloroplast divides before mitosis. Two pairs of centrioles are already present at the beginning of interphase. Then, in early prophase, the nuclear envelope becomes surrounded by one or two layers of **perinuclear endoplasmic reticulum**, which is rough, i.e. covered by ribosomes (Fig. 19.20 I*a*). Perinuclear microtubules appear around the nucleus and in late prophase microtubules proliferate within the nucleus to form a tilted mitotic spindle between the pairs of centrioles lying at the spindle poles.

At metaphase the nuclear envelope is still intact and surrounded by perinuclear ER, so that **mitosis is closed** (Fig. 19.20 I*b*). The fully condensed chromosomes become aligned to form a distinct metaphase plate and have plate-like layered kinetochores. At telophase the spindle soon degenerates (a **nonpersistent telophase spindle**) although a few microtubules can still be found around the re-formed nuclear envelopes. The pairs of centrioles migrate around the telophase nuclei, away from the former spindle poles and towards the centre of the equatorial plane, where they remain until after cytokinesis (Fig. 19.20 I*c*: arrows indicate the direction of movement of the centrioles).

Cytokinesis

Cisternae of rough endoplasmic reticulum proliferate in the narrow zone of cytoplasm lying in the centre of the cell, between the two daughter nuclei (Fig. 19.20 I*c*). They then presumably bleb off smooth ER vesicles, which become aligned in the equatorial plane to form a **cell plate of smooth vesicles**, probably derived from the ER. As in other kinds of cell plate the vesicles coalesce to form a transverse system separating the daughter cells. Here, the vesicles accumulate within a **phycoplast**, i.e. a plate of microtubules lying in the future plane of division (Fig. 19.20 I*c*).

After completion of the transverse septum and the resultant separation of the daughter cells, the golgi

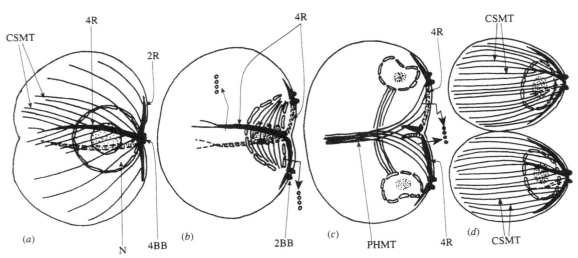

Figure 19.19. Phycoplast formation in a *Chlamydomonas*-like cell (compare with Fig. 19.17 II). (*a*) Cell just before mitosis. Four basal bodies are present following replication of the original pair. The cytoskeletal microtubules (lying just under the plasmalemma) converge on the microtubular roots of the flagella. (*b*) Metaphase. The four-stranded microtubular flagellar roots slide past each other, thus pushing the pairs of basal bodies apart. The cytoskeletal microtubules have disassembled. (*c*) Late telophase. Phycoplast microtubules arise from the four-stranded microtubular roots and interdigitate in the plane where cleavage will take place. (*d*) Just after cytokinesis: cytoskeletal microtubules arise again from the four microtubular roots. 2BB = two basal bodies; 4BB = four basal bodies, produced by replication of the original pair; CSMT = cytoskeletal microtubules; N = nucleus; PHMT = phycoplast microtubules; 2R = two-stranded microtubular root; 4R = four-stranded microtubular root. (Based on [1615].)

bodies become active and a **new cell wall is secreted around each daughter protoplast** by exocytosis of golgi-derived vesicles containing wall material (Fig. 19.20 I*d*). Each daughter cell thus gains a complete new wall. In the case of *Cylindrocapsa* the parental walls are persistent, so that the daughter cells remain united to form filaments. In most other green algae with this kind of mitosis and cytokinesis, however, the daughter cells are liberated from the parent cell wall as autospores, when they are non-flagellate, or as zoospores, when the two centrioles go on to generate flagella ([1646]). An example of this is in the non-motile green alga *Kirchneriella* (Figs. 21.11, 21.12), which is unicellular and forms autospores; it is very similar to *Cylindrocapsa* in all the details of mitosis and cytokinesis, except that deposition of new wall material into the transverse septa begins before the septa are complete.

Types of mitosis and cytokinesis in the Chlorophyta IV. *Uronema*, an example of the order Chaetophorales: closed mitosis with a non-persistent telophase spindle; cytokinesis effected by a cell plate of golgi-derived vesicles within a phycoplast (Fig. 19.20 II; [426, as *Ulothrix*])

Uronema is a freshwater green alga, which forms unbranched filaments (p. 380, Fig. 21.22*a*). The order Chaetophorales includes both unbranched and branched, filamentous species. They occur in fresh water and are composed of uninucleate cells.

Mitosis

The single parietal chloroplast begins to divide at early prophase (Fig. 19.20 II*a*). A pair of centrioles is pre-

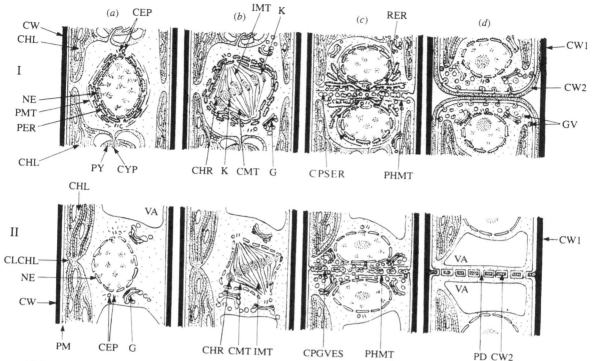

Figure 19.20. Mitosis and cytokinesis in the class Chlorophyceae. I. *Cylindrocapsa,* an example of the order Chlorococcales: closed mitosis with a non-persistent telophase spindle, cytokinesis achieved by the formation of a cell plate of smooth ER vesicles lying within a phycoplast. II. *Uronema,* an example of the order Chaetophorales: closed mitosis with a non-persistent telophase spindle, cytokinesis brought about by a cell plate of golgi vesicles lying within a phycoplast. See text for further explanation.
(a) Early prophase. (b) Metaphase. (c) Late telophase. (d) Early interphase. CEP = pair of centrioles; CHL = chloroplast; CHR = chromosome; CLCHL = cleaving chloroplast; CMT = chromosomal spindle microtubule; CPGVES = cell plate of golgi vesicles; CPSER = cell plate of smooth ER vesicles; CW = cell wall; CW1 = old cell wall; CW2 = young cell wall; CYP = cytoplasmic channel within pyrenoid; G = golgi body; GV = golgi vesicles; IMT = interzonal spindle microtubule; K = kinetochore; NE = nuclear envelope; PD = plasmodesma; PER = perinuclear endoplasmic reticulum; PHMT = phycoplast microtubule; PM = plasma membrane (plasmalemma); PMT = perinuclear microtubule; PY = pyrenoid; RER = rough endoplasmic reticulum; VA = vacuole. (I based on [1642–1644]; II on [426].)

sent at each pole of the cell and at late prophase microtubules proliferate within the nuclear envelope, forming a tilted spindle between the centrioles.

At metaphase the nuclear envelope does not break down, although it tends to become somewhat dispersed and vesiculated; *Uronema* therefore has a **closed mitosis** (Fig. 19.20 II*b*). The chromosomes become aligned in a distinct metaphase plate. Distinct kinetochores are lacking. At telophase the spindle soon degenerates and the young daughter nuclei move

back towards each other and lie close together during cytokinesis (a **non-persistent telophase spindle**).

Cytokinesis

A **cell plate of vesicles**, derived from the **golgi apparatus**, forms in the narrow equatorial zone of cytoplasm lying between the daughter nuclei. The vesicles are aligned by a **phycoplast**, i.e. a plate of microtubules lying in the future plane of division (Fig. 19.20

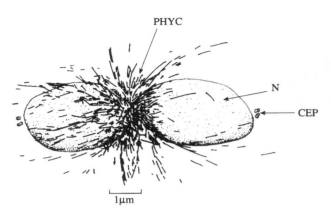

Figure 19.21. *Aphanochaete*, a member of the order Chaetophorales, class Chlorophyceae: the phycoplast immediately before the formation of the septum, with microtubules radiating out over the surfaces of the daughter nuclei. CEP = pair of centrioles; N = nucleus; PHYC = phycoplast. (Based on [1617].)

II*c*). They contain cell wall material and when they coalesce the result is a transverse septum composed of two plasmalemmas with the new transverse cell wall between them. Coalescence is not complete, however, and the narrow connections left between the daughter cells develop into **plasmodesmata**.

In thin sections prepared for transmission electron microscopy (TEM), the phycoplast appears to consist of dispersed microtubules lying in the plane of division (this is illustrated diagrammatically in Fig. 19.20 II*c*). It is now possible, however, to view the whole phycoplast using fluorescence microscopy, after the tubulin has been stained with tubulin-specific fluorescent antibodies; the spatial organization of the phycoplast can also be investigated in computer reconstructions of the phycoplast, made from TEM micrographs of serial sections. These techniques reveal that the phycoplast consists of a dense array of criss-crossing microtubules lying in the prospective plane of division; from here numerous microtubules radiate out from the middle of the telophase spindle, some along the sides of the two daughter nuclei (Figs. 19.21*a*, 21.21; [1617]).

Types of mitosis and cytokinesis in the Chlorophyta V. *Ulothrix*, an example of the class Ulvophyceae with uninucleate cells: closed mitosis with a persistent telophase spindle; cytokinesis effected by a cleavage furrow, to which golgi-derived vesicles are added (Fig. 19.22 I; [1030, 1031, 1651])

Ulothrix is a genus of unbranched filamentous green algae, many of which are marine (p. 394; Fig. 22.2). The class Ulvophyceae is predominantly marine and encompasses a great diversity of algae, from unicellular uninucleate species to blade-like multicellular forms and algae with siphonous thalli, composed of a series of multinucleate compartments.

Mitosis

A rudimentary cleavage furrow is present even before mitosis, during interphase (Fig. 19.22 I*a*); the leading edge of the furrow is accompanied by a few microtubules. Division of the parietal chloroplast has also occurred by the beginning of mitosis. The single lateral pair of centrioles present during interphase (Fig. 19.22 I*d*) replicates and one daughter pair moves to each of the future poles of the spindle. They remain slightly lateral, offset from the spindle axis (Fig. 19.22 I*a, b*).

At metaphase the nuclear envelope remains intact, so that **mitosis is closed** (Fig. 19.22 I*b*). The chromosomes align to form a distinct metaphase plate but kinetochores have not been observed. At telophase the spindle microtubules persist for some time, so that the daughter nuclei are held apart and do not approach each other, i.e. there is a **persistent telophase spindle**.

Cytokinesis

The zone of cytoplasm between the daughter nuclei, which is rather broad as a result of the persistent spindle, becomes highly vesiculate, through the formation of numerous golgi vesicles. A transverse septum is then produced by the addition of these vesicles to the pre-formed cleavage furrow (Fig. 19.22 I*c*). Further wall material is deposited onto the septum until a continuous transverse **cell wall** is produced, and this **lacks plasmodesmata** (Fig. 19.22 I*d*). **No phycoplast or phragmoplast** are involved in the formation of the

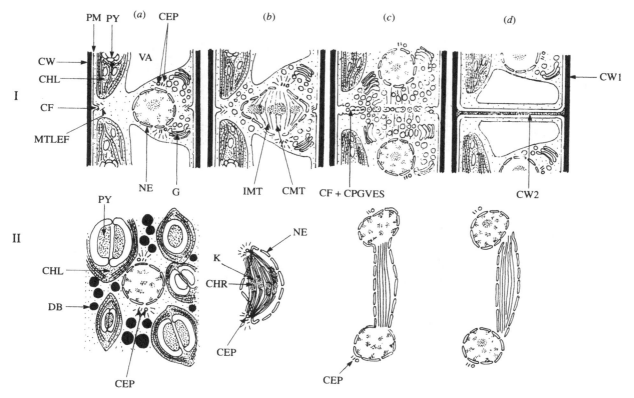

Figure 19.22. Mitosis and cytokinesis in the class Ulvophyceae (I) and the class Cladophorophyceae (II). I. *Ulothrix,* an example of a multicellular alga with uninucleate cells: closed mitosis with a persistent telophase spindle, cytokinesis brought about by a cleavage furrow, to which golgi vesicles are added, with no phycoplast. II. *Valonia,* an example with multinucleate cells: closed mitosis with a persistent telophase spindle (giving the telophase nucleus a characteristic dumbbell shape), cytokinesis decoupled from mitosis. See text for further explanation.
(*a*) Early prophase. (*b*) Metaphase. (*c*) Late telophase. (*d*) Early interphase. CEP = pair of centrioles; CF = cleavage furrow; CHL = chloroplast; CHR = chromosome; CMT = chromosomal spindle microtubule; CPGVES = cell plate of golgi vesicles; CW = cell wall; CW1 = old cell wall; CW2 = young cell wall; DB = dark-staining bodies; G = golgi body; IMT = interzonal spindle microtubule; K = kinetochore; MTLEF = microtubules along the leading edge of the cleavage furrow; NE = nuclear envelope; PM = plasma membrane (plasmalemma); PY = pyrenoid; VA = vacuole. (I based on [1651]; II on [740].)

transverse septum and wall. A phycoplast is an array of microtubules in the plane of the future transverse wall (see p. 328: type IV mitosis and cytokinesis), while a phragmoplast is an array of microtubules oriented perpendicular to the plane of the transverse walls (see p. 334: type VIII mitosis and cytokinesis).

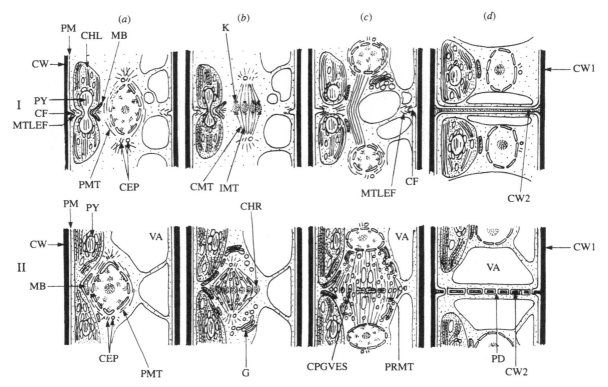

Figure 19.23. Mitosis and cytokinesis in the class Klebsormidiophyceae. I. *Klebsormidium:* open mitosis
with a persistent telophase spindle, cytokinesis
brought about by a cleavage furrow. II. *Coleochaete:*
open mitosis with a persistent telophase spindle,
cytokinesis achieved by formation of a cell plate of
golgi vesicles within a phragmoplast. See text for further information.
(a) Early prophase. (b) Metaphase. (c) Late telophase. (d)
Early interphase. CEP = pair of centrioles; CF =
cleavage furrow; CHL = chloroplast; CHR = chromosome; CMT = chromosomal spindle microtubule;
CPGVES = cell plate of golgi vesicles; CW = cell
wall; CW1 = old cell wall; CW2 = young cell wall;
G = golgi body; IMT = interzonal spindle microtubule; K = kinetochore; MB = microbody; MTLEF =
microtubules along the leading edge of the cleavage
furrow; PD = plasmodesma; PM = plasma membrane
(plasmalemma); PMT = perinuclear microtubule;
PRMT = phragmoplast microtubule; PY = pyrenoid;
VA = vacuole. (I based on [1036]; II on [1119].)

Types of mitosis and cytokinesis in the Chlorophyta VI. *Valonia,* an example of the class Cladophorophyceae with multinucleate cells: closed mitosis with a prominent persistent telophase spindle, which gives the telophase nucleus a characteristic dumbbell shape; mitosis not immediately followed by cytokinesis (Fig. 19.22 II; [740, 958])

Valonia plants consist of large vesicles, up to one or
two centimetres in diameter, each of which is a single

multinucleate cell with a large central vacuole and a
thin peripheral layer of protoplasm, containing the
organelles and nuclei (Fig. 23.8b, p. 417).

Mitosis

During prophase centrioles appear close to the
nucleus, at the poles of the future spindle (Fig. 19.22
IIa). At metaphase the nuclear envelope remains
intact, so that **mitosis is closed** (Fig. 19.22 IIb). The
metaphase spindle is distinctly curved and the spindle
microtubules converge upon the centrioles lying outside the nuclear envelope, passing through it via tiny

gaps; polar fenestrae are not present. The chromosomes do not align to form a distinct metaphase plate. The chromosome microtubules attach in groups to distinct, plate-like kinetochores (Fig. 19.22 II*b*). During anaphase and telophase the interzonal microtubules continue to grow, pushing the daughter nuclei far apart (Fig. 19.22 II*c*), but both the nuclei and spindle remain entirely surrounded by a common nuclear envelope, so that the telophase nuclei, together with the elongate spindle connecting them, have a characteristic dumbbell-like shape (Fig. 19.22 II*c*). *Valonia* thus has a very conspicuous **persistent telophase spindle**. At the end of telophase, or in early interphase, the nuclei 'bud off' from the remnant of the spindle, and their own nuclear envelopes are completed (Fig. 19.22 II*d*).

In multinucleate cells mitosis is not usually followed immediately by cytokinesis. In *Chaetomorpha*, a close relative of *Valonia*, the multinucleate cells are divided by ingrowth of diaphragm-like transverse walls (Fig. 23.7, p. 416).

This type of mitosis or something similar, again producing a curious dumbbell-like shape of the nucleus at telophase, seems to be characteristic of many chlorophytes with multinucleate compartments, though it is not found in all of them. It occurs in the classes Cladophorophyceae (to which *Valonia* belongs: see p. 410) and Bryopsidophyceae ([739]; see also p. 422). However, there is some variation in these groups; for instance, centrioles are not always involved in the assembly of the mitotic spindle (e.g. [739]), and their presence in the example we have described (*Valonia*) may reflect the fact that mitoses in this organism occur in preparation for the formation of **zoids**, i.e. cells that need centrioles to function as flagellar basal bodies (cf. p. 308).

Types of mitosis and cytokinesis in the Chlorophyta VII. *Klebsormidium*, an example of the class Klebsormidiophyceae (order Klebsormidiales): open mitosis with a prominent persistent telophase spindle; cytokinesis effected by a cleavage furrow (Fig. 19.23 I; [1036])

Klebsormidium is an unbranched filamentous chlorophyte, which occurs in freshwater or subaerial habitats (p. 459, Fig. 28.2*g–j*). Without electron microscopical investigation of nuclear and cell division, or of the zoospores, it is virtually impossible to distinguish *Klebsormidium* from the genera *Ulothrix* (p. 394, Fig. 22.2) and *Uronema* (p. 380, Fig. 21.22*a*).

Mitosis

By the end of interphase a rudimentary cleavage furrow can already be detected, the leading edge of the furrow being accompanied by a few microtubules. The parietal chloroplast, together with the pyrenoid contained within it, begins to divide, by constriction (Fig. 19.23 I*a*). The single pair of centrioles, which is located at the side of the nucleus during interphase (Fig. 19.23 I*d*), now replicates, each daughter pair moving to one pole of the future spindle. Microtubules are then formed outside the nuclear envelope, between the centriolar pairs (Fig. 19.23 I*a*), while a conspicuous microbody (peroxisome) can be seen lying between the nucleus and chloroplast.

During metaphase the nuclear envelope breaks down completely, so that **mitosis is open**. The metaphase spindle is characteristically elongate and the chromosomes align to form a distinct metaphase plate (Fig. 19.23 I*b*). The chromosome microtubules attach to plate-like kinetochores, which are distinctly layered in structure.

At anaphase (not shown) and early telophase the daughter chromosomes move far apart, mainly through a great elongation of the spindle, but to a lesser extent by a decrease in the distance from the chromosomes to the poles. At telophase (Fig. 19.23 I*c*) the nuclei are held far apart by a prominent and **persistent telophase spindle**. This is supported in the cell by large vacuoles, which accumulate in the cytoplasm around and among the spindle microtubules, between the daughter nuclei.

Cytokinesis

The incipient **cleavage furrow**, present from before prophase, does not develop any further until telophase. Then, however, the cleavage furrow resumes its growth inwards, bisecting the cell and thus also the persistent spindle (Fig. 19.23 I*c, d*). Just before this the chloroplast and pyrenoid, together with the microbody, finish their division. The leading edge of the furrow is lined and preceded by microtubules but this collection of microtubules, and the remaining spindle microtubules, with their various orientations do **not** resemble a true phycoplast, as is present for example in *Uronema* (types of mitosis and cytokinesis IV, p. 328). The transverse wall in *Klebsormidium* seems to arise entirely through the ingrowth of the cleavage furrow, wall material being added between the two plasmamembranes; there are **no plasmodesmata** (Fig. 19.23 I*d*).

Types of mitosis and cytokinesis in the Chlorophyta VIII. *Coleochaete,* a second example of the class Klebsormidiophyceae (order Coleochaetales): open mitosis with a prominent persistent telophase spindle; cytokinesis effected through the formation of a cell plate of golgi vesicles in a phragmoplast (Fig. 19.23 II) [1119, 1419]

Coleochaete forms small disc- or cushion-like thalli, which occur as epiphytes on larger algae or aquatic angiosperms in freshwater. They are composed of densely branched, cohering filaments, and bear a characteristic type of hair with a basal sheath (p. 460, Fig. 28.3).

Mitosis

At prophase the parietal chloroplast begins to cleave. There is a conspicuous microbody between the chloroplast and the nucleus. During interphase there is a single centriolar pair and at prophase this replicates and each of the two new pairs takes up a position at one pole of the future spindle. Microtubules then form between the centriolar pairs, outside the envelope of the prophase nucleus, which is somewhat elongate (Fig. 19.23 II*a*).

In the course of metaphase the nuclear envelope disperses completely, so that **mitosis is open**; vesicles and endoplasmic reticulum are to be found among the spindle microtubules (Fig. 19.23 II*b*). The chromosomes become aligned in a distinct metaphase plate but the chromosomal microtubules do not attach to clearly defined kinetochores (Fig. 19.23 II*b*). At anaphase (not shown) and early telophase, the daughter chromosomes are separated from each other mainly through the elongation of the spindle, though shortening of the chromosome–pole distance also plays a part, as in *Klebsormidium*.

The telophase nuclei are held far apart by a prominent **persistent telophase spindle**.

Cytokinesis

New microtubules proliferate so that by the end of telophase the spindle microtubules are surrounded by many other microtubules running parallel to them. The whole complex of microtubules from the old spindle and the peripheral arrays of new microtubules is termed a **phragmoplast**, and it also includes **actin filaments** [16]. Numerous vesicles appear within the phragmoplast, derived from the golgi apparatus. They seem to be 'guided' by the microtubules or actin filaments (or both) to the future plane of division, where they become arranged to form a **cell plate of golgi-derived vesicles** (Fig. 19.23 II*c*). The vesicles contain cell wall material; their coalescence results in the formation of a transverse septum, consisting of two plasma membranes with the new transverse wall sandwiched between. The coalescence is not complete. Connections are left between the daughter cells and these develop into **plasmodesmata**.

This type of mitosis and cytokinesis is comparatively rare in the green algae but it is, of course, the usual mode of division in bryophytes and tracheophytes. There is a difference, however, in that centrioles are generally not involved in mitosis in the two groups of higher plants.

Levels of organization of the chlorophyte thallus

In the Chlorophyta various kinds of thallus organization can be found; these have already been listed on p. 119 and in Table 6.1. The following levels of organization can be distinguished in the green algae.

unicellular flagellates or **monads** (e.g. *Chlamydomonas*; Fig. 19.1)

colonial flagellates (e.g. *Volvox, Gonium, Eudorina*; Figs. 21.4*a–d*, 21.5)

palmelloid (or **tetrasporal**) colonies (e.g. *Pseudosphaerocystis, Sphaerocystis, Coccomyxa*; Figs. 21.4*f*, 21.14)

coccoid organisms (e.g. *Chlorococcum, Chodatella, Oocystis*; Figs. 21.7, 21.10)

sarcinoid (= packet-like) organization (e.g.

Chlorosarcinopsis; Fig. 21.17)

filamentous organization (e.g. *Ulothrix, Stigeoclonium, Oedogonium, Spirogyra*; Figs. 21.23, 21.25, 22.2, 29.1)

thallose organization (e.g. *Ulva*; Fig. 22.10)

siphonous organization (e.g. *Bryopsis, Codium, Caulerpa*; Figs. 24.7, 24.10, 24.16)

Of the levels of organization listed in Table 6.1 only the amoeboid type is missing, for there are no green algae that live as amoeboid cells during the vegetative phase of the life cycle. Reproductive cells can sometimes be amoeboid, however, as for instance in some Chaetophorales and Zygnematales ([377]).

Within the chlorophytes the sarcinoid level of organization has received much attention, since it is considered by some authors (e.g. [100, 577]) that this represents the most primitive multicellular condition.

In the traditional systems of classification (e.g. [100, 440, 464, 703]), thallus organization was used as the principal basis for distinguishing orders within the Chlorophyta. For instance, Bold & Wynne ([100]) distinguished the following orders on the basis of organizational level.

Volvocales: unicellular and colonial flagellates (e.g. *Chlamydomonas*, Fig. 19.1; *Pyramimonas*, Fig. 19.9; *Nephroselmis*, Fig. 20.2; *Gonium*, Fig. 21.4a; *Volvox*, Fig. 21.5).

Tetrasporales: palmelloid chlorophytes, characterized by having immobile, *Chlamydomonas*-like cells embedded in a gelatinous matrix (Fig. 21.4*e, f*).

Chlorococcales: coccoid chlorophytes (e.g. *Chlorococcum*, Fig. 21.7; *Chlorella*, Fig. 21.10; *Kirchneriella*, Fig. 21.11).

Chlorosarcinales: characterized by the sarcinoid (packet-like) level of organization (e.g. *Chlorosarcinopsis*, Fig. 21.17).

Ulotrichales: unbranched, filamentous chlorophytes (e.g. *Ulothrix*, Fig. 22.2; *Uronema*, Fig. 21.22a, *Cylindrocapsa*, Fig. 21.18; *Klebsormidium*, Fig. 28.2*g*).

Chaetophorales: chlorophytes with branching filaments (e.g. *Stigeoclonium*, Fig. 21.23).

Ulvales: thallose chlorophytes (e.g. *Ulva*, Fig. 22.10; *Enteromorpha*, Fig. 22.11).

Cladophorales, Siphonocladales, and **Acro-**

siphoniales: all with siphonocladous organization, composed of multinucleate cells; this is a special type of siphonous organization (e.g. *Chaetomorpha*, Fig. 23.7). Bold & Wynne ([100]) separated these orders on the basis of differences in reproduction and cytology.

Caulerpales and **Dasycladales**: siphonous chlorophytes (e.g. *Caulerpa*, Fig. 24.16; *Acetabularia*, Fig. 25.1). These orders differ in their vegetative structure, the Dasycladales having a pronounced radial symmetry.

Oedogoniales: these have branched or unbranched filaments, but in addition they have a highly characteristic vegetative structure and mode of reproduction (see p. 382).

Trentepohliales: branched filamentous chlorophytes, additionally characterized by special features of the filamentous thallus and by the method of reproduction (see p. 445).

Zygnematales: this order encompasses species that either are coccoid or have an unbranched, filamentous level of organization; all have a similar, very characteristic cytology and reproduction (see p. 461).

Charales: these algae, with their unique vegetative structure and reproduction, are put by Bold & Wynne ([100]) in a separate division, the Charophyta.

The subdivision of the Chlorophyta outlined above (with some slight modifications) is still widely used, for two reasons.

1 It is desirable, for practical purposes, for a classification to be simple and stable. Researchers and other users of classifications therefore hesitate to adopt radical taxonomic rearrangements.

2 Because the traditional system of classification is essentially so simple, it is not difficult to find a place in it for almost any known green alga.

However, in the past 20 years, electron microscopical observations have revealed many new ultrastructural features, which have enabled us to understand much better how the various groups of green algae are interrelated. The ultrastructure of the flagellate cells (zoids) and the pattern of mitosis and cytokinesis, in particular, have given important information about the evolution of the main lineages. The new data indicate that many traditional orders are heterogeneous, harbouring quite unrelated green algae, with quite different types of cell division and zoids.

Thus, for instance, the order Volvocales has traditionally included both *Chlamydomonas* (Fig. 19.1) and *Pyramimonas* (Fig. 19.9), while recent research suggests that these two genera belong to different evolutionary lineages (recognized as classes), which diverged from each other long ago; in this account, therefore, they are placed in the classes Chlorophyceae and Prasinophyceae, respectively. The traditional order Chlorococcales is also unnatural. The kind of zoid formed by most coccoid green algae seems to be the *Chlamydomonas* type, with a cruciate arrangement of microtubular roots in a 1 o'clock – 7 o'clock configuration (Fig. 19.14c). However, at least one genus, *Trebouxia*, has zoids with an 11 o'clock – 5 o'clock cruciate arrangement, and so it has now been removed from the Chlorococcales. *Trebouxia* (p. 449, Fig. 27.1a) is an extremely common aerophytic alga, and is also found widely as the phycobiont of many lichens ([1140]).

An even more striking example of heterogeneity is given by the 'old' order Chlorosarcinales. The sarcinoid soil alga *Friedmannia* (Fig. 27.1d–h) has zoids with a cruciate 11 o'clock – 5 o'clock arrangement of microtubular roots (Fig. 19.14b; [1180]), while in another sarcinoid soil alga, *Chlorokybus* (Fig. 28.2c–f) the flagellar roots do not form a cruciate configuration at all; instead they have a unilateral system of roots (Fig. 19.15; [1521]). Yet other sarcinoid genera have zoids with a 1 o'clock – 7 o'clock cruciate arrangement of flagellar roots (Fig. 19.14c; [1140]).

A comparable spread of different, unrelated forms occurs among the unbranched filamentous green algae previously classified in the 'old' Ulotrichales. *Ulothrix* (Fig. 22.2) has zoids with a cruciate 11 o'clock – 5 o'clock arrangement of rootlets (Fig. 19.14b; [1031, 1644, 1645]) and type V mitosis–cytokinesis (Fig. 19.22 I). *Uronema* (Fig. 21.22a) has zoids with a 1 o'clock – 7 o'clock configuration and type IV mitosis–cytokinesis (Figs. 19.14c, 19.20 II; [423, 426]). *Klebsormidium* (Fig. 28.2g), on the other hand, has zoospores of the unilateral type (Fig. 19.15; [1119, 1419]) and type VII mitosis–cytokinesis (p. 333, Fig. 19.23 I; [1036, 1417]). Yet in the light microscope the filaments of *Ulothrix*, *Uronema* and *Klebsormidium* look so simi-

lar that all have often been identified as *Ulothrix* ([1031]). Convergent evolution has apparently produced a very similar plant habit, with unbranched, parallel-sided filaments, in three distantly related phylogenetic lineages of the Chlorophyta, namely the classes Ulvophyceae (*Ulothrix*), Chlorophyceae (*Uronema*) and Klebsormidiophyceae (*Klebsormidium*).

The Chaetophorales, which traditionally accommodates those chlorophytes with branched filaments, has also been shown by recent work to contain members of quite different lineages. *Acrochaete* (Fig. 22.13), a tiny marine alga, has zoids with a cruciate 11 o'clock – 5 o'clock configuration of flagellar roots (Fig. 19.14b; [1326]). *Stigeoclonium*, which has thalli that consist of erect branched filaments arising from a prostrate system of filaments (Fig. 21.23), is a freshwater chlorophyte that produces zoids with a cruciate 1 o'clock – 7 o'clock configuration (Fig. 19.14 c-2; [1091]) and type IV mitosis–cytokinesis (p. 328, Fig. 19.20 II; [426, 1419]). Finally, there is *Coleochaete*, a freshwater alga that forms discs or cushions of densely branched filaments, which produces zoids of the unilateral, charophycean type (Fig. 19.15 [1419, 1641]); its mitosis–cytokinesis conforms to type VIII (p. 334, Fig. 19.23 II), which is common in bryophytes and vascular plants. It is clear, then, that the branched filamentous level of organization, which has traditionally been considered characteristic of the Chaetophorales, has arisen independently in at least three different evolutionary lineages of chlorophytes. As in the Ulotrichales, the degree of convergence undermines the traditional concept of the order.

What about the thallose organization traditionally characteristic of the Ulvales? Has this too arisen several times by convergent evolution, so that the Ulvales too are heterogeneous? The answer must be yes. *Schizomeris* (Fig. 21.22b–e) has a cylindrical thallus, which can be constricted at intervals and which is solid, not hollow as in *Enteromorpha* (Fig. 22.11c). It is a freshwater alga and its zoids have a 1 o'clock – 7 o'clock cruciate arrangement of roots (Fig. 19.14c; [422a]) and type IV mitosis–cytokinesis (p. 328, Fig. 19.20 II; [1141]). The zoids of *Ulva* (Fig. 22.10) and *Enteromorpha* (Fig. 22.11), on the other hand, have an 11 o'clock – 5 o'clock configuration (Fig. 19.14b; [424, 1727]), while their mitosis–cytokinesis accords with type V (p. 330, Fig. 19.22 I; [1044, 1143]).

Some other orders have emerged more or less unscathed from the close scrutiny of electron microscopists. These are the orders that were characterized not only by the level of organization of the thalli but also by particular features of their vegetation structure, reproduction or biochemistry. They comprise the Cladophorales (p. 408), Caulerpales (here equivalent to the class Bryopsidophyceae, p. 419), Dasycladales (p. 436), Oedogoniales (p. 382), Trentepohliales (p. 445), Zygnematales (p. 463) and Charales (p. 474). The other orders – the Volvocales, Tetrasporales, Chlorococcales, Chlorosarcinales, Ulotrichales, Chaetophorales and Ulvales – which have all been revealed by electron microscopy to be heterogeneous, must be abandoned or redefined in such a way that they become truly natural groupings.

It must be admitted, however, that the adoption of a new, natural system has one considerable disadvantage: it is not possible to assign a great many green algae to any of the new or redefined classes and orders, except perhaps tentatively, because their ultrastructure has not yet been investigated. Of course, this is not an unusual problem in taxonomy and there are several possible solutions to it. One is to put the uninvestigated forms in a special category, 'incertae sedis' (= of uncertain position), within the Chlorophyta. Another is to classify them provisionally, assigning them to the class and order where they seem to belong on the basis of light microscope observations; the provisional nature of the classification should be clearly indicated. This second solution will undoubtedly be more popular.

Pigments and chloroplasts

The green algae owe their colour to the fact that the green of the chlorophylls is not masked by accessory pigments, even though several carotenoids are always present: β-carotene is present, and also the xanthophylls lutein, violaxanthin, neoxanthin, antheraxanthin and zeaxanthin, of which lutein is usually the most important (Table 1.2), although it may be replaced by prasinoxanthin in certain members of the Prasinophyceae [332, 437a, 725]. In members of the class Bryopsidophyceae lutein is scarce or absent and the xanthophylls siphonein and siphonoxanthin are to be found instead. Siphonoxanthin or loroxanthin has also been found instead of lutein in a few species in the order Cladophorales [544] and in some, but not all, *Ulva* species [776, 815, 1929, 1930, 1931]. It is important in

evaluating the taxonomic significance of this variation to realize that lutein is a biochemical precursor of loroxanthin and siphonoxanthin. In the Cladophorales and Ulvales the possession of these two pigments is thought to be an adaptation to life in deep water, because they are well suited to the harvesting of the green light found there [816, 1929, 1930].

In some chlorophytes the chlorophyll is masked by 'haematochrome', which is red and consists of a mixture of carotenoid pigments. It occurs outside the chloroplasts in droplets of lipid. The aerophytic species *Chlamydomonas nivalis* can colour snow red, as has already been mentioned, while *Haematococcus pluvialis* (Fig. 21.3*d*) is sometimes responsible for giving puddles a red hue [276, 330]. The filamentous chlorophyte *Trentepohlia* (Figs. 26.1, 26.3) also accumulates haematochrome, forming red or brown velvety growths on tree trunks and damp rock-faces. Elsewhere carotenoids often accumulate within the cells in cultures that have become depleted in nutrients.

The chloroplasts contain chlorophyll b as well as chlorophyll a, and recently a pigment that resembles chlorophyll c has been discovered in at least two species of the class Prasinophyceae [332, 1897], where it occurs in addition to chlorophylls a and b. Chlorophyll c is generally considered characteristic of the divisions Heterokontophyta, Haptophyta, Cryptophyta and Dinophyta (Table 1.2), and so its appearance in green algae was rather unexpected. Other investigations indicate, however, that the chlorophyll c-like pigment is MgDVP (magnesium 2,4-divinylphaeoporphyrin a_5 monomethyl ester), an important intermediate in the synthesis of chlorophyll [794], but the evidence remains controversial [1532a].

The chloroplasts vary greatly in shape and size. In unicellular forms the chloroplast often takes the form of a cup with a thick base (Figs. 19.1, 21.7). In filamentous green algae, on the other hand, the chloroplast is often annular (ring-like) or reticulate (net-like; Figs. 21.25, 22.2); in either case it lies against the cell wall. In yet other green algae there are many small discoid chloroplasts, which again are parietal (i.e. lying against the cell wall; Figs. 21.3*s*, 24.4*a*). More massive and elaborate plastids, lying along the longitudinal axis of the cell and having lobed margins, are particularly characteristic of members of the orders Prasiolales and Zygnematales (Figs. 27.4, 29.4*d*), although they do occasionally occur also in other orders, e.g. in some *Chlamydomonas* species (order Volvocales).

Each chloroplast often contains one to several pyrenoids. With the light microscope pyrenoids appear as round or oval bodies within the chloroplast and in the Chlorophyta plates of starch can always be found lying against them; these stain blue-violet with iodine (Figs. 19.1*a*, 21.7*a*). The starch grains lie within the chloroplast, whereas in all the other divisions of the algae the reserve polysaccharides (of which there are several different kinds besides starch) are stored outside, in the cytoplasm. The function of the pyrenoid in photosynthetic CO_2 fixation is discussed on p. 310.

In contrast to the Rhodophyta (p. 48) and Heterokontophyta (p. 102), the Chlorophyta are not uniform in the ultrastructure of the chloroplasts; there is no plan common to the whole group. However, the following generalizations can be made:

the number of thylakoids per stack (lamella) is variable, from 2 to 6, or sometimes more (Figs. 19.7*c, e*, 19.8, 23.3*b*). In several other divisions the number is constant, at two or three thylakoids per lamella;

there is no peripheral, girdle lamella surrounding the other lamellae: contrast the Heterokontophyta (p. 112)

the chloroplast is surrounded only by its own double membrane (Figs. 19.1, 19.8). There is no extra fold of endoplasmic reticulum as in the Heterokontophyta, Haptophyta, Eustigmatophyta, and Cryptophyta.

Electron microscopical investigations show that the pyrenoid consists of a homogeneous stroma, which stains rather more heavily than the stroma of the chloroplast itself. In many cases the pyrenoid stroma is penetrated by several thylakoids, which sometimes narrow within it to form small tubes (Fig. 19.7*e* ; [319, 508, 575]).

Within the Chlorophyta some of the classes and orders seem to have characteristic types of chloroplast and pyrenoid ultrastructure. There are differences, for example, in the stacking of the thylakoids, in the way the thylakoids penetrate into the pyrenoid, and in the arrangement of the starch grains around the pyrenoid ([749]). Elsewhere, however, there can be variation in such features even between species of the same genus ([381, 1031, 1034]).

The chloroplast DNA is organized in numerous small (*ca.* 1–2 µm) aggregates, referred to as nucleoids, which are scattered throughout the chloroplast ([254]; see also pp. 51, 112). Each aggregate consists of a number of circular molecules of chloroplast DNA, all the same size, each of which contains a complete chloroplast genome ([198, 1354]).

Storage products

The most important storage product of photosynthesis is starch, an α-1,4-linked glucan; in the Dasycladales and Cladophorales, however, there is also a fructan. The starch lies within the chloroplast in the form of grains, which are either distributed through the chloroplast stroma or appressed to the pyrenoid (Fig. 19.1). Besides starch, there are also lipids, which occur inside and outside the chloroplasts in the form of small globules.

Cell wall structure

In many Chlorophyta, just as in the red and brown algae (pp. 51, 169), the cell wall consists of a structural, fibrillar component and an amorphous matrix component. The fibrillar part, which is rigid and gives the wall its strength, lies embedded in the matrix. In most cases the fibrillar component forms a layer lying directly against the plasmalemma. The amorphous part of the wall, on the other hand, is predominantly on the outer side of the wall, forming a slimy outer layer, although fibrillar material does extend out into this.

Electron microscopical investigations have shown that the fibrillar layer consists for the most part of 'microfibrils', with diameters varying from 3 to 35 nm. In the classes Cladophorophyceae, Zygnematophyceae and Charophyceae, in certain representatives of other classes of green algae, and in the bryophytes and vascular plants, the microfibrils consist of crystalline cellulose. The cellulose microfibrils of the Cladophorophyceae are synthesized by linear arrays of particles ('cellulose synthase'), which are free to move within the plasmalemma (Fig. 19.24). In the Zygnematophyceae and Charophyceae, on the other hand, microfibril synthesis is performed by rosette-

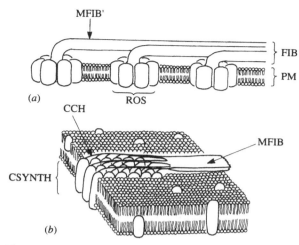

Fig. 19.24. (*a*) Synthesis of cellulose microfibrils in a member of the class Zygnematophyceae, by rosette-like cellulose synthase complexes. (*b*) Synthesis of cellulose microfibrils in a member of the class Cladophorophyceae, by rows of cellulose synthesizing units. CCH = cellulose chain; CSYNTH = cellulose synthase complex; FIB = large cellulose fibril; MFIB = cellulose microfibril; MFIB′ = 5 nm diameter cellulose microfibril; PM = plasma membrane (plasmalemma); ROS = rosette-like cellulose synthase complex. (*a* based on [518]; *b* on [784a].)

like complexes of cellulose synthase particles, as in vascular plants (Fig. 19.24; [16, 518, 754, 1206, 1207, 1208]).

In the green algae as a whole, the chemical composition of the microfibrillar and amorphous fractions of the cell wall varies greatly; in many groups, the composition has yet to be investigated. It is likely that proteins pervade the cell walls of green algae, just as they do the walls of higher plants, binding to the polysaccharides to form glycoprotein. Unfortunately there is as yet little information on this topic ([1148]). It is known, however, that the cell envelopes ('walls') of *Chlamydomonas* and related flagellates in the order Volvocales consist of glycoprotein and that this includes a crystalline layer (see p. 303).

An outer coat of sporopollenin-like substances has been demonstrated in the walls of several coccoid green algae, such as *Chlorella* (Fig. 21.10*a–c*), *Scenedesmus* (Fig. 21.13*d, e*) and *Pediastrum* (Fig. 21.16; [1419]), and a similar covering has also been found in two genera of the order Trentepohliales ([212]). Sporopollenin itself occurs, of course, in the walls of the spores and pollen grains produced by land plants,

where it helps protect the cells from desiccation. Perhaps the sporopollenin-like layer acts in a similar way in coccoid green algae, enabling the airborne dispersal of these freshwater algae from one water body to another (as observed for instance by [1563]). The presence of such layers in the aerophytic members of the order Trentepohliales could also be interpreted as an adaptation to terrestrial life.

Types of life history in green algae

Meiosis is thought to have arisen at an early stage in the evolution of the primaeval Eukaryota. One important argument for this is the fundamental similarity of the process in living eukaryotes, and this is discussed further in Chapter 5 ('Division Rhodophyta', p. 55). The positions of meiosis and sexual reproduction in the life cycle are thought to be conservative features, changing only slowly during evolution, so that they generally characterize taxa at a high level of the hierarchy (e.g. classes, orders). Our knowledge of life cycles is still very poor for many green algae, however, especially with regard to the exact position of meiosis and consequently also the ploidy of the different stages.

On the basis of the evidence available at present, it seems that most green algal groups have a **haplontic life cycle**; only the nucleus of the zygote is diploid (Fig. 1.4). In the freshwater classes Chlorophyceae, Zygnematophyceae, Klebsormidiophyceae and Charophyceae, the zygote is also a resting stage, a **hypnozygote** (Figs. 21.1*f*, 28.3*c*, 29.8, 30.3*q*). Hypnozygotes are thick-walled and only germinate after a period of obligate dormancy. They are probably an adaptation to life in freshwater, where they enable algae to survive adverse circumstances, such as temporary drying out of the habitat or the anoxic conditions in decaying organic matter on lake bottoms. Many hypnozygotes can also be dispersed from one body of freshwater to another, by water fowl, insects, the wind, or some other agency. In this connection it is important to realize that, in geological terms, freshwater habitats are ephemeral compared with the world's oceans; many of them will only develop an algal flora if algae are transported to them through the air.

In the classes Bryopsidophyceae and Dasycladophyceae, and in the order Codiolales of the Ulvophyceae, all of them marine groups, the zygote nuclei are again probably the only diploid nuclei of the life cycle, although the evidence for this is limited. Hypnozygotes are not formed in these algae and the zygotes are merely non-dormant, unicellular stages. For a long time the Bryopsidophyceae and Dasycladophyceae were thought to be basically diplontic (Fig. 1.4), with meiosis preceding the formation of gametes: in a diplontic life cycle the only haploid cells are the gametes. The early karyological evidence on which this was based has now been called into question, however, and the occurrence of diplontic life cycles in green algae is now thought unlikely (for further discussion, see [704]).

Diplohaplontic life cycles (Fig. 1.4) seem to have evolved at least four times in green plants, in the classes Ulvophyceae (order Ulvales), Cladophorophyceae and Trentepohliophyceae, and in the 'higher plants' (Bryophyta and Tracheophyta).

Subdivision of the Chlorophyta into classes and orders

We subdivide the division (phylum) Chlorophyta into eleven classes.

1. Class **Prasinophyceae***
   Orders **Mamiellales***,
   Pseudoscourfeldiales*, **Pyramimonadales***,
   Chlorodendrales*
2. Class **Chlorophyceae***
   Orders **Volvocales**, **Chlorococcales***,
   Chaetophorales, **Oedogoniales**
3. Class **Ulvophyceae**
   Orders **Codiolales**, **Ulvales**
4. Class **Cladophorophyceae**
   Order **Cladophorales**
5. Class **Bryopsidophyceae**
   Orders **Bryopsidales**, **Halimedales**
6. Class **Dasycladophyceae**
   Order **Dasycladales**
7. Class **Trentepohliophyceae**
   Order **Trentepohliales**
8. Class **Pleurastrophyceae**
   Order **Pleurastrales**
   One order, the **Prasiolales***, whose true position is uncertain, is placed here provisionally.
9. Class **Klebsormidiophyceae**
   Orders **Klebsormidiales**, **Coleochaetales**
10. Class **Zygnematophyceae**
    Orders **Zygnematales**, **Desmidiales**
11. Class **Charophyceae**
    Order **Charales**

The status of the taxa (two classes and six orders) marked with an asterisk (*) is uncertain.

Once it had been discovered that there are at least four fundamentally different types of flagellate cell architecture in the Chlorophyta, it was proposed that each of the four might represent a major phylogenetic lineage, and hence that each should perhaps be recognized as a class within the Chlorophyta. Unicellular flagellate chlorophytes with organic body scales were placed in the class Prasinophyceae; chlorophytes whose zoids had a cruciate type of flagellar root system, with a 1 o'clock – 7 o'clock configuration, were placed in the Chlorophyceae; chlorophytes with a cruciate 11 o'clock – 5 o'clock configuration were assigned to the Ulvophyceae; and the chlorophytes with a unilateral arrangement of flagellar roots were put in the Charophyceae [704, 1140, 1175, 1644, 1645]. As conceived in this way, however, each class would encompass green algae with extremely diverse vegetative cell structure, cell wall composition, patterns of mitosis and cell division, and life history. We take the view that classes of algae should be distinguished by *sets* of derived characters, common to the members of the class. The features of the flagellate cell are very important, of course, but they should also correlate with other characters. We have had to retain the classes Prasinophyceae and Chlorophyceae in the broad sense outlined above, because there is as yet no better alternative; in any case, the classes probably do each contain a core of closely related genera. With the Ulvophyceae and Charophyceae, we have been more radical, using these names in a much more restricted way than in the four-class system. We have characterized them not only by the architecture of the zoids, but also by the pattern of mitosis and cell division, the cell wall composition, the architecture of the protoplast, and the life cycle.

Note added in proof

We have defined the class Chlorophyceae much more narrowly than has been usual hitherto (traditionally, it has been taken to include almost all green algae), but Kouwets [907a] argues persuasively that even our restricted concept of this class is incorrect, because the Chlorophyceae would still be phylogenetically heterogeneous. According to Kouwets, it should be split into at least two classes: the **Chlamydophyceae** and the **Chlorophyceae** (which would thus be even more narrowly circumscribed than by us). The two classes are characterized principally as follows.

Class **Chlamydophyceae**

1. The zoids are of the **cruciate 1 o'clock – 7 o'clock type**, as in *Chlamydomonas* (Figs. 19.1, 19.14c).
2. Each zoid possesses a 'wall' (not a true wall, since it is pierced by the pores through which the flagella emerge), although this is sometimes inconspicuous.
3. Four centrioles (two pairs) are associated with the interphase nucleus; during mitosis the pairs can immediately be mobilized to function at the spindle poles.
4. Zoids or other spores are formed through **centripetal cleavage** within a phycoplast (Fig. 19.17 II).

Class **Chlorophyceae**

1. The zoids are of the **cruciate 12 o'clock – 6 o'clock type** (Fig. 19.14a).
2. The zoids are naked, lacking any wall.
3. Two centrioles (one pair) are associated with the interphase nucleus; replication takes place immediately before mitosis.
4. Zoids or other spores are formed through **centrifugal cleavage** within a phycoplast (Fig. 21.12g, h).

The class **Chlamydophyceae** contains the following green algae among those treated in this book: the orders **Volvocales** (p. 350) and **Chaetophorales** (p. 378), and the **Chlorococcales** [but only part of this order as we have described it, including, for example, *Chlorococcum* (p. 362), *Chlorosarcinopsis* (p. 374), *Cylindrocapsa* (?) (p. 376)].

Of the other green algae we describe, the following belong to the class Chlorophyceae, *sensu* Kouwets: *Chlorella* (p. 365), *Kirchneriella* (p. 366), *Scenedesmus* (p. 370), *Hydrodictyon* (p. 371), *Pediastrum* (p. 374), *Sphaeroplea* (p. 377) and *Atractomorpha* (p. 377). These algae, which will be found within the Chlorococcales in our account, are placed by Kouwets in the order **Chlorellales**.

Not all of the examples given in this book can yet be assigned to one of the classes recognized by Kouwets,

because the ultrastructural characteristics needed for their classification have not been studied.

If Kouwets' proposals are accepted, it would be logical to treat the order Oedogoniales as a separate class, in view of the highly characteristic ultrastructure of its stephanokont zoids, and the type of mitosis and cytokinesis (p. 382).

The classes Chlamydophyceae, Chlorophyceae (in the very restricted sense used by Kouwets) and Oedogoniophyceae had already been proposed by Ettl and Komarek ([385–387]; see also [1526]), on the basis of light microscopical characteristics. They are now confirmed in part, and also modified, by observations of ultrastructure made with the electron microscope.

20

Chlorophyta: Class 1. Prasinophyceae

The principal characteristics of the Prasinophyceae

1 The Prasinophyceae are free-living, flagellate green algae.

2 The cell body and flagella are covered by one to several layers of more or less elaborate organic scales, which are produced in the Golgi apparatus (Figs. 19.9, 19.10, 20.1 – 20.3; see p. 313 for information on the unusual chemical composition of the scales).

3 The cells bear 1–8 flagella, which are laterally or apically inserted.

4 The flagella usually (but not always) arise from the base of a more or less pronounced depression (Figs. 19.9, 20.1).

5 The flagellar root systems vary from cruciate to unilateral; in this variation the Prasinophyceae differ from the other chlorophyte classes, each of which is characterized by a particular type of root architecture. Distinct rhizoplasts are usually present (Figs. 19.9, 19.10*j*, 19.11, 19.12) and the basal bodies are unusually long (Fig. 19.10*h*).

6 Mitosis and cytokinesis also vary within the class (in this too the Prasinophyceae are set apart from the other classes): mitosis is open or closed, with or without a persistent telophase spindle; cytokinesis is achieved either by a cleavage furrow or by a cell plate of vesicles within a phycoplast.

7 Species of the class occur in marine and fresh waters.

The anchorage of the flagellar apparatus is highly variable within the Prasinophyceae ([1218]). For instance, in *Pyramimonas* (Fig. 19.11; [1171, 1433]) and *Tetraselmis* ([1167]) the basal bodies are anchored by four cruciately arranged microtubular roots, in a 4–2–4–2 pattern. *Nephroselmis*, on the other hand, has only three microtubular roots, containing 3, 4 and 7–11 microtubules, respectively ([1221]); a peculiar structure, resembling the multilayered structure (MLS) of the unilateral type of flagellar root system (cf. Fig. 19.15 and p. 323), is associated with the broadest microtubular root. As a result of this similarity, *Nephroselmis* has been suggested to be related to the ancestors of the green algae with unilateral root systems (in the Klebsormidiophyceae; [1218, 1221]). However, at least one genus (*Mesostigma*) with a typical 'cruciate prasinophycean type of flagellate cell' (p. 313, Figs. 19.9, 19.11) has multilayered structures (MLS) associated with two of the four microtubular roots ([1176]), while the cruciate zoids of two other genera (*Halosphaera* and *Pterosperma*: see p. 347, Fig. 20.4) have a MLS associated with one microtubular root ([746, 1176]). This suggests that MLSs are ancient structures, which were present in the ancestral flagellate green algae. They have survived in some lineages of Prasinophyceae, some of them with cruciate root systems, others with unilateral root systems, and also in the Klebsormidiophyceae, the bryophytes and some vascular plants, but in most other green algae they have been lost in the course of evolution.

Mitosis and cytokinesis also vary greatly within the class. *Pyramimonas* has open mitosis and a persistent telophase spindle, while cytokinesis is effected by a cleavage furrow (p. 323, Fig. 19.17 I; [1919]). *Tetraselmis*, on the other hand, has closed mitosis and a collapsing (non-persistent) telophase spindle; cytokinesis is achieved via a cell plate, possibly of smooth ER vesicles, which lies within a phycoplast ([1642, 1701]: compare Fig. 19.20 I). In *Nephroselmis* and *Mantoniella* mitosis is closed, as in *Tetraselmis*, but the telophase spindle is persistent; cytokinesis is brought about by invagination of the plasmalemma ([47, 1139]: compare Fig. 19.22 I).

This great diversity in the architecture of the flagellar apparatus and the different modes of mitosis and cytokinesis are interpreted as reflecting the great age and primitiveness of the Prasinophyceae ([1301]). If so, the class can perhaps be thought of as a kind of laboratory for the evolution of the various kinds of flagellate cell types found in the green algae. In the course of its long history, many lineages may have evolved within the Prasinophyceae, each with its own flagellar apparatus and method of mitosis and cytokinesis, and some of these lineages may have been ancestral to other chlorophyte classes (see also Chapter 31 'Reflections on evolutionary relationships in the Chlorophyta', p. 483).

Few characters are uniform throughout the Prasinophyceae and the class is separated from other green algal classes essentially by the combination of a unicellular, flagellate life-form and the presence of organic scales on the cell body and flagella. However, there are exceptions even to these characters. For instance, a number of flagellate green algae are classified in the Prasinophyceae, even though they lack scales, because in other respects they resemble certain of the more typical, scaly members of the class (sometimes, however, these organisms are treated as a separate class, the Loxophyceae: see [1218]). Furthermore, organic body scales are also found on the reproductive zoids of a variety of other green algae, including representatives of the classes Chlorophyceae ([1328]), Ulvophyceae (p. 393), Klebsormidiophyceae (Fig. 19.15) and Charophyceae (p. 474). This suggests that organic body scales, like the multilayered structures (MLSs) associated with the flagellar roots, are primitive features; they were present in the ancestral green algae and have been retained in the Prasinophyceae and in a few other chlorophyte lineages, but have been lost in the majority of green algae. If this is so, then it would appear that the Prasinophyceae are a class of green algae that have no derived characters in common with each other; the Prasinophyceae would therefore be an unnatural group, less closely related to each other than they are to members of other classes within the Chlorophyta. As has already been mentioned, certain Prasinophyceae have been suggested to represent lineages ancestral to the other chlorophyte classes. The *Nephroselmis* lineage has been suggested to have been ancestral to the Klebsormidiophyceae, with their unilateral flagellar root systems. *Nephro-*

selmis would thus be more closely related to the Klebsormidiophyceae than to other members of the Prasinophyceae.

Nonetheless, the bizarre complexity of the scales found in many Prasinophyceae, which seem in most cases to be variations on just a few basic ground plans (Figs. 19.9, 19.10), have convinced many specialists that the Prasinophyceae constitute a natural group. Here the characters shared between different Prasinophyceae, and interpreted to be derived, are the characteristic elaboration of the body scales into complex, exuberant morphologies; the presence of special scales on the flagella and their arrangement; the presence of two rows of stiff, hair-like scales on the flagella; and the great length of the basal bodies ([1227]).

Until recently the only methods of reproduction known in the Prasinophyceae were asexual. Now, however, a freshwater species of the genus *Nephroselmis* (Fig. 20.2) has been demonstrated to have a **haplontic life cycle**; this organism is heterothallic and isogamous ([1731]). Two morphologically indistinguishable gametes, a (+) gamete and a (−) gamete, fuse to produce a diploid zygote. This develops into a hypnozygote (i.e. a thick-walled resting stage) which, after a period of dormancy, undergoes meiosis and produces four meiospores; these then give rise to cells of the new haploid gametophyte generation, some (+), others (−). This type of life cycle is also to be found in *Chlamydomonas* species (class Chlorophyceae; Figs. 1.4, 21.1).

Size and distribution of the class

The Prasinophyceae contains about 16 genera, with around 180 species; they occur in marine, brackish and freshwater habitats ([1302]). Minute prasinophyceans belonging to the genus *Bathycoccus*, 0.5 to a few micrometres in diameter, appear to form an important part of the photosynthetic picoplankton (= plankton < 2 μm in diameter) in the euphotic zone of the oceans (Fig. 20.3a, b; [365a, 375, 803]). These organisms, together with tiny coccoid cyanophytes, prochlorophytes, heterokontophytes and haptophytes, probably contribute greatly to oceanic primary production, much more than was previously thought.

There are other, more conspicuous prasinophyceans in the marine phytoplankton, belonging to the genera *Halosphaera* ([746, 1364]) and *Pterosperma* ([1362]; Fig.

20.4). These algae form large cyst-like stages, 100–800 µm in diameter, in the phytoplankton; these are called 'phycomata' (singular phycoma). These structures have thick walls composed of two layers, of which the outer is resistant to microbial degradation and consequently fossilizes readily. Fossils of cysts similar to those formed by the extant genus *Pterosperma* are known from the Precambrian (*ca.* 1.2 × 10⁹ years old) as well as from more recent geological eras ([92, 249, 590, 591, 1751]); they indicate extreme age for the class as a whole.

Prasinophyceans are known too as photosynthetic endosymbionts of various heterotrophic organisms. *Tetraselmis convolutae*, for instance, is the endosymbiont of the intertidal turbellarian worm *Convoluta roscoffensis* ([161, 1368]). Tiny prasinophycean species have also been found in various radiolarians, as endosymbionts in the rhizopodia that extend out into the jelly surrounding the radiolarian capsule ([29, 181]); radiolarians (class Polycystinea, cf. Table 1.1) are marine plantonic protozoans with stiff radiating rhizopods and rather attractive siliceous skeletons with a radial organization. Another species of the group lives as an endosymbiont within the large vacuole of the phagotrophic dinoflagellate *Noctiluca* ([1738, 1739]; see p. 255).

Examples of Prasinophyceae

Pyramimonas (Figs. 19.9 – 19.10)
See p. 313 for a description.

Tetraselmis suecica (Figs. 19.12, 20.1; [172, 748, 1111])

The cells are green, ovoid and slightly flattened; they measure 9–11 µm × 7–8 µm × 4.5–6 µm. Four equal flagella arise from the bottom of a fissure-like invagination at the apex of the cell. The chloroplast is four-lobed and has a basal pyrenoid, and at the posterior end of the cell there is a stigma. Electron microscopical investigations demonstrate that the flagella are covered with two layers of small scales and also by brittle tubular hairs, which are easily detached (Fig. 20.1*b–d*). The body of the cell is surrounded by a theca, consisting of many stellate scales cemented together, which are formed within and secreted by the golgi apparatus (Fig. 20.1*g*). The theca has a most unusual carbohydrate composition, the main constituent being 3-deoxy-manno-2-octulosonic acid ([56]). It therefore differs greatly in its composition from the glycoprotein wall of *Chlamydomonas* (class Chloro-phyceae), underlining the wide phylogenetic separation between the two genera. During cell division a new theca is formed around each daughter cell, within the theca of the parent cell (Fig. 20.1*f*). The pyrenoid is penetrated by a branching cytoplasmic canal (Fig. 20.1*e*).

Tetraselmis suecica was initially isolated from sea-water off the English and Swedish coasts, but later research has suggested that it is probably cosmopolitan ([748]). Related species are known from both marine and fresh waters.

Nephroselmis rotunda (Fig. 20.2; [172, 1113])

The yellow-green cells of this species are elliptical and strongly compressed (± bean-shaped); they measure 4.5 – 8 µm × 4.5 – 6.5 µm × 2 – 2.5 µm. Two flagella are present. They are unequal in length and arise laterally on the cell. There is a single crescent-shaped chloroplast, which contains a pyrenoid at its centre and a stigma near the anterior end of the cell; the pyrenoid is surrounded by a sheath of starch grains. The flagellar bases are connected to the middle of the concave face of the chloroplast by a rhizoplast, while close to the flagellar bases themselves are several dictyosomes (golgi apparatus). There is usually a single long mitochondrion, which lies against the concave side of the chloroplast.

The surface of the cell is covered with three layers of scales. Immediately adjacent to the plasmalemma is a layer of closely packed rectangular scales, each about 50 nm long, in orderly rows (Fig. 20.2*g*). Above this layer is a layer of stellate scales, which are approximately the same size as the rectangular scales beneath, each one lying above the interstice between four adjacent rectangular scales (Fig. 20.2*g, h*). The outermost layer of scales again contains stellate scales, but these are about ten times larger than the scales in either of the two underlying layers (Fig. 20.2*e, f, h*). The flagella are covered with two layers of small scales and also bear hairs very similar to those in *Tetraselmis* and *Pyramimonas*. The three types of scales and also the flagellar hairs are formed in the golgi apparatus and then secreted. It is possible to be certain that the formation of the scales or the components of the theca occurs in the golgi apparatus, in *Nephroselmis*, *Tetraselmis* and *Pyramimonas* ([1224]),

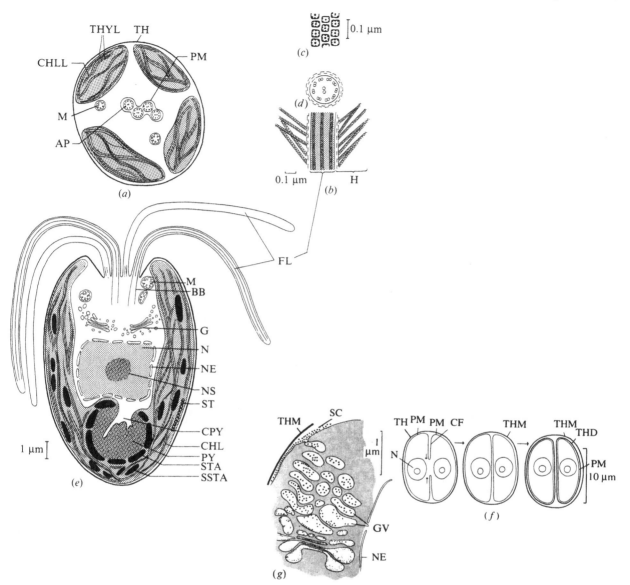

Figure 20.1. *Tetraselmis suecica.* (*a*) Cross section through a cell, just above the base of the flagellar pit. (*b*) Longitudinal section through part of a flagellum. (*c*) Surface view of the outer layer of flagellar scales. (*d*) Cross section though flagellum, showing the 9 + 2 structure of the axoneme. (*e*) Longitudinal section through a cell, based on EM observations. (*f*) The later stages of cell division. (*g*) An active golgi body, delivering new star-shaped scales to the cell surface, where they are assembled together to form the theca. AP = apical pit; BB = basal body; CF = cleavage furrow; CHL = chloroplast; CHLL = one of the four lobes of the chloroplast; CPY = cytoplasmic channel within the pyrenoid; FL = flagellum, bearing two layers of overlapping scales and stiff, brittle hairs; G = golgi body; GV = golgi vesicles; H = stiff hairs on flagellum, underlain by scales; M = mitochondrion; N = nucleus; NE = nuclear envelope; NS = nucleolus; PM = plasma membrane (plasmalemma); PY = pyrenoid; SC = star-shaped scales being assembled to form the theca; SSTA = stroma starch; ST = stigma (eyespot), lying within the chloroplast; STA = starch grain appressed to the pyrenoid; TH = theca; THD = theca of daughter cell; THM = theca of mother cell; THYL = stacked thylakoids. (After [1111].)

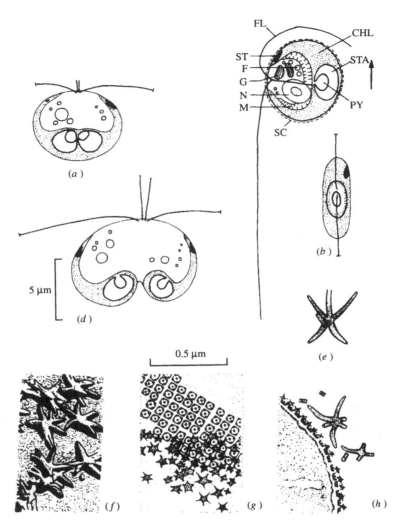

Figure 20.2. *Nephroselmis rotunda.* (*a*) Cell ready for rapid swimming in the direction of the arrow. (*b*) Anterior view of cell. (*c, d*) Stages in division. (*e, f*) Large stellate scales. (*g*) Tangential section through the cell surface, showing the underlayer of diamond-shaped scales and the upper stellate scales, which lie above the interstices between the diamond-shaped scales.

(*h*) Transverse section through the cell surface, showing the layers of small plate-like scales (innermost), small stellate scales and large stellate scales. CHL = chloroplast; F = lipid droplets; FL = flagellum; G = golgi apparatus; M = mitochondrion; N = nucleus; PY = pyrenoid; SC = scales; ST = stigma (eyespot); STA = starch sheath around pyrenoid. (After [1113].)

because the scales have a very characteristic structure and are recognizable from an early stage of development in the golgi cisternae (Fig. 19.10*g*).

Nephroselmis rotunda has been isolated a number of times from estuaries and other marine habitats around the English coast. There are also two freshwater species of *Nephroselmis.*

Bathycoccus, a tiny coccoid prasinophycean (Fig. 20.3)

This form, about the same size as a bacterium, appears to be common in the N Atlantic Ocean ([365a, 803]). The cells are covered by delicate overlapping scales, which have a spider's-web structure and are formed within vesicles (probably golgi vesicles). The organelles are

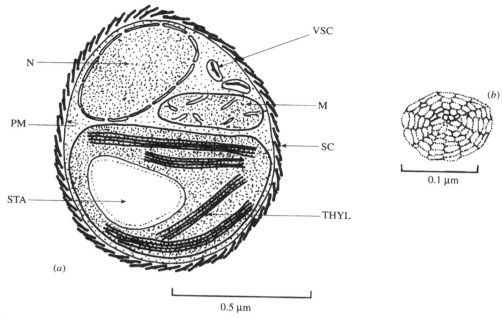

Figure 20.3. *Bathycoccus*, a coccoid member of the Prasinophyceae, from the picoplankton of the N Atlantic; note the tiny size, comparable to many bacteria, and the compact arrangement of the organelles. (*a*) Cell. (*b*) Body scale. M = mitochondrion; N = nucleus; PM = plasma membrane (plasmalemma); SC = body scale; STA = starch; THYL = thylakoids, in stacks of four; VSC = (golgi?) vesicle, containing scale. (Based on [803].)

tightly packed within the cell. This alga closely resembles *Mamiella gilva*, a tiny biflagellate green alga which is also covered by spider's-web type scales ([1219]).

Pterosperma (Fig. 20.4)

Pterosperma is one of the Prasinophyceae with a long-lasting **cyst** or **phycoma stage**, and a free-living flagellate stage of lesser duration. The phycoma can be quite large (up to 230 μm in diameter), is more or less globose and bears wings; in the example illustrated there is a single equatorial wing (Fig. 20.4). Inside the phycoma there is a nucleus, together with numerous discoid chloroplasts, each containing a pyrenoid. The wall of the cell consists of two layers, a delicate inner layer and a thicker outer one, which is resistant to bacterial decay. *Pterosperma* reproduces through division of its contents into numerous flagellate cells (zoids), which are at first enclosed in a vesicle formed by the delicate inner wall. The vesicle is extruded through a slit in the outer wall and contains the zoids until they

are mature, when it bursts, releasing them. The zoids themselves can reproduce by fission. Each zoid bears four lateral flagella and both its body and its flagella are covered with various kinds of scale. Within a few weeks a flagellate cell can develop back into a phycoma.

Pterosperma species are widely distributed through the world's oceans ([1362]). There are other genera with similar life cycles, such as *Pachysphaera* ([1359]) and *Halosphaera* ([1364]). These too have a dominant phycoma stage, but whereas *Pachysphaera* has the same type of zoid as *Pterosperma*, *Halosphaera* has *Pyramimonas*-like flagellate cells (cf. Fig. 19.9); it has been shown, however, that *Halosphaera* zoids and *Pyramimonas* cells do differ in various points of detail ([746]).

The resistant outer wall of the phycoma is well preserved in fossil deposits and fossil relatives of the three genera mentioned above are known from as early as the Precambrian (*ca.* 1.2×10^9 y ago). In the Palaeozoic era ($600–225 \times 10^6$ y ago) they became

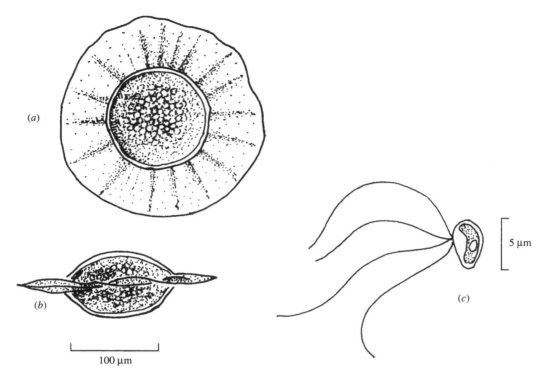

Figure 20.4. *Pterosperma*. (*a*) A phycoma bearing a single wing: top view. (*b*) As (*a*): side view. (*c*) Flagellate stage. (Based on [1362, 1751].)

widespread and very diverse. Examples from the Palaeozoic include *Tasmanites*, which is quite similar to the recent genus *Pachysphaera*, and *Pterospermella*, which, as its name implies, is like the modern *Pterosperma* ([249, 590, 591, 1751]).

The subdivision of the Prasinophyceae into orders

A new classification of the Prasinophyceae has recently been produced ([1178a]), based on differences in cell architecture, the kinds of organic body scales present, and the processes of mitosis and cytokinesis. The following four orders are distinguished.

Mamiellales: cells tiny, with one or two laterally inserted flagella, anchored by two microtubular roots; there is only one layer of delicate body scales, which resemble a spider's web (e.g. *Mamiella*, *Bathycoccus*).

Pseudoscourfeldiales: cells with two unequal, laterally inserted flagella, which are anchored by three microtubular roots; there are two or three layers of different body scales (e.g. *Nephroselmis*).

Pyramimonadales: four (rarely eight) flagella arise from the bottom of a pit at the apex of the cell (except in *Pterosperma*, where they are laterally inserted); there are three layers of body scales, including an outer layer of spectacular complex scales; mitosis and cytokinesis corresponding to type I (p. 321) (e.g. *Pyramimonas*, *Halosphaera*, *Pachysphaera* [?], *Pterosperma* [?], *Mesostigma* [?]).

Chlorodendrales: cells compressed, with four flagella arising from the bottom of an apical pit; body scales coalesced to form a theca; mitosis and cytokinesis more or less as in the class Pleurastrophyceae (Fig. 27.2*f–i*) (e.g. *Tetraselmis*).

Tiny chlorophytes (less than 10 μm long) of the genus *Pedinomonas*, with one laterally inserted flagellum but without body scales, are classified either in the Prasinophyceae or in their own class, the Pedinophyceae (or Loxophyceae) ([1220a]). *Pedinomonas* looks like *Mantoniella* (a member of the Mamiellales), but without its body scales. These two genera are considered to be the direct, little-changed descendants of the first primitive chlorophytes (cf. Figs. 31.2, 31.3 and p. 487).

21

Chlorophyta: Class 2. Chlorophyceae

The principal characteristics of the Chlorophyceae

1 The members of this class exhibit a great variety of levels of organization. Some are free-living flagellates, either unicellular (monads) or colonial; others are coccoid or palmelloid, and hence non-motile; others again are multicellular (filamentous or thallose); yet others are siphonous.

2 In the flagellate representatives of the class the body of the cell is surrounded by a glycoprotein envelope. The non-flagellate forms have firm polysaccharide walls. The presence of cellulose has been demonstrated in some coccoid and filamentous species ([292]).

3 Reproduction is usually brought about through the formation of flagellate reproductive cells, which usually have two or four apically inserted flagella; a few genera produce zoids with many flagella. The reproductive zoids resemble the free-living flagellate members of the class. Some Chlorophyceae only produce non-flagellate reproductive cells, while others produce both non-flagellate and flagellate reproductive cells.

4 The zoids have a cruciate type of flagellar root system, with a 1 o'clock – 7 o'clock or 12 o'clock – 6 o'clock configuration of the basal

bodies (Figs. 19.6, 19.14, 21.17h, p. 302; [293, 428, 704, 1175, 1328, 1856, 1857, 1894]). The stephanokont zoids of one order, which have a crown of flagella around the anterior of the cell, are considered to have been derived from the simpler cruciate types of zoid (Figs. 21.28, 21.30, p. 386).

5   Mitosis is closed, the telophase spindle is not persistent, and cytokinesis is brought about via the formation of a transverse septum, which develops within a phycoplast. The septum is produced either through the activities of a cleavage furrow (an invagination of the plasmalemma; Fig. 19.17 II), or by the coalescence of vesicles within a cell plate (Fig. 19.20 I, II, p. 329).

6   Species that reproduce sexually have a haplontic life cycle (Fig. 1.4), including a hypnozygote stage (i.e. a thick-walled resting zygote). Copulation can be isogamous, anisogamous or oogamous.

7   The Chlorophyceae are almost entirely restricted to freshwater habitats.

There may also be other features of the flagellar apparatus that are characteristic of the Chlorophyceae, besides those mentioned under 4 above. For instance, members of the Chlorophyceae have an upper connective between the basal bodies, which is transversely striated, and also two lower basal body connectives, also transversely striated (Fig. 19.6b).

The class Chlorophyceae has traditionally been taken to include almost all the green algae (e.g. [100, 703]), but we define it much more narrowly.

Size and distribution of the class

About 355 genera, encompassing 2650 species, are included within the Chlorophyceae as we define it. The great majority of the species occur in freshwater, but there are also a fair number of terrestrial forms and just a few species that live in brackish or marine habitats.

Order Volvocales

1   This order consists of unicellular (Figs. 19.1, 21.3) and colonial flagellates (Figs. 21.4 – 21.6).

2   Mitosis is closed, the spindle does not persist at telophase, and cytokinesis takes place via a cleavage furrow (type II mitosis and cytokinesis: p. 325, Figs. 19.17 II, 19.19).

3   After cytokinesis each daughter cell becomes surrounded by its own glycoprotein envelope, composed mainly of hydroxyproline but with galactose, arabinose, mannose and glucose residues attached to it (p. 303). In some representatives of the class the glycoprotein envelope is vestigial, so that the flagellate cells appear to be naked ([223]). Walls containing cellulose are never present ([292, 293, 1502, 1503, 1504]).

Size and distribution of the order

About 110 genera, containing between them almost 1000 species, are included within the Volvocales ([1630]). The vast majority of the species occur in freshwater, but there are also terrestrial species and a few marine forms. A limited number are found on snow ([716]). Water bodies with elevated levels of nutrients (nitrate, ammonium, phosphate) are often especially rich in Volvocales, but there are also many specialist forms that are restricted to nutrient-poor and acidic freshwaters ([988, 1630]). Some marine *Chlamydomonas* species are endosymbionts of large (0.5–1 cm) tropical benthic foraminifera, although their numbers are always small compared with those of the dominant endosymbionts, which are diatoms ([973]).

A few members of the Volvocales are colourless and heterotrophic. They are placed in this order of the green algae because of their morphological and ultrastructural similarity to pigmented, photosynthetic representatives of the order. Examples are *Polytoma* (Fig. 21.3q), a colourless version of *Chlamydomonas*, and *Hyalogonium*, which closely resembles *Chlorogonium* (Fig. 21.3a, b).

Examples of Volvocales

Chlamydomonas (Figs. 19.1, 19.2, 19.4 – 19.8, 19.17 II, 19.18)

A detailed description of *Chlamydomonas* is given on p. 302.

The genus is large, containing more than 600 species. They occur in freshwater and on damp soil, and a few occur in the sea. Species of *Chlamydomonas* and related genera are common in highly eutrophic and even in organically polluted waters, although there are also species that are characteristic of the oligotrophic, acid waters of bogs ([988]). The terrestrial species are well adapted to the drying out of their habitat and they probably survive in the form of hypnozygotes (see below). Two species of *Chlamydomonas* were found to have survived for 25 years in desiccated soil samples from a corn field ([1782]).

The characteristics used to separate different species include the shape and size of the cell, the shape of the apical papilla, the number of contractile vacuoles present (if any), and the number and shape of the chloroplasts and pyrenoids ([378, 381, 382, 758]). Certain species of the genus (*Chlamydomonas eugametos*, *C. reinhardtii*) are used extensively in laboratory investigations of molecular genetics and photosynthesis ([159, 355, 537, 612, 988, 993, 994, 1538, 1539, 1730, 1784]).

The life cycle of Chlamydomonas eugametos

Sexual reproduction is known in relatively few (around 10%) of the many *Chlamydomonas* species. Here we will discuss the reproduction of *C. eugametos*, which is well-known as a 'laboratory' organism but was originally isolated from soil.

Under the light microscope the gametes are indistinguishable from vegetative cells; just like the vegetative cells, their formation follows one to several cell divisions, which occur one after another within the envelope of the parent cell (Fig. 19.17 II). The gametes are set free through the partial degradation of the parent cell envelope by an '**autolysin**', an enzyme released by the young daughter cells shortly after cytokinesis. The autolysin only degrades cell walls of the same or related species ([612, 1564, 1565, 1566]).

When observed by transmission electron microscopy, gametes can be seen to differ from vegetative cells in two rather subtle ways: the gametes possess **mating structures** (at least in *Chlamydomonas reinhardtii*; Fig. 19.7a, b), and they bear numerous **agglutinin** molecules on their flagella. The agglutinin molecules are linear and hair-like, ca. 250–300 nm long, and occur among the 0.9 μm long flagellar hairs (Fig. 19.2e). They are involved in the adhesion of flagella of opposite mating types (see below). The mating structures are specialized areas of the plasmalemma, which bulge out slightly and are located close

to the tip of the cell, where gamete fusion is initiated (p. 312).

During the sexual phase of the life cycle (Fig. 21.1), two gametes come together and become attached by their anterior ends. They then fuse to form a zygote, which at first has two eyespots, one from each gamete. Because the gametes are alike morphologically they are called **isogametes**; their fusion is thus an isogamous copulation or isogamy.

After some time the gametic nuclei fuse within the zygote to form a diploid zygotic nucleus. The diploid ($2n$) zygote secretes a thick, somewhat spiny wall and becomes dormant: such thick-walled, dormant zygotes are termed **hypnozygotes**. After the dormant period the hypnozygote germinates and the diploid zygote nucleus divides meiotically to give four haploid (n) daughter nuclei. Hence four haploid daughter cells emerge from the hypnozygote and these swim away: the sexual cycle is completed. We can summarize the life cycle of *C. eugametos* by saying that this species is an isogamous haplont; it is also heterothallic (see below).

In fact, however, the sexual cycle of *Chlamydomonas eugametos*, at first sight so simple, is a complicated process, consisting of a whole series of interdependent events ([157, 251, 367, 368, 612, 994, 1784, 1891]). The same is true for almost all apparently simple biological processes: closer examination reveals an almost bewildering complexity (compare, for example, the sexual reproduction of the diatoms; p. 152). In the following account we attempt to convey some impression of what lies behind the simple summary of sexuality given above for *Chlamydomonas eugametos*. The sexual cycle of this species is particularly well known because it is so often used as an experimental organism. Sexual reproduction will no doubt be equally complex in many other 'simple' algae, but the details will undoubtedly vary from one species to another: the account given below may well apply to other green algae only in its general principles.

Although all the gametes produced by the vegetative cells of *C. eugametos* are morphologically identical, we can nevertheless separate them into two groups, called '+' and '-'. Cells derived from a single cell by vegetative multiplication produce gametes that cannot copulate with one another: in other words gametes produced by a clone are incompatible. If gametes from one clone are mixed with gametes from another clone, sometimes they copulate and some-

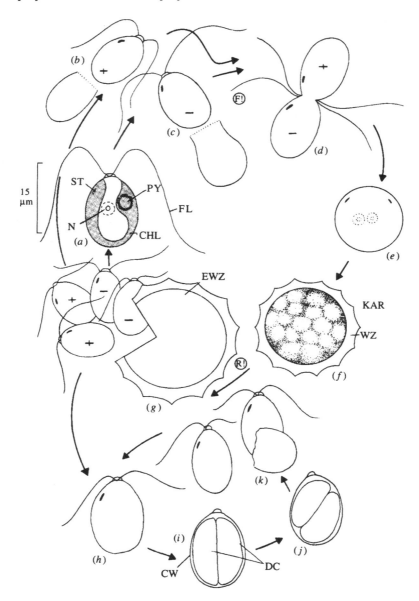

Figure 21.1. The life cycle of *Chlamydomonas eugametos*. (a) Vegetative cell. (b, c) (+) and (–) gametes. (d) Plasmogamy. (e) Young zygote containing two unfused gametic nuclei. (f) Thick-walled hypnozygote. (g) Germinating hypnozygote, undergoing meiosis to form four haploid zoids. (h) Vegetative cell. (i, j) Dividing cell. (k) Release of two daughter cells, following breakdown of the parent cell enve-lope. For further explanation, see text. CHL = chloroplast; CW = wall-like envelope of (parent) cell; DC = daughter cells; EWZ = empty wall of hypnozygote; F! = fertilization; FL = flagellum; KAR = karyogamy; N = nucleus; PY = pyrenoid; R! = reduction division (meiosis); ST = stigma; WZ = thick spiny wall of the hypnozygote.

times they do not. Clones that copulate belong to different 'sexes', while those that do not belong to the same 'sex'. One sex is designated '+', although since all the gametes are morphologically identical (isogametes) the designation is quite arbitrary. All the clones that cannot copulate with a '+' clone are also '+'

clones, while those that can are termed '–' clones. The (+) clones are often called male and the (–) clones female, but there is no biological basis for this.

The haploid vegetative cells can be cultivated in a liquid medium containing nutrient salts, or on a medium solidified with agar, when they fail to form flagella. If distilled water is added to an agar culture and this is then illuminated, the cells produce flagella. Within two to four hours flagellate male (+) cells arising in this way are capable of copulating with flagellate female (–) cells.

The series of cell divisions leading to gamete formation are initiated only when the vegetative cells are depleted of nutrients, for instance, after transfer from nitrogen-rich to nitrogen-poor media. When nutrients are abundant the vegetative cells do not differentiate into gametes, ammonium ions in particular being inhibitory to gamete formation. If gametes are transferred back into nutrient-rich medium they dedifferentiate and become vegetative again.

When (+) and (–) sexualized cells are brought together a very characteristic phenomenon can be observed, called 'clumping' (Fig. 21.2a). The gametes unite into groups very quickly, often within a minute; the thicker the suspension of gametes, the more pronounced the effect. Each clump begins with the association of a (+) cell with a (–) cell, via their flagella, following which other gametes also attach themselves to the pair, producing the clump.

The flagella of each (+) gamete are covered with an agglutinin ('glue'), which is characteristic for the (+) sex. The (–) gametes correspondingly have an agglutinin typical of the (–) sex. The (+) and (–) agglutinins are complementary, so that if the flagella of a (+) gamete come into contact with those of a (–) gamete swimming by, they will stick together. Thus, as more and more gametes attach themselves to the original pair, a group of gametes arises, linked by their flagellar tips (Fig. 21.2a).

The agglutinins are large linear glycoproteins, which can be seen in the transmission electron microscope. The (+) agglutinin is 245 nm long, the (–) agglutinin 340 nm. Both are attached to the membrane of the flagellum via a tapered base and they end distally in a globular head. Agglutination is probably brought about by cross-linking between complementary sites on the globular heads; subtle differences in the carbohydrate portions of the agglutinin molecules seem to be essential for this.

Compatible gametes come into contact through chance encounter. Long-distance attraction via pheromones, such as occurs between the gametes of brown algae (p. 178), does not occur in *Chlamydomonas eugametos*. Immediately after the gametes have come into contact, the ciliary beating of the flagella ceases (Fig. 21.2p), so that normal swimming stops and the agglutination is stabilized. Other gametes may collide randomly with the initial pair and become trapped via their sticky flagella, so that a clump begins to form. Furthermore, since agglutinin production is stimulated when gametes become attached to each other, the flagella become progressively more sticky, so that addition of new gametes to an existing clump becomes easier and easier.

Before agglutination the agglutinins are distributed evenly over the whole of each flagellum. Once gametes have begun to adhere, however, the agglutinins become concentrated at the flagellar tips, as a result of transport along the flagellum surface. The flagella subsequently become glued together over their whole length, from the tips (where adhesion is strongest) downwards (Fig. 21.2p–s). The tips of the gametes themselves are thus brought close together and also precisely opposite each other, making it possible for mating papillae to grow out and establish a protoplasmic connection between the gametes, via a copulation canal (Fig. 21.2s). In *Chlamydomonas reinhardtii* the mating papillae develop from the mating structures mentioned earlier (p. 312). At this stage the two pairs of flagella of the copulating gametes become reflexed along the body of the (–) gamete (Fig. 21.2r, s; [368, 1777]).

The narrow copulation tube is formed quickly and then the flagella disengage from each other (Fig. 21.2c). Only one pair of flagella remains active (always those of the (+) gamete) and these can propel the copulating cells around for several hours (as a 'vis-à-vis pair').

Fusion of the cells (cytogamy or plasmogamy) occurs via the bridge of cytoplasm of the copulation tube and can be completed within a few minutes (Fig. 21.2d, e). For plasmogamy light is necessary; in the dark the 'vis-à-vis pairs' swim around until they die. The fusion of the gametes is facilitated by the enzymatic digestion of the cell envelopes by a special autolysin, which is specific to the gametes [612, 1838]. Following fusion the zygote remains motile for some time, a motile flagellate zygote of this kind being

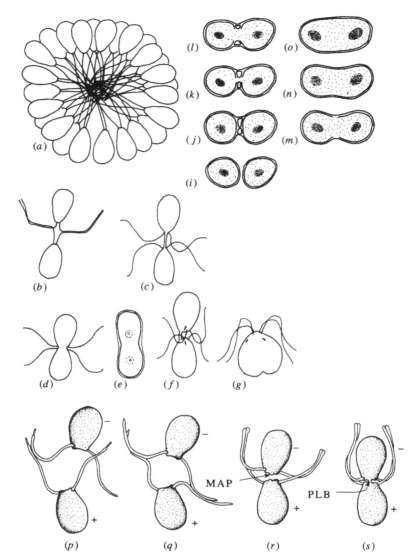

Figure 21.2. *Chlamydomonas*: stages during sexual reproduction. (*a*) Clump formation (aggregation). (*b*)
Agglutination between the flagella of two gametes.
(*c*) Formation of a cytoplasmic bridge between fusing
gametes in *C. eugametos*. (*d*) Planozygote. (*e*) Plasmogamy in *C. eugametos*. (*f*) Formation of a cytoplasmic bridge between the gametes in *C. reinhardtii*. (*g*)
Plasmogamy in *C. reinhardtii*. (*i–o*) Stages in karyogamy. (*p–s*) Stages in the activation of the gametes in
C. eugametos. (*p*) The flagella of complementary
gametes come into contact and cease to beat. (*q*)

Complementary flagella adhere over progressively
more of their length, as a result of the presence of
increasing amounts of agglutinins. (*r*) Concentration
of the agglutinins at the flagellar tips results in a
closer and more precise association between the tips
of the two gametes, where the mating papillae are
formed. (*s*) Fusion of the mating papillae to form a
protoplasmic bridge (fertilization canal) between the
gametes; the flagella flex back against the (–) gamete.
MAP = mating papilla; PLB = protoplasmic bridge.
(*i–o* based on [157]; *p–s* on [1777].)

termed a **planozygote**. Later the zygote loses its flagella, which disintegrate from the tips down. Shortly
after plasmogamy, the nuclei also fuse (karyogamy;
Fig. 21.2*i–o*). During this process the outer membranes
of the nuclear envelopes fuse first, and then the inner

membrane breaks and unites with that of the other
nucleus.

As it matures the zygote becomes invested by a thick,
warty wall, which resembles the envelopes of the vegetative cells in that it consists of hydroxy-

proline-rich glycoproteins, and then it becomes filled with much starch and lipid. After a dormant phase of around six days the hypnozygotes can be induced to germinate by transferring them to fresh agar medium at 25 °C; light is also necessary.

Germination begins with a reduction division (meiosis). The evidence for this includes the detection of synaptonemal complexes at prophase in the dividing zygote nucleus (compare p. 59 and Fig. 5.12) ([1792]). In *Chlamydomonas reinhardtii* light microscope observations indicate that the haploid chromosome number is 8, although genetic evidence suggests a much higher number, of 16 or more ([612]). For reviews of the life history of *Chlamydomonas*, see [100, 367, 612, 861, 988, 1784].

Sexual reproduction in some other species of Chlamydomonas

The gametes of *Chlamydomonas eugametos* are morphologically alike, as has been described, and the copulation of these gametes is therefore an instance of isogamy. *Chlamydomonas reinhardtii*, which is closely related to *C. eugametos*, is also isogamous. Here too a narrow bridge of cytoplasm is formed between the gametes, although this lies a bit to one side of the longitudinal axes of the cells and is formed between the (+) and (–) mating structures (Fig. 19.7a, b). Another minor difference is that the cells fuse with each other laterally during plasmogamy, instead of apically as in *C. eugametos* (Fig. 21.2f, g; [460]).

Some other species of *Chlamydomonas* (e.g. *Chlamydomonas braunii*; Fig. 21.3i, j) exhibit anisogamy: copulation occurs between relatively small 'male' gametes and larger 'female' gametes, both however being flagellate. In the soil-dwelling species *Chlamydomonas zimbabwaensis*, which is homothallic, tiny naked male gametes are formed through successive divisions of a vegetative cell. After their escape from the envelope of this cell, they produce a proteinaceous sex hormone, which induces vegetative cells to escape from their envelopes and function as naked female gametes ([633]). Still other *Chlamydomonas* species are oogamous (Fig. 21.3k–n): fusion takes place between small flagellate male cells and large non-motile female gametes (egg cells).

These three types of gamete differentiation and behaviour – isogamy, anisogamy and oogamy – can be found in various groups of plants, and it must be assumed that they have all arisen many times in the course of evolution. Thus, for instance, all members of

the brown algal order Fucales (p. 206) and all of the green algae in the order Oedogoniales (p. 382) are oogamous, as essentially are all vascular plants (Tracheophyta) and mosses and liverworts (Bryophyta). It is interesting, however, that such different types of gamete behaviour are found within the genus *Chlamydomonas*. It may perhaps reflect the great antiquity and primitiveness of the genus.

Examples of other unicellular representatives of the order Volvocales (Fig. 21.3)

Chlorogonium (Fig. 21.3b)
The body of this alga is fusiform (spindle-shaped). *Chlorogonium* has a massive chloroplast and two flagella, and each cell contains numerous contractile vacuoles. The species illustrated, *C. euchlorum*, occurs in slightly enriched freshwaters.

Hyalogonium (Fig. 21.3a)
This alga is a colourless, heterotrophic version of *Chlorogonium*. It lives in polluted waters.

Gloeomonas (Fig. 21.3s)
Gloeomonas is distinguished from *Chlamydomonas* by its very broad, flat apical papilla; the flagella arise near this, one on each side. The species illustrated, *G. ovalis*, occurs in ponds and puddles.

Diplostauron (Fig. 21.3r)
From the side the cells of *Diplostauron* are rectangular, with a fairly large wing at each corner. *D. angulosum* is a freshwater form.

Polytoma (Fig. 21.3q)
This alga is a colourless, heterotrophic variant of *Chlamydomonas*. In nature it is to be found in water between the rotting remains of plants.

Polytoma, which is distinguished from *Chlamydomonas* only by its lack of pigments, cannot photosynthesize and so can only grow heterotrophically; it requires an organic medium. Nevertheless, *Polytoma* does possess chloroplasts, though these are colourless and better termed plastids. The plastids do not possess thylakoids but contain instead an irregular system of tubes (Fig. 19.2b). Chloroplasts with a similar structure have been induced in one *Chlamydomonas* species by irradiating it with UV light, leading to the production of a yellow, non-photosynthetic mutant ([962, 1539, 1540]). The complex of tubes present in the plastids of the mutant and *Polytoma* should apparently be interpreted as an

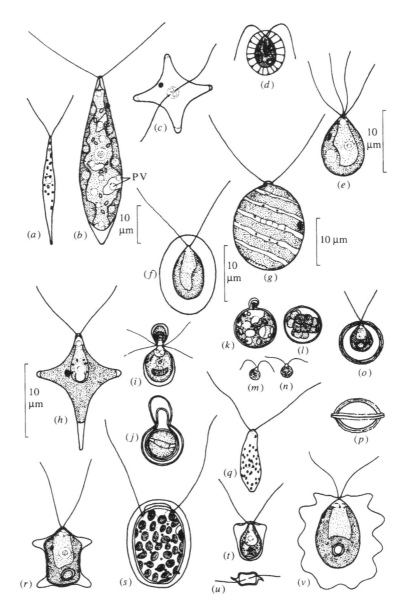

Figure 21.3. (a) *Hyalogonium klebsii.* (b) *Chlorogonium euchlorum.* (c) *Brachiomonas crux.* (d) *Haematococcus pluvialis.* (e) *Carteria gutta.* (f) *Sphaerellopsis lateralis.* (g) *Chlamydomonas spirogyroides.* (h) *Brachiomonas crux.* (i, j) *Chlamydomonas braunii:* anisogamy. (k–n) *Chlamydomonas coccifera:* oogamy. (o, p) *Phacotus lenticularis.* (q) *Polytoma uvella.* (r) *Diplostauron angulosum.* (s) *Gloeomonas ovalis.* (t, u) *Pteromonas cordiformis.* (v) *Lobomonas ampla.* PV = contractile (pulsing) vacuole. (a, d, i–v after [440]; b, c, e–h after [376].)

incompletely developed system of thylakoids. *Polytoma* seems in effect to be a '*Chlamydomonas*' that has lost the capacity for photosynthesis during the course of evolution.

Other classes of algae also contain colourless, heterotrophic variants of pigmented, photosynthetic forms. Numerous examples of such organisms, for instance, occur in the Dinophyta and Euglenophyta.

Astasia, for example, is the colourless equivalent of the green genus *Euglena* (division Euglenophyta; p. 295). It may well be, however, that some of the colourless Euglenophyceae and Dinophyceae are very primitive forms, which never took up photosynthetic prokaryotes or eukaryotes as endosymbionts and so have never possessed chloroplasts (p. 286).

Carteria (Fig. 21.3e)
Carteria resembles *Chlamydomonas* but the cells possess four flagella. The species shown, *Carteria gutta*, occurs in freshwater.

Brachiomonas (Fig. 21.3c, h)
The cells are pyramidal and also have a long, tapering tail. Most species live in marine or brackish waters, and they often occur too in pools that have become hypersaline through evaporation, as for instance in the upper part of the marine littoral. The species illustrated, however, *Brachiomonas crux*, occurs in polluted freshwaters.

Lobomonas (Fig. 21.3v)
This alga is distinguished from *Chlamydomonas* by its distended cell envelope, which has an irregularly undulate outline. It occurs in freshwater pools.

Sphaerellopsis (Fig. 21.3f)
As in *Lobomonas*, the cell envelope is distended. In *Sphaerellopsis*, however, the envelope is not undulate, so that the alga has a smooth, oval outline. Between the envelope and the protoplast is a layer of mucilage, the protoplast itself being spindle-shaped. *Sphaerellopsis* lives in freshwater.

Haematococcus (Fig. 21.3d)
Haematococcus is distinguished from *Sphaerellopsis* by the presence of delicate strands of protoplasm that radiate out from the cell into the layer of mucilage. In addition, the cells are usually coloured red by an abundance of carotenoid pigments ('haematochrome'), lying in the cytoplasm. Most species occur in puddles of rainwater, which they can turn blood-red.

Phacotus (Fig. 21.3o, p)
The cells of *Phacotus* species are similar to cells of *Chlamydomonas* but lie within a flat, lime-encrusted case, which consists of two watch-glass-shaped halves clasped together at their edges. The species illustrated, *Phacotus lenticularis*, occurs in freshwater pools rich in lime.

Pteromonas (Fig. 21.3t, u)
This alga, like *Phacotus*, possesses a case made of two halves. However, the case is not encrusted with lime and where the two halves join the cell bears a narrow wing. *Pteromonas* species live in the plankton of ponds and lakes.

Some colonial members of the order Volvocales (Figs. 21.4, 21.5)

Stephanosphaera (Fig. 21.4d)
Here 8–16 cells lie embedded in a common sphere of mucilage. The flagella of each cell project out from the mucilage and the cells also bear thin branched extensions. *Stephanosphaera pluvialis* is the only known species of the genus. Together with *Haematococcus* species, it can produce blood-red discolorations of rainwater puddles.

Gonium (Fig. 21.4a)
The cells of *Gonium* species are individually similar to *Chlamydomonas* cells but they are united into flat rectangular colonies, containing 4–16 cells. The seven known species, among which is the species illustrated, *Gonium formosum*, live in freshwater pools that are rich in organic material.

Pandorina (Fig. 21.4c)
The cells of the 8- to 16-celled colonies of *Pandorina* are embedded in a spherical or ellipsoidal mass of mucilage. All the cells are similar, except with respect to the eyespots, which are larger on one side of the colony than on the other. Two species are known and these live in freshwater.

Eudorina (Fig. 21.4b)
Eudorina species have disc-shaped colonies containing 16–64 (usually 32) cells. The cells are arranged in several rings around the periphery of the colony, the plane of each ring lying at right angles to the axis of the colony. The colonies can be polar, although this is only modestly developed: the cells at the posterior of the colony are sometimes larger than those at the anterior and may have larger eyespots. These algae occur in the freshwater phytoplankton.

Volvox (Figs. 21.5, 21.6)
The spherical colonies of *Volvox* can be up to 0.5 – 1.5

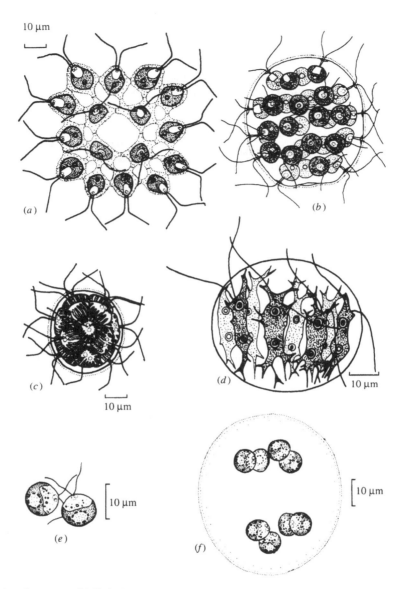

Figure 21.4. (a) *Gonium formosum.* (b) *Eudorina unicocca.* (c) *Pandorina morum.* (d) *Stephanosphaera pluvialis.* (e, f) *Pseudosphaerocystis lacustris.* (a, c, d after [121]; b after [758]; e, f after [440].)

mm in diameter. The individual cells are similar to those of *Chlamydomonas* but 500 to several thousand of them are present, arranged around the periphery of a spherical mass of mucilage, in which they are embedded. Each cell possesses its own separate mucilage envelope, which appears hexagonal when seen from above. The cells are connected to each other by protoplasmic strands (Fig. 21.5b).

Asexual reproduction takes place as follows. A relatively large cell (called a gonidium) at the posterior end of the colony (Fig. 21.6a–f) divides longitudinally many times. As a result of this a round daughter colony is produced, consisting of small cells, which lies below the surface of the parent colony (Fig. 21.6f). The anterior ends of the small cells point inwards, and hence so do the flagella they bear. In the

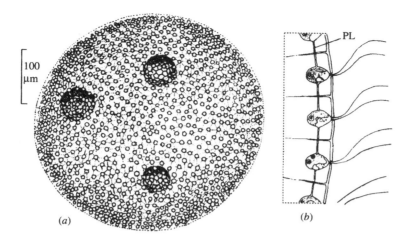

Figure 21.5. *Volvox globator.* (*a*) Colony with three daughter colonies. (*b*) Detail of a section through the colony surface, showing individual cells. PL = plasmodesma: a protoplasmic connection between cells. (*a* after [758]; *b* after [790].)

end the flagella must clearly be pointing outwards, if they are to be functional, and this is achieved through inversion of the daughter colonies (Fig. 21.6*g, h*). The daughter colonies are released when the parent colony breaks open.

Sexuality begins with the appearance of a few male colonies. How these are produced is not known, though it has been suggested that the first male is a mutant at a locus affecting sexuality ([523]). If the sex hormone produced by a male colony is present, the gonidia of *Volvox carteri* are induced to function as sexual colonies. The gonidia of female clones become female colonies and those of male clones become male colonies. The sex hormone is a glycoprotein ([1688]) and in its absence the gonidia continue to be asexual. For reviews of hormonal induction in various *Volvox* species, see [252, 367, 523, 861, 1866].

Sexual reproduction is oogamous. The egg cells are relatively large cells lying at the posterior of female colonies (Fig. 21.6*l*), the posterior end being fixed in relation to the direction in which the colony swims. The spermatozoids are formed in groups at the posterior of male colonies, in much the same way that asexual daughter colonies develop (Fig. 21.6*i–k*). Following fertilization (Fig. 21.6*m*) the egg cell develops into a thick-walled, spiny hypnozygote (Fig. 21.6*n*). The zygote germinates after a meiotic division and produces a zoid, which grows into a new colony

through repeated cell divisions. *Volvox* is therefore an oogamous haplont.

Each *Volvox* colony is thus a polar structure, with a well-differentiated anterior and posterior. There is a predominant direction of swimming and the cells at the forward, anterior end have larger eyespots; the coordination of flagellar activity between the individual cells is astonishing. Daughter colonies and sexual cells arise at the posterior.

The flagellar apparatus of immature, vegetative cells and of the male gametes in *Volvox* (and in other colonial members of the Volvocales) is similar to that of *Chlamydomonas* cells (Fig. 19.6). The basal bodies lie at an acute angle to each other, in the typical V-configuration. By the time the vegetative cells are mature, however, the flagellar apparatus has undergone a considerable rearrangement. First, the basal bodies become nearly parallel, so that the flagella emerge perpendicular to the colony surface; as a result neighbouring flagella are unlikely to become entangled. Second, the basal bodies rotate, so that both flagella beat in the same direction, instead of in opposite directions. This enables the colony as a whole to swim one way (Fig. 21.5*b*; [573, 728, 729]).

Volvox species frequently occur in the plankton of ponds and lakes. In small, nutrient-rich pools they sometimes grow explosively, giving rise to dense blooms.

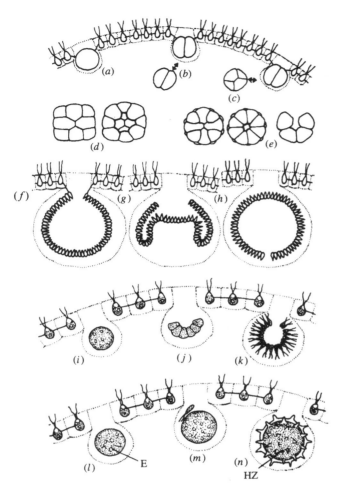

Figure 21.6. *Volvox*. (*a–h*) Successive stages in the formation of a daughter colony. (*i–k*) Development of a packet of spermatozoids; (*k*) shows the packet after inversion, with the flagella pointing outwards. (*l–n*) Oogamy. E = egg cell; F! = fertilization; HZ = hypnozygote. (After [1658].)

Capsular, 'palmelloid' (tetrasporal) members of the Volvocales

Colonial or unicellular green algae, which are non-motile but 'still' possess several characteristics of free-living flagellates, such as contractile vacuoles, eyespots, and prominent flagellate stages, are often classified in the order Tetrasporales. Many of these algae form gelatinous colonies and exhibit a capsular

or 'palmelloid' level of organization (Table 6.1). Many members of the Volvocales (e.g. *Chlamydomonas* species), however, can also form gelatinous, palmelloid stages, which are indistinguishable from those of the Tetrasporales. Thus, since the Tetrasporales possess no characteristics that clearly distinguish them from the Volvocales it is probably best to unite the two groups.

One example is *Pseudosphaerocystis lacustris* (Fig. 21.4*e*, *f*). Here the cells lie in pairs within a common mass of mucilage, which is spherical. The cells possess contractile vacuoles and can easily be induced to form two flagella. *P. lacustris* occurs in the plankton of lakes.

Order Chlorococcales

1 Mitosis is closed; the telophase spindle is not persistent; and cytokinesis is brought about by the formation of either a transverse septum (cleavage furrow; Fig. 19.17 II) or a cell plate, composed of coalescing vesicles (Fig. 19.20 I), within a phycoplast.

2 Following cytokinesis, each daughter cell becomes completely surrounded by its own new cell wall, secreted from golgi-derived vesicles (Fig. 19.20 I).

3 In some genera, the daughter cells remain confined within the parental cell wall (Fig. 19.20 I), thus producing multicellular sarcinoid (Fig. 21.17) or filamentous plants (Figs. 21.18, 21.19). In other genera, the daughter cells are released after formation, as non-flagellate or flagellate reproductive cells; they are liberated by enzymatic breakdown of the parent cell wall (Figs. 21.8, 21.10*a–c*).

The non-flagellate cells of the Chlorococcales, whether they are reproductive or vegetative, often contain a vestigial flagellar apparatus (which consists of the basal bodies with their connectives; [1646]), thus betraying their evolutionary origin as flagellate cells.

The possession of firm polysaccharide walls and the lack of a glycoprotein lattice are thought to differentiate the Chlorococcales from the Volvocales. However, the zoospores of one coccoid species of the Chlorophyceae seem to be covered by a crystalline glycoprotein envelope similar to that found in

Chlamydomonas ([1201]). When these zoospores become sessile and develop into spherical vegetative cells, a non-crystalline cellulose wall is deposited against the inside of the glycoprotein envelope, which is probably sloughed off. This example may perhaps illustrate how the non-flagellate Chlorococcales may have arisen from a *Chlamydomonas*-like ancestor.

The cell walls of some Chlorococcales are covered by a layer of sporopollenin-like material (p. 370, Figs. 21.10*a*–*c*, 21.13*d, e, g*, 21.16; [1419]).

In the multicellular species, some of the vegetative cells can become reproductive, in which case the cell contents divide up into reproductive daughter cells. These can be flagellate or non-flagellate and are released by enzymatic breakdown of the parent wall (Fig. 21.17).

Not long ago, Sluiman ([1642, 1643, 1646]) proposed that type III mitosis–cytokinesis is characteristic of all Chlorococcales (p. 327, Fig. 19.20 I). Here, cytokinesis is brought about by the formation of a plate of vesicles (possibly derived from the ER) within a phycoplast. However, it is now clear that type II mitosis–cytokinesis (the '*Chlamydomonas*' type: p. 325, Fig. 19.17 II) is also widespread in the Chlorococcales: a septum (cleavage furrow) develops centripetally, though again within a phycoplast ([297, 1419]). Yet another type of cytokinesis has been found, in which a septum appears in the centre of the division plane and grows out centrifugally until it reaches the periphery of the cell (e.g. in *Kirchneriella*: Fig. 21.12*g, h*; cf. note on p. 328;[1414]).

It used to be thought that there is a fundamental difference between the kind of cell division leading to the formation of reproductive cells that are subsequently released and the kind that leads to the formation of multicellular plant tissues. The type of cell division resulting in the production of reproductive cells was termed 'eleutheroschisis' or 'sporulation', while the type of division resulting in multicellular development was called 'desmoschisis' or 'vegetative cell division' ([100]). The evolution of 'desmoschisis' was therefore thought to be an essential, critical phase in the development of simple multicellular green algae from unicellular coccoid forms. We now know from electron microscopical observations, however, that there are many different modes of cell division in multicellular green algae (Figs. 19.17 II, 19.20 I, II, 19.22 I, 19.23 I, II). Two of these, types II and III mitosis–cytokinesis (see pp. 325–8, Figs. 19.17 II, 19.20 I), are found in a variety of coccoid, sarcinoid and filamentous green algae ([297, 490, 1642, 1643, 1646]) and this is an important reason for including all of these algae in the same order, the Chlorococcales *sensu lato*. The Chlorococcales, in turn, is placed in the class Chlorophyceae *sensu stricto*, which is characterized primarily by having a cruciate, 1 o'clock – 7 o'clock or 12 o'clock – 6 o'clock configuration of the flagellar apparatus in the reproductive zoids (p. 302, Figs. 19.6, 19.14*a, c*; [428, 1856, 1857, 1894]). We shall see later that the coccoid, sarcinoid and filamentous levels of organization have all evolved independently several times, in different classes of green algae (pp. 483, 494). In addition, there is no abrupt, absolute distinction between the pattern of development in those unicellular coccoid algae that release their daughter cells and the pattern exhibited by multicellular algae; indeed, there is a gradual transition from one to the other. For instance, in *Kirchneriella* (p. 366, Fig. 21.12) the daughter cells at first form a short filament and only then dissociate into single, independent cells; in *Pediastrum* (p. 374, Fig. 21.16) and *Hydrodictyon* (p. 371, Fig. 21.15), reproduction begins with the formation of flagellate reproductive cells (zoospores), which later associate and differentiate to form complex multicellular structures ('colonies' or 'coenobia'; see also the discussion under *Chlorosarcinopsis*, p. 374).

Non-flagellate, asexual reproductive cells in the Chlorococcales are often called **autospores**. Where the spores still retain features that are usually characteristic of flagellate cells, such as contractile vacuoles, they may also be termed **aplanospores**. Autospores are morphologically similar to the vegetative cells that produce them. In colonial members of the Chlorococcales the spores produced within one parent cell become united to form a miniature colony, which is then released; such a colony is often termed an **autocolony** or **coenobium** (e.g. Fig. 21.13*g*). In sexually reproducing species the type of gametic fusion varies from **isogamy**, through **anisogamy** to **oogamy** (Figs. 21.8*i*, 21.9*c*).

The order Chlorococcales contains species with the following levels of organization: **coccoid** (Figs. 21.7 – 21.10), **coccoid and colonial** (= coenobial) (Figs. 21.11 – 21.16), **sarcinoid** (Fig. 21.17), **filamentous** (Figs. 21.18, 21.19), and **siphonous** (Fig. 21.20). The order, as it is defined here, contains about 215 genera, with 1000 species ([874, 1630]), most of which occur in freshwater habitats. Only a tiny minority are marine but among them are the tiny (1–2 µm) *Chlorella*-like green algae found in the phytoplankton of the Atlantic Ocean ([802]), and the *Chlorella* species that functions as the photosynthetic endosymbiont of some large (0.5–1 cm) benthic tropical foraminifera ([973]).

In freshwater habitats, species of the Chlorococcales often abound where nutrient concentrations are high. Many Chlorococcales are terrestrial. Some, for example, form bright green streaks on the wind- and rain-swept sides of trees and walls; the algae responsible for these are often members of the aerophytic, sarcinoid genus *Apatococcus* (similar to *Chlorosarcinopsis*, see Fig. 21.17), or related genera. Other Chlorococcales inhabit damp soils, although they are capable of surviving prolonged desiccation (25 years in dry storage; [1782]). Here they often occur together with members of the Xanthophyceae ([1196, 1683]) and with species of the green algal genus *Klebsormidium* (class Klebsormidiophyceae; p. 455). Members of the Chlorococcales are also found as the algal partners in lichen symbioses ([1797]), although the commonest green algal symbiont of lichens is *Trebouxia*, a coccoid organism that has recently been placed in a quite different class of green algae, the Pleurastrophyceae, on the basis of ultrastructural evidence (p. 448).

In freshwater, as in the marine environment, coccoid Chlorococcales (e.g. *Chlorella* species, Fig. 21.10 *a–c*) can function as photosynthetic endosymbionts, being found in some hydroid polyps (e.g. *Chlorohydra*, phylum Cnidaria), freshwater sponges, and protozoa, of which the green *Paramecium* species are well-known examples ([161, 1483, 1656]). *Chlorohydra* appears to be capable of absorbing the photosynthetic produce of its endosymbiotic *Chlorella*.

A few species placed in the Chlorococcales are colourless and heterotrophic. They are included in the order because of their morphological and ultrastructural resemblance to green photosynthetic representatives of the order; thus *Prototheca*, for instance, is a colourless, heterotrophic version of *Chlorella* ([834]).

Examples of unicellular representatives of the order Chlorococcales: Chlorococcum

Chlorococcum (Figs. 21.7, 21.8)
These algae are spherical unicells and have polysaccharide walls. The chloroplast is cup-shaped and pari-

etal (placed against the wall of the cell), and contains a pyrenoid in its thickened, basal section. The zoids resemble *Chlamydomonas*.

Most species of *Chlorococcum* and related genera are found in freshwater, in the benthos. A proper understanding of the systematics of these algae can only be obtained by studying them in unialgal or axenic culture. Unialgal cultures contain only one algal species but may be contaminated with bacteria or fungi; axenic cultures, on the other hand, are free of bacteria and any other contaminant organism. Only a few species (around 20) are well known.

Although the structure of these algae is very simple, more and more new species keep being described. *Chlorococcum* species are encountered whenever soil samples are inoculated into liquid or solid media and the algae allowed to grow. Unialgal cultures can easily be isolated from such mixed cultures and it seems that it is often simpler to discover new species than it is to re-find old ones; the situation is similar in *Chlamydomonas*!

Some species can survive extreme environmental conditions. Thus, for instance, species have been isolated from the sands and rocks of deserts, while cultures of *Spongiochloris*, another spherical chlorococcalean alga, can survive for an hour at 100 °C ([1786]).

Sexual reproduction does not occur in the majority of *Chlorococcum* species, or at least has never been observed, just as in most *Chlamydomonas* species. *Chlorococcum echinozygotum*, a species that does reproduce sexually, is described in more detail below; it was isolated from a soil sample from Luzon in the Philippines.

The structure of *Chlorococcum echinozygotum* (Fig. 21.7)
Chlorococcum echinozygotum has been investigated both light and electron microscopically ([291, 1685]). The individual cells are spherical and are surrounded by a robust cell wall made of polysaccharide. The vegetative cells lack flagella but contractile vacuoles are present, though they are absent in most other species of *Chlorococcum* and related genera.

Asexual reproduction in *Chlorococcum echinozygotum*
During asexual reproduction the cells of *Chlorococcum* each divide up into several daughter cells (Fig. 21.8*a–g*), as in *Chlamydomonas*. The

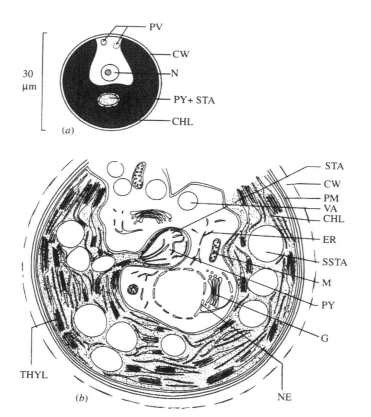

Figure 21.7. *Chlorococcum echinozygotum.* (*a*) Cell as seen with the light microscope. (*b*) Longitudinal section of the lower part of the cell, based on EM observations. CHL = chloroplast; CW = polysaccharide cell wall; ER = endoplasmic reticulum; G = golgi body; M = mitochondrion; N = nucleus; NE = nuclear envelope; PM = plasma membrane (plasmalemma); PV = contractile (pulsing) vacuole; PY = pyrenoid, which contains thylakoids; SSTA = stroma starch; STA = sheath of starch around the pyrenoid; THYL = thylakoids; VA = vacuole. (After [291].)

daughter cells may be non-motile spores (aplanospores: Fig. 21.8*d, e*), or flagellate spores (zoids: Fig. 21.8*f, g*); both subsequently grow into new, walled vegetative cells. Other members of the Chlorococcales often produce autospores too, as well as aplanospores. An aplanospore is like a zoospore without flagella, since it has both an eyespot and a contractile vacuole. An autospore, on the other hand, lacks these structures, which are generally found in free-living, flagellate cells, and it also lacks contractile vacuoles. Furthermore, autospores develop the characteristic shape of the vegetative cell before release, while they are still enclosed within the parent cell wall (see, for instance, *Kirchneriella*: Fig. 21.11).

Sexual reproduction in *Chlorococcum echinozygotum* (Fig. 21.8*a–c, f, h–m*)

A sexual response is stimulated by low concentrations of nitrogen (as ammonium-N or nitrate-N) and inhibited by high concentrations ([1322]). *Chlorococcum echinozygotum* is homothallic, so that the zoids from a single clone are able to copulate with one another. The zoids can also develop directly into new vegetative cells, as mentioned above; they are therefore facultative gametes.

The isogametes of *Chlorococcum echinozygotum* exhibit clumping, just as in *Chlamydomonas*. Pairs of gametes disengage themselves from the clumps and may swim around together for a long time before

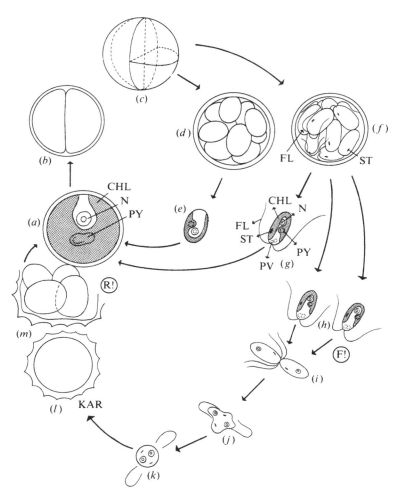

Figure 21.8. The life cycle of *Chlorococcum echinozygotum*. (*a*) Vegetative cell. (*b*) Division of a cell into two. (*c*) The planes of division during the formation of a tetrad. (*d, e*) Formation of aplanospores. (*f, g*) Formation of zoospores. (*h, i*) Gametes and copulation. (*j*) Loss of the cell envelopes around the gametes and plasmogamy. (*k*) Spherical zygote containing two unfused gametic nuclei. (*l*) Mature hypnozygote. (*m*) Germination of the hypnozygote, with the formation of four vegetative cells. CHL = chloroplast; F! = fertilization; FL = flagellum; KAR = probable position of karyogamy; N = nucleus; PV = contractile (pulsing) vacuole; PY = pyrenoid; R! = probable position of meiosis; ST = stigma (eyespot). (After [1585].)

finally fusing with each other, when the old cell envelopes are cast off. The zygote grows for some time and then forms a thick spiny wall, becoming dormant (as a hypnozygote). This resistant stage, which can remain dormant for a considerable time, probably enables the alga to survive unfavourable or extreme environmental conditions. In the laboratory, zygotes can be induced to germinate by transferring them to fresh agar medium at 37 °C; germination ensues within 48 h and four aplanospores are formed, probably following meiotic division of the zygote nucleus. The aplanospores then develop into vegetative cells and so the life cycle is completed.

Thus, although cytological and genetic evidence is

not yet available, it can be surmised that *Chlorococcum echinozygotum* has a haplontic life cycle.

Other examples of unicellular Chlorococcales

The order Chlorococcales also includes a number of other genera whose members are spherical unicells, like *Chlorococcum*. These genera are distinguished from each other by various criteria, among which are the structure of the chloroplasts and the presence or absence of pyrenoids, and to some extent also the structure of the pyrenoids. Thus *Spongiochloris*, unlike *Chlorococcum*, has a reticulate chloroplast. Also important in the classification of the unicellular Chlorococcales is the kind of zoid produced during reproduction. Some zoids, for instance, are naked, while others have an envelope: *Neochloris*, with naked zoids, can be distinguished from *Chlorococcum*, which has 'walled' zoids. Similar characteristics occur and are important in other genera [693, 1685].

Golenkinia (Fig. 21.9)

The solitary spherical cells of this genus are ornamented with many radiating spines. The single parietal chloroplast is cup-like and its basal part contains a pyrenoid. During asexual reproduction two, four or eight autospores are formed within the parent cell wall (Fig. 21.9b). *G. minutissima* exhibits oogamous sexual reproduction. Some cells divide up their contents into eight or sixteen biflagellate male gametes, which are at first walled but then naked, while other cells function as non-motile female gametes. After fertilization the zygotes develop thick walls and become hypnozygotes (Figs. 21.9c, d; [1687]). The three known species of *Golenkinia* occur throughout the world in freshwater [121].

Chlorella (Fig. 21.10a–c)

This genus contains about ten species, which have small (*ca.* 2–12 µm) spherical or ellipsoidal cells, very similar to those of *Chlorococcum*. *Chlorella*, however, does not form zoids and propagates itself only by autospores. *Chlorella* species generally occur on soil and in freshwater, but tiny (1–2 µm) *Chlorella*-like algae are also found in oceanic phytoplankton (cf. p. 121). They can also occur as endosymbionts in invertebrate animals, e.g. in the hydroid cnidarian *Chlorohydra*, some freshwater sponges, and the ciliate

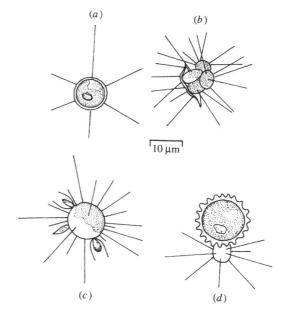

Figure 21.9. *Golenkinia minutissima.* (*a*) Vegetative cell. (*b*) Release of autospores from parent cell wall. (*c*) Oogamy between large non-motile egg cell and small flagellate male gametes. (*d*) Hypnozygote. (After [1687].)

Paramecium (see p. 362). *Chlorella* species are easy to grow in culture and are therefore frequently used in plant physiological and biochemical investigations. The cell wall consists in part of a sporopollenin-like substance, which also occurs in the walls of the pollen grains of higher plants [37].

The genus *Chlorella* appears to be highly diverse genetically [835], and many of its species are probably not at all closely related; recent DNA–DNA hybridization studies support this conclusion [766, 767, 768, 769; for an introduction to DNA hybridization, see p. 40]. '*Chlorella*' has probably arisen through the convergent evolution of cell morphology in several different evolutionary lineages of the Chlorococcales [443].

Chodatella (Fig. 21.10g)

The ellipsoidal cells of *Chodatella* bear thin spines at both poles of the cell; propagation takes place via autospores. *Chodatella* lives in the plankton of ponds and lakes.

Oocystis (Fig. 21.10d–f)

Oocystis cells are ellipsoidal and reproduce by autospores. This genus is in some ways intermediate

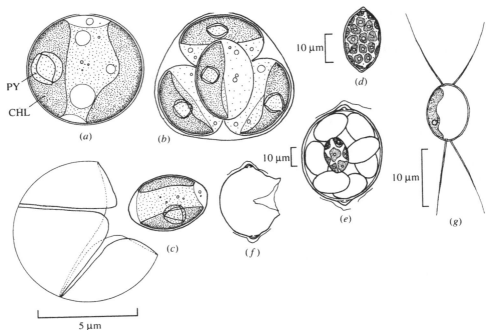

PY
CHL

10 μm
(d)

10 μm

10 μm

(a)   (b)

(c)   (f)   (e)   (g)

5 μm

Figure 21.10. Examples of unicellular coccoid Chloro-coc-cales. (*a–c*) *Chlorella vulgaris.* (*a*) Vegetative cell. (*b*, *c*) Formation and release of autospores.

(*d–f*) *Oocystis solitaria.* (*g*) *Chodatella quadriseta.* CHL = chloroplast; PY = pyrenoid. (*a–c* after [443]; *d–f* after [440]; *g* after [374].)

between the coccoid unicellular and coccoid colonial levels of organization, since the daughter cells can live separately, following their release from the parent cell wall, or they can live together as a group, contained within the parent cell wall. *Oocystis* species are found predominantly in the plankton of small freshwater lakes and ponds.

Examples of colonial representatives of the order Chlorococcales

Kirchneriella (Figs. 21.11, 21.12)

The cells of *Kirchneriella* are crescent-shaped and live within a rather diffuse mass of mucilage; they propagate via autospores. *Kirchneriella* is common in fresh-water.

Ultrastructural aspects of mitosis and cytokinesis in *Kirchneriella* are treated in some detail below, because they illustrate that it is impossible to distinguish clearly between unicellular and multicellular genera within the Chlorococcales. Mitosis resembles

that of *Chlamydomonas* (type II: p. 325, Fig. 19.17 II), but differs in that the septum (cleavage furrow) grows out centrifugally.

During the formation of the autospores the nucleus divides twice. The protoplast divides up around the four daughter nuclei, producing four autospores, each of which develops its own wall and becomes like a miniature version of the parent cell. As the autospores mature, they remain together within the parent cell wall. Finally the parent cell wall bursts open, releasing the four autospores (Fig. 21.11).

Autospore formation can be split into the following stages:

1 **Interphase in the vegetative cell** (Fig. 21.12*a*) The nucleus normally lies nearer one end of the cell. The single chloroplast is parietal and contains a pyrenoid, which usually lies at the tip of the cell. A long mitochondrion stretches along the inner face of the chloroplast, while on the inner side of the nucleus is a golgi apparatus. The cell is surrounded by a thin cell wall.

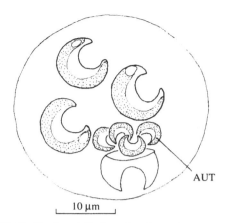

AUT

Figure 21.11. *Kirchneriella lunaris* colony. AUT = auto-spores being released from the parental cell wall. (After [1414].)

2 Prophase of the first mitosis (Fig. 21.12*b*) During prophase the nucleus moves to the centre of the cell. A centriole appears at each pole of the nucleus (compare p. 327) but the origin of the centrioles is unknown. They evidently play a role in mitosis in *Kirchneriella*, which is particularly interesting because flagellate stages, and hence also basal bodies, do not occur at any time in the life cycle of this alga.

Some microtubules are formed outside the nucleus during prophase, near the centrioles. A window develops in the nuclear envelope opposite each centriole; shortly afterwards, the centriole, together with several microtubules, moves through this into the nucleoplasm. The nucleolus disappears and the chromatin condenses, so that the chromosomes become visible, and a perinuclear sheet of endoplasmic reticulum develops around the nucleus, between it and the golgi apparatus.

3 Metaphase of the first mitosis (Fig. 21.12*c*) Both centrioles now lie within the nuclear envelope and between them lies the spindle. Some spindle microtubules extend from pole to pole, while others only reach from pole to chromosome. The nuclear envelope and the perinuclear endoplasmic reticulum remain intact, so that mitosis is intranuclear, as in *Chlamydomonas*: so-called 'closed mitosis'.

4 Late anaphase (Fig. 21.12*d*) The length of the spindle has increased through elongation of the continuous, pole-to-pole microtubules. This, together with shortening of the chromosome microtubules,

causes the daughter chromosomes to be segregated and drawn far apart. Nevertheless, the nuclear envelope and perinuclear endoplasmic reticulum remain intact.

5 Telophase (Fig. 21.12*e*) Each daughter nucleus is now surrounded by a new nuclear envelope, with the centriole outside. The envelope and perinuclear endoplasmic reticulum of the parent nucleus are still present but become discontinuous, and only a few microtubules remain of those that made up the spindle: the spindle is thus apparently not persistent. As a result of the previous elongation of the spindle, however, the daughter nuclei are as yet distant from each other.

6 The first cell division: organization of phycoplast microtubules in the division plane (Fig. 21.12*f*) Following the completion of mitosis and the collapse of the telophase spindle, the daughter nuclei move back towards each other. A golgi apparatus can be found by each nucleus. The centrioles move around the nuclei to lie close to where the transverse wall is to be formed. A complex system of criss-crossing microtubules (the phycoplast) develops in the plane where the wall is to form, while immediately beneath the plasmalemma but in the same plane are further microtubules, forming a hoop around the cell. These microtubules may have a skeletal function, reinforcing the shape of the cell in the zone where division takes place (see also p. 326).

7 Formation of the primary transverse wall (Fig. 21.12*g*) After the phycoplast has been formed in the plane of the prospective cell wall, the primary septum (cleavage furrow) is laid down within it. At the same time the chloroplast divides by constriction (Fig. 21.12*f, g*). Cell wall material is deposited in the primary septum, probably from golgi vesicles. The centrioles replicate and in one daughter cell (the lower one in the illustrations) a new pyrenoid is formed within the chloroplast.

8 The second mitosis and subsequent cell divisions The second mitosis takes place in essentially the same way as the first. Interestingly, the primary septum, together with the cell wall material it contains, largely disappears again. After the second round of mitosis is complete, new secondary septa are formed between all four daughter nuclei (Fig. 21.12*h*); only vestiges remain of the primary septum. Cell wall material is laid down in the secondary septa as it was in the primary septum.

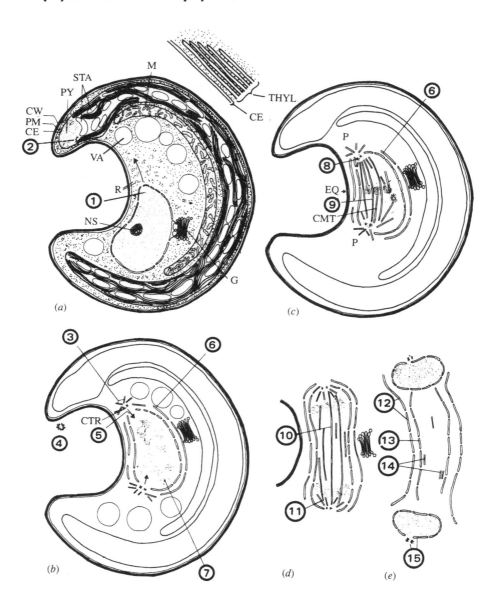

Figure 21.12. Cell division in *Kirchneriella lunaris*. (*a*) Interphase. (*b*) Prophase. (*c*) Metaphase. (*d*) Anaphase. (*e*) Telophase. (*f*) First cell division: an array of microtubules becomes organized in the plane of division. (*g*) First cell division: formation of the first septum. (*h*) Second cell division. (*i*) Four autospores within the parental cell wall.

Further explanation: 1. The nucleus moves (arrow) to the centre of the cell. 2. Part of a chloroplast (see detail above), showing a stack of thylakoids. 3. Microtubules are assembled outside the nucleus. 4. Cross section through a centriole.

5. Polar fenestra: a gap in the nuclear envelope, through which the centriole moves. 6. Perinuclear layer of ER. 7. The chromatin condenses so that individual chromosomes become visible. 8. Centriole now lying within the nucleus. 9. Pole-to pole (interzonal) microtubules. 10. The interzonal microtubules increase in length. 11. The chromosome microtubules shorten. 12. Remains of the perinuclear ER. 13. Remains of the original nuclear envelope. 14. Remains of the spindle. 15. The envelope of the new daughter nucleus forms, with the centriole outside. 16. The centrioles move around the nucleus to

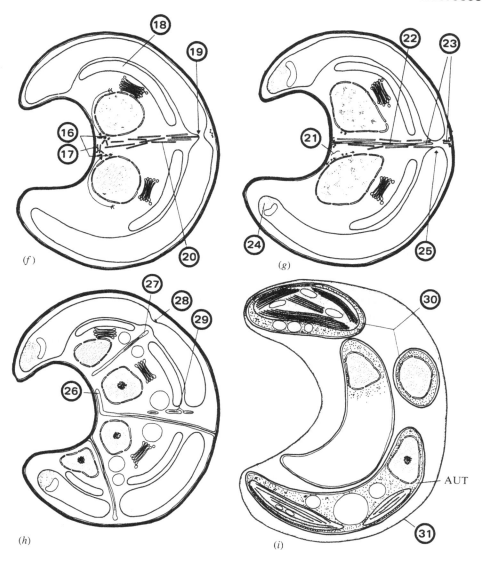

Caption for fig. 21.12 (cont.).

the plane of division. 17. Proliferation of microtubules beneath the plasmalemma. 18. Daughter mitochondrion. 19. Division of the chloroplast begins, through constriction. 20. Microtubules arranged in the plane of division. 21. The centrioles replicate and move to the poles of the nucleus in anticipation of the second division. 22. Cell wall material is deposited in the primary septum.
23. Arrows indicate the growth of the primary septum. 24. *De novo* origin of the pyrenoid in a daughter chloroplast. 25. The daughter chloroplasts separate. 26. Secondary septum growing around towards another secondary septum. 27. Secondary septum

containing cell wall material. 28. Constriction of the chloroplast. 29. Remains of the primary septum and wall material deposited in it. 30. The apices of the crescent-shaped autospores. 31. Wall of parent cell, now swollen and broken. AUT = autospore; CE = chloroplast envelope; CMT = chromosomal spindle microtubule; CTR = centriole complex; CW = cell wall; EQ = equator of spindle and cell at the first division; G = golgi body; M = mitochondrion; NS = nucleolus; P = pole of spindle; PM = plasma membrane (plasmalemma); PY = pyrenoid; R = ribosomes; STA = starch grains; THYL = stacked thylakoids; VA = vacuole. (Based on [1414].)

9   **Formation of the autospores** (Fig. 21.12*i*) The four daughter cells separate from each other only when the new cell walls are complete. Then the old cell wall swells up, so that a large space is formed in which the daughter cells each have room to assume the shape of the parent cell. However, before the daughter cells are able to separate from each other, the cell walls that have been formed must to some extent be broken down yet again.

Some conclusions:

1   In *Kirchneriella* the cell does not divide initially into separate naked protoplasts and then form new cell walls around each; instead it gives rise to a small four-celled thallus.

2   The first and second cell divisions both have the characteristics of vegetative cell division, because cell wall material is deposited directly into the septum. It is only later that the cells separate from each other, along the transverse walls that have already been laid down. If ontogeny is interpreted as a recapitulation of phylogeny, then in *Kirchneriella* vegetative cell division is more primitive than the formation of autospores and multicellular organization more primitive than unicellular organization!

From this account of cell division in *Kirchneriella* it can be seen that, without electron microscopical investigation, it is very difficult to get a correct picture of cell division in small algae. In addition, it seems that the distinction between unicellularity and multicellularity is not fundamental, and that unicellular algae cannot always, or with certainty, be assumed to be more primitive than multicellular forms.

Nephrocytium (Fig. 21.13*f*)
The kidney-shaped cells of this alga remain within the walls of their parent cells, which become swollen and mucilaginous, so that colonies are built up. Propagation occurs by autospores. *Nephrocytium* occurs in the freshwater phytoplankton.

Actinastrum (Fig. 21.13*b*)
The elongate, skittle-shaped or cylindrical cells of *Actinastrum* are attached to each other by their ends to form star-like (stellate) colonies. There is a single parietal chloroplast in each cell, which contain a pyrenoid. Reproduction takes place via autospores. *Actinastrum* occurs in slightly polluted or enriched waters.

Crucigenia (Fig. 21.13*c*)
In *Crucigenia* square colonies are produced, consisting of four cells. Daughter colonies remain united by the parent cell walls, which become mucilaginous. This alga is widely distributed in the freshwater phytoplankton.

Sphaerocystis (Fig. 21.14*a, b*)
Here the cells are spherical and contained within a sphere of mucilage. Inside each colony, younger daughter colonies of clustered cells can clearly be seen, reproduction occurring through the formation of autospores. *Sphaerocystis* is a member of the freshwater phytoplankton.

Coccomyxa (Fig. 21.14*c*)
Ellipsoidal or slightly reniform cells lie within an ill-defined common mass of mucilage. Propagation occurs by autospores. This alga lives aerophytically, on damp soil or on rock surfaces.

Scenedesmus (Fig. 21.13*d, e, g*)
The individual cells of this alga are elliptical to spindle-shaped and in many species they bear spines. The cells are connected together, usually 4, 8 or 16 of them in a row, to form a colony; sometimes they lie in two rows. Electron microscopical investigations have shown that the cell wall of *Scenedesmus* is a complex structure. On the inner side of the wall there is a robust supporting layer, containing a sporopollenin-like substance [319]. Outside this there is a net-like layer, which is supported by a series of small bars (columellae) and pierced at intervals by bristles, which have their own complex substructure [82, 85, 86, 1419]. The cells are clothed by large numbers of these bristles, which are long and delicate (100–200 µm × 25–40 nm). They seem to help keep the cells in suspension and discourage grazing zooplankton [1785].

Scenedesmus reproduces itself through the production of **autocolonies**. Each of these is a complete daughter colony (coenobium), which is formed by one of the cells of the parent colony. The contents of the parent cell divide up into a number of non-flagellate daughter cells, which subsequently regroup to form a new daughter colony: an autocolony (Fig. 21.13*g*; [1419, 1428]). In certain circumstances, for instance in conditions of nitrogen deficiency, *Scenedesmus* may also form zoids, which can copulate [1783].

Scenedesmus species are common in fresh and brackish waters, especially in fairly nutrient-rich con-

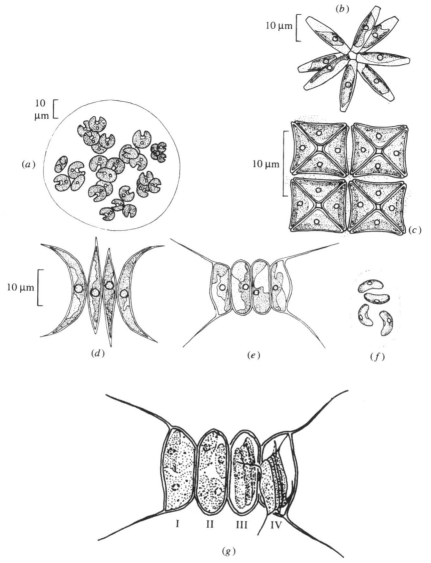

Figure 21.13. Examples of colonial Chlorococcales. (a)
Kirchneriella obesa. (b) *Actinastrum hantzschii*. (c)
Crucigenia tetrapedia. (d) *Scenedesmus falcatus*. (e)
Scenedesmus quadricauda. (f) *Nephrocytium agardhi-
anum*. (g) *Scenedesmus quadricauda*: autocolony

(coenobium) formation. I. Formation of two daughter
protoplasts; II. Formation of four daughter protoplasts;
III. Rearrangement of the protoplasts to form an autocolony; IV. Release of the autocolony through a slit in
the parental cell wall. (a–e, g after [374]; f after [440].)

ditions. More than 100 species and varieties have been
described ([631, 1807]), many of which are easy to grow in
culture; *Scenedesmus* is therefore often used in plant
physiological investigations. In culture the cells often
fail to produce colonies but remain separate, when
they resemble species of the genus *Chodatella*.

Hydrodictyon reticulatum: the water net (Fig. 21.15)

This alga is colonial, forming large cylindrical nets up
to around 20 cm long. The individual cells are also
cylindrical and can themselves be up to 1 cm long; at
each end they are connected to two other cells. Each

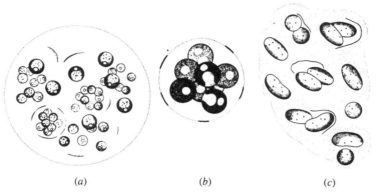

(a)   (b)   (c)

Figure 21.14. Examples of colonial Chlorococcales. (a) *Sphaerocystis schroeteri:* colony containing cells of different ages (generations).

(b) *Sphaerocystis schroeteri:* young colony.
(c) *Coccomyxa dispar.* (From [440].)

cell is multinucleate and contains an irregularly lobed, parietal chloroplast. Mitosis is intranuclear and during mitosis the nuclear envelope is surrounded by a special perinuclear endoplasmic reticulum, like that present in *Kirchneriella*; indeed, many aspects of mitosis are similar in *Hydrodictyon* and *Kirchneriella* (p. 366; [1115]).

Asexual reproduction occurs through the formation of autocolonies (Fig. 21.15*a–i*). The cytoplasm, which is restricted to the periphery of the cell by a large vacuole, divides up into many uninucleate protoplasts and these lie squashed together, so that each has a polygonal outline (Fig. 21.15*d*). Each protoplast develops into a zoid, and by the time differentiation is complete the cylindrical parent cell may contain up to 20 000 small flagellate cells. The zoids are biflagellate and exhibit only a few transient, convulsive movements. They soon become associated laterally to produce a net-like colony (Fig. 21.15*e–g*). They develop into cylindrical, uninucleate cells and subsequently grow to become the large, multinucleate cells of the mature colony (Fig. 21.15*h, i*). The young water net is liberated through the disintegration and dispersion of the parent cell wall.

After their formation, the zoids can also be liberated, instead of assembling within the parent cell to form a new colony. In this case asexual reproduction occurs by a different method (Fig. 21.15*n*). Zoospores produced in this way swim around freely, then come to rest and surround themselves with a thick wall. The resulting resting spore is termed a hypnospore (Fig. 21.15*o*) and this germinates by forming a new zoospore (Fig. 21.15*p*). Like the first set of zoospores, the new

zoospore settles but develops, not into a hypnospore, but into a **polyeder** (Fig. 21.15*q*), which is an irregularly shaped cell bearing pointed projections. The contents of the polyeder divide up into zoids and these are then discharged into a vesicle that the polyeder extrudes. Within the vesicle the zoids order themselves into a more or less spherical net, called the 'germination net' (Fig. 21.15*r*). Each cylindrical cell of the germination net subsequently produces a daughter net, by the same developmental process as has already been described above (illustrated in Fig. 21.15*a–i*), and so, because these daughter nets take on the cylindrical shape of the cells in which they form, we have now got back to our starting point: a cylindrical water net.

Sexual reproduction involves the formation of isogametes. These arise in the same way as the asexual zoospores but are smaller (Fig. 21.15*j*). Fusion of the gametes begins with the formation of a fertilization canal, like that in *Chlamydomonas reinhardtii* (Fig. 21.2*f*; [1116]). After copulation (isogamy) the zygote develops into a spherical resting stage, the hypnozygote (Fig. 21.15*k, l*). After a period of dormancy the hypnozygote germinates and produces several zoospores (Fig. 21.15*m*); meiosis may occur during this process. Each zoospore forms a polyeder (Fig. 21.15*q*) and this then develops as during asexual reproduction, in the manner described above. It is assumed that *Hydrodictyon* possesses a haplontic life cycle, in which the only diploid cell is the zygote, but this has yet to be proved.

Overviews of the life history of *Hydrodictyon*, cover-

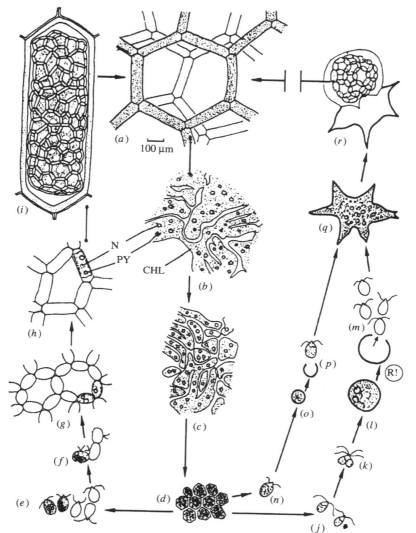

Figure 21.15. The life cycle of *Hydrodictyon reticulatum*.
(*a*) Part of the net-like coenobium. (*b*) Detail of the
parietal cytoplasm. (*c, d*) Division of the cytoplasm
into numerous small flagellate cells (zoids). (*e*) Zoids,
still enclosed within the parent cell wall. (*f*)
Assembly of the zoids to form a new net-like colony,
through lateral association. (*g, h*) The zoids lose their
flagella, the cells elongate and become cylindrical. (*i*)
Daughter colony still enclosed within parental cell
wall. (*j*) Gametes. (*k*) Plasmogamy. (*l*) Hypnozygote.

(*m*) Germination of hypnozygote with the release of
four zoids. (*n*) Asexual zoospore, following release
from the parent cell. (*o*) Hypnospore. (*p*) Germination
of hypnospore, with the release of a single secondary
zoospore. (*q*) Polyeder. (*r*) Germination of polyeder,
with the formation of a vesicle, within which a new
water-net is produced. See text for further explanation. CHL = chloroplast; N = nucleus; PY = pyrenoid;
R! = probable site of reduction division (meiosis).

ing both light and electron microscopical aspects, are
given by Pocock ([1434]) and Pickett-Heaps ([1419]).

The water net occurs all over the world in still or
slowly flowing freshwaters and it can form large
growths, particularly in nutrient-rich waters. In the
Zürichsee the massive blooms of *Hydrodictyon* can be
most unpleasant, since the wind collects it together into
thick mats, which can be driven onshore where they rot
([1770]).

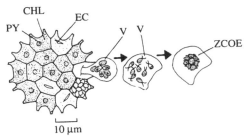

Figure 21.16. *Pediastrum boryanum* colony, showing in addition the formation of a new daughter colony. CHL = chloroplast; EC = empty cell, with a split in its wall marking where the vesicle emerged; PY = pyrenoid; V = vesicle containing zoids; ZCOE = zoids becoming organized into a new coenobium. (After [1658].)

Pediastrum (Fig. 21.16)

Pediastrum colonies are circular, flat and radially organized; they are usually one cell thick. The cells around the colony margin generally bear horn-like projections, while those in the centre do not.

Silica is an important component of the cell wall, which takes the form of a thin skin supported by a network of struts; there is also an outermost layer of sporopollenin-like material ([1202, 1230]). As in *Scenedesmus* the wall bears many delicate bristles, which help to keep the colonies in suspension ([492]). Vegetative reproduction occurs through the formation of biflagellate zoids, which are not released separately but discharged together into a vesicle extruded from the parent cell, which is formed from the innermost layer of the parent cell wall. Within the vesicle the zoids arrange themselves to form a complete daughter colony, as in *Hydrodictyon* ([624]).

The method of sexual reproduction also resembles that of *Hydrodictyon*. Isogametes fuse to give a hypnozygote, from which zoospores emerge on germination. Each zoospore develops into a polyeder, and when this germinates a daughter colony is formed by the lateral association and differentiation of biflagellate zoids. Just as in *Hydrodictyon*, polyeders can also arise asexually ([289, 1419]).

Species of *Pediastrum* are very common, particularly in nutrient-rich freshwaters. They are found in the plankton and also live on and between aquatic macrophytes.

Examples of multicellular representatives of the order Chlorococcales

Chlorosarcinopsis, a sarcinoid representative of the Chlorococcales (Fig. 21.17)

The cells of this alga are spherical or somewhat angular, as a result of mutual compression. The cells can be solitary and are then very similar to *Chlorococcum*, but they usually occur in more or less cubical, 'sarcinoid' groups or packets. After mitotic division the daughter cells remain enclosed by the parent cell wall and so, because the planes of successive divisions are perpendicular to each other, cubical packets of cells arise. Each cell has a single cup-shaped chloroplast containing a pyrenoid.

Sometimes the cells divide up their contents into naked, biflagellate zoids (Fig. 21.17*f, h*) with a cruciate, 1 o'clock – 7 o'clock type of flagellar apparatus (p. 302: [1165, 1166, 1328, 1329]), and in one species these can function as isogametes ([646]). There are about seven species in the genus (see [207, 1166]), all of them primarily being soil algae.

The difference in the mode of cell division between *Chlorosarcinopsis* (Fig. 21.17) and *Kirchneriella* (Fig. 21.12) lies mainly in the timing of cell wall deposition. In *Chlorosarcinopsis* cell walls are formed around the daughter cells after each mitotic division, whereas in *Kirchneriella* and other coccoid or colonial members of the Chlorococcales, the final deposition of wall material is delayed until after the parent cell has divided several times, into four or more daughter cells. In *Kirchneriella* the daughter cells are termed autospores and so the daughter cells formed by bipartition of *Chlorosarcinopsis* cells could also be considered as autospores ([1646]), the maximum number produced from each parent cell being just two in this case. In certain coccoid members of the Chlorococcales, e.g. *Coccomyxa* (Fig. 21.14*c*) the maximum number of autospores produced is also two, while in some *Scenedesmus* species (Fig. 21.13*d, e*) the number of autospores formed per parent cell varies from 2 to 4 to 8, producing 2- to 8-celled colonies ([1807]). Many sarcinoid green algae dissociate easily into single cells, probably through enzymatic breakdown of the walls of the parent cells in which the daughter cells ('autospores') are enclosed (for examples, see [121]). Enzymatic dissolution of the parent cell wall has also been demonstrated, however, in a filamentous representative of the Chlorococcales, *Geminella* (Fig. 21.19*d*; [1565, 1566]). It

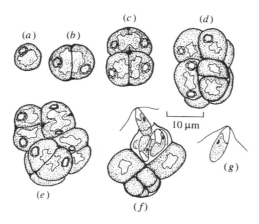

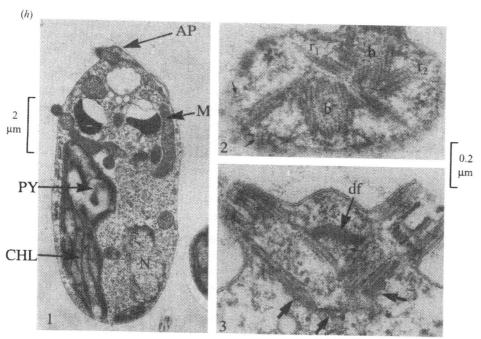

Figure 21.17. *Chlorosarcinopsis minor,* a sarcinoid member of the Chlorococcales. (*a–g*) Sarcinoid packets of cells (with zoospore formation in *f, g*). (*h*) Ultrastructure of the biflagellate zoospore, which has a cruciate 1 o'clock–7 o'clock construction. (*h-1*) Longitudinal section showing the general organization of the cell. Note the apical papilla where one of the two flagella appears in section. (*h-2*) Transverse section through the cell apex, showing the two basal bodies (b) in their 1 o'clock–7 o'clock positions, as well as the four microtubular roots, in 4–2–4–2 configuration. Two opposite roots (r1) have two microtubules, while the other two (r2) have four. (*h-3*) Median longitudinal section through the apical papilla showing the two basal bodies connected by the upper transversely striated connective (df). AP = apical papilla; b = basal body; CHL = chloroplast; df = upper transversely striated connective; M = mitochondrion; PY = pyrenoid; r_1 = two-stranded microtubular root; r_2 = four-stranded microtubular root. (*a–g* after [646]; *h* from [1166], with the permission of the author and Springer Verlag, Vienna.)

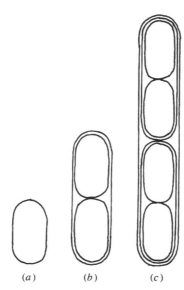

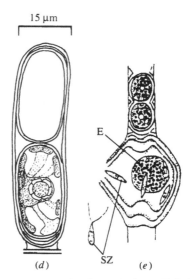

15 μm

Figure 21.18. *Cylindrocapsa,* a filamentous member of the Chlorococcales. (*a–c*) Diagrams illustrating how the filament grows (see text for further explanation). (*d*) A young, two-celled filament: the two daughter cells resulting from the first cell division remain enclosed within the parental cell wall. (*e*) Oogamy. E = egg cell; SZ = spermatozoid. (*a–d* after [440]; *e* after [464].)

must be concluded, therefore, that there is no clear-cut distinction between the coccoid, colonial, sarcinoid and filamentous levels of organization in the order Chlorococcales.

Cylindrocapsa, a filamentous representative of the Chlorococcales (Fig. 21.18)

The ellipsoidal cells of *Cylindrocapsa* are arranged in simple, unbranched filaments. Each cell contains one lobed parietal chloroplast, which bears an internal projection at the centre of the cell, containing a prominent pyrenoid ([1643]). The cell walls are thick, gelatinous and layered. Vegetative reproduction occurs by fragmentation of the filaments, or by the formation of biflagellate zoospores. Sexual reproduction is oogamous (Fig. 21.18*e*; [711,714]).

Mitosis and cytokinesis have recently been analysed in detail by Sluiman ([1642, 1643, 1644]). They conform to type III described on p. 327 (Fig. 19.20 I), which occurs in various Chlorococcales. Cytokinesis is accomplished by a cell plate of coalescing smooth vesicles, which may be derived from the ER. Following this new cell wall material is deposited around both daughter cells by golgi vesicles, while the two daughter cells remain imprisoned within the parent wall (Fig. 21.18*a–d*). Each of the daughter cells then divides into two further cells and so, because the planes of division are parallel,

a filament is produced. This is unbranched and has distinctly layered walls, each layer (lamella) representing a cell generation. The individual cells can be released through dissociation of the filament, probably following enzymatic breakdown of the wall. This again emphasizes that the vegetative cells of filamentous members of the Chlorococcales, such as *Cylindrocapsa,* are equivalent to the autospores of coccoid forms ([1644, 1646]). *Cylindrocapsa* includes five species, which occur in freshwater.

Geminella (Fig. 21.19*c*)

The filaments are surrounded by a thick sheath of mucilage. The cells often lie together in pairs and reproduction takes place through fragmentation of the filament, involving a species-specific enzyme (an autolysin; [1565]). *Geminella* occurs in the freshwater phytoplankton.

Binuclearia (Fig. 21.19*d–f*)

The cross walls of this alga are extremely thick and can clearly be seen to consist of several layers. *Binuclearia tectorum* lives in pools on bogs.

Radiofilum (Fig. 21.19*a, b*)

The cells of *Radiofilum* are spherical or somewhat compressed and have bipartite walls, consisting of two hemispherical pieces, which half enclose the daughter

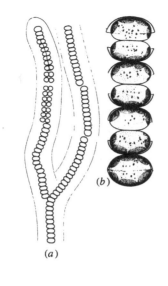

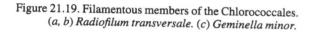

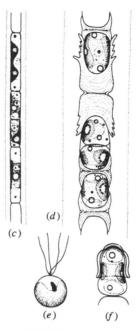

Figure 21.19. Filamentous members of the Chlorococcales. (a, b) *Radiofilum transversale.* (c) *Geminella minor.*

(d–f) *Binuclearia tectorum:* filament (d), zoospore (e) and terminal cell (f). (From [440].)

cells after division. The cells sometimes divide longitudinally and reproduction of the filaments takes place through fragmentation. The filaments possess a thick sheath of mucilage and false branching can occur, as a result of the growth of fragments within the same sheath. Fott ([440]) interprets *Radiofilum* as a row of autospores held together within a common sheath of mucilage.

Radiofilum is a freshwater genus.

Examples of siphonous representatives of the order Chlorococcales

Among the spherical unicellular species classified in the Chlorococcales are several that are multinucleate ([871]), including, for instance, one species of *Chlorococcum* ([295, 646, 871, 1685]). We would not generally say that these algae were 'siphonous', yet it would not be unreasonable to apply this term to the cylindrical, multinucleate cells of the *Hydrodictyon* coenobium (Fig. 21.15). The reason that it is not usually applied to *Hydrodictyon* is the apparently close relationship of *Hydrodictyon* to coenobial Chlorococcales with uninucleate cells, such as *Pediastrum*. The tiny freshwater alga *Characiosiphon* is another unmistak-

ably siphonous representative of the Chlorococcales ([1703]). The alga we describe in detail, however, is *Sphaeroplea*, a striking example of siphonous organization, although it should strictly be described perhaps as siphonocladous, since the thallus consists of unbranched filaments composed of many multinucleate cells. *Sphaeroplea* and its close relative *Atractomorpha* are often classified together in a separate order, the Sphaeropleales ([100, 1630]).

Sphaeroplea (Fig. 21.20)

This alga forms unbranched, free-floating filaments, which can grow several centimetres long and consist of elongate, cylindrical cells. The cells are multinucleate, and each contains a number of annular (ring-like) accumulations of cytoplasm, separated by large vacuoles. Each ring of cytoplasm harbours several nuclei, and an annular chloroplast containing several pyrenoids (Fig. 21.20a). The cells are separated from each other by rather thick transverse walls and are thought to divide like *Cylindrocapsa* cells, the daughter cells remaining enclosed by the parent cell wall (Fig. 22.18a–c; [177]). Mitosis is not coupled to cytokinesis in this multinucleate alga, but in other respects it follows the pattern exhibited by *Kirchneriella*: the

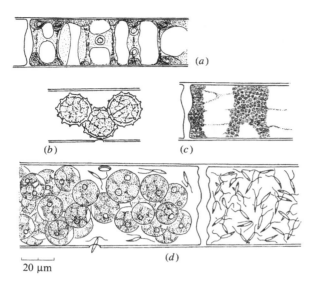

20 μm

Figure 21.20. *Sphaeroplea*, a siphonocladous member of the Chlorococcales. (*a*) Vegetative filament: a single cell with annular accumulations of cytoplasm, which contain the band-like parietal chloroplasts. (*b*) Female cell containing hypnozygotes. (*c*) Cell in the process of dividing up its contents into male gametes. (*d*) Left: a female gametangium containing eggs (non-motile female gametes) ready for fertilization. Right: a male gametangium containing small biflagellate spermatozoids (male gametes). (*a* after [121]; *b–d* after [1658].)

telophase spindle is not persistent (Fig. 21.12) and a phycoplast is formed between the two telophase nuclei, even though no cytokinesis is associated with it ([177]). The ultrastructural details of cytokinesis itself are not known.

Asexual reproduction takes place by fragmentation of the thallus, through dissociation of the cells. Sexual reproduction is oogamous. The cells divide either into many small biflagellate male cells or into a smaller number of eggs (Fig. 21.20*c, d*). Fertilized eggs develop into thick-walled hypnozygotes, which are thought to be the only diploid stage in the life cycle ([177]).

The biflagellate male gametes of *Sphaeroplea*, and those of the closely related genus *Atractomorpha*, have all the ultrastructural features that are characteristic of the class Chlorophyceae ([160a, 178, 712, 713, 1216]), with a cruciate 12 o'clock – 6 o'clock flagellar apparatus (Fig. 19.14*a*-1). There are about five species, which are all free-floating algae of freshwaters.

Order Chaetophorales *sensu stricto*

1 Mitosis is closed, the telophase spindle is not persistent, and cytokinesis is brought about by a cell plate of golgi vesicles containing cell wall material, which lie within a phycoplast; the daughter cells remain connected after division by plasmodesmata, which perforate the transverse wall between them (type IV mitosis–cytokinesis: see p. 328 and Fig. 19.20 II; [426, 1145, 1147, 1419, 1612, 1613, 1617]).

2 After cytokinesis each daughter cell does *not* become entirely surrounded by a new cell wall; the transverse wall between the daughter cells is the only new wall produced.

3 All the known representatives of the order are multicellular, which is a natural consequence of the mode of mitosis and cytokinesis. Members of the Chaetophorales have a filamentous organization (Figs. 21.22*a*, 21.23), or more rarely a thallose organization (Fig. 21.22*b–d*); the filamentous species can be branched or unbranched.

Other features of cytokinesis have recently been discovered, which also seem to be characteristic of the Chaetophorales. They were revealed by the use of indirect immunofluorescence microscopy, involving staining dividing cells with spindle- and tubulin-specific fluorescent antibodies; and by computer-aided, 3-dimensional reconstructions of microtubular arrays, made from TEM micrographs of serial sections. The results obtained from these two approaches are summarized in Fig. 21.21, which depicts the later stages of mitosis and cytokinesis ([1612, 1613, 1617]).

At late anaphase the nucleus is very elongated but is still surrounded by an intact envelope (Fig. 21.21*a*). Arrays of radiating microtubules (asters) are present around the pairs of centrioles. During late telophase, as the characteristic collapse of the telophase spindle begins, a phycoplast starts to form in the central region of the interzonal spindle (Fig. 21.21*b*), apparently under the control of a diffuse MTOC (microtubule organizing centre). At first the phycoplast takes the form of a simple radiating system of microtubules, but later it develops into a conspicuous stellate (star-shaped) array (Fig. 21.21*c*). This then becomes compressed between the daughter nuclei, which by now

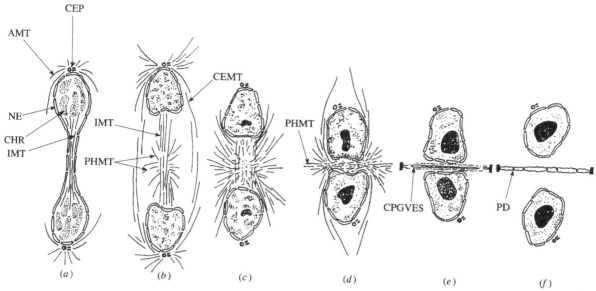

Figure 21.21. The later stages of mitosis and cytokinesis in a member of the Chaetophorales. (*a, b*) Late anaphase and telophase. (*c, d*) Collapse of the telophase spindle and formation of a phycoplast. (*e, f*) Formation of the a new cross-wall containing plasmodesmata. For further explanation, see text. AMT = astral microtubule; CEMT = microtubules connecting the centriolar pairs; CEP = centriolar pair; CHR = chromosome; CPGVES = cell plate of golgi vesicles; IMT = interzonal spindle microtubule; NE = nuclear envelope; PD = plasmodesma; PHMT = phycoplast microtubules. (Based on [1617].)

have collapsed back towards each other in the centre of the cell, forming a flat array of criss-crossing microtubules lying in the future plane of division, with radiating microtubules at the margin (Figs. 21.21*d*, 19.21). Vesicles produced by the golgi apparatus assemble within the phycoplast and fuse to form a cell plate, into which they deposit cell wall material (Fig. 21.21*e*), although the new transverse wall remains perforated by plasmodesmata (Fig. 21.21*f*). The method of formation of the phycoplast described is characteristic of the Chaetophorales but differs fundamentally from phycoplast formation in the Volvocales (p. 326, Figs. 19.17 II, 19.19).

As well as dividing in the way we have described, the vegetative cells may also give rise to flagellate cells. Here the contents of the cell may divide up into 2 to 16 biflagellate or quadriflagellate reproductive cells, but often the whole of the cytoplasm of a vegetative cell is transformed into a single flagellate cell, which is subsequently released. Each flagellate cell (zoid) has a cruciate 1 o'clock – 7 o'clock configuration of flagellar apparatus (Figs. 19.6, 19.14*c*; [422a, 423, 1328]). For the most part the zoids function as zoospores;

sexual reproduction is known in very few representatives of the order. The life cycles of the Chaetophorales are thus poorly understood; haplontic, diplohaplontic and diplontic life cycles have all been suggested to occur but the evidence for these is meagre (for reviews, see [100, 801, 1635]). Vegetative cells can also form thick walls and survive adverse conditions as akinetes.

A close phylogenetic relationship between 19 species of the order Chaetophorales, belonging to 6 different genera, has recently been demonstrated biochemically. It was observed that the cell wall autolysin produced by one of the species (a species of *Uronema*) could break down the walls of its own thalli and those of all the other species of Chaetophorales tested, but could not degrade the walls of 24 species drawn from the Chlorococcales, Codiolales, Trentepohliales and Klebsormidiales. The only member of the Chaetophorales, as we define the group, that did not react to the autolysin was the thallose alga *Schizomeris* (Fig. 21.22*b–e*). The natural functions of cell wall autolysins include the degradation of cell walls to allow the liberation of reproductive cells, as in the formation of exit pores in sporangia. Autolysins are generally effective only within a species, or within a group of closely related species ([1567]).

The Chaetophorales contains about 28 genera and 90 species. Most occur in freshwater habitats, while some of them are terrestrial ([1630]); none are marine.

Examples of the order Chaetophorales

Uronema (Fig. 21.22a)

The plants consist of unbranched filaments, each of which has at its tip a pointed and often slightly curved apical cell; the basal end of the filament is attached by an attachment disc, composed of cell wall material ([1445]). Each cell is uninucleate and possesses a single parietal chloroplast, which is annular and contains one to several pyrenoids. The nuclei and cells divide as in type IV mitosis–cytokinesis (p. 328, Fig. 19.20 II), which is characteristic of the order Chaetophorales ([426, 1419]; both authors refer to the organism as 'Ulothrix fimbriata'). Uronema reproduces asexually through the formation of quadriflagellate zoospores with a cruciate, 1 o'clock – 7 o'clock configuration of the flagellar apparatus (p. 302, Fig. 19.14c; [423]). One or two zoospores are formed per cell.

In the light microscope Uronema is almost indistinguishable from Ulothrix (class Ulvophyceae, p. 394) and Klebsormidium (class Klebsormidiophyceae, p. 459). The similarity of these three genera apparently results from convergent evolution in three quite separate evolutionary lineages within the division Chlorophyta. About 10 freshwater species have been described.

Stigeoclonium (Figs. 21.23a, 21.24)

In Stigeoclonium, branched upright filaments of cells arise from a system of prostrate filaments, which grow across the surface of the substratum. The cells of the main axis may bear one or two side branches and each cell contains one nucleus and an annular, parietal chloroplast, within which there are several pyrenoids. The upright filaments often end in thin, pale extensions. The formation of these hair-like structures is stimulated by deficiencies of nutrients – phosphate in particular, but also nitrate or iron – and they probably function in nutrient uptake ([516, 517, 1889]).

Stigeoclonium can reproduce asexually via quadriflagellate zoospores, which are similar to the cells of

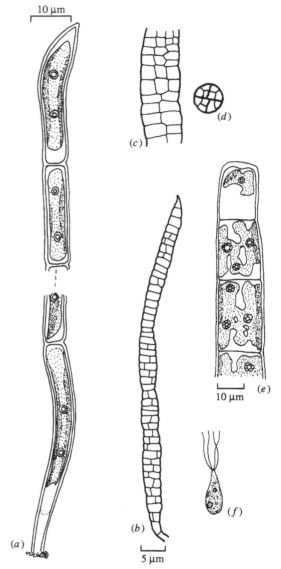

Figure 21.22. (a) Uronema elongatum. (b–f) Schizomeris leibleinii. (b) Young thallus, still partly uniseriate. (c) Older thallus, surface view. (d) Older thallus, cross section. (e) Uniseriate tip of thallus, showing the reticulate parietal chloroplasts, each containing pyrenoids. (f) Quadriflagellate zoospore. (a after [121]; b–f after [1445].)

Carteria (see Fig. 21.3e). The ultrastructure of the zoospores (Fig. 21.24) resembles that of Chlamydomonas cells (p. 302, Fig. 19.1). A set of the usual cell organelles can be distinguished: a nucleus with a

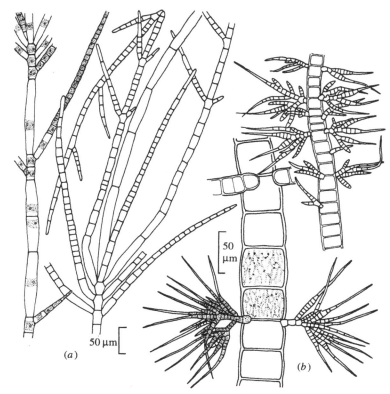

Figure 21.23. (a) *Stigeoclonium amoenum*. (b) *Draparnaldia platyzonata*. (After [1445].)

nucleolus, endoplasmic reticulum, ribosomes, mitochondria, vacuoles, and a golgi apparatus, which is enclosed by a fold of endoplasmic reticulum, just as in *Chlamydomonas*. In the chloroplast the thylakoids are united into stacks of various sizes and each zoospore has two prominent contractile vacuoles, which pulse alternately; in Fig. 21.24b the contractile vacuole is shown discharged. Associated with each contractile vacuole are several smaller, 'hairy' vesicles, which appear to deliver up their contents to it.

One difference from *Chlamydomonas* is the presence of numerous vesicles immediately under the plasmalemma, which are filled with material of some kind. The vesicles disappear when the zoospore becomes attached to a substratum via its anterior end, so perhaps they contain a sticky substance that aids attachment. Alternatively, they may be full of primary cell wall material, which is known to be secreted at the time of attachment. Newly attached zoospores are surrounded by a halo of flocculent matter ([1091]).

The basal bodies of the flagella are connected by an upper connective, which is transversely striated as in *Chlamydomonas*. Four microtubular roots arise below the connective, again as in *Chlamydomonas*, two of them containing five microtubules, the others two. The roots run beneath the plasmalemma towards the posterior of the zoospore and appear to be important in anchoring the flagellar apparatus in the cell.

Once the zoospore has attached itself, the flagella are not cast off but are absorbed back into the cell, and the basal bodies seem to play a role (as centrioles) in the first nuclear division of the germinating zoospore (see p. 378).

Stigeoclonium includes about 30 species, which are all restricted to freshwater.

Draparnaldia (Fig. 21.23b)

This alga is distinguished from *Stigeoclonium* by a much greater differentiation between the main axes and the side branches. The main axis and some of the

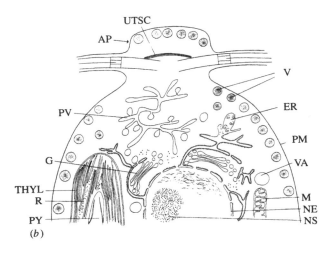

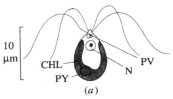

Figure 21.24. *Stigeoclonium* zoospore. (*a*) As seen with the light microscope, showing the four flagella, which arise around the sides of an apical papilla. (*b*) Longitudinal section through the apical part of the cell, based on EM observations. AP = apical papilla; CHL = chloroplast; ER = endoplasmic reticulum; G = perinuclear golgi body, enclosed by a fold of ER; M = mitochondrion; N = nucleus; NE = nuclear envelope; NS = nucleolus; PM = plasma membrane (plasmalemma); PV = contractile (pulsing) vacuole; PY = pyrenoid; R = ribosomes; THYL = thylakoid; UTSC = upper transversely striated connective; V = vesicle containing material for adhesion and/or primary cell wall components; VA = vacuole. (After [1091].)

larger side branches can continue to grow more or less indefinitely (they are axes of unlimited growth) and bear densely branched laterals, consisting of small cells. The laterals exhibit limited growth (they are sometimes called 'short shoots') and grow out from single cells of the main axes. The whole thallus is surrounded by a mucilage sheath. The construction of *Draparnaldia* is reminiscent of the red alga *Acrosymphyton* (p. 75, Fig. 5.21*a*), and certain members of the brown algal order Chordariales also have a similar structure.

Around twenty species of *Draparnaldia* are known, all from freshwater.

Schizomeris (Fig. 21.22*b–f*)

The *Schizomeris* thallus grows up to 2 cm long and consists of a solid cylinder of parenchyma, with ring-like constrictions at intervals along its length. It is superficially similar to *Enteromorpha* (Fig. 22.11*c*), but there the cylindrical thallus is hollow, not solid. Each cell contains a parietal reticulate chloroplast with several pyrenoids (Fig. 21.22*e*). During asexual reproduction quadriflagellate zoospores are produced (one per cell), which have the cruciate 1 o'clock – 7 o'clock configuration of the flagellar apparatus that is characteristic of the class Chlorophyceae *sensu stricto* ([1328, 1329]). Mitosis and cytokinesis are of type IV (p. 328, Fig. 19.20 II), which is typical of the order Chaetophorales ([1141]).

Schizomeris exhibits the greatest degree of parenchymatous development found in the class Chlorophyceae *sensu stricto*. Each cylindrical *Schizomeris* thallus begins in its earliest stages as a *Uronema*-like filament. Subsequently the formation of vertical cell walls (i.e. parallel to the long axis of the plant) and intercalary growth transform the initially uniseriate filament into a parenchymatous cylinder (Fig. 21.22*b, e*).

There are two species, which are widespread in fairly eutrophic freshwater.

Order Oedogoniales

1 Mitosis and cytokinesis superficially resemble type III mitosis-cytokinesis (p. 327, Fig. 19.20 I). Mitosis is closed, although no centrioles are associated with the spindle, in contrast to typical type III organisms (compare Fig. 21.27 with Fig. 19.20 I); and cytokinesis is brought about by a cell plate of numerous small vesicles lying within a phycoplast. The vesicles appear not to be derived from the golgi apparatus ([1419, 1422, 1424, 1425]) but probably come instead from ER ([1644]). A special ring of cell wall material is produced during the growth and division of the vegetative cells (Figs. 21.26, 21.27). Cell growth, mitosis and cytokinesis are integrated into a process that is highly characteristic of the order and will be described in detail below.

2 All members of the Oedogoniales are filamentous. The uniseriate filaments may be branched or unbranched.

3 Each uninucleate cell contains a parietal, reticulate chloroplast, within which there are numerous pyrenoids (Fig. 21.25).

4 The flagellate reproductive cells are stephanokont, each having a ring or crown of flagella near its anterior end (Fig. 21.28). The numerous basal bodies of the zoid are connected by a massive fibrous ring, which is transversely striated (Figs. 21.29, 21.30) and is considered to be homologous with the upper connective (also transversely striated) that links the two basal bodies in *Chlamydomonas*-type zoids (Figs. 19.4, 19.6*b*).

5 The life cycle is haplontic, involving a peculiar, characteristic type of oogamy (Figs. 21.31, 21.32).

Mitosis and cytokinesis in Oedogonium

Oedogonium exhibits a remarkable type of cell division, which is unique to the order. Growth of the filaments and cell division are intercalary. During mitosis a ring of cell wall material is deposited close to the upper end of the cell (Fig. 21.26*a*). Following telophase, a septum is formed between the two daughter nuclei and then moves upwards within the cell (Fig. 21.26*b, c*); this represents the embryonic cross-wall. Subsequently, the parent cell wall splits apart near the top of the cell, just outside the new ring of cell wall material, and the ring elongates parallel to the longitudinal axis of the filament, to become a cylinder (Fig. 21.26*d*). The place where the old cell wall splits apart remains visible in the form of two ridges or 'caps' around the cell, one facing upwards and the other down. The septum moves up within the cell to lie more or less level with the lower, upwardly pointing ridge and there the transverse wall is completed, separating the daughter cells.

It is usually the upper of the two daughter cells that divides again, so that after a while the upper end of the cell may bear a stack of overlapping caps, a characteristic feature of *Oedogonium* filaments (Fig. 21.25).

Investigations using both light and electron microscopy have brought to light several further interesting peculiarities of intercalary cell division in *Oedogonium* ([682, 1422, 1424]); these will therefore be dis-

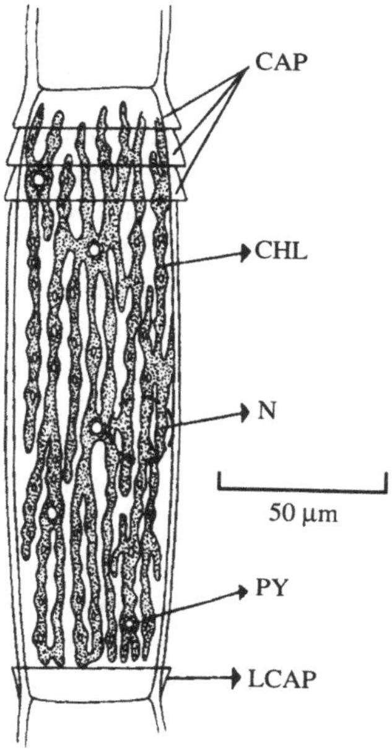

Figure 21.25. *Oedogonium* vegetative cell. CAP = caps of cell wall material; CHL = reticulate parietal chloroplast; LCAP = lower, upward-facing cap or rim of wall material; N = nucleus; PY = pyrenoid.

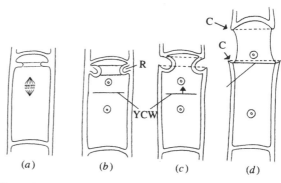

Figure 21.26. *Oedogonium:* cell division and elongation. (*a*) Anaphase and the deposition of a ring of wall material near the top of the cell. (*b*) Fully developed ring; formation of the new cross-wall. (*c*) Rupture of the cell wall near the top of the cell, just outside the ring of new wall material; upward movement of the new cross-wall. (*d*) Stretching upwards of the ring to form the cylindrical wall of the upper daughter cell. R = ring of cell wall material; C = caps of material left at the top and bottom of cells, as a result of ring formation; YCW = young cross-wall.

cussed in more detail, with the aid of the schematic diagrams shown in Fig. 21.27. Chloroplasts, mitochondria and endoplasmic reticulum are omitted from the diagrams to improve clarity. The following stages can be distinguished.

(a) Interphase. The nucleus lies roughly halfway along the cell, against the wall. The cell wall consists of a structural component and an outer, amorphous part, which appears slightly fibrillar under the electron microscope and stains with ruthenium red. The golgi apparatus shows no activity at this stage. Beneath the cell wall are microtubules, which run longitudinally, whereas in the cells of higher plants they usually lie oblique to the longitudinal axis.

(b) Prophase. The nucleus, which in the meantime has swollen, now lies in the centre of the cell, instead of against the wall; it has also moved higher in the cell. The nuclear envelope is drawn out into tube-like extensions at each pole and within the nucleus the chromatin begins to contract. Paired kinetochores appear, scattered through the nucleus, and are associated with bundles of microtubules. Other microtubules, not associated with kinetochores, also appear within the nucleus. Outside the nuclear envelope, longitudinally aligned microtubules can be found and these probably give the nucleus its shape. Mitosis takes place entirely within the nuclear envelope and is therefore closed (intranuclear). The kinetochores are disc-like and exhibit a complex substructure. There are no centrioles at the poles of the spindle; their absence in *Oedogonium*, despite the presence of large numbers of basal bodies in the zoids, shows that these organelles are not essential components of the mitotic apparatus. As the nucleus goes through prophase, a ring of wall material begins to be deposited at the upper end of the cell. It arises through the exocytosis of vesicles, which are almost certainly derived from the golgi apparatus [682].

(c) Metaphase. In the illustration the chromosomes have just divided; discoid kinetochores and continuous pole-to-pole microtubules are clearly visible at this stage. During anaphase the spindle elongates considerably, through growth of the interzonal microtubules. By now the wall ring has almost reached its final size and consists predominantly of the same material that makes up the amorphous fraction of the cell wall; only at its edges are there thin outgrowths or 'lips' of the material that makes up the structural layer of the wall. The position where the parent cell wall will later split apart is marked by a pre-formed break in the structural layer.

(d) The beginning of telophase. The spindle has now attained its maximum length and will shortly collapse. On the side of each nucleus facing the cell equator, many vesicles and microtubules appear. These are the progenitors of the cell plate, from which the cross-wall will eventually be formed. The vesicles are apparently derived, not from the golgi apparatus [1419, 1422, 1424, 1425], but probably from the ER [1644]. According to Sluiman [1644], mitosis–cytokinesis in the Oedogoniales resembles that in the Chlorococcales (type III mitosis–cytokinesis; p. 327, Fig. 19.20 I) and he therefore considers these two groups to be closely related.

(e) Completion of nuclear division and formation of the septum. After the collapse of the spindle, the daughter nuclei quickly move back towards each other, but between them a 'septum' is formed, which consists of a plate of vesicles together with a system of more or less transversely orientated microtubules (the phycoplast). It is from the septum that the new cross-wall develops. In the lower daughter cell the vacuoles swell greatly, displacing the septum upwards. The swelling is probably brought about by the golgi apparatus, which is now very active and delivers large vesicles to the vacuoles (a process comparable, perhaps, with osmoregulation in *Chlamydomonas*, p. 312). The parent cell wall is about to rupture above the ring of new wall material.

(f) The parent cell wall has now split and the ring has become transformed into a cylinder. This process and the elongation of the cell that ensues take place so rapidly and violently that the filaments themselves bend this way and that with the strain. The small 'lips' of structural wall material grow towards each other beneath the elongating mass of amorphous material, to form the structural, strength-giving layer of the wall

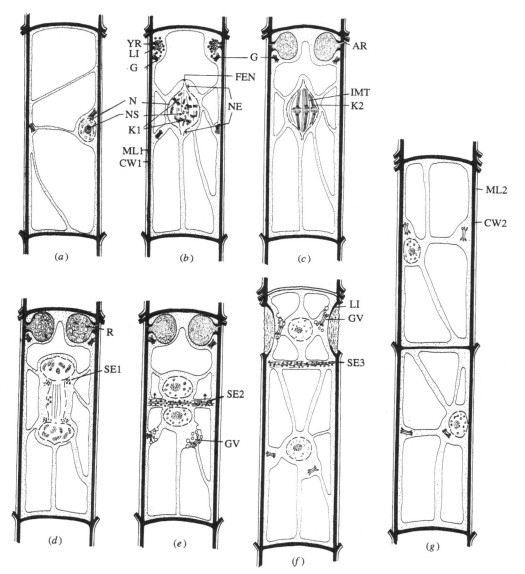

Figure 21.27. *Oedogonium:* stages in nuclear and cell division, based on EM observations. (*a*) Interphase. (*b*) Prophase. (*c*) Metaphase. (*d*) Beginning of telophase. (*e*) Completion of mitosis. (*f*) Elongation of the cell wall ring, after rupture of the parent cell wall. (*g*) Completion of cell division. AR = preformed position where the parent cell wall breaks during cell division; CW1 = structural layer of cell wall; CW2 = structural layer of new cell wall, formed from the lips of material on the inner side of the wall ring; FEN = polar fenestra in nuclear envelope; G = golgi body; GV = golgi body apparently producing vesicles that fuse with the vacuole membrane; IMT = interzonal spindle micro-tubule; K1 = scattered kinetochores; K2 = kineto-chores arranged in a plate; LI = inner lip of structural wall material in the wall ring; ML1 = layer of mucilage; ML2 = layer of amorphous mucilage produced by transformation of the wall ring; N = nucleus; NE = nuclear envelope, which is drawn out into tubes at the poles of the nucleus at prophase; NS = nucleolus; R = ring of cell wall material; SE1 = early stage in septum formation, with a horizontal array of vesicles and microtubules; SE2 = septum moving upwards within cell; SE3 = septum in its final position, just below the wall ring; VA = vacuole; YR = young ring of cell wall material. (After [682, 1422, 1424, 1425].)

in the upper daughter cell. The ring itself is destined to form the outer amorphous fraction of the new cell wall. At the upper and lower margins of the elongating ring, the edges of the original cell wall become bent outwards, because the new structural wall layer, formed by elongation of the 'lips' described above, extends and straightens, pushing the old wall aside. In this way the cell wall caps characteristic of *Oedogonium* are produced. In the upper daughter cell a marked enlargement of the vacuoles now takes place, probably through the addition of vesicles cut off from the golgi apparatus. In both daughter cells the nuclei are now central, while the septum, containing its vesicles and phycoplast microtubules, has reached its final position at the lower end of the expanded ring.

(g) Both daughter cells are complete, the upper cell having expanded to its final size. The golgi apparatus has returned to its inactive interphase condition, while the nuclei have moved to their interphase positions alongside the cell wall. The vesicles of the septum have fused with each other and cell wall polysaccharides are being deposited in the septum. The cross-wall subsequently thickens, but plasmodesmata with a distinctive substructure are left, connecting the daughter cells through the transverse wall (in the Chlorococcales the cross-walls do not contain plasmodesmata; [447]).

Stephanokont zoospores

Oedogonium and the genera related to it reproduce themselves asexually through the formation of stephanokont zoospores (Fig. 21.28), which are each formed from the contents of one vegetative cell. Zoospore formation usually occurs in cells that have been dividing actively, as is shown by the stack of caps at the upper ends of the cells. The protoplast of the vegetative cell contracts, the cell wall splits apart just below the stack of caps, and the cell contents extrude themselves as a hyaline vesicle, within which there is a single stephanokont zoospore. The vesicle lasts in this form for about 10 minutes; then it disappears and the zoospore swims away. The zoospores swim around for *ca.* 1–2 h, before attaching themselves to the substratum by their anterior ends and growing into new filaments.

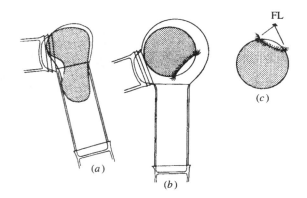

Figure 21.28. *Oedogonium:* asexual reproduction through the formation of stephanokont zoospores. (*a*) The cell wall breaks open, the protoplast contracts and bulges out in a vesicle. (*b*) A single zoospore is enclosed within the thin-walled vesicle. (*c*) Stephanokont zoospore after release. FL = ring of flagella around the anterior end of the zoospore.

The structure of the flagellar apparatus and its complicated root system has been investigated electron microscopically ([709, 1415]), and the ultrastructure of the flagellar apparatus is illustrated in Fig. 21.30. Its most striking feature is a massive band (Fig. 21.30), which is transversely striated and fibrous, and runs around the top of the zoospore just beneath the plasmalemma, at the base of the apical dome (Fig. 21.29). This fibrous band connects the flagellar bases, which lie in a whorl just below it (Fig. 21.30).

Microtubular roots, each composed of three microtubules (Fig. 21.30, MR), alternate with the basal bodies (Fig. 21.30, BB), which lie almost perpendicular to them. The roots extend downwards along the zoospore from the basal bodies, running just beneath the plasmalemma. In addition there are narrow, transversely striated components (Fig. 21.30, SR), which are closely associated with the microtubular roots. The whole basal apparatus of the flagella is embedded in fibrous supporting material (Fig. 21.30, SM).

The apical dome has a characteristic structure, consisting of two zones (Fig. 21.29). The lower zone lies just above the transversely striated annular fibre and contains numerous mitochondria, rough ER, golgi bodies, and a peripheral area with irregularly shaped vesicles containing granular material. Above this is an upper zone, in which there are many rounded vesicles with darkly staining contents. These vesicles contain

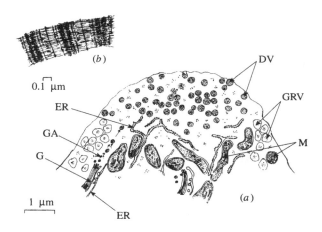

Figure 21.29. *Oedocladium:* zoospore ultrastructure. (*a*) Longitudinal section through the apical dome (i.e. the anterior part of the zoospore, above the whorl of flagella). The anterior region contains numerous vesicles, probably derived from the golgi apparatus; the posterior region is occupied predominantly by mitochondria and ER, but also contains golgi bodies. (*b*) Longitudinal section through the transversely striated fibrous band that connects the ring of basal bodies (see Fig. 21.30). DV = vesicles with electron-dense contents; ER = endoplasmic reticulum; G = golgi body; GA = arrows indicating the possible formation of dense vesicles from a golgi body; GRV = vesicles with granular contents; M = mitochondria. (After [1127].)

mucopolysaccharides, which act as an adhesive for the zoospore when it settles (comparable vesicles are found in the zoospore of *Stigeoclonium:* p. 381, Fig. 21.24*b*). The body of the zoospore contains many chloroplasts and contractile vacuoles ([1127, 1419]).

At first sight the structure and arrangement of the flagellar apparatus in *Oedogonium* seem to differ radically from the cruciate, 1 o'clock – 7 o'clock configuration found in other members of the class Chlorophyceae (compare Fig. 21.30 with Fig. 19.6), and it may therefore be wondered why we place the Oedogoniales in the Chlorophyceae. In fact, however, the flagellar apparatus of *Oedogonium* can be considered as a modification of the more typical, cruciate configuration of the Chlorophyceae *sensu stricto* ([1218]). The strongest evidence for such a derivation lies in the ultrastructure of the transversely striated fibrous ring, which is very similar to the upper transversely striated fibre connecting the basal bodies in the Chlorophyceae (compare Fig. 21.30 with Fig. 19.6). If

the *Oedogonium* zoospore has indeed developed from a *Chlamydomonas*-like zoid, the proliferation of the flagella and their basal bodies has presumably been accompanied by repetition of one of the two types of microtubular root present in the *Chlamydomonas* type of zoid; in addition, there has been an expansion of the upper transversely striated connective to form the ring fibre. The flagellar apparatus of the stephanokont zoospores of *Derbesia* in the class Bryopsidophyceae has presumably been derived in a similar way, but from the different type of cruciate zoid characteristic of this class (p. 429, Figs. 24.2, 24.8). In other words, stephanokont zoids have apparently evolved convergently in two different lineages of green algae, the Chlorophyceae and Bryopsidophyceae.

Sexual reproduction in Oedogonium *(Figs. 21.31, 21.32)*

Oedogonium species are oogamous haplonts. Hypnozygotes are produced after fertilization and they are retained within the wall of the oogonium. The spermatozoids are stephanokont like the zoospores, though they are much smaller. Sexual reproduction in this alga is a complex process, involving hormonal regulation at various points ([707, 1063, 1474]). The following stages may be distinguished in dioecious species (Fig. 21.31).

(*a*) Following meiosis in the diploid hypnozygote, four haploid stephanokont meiospores are produced ([708]). Meiosis is preceded by a period of dormancy. Two of the four meiospores give rise to relatively broad female filaments, the other two to thinner male filaments. Clearly haplogenotypic sex determination must occur during the reduction division. If the male or female plants are cultured in nutrient-rich media, vegetative cell division can continue indefinitely.

(*b*) Transfer to a poorer culture medium can lead to the formation of sexual organs within two weeks. The female filaments form large swollen cells (oogonium mother cells), which give rise to oogonia, while the male filaments produce small discoid androsporangia arranged in stacks. Each androsporangium forms a stephanokont androspore.

(*c*) The androspores are attracted by a substance, a pheromone, secreted by the oogonium mother

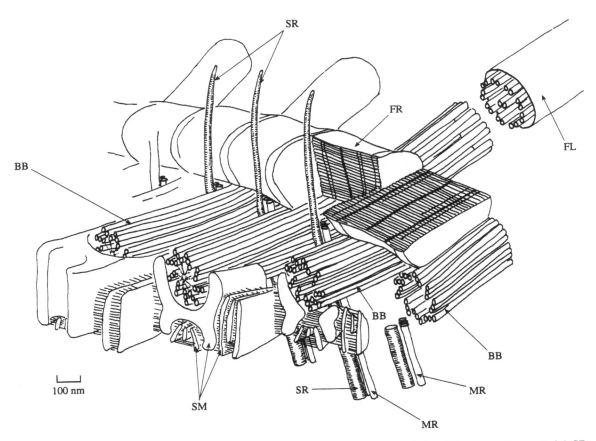

Figure 21.30. *Oedocladium* zoospore: three-dimensional reconstruction of part of the flagellar apparatus. BB = basal body; FL = flagellum; FR = transversely striated fibrous ring; MR = microtubular root, containing three microtubules; SM = supportive material; SR = transversely striated component associated with the microtubular root. (After [1127].)

cell (i.e. they exhibit chemotaxis). They swim to the oogonium mother cell and attach themselves to it or adjacent cells. Chemotaxis can be demonstrated by a simple experiment, in which a cotton thread is dipped into a culture containing sexualized female filaments with oogonium mother cells, and then transferred to a culture of male filaments with ripe androsporangia: androspores immediately congregate in enormous numbers around the cotton thread, which is saturated with female hormone from the female culture.

(d) The androspores, now attached to the female filaments, develop into small unicellular male plantlets: the dwarf males or nannandria. For this to occur it is not essential that androspores settle on oogonium mother cells. Spores that have settled elsewhere, e.g. on other cells of the female filament, can also develop into nannandria, although some of the androspores grow into new vegetative male filaments. It can be concluded, however, that no further induction by the oogonium mother cells is necessary for the development of the androspores into nannandria. Nevertheless, the oogonium mother cells do secrete other substances, which cause the nannandria to grow upwards or downwards,

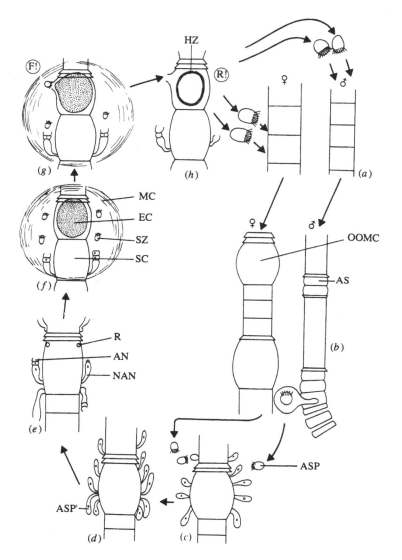

Figure 21.31. The life cycle of *Oedogonium*. (*a*) Male and female filaments. (*b*) Differentiation of oogonium mother cell and androsporangia (0 h). (*c*) Attraction of androspores to oogonium mother cell (3 h). (*d*) Germination of androspores (12 h). (*e*) Formation of nannandria with antheridia (22 h). (*f*) Formation of egg cell and a mucilage capsule that surrounds the sexual structures (24 h). (*g*) Fertilization of the egg cell by a stephanokont sperm. (*h*) Formation of a hyp-

nozygote, which later germinates meiotically to give haploid zoospores (meiospores). AN = antheridium; AS = androsporangium; ASP = stephanokont androspore; ASP′ = germinating androspore; EC = egg cell; F! = fertilization; HZ = hypnozygote; MC = mucilage capsule; NAN = nannandrium; OOMC = oogonium mother cell; R = wall ring; R! = reduction division (meiosis); SC = supporting cell; SZ = spermatozoid. (Based on [1474].)

depending on their position relative to the oogonium mother cell (see Fig. 21.31).

(*e*) Under the influence of hormones produced by the nannandria, the oogonium mother cell now

divides through the formation of a wall ring, just as in vegetative cell division. A lower, vegetative cell is produced, called the supporting cell, and an upper, sexual cell, which is the oogonium. Oogonium mother cells proceed to this division only if nannandria are attached to them. If female filaments with fully developed oogonium mother cells are transferred back into rich culture medium, however, they lose their sexual potency and divide vegetatively. In the meantime the nannandria cut off two small discoid cells from their upper ends, and these can be considered as antheridia. Each antheridium produces two spermatozoids (i.e. male flagellate sexual cells), which are stephanokont.

(*f*) The oogonium attracts the spermatozoids through chemotaxis, the spermatozoids moving through a sphere of mucilage secreted from the female cells.

(*g*) The oogonium forms a pore, and then a papilla of cytoplasm is suddenly thrust into it. Spermatozoids that are in the vicinity of the papilla attempt to make contact with it, and within a second the papilla is withdrawn again, dragging with it a spermatozoid; the spermatozoid then fertilizes the egg cell.

(*h*) The zygotes of *Oedogonium* remain enclosed within the walls of the oogonium for a long time and it is common to find filaments with hypnozygotes spaced at regular intervals along them. The hypnozygotes have thick walls, which are made up of three layers and bear species-specific structures and ornamentation; the hypnozygotes of one *Oedogonium* species have been found to remain viable for more than 20 years ([253]).

The *Oedogonium* species described here is dioecious. Other species are monoecious and form male and female sex organs on the same filament. Another characteristic of the species we have described is that it is nannandrous, i.e. the life cycle includes the formation of dwarf male plants (nannandria). In many species, however, nannandria are not produced. Instead, the discoid male cells do not form androspores but form spermatozoids directly: such species are termed macrandrous. The species of *Oedogonium* can also differ in the details of how the life cycle is regulated ([681]).

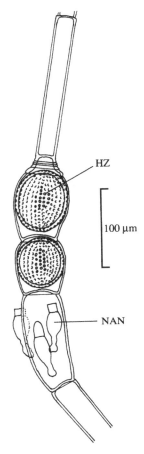

Figure 21.32. *Oedogonium concatenatum*: sexual reproduction. HZ = hypnozygote; NAN = nannandrium (dwarf male). (After [690].)

Size and distribution of the order Oedogoniales

The order contains three genera with about 550 species ([505, 690, 1775]); *ca.* 400 of these belong to the genus *Oedogonium*. The unbranched filaments of *Oedogonium*, with their cylindrical cells, are initially attached to other algae, aquatic macrophytes or other solid substrata. Later, however, they may become loose and float freely in the water. Species of *Oedogonium* can develop in great profusion in late spring and summer, particularly in more or less eutrophic water.

22

Chlorophyta: Class 3. Ulvophyceae

The principal characteristics of the Ulvophyceae

1 The class Ulvophyceae contains unicellular (Fig. 22.1), multicellular (Figs. 22.2, 22.10) and siphonocladous (Fig. 22.6a) **non-flagellate** green algae.

2 The reproductive zoids have two or four flagella, with a cruciate, 11 o'clock – 5 o'clock configuration of the flagellar apparatus; there is a distinct overlap between the basal bodies (Figs. 19.13, 19.14b, p. 320; [424, 1327]). The zoids produced by some representatives of one order (Codiolales) are covered by a layer of diamond-shaped organic scales, similar to the inner body scales of the Prasinophyceae (Fig. 19.10d, e).

3 The pattern of mitosis and cytokinesis conforms to type V (see p. 330): mitosis is closed and the telophase spindle is persistent (Fig. 19.22 I). In the vegetative cells cytokinesis is strictly coupled to mitosis and is accomplished through the ingrowth of a cleavage furrow, often with the addition of golgi vesicles, which coalesce with the furrow (Fig. 19.22 I). Microtubules are often associated with the leading edge of the furrow but a distinct phycoplast is not formed (cf. p. 326; [1031]). The cross-walls are not perforated by plasmodesmata.

4 Each cell contains one parietal chloroplast, which is cup-shaped or in the form of a band girdling the cell; it may or may not be perforated. The chloroplast contains one to several pyrenoids (Figs. 22.1a, 22.2, 22.6, 22.11b, h).

5 Species for which sexual reproduction is known either have a haplontic life cycle, in which the zygote is the only cell with a diploid nucleus, or an isomorphic diplohaplontic life cycle. Thick-walled hypnozygotes (resistant, dormant zygotes) are not formed. Sexual reproduction is isogamous or anisogamous.

6 The class is almost entirely restricted to marine habitats.

As in other multicellular algae, the **cell walls** of the Ulvophyceae consist of a structural fraction, made of microfibrils, embedded in an amorphous matrix. The exact chemical composition of the wall varies within the class and indeed is only poorly known. The microfibrils are usually irregularly arranged, forming a felt-like network. In the order Codiolales, mannan, xylan, glucan and rhamnan, in varying proportions, make up the structural part of the cell wall ([41, 189, 1148]). Glucan and xylan occur in the cell walls of *Ulva* and *Enteromorpha* (in the order Ulvales; [1148]). The relative amounts of the different polysaccharides can vary, not only between species, but also between different stages in the life cycle of a single species. Cell wall composition should therefore be thought of as dynamic, changing as the plant ages and as one phase gives way to another.

The amorphous, mucilaginous matrix of the cell wall in members of the Ulvophyceae is made of very complex heteropolysaccharides (i.e. polysaccharides composed of several different monosaccharides), in which at least some of the hydroxyl groups of the sugar residues have been replaced by half ester sulphate groups. These heteropolysaccharides are therefore strong acids and exist as salts of various metals. The monomers found in them are glucuronic acid, xylose, rhamnose, galactose and arabinose. The limited data available show that the composition of the sulphated heteropolysaccharides varies between the different orders within the Ulvophyceae ([1148, 1395]).

Besides the cruciate 11 o'clock – 5 o'clock configuration, several other features of the zoids characterize the Ulvophyceae, although they are more variable.

1 The upper connective linking the basal bodies is non-striated, or only partly striated. By contrast, in the Chlorophyceae, it has a distinct transverse striation (compare Fig. 19.6*b* with Fig. 19.13*a, c–e*).

2 Terminal caps are present, partly or wholly covering the ends of the basal bodies; these are absent in the Chlorophyceae (Fig. 19.6*a, b*).

3 There is a proximal sheath, made of darkly staining, amorphous material, which is appressed to the lower sides of the basal bodies (Fig. 19.13*b, d, e*); again, this is absent in the Chlorophyceae. Further information is given on p. 320, where the ultrastructure of one zoid, the gamete of *Acrosiphonia*, is described in detail (for overviews, see [424, 1327, 1644, 1645]).

Cytokinesis is achieved by the formation of a cleavage furrow. There may also be a cell plate, formed from golgi-derived vesicles (Fig. 19.22 I), but the extent to which such a plate participates in cytokinesis can vary even between the species of one genus (e.g. in *Ulothrix*: [1031]).

Vegetative cell division in the Ulvophyceae is always strictly coupled to mitosis, even in the siphono-cladous representatives with their multinucleate cells. For instance, in *Acrosiphonia*, all the nuclei migrate before mitosis to the future plane of cell division; the division of the nuclei is synchronous and the new cell wall is formed along the equatorial plane common to them all (Fig. 22.7). This mode of cell division contrasts with that of the multinucleate cells of the class Cladophorophyceae, where vegetative cell division is uncoupled from nuclear division (Fig. 23.7*e*).

The sexually reproducing members of the class Ulvophyceae have either a haplontic or a diplohaplontic life cycle, in contrast to the consistently haplontic cycles found in the classes Chlorophyceae, Zygnematophyceae and Charophyceae. As elsewhere, species that lack sexual reproduction are thought to have lost it secondarily.

The Ulvophyceae encompass genera with a great range of organizational levels: coccoid (Fig. 22.1), filamentous (Figs. 22.2, 22.3, 22.13), thallose (Figs. 22.8, 22.10, 22.11), and siphonocladous (Figs. 22.4*d*, 22.5, 22.6) representatives are known.

When it was first put forward, which happened only recently, the class Ulvophyceae was defined much more broadly than in our classification ([704, 1140, 1175, 1644, 1645, 1648]). It was understood to include all the green algae with zoids possessing an 11 o'clock – 5 o'clock configuration of the basal bodies (Fig. 19.14*b*), irrespective of other features. This concept of the Ulvophyceae would also include the classes Cladophorophyceae, Bryopsidophyceae, Dasycladophyceae and Trentepohliophyceae, as we have defined them here (pp. 408, 419, 436, 445). We contend that classes should be characterized not only by flagellate cell architecture, but also by features drawn from the structure of the vegetative cells, mitosis, the life cycle, and the composition of the cell wall. Furthermore, analyses of ribosomal RNAs in a variety of algae, previously classified together in the Ulvophyceae *sensu lato*, have shown that the broad concept of the Ulvophyceae (the '11 o'clock – 5 o'clock class') is untenable, since it appears to be phylogenetically heterogeneous ([1933]; see p. 37 for a brief introduction to the use of RNA sequence analysis in phylogenetic reconstruction).

Size and distribution of the class

The class Ulvophyceae is considered here to contain about 35 genera and 265 species ([1630]). The great majority of the species are marine or brackish; only a few species occur in freshwater, among them being *Ulothrix zonata* (Fig. 22.2) and several other *Ulothrix* species ([1039, 1040, 1041]), and a few *Enteromorpha* species.

Order Codiolales

1 Sexually reproducing species are haplontic, with a characteristic type of zygote: the '*Codiolum*' phase. This is club-shaped and has a basal stipe made of cell wall material, with annular constrictions (Figs. 22.1*j*, 22.2*l*, 22.3*h, i*, 22.8*e–g*). The zygote nucleus is the only diploid nucleus in the life cycle. The zygote stages which were formerly considered to be species of a separate genus, *Codiolum* (hence '*Codiolum*' phase), produce quadriflagellate spores (meiospores), which grow into new gametophytes (Figs. 22.2, 22.3; [807, 808]).

2 Each cell contains one parietal chloroplast, which is cup-shaped or takes the form of an

incomplete or complete cylinder; in this case it may or may not be perforated (Figs. 22.1a, 22.2a, 22.4a–d, 22.6). Within the chloroplast are one to several pyrenoids, each surrounded by a sheath of starch grains (Figs. 22.4a–d, 22.6). Pyrenoid shape and ultrastructure vary, even within one genus, e.g. in *Ulothrix*, where the pyrenoids can be bilenticular to polypyramidal ([1031, 1034]).

An 11 o'clock – 5 o'clock configuration of the flagellar apparatus has been shown to be present in the zoids of 18 species of the order Codiolales ([70, 424, 730, 810, 1030, 1031, 1331, 1649, 1650]). According to Floyd & O'Kelly ([424]) the Codiolales are also characterized by the presence of tiny organic body scales on the zoids, but not every representative of the order that has been scrutinized in detail has proved to have them; *Urospora* and *Acrosiphonia*, for example, lack scales. Where scales are present, they are very similar to the inner body scales of the Prasinophyceae (Fig. 19.10d) and they are therefore interpreted as a survival from the distant past, when the Ulvophyceae diverged from prasinophycean ancestors. The presence of type V mitosis and cytokinesis (p. 390, character 3) has been shown to be present in 10 members of the Codiolales ([760, 761, 1030, 1031, 1035, 1651]).

The principal feature of the order, the possession of a *Codiolum* type of zygote, is not generally found in species that lack sexual reproduction, but they can nevertheless be assigned to the Codiolales on the basis of morphological similarities to forms that do reproduce sexually and therefore have a *Codiolum*-phase. Thus, in the genus *Acrosiphonia*, which has a very characteristic morphology (Figs. 22.5, 22.6), several different types of life cycle have been demonstrated. In some species, all sexual forms, the life cycle includes a branched, siphonocladous gametophyte and a *Codiolum*-like zygote. In other species, only the siphonocladous stage is found, which reproduces itself asexually via biflagellate zoospores ([896, 897, 898]). It has even been shown that there can be a purely asexual alternation between a siphonocladous *Acrosiphonia*-phase and a *Codiolum*-phase. Here, as elsewhere, the absence of sexual reproduction is interpreted as secondary, sexuality having been lost in the course of evolution.

The *Codiolum*-phase has often been considered as a unicellular, independent sporophyte, and the life cycle of the Codiolales has therefore been thought of as strongly heteromorphic but diplohaplontic (e.g. [1750]). In the present account the *Codiolum*-phase is treated simply as a zygote, because the nucleus within it is the only diploid nucleus of the entire life cycle.

The order Codiolales as defined here was first recognized by Kornmann ([887], as the 'Ulotrichales'), who later even elevated it to class status (Codiolophyceae) ([899]). The ultrastructural features of the group have been listed by Floyd & O'Kelly ([424], again as the 'Ulotrichales').

Within the Codiolales the following levels of organization are represented: coccoid (Fig. 22.1), unbranched filamentous (Fig. 22.2), branched filamentous (Fig. 22.3), unbranched siphonocladous (Fig. 22.4c, d), branched siphonocladous (Figs. 22.5, 22.6), and thallose (Fig. 22.8).

The Codiolales includes about 10 genera and 90 species ([1630]). The great majority of species are marine but a few genera that are primarily marine, such as *Ulothrix* and *Monostroma*, also include several freshwater forms.

An example of a unicellular, coccoid member of the order Codiolales: Chlorocystis cohnii (Fig. 22.1)

Chlorocystis cohnii cells are spherical or slightly compressed and have a polysaccharide wall. The parietal, cup-shaped chloroplast bears finger-like lobes and contains a single pyrenoid. The cells are uninucleate. *C. cohnii* lives as an endophyte in the mucilage tubes produced by a colonial *Navicula* species (a diatom: class Bacillariophyceae) (Fig. 22.1a), or in the walls of various marine algae, such as *Enteromorpha* or *Polysiphonia*; it is always marine ([143, 282, 904]).

The life cycle of *Chlorocystis cohnii* has been investigated by Kornmann & Sahling ([904]) and appears to be haplontic, with a typical *Codiolum*-like zygote stage.

Fertile vegetative cells may divide up their contents either into quadriflagellate asexual zoospores, or into biflagellate gametes. In either case the zoids are at first discharged as a group, enclosed in a vesicle (Figs. 22.1b, b′, c, c′); only later are they liberated as individuals. The quadriflagellate zoospores grow into new vegetative cells as in *Ulothrix* (Fig. 22.2), a genus of the Codiolales containing unbranched filamentous forms.

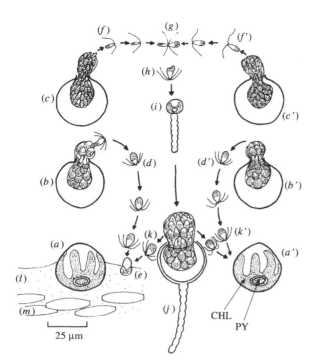

Figure 22.1. The life cycle of *Chlorocystis cohnii*. (*a, a'*)
Gametophytes. (*b, b'*) Division of the cell into asexual
quadriflagellate zoospores. (*c, c'*) Division of the cell
contents into biflagellate gametes: these are of two
sizes, *Chlorocystis* being anisogamous. (*d, d'*)
Asexual quadriflagellate zoospores. (*e*) Germling produced by a zoospore that has settled and lost its flagella. (*f*) Small male gametes. (*f'*) Larger female
gametes. (*g*) Anisogamous copulation. (*h*) Planozygote. (*i*) Young zygote. (*j*) Full-grown zygote,
which is stalked and releases many quadriflagellate
zoids. (*k, k'*) Quadriflagellate zoids released from the
zygote; these are presumably meiospores. (*l*) Gelatinous material secreted by tube-dwelling diatoms (*m*).
CHL = chloroplast; PY = pyrenoid. (Based on [904].)

Chlorocystis is slightly anisogamous and also heterothallic, the 'male' and 'female' gametes being produced by different cells (Fig. 22.1*f, f'*). The zygote is a
typical *Codiolum*-like cell, with a basal stipe composed of cell wall material (Fig. 22.1*i, j*). About a fort-
night after copulation, the zygotes mature and produce
quadriflagellate zoospores, which grow into new vegetative cells (Fig. 22.1*k, k', a, a'*). By analogy with the
life cycles of other Codiolales it is thought that meiosis takes place during the maturation of the *Codiolum*-
like zygote, but there is as yet no confirmation of this
from karyological observations.

Chlorocystis and the related genus *Halochloro-
coccum* are superficially very similar to *Chlorococcum* in the order Chlorococcales, class Chlorophyceae (p. 362, Fig. 21.7), and to *Trebouxia*, in the
order Pleurastrales, class Pleurastrophyceae (Fig.
27.1, p. 450). Indeed, until recently all four were
included together in the Chlorococcales. It now
appears, however, that their resemblance has come
about by convergent evolution in three different
classes of green algae.

An example of an unbranched, filamentous member of the order Codiolales: Ulothrix zonata (Fig. 22.2)

Ulothrix species consist of unbranched filaments of
cells. They grow by intercalary cell division, all cells
in the filament being capable of division. Each cell
contains a single nucleus and an annular (ring-like)
parietal chloroplast, in which there are one to several
pyrenoids. Several dozen species have been described
from freshwater and marine habitats, but in modern
treatments of the genus this number has been reduced,
at least for Western Europe, to five freshwater species
and five marine ones ([69, 1028, 1029, 1031, 1039, 1040, 1041]).
Ulothrix is found predominantly in the coldest periods
of the year, either in running water or in wave-swept
parts of the littoral zone in lakes and canals. The five
marine species occur on rocky shores and salt
marshes.

Among the freshwater species is *Ulothrix zonata*, a
robust alga which, especially in spring, can form large,
dark green or yellow-green masses, up to 30 cm long.
It lives attached to wave-washed stones in fairly nutrient-rich canals and lakes. Each cell of the filament
possesses an annular chloroplast, which girdles the
cell and contains many pyrenoids (Fig. 22.2*a, a'*).

The life cycle of *Ulothrix zonata* (Fig. 22.2)
([1039])

In both short-day (8 h light) and long-day conditions
(16 h light), the filaments produce asexual, quadriflagellate zoospores, which grow directly into new
vegetative filaments (Fig. 22.2*a, b, d, e*). High temperatures (*ca.* 10–20 °C) stimulate the formation of
zoospores ([552]), which in part explains why populations decline when temperatures rise above 10 °C in
the spring; 2–16 zoospores are produced per cell.

In long days the filaments produce biflagellate

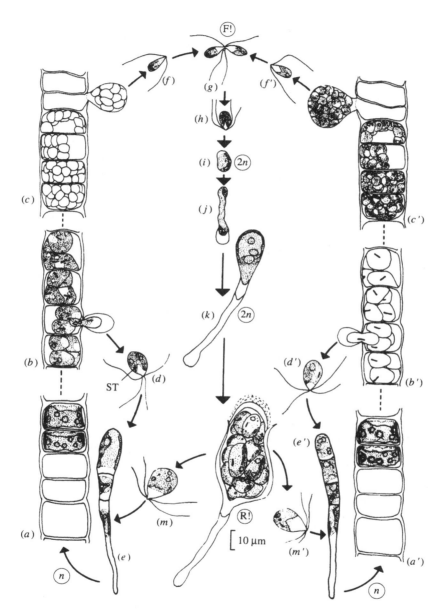

Figure 22.2. The life cycle of *Ulothrix zonata*. (*a, a'*) Gametophytes. (*b, b'*) Division of the cell contents into quadriflagellate zoospores. (*c, c'*) Division of the cell contents into biflagellate gametes; these are all of the same size. (*d, d'*) Asexual quadriflagellate zoospores. (*e, e'*) Germlings. (*f, f'*) Gametes. (*g*) Isogamous copulation. (*h*) Quadriflagellate planozygote. (*i*) Young zygote. (*j–l*) Development of the zygote, which becomes stalked and produces many zoids. (*m, m'*) Quadriflagellate zoids released from the zygote; these are presumably meiospores. F! = fertilization; R! = reduction division (meiosis); ST = stigma (eyespot); *n* = haploid; 2*n* = diploid. (After [1039].)

gametes, which are smaller than the zoospores; like the zoospores, they are not released directly from the parent cell but are initially discharged into a vesicle (Fig. 22.2c, f). Copulation is isogamous but takes place between gametes produced from different sexualized filaments (Fig. 22.2g). Whereas the gametes are positively phototactic, the quadriflagellate planozygotes arising through sexual reproduction are negatively phototactic (Fig. 22.2h); the zygote thus swims down and attaches itself to the substratum, and then becomes immobile.

Zygotes germinate only in short-day conditions (8 h light, 8 °C), when they swell up into large stalked cells. At a temperature of 4 °C, still in short day conditions, the contents of each expanded zygote divide up to give 4–16 (usually 8) quadriflagellate zoospores and it is apparently during this process that meiosis takes place. The zoospores grow into new *Ulothrix* filaments (Fig. 22.2l, m), which are probably haploid.

The life cycle of *Ulothrix zonata* can therefore be summarized as follows. The alga possesses a haplontic cycle, characterized by heterothallism, isogamy, and a stalked, *Codiolum*-like zygote, asexual reproduction taking place through the formation of quadriflagellate zoospores. *U. zonata* is a winter and spring form, which apparently survives the summer in the zygote stage. Several marine species of *Ulothrix* have been shown to have the same type of life cycle as *U. zonata* [69, 888, 1029].

The flagellar apparatus of the quadriflagellate zoospores of *U. zonata* has an 11 o'clock – 5 o'clock configuration and also several other features characteristic of ulvophycean zoids. The zoospores are covered with tiny body scales [1644, 1648]. Mitosis and cytokinesis are also typical for the Ulvophyceae (type V, p. 330, Fig. 19.22 I). Mitosis is closed, the telophase spindle is persistent, and cytokinesis is brought about by a cleavage furrow, with the involvement of vesicles derived from the golgi apparatus; microtubules are sometimes associated with the leading edge of the furrow [1031, 1035, 1651].

The unbranched, uniseriate filaments of *Ulothrix* are extremely similar to those of *Uronema*, in the class Chlorophyceae (p. 380, Fig. 21.22a) and *Klebsormidium*, in the class Klebsormidiophyceae (p. 459, Fig. 28.2g). *Uronema* and *Klebsormidium* have fundamentally different types of zoid and different patterns of mitosis and cytokinesis, yet until recently they were usually classified together in *Ulothrix*, along with

species such as *U. zonata*. It is now considered that the similarity between these three genera has come about through convergent evolution in three different classes of green algae [1036].

An example of a branched, filamentous member of the order Codiolales: Spongomorpha aeruginosa (Figs. 22.3, 22.4a, b; [806, 881, 889])

Spongomorpha plants resemble small yellow-green pompoms and grow one to a few centimetres high. They often live attached to the red alga *Polyides* and other large marine algae. The thallus consists of densely branched filaments of uninucleate cells and within each cell there is a single cylindrical chloroplast (Fig. 22.4a, b), which is more or less perforated and contains numerous pyrenoids. The starch grains are radially arranged around the periphery of the pyrenoid (Fig. 22.4a, b), this kind of pyrenoid being termed polypyramidal. Elongation of the thallus is brought about solely through the growth of the apical cells. Segments cut off from the apical cell are still able to divide when in an intercalary position, but they do not elongate at all, so that the filaments consist of cells of unequal size [894]. Side branches arise from just beneath cross walls formed during division of the apical cell. Many short, hooked side branches are formed, which curve back against the main axis, and it is this that produces the tangled, pompom-like appearance of the adult plants (Fig. 22.3c).

This species occurs on N Atlantic coasts in spring. During sexual reproduction intercalary cells divide up their contents into biflagellate isogametes (Fig. 22.3d, e). The gametes are released from the parent cells when a small, easily detached lid (operculum) opens in the cell wall, producing a pore. The gametes copulate isogamously and the zygote grows into a *Codiolum*-like, stalked zygote, which is how the alga spends the summer (Fig. 22.3h); the zygote lives embedded in the tissues of various red algae, such as the crustose alga *Petrocelis* (Fig. 22.3h, i) or the cylindrical *Polyides*. In winter the zygote germinates, apparently meiotically, and forms quadriflagellate meiospores, each of which can grow into a new *Spongomorpha* plant.

Spongomorpha aeruginosa, then, possesses a haplontic life cycle with a typical *Codiolum*-like zygote [806, 881, 889].

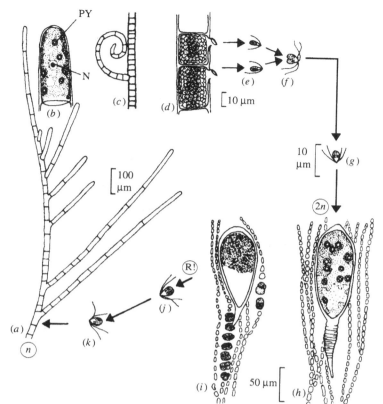

Figure 22.3. The life cycle of *Spongomorpha aeruginosa*. (*a*) Gametophyte. (*b*) Branch tip. (*c*) Hook-shaped side branch. (*d*) Gametangia; each releases biflagellate gametes through a pore at one end of the cell, following the shedding of an operculum. (*e–g*) Isogamous copulation between biflagellate gametes, producing a quadriflagellate planozygote. (*h, i*) Development of a stalked zygote within the tissues of the red alga *Petrocelis*. (*j, k*) Quadriflagellate zoids produced by the zygotes; these are presumably meiospores. N = nucleus; PY = pyrenoid; R! = reduction division (meiosis). (After [881, 889].)

An example of an unbranched, siphonocladous member of the order Codiolales: Urospora penicilliformis (Fig. 22.4c–g; [1038])

The unbranched filaments of *Urospora* are up to 6 cm long and 90 μm thick. They are attached to a substratum by several rhizoids, which grow down from the basal cells of the filament (Fig. 22.4*c*). Each cell contains several nuclei and one cylindrical, more or less perforate chloroplast with numerous polypyramidal pyrenoids (Figs. 22.4*d*, 22.6*b, c*). In young cells the chloroplast is not perforated and resembles the chloroplast of *Ulothrix* (Fig. 22.4*c*: see the lower cells). The filaments grow by intercalary cell division. *Urospora penicilliformis* occurs along the rocky coasts of NW Europe and NE America.

The life cycle of *Urospora penicilliformis* and other sexually reproducing species of the genus is very similar to that of *Ulothrix zonata* (Fig. 22.2). The cells of the filaments can divide up their contents into many quadriflagellate zoospores (Fig. 22.4*e*), which give rise to new *Urospora* filaments, or into biflagellate gametes (Fig. 22.4*f, g*). Male filaments produce male gametes (Fig. 22.4*f*). These are much smaller than the female gametes (Fig. 22.4*g*), which are produced by female filaments. Anisogamous copulation produces a zygote, which grows into a *Codiolum*-like plant. This

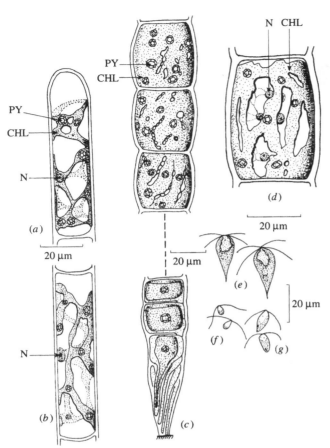

Figure 22.4. (*a, b*) *Spongomorpha aeruginosa*. (*a*) Apical cell. (*b*) Intercalary cell. The apical and intercalary cells have highly perforate (reticulate) chloroplasts and one nucleus per cell. (*c–g*) *Urospora penicilliformis*. (*c*) Intercalary (above) and basal sections of a filament. (*d*) Single cell. (*e*) Quadriflagellate zoospores. (*f*) Small biflagellate male gametes. (*g*) Larger biflagellate female gametes. CHL = chloroplast; N = nucleus; PY = pyrenoid. (*a–d* based on [806]; *e–g* on [1038].)

zygotic *Codiolum*-phase subsequently produces quadriflagellate zoospores, presumably following meiosis, and these then grow into new *Urospora* filaments. *Urospora* seems, therefore, to have a haplontic life cycle, with a *Codiolum*-like zygote stage; it is also heterothallic and anisogamous ([806, 812, 882, 893, 1038]).

Urospora differs from *Ulothrix* in its multinucleate cells and perforate chloroplasts, and also in the peculiar shape of its quadriflagellate zoospores. These have a stiff, tapering tail portion (Fig. 22.4*e*) and flagella that are held rather stiffly outwards. The flagellar

apparatus is highly specialized and its ultrastructure shows a number of unusual characteristics, although an 11 o'clock – 5 o'clock configuration of the basal bodies is clearly present ([424, 1644, 1650]). Mitosis is similar to that in *Acrosiphonia* (Fig. 22.7 and see below). Before mitosis numerous nuclei congregate in the plane where the cross wall will later be formed and here they divide, synchronously. Mitosis is closed and cytokinesis is achieved by ingrowth of a cleavage furrow, whose leading edge is lined by microtubules. This type of mitosis and cytokinesis is characteristic of the Ulvophyceae ([1035]).

Urospora gives the impression of being a multinucleate, rather coarse version of *Ulothrix*, just as *Acrosiphonia* seems like a multinucleate, coarse version of *Spongomorpha* (compare Fig. 22.3*a* with Fig. 22.5*a*, and see below). A close relationship between *Ulothrix* and *Urospora* is also indicated by the recent discovery of three intermediate species, with uninucleate cells, non-perforate chloroplasts and tail-bearing zoospores ([68]). The phyletic link between *Ulothrix* and *Urospora* is interesting and stressed in our account because it is customary to place them in separate orders (Ulotrichales and Acrosiphoniales, respectively: see, for example, [100, 703, 1630]).

Urospora has also converged morphologically with the genus *Chaetomorpha* (p. 416, Fig. 23.7), a member of the class Cladophorophyceae. The two genera are clearly separated, however, in the chemical composition of their cell walls, the structure of the chloroplasts, and the plan of the life cycle: compare the characters of the Codiolales (p. 392) and the Cladophorophyceae (p. 408).

An example of a branched, siphonocladous member of the order Codiolales: Acrosiphonia (Figs. 22.5, 22.6a)

The species of the genus *Acrosiphonia* bear a quite extraordinary resemblance to *Spongomorpha* in their vegetative structure and life cycle. The principal differences are that the filaments of cells are rather wider in *Acrosiphonia* and that the cells themselves are multinucleate. The nuclei of each cell undergo synchronous mitosis in the prospective plane of cytokinesis, as in *Urospora* (Fig. 22.7; [806, 892]), and then, after deposition of the new cross wall, the daughter nuclei move away from the wall into the cytoplasm, remain-

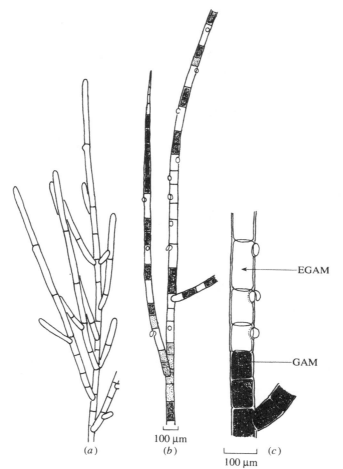

100 μm

(a)   *(b)*

EGAM

GAM

(c)

100 μm

Figure 22.5. *Acrosiphonia.* (*a*) The apical section of a vigorously growing plant. Note the long apical cells, which through their division bring about growth of the plant. (*b, c*) Part of a fertile plant. Note the pointed apex, which has stopped growing. Intercalary cells have divided into short gametangia, whose contents are released when an operculum opens near the top of the cell producing a circular pore; the opercula are not shed, in contrast to *Spongomorpha aeruginosa* (Fig. 22.3). EGAM = empty gametangium; GAM = full gametangium. (Based on [891, 892].)

ing 'in close order' (Fig. 22.7*b*). In other respects mitosis and cytokinesis are quite similar to those of *Urospora* ([760, 761]) and support the classification of *Acrosiphonia* in the Ulvophyceae. The gametes have a typical 11 o'clock – 5 o'clock configuration of the basal bodies and indeed we have used *Acrosiphonia* to illustrate this type of flagellar apparatus (cf. p. 320, Fig. 19.13; [424, 1205]). The gamete has a pointed tail, though it is not as pronounced as in the zoospores of *Urospora* (Fig. 19.13).

Acrosiphonia species occur along the rocky coasts of temperate and polar regions, in both hemispheres. In temperate latitudes they are generally found in spring.

An example of a multicellular, thalloid member of the order Codiolales: Monostroma grevillei *(Fig. 22.8)*

Monostroma thalli are green, leaf-like structures, only one layer of cells thick, each cell containing one cup-shaped chloroplast with a single pyrenoid. Several

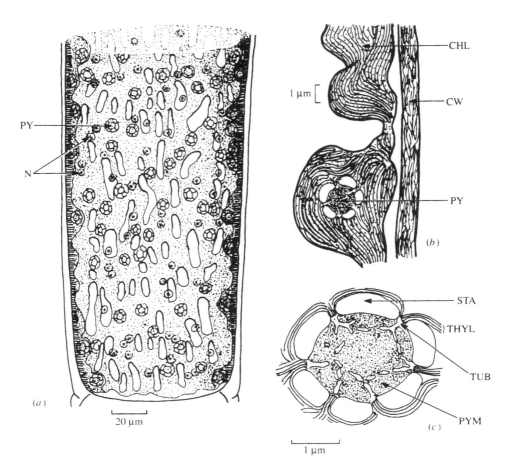

Figure 22.6. (*a*) *Acrosiphonia*: the lower part of an intercalary cell, showing the cylindrical perforate chloroplast, numerous nuclei and numerous polypyramidal pyrenoids. (*b*) *Urospora*: longitudinal section of part of a chloroplast, based on EM observations (the widths of the thylakoids are exaggerated). Note the polypyramidal pyrenoid. (*c*) *Urospora*: section through a polypyramidal pyrenoid. Tubules containing chloroplast matrix material penetrate into the pyrenoid, but thylakoids do not. CHL = chloroplast, containing thylakoids; CW = cell wall; N = nuclei; PY = pyrenoid; PYM = pyrenoid matrix; STA = starch sheath around pyrenoid; THYL = thylakoids; TUB = tubule of chloroplast matrix. (*a* based on [892]; *b, c* on [749, 1038].)

marine species are known, together with one freshwater species.

Fig. 22.8 shows the life cycle of *Monostroma grevillei* ([91, 883, 884, 902, 1752, 1753]). The thalli grow up to 20 cm high and are irregularly undulate and folded (Fig. 22.8*a, a'*); they arise through the rupture of sac-like juvenile stages (Fig. 22.8*j, j'*). *M. grevillei* occurs in the early part of the year on the Atlantic coasts of Europe and N America, and on N Pacific coasts, usually in the lower parts of the intertidal zone. The leaf-like thalli are gametophytes. The female thallus produces rather larger gametes than the male thallus, but in both cases the gametes are biflagellate (Fig. 22.8*c, c'*). Anisogamous copulation (Fig. 22.8*d*) produces a zygote, which develops in exactly the same way as the zygote of *Ulothrix zonata* (compare Figs. 22.8*e* and 22.2). The *Codiolum*-like cell bores into the calcareous shells of lamellibranchs and barnacles (cirripeds), taking on an irregular outline with a number of protrusions (Fig. 22.8*f*). In this form the zygote resembles

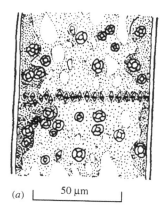
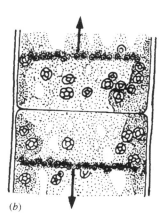

(a) ⊢ 50 μm ⊣

(b)

Figure 22.7. *Acrosiphonia*: nuclear and cell division. (*a*) Synchronous mitoses, with all the spindle equators aligned in the plane of cell division.

(*b*) Migration of daughter nuclei immediately after cytokinesis. (Based on [892].)

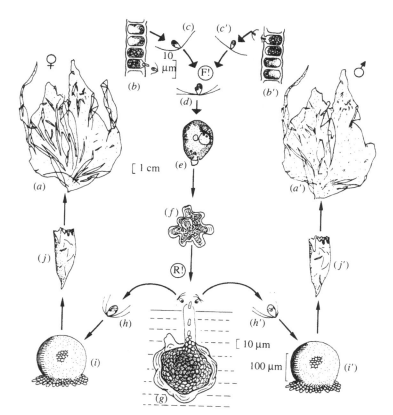

Figure 22.8. The life cycle of *Monostroma grevillei*. (*a*, *a*′) Flat, blade-like thalli. (*b*, *b*′, *c*, *c*′) The formation of biflagellate female and male gametes. (*d*) Aniso-gamous copulation to produce a quadriflagellate zygote. (*e*) Developing zygote. (*f*, *g*) Zygote boring into calcareous material and producing zoids (meio-spores). (*h*, *h*′) Quadriflagellate zoids (meiospores). (*i*, *i*′) Young female and male gametophytes. (*j*, *j*′) Sac-like stages. F! = fertilization; R! = reduction divi-sion (meiosis). (After [883, 884].)

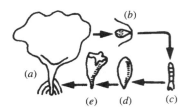

Figure 22.9. The life cycle of *Monostroma oxyspermum*. (*a*) Full-grown blade. (*b*) Asexual biflagellate zoospore. (*c*) Filamentous germling. (*d*) Tubular stage. (*e*) Sac-like stage (formed by splitting of the tube tip). (Based on [693].)

very much the chalk-boring green alga *Gomontia*. *Monostroma* spends the summer in this condition, safely concealed.

The zygote germinates with the formation of haploid, quadriflagellate zoids ([807]), which are released through a discharge tube (Fig. 22.8*g*). Each of these meiospores grows into a discoid plantlet, which is attached to the substratum. The discoid plantlet in its turn grows into a hollow spherical vesicle, by intercalary cell division (Fig. 22.8*i, i'*). This ruptures at its upper end and forms a sac-like thallus, which subsequently tears further to give the blade-like morphology of the adult plant (Fig. 22.8*j, j'*). On the basis of its possession of a *Codiolum*-like zygote, *Monostroma grevillei* can be assigned to the order Codiolales.

The *Codiolum*-phase of *M. grevillei* produces quadriflagellate meiospores only in short days (e.g. 8 h light) and at low temperatures (5–15 °C). Spore formation is inhibited by long days (16 h light), or by a light break during the long dark periods of a short-day regime ([1055]). This combination of effects is considered to indicate that *Monostroma* is measuring the length of the photoperiod (and of the dark period), rather than responding only to the amount of light received ([344]). The growth of the sac-like thalli and the splitting of the sacs into blades are not under photoperiodic control but are affected by temperature, the upper limit for them being 15 °C. The short-day response of the zygote and the low-temperature requirements of both zygote and gametophyte correlate well with the occurrence of the species in nature during the colder seasons.

Other types of life cycle are known in the genus *Monostroma*. '*Monostroma*' *obscurum* possesses an isomorphic, diplohaplontic cycle of the same type as

that present in *Ulva lactuca* (Fig. 22.10). This species has therefore been transferred into a separate genus, *Ulvaria*, which is at present classified in the order Ulvales (p. 405). *Monostroma oxyspermum* does not reproduce sexually but only asexually, by biflagellate zoospores. The zoospore grows into a filament, which develops into a small sac; the sac then splits open, forming a blade (Fig. 22.9). This species is cosmopolitan but is particularly common in lagoon habitats.

Indeed, on the basis of variation in life cycle and thallus ontogeny, it is possible to distinguish no less than 14 different types among those species that have at one time or another been referred to *Monostroma* ([91, 693, 1752]), and it has for long been unclear where some of the species really belong ([536, 1750, 1752, 1829, 1830]).

The biflagellate zoids of *Monostroma grevillei*, *M. oxyspermum* and *M. bullosum* all have an 11 o'clock – 5 o'clock configuration of the flagellar apparatus (p. 320, Fig. 19.14*b*). The zoids also have a covering of tiny organic scales, which are like the inner body scales of the Prasinophyceae (Fig. 19.10*d*). Within the Ulvophyceae, these scales are found only in certain members of the order Codiolales ([424, 730, 1329, 1331]).

Order Ulvales

1 In sexually reproducing species the life cycle is isomorphic and diplohaplontic. The haploid gametophytes produce biflagellate gametes of two types, large and small. Following anisogamous fusion of a small male gamete with a larger female gamete, the zygote grows into a diploid sporophyte, which is morphologically similar to the gametophyte. The sporophyte produces quadriflagellate meiospores, which grow into gametophytes (Fig. 22.10).

2 Each cell is uninucleate and contains one parietal chloroplast, which is cup-shaped or takes the form of a band girdling the cell. It is not usually perforated, although sometimes there is some slight degree of perforation. Each chloroplast contains one to several pyrenoids (Figs. 22.11*a, b, h*, 22.13*b*).

An 11 o'clock – 5 o'clock configuration of the flagellar apparatus (cf. Figs. 19.13, 19.14*b*; p. 391, character 2) has been demonstrated in the zoids of seven species of Ulvales ([424, 1168, 1169, 1326, 1329, 1331, 1727]). An additional feature which, according to Floyd & O'Kelly ([424]), distinguishes the Ulvales from the Codiolales, is the consistent absence of organic body scales on the zoids of Ulvales, although several of the Codiolales also lack scales, e.g. *Acrosiphonia* (Fig. 19.13).

Mitosis and cytokinesis have been investigated critically in only two species of the order Ulvales (one species of *Ulva* and one of *Enteromorpha*) but both exhibited ulvophycean characteristics, being of type V (p. 391, character 3; [132, 1043, 1044, 1143]).

The principal diagnostic character of the Ulvales, the possession of an isomorphic, diplohaplontic life cycle, can only be exhibited, of course, by species or varieties that reproduce sexually. However, many species and varieties in the genera *Enteromorpha* and *Ulva*, among others, are asexual, reproducing by biflagellate or quadriflagellate zoospores ([90a, 91, 862, 864, 865, 866, 867]). It is nevertheless easy to assign these species to the Ulvales, because their morphology allies them closely to sexual species of *Ulva* and *Enteromorpha* with a diplohaplontic life cycle. The asexual forms are thought to have lost their sexuality secondarily during evolution.

While the classification of *Ulva* and *Enteromorpha* in the Ulvales is uncontroversial, the inclusion of certain branched filamentous (marine) forms is more problematic. These algae have traditionally been placed in the order Chaetophorales (or in the Ulotrichales), which has in the past been used (e.g. by [100]) to include most green algae with a branched filamentous level of organization. We use the Chaetophorales in a much more restricted sense, defining it primarily by certain ultrastructural features (p. 378); with this narrower circumscription the order is restricted to fresh waters. In 1981, O'Kelly & Yarish ([1332]) discovered that two species of 'marine Chaetophorales', both belonging to the genus *Acrochaete* (Fig. 22.13; O'Kelly & Yarish referred them to *Entocladia*), have an isomorphic, diplohaplontic life cycle, which will be described in more detail below (p. 408). Subsequently, isomorphic diplohaplontic life cycles have been discovered in three other species, belonging to three related genera ([1292, 1323, 1324]). In addition, the gametes and zoospores of *Acrochaete* have an 11 o'clock – 5 o'clock configuration of the flagellar apparatus (p. 391, character 2: [424, 1326]). Thus, on the basis of the architecture of its zoids, *Acrochaete* apparently belongs to the class Ulvophyceae, while its isomorphic, diplohaplontic life

cycle relates it to *Ulva* and *Enteromorpha*, in the Ulvales. The strongly protruding, circular exit pores of the zoidangia in *Acrochaete* also indicate a close link with *Ulva* and *Enteromorpha*.

In addition to the four marine 'chaetophoralean' genera in which an isomorphic, diplohaplontic life cycle has been demonstrated, there are at least 11 other marine genera with branched filamentous thalli, whose ultrastructure has not yet been investigated and which are not known to reproduce sexually ([904, 1285, 1286, 1287, 1288, 1289, 1290, 1291, 1323, 1324, 1326, 1329]). At present, these 11 genera can be classified in the Ulvales only tentatively.

Only two levels of organization occur in the Ulvales: plants are either branched filaments (Fig. 22.13), or thalloid (Figs. 22.10, 22.11c).

The order Ulvales contains about 24 genera and 175 species ([1630]), almost all being marine, with just a few species of *Enteromorpha* penetrating into freshwater habitats ([862]). Species of *Ulva* and *Enteromorpha* can be found world-wide along sea coasts. They often form extensive swards in highly dynamic environments, for instance where rocks or boulders are frequently covered and then uncovered by shifting sands in the intertidal zone; their prolific and continuous reproduction fits them for the rapid, 'opportunistic' colonization of bare substrata. Species of both genera also form a conspicuous part of the vegetation in estuarine habitats, where they can create a continuous green cover not only on solid substrata, but also over the sediments in salt marshes. The taxonomy of *Ulva* and *Enteromorpha* is notoriously difficult ([90a, 705, 862, 864, 865, 866, 867, 1749]).

Examples of thalloid members of the order Ulvales

Ulva (Figs. 22.10, 22.11a, b)

The leaf-like thalli of sea lettuce can vary in length from several centimetres to more than a metre. The plants grow attached to solid substrata, anchored by an attachment disc. Many species, however, can continue to grow even when detached, such free-floating plants being found, for instance, in the Wadden Sea. The thallus is **distromatic**, i.e. it consists of two robust layers of cells, which are closely appressed. When they are young, however, the young germlings (Fig. 22.10f) resemble small *Ulothrix* plants, since they are

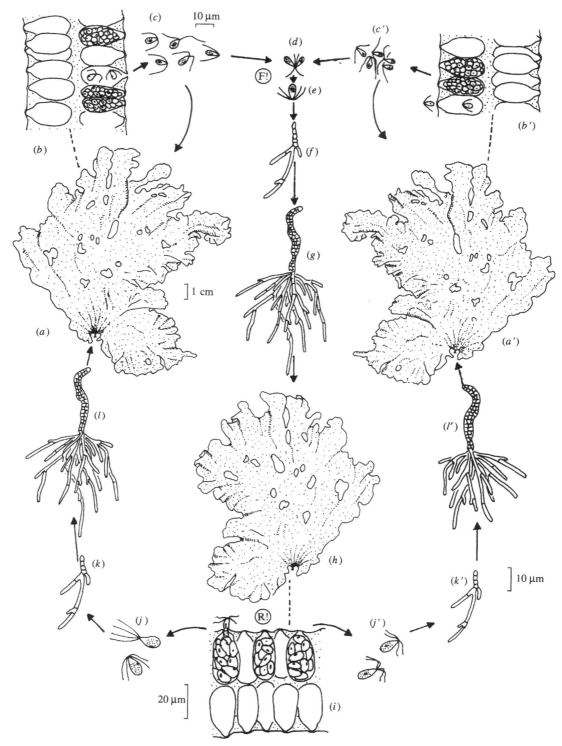

Figure 22.10. The life cycle of *Ulva lactuca*. (*a, a'*) Flat, blade-like gametophytes. (*b, b'*) Division of the cell contents into biflagellate gametes; these are unequal, copulation being anisogamous. (*c*) Female gametes. (*c'*) Male gametes. (*d*) Anisogamous copulation. (*e*) Quadriflagellate planozygote. (*f*) Uniseriate

filamentous and uniseriate; only at a later stage do they grow first into pluriseriate filaments and then into small hollow tubes (Fig. 22.10g), these finally 'collapsing' to produce the flat distromatic blades of the adult plants ([1749]). Each cell is uninucleate and contains a cup-shaped, parietal chloroplast, in which there are one or more pyrenoids (Fig. 22.11a, b).

The life cycle of *Ulva lactuca* (Fig. 22.10) includes a haploid gametophyte generation and a diploid sporophyte generation. This species has an isomorphic, diplohaplontic life cycle, with haplogenotypic sex determination; it is anisogamous ([91, 446]).

In the haploid thalli (the gametophytes), biflagellate gametes are formed in the marginal cells by mitotic cell division (Fig. 22.10a, a'). Gametes produced from the same gametophyte cannot copulate: they are incompatible. Copulation can only occur between male and female gametes, produced from male and female gametophytes, respectively. The male gametes are slightly smaller than the female gametes and fusion is therefore anisogamous. The diploid zygote (Fig. 22.10e) germinates immediately, with no period of dormancy, to give a *Ulothrix*-like germling (Fig. 22.10f), and this develops into a diploid sporophyte (Fig. 22.10h), which is morphologically similar to the gametophyte. Cells in the marginal parts of the sporophyte blade undergo meiosis and divide to produce a number of quadriflagellate, haploid meiospores (Fig. 22.10i). Half of the meiospores grow via *Ulothrix*-like germlings (Fig. 22.10k') into male gametophytes (Fig. 22.10a'), while the other half grow into female gametophytes (Fig. 22.10a). Haplogenotypic sex determination must therefore occur during meiosis. Several variations are known on the basic life cycle as described above ([1750]). The blade-like thalli of *Ulva* grow through intercalary cell division, in which the new cell walls are always laid down at right angles to the plane of the thallus (Fig. 22.11a, b).

In Europe there are about ten species of *Ulva*, of which *U. lactuca* is the best known ([91, 705, 864]). All *Ulva* species are marine. They can grow in great abundance on rocky coasts, sea-walls and quays, but can also form large free-floating masses in lagoons and brackish pools; great rafts of drifting sea lettuce are a characteristic feature, for instance, of the Wadden Sea.

The flagellar apparatus has been shown to have an 11 o'clock – 5 o'clock configuration ([424, 1168, 1169]), and mitosis and cytokinesis are of type V ([1043, 1044]).

Enteromorpha (Fig. 22.11c–h)

Enteromorpha thalli are tube-like, and may be branched or unbranched; they can be several centimetres to several decimetres long. The tube wall is one layer of cells thick. The structure of the cells is identical to that found in *Ulva*; indeed, these genera are closely related and intermediate forms have been found. As in *Ulva*, the younger stages in thallus development are uniseriate and resemble *Ulothrix* (Fig. 22.11g). Later the uniseriate filaments become pluriseriate and eventually hollow tubes are produced. The young plantlets have branched rhizoidal systems, which resemble the branched filamentous members of the Ulvales, such as *Acrochaete* (compare Figs. 22.11g and 22.13a).

About 25 species of *Enteromorpha* have been found in Europe, in brackish and marine waters. A few species penetrate into freshwater ([90a, 862, 865, 866, 867, 1829, 1830]). *Enteromorpha* occupies the same kinds of habitats as *Ulva* (see above), and they sometimes grow together in great abundance.

Species of *Enteromorpha* that reproduce sexually have an isomorphic, diplohaplontic life cycle, just as in *Ulva*. The flagellar apparatus has been shown to have an 11 o'clock – 5 o'clock configuration ([424, 1727]).

Ulvaria (Fig. 22.12)

The leaf-like thalli of *Ulvaria* are up to 30 cm long, dark green, and **monostromatic**. As in *Ulva* and *Enteromorpha*, the youngest stages are uniseriate filaments, resembling *Ulothrix* plants (Fig. 22.12d). These filaments become pluriseriate as a result of longitudinal cell divisions and eventually a hollow,

Caption for fig. 22.10 (cont.).
filamentous germling of sporophyte generation, attached via branched rhizoids. (g) Tubular germling of sporophyte generation. (h) Fully developed blade-like sporophyte (diploid). (i) Meiotic division of sporophyte cells to form haploid quadriflagellate zoids (meiospores). (j, j') Quadriflagellate meiospores. (k, k') Uniseriate filamentous germlings of the female and male gametophytes. (l, l') Tubular germlings of the female and male gametophytes. F! = fertilization; R! = reduction division (meiosis). (Based on [694, 864].)

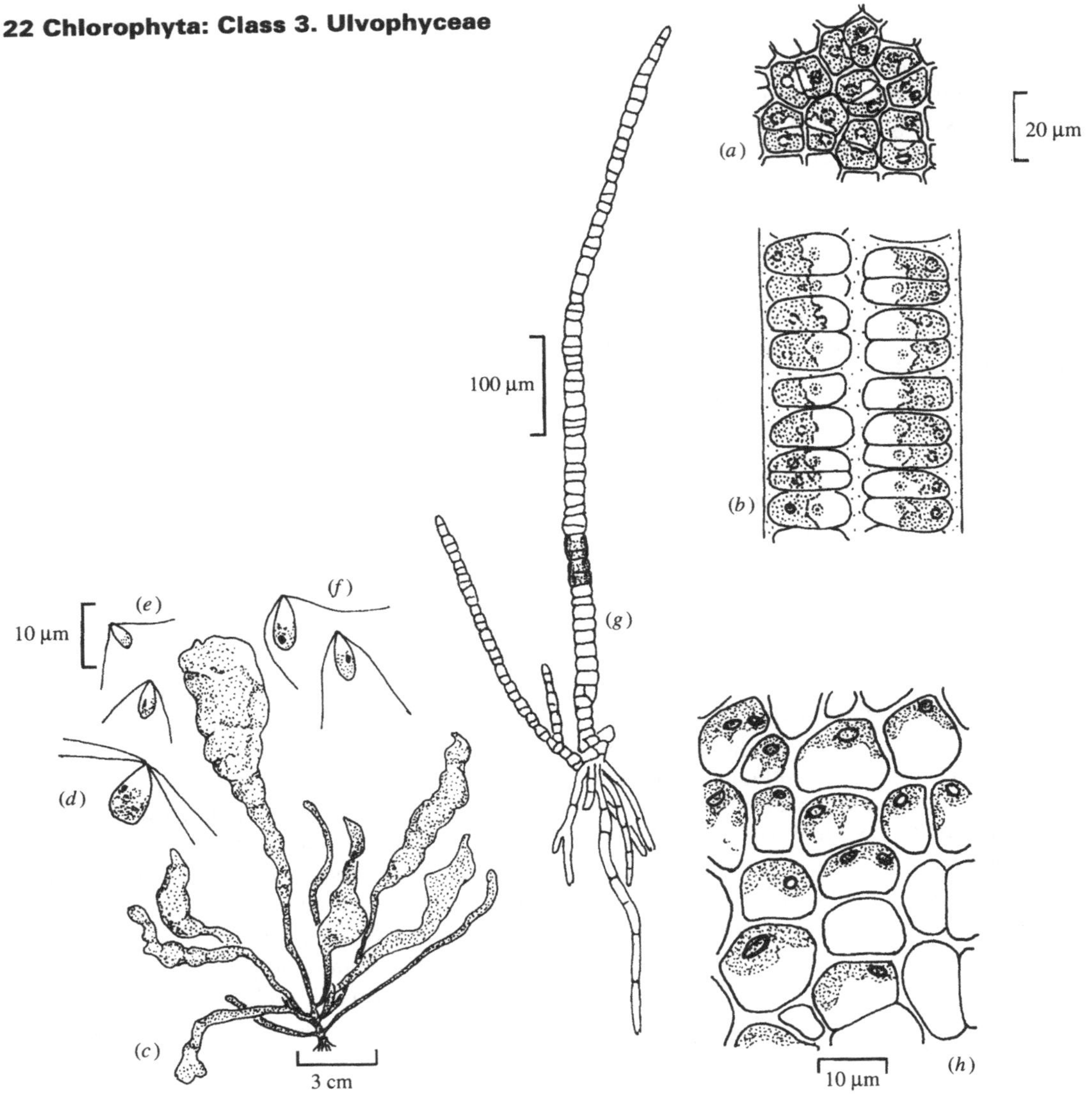

Figure 22.11. (*a, b*) *Ulva lactuca.* (*a*) Surface view of thallus, showing cells with cup-shaped chloroplasts and pyrenoids. Note the pairs of recently divided cells, with their chloroplasts on opposite sides. (*b*) Cross section through thallus, showing the two layers of cells with cup-shaped chloroplasts and pyrenoids. (*c–h*) *Enteromorpha compressa.* (*c*) Habit of whole plant. (*d*) Quadriflagellate meiospore. (*e*) Male gametes. (*f*) Female gametes. (*g*) Uniseriate filamentous germling. (*h*) Surface view of thallus. Note the cup-shaped chloroplasts; in this species they are appressed to the upper (apical) parts of the cell walls. Each chloroplast usually contains one pyrenoid. (*a, b* based on [1695]; *c–e* on [694, 865].)

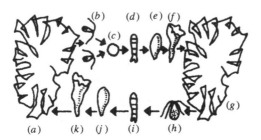

Figure 22.12. The life cycle of *Ulvaria obscura.* (*a*) Monostromatic, blade-like thallus. (*b*) Biflagellate gametes. (*c*) Zygote. (*d*) Uniseriate filamentous germling of sporophyte. (*e*) Tubular stage. (*f*) Sac-like stage. (*g*) Monostromatic, blade-like sporophyte. (*h*) Quadriflagellate meiospore. (*i*) Uniseriate filamentous germling of gametophyte. (*j*) Tubular stage. (*k*) Sac-like stage. (Based on [693].)

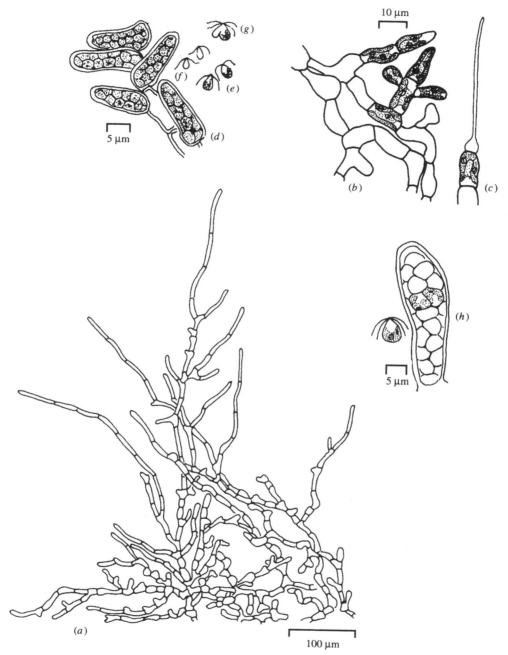

Figure 22.13. *Acrochaete*. (*a*) Habit of plant, which is endophytic in the cell walls of larger algae. (*b*) Detail of the thallus. The parietal chloroplasts take the form of incomplete cylinders and contain bilenticular pyrenoids. (*c*) Cell bearing a colourless hair with an inflated base. (*d*) Portion of a filament bearing flask-shaped gametangia. (*e*) Biflagellate female gametes. (*f*) Biflagellate male gametes. (*g*) Anisogamous copulation to form a quadriflagellate planozygote. (*h*) Meiosporangium, with quadriflagellate meiospore. (*a, b* based on [1763]; *c–h* on [1332].)

Enteromorpha-like, tubular thallus is produced (Fig. 22.12*e*). Finally, the tubes split open at their upper ends and continue growth as monostromatic blades (Fig. 22.12*f, g*). *Ulvaria* is isogamous and has an isomorphic, diplohaplontic life cycle (Fig. 22.12; [1750]).

Ulvaria occurs along the rocky coasts of the N Atlantic and N Pacific. It was formerly included within the genus *Monostroma* (p. 399) because of its monostromatic thalli. The zoids have been shown to have an 11 o'clock – 5 o'clock configuration of the flagellar apparatus ([424, 1331]).

An example of a branched, filamentous member of the order Ulvales: Acrochaete *(Fig. 22.13;* [1288, 1332, 1695]*)*

Acrochaete forms irregular spreading patches of branched filaments growing in and on the cell walls of other, larger marine algae. In the centre of a patch the filaments may be crowded closely together, forming a pseudoparenchyma. Each cell has one nucleus and one parietal chloroplast, which takes the form of an incomplete cylinder and contains one to several bilenticular pyrenoids (Fig. 22.13*b*). Colourless hairs are sometimes produced. They are borne singly on cells of the filaments and have basal inflations (Fig. 22.13*c*), and their formation is stimulated by nutrient deficiency ([1332]).

Acrochaete species have an isomorphic, diplohaplontic life cycle. Zoids are produced in flask-shaped zoidangia, each with a circular exit pore (Fig. 22.13*d, h*). The haploid gametophytes ($n = 8$) produce biflagellate anisogametes (Fig. 22.13*e, f*). Male and female gametes are produced in different gametangia on the same plant and this species is therefore homothallic. Fusion of a male with a female gamete produces a zygote, which develops into a diploid sporophyte ($2n = 16$). Quadriflagellate zoospores are formed by the sporophyte in flask-shaped sporangia (Fig. 22.13*h*), presumably following meiosis, and these grow into new gametophytes.

The ultrastructure of the flagellar apparatus has been investigated and shown to have an 11 o'clock – 5 o'clock configuration ([1326]).

23

Chlorophyta: Class 4. Cladophorophyceae

There is one order, the Cladophorales ([697]).

The principal characteristics of the Cladophorophyceae

1 The thalli always have a siphonocladous level of organization; this means that the filaments, which are uniseriate and can be branched or unbranched, are composed of multinucleate cells (Figs. 23.1*a*, 23.7*e*). Some Cladophorales have evolved complex thalli, in which the basically filamentous, branched organization can be difficult to recognize (Fig. 23.10).

2 The principal polysaccharide of the cell wall is highly crystalline cellulose I. The microfibrils of cellulose, each *ca.* 20 nm in diameter, are arranged parallel to each other in numerous lamellae, their orientation changing from one lamella to the next in a 'crossed fibril' arrangement (Figs. 23.1*b*, *c*, 23.2). The microfibrils are produced by linear arrays of cellulose synthase particles, 10 nm in diameter, located in the plasmalemma (Fig. 19.24*b*).

3 The reproductive zoids have two or four flagella. The basal bodies have an 11 o'clock – 5 o'clock configuration and exhibit a distinct overlap (Figs. 19.14*b*, 23.4; [45]).

4 Mitosis is of type VI (p. 328, Fig. 19.22 II):

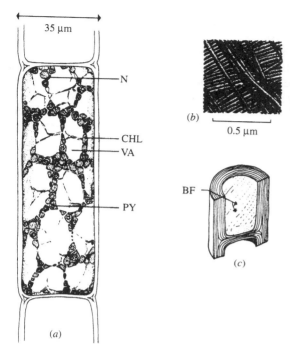

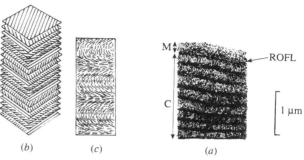

Figure 23.2. The helicoidal (crossed fibrillar) arrangement of microfibrils in the cell wall of a cladophoralean alga (*Boergesenia*). (*a*) Cross section through the wall, showing the festooned appearance that results from a regular, repeated shift in microfibrillar orientation. This illustration is based on a Pt–C shadowed EM preparation. (*b*) Diagram showing the shift in microfibrillar orientation between successive wall layers. (*c*) The pattern produced by the structure shown in (*b*) when it is seen in an ultrathin section. C = inner part of the cell wall, with helicoidal structure; M = matrix-rich outer layer; ROFL = layer of randomly orientated microfibrils. (*a* based on [1208].)

Figure 23.1. *Cladophora*. (*a*) Cell structure. (*b*) Cellulose microfibrils of the cell wall. (*c*) Three-dimensional reconstruction of part of the cell wall, showing the orientation of the bundles of microfibrils. BF = bundle of microfibrils; CHL = chloroplast; N = nucleus; PY = pyrenoid; VA = vacuole. (*b* based on [911]; *c* on [602a].)

mitosis is closed, while the telophase nucleus has a characteristic dumbbell shape because of the presence of a prominent, persistent telophase spindle. The spindle forms between polar pairs of centrioles (mitosis is **centric**). Vegetative cell division is uncoupled from mitosis and the cross-walls are not perforated by plasmodesmata.

5 Each cell of the gametophyte or sporophyte is multinucleate and contains numerous irregular, angular chloroplasts, which form a parietal network or a more or less continuous layer; they may also extend into the cell along the cytoplasmic strands that traverse the vacuole. The individual chloroplasts often appear to be interconnected by delicate strands (Figs. 23.1*a*,

23.3*a*). In many but not all of the chloroplasts in a cell, there is a single bilenticular pyrenoid, which is divided into two hemispheres by a thylakoid. Each hemisphere is capped by a bowl-shaped starch grain (Fig. 23.3*b*, *c*; [206, 749, 750]).

6 The cytoplasm does not stream as it does in the giant cells of the Bryopsidophyceae, Dasycladophyceae and Charophyceae. As a result, the chloroplasts have fixed positions.

7 The life cycles of sexually reproducing species are diplohaplontic and isomorphic. The haploid gametophytes produce biflagellate gametes. Following isogamous or anisogamous fusion of two gametes, the zygote grows into a diploid sporophyte, which is morphologically similar to the gametophyte. The sporophytes in turn produce quadriflagellate meiospores, which grow into gametophytes. Some reproduce, either additionally or exclusively, by means of asexual, biflagellate or quadriflagellate zoospores (Fig. 23.6; for reviews, see [64, 94, 694, 697, 1750]).

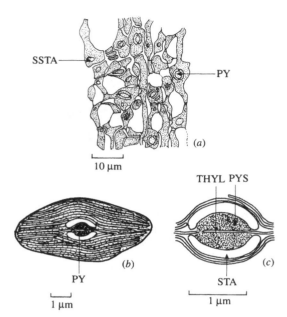

SSTA

PY

10 μm

THYL PYS

(a)

(b)   *(c)*

PY   STA

1 μm   1 μm

Figure 23.3. The parietal network of chloroplasts in a *Cladophora* species. (*a*) Surface view of the network as seen with the light microscope. (*b*) Cross section of an individual chloroplast, containing a bilenticular pyrenoid. Note the closely appressed thylakoids. (*c*) Cross section through a bilenticular pyrenoid. The pyrenoid is divided by a single thylakoid into two halves, each of which is covered by a bowl-shaped shell of starch. PY = pyrenoid; PYS = pyrenoid stroma; SSTA = stroma starch; STA = starch shell around pyrenoid; THYL = thylakoid. (*a* based on [806]; *b, c* on [750].)

An 11 o'clock – 5 o'clock configuration of the basal bodies has been demonstrated in the zoids of six species of the Cladophorophyceae, belonging to the genera *Cladophora* (Fig. 23.5) and *Chaetomorpha* (Fig. 23.7) ([45, 425, 689, 1750]). We will briefly describe the biflagellate zoids of a *Chaetomorpha* species (Fig. 23.4; [45]), for comparison with those of *Acrosiphonia* (p. 320, Fig. 19.13), which we have used as a 'model' of the 11 o'clock – 5 o'clock type of flagellar apparatus.

As in *Acrosiphonia*, the two flagella of *Chaetomorpha* zoids emerge at the base of a conspicuous apical papilla (Fig. 23.4a). They lie at a very obtuse angle to each other (almost 180°) and hence are almost perpendicular to the longitudinal axis of the zoid. The flagella are anchored in the cell by four cruciately

arranged microtubular roots (Fig. 23.4c), which exhibit the usual x–2–x–2 pattern; in both *Acrosiphonia* and *Chaetomorpha* the 'x' roots contain 3 microtubules. When viewed from the apex of the cell, the basal bodies show a distinct 11 o'clock – 5 o'clock displacement and they also overlap. Again, these are features found in *Acrosiphonia* (compare Fig. 23.4c with Fig. 19.13a, b). The genera differ, however, in the exact arrangement of microtubular roots, since in *Chaetomorpha* the roots make a much smaller angle with the basal bodies than in *Acrosiphonia*. This seems to be characteristic of the class Cladophorophyceae ([1645]), members of which have a flagellar apparatus that is somewhat compressed laterally. Another difference is that the upper basal body connective in *Chaetomorpha* shows a distinct transverse striation, whereas the equivalent connective in *Acrosiphonia* is not striated (compare Fig. 23.4b, c with Fig. 19.13a, c). The *Chaetomorpha* zoid also has two faintly fibrous strands not found in *Acrosiphonia*, which descend into the cell beneath the three-stranded microtubular roots (Fig. 23.4b). The *Acrosiphonia* zoid, on the other hand, has various structures not recorded in *Chaetomorpha*, including a second striated fibre linking the two basal bodies and two transversely striated lateral fibres connecting the three-stranded microtubular roots with the proximal sheaths (Fig. 19.13). In addition, the apical papilla of *Chaetomorpha* is strengthened by an umbrella-like cytoskeleton of microtubules (Fig. 23.4b), which is absent in *Acrosiphonia*, while the tail portion of the *Acrosiphonia* zoid is strengthened by a microtubular cytoskeleton (Fig. 19.13c) not seen in *Chaetomorpha*. On the other hand, the zoids of the two genera are alike in having terminal caps over the proximal ends of the basal bodies and also proximal sheaths of amorphous material, which are appressed to the lower sides of the basal bodies.

Type VI mitosis (p. 408, character 4) has been shown to be present in four members of the Cladophorophyceae ([740, 741, 742, 1152, 1611]). Mitosis is closed and there is a prominent, persistent telophase spindle, these features leading to a characteristic dumbbell shape of the nucleus at telophase (Fig. 19.22 II); cytokinesis does not immediately follow mitosis. This type of mitosis is very similar to that in the Bryopsidophyceae (Fig. 24.3). Centrioles are involved in the formation of the spindle, mitosis therefore being centric (Fig. 19.22 II).

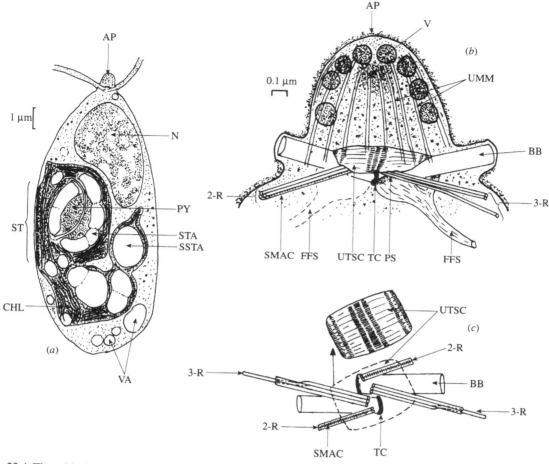

Figure 23.4. The zoid of a cladophoralean alga (*Chaetomorpha*). (*a*) Longitudinal section of the zoid, based on EM observations. (*b*) Three-dimensional reconstruction of the flagellar apparatus and apical papilla, seen from the side. (*c*) Flagellar apparatus, seen from the cell apex. AP = apical papilla; BB = basal body; CHL = chloroplast; FFS = faintly fibrous strand; N = nucleus; PS = proximal (= lower) sheath; PY = pyrenoid; SMAC = striated microtubule-associated component; SSTA = stroma starch; ST = stigma (eyespot); STA = starch grain appressed to the pyrenoid surface; TC = terminal cap on the lower (inner) end of the basal body; UMM = umbrella-like array of cytoskeletal microtubules; UTSC = upper transversely striated connective, linking the basal bodies; V = vesicle, probably containing sticky material for attachment of the zoid; VA = vacuole; 2-R = two-stranded microtubular root; 3-R = three-stranded (*x*-) root. (Based on [45].)

In cladophorophycean cells mitoses are mostly synchronous, but take place with the nuclei scattered throughout the cell (Fig. 23.7*e*; [1690]). This contrasts with the situation in *Acrosiphonia* (class Ulvophyceae), where the mitoses are again synchronous but take place in one plane, which corresponds to where the cell will later divide. Furthermore, in *Acrosiphonia* cytokinesis follows immediately after mitosis (p. 398, Fig. 22.7), whereas this does not occur in the Cladophorophyceae.

Vegetative cytokinesis usually takes place through the ingrowth of a diaphragm-like cross-wall (Fig. 23.7*c, d*); so far, however, there have been no investigations of this process at the ultrastructural level. During the formation of zoids, the parietal layer of cytoplasm is partitioned by a series of ramifying cleavage furrows, whose membranes are derived in part from golgi vesicles ([740]).

A few members of the Cladophorophyceae exhibit a different and rather curious mode of vegetative cell division, termed **segregative cell division**. Here the protoplast cleaves into rounded, walled portions, which later expand into new vegetative cells (Figs. 23.9, 23.10*a–f*). It has sometimes been suggested that the forms with segregative cell division should be classified in a separate group and this has been investigated in an immunological study by Olson-Stojkovich *et al.* ([1339]; see also [704, 1338]). Antibodies were raised in rabbits to the soluble protein fraction (antigens) of extracts obtained from 24 strains, belonging to 11 different species of Cladophorophyceae. The degree of binding between the antigens and the various antibodies (in rabbit blood serum) was then used to assess the degree of phylogenetic relatedness. The results showed clearly that the species with segregative cell division and the species without belong to one evolutionary group.

Segregative cell division has been examined in detail in *Dictyosphaeria* ([369]). During the night the parietal layer of protoplasm contracts into small granular portions, which soon fuse to form a network (Fig. 23.10*a–c*). This in turn breaks down into many spheres of protoplasm, which at first lack walls (Fig. 23.10*d*) but form them in the course of the following day (Fig. 23.10*e*). The young spheres contain many nuclei in various stages of mitosis. In the next three days the young daughter cells increase in size, pressing against each other and becoming polygonal (Fig. 23.10*f*). A parietal layer of daughter cells is thus produced within the parent cell wall and each daughter cell can then go on to repeat the process.

In various other representatives of the Cladophorophyceae, wounding the cells, by puncturing them, induces a rapid contraction of the protoplast into a larger or smaller number of segments, which pinch apart and pull away from each other within a few minutes. These segments may subsequently become walled and grow into new cells ([951, 955]). Calcium ions and ATP are necessary for this active contraction of the protoplast, which is mediated by actin filaments 5–9 nm thick ([952, 953, 954, 955]). The arrays of actin microfilaments can be made visible by staining them with actin-specific fluorescent antibodies and observing the cells by fluorescence microscopy. After the cells have been wounded a network of actin suddenly appears in the outermost (cortical) layer of cytoplasm; it is probably contraction of the bundles of actin filaments that brings about the contraction of the protoplast during the wounding reaction ([957]). Actin microfilaments, like microtubules, are a class of cytoskeletal elements found throughout the realm of the Eukaryota; they must have been present in the ancestral eukaryotes. They are involved in muscular contraction (through their interaction with the protein myosin), amoeboid movement, protoplasmic streaming (e.g. in cells of the green algal classes Bryopsidophyceae, Dasycladophyceae and Charophyceae), and in many other activities.

The rapid contraction of the actin bundles during the wounding reaction is accompanied by passive contortion and convolution of the arrays of microtubules present in the cortical cytoplasm; normally these are parallel and oriented longitudinally ([956, 957]). The microtubule arrays are probably responsible for the firm anchoring of the chloroplasts in the cortical cytoplasm and hence for the rigidity of the cytoplasm so typical of the Cladophorophyceae. In turn, the nuclei are anchored to the chloroplasts by radial arrays of microtubules, which ensheath them. The nuclei are always positioned below the chloroplasts ([1623]). While, in the Cladophorophyceae, the arrays of microtubules are thought to be responsible for stability of the cytoplasm, in the Bryopsidophyceae (p. 419) and Dasycladophyceae (p. 436) bundles of microtubules seem to be instrumental in bringing about protoplasmic streaming, albeit through their interaction with actin microfilaments.

The excess of plasma membrane brought about by the contraction of the protoplast is recycled through the formation of numerous 'coated' vesicles, which are then gradually resorbed into the protoplasm ([955]).

The wounding reaction described above resembles segregative cell division, which might perhaps therefore be viewed as a 'slowed down' version of the wounding response; it remains to be seen, however, whether the resemblance is any more than superficial.

The **ultrastructure of the pyrenoid** is highly constant within the Cladophorophyceae and characteristic of it. This contrasts with the class Ulvophyceae, where various types of pyrenoid can be found even within one genus (e.g. in *Ulothrix*: [1034]). In the Cladophorales the pyrenoid is 'bilenticular', i.e. divided into two hemispheres by a single thylakoid, and each hemisphere is covered by a bowl-shaped starch grain (Fig. 23.3*b, c*). The grains are easily seen, even under the light microscope (Fig. 23.3*a*). Each chloroplast is densely packed with tightly appressed thylakoids, which are often paired (Fig. 23.3*b*). Grains of starch are often found distributed through the stroma of the chloroplast ([206, 749, 750]).

The structural fraction of the cell walls in the Cladophorophyceae is composed of microfibrils of cellulose I, which is the kind of cellulose that forms the greater part of the cell wall in higher plants (Tracheophyta). Cellulose is a β-1,4-linked glucan. The microfibrils have a diameter of 10–25 nm and are arranged parallel to each other in layers, the orientation of the microfibrils changing by *ca*. 30° from one layer to the next in a 'helicoid' (Fig. 23.2*b*; [1282]). This arrangement of the microfibrils is sometimes termed a 'crossed fibrillar pattern'. The gradual change in the orientation of the microfibrils across the wall produces a festooned appearance in transverse sections, and this is shown and explained in Fig. 23.2 ([1208, 1282, 1335, 1386]). The fibrillar nature of the cell wall can even be made out under the light microscope (Figs. 23.1*c*, 23.7*a, b*), which suggests that the fibrils are grouped into in bundles ([602a, 911, 1148, 1297, 1396]).

The amorphous matrix fraction of the cell wall consists predominantly of a complexly branched arabino-galactan (a polymer of arabinose and galactose, together with some xylose), which is highly sulphated ([1396]). The outermost part of the cell wall is a layer *ca.* 0.2 μm thick, consisting predominantly of amorphous (matrix) wall material, with relatively few and randomly orientated microfibrils (Fig. 23.2*a*; [1208]).

Freeze–etch studies reveal arrays of granules in the plasmalemmas of actively growing cells of *Cladophora* and other members of the Cladophorophyceae ([48, 1207]); the diameter of each granule is approximately 10 nm. These granules may be cellulose synthase, the enzyme responsible for the polymerization and orientation of the cellulose microfibrils. The linear arrays of cellulose synthase particles in the Cladophorophyceae contrast with the rosettes of cellulose synthase present in the Zygnematophyceae, Charophyceae and higher plants (p. 338, Fig. 19.24).

In contrast to the classes of green algae described in previous chapters (the Chlorophyceae and Ulvophyceae), the Cladophorophyceae exhibit only one level of organization: the **siphonocladous** level.

The number of genera included in the Cladophorophyceae is about 32, the number of species *ca.* 420 ([1630]). The great majority of the Cladophorales are marine ([697]).

Examples of the class Cladophorophyceae

Cladophora (Figs. 23.5, 23.6)

Each cell in the branching filaments of *Cladophora* is multinucleate and contains many angular, discoid chloroplasts around its periphery; these are united to form a reticulum (Figs. 23.1*a*, 23.3*a*). The genus includes both freshwater and marine species. In Europe there are 9 freshwater species and 25 marine species ([692]), while 31 species are known from the coasts of NE America ([695]). *Cladophora* is widespread in temperate and tropical seas but it is virtually absent from polar waters. Most species grow attached to rocky substrata, but a few can form extensive, free-floating masses in more or less stagnant, eutrophic waters, such as in coastal lagoons or freshwater ponds.

The vegetative structure of *Cladophora vagabunda* (Fig. 23.5*a, b*)

This species is common along all temperate and tropical seashores. It forms dense fluffy or pompom-like thalli, which are yellow-green in colour and occur, for instance, in intertidal pools on rocky shores or in salt marsh ponds.

Young, vigorously growing plants of *Cladophora vagabunda* have an acropetal organization, the side branches being formed in an acropetal succession (Fig. 23.5*a*). In other words, the most recently formed branch is the one closest to the apex, while the branch furthest from the apex is the oldest; the side branches become progressively younger and shorter towards the tip. This type of arrangement is closely correlated with the fact that the plants grow apically, essentially through the division of the apical cell itself and through elongation of the daughter cells that arise from it.

Beneath the apical cell is the subapical cell, which resembles the apical cell in many of its characteristics, such as its capacity for elongation, especially in the apical part of the cell. However, while elongation of the apical cell takes place along its longitudinal axis, in the subapical cell the stretching finds an 'outlet' in lateral growth, thus initiating a side branch (Fig. 23.5*c–g*). When the initial cell of the new side branch has grown out far enough, it is cut off from the main axis by a cross-wall. The apical cells of the side branches possess essentially the same potential for

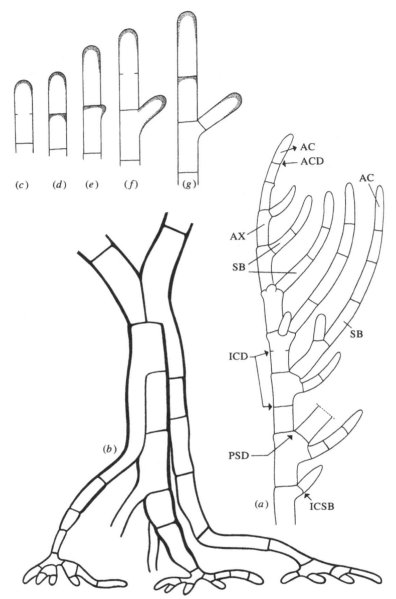

Figure 23.5. *Cladophora vagabunda:* the construction of the vegetative thallus. (*a*) Apical portion of thallus. (*b*) Base of plant, showing rhizoidal attachment. (*c–g*) Pattern of apical growth and branching: the zones where the greatest growth of the wall occurs are stippled. AC = apical cell; ACD = apical cell division; AX = main axis; ICD = intercalary cell division; ICSB = side branch from below a cell wall produced at an intercalary cell division; PSD = pseudodichotomy; SB = primary side branch.

growth as the apical cell of the main axis, and so the side branches can recapitulate the development of the main axis, producing a second-order, acropetal system of branching. The growth of the side branches is basically indeterminate, just like the growth of the main axis; the side branches can therefore be said to be indeterminate laterals, or branches of unlimited growth.

It might be thought from the above account that

higher-order acropetal branching systems could be produced indefinitely in the same way, but this does not occur. Plants do have a maximum size, although in *Cladophora vagabunda* this is very variable and highly dependent on environmental conditions. The maximum is determined mainly by when the plants become fertile, since at that stage the cells in the outer, peripheral branch systems divide up their contents into zoids and the plants disintegrate back to the lowest parts of the main axis and some of its side branches. In exposed areas, where currents and wave action are severe (e.g. in tidal pools on some rocky shores), the formation of zoids begins earlier and is more complete than in sheltered places. Consequently, in exposed places the plants are much smaller (several centimetres to several decimetres) than in still conditions, where the thalli can be more than a metre long and often give rise to free-floating masses.

Cladophora vagabunda exhibits intercalary growth as well as apical growth (Fig. 23.5a). Intercalary cells lying some distance from the apex can divide and indeed, towards the base of the plant, the number of intercalary divisions increases, so that the distance between the primary side branches becomes wider and wider. This feature may be obscured, however, by secondary side branches, which grow out from below the cross walls produced following intercalary cell division.

The balance between apical and intercalary growth can vary greatly in *Cladophora vagabunda*. If apical growth predominates, plants with a distinctly acropetal organization develop; if intercalary growth predominates, the acropetal organization becomes difficult to recognize or disappears. Plants that have been reduced to their main axes through sporulation sometimes continue to grow through intercalary division to give long, scarcely branched filaments: very different from the same plants when they were young, with their acropetal branching systems.

From this it can be seen that *Cladophora vagabunda* is extremely plastic in its morphology, and the same goes for most other *Cladophora* species. The result has been great confusion in the systematics of the genus, so that, for instance, of the 800 or so species and infraspecific taxa described for Europe, only 34 remained after a thorough taxonomic revision ([692]).

The plants are attached to substrata by branched rhizoids (Fig. 23.5b), which grow out from the base of the main axis itself and from a few of the cells imme-

diately above this. Rhizoids can also develop and grow down from the lowest cells of the side branches, even when these are not at the base of the plant.

Life cycle of *Cladophora vagabunda* (Fig. 23.6)

In a fertile plant vegetative growth ceases in the outer, peripheral branches, the cells swell somewhat, and their contents divide up into zoids; these then make their exit through a pore at the upper end of the zoidan-

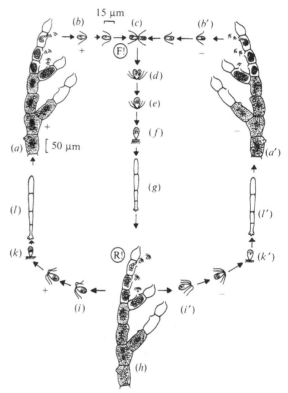

Figure 23.6. The life cycle of *Cladophora vagabunda*. (*a, a'*) Fertile gametophytes (haploid), in which all the cells in the apical zone divide up into biflagellate gametes. (*b*) Biflagellate (+) gamete. (*b'*) Biflagellate (−) gamete. (*c, d*) Copulation between (+) and (−) gametes. (*e*) Quadriflagellate planozygote. (*f*) Recently settled zygote. (*g*) Uniseriate filamentous germling of the sporophyte generation. (*h*) Mature sporophyte. The tips of the thallus are fertile and the cells contents have divided up into quadriflagellate zoids (meiospores). (*i, i'*) Quadriflagellate meiospores. (*k, k'*) Recently settled meiospores. (*l, l'*) Uniseriate filamentous germlings of the gametophyte generation. F! = fertilization; R! = reduction division (meiosis).

gium. In principle, any vegetative cell can develop into a zoidangium.

Cladophora vagabunda is an isomorphic diplohaplont, which exhibits isogamy and haplogenotypic sex determination. The diploid (*2n*) sporophyte (Fig. 23.6*h*) gives rise, following meiosis, to quadriflagellate haploid zoospores (Fig. 23.6*i, i′*). These give rise to haploid (*n*) gametophytes, of which 50% are '+' and 50% are '−' (Fig. 23.6*a, a′*). The gametophytes are morphologically identical to the sporophytes and, after a number of mitoses, produce biflagellate gametes (Fig. 23.6*b, b′*). A (+) gamete copulates with a (−) gamete, this being an instance of isogamy, since the gametes are morphologically alike (Fig. 23.6*c, d*). Following plasmogamy the quadriflagellate planozygote (Fig. 23.6*e*) becomes attached (Fig. 23.6*f*) and grows directly into a diploid sporophyte, without an intervening period of dormancy (Fig 23.6*g, h*): the cycle is complete.

During unfavourable conditions (e.g. when nutrients are scarce) the vegetative cells form thick walls and accumulate great quantities of reserve starch. These thick-walled cells are termed **akinetes**. When conditions improve, the akinetes give rise to new *Cladophora* plants. In addition, filaments composed of akinetes can fragment.

Other *Cladophora* species have the same kind of life cycle ([694, 1750, 1892]).

Cladophora glomerata

Cladophora glomerata is a very common freshwater alga, which grows on stones and other solid substrata in eutrophic waters, just beneath the water surface (e.g. in the wave-washed zone on the banks of lakes and canals). It can cover the surface of ditches and ponds with thick, free-floating mats.

Cladophora glomerata is virtually identical in its morphology to *C. vagabunda*, but it lacks sexual reproduction. As far as is known, *C. glomerata* reproduces only by the asexual production of biflagellate zoospores. The formation of zoosporangia is favoured by short-day conditions (8 h light, 16 h dark; [706]).

Chaetomorpha (Fig. 23.7)

The thalli of *Chaetomorpha* consist of thick unbranched filaments, made of short squat cells. The filaments grow mainly through intercalary cell division (Fig. 23.7*a–d*). Species with sexual reproduction have an isomorphic, diplohaplontic life cycle ([94, 694,

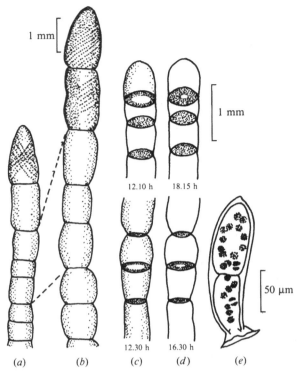

Figure 23.7. *Chaetomorpha darwinii*. (*a, b*) Intercalary growth of filaments by cell enlargement and elongation; the upper two cells are fertile. Note the spiralling bundles of microfibrils, which are just visible using the light microscope. (*c, d*) The division of apical and intercalary cells through the formation of cross walls, which develop inwards like the closing of an iris diaphragm. (*e*) Germling. The many nuclei exhibit virtually simultaneous division, though they are spread throughout the cell (contrast Fig. 22.7). (Based on [895].)

1750]). *Chaetomorpha linum*, with filaments 100–300 µm wide, forms curly, hair-like growths, which float around freely in brackish water (e.g. in the Wadden Sea).

Rhizoclonium

This alga consists of thin, unbranched filaments, 10–50 µm wide. Sexually reproducing species have an isomorphic, diplohaplontic life cycle ([694, 1750]). *Rhizoclonium riparium* is very common in marine and brackish environments, growing for instance on the damp mud of salt marshes.

Struvea (Figs. 23.8*a*, 23.10*i, j*)

In *Struvea* the plants have a large-celled axis bearing side branches. The axis and the laterals both bear triangular 'leaves' at their tips, which are composed of a dense mass of crowded branches containing relatively small cells. Within each 'leaf' the apical cells of the branches are linked to each other or to other cells by tiny rhizoidal structures (Fig. 23.10*i, j*). *Struvea* is a marine genus, occurring in the tropics.

Valonia (Fig. 23.8*b*)

Valonia consists of large club-shaped cells, which can grow to several centimetres in size and can bear a number of other cells laterally. During cell division a local accumulation of nuclei and chloroplasts is cut off by a domed cell wall, forming a small lens-shaped cell. If this is formed from the apical part of the mother cell, it will develop into a lateral cell. If, on the other hand, it arises basally, it will develop into a rhizoid. One species of *Valonia* is known to have an isomorphic and presumably diplohaplontic life cycle ([64, 228]). *Valonia* is common in tropical and subtropical seas.

Siphonocladus (Fig. 23.9)

Siphonocladus plants are brush-like and up to *ca.* 5 cm high. During growth, a large elongate primary cell divides up its contents into walled spherical portions, which grow into a dense tuft of secondary cells (segregative cell division: see p. 412) (Fig. 23.9*b*). This process may then be repeated in the secondary cells. *Siphonocladus* occurs along the coasts of tropical and subtropical seas.

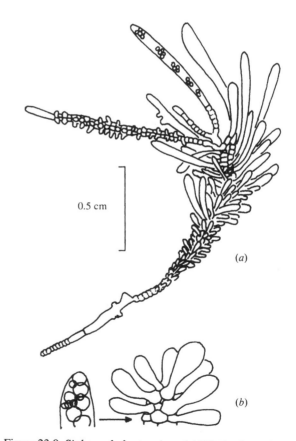

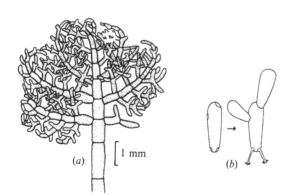

Figure 23.8. (*a*) *Struvea anastomosans.* Apical portion of thallus. (*b*) *Valonia.* Lens-shaped cells are formed around the periphery of the mother cell. Towards the top of the plant these develop into side branches, while towards the base they develop into rhizoids. (*a* based on [1826].)

Figure 23.9. *Siphonocladus tropicus.* (*a*) Whole plant. (*b*) Segregative cell division and development of the newly walled-off portions of the mother cell into lateral branches. (*a* based on [1826]; *b* on [694].)

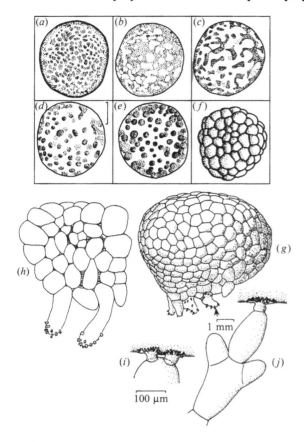

Dictyosphaeria (Fig. 23.10*a–h*)

Dictyosphaeria forms irregular hollow spheres, which grow up to *ca.* 5 cm in diameter. The thallus consists of a peripheral layer of cells, which are tightly packed and mutually compressed, and it is attached to substrate by tiny rhizoids. Each cell is capable of dividing up into spherical, walled portions, which then expand and form the mutually compressed cells around the periphery of a new spherical thallus (segregative cell division: see p. 412, Fig. 23.10*a–f*). The cells subsequently become attached to each other by special tiny rhizoidal cells (Fig. 23.10*h*). One species has been shown to possess an isomorphic and presumably diplohaplontic life cycle ([370]). *Dictyosphaeria* occurs along tropical sea-coasts.

Figure 23.10. (*a–h*) *Dictyosphaeria cavernosa.* (*a–f*) Segregative cell division. The stages shown in *a–d* take place during the dark period of a 14 h light : 10 h dark photoregime. (Scale bar = 1 mm.) (*a*) 10–30 min after the beginning of segregative cell division: the peripheral protoplasm contracts into small granular portions. (*b*) *ca.* 2 h: the granular portions of protoplasm have fused to form a network. (*c*) 3 h: condensation and simplification of the network, which begins to break down in several places. (*d*) 3.5 h: further breakdown of the network so that almost spherical, naked masses of protoplasm are produced. (*e*) 5.5 h: quite spherical bodies now lie around the periphery of the primary vesicle. (*f*) *ca.* 2–3 days: the young daughter cells have expanded and now have a polygonal outline, as a result of mutual compression. (*g*) Full-grown plant with tiny rhizoidal cells at the base, which attach the plant to the substratum. (*h*) Full-grown plant: longitudinal section, showing the presence of some tiny rhizoidal cells within the body of the plant, linking the normal vegetative cells, and others at the base, anchoring the plant to the substratum. (*i, j*) *Struvea:* tiny rhizoidal cells at the apices link the branches together within the blade (see also Fig. 23.8 (*a*)). (*a–f* based on [369]; *g–j* on [1340].)

24

Chlorophyta: Class 5. Bryopsidophyceae

The principal characteristics of the Bryopsidophyceae

1 The organization of the thallus is always siphonous, which means that each plant is essentially a single giant multinucleate cell, which usually takes the form of a branching tube or siphon. This contains a thin parietal layer of cytoplasm, containing many nuclei, and a huge central vacuole (Figs. 24.7 *a, b, m, n*, 24.15*c–e*). In many members of the class the multinucleate siphons combine to form fairly complex tissues (Figs. 24.10*a, b*, 24.11*a, a′*, 24.12, 24.14*a, c*).

2 The principal polysaccharides found in the fibrillar, structural fraction of the cell wall are mannan, xylan and glucan ('cellulose'), which occur in varying proportions. The glucan ('cellulose') is never found in a highly crystalline form, in contrast to the glucan of the Cladophorophyceae (cf. p. 408; [762, 763, 1297, 1921]).

3 The reproductive zoids have two or four flagella. The flagellar apparatus has a cruciate, 11 o'clock – 5 o'clock configuration, the basal bodies exhibiting a marked overlap (Figs. 19.14*b*, 24.1; [739a, 1513, 1514]). Some members of the class also produce reproductive zoids with many flagella arranged in a whorl near the anterior end of the cell (**stephanokont** zoids; Fig. 24.8*l, m*).

4 Mitosis is of type VI (p. 332, Figs. 19.22 II, 24.3). Mitosis is closed and there is a prominent, persistent telophase spindle, which gives the telophase nucleus a characteristic dumbbell shape. Mitosis can be either centric ([169, 1333]) or acentric ([739, 740, 1333]), i.e. with or without centrioles at the poles of the spindle.

5 The multinucleate siphons (coenocytes) contain numerous fusiform (Fig. 24.4*a*) or ellipsoidal (Fig. 24.5*a*) chloroplasts in the parietal layer of protoplasm. Two types of Bryopsidophyceae can be distinguished, according to the kinds of plastids they contain. In **homoplastidic** forms, the only plastids present are chloroplasts, which may or may not contain pyrenoids (Fig. 24.4*a–c*). **Heteroplastidic** forms, however, contain amyloplasts as well as chloroplasts (Fig. 24.5*a–e*). Siphonoxanthin and siphonein occur as accessory photosynthetic pigments in the chloroplasts (Table 1.2).

6 The cytoplasm exhibits vigorous streaming, which takes place along narrow lanes parallel to the long axis of the thallus. Organelles move with the cytoplasm, especially the chloroplasts and amyloplasts ([1188, 1190, 1193, 1194]).

7 Sexually reproducing species seem usually to have a haplontic life cycle, in which a multinucleate and presumably haploid gametophyte alternates with a microscopic zygote stage, containing a giant diploid nucleus. The zygote may divide up its contents into stephanokont zoospores, which then grow into gametophytes, or it may itself bud off gametophytes directly (Figs 24.7, 24.11). Evidence concerning the ploidy of the various stages in the life cycle is incomplete. Sexual fusion is anisogamous.

8 The class is almost completely marine.

An 11 o'clock – 5 o'clock configuration of the flagellar apparatus has been demonstrated in the zoids of seven members of the class ([547, 737, 739a, 747, 1172, 1513, 1515]). We will take the biflagellate male and female gametes of *Pseudobryopsis* as an example ([1515]), although reference should also be made to the light micrographs of the male and female gametes of *Bryopsis* (Fig. 24.7*c, d*), which are similar to those of *Pseudobryopsis*.

In its ultrastructure the flagellar apparatus of the *Pseudobryopsis* male gamete is quite similar to that of

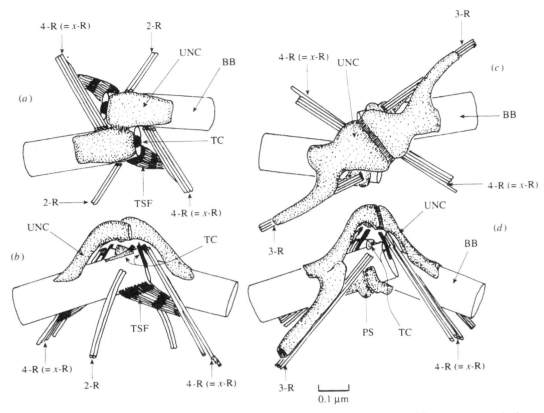

Figure 24.1. The flagellar apparatus of the male and female gametes of *Bryopsis* (*e–g*) and its close relative *Pseudobryopsis* (*a–d*), which have cruciate zoids of the 11 o'clock – 5 o'clock type. (*a*) Top view of the flagellar apparatus of a male gamete, three-dimensional reconstruction. (*b*) Three-dimensional reconstruction of the flagellar apparatus of a male gamete, seen from the side. (*c*) Top view of the flagellar apparatus of a female gamete. (*d*) Three-dimensional reconstruction of the flagellar apparatus of a female gamete, seen from the side. (*e–g*) Transmission electron micrographs. (*e*) Median longitudinal section of male gamete. (*f*) Male gamete: cross section through the cell apex, showing the two basal bodies at 11 o'clock and 5 o'clock. (*g*) Cross section just below the cell apex. Four ridges are present; in the upper left and lower right ridges there are two-stranded roots, while the other two ridges contain five-stranded roots (arrows). BB = basal body; c = chloroplast; g = golgi apparatus; m = mitochondrion; n = nucleus; PS = proximal sheath; TC = terminal cap over the lower (inner) end of the basal body; TSF = transversely striated fibre; UNC = upper non-striated connective linking the basal bodies; 2-R = two-stranded microtubular root; 3-R = three-stranded microtubular root (this replaces the two-stranded root in the female gamete); 4-R (= *x*-R) = four-stranded microtubular root (*x* root). (*a–d* based on [1515]; *e–g* from [739a], with the permission of the author and the editor of the *Japanese Journal of Phycology*.)

Acrosiphonia gametes (compare Fig. 24.1*a, b* with Fig. 19.13), which we have taken as a 'model' to illustrate the 11 o'clock – 5 o'clock type of configuration. As in *Acrosiphonia*, the two basal bodies lie at a very wide angle (about 180°) to each other; in *Pseudobryopsis* they may even point slightly backwards (Fig. 24.1*b*). The flagellar apparatus is anchored in the cell by four cruciately-arranged microtubular roots (Fig. 24.1*a, g*), which follow the usual *x*–2–*x*–2 pattern (cf. p. 320), the *x* roots of *Pseudobryopsis* containing four microtubules (*Acrosiphonia* has three). As in *Acrosiphonia* gametes, the basal bodies are placed in an 11 o'clock–5 o'clock configuration (when viewed from the cell anterior) and exhibit a clear

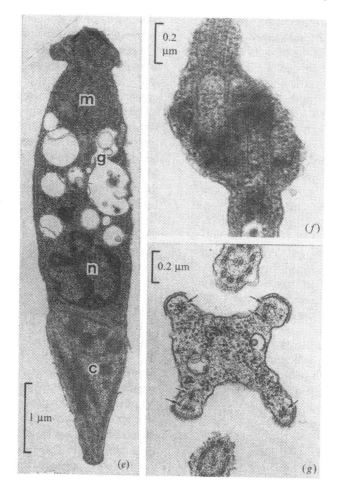

For legend see opposite.

'basal body overlap' (Fig. 24.1f). In both zoids the basal bodies are connected anteriorly by an upper connective, which is not striated and consists of two distinct halves. In the *Pseudobryopsis* male gamete the halves of the upper connective are linked by finely striated material, whereas in *Acrosiphonia* this role is played by a non-striated linking zone. In addition, the basal bodies of both *Pseudobryopsis* and *Acrosiphonia* are connected by a tiny second fibre, which is striated and lies beneath the upper non-striated connective (Fig. 19.13e, SF; it is omitted in Fig. 24.1b, for clarity). In both genera the ends of the basal bodies are covered by terminal caps, though

there are some small differences in structure. Two short, transversely striated fibres are present below the *x* roots.

The female gametes of *Pseudobryopsis* have also been investigated in some species ([1515]; Fig. 24.1c, d) and there are a number of differences from the flagellar apparatus of the male gametes. Thus, instead of the usual *x*–2–*x*–2 arrangement of roots, there is an *x*–3–*x*–3 arrangement, though *x* is 4, just as in the male gametes. Furthermore, the upper non-striated connective linking the basal bodies has two extensions, which overlie the 3-stranded roots, while the two short transversely striated fibres that lie beneath the *x* roots in the male gametes are missing in the female gametes. A proximal sheath, bearing a crescent-shaped structure, is appressed to the underside of the basal body. Thus, even within a single species there can be variations in the structure of the flagellar apparatus, reflecting functional differences between zoids of different types, here between the male and female gametes.

But that is not the end of the story. Further variation of the flagellar apparatus occurs within those species that produce stephanokont zoospores ([747]). In the life cycle of *Pseudobryopsis* the stephanokont zoids probably represent meiospores (see Fig. 24.7i, j, which illustrates the life cycle of the closely related genus *Bryopsis*). Each stephanokont cell possesses about 35 flagella, which emerge around the base of an apical dome. Corresponding to these are 35 basal bodies, connected by a non-striated upper ring (Fig. 24.2), which has a fibrous texture. This may be homologous with, and equivalent to, a large number of non-striated upper connectives, as found in the biflagellate gametes (Fig. 24.1), all fused together.

Each basal body is held in a socket-like structure, which in turn is connected by a short stalk to the non-striated ring. Appressed to and partially enclosing the inner ends of the basal bodies is a second, lower ring,

composed of amorphous material; this can perhaps be interpreted as the fused proximal sheaths of the female gametes (Fig. 24.1c, d). Four- and six-stranded microtubular roots extend out from between the basal bodies.

It is interesting to compare the flagellar apparatus of the stephanokont zoospore of *Pseudobryopsis* (class Bryopsidophyceae) with that of the superficially similar stephanokont zoospore formed by *Oedogonium* and its relatives (class Chlorophyceae): compare Fig. 21.30 with Fig. 24.2. The most obvious difference is in the structure of the upper ring connecting the whorl of basal bodies. In *Oedogonium* this has a distinct transverse striation, a feature considered characteristic of chlorophycean upper basal body connectives; in *Pseudobryopsis* there is no striation. It is thought, therefore, that the stephanokont type of zoid must have evolved at least twice, in two independent evolutionary lineages: once in the Chlorophyceae and once in the Bryopsidophyceae.

A variant of type VI mitosis (p. 419, character 4) has been shown to be present in the Bryopsidophyceae but only three species have been investigated. The closed type of mitosis found closely resembles that present in the Cladophorophyceae (Fig. 19.22 II: type VI mitosis); in both groups there is a prominent persistent spindle, which leads to a characteristic dumbbell shape of the nucleus at telophase (Fig. 24.3). In the example we illustrate (*Caulerpa*), mitosis is acentric, i.e. without centrioles (Fig. 24.3; [739]), but in *Pseudobryopsis* the early mitoses, leading to the formation of biflagellate gametes, are acentric, while later mitoses are centric. In centric mitosis pairs of centrioles are formed *de novo*, each one close to an interphase nucleus. During prophase the pair replicates and one daughter pair moves to the opposite pole of the spindle. Only at this stage do cleavage furrows appear and divide the multinucleate cytoplasm into uninucleate gametic units. Cytoplasmic vesicles and vacuoles are incorporated into the cleavage furrows, which seem to be guided in their growth by tangential arrays of microtubules associated with their edges. Thus, the centriolar pairs appear when they are needed, together with the MTOCs (microtubule organizing centres) associated with them, which take the form of amorphous masses of material surrounding the centrioles. They are involved in assembling the arrays of microtubules that guide the ingrowing cleavage furrows, and then in the production of the flagella and flagellar

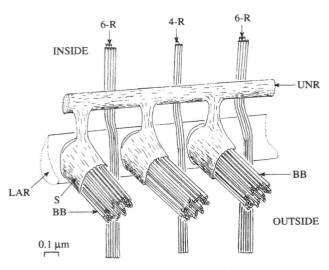

Figure 24.2. Part of the flagellar apparatus of the stephanokont zoospore of *Pseudobryopsis:* three-dimensional reconstruction, seen from the side. BB = basal body; LAR = lower amorphous ring; S = socket-like structure; UNR = upper non-striated ring, with fibrous texture; 4-R = four-stranded microtubular root; 6-R = six-stranded microtubular root. (Based on [747].)

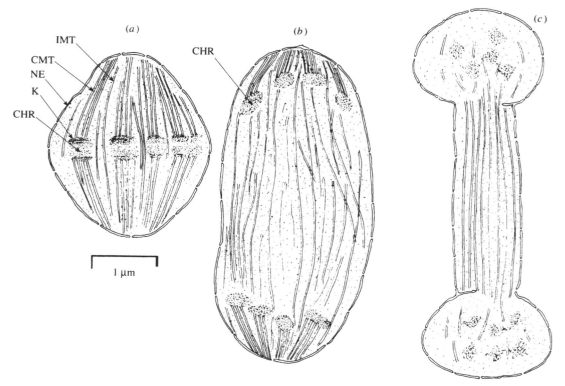

Figure 24.3. Closed mitosis in *Caulerpa*. (*a*) Metaphase. (*b*) Anaphase. (*c*) Dumbbell-shaped telophase configuration. CHR = chromosome; CMT = chromosomal spindle microtubule; IMT = interzonal spindle microtubule; K = (indistinct) kinetochore; NE = nuclear envelope. (Based on [739].)

apparatus in the gametes ([169, 1333]); it should be remembered that centrioles and basal bodies are essentially the same, and that they are required for the assembly of the flagellar axoneme (cf. p. 307).

The many small chloroplasts (Figs. 24.4*a*, 24.5*a*) are fusiform or ellipsoidal, and filled with lamellae (stacks) containing a variable number of thylakoids (Figs. 24.4*b*, 24.5*b*, *d*). **Homoplastidic** Bryopsidophyceae contain only one kind of plastid: chloroplasts. In some *Derbesia* species and in *Bryopsis* the chloroplasts contain pyrenoids (Fig. 24.4*a*, *b*), whose stroma is partitioned by several thylakoids (Fig. 24.4*c*). **Heteroplastidic** Bryopsidophyceae, such as *Udotea* (Fig. 24.5*a–c*) and *Caulerpa* (Fig. 24.5*d*, *e*) contain both chloroplasts and amyloplasts. As in vascular plants the amyloplasts are modified chloroplasts, specialized for starch storage. Both the chloroplasts and the amyloplasts, especially in young, growing regions

of the thallus, characteristically contain a 'thylakoid organizing body' at one end of the plastid (Figs. 24.5*b–e*, 24.6), which consists of concentrically arranged sets of double membranes. The formation of the thylakoids in young chloroplasts begins from these organizing bodies ([108, 736, 749, 750]). The presence of pyrenoids is something of an exception within the heteroplastidic group, but does occur, for instance, in *Caulerpa* chloroplasts (Fig. 24.5*d*; [1524]).

Another characteristic of the class Bryopsidophyceae is the occurrence of both siphonein and siphonoxanthin in the chloroplasts ([544]), as accessory photosynthetic pigments. Siphonoxanthin has been found on its own in isolated species of the Cladophorophyceae and Ulvophyceae (p. 337).

The Bryopsidophyceae exhibit vigorous cytoplasmic streaming, which occurs along an interconnected network of narrow lanes aligned parallel to the long

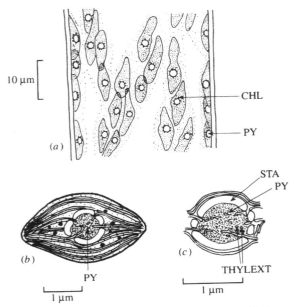

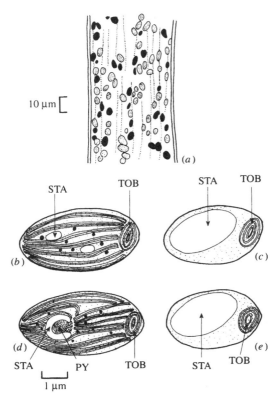

Figure 24.4. (a) *Derbesia:* detail of a cell as seen with the light microscope, showing the fusiform chloroplasts in the parietal cytoplasm. (b, c) *Bryopsis.* (b) Cross section of a fusiform chloroplast, based on EM observations. Note the stacks (lamellae) of thylakoids. (c) Cross section through a pyrenoid, showing several extensions of the thylakoids penetrating into the pyrenoid stroma. CHL = chloroplast; PY = pyrenoid; STA = starch shell around the pyrenoid; THYLEXT = extensions of the thylakoids within the pyrenoid. (a based on [412]; b, c on [750].)

Figure 24.5. Elliptical chloroplasts and amyloplasts in heteroplastidic members of the Bryopsidophyceae. (a) Part of a siphon of *Udotea*, as seen with the light microscope, showing chloroplasts and amyloplasts (stained dark violet with Lugol's iodine) in the parietal layer of cytoplasm. (b) Cross section through a chloroplast of *Udotea*. Note the stacks (lamellae) of thylakoids and the concentrically structured thylakoid organizing body. (c) Amyloplast of *Udotea*. (d) Cross section through a chloroplast of *Caulerpa;* note the reduced pyrenoid. (e) Amyloplast of *Caulerpa*. PY = pyrenoid; STA = starch; TOB = thylakoid-organizing body. (a based on [412]; b–e on [750].)

axis of the thallus. When the thalli are stained with fluorescent antibodies specific for tubulin and actin and then viewed with fluorescence microscopy, bundles of microtubules can be seen lying along the lanes of streaming, associated with actin filaments. Since actin filaments and microtubules are known to be involved in various types of cell movement – actin filaments in muscle contraction, for instance, and microtubules in flagellar bending – it is likely that the bundles of microtubules and actin filaments are responsible in some way for protoplasmic streaming in the Bryopsidophyceae. In *Bryopsis* (Fig. 24.7) fine bundles are present in the cortical cytoplasm (around the outside of the siphons) and chloroplasts move along them at speeds of up to 60 μm min^{-1}. In larger, coarser members of the class, such as *Caulerpa* (Fig. 24.16), the axial bundles combine to form pathways

for mass transport in the centre of the cell, which can be seen even with the naked eye. Various cell inclusions move along the bundles, but especially amyloplasts (Fig. 24.5c, e). Both the chloroplasts and the amyloplasts slide along with their flat ventral sides appressed to the bundles, not their more convex dorsal sides ([1188, 1190, 1193, 1194]).

Cytoplasmic streaming also occurs in the large multinucleate cells of the Dasycladophyceae (p. 436) and Charophyceae (p. 474), and also in the cells of

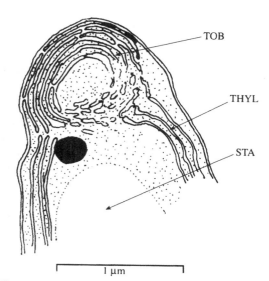

Figure 24.6. Section through part of a young plastid of *Halimeda,* based on EM observations. Note the thylakoid organizing body. STA = starch; THYL = thylakoid; TOB = thylakoid organizing body. (Based on [108].)

higher plants. It is absent, however, in the multinucleate cells both of the Cladophorophyceae (p. 409) and of certain Ulvophyceae (e.g. *Acrosiphonia*).

We interpret the **life cycles** of most Bryopsidales as being **haplontic**. The only diploid nucleus is probably the giant zygote nucleus present in the zygote, which is a microscopic structure and either filamentous (Fig. 24.7*g*) or spherical (Fig. 24.11*h*). The zygote is not a resting stage of the type found in the class Chlorophyceae, however, where hypnozygotes with thick, resistant, sculptured walls are formed (e.g. Figs. 21.1*f*, 21.9*d*, p. 351). In at least one genus (*Derbesia*; Fig. 24.8) the fused male and female gametes develop into a heterokaryotic sporophyte stage, in which karyogamy is 'postponed', occurring in the young meiosporangia. The zygotic nuclei resulting from karyogamy, and lying within the meiosporangia, are the only diploid nuclei found in *Derbesia*, and so the life cycle can again be characterized as haplontic, though with the intercalation of a heterokaryotic sporophyte stage. It must be admitted, however, that in most Bryopsidales evidence for ploidy levels and the site of meiosis is scanty, so that the general interpretation of life cycles in the Bryopsidophyceae that we have given remains somewhat speculative.

Further discussion will be found in the sections devoted to the life cycles of the various genera (see below).

Unlike the orders Codiolales and Ulvales of the Ulvophyceae, members of the class Bryopsidophyceae exhibit only one level of organization: **siphonous** organization. Each plant consists essentially of a single giant cell, containing a huge central vacuole with a thin layer of cytoplasm around it. The cell is multinucleate: it is a **coenocyte**. Parts of the coenocyte, however, are sometimes sealed off by plugs of cell wall material, as occurs for instance during the formation of the gametangia in *Bryopsis* (Fig. 24.7*a, b*) and *Codium* (Fig. 24.10*b*), and during the formation of the sporangia in *Derbesia* (Fig. 24.8*g, k*).

Wounds too can be sealed off by plugs, this having been observed in the genera *Bryopsis*, *Derbesia* and *Caulerpa* ([170, 335, 757, 1187]). The wound reaction of the Bryopsidophyceae is quite similar to that of the Cladophorophyceae, except that it occurs much more quickly than in the Cladophorophyceae (within seconds instead of within minutes). In both classes the wound is closed first by a contracting network of actin filaments (p. 412). Then, in the Bryopsidophyceae, plug precursors are squeezed from the central vacuole (like toothpaste from a tube) and cling to the cell wall around the margins of the injured section, where they polymerize to form a plug. Later, a new cell wall is deposited, up against the inside of the plug ([1191]). Such reactions are important, of course, in the protection of the plants against injuries caused by grazing animals, sand scour, surf, etc.

The number of genera included in the Bryopsidophyceae is about 25 and the number of species around 150 ([1630]). The Bryopsidophyceae are almost all marine and most of the genera are tropical or extend from the tropics into warm temperate waters. The marine genera *Caulerpa* (Fig. 24.15*c–e*), *Udotea* (Fig. 24.11*a, a'*), *Penicillus* (Fig. 24.12) and *Halimeda* (Fig. 24.15*a, b*), for instance, together with some related genera, are predominantly tropical. There is only one freshwater genus, *Dichotomosiphon* ([100]), and this is rare. *Dichotomosiphon* is the only oogamous representative among the Bryopsidales, but its position within the order is confirmed by the 11 o'clock – 5 o'clock configuration of the flagellar apparatus in the male gametes ([1222]).

The Bryopsidophyceae includes not only species that grow attached to rocky substrata by means of rhizoids, but also forms that grow in sand, anchored by creeping 'rhizomes' (e.g. *Caulerpa*, Fig. 24.15*c–e*), bulbous bases (e.g. *Halimeda*, Fig. 22.15*a*) or both (e.g. *Penicillus*, Fig. 24.12).

Some species of *Penicillus* and *Udotea*, and almost all species of *Halimeda* are encrusted with aragonite crystals (a form of calcium carbonate) and are among the most important contributors to calcium carbonate deposition on tropical reefs. Other important contributors are the reef corals (p. 276) and coralline algae (p. 83).

Order Bryopsidales [685]

1 The thalli are homoplastidic, i.e. chloroplasts are present, but not amyloplasts (Fig. 24.4).

2 Concentrically organized 'thylakoid organizing bodies' are absent from the chloroplasts (Fig. 24.4*b*; cf. Fig. 24.5*b–e*).

3 The production of the reproductive zoids is non-holocarpic, occurring within special, delimited zones within the thallus (gametangia or sporangia): it does not involve the whole thallus (Figs. 24.7–24.10).

4 Many, though not all, members of the class produce stephanokont zoids at some stage in their life cycle (Figs. 24.7*i, j*, 24.8*l, m*, 24.9*h, i*).

5 The main cell wall polysaccharides are mannan, xylan and cellulose.

Examples of the order Bryopsidales

Bryopsis (Fig. 24.7)

In *Bryopsis*, upright siphons bearing fairly regularly pinnate systems of branches arise from prostrate, tube-like siphons, which creep over the substratum. The pinnae grow to around 10 cm high. The protoplasm forms a thin peripheral layer within the siphons and contains nuclei towards the outside and discoid chloroplasts towards the inside. The chloroplasts usually contain pyrenoids. The centre of the tube-like siphon is occupied by a large vacuole. Small side branches, destined to be gametangia, become separated from the main axis, but only some considerable time after their initiation.

Two *Bryopsis* species are commonly found on the Atlantic coasts of Europe; one of them, *B. plumosa*, will be described in more detail. In this species the main axes bear two opposite rows of short side branches and so resemble tiny feathers (Fig. 24.7*a, b, m, n*).

Fig. 24.7 shows the life cycle of *Bryopsis plumosa* ([700, 1279, 1489, 1490, 1491]).

1 There are female plants of *Bryopsis plumosa* and also male plants. In the female plants (Fig. 24.7*a*), short side branches become transformed into dark-green female gametangia, whose contents are liberated in the form of relatively large biflagellate gametes (Fig. 24.7*c*). Male plants (Fig. 24.7*b*) produce gametes in a similar way, except that the male gametangia are yellowish and bleached in appearance and the biflagellate male gametes (Fig. 24.7*d*) are relatively small and pale.

2 If male and female gametes come into contact, they may copulate (Fig. 24.7*e*) and form a planozygote. This attaches itself to a substratum and grows (Fig. 24.7*f*).

3 In the course of two to three months the zygote grows slowly into a tiny branched filament, which initially contains an enormous nucleus with a conspicuous, elongate nucleolus (Fig. 24.7*g*). In its ultrastructure this nucleus greatly resembles the giant zygotic nucleus of the Dasycladophyceae (Figs. 25.3–25.5). Zygotes grown in the laboratory in fresh culture medium can develop further in one of two different ways (pathways A and B in Fig. 24.7): material from Brittany was found to follow pathway A, while plants from the Dutch coast followed pathway B.

4 In developmental pathway A the giant nucleus divides many times to give a large number of small nuclei and then the zygotic cell itself cleaves up into stephanokont zoospores (Fig. 24.7*h–j*). Meiosis probably takes place during the formation of the zoospores. This has not been confirmed cytologically but seems almost certain, since about half of the zoospores grow up into male plants (Fig. 24.7*n, b*) and half into female plants (Fig. 24.7*m, a*) (haplogenotypic sex determination).

5 In developmental pathway B, too, the giant nucleus gives rise to many small nuclei. Here, however, the branched filament gives rise

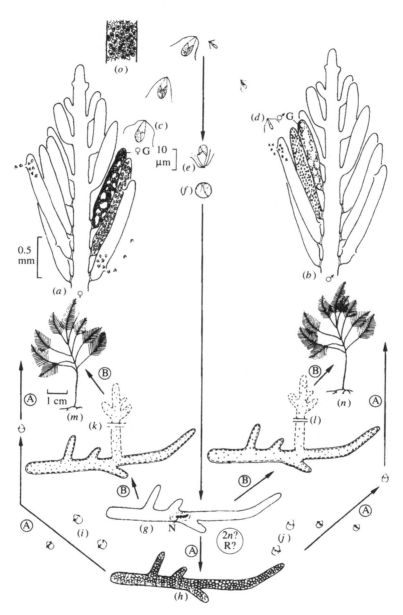

Figure 24.7. The life cycle of *Bryopsis plumosa*. There are two possible pathways (A and B): for explanation, see text. (*a, b*) The feather-like tips (pinnae) of female (*a*) and male (*b*) plants. (*c, d*) Biflagellate female and male gametes. (*e*) Anisogamous copulation. (*f*) Young zygote. (*g*) Filamentous zygote, containing a giant nucleus. (*h*) The contents of the filamentous zygote divide up into stephanokont zoospores. (*i, j*) Stephanokont zoospores. (*k, l*) Buds formed by the zygote develop directly into new gametophytes; the mannan–glucan (cellulose) wall of the zygote is indicated by a continuous line, the xylan–cellulose wall of the gametophyte by a dashed line. (*m, n*) Full-grown, mature gametophytes. (*o*) Detail of the multi-nucleate vegetative gametophyte (*a, b*), showing the chloroplasts and pyrenoids. G = gametangium; N = giant nucleus within the zygote. (Based on [1494].)

directly to a new *Bryopsis* plant (Fig. 24.7*k, l*). About half of the *Bryopsis* plants produced in this way are male and half female, so that meiosis must presumably take place before the new *Bryopsis* plants begin to develop from the filamentous zygote.

In developmental pathway B the small creeping filaments are interpreted as zygotes that have lost the ability to produce zoospores. Material of *Bryopsis plumosa* from the Mediterranean can develop along either of the two pathways outlined above.

The life cycle can be summarized as follows. *Bryopsis plumosa* is dioecious (heterothallic). It exhibits a haplontic life cycle and anisogamy, the gametes being biflagellate. The zygote is filamentous, containing a giant nucleus, and can either form stephanokont zoospores or grow directly into a new *Bryopsis* plant. The giant zygote nucleus is probably the only diploid nucleus in the life cycle. If, on the other hand, the tiny filamentous zygote is interpreted as a sporophyte (e.g. see [694, 703, 1750]), then the life cycle would be strongly heteromorphic and diplohaplontic.

Traditionally, *Bryopsis* and other members of the Bryopsidophyceae have been interpreted as diplonts, with gametic meiosis. This view was based on old karyological studies ([1594, 1595, 1596, 1597, 1598, 1599, 1900, 1936]), which are now considered unreliable ([700, 1490, 1492, 1750]). A more recent paper supporting the idea of gametic meiosis in the Bryopsidales ([833]) is also unconvincing. Here line drawings are presented of nuclei supposed to be undergoing meiosis and mitosis, but the nuclei measure 2.1 – 2.7 µm in diameter and individual chromosomes are about 0.15 – 0.3 µm, which is at the limit of resolution of the light microscope. It is unlikely that typical meiotic configurations like diakinesis could be recognized reliably with such tiny nuclei and chromosomes, especially since it is thought that the meiotic nuclei are few in number and dispersed among a much larger number of mitotic nuclei.

Division has been observed in the giant zygote nuclei only once, the stage observed being prophase; unfortunately, it is very difficult or impossible to know whether this was prophase of mitosis or of meiosis ([1279]).

A similar uncertainty existed until recently concerning the timing of meiosis in the Dasycladophyceae, which were also thought originally to have gametic meiosis. It was only after estimates were made of the amount of DNA in the nucleus at various stages of the life cycle that it was finally established that meiosis takes place in the giant zygote nucleus. The estimates were obtained by treating plants of the Dasycladophyceae with Feulgen reagent, which is specific for DNA, followed by microspectrophotometric scanning of the stained nuclei. The giant zygote nucleus was the only nucleus that appeared to be diploid, all the other nuclei tested being haploid ([875]; p. 443). The same method has recently been used to demonstrate that the vegetative nuclei of the gametophyte and the gamete nuclei of *Pseudobryopsis* (a close relative of *Bryopsis*) contain the same amounts of DNA, thus precluding the possibility of gametic meiosis; this leaves the giant zygote nucleus as the only possible site for meiosis ([1582]).

A second species of *Bryopsis* occurring in Europe, *Bryopsis hypnoides*, possesses the same life cycle as *Bryopsis plumosa*, except that it is monoecious (homothallic); the male and female gametes are formed on the same plant. The zygote has been found to be able to produce gametes (in material from Newfoundland), or it can grow directly into a new *Bryopsis* plant ([50]).

Interestingly, the cell walls of the gametophytes have a different chemical composition from those of the zygote. In the gametophytes the principal polysaccharide in the structural part of the cell wall is a xylan; cellulose is also present ([762, 1491, 1494]). The structural fraction of the zygote wall, on the other hand, consists predominantly of mannan. This difference is reflected in staining reactions: the cellulose of the gametophyte walls can be stained with chlor-zinc-iodine or with the vital stain Congo red, whereas the zygote wall remains unstained. Even so, the cell walls of the zygote do contain cellulose (or at least a glucan), though apparently in a form that does not stain with chlor-zinc-iodine or Congo red ([763]). Where a zygote develops directly into a gametophyte instead of producing zoospores, the gametophyte walls acquire a cellulose staining-reaction: an additional wall layer is deposited against the inner side of the zygote wall, and it is this that is stained. The extra layer is indicated by a dashed line in Fig. 24.7*k, l*.

Pseudobryopsis

This genus has feather-like thalli and is closely related to *Bryopsis*, from which it is distinguished by having gametangia that are shorter than the vegetative branchlets. Its life cycle is like that of *Bryopsis*. The tiny filamentous zygote can either produce stephanokont zoospores ([860, 1334]) or bud off gametophytes directly ([1281]). The ultrastructure of the male and female gametes, and of the stephanokont zoospores, has already been described (p. 419, and Figs. 24.1, 24.2).

Derbesia marina (Fig. 24.8)

The thallus of *Derbesia* consists of a prostrate system of tubes or siphons (p. 425) creeping across the substratum, from which there arise erect, branching tubes about 1–10 cm high. The older side branches are cut off at their bases by plugs of material. The protoplasm forms a thin peripheral lining to the siphons and contains numerous nuclei towards the outside, with discoid chloroplasts beneath. There are no pyrenoids in the chloroplasts, except in *Derbesia tenuissima* (Fig. 24.4*a*). The centre of each siphon is occupied by large vacuoles. *Derbesia marina* is a cosmopolitan species of temperate coasts.

Fig. 24.8 summarizes the life cycle of *Derbesia marina* ([722, 723, 879, 1069, 1279]). The plant generally known as *Derbesia marina* (Fig. 24.8*g*) has proved to be a sporophyte, the corresponding gametophyte being a small vesicular structure, up to 5 mm or so in diameter. The vesicles were known before the life cycle was understood, and were named separately, as '*Halicystis ovalis*' (Fig. 24.8*a, b*). As in the tubular thalli of *Derbesia*, the protoplasm forms a thin parietal layer, containing numerous chloroplasts (without pyrenoids) and nuclei; in the centre there is a large vacuole, containing cell sap.

The gametophytes ('*Halicystis* plants') can be male or female. Fertile male vesicles (Fig. 24.8*a*) bear pale yellow-green patches of gametes; the pallid male gametes, which are biflagellate (Fig. 24.8*c*), are expelled through one to several pores. Fertile female vesicles (Fig. 24.8*b*) produce dark green parietal patches of gametes. The female gametes are again biflagellate, contain several chloroplasts, and are released in the same way as the male gametes, through one to several pores (Fig. 24.8*b*).

Copulation between a male and a female gamete (Fig. 24.8*e*) results in the formation of a binucleate cell containing one male and one female nucleus (Fig. 24.8*f*). These nuclei do not immediately fuse: in other words, plasmogamy occurs but not karyogamy. The fusion cell grows into a heterokaryotic (dikaryotic)

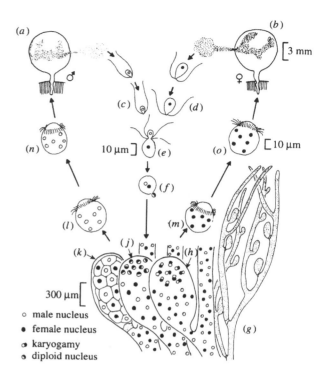

Figure 24.8. The life cycle of *Derbesia marina*. (*a*, *b*) Male (*a*) and female (*b*) gametophytes (the '*Halicystis*' phase). (*c*) Biflagellate male gametes. (*d*) Biflagellate female gametes. (*e*) Anisogamous copulation. (*f*) Heterokaryon (dikaryon) produced after fusion of the cells (cytogamy, plasmogamy). (*g*) Sporophyte (the '*Derbesia*' phase). (*h*) Detail of the heterokaryotic sporophyte with a young sporangium. Towards the apex of the young sporangium, fusion (karyogamy) is occurring between male and female nuclei. (*j*) As (*h*), but with diploid, zygotic nuclei towards the apex of the sporangium. (*k*) Detail of a mature sporangium, following meiosis. Half of the young meiospores contain male nuclei, while the other half contain female nuclei. Note the basal plug (stippled) that separates the sporangium from the vegetative part of the thallus. (*l*, *n*) Multinucleate stephanokont meiospores containing male nuclei. (*m*, *o*) Multinucleate stephanokont meiospores containing female nuclei. (Based on [359].)

sporophyte of the '*Derbesia*' type, with numerous haploid male and female nuclei (Fig. 24.8*h*; [358, 359, 1582, 1583, 1584]). The fertile sporophyte bears pear-shaped sporangia (Fig. 24.8*g–k*) and it is in these that the 'postponed' karyogamy finally takes place; a few male and female nuclei fuse in the young sporangia, producing diploid zygote nuclei that immediately undergo meiosis. Stephanokont meiospores are then formed (Fig. 24.8*j, k*), each containing several nuclei (Fig. 24.8*l, m*). About half of the meiospores develop into male gametophytes and half into female gametophytes.

The ploidy of the nuclei in the gametophytes and sporophytes has been determined by estimating the DNA content, using Feulgen stain and microspectrophotometry. This method allows diploid nuclei to be distinguished from haploid nuclei and demonstrates that the only diploid nuclei in *Derbesia* are the fusion nuclei present in the young sporangia. A comparable method is to stain the nuclei with a DNA-specific fluorescent dye and determine the DNA content by microfluorometry ([359, 1583]).

In summary, the life cycle of *Derbesia marina* can be characterized as being haplontic, with the intercalation of a heterokaryotic (dikaryotic) vegetative sporophyte and the postponement of karyogamy to the meiosporangia. Only the zygote nuclei are diploid. This type of life cycle is very similar to that found in the Ascomycetes and Basidiomycetes (cf. Fig. 1.4), the two most important groups of fungi. *Derbesia* is the only known example of an alga with a heterokaryotic stage in its life cycle. *Derbesia tenuissima*, another species found on south European coasts, has been shown to have exactly the same type of life history as *Derbesia marina* ([359, 407, 1493, 1934]).

Derbesia resembles *Bryopsis* in that the cell walls of the gametophytes and sporophytes differ in their chemical composition. As in *Bryopsis*, the most important polysaccharide in the structural fraction of the gametophyte cell walls is a xylan, with cellulose also present. The predominant polysaccharide in the equivalent part of the sporophyte walls (or of the zygote walls in *Bryopsis*) is a mannan, with very little cellulose present ([762, 763, 1870]).

Unmated female gametes of *Derbesia* can grow into haploid, homokaryotic sporophytes, in which all the haploid nuclei have identical genomes. These parthenogenetically produced sporophytes have mannan as the main wall polysaccharide, not xylan, and so it is clear that the formation of a heterokaryon is not a necessary prerequisite for the change-over in morphology and cell wall composition during the gametophyte–sporophyte transition ([763]).

The genera *Bryopsis* and *Derbesia* used to be classified in different families, suborders, orders ([220, 1527]) or

even classes, since their life cycles were thought to be quite different. As we have noted, however, recent investigations have shown that these genera are closely related. In both, the gametophyte cell walls contain xylan and cellulose, while in the sporophyte of *Derbesia* and the zygote of *Bryopsis* the walls are composed of mannan, with a little cellulose. In addition both genera produce stephanokont meiospores.

A close relationship between *Derbesia* and *Bryopsis* is made even more likely by the existence of a transitional form, *Bryopsidella* (= *Derbesia*) *neglecta*. After meiosis this forms stephanokont zoospores ([1492]), which grow into gametophytes known originally as '*Bryopsis halymeniae*' ([770, 771]; Fig. 24.9). The sporophyte of *Bryopsidella* is diploid, not heterokaryotic, and so its life cycle is **diplohaplontic** ([185]). *Bryopsidella neglecta* is a Mediterranean species, with the gametophytes epiphytic on the red alga *Halymenia*.

Codium (Fig. 24.10)

Codium plants are branched and can grow more than a metre long. The thalli are cylindrical or form rather irregular masses, and are spongy, consisting of interwoven coenocytic (multinucleate) tubes subdivided into compartments by rings of cell wall material. The centre of the thallus is composed of a dense mass of intertwined tubes, which are almost colourless. Outside this the siphons are dilated into large, green, club-shaped compartments (utricles), which contain numerous chloroplasts and form a palisade-like layer around the periphery of the thallus. *Codium* is homoplastidic and the chloroplasts do not contain pyrenoids ([750]). The structural fraction of the cell wall consists mainly of a mannan (β-1,4-linked D-mannose), while the amorphous matrix fraction is for the most part made of sulphated arabinogalactan ([1396]).

There are around 50 known species of *Codium*, which occur on rocky coasts in tropical and temperate seas.

The gametangia are club-shaped (Fig. 24.10*b*) and arise as evaginations from the utricles. The male gametangia are yellowish, their contents dividing up into tiny biflagellate male gametes (Fig. 24.10*d*). The female gametangia, on the other hand, are dark green and divide up into large biflagellate gametes, each containing many chloroplasts (Fig. 24.10*c*). *Codium* exhibits marked anisogamy (Fig. 24.10*e*).

After attachment, the zygote grows into a filamen-

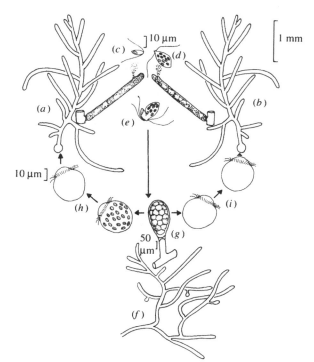

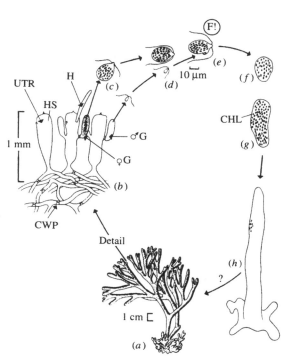

Figure 24.9. The life cycle of *Bryopsidella neglecta*. (*a, b*) Male (*a*) and female (*b*) gametophytes (the '*Bryopsis halymeniae*' phase). (*c*) Male gamete. (*d*) Female gamete. (*e*) Anisogamous copulation. (*f*) Sporophyte (the '*Derbesia neglecta*' phase). (*g*) Meiosporangium. (*h, i*) Stephanokont meiospores. (Based on [1494].)

Figure 24.10. The life cycle of *Codium fragile*. (*a*) Full-grown plant. (*b*) Detail of a transverse section through one of the finger-like branches of the thallus. (*c–e*) Biflagellate male and female gametes and anisogamous copulation. (*f*) Zygote. (*g, h*) Development of the filamentous germling. CHL = chloroplast (without pyrenoids); CWP = plug of cell wall material; F! = fertilization; G = gametangium; H = hair; HS = hair scar; UTR = utricle, containing chloroplasts.

tous germling (Fig. 24.10*h*) comparable, perhaps, with the filamentous zygote of *Bryopsis*. *Codium* has traditionally been considered to have gametic meiosis, but the evidence for this is not convincing ([822]). It has never yet been possible to obtain full-grown plants in culture and so the arrow from (*h*) to (*a*) in Fig. 24.10 is marked with a question-mark.

Some populations of *Codium* only produce large biflagellate zoids, which germinate directly without copulating. These are interpreted as female gametes that develop parthenogenetically ([281, 283, 302, 410]).

The gametophytes consist at first of an undifferentiated tangle of siphons. Later this gives rise to the interwoven siphons of the adult frond, providing a contrast to the equally 'multiaxial' thalli of *Penicillus* (order Halimedales; Fig. 24.12), where the upright frond begins as a discrete uniaxial primordium, formed by the swollen tip of a stolon (Fig. 24.13; [456]).

Order Halimedales ([685])

1 The thalli are heteroplastidic: chloroplasts and amyloplasts are both present (Fig. 24.5).

2 Concentrically-structured 'thylakoid organizing bodies' are present in the chloroplasts and amyloplasts (Fig. 24.5*b–e*).

3 The production of reproductive zoids (gametes) is holocarpic. The fertile thallus is entirely transformed into gametes, so that all that is left after gamete release is a dead 'ghost', composed of empty cell walls.

4 Stephanokont zoids are never produced at any stage in the life cycle.

5 The main cell wall polysaccharide is xylan, with little or no cellulose.

Udotea (Fig. 24.11)

Udotea, like *Codium*, consists of intertwined siphons. The fan-shaped thalli are heteroplastidic, containing both chloroplasts and amyloplasts (Fig. 24.5a–c). The most important polysaccharide in the cell wall is a xylan. There are *ca.* 15 species, which are to be found in tropical and subtropical seas.

Reproduction was first observed comparatively recently, in the Mediterranean species *Udotea petiolata* ([1161, 1164]). This species is holocarpic. The contents of the whole plant divide up either into small male gametes or into large female gametes. The gametes are biflagellate and are liberated through papillae at the edge of the fan (Fig. 24.11b, b'). The young zygote grows into a uninucleate, spherical plant (the protosphere), 50–90 μm in diameter. The fully-grown protosphere contains a large primary zygote nucleus (Fig. 24.11g, h) and is not heteroplastidic but homoplastidic; the numerous parietal chloroplasts are rounded and contain one or two starch grains. After division of the primary nucleus, however, the protosphere becomes heteroplastidic. Amyloplasts appear and the chloroplasts become more elongate.

The protosphere now gives rise to an erect filament (Fig. 24.11i) and a prostrate filament. The erect one develops into a small plant, up to 1.5 cm high, composed of dichotomously branched siphons (Fig. 24.11k, k'), with a constriction at the base of each dichotomy. These small plants do not differentiate into fan-like fronds and similar dichotomously branched plants continue to be formed from the stolons, even in the adult thallus.

At a later stage (in culture, 16 months after the germination of the protosphere), typical *Udotea* plants begin to develop from the prostrate filaments. Each *Udotea* plant starts as a small, swollen, uniaxial primordium, which soon gives rise to upwardly and downwardly growing lateral siphons (Figs 24.11l, l'). Then the primordium gradually develops the complex multiaxial structure of the fan-like *Udotea* frond (see also *Penicillus*).

The protosphere stage of *Udotea* is probably homologous to the filamentous zygote stage in *Bryopsis*. Both contain one large primary nucleus, which is probably the only diploid nucleus in the life cycle. The first division of this nucleus may be mei-

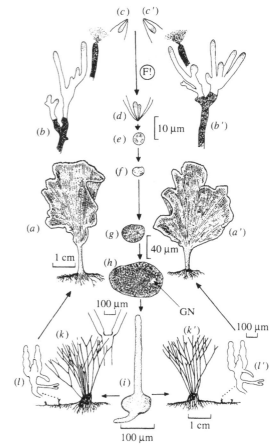

Figure 24.11. The life cycle of *Udotea petiolata*. (*a, a'*) Fan-shaped gametophytes. (*b, b'*) Margins of the holocarpic thalli, showing the release of gametes through exit papillae. (*c*) Biflagellate male gamete. (*c'*) Biflagellate female gamete. (*d*) Anisogamous copulation. (*e*) Young zygote. (*f–h*) Development of the zygote into a large spherical structure (the protosphere), which contains a conspicuous primary nucleus. (*i*) Following division of the zygote nucleus, the protosphere gives rise to an erect siphon (filament) and a prostrate siphon. (*k, k'*) Development of dichotomously branching plants from the protosphere. (*l, l'*) Initiation of fan-shaped fronds from special swollen primordia, which develop on the stolons (prostrate siphons) produced by the protosphere. F! = fertilization; GN = giant zygotic nucleus of the protosphere. (Based on [1164].)

otic, although karyological evidence is as yet lacking (see also p. 430). If so, the protosphere should be considered perhaps as a zygote that has lost the capacity to produce meiospores, the gametophytes being budded off instead from the zygote stage, following vegetative meiosis. This is certainly what happens in the related class Dasycladophyceae (p. 443). Vegetative propagation takes place as the stolons grow across the substratum, giving off new upright fronds.

In several *Udotea* species the thallus is encrusted with calcium carbonate, in the form of needle-like crystals of aragonite. These are deposited outside the cell walls, in the interstices between the tightly interwoven siphons ([109]). Photosynthetic CO_2 uptake from the interstices is thought to result in a rise in pH, and hence in the concentration of carbonate ions, due to the slow diffusion of CO_2 across the outer walls of the tissue. The rise in carbonate ion concentration in turn brings about calcium carbonate precipitation.

Penicillus (Fig. 24.12)

The thallus consists of a simple stalk, bearing a brush-like head of dichotomizing siphons. The stalk has a multiaxial construction and is composed of tightly interwoven, parallel siphons (Fig. 24.12*b*). The brush-like plants develop from small swollen primordia, which are uniaxial and arise from creeping stolons (Fig. 24.12*d–f*). Upwardly and downwardly growing lateral siphons grow out from the primordium and in their turn give off new laterals, in this way gradually producing the multiaxial construction of the adult plant (Fig. 24.13; [456, 1164]).

The sexual reproduction of *Penicillus* is similar to that of *Udotea* ([1164]). Vegetative multiplication is brought about by the growth of stolons, which creep through the surface of sediments, giving rise at intervals to new upright plants (Fig. 24.12).

Penicillus plants are lightly encrusted with calcium carbonate, in the form of needles of aragonite ([109]). There are about five species of *Penicillus*. They occur in tropical seas, for instance in lagoons, where they live anchored in the sandy sediments by bulbous bases composed of branched, rhizoidal siphons (Fig. 24.12*g, h*).

Halimeda (Figs. 24.14, 24.15*a, b*)

In the structure of its thalli, *Halimeda* resembles *Penicillus*. There is an inner tissue of coenocytic hyphae, which to the outside bear utricles containing numerous chloroplasts (Fig. 24.14*c*). During the night the chloroplasts are withdrawn from the utricles into the medullary filaments deep within the calcium car-

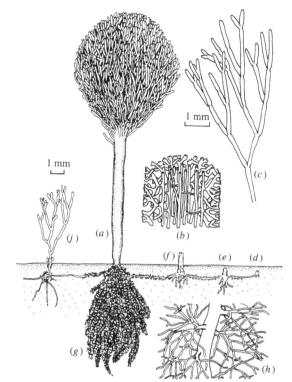

Figure 24.12. *Penicillus capitatus*. (*a*) Adult plant composed of a multiaxial stipe, which bears a brush-like tuft of dichotomous siphons. (*b*) Structure of the multiaxial stipe. (*c*) Detail of the brush-like part of the thallus, showing the dichotomously branching siphons. (*d–f*) Progressively later stages in the development of erect plant primordia. (*g*) The clustered rhizoidal siphons that anchor the adult plant in the sediment. (*h*) Detail of the rhizoidal system shown in (*g*). (*j*) An undifferentiated plant, consisting of dichotomous siphons, sprouting from a prostrate siphon (stolon). (Based on [456].)

bonate skeleton. This probably helps to protect them from nocturnal grazers. The chloroplasts move in tracks, along the microtubules responsible for protoplasmic streaming (cf. p. 424; [339]).

Each *Halimeda* plant consists of a great many heart- or kidney-shaped segments and can grow several decimetres high. The segments can be somewhat flattened and are heavily encrusted with calcium carbonate, in the form of needle-like crystals of aragonite ([109, 684]), except at the junction with neighbouring segments, where they remain uncalcified, allowing the thallus to bend.

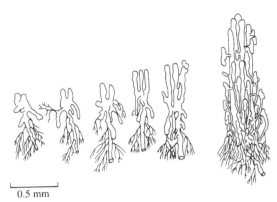

Figure 24.13. *Penicillus capitatus.* Stages in the development of the plant primordium. Note the progressive change from uniaxial to multiaxial construction as upwardly and downwardly growing siphons sprout from the existing structure. (Based on [1164].)

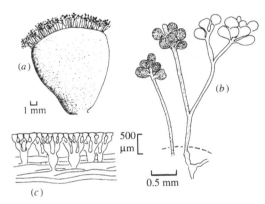

Figure 24.14. *Halimeda.* (*a*) Fertile segment, bearing a fringe of stalked gametangial branches. (*b*) Detail of (*a*), showing stalked bunches of gametangia. (*c*) Section through the cortex, which consists of tightly appressed vesicles. (*a* based on [684]; *b* on [1164]; *c* on [683].)

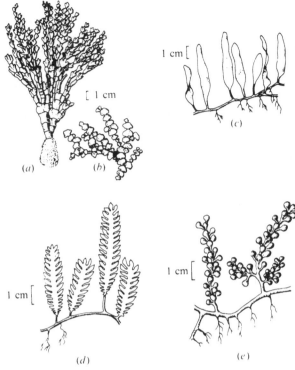

Figure 24.15. (*a*) *Halimeda incrassata.* (*b*) *Halimeda opuntia.* (*c*) *Caulerpa prolifera.* (*d*) *Caulerpa mexicana.* (*e*) *Caulerpa racemosa.* (*a–c* based on [1764]; *d, e* on [1826].)

The structural fraction of the *Halimeda* cell wall consists predominantly of a β-1,3-linked xylan, as in the cell walls of *Caulerpa*, *Udotea*, and the gametophytes of *Bryopsis* ([1396]).

The 30 or so species of *Halimeda* are marine and to be found on tropical and subtropical coasts ([683, 684]). Certain species grow so luxuriantly in tropical lagoons that the sediments are composed largely of dead *Halimeda* plants, forming a calcareous sand. Indeed, tropical reef systems, such as atolls, consist to a great extent of *Halimeda* sand, laid down over the course of their geological history. Other important contributors to reef structure are the reef corals and crustose coralline algae (p. 52); these form the solid framework of the reef ([684]). As an adaptation to life in lagoons, several species have a conspicuous bulbous base (Fig. 24.15*a*), which anchors the plant in the sandy bottom.

Halimeda is anisogamous, the male and female gametes being borne on different plants. The gametangia are produced in stalked bunches in a fringe along the upper margins of the segments (Fig. 24.14*a, b*; [227, 409, 684, 1164]). *Halimeda* is holocarpic and after the gametes have been released only a 'ghost' thallus remains, consisting of the calcium carbonate-encrusted cell walls. The zygote develops first into a spherical plant, the protosphere, which contains a large primary nucleus. The protosphere then produces filaments, from which new *Halimeda* plants arise. The life cycle of *Halimeda* is thus identical to that of *Udotea* (Fig. 24.11) and, again as in *Udotea*, vegetative propagation takes place via stolons ([684]).

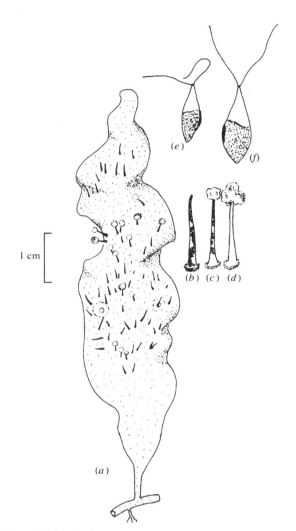

Figure 24.16. *Caulerpa prolifera:* sexual reproduction. (*a*)
Blade like portion of thallus, with numerous exit
papillae through which the gametes are released.
(*b–d*) Exit papillae at three different stages of gamete
discharge. (*e, f*) Anisogametes. (Based on [464].)

Caulerpa (Figs. 24.15*c–e*, 24.16)

This alga consists of creeping tube-like stolons, from
which there arise upright photosynthetic 'shoots',
these being very varied in form: leaf-like, feathery,
knobbly, etc. The stolons are anchored by bundles of
rhizoids. Each plant, which can grow to several
decimetres high and is thus comparable in size to
small herbaceous angiosperms, consists of a single
immense cell, which is multinucleate and contains one
to several central vacuoles and a thin peripheral layer
of protoplasm. Chloroplasts and amyloplasts (specialized for starch accumulation) lie in the peripheral protoplasm together with the nuclei, *Caulerpa* thus being
heteroplastidic (Fig. 24.5*d, e*).

The form of the giant cell is supported and maintained by numerous bars of cell wall material (trabeculae), which traverse the cell lumen from wall to wall.
The structural fraction of the *Caulerpa* wall consists
predominantly of a β-1,3-linked xylan, which probably forms microfibrils. The xylan fibrils seem to be
embedded in a β-1,3-glucan matrix ([756, 1396]).

All *Caulerpa* species are marine and occur in tropical and subtropical regions; there are about 60 of them.
In many species the stolons grow through the surface
layers of sandy or muddy sediments, the plants forming dense swards on the bottom of tropical lagoons.
Other species creep over rocks.

The erect parts of the thallus can produce biflagellate anisogametes, which are liberated through papillae ([1658]). *Caulerpa* is holocarpic and after the gametes
(Fig. 24.16) have been released only the empty cell
walls remain. The young zygote develops into a spherical structure (protosphere), containing a large primary zygote nucleus. Then multinucleate filaments
sprout from the protosphere and branch, giving rise to
new *Caulerpa* fronds ([371, 1443]). In short, the life cycle
of *Caulerpa* is of the *Udotea* type (Fig. 24.11; [1164]).

25

Chlorophyta: Class 6. Dasycladophyceae

The Dasycladophyceae contains only one order, the Dasycladales.

The principal characteristics of the Dasycladophyceae

1 The thalli are siphonous. Each full-grown plant is a single giant, multinucleate cell, containing a thin parietal layer of cytoplasm and a huge central vacuole. Its architecture is highly characteristic, consisting of a central axis bearing whorls of determinate laterals (laterals of limited growth). Most Dasycladales are encrusted with calcium carbonate (Figs. 25.1, 25.7, 25.8).

2 The principal polysaccharide in the fibrillar, structural fraction of the cell wall is a β-1,4-linked mannan, but cellulose is the dominant component in the walls of the gametangial cysts [649, 858, 1295].

3 The reproductive zoids (gametes) have two flagella and have a cruciate, 11 o'clock – 5 o'clock configuration of the flagellar apparatus; the basal bodies show a distinct overlap (Fig. 19.14*b*; [1506]).

4 The Dasycladophyceae exhibit type VI mitosis (Fig. 19.22 II, p. 331). Mitosis is closed and the telophase spindle is prominent and persistent. As a result, the telophase nucleus has a charac-

teristic dumbbell shape (Fig. 25.3 B5). No centrioles are involved at any stage, so that mitosis is acentric [1008].

5 The multinucleate siphons (coenocytes) contain numerous fusiform or ellipsoidal chloroplasts (Fig. 25.2), which never contain pyrenoids but do often contain grains of reserve polysaccharide: mostly fructan, but also starch [1395]. In contrast to other groups of green algae, the Dasycladophyceae also have grains of reserve polysaccharide in the cytoplasm (Fig. 25.2*b, c*; [750]).

6 Vigorous streaming of the cytoplasm occurs along numerous narrow lanes (striae) orientated parallel to the longitudinal axis of the cell. Organelles, including chloroplasts and nuclei, move along in the streams of cytoplasm [102, 858].

7 The species of the Dasycladophyceae have a life cycle that we interpret as haplontic. A macroscopic, multinucleate gametophyte stage, which is haploid, alternates with a zygote stage containing one giant diploid nucleus; this is the only diploid nucleus in the life cycle. The zygote stage develops vegetatively into the gametophyte, meiosis taking place at some stage in this transformation and being followed by numerous mitoses to produce many haploid nuclei. Sexual fusion takes place isogamously, between biflagellate gametes (Fig. 25.1).

8 The class is entirely marine.

An 11 o'clock – 5 o'clock configuration of the basal bodies has been demonstrated to be present in the zoids (in this case, the biflagellate gametes) of two species [648, 1505, 1516]. The ultrastructure of the flagellar apparatus is quite similar to that in the *Acrosiphonia* gamete, which we have used as the model '11 o'clock – 5 o'clock zoid' (p. 320, Fig. 19.13), but it is even more like that of the biflagellate gametes of *Pseudobryopsis* (class Bryopsidophyceae; Fig. 24.1, p. 419). Dasycladalean zoids differ from both *Acrosiphonia* and *Pseudobryopsis*, however, in the absence of terminal caps over the ends of the basal bodies, and in a few other details that will not be treated any further here.

Type VI mitosis has been shown to occur in one species [1008]. The closed type of mitosis present is similar to mitosis in the Bryopsidophyceae (Fig. 24.3)

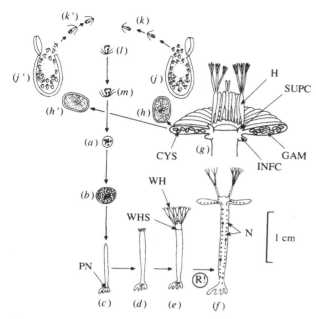

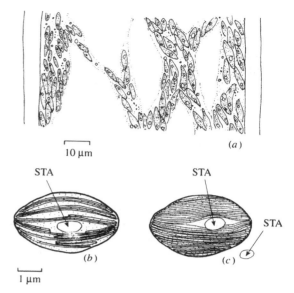

Figure 25.1. The life cycle of *Acetabularia acetabulum*. (*a*) Young zygote, with a single diploid nucleus. (*b*) Older zygote, with larger, growing diploid nucleus. (*c*) Young erect plant with giant diploid nucleus located in the rhizoidal base of the plant. (*d, e*) Development of whorls of sterile hairs at the apex of the erect stipe; the giant diploid nucleus is still present in the rhizoidal section of the thallus. (*f*) Following meiotic division of the giant nucleus, numerous small haploid nuclei are formed, which are transported to other parts of the plant by protoplasmic streaming; an umbrella- or cap-like whorl of gametangia forms at the top of the stipe. (*g*) Formation of numerous gametangial cysts within the whorled gametangia. (*h, h′*) Two cysts, each containing a single haploid nucleus. (*j, j′*) Production of biflagellate gametes by the cysts and their release through the opening of an operculum. (*k, k′*) Gametes. These are similar in size but of opposite sexes. (*l, m*) Isogamous copulation. CYS = gametangial cyst; GAM = gametangia, arranged in an umbrella-like whorl; H = hair; INFC = inferior corona; N = migrating secondary nuclei (haploid); PN = giant primary nucleus (diploid); R! = reduction division (meiosis); SUPC = superior corona; WH = whorl of hairs; WHS = whorl of hair scars.

Figure 25.2. (*a*) Fusiform chloroplasts in the stipe of *Batophora*. Note the strands of cytoplasm containing the chloroplasts and the large vacuoles. (*b, c*) Cross sections through the fusiform chloroplasts of *Acetabularia* (*b*) and *Cymopolia* (*c*), based on EM observations. Note the absence of pyrenoids and the presence of starch grains both inside and outside the chloroplasts. The thylakoids are stacked to various extents. STA = starch grain. (*a* based on [1458]; *b, c* on [750].)

and also to mitosis in the Cladophorophyceae (Fig. 19.22 II), though to a lesser extent. The telophase spindle is persistent, prominent and elongate, and gives the telophase nucleus a characteristic dumb-bell shape (Fig. 25.3 B5). No centrioles are to be found associated with the nucleus during vegetative mitoses ([1008]).

The numerous small chloroplasts (Fig. 25.2) are fusiform or ellipsoidal and always lack pyrenoids. The thylakoids may combine to form stacks of various sizes (Fig. 25.2*b*) or may completely fill the chloroplast (Fig. 25.2*c*). Chloroplasts of the latter type are concentrated towards the apex of the thallus and also near the primary nucleus ([750, 858]).

Chloroplasts are transported along the thallus at rates of about 60 to 120 μm min⁻¹ by cytoplasmic streaming, which takes place along numerous narrow 'traffic lanes' lying parallel to the longitudinal axis of the cell. This is the same speed with which the chloroplasts are transported along the siphons of the Bryopsidophyceae, again by cytoplasmic streaming (p. 424). The direction of streaming is not uniform, some streams moving in the opposite direction to others ([858]). Cytoplasmic streaming is not found in all the green algae that have large multinucleate cells; it does not occur, for instance, in the multinucleate cells of the

Cladophorophyceae and certain Ulvophyceae, e.g. *Acrosiphonia* (pp. 409, 398).

In the Dasycladophyceae the lanes contain bundles of actin filaments. These are clearly involved in some way with generating the movement of the cytoplasm, since treatment with drugs known to interfere with actin function, such as cytochalasin B, causes streaming to stop ([858, 1189, 1192]). In the Bryopsidophyceae, on the other hand, the narrow streams of cytoplasm are associated not only with actin microfilaments but also with bundles of microtubules, and both are necessary for streaming to occur (p. 424).

The Dasycladophyceae also possess a second, broader type of 'traffic lane', in which movement is faster than in the narrow lanes (*ca.* 200–600 µm min^{-1}). The numerous small haploid nuclei produced following meiosis of the diploid primary nucleus are transported rapidly along the 'fast traffic lanes', so that they become distributed throughout the rest of the giant cell, with a particular concentration in the tip ([1192]). The nuclei are surrounded by radial arrays of microtubules, which are thought to interact with the actin bundles of the cytoplasmic 'traffic lanes', although the mechanism of streaming remains unclear.

The arrays of microtubules and actin microfila-ments described above were made visible by staining them with actin- or tubulin-specific fluorescent antibodies and viewing the stained thalli by fluorescence microscopy ([1189, 1192]).

The Dasycladophyceae display wounding reactions quite similar to those of the Bryopsidophyceae (p. 425). Wounding is followed by a rapid contraction of the cytoplasm, mediated by actin ([1191]), and by the formation of wound plugs.

We interpret the life cycles of the Dasycladophyceae to be haplontic, the only diploid nucleus being that of the zygote (Fig. 25.1). Following its formation, the uninucleate zygote soon begins to develop into an upright axis with whorls of branches. As this occurs the diploid zygote nucleus increases enormously to form a giant 'primary nucleus' (Fig. 25.3 B), which lies in the rhizoidal basal part of the plant (Fig. 25.1*c–e*). In *Acetabularia* the primary nucleus divides meiotically ([858, 875, 876, 1624, 1674]), but only after the plant is fully grown and has already formed young gametangia. Here meiosis, together with the mitoses involved in the subsequent production of many small, haploid 'secondary' nuclei, is the prelude to sexual reproduction, which entails the death of the parent plant (see below, under *Acetabularia*, for a more detailed treatment of the life cycle). It could be argued,

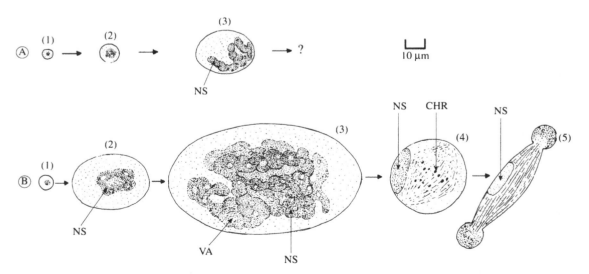

Figure 25.3. Development of the giant zygote nucleus (= primary nucleus) in *Bryopsis* (A) and *Acetabularia* (B). 1. The small zygotic nucleus immediately after fusion of the gametes and karyogamy. 2. Two weeks later. 3. Four weeks later. 4. Six weeks later: anaphase of the first meiotic division. 5. Telophase of the first meiotic division. CHR = chromosome; NS = nucleolus; VA = 'vacuole' within the nucleolus of the giant primary nucleus. (A based on [1279]; B1–3 based on [1458]; B4 based on [878]; B5 based on [876, 1008].)

therefore, that the whole vegetative episode, during which the erect *Acetabularia* plant develops and functions, is under the control of the diploid primary nucleus and that the life cycle should therefore be considered as diplontic. In this case *Acetabularia* could not be said to have a siphonous organization, since the multinucleate stage would only be a step in reproduction; the vegetative phase would be the unicellular, uninucleate plant, which is diploid. However, other Dasycladophyceae have a multinucleate thallus that continues to grow vegetatively after it has formed the first gametangia ([1007, 1009]). *Cymopolia*, for example (Figs. 25.7*d*, 25.8*b*), is apparently truly siphonous (coenocytic). Here the multinucleate plants exhibit indeterminate vegetative growth and continue to form new gametangia as the apices of the thallus extend. We consider, therefore, that *Acetabularia* has a highly modified haplontic life cycle, having been derived from dasycladalean ancestors with a truly vegetative, multinucleate gametophyte. During evolution, *Acetabularia* has lost the capacity to continue vegetative growth after producing the first whorl of gametangia. Unfortunately, nothing is known about the position of meiosis in the life cycle or the ploidy of the nuclei in *Cymopolia* and other truly siphonous Dasycladophyceae ([1007, 1009]).

The available data suggest, therefore, but do not prove, that the life cycles of the Dasycladophyceae are similar to those of some Bryopsidophyceae (compare Fig. 25.1 with Fig. 24.7 route B and Fig. 24.11, which show the life cycles of *Bryopsis* and *Udotea*). The following common plan emerges. The life cycle is haplontic. There is a multinucleate, vegetative gametophyte, which is haploid and siphonous (= coenocytic). The gametophyte produces biflagellate gametes, which pair and form zygotes. The zygote nucleus is the only diploid nucleus in the life cycle and increases greatly in size to become a giant 'primary' nucleus. The ultrastructure of the giant nucleus is very similar in the Bryopsidophyceae and Dasycladophyceae (Fig. 25.3), and will be described more fully with reference to *Acetabularia* (see below). Meiosis and the subsequent mitoses lead to the formation of many small haploid nuclei, termed the 'secondary' nuclei. These are incorporated into the gametophyte, which sprouts from the zygote; in some *Bryopsis* strains, however, secondary nuclei are incorporated into stephanokont meiospores (Fig. 24.7, pathway A).

In contrast to many other groups of green algae,

such as the orders Codiolales and Ulvales in the class Ulvophyceae, the Dasycladophyceae exhibit only one level of organization: the **siphonous** level. In this they resemble the Bryopsidophyceae. Essentially, each adult plant consists of a single, multinucleate cell. However, since meiosis of the zygote nucleus is postponed until a late stage in the development of the thallus, the plant is uninucleate for a considerable proportion of its life.

The number of extant genera in the Dasycladophyceae is about 11, with *ca.* 50 species ([1630]). Almost all are marine and restricted to tropical and subtropical coasts; one species is to be found in inland brackish waters. The cells of almost all Dasycladophyceae are heavily encrusted with calcium carbonate, in the form of aragonite crystals, and it is because of this that members of the order have often become fossilized. More than 150 fossil genera have been described, the oldest dating from the Cambrian (*ca.* 550 million years ago) or even the late Precambrian (*ca.* 1200 million years ago) ([430, 1751]).

Living members of the Dasycladophyceae form a rather inconspicuous, though widespread and common element of tropical marine, shallow-water floras. In the geological past, however, the diversity and abundance of the Dasycladophyceae seem to have been much greater, especially in the Permian (*ca.* 250 m.y. ago), the lower Cretaceous (*ca.* 130 m.y. ago) and the lower Tertiary (*ca.* 55 m.y. ago) ([430]). In these periods the sea level was much higher than at present and vast epicontinental seas stretched over large parts of the continents. The Dasycladophyceae were then widespread and abundant, and were important contributors to the thick deposits of calcium carbonate that were laid down, which today form the limestone mountains in parts of the Alps and other areas ([51, 52]).

Examples of the order Dasycladales

Acetabularia

Acetabularia acetabulum (= *mediterranea*) is an attractive small alga, five to ten centimetres high, which grows in clusters in sheltered spots along the rocky coasts of the Mediterranean. It also occurs in sandy lagoons in the Mediterranean, where it is to be found attached to mollusc shells. Each plant is shaped like an umbrella and is white, as a result of the encrustation of lime.

The life cycle of *Acetabularia acetabulum*

The morphology and structure of the *Acetabularia* thallus are best described in connection with the life cycle (see Fig. 25.1; [858, 875, 876, 878, 1458, 1459]).

1 The planozygote germinates immediately, without a period of dormancy, and grows into a young plant. This is a single cell, but it is differentiated into an upright portion and a creeping system of rhizoids. Growth is apical: at the tip of the plant new cell wall material is continuously being inserted and intercalated into the existing wall, while nearer the base the wall grows in thickness, through apposition of new wall material (Fig. 25.1a–c).

The zygote nucleus, tiny at first (*ca.* 5 μm in diameter) expands enormously, to more than 100 μm in diameter, and becomes the giant 'primary' nucleus. At the same time the single nucleolus present initially is replaced by a large number of sausage-shaped nucleoli, which contain vacuole-like spaces and twist around each other in a skein-like mass (Fig. 25.3 B). The development of the giant primary nucleus in *Acetabularia* greatly resembles that of the giant nucleus in *Bryopsis* (p. 426), but the final size of the nucleus in *Bryopsis*, though large, is much smaller than in *Acetabularia* (compare Fig. 25.3 A with Fig. 25.3 B). The giant nucleus of *Acetabularia* remains in the rhizoidal base of the plant (Fig. 25.1c).

Nucleoli are known to be ribosome-producing organelles ([16]), and the enormous increase in nucleolar mass within the giant nucleus is apparently related to an enormous increase in the production of cytoplasmic ribosomes. These are transported to the growing apex of the cell, where they are needed for protein synthesis ([858]). The increased production of ribosomes begins with rapid transcription of a huge number of rRNA (= ribosomal RNA) genes on the chromosomal DNA. This transcription can be visualized if the contents of lysed nuclei are spread out thinly and examined with the electron microscope (Fig. 25.6). The product of transcription is a precursor of the rRNA and this, together with ribosomal protein, is used in the construction of the cytoplasmic ribosomes.

The ultrastructure of the active giant nucleus of *Acetabularia* is very similar to that of *Bryopsis* (class Bryopsidophyceae, p. 426) (Figs. 25.4, 25.5). The zone of active exchange between nucleus and cytoplasm, in particular, has a number of characteristic features common to both genera. The nucleus is surrounded by a thin layer of cytoplasm without organelles, termed the **intermediate zone**. This is separated from the rest of the cytoplasm by a layer of vacuoles, the '**lacunar labyrinth**'; cytoplasmic **junction channels** connect the intermediate zone with the cytoplasm and these are thought to regulate the exchange of material between the nucleus and the rest of the cell. Just outside the nucleus there are numerous **perinuclear dense bodies**, which resemble the nucleoli in their structure and are probably also involved in the synthesis of ribosomes. Systems of granules, globules and fibres seem to extend out from the nucleolar mass through the nuclear pores, the intermediate zone and the junction channels, and probably consist of ribosome precursors ([67, 171, 858, 1008]). The nuclear envelope is pierced by an enormous number of closely spaced nuclear pores, and this too may reflect the high activity of the nucleus. Each pore is surrounded by eight peripheral granules and contain a single central granule (Fig. 25.5), this being the typical structure of the nuclear pores in eukaryotes. In the giant nucleus of *Bryopsis*, the nuclear envelope is underlain by a **peripheral fibrillar reticulum**, which is absent in *Acetabularia* (Fig. 25.5; [171]). In the past 25 years a great amount of information has been accumulated concerning the various interactions between nucleus, cytoplasm, chloroplasts and mitochondria in *Acetabularia* (for reviews, see [102, 103, 128, 858, 1460, 1601, 1602, 1918]).

Once the upright axis has reached a certain height, a whorl of brittle, dichotomously branched hairs (determinate laterals) is initiated. The axis itself continues to grow, and at some distance above the first whorl of hairs a second whorl is initiated, whereupon the first whorl is gradually shed, leaving only scars behind (Fig. 25.1d, e).

In *Acetabularia acetabulum* the stalk grows to a height of about a centimetre during the first growing season (summer), and produces one to three whorls of hairs. In the following winter the plant is reduced to several rhizoids, containing

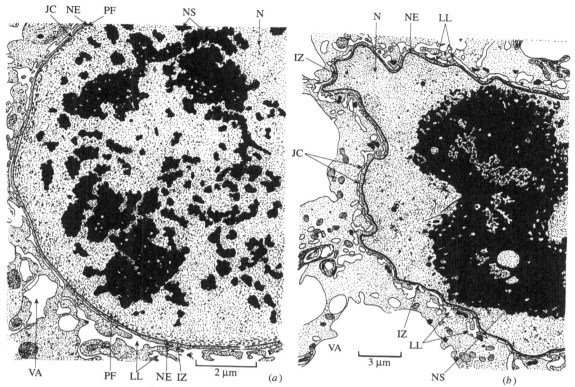

Figure 25.4. Parts of cross sections through the giant primary nuclei of *Bryopsis* (*a*) and *Acetabularia* (*b*), based on EM observations. IZ = intermediate zone; JC = junction channel; LL = lacunar labyrinthum; N = nucleus; NE = nuclear envelope; NS = nucleolus; PF = peripheral fibrillar reticulum; VA = vacuole. (Based on [171].)

the nucleus, but during spring the stalk grows again and, drawing upon reserve material stored in the rhizoids, attains a greater height than in the first year (2–3 cm). Then in winter the plant is again reduced to the rhizoidal base, which is packed with reserve material. In the third year the stalk first shoots up rapidly, then forms several whorls of hairs, and finally develops the reproductive umbel (Fig. 25.1*f, g*; [1458, 1459]).

Laboratory cultures can be made to behave quite differently. Fertile plants can be grown from zygotes in just two or three months. For this, however, the plants must be subjected to light of relatively high intensity (more than 2500 lux, approximately 50 mE m^{-2} s^{-1}); if lower intensities are used (500 lux, approximately 10 mE m^{-2} s^{-1}, or lower), the upright axis continues to grow vegetatively, producing whorl after whorl of sterile hairs.

2 The reproductive umbel (Fig. 25.1*g*) consists of a whorl of fused gametangia, which can be considered as fertile, determinate laterals (short shoots).

When the umbel has achieved its final diameter, the giant nucleus gradually decreases in size, from a diameter of over 100 μm to about 30–50 μm, and the number of nucleoli drops to one or two (Fig. 25.3 B4). The drop in size apparently reflects the end of the hectic regulatory activity of the primary nucleus, and marks its preparation for meiosis. During the first meiotic division a huge intranuclear spindle is formed (Fig. 25.3 B4; [878]), and at anaphase haploid sets of about 10 chromosomes are segregated to the

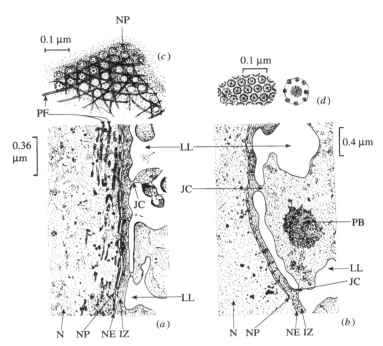

Figure 25.5. (*a, b*) The periphery of the giant primary nucleus, in cross section, in *Bryopsis* (*a*) and *Acetabularia* (*b*). (*c*) Grazing section through the nuclear envelope of *Bryopsis,* showing the nuclear pores and associated fibrillar elements. (*d*) Nuclear pores of *Acetabularia;* one is shown in detail, with eight peripheral granules and one central granule. IZ = intermediate zone; JC = junction channel; LL = lacunar labyrinthum; N = nucleus; NE = nuclear envelope; NP = nuclear pore; PB = dense perinuclear body; PF = peripheral fibrillar reticulum. (*a–c* based on [171]; *d* on [67].)

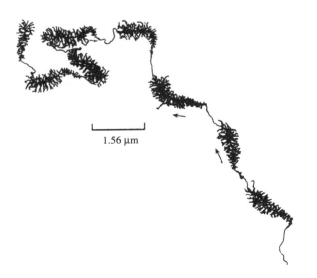

Figure 25.6. A stretch of nucleolar DNA in *Acetabularia major,* with evenly spaced regions of active ribosomal RNA synthesis, based on an electron micrograph. The active regions, marked by the presence of growing rRNA transcripts growing out at the sides of the DNA, alternate with inactive stretches of spacer DNA. The arrows indicate the direction of transcription of the rDNA (the DNA that codes for the rRNA) to form rRNA. Many transcripts are visible coming from the same strip of rDNA: the tip of each 'Christmas tree' is where transcription begins, while the base of the 'tree' marks where transcription is completed. (Based on [1602].)

poles. The telophase nuclei are small and are connected by an elongate spindle, which contains the remains of the nucleolus (Fig. 25.3 B5). Mitosis is closed, the dumbbell-like telophase nucleus being surrounded by a persistent nuclear envelope.

The small haploid daughter nuclei produced by meiosis are the first 'secondary' nuclei. Subsequent rounds of mitosis lead to the production of up to *ca.* 20 000 tiny secondary nuclei, which become distributed throughout the stipe and the reproductive cap or umbel (Fig. 25.1*f*) by cytoplasmic streaming. Finally, the greater part of the cytoplasm, together with the secondary nuclei contained in it, becomes concentrated in the rays of the reproductive umbel (i.e. in the gametangia).

3 The development of the reproductive umbel continues with the division of the gametangial contents into uninucleate protoplasts, each of which surrounds itself with a thick, rigid wall. These structures are termed gametangial cysts (Fig. 25.1*g, h, h′*). The contents of the stem are almost wholly used up during the formation of the cysts, so that the thallus subsequently withers and disappears; in nature this takes place from July to September.

4 The gametangial cysts of *Acetabularia acetabulum* require a period of dormancy before they can germinate, although in *Acetabularia moebii*, *A. wettsteinii* and *Batophora*, the cysts can germinate immediately. In nature, the cysts of *Acetabularia acetabulum* overwinter; in the laboratory they must be stored in the dark for 0.5 to 2 months. They are liberated when the umbel perishes but in the meantime they have become multinucleate. Upon germination the cyst contents divide up into numerous biflagellate zoids (Fig. 25.1*j, j′*); these are the gametes and they are set free through the opening of an operculum.

5 Copulation is isogamous and occurs between zoids produced from different cysts (Fig. 25.1*l*). Nuclear fusion has been studied with the electron microscope ([1460]). The zygote grows into a new *Acetabularia* plant, its nucleus gradually swelling and developing into the giant primary nucleus.

Originally, meiosis was thought to take place in the gametangial cysts, just before the formation of the gametes (gametic meiosis; [1593]). The life cycle was therefore considered to be diplontic. Evidence gathered in the past 15 years, however, shows that meiosis occurs during the division of the primary nucleus. The ploidy of the nuclei was determined by microspectrophotometry after specific staining of the DNA using the Feulgen technique. The zygote nucleus alone proved to be diploid, the secondary nuclei, cyst nuclei and gamete nuclei all being haploid ([875]). More recently, observations of dividing giant nuclei stained with the DNA-specific fluorescent probe DAPI have revealed meiotic stages ([1624]). Furthermore, meiotic pairing of homologous chromosomes (involving synaptonemal complexes; see p. 59) has been detected with the electron microscope in the giant nuclei of the closely related genus *Batophora* ([1008]). Reviews of the evidence concerning the position of meiosis in the life cycle of *Acetabularia* are given by Koop ([876]) and Bonotto ([102]). Since the only diploid nucleus seems to be the zygote nucleus, we interpret the life cycle as haplontic (see p. 428 for a further discussion of the life cycle in the Dasycladophyceae, as compared with that of the Bryopsidophyceae).

Batophora (Fig. 25.7*f, g*)

The plants of *Batophora* grow 3–10 cm high and consist of a long upright axis bearing whorls of branched determinate laterals. The whorls lie so far apart that they are visibly separate, even to the naked eye. Spherical zoidangia are produced at the branching points of the laterals (Fig. 25.7*f*). The plants are pale green and only sparsely, if at all, encrusted with lime.

Batophora lives in tropical lagoons. It can occur in brackish or almost fresh waters but it is also found in hypersaline conditions (i.e. in salt concentrations greater than that of the sea).

Dasycladus (Fig. 25.7*h*)

Dasycladus vermicularis plants are 2–6 cm tall. The axis is covered with closely spaced whorls of dichotomously branched determinate laterals. As in *Batophora*, there is only a light encrustation of lime. A spherical zoidangium develops at the base of each determinate lateral. *Dasycladus vermicularis* grows in

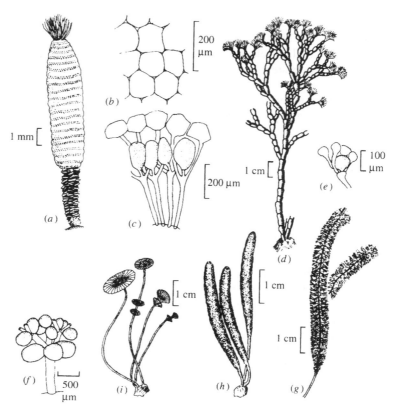

Figure 25.7. Examples of the order Dasycladales. (*a*) *Neomeris annulata:* whole plant. (*b*) *Neomeris:* detail of surface. (*c*) *Neomeris* gametangia. (*d, e*) *Cymopolia barbata.* (*f*) *Batophora oerstedii* gametangia.

(*g*) *Batophora oerstedii* plant. (*h*) *Dasycladus vermicularis.* (*i*) *Acetabularia crenulata.* (*a, b, d–i* after [1764]; *c* after [805].)

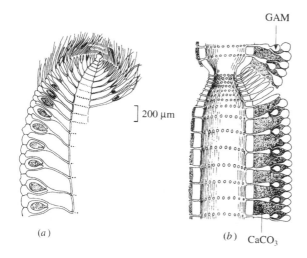

Figure 25.8. (*a*) *Neomeris:* longitudinal section through the tip of a plant. (*b*) *Cymopolia:* longitudinal section through a node and part of the adjacent internode. $CaCO_3$ = calcium carbonate deposited around the siphons; GAM = gametangium. (Based on [1340].)

shallow water on moderately exposed rocky coasts in the Caribbean.

Neomeris (Figs. 25.7a–c, 25.8a)

The thalli of *Neomeris* are 0.5 – 2.5 cm high. The axis ends in a cluster of pale green hairs and is clothed with a dense covering of dichotomously branched, determinate laterals, whose flattened ends attach to each other to form a thick cortex. The sporangia are arranged in whorls, which are easily seen (the double whorls of dark dots in Fig. 25.7a), each sporangium being club-shaped and borne at the base of a determinate lateral. *Neomeris annulata* is heavily encrusted with lime and occurs in shallow tidal pools on rocky coasts in the Caribbean.

Cymopolia (Figs. 25.7d, e, 25.8b)

The branching axes of *Cymopolia* can attain heights of 10–20 cm. They are made up of segments, between which are articulations allowing the thallus to bend and flex. At the end of each axis there is a cluster of trichotomously branched, pale green hairs. The axes themselves are covered with whorls of determinate lateral branches, whose outer cells become attached to each other, forming a 'rind', as in *Neomeris*. This cortical tissue is white, as a result of the lime encrusting it. The basal cell of each determinate lateral bears a spherical zoidangium.

Cymopolia inhabits warm, shallow waters in the tropics, growing attached to rocks and fragments of coral.

26

Chlorophyta: Class 7. Trentepohlio- phyceae

This class contains only one order, the Trentepohliales.

The principal characteristics of the Trentepohliophyceae [210, 211, 212, 213, 214, 215, 216, 217, 218]

1 In all of the Trentepohliophyceae the thalli are filamentous and consist of uninucleate cells. Some thalli are differentiated into two systems of branched filaments, one creeping and one erect, as in *Trentepohlia* (Fig. 26.1). Elsewhere there is only a creeping system of filaments, which are united to form a prostrate disc; this is found, for instance, in *Cephaleuros*. In two genera the polysaccharide cell walls have been found to have an outer covering of sporopollenin-like material (p. 339; [212]).

2. The reproductive zoids (flagellate cells) bear two or four flagella, and have four microtubular roots in a cruciate arrangement. The basal bodies have an 11 o'clock – 5 o'clock configuration and overlap each other quite distinctly (Fig. 19.14b). The flagellar apparatus also exhibits a number of other features that seem to be unique to the Trentepohliophyceae, such as the 'columnar structures' that subtend two of the four microtubular roots (Fig. 26.2; further explanation is given below).

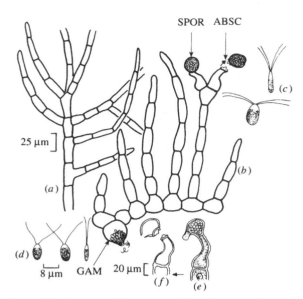

Figure 26.1. *Trentepohlia aurea*. (*a*) Erect branched filament. (*b*) A creeping, prostrate filament bearing a
gametangium (left) and a row of erect filaments, one
of which has produced two sporangia. (*c*) Quadriflagellate zoospores in side (above) and face views.
(*d*) Biflagellate gametes in side (right) and face
views. (*e*) Sporangium, borne on a hooked stalk cell.
(*f*) Sporangium just after abscission from the stalk
cell. ABSC = abscission of sporangium from the
hooked stalk cell; GAM = gametangium; SPOR =
sporangium. (*a* based on [464]; *b* on [440]; *e*, *f* on [1340].)

3. In dividing vegetative cells, cytokinesis is
brought about through the formation of a phragmoplast (p. 334, Fig. 19.23 II). A corollary of
this is that the cross walls between sibling cells
are perforated by fields of plasmodesmata ([214,
218]).

4. The chloroplasts are parietal, and are either ribbon-like or appear as chains of discs (Fig. 26.3).
Starch grains are present within them ([215]). An
orange-red pigment, called haematochrome,
accumulates in the cytoplasm and gives a yellow
or orange colour to the thalli ([100, 121]); haematochrome consists mainly of β-carotene ([544]).
Polyhydroxyalcohols (polyols and alditols) are
also present and this seems to be a unique feature of the group ([404a]).

5. The life cycles of most members of the class are
probably diplohaplontic and isomorphic. It is

thought that there is a diploid sporophyte, producing quadriflagellate meiospores, and a haploid gametophyte, producing biflagellate
gametes which fuse isogamously. The evidence
for this, however, is inconclusive ([211, 212, 216, 217,
553, 554, 1506, 1645]). The gametophytes also reproduce asexually, through the formation of quadriflagellate zoospores (Fig. 26.1*c*). The zoosporangia, which are spherical or ellipsoidal, can
also function as propagules, since they can
abscise and be dispersed by insects, wind or
water (Fig. 26.1*b*, *e*, *f*).

6. The Trentepohliophyceae all grow in subaerial
habitats.

The flagellate cells are strongly compressed dorsiventrally. Each bears two or four flagella and has a cruciate type of flagellar apparatus, with the basal bodies in
an 11 o'clock – 5 o'clock configuration (Figs. 26.1*c*, *d*,
26.2). The four microtubular roots do *not* show the
x–2–*x*–2 pattern (Fig. 19.14) characteristic of most
green algae with cruciately-arranged flagellar roots. In
Trentepohlia we find instead a 6–4–6–4 arrangement,
while in other genera the numbers are different again.
Another unusual feature is that, because of the compressed form of the zoids, the microtubular roots are
appressed to the basal bodies (Fig. 26.2*a*).

The 6-membered microtubular roots of *Trentepohlia* emanate from a mass of darkly staining material, which is faintly striated and covers the ends of the
basal bodies; this should perhaps be considered as
equivalent to the terminal caps present in the
Ulvophyceae, Cladophorophyceae and Bryopsidophyceae (compare Fig. 26.2 with Fig. 19.13*a*, *b*).

The two basal bodies are connected by a tiny upper
connective, which is reduced and non-striated. The
terminal part of each 4-membered microtubular root is
subtended by a **columnar structure** (Fig. 26.2),
which shows a superficial similarity to the multilayered structure (MLS) present in zoids of the unilateral
type (Figs. 19.15, 19.16; [211, 212, 216, 217, 553, 554, 1505, 1641]).
Note that in the Trentepohliophyceae the columnar
structure is associated with the spatial equivalent of
the 2-membered microtubular root, while in the
Pleurastrales, the MLS-like structure is associated
with the '*x*' root (compare Fig. 26.2*a* with Fig. 27.2*c*,
d and Fig. 19.14*b*). The flagella bear a wing-like keel
on each side.

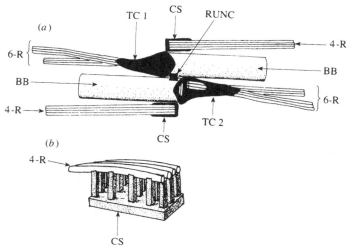

Figure 26.2. The flagellar apparatus of *Trentepohlia*. (*a*) Top view. (*b*) Three-dimensional reconstruction of the columnar structure associated with the four-stranded microtubular roots, seen from the side. BB = basal body; CS = columnar structure; RUNC = reduced upper non-striated connective; TC1 = terminal cap of dark-staining, faintly striated material; TC2 = terminal cap as TC1, cut away in places to show its position in relation to the six-stranded microtubular root; 4-R = four-stranded microtubular root; 6-R = six-stranded microtubular root (= *x* root). (Based on [1506].)

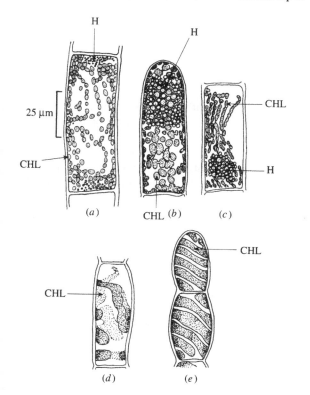

Figure 26.3. *Trentepohlia*: chloroplast morphology in *T. aurea* (*a*–*c*), *T. iolithus* (*d*) and *T. umbrina* (*e*). CHL = chloroplast; H = haematochrome. (*a* based on [412]; *b*–*e* on [464].)

The unique type of flagellar apparatus, the way the vegetative cells divide, the structure of the vegetative cells, and the life cycle, all suggest that it is appropriate for these algae to be placed in a separate class, the Trentepohliophyceae.

The class contains four genera, with about 60 species. Species of *Trentepohlia* form felty growths on rocks and tree trunks, or even on leaves. They are often yellow or orange. *Trentepohlia* species can also be the algal partners (phycobionts) in lichens ([643]). Other genera, such as *Cephaleuros*, grow on the leaves of higher plants in tropical or subtropical regions, as disc-like epiphytes. Here they can cause significant damage to economically important crops, such as tea, coffee, citrus and others ([215]).

Trentepohlia (Figs. 26.1 – 26.3)
Trentepohlia forms two types of filaments: creeping and erect. The creeping filaments are branched and grow over the surfaces of rocks, tree trunks and leaves. They give rise to erect filaments, which may be branched or unbranched and form a dense, velvety felt, yellow or orange in colour.

The creeping filaments produce rounded gametangia, each with a single exit pore (Fig. 26.1*b*), through which biflagellate isogametes emerge (Fig. 26.1*d*). The erect filaments, on the other hand, produce rounded sporangia, each borne on a special hooked stalk cell (Fig. 26.1*b, e, f*). The wall separating the sporangium from the stalk cell exhibits special features which facilitate abscission of the sporangium as a single unit ([215]); this can then be dispersed by insects, rain or wind. In moist conditions the sporangia release quadriflagellate zoospores through an exit pore.

Trentepohlia contains about 40 species, most of which are tropical or subtropical.

27

Chlorophyta: Class 8. Pleurastrophyceae, and the order Prasiolales (Appendix to the classes with an 11 o'clock – 5 o'clock configuration of the basal bodies)

This chapter deals with two orders, the Pleurastrales and Prasiolales, whose members occur predominantly in subaerial habitats.

The flagellate cells produced by these algae have four microtubular roots in a cruciate arrangement, and basal bodies that clearly overlap, in an 11 o'clock – 5 o'clock configuration (Fig. 19.14*b*). This type of flagellar apparatus is also to be found in the class Ulvophyceae (p. 391) and so the Pleurastrales and Prasiolales are put in this class by some authors ([1180, 1645]). Several things, however, including the architecture of the cells, details of mitosis and cytokinesis, the plan of the life cycle, and the essentially non-marine distribution of the two orders, suggest that classification in the Ulvophyceae is unwise; thus, for instance, the Ulvophyceae are almost all marine. It may well be that the Pleurastrales and Prasiolales are quite separate evolutionary lineages, which themselves deserve to be recognized as classes.

Class 8. Pleurastrophyceae: one order (Pleurastrales)

1 Members of the Pleurastrales exhibit three levels of organization. Some are coccoid (Fig. 27.1a–c), others are sarcinoid (Fig. 27.1f), while yet others form branched filaments ([296, 1170, 1173, 1180, 1182, 1645, 1645a, 1647, 1798, 1860]).

2 The flagellate cells are strongly compressed (Fig. 27.2a, b); they have four microtubular roots in a cruciate arrangement and basal bodies that exhibit a distinct overlap (Fig. 27.2c; compare this with Fig. 19.13a). The microtubular roots show the usual x–2–x–2 pattern (see also p. 320), the 'x' roots containing four or five microtubules. The tips of the 'x' roots overlie a faintly layered structure (Fig. 27.2c, d), which shows some resemblance to the multilayered structure (MLS) found in the unilateral type of zoid (Figs. 19.15, 19.16; [296, 1180, 1182]).

3 Contrary to what one might expect, the pair of nuclear centrioles is *not* involved in the formation of the mitotic spindle, but in the assembly of a phycoplast. Cytokinesis is brought about by a cleavage furrow, which grows in from one side only. Mitosis is semi-closed and the telophase spindle is non-persistent (Fig. 27.2f–j).

4 After cytokinesis each daughter cell becomes completely surrounded by a new cell wall (Fig. 27.2i). Two to several daughter cells thus can remain enclosed in the parent cell wall, forming a multicellular, sarcinoid (packet-like; Fig. 27.1f) thallus, or a filament. Alternatively, they may be released as reproductive cells, either as non-flagellate, walled cells (autospores; Fig. 27.1b), or as naked flagellate cells (zoospores, gametes; Fig. 27.1g, h). These outcomes of cytokinesis are very similar to what occurs in the order Chlorococcales (class Chlorophyceae; p. 360). The processes of mitosis and cytokinesis, however, are quite different in these two groups (compare Fig. 27.2f–i with Figs. 19.20 I and 19.17 II).

The class is characterized by a distinctive type of mitosis and cytokinesis (Fig. 27.2h, i; [296, 298, 1032, 1140, 1229, 1645]). During interphase a pair of centrioles lies against the nuclear envelope. They are arranged as if they were flagellar basal bodies lying in an 11 o'clock–5 o'clock configuration and they are even accompanied by a vestigial set of microtubular roots.

During early prophase the pair of centrioles replicates and migrates to the side of the cell (Fig. 27.2f, g). Here the plasmalemma begins to be formed into a cleavage furrow, between the two centriolar pairs (Fig. 27.2g). Meanwhile, a spindle develops with broad, flat poles that are formed from parts of the nuclear envelope, which is only partly retained (mitosis is semi-closed). At metaphase the chromosomes are arranged in a distinct plate and are attached to chromosome microtubules by kinetochores (Fig. 27.2g). A phycoplast (a plate of microtubules) is formed from the centrioles in the prospective plane of division of the cell (Fig. 27.2h) and sheaths of microtubules also radiate out over the daughter nuclei (Fig. 27.2h). It is only at late telophase (Fig. 27.2h) that the cleavage furrow resumes its inward growth, which is brought about through the addition of membrane vesicles derived from at least three different sources (one of which is the golgi apparatus). At a later stage a new cell wall is formed around each daughter cell, as a result of the secretion of wall material by the same kinds of vesicles as were earlier involved in the growth of the cleavage furrow. The result is that two (Fig. 27.2i) or more (Fig. 27.2j) daughter cells, each with its own wall, lie surrounded by a common wall, derived from the parent cell; in this outcome of mitosis and cytokinesis the Pleurastrophyceae resemble the order Chlorococcales of the Chlorophyceae (p. 360).

The chloroplasts are either parietal, in which case they are cup- or band-shaped, or they are central and stellate. Each may contain a single pyrenoid, or pyrenoids may be entirely absent (Fig. 27.1a, e).

At present only six genera are known to belong to the Pleurastrales and these are *Trebouxia*, *Myrmecia*, *Friedmannia*, *Pleurastrosarcina*, *Pleurastrum* and *Microthamnion* ([294, 296, 1182, 1645, 1645a]). It is likely that many other coccoid, sarcinoid and branched, filamentous green algae will prove to belong to the order, but confirmation of this will have to await ultrastructural investigations of the flagellar apparatus, mitosis and cytokinesis.

Two examples of the order Pleurastrales

Trebouxia (Fig. 27.1a–c)

This is a genus of unicellular, coccoid green algae, although some species also form sarcinoid packets of

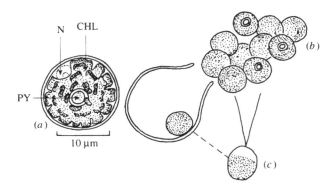

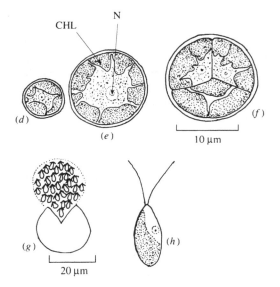

Figure 27.1. (*a–c*) *Trebouxia parmeliae.* (*a*) Adult cell. (*b*) Formation of autospores. (*c*) Biflagellate zoospore. (*d–h*) *Friedmannia israelensis.* (*d*) Young cell, which has arisen from a zoospore. (*e*) Adult cell. (*f*) Tetrahedron of daughter cells within the parental cell wall. (*g*) Formation of zoospores. (*h*) Biflagellate zoospore. CHL = chloroplast; N = nucleus; PY = pyrenoid. (Based on [121].)

Figure 27.2. *Friedmannia:* zoospore (*a–e*), and mitosis and cytokinesis (*f–j*). (*a*) Face view of zoospore, as seen with the light microscope; note the absence of an eye-spot. (*b*) As (*a*), but in side view, showing the slight curvature of the cell body. (*c*) Top view of the flagellar apparatus. (*d*) Three-dimensional detail of the five-stranded microtubular root, subtended by a faintly lay-ered structure. (*e*) Cross section through the flagellar apparatus, taken perpendicular to the basal bodies. (*f*) Early prophase. (*g*) Metaphase. (*h*) Late telophase. (*i, j*) Interphase. BB = basal body; BB(CA) = cart-wheel structure within basal body; BB(TRIP) = basal body triplets: the faintly layered structure is connected to two of these; CEP = pair of centrioles; 2CEP = two centriolar pairs; CF = cleavage furrow; CHL = chloro-plast; CHR = chromosome; CW = cell wall; CW1 = parental cell wall; CW2 = daughter cell wall; FLS = faintly layered structure, within which three faint darker-staining layers can be distinguished; the whole structure is composed of delicate vertical sheets of material; G = golgi body; K = kinetochore; MTSH = sheath of microtubules radiating out from a centriolar pair over the surface of the nucleus; NE = nuclear envelope; PHMT = phycoplast microtubules; PM = plasma membrane (plasmalemma); RTSF = rudimen-tary transversely striated fibre; SF = striated fibre, one of two connecting the basal bodies; UNC = upper non-striated connective linking the basal bodies, consisting of two overlapping halves; 2-R = two-stranded micro-tubular root; 5-R = five-stranded microtubular root. (*a–e*: interpretation based on [1180]; *f–j* on [1032].)

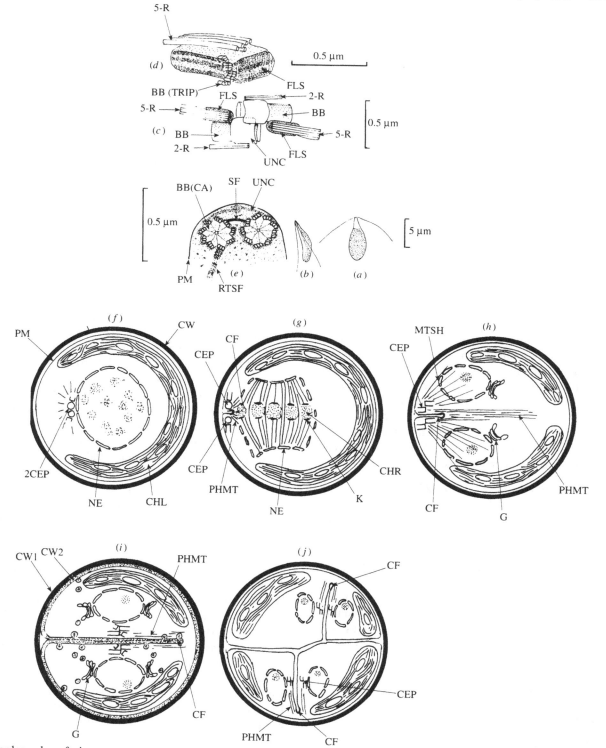

For legend see facing page.

cells. The cells are spherical and possess a massive central chloroplast, which is stellate and contains a central pyrenoid. The nucleus lies near the periphery of the cell. The cells reproduce through the formation of autospores and biflagellate zoospores.

Trebouxia and *Myrmecia* species occur widely in subaerial habitats and form the phycobionts (algal partners) in many lichen symbioses ([453, 489, 1796, 1797]); the fungi involved in the symbioses, which are usually Ascomycetes, use the algal cells as photosynthetic organs. In many ways a lichen is a controlled parasitism rather than a symbiosis, since *ca.* 70–80% of the carbon fixed by the alga during photosynthesis is transferred to the fungus. There is no clear advantage to the alga, which captures its nutrients from water. The alga holds the fungal attack in check by producing antibiotic substances (phytoalexins; [13]).

Trebouxia and *Myrmecia* have also been found living free on the bark of trees ([489, 1796]). Sporopollenin-like substances are found in the cell walls and this can be considered as an adaptation to a terrestrial or subaerial way of life, hindering desiccation ([489]). Both genera are very similar to *Chlorococcum* (class Chlorophyceae, order Chlorococcales; p. 362, Fig. 21.7) and to *Chlorocystis* (class Ulvophyceae, order Codiolales; p. 393, Fig. 22.1), and until recently all four genera were classified close together, within the Chlorococcales. It is now thought that their similarity reflects convergent evolution in three quite different lineages (classes) of green algae.

Friedmannia (Figs. 27.1d–h, 27.2)

The spherical cells of *Friedmannia* have an irregularly lobed, parietal chloroplast, which lacks pyrenoids. Each cell can divide to form a tetrahedral cluster, producing a sarcinoid level of organization, while reproduction takes place via autospores and biflagellate zoospores.

Only one species is known and this was isolated from soil from the Negev desert, in Israel. In culture *Friedmannia* can easily be induced to become associated with a fungus in a lichen symbiosis ([13]) but it has not yet been found as a phycobiont in nature.

Order Prasiolales (classification of this group at the class level is as yet impossible)

1 The flagellate cells produced by members of the Prasiolales (i.e. the biflagellate male gametes)

have four microtubular roots in a cruciate arrangement; the basal bodies lie in an 11 o'clock – 5 o'clock configuration and exhibit a distinct overlap ([1099]; this early EM paper does not reveal enough of the ultrastructure of the flagellar apparatus to allow a full evaluation).

2 The thalli are multicellular but very simply constructed, consisting of small clusters or filaments of cells, or small, flat leaf-like structures.

3 Each cell contains a nucleus and a central, stellate chloroplast; its architecture is very similar to that of the unicellular, coccoid alga *Trebouxia* (order Pleurastrales; p. 449, Fig. 27.1a).

Prasiola (Figs. 27.3, 27.4)

The crinkled, leaf-like thalli of *Prasiola* are small, reaching heights of up to 1.5 cm, and only one layer of cells thick. In their youngest stages the thalli are uniseriate filaments; later they become flat sheets and in older plants the cells are organized into rectangular groups (Fig. 27.4), which look like sarcinoid packets of *Trebouxia* cells. The pattern of mitosis and cytokinesis, however, is quite similar to that of the Ulvophyceae (type V mitosis and cytokinesis; p. 329, Fig. 19.22 I) and differs from that in the Pleurastrales ([1032, 1037]). In one species at least, the cell walls consist predominantly of xylomannan ([1745, 1746]).

There are about 20 species of *Prasiola*. They grow on damp rocks, walls, tree trunks and sea coasts, here often preferring places that have been enriched with nitrogen, through bird droppings. This is true, for example, of *Prasiola stipitata*, which grows on European coasts, on rocks around the high water mark that are kept damp by salt spray.

The life cycle of *Prasiola stipitata* (Fig. 27.3b; 457, 458, 459, 469, 1099)

The vegetative, leaf-like thallus is diploid. Vegetative reproduction involves the formation of diploid aplanospores (Fig. 27.3b, right). This begins with periclinal divisions of the cells (parallel to the thallus surface) in fertile parts of the thallus, which are often located towards its upper edge. The thallus thus becomes two- or four-layered in the fertile regions. The cell contents then round up to form aplanospores, swell, and are set free when the anticlinal cell walls rupture (Fig. 27.3b, right).

The gametes are produced in a curious way, which

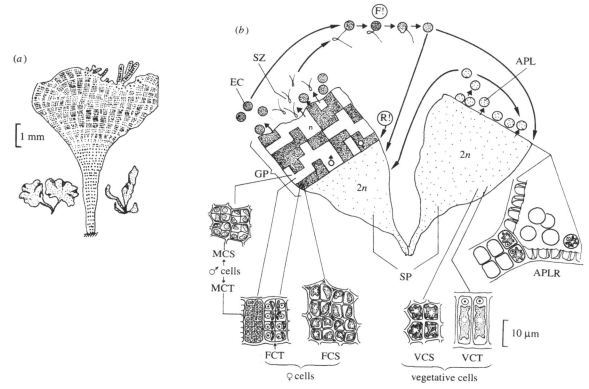

Figure 27.3. *Prasiola stipitata*. (*a*) Habit. (*b*) Life cycle.
APL = aplanospore; APLR = release of aplanospores;
EC = egg cell; F! = fertilization, through oogamy;
FCS = female cells in surface view; FCT = female
cells in transverse section; GP = gametophyte (haploid); MCS = male cells in surface view; MCT = male
cells in transverse section; R! = reduction division
(meiosis); SP = sporophyte; SZ = spermatozoid;
VCS = vegetative cells in surface view; VCT = vegetative cells in transverse section; n = haploid; $2n$ =
diploid. (*a* after [600]; *b* after [457].)

appears to be unique to *Prasiola*. Vegetative meiosis
takes place more or less synchronously in the upper
part of a sexualized diploid thallus, followed by several rounds of mitosis in the haploid tissue that has
been produced. Half of the haploid tissue divides into
very small pale cells, with pale chloroplasts; these are
considered as male cells. The other half divides up into
larger, darker cells, which have larger chloroplasts;
these are the female cells (Fig. 27.3*b*). The upper part
of the sexually mature thallus thus consists of a mosaic
of patches, all haploid, some dark and female, others
lighter and male. Since the same diploid thallus gives
rise to male and female sectors, it can be taken that sex
determination is haplogenotypic. Once mature, the
whole content of each haploid cell is set free, as a gamete. The gametes are generally discharged together in
large numbers, simultaneously.

The male gametes are motile biflagellate cells (spermatozoids), measuring 2–7 µm × 1.8–4 µm, while the
female gametes are non-motile and larger, 3.2–5 µm ×
4–6.8 µm. When a spermatozoid touches an egg cell
via the tip of one of its flagella, the egg cell and the flagellum stick together. Then this flagellum, together
with the body of the spermatozoid, is absorbed into the
egg cell, so that a uniflagellate zygote is produced. The
zygote can swim around for some time, with the flagellum trailing at the posterior. After a few days karyogamy occurs within the zygote, which by now has
come to rest. The zygote germinates immediately, with
no period of dormancy, to give a new *Prasiola* plant.

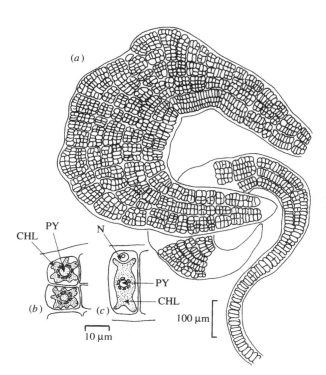

Figure 27.4. *Prasiola crispa.* (*a*) A young plant: note the rectangular 'sarcinoid' packets of cells. (*b*) Detail of the thallus, in surface view, showing the *Trebouxia*-like cells. (*c*) Cross section of single cell. CHL = chloroplast; N = nucleus; PY = pyrenoid. (*a* based on Imhäuser in [1340].)

Prasiola stipitata thus possesses a life cycle that can be summarized as strongly heteromorphic and diplohaplontic, the haploid gametophytes remaining part of the original diploid thallus after meiosis; sexual reproduction is oogamous. It might be possible, however, to interpret the haploid male and female parts of the thallus as plurilocular gametangia (compare the Phaeophyceae; p. 173, Fig. 12.8), in which case the life cycle would be diplontic. Which of these interpretations is correct depends on how the gametophyte is defined (see discussion of the Codiolales life cycle, p. 393). The matter is complicated by reports of a quite different type of life cycle in two other members of the Prasiolales, *Prasiola japonica* ([469]) and *Rosenvingiella constricta* ([903]). Here the reproductive structures are very similar to those in *Prasiola stipitata*, and again sexual reproduction is oogamous, but the evidence available so far indicates that the life cycle is haplontic, with zygotic meiosis. It seems unlikely that such different types of life cycle would exist in species that are so closely related as these, and the life cycles of the Prasiolales should therefore be re-investigated.

28

Chlorophyta: Class 9. Klebsormidiophyceae

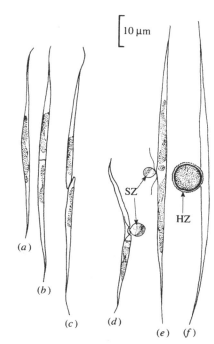

Figure 28.1. *Raphidonema longiseta.* (*a*) Single cell. (*b*) Two-celled 'filament' produced by cell division, through the formation of a cross-wall. (*c*) Fragmentation of a two-celled filament to produce two unicells. (*d*) Two-celled filament in which one cell has released a biflagellate male gamete. (*e*) Oogamous copulation. (*f*) Hypnozygote. HZ = hypnozygote; SZ = spermatozoid (male gamete). (Based on [905].)

The principal characteristics of the Klebsormidiophyceae

1 The members of this class exhibit three different levels of organization. Some are coccoid (Figs. 28.1, 28.2*a*) and others sarcinoid (Fig. 28.2*c–f*); in a third group the thalli are filamentous and these may be branched or unbranched (Figs. 28.2*g*, 28.3).

2 The main polysaccharide in the fibrillar, structural component of the cell wall is crystalline cellulose ([329, 755]).

3 The flagellate cells (zoids) produced during reproduction have two flagella. The flagellar apparatus has a unilateral construction and includes a distinct multilayered structure (MLS) (p. 323, Figs. 19.15, 19.16, 28.4). The zoids are usually covered with diamond-shaped organic scales (Figs. 19.15*b*, 28.4*b*, *d*), which are similar to the inner body scales in the Prasinophyceae (Fig. 19.10*d*).

4 Mitosis is open and the telophase spindle is persistent. Cytokinesis is brought about either through the ingrowth of the plasmalemma as a cleavage furrow, or by the formation of a cell plate, which lies within a phragmoplast (types VII and VIII mitosis–cytokinesis; pp. 333, 334, Fig. 19.23 I and II).

5 The cells are uninucleate. Each has a cup- or band-shaped chloroplast, which is parietal and usually contains a single pyrenoid (Figs. 28.1, 28.2, 28.3*a*).

6 In those species in which sexual reproduction is known to occur, the life cycle is haplontic and includes a hypnozygote stage (a thick-walled, dormant zygote; Figs. 28.1*d–f*, 28.3).

7 The Klebsormidiophyceae are restricted to freshwaters and moist subaerial habitats.

It is now thought by many that the architecture of the flagellate cell (zoid) provides the most important source of characters for distinguishing the main evolutionary lineages (the classes) within the green algae; the zoid is considered to be a repository for primitive characters. The organic scales present on the body of the zoid in the Klebsormidiophyceae are very similar

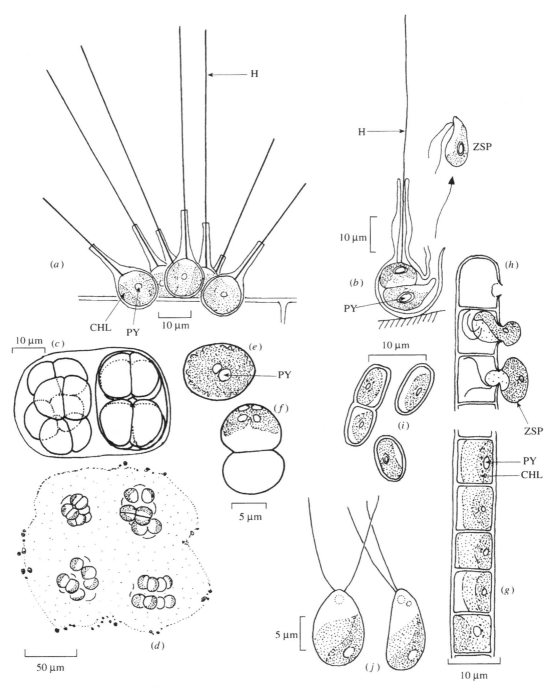

Figure 28.2. (*a, b*) *Chaetosphaeridium.* (*a*) Cluster of cells epiphytic on a filamentous alga. (*b*) Formation of a biflagellate zoospore. (*c–f*) *Chlorokybus atmophyticus.* (*c*) Sarcinoid packets of cells. (*d*) Mucilaginous colony containing sarcinoid packets of cells. (*e, f*) Detail of individual cells, as seen with the light microscope.

(*g–j*) *Klebsormidium.* (*g*) Filament. (*h*) Release of biflagellate zoospores, one from each cell. (*i*) Fragmentation of the filament into unicells. (*j*) Face (left) and side views of a zoospore. CHL = chloroplast; H = cytoplasmic hair; PY = pyrenoid; ZSP = zoospore. (*a* based on [1657]; *b–g, i* on [121]; *h* on [1419]; *j* on [440].)

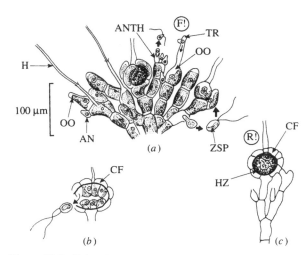

Figure 28.3. *Coleochaete pulvinata*. (*a*) Part of the tiny cushion-like plant, showing the systems of branched radiating filaments. (*b*) Germinating hypnozygote, producing zoospore. (*c*) Hypnozygote surrounded by corticating filaments. ANTH = antheridium; CF = corticating filaments enclosing the hypnozygote; F! = fertilization, involving oogamy; H = cytoplasmic hair; HZ = hypnozygote; OO = oogonium; R! = reduction division (meiosis); TR = trichogyne; ZSP = biflagellate zoospore. (Based on [1445].)

indeed to the inner body scales of the Prasinophyceae (compare Fig. 19.15*b* with Fig. 19.10*d* and Fig. 28.4*d*), and this is interpreted as showing that, long ago, the Klebsormidiophyceae diverged from prasinophycean ancestors (see also the discussion of the body scales present in the Ulvophyceae, p. 393).

Another link is demonstrated by the structure of the flagellar apparatus. Unilateral construction, including a multilayered structure, is also found in the Charophyceae (Chapter 30), the mosses and liverworts, and the 'lower' vascular plants, and these are therefore thought to have evolved from the same evolutionary lineage that gave rise to the Klebsormidiophyceae. This idea is supported by the presence of type VIII mitosis and cytokinesis in the klebsormidiophycean alga *Coleochaete*. Here mitosis is open, the telophase spindle is persistent, and cytokinesis involves the formation of a phragmoplast. The highly specialized stoneworts (class Charophyceae), the bryophytes, and the vascular plants have almost exactly the same type of mitosis and cytokinesis as

Coleochaete, except that centrioles are generally absent in the land plants but present during division in *Coleochaete*.

There are several differences, however, between the two groups of green algae, the Klebsormidiophyceae and the Charophyceae, and the land plants (the mosses, liverworts and vascular plants). Thus, the architecture of the zoids is much more complicated in land plants, though still based on the unilateral plan and still containing a multilayered structure; and the land plants have a strongly heteromorphic, diplohaplontic life cycle, in contrast to the haplontic life cycle of the Klebsormidiophyceae and Charophyceae. A fuller treatment of evolution within the green plants is given on p. 483 ([1218, 1641, 1644]).

At present the Klebsormidiophyceae includes 7 genera with about 45 species, although more taxa may well be assigned to the class as more green algae are investigated in detail.

Order Klebsormidiales

1 Mitosis is open, the telophase spindle is persistent, and cytokinesis is brought about by a cleavage furrow (type VII mitosis and cytokinesis; p. 333, Fig. 19.23 I). The transverse walls lack plasmodesmata.

2 The members of the order are either coccoid (Fig. 28.1) or sarcinoid (Fig. 28.2*c*, *f*), or they form unbranched filaments (Fig. 28.2*g*).

3 The chloroplast is parietal, band- or cup-shaped, and usually contains a single pyrenoid (Figs. 28.1, 28.2).

The unilateral construction of the flagellar apparatus has been demonstrated in two genera, *Chlorokybus* ([1521]) and *Klebsormidium* ([1120, 1419]), while type VII mitosis and cytokinesis has been shown to occur in six species, belonging to the genera *Chlorokybus*, *Klebsormidium*, *Raphidonema* and *Stichococcus* ([222, 427, 1033, 1036, 1417, 1418, 1420]).

Oogamous sexual reproduction, in which a biflagellate zoid functions as the male gamete, is known in one species of *Raphidonema* ([905]; Fig. 28.1*d–f*). Asexual reproduction by biflagellate zoospores occurs in *Chlorokybus* and *Klebsormidium* (Fig. 28.2*h*, *j*), each vegetative cell producing only one spore. The

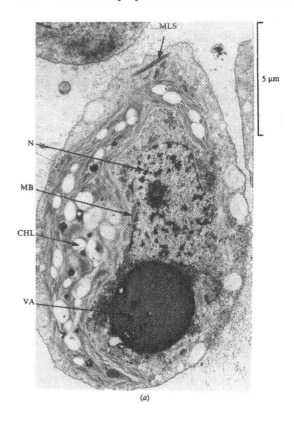

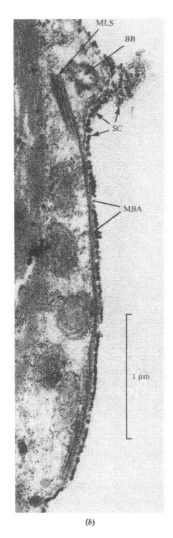

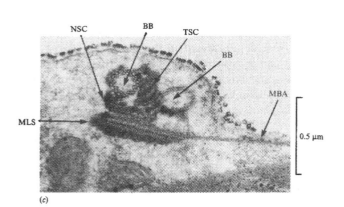

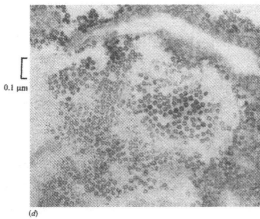

For legend see facing page.

predominant mode of reproduction, however, is fragmentation, the vegetative filaments or thalli breaking apart at the cross-walls (Figs. 28.1*b, c*, 28.2*d, i*). In *Chlorokybus, Raphidonema* and *Stichococcus* the formation of each cross-wall is followed almost immediately by the development of a split in the plane of the newly formed cross-wall, resulting in a predominantly unicellular, coccoid level of organization (see [1033]).

The three levels of organization found in the Klebsormidiophyceae (coccoid, sarcinoid and filamentous) are also found in two other groups of green algae, the Chlorococcales, which belongs to the class Chlorophyceae, and the Pleurastrales, which belongs to a separate class, the Pleurastrophyceae (pp. 360, 448). The Chlorococcales, Pleurastrales and Klebsormidiales appear therefore to have evolved in parallel, or convergently, so that similar types of thallus morphology have been produced in quite different lineages of green algae.

For many coccoid, sarcinoid and filamentous green algae it is at present difficult, if not impossible, to determine the order or even the class to which they belong, since we have no information about the ultrastructure of their zoids and the pattern of mitosis and cytokinesis.

Three examples of the order Klebsormidiales

Chlorokybus (Fig. 28.2c–f)

The cells of *Chlorokybus* are spherical or ellipsoidal, which are grouped into more or less cubical packets and embedded in a common gelatinous matrix (a sarcinoid level of organization). Each cell contains a lobed parietal chloroplast, with one or two pyrenoids. Reproduction takes place through the formation of zoospores, which have a unilateral flagellar apparatus and a MLS ([1521]). The only known species grows on rocky substrata, in subaerial habitats ([1499]).

Raphidonema (Fig. 28.1a–f)

This alga produces short, unattached filaments with two pointed end-cells, but the filaments fragment so easily into spindle-shaped unicells that the level of organization is really coccoid. Each cell contains one parietal chloroplast, which may or may not have a pyrenoid. Oogamous sexual reproduction has been observed in one *Raphidonema* species (Fig. 28.1*d–f*). A whole vegetative cell functions as a female gamete and this is fertilized by a biflagellate male gamete; it is interesting that with the male gametes too, only one gamete is produced per vegetative cell. Other *Raphidonema* species reproduce asexually, through the formation of biflagellate zoospores.

Raphidonema contains about 20 species, some of which grow in freshwater, while others live in the surface layers of alpine glaciers and snow ([688]).

Klebsormidium (Fig. 28.2g–j)

The filaments of *Klebsormidium* grow unattached and have rounded end-cells. They do not branch and dissociate easily into fragments containing one to a few cells. Within each cell there is a single parietal chloroplast, which is relatively narrow, extending around less than half of the cell's circumference; it contains a pyrenoid. Asexual reproduction involves the formation of biflagellate zoospores, which have a unilateral type of flagellar apparatus (Fig. 19.15; [1120, 1419]). Each vegetative cell produces only one zoospore and this is released through a break in the cell wall (Fig. 28.2*h*).

About 15 species of *Klebsormidium* have been described; they live in subaerial and freshwater habitats.

Figure 28.4. The ultrastructure of the biflagellate zoospore of *Coleochaete*, which exhibits the characteristics of the unilateral type of zoid construction (compare with Figs. 19.15, 19.16). (*a*) Longitudinal section, showing the general organization of the cell. (*b*) Transverse section of the broad microtubular band of the flagellar apparatus, just below the multilayered structure (which is just grazed by the section) (compare with Fig. 19.15*b*). (*c*) Approximately longitudinal section through the multilayered structure; the two basal bodies and the connectives that link them are also visible (compare with Fig. 19.15*a* and Fig. 19.16). (*d*) Glancing section showing the organic, diamond-shaped scales that cover the cell. BB = basal body; CHL = chloroplast; MB = microbody; MBA = microtubular band of the flagellar apparatus; MLS = multilayered structure; N = nucleus; NSC = non-striated connective; SC = organic scales; TSC = transversely striated connective; VA = vacuole. (From [1641], with the permission of the author and Springer-Verlag, Vienna.)

Order Coleochaetales

1   Mitosis is open and the telophase spindle is persistent. Cytokinesis is brought about through the formation of a cell plate, which consists of vesicles derived from the golgi apparatus lying within a phragmoplast (type VIII mitosis and cytokinesis; p. 334, Fig. 19.23 II). The cross walls are perforated by plasmodesmata.

2   The thalli of the Coleochaetales are branched filaments, which in some species readily dissociate into groups of unicells. Most cells bear one or more setae (hairs), which have a basal sheath and contain cytoplasm (Figs. 28.2a, b, 28.3).

3   The chloroplast is parietal, cup- or band-shaped, and contains a pyrenoid (Figs. 28.2a, b, 28.3).

The zoids have been shown to have a unilaterally constructed flagellar apparatus in one species of *Chaetosphaeridium* ([1215]) and two species of *Coleochaete* (Fig. 28.4; [555, 556, 1641]). Mitosis and cytokinesis have been investigated in detail and shown to be of type VIII (see above and p. 334) in a *Coleochaete* species ([1119, 1419]).

Oogamous sexual reproduction, in which biflagellate zoids function as the male gametes, is known to occur in both *Chaetosphaeridium* ([1771]) and *Coleochaete* ([100, 440, 464, 1340]). Both genera also exhibit asexual reproduction, involving biflagellate zoospores. As in the Klebsormidiales, each vegetative cell only produces one zoospore or male gamete (Figs. 28.2b, 28.3).

The Coleochaetales includes about 3 genera and 15 species. Other genera may also need to be transferred to the order, but it is difficult to be sure, since we do not yet have sufficient information about them, especially about the ultrastructure of the zoids and about mitosis and cytokinesis.

Two examples of the order Coleochaetales

Chaetosphaeridium (Figs. 19.15, 28.2*a*, *b*)

Chaetosphaeridium occurs as an epiphyte on larger freshwater algae. The cells are spherical and are united into dense clusters. Each has a single parietal chloroplast, which contains a pyrenoid, and it bears a hair, filled with cytoplasm and possessing a prominent basal sheath. Oogamy has been demonstrated in one species ([1771]), while asexual reproduction also occurs, through the formation of biflagellate zoospores with a unilateral flagellar apparatus (Figs. 19.15a, b, 19.16). It should be emphasized, perhaps, that mitosis and cytokinesis have not yet been investigated at the ultrastructural level.

Coleochaete (Figs. 28.3*a–c*, 28.4)

These tiny discoid or cushion-like plants consist of densely branched filaments of cells and live as epiphytes on aquatic macrophytes and larger algae in freshwaters. Each cell contains a parietal chloroplast, in which there are one or two pyrenoids, and many of the cells bear colourless hairs with basal sheaths. Asexual reproduction takes place via biflagellate zoospores with a unilateral type of flagellar apparatus ([1641]), each vegetative cell producing only one spore.

Sexual reproduction is oogamous. The vegetative cells bud off small, colourless antheridia, which are flask-shaped, and each of these produces a small, colourless, biflagellate spermatozoid, which has a unilateral flagellar apparatus ([555]), like the zoospores. Each spermatozoid contains a minute chloroplast. The oogonia are also flask-shaped but bear a long trichogyne, which receives the nucleus from a spermatozoid after its own wall has become gelatinous. Following fertilization the zygote swells and becomes more rounded. The filaments of cells nearby grow up to form a pseudoparenchyma surrounding the zygote, which becomes dormant. After a time the hypnozygote germinates, undergoes meiosis ([18, 732]), and divides up into 16–32 cells, each of which forms one biflagellate, haploid zoospore. The zoospores are set free when the zygote wall and the surrounding pseudoparenchyma split open; they later give rise to new haploid thalli. *Coleochaete* thus has a haplontic life cycle ([1340]).

Cytokinesis is brought about through the formation of a cell plate lying within a phragmoplast (type VIII mitosis and cytokinesis; p. 334, Fig. 19.23 II: [1119, 1419]).

29

Chlorophyta: Class 10. Zygnematophyceae

The principal characteristics of the Zygnematophyceae [753]

1 The Zygnematophyceae exhibit only two levels of organization: species are either coccoid (Figs. 29.5, 29.9) or filamentous (Figs. 29.3, 29.4). The filaments are always unbranched.

2 The fibrillar, structural component of the cell walls is crystalline cellulose, which occurs in the form of microfibrils (Fig. 29.2). Synthesis of the cellulose microfibrils takes place at the plasmalemma, which contains rosette-like arrays of 6 granules of cellulose synthase, each one with a diameter of 10 nm (Fig. 19.24a; [518, 755]).

3 Flagellate reproductive cells are never formed. Sexual reproduction takes place by conjugation, involving the fusion of two amoeboid gametes, in a manner characteristic of the class (Figs. 29.3, 29.7); this is described in more detail below.

4 Mitosis and cytokinesis exhibit features of both type VII and type VIII mitosis–cytokinesis (pp. 333, 334, Fig. 19.23 I, II). Mitosis is semi-closed and there is a persistent telophase spindle. Cytokinesis is brought through the ingrowth of a cleavage furrow, together in many cases with a cell plate, which is formed within a phragmoplast (Fig. 29.1). A cross-wall is deposited within the cell plate; this does not contain plasmodesmata.

5 Each cell is uninucleate. The chloroplasts take various forms. Sometimes the cell contains one to several spiral chloroplasts (Figs. 29.1, 29.5b); elsewhere there is one axial, plate-like chloroplast (Figs. 29.4, 29.5a), or two massive chloroplasts, which are often more or less stellate (Figs. 29.4d, 29.5f). The chloroplasts contain pyrenoids.

6 The Zygnematophyceae are haplontic. The life cycle includes formation of a thick-walled hypnozygote (Figs. 29.3d–g, k–m, 29.7d, 29.8).

7 The class is restricted to freshwater habitats.

An important characteristic of this class is the total absence of flagellate stages, at any stage of the life cycle. Correlated with this is the total absence of centrioles at mitosis ([1419]); centrioles are thought to represent the rudimentary, self-duplicating templates for basal bodies and flagellar axonemes (cf. p. 307).

The Zygnematophyceae probably diverged from one of the other main lineages of green algae by the loss of flagellate cells. However, since the structure of flagellate cells seems to change only slowly during evolution, so that they act as repositories for primitive characters, and since it is therefore these sets of conservative characters that are used to distinguish the main groups of algae, it is difficult to decide exactly where the Zygnematophyceae should be placed. Certain features of mitosis and cytokinesis (see below, under *Spirogyra*, for a fuller treatment) resemble what occurs in *Klebsormidium* and *Coleochaete*, which belong to the Klebsormidiophyceae (these two genera exhibit types VII and VIII of mitosis and cytokinesis: pp. 333, 334, Fig. 19.23 I, II). But even then, there are many differences of detail.

The cell walls are composed of three layers: an outermost layer of mucilage, composed of complex polysaccharides, and two inner layers, consisting of microfibrillar cellulose. In the outer of the two microfibrillar layers the cellulose microfibrils tend to be orientated parallel to the long axis of the cell, while in the inner one they tend to be aligned transversely ([290, 755, 911, 1064]). The longitudinally aligned microfibrils initially also have a transverse orientation, but this is lost as the cell extends.

The cellulose microfibrils are synthesized by

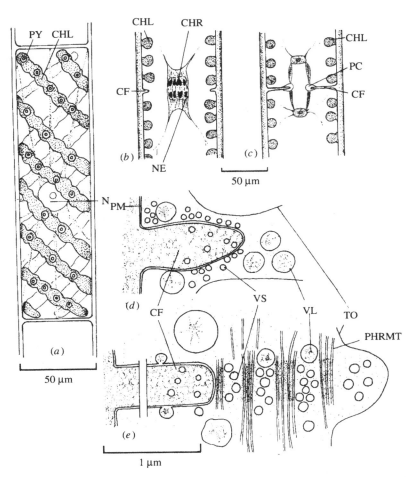

Figure 29.1. *Spirogyra.* (*a*) Vegetative cell. (*b*) Early anaphase, as seen with the light microscope. (*c*) Telophase, as seen with the light microscope. (*d*) Detail of the forming cleavage furrow, containing the young cross-wall, at early anaphase, from EM observations. (*e*) Detail of the cleavage furrow, young cross-wall and phragmoplast at telophase, from EM observations. CF = cleavage furrow, containing the young cross-wall; CHL = chloroplast; CHR = chromosome; N = nucleus; NE = nuclear envelope; PC = cap of protoplasm; PHRMT = phragmoplast microtubules; PM = plasma membrane (plasmalemma); PY = pyrenoid; TO = tonoplast; VL = large vesicle; VS = small vesicle. (*b–e* after [444, 445].)

rosette-like arrays of six particles ('cellulose synthase complexes'; Fig. 19.24*a*). These are situated in the plasmalemma, within which they are free to move ([518, 755]). Rosette-like arrays of cellulose synthase complexes also occur in the green algal class Charophyceae, and in mosses, liverworts and vascular plants (p. 339). The cell wall composition of the Zygnematophyceae resembles that of *Klebsormidium* ([755]), which supports the idea of a phylogenetic link between the Zygnematophyceae and the Klebsormidio-

phyceae. Unfortunately, no-one has yet examined the Klebsormidiophyceae for the presence of rosette-like arrays of cellulose synthase.

In the unicellular Desmidiales the innermost, secondary layer of microfibrils consists of characteristic flat bands of 8–12 cellulose microfibrils, each *ca*. 30 nm in diameter, embedded in an amorphous matrix (Fig. 29.2). These bands are either formed within elongate vesicles (probably derived from the golgi apparatus) and delivered to the cell surface by exocytosis

Figure 29.2. Detail of the secondary wall of a desmid, as revealed by freeze etching (EM), showing bands of cellulose microfibrils with different orientations. (After [1204].)

(¹²⁰³, ¹²⁰⁴); or they are synthesized by arrays of cellulose synthase rosettes in the plasmalemma, the arrays having come from the same elongate vesicles ([312, 836]).

One consequence of the absence of flagellate cells is that sexual reproduction has to be accomplished via non-flagellate gametes. The details of the sexual process involved, termed conjugation, will be described for a filamentous representative of the class, *Spirogyra*, and a unicellular representative, *Cosmarium*.

Size and distribution of the class

The Zygnematophyceae live in freshwater, with only a few (some *Spirogyra* species) being able to tolerate slightly brackish conditions. A few members of the group are terrestrial. About 50 genera are known, containing 4000–6000 species, the majority being unicellular forms. Fossil hypnozygotes of four genera that are still extant, including *Spirogyra*, *Mougeotia* and *Zygnema*, have been found in deposits dating back to the Carboniferous ([753]). The sporopollenin-like layer of the hypnozygote wall is particularly resistant to decay and therefore fossilizes easily, like the sporopollenin layer in the spores and pollen grains of vascular plants. Thus the Zygnematales were present, much as we know them today, in the Carboniferous period (*ca.* 300 million years ago). Certain other classes of green algae have an even longer fossil record (Fig. 32.1).

Order Zygnematales

1 The algae of this order are unicellular or form simple uniseriate filaments, which are unbranched.

2 The wall of each cell is a single entity: it is not divided into two more or less equal, slightly overlapping segments (semicells). The walls are covered by a smooth mucilaginous layer, which makes the filamentous forms slippery to the touch (¹⁵³).

The *ca.* 18 genera and 900 species of this order are all inhabitants of freshwater, though some, e.g. *Zygogonium* species, also occur on damp soil. Most of them prefer stagnant pools, ponds and ditches, but some are found in fast-flowing mountain streams. The genera, and even many of the species, generally have a worldwide distribution (⁷⁵²).

Spirogyra *(Fig. 29.1a)*

Each cell contains one to several spiral chloroplasts, which are parietal and contain pyrenoids spaced at regular intervals along their length. The nucleus, which is often clearly visible in the living cell, lies at the centre of the cell, suspended by strands of protoplasm, which traverse the large vacuole.

The filaments of many species fragment readily, coming apart at the cross-walls; they grow through intercalary cell division. Mitosis is acentric (without centrioles) and mostly intranuclear, the nuclear envelope remaining intact most of the time (Fig. 29.1b; ⁴⁴⁴); it is only during anaphase that the envelope disperses completely. The cross-walls are formed partly from a cell plate lying in a phragmoplast, but mostly as a result of the inward development of a diaphragm-like cleavage furrow (⁴⁴⁵). The formation of the cleavage furrow begins at early anaphase (Fig. 29.1b, d) and involves vesicles of two types: small vesicles like those observed to be cut off from the golgi bodies, and larger ones with fluffy, fibrous contents, which seem to be cell wall material. The small vesicles can later be found, apparently intact, within the septum itself.

During late telophase the ingrowing septum intercepts the mitotic spindle, which up to this point has been hollow (Fig. 29.1c). At this stage a phragmoplast begins to form (Fig. 29.1e), consisting of longitudinal bundles of microtubules, which no longer extend as far as the daughter nuclei. They are embedded in dark-staining material and between them golgi vesicles collect, forming a cell plate. *Mougeotia* (Fig. 29.4*a*) has the same type of mitosis and cytokinesis as in *Spirogyra* ([55, 444, 445, 1430]), but in the desmid *Closterium* (Fig. 29.5*f*) there is no phragmoplast and cytokinesis is brought about solely by the formation of a cleavage furrow ([1423]).

Sexual reproduction in *Spirogyra* (Fig. 29.3)

The method of sexual reproduction found in the Zygnematales is very unusual and is highly characteristic of the order. It involves **conjugation** and is promoted by low nitrogen concentrations and generally occurs within a narrow range of pH ([579]). The following stages can be distinguished during conjugation in *Spirogyra*.

1 The filaments lie next to each other and may exhibit gliding movements, although it is not yet clear whether these can strictly be regarded as true, autonomous motility. They adhere in pairs (Fig. 29.3*a*). At this stage the cells ('progametes') are not ready for conjugation. Hormonal interactions between the paired filaments induce one last division of each progamete, producing two gametes ([580]).

2 The cells of the paired filaments lie opposite one another, and each cell (gametangium) produces a papilla, which grows out and comes into contact with the papilla growing out from an adjacent cell in the other filament (Fig. 29.3*b*). Sometimes the papillae produced by one filament (the 'male' filament) are somewhat larger than those produced by the other (the 'female' filament). Since most or all of the cells in the filaments produce papillae, the filaments are slowly pushed apart.

In one species at least, induction of the papilla formation is under hormonal control: when a slip of mica is inserted between two paired filaments over part of their length, only the parts not separated by mica form papillae ([580]; see also [753]).

3 The walls between the papillae break down in the area of contact, so that a canal is established connecting the two gametangia. The protoplasts contract, through expulsion of water by contractile vacuoles.

4 One of the two protoplasts, which can be designated as the male gamete, moves out of its gametangium and through the copulation canal, like an amoeba, towards the immobile female protoplast (Fig. 29.3*c*, left).

5 The male and female protoplasts fuse (Fig. 29.3*c*, right).

6 After karyogamy, the ellipsoidal zygote surrounds itself with a thick three-layered wall, consisting of endo- , meso- and exospore (Fig. 29.3*d*). The wall of the hypnozygote has a suture, which allows the cell inside to break out at germination. The thick central mesospore is always brown and often furnished with species-specific ornamentation, and it also contains sporopollenin-like material, which is responsible for the resistance of the hypnozygote to desiccation ([838, 839]). The dormant hypnozygotes contain reserves of starch and fatty material and have been kept alive for more than 20 years, stored dry ([253]).

7 After a period of dormancy the hypnozygote germinates (Fig. 29.3*e–i*). This is preceded by a reduction division (meiosis), following which three of the four haploid nuclei degenerate ([532, 609]). The zygote wall splits apart along the suture and the single-celled, haploid germling grows out.

Spirogyra is therefore a haplontic organism, only the zygote being diploid. From the description of the life cycle given above it might be expected that *Spirogyra* would exhibit haplogenotypic sex determination. In at least one species, however, this does not appear to be the case, since filaments grown from one germling, or even from vegetative cells broken off the same filament, are capable of conjugating with each other ([580]). It is conceivable, however, that other species may prove to have haplogenotypic sex determination, especially since this has been found in some *Zygnema* species and in certain members of the Desmidiales, such as *Cosmarium botrytis* (p. 470; [752]).

The type of conjugation described above is referred to as scalariform (ladder-like) conjugation. For this kind of conjugation two filaments are necessary, the numerous conjugation tubes between them forming the rungs of the ladder. Another kind of conjugation found in filamentous Zygnematales is lateral conjugation (Fig. 29.3*j, k*). Here adjacent cells in the same fila-

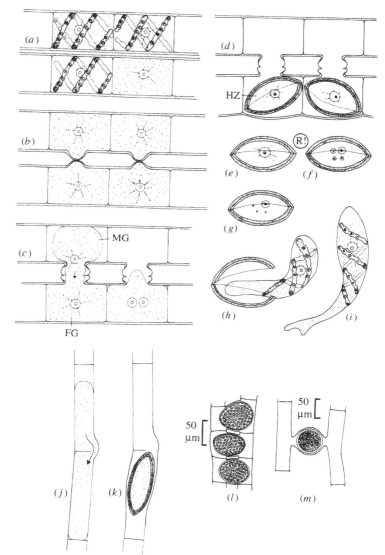

Figure 29.3. (*a–d*) *Spirogyra:* stages in scalariform conjugation. (*e–g*) Meiosis in the zygote of *Spirogyra,* with degeneration of three of the four haploid nuclei. (*h, i*) Germination of the hypnozygote in *Spirogyra.* (*j, k*) *Spirogyra:* lateral conjugation. (*l*) *Zygnema kiangsiense:* zygotes lying in the bridges (canals) between the filaments. (*m*) *Mougeotia sanfordiana:* a zygote in the bridge between two cells. FG = 'female' gamete; HZ = hypnozygote; MG = 'male' gamete; R! = reduction division (meiosis). (*l, m* after [868].)

ment become connected by longitudinally aligned conjugation tubes. The contents of one cell migrate through the tube into the other cell to effect fertilization. Some species exhibit only one type of conjugation, while in others both can occur.

The development of a population of *Spirogyra maxima* has been followed in nature ([1294]) and the following phases distinguished.

1 At the beginning of June, the hypnozygotes germinated.

2 After 4 weeks, two plate-sized masses of vegetative filaments were present.

3 After 5 weeks, the ditch under investigation was full of *Spirogyra maxima*, as a result of vegetative growth. The initial stages of copulation were observed.

4 After 6 weeks, zygotes were beginning to be formed. They were still dark green because the zygote walls were thin and colourless.

5 After 7 weeks, the zygotes had brown mesospores.

6 After 9 weeks, the masses of *Spirogyra* filaments, together with the zygotes in them, had sunk to the bottom of the ditch and the empty cell walls then disappeared.

In nature, therefore, the whole vegetative development of *Spirogyra maxima* can be completed in two months. In this case the various developmental events occurred almost simultaneously.

The dormancy and survival of the zygotes has also been investigated ([1294]). It was shown that zygotes are well able to withstand the decay processes that occur in the muds where the alga lives. The length of the dormant period depends on the temperature. At 4 °C *Spirogyra maxima* zygotes remain dormant for 14 months, but at 18–20 °C they are dormant for only 3.5 months. For germination to occur, it is also necessary for the zygotes to be exposed to light for 2–3 days.

In other species, with thinner walls, the obligate period of dormancy can be much shorter and may amount to only three or four weeks at a temperature of 18–20 °C. It is possible that such species may have several periods of vegetative growth per year.

This species-rich genus – about 380 species are known – is widely distributed in freshwater habitats ([814, 917, 1470, 1787]). The surfaces of small nutrient-rich ditches and ponds can become completely covered with thick, slimy, yellow-green masses of *Spirogyra*, especially in late spring and early summer.

Some other filamentous representatives of the Zygnematales

Mougeotia (Figs. 29.3*m*, 29.4*a–c*)
Each cell contains an axial plate-like chloroplast with several pyrenoids, which can alter its position in the

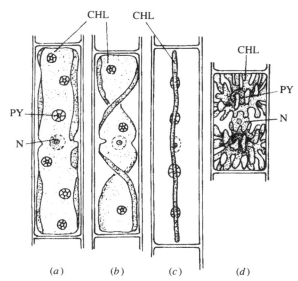

Figure 29.4. (*a–c*) *Mougeotia*: light-induced reorientation of the chloroplast. (*d*) *Zygnema* cell. CHL = chloroplast (plate-like in *Mougeotia*; stellate in *Zygnema*); N = nucleus; PY = pyrenoid. (After [917].)

cell with respect to light. In dim light the chloroplast positions itself at right angles to the incident light, while in strong light it becomes aligned parallel to the incident light ([618, 1308]). In this genus the zygotes are formed within the conjugation canals. About 125 species have been described from freshwater ([814]).

Zygnema (Figs. 29.3*l*, 29.4*d*)
Zygnema cells contain two stellate, axial chloroplasts, each possessing a single pyrenoid. Again the zygote often lies in the conjugation canal. About 140 species are known, all occurring in freshwater ([814]).

Some unicellular representatives of the Zygnematales

In contrast to the Desmidiales (for which, see below), the cell walls of unicellular Zygnematales do not consist of two halves (semicells) separated by a suture or isthmus.

Spirotaenia (Fig. 29.5*b*)
The cells of *Spirotaenia* are short and cylindrical, with rounded ends. The chloroplast is spiral, as in *Spirogyra*. Around 20 species are known.

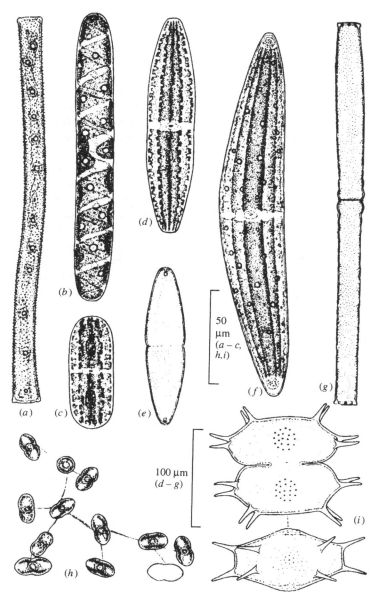

Figure 29.5. Unicellular Zygnematales (*b–d*) and Desmidiales (*a, e–i*). (*a*) *Gonatozygon brebissonii*. (*b*) *Spirotaenia condensata*. (*c*) *Cylindrocystis brebissonii*. (*d*) *Netrium digitus*. (*e*) *Tetmemorus granulatus*. (*f*) *Closterium lunula*. (*g*) *Pleurotaenium ehrenbergii*. (*h*) *Cosmocladium constrictum*. (*i*) *Xanthidium antilopaeum*. (From [440].)

Cylindrocystis (Fig. 29.5*c*)

This alga also has cylindrical cells with rounded ends. There are two chloroplasts, one lying towards each end of the cell. Each chloroplast lies axially, contains a rounded central pyrenoid, and is stellate in transverse section. About 5 species are known. *Cylindrocystis brebissonii* occurs among *Sphagnum* in bog pools.

Netrium (Fig. 29.5*d*)

Netrium cells are elongate and elliptical in outline. The cell wall is smooth and, as in *Cylindrocystis*, there are two chloroplasts, one in each half of the cell. The chloroplasts are axial and stellate in section, but are more elaborate than in *Cylindrocystis* and contain an elongate pyrenoid.

Order Desmidiales

1 The cells are generally solitary, but sometimes form amorphous colonies or are united to form simple, unbranched filaments.

2 The wall of each cell consists of two symmetrical halves, which overlap slightly (in some genera there are also several small wall segments lying between the two principal pieces). The overlap is usually accompanied by a marked constriction of the cell, creating two semicells joined by a narrow isthmus. The cell walls are often ornamented in various ways. Pores are present in the wall, or pore-like modifications ([152, 153]), through which mucilage is often secreted.

The order contains about 30 genera and 5000 species ([906, 907, 916, 918, 1439, 1440, 1535, 1536, 1875, 1876]). These are particularly beautiful algae but their systematics are mastered by very few. Rich, diverse desmid floras are particularly characteristic of freshwaters of low pH (4–7), such as occur in bog pools or in acid ponds lying over leached sands and gravels ([632]). Most species are benthic and live on or between higher plants around the margins of the water-body. However, from here they may at times give rise to free-floating populations, while a few species are truly planktonic; these are usually small forms (9–20 μm), presumably because of their lower sinking rate ([152]).

Waters with low pH are often also oligotrophic (poor in nitrates and phosphates). Waters with pHs of 7–9, on the other hand, are often eutrophic (more or less rich in nitrate and phosphate), allowing a greater biomass of algae to develop. In addition there are dystrophic waters, such as those found in very acid bog pools, where the water is poor in nutrients and coloured brown by dissolved peaty (humic) material. These are very general categories disguising much other important variation in water quality, but the Danish hydrobiologist Nygaard has designed a compound quotient, t, which makes it possible to convey an overall impression of the trophic status of a water-body ([1309]):

t = (No. of species of Cyanophyta + centric diatoms + Chlorococcales)/(No. of species of Desmidiales).

In oligotrophic lakes $t < 1$;

In dystrophic lakes $t = 0$–0.3;

In eutrophic lakes $t > 1.0$;

In highly eutrophic (hypertrophic) lakes $t = 5$–20.

An investigation of a number of ponds in Scotland indicated that these correlations are broadly valid ([151, 152]). Of about 50 species of Desmidiales recorded, 59% were found in oligotrophic waters, 8% in mesotrophic waters, and 24% in eutrophic waters.

Various investigators think that the abundance and diversity of desmids in relatively oligotrophic waters are brought about by the effects of low pH, rather than by low nutrient concentrations. Moss ([1236, 1237, 1238]), for instance, believes that there is an indirect relationship with the carbon dioxide–bicarbonate system. He found that both 'oligotrophic' and 'eutrophic' desmids had a pH minimum of 4 for growth, but that the maximum pH tolerated by 'eutrophic' species was higher than that tolerated by 'oligotrophic' forms (9 as against 8–8.5). From his work Moss concluded that the 'oligotrophic' species may only be able to take up and use free CO_2 as a carbon source for photosynthesis, which is present in appreciable amounts in freshwaters only below a pH of 8 to 8.5; 'eutrophic' species, on the other hand, may be able to use bicarbonate as well as free CO_2, bicarbonate being present in quantity at pHs of 8–9. This would give the 'eutrophic' species a competitive advantage over 'oligotrophic' species at high pH. Coesel ([243]) considers that subtle, small-scale patchiness in nutrient concentration within natural habitats may also be important in producing a diverse desmid flora. For instance, where mixing between relatively eutrophic ground water and oligotrophic rain water is restricted and incomplete, as may occur in mires perhaps, or small ponds, small-scale patchiness may be brought about in nutrient concentrations, producing a variety of different microenvironments. These might support a variety of different algal communities and hence, overall, a rich desmid flora. Excessive nutrient enrichment could swamp the subtle differences between the microhabitats and so cause a decline in diversity. Long-term observations of the desmid flora in one pond (made in 1925, 1955 and 1975) showed a decline from 195 to 123 species as the pond, initially oligotrophic, became more eutrophic between 1925 and 1955. The eutrophication, brought about by enrichment from domestic sewage, was halted after 1955, but the decline in diversity continued (from 123 to 68 species). Surprisingly, this appears to have been caused by 'oligotrophication', or rather by the acidification caused by acid rain; the acid rain in turn results from emissions of sulphur dioxide and nitrous oxide into the atmosphere from industrial areas ([245]).

Cosmarium botrytis (Figs. 29.6, 29.7, 29.9d)

In this desmid the two half cells (semicells) are separated by a marked constriction. The cell is compressed (Fig. 29.6*b, c*) each semicell being trapezoidal in face view (Fig. 29.6*a*).

The cell wall consists of two halves, which overlap slightly at the isthmus. The suture between them is difficult to discern, however, and only in conjugating (Fig. 29.7) or dead cells does it become obvious. The cell wall is garnished with warts; similar or even more elaborate ornamentation is characteristic of many Desmidiales.

The cell wall is pierced by many pores, through which mucilage is secreted. Some desmids execute sluggish movements, which are apparently brought about by mucilage secretion, through particularly

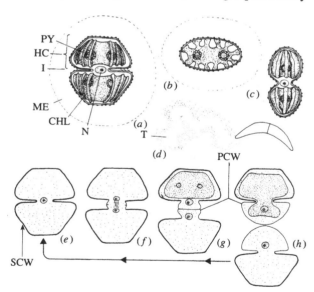

Figure 29.6. (*a–c*) *Cosmarium botrytis*. (*a*) Side view: broad aspect. (*b*) End view. (*c*) Side view: narrow aspect (seen at right angles to (*a*)). (*d*) *Closterium* movement. (*e–h*) *Cosmarium*: stages in cell division and the formation of new semicells. CHL = chloroplast; HC = half cell or semicell; I = isthmus; ME = mucilage envelope; N = nucleus; PCW = primary cell wall; PY = pyrenoid; SCW = secondary cell wall; T = trail of mucilage.

large pores at the cell apices (Fig. 29.6*d*). As they move, desmids leave behind them a trail of slime, which can be made visible in microscopical preparations by adding Indian ink, when the trails appear as pale tracks in a dark field. Movement is phototactic: Desmidiales move towards dim light and away from bright light.

The nucleus lies in the isthmus linking the two semicells. Each semicell contains a massive central chloroplast, which, indeed, virtually fills it. The chloroplasts each contain two pyrenoids and bear eight to twelve ridges.

Cell division

Cell division (Fig. 29.6*e–h*) is preceded by mitosis, which is not intranuclear, in contrast to mitosis in *Spirogyra* and many other green algae ([1416, 1423]), since the nuclear envelope fragments during prophase. During mitosis the isthmus begins to elongate, and as it does so a cross-wall develops, centripetally, between the two daughter cells (Fig. 29.6*f*). The cross-wall grows through the addition of vesicles containing wall material, which are probably derived from the golgi apparatus. Neither a phycoplast nor a phragmoplast is present (contrast cell division in *Spirogyra*, p. 463).

Once cell division is complete the two halves of the isthmus, now separated from each other by the new cross-wall, both grow out to form new semicells. At the same time the new semicells separate from each other along the cross wall (Fig. 29.6*g, h*). The young wall of each new semicell is a finely fibrillar, primary wall. As the new semicell grows, further material is added to the primary wall from golgi vesicles, until expansion is complete. Then a secondary wall is deposited against the inner face of the mature primary wall, consisting for the most part of flat bands of 8–12 cellulose microfibrils, each 30 nm thick (Fig. 29.2, p. 462; [837, 1042]).

During the division of *Cosmarium* two unicellular individuals arise from a short-lived individual with two cells. Hence, if ontogeny recapitulates phylogeny, the unicellular Desmidiales may perhaps have been derived from the multicellular Zygnematales. In this respect *Cosmarium* should be compared with *Kirchneriella* (p. 370).

The single chloroplast inherited by each daughter cell moves into the new semicell until it is symmetrically positioned with respect to the isthmus, and then it divides. The complicated reorganization of the cell contents during division has been investigated in *Cosmarium* and also in *Closterium* ([1416, 1423]).

Sexual reproduction: conjugation (Fig. 29.7)

Desmids can be either heterothallic or homothallic ([152]). *Cosmarium botrytis* is heterothallic ([1684, 1686]); its life cycle has been investigated using unialgal cultures, although the main features of conjugation were already known from nature (see also Fig. 29.8, showing conjugation in *Closterium*).

All the stages of conjugation can be observed within 24–48 h of mixing a (+) clone with a (−) clone. The following stages can be distinguished.

1   When they are ready for copulation the cells seek each other actively and pair, leaving slime trails behind them as they move. How the cells find each other is as yet unknown. For the vegetative cells to become sexual, it is necessary not only that environmental conditions are suitable (e.g. low nitrogen concentrations), but also that cells of both mating types are present. Cells belonging to one clone, and thus having the same mating type as each other, continue to divide vegetatively even when they are placed in low nitrogen concentrations. This suggests perhaps that a sexual hormone secreted by one clone induces sexuality in the cells of the other ([775]).

In one *Closterium* species the (+) cells are able to move through thin strips of agar towards (−) cells, by secreting mucilage. Sometimes both the (+) and the (−) cells move towards each other and conjugate halfway across the strip, and it seems that the (+) and (−) cells must be attracted to each other via sexual hormones diffusing through the agar ([244]).

2   The paired cells align themselves with their long axes at right angles to each other and surround themselves with mucilage.

3   The wall of each cell splits apart at the isthmus and an amoeboid gamete emerges; the gametes move towards each other (Fig. 29.7a).

4   As soon as the gametes come into contact, they quickly abandon the parent cell walls and fuse with each other, this being completed within about 5 minutes. An irregularly shaped zygote is produced, which then rounds up (Fig. 29.7b, c). Numerous contractile vacuoles appear while the

zygote is rounding up and then disappear again afterwards.

5   After about an hour the first ornamentation is visible on the zygote wall, in the form of small spines. In the course of the following three weeks a thick brown middle wall (mesospore) and an inner wall (endospore) develop inside the hyaline outer wall (exospore); it is the exospore that bears the spines (Fig. 29.7d). The exospore and endospore consist of cellulose microfibrils lying in a matrix of polysaccharide. The thick mesospore, however, is built of a reticulum of cellulose microfibrils embedded in sporopollenin-like material, which makes the zygote resistant to desiccation, as does the sporopollenin in the walls of higher plant pollen ([838, 839]).

6   The hypnozygotes (resting zygotes) remain dormant for at least three months before they can be made to germinate, and during this time they can be stored dry. If after three months they are transferred to fresh medium and exposed to light, they will germinate in profusion after two to three days.

7   Upon germination the zygote wall splits apart and the protoplast, still undivided and naked, is liberated into the surrounding medium. It swells greatly through the uptake of water but subsequently becomes enclosed by a thin wall (Fig. 29.7f); it contains a single diploid nucleus.

8   Within two hours of release the cell shrinks again by losing water. During this time the nucleus divides meiotically, producing four haploid nuclei ([825]), although according to some authors meiosis takes place *within* the hypnozygote ([129]). The protoplast now divides, to give two binucleate cells (Fig. 29.7g). One nucleus in each daughter cell then degenerates, so that two uninucleate, haploid cells are produced from each hypnozygote; these give rise to two clones, one of the (+) mating type and one of the (−) mating type. Sex determination is thus haplogenotypic (cf. [825]).

9   Each haploid daughter cell arising from the zygote constricts, taking on the general form of a desmid cell (Fig. 29.7h). As yet, however, they do not possess the characteristic shape of *Cosmarium botrytis*.

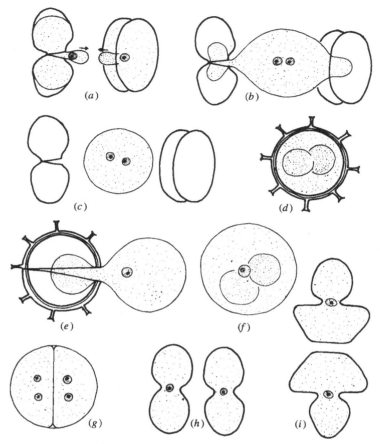

Figure 29.7. *Cosmarium botrytis:* conjugation. (*a*) Formation of papillae by the two gametangia, the contents of which act as isogametes. (*b*) Plasmogamy. (*c*) Rounding off of the zygote. (*d*) Mature hypnozygote, with thick spiny wall. (*e*) Germination of the hypnozygote. (*f*) Swelling of the protoplast released after germination. (*g*) Meiosis and cell division produce two daughter cells, each containing two haploid nuclei; one of the nuclei then degenerates in each cell. (*h*) Development of each daughter into a constricted cell, which has a morphology unlike that of normal vegetative cells. (*i*) After division of this initial cell, new semicells are produced that have a normal morphology.

10 The new semicells formed after the next cell division develop the typical *C. botrytis* morphology (Fig. 29.7*i*), and in subsequent divisions cells are produced that have two normal *C. botrytis* semicells.

In summary, we can say that *Cosmarium botrytis* is a haplont with isogamous copulation and haplogenotypic sex determination.

In desmids, sexual reproduction has been observed only sporadically in nature; Coesel([243]) thinks that this reflects sexual incompatibility rather than unsuitable environmental conditions (see also [246]). Most desmids must therefore survive adverse conditions (low temperature, freezing, low light intensities, partial desiccation, etc.) as vegetative cells rather than as hypnozygotes, and several investigations suggest that this is indeed possible ([152, 243]).

Some other representatives of the Desmidiales

Gonatozygon (Fig. 29.5*a*)

The cells of *Gonatozygon* are elongate, cylindrical or spindle-shaped, and they have flat, truncate ends. The wall is usually rough, bearing granules or small spines.

There is a single, axile chloroplast, which is ribbon-like and contains many pyrenoids. About seven species are known.

Closterium (Fig. 29.5f, 29.8)

Closterium cells are curved, coming to a sharp point at each end. They are circular in cross section and possess no isthmus. The cell wall often bears fine longitudinal striations and small pores, while at the ends of the cell it is pierced by larger pores, through which mucilage is secreted during locomotion (Fig. 29.6d). In Europe 85 species have been found, growing in acid to basic waters.

Pleurotaenium (Fig. 29.5g)

Pleurotaenium cells are cylindrical or almost so. Each end of the cell is truncate and bears a ring of warts, while near the ends there are vacuoles containing crystals of gypsum ($CaSO_4$). An isthmus is present but it is only shallow. About 200 species have been described.

Tetmemorus (Fig. 29.5e)

The cells are straight and taper towards the ends, where there is a notch. The isthmus is shallow. About 24 species are known.

Euastrum (Fig. 29.9a)

Euastrum cells are compressed, about twice as long as broad, and have a narrow but deep central isthmus. The semicells are trapezoidal and their margins bear two or four, broad indentations, which are symmetrically placed. At each end of the cell there is a prominent notch. About 150 species are known, almost all of them living in acid water.

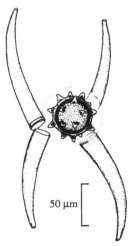

Figure 29.8. *Closterium calosporum* zygote. (After [1638].)

Micrasterias (Fig. 29.9i, j)

In this genus the cells are strongly flattened and possess a deep isthmus. Each semicell is divided into five lobes by four deep indentations, which are symmetrically positioned about the cell's axis. The individual lobes are themselves subdivided by shallower indentations. The margins of the cell often bear spines or teeth and the cell wall can be smooth, warty or spiny. Most *Micrasterias* species live in acid waters.

Cosmarium (Fig. 29.9d)

Cosmarium cells have flat ends and a deep isthmus. The semicells are semicircular, semielliptical, reniform or trapezoidal; the margins never have notches or invaginations. The cell wall is smooth or warty but never bears spines. This genus is very rich in species, about 1000 having been described.

Cosmocladium (Fig. 29.5h)

In *Cosmocladium* the individual cells resemble *Cosmarium*, but they are united into colonies by strands of mucilage. There are only a few species.

Xanthidium (Fig. 29.5i)

Xanthidium cells resemble those of *Cosmarium* in their shape, but they can be distinguished by the presence of simple or double spines, which are positioned on the cell margin.

Staurastrum (Fig. 29.9b)

In end view the cells are usually 3-, 4- or 5-angled, the corners often being extended into one or more horn-like projections. Sometimes the cells are flattened and bear only two projections (biradiate organization). The cell wall can be smooth with pores, or they can be warty or spiny. *Staurastrum* contains several hundred species, among which are some particularly bizarre forms.

Desmidium (Fig. 29.9h)

Desmidium cells are linked to form unbranched filaments, which have a spiral twist and are enclosed within mucilage sheaths. In end view the cells are three-cornered. *Desmidium* contain a few species.

Hyalotheca (Fig. 29.9c)

The cells of this genus are united into unbranched, filamentous colonies, as in *Desmidium*. Each cell has an indistinct isthmus and the colony lies within a sheath of mucilage. *Hyalotheca dissiliens* is commonly encountered in bog pools.

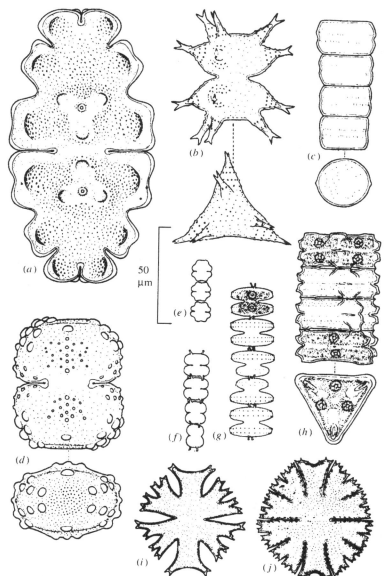

Figure 29.9. Desmidiales. (*a*) *Euastrum oblongum*. (*b*) *Staurastrum furcigerum*. (*c*) *Hyalotheca dissiliens*. (*d*) *Cosmarium ungerianum*. (*e*) *Spondylosium pulchellum*. (*f*) *Onychonema filiforme*.

(*g*) *Sphaerozosma aubertianum*. (*h*) *Desmidium schwartzii*. (*i*) *Micrasterias crux-melitensis*. (*j*) *Micrasterias papillifera*. (From [440].)

Spondylosium (Fig. 29.9*e*)

Individual *Spondylosium* cells resemble *Cosmarium* but they occur in chains, linked by mucilage. About 30 species are known.

Sphaerozosma (Fig. 29.9*f, g*) (including *Onychonema*)

In *Sphaerozosma*, *Cosmarium*-like cells are united to form helical chains. Each end of the cell bears two spines, which mesh with the spines of the adjacent cell to link the cells together. Each spine ends in a small knob. About 10 species are known.

30

Chlorophyta: Class 11. Charophyceae

The class Charophyceae contains only one order, the Charales.

The principal characteristics of the Charophyceae

1 The thalli are macroscopic, growing several decimetres high, and are differentiated into a series of nodes and internodes, which alternate along the axis of the plant. The nodes bear whorls of branches, each of limited growth; arising from the axils of some of these determinate laterals are side branches with unlimited growth, like the main axis (Figs. 30.1, 30.5).

2 Young, dividing cells are uninucleate, whereas the older cells become multinucleate. The thallus therefore exhibits the characteristics of both the filamentous and siphonocladous levels of organization.

3 The structural fraction of the cell wall is fibrillar, consisting of microfibrils of crystalline cellulose (Fig. 30.2; [571, 911]). The cellulose microfibrils are arranged in a helicoidal, 'crossed fibrillar pattern', which appears as a series of festoons when the wall is seen in transverse section (p. 411, Figs. 23.2, 30.2b; [1282]). As in the Zygnematophyceae, mosses and liverworts, and vascular plants, the microfibrils are synthesized by rosette-like complexes of cellulose synthase molecules, which lie in the plasmalemma (Fig. 19.24a; [754]).

4 Flagellate cells are produced during the life cycle, in the form of biflagellate male gametes, and these are a highly specialized version of the unilateral type of zoid (p. 321; compare Fig. 30.3p with Fig. 19.15). The zoids are covered with tiny organic scales, which are diamond-shaped and resemble the inner body scales of the Prasinophyceae (Figs. 19.15b, 19.10d; [1213, 1412, 1419, 1804]).

5 Mitosis is open, the telophase spindle is persistent, and cytokinesis is brought about by the formation of a cell plate, which is derived from golgi vesicles and lies within a phragmoplast (type VIII mitosis and cytokinesis; p. 334, Fig. 19.23 II). The cross-walls are pierced by plasmodesmata ([1411, 1419]).

6 Countless round, discoid chloroplasts are present in the peripheral layer of cytoplasm (Fig. 30.2). The chloroplasts lack pyrenoids and, in cells that are elongating, they divide continuously ([572]).

7 In the centre of each cell, when it is fully grown, there is a large vacuole. The cytoplasm close to the vacuole exhibits an incessant and remarkable streaming around the cell, in a longitudinal direction (Fig. 30.2).

8 All of the Charophyceae are oogamous haplonts. The ovoid oogonium, which is always borne on a determinate lateral branch, consists of a large egg cell surrounded by narrow sterile cells (Figs. 30.1c–e, 30.3f, g, 30.5b, c). The antheridia are also borne on determinate laterals. They are spherical and contain numerous multicellular, spermatogenous threads, each cell of which gives rise to a single spermatozoid. Around the outside of the antheridium is an envelope of sterile cells (Figs. 30.2a, 30.3m–o).

9 The class is almost entirely restricted to freshwater habitats; there are just a few species that occur in brackish waters.

The Charophyceae (stoneworts) form a distinct and easily recognized group, characterized by unique types of vegetative structure and reproductive organs.

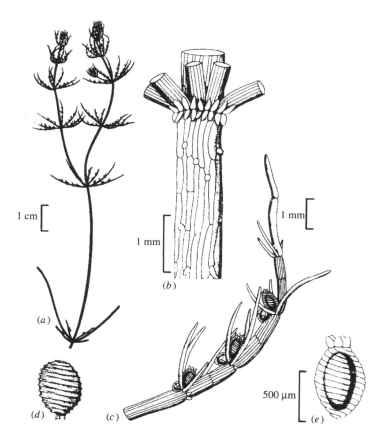

Figure 30.1. *Chara vulgaris.* (*a*) Habit of plant. (*b*) Part of the
axis. (*c*) Leaf (determinate lateral) with oogonia and
antheridia. (*d*) Oospore. (*e*) Oogonium. (From [1917].)

Recently, however, the name has been used in a much
broader sense, to refer to all the green algae with the
unilateral kind of zoid architecture and with type VII
or type VIII mitosis and cytokinesis (pp. 333, 334, Fig.
19.23 I, II; [704, 1140, 1175, 1644, 1645]). This concept of the
Charophyceae would include not only the stoneworts,
but also the Klebsormidiophyceae and Zygnematophyceae, as we have circumscribed them here. Each of
these three classes is 'natural' (in other words, the genera within them are closely related to each other) and
very distinct from the other two, differing markedly in
cell structure, thallus morphology, and life cycle. It is
therefore undesirable to merge them all in a single, diffuse class (see also p. 485), especially since the fossil
record shows clearly that the Zygnematophyceae and
Charophyceae, as we define them, are ancient lineages, which have existed for at least 300 and 420 mil-

lion years, respectively (p. 489, Fig. 32.1). This does
not preclude the possibility, however, that all three
classes are descended from a single ancestral group
with unilateral zoids; this group might also have given
rise to the bryophytes and vascular plants, since these
too have zoids with a unilateral configuration of the
flagellar apparatus (see p. 457 and Chapter 31).

A distinctive feature of the Charophyceae is the
rapid streaming of the cytoplasm around the cell,
which must lead to continuous mixing of the cell contents. It is particularly impressive in the long cells of
the internodes and the determinate laterals (Fig. 30.2),
where is a huge central vacuole, surrounded by a thin
peripheral layer of cytoplasm. The cytoplasm is subdivided into an outer, stationary ectoplasm, containing
closely packed rows of lenticular chloroplasts, and an
inner layer of endoplasm, which is mobile and streams

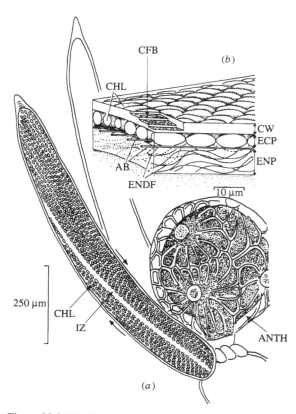

Figure 30.2. *Nitella.* (*a*) Antheridium and two 'leaflets'. In one of the leaflets the rows of chloroplasts are shown; the arrows indicate the directions in which the cytoplasm streams around the cell. (*b*) Three-dimensional reconstruction of part of the cell periphery, showing the rigid layer of ectoplasm containing the chloroplasts and the endoplasm that moves over it. AB = bundles of actin filaments; ANTH = antheridium; CFB = crossed fibrillar (helicoidal), crystalline structure of the cellulose in the cell wall; CHL = chloroplast; CW = cell wall; ECP = rigid ectoplasm containing chloroplasts; ENDF = motile endoplasmic fibres; ENP = streaming layer of endoplasm; IZ = indifferent zone (the boundary strip, lacking chloroplasts, between the upwardly and downwardly moving streams of cytoplasm. (*a* based on [1340]; *b* on [1691].)

parallel to the rows of chloroplasts, at speeds of about 50–100 µm s⁻¹. The boundary between the upwardly and downwardly moving streams of cytoplasm is marked by a narrow clear strip lacking chloroplasts, which is called the **indifferent zone**.

Just below the rigid ectoplasm there are 0.2 µm diameter bundles of actin filaments, each 5 nm thick.

These run parallel to the rows of chloroplasts and one of their functions is apparently to fix the chloroplasts in place. In addition they are involved in generating the motion of the endoplasm, through interactions with myosin molecules attached to the membranes of mitochondria, nuclei, endoplasmic reticulum, etc. The myosin molecules slide along the actin filaments ([16]), as during muscle contraction in animals, although exactly how streaming is brought about is unclear. The moving endoplasm contains mobile, undulating fibrils, which are visible with the light microscope and contain microfilaments (Fig. 30.2*b*; [16, 19, 1691, 1901, 1902]).

Vigorous cytoplasmic streaming can also be observed in the siphons of the Bryopsidophyceae and Dasycladophyceae. The mechanisms involved in generating motion differ from that present in the Charophyceae, although actin, and possibly also myosin, are again involved (pp. 424, 437).

Size and distribution of the class

Most stoneworts grow in fairly still, clear freshwaters, such as ditches, ponds and lakes, where they can form extensive underwater swards, anchored in the sediments by their rhizoids. They are particularly abundant in hard, basic waters (pH ≥ 7), where the cell walls often become encrusted with lime. It has been shown that some species cannot tolerate high phosphate concentrations (> 20 µg l⁻¹), and they disappear from lakes that have been polluted and made more eutrophic by sewage ([435, 436]), although this is often caused primarily by shading, through the luxuriant growth of other algae, duckweed, and so on. Some stoneworts grow abundantly in still brackish waters, such as around the shores of the Baltic, in the brackish lagoons of the Mediterranean, or in non-tidal river estuaries.

The Charales are a very ancient group. The calcified envelopes of the zygotes, known as 'gyrogonites', have been found in sedimentary rocks from the Silurian period, around 420 million years ago ([557, 558]), and they occur too in deposits from almost all later periods. The genera present today date back to the Mesozoic era (130–200 million years ago) and seem to be very conservative in their morphology ([1664]; Fig. 32.1). According to one revision, carried out on a global basis ([1917]), the order consists of six genera and 81 species, although these were split up into about 400 infraspecific taxa ([121, 1078]). There has been severe criticism, however, of the species concept underlying this work ([1446]).

Five examples of the order Charales

Chara (Figs. 30.1, 30.3, 30.4)

Here each **internode** consists of a very large, elongate cell, surrounded by longitudinally orientated rows of small cells, which form a cortex. Just below each whorl of 'leaves' (the determinate laterals), there is a whorl of spine cells, which are termed **stipulae** ('stipules'; Figs. 30.1*b*, 30.3*a*). Terms like 'node', 'internode', 'leaf' and 'stipule' are drawn from the morphology of angiosperms, but of course, the organs of *Chara* have very little in common with the organs of higher plants.

The 'leaves' of *Chara* are differentiated into nodes and internodes, just like the main axes. Instead of bearing determinate laterals, however, the nodes give rise to whorls of unicellular spines, sometimes referred to as 'leaflets', which are very unequal in size (Figs. 30.1*c*, 30.3*a*). In monoecious species the spherical antheridia and flask-shaped oogonia are paired and lie on the adaxial sides of the 'leaves'. They become more or less encased by two special 'leaflets', which are called 'bracteoles' (Fig. 30.1*c*). The coronula of the oogonium (i.e. the apical tips of the corticating cells that surround the oogonium) consists of five cells (Figs. 30.1*e*, 30.3*g*).

The plants are anchored in sediments by rhizoids. The genus contains about 20 species (according to [1917]), although the number of infraspecific taxa is much larger ([121, 1078]).

The life cycle of *Chara*

In the following account we attempt to convey something of the complexity and specialization of the stoneworts, in a detailed account of the life cycle, including descriptions of the structure and development of the vegetative and reproductive organs ([1340, 1658]).

The structure of the male and female reproductive organs (the antheridia and oogonia) is extremely complicated, but characteristic of the whole class. Both reproductive organs arise on the adaxial side of a leaf node; in *Chara* the antheridium lies below the oogonium, but in other genera the arrangement is different.

The antheridium and oogonium initials each arise through the division of a cell that has been cut off from a peripheral, adaxial cell of the leaf node (Fig. 30.3*h*). The first cell cut off from the antheridium initial is the **stalk cell** (Fig. 30.3*h*). The other cell, distal to the leaf node, divides into four, through the formation of longitudinal walls, and then these four cells themselves divide up, this time by transverse walls, to form a group of eight cells (Fig. 30.3*i*). Each cell of these cells divides periclinally, as do the eight outer daughter cells produced from this round of cell division, so that each cell of the original eight gives rise to an outer cell, called the **shield cell**; a central cell, called the **manubrium**; and an inner cell, called the **primary capitulum cell** (Fig. 30.3*j*, *k*). The shield cells grow out laterally and as this happens, the manubrium cells and primary capitulum cells are drawn apart, producing cavities inside the young antheridium. The manubrium cells elongate in a radial direction, while the primary capitulum cells continue to divide. Each primary capitulum cell cuts off six **secondary capitulum cells** (Fig. 30.3*l*), and these cut off **tertiary capitulum cells**. Then the capitulum cells give rise to **spermatogenous filaments** containing between 5 and 50 cells (Fig. 30.3*m*), each of which produces a single spermatozoid (Fig. 30.3*n–p*). Meanwhile, in each of the shield cells, partition-like walls grow out from the anticlinal walls of the cell into the cell lumen (Fig. 30.3*n*).

The mature spermatozoid has a characteristic spiral shape (Fig. 30.3*p*), with the flagella inserted subapically. The body of the cell is largely filled a long, spiral nucleus, behind which there are several plastids, full of starch. The flagella and the cell body are both covered with tiny (60–75 nm) diamond-shaped scales, which are similar to the inner body scales of the Prasinophyceae (p. 313; [1213, 1412]).

The basal node bearing the antheridium also produces the adaxial cell that serves as the initial for an oogonium. This initial divides into three cells. The uppermost one, which is an internode cell, develops into the egg cell; the central one, which is nodal, gives rise to the cortication around the egg; and the basal cell, another internode cell, develops into the oogonium stalk (Fig. 30.3*b–d*, *h*). The nodal cell divides to form a central cell surrounded by five peripheral cells, which then grow up to form the strongly spiralled (laevorotatory) cortical cells of the oogonium; each of them ends in a **coronula cell** (Fig. 30.3*f*, *g*).

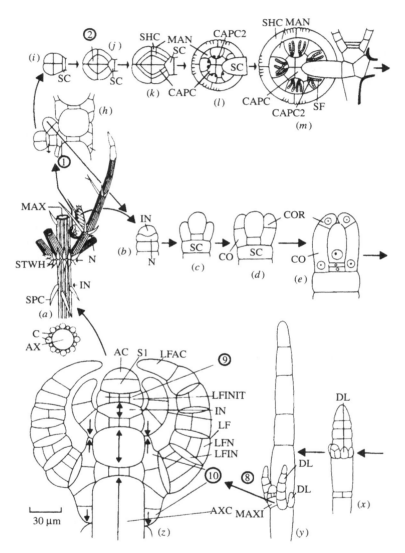

Figure 30.3. The life cycle of *Chara*. (*a*) Part of the plant, showing a node and internode of the main axis, and whorled branches. (*b–f*) Formation of the oogonium. (*h–m*) Formation of the antheridium. (*n–p*) Form-ation of spermatozoids. (*g*) Fertilization, involving oogamy. (*q–u*) Meiosis and germination of the zygote. (*v–z*) Development of the germling and vegetative growth. For further explanation, see text.

1 = a peripheral, adaxial node cell, which bears a condensed, fertile, short shoot; 2 = periclinal divisions of each cell in the octet; 3 = remnants (the inner walls) of the corticating filaments around the oogonium; 4 = four haploid nuclei are produced through meiosis in the zygote; 5 = three nuclei degenerate; 6 = functional nucleus; 7 = spermatozoids are able to penetrate into the oogonium through openings between the coronula cells and the ends of the cortical cells; 8 = a long shoot borne by the germling develops into a new plant; 9 = a node: the longitudinal section shows the two central cells and two peripheral leaf (branch) initials; 10 = a cortex is formed around the main axis and branches through the development of filaments that

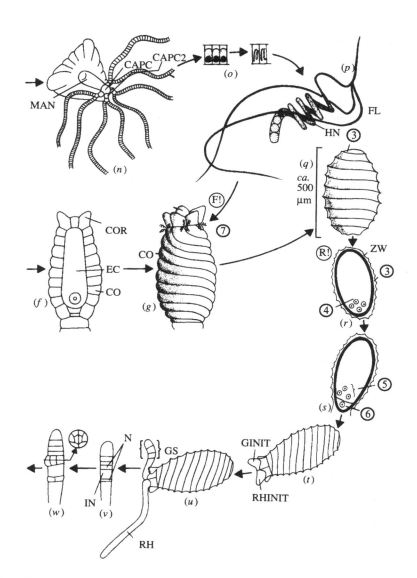

Caption for fig. 30.3 *(cont.)*.

grow downwards and upwards from the node. AC = apical cell; AX = axis; AXC = elongating axial cell; C = cortex; CAPC = capitulum cell; CAPC2 = secondary capitulum cell; CO = cortication around the egg cell; COR = coronula; DL = determinate lateral branch (short shoot) borne by the germling; EC = egg cell; F! = fertilization; FL = flagellum; GINIT = initial of the shoot of the germling; GS = upwardly growing shoot of the germling; HN = helical nucleus; IN = internode; LF = leaf; LFAC = leaf apical cell; LFIN = leaf internode; LFINIT = leaf initial; LFN = leaf node; MAN = manubrium cell; MAX = main axis; MAXI = initial of main axis; N = node; R! = reduction division (meiosis); RH = rhizoid; RHINIT = rhizoid initial; S1 = primary segment, which divides into a biconcave node cell and a biconvex internode cell; SC = stalk cell; SF = spermatogenous filaments (antheridial filaments); SHC = shield cell; SPC = spine cell; STWH = double whorl of stipules; ZW = zygote wall.

Near the oogonium, the basal node of the antheridium also forms two bracteoles (Fig. 30.1c).

Spermatozoids are able to penetrate the narrow fissures between the coronula cells and the upper ends of the cortical filaments; the apical part of the egg cell wall becomes gelatinous and one of the spermatozoids passes through this and fertilizes the egg. The zygote secretes a thick wall and at the same time the inner walls of the cortical cells thicken and become encrusted with lime. The rest of the cortex surrounding the oogonium decays; the zygote, together with the thickened inner walls of the cortical cells which spiral around it, is all that is left (Fig. 30.3q).

The mature zygote sinks onto the sediments and later germinates, after a short or long period of dormancy. The zygotes of some *Chara* species germinate best under anaerobic conditions, particularly in sediments that are sufficiently rich in organic material to be anoxic close to the surface. This requirement is significant, since germination also requires light, which will not penetrate far into the sediments, even when the water above is clear. The necessary combination of organic sediments and clear water exists in the moderately eutrophic lakes in which *Chara* is to be found ([436]). Germination of the zygote is induced by red light (wavelength 660 nm) and even a short period of irradiation is enough to elicit a response. The effects of red light are reversed, however, by irradiation with infrared (wavelength 730 nm), suggesting that phytochrome may play a part in the control of germination ([1744]), as in the germination of the seeds of many flowering plants.

Meiosis almost certainly takes place during germination (Fig. 30.3r, s), producing a quadrinucleate cell. Then the zygote divides up into a small outer cell, with one nucleus, and a large inner cell, which is trinucleate; the three nuclei of the inner cell subsequently degenerate (Fig. 30.3s). The uninucleate cell is the initial of a new vegetative plant, and it divides into a shoot initial and a rhizoid initial (Fig. 30.3t, u). The shoot of the young germling consists of a short axis, of determinate growth, with a limited number of nodes (two in Fig. 30.3v–x). At one node a whorl of six small determinate laterals ('leaves') is formed, and the main axis of the new plant develops from one of these (Fig. 30.3x–z); thus, the main axis of the vegetative plant is generated as the side branch of the germling.

The main axis grows predominantly through the activity of a domed apical cell (Fig. 30.3z), which cuts off segments at its base. Each segment divides while it is still near the apex, to form a biconcave upper cell and a biconvex lower cell. The biconcave cell continues to divide and develops into a node, while the biconvex cell divides no more but elongates enormously into a long internodal cell.

The nodal cell divides first into two equal halves, via the formation of a vertical wall. Several divisions follow (Fig. 30.4a), producing two central cells and six peripheral cells, which are the initials of six whorled 'leaves'. The leaves grow apically, just like the main axis, but the apical cell soon ceases activity, after it has cut off five to fifteen cells; it then becomes conical (Fig. 30.3z). The peripheral cells of the leaf nodes grow into unicellular spines: the 'leaflets'.

Side axes are formed, with unlimited growth like the main axis. Each arises from a peripheral cell in the basal node of one of the leaves in a whorl, always the first leaf that was initiated (Fig. 30.1a).

The rows of corticating cells also develop from the basal nodes of the leaves. One row arises from the peripheral cell that lies on the upper side of the leaf base, while another arises on the opposite side (Fig. 30.3z). Adjacent rows of cells fit closely against each other and their growth keeps pace with the elongation of the internode cell beneath, so that at all stages the plant is provided with a complete covering of cortical tissue. The rows extending upwards and downwards from adjacent nodes meet each other in the middle of the internode.

The cortical filaments show essentially the same pattern of growth as the main axis and the 'leaves'. At the tip of each filament is an apical cell, which cuts off segments, and these in their turn divide into node and internode (Fig. 30.4b, c). The nodal cell divides into three (a central cell and two peripheral cells), through the formation of two radial walls (Fig. 30.4c, d), while the internodal cell remains undivided. In *Chara globularis* the peripheral nodal cells and the internodal cells elongate simultaneously, matching the elongation of the internodes in the main axis beneath. In this way a cortex arises that contains three times as many rows of cells as there are leaves in a whorl; this is called a triplostichous cortex. In other species, however, the peripheral node cells of the cortex remain small, so that here the cortex consists largely of the elongated internodal cells. In this case there will be only as many rows of cells in the cortex as there are leaves in a whorl, and this is called a haplostichous cortex.

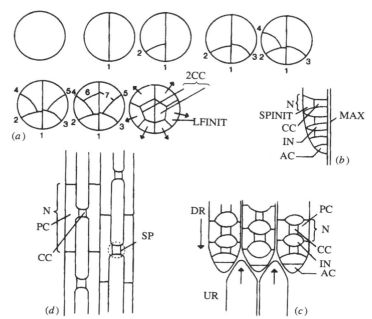

Figure 30.4. *Chara*. (*a*) The primary node cell sectioned transverse to the shoot axis, showing the order of formation of segments (numbers). The arrows indicate the directions of growth of the leaves. (*b*) Longitudinal section through the young cortex, just beneath the apical zone. (*c*) Surface view of the young cortex. (*d*) Surface view of the almost fully developed cortex.

AC = apical cell (of corticating filament); CC = central cell; DR = downwardly growing filaments of cells; IN = internode; LFINIT = leaf initial; MAX = main axis; N = node; PC = peripheral cell; SP = spine; SPINIT = spine initial; UR = upwardly growing filaments of cells; 2CC = two central cells.

The central cell of the cortical node can cut off a small cell to the outside, which in certain circumstances will develop into a spine (Fig. 30.4*b* shows the initials of the spine cells, while Fig. 30.3*a* shows the spine cells themselves).

Branched rhizoids develop from the lower nodes of the main axis and from the basal nodes of the leaves. They too grow through the activity of an apical cell but they are not subdivided into nodes and internodes. It has sometimes been suggested that the rhizoids are important not only in anchoring the plants in sediment but also in the uptake of nutrients. This has not been confirmed by experiments using labelled phosphate [1017]. All parts of the plant were found to be equally effective in taking up phosphate, and phosphate ions were transported uniformly to all parts of the plant, regardless of whether they had been supplied to the rhizoids or to the shoot apices.

Lamprothamnium

This genus is similar to *Chara*, but the plants possess no cortex. Beneath the leaves there is a whorl of stipules. As in *Chara* the coronula consists of five cells, but whereas in *Chara* the oogonia are attached above the antheridia, in *Lamprothamnium* the arrangement is the other way around. Three species are known and all are inhabitants of fairly still, brackish waters (such as Mediterranean lagoons).

Nitellopsis

These stoneworts have no cortex and no stipules, but again the coronula consists of five cells. *Nitellopsis obtusa* can reproduce vegetatively, through the formation of small star-shaped structures (bulbils). *Nitellopsis* contains three species; *Nitellopsis obtusa* extends into Europe.

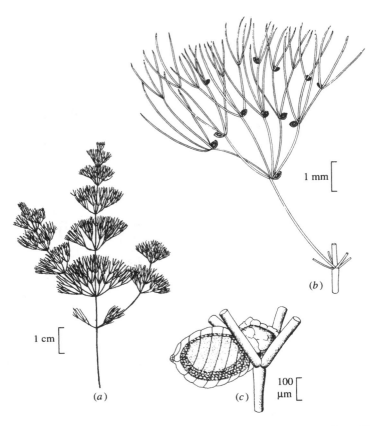

Figure 30.5. *Nitella gracilis.* (*a*) Habit of plant. (*b*) Part of the axis. (*c*) Oogonium and antheridium. (From [1917].)

Nitella (Fig. 30.5)

In *Nitella* there are no stipules and no cortex. The leaves bear forked branches, while the coronula contains two rows of cells, with five cells in each. In monoecious species the antheridia lie above the oogonia. The genus includes 53 species, while around 200 infraspecific taxa are also recognized.

Tolypella

Again, cortex and stipules are absent. The leaves are numerous, of unequal length, and either dichotomously branched or unbranched. The coronula consists of two rows of five cells, as in *Nitella.* Two species are known, containing 10 infraspecific taxa.

31

Reflections on the phylogeny of the Chlorophyta

Traditional classifications of the Chlorophyta

The principal feature used for distinguishing the major groups (orders, classes) within the Chlorophyta has traditionally been the level of organization exhibited by the thallus ([99, 100, 440, 464, 703]). To illustrate this, we reproduce Fott's classification of 1971 (Table 31.1), which reflects the hypothesis that unicellular flagellates are primitive within the Chlorophyta, and that they evolved initially into coccoid and sarcinoid green algae, and later into filamentous and siphonous forms. This hypothesis is shown in Fig. 31.1. It builds on ideas advanced many years ago, by Blackman ([89]) and Pascher ([1380]), and shows the Bryophyta (mosses and liverworts) and Tracheophyta (vascular plants) as having been derived from branched filamentous green algae.

Since 1971 an enormous amount of new information has gradually accumulated, mainly from ultrastructural investigations, which shows that the traditional system of classification is unsatisfactory. It has become clear that the main evolutionary lineages of the green algae cut across the taxonomic divisions made on the basis of thallus organization. New classifications have therefore been put forward, which attempt to reflect phylogeny more accurately ([704, 704a, 1140, 1173, 1328, 1644, 1645, 1648, 1700]).

A new classification of the Chlorophyta

Fig. 31.2 summarizes the classification we have adopted for this text and also some of the hypotheses that underlie it. Note that this phylogenetic tree no longer implies a step-wise evolutionary progression through the various organizational levels, in which the flagellate level represents one lineage (the most primitive), the coccoid and sarcinoid levels of organization represent two lineages of intermediate derivation, while the filamentous, siphonocladous and siphonous levels represent the three most derived (most 'advanced') lineages (Fig. 31.1). In the new phylogeny the first radiation of the Chlorophyta is thought to have taken place at the flagellate level, resulting in a multitude of ancient lineages of flagellates, some of which then went on to give rise to non-flagellate coccoid, sarcinoid, filamentous, siphonocladous or siphonous representatives. An implication of this hypotheti-

Table 31.1. *Subdivision of Chlorophyta according to Fott (1971)*

(I) Class Chlorophyceae

Organizational level	Order Suborder
FLAGELLATE	VOLVOCALES
PALMELLOID	TETRASPORALES
COCCOID	CHLOROCOCCALES
FILAMENTOUS	ULOTRICHALES
sarcinoid	Chlorosarcinineae
unbranched filamentous	Ulotrichineae
unbranched filamentous; cell wall of H-pieces	Microsporineae
unbranched filamentous; special features of cell division and reproduction	Oedogoniineae
branched filamentous	Chaetophorineae
SIPHONOCLADOUS	SIPHONOCLADALES
SIPHONOUS	BRYOPSIDALES

(II) Class Conjugatophyceae
Essentially with coccoid organizational level; special features of reproduction (conjugation)

(III) Class Charophyceae
Special vegetative and reproductive architecture

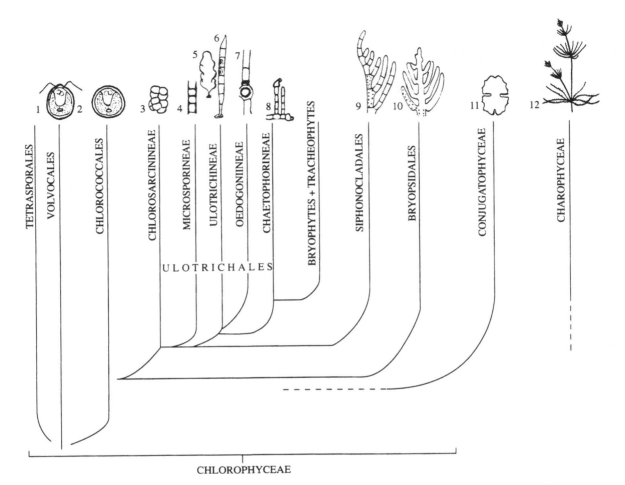

Figure 31.1. The phylogeny and subdivision of the Chlorophyta according to Fott [440], based largely on levels of organization, namely: 1. Flagellate (*Chlamydomonas*). 2. Coccoid (*Chlorococcum*). 3. Sarcinoid (*Chlorosarcinopsis*). 4. Filamentous (*Microspora*). 5. Thallose or foliose, derived from the filamentous level (*Ulva*). 6. Filamentous (*Uronema*). 7. Filamentous (*Oedogonium*). 8. Branched filamentous (*Trentepohlia*). 9. Siphonocladous (*Cladophora*). 10. Siphonous (*Bryopsis*). 11. Coccoid or filamentous (with special reproductive features: *Euastrum*). 12. Complex multicellular (charophycean) construction (*Chara*).

cal early radiation of the green algae at the flagellate level is that the various flagellate chlorophytes alive today may represent several ancient, relatively distantly related lineages.

The more elaborate types of thallus seem to have evolved many times in parallel in the main lineages (classes). Thus, for instance, unbranched *Ulothrix*-like filaments have evolved in the Ulvophyceae (in *Ulothrix* itself, within the order Codiolales), in the Chlorophyceae (in *Uronema*, order Chaetophorales),

and in the Klebsormidiophyceae (in *Klebsormidium*, order Klebsormidiales). The phylogenetic separation between these green algae, which are superficially very similar, is shown by differences in zoid architecture and in the ultrastructural detail of mitosis and cytokinesis. In addition, it has recently been demonstrated by Schlösser ([1567]) that *Uronema* autolysins are effective in other filamentous genera of the Chaetophorales (such as *Stigeoclonium*, *Draparnaldia* and *Chaetophora*), which belongs to the class Chlorophyceae, but not in *Ulothrix* (class Ulvophyceae) or *Klebsormidium* (class *Klebsormidiophyceae*); autolysins are enzymes that degrade cell wall polysaccharides during the fragmentation of filaments into separate cells, or during the formation of exit pores for zoids, etc.

Parallelism is not restricted to the filamentous level of organization. Coccoid representatives are known in the Chlorophyceae (e.g. *Golenkinia* and *Chlorococcum,* order Chlorococcales), Ulvophyceae (e.g. *Chlorocystis*, order Codiolales), Pleurastrophyceae (e.g. *Trebouxia*, order Pleurastrales, cf. [428]) and Klebsormidiophyceae (e.g. *Raphidonema*, order Klebsormidiales), while sarcinoid genera occur in the Chlorophyceae (e.g. *Chlorosarcinopsis*, order Chlorococcales), Pleurastrophyceae (e.g. *Friedmannia*, order Pleurastrales), and Klebsormidiophyceae (e.g. *Chlorokybus*, order Klebsormidiales).

The Ulvophyceae, Chlorophyceae and Klebsormidiophyceae each contain one order that exhibits considerable diversity in thallus organization. These three orders, the Codiolales, Chlorococcales and Klebsormidiales, can perhaps be considered to be primitive within their classes, since each contains some representatives with coccoid or sarcinoid organization, which can presumably be interpreted as primitive. But even within a single class the coccoid and sarcinoid forms probably do not represent a homogeneous, natural group, since they vary in chloroplast structure or in some other aspect of cell architecture ([577, 874]); they are themselves the product of parallel evolution. So, for instance, within the Chlorophyceae (order Chlorococcales), the coccoid genera *Neochloris* ([1002]) and *Chlorella* appear to be genetically highly heterogeneous ([766,767,768,769,835]), as indeed are some of the 'species' within *Chlorella*, suggesting that the coccoid morphology may be the result of parallel evolution. It may even be that some coccoid forms have evolved convergently, through evolutionary simplification and reduction from multicellular green algae. The Codiolales, Chlorococcales and Klebsormidiales are not the only orders that exhibit several different levels of organization; the order Ulvales (class Ulvophyceae), for instance, contains species that form branched filaments and also leafy, thallose algae.

Some of the classes are more homogeneous with respect to the level of organization of the thallus and have many unique features, which show them to be internally consistent; these include the Cladophoro-

phyceae, Bryopsidophyceae, Dasycladophyceae, Trentepohliophyceae, Zygnematophyceae and Charophyceae.

The new system of classification has at its heart the idea that there are at least four main evolutionary lineages, each characterized by its own type of flagellate cell (zoid). These four types are:

1 zoids with organic body scales (Fig. 19.9);
2 zoids with four microtubular flagellar roots in a cruciate arrangement and a 1 o'clock – 7 o'clock configuration of the basal bodies (Figs. 19.1, 19.14c);
3 zoids with four microtubular flagellar roots in a cruciate arrangement and an 11 o'clock – 5 o'clock configuration of the basal bodies (Figs. 19.13, 19.14b); and
4 zoids with a unilateral arrangement of the flagellar apparatus (Fig. 19.15).

Originally it was suggested that these four lineages should be recognized as four classes, called the Prasinophyceae, Chlorophyceae, Ulvophyceae and Charophyceae, respectively. These were broadly defined and do not correspond to the groups as they are circumscribed here. We consider that the traits of the flagellate cell are insufficient, on their own, to characterize classes within the green algae. Other features must also be taken into account, such as the structure of the vegetative cells, mitosis and cell division, the composition of the cell walls, and the life cycle. The result of this approach is that our classes are more narrowly circumscribed and probably more 'natural' (pp. 8, 9) than in the four-class system. Most of our classes (the Cladophorophyceae, Bryopsidophyceae, Dasycladophyceae, Trentepohliophyceae, Zygnematophyceae, and Charophyceae) are so distinctive that they have long been considered natural, but they have hitherto been recognized generally as orders, not classes. In our system the 'cruciate 1 o'clock – 7 o'clock lineage' (with zoids as described above under 2) has given rise to just one class, the Chlorophyceae (which, however, according to a recent idea, may encompass two separate classes: see p. 340); the 'cruciate 11 o'clock – 5 o'clock lineage' (with zoids as described above under 3) to six classes, the Ulvophyceae, Cladophorophyceae, Bryopsidophyceae, Dasycladophyceae, Trentepohliophyceae and Pleurastrophyceae; and the 'unilateral lineage' (with

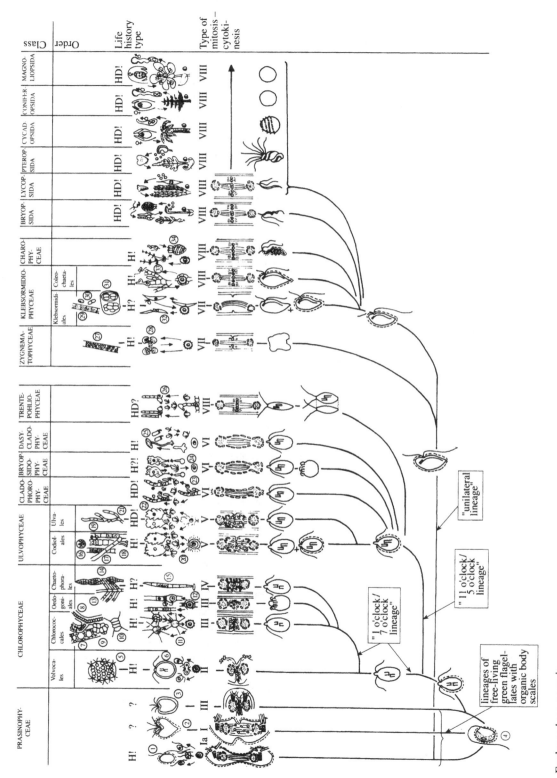

For legend see opposite page.

zoids as described above under 4) to three, the Zygnematophyceae, Klebsormidiophyceae and Charophyceae, as well as to the various classes of mosses, liverworts and vascular plants (Fig. 31.2).

Zoids are thought to act as repositories for evolutionarily old characters, because they occur in widely different groups of eukaryotes and the flagella they bear almost always have the familiar '9 + 2' structure. The implication of this is that the free-living flagellates in each major group, such as the Chlorophyta, are more primitive (have retained more ancestral characteristics) than their non-flagellate relatives, and that all of the non-flagellate representatives have ultimately been derived from flagellate ancestors. In the older classifications the flagellate forms were often classified together in one group (in the green algae this was the Volvocales), which was considered as ancestral to all other groups.

In the green algae it has gradually become clear, however, that the Volvocales are not the only lineage of free-living flagellates; there is at least one other major lineage, which is now generally referred to as the class Prasinophyceae. The Prasinophyceae are characterized by the highly elaborate scales they bear, both on the body of the cell and on the flagella (cf. [1301]). They are thought to be the most primitive algae within the Chlorophyta ([1301]), one argument for this being the great diversity of cellular architecture within the group, which seems to represent a pool from which the other types of green algal zoid have evolved; we illustrate this diversity in Fig. 31.2.

The ancestral prasinophycean alga is suggested to have been scaly and to have had one flagellum; the present-day genus *Mantoniella* acts as a model for this organism. This uniflagellate ancestor is then supposed to have given rise to biflagellate, quadriflagellate, and even octoflagellate Prasinophyceae, through a shift in the timing of cytokinesis relative to the semi-conservative replication of the basal bodies, and hence of the flagella themselves (cf. M. Melkonian, personal communication, [1184, 1301]); replication is termed semi-conservative because an existing basal body is conserved while a new one is produced alongside it.

Another argument for the primitiveness of the

Figure 31.2. The phylogeny and subdivision of the Chlorophyta as put forward in the present account. 1. *Nephroselmis* (with a scaly covering). 2. *Pyramimonas* (with a scaly covering). 3. *Tetraselmis* (with a theca). 4. Hypothetical *Mantoniella*-like ancestral prasinophycean green alga. 5. *Eudorina*. 6. *Chlamydomonas* (with wall-like envelope). 7. *Sphaeroplea*. 8. *Radiofilum*. 9. *Chlorosarcinopsis*. 10. *Scenedesmus*. 11. *Golenkinia*. 12. *Oedogonium*. 13. *Stigeoclonium*. 14. *Schizomeris*. 15. *Uronema*. 16. *Chlorocystis*. 17. *Ulothrix*. 18. *Urospora*. 19. *Acrosiphonia*. 20. *Monostroma*. 21. *Acrochaete*. 22. *Ulva*. 23. *Cladophora*. 24. *Udotea*. 25. *Acetabularia*. 26. *Trentepohlia*. 27. *Spirogyra*. 28. *Cosmarium*. 29, 30. *Klebsormidium*. 31. *Chlorokybus*. 32. *Raphidonema*. 33. *Coleochaete*. 34. *Chara*.

Types of life cycle: ? = unknown; H! = haplontic, karyological evidence available; H? = probably haplontic, but little or no supporting karyological evidence; HD! = haplodiplontic, karyological evidence available; HD? = probably haplodiplontic, but little or no supporting karyological evidence.

Types of mitosis and cytokinesis (see also chapter 19): I. Open mitosis with a persistent telophase spindle; cytokinesis effected by a cleavage furrow. Ia. Closed mitosis with a persistent telophase spindle; cytokinesis effected by a cleavage furrow. II. Closed mitosis with a non-persistent telophase spindle; cytokinesis effected by a cleavage furrow operating within a phycoplast. III. Closed mitosis with a non-persistent telophase spindle; cytokinesis effected by formation of a cell plate of vesicles within a phycoplast. IV. Closed mitosis with a non-persistent telophase spindle; cytokinesis effected by formation of a cell plate of golgi vesicles within a phycoplast. V. Closed mitosis with a persistent telophase spindle; cytokinesis effected by a cleavage furrow, to which golgi vesicles are added. VI. Closed mitosis with a prominent persistent telophase spindle, which gives the telophase nucleus a characteristic dumbbell shape; mitosis not immediately followed by cytokinesis. VII. Open mitosis with a prominent persistent telophase spindle; cytokinesis effected by a cleavage furrow. VIII. Open mitosis with a prominent persistent telophase spindle; cytokinesis effected by the formation of a cell plate of golgi vesicles within a phragmoplast.

Zoid architecture: the pictures of cruciate zoids indicate the rotation of the basal bodies via a small top-view diagram within the zoid. In the Ulvophyceae, Cladophorophyceae, Bryopsidophyceae, Dasycladophyceae and Trentepohliophyceae the rotation is anticlockwise (11 o'clock – 5 o'clock configuration); in the Chlorophyceae the rotation is clockwise (1 o'clock – 7 o'clock configuration). Note the scaly coverings of the zoids in the Prasinophyceae, Ulvophyceae (Codiolales), Klebsormidiophyceae and Charophyceae. Note also the hypothetical prasinophycean ancestor (bottom left), which is scaly and uniflagellate; the present day species *Mantoniella squamata* is the best available model for this ancestor ([386, 1109]).

Prasinophyceae, besides the diversity in zoid architecture, is that the main character defining the class, the presence of body scales, is shared with the members of several other classes of green algae, which have scales on their reproductive zoids (Fig. 31.2). The retention of scales in very distantly related, multicellular green algae is interpreted as showing that the scales evolved long ago, before the divergence of the classes from each other. In a similar way, the presence of '9 + 2' flagella in such different eukaryotes as mammals, chytrids and chlorophytes is thought to reflect the fact that flagella arose at an extremely early stage in eukaryote evolution.

This highlights a major problem with the Prasinophyceae. It is defined by the presence of a primitive trait and by the absence of more advanced traits. But primitive, ancestral traits, such as the possession of organic body scales and flagellar scales, should not be used to characterize particular groups within the Chlorophyta, since they are characteristic of the green algae as a whole; they have not been retained in all the lineages of green algae but where they have, their presence only reflects the basic chlorophyte nature of the algae. Similarly, the possession of flagella is a characteristic that defines (almost) the whole realm of the eukaryotes; it is not a characteristic that can be used to define any particular group within the eukaryotes. In some cases, however, the absence of flagella can be a useful taxonomic character, as for instance in the Zygnematophyceae and the flowering plants, where secondary loss has produced whole lineages of plants with no trace of flagella.

So the whole basis of the class Prasinophyceae seems to be undermined and this idea is reinforced by further analysis of the phylogeny shown in Fig. 31.2. Consider, for instance, the evolution of the cruciate and unilateral types of zoid architecture. Cruciate reproductive zoids are thought to have evolved from a free-living, prasinophycean ancestor [730, 1700], whose closest living relative has been suggested to be *Tetraselmis* (Fig. 20.1;[1218, 1648, 1698]). This could have come about as follows. During the diversification of the first flagellate green algae, scaly *Tetraselmis*-like forms gave rise to an alga not unlike *Chlamydomonas*, which had a 12 o'clock – 6 o'clock configuration of the basal bodies and still possessed a scaly covering. This was the common ancestor of both the 'cruciate 1 o'clock – 7 o'clock lineage' and the 'cruciate 11 o'clock – 5 o'clock lineage' (Fig. 31.2). The unilateral

type of zoid, on the other hand, probably evolved from a different free-living prasinophycean ancestor, whose closest living relative has been suggested to be *Nephroselmis* [1221]. *Nephroselmis* resembles the unilateral type of reproductive zoid in having a broad, lateral microtubular root, an MLS-like structure, and a scaly covering (Figs. 19.15, 20.2). If these two hypotheses are correct, however, *Tetraselmis* would be more closely related to the green algae with cruciate zoid architecture, and *Nephroselmis* would be more closely related to the green algae with unilateral zoid architecture, than either genus would be to other Prasinophyceae or to each other.

This phylogeny, in which the cruciate zoid is derived from a *Tetraselmis*-like ancestor and the unilateral zoid from a *Nephroselmis*-like ancestor, requires that these two modern genera of free-living flagellates have survived almost unchanged since the early radiation of the green algae to give non-flagellate forms. This accords with the basic hypothesis that the structure of flagellate cells is evolutionarily conservative. The Prasinophyceae would thus appear to be a cluster of ancient lineages (each of which should perhaps be recognized as a separate class?), which have retained ancestral features, such as the presence of organic body scales and flagellar scales. The great diversity within the class in zoid architecture (e.g. [1221]: table 1, p. 97), flagellar root systems [1175, 1218, 1220, 1301], and patterns of mitosis and cytokinesis [47, 1139, 1301, 1387, 1701, 1919], further underline its phylogenetic heterogeneity (see Fig. 31.2).

There are other groups besides the Prasinophyceae that contain several lineages that diverged from each other long ago. The Volvocales (class Chlorophyceae) is an order of free-living flagellates characterized by a cruciate 1 o'clock – 7 o'clock configuration of the flagellar apparatus, closed mitosis with a non-persistent telophase spindle, a glycoprotein envelope or theca around the cell, and cytokinesis via a cleavage furrow, which develops within a phycoplast (Fig. 31.2). The order harbours some very diverse forms, however, especially with respect to chloroplast structure, and this suggests that it consists of an aggregate of ancient lineages, which have retained the characteristics of the ancestral flagellate in all their cells, vegetative as well as reproductive; unfortunately, the ultrastructure of many of these flagellates is still unknown [386]. Similar reasoning could also be applied to the orders Codiolales (class Ulvophyceae), Chlorococcales (class

Chlorophyceae) and Klebsormidiales (class Klebsormidiophyceae). In each case the order is thought to be primitive and so must contain relatively conservative genera; they can therefore be considered as clusters of ancient lineages.

We have argued, then, that the class Prasinophyceae contains several major lineages, which diverged from each other long ago and have remained very conservative in their anatomy and morphology during evolution; the same is true for several other groups of simple green algae. In contrast, in the most derived and highly diversified groups of green plants, such as in the flowering plants, each major lineage should be relatively young, the product of rapid phenotypic evolution. In groups of intermediate character, such as in the classes Cladophorophyceae, Bryopsidophyceae, Dasycladophyceae, Zygnematophyceae and Charophyceae, the lineages will be of intermediate age. Elaborating further upon this idea, within the most conservative lineages, the genera and species can themselves be expected to be phenotypically conservative; phenotypically defined genera and species should therefore be 'old'. In contrast, within the most advanced and highly diversified groups, phenotypically defined genera and species will be 'young', because here phenotypic change has been relatively rapid.

These predictions can be tested in two ways; first, by inspecting the fossil record, and second, by estimating when lineages diverged from each other, through comparisons of macromolecules containing genetic information.

Fossil evidence

In Fig. 32.1 we have summarized what is known about the occurrence of the main groups of algae in the geological record. Solid lines indicate fairly certain identifications, while dashed lines indicate where the interpretation is more speculative. Within the green algae, there is abundant, reliable fossil evidence only for the Prasinophyceae, Bryopsidophyceae, Dasycladophyceae, Charophyceae and, as has recently been shown, the Zygnematophyceae [753]. The vascular plants are well represented in the fossil record from *ca.* 400 million years ago onwards, while the remains of flowering plants begin to be abundant around 115 million years ago (not shown in Fig. 32.1).

The fossil evidence suggests that the Prasino-

phyceae are very ancient, dating back at least 600 million years, perhaps 1400 million years. The oldest reliable records of the classes Bryopsidophyceae, Dasycladophyceae and Charophyceae, which are all relatively advanced, derived groups of green algae, are 400–500 million years old, while fossils of the Zygnematophyceae occur in deposits 250–300 million years in age; as we have already mentioned, the oldest vascular plants are *ca.* 400 million years old. These data, taken together, suggest that the major radiation of the green algae, which produced the classes present today, had occurred by 500 million years ago and probably took place much earlier.

The geological record contains some striking evidence about the origins of modern genera. Among the Prasinophyceae the genera *Pterosperma* and *Pachysphaera* must be at least 600 million years old, assuming that they are equivalent to the two fossil genera *Pterospermella* and *Tasmanites* [92, 590, 1362]. In the Bryopsidophyceae and Dasycladophyceae, some extant genera seem to be at least 230–280 million years old, while in the Charophyceae some date back 250–280 million years (Fig. 32.1); three extant genera of Zygnematophyceae are at least 250–300 million years old [753]. Extant genera of conifers and flowering plants are younger: 50–150 million years for some conifers and 5–60 million years for angiosperms [1197, 1276, 1769].

It seems therefore that phenotypic change is much slower and smaller in the green algae than in vascular plants, and this is suggested also by the numbers of taxa in the two groups. Thus the green algae have only 7000–8000 species, while the vascular plants are much more diverse, with around 250 000 species, of which more than 200 000 are angiosperms.

Macromolecular evidence

After two lineages have diverged from each other during evolution their genomes, initially alike, become more and more dissimilar as time passes. This process is inevitable and inexorable, even when the lineages remain morphologically very similar [38, 1278, 1772]. The differences between the genomes can be quantified by comparing nucleotide sequences in selected sections of the nuclear, chloroplast or mitochondrial DNA, or in ribosomal RNA, or by comparing amino acid sequences in selected proteins. Thus it is possible to estimate which lineages are closely related geneti-cally, having diverged from each other only recently, and which are more distantly related, having diverged long ago. A short introduction to the methods involved in these calculations is given on pp. 37–9.

The macromolecules most often chosen for sequencing in evolutionary studies are the 5S, 18S and 28S components of cytoplasmic ribosomal RNA (rRNA) or their nuclear genes. The first measurements of relationships among the green plants (Chlorophyta, mosses, liverworts and vascular plants) were based on 5S rRNA sequences ([733, 734, 735]) but, because of the small number of nucleotides in this molecule (*ca.* 120), evolutionary studies based on this subunit are statistically unreliable. 18S and 28S rRNA molecules are much larger, with about 2000 and 5000 nucleo-tides respectively, and give more useful information.

The first 18S and 28S rRNA studies, which covered a broad selection of eukaryotes, confirmed the phylo-genetic link between the Chlorophyta and the higher plants (Figs. 32.2, 32.3; [589, 1393, 1394, 1471]), but unfortu-nately they included only a few green algae and so did not reveal relationships within the group.

In a recent study, combining analyses of 18S and 28S ribosomal RNAs ([1933]), phylogenetic relationships were investigated among a wide spectrum of green algae. The results, based on a comparison of 285 phy-logenetically informative nucleotide sites (out of a total of around 1200 nucleotides per species), are sum-marized in a cladogram (Fig. 31.3), which suggests the following conclusions.

1 The 'cruciate 11 o'clock – 5 o'clock lineage' (the Ulvophyceae, taken in its widest sense rather than as we have defined it here: see p. 340) (Fig. 31.2) is phylogenetically hetero-geneous, since green algae with 11 o'clock – 5 o'clock type reproductive zoids emerge three times: in the **Ulvophyceae** *sensu stricto* (i.e. defined in the narrower sense we have adopted here), in the **Pleurastrophyceae**, and in the complex that contains the **Trentepohlio-phyceae, Dasycladophyceae, Bryopsido-phyceae** and **Cladophorophyceae**. Each of these six classes seems to be an internally coher-ent, natural group. The tree of Fig. 31.3 thus suggests that the cruciate 11 o'clock – 5 o'clock type of zoid may have evolved several times from the cruciate 12 o'clock – 6 o'clock type.

Alternatively, the 11 o'clock – 5 o'clock arrange-ment of the basal bodies may be a primitive trait: it may have been the configuration present in the ancestral green algal flagellate, which has been retained in various unrelated lineages of Chlorophyta but transformed into the 12 o'clock – 6 o'clock and 1 o'clock – 7 o'clock configura-tions in other lineages. This hypothesis gains some support from the recent discovery that the basal bodies of *Pedinomonas* (the most primi-tive green flagellate in Fig. 31.3) are shifted into 11 o'clock – 5 o'clock positions with respect to each other ([1179, 1220a]).

2 The 'cruciate 1 o'clock – 7 o'clock lineage' (the class Chlorophyceae) is also phylogenetically heterogeneous, since flagellate cells with this configuration of the flagellar apparatus emerge twice in the tree (Fig. 31.3). *Chlamydomonas, Chloromonas* (order Volvocales) and *Uronema* (order Chaetophorales) appear to be closely related to each other, but are relatively distantly related to *Chlorella* and *Atractomorpha* (order Chlorococcales).

3 The great age of the phylogenetic divergence between a 'unilateral lineage' (with zoids that have a unilateral type of flagellar apparatus) and a 'cruciate lineage' (Fig. 31.2) is confirmed by the 18S/28S rRNA data (Fig. 31.3). Also con-firmed is the close link between the 'unilateral lineage', the Zygnematophyceae and vascular plants.

4 The two flagellate chlorophytes used in the study (*Pedinomonas* and *Chlamydomonas*) emerge far apart on the tree, in agreement with the idea that extant green algal flagellates repre-sent several unrelated lineages (cf. p. 487). *Pedinomonas* is a uniflagellate green alga of uncertain taxonomic position, whose flagellar apparatus contains two basal bodies in a cruciate 11 o'clock – 5 o'clock configuration ([1179, 1220a]), representing a further '11 o'clock – 5 o'clock' lineage to add to those listed above (see 1). Among the species studied so far it appears to be the closest relative of the hypothetical ancestral green alga.

The polyphyletic evolution of flagellate green algae is further supported by recent reports on a series of 18S and 28S rRNA studies and other molecular investigations, which reveal the following points of interest.

1 The Prasinophyceae seem to be polyphyletic, in accordance with the hypothesis developed here and illustrated in Fig. 31.2. This class is therefore artificial. Quite unexpectedly, the 'prasinophycean' genera *Pyramimonas* (Fig. 19.9) and *Tetraselmis* (Fig. 20.1) appear to belong to the class Pleurastrophyceae, while other 'prasinophycean' genera emerge at various, widely separated positions in the phylogenetic tree ([213a, 818, 819, 819a]).

2 The genus *Chlamydomonas* (belonging to the order Volvocales) seems to contain more than one major line of evolution ([160, 160b, 213a]). This supports the idea put forward here that the various lineages of free-living flagellates retain primitive features of cell architecture, since *Chlamydomonas* is itself highly diverse in cell structure. Furthermore, some *Chlamydomonas* species seem to be more closely related to certain colonial Volvocales than they are to other *Chlamydomonas* species. For example, *Chlamydomonas reinhardtii* is closely related to *Volvox carteri* (cf. *V. globator*, Fig. 21.5; [160b, 1471]), *Pandorina morum* (Fig. 21.4c) and *Eudorina elegans* (cf. *E. unicocca*, Fig. 21.4b), but not to many other species of *Chlamydomonas* or species of other genera in the Volvocales, judging by the cross-reactivity of the gamete wall autolysin of *C. reinhardtii* with the cell walls of other flagellate green algae ([1133, 1134]). The colonial Volvocales are also polyphyletic ([1144]).

3 The internal phylogenetic coherence ('naturalness') of the lineage with unilateral reproductive zoids (Fig. 31.2) gains further support from studies that have shown sequence similarities in the chloroplast gene that encodes the large subunit of the enzyme ribulose 1,5-bisphosphate carboxylase–oxygenase ([1088]); these studies also indicate that the Zygnematophyceae belongs to this lineage. Several other biochemical features also support the naturalness of the 'unilateral lineage' (including the Zygnematophyceae), such as the synthesis of the cellulose micro-fibrils in the cell wall by rosette-like cellulose synthase complexes located in the plasmalemma

(Fig. 19.24a, p. 339); the oxidation of glycolate by the enzyme glycolate oxidase, located in microbodies (instead of glycolate dehydrogenase located in the mitochondria, as in other green algae; [753, 1472]); and the presence of Cu/Zn superoxide dismutase in the lineage with unilateral zoids (including the vascular plants) but its absence in other green algae ([798, 1472]).

By comparing the genomes of algae that appear to be close relatives, judging by their phenotypes, one could in principle test the hypothesis that extant genera and species in ancient lineages are on average older (i.e. they diverged from each other longer ago) than genera and species in young, derived lineages. The literature contains a number of scattered reports that seem to be relevant here and these are discussed below; they include studies of chloroplast genomes, DNA–DNA hybridization and immunological cross-reactivity.

Chloroplast genomes in green plants

The organization of the chloroplast genome has been investigated in over 200 flowering plants, but only a few gymnosperms, ferns, bryophytes, and green algae; among these are four species of *Chlamydomonas* ([1354]).

The angiosperms and other land plants all share the same overall arrangement of the chloroplast genome, which has therefore been highly conserved during evolution. Thus, for instance, the liverwort *Marchantia polymorpha* has the same genome structure as in most angiosperms, implying that the characteristic arrangement of the chloroplast genes found in land plants evolved before the divergence of the vascular plants and bryophytes some 400 million years ago ([1354, 1355]).

In contrast to the great uniformity of the chloroplast genomes in land plants, in the green algae the structure of the chloroplast genome can vary even within a genus. In *Chlamydomonas* the order of the genes is quite different in *C. eugametos* and *C. reinhardtii* ([990, 1354]), and Lemieux and his co-workers suggest that these two distantly related species therefore represent lineages that diverged from each other much earlier than the land plant lineages. This suggests a minimum age of 400–500 million years for the genus *Chlamydo-*

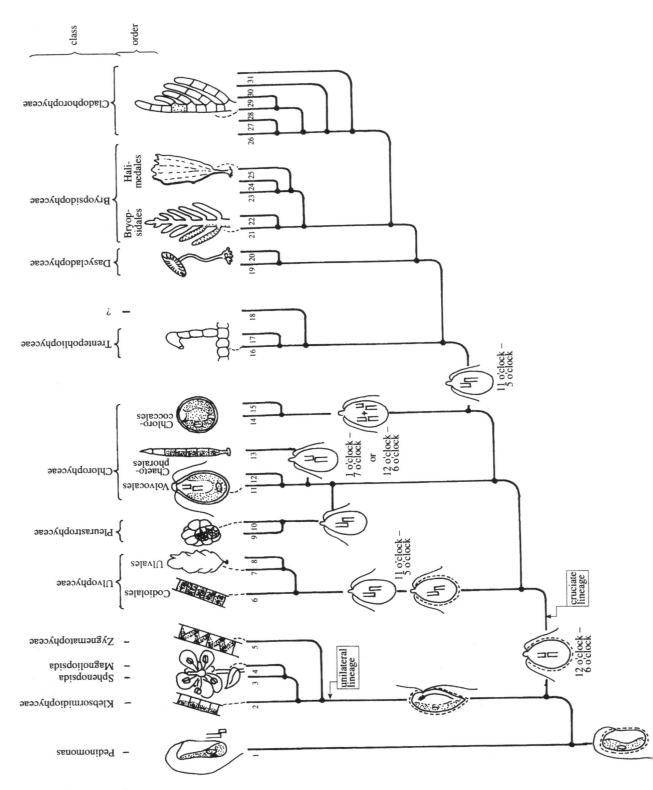

For legend see opposite page.

monas, which supports the basic hypothesis that free-living flagellates evolve very slowly in their morphology and represent very conservative lineages.

A further interesting point that emerges from the few studies of chlorophyte chloroplast genomes undertaken so far is that phenotypically similar pairs of species that are closely related and still at least partly interfertile, such as *Chlamydomonas reinhardtii* and *C. smithii* or *C. eugametos* and *C. moewusii*, have essentially the same arrangement of common sequences. There are minor differences between them, however, just as there are between the chloroplast genomes of land plants.

Single copy DNA–DNA hybridization

Some seaweeds have highly disjunct distributions, which suggest a minimum age for the species involved. Many tropical species, for instance, occur in the Caribbean, the Indian Ocean and the western Pacific, and this distribution can be explained as a relict Tethyan distribution [366, 684, 686, 698, 811]. The Tethys was originally continuous from what is now the Caribbean, between the European and African continental plates, to the Indo-Pacific region. The western and eastern parts of this finally became separated from each other with the closing and uplift of the Middle East, which took place in the Miocene (*ca.* 20 million years ago), although there had also been earlier, temporary separations. Species with a relict Tethyan distribution can therefore be suggested to

have a minimum age of 20 million years. A considerable number of genera and species within the classes Cladophorophyceae, Bryopsidophyceae and Dasycladophyceae exhibit disjunct distributions of this type, and fossil representatives of the extant Dasycladophycean genera *Dasycladus*, *Cymopolia*, *Neomeris* and *Acetabularia* (see Fig. 32.1) did indeed have continuous distributions around the Tethys Ocean throughout the Cretaceous and early Cenozoic periods [366].

The time when different geographical populations of the same morphospecies diverged from each other can be estimated tentatively from studies using single copy DNA–DNA hybridization. Here the difference in thermal stability between homoduplexes and heteroduplexes, as indicated by thermal elution profiles, gives a measure of genotypic similarity (see p. 40). The temperatures are determined at which 50% of the hybrid DNA molecules are eluted. A difference of 1 °C between the temperatures for the homoduplexes and heteroduplexes ($\Delta T_{m(e)} = 1$ °C) has been estimated to be equivalent on average to a time of 5.5 million years since divergence [1680], although there is much debate about whether this and similar estimates are valid [111]. Using this approach, however, two *Dictyosphaeria cavernosa* isolates (*Dictyosphaeria* belongs to the Cladophorophyceae), one from Hawaii and the other from the Virgin Islands, were estimated to have diverged from each other 55 million years ago, while *D. cavernosa* and *D. versluysii* isolates appeared to have diverged somewhat earlier, at *ca.* 70 million years ago [1336]. This would indicate a high degree of

Figure 31.3. A phylogenetic tree of the green algae and higher green plants (*Equisetum*, *Glycine*), based on comparisons of nucleotide sequences in the 18S and 28S rRNAs of 31 species. It is a 'maximum parsimony tree' [1278], which gives the relative positions of taxa within the tree but no information about the degree of divergence (as is presented, on the other hand, in distance trees, e.g. Figs. 32.1, 32.2). The pictures of flagellate cells towards the bottom of the figure illustrate how the primary radiation of the green algae may have occurred at the cellular, flagellate level. As in Fig. 31.2, a hypothetical scaly unicellular flagellate, like the present-day *Mantoniella*, is placed at the base of the tree. The pictures of cruciate zoids indicate the rotation of the basal bodies via a small top-view diagram within the zoid: the configurations are 12 o'clock – 6 o'clock, 1 o'clock – 7 o'clock, or 11 o'clock – 5 o'clock (cf. Fig. 19.14).

1. *Pedinomonas minutissima*. 2. *Klebsormidium flaccidum*. 3. *Equisetum* sp. 4. *Glycine max*. 5. *Spirogyra maxima*. 6. *Ulothrix zonata*. 7. *Ulva fasciata*. 8. *Enteromorpha intestinalis*. 9. *Pleurastrum terrestre*. 10. *Pseudotrebouxia gigantea*. 11. *Chlamydomonas eugametos*. 12. *Chlorogonium elongatum*. 13. *Uronema belkae*. 14. *Chlorella vulgaris*. 15. *Atractomorpha echinata*. 16. *Trentepohlia* sp. 17. *Cephaleuros virescens*. 18. *Blastophysa rhizopus*. 19. *Batophora oerstedii*. 20. *Cymopolia barbata*. 21. *Bryopsis plumosa*. 22. *Codium decorticatum*. 23. *Caulerpa prolifera*. 24. *Halimeda discoidea*. 25. *Udotea occidentalis*. 26. *Anadyomene stellata*. 27. *Microdictyon boergesenii*. 28. *Cladophora albida*. 29. *Chaetomorpha linum*. 30. *Cladophoropsis membranacea*. 31. *Dictyosphaeria versluysii*. (Based on fig. 1 of [1933].)

morphological conservatism in *Dictyosphaeria*, with the *D. cavernosa* morphology persisting, apparently unchanged, for 50–70 million years until the present day. Comparable results have been obtained from highly disjunct isolates of *Cladophora* morphospecies or species complexes ([111]). In *Chlorella*, low DNA homology, similar to that found between the *Dictyosphaeria* and *Cladophora* isolates, can exist between strains of the same, morphologically defined species, while between different *Chlorella* species the homology may be so low that it cannot be detected by the DNA hybridization method ([766, 767, 768, 769]).

The *Dictyosphaeria* isolates mentioned above were also included in a broader study, concerned with the phylogeny of the Cladophorophyceae, where phylogenetic relationships were estimated using immunological techniques ([1338, 1339]). The relative times estimated for the divergence of the three isolates were the same as were obtained from the DNA–DNA hybridization experiments. The immunological study also indicated (through application to 43 isolates, belonging to 26 species in 16 genera) that there is a high degree of conservatism in morphology within the Cladophorophyceae as a whole, and in individual genera.

Conclusions

The fossil and macromolecular evidence we have listed is patchy but enables us to put forward some tentative conclusions concerning the phylogeny of the green plants.

1 The first phylogenetic radiation of the Chlorophyta took place at the flagellate level, resulting in the evolution of a plethora of ancient lineages of flagellates, some of which then gave rise to non-flagellate coccoid, sarcinoid, filamentous, siphonocladous and siphonous green algae. This idea is based on morphological, ultrastructural and life cycle evidence, but it also receives support from rRNA sequence studies and other molecular data.

2 One implication of this is that extant genera and species of flagellate green algae can be expected, on average, to be more ancient and phenotypically conservative than genera and species in derived, non-flagellate lineages. The fossil evidence indicates, for instance, that the

extant prasinophycean genera *Pterosperma* and *Pachysphaera* are probably at least 600 million years old. Comparisons of chloroplast genomes suggest that the 'genus' *Chlamydomonas* may date back more than 400–500 million years. However, comparisons of 16S and 28S rRNA sequences within *Chlamydomonas* show a level of divergence comparable to that between angiosperms and gymnosperms ([160]), which are estimated from molecular data to have diverged from each other *ca.* 340 million years ago ([1915]).

3 A second implication of conclusion 1. is that extant genera and species in the most advanced (most derived) green plants, the angiosperms, can be expected, on average, to be much younger than flagellate lineages and to exhibit more rapid morphological change. Fossil evidence indicates that many extant genera of advanced green plants are around 5–60 million years old, perhaps a little older, while DNA–DNA hybridization studies on *Atriplex* species (a genus of flowering plants in the family Chenopodiaceae) suggest that some species separated from each other between 20 and 40 million years ago ([62]). Numerous flowering plant families, such as the Brassicaceae (Cruciferae), Lamiaceae (Labiatae) and Fabaceae (Leguminosae), seem to have arisen as late as the Miocene, 5–10 million years ago ([1276]), while their genera and species must be even younger.

4 The third implication, of course, is that extant genera and species in those green algae that are of intermediate derivation (such as the Cladophorophyceae, Bryopsidophyceae, Dasycladophyceae, Zygnematophyceae and Charophyceae) can be expected to be of intermediate age and to have only a moderate degree of morphological conservatism. Fossil evidence suggests that six extant genera of Bryopsidophyceae and Dasycladophyceae are at least 230–280 million years old, three extant genera in the Zygnematophyceae are at least 250–300 million years old, while seven genera in the Charophyceae are at least 250–280 million years old. In addition, the genus *Dictyosphaeria* (Cladophorophyceae) seems from DNA–DNA hybridization studies to be *ca.* 70 million years

Table 31.2. *Summary of the estimated minimum ages of extant genera and species in some chlorophytan classes*

In brackets: number of genera/species for which estimates are available; (f) = fossil evidence; (m) = macromolecular evidence.

Class	Minimum age of extant genera (million years)		Minimum age of extant species (million years)	
Prasinophyceae	600	(2) (f)[a]	—	
Chlorophyceae (Volvocales)	400–500	(1) (m)[b]	400–500	(1) (m)[c]
Bryopsidophyceae	75–230	(2) (f)[d]	—	
Dasycladophyceae	80–220	(4) (f)[e]	—	
Cladophorophyceae	70	(1) (m)[f]	55–70	(1) (m)[g]
Zygnematophyceae	250–300	(3) (f)[h]	—	
Charophyceae	80–250	(7) (f)[i]	—	
Angiosperms (Magnoliopsida)	5–60	(many) (f)[j]	20–40	(14) (m)[k]
			<5–10	(many) (f)[l]

Sources: [a] 249, 1362, 1751; [b, c] 990, 1354, 1355; [d] 366, 684, 1751; [e] 51, 366; [f, g] 1336; [h] 753; [i] 1664; [j, l] 1276; [k] 62.

old, while the morphologically defined species *D. cavernosa* is thought to be 55–70 million years old (Table 31.2 summarizes the points raised in conclusions 1–4).

5 The main phylogenetic lineages in the Chloro-phyta are not characterized by progressively more complex levels of organization (flagellate, coccoid, sarcinoid, filamentous, siphono-cladous, siphonous) and so the traditional view of chlorophyte evolution should be abandoned.

32

Phylogenetic reflections on the algae

The fan-shaped phylogenetic tree shown in Fig. 1.3 ([982]) illustrates the idea that the first unicellular eukaryotes had a monophyletic origin. After this there was a large-scale diversification of the eukaryotes at the cellular level, resulting in a proliferation of phyla, each with its own cellular body plan. Later, some of these gave rise independently to multicellular or multi-inucleate organisms. The phylogenetic tree does not indicate any distant, ancient phylogenetic relationships there may be between the main phyla of eukaryotes; for instance, it does not indicate whether the Chlorophyta are more distantly related to the Heterokontophyta than to the Eumetazoa, or less so. The reason for this is the near impossibility of detecting ancient relationships on the basis of shared morphological characteristics or other features. Most of the features we observe today are more-or-less derived and characteristic of a particular phylum, and we have listed these for each algal phylum (division) at the head of the chapter devoted to it. The only morphological and anatomical features shared *between* different eukaryotic phyla are for the most part those common to all eukaryotes: they are basic features of the generalized eukaryote cell, such as the typical eukaryote organelles (nucleus, golgi apparatus, endoplasmic reticulum, flagella, mitochondria). These characteristics reflect the monophyletic origin of all eukaryotes and yield very little information about phylogenetic relationships between the phyla.

The fossil record

The fossil record too is insufficient to allow us to make inferences about phylogenetic relationships between individual phyla. Fig. 32.1 summarizes the geological occurrence of the phyla of eukaryotic algae, and of some genera within these phyla, as shown by the fossil record, together with some tentative minimum or maximum geological ages that have been inferred from macromolecular data. The fossil evidence covers only a fraction of the organisms included in the various phyla, since it is biased heavily towards those organisms that are particularly suited to fossilization, mostly because their cell walls are calcified (indicated by 'c' in Fig. 32.1) or silicified ('s' in Fig. 32.1); in other cases the cell walls may contain especially resistant organic compounds ('o' in Fig. 32.1). Fossils only give minimum geological ages for algal phyla and it is possible, indeed quite likely, that representatives of the different groups were present earlier than the fossil record indicates, but they were not preserved because they lacked calcified or silicified cell walls.

The fossil data summarized in Fig. 32.1 indicate that the **Rhodophyta**, **Chlorophyta** and **Dinophyta** were already in existence by the end of the Precambrian, some 600 million years ago, as were marine invertebrates (Eumetazoa). Unmistakable evidence of the **Heterokontophyta** (in the form of fossil diatoms, class **Bacillariophyceae**) does not appear until much later, around 120 million years ago. This does not, of course, preclude the possibility that they may have been present earlier, perhaps in the form of organisms without silicified walls.

The earliest known fossil remains of unicellular organisms that appear to have been eukaryotic are 1900 million years old, while foliose organisms resembling algae can be found in deposits dating back 1300 million years (Figs. 2.7, 32.1; cf. pp. 95–6; [715, 1751, 1827]). Unfortunately, however, these microscopic and macroscopic remains have no features that are distinctive enough to allow them to be classified in any particular algal phylum.

In conclusion, the fossil record suggests that the evolutionary radiation and diversification of eukaryote unicells began some 2000 million years ago and intensified around 1000 million years ago, so that by the end of the Precambrian (600 million years ago), and probably rather earlier than this, the main phylogenetic lineages had arisen, including the Chlorophyta,

Rhodophyta, Dinophyta, and the multicellular animals (Eumetazoa). The fossil record tells us no more about the phylogenetic relationships between these phyla than do comparisons based on morphology or other traditional sources of information.

An 18S rRNA phylogenetic tree

Fortunately, it has recently become possible to use various molecular biological techniques to delve into the 'historical archives' stored in the genomes of organisms. Where two organisms have similar sequences of nucleotides in their RNA or DNA, or similar sequences of amino acids in their proteins, then it is likely that they have a relatively close phylogenetic relationship; they are of recent common descent. Ribosomal RNA (rRNA) sequences, or sequences within nuclear genes that code for rRNA, have been of particular use in unravelling phylogenetic relationships and the basics of the method have already been introduced in Chapter 2 (p. 37), where it was used to explore relationships between various blue-green algae (Cyanophyta or Cyanobacteria) (Fig. 2.8). The small 18S and the large 25–28S rRNAs are the molecules best suited for these studies.

Fig. 32.2 presents a phylogenetic tree that has recently been constructed, based on the 18S rRNA sequences of a number of representative species drawn from a wide range of eukaryotic phyla ([589, 1471, 1661]). A simplified tree of the prokaryotes, based on studies of prokaryotic 16S rRNA ([526]), is appended to the tree to facilitate comparison between the prokaryotes (Archaebacteria and Eubacteria, the latter including the blue-green algae) and the eukaryotes. The vertical axis denotes the evolutionary distance between taxa, as the estimated average number of point mutations that have become fixed and have accumulated per sequence position since the divergence of the three realms of living organisms, namely the Archaebacteria, Eubacteria and Eukaryota (on the assumption that the branching point they have in common represents their common ancestor: this need not be the case). Horizontal distances are arbitrary and are introduced for clarity, to allow close branchings to be separated and seen. The evolutionary distance between two species is thus the sum of the two vertical heights, down to the common branch point. For instance, the evolutionary distance between *Chlamydomonas*

(Chlorophyta) and *Zea mais* (maize, a vascular plant) is 0.10 units; between *Chlamydomonas* and *Rattus* (multicellular animals), 0.21 units; and between *Chlamydomonas* and *Euglena* (Euglenophyta), 0.46 units. These few examples illustrate that some algal phyla (divisions) are much more distantly related to each other than they are to multicellular animals. Thus for instance, the Chlorophyta (green algae) are less closely related to the Euglenophyta than they are to animals, while they are also closely related to the bryophytes and vascular plants.

The 18S rRNA tree (Fig. 32.2) demonstrates or suggests a number of interesting points, including the following.

1 The various algal phyla (marked by asterisks in Fig. 32.2) are **not** closely related and do not form a coherent group. They emerge interspersed with various phyla of heterotrophs.

2 The 'oldest' algal phylum is the **Euglenophyta**, which is related, though only very distantly, to the **Kinetoplasta**, which is a phylum of heterotrophic protozoans that includes *Trypanosoma brucei*, the cause of sleeping sickness. This relationship had already been suggested on the basis of features of the nuclei, mitochondria and flagella ([202, 261, 1848]).

3 The algal phylum **Dinophyta** emerges close to another group of heterotrophic protozoans, the **Ciliophora** (the ciliates).

4 The algal phylum **Heterokontophyta** includes the fungal class **Oomycetes**, which includes for instance the water mould *Achlya bisexualis* (Fig. 32.2, 22) and the downy mildews, important pathogens of agricultural crops. The Oomycetes had already been placed close to the Heterokontophyta on the basis of similarities in flagellum structure, both groups having the typical heterokontophyte flagellum with its stiff mastigonemes ([57, 1640, 1862]).

5 The algal phylum **Chlorophyta** and the vascular plants (phylum **Tracheophyta**) belong to the same phylogenetic lineage, confirming the hypothesis that the vascular plants evolved from a green algal ancestor.

6 Quite amazingly, the fungal phylum **Ascomycota**, the **green plants** (including the Chlorophyta *and* the vascular plants), and the

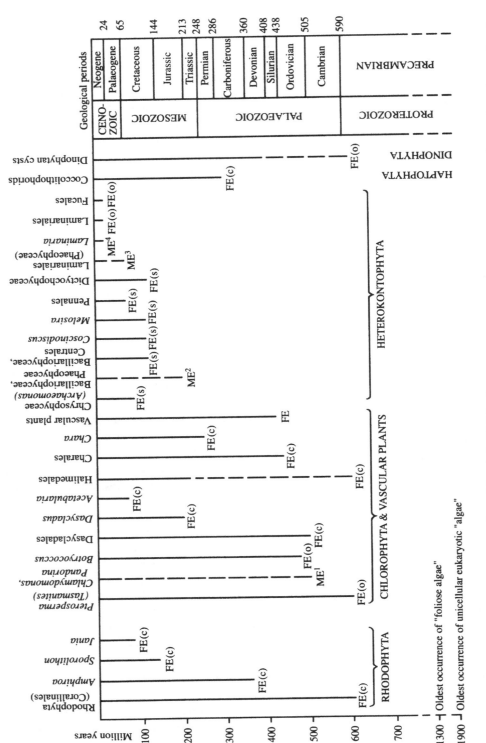

Figure 32.1. Geological occurrence of representatives of five phyla (divisions) of algae (based on information in [51, 249, 366, 684, 715, 1362, 1376, 1586, 1664, 1751, 1827]). Tentative estimates of geological ages, based on molecular data, are indicated for a few taxa. *Continuous lines* = reasonably firm evidence; *dashed lines* = more speculative evidence. FE = fossil evidence: c = calcareous fossils, o = organic fossils, s = siliceous fossils. ME = macromolecular evidence: [1] Minimum age estimated on the basis of divergence between chloroplast genomes in *Chlamydomonas* [990].

[2] Maximum age of the Bacillariophyceae and Phaeophyceae, based on the divergence time indicated by 5S rRNA homology [1011].

[3] Minimum age of the Laminariales (Phaeophyceae), from the estimated time of divergence between *Laminaria* and *Chorda*, based on DNA homology. [4] The minimum age of *Laminaria*, based on the time of divergence between two *Laminaria* species, estimated from DNA homology [1680].

Eumetazoa (multicellular animals) appear close together, forming the last main evolutionary lineages to emerge. Of these three groups, the green plant (chlorophyte) lineage and the animal lineage diverge more recently than the ascomycete lineage. This unexpectedly close phylogenetic relationship between the green algae (together with the higher plants) and the higher animals has now been confirmed in several studies involving comparisons of gene or amino acid sequences ([40, 549, 636]).

7 By and large, the 18S rRNA phylogenetic tree supports the idea (expressed in the fan-shaped tree of Fig. 1.3) that the first extensive evolutionary radiation of the Eukaryota took place at the unicellular level and resulted in a multitude of different types of unicell, both heterotrophic and photoautotrophic, each with its own body plan. A particularly rapid diversification of phyla seems to have taken place after the emergence of the ancestors of the Kinetoplasta and Euglenophyta, which are very ancient groups. This explosive diversification is shown by the very small vertical separation between the branch points (nodes) in the lower part of the tree (remember that in Fig. 32.2 horizontal distances have no meaning), which are so close that they almost form a single node, from which the different phyla radiate out, just as in the fan-shaped phylogenetic tree of Fig. 1.3.

8 The ancestors of all the main evolutionary lineages (of the various algal, protozoan and fungal phyla, and of the cluster of multicellular animal phyla) were probably unicellular flagellates, even in those lineages that today lack unicellular flagellate representatives, such as the Ascomycota and the multicellular animals. The argument supporting this hypothesis is that the rRNA evidence shows that the Ascomycota and the multicellular animals are parts of a lineage that also includes the green algae (Division Chlorophyta), which is a group that contains unicellular flagellates. Hence, unless there has been a reversal within the green algae from a multicellular, non-flagellate type of body plan to a unicellular flagellate body plan, which is extremely unlikely, the common ancestors of the Ascomycota and the Chlorophyta must have

been unicellular flagellates, as must the common ancestors of the Chlorophyta and the Eumetazoa. The presence in the Eumetazoa of tissues containing flagellate cells, and the occurrence of flagellate male gametes, also suggest that the common ancestor of green algae and multicellular animals must have been flagellate.

9 Phyla in which several representatives have been investigated appear to be coherent entities; on the basis of 18S rRNA sequences, the species of one phylum are much more closely related to each other than they are to species of other phyla. This confirms that the phyla are 'natural', even though they were originally defined on the basis of morphology alone (see also p. 211). Examples shown in Fig. 32.2 are the Ciliophora; the Heterokontophyta; the Ascomycota; the Chlorophyta, together with the Tracheophyta (vascular plants); and the Eumetazoa. Other studies of nucleotide sequences confirm and extend this idea ([636]). For instance, 18S rRNA sequences show that the kelp *Costaria* (Phaeophyceae) is closely related to the two representatives of the Heterokontophyta included in Fig. 32.2, namely *Ochromonas* (Chrysophyceae) and *Achlya* (Oomycetes), confirming that the concept of the Heterokontophyta, originally developed on the basis of morphological evidence, is sound ([73]); in other words, this phylum (division) is 'natural'. Studies of 5S rRNA also confirm the internal phylogenetic coherence of the Rhodophyta; the Chlorophyta, together with the Bryophyta (the mosses and liverworts) and the Tracheophyta; the Heterokontophyta; the Ascomycota; the Basidiomycota; and the Eumetazoa (5S rRNA studies are not suited to the detection of phylogenetic relationships *between* phyla; cf. p. 39) ([735]).

A 28S rRNA phylogenetic tree

Recently, a phylogenetic tree of the eukaryotes has been constructed from nucleotide sequences of large (28S) ribosomal RNA (Fig. 32.3; [1393, 1394]). Various eukaryote phyla were included in the study and, to facilitate comparison with the 18S rRNA tree, the same species are pictured in Fig 32.3 as in Fig. 32.2, although in fact the species chosen to represent the

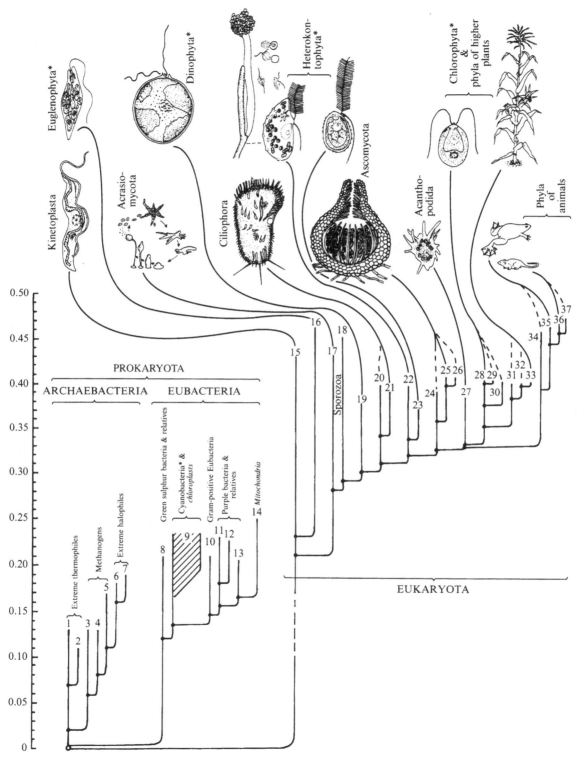

For legend see facing page.

various phyla in the 18S and 28S studies were not always the same (see the caption to Fig. 32.3). In addition, the 28S rRNA tree includes representatives of four phyla not included in the 18S rRNA study, namely the **Parabasalia** (a group of flagellate protozoans, all heterotrophic, which live in the guts of higher animals) and the algal phyla **Haptophyta**, **Cryptophyta** and **Rhodophyta**. Conversely, the Euglenophyta and Dinophyta were included in the 18S rRNA study, but not in the 28S rRNA study. Despite the differences in the organisms and phyla chosen for study, there is a striking overall resemblance between the two phylogenetic trees, including the order in which the phyla emerge, from left to right. Note that in the 28S rRNA tree the green plants (including both the green algae and the higher plants) and the metazoan animals are again the last lineages to diverge. It should be stressed, however, that the final form of the phylogenetic tree depends very much upon the mathematical methods used to construct the tree. The deeper bifurcations are particularly strongly affected, and hence also the order in which the phyla seem to emerge. This is not surprising in view of the very small genetic distances between most of the deeper nodes.

The 28S rRNA phylogenetic tree (Fig. 32.3) exhibits a number of interesting features, which add the following to what had been deduced from the 18S rRNA tree.

1 The **Rhodophyta** and **Cryptophyta** emerge quite late and close to each other, and also quite close to the **Chlorophyta**. This late phylogenetic origin of the Rhodophyta is quite unexpected, since it contradicts the earlier and widely accepted view that the Rhodophyta are one of the most ancient and primitive of eukaryote lineages. Since the red algae are the only phylum of algae where 9 + 2 flagella are completely absent, it had been suggested that the Rhodophyta diverged from other primaeval eukaryotes before 9 + 2 flagella evolved ([200, 201, 231, 232, 440, 1556, 1665, 1751]). The 28S rRNA tree, however, suggests that the ancestors of the Rhodophyta did possess flagella and that these were subsequently lost, secondarily. It may be that the algal phylum Glaucophyta, which contains flagellate members (see p. 45), can be considered as having descended from the primitive, flagellate ancestors of the Rhodophyta, since the Glaucophyta is the only other algal phylum with

Figure 32.2. A phylogenetic tree of the main groups of organisms within the three realms of organisms: the **Archaebacteria, Eubacteria** and **Eukaryota**. The groups indicated by asterisks are phyla (= divisions) of algae. The tree is composite and based on similarities in the nucleotide sequences of 16S rRNAs in the Archaebacteria and Eubacteria and the similar 18S rRNAs in the Eukaryota. The part of the tree containing the prokaryotes is based on *ca.* 920 nucleotides ([526]), that containing the eukaryotes on *ca.* 1530 nucleotides ([589]). The vertical axis gives an estimate of the evolutionary distance between taxa, as the estimated average number of fixed point mutations per sequence position; the distance between two taxa is the sum of the two vertical distances down to the first common branch point. Horizontal distances have no significance other than clarity, especially where there are dense knots of branch points.

The tree is based on analyses of representative species. 1 = *Sulfolobus solfatarius*. 2 = *Thermoproteus tenax*. 3 = *Methanococcus vannielii*. 4 = *Methanobacterium formicicum*. 5 = *Methanospiril-* *lum hungatei*. 6 = *Halobacterium volcanii*. 7 = *Halococcus morrhua*. 8 = *Thermomicrobium roseum*. 9 = Blue-green algae (Cyanobacteria, Cyanophyta) and chloroplasts. 10. *Bacillus subtilis*. 11 = *Pseudomonas testosteroni*. 12 = *Escherichia coli*. 13 = *Agrobacterium tumefaciens*. 14 = mitochondrion of maize (*Zea mais*). 15 = *Trypanosoma brucei* (the cause of human sleeping sickness). 16 = *Euglena gracilis*. 17 = *Dictyostelium discoideum*. 18 = *Plasmodium berghei* (causes malaria in rats and mice). 19 = *Prorocentrum micans*. 20 = *Paramecium tetraurelia*. 21 = *Stylonichia pustulata*. 22 = *Achlya bisexualis*. 23 = *Ochromonas danica*. 24 = *Saccharomyces cerevisiae*. 25 = *Neurospora crassa*. 26 = *Podospora anserina*. 27 = *Acanthamoeba castellani* (a soil amoeba). 28 = *Chlamydomonas reinhardtii*. 29 = *Volvox carteri*. 30 = *Nanochlorum eukaryotum*. 31 = *Glycine max* (soy bean). 32 = *Oryza sativa* (rice). 33 = *Zea mais* (maize). 34 = *Artemia salina* (brine shrimp). 35 = *Xenopus laevis*. 36 = *Rattus norvegicus* (rat). 37 = *Oryctolagus cuniculus* (rabbit). (Based on [526, 589, 1471].)

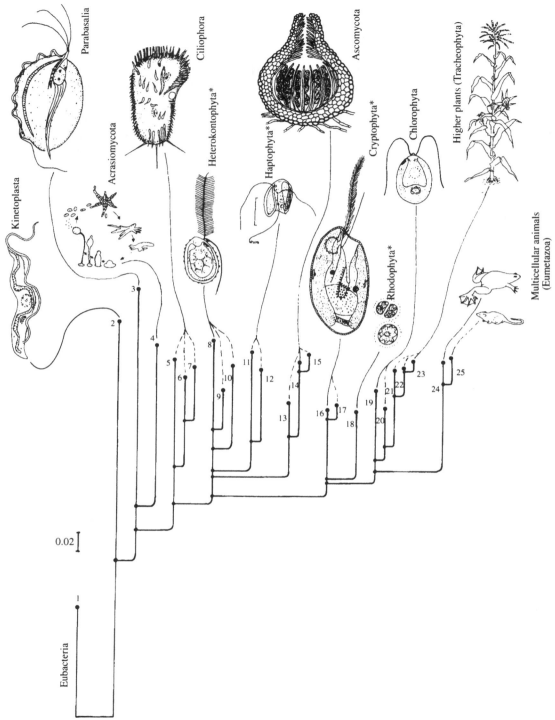

Figure 32.3. A phylogenetic tree of the main groups of the Eukaryota, based on similarities in the nucleotide sequences (*ca.* 450 nucleotides) of 28S rRNAs. The groups indicated by asterisks are phyla (= divisions) of algae. The scale bar gives a measure of relative genetic dissimilarity and evolutionary distance (see Fig. 32.2). The evolutionary distance between two taxa is the sum of the two vertical distances down to

chloroplasts of the type found in the red algae (with equally spaced, distant thylakoids bearing phycobilisomes). In a more recently constructed 18S rRNA tree, the relatively late emergence of the Rhodophyta is confirmed, although its position with respect to the other phyla is quite different from that shown in Fig. 32.3 ([331a]).

2 The algal phylum **Haptophyta** emerges close to the phylum **Heterokontophyta**.

3 The 28S rRNA study summarized in Fig. 32.3 did not include the algal phyla Euglenophyta and Dinophyta. However, in another 28S rRNA study ([991]), the **Dinophyta** were found to emerge close to the **Ciliophora**, just as in the 18S rRNA phylogenetic tree (Fig. 32.2).

The endosymbiont hypothesis

The hypothesis of the **endosymbiotic origin of chloroplasts and mitochondria** (cf. pp. 2, 7, 39), initially considered as wild speculation, has gained so much supporting evidence in the last decade that its validity is now scarcely questioned ([16, 513, 1622, 1854]). The **endosymbiotic origin of flagella**, on the other hand, has generally been considered unlikely, since no prokaryotes are known that possess microtubules. Even this hypothesis has recently become more attractive, however, gaining credence from the discovery that there seems to be a small semi-autonomous flagellar genome in the flagellar basal bodies of the green alga *Chlamydomonas* ([539, 596, 1466]).

It is now recognized that there have been profound changes in mitochondria and chloroplasts since their eubacterial forebears were engulfed by primitive eukaryotes, during their 'taming' as organelles. They have lost most of their DNA and retain only a small portion of the original bacterial DNA, which codes for some of the organelle proteins. Most of the molecules from which mitochondria and chloroplasts are constructed are synthesized elsewhere in the eukaryote cell, under the control of nuclear genes, and they are then imported into the organelles. There seems, therefore, to have been extensive transference of genes originally in the organelles, from the organelle genomes to the nuclear genome, including for instance many of the genes coding for chloroplast ribosome proteins.

Biosynthesis of chloroplast components is regulated by close cooperation between the genetic systems of chloroplast and nucleus. The photosynthetic apparatus and several of the chloroplast protein complexes each consist of a large number of polypeptides. Some of these are encoded within the chloroplast genome, while others are encoded by the nuclear genome and have to be imported into the chloroplast. Here they assemble with their partner polypeptides, synthesized within the chloroplast, to form the final, functional protein complexes. One example is the enzyme ribulose 1,5-bisphosphate carboxylase–oxygenase (RuBisCO), which catalyses the initial step of the 'dark' reactions of photosynthesis, during which CO_2 is reduced to carbohydrate, $(CH_2O)_n$. RuBisCO is present in large amounts in chloroplasts, especially in pyrenoids, and consists of eight identical large subunits and eight identical small subunits. In the green algae and higher plants the large subunits are encoded by the chloroplast genome, while the small subunits are encoded by the nuclear genome ([1354, 1519]). In other phyla of algae, both the large and the small subunits are encoded by the chloroplast genome ([908a]).

Caption for fig. 32.3 *(cont.)*.

the first common branch point. Horizontal distances have no significance other than for clarity, especially where there are dense knots of branch points. To facilitate comparison with the 18S rRNA tree shown in Fig. 32.2, the same species are illustrated for each phylum (division) in the two figures, even though in some cases the analyses were based on different species. 1 = *Escherichia coli*. 2 = *Crithidia fasciculata*. 3 = *Trichomonas vaginalis*. 4 = *Dictyostelium discoideum*. 5 = *Paramecium primaurelia*. 6 = *Blepharisma japonicum*. 7 = *Stentor coeruleus*.

8 = *Ochromonas danica* (Chrysophyceae). 9 = *Synura petersenii* (Chrysophyceae). 10 = *Vacuolaria virescens* (Raphidophyceae). 11 = *Prymnesium parvum*. 12 = *Crico-sphaera roscoffensis*. 13 = *Saccharomyces cerevisiae*. 14 = *Neurospora crassa*. 15 = *Fusarium oxysporum*. 16 = *Cryptomonas ovata*. 17 = *Chilomonas paramecium*. 18 = *Porphyridium purpureum*. 19 = *Chlorogonium elongatum*. 20 = *Pyramimonas parkeae*. 21 = *Nicotiana tabacum*. 22 = *Oryza sativa*. 23 = *Zea mais*. 24 = *Xenopus laevis*. 25 = *Mus musculus*. (Based on [1394].)

Persuasive evidence in support of the endosymbiont hypothesis is provided by studies of small (16S) rRNA, which is a size class of ribosomal RNA characteristic of both prokaryotes and the mitochondria and chloroplasts of eukaryotes (cf. p. 37). Sequencing of the RNA shows that there is a fundamental similarity (homology) between the 16S rRNA of the organelles and the 16S rRNA of certain groups of Eubacteria. Mitochondria share most homologous sequences with the purple bacteria and their relatives, while chloroplast 16S rRNA is most similar to that of the cyanobacteria (blue-green algae) (Figs. 32.2, 2.8; [526, 1806, 1913, 1914]). A close phylogenetic relationship between chloroplasts and cyanobacteria is also indicated by resemblances in the arrangement and nucleotide sequences of certain genes present in the genomes of both, such as the genes coding for ATP synthase subunits ([268, 938]). The ATP synthase complex, which is anchored in the thylakoid, produces stored energy in the form of ATP, the energy for this being provided by the photosynthetic electron transport chain. Other examples of genes whose arrangement and structure support a link between chloroplasts and cyanobacteria are the genes coding for thylakoid proteins of photosystems I and II ([275, 1697]).

The origin of chloroplasts: monophyletic or polyphyletic?

One highly intriguing question that has not been settled as yet is whether mitochondria and chloroplasts are monophyletic or polyphyletic. In other words, are the mitochondria of all living eukaryotes descended from a single engulfed aerobic bacterium, or are they descended from several different endosymbiotic bacteria, each taken up separately? Are the chloroplasts of all living eukaryotes derived from a single endosymbiotic cyanobacterium, or are they descendants of several, independently engulfed cyanobacteria? The phylogenetic tree derived from studies of prokaryotic and organellar 16S rRNAs suggests strongly that mitochondria are monophyletic, all having been derived from a single aerobic, heterotrophic eubacterium ([204, 549, 764]); it also suggests that chloroplasts are also monophyletic, descendants of a single cyanobacterium (Figs. 2.8, 32.2; [204, 526]).

Let us examine more closely the phylogenetic tree shown in Fig. 2.8. This tree, which includes the cyanobacteria and various kinds of chloroplasts, indicates that the chloroplasts of *Cyanophora* (Glaucophyta), *Chlamydomonas* (Chlorophyta), *Euglena* (Euglenophyta), *Marchantia* (Bryophyta), tobacco and maize (*Nicotiana* and *Zea*, respectively: Tracheophyta) had a common origin from one ancestral, free-living cyanobacterium ([526, 1806]). Other evidence shows that the ancestral chloroplasts of *Ochromonas* (Heterokontophyta) also diverged from other chloroplasts *after* the common origin of all from an ancestral, free-living cyanobacterium ([1910]). What the tree does not indicate, however, is whether the diversification of the ancestral cyanobacterium took place before or after uptake into host cells. If uptake occurred after diversification, then several separate endosymbioses have been involved in the evolution of chloroplasts, involving several closely related cyanobacteria.

In earlier versions of the endosymbiont theory ([1473]), chloroplasts were considered to have had a polyphyletic origin. With respect to pigmentation, there are three basic types of chloroplast in eukaryotes: the red type (with chlorophyll a and phycobilins); the brown type (with chlorophyll a and chlorophyll c and fucoxanthin); and the green type (with chlorophyll a and chlorophyll b) (Table 1.2). Each of these was suggested to have arisen from its own prokaryotic ancestor, which possessed a similar set of pigments. When this hypothesis was put forward, the only chloroplast for which an equivalent free-living prokaryote was known was the red algal chloroplast. This shows several similarities to the cyanobacterial cell: both have unstacked, equally spaced thylakoids, which bear phycobilisomes, and both lack any chlorophyll apart from chlorophyll a (Table 1.2). Initially, no prokaryotic algae were known that could be considered as present-day relatives of the ancestors of brown and green chloroplasts; the free-living brown and green prokaryotic ancestors were only imaginary. It was no wonder, therefore, that the discovery of *Prochloron* in the early 1970s caused so much excitement, since this green prokaryote seemed to be just the kind of organism that had been hypothesized as the ancestor of green chloroplasts ([1001, 1589]). The very name given to the new organism expressed the opinion that it is related to the ancestors of green chloroplasts: *Prochloron* (= primitive green thing). *Prochloron* and green chloroplasts resemble each other in having stacked thylakoids and chlorophylls a *and* b, while both lack phycobilins and consequently also phycobilisomes (Table 1.2; p. 42).

Later, yet another green prokaryote was discovered, again having stacked thylakoids and chlorophylls a and b; this was the unbranched, filamentous alga *Prochlorothrix* ([168]), which has been included in a study of 16S rRNA sequences in chloroplasts and prokaryotes ([1806]). The 16S rRNA phylogenetic tree (Fig. 2.8) indicates that *Prochlorothrix* is a 'green cyanobacterium', which emerges from the tree quite far away from the chloroplast cluster (including *Chlamydomonas*, *Euglena*, *Marchantia*, tobacco and maize). It seems from this that *Prochlorothrix* cannot be considered as a close phylogenetic relative of green chloroplasts. Not all the evidence points in the same direction, however, since the amino acid sequences of one of the thylakoid proteins of photosystem II suggest a closer relationship between *Prochlorothrix* and green chloroplasts than do the 16S rRNA data ([1233]).

A suggestion that the brown photosynthetic eubacterium *Heliobacterium* might represent the ancestral free-living 'brown chloroplast' ([506, 1125]) must be rejected, as 16S rRNA sequences indicate that this prokaryote is related neither to the brown chloroplasts of *Ochromonas*, nor to any other chloroplast ([1910]).

The 16S rRNA tree shown in Fig. 2.8 suggests that the evolution of chlorophyll a + phycobilin photosynthesis into chlorophyll a + b photosynthesis (involving the loss of phycobilins and their replacement by chlorophyll b as an antenna pigment) has occurred at least twice, once when *Prochlorothrix* evolved from a cyanobacterial ancestor (with chlorophyll a and phycobilins), and once when the chlorophyll a + b type of chloroplast evolved from chloroplasts containing chlorophyll a and phycobilins. It is possible that this transformation also took place in other lineages, such as in other 'green cyanobacteria' (prochlorophytes, cf. p. 44), if these evolved independently from different cyanobacterial ancestors, each containing chlorophyll a and phycobilins. Multiple evolution of chlorophyll b (or of chlorophyll c) from chlorophyll a is certainly plausible, since they are quite similar chemically ([203]).

The recent discovery that a chlorophyll c-like pigment occurs, in additon to chlorophylls a and b, in certain green algae of the class Prasinophyceae ([794, 1897, 1898]) also suggests that the difference between chlorophyll a + c chloroplasts and chlorophyll a + b chloroplasts may not be as fundamental as has been thought until recently. The presence of chlorophyll c, which is derived biochemically from a precursor of chlorophyll a, might in fact be a primitive character ([1898]).

However, the exact nature of the chlorophyll c-like pigment of the Prasinophyceae is still controversial (see discussion in [1532a] and p. 337).

On the whole, the phylogenetic relationships inferred between chloroplasts and cyanobacteria from 16S rRNA sequences tend to suggest that the different types of chloroplast are monophyletic, all having arisen from a single common ancestor, which was a cyanobacterium. Comparison between the genomes of various types of chloroplast and those of cyanobacteria also supports a monophyletic origin of chloroplasts, rather than a polyphyletic origin from three different prokaryotic ancestors, with different sets of photosynthetic pigments. There are many basic similarities (homologies) in the arrangements of genes in these genomes, which point to a monophyletic origin of the chloroplasts of groups as diverse as the Glaucophyta, Euglenophyta, Heterokontophyta, Chlorophyta and the higher plants, although extensive rearrangements of the genome indicate long periods of independent evolution ([331b, 908a, 938]).

Comparisons of chloroplast genomes also suggest that the common ancestor of chloroplasts underwent a phase of development as a primaeval chloroplast, after its uptake and incorporation as an endosymbiont but before its evolutionary diversification into the various types of chloroplast present today (for a review, see [938]). Thus, for instance, most chloroplast genomes differ from cyanobacterial genomes in the presence of two **inverted repeats**. Inverted repeats are two sections of the circular chloroplast genome, which are identical but inverted, being transcribed in opposite directions. They separate two sections of DNA present in single copy and contain the genes for the chloroplast ribosomal RNA, together with various other genes, exactly which depending on the group. Inverted repeats have been observed in the chloroplast genomes of algae belonging to the Glaucophyta ([96, 1854]), Cryptophyta ([331]), Heterokontophyta ([938, 939, 1004, 1016, 1484]) and Chlorophyta ([1354, 1519]). Among higher plants, the liverwort *Marchantia* and numerous vascular plants have been found to have chloroplasts containing inverted repeats ([938, 1354]). Chloroplasts without inverted repeats seem to be the exceptions to the rule, occurring only in a few vascular plants ([938, 1354]) and in two red algae ([1004, 1627]). The *Euglena* chloroplast genome contains between one and five **tandem repeats**, which are transcribed in the same direction; these contain the chloroplast rRNA genes ([1354]).

The widespread occurrence of inverted repeats in the chloroplasts of various eukaryotic algae, drawn from a great diversity of phyla, and their absence from cyanobacteria, suggests that inverted repeats are a primitive feature of chloroplast genomes; they have been inherited from the ancestral chloroplast from which the various other types of chloroplast later evolved. If so, the lack of inverted repeats in certain vascular plants and in two red algae must be ascribed to secondary loss ([938]).

More support for the monophyletic origin of chloroplasts and an early period of common evolutionary development of this organelle comes from studies of nucleotide sequences in the genes coding for polypeptides of the ATPase and cytochrome b_6 – cytochrome f complexes of photosystem II, and the genes for 16S rRNA ([331a, b, e, 908a, 938, 986a]). However, in contrast to this, a phylogenetic tree based on the sequences of the chloroplast genes coding for the large and small subunits of RuBisCO (ribulose 1,5-bisphosphate carboxylase–oxygenase) indicates that there are two main evolutionary lineages of chloroplasts. One lineage is more closely allied to the β-purple bacteria and encompasses the chloroplasts of the Rhodophyta, Cryptophyta and Heterokontophyta. The other is related to the cyanobacteria and contains the chloroplasts of the Glaucophyta, Euglenophyta, Chlorophyta and higher plants ([36a, 331b, c, 1027a, 1127a, b]). These results therefore seem to support a polyphyletic (more precisely, a biphyletic) origin of chloroplasts.

When we try to reconcile these apparently contradictory results, we should always be aware of the fact that we are comparing the phylogenetic trees, not of whole organisms, but of individual genes. It is possible that different genes in one and the same organism have had different evolutionary histories. This is clearly true for eukaryotic algae, where we now know that the chloroplast genes have not had the same evolutionary history as those coding for components of the cell outside the chloroplast; each plant cell is itself a chimaera. Furthermore, the endosymbiotic origin of the chloroplast as a subjugated cyanobacterium within a host eukaryote must have involved extensive **lateral gene transfer**. Lateral gene transfer can perhaps also be invoked to explain the presence, in the same chloroplast (in the Rhodophyta, Cryptophyta and Heterokontophyta), of several genes derived from a cyanobacterial ancestor together with one from a β-purple bacterial ancestor. One possibility is that the ancestral eukaryotic plant cell had engulfed and tamed both a cyanobacterium and a β-purple bacterium in a multiple endosymbiosis. Then, during the primaeval divergence between the two principal chloroplast lineages, the rhodophyte–cryptophyte–heterokontophyte lineage retained the β-purple bacterium type of RuBisCO gene (which was transferred to the chloroplast) and lost the cyanobacterial type, while the chlorophyte–higher plant lineage retained the cyanobacterial type and lost the β-purple bacterial type. Alternatively, the primitive eukaryotic ancestor of the rhodophyte–cryptophyte–heterokontophyte lineage (possibly a phagotrophic but photosynthetic flagellate resembling a glaucophyte) may have engulfed and tamed a β-purple bacterium, from which it obtained a replacement for its own cyanobacterial RuBisCO gene ([331b, 908a]).

In the present context it is perhaps appropriate to stress that molecular phylogenies like those discussed here do not represent the absolute truth about relationships. Hypothetical reconstructions of evolution should be based on a diversity of evidence, including morphological data. Analysis of the sequences of nucleotides in different genes can lead, for the same organisms, to conflicting phylogenies, as shown in the above example, although these can sometimes be 'explained away'. But some molecular phylogenies are so incongruent with all other data that they must even be rejected. One example is a phylogeny of algal chloroplasts based on sequences in the gene coding for the $F_I/CF_{1-\alpha}$ subunit of chloroplast ATPase. According to this tree, cyanobacteria have evolved from heterokontophyte chloroplasts, which is absurd. Such incongruities may be caused by differences in the nucleotide substitution rates in the organisms being compared, at least for a particular gene ([908a]). On the other hand, a phylogeny based on the gene for the $F_I/CF_{1-\beta}$ subunit of chloroplast ATPase supports the hypothesis of a monophyletic evolutionary origin of heterokontophyte and chlorophyte chloroplasts ([908a, 986a]), which is plausible because it agrees with other data.

Synthesis: an integrated phylogenetic tree for eukaryotes and chloroplasts

The information summarized in the previous section supports in general the idea that eukaryotic chloroplasts are monophyletic; they arose once, from a cyanobacterial ancestor. After its incorporation into a host cell, the ancestral chloroplast first underwent a period of evolution in which inverted repeats arose and the size of its genome was reduced tenfold, and then it diversified into the various types of chloroplast present today.

The notion of a monophyletic origin of chloroplasts is most easily and economically integrated into the 18S rRNA phylogenetic tree of the eukaryotes (Fig. 32.2) by postulating that all extant groups of eukaryotes were originally photosynthetic. In this simplest of hypotheses, the ancient ancestral eukaryote took up a cyanobacterium and transformed it into a chloroplast; during the subsequent phylogenetic radiation of the eukaryotes, some lineages retained chloroplasts and developed different assortments of photosynthetic pigments, while other lineages lost them and became heterotrophic. There are two compelling arguments against this. Firstly, the eukaryotic algae *Euglena* (Euglenophyta) and *Chlamydomonas* (Chlorophyta), both with green chloroplasts, are very distantly related on the basis of their cytoplasmic 18S rRNA sequences (cf. Fig. 32.2), but closely related on the basis of chloroplast 16S rRNA sequences (cf. Fig. 2.8). Secondly, the existence of many symbiotic associations between photoautotrophic organisms (some of them prokaryotes but most of them eukaryotes) and heterotrophic eukaryotes suggests that the capture and incorporation of photoautotrophs by heterotrophs, and their transformation into photosynthetic organelles, has occurred over and over again in the course of evolution ([1656]); many examples of this have been given in the preceding chapters. In the fan-shaped phylogenetic tree of Fig. 1.3, ten phyla are marked (with an 's') that contain heterotrophic organisms capable of forming close symbiotic associations with photoautotrophs. The photosynthetic partners in these symbioses vary from loosely associated algal cells still capable of independent existence, to cells that are highly integrated with their host and are in fact functionally equivalent to chloroplasts.

The phylogeny shown in Fig. 32.4 represents an attempt to reconcile the apparently conflicting ideas and data mentioned above, namely the monophyletic origin of chloroplasts; the multiple origin of photosynthetic symbioses; the close relationship between the chloroplasts of *Euglena* and *Chlamydomonas*, and the distant relationship between their cytoplasts. Fig. 32.4

shows a phylogenetic tree of the Eukaryota (continuous lines), on which is superimposed a phylogenetic tree of chloroplasts. The eukaryote tree, which is based largely on the RNA sequence data summarized in Figs. 32.2 and 32.3, illustrates the hypothesis that the first large-scale evolutionary radiation took place at the cellular level, among heterotrophic, phagotrophic flagellates. This resulted in a multitude of different types of heterotroph, each with its own unicellular body plan. Multicellular fungi, such as the Ascomycota, and multicellular animals probably arose from heterotrophic, flagellate ancestors. The various lineages of eukaryotic algae were also derived from heterotrophic ancestors, but subsequently obtained chloroplasts by a series of steps, beginning with the phagotrophic uptake of photoautotrophs into food vacuoles. The main evolutionary events leading to the incorporation of chloroplasts are numbered 1 to 6 in Fig. 32.4 (and are shown by thick dashed lines), while other more minor events, leading to the evolution of smaller and more specialized groups of algae and other photosynthetic organisms, are numbered 7 to 17.

Event 1. The main prey of the primitive phagotrophic flagellates of the Precambrian were probably **cyanobacteria** (cf. Fig. 2.7). Initially the prey were always digested, but in one of the last major lineages of phagotrophic flagellates to emerge, one flagellate evolved in which the cyanobacteria were taken up but not digested, being transformed instead into photosynthetic organelles ('1' in Fig. 32.4); these had a reduced genome containing inverted repeats (see above). In this way the first **primaeval photosynthetic flagellate** arose. The present-day **Glaucophyta** may perhaps be the direct, little-changed descendants of the primaeval flagellates: glaucophyte chloroplasts are in several ways intermediate between cyanobacteria and the chloroplasts of other algae, with respect both to their morphology and structure, and to aspects of their molecular biology (Chapter 4, p. 45). Thus, for instance, the chloroplasts of glaucophytes, with their equidistant, phycobilisome-bearing thylakoids, are very similar to free-living coccoid cyanobacteria but also to the chloroplasts of red algae (Rhodophyta). Another interesting, apparently primitive character is the presence, in the chloroplast genome of the glaucophyte *Cyanophora*, of the genes coding for *both* types

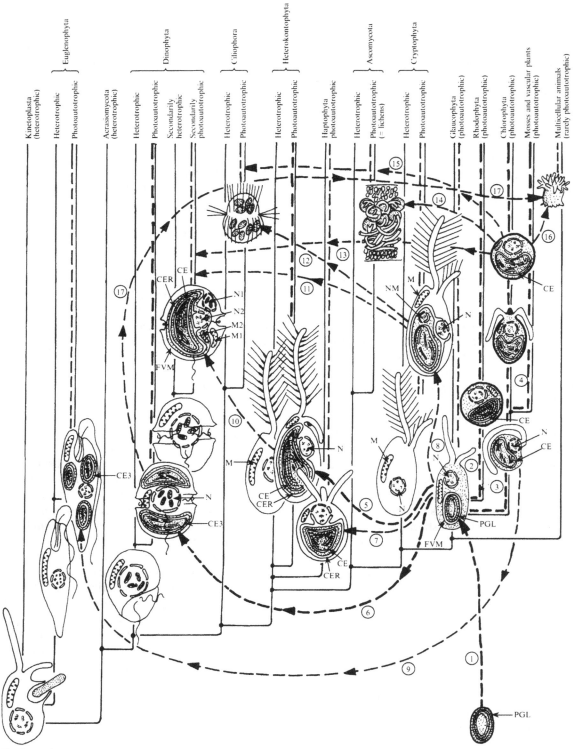

For legend see facing page.

of subunit, large and small, of the enzyme ribulose 1,5-bisphosphate carboxylase–oxygenase [96, 634, 1854]. *Cyanophora* chloroplasts share this feature with the cyanobacteria, as well as with the chloroplasts of the Rhodophyta, Cryptophyta and Heterokonto-phyta [908a]. On the other hand, in the Chloro-phyta and higher plants, the chloroplast genome codes only for the large subunit of RuBisCO; the genes for the small subunits have been transferred to the nuclear genome.

The chloroplast of the primaeval, glaucophyte-like flagellate may be transitional, derived from the bifurcation between the two principal chloroplast lineages mentioned in the previous section, one with the β-purple bacterium type of RuBisCO genes (large *and* small subunit genes; as in the chloroplasts of Rhodophyta, Cryptophyta and Heterokontophyta) and the other with the cyanobacterial type of RuBisCO genes (large subunits only; as in the chloroplasts of Chlorophyta and higher plants). The primitive nature of the glaucophyte chloroplast is confirmed by the 16S rRNA phylogenetic tree of cyanobacteria and chloroplasts (Fig. 2.8: *Cyanophora*). More recent 16S rRNA sequence data on the chloroplasts of Rhodophyta, Cryptophyta and Heterokontophyta also support the idea that the glaucophyte chloroplast is primitive and its position at the divergence between the two main chloroplast lineages [331b, e]. This is further confirmed by a phylogenetic tree constructed from sequences of the $F_1/CF_{1-\beta}$ subunit of chloroplast ATPase [908a]. Unfortunately, no sequence data are yet available from nuclear genes in the Glaucophyta, so that the phylogenetic position of the eukaryotic compartment in these organisms remains uncertain.

Yet another primitive trait of the Glaucophyta is the presence of a vestigial peptidoglycan wall around the chloroplast, which is considered as a relic or vestige of its origin as a cyanobacterium (cyanobacteria typically have a peptidoglycan wall layer; cf. pp. 28, 46).

Event 2. The **Rhodophyta** arose from a primaeval, glaucophyte-like alga, through the loss of flagella. They retained several primitive features of the cyanobacteria and Glaucophyta, such as equidistant thylakoids and the presence of phycobilisomes. In the primaeval glaucophyte-like alga the cyanobacterial type of chloroplast genes for the large and small subunits of RuBisCO were replaced, possibly through lateral gene transfer, by the β-purple bacterium type (see above, section 1). This alga may also have been ancestral to the chloroplasts compartments of the Heterokontophyta and Cryptophyta (see below, events 5 and 8). Inverted repeats are not present in the chloroplast genome and must have been lost secondarily (cf. [938, 1004, 1627]). The chloroplasts are surrounded by the standard double chloroplast envelope, the inner membrane being interpreted as representing the plasmalemma of the original endosymbiotic cyanobacterium, the outer as the original host's food vacuole membrane.

Note that in this hypothesis the red algae are considered to have arisen through the evolutionary transformation of an existing photosynthetic eukaryote, not through an independent symbiotic event.

Event 3. The **Chlorophyta** arose from the primaeval glaucophytes by the transformation of the photosynthetic apparatus from one based on chlorophyll a and phycobilins, to one based on chlorophyll a and chlorophyll b. Phycobilisomes were lost and stacking of the thylakoids became possible. Flagella have been retained (except in several lineages within the green algae, where they

Figure 32.4. A phylogenetic tree of the Eukaryota, based on the trees in Figs 32.1 and 32.2. Superimposed upon it is a suggested phylogeny of chloroplasts; for further explanation of steps 1–17, see text. CE = two-membrane chloroplast envelope; CE3 = three-membrane chloroplast envelope; CER = chloroplast endoplasmic reticulum, composed of two concentric membranes; FVM = food vacuole membrane; M = mitochondrion; M1 = mitochondrion of host cell; M2 = mitochondrion of endosymbiont cell; N = nucleus; N1 = nucleus of host cell; N2 = nucleus of endosymbiont cell; NM = nucleomorph (vestigial nucleus); PGL = peptidoglycan layer.

have been lost secondarily), and so have inverted repeats within the chloroplast genome, but the genes coding for the small subunits of ribulose 1,5-bisphosphate carboxylase–oxygenase have been transferred to the nuclear genome. The chloroplasts are surrounded only by the standard double chloroplast envelope.

Like the red algae, the green algae are thought to have arisen through evolutionary transformation of a pre-existing eukaryotic alga, not through separate endosymbioses. As we shall see, however, all the remaining phyla of eukaryotic algae probably obtained their chloroplasts by a different process, involving the capture and subjugation of **eukaryotic** algae ([511]).

Event 4. The higher plants (mosses and liverworts, and vascular plants) evolved from the green algae between 400 and 500 million years ago, as highly specialized lineages, adapted to terrestrial life (Figs. 32.2, 32.3).

Event 5. The **photosynthetic** members of the **Heterokontophyta** may have evolved when a primaeval heterotrophic heterokontophyte (perhaps resembling the recently described *Cafeteria*: [416]) ingested one of the early glaucophyte-like algae and incorporated it into its cell, first as an endosymbiont and later as a chloroplast; it may have been in this glaucophyte-like alga that the type of RuBisCO genes found in cyanobacteria (coding for large and small subunits) was replaced, though lateral transfer, by the β-purple bacterium type (see above). The presence of four membranes surrounding the chloroplast is consistent with this idea. The innermost two membranes can be interpreted as representing the standard double membrane envelope of the endosymbiont's own chloroplast; the inner membrane of the chloroplast endoplasmic reticulum (ER) would then be equivalent to the plasmalemma of the endosymbiont alga, while the outer membrane of the chloroplast ER would represent the food vacuole membrane of the host. The cytoplasm between the chloroplast envelope and the chloroplast ER could thus be seen as vestigial, representing the cytoplasm of the original endosymbiotic eukaryote; all the organelles originally within it have been lost, however, except for the chloroplasts ([511, 1880]).

The photosynthetic apparatus of the glaucophytes, which is based on chlorophyll a and phycobilins, has been replaced by one based on chlorophylls a and c. The inverted repeats of the chloroplast genome have been retained but in an extremely compact form ([908, 938]).

Event 6. Another endosymbiosis, involving the independent capture and transformation of another primaeval glaucophyte by an ancient heterotrophic dinophyte, led to the evolution of typical photosynthetic **Dinophyta**, with their triple chloroplast envelope. The innermost pair of membranes are interpreted as representing the standard double membrane of the endosymbiont's chloroplast, while the outermost membrane may represent the host's food vacuole membrane. The absence of a membrane equivalent to the plasmalemma of the endosymbiont may be explicable as follows. Many phagotrophic dinophytes are known to feed by puncturing the plasmalemma of the prey cell and sucking up its cytoplasm (cf. p. 257). As a result the plasmalemma is not taken in and the ingested prey cytoplasm is surrounded only by the food vacuole membrane of the host. During the evolution of the Dinophyta, photosynthesis using chlorophyll a and phycobilins has been replaced by a system based on chlorophylls a and c, but this differs in several ways (e.g. in the other accessory pigments present) from the chlorophyll a + c photosynthetic apparatus of the Heterokontophyta (cf. pp. 102 and 251).

Sometimes the three-membrane-bound chloroplast is interpreted as a eukaryotic prey chloroplast (with two membranes) that has been taken up directly into the host's food vacuole; the vacuole provides the third and outermost membrane of the chloroplast envelope ([977]). This would be impossible, however, because the biosynthesis of chloroplast components is regulated through close 'cooperation' between the chloroplast and nuclear genomes. The only way in which a chloroplast could be captured would be for the prey nucleus to be retained for a long period alongside the chloroplast, permitting the gradual transfer of nuclear chloroplast genes from the prey nucleus to the host nucleus; only then could the prey nucleus be lost (cf. p. 255).

Event 7. A third independent incorporation of a primaeval glaucophyte may have been involved in the evolution of the algal phylum **Haptophyta**: as in the Heterokontophyta, the chloroplasts are surrounded by four membranes. However, the two phyla also resemble each other in the photosynthetic pigments present, and this suggests that the ingestion of the endosymbiotic glaucophyte and the transformation of the photosynthetic apparatus (from one based on chlorophyll a and phycobilins to one based on chlorophylls a and c) may have taken place before the haptophyte and heterokontophyte lineages diverged from each other.

Event 8. A fourth independent engulfment of a primaeval glaucophyte-like alga with the β-purple bacterium type of RuBisCO genes (see above, events 2 and 5), this time by an ancient heterotrophic cryptophyte (perhaps comparable to the present-day genus *Cyathomonas*), may have been involved in the origin of the photoautotrophic **Cryptophyta**. As in the Heterokontophyta and Haptophyta, the chloroplasts of the Cryptophyta are each surrounded by four membranes, of which the innermost pair are interpreted as the standard double chloroplast envelope, while the outer two (together making up the chloroplast endoplasmic reticulum) are thought to represent the plasmalemma of the ingested glaucophyte and the food vacuole membrane of the host cryptophyte. The cytoplasm lying in the narrow space between the double chloroplast envelope and the chloroplast ER, interpreted as the vestigial cytoplasm of the glaucophyte, harbours a vestigial nucleus containing DNA, the 'nucleomorph' (cf. p. 237); the presence of the nucleomorph is strong evidence in support of the idea that the four-membrane-bound chloroplast has been derived from a eukaryotic algal endosymbiont. A recent phylogenetic analysis of the 18S rRNA genes in the nucleus and nucleomorph [331, 331a, d] has confirmed that each cryptophyte cell is a chimaera, containing two unrelated eukaryotes. The compartment containing the nucleomorph and chloroplast is more closely related to the rhodophytes, suggesting that it is derived from a primaeval alga ancestral to this group; 16S rRNA

sequences in the chloroplasts give further support to this idea [331e]. The cryptophyte 'host cell', on the other hand, seems to be more closely related to the common ancestor of the heterotrophic protist *Acanthamoeba* and the chlorophytes (cf. Figs. 32.2, 32.3).

The ingestion and incorporation of a glaucophyte by a cryptophyte has been accompanied by a partial transformation of the photosynthetic apparatus. The chlorophyll a and phycobilins of the glaucophytes have been retained, but chlorophyll c is also present. The cryptophytes are the only algae whose chloroplasts contain chlorophylls a and c *and* phycobilins, although the phycobilins are not borne on the outside of the thylakoids in phycobilisomes (as in other phycobilin-containing forms), but are located within the thylakoids (cf. p. 237). The chloroplast genome has retained inverted repeats.

Event 9. The photoautotrophic **Euglenophyta** may have arisen through the incorporation and transformation of an ancient chlorophyte by a heterotrophic euglenophyte. The chloroplasts are surrounded by three membranes, which can be interpreted in the same way as the three membranes around the chloroplasts of the Dinophyta (see above, event 6). During the subjugation of the chlorophyte, its assortment of photosynthetic pigments has been retained, while the inverted repeats of the chloroplast genome have changed into tandem repeats (see the section above on 'The origin of chloroplasts: monophyletic or polyphyletic?'). The 16S rRNA phylogenetic tree of the cyanobacteria and chloroplasts supports the idea that euglenophyte chloroplasts have been derived from chlorophyte chloroplasts (Fig. 2.8). However, additional 16S rRNA sequences that have recently been analysed suggest that euglenophyte chloroplasts are phylogenetically close to heterokontophyte chloroplasts. Sequences in the gene for the large subunit of RuBisCO, on the other hand, support the link between the chloroplasts of euglenophytes and chlorophytes [331a, 331e].

Event 10. The ingestion of a heterokontophyte by a secondarily heterotrophic dinophyte resulted in the evolution of photoautotrophic **Dinophyta** with heterokontophyte photosynthetic pigments (cf. p. 253). The endosymbiont, though fully integrated into the dinophyte cell, is still recognizable as a heterokontophyte: it has its own complete nucleus, and even mitochondria. The chloroplasts are surrounded by five membranes, namely (from the inside outwards) the standard double chloroplast envelope, the inner and outer membranes of the chloroplast ER, and the host food vacuole membrane (for an evolutionary interpretation of the chloroplast ER membranes, see above, event 5).

Event 11. Uptake and incorporation of a cryptophyte by another secondarily heterotrophic dinophyte gave rise to photoautotrophic **Dinophyta** with cryptophyte photosynthetic pigments (cf. p. 253). Although the endosymbiont is fully integrated into the host cell, it is still recognizable as a cryptophyte.

Event 12. Ingestion and incorporation of a cryptophyte by the heterotrophic protozoan *Mesodinium*, a ciliate, led to the evolution of photoautotrophic *Mesodinium* (cf. p. 241). Here again, the endosymbiont is fully integrated but recognizable as a cryptophyte.

Event 13. Ingestion of a chlorophyte by a secondarily heterotrophic dinophyte resulted in the evolution of photoautotrophic **Dinophyta** with chlorophyte photosynthetic pigments. The endosymbionts are highly reduced, though they still contain vestigial cytoplasm and a vestigial nucleus (nucleomorph; cf. p. 253).

Event 14. A close extracellular association between chlorophytes and ascomycete fungi (or rarely with basidiomycete fungi) led to the origin of photoautotrophic **Ascomycota**, i.e. **lichens**. The association is still rather loose. Each partner can be grown in isolation from the other, although the characteristic thallus of the lichen is only formed by the complete association.

Event 15. Engulfment of unicellular chlorophytes (*Chlorella*) by heterotrophic ciliate protozoans (e.g. *Paramecium*) resulted in the evolution of a number of photoautotrophic members of the **Ciliophora**. The association is still rather loose and each partner can be cultured without the other ([1656]).

Event 16. Ingestion and retention of unicellular chlorophytes by the digestive cells of freshwater *Hydra* (phylum Cnidaria, a group of multicellular animals) led to the origin of photoautotrophic multicellular animals, in this case *Hydra viridis*. This association too is fairly loose, since both partners can be cultured separately ([1656]).

Event 17. The uptake and retention of unicellular dinophytes by the digestive cells of **anthozoans** (phylum Cnidaria), particularly the stony corals, gave rise to another group of photoautotrophic multicellular animals (cf. p. 275). The associations are rather loose and the participants still have some (limited) capacity for independent life.

Some of the events are speculative, though plausible. In events 5, 6, 7 and 9, for instance, it has been suggested that chloroplasts arose as eukaryotic endosymbionts and this might explain the presence of more than two membranes around them. In events 8 and 13 the origin of chloroplasts from eukaryotic endosymbionts is made more plausible by the presence of vestigial nuclei in the appropriate compartment of the chloroplast, while in events 10, 11, 12, 14, 15, 16 and 17, the origin of the photosynthetic component is unmistakable, because the symbiont is still recognizable as an algal cell. There are also many other symbioses between photosynthetic and heterotrophic eukaryotes which have been omitted from Fig. 32.4 ([1656]; see pp. 136, 344), and their existence strengthens the argument that certain algal chloroplasts may have evolved, long ago, as endosymbiotic eukaryotic algae.

In summary, the Rhodophyta, Glaucophyta and Chlorophyta (including their offshoots, the higher plants) probably evolved from a common eukaryotic ancestor, which was a photoautotrophic flagellate. This in turn arose through the endosymbiosis of a cyanobacterium with a heterotrophic flagellate. The remaining algal phyla arose from different heterotrophic flagellate ancestors, through the ingestion and incorporation of a primaeval eukaryotic alga.

Glossary

A-tubule (of one of the 9 peripheral doublets in an axoneme): a complete microtubule composed of 13 rows of tubulin filaments. Linked to the A-tubule is an incomplete microtubule consisting of 10 tubulin filaments (the B-tubule)

Å: an Ångstrom unit (10^{-10} m)

Abaxial side: the side of an organ facing away from the main axis

Accessory pigment: a pigment that absorbs light energy and transfers it to chlorophyll for use in photosynthesis

Acentric mitosis: mitosis where no centrioles are present at the spindle poles

Acritarch: a hollow organic microfossil, often bearing spines; the systematic positions of many acritarchs are unknown or uncertain

Acronema: a fine hair-like projection from the end of a flagellum, containing the central pair of microtubules of the *axoneme*

Acropetal organization: a branching system in which the side branches are produced in acropetal succession, i.e. with the youngest and shortest side branches closest to the apex

Actin filaments: intracellular filaments of protein *ca.* 8 nm wide, each consisting of a tight helix of actin monomers, all with the same orientation. Actin filaments are often visible in thin sections as *microfilaments* and are important components of the cytoskeleton, together with microtubules; they are also present in muscles

Adaxial side: the side of an organ facing the main axis

Aerobic: to do with an oxygen-rich environment

Aerophytic: living in the air on rocks, leaves, stems, etc., though sometimes covered by a film of water; an alternative term is *subaerial*.

Agar: the gelatinous fraction of the cell wall of certain red algae, consisting of a sulphated complex polysaccharide composed mainly of β-1,3-linked D-galactose and 1,4-linked anhydro-L-galactose. Used for the preparation of gelatinous culture media for bacteria and other microorganisms

Agglutinins: large (*ca.* 250–350 nm long) glycoprotein molecules occurring, for instance, on the flagella of gametes (e.g. in *Chlamydomonas*) and causing the adhesion of gametes of opposite sex (by cross-linking between the (+) agglutinin on the flagella of (+) gametes and the (–) agglutinin on the flagella of (–) gametes)

Akinete: a thick-walled resting spore, produced through the differentiation of a vegetative cell

Alginic acid: a complex acid polysaccharide composed of β-1,4-linked mannuronic acid units and α-1,4-linked L-guluronic acid units, in varying proportions. Alginic acid is an important constituent of brown algal cell walls but also occurs in the cell walls of some red algae

Amoeboid organism: an organism without a cell wall but with pseudopodia, which are mobile, plastically deformable projections of the protoplast that are involved in locomotion and the uptake of solid food particles

Ampulla (in Euglenophyta)*:* a flask-shaped invagination at the anterior end of the cell

Amyloplast: a colourless plastid (*leucoplast*), whose function is to store starch

Anaerobic: to do with an oxygen-free environment

Anaphase: the stage of mitosis during which the chromatids (daughter chromosomes) begin to move towards the poles of the spindle

Anastomosis: point of fusion, e.g. between the cells of two filaments

Anisogametes: gametes of different sexes, the females being larger than the males

Anisogamy (= heterogamy): copulation (fusion) of anisogametes

Anoxic: without oxygen

Anoxygenic: without the production of oxygen. Anoxygenic photosynthesis is carried out by photosynthetic bacteria (other than the 'cyanobacteria'), which are incapable of splitting water and use other reduced substrates (H_2S, H_2, organic compounds) as electron donors (see also *oxygenic photosynthesis*)

Antapical half (of the dinoflagellate cell): posterior half of the cell (= hypocone)

Antenna pigments: photosynthetic pigments involved in light harvesting (the main accessory pigments, together with a large proportion of the chlorophyll a)

Antheridium: cell whose contents divide up or differentiate to form male gametes

Antherozoid = spermatozoid

Antiapex (in dinoflagellate cells): the back end of the cell

Anticlinal: at right angles to the surface

Anticlockwise (counter-clockwise) rotation of the basal bodies (in Chlorophyta): see *cruciate 11 o'clock–5 o'clock type of zoid*

Apex (in dinoflagellate cells): the tip or front end of the cell

Apical cell: the cell at the tip of a filament or thallus. The apical cell is often meristematic and responsible for apical growth; it is also, then, an initial cell. Some apical cells cut off cells only from one face; others cut off cells from two or more faces

Apical growth: growth at the tip of a thallus brought about through the activity of an apical cell or apical meristem

Apical half (of the dinoflagellate cell): anterior half of the cell (= epicone)

Aplanospores: non-motile spores, produced through subdivision of the protoplast of a cell (sporangium). Aplanospores have no flagella but possess certain of the characteristics of flagellate cells, such as contractile vacuoles or eyespots

Apposition: thickening of the cell wall brought about through deposition of material onto its inner face

Arabinogalactan: a polysaccharide – a polymer of arabinose and galactose

Aragonite: a form of calcium carbonate with needle-like orthorhombic crystals

Archaean Era: the oldest geological era of the earth's history (2500–4500 million years ago), during which life originated and towards the end of which anaerobic microbes inhabited what was presumably an anoxic ocean

Archaeopyle (in Dinophyta): the exit hole of a germinating cyst

Areola (plural: *areolae*): a perforation through the siliceous frustule of a diatom. The areolae are usually very numerous and arranged in regular patterns

Assimilator (in Phaeophyceae): filaments of cells containing many chloroplasts and involved in photosynthesis

Aster: a star-shaped array of microtubules radiating from a centriole at the pole of the spindle during mitosis; present in many eukaryotes

ATP: adenosine triphosphate, a nucleotide made up of adenosine and three phosphate groups, important in many biochemical reactions because of its role in energy transfer

Autocolony: a daughter colony (daughter coenobium) formed within the cell of the parent (mother) colony (mother coenobium) and resembling a miniature version of the parent colony

Autolysin: an enzyme that degrades the cell wall of the alga producing it. Hence a *vegetative autolysin* is one that releases asexual spores from a sporangial wall (or vegetative cells from their walls), while a *gametic autolysin* releases gametes from the gametangial wall

Autospores: non-motile spores produced within a parent cell, which develop the same shape as the parent cell at an early stage, before release

Autotrophic: with the capacity to synthesize organic compounds from inorganic substrates, using light energy (photoautotrophs) or chemical energy (chemoautotrophs)

Auxiliary cell (in Rhodophyta): a cell rich in cytoplasm into which the diploid zygotic nucleus itself, or a diploid nucleus produced after one or several divisions of the zygotic nucleus, is injected. The auxiliary cell gives rise to the *gonimocarp*

Auxiliary mother cell (in Rhodophyta): a cell that cuts off the auxiliary cell

Auxospore (in Bacillariophyceae): the special cell produced by diatoms, which expands and in which a much enlarged but normal cell is formed, thus compensating for the diminution in cell size that occurred during the previous phase of vegetative cell division. The auxospore is often also the zygote

Axenic culture: culture of an organism in isolation, free from all other kinds of organism, including bacteria

Axial: to do with the axis; forming the axis

Axial or *axile chloroplast:* a chloroplast lying along the longitudinal axis of a cell or filament of cells

Axial filament: the line of cell forming the main axis in a branching system of filaments

Axoneme: the cylindrical arrangement of microtubules, with 9 doublets around the periphery and two single microtubules at the centre, that is characteristic of the flagella in eukaryotes

Axosome (in certain Haptophyta): a hat-like plug in the transition zone between the flagellum and the basal body

B-tubule: see *A-tubule*

Basal body: the basal section of the flagellum, lying within the cell and consisting of a short cylinder of 9 triplets of microtubules; characteristic of eukaryote flagella

Benthic: belonging to, or to do with the benthos

Benthos: organisms that live at the bottom of aquatic habitats (as opposed to being suspended in the water itself)

Biflagellate: with two flagella

Bilenticular pyrenoid: a pyrenoid composed of two halves, which are covered by two bowl-shaped starch grains and thus appear in the light microscope like two plano-convex lenses appressed to each other

Biogenic: produced by or originating from living organisms

Bioluminescence: production of light by living organisms

Bracteoles (in Charophyceae): 'leaflets' positioned near the oogonia and antheridia

Calcite: a form of calcium carbonate with rhombohedral crystals (appearing lozenge-shaped in outline)

Callose: an amorphous polysaccharide, consisting of glucose residues linked β-1,3. Found blocking the older sieve plates of vascular plants and Laminariales

Cambrian: the earliest geological period (505–590 million years ago) of the Palaeozoic Era (248–590 million years ago), characterized by the appearance of many conspicuous invertebrate fossils

Canal raphe (in the valves of certain pennate Bacillariophyceae): a tube-like structure running longitudinally along the valve, opening externally via the raphe slit and to the inside by several to many apertures. Like the simple raphe, it functions in locomotion

Capitulum cell (in Charophyceae): a cell within the antheridium bearing the spermatogenous threads

Capsular = tetrasporal

Carboniferous: a late period (286–360 million years ago) of the Palaeozoic Era (248–590 million years ago), characterized by the deposition of huge deposits of coal (the fossil remains of forests)

Carboxysome (= polyhedral body): a polyhedral organelle present in blue-green algal (cyanobacterial) cells, containing the enzyme RuBisCO (ribulose 1,5-bisphosphate carboxylase–oxygenase), which is responsible for CO_2 fixation during the dark reactions of photosynthesis

Carpogonium (in Rhodophyta): an oogonium, mostly consisting of a swollen basal portion (containing the female nucleus) and an elongate, colourless tip (the trichogyne) with which the male gamete (spermatium) fuses

Carposporangium (in Rhodophyta): a diploid sporangium produced directly or indirectly from the zygote. Each carposporangium generally produces one diploid, non-flagellate spore (the *carpospore*), though sometimes several are formed

Carpospore (in Rhodophyta): a diploid spore produced by the carposporangium

Carposporophyte (in Rhodophyta): the *gonimocarp*, where this is interpreted as a separate phase of the life cycle, parasitic on the gametophyte

Carrageenan: the gelatinous fraction of the cell wall in certain Rhodophyta, consisting of a sulphated complex polysaccharide composed mainly of α-1,3- and β-1,4-linked D-galactopyranose units. Used for the preparation of gels in the food industry

Cartwheel structure: a structure composed of the nine tilted triplets of the basal body connected by radial spokes, lying at the lower end of the flagellar basal body

Cell equator: the plane in the centre of the cell, which coincides with the spindle equator at mitosis and in which the new wall is formed between the daughter cells

Cell lumen: the space within the cell wall

Cell plate: a flat, plate-like array of vesicles containing wall material, which develops during cell division and later gives rise to the new cross-wall when the vesicles fuse

Cellulose: the structural polysaccharide of the cell walls in many algae and also of vascular plants. Cellulose forms microfibrils and consists of β-1,4-linked glucose units

Cellulose synthase: an enzyme complex bound to the plasmalemma that produces cellulose microfibrils outside the plasmalemma by polymerizing glucose present within the cytoplasm

Cenozoic Era: the geological era from 65 million years ago to the present, characterized by among other things a great diversification of the mammals

Central cell: the central (axial) cell, where this is surrounded by several pericentral cells

Central filament type of structure = uniaxial construction

Central nodule (in Bacillariophyceae): a thickening at the centre of the valve in those pennate diatoms that possess a raphe

Centric mitosis: mitosis where pairs of centrioles are present at the spindle poles

Centrin: see *rhizoplast*

Centriole: a cell organelle with the same structure as *basal bodies*. Centrioles lie at the poles of the mitotic spindle in many eukaryotes and are apparently involved in the formation of the spindle: see also *microtubule organizing centre (MTOC)*

Centromere (= kinetochore): the structure by which a chromosome is attached to its chromosome microtubule(s) during nuclear division

Centroplasm (in Cyanophyta): the central, unpigmented part of the cytoplasm

Chemokinesis: non-directional movements of motile gametes, triggered by chemicals secreted by gametes of the opposite sex

Chemotaxis: movement in a direction determined by a chemical gradient

Chitin: a linear polymer composed of β-1,4-linked *N*-acetylglucosamine units. Chitin is the main constituent of arthropod exoskeletons and the cell walls of most fungi

Chloroplast: plastid containing chlorophyll, which is contained within the thylakoid membranes. Chloroplasts can also contain various accessory pigments

Chondriome: the whole complement of mitochondria present in a cell

Chromatin: the nuclear DNA of eukaryotes, with its associated histones (histoproteins), which exhibits characteristic staining properties

Chromatoplasm (in Cyanophyta): the peripheral cytoplasm of the cell, containing thylakoids and the photosynthetic pigments associated with them

Chromosome microtubules: see *spindle*

Chrysolaminaran: a storage polysaccharide composed mainly of β-1,3-linked glucose residues

Ciliates: the informal name for organisms belonging to the protozoan phylum Ciliophora, which are characterized by their numerous cilia (locomotory organelles; = flagella), the possession of two nuclei (a large 'macronucleus' and a smaller 'micronucleus') and by the presence of a cell mouth (cytostome)

Cilia = flagella

Circadian rhythm: see *endogenous rhythm*

Cisterna: a flat vesicle bounded by a plasma membrane (e.g. golgi cisternae, ER cisternae)

Cladocera: an order of planktonic crustaceans, including the water fleas, some of which graze on phytoplankton

Cladogram: a tree diagram expressing a hypothesis about phylogeny and constructed according to the highly formalized methods of cladistics, in which the branches (clades) are positioned close to each other when they share common derived traits

Cleavage furrow: a ring-shaped invagination that brings about cell division (cytokinesis)

Clockwise rotation of the flagellar basal bodies (in Chlorophyta): see *cruciate 1 o'clock – 7 o'clock type of zoid*

Clone: a group of individuals derived, through vegetative propagation or asexual reproduction, from one ancestral individual. All the individuals belonging to the same clone are virtually identical genetically

Closed mitosis (= intranuclear mitosis): mitosis that takes place within an intact nuclear envelope

Clumping: the formation of dense clusters of flagellate gametes (zoogametes) of two sexes as a result of adhesion between their flagella, immediately before fusion of the gametes

Coated vesicle: a spherical vesicle surrounded by a dark-staining layer composed of the protein clathrin. By forming an ephemeral, rigid basket-like structure around a portion of membrane, clathrin can pinch off a membrane vesicle from the plasmalemma (thus causing *endocytosis*) or from an organelle, e.g. from a golgi cisterna (the resulting golgi vesicle may then be transported to the exterior, where *exocytosis* takes place)

Coccoid (= coccal): adjective applied to unicellular, non-flagellate organisms possessing a cell wall, often though not always with a rounded morphology

Coccolithosomes: small granules, 25 nm in diameter, occurring in the golgi bodies of coccolithophorids (Haptophyta); they are thought to be the precursors of the matrix of acidic polysaccharide that imprints a characteristic shape on the coccoliths

Coccoliths (in Coccolithophoraceae): calcareous scales covering the surface of certain unicellular flagellates

Codiolum phase (in Chlorophyta): a unicellular diploid stage in the life cycle of the order Codiolales (Chlorophyta). The single cells are club-shaped to spherical, or sometimes rather irregular in shape and contain the only diploid nucleus in the life cycles of sexually reproducing species; the *Codiolum* phase is thus a zygote

Coenobium: see *colony*

Coenocyte: a huge multinucleate cell without septa, constituting the whole thallus

Colony (= *coenobium*): a well-defined group of individual cells, usually with a distinct morphology, which can be held together in various ways, e.g. by a common envelope of mucilage

Compatible strains: strains that are able to mate with each other, because of genetically determined traits

Compatible: see *homothallic, heterothallic*

Conceptacle: a cavity in the thallus in which gametangia or sporangia are formed

Conchospore: spore produced by the sporophytes of the red algae *Porphyra* and *Bangia*, which inhabit the calcium carbonate shells of molluscs and other calcareous material

Conjugation: 1. the formation of a bridge between two cells during sexual reproduction, often between a donor (male) cell and a recipient (female) cell; the male cell injects genetic material into the female cell through the bridge. Conjugation occurs in certain bacteria and in the green algal class Zygnematophyceae. 2. fusion of two gametes of opposite sex

Conjunctor cell (in Rhodophyta): a small cell cut off from one large cell that subsequently fuses with another large cell, thus transferring a nucleus from one to the other

Connective (in a flagellate cell): a component of the flagellar apparatus consisting of a fibrous band of material (probably composed of the ubiquitous contractile protein centrin), which connects the microtubular roots just below the insertion of the flagella. See also *transversely striated connective*

Continuous microtubules = interzonal spindle microtubules

Contractile vacuole: a rhythmically contracting vesicle, which expels fluid (possibly containing excretory products) from the cell (see *osmoregulation*)

Convergent evolution: the evolution of similar features in different, unrelated taxa

Copula: girdle band of a diatom

Copulation: association and fusion of two flagellate gametes, or of a flagellate with a non-flagellate gamete

Coronula (in Charophyceae): a miniature 'crown' at the upper end of an oogonium, consisting of the end cells of a series of filaments that enclose and cover the oogonium itself

Cortex: the peripheral tissue of a thallus, lying outside the medulla (pith)

Cortical cytoplasm: the outermost layer of cytoplasm in a cell

Costa: rib or strip of material

Counter-clockwise (anticlockwise) rotation of the basal bodies (in Chlorophyta): see *cruciate 11 o'clock – 5 o'clock type of zoid*

Cretaceous: the last geological period (65–144 million years ago) of the Mesozoic era (65–248 million years ago), characterized among other things by the formation of massive deposits of chalk (which is composed for the most part of the calcareous scales of coccolithophorids, algae of the division Haptophyta)

Cribrum (plural cribra): a delicate siliceous plate perforated by many tiny holes that occludes one of the many simple or chambered pores through a diatom frustule

Critical daylength: see *short-day response*

Cruciate 11 o'clock – 5 o'clock type of zoid (in Chlorophyta): a type of zoid with apically inserted, almost opposite flagella, in which (when the zoid is seen from the anterior end) the basal bodies of the two flagella are slightly displaced anticlockwise (counterclockwise). Thus, by analogy with a clock-face, exactly opposite flagella would have a 12 o'clock – 6 o'clock configuration, while an imaginary anticlockwise rotation would bring about an 11 o'clock – 5 o'clock configuration. The two basal bodies are linked to four *cruciate microtubular roots.* An 11 o'clock – 5 o'clock configuration can also occur in quadriflagellate zoids, but only for two of the four flagella

Cruciate 1 o'clock – 7 o'clock type of zoid (in Chlorophyta): a type of zoid like the *cruciate 11 o'clock – 5 o'clock type* but with anticlockwise rotation (counter-clockwise). Again, quadriflagellate zoids can also occur, in which the basal bodies of two of the flagella occupy the 1 o'clock and 7 o'clock positions

Cruciate microtubular roots (in Chlorophyta): four microtubular roots that anchor the flagella in the cell and form a cross when seen from the apex of the cell (see also *microtubules* and *microtubular roots*). The four roots generally exhibit an *x*–2–*x*–2 arrangement, which means that two roots, lying opposite one another, each contain two microtubules, while the other two roots, also lying opposite one another, are composed of a varying number of microtubules (*ca.* 3–8).

Cryptostoma (in Fucales, Phaeophyceae): a cavity sunk into the surface of a thallus and bearing a bundle of phaeophycean hairs from its floor

Cuticle: a layer of waxy material (cutin) covering the epidermis of land plants. Sometimes the term is also applied to a similar, but biochemically different outer layer covering a multicellular alga

Cyanelle: an intracellular structure presumed to represent an endosymbiotic blue-green alga (cyanobacterium)

Cyanophycin granule (in Cyanophyta): a granule of proteinaceous reserve material, consisting exclusively of a polymer of the two amino acids arginine and asparagine

Cyst: a cell protected from unfavourable environmental conditions (drought, cold heat, nutrient deficiency) by a thick wall

Cystocarp (in Rhodophyta): a *gonimocarp* enclosed within an envelope of tissue (*pericarp*)

Cytogamy = *plasmogamy*

Cytokinesis: division of the cytoplasm, usually directly after division of the nucleus

Cytopharynx: a permanent invagination of the cell surface, through which food is taken up and incorporated into food vacuoles (in some protists)

Cytoskeleton: the internal skeleton of a cell that maintains cell shape and the proper arrangement of the cell organelles, and also the capacity for cell movement and intracellular transport. Composed of *microtubules*, *actin filaments* and other filaments, *myosin* molecules, etc.

Cytostome: a permanent mouth-like organelle present in the cells of certain unicellular protozoa and algae (e.g. *Noctiluca*), through which food is taken up

DAPI: 4′,6-diamidino-2-phenylindole, a DNA-specific fluorescent dye

Determinate lateral (= *short shoot*): side branch of limited growth, which quickly reaches its maximum length and often also has a characteristic structure

Devonian: a geological period (360–408 million years ago) in the Palaeozoic Era (248–590 million years ago)

Dichotomy: a forked branching, reflecting the activity of two equal apical cells after they have been formed through longitudinal division of a single pre-existing apical cell

Dicotyledon: a vascular plant with two seed leaves (cotyledons)

Dikaryotic thallus: usually = *heterokaryotic thallus*

Dinokaryon (in Dinophyta): a type of nucleus in which the chromosomes remain condensed and exhibit a characteristic 'garland structure' (helicoidal structure) throughout interphase

Dioecious: with the male and female sex organs on separate gametophytes. (In vascular plants: with microsporangia and macrosporangia on separate plants, or with male and female unisexual flowers on separate plants)

Diplohaplontic life cycle: a life cycle containing two vegetative phases, one diploid and one haploid. The diploid phase arises through the growth and division of a diploid zygote, itself formed by the fusion of two haploid gametes. The haploid phase develops from a haploid meispore, produced following meiosis in a cell of the diploid phase.

Diploid: with two homologous sets of chromosomes (= with two homologous genomes)

Diplontic life cycle: a life cycle containing only one vegetative phase, which is diploid. The gametes, produced following meiosis, are the only haploid cells of the life cycle

Diplophase: the diploid vegetative phase of a life cycle

Discobolocyst (in certain Chrysophyceae): tiny discoid structures lying just beneath the cell surface, which shoot out their contents upon stimulation

Distromatic: composed of two layers of cells

DNA–DNA hybridization: a method of estimating genetic (and hence phylogenetic) relationship, based on the principle that single strands of DNA, separated by heating, will associate into double-stranded DNA when they cool, and that single strands from related species will associate better than those of unrelated species

Dormancy: the resting state of an organism, in which life processes are slowed down in order for the organism to survive adverse conditions, such as high summer temperatures, low winter temperatures, drought, etc. Thus, for instance, dormancy occurs in hypnospores and hypnozygotes (resting spores and resting zygotes, respectively) and also in seeds

Dorsiventral: with distinct front (ventral) and back (dorsal) sides; these are often concave or flat and convex, respectively

Doublet: see *axoneme*

Dwarf males: see *nannandrous*

Dynein arms (in the axoneme of a flagellum): protein arms borne by the A-tubule of each peripheral doublet, which 'walk' along the B-tubule of the adjacent doublet and thus cause the doublets to slide over one another

Dystrophic waters: the acid, oligotrophic waters of peaty areas, coloured brown by humic acids

Ecological niche: the particular role of a species in a biocoenosis (= a community of organisms), expressing its place in the network of relationships between all species present

Ecosystem: an ecological system, composed of all the interacting biotic and abiotic elements in a particular part of the biosphere and which is supposed to be at least partly self-sustaining and self-regulating

Ectoplasm: a peripheral layer of cytoplasm in the cells of some eukaryotes (e.g. amoebae, Charophyceae) that is relatively rigid and non-granular

Egg cell: non-motile female gamete that is relatively large compared with the corresponding male gametes, which may be flagellate or non-flagellate

Ejectosome (in Cryptophyta): a tiny body lying beneath the cell surface, which discharges explosively upon stimulation. It contains a tightly wound band of material, which unrolls during discharge

Embryonic: pertaining to an embryo (i.e. a young organism, in its early developmental stages)

Endocytosis: uptake of material by a cell, through its incorporation into vesicles pinched in from the plasmalemma. See also *phagocytosis, pinocytosis, coated vesicle*

Endogenous cyst (in Chryso- and Xanthophyceae): a cyst whose wall is formed within the protoplast of a unicellular alga

Endogenous rhythm: cyclic changes in an organism maintained by the organism itself: the rhythm persists even after transfer of the organism to constant external conditions (e.g. continuous light and constant temperature), although there may be a slight change in the length of the cycle. A circadian endogenous rhythm has a cycle of *approximately* 24 h

Endolithic: living within rock

Endophyte: a plant that lives within the tissues of other plants, without being parasitic

Endoplasm: cytoplasm that is granular and streams actively and lies in the interior of the cell, surrounded by a thin peripheral layer of rigid, non-granular ectoplasm; present in some eukaryotes (e.g. amoebae, Charophyceae)

Endoplasmic reticulum (ER): a net-like system of flat and tubular vesicles, bounded by membranes, lying in the cytoplasm. Occurs as *rough ER* and *smooth ER*

Endospore: the innermost layer of the wall in a thick-walled spore or zygote

Endospores (in Cyanophyta): spores that form following division of the protoplast, enclosed within the parent cell wall

Endosymbiont: the partner in a symbiosis that lives within the tissues or cells of the other partner

Envelope: it is useful to use 'envelope' to refer to the wall-like covering around the cells of unicellular or colonial flagellates (e.g. *Chlamydomonas*), which cannot be fully functional in osmoregulation because the flagella pass through it (see also *lorica*)

Eocene: a geological epoch (37–58 million years ago) early in the Cenozoic Era (65 million years ago to the present)

Epicingulum (in Bacillariophyceae): the ring-like side wall of the *epitheca*

Epicone: the apical half of the dinoflagellate cell

Epilimnion: the upper layer in a freshwater lake, where the lake water is separated into a relatively warm, less dense upper layer, and a cold, deep layer (the *hypolimnion*). The boundary with the hypolimnion is marked by a *thermocline* (where temperature drops rapidly, strictly maximally, with depth) and a *pycnocline* (where density increases rapidly)

Epilithic: growing attached to rocks or stones

Epiphytic: growing attached to other plants, but not parasitizing them

Epithallus: see *hypothallus*

Epitheca: the upper, apical half of the cellulose armour in Dinophyta or the upper (older) half of the silica shell (frustule) in Bacillariophyceae

Epivalve (in Bacillariophyceae): the principal element of the epitheca, covering one end of the cell

ER: see *endoplasmic reticulum*

Estuary: a bay or a partly enclosed body of seawater, normally with an inflow of fresh water

Eukaryotic: with the characteristics of the Eukaryota (with nucleus, mitochondria, endoplasmic reticulum, golgi apparatus, 9 + 2 flagellum structure)

Euphotic zone: the upper layer of a lake or sea, in which there is sufficient light for photosynthesis

Eutrophic: nutrient-rich (can mean 'rich in nutrient salts' or, by extension, 'with high primary production')

Eutrophicated waters: waters that have become eutrophic (mostly) through pollution

Exocytosis: secretion of material from a cell, through the fusion of the vesicle containing the material with the plasmalemma (see also *endocytosis*)

Exogenous cyst (in Chryso- and Xanthophyceae): a cyst whose wall is laid down against the outside of the protoplast of a unicellular alga

Exospores (in Cyanophyta): spores cut off externally by a spore mother cell

Extension growth: growth brought about by elongation of the cells rather than through cell division

Eyespot (stigma): a red spot, usually found in unicellular or colonial flagellate algae and involved in light perception; consisting of lipid globules containing dissolved carotenoid pigments

False branching: a type of branching occurring in some types of filamentous algae, where the filaments are surrounded by a mucilage sheath. A filament breaks and then one or both ends grow out laterally from the sheath

Fenestra (plural *fenestrae*): opening, window. Thus, the polar fenestrae are openings in the nuclear envelope at the two poles of the spindle in a closed mitosis

Fibulae (singular *fibula*; in pennate diatoms with a canal raphe): bridges of silica that lie between the pores connecting the cell lumen with the canal beneath the raphe

Filament: a line of cells connected together, or an elongate thread-like structure

Filamentous: thread-like, usually referring to a thallus composed of a single row of linked cells, but sometimes also used for thalli composed of several rows of cells

Filopodium: a fine, thread-like *pseudopodium*

Flagellar apparatus: the whole complex of flagellar basal bodies, microtubular roots and their associated structures, and rhizoplasts (if any) present in a flagellate cell

Flagellar canal: a narrow invagination of the plasmalemma from the floor of which a flagellum arises (in Dinophyta), or a canal in the cell envelope through which the flagellum runs and emerges to the exterior (in *Chlamydomonas* and other Chlorophyceae)

Flagellar pit (in a flagellate alga): a depression in the cell surface from the bottom of which the flagella arise

Flagellar pore (in Dinophyta): the outer aperture of the flagellar canal

Flagellar roots: root-like structures composed of microtubules and striated fibres and connected to the flagella inside the cell. Their functions are largely unknown but include controlling the conformation of the flagellar apparatus and anchorage within the cell

Flagellar swelling (= paraflagellar body): a swelling at the base of a flagellum, which often lies appressed to the eyespot. It is presumed that the swelling is involved in light perception (see also *photoreceptor apparatus*)

Flagellate (monadoid): bearing flagella

Flagellum (in Eukaryota): an elongate, cylindrical projection from the cell, with a characteristic internal structure (the axoneme) consisting of 9 peripheral doublet microtubules and 2 central microtubules (there are rare exceptions with a different structure, e.g. with the central tubules missing). Its function is in motility or producing water movements

Flimmer flagellum = pleuronematic flagellum

Flimmers = mastigonemes

Floridean starch: the reserve polysaccharide produced by red algae, consisting of an α-1,4-linked glucan. It differs from green algal (and higher plant) starch by lacking amylose, the unbranched fraction of starches, and resembles the branched amylopectin fraction of green algal starch

Foliose: leafy or leaf-like

Food vacuole: a vacuole into which solid food particles are taken up by phagotrophy and where they are digested

Foramen: an opening, hole, or pore

Foraminifera: a phylum of protozoans characterized by their possession of a calcareous shell (often resembling a miniature snail shell), which is porous. Systems of anastomosing filopodia extend through the pores. The foraminifera are highly diverse and are widespread in the world's oceans

Forming face (of a golgi body): the side on which cisternae of the golgi body are assembled through fusion of vesicles derived from the endoplasmic reticulum or nuclear envelope

Fossil: the remains or traces of an organism from the geological past, found embedded in rocks or sediments. *Microfossils* are the fossils of microscopic organisms, or the pollen or spores of organisms

Fountain-type structure: see *multiaxial structure*

Front (in the sea): a boundary between different water masses

Fructan: a polysaccharide – a polymer of fructose

Frustule (in Bacillariophyceae): the silica shell of a diatom

Fucoidan: a complex sulphated polysaccharide found in the mucilaginous fraction of the cell walls of the Phaeophyceae. It is water-soluble and composed of the monosaccharide fucose and varying proportions of other monosaccharides.

Fusion cell (in Rhodophyta): the cell produced through the fusion of the *auxiliary cell* with one or more neighbouring cells. The *gonimocarp* develops from the fusion cell

Galactan: a polysaccharide – a polymer of galactose

Gametangium: a cell (often with a characteristic shape and structure) whose contents divide up into gametes

Gamete: a haploid sexual cell. Fusion of two haploid gametes produces a diploid zygote

Gametic meiosis: meiosis that leads directly to the formation of gametes

Gametophyte: the gamete-producing phase of the life cycle

-gamy: fusion of gametes, as in *plasmogamy* and *karyogamy*

Gas vacuoles (in Cyanophyta): irregularly shaped, gas-filled structures in the cell, composed of aggregates of closely packed gas vesicles

Gas vesicles (in Cyanophyta): small cylindrical structures, with proteinaceous walls and filled with gas, which occur in clusters in the cytoplasm (forming gas vacuoles)

Geniculum: a non-calcified zone between calcified segments in bushy calcareous red algae and also in the calcareous green alga *Halimeda*

Genome: the sum total of the genes contained either in the nucleus or in the nucleoid of an organelle (mitochondria, chloroplasts) in eukaryotes, or in the nucleoid of a prokaryote

Geotaxis: movement in response to gravity: in the direction of the gravitational force (positive geotaxis) or away from it (negative geotaxis)

Girdle lamella: a lamella composed of three thylakoids that runs around the periphery of a chloroplast, parallel and close to the chloroplast envelope

Girdle: 1. the transverse furrow of dinoflagellates (Dinophyta); 2. the side wall of the box-like shell (frustule) of diatoms (Bacillariophyceae)

Glucan: a polysaccharide – a polymer of glucose

Glycoprotein: a protein with carbohydrates attached to it

Golgi apparatus: a complex of golgi bodies or the whole complement of golgi bodies within a cell

Golgi body: a cell organelle typical of the Eukaryota, consisting of a stack of flat, disc-like cisternae, whose edges are generally slightly to greatly inflated. The cisternae cut off vesicles containing various substances (e.g. wall material)

Gonidium: a reproductive cell; in Volvocales (Chlorophyceae) a gonidium is an enlarged cell that gives rise to a daughter colony

Gonimoblast (in Rhodophyta): a filament of diploid cells that produces *carpospores*. It develops from the zygote or from an *auxiliary* cell that has acquired the zygote nucleus or a diploid nucleus derived from the zygote nucleus

Gonimocarp (in Rhodophyta): the collective name for the structure formed by a group of gonimoblasts

Gram stain (for bacterial cell walls): a stain containing crystal violet and iodine, which, following treatment with alcohol, is retained by the walls of gram-positive bacteria but not by those of gram-negative bacteria

Granum (plural *grana*): a stack of thylakoids that resembles a pile of coins. The membranes of adjacent thylakoids are fused

Gullet: a deep depression present at the anterior of the cell in some unicellular flagellate, from which the flagella arise

Haplogenotypic sex determination: separation of the different sexes during meiosis, such that the homologous chromosomes with the alleles for 'maleness' (+ alleles) are segregated from those for 'femaleness' (– alleles). The meiospores inheriting male (+) alleles grow into haploid 'male' (+) plants, while those inheriting female (–) alleles grow into haploid 'female' (–) plants; 50% of the plants are male and 50% female

Haploid: with one set of chromosomes and therefore with a single genome

Haplontic life cycle: a life cycle containing only one vegetative phase, which is haploid; only the zygote is diploid

Haplophase: the haploid vegetative phase of a life cycle

Hapteron (plural *haptera*): a branched, root-like or unbranched disc-like attachment organ (holdfast)

Haptonema (in Haptophyta): a thread-like appendage arising near the flagella, containing 6 or 7 simple microtubules (arranged in section in a crescent) and a fold of endoplasmic reticulum

Heterocyst (in Cyanophyta): a cell distinguished from normal vegetative cells by its glassy, often yellowish appearance and thick wall; where it adjoins other cells the wall is often thickened even further internally. Nitrogen is fixed in heterocysts

Heterogamy = anisogamy

Heterokaryotic thallus: a thallus containing genetically different haploid nuclei, e.g. with nuclei bearing the male genetic factor and nuclei bearing the female genetic factor. Heterokaryotic thalli are common in some groups of fungi (Basidiomycota, Ascomycota), but rare in algae

Heterokont zoids: zoids with two flagella that behave differently and have a different structure; usually used in relation to the zoids of the Heterokontophyta, where each cell bears a forwardly directed pleuronematic flagellum and a backwardly directed smooth flagellum

Heteromorphic diplohaplontic life cycle: a diplohaplontic life cycle in which the diploid vegetative phase differs morphologically from the haploid vegetative phase

Heteroplastidic (in Bryopsidophyceae): possessing both chloroplasts and amyloplasts (see also *homoplastidic*)

Heterospory: the production, in certain vascular plants, of two kinds of meiospores: relatively small microspores (which grow into reduced male gametophytes) and relatively large megaspores or macrospores (which grow into reduced female gametophytes)

Heterothallic: of organisms where the gametes produced by a single haploid plant are unable to copulate with each other, because they are incompatible (i.e. the plant is *self-incompatible*). For copulation it is necessary for the gametes to come from two plants of different sexes. Thus, for example, one of the two plants may produce small male gametes (microgametes), while the other forms large female gametes (macrogametes). Elsewhere the gametes may be morphologically indistinguishable, in which case the sexes may be referred to as (+) and (−)

Heterotrophic: gaining nutrients through the uptake of organic substances produced by other organisms

Histones (= *histoproteins* = *nucleohistones*): structural proteins present in eukaryote chromosomes, containing very high proportions of positively charged amino acids (lysine and arginine), which bind tightly to DNA. The histones are responsible for the coiling and packing of the chromosomal DNA

Histoprotein: see *histones*

Holdfast: see *hapteron*

Holocarpic: of organisms where the whole contents of the vegetative plant divides up into reproductive cells

Hologamy: the process in which two whole organisms fuse with each other during sexual reproduction

Homokaryotic thallus: a thallus containing genetically identical haploid nuclei: contrast *heterokaryotic thallus*

Homologous: similar as a result of common evolutionary descent

Homology: a fundamental similarity of traits, reflecting common evolutionary descent

Homoplastidic (in Bryopsidophyceae): possessing chloroplasts but not amyloplasts (see also *heteroplastidic*)

Homothallic: of organisms where the gametes produced by a single haploid plant can copulate with each other, because they are compatible. The gametes can be morphologically identical, or they may be differentiated into small males (microgametes) and large females (macrogametes)

Hormogonium (in Cyanophyta): a multicellular fragment of a filament, which serves in vegetative reproduction and often performs active gliding movements

Hypha: the colourless filament of a fungal mycelium; also used to refer to the colourless filaments of cells present in the central parts (medulla) of *Laminaria* and other Laminariales (Phaeophyceae)

Hypnospore: resting spore; a thick-walled resting stage, which can germinate only after an obligatory period of dormancy

Hypnozygote: a thick-walled resting zygote, which germinates after an obligatory period of dormancy

Hypocingulum (in Bacillariophyceae): the ring-like side wall of the *hypotheca*

Hypocone = antapical half of the dinophycean cell

Hypogenous cell (in Rhodophyta): the cell lying beneath the carpogonium

Hypolimnion: see *epilimnion*

Hypothallus (in Rhodophyta): the basal layer of a crust-like thallus or part of a thallus, composed of one or more layers of densely packed, fused filaments (the *primigenous filaments*). These grow parallel to the substratum through division of apical cells, which together form the margin of the crust. Other densely packed, fused filaments arch upwards (the *postigenous filaments*), forming the *perithallus* of the crust; this grows in thickness through division of the uppermost (intercalary) perithallus cells, which in turn are covered by one or more layers of non-dividing *epithallus* cells

Hypotheca: 1. the lower, antapical half of the cellulose armour in Dinophyta; 2. the lower (younger) half of the silica shell (frustule) in Bacillariophyceae

Hypovalve (in Bacillariophyceae): the principal element of the hypotheca, covering one end of the cell

Hystrichosphere: a spherical or ellipsoidal microfossil with spiny projections (often the fossil cyst of a species of Dinophyta)

Incompatible strains: strains that are unable to mate with each other, because of genetically determined traits

Incompatible: see *heterothallic*

Indeterminate lateral (= long shoot): a side branch with unlimited (indeterminate) growth, which often exhibits the same structure and mode of growth as the main axis

Initial, initial cell: the first cell of a plant or tissue, from which the plant or tissue develops; in Bacillario-phyceae, the first cell of the new vegetative phase, produced within the auxospore and often having a unique morphology

Inoculum: a group of living cells or organisms used to begin a new culture of algae after transfer to a new culture medium, or acting to initiate a new population in nature

Intercalary growth: growth in the middle of a tissue or fila-ment of cells, i.e. not at the tip (= *apical growth*), nor at the base

Intergeneric: between genera

Internode (in Charophyceae, Bryophyta, vascular plants): the part of the axis between two nodes

Interphase: the period in the nuclear cycle between two nuclear divisions

Interspecific: between species

Intertidal: see *littoral*

Interzonal spindle microtubules (continuous spindle micro-tubules): microtubules that extend from one pole of the mitotic spindle to the other. During anaphase they appear to increase in length, thus separating the chro-matids, but in fact separation seems to be achieved more by the microtubules sliding over one another

Intranuclear mitosis = closed mitosis

Intussusception: the growth of something through the depo-sition of new material within the existing structure

Inverted repeats: two identical sections of the circular chloroplast genome, containing the genes for chloro-plast ribosomal RNA, which are transcribed in oppo-site directions (i.e. inverted)

Isogametes: gametes that are morphologically identical, even though they may belong to different sexes (+ and –)

Isogamy: copulation (fusion) of isogametes

Isokont: possessing two equal and similarly structured fla-gella

Isomorphic diplohaplontic life cycle: a diplohaplontic life cycle in which the diploid vegetative phase and the haploid vegetative phase appear identical

Isthmus (in the order Desmidiales, class Zygnematophyceae): a constriction between two semicells

Jurassic: a geological period (144–213 million years ago) in the middle of the Mesozoic Era (65–248 million years ago)

Karyogamy: the fusion of the nuclei of two gametes (see also *plasmogamy*)

Kinetochore = centromere

Kinetome: the whole complement of centrioles, basal bodies and flagella present in a cell

Labiate process (= rimoportula): a tubular structure in the valve of a diatom frustule, which opens externally by a simple pore or may be extended outwards and opens

internally via a slit resembling a mouth flanked by two lips (labiate = lip-like)

Lagoon: shallow lake of salt or brackish water separated from the sea

Lamella (in a chloroplast): a stack of thylakoids that extends along the whole length of the chloroplast

Lateral filament: a side branch from a filament of cells

Leaf (in Charophyceae): one of the whorled short shoots of a charophycean thallus

Leaflets (in Charophyceae): small whorled side branches borne by a *leaf*

Leucoplast: a colourless plastid that contains no thylakoids or only vestigial ones, and which is homologous to a chloroplast. Its function is the synthesis of reserve polysaccharide

Levels of organization: different levels of complexity of thallus structure, representing increasing degrees of evolutionary advancement. In order of evolutionary advancement, the following levels can be distin-guished: the monadoid level (unicellular flagellates); the colonial monadoid level (colonial flagellates); the amoeboid level; the capsal (= encapsuled = tetraspo-ral = palmelloid) level; the coccal (= coccoid) level; the trichal (= filamentous) level; the thallose (= thal-loid) level; and the siphonous level. According to some theories these levels of organization have arisen independently in different algal phyla (divisions)

Lipid: the ester of a fatty acid, insoluble in water

Lipopolysaccharide: a molecule consisting of lipid linked to polysaccharide. Lipopolysaccharides are important constituents of blue-green algal (cyanobacterial) cell walls

Littoral (= intertidal): occurring between the levels of high and low water on the sea-shore

Loculate: chambered

Loculus: a small chamber, e.g. one of the chambers in the plurilocular zoidangia of Phaeophyceae

Long shoot = indeterminate lateral

Long-day response: see *short-day response*

Longitudinal flagellum: see *longitudinal furrow*

Longitudinal furrow (in Dinophyta) (= sulcus): a furrow in the cell surface, running from the anterior end or the centre of the cell towards the posterior, in which the longitudinal flagellum lies

Lorica: a protective case containing a naked (non-walled) cell

Lysosome: a vesicle containing enzymes capable of decom-posing various types of compound; sometimes also used to refer to vesicles containing the remains of organelles (often membrane profiles) that have been broken down

Macrandrous (in Oedogoniales, Chlorophyta): without dwarf males (nannandria). The sexual zoids formed by the cells of the male filaments function directly as male gametes and do not first give rise to tiny male plants (dwarf males)

Macrogamete: a relatively large female gamete

Macrothallus phase: the phase of a heteromorphic life cycle in which a relatively large, usually well-differentiated thallus is produced

Mannan: a polysaccharide – a polymer of mannose

Mannitol: a polyhydroxyalcohol derived from the hexose monosaccharide mannose

Manubrium cells (in Charophyceae): columnar or fist-shaped, radially oriented cells in the antheridium, lying on the inner side of the shield cells

Mastigonemes: stiff lateral hairs borne by a flagellum, each one *ca.* 15 nm thick and consisting of a base, a tubular shaft, and several terminal hairs; occurring in the Heterokontophyta and Cryptophyta

Mating structure (in flagellate gametes of the Chlorophyta): a special portion of the plasmalemma (overlying one of the two 2-membered microtubular flagellar roots and a single or double plate of dark-staining material) where fusion begins between gametes of the opposite sex

Maturing face (secretory face) (of a golgi body): the side on which golgi vesicles are cut off from the cisternae of a golgi body

Maupas bodies (in Cryptophyta): vesicles lying at the anterior of the cell, filled with the remnants of membranes; probably lysosomes

Medulla: the tissue lying in the centre of a thallus

Meiosis: the process of nuclear division that results in the halving of the chromosome number, from the diploid number ($2n$) to the haploid number (n), so that each haploid nucleus receives a complete set of chromosomes, homologous to the sets received by the others. Meiosis consists of two successive divisions, so that four haploid nuclei arise from each diploid nucleus

Meiosporangium: a cell, often with a particular, characteristic shape and structure, whose contents divide up into meiospores

Meiospores: spores that arise through meiosis and are therefore haploid

Meristem: a tissue in which the cell or cells divide frequently

Meristoderm: a tissue at the surface of a thallus (i.e. an epidermis) that behaves meristematically, i.e. in which the cells divide frequently

Mesospore: the central layer of the wall in thick-walled spores or zygotes

Mesotrophic: (of running or standing waters): intermediate between eutrophic and oligotrophic

Metaphase: the stage of nuclear division when the chromosomes are maximally contracted and become arranged at the equator of the spindle, shortly before the chromatids move apart to the spindle poles

Metaphase plate: the plate-like arrangement of chromosomes at the equator of the spindle at metaphase

Microbody: see *peroxisome*

Microfilaments: submicroscopic protein filaments in eukaryote cells (visible with the electron microscope), including *actin filaments*

Microfossil: see *fossil* and *micropalaeontology*

Microgamete: a small, male gamete

Micrometre = μm = 10^{-6} m

Micropalaeontology: the study of microfossils (see *fossils*)

Microplankton: plankton in the size category 20–200 μm. Compare *nannoplankton* (2–20 μm) and *picoplankton* (0.2–2 μm)

Microthallus phase: the phase of a heteromorphic life cycle in which a relatively small and relatively undifferentiated thallus is produced

Microtubular roots: bundles of one to many parallel microtubules that extend down into the cell from the flagellar basal bodies (see *flagellar roots*)

Microtubule organizing centre (MTOC): an area within the cell from which microtubules arise and grow. MTOCs often appear in thin sections (electron microscope observations) as diffuse darker-staining areas ('clouds') and may operate at various positions in the cell; those situated at the poles of the mitotic spindle often contain centrioles or polar rings (in Rhodophyta)

Microtubules: very fine, tubular structures (diameter 25 nm) in the protoplasm, which can be resolved with the electron microscope. Each consists of 13 rows (*protofilaments*) of globular protein (tubulin) molecules, closely associated together laterally to form a cylinder. Microtubules are part of the cell skeleton (cytoskeleton) and also play a part in certain cellular movements, such as flagellar bending (when microtubules of the axoneme slide along each other) and in the movement of chromosomes in the mitotic spindle, which also consists of microtubules

Miocene: a geological epoch (5–24 million years ago) within the Cenozoic Era (65 million years ago to the present)

Mitochondrion: a characteristic organelle of eukaryotic cells that is surrounded by a double membrane and is responsible for respiration; the inner membrane projects into the lumen of the mitochondrion in a series of folds (cristae) or tubes

Mitosis: the process of nuclear division that results in both daughter nuclei receiving identical sets of chromosomes, following replication of the chromosomes during the preceding cell cycle; the sets inherited by the daughter cells are also identical to the set possessed by the parent cell

Mitospores: spores formed through mitosis

MLS: see *multilayered structure*

Monad: a solitary flagellate cell (unicellular flagellate)

Monadoid: pertaining to a flagellate cell (monad): see *flagellate*

Monoecious: with male and female sex organs on the same gametophyte. (In vascular plants: with microsporangia and macrosporangia on the same plant, or with male and female unisexual flowers on the same plant)

Monophyletic: descended from a single ancestor

Monosporangium: a sporangium in which only one spore (a *monospore*) is produced

Monospore: the single spore produced by a monosporangium

Monostromatic: composed of one layer of cells

MTOC: see *microtubule organizing centre*

Mucilage bodies (in unicellular, flagellate algae): vesicles containing mucilage, which lie beneath the plasmalemma and often discharge upon stimulation

Mucopolysaccharides (= glycosaminoglycans): polysaccharides containing amino sugars and uronic acids. Mucopolysaccharides attract much water, which is bound in a mucilaginous slime

Multiaxial structure (= fountain-type structure): a type of thallus construction, in which the central part of the axis is composed of numerous filaments, all alike and running roughly parallel to each other

Multilayered structure (MLS) (in some Chlorophyta, vascular plants, Glaucophyta, Dinophyta): a flat, layered structure situated below the flagellar basal bodies and associated with a microtubular flagellar root. It is composed of two laminate layers containing differently oriented platelets and also incorporates the apical portion of a microtubular root, containing many microtubules

Murein: the peptidoglycan that forms the supportive fibrillar layer of bacterial cell walls. It is a polymer composed of polysaccharide chains (in which there are alternating units of *N*-acetylglucosamine and *N*-acetylmuramic acid, linked by β-1,4-glucosidic linkages), linked by peptide bridges

Mycobiont: the fungal partner in a lichen

Myosin: a cytoskeletal protein, composed of two globular heads and a 150 nm long double helix, which forms a rod-like tail. Myosin molecules associate to form the thick filaments found in animal muscles. Muscle contraction is caused by the sliding of actin filaments (the thin filaments of muscles) along the myosin heads. Interaction between actin and myosin is also involved in generating cytoplasmic streaming in certain algal cells (e.g. of the Bryopsidophyceae), but the details of the mechanism are unknown

Nannandrium: see *nannandrous*

Nannandrous (in Oedogoniales, Chlorophyta): possessing dwarf males (nannandria). The sexual zoids produced by the male filaments function as spores (androspores), which grow into tiny male plantlets (nannandria). These then produce the male gametes (spermatozoids)

Nannoplankton: see *microplankton*

Nanocytes (in Cyanophyta): dwarf cells formed from normal cells following a series of cell divisions, between which there is no significant growth

Nanometre = nm = 10^{-9} m

Nematocyst: a cell organelle that shoots out a harpoon-like spine when stimulated

Neritic zone: the area of continental shelf where the sea bottom is no deeper than 200 m

Nexin links (in the axoneme): protein links present between the 9 peripheral doublets

nm: see *nanometre*

Node (in Charophyceae, Bryophyta and vascular plants): the part of an axis that bears one or more leaves or side branches

Non-persistent (collapsing) telophase spindle: a mitotic spindle that collapses (disintegrates) in early telophase, long before cytokinesis. See also *persistent telophase spindle*

Non-striated connective (in flagellate cells): see *transversely striated connective*

Nori (Japanese): edible sheets of dried *Porphyra* (Rhodophyta)

Nucleohistone: see *histones*

Nucleoid (in prokaryotes and in the mitochondria and chloroplasts of eukaryotes): an aggregation of DNA that somewhat resembles a nucleus but lacks a nuclear envelope and histones; see also *nucleoplasm*

Nucleolus: a spherical body within the nucleus, whose function is the production of cytoplasmic ribosomes. It consists of proteins and RNA, the components of ribosomes

Nucleomorph (in Cryptophyta, Chlorarachniophyta and some Dinophyta): an organelle closely associated with a chloroplast, which contains DNA and is enclosed by a double membrane envelope. The nucleomorph is interpreted as the vestigial nucleus of a photosynthetic, eukaryotic endosymbiont

Nucleoplasm (in Cyanophyta): the part of the centroplasm containing the DNA

Oligotrophic: nutrient-poor (can mean 'poor in nutrient salts' or, by extension, 'with low primary production')

Ontogeny: the process by which the adult organism develops from the very youngest stage

Oogamous: where sexual reproduction involves oogamy

Oogamy: fusion between a relatively small male gamete with a relatively large, non-motile female gamete (egg cell)

Oogonium: a cell (often with a characteristic shape and structure) whose contents divide up into egg cells, which may remain within the oogonium or be released

Oogonium mother cell: a cell that cuts off an oogonium

Open mitosis: mitosis in which the nuclear membrane disperses or disappears

Organelle: a differentiated structure within a eukaryotic cell, often membrane-bound (e.g. nucleus, chloroplast, pyrenoid)

Organizational levels: see *levels of organization*

Osmoregulation: regulation of the water content of the cell. If the cell sap of a wall-less cell is hypertonic with respect to the surrounding water (i.e. is more concentrated), water will tend to enter the cell and must be removed, e.g. via contractile vacuoles

Ostiole: an opening, e.g. of the cystocarp in Rhodophyta

Oxygenic: producing oxygen. In oxygenic photosynthesis, summarized thus:

$$CO_2 + 2H_2O \rightarrow [CH_2O] + H_2O + O_2.$$

Water is used as a donor of high-energy electrons and hydrogen (protons), with the formation of oxygen as a by-product. Oxygenic photosynthesis is exhibited by the prokaryotic blue-green algae (cyanobacteria) and by photosynthetic eukaryotes (see also *anoxygenic*)

Pachytene: the stage of meiotic prophase during which homologous chromosomes are linked together in pairs by 'synaptonemal complexes' and begin to shorten through supercoiling. The synaptonemal complex is a zip-like structure formed between the homologues, which can be observed with the electron microscope (it can also be detected in the light microscope after special staining)

Palmelloid = tetrasporal

Papilla: a protuberance borne by a cell wall or envelope (e.g. the apical papilla of *Chlamydomonas*)

Paraflagellar body = flagellar swelling

Parallel evolution: evolution in a similar way, or of similar traits, in two or more different groups.

Paramylon: a storage polysaccharide composed of β-1,3-linked glucose residues

Paraphyses: sterile filaments of cells lying between reproductive structures

Parasexual recombination: a process that brings about genetic recombination without involving karyogamy and meiosis, the characteristic processes bringing about recombination in a sexual life cycle

Parasite: an organism that lives and grows at the expense of a host organism

Parenchyma: relatively undifferentiated plant tissue, consisting for the most part of a more or less homogeneous mass of isodiametric or slightly elongate, living cells

Parietal chloroplast: a chloroplast that lies against the wall of the cell

Parthenogenesis: development of a female gamete into an adult organism without fertilization by a male gamete. The term is also used to refer to the development of male gametes or isogametes into adult organisms without the intervention of sexual fusion

Peduncle (in Dinophyta): an extensible pseudopod used to catch and either suck out or engulf a prey organism (another alga or a protozoan)

Pellicle (= periplast): a skin-like layer, composed principally of protein, found around the cells of certain unicellular algae (Raphidophyceae, Euglenophyceae, Cryptophyceae). In Dinophyta: a thin additional wall layer or envelope, made of cellulose and sporopollenin-like material, lying below the theca

Peptidoglycans: polymers consisting of cross-linked polysaccharide and polypeptide chains. Peptidoglycans are the main constituents of the cell walls of blue-green algae (Cyanophyta = Cyanobacteria) and some bacteria

Perennating: living for several years

Pericarp (in Rhodophyta): the envelope of tissue surrounding the *gonimocarp* in a cystocarp

Pericentral cells: cells that lie around a central (axial) cell

Periclinal: parallel to the surface

Perinuclear: lying around the nucleus

Periplast = pellicle ('periplast' is often used in Cryptophyta)

Periplastidial compartment: the narrow space between the chloroplast and the chloroplast endoplasmic reticulum in the Heterokontophyta, Cryptophyta and Chlorarachniophyta

Periplastidial reticulum (= periplastidial network): a network of interconnected tubules found in the narrow space (periplastidial compartment) between the chloroplast and the chloroplast endoplasmic reticulum in Heterokontophyta and Haptophyta. The reticulum may serve to transport polypeptides from nucleus to chloroplast

Perithallus: see *hypothallus*

Perizonium (in pennate diatoms, Bacillariophyceae): part of the auxospore wall, consisting of silicified bands in two series, one transverse to the auxospore axis and one longitudinal

Permian: the last geological period (248–286 million years ago) of the Palaeozoic Era (248–590 million years ago)

Peroxisome (= microbody): an organelle bounded by a single membrane, which is the site of oxidation of a variety of substrates. Molecular oxygen is used to oxidize material, with the production of hydrogen peroxide (H_2O_2); this is then used by the enzyme catalase for the oxidation of various other substrates, with the formation of H_2O

Persistent telophase spindle: a mitotic spindle that persists through telophase until cytokinesis. See also *non-persistent (collapsing) telophase spindle*

Phaeophycean hair: a fragile hair with a basal meristem and often also with a basal collar. The hair is almost colourless, because the chloroplasts in it are highly reduced

Phagocytosis: uptake of a solid food particle or a prey organism by a cell, through incorporation into vesicles pinched in from the plasmalemma. See also *endocytosis*

Phagotrophic unicellular organism: an organism that feeds on solid particles of food, which are taken up into a food vacuole, often with the help of pseudopodia

Pheromone: a substance produced by one organism that acts as a chemical messenger in communication with another organism; for example, a sexual attractant given off by a female to attract a male

Phlorotannins: polymers of phloroglucinol (1,3,5-trihydroxybenzene), known only from the Phaeophyceae. Phlorotannins exhibit the properties of tannins, precipitating proteins from solution and binding metal ions; they also have an astringent taste

Photoassimilates (= photosynthates): simple, low-molecular-mass sugars formed through photosynthesis

Photoautotrophic: using light as a source of energy (capturing it with photosynthetic pigments) and deriving carbon from inorganic sources, principally carbon dioxide or bicarbonate

Photoautotrophy: a form of nutrition involving the formation of organic compounds, the energy for this coming from light harvested by photosynthetic pigments

Photoheterotrophic: using light as a source of energy (capturing it with photosynthetic pigments), but deriving carbon from organic compounds

Photoinhibition: the inhibition of photosynthesis by high light intensities

Photokinesis: light-stimulated movement of an alga, the speed of movement increasing with light intensity (within certain limits)

Photophobic response: a sudden reversal in the movement of an alga, as a result of a sudden increase or decrease of light intensity

Photoreceptor apparatus: the whole complex of eyespot (stigma) and photoreceptor in flagellate algal cells. The photoreceptor contains a light-sensitive pigment and is situated either in a flagellar swelling (Heterokontophyta, Euglenophyta) or in a specialized area of the plasmalemma overlying the eyespot (Chlorophyta)

Photosynthates: see *photoassimilates*

Phototaxis: movement in response to light: towards light (positive phototaxis) or away from it (negative phototaxis)

Phototrophic: requiring light as a source of energy (see also *photoautotrophic* and *photoheterotrophic*)

Phragmoplast: a structure composed of the interzonal (continuous) spindle microtubules, together with various other microtubules around the periphery of the spindle and lying parallel to it, which is involved in the assembly of a cell plate and hence also in the formation of the new cell wall, in the plane of the spindle equator

Phycobilisomes (in Cyanophyta and Rhodophyta): tiny spherical or discoid bodies attached to the thylakoids, containing the accessory pigments phycoerythrin and phycocyanin

Phycobiont: the algal partner in a lichen

Phycoma: a cyst-like stage in the life cycles of certain Prasinophyceae. It has a wall that is resistant to bacterial degradation and probably contains sporopollenin-like material

Phycoplast: an assembly of microtubules at the equator of the spindle during telophase; the microtubules are orientated with their long axes approximately in the equatorial plane, at right angles to the spindle axis (contrast the *phragmoplast*). Cell division takes place in the plane of the phycoplast, e.g. through the formation of a wall via a cell plate

Phylloid: a leaf-like organ

Phylogeny: the evolutionary origin and derivation of organisms. In a narrower sense: the evolution of phyla, the principal taxonomic groups in the animal kingdom

Physiological anisogamy: the fusion of two gametes that appear the same morphologically, but behave differently: the male gamete moves towards the female

Phytochrome: a pigment that occurs in two forms, one sensitive to red light and the other to far-red light. Phytochrome is involved in the perception of daylength and the control of various developmental processes in higher plants and diverse algae

Phytopathogen: an organism causing a disease of plants

Phytoplankton: microscopic algae that live free, suspended (or swimming feebly) in water

Picoplankton: see *microplankton*

Pinocytosis: uptake of fluid by a cell, through incorporation into vesicles pinched in from the plasmalemma

Pit plug (in Rhodophyta): a plug of proteinaceous material deposited in a pore (= pit) between adjacent cells, the pore resulting from incomplete wall formation at cell division

Pit: a break in the cell wall through which strands of cytoplasm extend, connecting adjacent cells

Plankton: microscopic organisms that live free, suspended (or swimming feebly) in water

Planktonic: belonging to the plankton

Planozygote: a zygote that swims using flagella. The flagella are derived from the gametes that fused to produce the zygote

Plasmalemma: the membrane bounding the cell

Plasmid: a small circular molecule of DNA, capable of independent replication. Plasmids are of general occurrence in prokaryotes, but also occur in eukaryotic cells

Plasmodesmata: thin protoplasmic connections between two cells

Plasmodium: a multinucleate protoplast without a cell wall and exhibiting amoeboid movement

Plasmogamy: the fusion of the protoplasts of two gametes (cf. *karyogamy*)

Plastid: an organelle, enclosed by a double membrane, that either contains thylakoids and photosynthetic pigments (chloroplasts) or stores carbohydrate (amyloplasts); plastids are often discoid or band-shaped

Plastidome: the whole complement of plastids in a cell

Pleuronematic flagellum: a flagellum bearing hairs, especially the stiff hairs (mastigonemes) characteristic of the Cryptophyta and Heterokontophyta

Ploidy: the number of complete sets of chromosomes in a cell

Plurilocular zoidangium (in Phaeophyceae): an organ containing many chambers (loculi), each one of which produces a single zoid

Pluriseriate (= multiseriate): composed of a few or many rows of cells (or other structures)

Plurizoids (in Phaeophyceae): the zoids produced by a plurilocular zoidangium

Polar fenestrae: openings in the nuclear envelope at the poles of the spindle during closed mitosis

Polar nodule: 1. a thickening of the cell wall of a heterocyst in Cyanophyta; 2. a thickening near the end of the valve in a raphid (raphe-bearing) pennate diatom

Polar plates (in Bacillariophyceae): dark-staining plate-like structures found at the poles of the mitotic spindle

Polar rings (in Rhodophyta): dark-staining, ring-like bodies found at the poles of the mitotic spindle. They probably form part of the microtubule organizing centres (MTOCs)

Polyeder: an irregularly shaped polyhedral cell formed during the life cycle of certain members of the Chlorococcales (e.g. *Hydrodictyon, Pediastrum*), which develops from a meiospore and gives rise to young colonies

Polyhedral body: see *carboxysome*

Polyphosphate granule: a microscopic granule of highly polymeric phosphate

Polyphyletic: descended from several or many different ancestors

Polypyramidal pyrenoid: a radially subdivided pyrenoid covered by a number of radially arranged starch grains

Polysaccharide: a macromolecule composed of sugar monomers

Polysiphonous: made of many tubes or siphons, i.e. consisting of parallel rows of elongate cells, packed close together

Postigenous filaments: see *hypothallus*

Precambrian: the long period of time (590–4500 million years ago) before the appearance *en masse* of invertebrate fossils. It comprises the Archaean and Proterozoic Eras

Precursor: a compound or structure that precedes another in a chemical or developmental pathway and is transformed or incorporated into it

Primary consumer (= herbivore): a consumer of primary producers (in most cases, therefore, of plants)

Primary production: the production of organic material by photosynthetic plants; when expressed per unit time and per unit horizontal area (or volume), the result is the *primary productivity*

Primigenous filaments: see *hypothallus*

Primordium: an embryonic structure, which will ultimately grow into an adult structure or organ

Proboscis: a snout-like projection at the anterior end of the spermatozoids of *Fucus* (Phaeophyceae) and *Vaucheria* (Xanthophyceae), whose shape is maintained by microtubules

Procarp (in certain Rhodophyta): a compact female reproductive tissue, consisting of a short carpogonial branch borne by a supporting cell. This is at the same time the auxiliary cell or bears a short auxiliary cell branch

Progressive cleavage: a form of cell division. Several rounds of nuclear division occur first, producing a multinucleate cell, which is then divided into uninucleate daughter cells by branching invaginations of the plasmalemma; finally, each daughter cell becomes surrounded by its own cell wall

Prokaryotic: possessing the characteristics of the Prokaryota (DNA and thylakoids lying free in the cytoplasm, not surrounded by a nuclear or chloroplast membrane; no mitochondria, golgi apparatus or ER)

Propagule: a morphologically specialized vegetative structure involved in vegetative propagation

Prophase: the earliest stage of mitosis and meiosis, during which the chromosomes become visible; in the preceding *interphase* the chromosomes are usually not distinguishable because they unspiral

Proterozoic Era: an early geological era (590–2500 million years ago), whose rocks contain microfossils of cyanobacteria and bacteria but few other fossils, except towards the end, when invertebrates appear

Protofilament: see *microtubules*

Protosphere (in Bryopsidophyceae, Chlorophyta): a spherical stage in the life cycles of certain siphonous green algae, containing a giant zygotic nucleus

Protozoa, protozoans: informal names for heterotrophic unicellular eukaryotes. Protozoa are phylogenetically heterogeneous, so that this is not a natural group

Proximal sheath (in flagellate cells of certain Chlorophyta): a sheath of amorphous, dark-staining material that lies appressed to the lower side (= the proximal side, i.e. nearest the body of the cell) of each of the basal bodies

Pseudodichotomy: a false dichotomy. One of the branches of the fork arises as a side branch from the main axis; the apparently equal dichotomy arises as a result of subsequent equal development of the main axis and side branch

Pseudofilament: a uniseriate row of cells spaced relatively distantly within a gelatinous sheath

Pseudogranum: a granum-like stack, formed by the partial overlap of a number of thylakoids

Pseudoparenchyma: a tissue composed of closely appressed filaments of cells, which in transverse section resembles a parenchyma

Pseudopodium: a plastically deformable protrusion of a naked cell, functioning in cell motility or the uptake of solid particles of food

Puncta (plural of *punctum*): small dots. Often used for pores or other structures in the walls of diatoms, as seen with the light microscope, whose true nature can be revealed through electron microscope observations

Pusule (in Dinophyta): a more or less branched system of tubes, lined by the plasmalemma, opening to the exterior of the cell

Pycnocline: see *epilimnion*

Pyknotic nucleus: a nucleus whose contents are degenerating and have become condensed

Pyrenoid: a structure lying in the chloroplast, which is visible in the light microscope and is usually spherical or ellipsoidal. It can be embedded in the chloroplast or lie beneath its surface and contains few or no thylakoids. Pyrenoids contain the enzyme *RuBisCO*. Reserve polysaccharides are formed near them (within the chloroplast in the Chlorophyta but outside in other groups)

Quadriflagellate: with four flagella

Radial spokes (in an axoneme): radial links, consisting of protein, between the 9 peripheral doublets and the central pair of microtubules

Radiolarians: marine planktonic protozoans (belonging to the class Polycystinea, phylum Actinopoda) with stiff radiating rhizopods and elegant siliceous skeletons, which have radial symmetry

Raphe (in pennate diatoms, Bacillariophyceae): a longitudinal fissure through the valve in some pennate diatoms, associated with and involved in gliding locomotion

Receptacle: a specialized structure bearing reproductive

organs. In the Fucales (Phaeophyceae) the receptacles are swollen regions at the ends of the thalli, in which the conceptacles are embedded

Red tide: see *water bloom*

Reduction division = *meiosis*

Resting spore = *hypnospore*

Rhizoid: a root-like filament of cells, which may be unicellular or multicellular and grows downwards, involved in attachment

Rhizoplast: a root-like, often transversely striated structure that connects the flagellar basal bodies and the nucleus; a contractile organelle, capable of supercoiling, composed of the ubiquitous contractile protein centrin

Rhizopodium: a thin thread-like *pseudopodium*

Rhizostyle (in Cryptophyta): a straight, longitudinal microtubular root (composed of 6–10 microtubules), which descends from the basal body of the longer flagellum towards the posterior end of the cell

Ribosomes: tiny granular structures (*ca.* 20–30 nm in diameter), composed of RNA (ribonucleic acid) and proteins; their function is the synthesis of proteins. The membranes of the endoplasmic reticulum are often studded with ribosomes engaged in protein synthesis (rough endoplasmic reticulum)

Rootlet: sometimes used to refer to root-like components of the flagellar apparatus

Rough ER: endoplasmic reticulum studded with ribosomes

RuBisCO: ribulose 1,5-bisphosphate carboxylase–oxygenase, the enzyme catalysing the primary dark reaction of photosynthesis, involving the fixation of CO_2 into carbohydrate

Saprotrophic: obtaining nutrition by taking up through the plasmalemma organic substances that have already been partly broken down outside the cell

Sarcinoid: composed of three-dimensional packets of cells

Scale reservoir (in unicellular or colonial algae where the cells are covered by scales): an invagination of the plasmalemma into which scales are secreted after being manufactured in golgi cisternae. From the reservoir the scales are distributed over the cell surface

SDV: see *silica deposition vesicle*

Secondary consumer: a carnivore that eats herbivores (= primary consumers)

Sediment: material deposited by water, ice or air (sand, silt, gravel, etc)

Sedimentary rock: rock formed from sedimented (settled) sand, silt, gravel, etc, through consolidation

Segregative cell division (in Chlorophyta): a form of cell division in which a multinucleate protoplast divides up into several, often rounded daughter protoplasts, which subsequently become surrounded by a wall. Each daughter cell then swells into an adult cell

Self-incompatible: see *heterothallic*

Semicell (in the order Desmidiales, class Zygnematophyceae): one of the two halves of the desmid cell, which are usually virtually equal

Semiconservative replication: (of DNA) where the double helix unwinds and each half acts as a template for a new half-helix; (of basal bodies) where a new basal body is manufactured close to an existing one, which seems to act as a template for the new one

Septum: a partition that completely or partially separates two compartments or spaces

Shield cell (in Charophyceae): a shield-shaped cell forming the outer wall of an antheridium

Short-day response: a response to the perception of relatively short daily periods of light, shorter than a *critical daylength* (for instance, of 14 h light per day). A *long-day response* is a response to the perception of long periods of light per day (e.g. longer than a critical daylength of, for instance, 12 h)

Short shoot = determinate lateral

Sieve plate: a plate perforated by many pores

Sieve tube: a tube in the phloem of a vascular plant (Tracheophyta), which is composed of separate sieve tube elements separated by sieve plates. Each sieve plate is traversed by a large number of protoplasmic strands. Sieve tubes function in the transport of organic material

Silica deposition vesicle (SDV): a membrane-bound vesicle within a cell, in which silica is deposited (e.g. individual elements of the frustule in diatoms, the siliceous cyst wall of Chrysophyceae)

Silurian: a geological period (408–438 million years ago) within the Palaeozoic Era (248–590 million years ago)

Siphonocladous: composed of multinucleate compartments (cells)

Siphonous: with a thallus formed of multinucleate tubular cells (siphons)

Smooth ER: endoplasmic reticulum without ribosomes

Sorus: a group of sporangia or gametangia

Spermatangiophore (in Rhodophyta): a structure that bears spermatangia

Spermatangium (in Rhodophyta): a cell whose contents differentiate into a spermatium

Spermatangium mother cell (in Rhodophyta): the cell that cuts off the spermatangium

Spermatium (in Rhodophyta): a non-motile or slightly amoeboid male gamete

Spermatogenous threads (in Charophyceae): filaments of cells, each of which gives rise to a single spermatozoid. The spermatogenous threads are enclosed in the antheridium

Spermatozoid (= antherozoid): a flagellate male gamete, produced in an antheridium

Spindle: an ellipsoidal or cylindrical bundle of spindle microtubules (seen in the light microscope as the spindle fibres) that converge towards each of the two spindle poles and which is present at mitosis and meiosis. The spindle consists of interzonal (continuous) microtubules, which run from pole to pole, and chromosome microtubules, which run from pole to chromosome

Spindle equator: the plane equidistant from the two spindle poles, lying between the daughter sets of chromosomes during anaphase and telophase

Spindle fibres (= spindle microtubules): see *spindle*

Sporangium: a cell (often with a particular, characteristic shape), whose contents divide up to form spores. The spores remain for some time within the sporangium before they are set free

Spore: a general term for asexual reproductive cells (or clusters of cells) in plants or fungi

Sporogenous: giving rise to spores

Sporophyte: the phase of the life cycle in which meiospores are produced

Sporopollenin: a very resistant, inert material found in the cell walls of spores and pollen grains of higher land plants. Certain unicellular algae (e.g. *Chlorella*) and colonial algae (e.g. *Scenedesmus*) contain sporopollenin-like material. Sporopollenins are complex polymers derived from carotenoids; they protect the cell from drought

Starch: a storage polysaccharide composed of α-1,4- and α-1,6-linked glucose residues

Statospore (in Chrysophyceae): see *endogenous cyst*

Stellate pattern (in Chlorophyta): a nine-pointed star visible (using the electron microscope) in transverse sections of the flagellar transition zone. Centripetal contraction of the stellate structure (which contains the contractile protein centrin) may bring about abscission of the flagellum

Stephanokont: bearing many equal flagella, arranged in a ring near one end of the cell, like a crown

Stigma = eyespot

Stipules (in Charophyceae): spine-like cells borne in a ring beneath a whorl of 'leaves'

Stolon: a creeping section of stem or creeping filaments of cells

Striated strand (in Dinophyta): a taut band of transversely striated material, which keeps the transverse flagellum in place within the transverse groove. It contains the contractile protein centrin

Stroma starch: starch grains lying in the stroma of the chloroplast, not in close association with the pyrenoid

Stromatolite: a finely layered calcareous structure, which is irregularly columnar, formed usually by mats of blue-green algae (cyanobacteria)

Subaerial: see *aerophytic*

Subapical cell: a cell lying beneath the apical cell

Successive bipartition: successive divisions of a uninucleate cell, in which each division of the nucleus is followed by division of the cytoplasm, but the daughter cells only later become surrounded by their own cell walls

Sulcus = longitudinal furrow

Summer annual: a plant where the whole of development, from spore or zygote to the death of the plant, takes place in a single summer

Supporting cell (of the carpogonial branch in the Rhodophyta): the characteristically shaped cell that bears the carpogonial branch

Symbiont: an organism that lives symbiotically with another organism

Symbiosis: a very close association between two organisms (as between fungus and alga in a lichen); often used in the narrower sense of an association in which both partners derive some benefit

Synaptonemal complex: see *pachytene*

Synistosome (in Prasinophyceae): a fibrous rectangular bar, striated longitudinally, which lies between the basal bodies

Synzoospore (in *Vaucheria,* Xanthophyceae): a large multinucleate zoospore bearing may pairs of flagella

Tannins: see *phlorotannins*

Taxon (plural *taxa*): the general term for any systematic category (e.g. species, families, divisions are all taxa)

Telophase: the last stage of nuclear division, during which the new daughter nuclei are formed at the poles of the spindle

Template: a mould, complementary in shape or structure to the organelle or macromolecule formed in or against it

Terminal cap (in the flagellate cells of certain Chlorophyta): a cap of dark-staining material that partly covers and occludes the lower end (= the proximal end, nearest the body of the cell) of a flagellar basal body

Terrestrial: living on land

Tertiary: the first and by far the longest geological period (1.8–65 million years ago) of the Cenozoic Era (65 million years ago until the present)

Tethys Sea: the elongate, largely tropical seaway, oriented E–W, that separated the northern continents from the southern continents and connected the Indo-Pacific and Atlantic Oceans from the early Palaeozoic Era until the Miocene epoch

Tetrasporal (= capsular, = palmelloid): resembling *Tetraspora* (Chlorophyta), i.e. with cells that are separate but remain enclosed within a common mucilage envelope

Tetrasporangium: a meiosporangium containing four meiospores

Tetraspore: one of the four meiospores produced by a tetrasporangium

Tetrasporophyte: the tetraspore-producing phase of the life cycle

Thallose: having a thallus, or exhibiting a thalloid organization

Thallus: a relatively undifferentiated plant body, lacking true leaves, stems and roots. 'Thallus' can thus be applied to all algae and fungi, even though some have organs that resemble leaves and stems

Theca: the envelope or armour of certain unicellular algae (Dinophyta, Prasinophyceae); half of the silica cell wall (frustule) in diatoms (Bacillariophyceae)

Thecal vesicles (in Dinophyta): flat polygonal vesicles forming a superficial layer just beneath the plasmalemma, which may be empty or contain thecal plates composed of cellulose

Thermocline: see *epilimnion*

Thylakoid organizing body (in the chloroplasts and amyloplasts of certain Bryopsidophyceae): a rounded body consisting of concentric double membranes, from which thylakoids are formed in young chloroplasts

Thylakoid: a flat, disc-like vesicle, bounded on each side by plasma membranes, which run parallel to each other and close together, and contain the photosynthetic pigments

Tonoplast: the plasma membrane containing the vacuole

Trabeculae (in *Caulerpa,* Chlorophyta): struts of cell wall material, which traverse and support the spherical or leaf-like, multinucleate thalli of *Caulerpa*

Transformation (when used to refer to a parasexual process in prokaryotes): the transfer of genetic information by means of 'naked' extracellular DNA

Transition zone (transition region): the zone between the flagellum and its basal body, just below the basal ends of the central pair of microtubules of the axoneme

Transitional helix (in many Heterokontophyta): a coiled fibre present in the transition zone between the flagellum itself and the basal body

Transverse flagellum (in Dinophyta): see *transverse furrow*

Transverse furrow (in Dinophyta): the *girdle*: a groove lying between the anterior and posterior ends of the cell, which houses the transverse flagellum

Transversely striated connective (in flagellate cells): a transversely striated band (probably composed of the ubiquitous contractile protein centrin) forming part of the flagellar apparatus and which connects the basal bodies just below the insertion of the flagella. Connectives in this position are often not striated

Triassic: the oldest geological period (213–248 million years ago) of the Mesozoic Era (65–248 million years ago)

Trichal: composed of filaments of cells; see *filamentous*

Trichoblast (in Rhodophyta): a branched filament of colourless or almost colourless cells, resembling a tuft of hairs

Trichocysts (in Raphidophyceae, Dinophyta): elongate organelles positioned beneath the cell surface, each surrounded by membrane, which shoot out threads of mucilage upon stimulation of the cell

Trichogyne: a hairlike extension of the oogonium in Rhodophyta and some Ascomycetes. It is via the trichogyne that the male nucleus is taken up during sexual reproduction

Trichome (in Cyanophyta): a filament of cells (not including any mucilage sheath that may be present)

Trichothallic growth: growth of a filament of cells through the activity of a discrete intercalary meristem (recognizable as a stack of short cells packed with cytoplasm)

Trichotomy: a branching that resembles a three-pronged fork

Triplet: see *basal body*

Trumpet hyphae (in Laminariales, Phaeophyceae): hyphalike filaments of cells in the medulla that are swollen, like trumpets, at each cross-wall

Tubulin: see *microtubule*

Turbulence: motion of a fluid in which irregular eddies cause mixing

Turgor pressure: the pressure exerted by a plant cell on its wall, as a result of the tendency of the cell to take up water and swell. The greater the concentration of solutes in the cell sap, the higher is the turgor pressure at equilibrium

Ultrastructure: the fine structure of cells or other structures as revealed using the electron microscope

Unialgal culture: a culture containing one species or race of alga, but which also contains bacteria

Uniaxial construction (= central filament type of structure): a thallus architecture in which the central part of the axis consists of just one axial filament

Unilateral type of zoid architecture (in Chlorophyta): the zoid architecture in which two equal flagella emerge on one side of the cell, just below the apex. The flagella are anchored in the cell by one broad, unilateral band of microtubules, which, near the flagellar basal bodies, forms part of a *multilayered structure* (MLS)

Unilocular zoidangium (in Phaeophyceae): a zoidangium with one chamber, whose contents divide up into many zoids. The unilocular zoidangium is usually a meiosporangium

Uniseriate: with a single, linear row of cells (or other structures)

Unizoids (in Phaeophyceae): the zoids formed by a unilocular zoidangium

Upwelling: the ascent of water, often containing high concentrations of nutrient salts, from the depths of oceans or lakes to the surface

Utricle: a swollen, vesicular part of a thallus. In some Bryopsidophyceae the utricles are the dilated tips of siphons, which contain numerous chloroplasts and are united to form a palisade-like layer

Vacuole: a large cavity within the cell, filled with cell sap and surrounded by a plasma membrane (tonoplast)

Valve (in Bacillariophyceae): one of the two major pieces of the frustule. Each valve covers one end of the cell; between the two valves is the *girdle*

Valve view (in Bacillariophyceae): the diatom cell or frustule seen with the valves in face view, i.e. at right angles to the line of sight

Vegetative cell division: cell division that results in the formation of vegetative (non-reproductive) cells

Ventral chamber (in Dinophyta): an indentation on the ventral side of the cell, at the intersection of the transverse and longitudinal furrows, from which the flagella arise

Vesicle: a small sac-like organelle within the cytoplasm, bounded by a single plasma membrane

Water bloom: a massive growth of phytoplankton, visible to the naked eye, in which the water becomes noticeably coloured (often red or green). A red water bloom in the sea is often called a *red tide*

Xylan: a polysaccharide – a polymer of xylose

Xylomannan: a polysaccharide – a polymer of xylose and mannose

Zoid: a reproductive cell that bears flagella and is hence free-swimming

Zoidangium: a cell (often with a particular, characteristic morphology) whose contents divide up to give zoids. The zoids remain enclosed within the wall of the zoidangium for a short time before release

Zoochlorella: a unicellular, endosymbiotic green algae that lives within an animal (e.g. *Chlorella* in *Chlorohydra*)

Zoogamete: a flagellate gamete

Zooplankton: animal plankton

Zoospore: a flagellate spore

Zooxanthella: a unicellular, endosymbiotic dinophyte (rarely a heterokontophyte) that lives within an animal (e.g. *Symbiodinium* in reef-building corals)

Zygote: the diploid cell produced through the fusion of two gametes

Zygotene: the stage of meiotic prophase during which homologous chromosomes become paired

μm: see *micrometre*

References

1 Abbott, B.C. & D. Ballantine (1957). The toxin from *Gymnodinium venificum* Ballantine. *J. Mar. Biol. Ass. U.K.* **36**: 169–89.

2 Abdel-Rahman, M.H. (1980). La morphologie et le cycle de développement de l'*Acrochaetium subtilissimum* (Rhodophycées, Acrochaetiales). *Crypt. Algol.* **1**: 99–110.

3 Abdel-Rahman, M.H. (1982a). Photopériodisme chez *Acrochaetium asparagopsis* (Rhodophycées). I. Réponse à une photopériode de jours courts au cours de la formation des tétrasporocystes. *Physiol. Végét.* **20**: 155–64.

4 Abdel-Rahman, M.H. (1982b). Photopériodisme chez *Acrochaetium asparagopsis* (Rhodophycées, Acrochaetiales). Influence de l'interruption de la nyctipériode, par un éclairement blanc ou monochromatique, sur la formation des tétrasporocystes. *C.R. Acad. Sci. Paris*, sér. III, **294**: 389–400.

5 Abdel-Rahman, M.H. (1982c). The involvement of an endogenous circadian rhythm in photoperiodic timing in *Acrochaetium asparagopsis* (Rhodophyta, Acrochaetiales). *Br. Phycol. J.* **17**: 389–400.

6 Abdel-Rahman, M.H. (1985). Le cycle de développement de l'*Acrochaetium gynandrum* (Rhodophycées, Acrochaetiales). *Crypt. Algol.* **6**: 1–12.

7 Abdel-Rahman, M.H. & F. Magne (1983). Existence d'un nouveau type de cycle de développement chez les Rhodophycées. *C.R. Acad. Sci. Paris*, sér. III, **296**: 641–44.

8 Abe, K. (1938). Entwicklung der Fortpflanzungsorgane und Keimungsgeschichte von *Desmarestia viridis* (Müll.) Lamour. *Sci. Rep. Tohoku Imp. Univ. Ser. IV*, **12**: 475–82.

9 Adams, J.A., D.D. Seaton, J.B. Buchanan & M.R. Longbottom (1968). Biological observations associated with the toxic phytoplankton bloom off the East coast. *Nature* **220**: 24–5.

10 Adey, W.H. & I.G. MacIntyre (1973). Crustose coralline algae: a re-evaluation in the geological sciences. *Geol. Soc. Am. Bull.* **84**: 883–904.

11 Admiraal, W. (1980). *Experiments on the ecology of benthic diatoms in the Eems-Dollard Estuary*. Biologisch Onderzoek Eems-Dollard Estuarium. Publicaties en Verslagen no. 3 1980. Thesis, University Groningen, Netherlands: 1–125.

12 Admiraal, W. & H. Peletier (1979). Influence of organic compounds and light limitation on the growth rate of estuarine benthic diatoms. *Br. Phycol. J.* **14**: 197–206.

13 Ahmadjian, V. & J.B. Jacobs (1983). Algal-fungal relationships in lichens: recognition, synthesis, and development. In *Algal Symbiosis, a Continuum of Interaction Strategies*, ed. L.J. Goff, pp. 147–72. Cambridge University Press.

14 Akatsuka, I. (1986). Japanese Gelidiales (Rhodophyta) especially *Gelidium*. *Oceanogr. Mar. Biol. Ann. Rev.* **24**: 171–263.

15 Alberte, R.S. (1989). Physiological and cellular features of *Prochloron*. In *Prochloron, a Microbial Enigma*, ed. R.A. Lewin & L. Cheng, pp. 31–52. Chapman & Hall, New York.

16 Alberts, B., D. Bray, J. Lewis, M. Raff, K. Roberts & J.D. Watson (1989). *Molecular Biology of the Cell*. 2nd Ed. Garland, New York & London.

17 Al-Kubaisi, K.H. & H.O. Schwantes (1981). Cytophotometrische Untersuchungen zum Generationswechsel autotropher und heterotropher siphonaler Organismen (*Vaucheria sessilis* und *Saprolegnia ferax*). *Nova Hedwigia* **34**: 301–16.

18 Allen, C.E. (1905). Die Keimung der Zygote bei *Coleochaete*. *Ber. Dtsch. Bot. Ges.* **23**: 285–92.

19 Allen, N.S. (1980). Cytoplasmic streaming and transport in the characean alga *Nitella*. *Can. J. Bot.* **58**: 786–96.

20 Allsop, A. (1969). Phylogenetic relationships of the Prokaryota and the origin of the eucaryotic cell. *New Phytol.* **68**: 591–612.

21 Anagnostidis, K. & J. Komárek (1985). Modern approach to the classification system of the Cyano-

phytes 1 – Introduction. *Algol. Stud.* **38/39**: 291–302.

22 Anagnostidis, K. & J. Komárek (1988). Modern approach to the classification system of the Cyanophytes 3 – Oscillatoriales. *Algol. Stud.* **50–53**: 327–472.

23 Anagnostidis, K. & J. Komárek (1990). Modern approach to the classification system of Cyanophytes 5 – Stigonematales. *Algol. Stud.* **59**: 1–73.

24 Andersen, R.A. (1987a). Synurophyceae classis nov., a new class of algae. *Am. J. Bot.* **74**: 337–53.

25 Andersen, R.A. (1987b). Structure and evolution of the Chrysophyceae. *J. Phycol.* **23** (suppl.): 11.

26 Andersen, R.A. (1990). The three-dimensional structure of the flagellar apparatus of *Chrysosphaerella brevispina* (Chrysophyceae) as viewed by high voltage electron microscopy stereo pairs. *Phycologia* **29**: 86–97.

27 Andersen, R.A. & T.J. Mulkey (1983). The occurrence of chlorophylls c_1 and c_2 in the Chrysophyceae. *J. Phycol.* **19**: 289–294.

28 Anderson, D.M. & D. Wall (1978). Potential importance of benthic cysts of *Gonyaulax tamarensis* and *G. excavata* in initiating toxic dinoflagellate blooms. *J. Phycol.* **14**: 224–34.

29 Anderson, O.R. (1983). The radiolarian symbiosis. In *Algal Symbiosis*, ed. L.J. Goff, pp. 69–89. Cambridge University Press.

30 Anderson, L.W.J. & B.M. Sweeney (1978). Role of inorganic ions in controlling sedimentation rate of a marine centric diatom *Ditylum brightwelli*. *J. Phycol.* **14**: 204–14.

31 Andreas, Ch.H. (1972). *Experimentele Plantensystematiek*. Oosthoek, Utrecht.

32 Antia, N.J. & J.Y. Cheng (1982). The ketocarotenoids of two marine coccoid members of the Eustigmatophyceae. *Br. Phycol. J.* **17**: 39–50.

33 Antia, N.J., J.Y. Cheng, R.A.J. Foyle & E. Percival (1979). Marine cryptomonad starch from autolysis of glycerol-grown *Chroomonas salina*. *J. Phycol.* **15**: 57–62.

34 Ardré, F. (1978). Sur les cycles morphologiques du *Gymnogongrus crenulatus* (Turn.) J. Ag. et du *Gymnogongrus devoniensis* (Grev.) Schott. (Gigartinales, Phyllophoracées) en culture. *Rev. Algol.* N.S. **13**: 151–76.

34a Ariztia, E.V., R.A. Andersen & M.L. Sogin (1991). A new phylogeny of chromophyte algae using 16S-like rRNA sequences from *Mallomonas*

papillosa (Synurophyceae) and *Tribonema aequale* (Xanthophyceae). *J. Phycol.* **27**: 428–36.

35 Arnott, H.J. (1970). Structure and function of the algal pyrenoid I. Ultrastructure and cytochemistry during zoosporogenesis. *J. Phycol.* **6**: 14–22.

36 Arpin, N., W.A. Svec & S. Liaaen-Jensen (1976). New fucoxanthin-related carotenoids from *Coccolithus huxleyi*. *Phytochemistry* **15**: 529–32.

36a Assali, N.-E., W.F. Martin, C.S. Sommerville & S. Loiseaux-de Goër (1991). Evolution of the Rubisco operon from prokaryotes to algae: structure and analysis of the rbcS gene of the brown alga *Pylaiella littoralis*. *Plant Mol. Biol.* **17**: 853–63.

37 Atkinson, A.W., B.E.S. Gunning & P.L.C. John (1972). Sporopollenin in the cell wall of *Chlorella* and other algae: ultrastructure, chemistry and incorporation of 14C acetate, studied in synchronous cultures. *Planta* **107**: 1–32.

38 Ayala, F.J. (1986). On the virtues and pitfalls of the molecular evolutionary clock. *Heredity* **77**: 226–35.

39 Baardseth, E. (1966). Localization and structure of alginate gels. *Proc. 5th Int. Seaweed Symp.*, 19–28.

40 Baba, M., L.L. Darga, M. Goodman & J. Czeluzniak (1981). Evolution of cytochrome c investigated by the maximum parsimony method. *J. Molec. Evol.* **17**: 197–213.

41 Bachmann, P., P. Kornmann & K. Zetsche (1976). Regulation der Entwicklung und des Stoffwechsels der Grünalge *Urospora* durch die Temperatur. *Planta* **128**: 241–5.

42 Bajer, A. (1968). Fine structure studies on phragmoplast in cell plate formation. *Chromosoma (Berl.)* **24**: 383–417.

43 Bakker, C. (1966). Een protozo in symbiose met algen in het Veerse Meer. *Lev. Natuur* **69**: 180–7.

44 Bakker, C. (1967). Massale ontwikkeling van ciliaten met symbiotische algen in het Veerse Meer. *Lev. Natuur* **70**: 166–73.

45 Bakker, M.E. & G.M. Lokhorst (1985). The ultrastructure of the flagellar apparatus of the zoospore of *Chaetomorpha melagonium* (Web. & Mohr) Kützing (Chlorophyta). *Phycologia* **24**: 275–88.

46 Balakrishnan, M.S. & B.B. Chaugule (1980). Cytology and life history of *Batrachospermum mahabaleshwarensis* Balakrishnan et Chaugule. *Crypt. Algol.* **1**: 83–97.

47 Barlow, S.B. & R.A. Cattolico (1981). Mitosis

and cytokinesis in the Prasinophyceae. I. *Mantoniella squamata* (Manton and Parke) Desikachary. *Am. J. Bot.* **68**: 606–15.

48   Barnett, J.R. & R.D. Preston (1970). Arrays of granules with the plasmalemma in swarmers of *Cladophora. Ann. Bot.* **34**: 1011–17.

49   Barr, D.J.S. & N.L. Désaulniers (1989). The flagellar apparatus of the Oomycetes and Hyphochytriomycetes. In *The Chromophyte Algae*, ed. J.C. Green, B.S.C. Leadbeater & W.L. Diver, pp. 343–55. Clarendon Press, Oxford.

50   Bartlett, R.B. & G.R. South (1973). Observations on the life-history of *Bryopsis hypnoides* Lamour. from Newfoundland: a new variation in culture. *Acta Bot. Neerl.* **22**: 1–5.

51   Bassoulet, J.P., P. Bernier, M.A. Conrad, R. Deloffre & M. Jaffrezo (1978). Les algues Dasycladales du Jurassique et du Crétacé. *Géobios*, mém. spéc. **2**: 1–330.

52   Bassoulet, J.P., P. Bernier, R. Deloffre, P. Génot, M. Jaffrezo & D. Vachard (1979). Essai de classification des Dasycladales en tribus. 2ème Symposium international sur les algues fossiles. *Bull. Cent. Rech. Explor.-Prod. Elf-Aquitaine* **3** (2): 429–42.

53   Bazin, M.J. (1968). Sexuality in a blue-green alga: genetic recombination in *Anacystis nidulans. Nature* **218**: 282–3.

54   Beakes, G.W. (1989). Oomycete fungi: their phylogeny and relationship to chromophyte algae. In *The Chromophyte Algae*, ed. J.C. Green, B.S.C. Leadbeater & W.L. Diver, pp. 325–42. Clarendon Press, Oxford.

55   Bech-Hansen, C.W. & L.C. Fowke (1972). Mitosis in *Mougeotia* sp. *Can. J. Bot.* **50**: 1811–16.

56   Becker, B., K. Hard, M. Melkonian, J.P. Kamerling & J.F.G. Vliegenthart (1989). Identification of 3-deoxy-manno-2-octulosonic acid, 3-deoxy-5-O-methyl-manno-2-octulosonic acid and 3-deoxy-lyxo-2-heptulosaric acid in the cell wall (theca) of the green alga *Tetraselmis striata* Butcher (Prasinophyceae). *Eur. J. Biochem.* **182**: 153–60.

57   Beckett, A., I.B. Heath & D.J. McLaughlin (1974). *An Atlas of Fungal Ultrastructure.* Longman, London.

58   Beech, P.L. & R. Wetherbee (1988). Observations on the flagellar apparatus and peripheral endoplasmic reticulum of the coccolithophorid, *Pleurochrysis carterae* (Prymnesiophyceae). *Phycologia* **27**: 142–58.

59   Beech, P.L. & R. Wetherbee (1990). The flagellar apparatus of *Mallomonas splendens* (Synurophyceae) at interphase and its development during the cell cycle. *J. Phycol.* **26**: 95–111.

60   Belcher, J.H. (1968a). A study of *Pyramimonas reticulata* Korshikov (Prasinophyceae) in culture. *Nova Hedwigia* **15**: 179–90.

61   Belcher, J.H. (1968b). A morphological study of *Pedinomonas major* Korschikov. *Nova Hedwigia* **16**: 131–39.

62   Belford, H.S. & W.F. Thompson (1981). Single copy DNA homologies in *Atriplex*. II. Hybrid thermal stabilities and molecular phylogeny. *Heredity* **46**: 109–22.

63   Bennoun, P. (1982). Evidence for a respiratory chain in the chloroplast. *Proc. Natl. Acad. Sci. USA* **79**: 4352–6.

64   Bentlich, A., B. Borstelmann, R. Reddemann, K. Speckenbach & R. Schnetter (1990). Notes on the life histories of *Boergesenia* and *Valonia* (Siphonocladales, Chlorophyta). *Hydrobiologia* **204/205**: 425–34.

65   Berdach, J.T. (1977). In situ preservation of the transverse flagellum of *Peridinium cinctum* (Dinophyceae) for scanning electron microscopy. *J. Phycol.* **13**: 243–51.

66   Berger, R., S. Liaaen-Jensen, V. McAllister & R.R.L. Guillard (1977). Carotenoids of Prymnesiophyceae (Haptophyceae). *Biochem. Syst. Ecol.* **5**: 71–5.

67   Berger, S. & H.G. Schweiger (1975). The ultrastructure of the nucleocytoplasmic interface in *Acetabularia*. In *Molecular Biology of Nucleocytoplasmic Relationships*, ed. S. Puiseux-Dao, pp. 243–50. Elsevier, Amsterdam.

68   Berger-Perrot, Y. (1980a). Trois nouvelles espèces d'*Urospora* à cellules uninuclées sur les côtes de Bretagne. *Crypt. Algol.* **1**: 141–60.

69   Berger-Perrot, Y. (1980b). *Ulothrix flacca* (Dillwyn) Thuret (Chlorophycée, Ulotrichale) des côtes de Bretagne et son polymorphisme. *Crypt. Algol.* **1**: 229–48.

70   Berger-Perrot, Y., J. C. Thomas & M.Th. L'Hardy-Halos (1986). Fine structure of the flagellar apparatus of gametes in situ and motile zygotes of the green alga *Ulothrix flacca* var. *roscoffensis* (Ulothrichales) (Chlorophyta). *Protoplasma* **134**: 17–29.

71   Berkaloff, C. & B. Rousseau (1979).

Ultrastructure of male gametogenesis in *Fucus serratus* (Phaeophyceae). *J. Phycol.* **15**: 163–73.

72 Berthold, W.U. (1978). Ultrastrukturanalyse der endoplasmatischen Algen von *Amphistegina lessonii* d'Orbigny, Foraminifera (Protozoa) und ihre systematische Stellung. *Arch. Protistenk.* **120**: 16–62.

73 Bhattacharya, D. & L.D. Druehl (1988). Phylogenetic comparison of the small-subunit ribosomal DNA sequence of *Costaria costata* (Phaeophyta) with those of other algae, vascular plants and Oomycetes. *J. Phycol.* **24**: 539–43.

73a Bhattacharya, D., S.K. Stickle & M.L. Sogin (1991). Molecular phylogenetic analysis of actin gene regions from *Achlya bisexualis* (Oomycota) and *Costaria costata* (Chromophyta). *J. Molec. Evol.* **33**: 525–36.

74 Bicudo, C.E.M. (1966). *Bjornbergiella*, a new genus of Cryptophyceae from Hawaiian soil. *Phycologia* **5**: 217–21.

75 Bidoux, C. & F. Magne (1989). Etude de quelques Acrochaetiales (Rhodophyta) devant être rapportées au genre *Rhodothamniella*. *Crypt. Algol.* **10**: 33–55.

76 Billard, C. (1985). Le complexe nucleoplastidial chez les Chromophytes: structure, fonction et intérêt dans une perspective phylogénétique. *Crypt. Algol.* **6**: 191–211.

77 Billard, C. & J. Fresnel (1980). Nouvelles observations sur les ceintures supralittorales de Chrysophycophytes des côtes de la Manche. *C.R. 105e Congrès National des Sociétés Savantes, Caen, Sciences* **III**: 213–24.

78 Billard, C. & P. Gayral (1972). Two new species of *Isochrysis* with remarks on the genus *Ruttnera*. *Br. Phycol. J.* **7**: 289–97.

79 Binder, B.J. & D.M. Anderson (1986). Green light-mediated photomorphogenesis in a dinoflagellate resting cyst. *Nature* **322**: 659–61.

80 Binder, B.J. & D.M. Anderson (1987). Physiological and environmental control of germination in *Scrippsiella trochoidea* (Dinophyceae) resting cysts. *J. Phycol.* **23**: 99–107.

81 Bird, C.J. (1973). Aspects of the life-history and ecology of *Porphyra linearis* (Bangiales, Rhodophyceae) in nature. *Can. J. Bot.* **51**: 2371–9.

81a Bird, C.J., E.L. Rice, C.A. Murphy & M.A. Ragan (1992). Phylogenetic relationships in the Gracilariales (Rhodophyta) as determined by 18S rRNA sequences. *Phycologia* **31**: 510–22.

82 Bisalputra, T. (1965). The origin of the pectic layer of the cell wall of *Scenedesmus quadricauda*. *Can. J. Bot.* **43**: 1549–52.

83 Bisalputra, T. (1974). Plastids. In *Algal Physiology and Biochemistry*, ed. W.D.P. Stewart, pp. 124–60. Blackwell, Oxford.

84 Bisalputra, T. & A.A. Bisalputra (1969). The ultra-structure of chloroplast of a brown alga *Sphacelaria* sp. I. Plastid DNA configuration - the chloroplast genophore. *J. Ultrastruct. Res.* **29**: 151–70.

85 Bisalputra, T. & T.E. Weier (1963). The cell-wall of *Scenedesmus quadricauda*. *Am. J. Bot.* **50**: 1011–9.

86 Bisalputra, T., T.E. Weier, E.B. Risley & A.H.P. Engelbrecht (1964). The pectic layer of the cell wall of *Scenedesmus quadricauda*. *Am. J. Bot.* **51**: 548–51.

87 Bjørnland, T. & M. Aguilar-Martinez (1976). Carotenoids in red algae. *Phytochemistry* **15**: 291–6.

88 Bjørnland, T. & S. Liaaen-Jensen (1989). Distribution patterns of carotenoids in relation to chromophyte phylogeny and systematics. In *The Chromophyte Algae*, ed. J.C. Green, B.S.C. Leadbeater & W.L. Diver, pp. 37–61. Clarendon Press, Oxford.

89 Blackman, F. (1900). The primitive algae and the Flagellata. *Ann. Bot.* **14**: 647–88.

90 Blank, R.J. (1987). Evolutionary differentiation in gymnodinioid zooxanthellae. *Ann. New York Acad. Sci.* **503**: 530–3.

90a Bliding, C. (1963). A critical survey of European taxa in Ulvales. Part I. *Opera Bot.* **3**: 1–160.

91 Bliding, C. (1968). A critical survey of European taxa in Ulvales. Part II. *Bot. Not.* **121**: 535–629.

92 Boalch, G.T. & M. Parke (1971). The prasinophycean genera (Chlorophyta) possibly related to fossil genera, in particular the genus *Tasmanites*. In *Proceedings of the Second Plankton Conference, Roma, 1970*, ed. A. Farinacci, pp. 99–105. Tecnoscienza, Rome.

93 Boardmann, N.K., A.W. Linnane & R.M. Smillie (1971). *Autonomy and Biogenesis of Mitochondria and Chloroplasts*. North-Holland, Amsterdam.

94 Bodenbender, S. & R. Schnetter (1990). Nuclear behaviour during the life cycles of *Chaetomorpha*, *Ernodesmis* and *Struvea* (Ulvophyceae,

Chlorophyta) under culture conditions. *Crypt. Bot.* **1**: 340–54.

95   Bohnert, H.J. & W. Löffelhardt (1984). Genome and gene organization of the cyanelle DNA from *Cyanophora paradoxa* in relation to the common organization in chloroplasts. In *Compartments in Algal Cells and their Interaction*, ed. W. Wiesner, D. Robinson & R.C. Starr, pp. 58–67. Springer-Verlag, Berlin.

96   Bohnert, H.J., C. Michalowski, S. Bevacqa, H. Mucke & W. Löffelhardt (1985). Cyanelle DNA from *Cyanophora paradoxa. Molec. Gen. Genet.* **201**: 565–74.

97   Boillot, A. (1975). Cycle biologique de *Rhodochaete parvula* Thuret (Rhodophycées, Bangiophycidées). *Publ. Staz. Zool. Napoli*, Suppl. **39**: 67–83.

98   Boillot, A. (1984). Ultrastructure des racines striées contractiles d'un *Tetraselmis* marin. *Crypt. Algol.* **4**: 191–204.

99   Bold, H.C., C.J. Alexopoulos & T. Delevoryas (1987). *Morphology of Plants and Fungi.* Harper & Row, New York.

100   Bold, H.C. & M.J. Wynne (1985). *Introduction to the Algae, Structure and Reproduction.* Prentice Hall, Englewood Cliffs, New Jersey.

101   Bolton, J.J. & K. Lüning (1982). Optimal growth and maximal survival temperatures of Atlantic *Laminaria* species (Phaeophyta) in culture. *Mar. Biol.* **66**: 89–94.

102   Bonotto, S. (1988). Recent progress in research on *Acetabularia* and related Dasycladales. In *Progress in Phycological Research*, Vol. 6, ed. F.E. Round & D.J. Chapman, pp. 59–235. Biopress, Bristol.

103   Bonotto, S., P. Lurquin & A. Mazza (1976). Recent advances in research on the marine alga, *Acetabularia. Adv. Mar. Biol.* **14**: 123–250.

104   Booth, B.C. & H.J. Marchant (1987). Parmales, a new order of marine chrysophytes, with descriptions of three new genera and seven new species. *J. Phycol.* **23**: 245–60.

105   Børgesen, F. (1917). The marine algae of the Danish West Indies, Vol. 3: Rhodophyceae. *Dansk Bot. Ark.* **3**: 145–240.

106   Børgesen, F. (1952). Some marine algae from Mauritius. Addition to the parts previously published, IV. *Kgl. Danske Vidensk. Selsk. Biol. Medd.* **18**: 1–72.

107   Borman, A.H., E.W. de Jong, R. Thierry, P. Westbroek, L. Bosch, M. Gruter & J.P. Kamerling (1987). Coccolith-associated polysaccharides from cells of *Emiliania huxleyi* (Haptophyceae). *J. Phycol.* **23**: 118–23.

108   Borowitzka, M. (1976). Some unusual features of the ultrastructure of the chloroplasts of the green algal order Caulerpales and their development. *Protoplasma* **89**: 129–47.

109   Borowitzka, M.A. (1982). Mechanisms in algal calcification. In *Progress in Phycological Research*, Vol. 1., ed. F.E. Round & D.J. Chapman, pp. 137–77. Elsevier Biomedical Press, Amsterdam.

110   Bosence, D.W.J. (1985). The 'coralligène' of the Mediterranean – a recent analog for tertiary coralline algal limestones. In *Paleoalgologie, Contemporary Research and Applications*, ed. D.F. Toomey & M.H. Nitecki, pp. 216–25. Springer, Berlin.

111   Bot, P.V.M. , R.W. Holton, W.T. Stam & C. van den Hoek (1989). Molecular divergence between North Atlantic and Indo-West Pacific *Cladophora albida* (Cladophorales: Chlorophyta) isolates as indicated by DNA–DNA hybridization. *Mar. Biol.* **102**: 307–13.

112   Bouck, G.B. (1962). Chromatophore development, pits, and other fine structure in the red alga, *Lomentaria bayleyana* (Harv.) Farlow. *J. Cell Biol.* **12**: 553–70.

113   Bouck, G.B. (1965). Fine structure and organelle associations in brown algae. *J. Cell Biol.* **26**: 523–37.

114   Bouck, G.B. (1969). Extracellular microtubules. The origin, structure and attachment of flagellar hairs in *Fucus* and *Ascophyllum* antherozoids. *J. Cell Biol.* **4**: 65–86.

115   Bouck, G.B. (1971). The structure, origin, isolation and composition of the tubular mastigonemes of the *Ochromonas* flagellum. *J. Cell Biol.* **50**: 362–84.

116   Bouck, G.B. & D.L. Brown (1973). Microtubule biogenesis and cell shape in *Ochromonas*. I. The distribution of cytoplasmic and mitotic microtubules. *J. Cell Biol.* **56**: 340–59.

117   Bouck, G.B. (1982). Flagella and the cell surface. In *The Biology of Euglena*, Vol. III: *Physiology*, ed. D.E. Buetow, pp. 29–51. Academic Press, New York.

118   Bouck, G.B., A. Rogalski & A. Valaitis (1978).

Surface organization and composition of *Euglena*. II. Flagellar mastigonemes. *J. Cell Biol.* **77**: 805–26.

119 Bourne, V.L., E. Conway & K. Cole (1970). On the ultrastructure of pit connections in the *Conchocelis* phase of the red alga *Porphyra perforata*. *Phycologia* **9**: 79–82.

120 Bourrelly, P. (1957). Recherches sur les Chrysophycées. *Rev. Algol., Mém. h.s.* **1**: 1–412.

121 Bourrelly, P. (1966). *Les Algues d'Eau Douce*. Vol. I: *Les Algues Vertes*. Boubée, Paris.

122 Bourrelly, P. (1968). *Les Algues d'Eau Douce*. Vol. II: *Les Algues Jaunes et Brunes*. Boubée, Paris.

123 Bourrelly, P. (1970). *Les Algues d'Eau Douce*. Vol. III: *Les Algues Bleues et Rouges*. Boubée, Paris.

124 Bourrelly, P. (1981). *Les Algues d'Eau Douce*. Vol. II: *Les Algues Jaunes et Brunes*. Réimpression revue et augmentée. Boubée, Paris.

125 Bourrelly, P. (1985). *Les Algues d'Eau Douce*. Vol. III. *Les Algues Bleues et Rouges*. Réimpression revue et augmentée. Boubée, Paris.

126 Bovee, E.C. (1982). Movement and locomotion of *Euglena*. In *The Biology of Euglena*, Vol. III: *Physiology*, ed. D.E. Buetow, pp. 143–68. Academic Press, New York.

127 Boyle, J.A., J.D. Pickett-Heaps & D.B. Czarnecki (1984). Valve morphogenesis in the pennate diatom *Achnanthes coarctata*. *J. Phycol.* **20**: 563–73.

128 Brachet, J. & S. Bonotto (1970). *Biology of Acetabularia*. Academic Press, New York.

129 Brandham, P. & M.B.E. Godward (1965). Meiosis in *Cosmarium botrytis*. *Can. J. Bot.* **43**: 1379–86.

130 Brandt, P. (1984). Aspects of translational coordination during chloroplast development. In *Compartments in Algal Cells*, ed. W. Wiessner, D.G. Robinson & R.C. Starr, pp. 47–57. Springer-Verlag, Berlin.

131 Brandt, P., J. Winter, B. von Kessel & B. Kohnke (1987). Regulation of chloroplast differentiation: cooperation between light-induced processes and internal adaptation. In *Algal Development*, ed. W. Wiessner, D.G. Robinson & R.C. Starr, pp. 134–41. Springer-Verlag, Berlin.

132 Bråten, T. & Nordby, Ø. (1973). Ultrastructure of meiosis and centriole behaviour in *Ulva mutabilis* Føyn. *J. Cell Sci.* **13**: 69–81.

133 Bravo, L.M. (1965). Studies on the life history of *Prasiola meridionalis*. *Phycologia* **4**: 177–94.

134 Breeman, A.M. (1979). The caryological phases in the life history of *Acrosymphyton purpuriferum* (J. Ag.) Sjöst. (Rhodophyceae, Cryptonemiales). *Phycologia* **12**: 146–8.

135 Breeman, A.M. (1988). Relative importance of temperature and other factors in determining geographic boundaries of seaweeds: experimental and phenological evidence. *Helgol. Meeresunters.* **42**: 199–241.

136 Breeman, A.M., S. Bos, S. van Essen & L.L. van Mulekom (1984). Light-dark regimes in the intertidal zone and tetrasporangial periodicity in the red alga *Rhodochorton purpureum*. *Helgol. Meeresunters.* **38**: 365–87.

137 Breeman, A.M. & A. ten Hoopen (1981). Ecology and distribution of the subtidal red alga *Acrosymphyton purpuriferum* (J. Ag.) Sjöst. (Rhodophyceae, Cryptonemiales). *Aquat. Bot.* **11**: 143–66.

138 Breeman, A.M. & A. ten Hoopen (1984). Adaptation of photosynthesis to irradiance and daylength in the red alga *Acrosymphyton purpuriferum* (J. Ag.) Sjöst. (Rhodophyceae, Cryptonemiales), a species from the deep sublittoral region. *Phycologia* **23**: 223–31.

139 Breeman, A.M. & A. ten Hoopen (1987). The mechanism of daylength perception in the red alga *Acrosymphyton purpuriferum*. *J. Phycol.* **23**: 36–42.

140 Brent Heath, I. (1986). Nuclear division: a marker for protist phylogeny? In *Progress in Protistology*, Vol. 1, ed. J.O. Corliss & D.J. Patterson, pp. 115–62. Biopress, Bristol.

141 Brett, S.J. & R. Wetherbee (1986). A comparative study of periplast structure in *Cryptomonas cryophila* and *C. ovata* (Cryptophyceae). *Protoplasma* **131**: 23–31.

142 Brett, S.J. & R. Wetherbee (1988). Periplast structure and development in the Cryptophyceae. *3rd International Phycological Congress, Monash University, Melbourne, Abstracts*: 5.

143 Bristol, B.M. (1920). A review of the genus *Chlorochytrium* Cohn. *J. Linn. Soc. Bot.* **45**: 1–28.

144 Britton, R.J. (1986). Rates of DNA sequence evolution differ between taxonomic groups. *Science* **231**: 1393–8.

145 Broadwater, S.T. & J. Scott (1982). Ultrastructure of early development in the female

reproductive systems of *Polysiphonia harveyi* Bailey (Ceramiales, Rhodophyta). *J. Phycol.* **18**: 427–41.

146   Broadwater, S. & J. Scott (1983). Fibrous vacuole associated organelles (FVAOs) in the Florideophyceae: a new interpretation of the 'appareil cinétique'. *Phycologia* **22**: 225–33.

147   Broadwater, S., J. Scott & B. Pobiner (1986). Ultrastructure of meiosis in *Dasya baillouviana* (Rhodophyta). I. Prophase I. *J. Phycol.* **22**: 490–500.

148   Brock, T.D. (1973). Evolutionary and ecological aspects of the Cyanophytes. In *The Biology of Blue-green Algae*, ed. N.G. Carr & B.A. Whitton, pp. 487–500. Blackwell, Oxford.

149   Brokaw, C.J. (1962). Flagella. In *Physiology and Biochemistry of Algae*, ed. R.A. Lewin, pp. 595–602. Academic Press, New York.

150   Brongersma-Sanders, M. (1958). Mass mortality in the sea. In J.W. Hedgpeth (Ed.). Treatise on Marine Ecology and Paleo-ecology. I. *Geol. Soc. Am., Memoirs* **67**: 941–1010.

151   Brook, A.J. (1965). Planktonic algae as indicators of lake types, with special reference to the Desmidiaceae. *Limnol. Oceanogr.* **10**: 401–11.

152   Brook, A.J. (1981). *The Biology of Desmids.* Blackwell Scientific Publications, Oxford.

153   Brook, A.J. (1984). Comparative studies in a polyphyletic group, the Desmidiaceae – 30 years on. In *Systematics of the Green Algae*, ed. D.E.G. Irvine & D.M. John, pp. 251–69. Academic Press, London.

154   Brown, D.L., A. Massalski & R. Patenaude (1976). Organization of the flagellar apparatus and associated cytoplasmic microtubules in the quadriflagellate alga, *Polytomella agilis. J. Cell Biol.* **69**: 106–25.

155   Brown, D.L. & K.A. Rogers (1978). Hydrostatic pressure-induced internalization of flagellar axonemes, disassembly, and reutilization during flagellar regeneration in *Polytomella. Exp. Cell Res.* **117**: 313–24.

156   Brown, L.M. & J. McLachlan (1982). Atypical carotenoids for the Rhodophyceae in the genus *Gracilaria* (Gigartinales). *Phycologia* **21**: 9–16.

157   Brown, R., C. Sister, O.P. Johnson & H.C. Bold (1968). Electron and phasecontrast microscopy of sexual reproduction in *Chlamydomonas moewusii. J. Phycol.* **4**: 100–20.

158   Brown, R.M., W.W. Franke, H. Kleinig, H. Falk & P. Sitte (1970). Scale formation in Chrysophycean algae I. Cellulosic and non cellulosic components made by the Golgi-apparatus. *J. Cell Biol.* **45**: 246–71.

159   Brunke, K., J. Anthony, E. Sternberg & D. Weeks (1984). Regulation of tubulin gene expression in *Chlamydomonas reinhardii* following flagellar excision. In *Compartments in Algal Cells and their Interaction,* ed. W. Wiessner, D.G. Robinson & R.C. Starr, pp. 88–95. Springer, Berlin.

160   Buchheim, M.A., R.L. Chapman & E.A. Zimmer (1989). Cytoplasmic rRNA sequence data and the systematics of the genus *Chlamydomonas. J. Phycol.* **25** (suppl.): 7.

160a   Buchheim, M.A. & L.R. Hoffman (1986). Ultrastructure of the male gametes of *Sphaeroplea robusta* (Chlorophyceae). *J. Phycol.* **22**: 176–85.

160b   Buchheim, M.A., M. Turmel, E.A. Zimmer & R.L. Chapman (1990). Phylogeny of *Chlamydomonas* (Chlorophyta) based on cladistic analysis of nuclear rRNA sequence data. *J. Phycol.* **26**: 689–99.

161   Buchner, P. (1953). *Endosymbiose der Tiere mit pflanzlichen Mikroorganismen.* Birkhauer, Basel.

162   Buetow, D.E. (ed.) (1982). *The Biology of Euglena,* vol. III: *Physiology.* Academic Press, New York.

163   Buggeln, R.G. (1983). Photoassimilate translocation in brown algae. In *Progress in Phycological Research,* Vol. 2, ed. F.E. Round & D.J. Chapman, pp. 283–332. Elsevier, Amsterdam.

164   Buggeln, R.G. (1983). The cross-wing translocation pathway in the blade of *Alaria esculenta* (Laminariales, Phaeophyceae). *Phycologia* **22**: 205–9.

165   Buggeln, R.G., D.S. Fenson & C.J. Emerson (1985). Translocation of ^{11}C-photoassimalate in the blade of *Macrocystis pyrifera* (Phaeophyceae). *J. Phycol.* **21**: 35–40.

166   Bullman, V. & K.R. Roberts (1986). Structure of the flagellar apparatus in *Heterocapsa pygmaea* (Pyrrophyta). *Phycologia* **25**: 558–71.

167   Burger-Wiersma, T. & L.R. Mur (1989). Genus '*Prochlorothrix*' Burger-Wiersma, Veenhuis, Korthals, van de Wiel and Mur 1986. In *Bergey's Manual of Systematic Bacteriology,* Vol. 3, Section 19: *Oxygenic photosynthetic bacteria,* ed. J.T.

Staley, M.P. Bryant, N.F. Pfennig & J.H. Holt, pp. 1805–6. Williams & Wilkins, Baltimore.

168 Burger-Wiersma, T., M. Veenhuis, H.J. Korthals, C.C.M. van de Wiel & L.R. Mur (1986). A new prokaryote containing chlorophylls a and b. *Nature* **320**: 262–4.

169 Burr, F.A. & J.A. West (1970). Light and electron microscope observations on the vegetative and reproductive structures of *Bryopsis hypnoides.* *Phycologia* **9**: 17–37.

170 Burr, F.A. & J.A. West (1971a). Protein bodies in *Bryopsis hypnoides:* their relationship to wound-healing and branch septum development. *J. Ultrastruct. Res.* **35**: 476–98.

171 Burr, F.A. & J.A. West (1971b). Comparative ultrastructure of the primary nucleus in *Bryopsis* and *Acetabularia*. *J. Phycol.* **7**: 108–13.

172 Butcher, R.W. (1959). *An Introductory Account of the Smaller Algae of the British Coastal Waters.* Part I: *Introduction and Chlorophyceae.* Her Majesty's Stationery Office, London.

173 Butcher, R.W. (1967). *An Introductory Account of the Smaller Algae of British Coastal Waters.* Part IV: *Crytophyceae.* Her Majesty's Stationery Office, London.

174 Cabioch, J. (1972). Etude sur les Corallinacées. II. La morphogénèse: conséquences systématiques et biologiques. *Cah. Biol. Mar. Roscoff* **13**: 137–288.

175 Cabioch, J. (1988). Morphogenesis and generic concepts in coralline algae – a reappraisal. *Helgol. Meeresunters.* **42**: 493–509.

176 Cabioch, J. & G. Giraud (1986). Structural aspects of biomineralization in the coralline algae (calcified Rhodophyceae). In *Biomineralization in Lower Plants and Animals,* ed. B.S.C. Leadbeater & R. Reading, pp. 141–56. Clarendon Press, Oxford.

177 Cáceres, E.J. & D.G. Robinson (1980). Ultrastructural studies on *Sphaeroplea annulina* (Chlorophyceae). Vegetative structure and mitosis. *J. Phycol.* **16**: 313–20.

178 Cáceres, E.J. & D.G. Robinson (1981). Ultrastructural studies on *Sphaeroplea annulina* (Chlorophyceae). II. Spermatogenesis and male gamete structure. *J. Phycol.* **17**: 173–80.

179 Cachon, J. & M. Cachon (1985). Class Polycistinea Ehrenberg 1838, emend. Riedel 1967. In *An Illustrated Guide to the Protozoa,* ed. J.J. Lee, S.H. Hutner & E.C. Bovee, pp. 283–95. Society of Protozoologists, Lawrence, Kansas.

180 Cachon, J. & M. Cachon (1987). Parasitic dinoflagellates. In *The Biology of Dinoflagellates,* ed. F.J.R. Taylor, pp. 571–610. Blackwell Scientific Publications, Oxford.

181 Cachon, M. & B. Caram (1979). A symbiotic green alga, *Pedinomonas symbiotica* sp. nov. (Prasinophyceae), in the radiolarian *Thalassolampe margarodes. Phycologia* **18**: 177–84.

182 Cadée, G.C. (1990). Increase of *Phaeocystis* blooms in the westernmost inlet of the Wadden Sea, the Marsdiep, since 1973. In *Eutrophication and Algal Blooms in North Sea Coastal Zones, the Baltic and Adjacent Areas (Water Pollution Research Report 12),* ed. C. Lancelot, G. Billen & H. Barth, pp. 105–12. Brussels.

183 Cadée, G.C. & J. Hegeman (1974). Primary production of the benthic microflora living on tidal flats in the Dutch Wadden Sea. *Neth. J. Sea Res.* **8**: 260–91.

184 Calderón-Sáenz, E. & R. Schnetter (1987). *Cryptochlora perforans,* a new genus and species of algae (Chlorarachniophyta) capable of penetrating dead algal filaments. *Pl. Syst. Evol.* **158**: 69–71.

185 Calderón-Sáenz, E. & R. Schnetter (1989). Life cyle and morphology of *Bryopsidella ostreobiformis* spec. nov. (Bryopsidaceae, Chlorophyta) from the Mediterranean, under culture conditions, with comments on the phylogeny of the *Bryopsis/Derbesia* complex. *Botanica Acta* **102**: 249–60.

186 Calvin, M. (1969). *Chemical Evolution.* Oxford University Press, London.

187 Campbell, S.E. (1980). *Paleoconchocelis starmachii,* a carbonate boring microfossil from the Upper Silurian of Poland (425 million years old): implications for the evolution of the Bangiaceae (Rhodophyta). *Phycologia* **19**: 25–36.

188 Caram, B. (1965). Recherches sur la reproduction et le cycle sexué de quelques Phéophycées. *Vie Milieu* **16**: 21–221.

189 Carlberg, G.E. & E. Percival (1977). The carbohydrates of the green seaweeds *Urospora wormskioldii* and *Codiolum pusillum. Carbohydr. Res.* **57**: 223–34.

190 Carr, N.G. (1989). Nitrogen reserves and dynamic reservoirs in Cyanobacteria. In *Biochemistry of the Algae and Cyanobacteria,* ed. L.J. Rogers & J.R. Gallon, pp. 13–21. Clarendon Press, Oxford.

191   Carr, N.G. & B.A. Whitton (eds) (1973). *The Biology of Blue-green Algae.* Blackwell, Oxford.

192   Carr, N.G. & B.A. Whitton (eds) (1982). *The Biology of Cyanobacteria.* Blackwell, Oxford.

193   Carrothers, Z.B. & J.G. Duckett (1988). The bryophyte spermatozoid: a source of new phylogenetic information. *Bull. Torrey Bot. Club* **107**: 281–97.

194   Castenholz, R.W. (1989). Subsection III. Order Oscillatoriales. Subsection IV. Order Nostocales. Subsection V. Order Stigonematales. In *Bergey's Manual of Systematic Bacteriology,* Vol. 3. Section 19: *Oxygenic photosynthetic bacteria,* ed. J.T. Staley, M.P. Bryant, N. Pfennig & J.H. Holt, pp. 1771–99. Williams & Wilkins, Baltimore.

195   Castenholz, R.W. & J.B. Waterbury (1989). Oxygenic photosynthetic bacteria. Group I. Cyanobacteria. In *Bergey's Manual of Systematic Bacteriology,* Vol. 3. Section 19: *Oxygenic photosynthetic bacteria,* ed. J.T. Staley, M.P. Bryant, N. Pfennig & J.H. Holt, pp. 1710–806. Williams & Wilkins, Baltimore.

196   Catt, J.W., G.J. Hills & K. Roberts (1976). A structural glycoprotein containing hydroxyproline, isolated from the cell wall of *Chlamydomonas reinhardtii. Planta* **131**: 165–71.

197   Catt, J.W., G.J. Hills & K. Roberts (1978). Cell wall glycoproteins from *Chlamydomonas reinhardtii,* and their self-assembly. *Planta* **138**: 91–8.

198   Cattolico, R.A. (1985). Chloroplast biosystematics: chloroplast DNA as a molecular probe. *BioSystems* **18**: 299–306.

199   Cavalier-Smith, T. (1974). Basal body and flagellar development during the vegetative cell cycle and the sexual cycle of *Chlamydomonas reinhardtii. J. Cell Sci.* **16**: 529–56.

200   Cavalier-Smith, T. (1975). The origin of nuclei and of eukaryotic cells. *Nature* **256**: 463–8.

201   Cavalier-Smith, T. (1978). The evolutionary origin and phylogeny of microtubules, mitotic spindles, and eukaryote flagella. *BioSystems* **10**: 93–114.

202   Cavalier-Smith, T. (1981). The origin and early evolution of the eukaryotic cell. *Symp. Soc. Gen. Microbiol.* **32**: 33–84.

203   Cavalier-Smith, T. (1982). The origin of plastids. *Biol. J. Linn. Soc.* **17**: 289–306.

204   Cedergren, R., M.W. Gray , Y. Abel & D. Sankoff (1988). The evolutionary relationships among known life forms. *J. Molec. Evol.* **28**: 98–112.

205   Chalker, B.E. & D.L. Taylor (1975). Light enhanced calcification and the role of oxidative phosphorylation in calcification of the coral *Acropora cervicornis. Proc. R. Soc. Lond.* B**190**: 323–31.

206   Chan, K.-Y., S.L.L. Wong & M.H. Wong (1978). Observations on *Chaetomorpha brachygona* Harv. (Chlorophyta, Cladophorales). 1. Ultrastructure of the vegetative cells. *Phycologia* **17**: 419–29.

207   Chantanachat, S. & H.C. Bold (1962). Phycological Studies II. Some algae from arid soils. *Univ. Texas Publ.* **6218**: 1–75.

208   Chapman, D.J. (1966). The pigments of symbiotic algae of *Cyanophora paradoxa, Glaucocystis nostochinearum* and two Rhodophyceae, *Porphyridium aeruginosum* and *Asterocystis ramosa. Arch. Mikrobiol.* **55**: 17–25.

209   Chapman, D.J. (1973). Biliproteins and bilipigments. In *The Biology of Blue-green Algae,* ed. N.G. Carr & B.A. Whitton, pp. 162–85. Blackwell, Oxford.

210   Chapman, R.L. (1980). Ultrastructure of *Cephaleuros virescens* (Chroolepidaceae; Chlorophyta). II. Gametes. *Am. J. Bot.* **67**: 10–17.

211   Chapman, R.L. (1981). Ultrastructure of *Cephaleuros virescens* (Chroolepidaceae; Chlorophyta). III. Zoospores. *Am. J. Bot* **68**: 544–56.

212   Chapman, R.L. (1984). An assessment of the current state of our knowledge of the Trentepohliaceae. In *Systematics of the Green Algae,* ed. D.E.G. Irvine & D.M. John, pp. 233–50. Academic Press, London.

213   Chapman, R.L., D.W. Avery & E.A. Zimmer (1989). Nuclear ribosomal RNA genes and the phylogeny of the Trentepohliales. *J. Phycol.* **25** (suppl.): 8.

213a Chapman, R.L. & M.A. Buchheim (1991). Ribosomal RNA gene sequences: analysis and significance in the phylogeny and taxonomy of green algae. *Critical Reviews in Plant Sciences* **10**: 343–68.

214   Chapman, R.L. & B.H. Good (1978). Ultrastructure of plasmodesmata and crosswalls in *Cephaleuros, Phycopeltis* and *Trentepohlia* (Chroolepidaceae; Chlorophyta). *Br. Phycol. J.* **13**: 241–6.

215   Chapman, R.L. & B.H. Good (1983). Subaerial

symbiotic green algae: interactions with vascular plant hosts. In *Algal Symbiosis*, ed. L.J. Goff, pp. 173–204. Cambridge University Press.

216   Chapman, R.L. & M.C. Henk (1983). Ultrastructure of *Cephaleuros virescens* (Chroolepidaceae; Chlorophyta). IV. Absolute configuration analysis of the cruciate flagellar apparatus and multilayered structures in the pre- and post-release gametes. *Am. J. Bot.* **70**: 1340–55.

217   Chapman, R.L. & M.C. Henk (1985). Observations on the habit, morphology and ultrastructure of *Cephaleuros parasiticus* (Chlorophyta) and a comparison with *C. virescens*. *J. Phycol.* **21**: 513–22.

218   Chapman, R.L. & M.C. Henk (1986). Phragmoplasts in cytokinesis of *Cephaleuros parasiticus* (Chlorophyta) vegetative cells. *J. Phycol.* **22**: 83–8.

219   Chapman, V.J. (1970). *Seaweeds and Their Uses*. 2nd Ed. Methuen, London.

220   Chapman, V.J. & D.J. Chapman (1973). *The Algae*. Macmillan, London.

221   Chapman, V.J. & Chapman, D.J. (1980). *Seaweeds and their Uses*. 3rd Ed. Chapman & Hall, London.

222   Chappell, D.F. & G.L. Floyd (1981). Cell division in the weakly filamentous *Raphidonema sessile* (= *Raphidonemopsis sessilis*) (Chlorophyta). *Trans. Am. Microsc. Soc.* **100**: 74–82.

223   Chardard, R. (1987). L'infrastructure du plasmalemme de *Dunaliella bioculata* (algue verte). Mise en évidence d'un cell coat; essai de localisation de charges négatives. *Crypt. Algol.* **8**: 173–90.

224   Chen, L.C.-M., T. Edelstein & J. McLachlan (1974). The life history of *Gigartina stellata* (Stackh.) Batt. (Rhodophyceae, Gigartinales) in culture. *Phycologia* **13**: 287–94.

225   Chen, L.C.-M. & J. McLachlan (1972). The life history of *Chondrus crispus* in culture. *Can. J. Bot.* **50**: 1055–60.

226   Chesnick, J.M. & E.R. Cox (1987). Ultrastructure of sexual stages in the binucleate flagellate *Peridinium balticum*. *J. Phycol.* **23** (suppl.): 16.

226a   Chiappino, M.L. & B.E. Volcani (1977). Studies on the biochemistry and fine structure of silica shell formation in diatoms. VII. Sequential cell wall development in the pennate *Navicula pelliculosa*. *Protoplasma* **93**: 205–21.

227   Chihara, M. (1956). Studies on the life history of green algae in the warm seas around Japan (4). On the life history of *Halimeda cuneata* Hernig. *J. Jap. Bot.* **3**: 102–10.

228   Chihara, M. (1959). Studies on the life history of the green algae in the warm seas around Japan (9). Supplementary note on the life history of *Valonia*. *J. Jap. Bot.* **34**: 257–66.

229   Chisholm, S.W., R.J. Olsen, E.R. Zettler, R. Goericke, J.B. Waterbury & N.A. Welschmeyer (1988). A novel free-living prochlorophyte abundant in the oceanic euphotic zone. *Nature* **334**: 340–3.

230   Chorin-Kirsh, I. & A.M. Mayer (1964). ATP-ase activity in isolated flagella of *Chlamydomonas snowiae*. *Plant Cell Physiol.* **5**: 441–5.

230a   Chrétiennot-Dinet, M.J. (1990). *Atlas du Phytoplankton Marin*, Vol. 3. Centre National de la Recherche Scientifique, Paris.

231   Christensen, T. (1962). Alger. In *Botanik*, Vol. II/2, ed. T.W. Böcher, M. Lange & T. Sørensen, pp. 1–178. Munksgaard, Copenhagen.

232   Christensen, T. (1964). The gross classification of algae. In *Algae and Man*, ed. D.F. Jackson, pp. 59–64. Plenum Press, New York.

233   Christensen, T. (1987). *Seaweeds of the British Isles*, Vol. 4: *Tribophyceae (Xanthophyceae)*. British Museum (Natural History), London.

234   Clayton, M.N. (1980). Sexual reproduction – a rare occurrence in the life history of the complanate form of *Scytosiphon* (Scytosiphonaceae, Phaeophyta) from southern Australia. *Br. Phycol. J.* **15**: 105–18.

235   Clayton, M.N. (1981a). Experimental analysis of the life history of the complanate form of *Scytosiphon* (Scytosiphonaceae, Phaeophyta) in southern Australia. *Phycologia* **20**: 358–64.

236   Clayton, M.N. (1981b). Observations on the factors controlling the reproduction of two common species of brown algae, *Colpomenia peregrina* and *Scytosiphon* sp. (Scytosiphonaceae), in Victoria. *Proc. Roy. Soc. Vict.* **92**: 113–18.

237   Clayton, M.N. (1984a). An electron microscope study of gamete release and settling in the complanate form of *Scytosiphon* (Scytosiphonaceae, Phaeophyta). *J. Phycol.* **20**: 276–85.

238   Clayton, M.N. (1984b). Evolution of the Phaeophyta with particular reference to the Fucales. In *Progress in Phycological Research*, Vol. 3, ed.

F.E. Round & D.J. Chapman, pp. 11–46. Biopress, Bristol.

239   Clayton, M.N. (1987). Isogamy and a fucalean type of life history in the Antarctic brown alga *Ascoseira mirabilis* (Ascoseirales, Phaeophyta). *Botanica Mar.* **30**: 447–54.

240   Clayton, M.N. (1988). Evolution and life histories of brown algae. *Botanica Mar.* **31**: 379–87.

241   Clayton, M.N., N.D. Hallam & C.M. Shankley (1987). The seasonal pattern of conceptacle development and gamete maturation in *Durvillaea potatorum* (Durvillaeales, Phaeophyta). *Phycologia* **26**: 35–45.

241a   Cmiech, H.A., G.F. Leedale & C.S. Reynolds (1987). Morphological and ultrastructural variability of planktonic Cyanophyceae in relation to seasonal periodicity. III. *Gomphosphaeria naegeliana*. *Br. Phycol. J.* **22**: 339–43.

242   Codd, G.A. & G.K. Poon (1989). Cyanobacterial toxins. In *Biochemistry of the Algae and Cyanobacteria*, ed. L.J. Rogers & J.R. Gallon, pp. 283–96. Oxford Scientific Publications, Clarendon Press, Oxford.

243   Coesel, P.F.M. (1981). *Distribution and ecology of desmids in a Dutch broads area*. Thesis, University of Amsterdam.

244   Coesel, P.F.M. & W. de Jong (1986). Vigorous chemotactic attraction as a sexual response in *Closterium ehrenbergii* Meneghini (Desmidiaceae, Chlorophyta). *Phycologia* **25**: 405–8.

245   Coesel, P.F.M., R. Kwakkestein & A. Verschoor (1978). Oligotrophication and eutrophication tendencies in some Dutch moorland pools, as reflected in their desmid flora. *Hydrobiologia* **61**: 21–31.

246   Coesel, P.F.M. & R.M.V. Teixeira (1974). Notes on sexual reproduction in desmids. II. Experiences with conjugating experiments in unialgal cultures. *Acta Bot. Neerl.* **23**: 603–11.

247   Cogburn, J.N. & J.A. Schiff (1984). Purification and properties of the mucus of *Euglena gracilis* (Euglenophyceae). *J. Phycol.* **20**: 533–44.

248   Cohen-Bazire, G. & D.A. Bryant (1982). Phycobilisomes: Composition and structure. In *The Biology of Cyanobacteria*, ed. N.G. Carr & B.A. Whitton, pp. 143–90. Blackwell Scientific Publications, Oxford.

249   Colbath, G.K. (1983). Fossil prasinophycean phycomata (Chlorophyta) from the Silurian Bainbridge formation, Missouri, USA. *Phycologia* **22**: 249–65.

250   Cole, K. & S. Akintobi (1963). The life-cycle of *Prasiola meridionalis* Setchell and Gardner. *Can J. Bot.* **41**: 661–8.

251   Coleman, A.W. (1962). Sexuality. In *Physiology and Biochemistry of Algae*, ed. R.A. Lewin, pp. 711–29. Academic Press, New York.

252   Coleman, A.W. (1979). Sexuality in colonial green flagellates. In *Physiology and Biochemistry of the Protozoa*, Vol.1. 2nd Ed, ed. S.H. Hutner & M. Levandowsky, pp. 307–40. Academic Press, New York.

253   Coleman, A.W. (1983). The roles of resting spores and akinetes in chlorophyte survival. In *Survival Strategies of the Algae*, ed. G.A. Fryxell, pp. 1–21. Cambridge University Press.

254   Coleman, A.W. (1985). Diversity of plastid DNA configuration among classes of eukaryote algae. *J. Phycol.* **21**: 1–16.

255   Coleman, A.W. & P. Heywood (1981). Structure of the chloroplast and its DNA in chloromonadophycean algae. *J. Cell Sci.* **49**: 401–9.

256   Coleman, A.W., L.J. Moore & L.J. Goff (1987). The many applications of results from molecular analysis of organelle genomes in chrysophytes, chlorophytes and rhodophytes. *14th International Botanical Congress Berlin (West), Abstracts:* 156. (Collated and edited by W. Greuter, B. Zimmer & H.D. Behnke; produced with the assistance of M.I. Hakki, H. Sipman and staff members of the Botanical Museum Berlin-Dahlem.)

257   Colijn, F. (1983). *Primary production in the Ems-Dollard Estuary.* Biologisch Onderzoek Eems-Dollard Estuarium, Vakgroep Mariene Biologie, Publicaties en Verslagen no. 2 1983. Thesis, University of Groningen: 1–123.

258   Colijn, F. & C. van den Hoek (1971). The life-history of *Sphacelaria furcigera* Kütz. (Phaeophyceae). II. The influence of day-length and temperature on sexual and vegetative reproduction. *Nova Hedwigia* **21**: 899–922.

259   Colombetti, G., F. Lenci & B. Diehn (1982). Responses to photic, chemical and mechanical stimuli. In *The Biology of Euglena*, ed. D.E. Buetow, pp. 143–68. Academic Press, New York.

260   Coombs, J. & B.E. Volcani (1968). Studies on the biochemistry and fine structure of silica-shell formation in diatoms. Chemical changes in the wall

of *Navicula pelliculosa* during its formation. *Planta* **82**: 280–92.

261   Corliss, J.O. (1984). The kingdom Protista and its 45 phyla. *BioSystems* **17**: 87–126.

262   Correa, J., I. Novaczek & J. McLachlan (1986). Effect of temperature and daylength on morphogenesis of *Scytosiphon lomentaria* (Scytosiphonales, Phaeophyta) from eastern Canada. *Phycologia* **25**: 469–75.

263   Cortel-Breeman, A.M. (1975). The life-history of *Acrosymphyton purpuriferum* (J. Ag.) Sjöst. (Rhodophyceae, Cryptonemiales). Isolation of tetrasporophytes. With some remarks on the tetrasporophyte of *Bonnemaisonia asparagoides* (Woodw.) C. Ag. (Nemalionales). *Acta Bot. Neerl.* **24**: 111–27.

264   Cortel-Breeman, A.M. & C. van den Hoek (1970). Life-history studies on Rhodophyceae. I. *Acrosymphyton purpurifereum* (J. Ag.) Kyl. *Acta Bot. Neerl.* **19**: 265–84.

265   Cortel-Breeman, A.M. & A. ten Hoopen (1978). The short-day response in *Acrosymphyton purpuriferum* (J. Ag.) Sjöst. (Rhodophyceae, Cryptonemiales). *Phycologia* **17**: 125–32.

266   Cote, G.T. & M.J. Wynne (1974). Endocytosis of *Microcystis aeruginosa* by *Ochromonas danica*. *J. Phycol.* **10**: 397–410.

267   Coulson, J.C., G.K. Potts, I.R. Deans & S.M. Fraser (1968). Mortality of shags and other seabirds caused by paralytic shellfish poison. *Nature* **220**: 23–4.

268   Cozens, A.L. & J.E. Walker (1987). The organization and sequence of the genes for ATP synthase subunits in the cyanobacterium *Synechococcus* 6301. Support for an endosymbiotic origin of chloroplasts. *J. Molec. Biol.* **194**: 359–83.

269   Craigie, J.S. (1974). Storage products. In *Algal Physiology and Biochemistry*, ed. W.D.P. Stewart, pp. 206–35. Blackwell, Oxford.

270   Crawford, R.M. (1973). The organic component of the cell wall of the marine diatom *Melosira nummuloides* (Dillw.) C. Ag. *Br. Phycol. J.* **8**: 257–66.

271   Crayton, M.A. (1980). Presence of a sulphated polysaccharide in the extracellular matrix of *Platydorina caudata* (Volvocales, Chlorophyta). *J. Phycol.* **16**: 80–7.

272   Crayton, M.A. (1982). Comparative cytochemical study of Volvocalean matrix polysaccharides. *J. Phycol.* **18**: 336–44.

273   Cronberg, G. (1986). Chrysophycean cysts and scales in lake sediments: a review. In *Chrysophytes: Aspects and Problems*, ed. J. Kristiansen & R.A. Andersen, pp. 281–315. Cambridge University Press.

274   Cunningham, E.M. & M.D. Guiry (1989). A circadian rhythm in the long-day photoperiodic induction of erect axis development in the marine red alga *Nemalion helminthoides*. *J. Phycol.* **25**: 705–12.

275   Cushman, J.C., R.B. Hallick & C.A. Price (1988). The two genes for the P700 chlorophyll a apoproteins on the *Euglena gracilis* chloroplast genome contain multiple introns. *Curr. Genet.* **13**: 159–71.

276   Czygan, F. (1970). Blutregen und Blutschnee: Stickstoffmangel-Zellen von *Haematococcus pluvialis* und *Chlamydomonas nivalis*. *Arch. Mikrobiol.* **74**: 69–76.

277   Daily, F.K. (1982). Charophyceae. In *Synopsis and Classification of Living Organisms*, Vol. I, ed. S.P. Parker, pp. 161–2. McGraw-Hill, New York.

278   Dale, B. (1976). Cyst formation, sedimentation, and preservation: factors affecting dinoflagellate assemblages in recent sediments from Trondheimsfjord, Norway. *Rev. Palaeobot. Palynol.* **22**: 39–60.

279   Dale, B. (1983). Dinoflagellate resting cysts: 'benthic plankton'. In *Survival Strategies of the Algae*, ed. G.A. Fryxell, pp. 69–136. Cambridge University Press.

280   Dale, B. (1986). Life cycle strategies of oceanic dinoflagellates. In *Pelagic Biogeography*, ed. A.C. Pierrot-Bults, S. van der Spoel, B.J. Zahuranec & R.K. Johnson, pp. 65–72. UNESCO technical papers in marine science **49**.

281   Dangeard, P. (1959). Recherches sur quelques 'Codium'. Leur reproduction et leur parthenogénèse. *Botaniste* **42**: 66–8.

282   Dangeard, P. (1965). Sur deux Chlorococcales marines. *Botaniste* **48**: 65–74.

283   Dangeard, P. & H. Parriaud (1956). Sur quelques cas de développement apogamique chex deux espèces de *Codium* de la région Sud-Ouest. *C.R. Acad. Sci.* **243**: 1981–3.

284   Daniel, G.F., A.H.L. Chamberlain & E.B.G. Jones (1987). Cytochemical and electron microscopical observations on the adhesive materials of marine fouling diatoms. *Br. Phycol. J.* **22**: 101–18.

285   Darley, W.M. (1974). Silicification and calcifi-

cation. In *Algal Physiology and Biochemistry*, ed. W.D.P. Stewart, pp. 655–75. Blackwell, London.

286 Darling, R.B., E.I. Friedmann & P.A. Broady (1987). *Heterococcus endolithicus* sp. nov. (Xanthophyceae) and other terrestrial *Heterococcus* species from Antarctica: morphological changes during life history and response to temperature. *J. Phycol.* **23**: 598–607.

287 Darwin, C. (1859). *On the Origin of Species by Natural Selection.* John Murray, London.

288 Dave, A.J. & M.B.E. Godward (1982). Ultrastructural studies in the Rhodophyta. I. Development of mitotic spindle poles in *Apoglossum ruscifolium*, Kylin. *J. Cell Sci.* **58**: 345–362.

289 Davis, J.S. (1967). The life cycle of *Pediastrum simplex*. *J. Phycol.* **3**: 95–103.

290 Dawes, C.J. (1966). A light and electron microscope survey of algal cell walls II. Chlorophyceae. *Ohio J. Sci.* **66**: 317–26.

291 Deason, T.R. (1965). Some observations on the fine structure of vegetative and dividing cells of *Chlorococcum echinozygotum* Starr. *J. Phycol.* **1**: 97–101.

292 Deason, T.R. (1983). Cell wall structure and composition as taxonomic characters in the coccoid Chlorophyceae. *J. Phycol.* **19**: 248–51.

293 Deason, T.R. (1984). A discussion of the classes Chlamydophyceae and Chlorophyceae and their subordinate taxa. *Pl. Syst. Evol.* **146**: 75–81.

294 Deason, T.R. (1987). An ultrastructural comparison of two coccoid green algae. *J. Phycol.* **23** (suppl.): 14.

295 Deason, T.R. & H.C. Bold (1960). Phycological studies. I. Exploratory studies of Texal soil algae. *Univ. Texas Publ.* **6022**: 1–72.

296 Deason, T.R. & G.L. Floyd (1987). Comparative ultrastructure of three species of *Chlorosarcina* (Chlorosarcinaceae, Chlorophyta). *J. Phycol.* **23**: 187–95.

297 Deason, T.R. & C.J. O'Kelly (1979). Mitosis and cleavage during zoosporogenesis in several coccoid green algae. *J. Phycol.* **15**: 371–8.

298 Deason, T.R., P.E. Ryals, C.J. O'Kelly & K.W. Bullock (1979). Fine structure of mitosis and cleavage in *Friedmannia israelensis*. *J. Phycol.* **15**: 452–7.

299 De Cew, T.C. & J.A. West (1981). Life histories in the Phyllophoraceae (Rhodophyta: Gigartinales) from the Pacific coast of North America. I. *Gymnogongrus linearis* and *G. leptophyllus*. *J. Phycol.* **17**: 240–50.

300 De Cew, T.C. & J.A. West (1982). A sexual life history in *Rhodophysema elegans* (Rhodophyceae): a re-interpretation. *Phycologia* **21**: 67–74.

300a Deflandre, G. (1952a). Classe des Silicoflagellidés. In *Traité de Zoologie*, Vol. I, part 1, ed. P.P. Grassé, pp. 425–38. Masson, Paris.

301 Deflandre, G. (1952b). Classe des Coccolithophoridés. In *Traité de Zoologie*, Vol. I, part 1, ed. P.P. Grassé, pp. 439–70. Masson, Paris.

302 Delépine, R. (1959). Observations sur quelques *Codium* (Chlorophycées) des côtes françaises. *Rev. Gén. Bot.* **66**: 366–94.

303 Dentler, W.L. & J.L. Rosenbaum (1977). Flagellar elongation and shortening in *Chlamydomonas*. III. Structures attached to the tips of flagellar microtubules and their relationship to the directionality of flagellar microtubule assembly. *J. Cell Biol.* **74**: 747–59.

304 Dick, M.W. (1990). Phylum Oomycota. In *Handbook of Protoctista*, ed. L. Margulis, J.O. Corliss, M. Melkonian & D.J. Chapman, pp. 661–85. Jones & Bartlett, Boston.

305 Dieck, I. tom (1987). Temperature tolerance and daylength effects in isolates of *Scytosiphon lomentaria* (Phaeophyceae) of the North Atlantic and Pacific Ocean. *Helgol. Meeresunters.* **41**: 307–21.

306 Dion, P. & R. Delépine (1979). Cycles de développement de *Gigartina stellata* et *Petrocelis cruenta* (Rhodophyceae, Gigartinales). *Rev. Algol.* N.S. **14**: 327–41.

307 Diwald, K. (1938). Die ungeschlechtliche und geschlechtliche Fortpflanzung von *Glenodinium lubinensiforme* sp. nova. *Flora* **32**: 174–92.

308 Dixon, P.S. (1959). The structure and development of the reproductive organs and carposporophyte in two British species of *Gelidium*. *Ann. Bot.* N.S. **23**: 397–407.

309 Dixon, P.S. (1973). *Biology of the Rhodophyta.* Oliver & Boyd, Edinburgh.

310 Dixon, P.S. & L.M. Irvine (1977). *Seaweeds of the British Isles*, Vol. 1. *Rhodophyta*, Part 1.: *Introduction, Nemaliales, Gigartinales*. British Museum (Natural History), London.

311 Dixon, P.S. & W.N. Richardson (1969). The life-histories of *Bangia* and *Porphyra* and the photoperiodic control of spore production. *Proc. 6th Int. Seaweed Symp.*, 133–9.

312 Dobberstein, B. & O. Kiermayer (1972). Das Auftreten eines besonderen Typs von Golgivesikeln während der Sekundärwandbildung von *Micrasterias denticulata* Bréb. *Protoplasma* 75: 185–94.

313 Dodge, J.D. (1966). The Dinophyceae. In *The Chromosomes of Algae*, ed. M.B.E. Godward, pp. 96–115. Arnold, London.

314 Dodge, J.D. (1968). The fine structure of chloroplasts and pyrenoids in some marine dinoflagellates. *J. Cell Sci.* 3: 4–48.

315 Dodge, J.D. (1969). A review of the fine structure of algal eyespots. *Br. Phycol. J.* 4: 199–210.

316 Dodge, J.D. (1969). The ultrastructure of *Chroomonas mesostigmatica* Butcher (Cryptophyceae). *Arch. Mikrobiol.* 69: 206–80.

317 Dodge, J.D. (1971). Fine structure of the Pyrrophyta. *Bot. Rev.* 37: 481–507.

318 Dodge, J.D. (1972). The ultrastructure of the dinoflagellate pusule: a unique osmo-regulatory organelle. *Protoplasma* 75: 285–302.

319 Dodge, J.D. (1973). *The Fine Structure of Algal Cells.* Academic Press, London.

320 Dodge, J.D. (1975). A survey of chloroplast ultrastructure in the Dinophyceae. *Phycologia* 14: 253–63.

321 Dodge, J.D. (1983). Dinoflagellates: investigation and phylogenetic speculation. *Br. Phycol. J.* 18: 335–56.

322 Dodge, J.D. (1984). Dinoflagellate taxonomy. In *Dinoflagellates*, ed. D.L. Spector, pp. 17–42. Academic Press, Orlando.

323 Dodge, J.D. (1982). *Marine Dinoflagellates of the British Isles.* Her Majesty's Stationery Office, London.

324 Dodge, J.D. (1987). General ultrastructure. In *The Biology of Dinoflagellates*, ed. F.J.R. Taylor, pp. 93–119. Blackwell Scientific Publications, Oxford.

325 Dodge, J.D. & R.M. Crawford (1970a). The morphology and fine structure of *Ceratium hirundinella* (Dinophyceae). *J. Phycol.* 6: 137–49.

326 Dodge, J.D. & R.M. Crawford (1970b). A survey of thecal fine structure in the Dinophyceae. *Bot. J. Linn. Soc.* 63: 53–67.

327 Dodge, J.D. & J.J. Lee (1985). Order 2. Dinoflagellida Bütchli, 1885. In *An Illustrated Guide to the Protozoa*, ed. J.J. Lee, S.H. Hutner & E.C. Bovee, pp. 22–41. Society of Protozoologists, Lawrence, Kansas.

328 Domozych, D.S. (1984). The crystalline cell wall of *Tetraselmis convolutae* (Chlorophyta): a freeze fracture analysis. *J. Phycol.* 20: 415–18.

329 Domozych, D.S., K.D. Stewart & K.R. Mattox (1980). The comparative aspects of cell wall chemistry in the green algae (Chlorophyta). *J. Molec. Evol.* 15: 1–12.

330 Donkin, P. (1976). Ketocarotenoid biosynthesis by *Haematococcus lacustris*. *Phytochemistry* 15: 711–15.

331 Douglas, S.E. (1988). Restriction analysis of the genome of the marine chromopyte alga, *Cryptomonas*. *J. Phycol.* 24 (suppl.): 23.

331a Douglas, S.E. (1992). Probable evolutionary history of cryptomonad algae. In *Origins of Plastids*, ed. R.A. Lewin, pp. 265–90. Chapman & Hall, New York.

331b Douglas, S.E. (1992). Eukaryote-eukaryote endosymbioses: insights from studies of a cryptomonad alga. *BioSystems* 25.

331c Douglas, S.E., D.G. Durnford & C.W. Morden (1990). Nucleotide sequence of the gene for the large subunit of ribulose 1,5 bisphosphate carboxylase/oxygenase from *Cryptomonas* Φ: evidence supporting the polyphyletic origin of plastids. *J. Phycol.* 26: 500–8.

331d Douglas, S.E., C.A. Murphy, D.F. Spencer & M.W. Gray (1991). Cryptomonad algae are evolutionary chimaeras of two phylogenetically distinct unicellular eukaryotes. *Nature* 350: 148–51.

331e Douglas, S.E. & S. Turner (1991). Molecular evidence for the origin of plastids from a cyanobacterium-like ancestor. *J. Molec. Evol.* 33: 267–73.

332 Down, K., J.A. Raven, R. Fauzi, C. Mantoura & C. Llewellyn (1988). Chlorophyll c-like chromophore and prasinoxanthin in light harvesting by the picoplanktonic Ω 48–23 (Micromonadophyceae). *Third International Phycological Congress, Monash University, Melbourne, Abstracts:* 11.

333 Drebes, G. (1977). Sexuality. In *The Biology of Diatoms*, ed. D. Werner, pp. 250–83. Blackwell, Oxford.

334 Drebes, G. (1978). *Dissodinium pseudolunula* (Dinophyta), a parasite on copepod eggs. *Br. Phycol. J.* 13: 319–27.

335 Dreher, T., B.R. Grant & R. Wetherbee (1978). The wound response in the siphonous alga *Caulerpa simpliciuscula* C. Ag.: fine structure and cytology. *Protoplasma* 96: 189–203.

336 Drew, K.M. (1949). *Conchocelis*-phase in the life-history of *Porphyra umbilicalis* (L.) Kütz. *Nature* **164**: 748.

337 Drew, K.M. (1951). Rhodophyta. In *Manual of Phycology*, ed. G.M. Smith, pp. 167–91. Blaisdell, Waltham, Massachusetts.

338 Drew, K.M. (1954). Studies in the Bangioideae III. The life-history of *Porphyra umbilicalis* (L.) Kütz. var. *laciniata* (Lightf.) J. Ag. The *Conchocelis*-phase in culture. *Ann. Bot.* N.S. **18**: 183–211.

339 Drew, E.A. & K.M. Abel (1988). The greening of *Halimeda*. *Third International Phycological Congress, Abstracts:* 12.

340 Drews, G. (1973). Fine structure and chemical composition of the cell envelopes. In *The Biology of Blue-green Algae*, ed. N.G. Carr & B.A. Whitton, pp. 99–116. Blackwell, Oxford.

340a Drews, G. & J. Weckesser (1982). Function, structure and composition of cell walls and external layers. In *The Biology of Cyanobacteria*, ed. N.G. Carr & B.A. Whitton, pp. 333–57. Blackwell, Oxford.

341 Dring, M.J. (1967a). Effects of day-length on growth and reproduction of the *Conchocelis* phase of *Porphyra tenera*. *J. Mar. Biol. Ass. U.K.* **47**: 501–10.

342 Dring, M.J. (1967b). Phytochrome in red alga *Porphyra tenera*. *Nature* **215**: 1411–12.

343 Dring, M.J. (1982). *The Biology of Marine Plants*. Arnold, London.

344 Dring, M.J. (1984). Photoperiodism and phycology. In *Progress in Phycological Research*, Vol. 3, ed. F.E. Round & D.J. Chapman, pp. 159–92. Biopress, Bristol.

345 Dring, M.J. (1988). Photocontrol of development in algae. *Ann. Rev. Plant Physiol.* **39**: 157–74.

346 Dring, M.J. & K. Lüning (1975). A photoperiodic response mediated by blue light in the brown alga *Scytosiphon lomentaria*. *Planta* **125**: 25–32.

347 Dring, M.J. & J.A. West (1983). Photoperiodic control of tetrasporangium formation in the red alga *Rhodochorton purpureum*. *Planta* **159**: 143–50.

347a Druehl, L.D. & G.W. Saunders (1992). Molecular explorations in kelp evolution. In *Progress in Phycological Research*, Vol. 8, ed. F.E. Round & D.J. Chapman, pp. 47–83. Biopress, Bristol.

348 Drum, R.W. & J.T. Hopkins (1966). Diatom locomotion: an explanation. *Protoplasma* **62**: 1–33.

349 Drum, R.W. & H.S. Pankratz (1966). Locomotion and raphe structure of the diatom *Bacillaria*. *Nova Hedwigia* **10**: 315–17.

350 Dubertret, G. & M. Lefort-Tran (1982). Chloroplast molecular structure with particular reference to the thylakoids and envelopes. In *The Biology of Euglena*, Vol. III: *Physiology*, ed. D.E. Buetow, pp. 253–312. Academic Press, New York.

351 Dürr, G. (1979). Elektronenmikroskopische Untersuchungen am Panzer von Dinoflagellaten II. *Peridinium cinctum. Arch. Protistenk.* **122**: 88–120.

352 Dustin, P. (1980). Microtubules. *Sci. Am.* **243** (2): 59–68.

353 Dwarte, D.M. & M. Vesk (1987). Immunocytochemical labelling of light-harvesting pigment protein complexes in cryptophyte thylakoids. *14th International Botanical Congress, Berlin, Abstracts:* 87. (Collated and edited by W. Greuter, B. Zimmer & H.D. Behnke; produced with the assistance of M.I. Hakki, H. Sipman and staff members of the Botanical Museum Berlin-Dahlem.)

354 Dyer, B.D. (1990). Phylum Zoomastigina, Class Bicoecids. In *Handbook of Protoctista*, ed. L. Margulis, J.O. Corliss, M. Melkonian & D.J. Chapman, pp. 191–3. Jones & Bartlett Publishers, Boston.

355 Ebersold, W.T. (1962). Biochemical genetics. In *Physiology and Biochemistry of Algae*, ed. R.A. Lewin, pp. 731–9. Academic Press, New York.

356 Echlin, P. (1967). The biology of *Glaucocystis nostochinearum* I. The morphology and fine structure. *Br. Phycol. Bull.* **3**: 225–39.

357 Eckert, R. (1965). Bioelectric control of bioluminescence in the dinoflagellate *Noctiluca*. *Science* **147**: 1140–5.

358 Eckhardt, R. & R. Schnetter (1984). Failure of karyogamy after gamete mating in *Derbesia tenuissima*. *Naturwissenschaften* **71**: 640–1.

359 Eckhardt, R., R. Schnetter & G. Seibold (1986). Nuclear behaviour during the life cycle of *Derbesia* (Chlorophyceae). *Br. Phycol. J.* **21**: 287–95.

360 Edgar, L.A. & J.D. Pickett-Heaps (1984a). Diatom locomotion. In *Progress in Phycological Research*, Vol. 3, ed. F.E. Round & D.J. Chapman, pp. 47–88. Biopress, Bristol.

361 Edgar, L.A. & J.D. Pickett-Heaps (1984b). Valve morphogenesis in the pennate diatom *Navicula cuspidata*. *J. Phycol.* **20**: 47–61.

362 Edmunds, L.N. (1982). Circadian and infradian rhythms. In *The Biology of Euglena,* Vol. III: *Physiology,* ed. D.E. Buetow, pp. 54–142. Academic Press, New York.

363 Edmunds, L.N. (1987). Interactions of circadian oscillators and the cell developmental cycle in *Euglena.* In *Algal Development,* ed. W. Wiessner, D.G. Robinson & R.C. Starr, pp. 1–8. Springer-Verlag, Berlin.

364 Edwards, P. (1969). The life history of *Callithamnion byssoides* in culture. *J. Phycol.* 5: 266–8.

365 Eichler, A. (1883). *Syllabus der Vorlesungen über specielle und medicinish-pharmaceutische Botanik,* 3rd Ed. Berlin.

365a Eikrem, W. & J. Throndsen (1990). The ultrastructure of *Bathycoccus* gen. nov. and *B. prasinos* sp. nov., a non-motile picoplanktonic alga (Chlorophyta, Prasinophyceae) from the Mediterranean and Atlantic. *Phycologia* 29: 344–50.

366 Elliott, G.F. (1981). The Tethyan dispersal of some chlorophyte algae subsequent to the Paleozoic. *Palaeogeogr. Palaeoclimat. Palaeoecol.* 32: 341–58.

367 Ende, H. van den (1976). *Sexual Interactions in Plants.* Academic Press, London.

368 Ende, H. van den, F.M. Klis & A. Musgrave (1988). The role of flagella in sexual reproduction of *Chlamydomonas eugametos. Acta Bot. Neerl.* 37: 327–50.

369 Enomoto, S., T. Hori & K. Okuda (1982). Culture studies of *Dictyosphaeria* (Chlorophyceae, Siphonocladales). II. Morphological analysis of segregative cell division in *Dictyosphaeria cavernosa. Jap. J. Phycol.* 30: 103–12.

370 Enomoto, S. & K. Okuda (1981). Culture studies of *Dictyosphaeria* (Chlorophyceae, Siphonocladales). I. Life history and morphogenesis of *Dictyosphaeria cavernosa. Jap. J. Phycol.* 29: 225–36.

371 Enomoto, S. & H. Ohba (1987). Culture studies on *Caulerpa* (Caulerpales, Chlorophyceae) I. Reproduction and development of *C. racemosa* var. *laetevirens. Jap. J. Phycol.* 35: 167–77.

372 Eppley, R.W., O. Holm-Hansen & J.D.H. Strickland (1968). Some observations on the vertical migration of dinoflagellates. *J. Phycol.* 4: 333–40.

373 Erata, M. & M. Chihara (1989). Re-examination of *Pyrenomonas* and *Rhodomonas* (Class Cryptophyceae) through ultrastructural survey of red pigmented Cryptomonads. *Bot. Mag. Tokyo* 102: 429–43.

374 Essen, A. van (1974). De Chlorococcales, een belangrijke orde van de groenwieren. *Wet. Meded. K.N.N.V.* 100: 1–87.

375 Estep, K.W., P.G. Davis, P.E. Hargraves & J.M. Sieburth (1984). Chloroplast containing microflagellates in natural populations of North Atlantic nanoplankton, their identification and distribution, including a description of five new species of *Chrysochromulina* (Prymnesiophyceae). *Protistologica* 20: 613–34.

376 Ettl, H. (1958). Zur Kenntnis der Klasse Volvophyceae. In *Algologische Studien,* ed. J. Komárek & H. Ettl, pp. 207–89. Verlag der Tschechoslowakischen Akademie der Wissenschaften, Prague.

377 Ettl, H. (1961). Über pulsierende Vakuolen bei Chlorophyceen. *Flora* 151: 88–98.

378 Ettl, H. (1965). Beitrag zur Kenntnis der Morphologie der Gattung *Chlamydomonas* Ehrenberg. *Arch. Protistenk.* 108: 271–430.

379 Ettl, H. (1966). Vergleichende Untersuchungen der Feinstruktur einiger *Chlamydomonas*-Arten. *Öst. bot. Z.* 113: 477–510.

380 Ettl, H. (1967). Die Feinstruktur von *Chloromonas rosae* Ettl. *Protoplasma* 64: 134–46.

381 Ettl, H. (1971). *Chlamydomonas* als geeigneter Modellorganismus für vergleichende cytomorphologische Untersuchungen. *Arch. Hydrobiol.,* Suppl. 39 (*Algol. Stud.* 5): 259–300.

382 Ettl, H. (1976). Die Gattung *Chlamydomonas* Ehrenberg. *Nova Hedwigia, Beih.* 49: 1–1122.

383 Ettl, H. (1978). Xanthophyceae. 1. Teil. *Süßwasserflora von Mitteleuropa,* Vol. 3, ed. H. Ettl, J. Gerloff & H. Heinig. Gustav Fischer, Stuttgart.

384 Ettl, H. (1980). *Grundriß der allgemeinen Algologie.* VEB Gustav Fischer Verlag, Jena.

385 Ettl, H. (1981). Die neue Klasse Chlamydophyceae, eine natürliche Gruppe der Grünalgen (Chlorophyta). *Pl. Syst. Evol.* 137: 107–26.

386 Ettl, H. (1983). Chlorophyta I. Phytomonadina. *Süßwasserflora von Mitteleuropa,* Vol. 9, ed. H. Ettl, J. Gerloff, H. Heynig & D. Mollenhauer. Gustav Fischer, Stuttgart.

387 Ettl, H. & J. Komárek (1982). Was versteht man unter dem Begriff 'coccale Grünalgen'? (System-

atische Bemerkungen zu den Grünalgen II). *Arch. Hydrobiol.* Suppl. **60** (*Algol. Stud.* **29**): 345–74.

388 Ettl, H. & I. Manton (1964). Die feinere Struktur von *Pedinomonas minor* Korschikoff. *Nova Hedwigia* **8**: 421–44.

389 Evans, L.V. (1966). Distribution of pyrenoids among some brown algae. *J. Cell Sci.* **1**: 449–54.

390 Evans, L.V. (1974). Cytoplasmic organelles. In *Algal Physiology and Biochemistry*, ed. W.D.P. Stewart, pp. 86–123. Blackwell, Oxford.

391 Evans, L.V., J.A. Callow & M.E. Callow (1978). Parasitic red algae: an appraisal. In *Modern Approaches to the Taxonomy of Red and Brown Algae*, ed. D.E.G. Irvine & J.H. Price, pp. 87–110. Academic Press, New York.

392 Evans, L.V. & M.S. Holligan (1972a). Correlated light and electron microscope studies on brown algae. I. Localization of alginic acid and sulphated polysaccharides in *Dictyota. New Phytol.* **71**: 1161–72.

393 Evans, L.V. & M.S. Holligan (1972b). Correlated light and electron microscope studies on brown algae. II. Physode production in *Dictyota. New Phytol.* **71**: 1173–80.

394 Eyden, B.P. (1975). Light and electron microscope study of *Dunaliella primolecta* Butcher (Volvocida). *J. Protozool.* **22**: 336–44.

395 Falkenberg, P. (1879). Die Befruchtung und der Generationswechsel von *Cutleria. Mitt. Zool. Stat. Neapel* **1**: 420–47.

396 Fan, K.C. (1961). Morphological studies of the Gelidiales. *Univ. Calif. Publ. Bot.* **32**: 315–68.

397 Farmer, M.A. & K.R. Roberts (1989). Organelle loss in the endosymbiont of a dinoflagellate. *J. Phycol.* **25** (suppl.): 9.

398 Farmer, M.A. & K.R. Roberts (1990). Comparative analysis of the dinoflagellate flagellar apparatus. IV. *Gymnodinium acidotum. J. Phycol.* **26**: 122–31.

399 Faust, M.A. (1974). Structure of the periplast of *Cryptomonas ovata* var. *palustris. J. Phycol.* **10**: 121–4.

400 Fawley, M.W. (1989). Detection of chlorophylls c_1, c_2 and c_3 in pigment extracts of *Prymnesium parvum* (Prymnesiophyceae). *J. Phycol.* **25**: 601–4.

401 Fay, P. (1973). The heterocyst. In *The Biology of Blue-green Algae*, ed. N.G. Carr & B.A. Whitton, pp. 238–59. Blackwell, Oxford.

402 Fay, P. (1983). *The Blue-greens*. Edward Arnold, London.

403 Fay, P. & C. Van Baalen (Eds) (1987). *The Cyanobacteria*. Elsevier, Amsterdam.

404 Febvre, J. & C. Febvre-Chevalier (1982). Motility processes in Acantharia (Protozoa). 1. Cinematographic and cytological study of the myonemes. Evidence for a helix-coil mechanism of the constituent filaments. *Biol. Cell* **44**: 283–304.

404a Feige, G.B. & B.P. Kremer (1980). Unusual carbohydrate pattern in *Trentepohlia* species. *Phytochemistry* **19**: 1844–5.

405 Feldmann, G. (1965). Le développement des tétraspores de *Falkenbergia rufolanosa* et le cycle des Bonnemaisoniales. *Rev. Gén. Bot.* **72**: 621–6.

406 Feldmann, J. (1949). L'ordre des Scytosiphonales. Traveaux botaniques dédiés à R. Maire. *Mém. h.s. Soc. Hist. Nat. Afr. Nord* **11**: 103–15.

407 Feldmann, J. (1950). Sur l'existence d'une alternance de générations entre l'*Halicystis parvula* et le *Derbesia tenuissima* (De Not.) Crn. *C.R. Acad. Sci. Paris* **230**: 322–3.

408 Feldmann, J. (1951a). Ecology of marine algae. In *Manual of Phycology*, ed. G.M. Smith, pp. 313–34. Blaidell, Waltham, Massachusetts.

409 Feldmann, J. (1951b). Sur la reproduction sexuée de l'*Halimeda tuna* (Ell. et Sol.) Lamour. f. *platydisca* (Decaisne) Barton. *C.R. Acad. Sci. Paris* **233**: 1309–10.

410 Feldmann, J. (1956). Sur la parthénogénèse du *Codium fragile* (Sur.) Hariot dans la Méditerranée. *C.R. Acad. Sci. Paris* **243**: 305–7.

411 Feldmann, J. (1972). Les problèmes actuels de l'alternance de générations chez les algues. *Soc. Bot. France, Mémoires*: 7–38.

412 Feldmann, J. (1978). Les algues. In *Précis de Botanique*, Vol. 1, *Végétaux Inférieurs*, ed. H. des Abbayes, M. Chadefaud, J. Feldmann, Y. de Ferré, H. Gaussen, P.–P. Grassé & A.R. Prévot, pp. 95–320. Masson, Paris.

413 Feldmann, J. & L. Codomier (1974). Sur le développement des zoospores d'une chlorophycée marine: *Derbesia lamourouxii* (J. Ag.) Solier. *C.R. Acad. Sci. Paris* **278**: 1845–8.

414 Feldmann-Mazoyer, G. (1940). *Recherches sur les Céramiacées de la Méditerranée Occidentale*. Alger, Imprimerie Minerva.

415 Fenchel, T. (1987). *Ecology of Protozoa*. Science Tech Publishers, Madison, Wisconsin/ Springer-Verlag, Berlin.

416 Fenchel, T. & D.J. Patterson (1988). *Cafeteria*

roenbergensis nov. gen., nov. sp., a heterotrophic microflagellate from marine plankton. *Marine Microbial Food Webs* **3**: 9–19.

417 Fetter, R. & M. Neushul (1981). Studies on developing and released spermatia in the red alga, *Tiffaniella snyderae* (Rhodophyta). *J. Phycol.* **17**: 141–59.

418 Fiksdahl, A., S. Liaaen-Jensen & H.W. Siegelman (1978). Carotenoids of *Coccolithus pelagicus*. *Biochem. Syst. Ecol.* **7**: 47–8.

419 Fiksdahl, F., N. Withers, R.R.L. Guillard & S. Liaaen-Jensen (1984). Carotenoids of the Raphidophyceae – a chemosystematic contribution. *Comp. Biochem. Physiol.* **78b**: 265–71.

420 Fiore, J. (1977). Life history and taxonomy of *Stictyosiphon subsimplex* Holden (Phaeophyta, Dictyosiphonales) and *Farlowiella onusta* (Kützing) Kornmann in Kuckuck (Phaeophyta, Ectocarpales). *Phycologia* **16**: 301–11.

421 Firth, F.E. (1969). *The Encyclopedia of Marine Resources.* Van Nostrand, New York.

422 Fitt, W.K. (1985). Chemosensory responses of the symbiotic dinoflagellate *Symbiodinium microadriaticum* (Dinophyceae). *J. Phycol.* **21**: 62–7.

423 Floyd, G.L., H.J. Hoops & J.A. Swanson (1980). Fine structure of the zoospore of *Ulothrix belkae* with emphasis on the flagellar apparatus. *Protoplasma* **104**: 17–31.

424 Floyd, G.L. & C.J. O'Kelly (1984). Motile cell ultrastructure and the circumscription of the orders Ulotrichales and Ulvales (Ulvophyceae, Chlorophyta). *Am. J. Bot.* **71**: 111–20.

425 Floyd, G.L., C.J. O'Kelly & D.F. Chappell (1985). Absolute configuration analysis of the flagellar apparatus in *Cladophora* and *Chaetomorpha* motile cells, with an assessment of the phylogenetic position of the Cladophoraceae (Ulvophyceae, Chlorophyta). *Am. J. Bot.* **72**: 615–25.

426 Floyd, G.L., K.D. Stewart & K.R. Mattox (1972a). Comparative cytology of *Ulothrix* and *Stigeoclonium. J. Phycol.* **8**: 68–81.

427 Floyd, G.L., K.D. Stewart & K.R. Mattox (1972b). Cellular organization, mitosis, and cytokinesis in the ulotrichalean alga, *Klebsormidium. J. Phycol.* **8**: 170–84.

428 Floyd, G.L. & S. Watanabe (1989). Comparative fine structure of the zoospores of nine species of *Neochloris* (Chlorophyceae). *J. Phycol.* **25** (suppl.): 4.

429 Floyd, G.L. & H.J. Hoops (1980). *Schizomeris leibleinii* revisited: ultrastructure of the flagellar apparatus. *J. Phycol.* **16** (suppl.): 11.

430 Flügel, E. (1985). Diversity and environments of Permian and Triassic dasycladalean algae. In *Paleoalgology*, ed. D.F. Toomey & M.H. Nitecki, pp. 341–51. Springer-Verlag, Berlin.

431 Fogg, G.E. (1965). *Algal Cultures and Phytoplankton Ecology.* Athlone Press, London.

432 Fogg, G.E. (1987). Marine planktonic Cyanobacteria. In *The Cyanobacteria,* ed. P. Fay & C. Van Baalen, pp. 393–414. Elsevier, Amsterdam.

433 Fogg, G.E., W.D.P. Stewart, P. Fay & A.E. Walsby (Eds) (1973). *The Bluegreen Algae.* Academic Press, New York.

434 Fogg, G.E. & B. Thake (1987). *Algal Cultures and Phytoplankton Ecology.* 3rd ed. The University of Wisconsin Press, Madison, Wisconsin.

435 Forsberg, C. (1964). The vegetation changes in Lake Tåkern. *Svensk bot. Tidskr.* **58**: 44–54.

436 Forsberg, C. (1965). Sterile germination of oospores of *Chara* and seeds of *Najas marina. Physiol. Plant.* **18**: 128–37.

437 Forsberg, C. (1965). Nutritional studies of *Chara* in axenic cultures. *Physiol. Plant.* **18**: 275–90.

437a Foss, P., R.R.L. Guillard & S. Liaaen-Jensen (1984). Prasinoxanthin – a chemosystematic marker for algae. *Phytochemistry* **23**: 1629–33.

438 Fott, B. (1959). Zur Frage der Sexualität bei den Chrysomonaden. *Nova Hedwigia* **1**: 115–30.

439 Fott, B. (1968). Chloromonadophyceae. In *Das Phytoplankton des Süßwassers,* 2nd Ed., part 3, ed. G. Huber-Pestalozzi, pp. 79–93. Schweizerbart, Stuttgart.

440 Fott, B. (1971). *Algenkunde.* 2nd Ed. VEB Fischer, Jena.

441 Fott, B. (1972). Tetrasporales. In *Das Phytoplankton des Süßwassers,* part 6: *Chlorophyceae,* ed. G. Huber-Pestalozzi, pp. I–X, 1–116, table 1–47. Schweizerbart, Stuttgart.

442 Fott, B. & J. Ludvik (1956). Über den submikroskopischen Bau des Panzers von *Ceratium hirundinella. Preslia* **28**: 278–80.

443 Fott, B. & M. Nováková (1969). A monograph of the genus *Chlorella.* The freshwater species. In *Studies in Phycology,* ed. B. Fott, pp. 10–74. Schweizerbart, Stuttgart.

444 Fowke, L.C. & J.D. Pickett-Heaps (1969a).

Cell-division in *Spirogyra*. I. Mitosis. *J. Phycol.* 5: 240–59.

445 Fowke, L.C. & J.D. Pickett-Heaps (1969b). Cell-division in *Spirogyra*. II. Cytokinesis. *J. Phycol.* 5: 273–81.

446 Föyn, B. (1934). Lebenszyklus und Sexualität der Chlorophycee *Ulva lactuca* L. *Arch. Protistenk.* 83: 154–77.

447 Fraser, T.W. & B.E.S. Gunning (1969). The ultrastructure of the plasmodesmata in the filamentous green alga *Bulbochaete hiloensis* (Nordst.) Tiffany. *Planta* 88: 244–54.

448 Fredericq, S. & M.H. Hommersand (1989). Proposal of the Gracilariales ord. nov. (Rhodophyta) based on an analysis of the reproductive development of *Gracilaria verrucosa*. *J. Phycol.* 25: 213–27.

449 Fredericq, S. & M.H. Hommersand (1989). Comparative morphology and taxonomic status of *Gracilariopsis* (Gracilariales, Rhodophyta). *J. Phycol.* 25: 228–41.

450 French III, F.W. & P.E. Hargraves (1985). Spore formation in the life cycles of the diatoms *Chaetoceros diadema* and *Leptocylindrus danicus*. *J. Phycol.* 21: 477–83.

451 Freshwater, D.W. & D.F. Kapraun (1986). Field, culture and cytological studies of *Porphyra carolinensis* Coll et Cox (Bangiales, Rhodophyta) from North Carolina. *Jap. J. Phycol.* 34: 251–62.

451a Fresnel, J. (1989). *Les Coccolithophoridés (Prymnesiophyceae) du Littoral.* Thesis, University of Caen, France: 1–218.

452 Fresnel, J. & C. Billard (1987). Contribution à la connaissance du genre *Rhodella* (Porphyridiales, Rhodophyceae). *Crypt. Algol.* 8: 49–60.

453 Friedl, T. (1989). *Systematik und Biologie von Trebouxia (Microthamniales, Chlorophyta) als Phycobiont der Parmeliaceae (lichenisierte Ascomyceten).* Thesis, University of Bayreuth, Germany: 1–218.

454 Friedman, A.L. & R.S. Alberte (1987). Phylogenetic distribution of the major diatom light-harvesting pigment-protein determined by immunological methods. *J. Phycol.* 23: 427–33.

455 Friedmann, E.I. (1982). Cyanophycota. In *Synopsis and Classification of Living Organisms,* Vol. I, ed. S.P. Parker, pp. 45–52. McGraw-Hill Book Company, New York.

456 Friedmann, E.I. & W.C. Roth (1977).

457 Friedmann, I. (1959). Structure, life-history, and sex determination of *Prasiola stipitata* Suhr. *Ann. Bot.* N.S. 23: 571–94.

458 Friedmann, I. (1964). Ecological aspects of the occurrence of meiosis in *Prasiola stipitata* Suhr. *Proc. 4th Int. Seaweed Symp.* 186–90.

459 Friedmann, I. (1969). Geographic and environmental factors controlling life-history and morphology in *Prasiola stipitata* Suhr. *Öst. bot. Z.* 116: 203–25.

460 Friedmann, I., A.L. Colwin & L.H. Colwin (1968). Fine-structural aspects of fertilization in *Chlamydomonas reinhardii. J. Cell Sci.* 3: 115–28.

461 Friedmann, I. & I. Manton (1960). Gametes, fertilization and zygote development in *Prasiola stipitata* Suhr. I. *Nova Hedwigia* 1: 333–44.

462 Fries, L. (1967). The sporophyte of *Nemalion multifidum* (Weber et Mohr) J. Ag. *Svensk bot. Tidskr.* 61: 457–62.

463 Fries, L. (1969). The sporophyte of *Nemalion multifidum* (Weber et Mohr) J. Ag. found on the Swedish West coast. *Svensk bot. Tidskr.* 63: 139–41.

464 Fritsch, F.E. (1935). *The Structure and Reproduction of the Algae,* Vol. I. Cambridge University Press, London.

465 Fritsch, F.E. (1945). *The Structure and Reproduction of the Algae,* Vol. II. Cambridge University Press, London.

466 Fuhs, G.W. (1958). Bau, Verhalten und Bedeutung der kernäquivalenten Strukturen bei *Oscillatoria amoena* (Kütz.) Gomont. *Arch. Mikrobiol.* 28: 270–302.

467 Fuhs, G.W. (1968). Cytology of blue-green algae: light microscopic aspects. In *Algae, Man, and the Environment,* ed. D.F. Jackson, pp. 213–33. Syracuse University Press, New York.

468 Fuhs, G.E. (1973). Cytochemical examination. In *The Biology of Blue-green Algae,* ed. N.G. Carr & B.A. Whitton, pp. 117–43. Blackwell, Oxford.

469 Fujiyama, T. (1955). On the life-history of *Prasiola japonica. J. Fac. Fish. Animal Husbandry Hiroshima Univ.* 1: 15–37.

470 Fuller, M.S. (1990). Phylum Hyphochytriomycota. In *Handbook of Protoctista,* ed. L. Margulis, J.O. Corliss, M. Melkonian and D.J. Chapman, pp. 380–7. Jones & Bartlett, Boston.

Development of the siphonous green alga *Penicillus* and the Espera state. *Bot. J. Linn. Soc.* 74: 189–214.

470a Gabrielson, P.W., D.J. Garbary & R.F. Scagel (1985). The nature of the ancestral red alga: inferences from cladistic analysis. *BioSystems* **18**: 335–46.

471 Gabrielson, P.W. & D.J. Garbary (1986). Systematics of red algae (Rhodophyta). *CRC Crit. Rev. Plant Sci.* **3**: 325–66.

472 Gabrielson, P.W. & D.J. Garbary (1987). A cladistic analysis of Rhodophyta: florideophycidean orders. *Br. Phycol. J.* **22**: 125–38.

473 Gaillard, J. & M.-Th. L'Hardy-Halos (1984). Morphogénèse du *Dictyota dichotoma* (Huds.) Lamouroux (Pheophycée, Dictyotale). *Ann. Sci. Nat. Bot. Paris,* 13 ser. **6**: 111–33.

474 Gaillard, J., M.Th. L'Hardy-Halos & L. Pellegrini (1986). Morphogénèse du *Dictyota dichotoma* (Huds.) Lamouroux. II. Ontogénèse du thalle et cytologie ultrastructurale des différents types de cellules. *Phycologia* **25**: 340–57.

475 Gaines, G. & M. Elbrächter (1987). Heterotrophic nutrition. In *The Biology of Dinoflagellates*, ed. F.J.R. Taylor, pp. 224–68. Blackwell Scientific Publications, Oxford.

476 Galatis, B., C. Katsaros & K. Mitrakos (1973). Ultrastructure of the mitotic apparatus in *Dictyota dichotoma*. *Rapp. Com. int. Mer Medit.* **22** (4): 53–4.

477 Gallagher, J.C. (1983). Cell enlargement in *Skeletonema costatum* (Bacillariophyceae). *J. Phycol.* **19**: 539–42.

478 Gallo, J.-M. & J. Schrevel (1982). Euglenoid movement in *Distigma proteus*. I. Cortical rotational motion. *Biol. Cell* **44**: 139–48.

479 Gallon, J.R. & A.E. Chaplin (1989). Nitrogen fixation. In *Biochemistry of the Algae and Cyanobacteria*, ed. L.J. Rogers & J.R. Gallon, pp. 147–73. Clarendon Press, Oxford.

480 Gantt, E. (1971). Micromorphology of the periplast of *Chroomonas* sp. (Cryptophyceae). *J. Phycol.* **7**: 177–84.

481 Gantt, E. (1980). Photosynthetic cryptophytes. In *Phytoflagellates*, ed. E.R. Cox, pp. 381–405. Elsevier/North-Holland, Amsterdam.

482 Gantt, E. (1981). Phycobilisomes. *Ann. Rev. Plant Physiol.* **32**: 327–47.

483 Gantt, E., M.R. Edwards & S.F. Conti (1968). Ultrastructure of *Porphyridium aerugineum*, a blue-green colored Rhodophytan. *J. Phycol.* **4**: 65–71.

484 Gantt, E., M.R. Edwards & L. Provasoli (1971). Chloroplast structure of the Cryptophyceae: evidence for phycobiliproteins within intrathylakoidal spaces. *J. Cell Biol.* **48**: 280–90.

485 Gantt, E., C.A. Lipschultz & T. Redlinger (1985). Phycobilisomes: a terminal acceptor pigment in cyanobacteria and red algae. In *Molecular Biology of the Photosynthetic Apparatus*, ed. K. Steinback, S. Bonitz, C. Arntzen & L. Bogorad, pp. 223–9. Cold Spring Harbor Laboratory, New York.

486 Gantt, E., J. Scott & C. Lipschultz (1986). Phycobiliprotein composition and chloroplast structure in the freshwater red alga *Compsopogon coeruleus* (Rhodophyta). *J. Phycol.* **22**: 480–4.

487 Gao Xiaoping, J.D. Dodge & J. Lewis (1989). Gamete mating and fusion in the marine dinoflagellate *Scrippsiella*. *Phycologia* **28**: 342–51.

488 Garbary, D.J. & P.W. Gabrielson (1987). Acrochaetiales (Rhodophyta): taxonomy and evolution. *Crypt. Algol.* **8**: 241–52.

489 Gärtner, G. (1985). Die Gattung *Trebouxia* Puymaly (Chlorellales, Chlorophyceae). *Arch. Hydrobiol.* Suppl. **64** (*Algol. Stud.* **41**): 495–548.

490 Gärtner, G., A. Hofer & E. Ingolic (1987). Contribution to cytology and taxonomy of some Chlorosarcinales with special reference to 'vegetative cell division'. *Progress in algal taxonomy, international symposium, Smolenice, Czechoslovakia, Abstracts:* 27.

491 Gastrich, M.D. (1987). Ultrastructure of a new intracellular symbiotic alga found within planktonic Foraminifera. *J. Phycol.* **23**: 623–32.

492 Gawlik, S.R. & W.F. Millington (1988). Structure and function of the bristles of *Pediastrum boryanum* (Chlorophyta). *J. Phycol.* **24**: 474–82.

493 Gayral, P. & C. Billard (1977). Synopsis du nouvel ordre des Sarcinochrysidales (Chrysophyceae). *Taxon* **26**: 241–5.

493a Gayral, P. & C. Billard (1986). A survey of the marine Chrysophyceae with special reference to the Sarcinochrysidales. In *Chrysophytes: Aspects and Problems*, ed. J. Kristiansen & R.A. Andersen, pp. 37–48. Cambridge University Press, Cambridge.

494 Gayral, P. & J. Fresnel (1983). Description, sexualité et cycle de développement d'une nouvelle coccolithophoracée (Prymnesiophyceae): *Pleurochrysis pseudoroscoffensis* sp. nov. *Protistologica* **19**: 245–61.

495 Gayral, P., C. Haas & H. Lepailleur (1972). Alternance morphologique de générations et alter-

nance de phases chex les Chrysophycées. *Soc. Bot. France, Mémoires*: 215–29.

496   Geider, R.J. & P.A. Gunter (1989). Evidence for the presence of phycoerythrin in *Dinophysis norvegica*, a pink dinoflagellate. *Br. Phycol. J.* **24**: 195–8.

497   Geitler, L. (1923). Der Zellbau von *Glaucocystis nostochinearum* und *Gloeochaete wittrockiana* und die Chromatophoren-Symbiosetheorie von Mereschkowsky. *Arch. Protistenk.* **47**: 1–24.

498   Geitler, L. (1930). Ein grünes Filarplasmodium und andere neue Protisten. *Arch. Protistenk.* **69**: 615–36.

499   Geitler, L. (1932). Der Formwechsel der pennaten Diatomeen. *Arch. Protistenk.* **78**: 1–226.

500   Geitler, L. (1932). Cyanophyceae. *Dr L. Rabenhorst's Kryptogamen-Flora von Deutschland, Österreich und der Schweiz*, Vol. XIV. Akademische Verlagsgesellschaft, Leipzig.

501   Geitler, L. (1951). Kopulation und Formwechsel von *Eunotia arcus*. *Öst. bot. Z.* **98**: 292–337.

502   Geitler, L. (1957). Sie sexuelle Fortpflanzung der pennaten Diatomeen. *Biol. Rev.* **32**: 261–95.

503   Geitler, L. (1960). Schizophyzeen. In *Handbuch der Pflanzenanatomie*, Vol. VI, part 1, ed. W. Zimmermann & P. Ozenda, pp. V–VII, 1–131. Borntraeger, Berlin.

503a   Geitler, L. (1973). Auxosporenbildung und Systematik bei pennaten Diatomeen, und die Cytologie von *Cocconeis*-Sippen. *Öst. bot. Z.* **122**: 299–321.

503b   Geitler, L. (1979). Einige kritische Bemerkungen zur neuen zusammenfassenden Darstellung der Morphologie und Systematik der Cyanophyceen. *Plant Syst. Evol.* **132**: 153–60.

504   Geller, A. & D.G. Müller (1981). Analysis of the flagellar beat pattern of male *Ectocarpus siliculosus* gametes (Phaeophyta) in relation to chemotactic stimulation by female cells. *J. Exp. Biol.* **92**: 53–66.

505   Gemeinhardt, K. (1939). Oedogoniales. *Dr L. Rabenhorst's Kryptogamen-Flora von Deutschland, Österreich und der Schweiz*, Vol. XII. Akademische Verlagsgesellschaft, Leipzig.

506   Gest, H. & J.C. Favinger (1983). *Heliobacterium chlorum*, an anoxygenic brownish-green photosynthetic bacterium containing a 'new' form of bacteriochlorophyll. *Arch. Microbiol.* **136**: 11–16.

507   Gibbs, S.P. (1962a). Nuclear envelope chloroplast relationships in algae. *J. Cell Biol.* **14**: 433–44.

508   Gibbs, S.P. (1962b). The ultrastructure of the pyrenoids of green algae. *J. Ultrastruct. Res.* **7**: 262–72.

509   Gibbs, S.P. (1962c). The ultrastructure of the chloroplasts of algae. *J. Ultrastruct. Res.* **7**: 418–35.

509a   Gibbs, S.P. (1970). The comparative ultrastructure of the algal chloroplast. *Ann. NY Acad. Sci.* **175**: 454–73.

510   Gibbs, S.P. (1979). The route of entry of cytoplasmically synthesized proteins into chloroplasts of algae possessing chloroplast ER. *J. Cell Sci.* **35**: 253–66.

511   Gibbs, S.P. (1981a). The chloroplasts of some algal groups may have evolved from endosymbiotic eukaryotic algae. *Ann. NY Acad. Sci.* **361**: 193–207.

512   Gibbs S.P. (1981b). The chloroplast endoplasmic reticulum: structure, function and evolutionary significance. *Int. Rev. Cytol.* **72**: 49–99.

513   Gibbs, S.P. (1990). The evolution of algal chloroplasts. In *Experimental Phycology 1. Cell Walls and Surfaces, Reproduction, Photosynthesis*, ed. W. Wiessner, D.G. Robinson & R.C. Starr, pp. 145–57. Springer-Verlag, Berlin.

514   Gibbs, S.P., D. Cheng & T. Slankis (1974). The chloroplast nucleoid in *Ochromonas danica*. *J. Cell Sci.* **16**: 557–77.

515   Gibson, G. & M.N. Clayton (1987). Sexual reproduction, early development and branching in *Notheia anomala* (Phaeophyta) and its classification in the Fucales. *Phycologia* **26**: 363–73.

516   Gibson, M.T. & B.A. Whitton (1987a). Hairs, phosphatase activity and environmental chemistry in *Stigeoclonium, Chaetophora* and *Draparnaldia* (Chaetophorales). *Br. Phycol. J.* **22**: 11–22.

517   Gibson, M.T. & B.A. Whitton (1987b). Influence of phosphorus on morphology and physiology of freshwater *Chaetophora, Draparnaldia* and *Stigeoclonium* (Chaetophorales, Chlorophyta). *Phycologia* **26**: 59–69.

518   Giddings, T.H., D.L. Brower & L.H. Staehelin (1980). Visualization of particle complexes in the plasma membrane of *Micrasterias denticulata* associated with the formation of cellulose fibrils in primary and secondary cell walls. *J. Cell Biol.* **84**: 327–39.

519   Gieskes, W.W.C. & Elbrächter, M. (1986). Abundance of nanoplankton-size chlorophyll-containing particles caused by diatom disruption in surface waters of the Southern Ocean (Antarctic Peninsula region). *Neth. J. Sea Res.* **20**: 291–303.

520 Gieskes, W.W.C. & G.W. Kraay (1983). Dominance of Cryptophyceae during the phytoplankton spring bloom in the central North Sea detected by HPLC analysis of pigments. *Mar. Biol.* **75**: 179–85.

521 Gieskes, W.W.C. & G.W. Kraay (1986). Analysis of phytoplankton pigments by HPLC before, during and after mass occurrence of the microflagellate *Corymbellus aureus* during the spring bloom in the open northern North Sea in 1983. *Mar. Biol.* **92**: 45–52.

522 Gieskes, W.W.C., G.W. Kraay, A. Nontji, D. Setiapermana & Sutomo (1988). Monsoonal alternation of a mixed and a layered structure in the phytoplankton of the euphotic zone of the Banda Sea (Indonesia): a mathematical analysis of algal pigment fingerprints. *Neth. J. Sea Res.* **22**: 123–37.

523 Gilles, R., D. Balshülseman & L. Jaenicke (1987). Molecular signals during sexual induction of *Volvox carteri* f. *nagariensis.* In *Algal Development*, ed. W. Wiessner, D.G. Robinson & R.C. Starr, pp. 50–7. Springer-Verlag, Berlin.

524 Gillott, M. (1990). Phylum Cryptophyta. In *Handbook of Protoctista*, ed. L. Margulis, J.O. Corliss, M. Melkonian & D.J. Chapman, pp. 139–51. Jones & Bartlett, Boston.

525 Gillott, M. & R.E. Triemer (1978). The ultrastructure of cell division in *Euglena gracilis. J. Cell Sci.* **31**: 25–35.

526 Giovannoni, S.J., S. Turner, G.J. Olsen, S. Barns, D.J. Lane & N.R. Pace (1988). Evolutionary relationships among Cyanobacteria and green chloroplasts. *J. Bacteriol.* **170**: 3584–92.

527 Giraud, A. & M. Magne (1968). La place de la méiose dans le cycle de développement de *Porphyra umbilicalis. C.R. Acad. Sci. Paris* **267**: 586–8.

528 Glazer, A.N. (1987). Phycobilisomes: assembly and attachment. In *The Cyanobacteria*, ed. P. Fay & C. Van Baalen, pp. 71–94. Elsevier, Amsterdam.

529 Glazer, A.N., J.A. West & C. Chan (1982). Phycoerythrins as chemotaxonomic markers in red algae: a survey. *Biochem. Syst. Ecol.* **10**: 203–15.

530 Gleason, F.K. & J.M. Wood (1987). Secondary metabolism in the Cyanobacteria. In *The Cyanobacteria*, ed. P. Fay & C. Van Baalen, pp. 437–52. Elsevier, Amsterdam.

531 Glicksman, M. (1987). Utilization of seaweed hydrocolloids in the food industry. *Hydrobiologia* **151/152**: 31–47.

531a Godward, M.B.E. (1942). The life-cycle of *Stigeoclonium amoenum. New Phytol.* **41**: 293–301.

532 Godward, M.B.E. (1966). The Chlorophyceae. In *The Chromosomes of Algae*, ed. M.B.E. Godward, pp. 1–77. Arnold, London.

533 Goff, L.J. (1982). Biology of parasitic red algae. In *Progress in Phycological Research*, Vol. 1, ed. F.E. Round & D.J. Chapman, pp. 289–369. Elsevier, Amsterdam.

534 Goff, L.J. & K. Cole (1975). The biology of *Harveyella mirabilis* (Cryptonemiales, Rhodophyceae). II. Carposporophyte development as related to the taxonomic affiliation of the parasitic alga, *Harveyella mirabilis. Phycologia* **14**: 227–38.

535 Goff, L.J. & A.W. Coleman (1985). The role of secondary pit connections in red algal parasitism. *J. Phycol.* **21**: 483–508.

536 Golden, L. & D.J. Garbary (1984). Studies on *Monostroma* (Monostromataceae, Chlorophyta) in British Columbia with emphasis on spore release. *Jap. J. Phycol.* **32**: 319–32.

537 Goldschmidt-Clermont, M., M. Dron, J.M. Erickson, J.-D. Rochaix, M. Schneider, R. Spreitzer & J.M. Vallet (1984). Structure and expression of chloroplast and nuclear genes in *Chlamydomonas reinhardtii.* In *Compartments in Algal Cells and their Interaction*, ed. W. Wiessner, D.G. Robinson & R.C. Starr, pp. 23–7. Springer-Verlag, Berlin.

538 Goodenough, U.W. (1970). Chloroplast division and pyrenoid formation in *Chlamydomonas reinhardtii. J. Phycol.* **6**: 1–6.

539 Goodenough, U.W. (1989). Basal body chromosomes? *Cell* **59**: 1–3.

540 Goodenough, U.W. & J.E. Heuser (1985). The *Chlamydomonas* cell wall and its constituent glycoproteins analysed by the quick-freeze, deep-etch technique. *J. Cell Biol.* **101**: 1550–68.

541 Goodenough, U.W. & R.L. Weiss (1975). Gametic differentiation in *Chlamydomonas reinhardtii.* III. Cell wall lysis and microfilament-associated mating structure activation in wild-type and mutant strains. *J. Cell Biol.* **67**: 623–37.

542 Goodenough, U.W. & R.L. Weiss (1978). Interrelationships between microtubules, a striated fiber, and the gametic mating structure of *Chlamydomonas reinhardtii. J. Cell Biol.* **76**: 430–8.

543 Goodman, D.K. (1987). Dinoflagellate cysts in ancient and modern sediments. In *The Biology of*

Dinoflagellates, ed. F.J.R. Taylor, pp. 649–722. Blackwell Scientific Publications, Oxford.

544   Goodwin, T.W. (1974). Carotenoids and biliproteins. In *Algal Physiology and Biochemistry*, ed. W.D.P. Stewart, pp. 176–205. Blackwell, Oxford.

545   Goreau, T.F. & N.I. Goreau (1959). The physiology of skeleton formation in corals. II. Calcium deposition by hermatypic corals under various conditions on the reef. *Biol. Bull. Woods Hole* 117: 239–50.

546   Gorham, P.R. (1964). Toxic algae. In *Algae and Man*, ed. D.F. Jackson, pp. 307–36. Plenum Press, New York.

547   Gori, P. (1979). Ultrastructure of the spermatozoid in *Halimeda tuna* (Chlorophyceae). *Gam. Res.* 2: 345–55.

548   Gorkom, H.J. van & M. Donze (1971). Localization of nitrogen fixation in *Anabaena*. *Nature* 234: 231–2.

549   Gouy, M. & W.-H. Li (1989). Molecular phylogeny of the kingdoms Animalia, Plantae and Fungi. *Molec. Biol. Evol.* 6: 109–22.

550   Gradinger, R. & J. Lenz (1989). Picocyanobacteria in the high Arctic. *Mar. Ecol. Prog. Ser.* 52: 99–101.

551   Graham, H.W. (1951). Pyrrophyta. In *Manual of Phycology*, ed. G.M. Smith, pp. 105–18. Blaisdell, Waltham, Massachusetts.

552   Graham, J.M., L.E. Graham & J.A. Kranzfelder (1985). Light, temperature and photoperiod as factors controlling reproduction in *Ulothrix zonata* (Ulvophyceae). *J. Phycol.* 21: 235–9.

553   Graham, L.E. (1984). An ultrastructural re-examination of putative multilayered structures in *Trentepohlia aurea*. *Protoplasma* 123: 1–7.

554   Graham, L.E. & G.E. McBride (1975). The ultrastructure of multilayered structures associated with flagellar bases in motile cells of *Trentepohlia aurea*. *J. Phycol.* 11: 86–96.

555   Graham, L.E. & G.E. McBride (1979). The occurrence and phylogenetic significance of a multi-layered structure in *Coleochaete* spermatozoids. *Am. J. Bot.* 66: 887–94.

556   Graham, L.E. & G.J. Wedemeyer (1984). Spermatogenesis in *Coleochaete pulvinata* (Charophyceae): sperm maturation. *J. Phycol.* 20: 302–9.

557   Grambast, L.I. (1965). Précisions nouvelles sur la phylogénie des Charophytes. *Nat. monspel.*, Ser. bot. 16: 71–7.

558   Grambast, L.J. (1974). Phylogeny of the Charophyta. *Taxon* 23: 463–81.

559   Grassé, P.-P. (1952). *Traité de Zoologie*, Vol. 1. *Phylogénie, Protozoaires: généralités. Flagellés. Premier fascicule*. Masson, Paris.

560   Green, J.C. (1967). A new species of *Pavlova* from Madeira. *Br. Phycol. Bull.* 3: 299–303.

561   Green, J.C. (1973). Studies on the fine structure and taxonomy of flagellates in the genus *Pavlova* II. A freshwater representative, *Pavlova granifera* (Mack) comb. nov. *Br. Phycol. J.* 8: 1–12.

562   Green, J.C. (1976). *Corymbellus aureus* gen. et sp. nov., a new colonial member of the Haptophyceae. *J. Mar. Biol. Ass. U.K.* 56: 31–8.

563   Green, J.C. (1980). The fine structure of *Pavlova pinguis* Green and a preliminary survey of the order Pavlovales (Prymnesiophyceae). *Br. Phycol. J.* 15: 151–91.

563a   Green, J.C., D.J. Hibberd & R.N. Pienaar (1982). The taxonomy of *Prymnesium* (Prymnesiophyceae) including a description of a new cosmopolitan species, *P. patellifera* sp. nov. and further observations on *P. parvum* N. Carter. *Br. Phycol. J.* 17: 363–82.

564   Green, J.C. & T. Hori (1986). The ultrastructure of the flagellar root system of *Imantonia rotunda* (Prymnesiophyceae). *Br. Phycol. J.* 21: 5–18.

565   Green, J.C. & T. Hori (1988). The fine structure of mitosis in *Pavlova* (Prymnesiophyceae). *Can. J. Bot.* 66: 1497–509.

566   Green, J.C., T. Hori & P.A. Course (1989). An ultrastructural study of mitosis in *Chrysochromulina chiton* (Prymnesiophyceae). *Phycologia* 28: 318–30.

567   Green, J.C. & I. Manton (1970). Studies on the fine structure and taxonomy of flagellates in the genus *Pavlova*. I. A revision of *Pavlova gyrans*, the type species. *J. Mar. Biol. Ass. U.K.* 50: 1113–30.

568   Green, J.C. & M. Parke (1975). New observations upon members of the genus *Chrysotila* Anand, with remarks upon their relationships within the Haptophyceae. *J. Mar. Biol. Ass. U.K.* 55: 109–21.

569   Green, J.C., K. Perch-Nielsen & P. Westbroek (1990). Phylum Prymnesiophyta. In *Handbook of Protoctista*, ed. L. Margulis, J.D. Corliss, M. Melkonian & D.J. Chapman, pp. 293–317. Jones & Bartlett, Boston.

570   Green, J.C. & R.N. Pienaar (1977). The taxonomy of the order Isochrysidales (Prymnesiophyceae) with special reference to the genera *Isochrysis* Parke, *Dicrateria* Parke and *Imantonia* Reynolds. *J. Mar. Biol. Ass. U.K.* 57: 7–17.

571 Green, P.B. (1962). Cell expansion. In *Physiology and Biochemistry of Algae*, ed. R.A. Lewin, pp. 625–32. Academic Press, New York.

572 Green, P.B. (1964). Cinematic observations on the growth and division of chloroplasts in *Nitella*. *Am. J. Bot.* **51**: 334–42.

573 Greuel, B.T. & G.L. Floyd (1985). Development of the flagellar apparatus and flagellar orientation in the colonial green alga *Gonium pectorale* (Volvocales). *J. Phycol.* **21**: 358–71.

574 Greuet, C. (1987). Complex organelles. In *The Biology of Dinoflagellates*, ed. F.J.R. Taylor, pp. 119–42. Blackwell Scientific Publications, Oxford.

575 Griffiths, D.J. (1970). The pyrenoid. *Bot. Rev.* **36**: 29–58.

576 Griffiths, D.J. & Luong-Van Thinh (1989). Current status of the taxonomy of the genus *Prochloron*. In *Bergey's Manual of Systematic Bacteriology*, Vol. 3. Section 19: *Oxygenic Photosynthetic Bacteria*, ed. J.T. Staley, M.P. Bryant, N. Pfennig & J.H. Holt, pp. 1802–5. Williams & Wilkins, Baltimore.

577 Groover, R.D. & H.C. Bold (1969). Phycological studies VIII. The taxonomy and comparative physiology of the Chlorosarcinales and certain other edaphic algae. *Univ. Texas Publ.* **6907**: 1–165.

578 Gross, F. & E. Zeuthen (1948). The buoyancy of plankton diatoms: a problem of cell physiology. *Proc. R. Soc. Lond.* **B135**: 382–9.

579 Grote, M. (1977a). Über die Auslösung der generativen Fortpflanzung unter kontrollierten Bedingungen bei der Grünalge *Spirogyra majuscula*. *Z. Pflanzenphysiol.* **83**: 95–117.

580 Grote, M. (1977b). Untersuchungen zum Kopulationsverlauf bei der Grünalge *Spirogyra majuscula*. *Protoplasma* **91**: 71–82.

581 Guillard, R.R.L. & P. Kilham (1977). The ecology of marine planktonic diatoms. In *The Biology of Diatoms*, ed. D. Werner, pp. 372–469. Blackwell, Oxford.

582 Guillard, R.R.L. & C.J. Lorenzen (1972). Yellow-green algae with chlorophyllide c. *J. Phycol.* **8**: 10–14.

583 Guiry, M.D. (1974). A preliminary consideration of the taxonomic position of *Palmaria palmata* (Linnaeus) Stackhouse = *Rhodymenia palmata* (Linnaeus) Greville. *J. Mar. Biol. Ass. U.K.* **54**: 509–28.

584 Guiry, M.D. (1975). An assessment of *Palmaria palmata* forma *mollis* (S. et G.) comb. nov. (= *Rhodymenia palmata* forma *mollis* S. et G.) in the eastern North Pacific. *Syesis* **8**: 245–61.

585 Guiry, M.D. (1978). The importance of sporangia in the classification of the Florideophyceae. In *Modern Approaches to the Taxonomy of Red and Brown Algae*, ed. D.E.G. Irvine & J.H. Price, pp. 111–44. Academic Press, London.

586 Guiry, M.D. (1987). The evolution of life history types in the Rhodophyta: an appraisal. *Crypt. Algol.* **8**: 1–12.

587 Guiry, M.D. & J.A. West (1983). Life history and hybridization studies on *Gigartina stellata* and *Petrocelis cruenta* (Rhodophyta) in the North Atlantic. *J. Phycol.* **19**: 474–94.

588 Guiry, M.D., J.A. West, D.-H Kimm & M. Masuda (1984). Reinstatement of the genus *Mastocarpus* Kützing (Rhodophyta). *Taxon* **33**: 53–63.

589 Gunderson, J.H., H. Elwood, A. Ingold, K. Kindle & M.L. Sogin (1987). Phylogenetic relationships between chlorophytes, chrysophytes, and Oomycetes. *Proc. Natl. Acad. Sci. USA* **84**: 5823–7.

590 Guy-Ohlson, D. (1988). Developmental stages in the life cycle of Mesozoic *Tasmanites*. *Botanica Mar.* **31**: 447–56.

591 Guy-Ohlson, D., N.G. Ohlson & B. Lindquist (1988). Fossil palynomorph deformation and its relationship to sedimentary deposition. *Geol. För. Stockholm Förh.* **110**: 111–9.

592 Häder, D.-P. (1987). Photomovement. In *The Cyanobacteria*, ed. P. Fay & C. Van Baalen, pp. 325–45. Elsevier, Amsterdam.

593 Hager, A. & H. Stransky (1970a). Das Carotinoidmuster und die Verbreitung des lichtinduzierten Xanthophyll-cyclus in verschiedenen Algenklassen. III. Grünalgen. *Arch. Mikrobiol.* **72**: 68–83.

594 Hager, A. & H. Stransky (1970b). Das Carotinoidmuster und die Verbreitung des lichtinduzierten Xanthophyll-cyclus in verschiedenen Algenklassen. V. Einzelne Vertreter der Cryptophyceae, Euglenophyceae, Bacillariophyceae, Chrysophyceae und Phaeophyceae. *Arch. Mikrobiol.* **73**: 77–89.

595 Halfen, L.N. (1973). Gliding motility of *Oscillatoria*: ultrastructural and chemical characterization of the fibrillar layer. *J. Phycol.* **9**: 248–53.

596   Hall, J.L., Z. Ramanis & D.J.L. Luck (1989). Basal body/centriolar DNA: molecular genetic studies in *Chlamydomonas*. *Cell* **59**: 121–32.

597   Halldall, P. (1958). Action spectra of phototaxis and related problems in Volvocales, *Ulva*-gametes and Dinophyceae. *Physiol. Plant.* **11**: 118–53.

597a   Hallegraeff, G. M. (1988). *Plankton, a microscopic world.* CSIRO in association with E. J. Brill/Robert Brown & Associates, Bathurst, Australia.

598   Hallegraeff, G.M. & S.W. Jeffrey (1984). Tropical phytoplankton species and pigments of continental shelf waters of North and North-West Australia. *Mar. Ecol. Prog. Ser.* **20**: 59–74.

599   Hallegraeff, G.M. & I.A.N. Lucas (1988). The marine dinoflagellate genus *Dinophysis* (Dinophyceae): photosynthetic, neritic and non-photosynthetic, oceanic species. *Phycologia* **27**: 25–42.

600   Hamel, G. (1930–32). Chlorophycées des côtes françaises. *Rev. Algol.* **5**: 1–54, 383–430; **6**: 9–73.

601   Hamel, G. & P. Lemoine (1952). Corallinacées de France et d'Afrique du Nord. *Arch. Mus. Nat. Hist. Nat.*, 7e sér. **1**: 17–136.

602   Hämmerling, J. (1934). Über die Geschlechtsverhältnisse von *Acetabularia mediterranea* und *A. wettsteinii*. *Arch. Protistenk.* **83**: 57–97.

602a   Hanic, L.A. & J.S. Craigie (1969). Studies on the algal cuticle. *J. Phycol.* **5**: 89–102.

603   Hansen, G. & Ø. Moestrup (1988). The formation and phylogenetic significance of body scales in the dinoflagellate *Katodinium rotundatum* (Lohm.) Loeblich. *Third International Phycological Congress, Monash University, Melbourne, Abstracts:* 29.

604   Happach-Kazan, C. & H.A. von Stosch (1978). [Paper on the life history of *Ceratium cornutum* presented to the 'Botanikertagung' at Marburg, 19 September 1978].

605   Hara, Y. & M. Chihara (1974). Comparative studies on the chloroplast ultrastructure in the Rhodophyta with special reference to their taxonomic significance. *Sci. Rep. Tokyo Kyoiku Daigaku*, Sect. B **15**: 209–35.

606   Hara, Y. & M. Chihara (1982). Ultrastructure and taxonomy of *Chattonella* (Class Raphidophyceae) in Japan. *Jap. J. Phycol.* **30**: 47–56.

607   Hara, Y. & M. Chihara (1985). Ultrastructure and taxonomy of *Fibrocapsa japonica* (class Raphidophyceae). *Arch. Protistenk.* **130**: 133–41.

608   Hara, Y., I. Inouye & M. Chihara (1985). Morphology and ultrastructure of *Olisthodiscus luteus* (Raphidophyceae) with special reference to the taxonomy. *Bot. Mag. Tokyo* **98**: 251–62.

609   Harada, A. & T. Yamagishi (1984). Meiosis in *Spirogyra* (Chlorophyceae). *Jap. J. Phycol.* **32**: 10–18.

610   Hargraves, P. & F.W. French (1983). Diatom resting spores: significance and strategies. In *Survival Strategies of the Algae*, ed. G.A. Fryxell, pp. 49–68. Cambridge University Press.

611   Harold, F.M. (1966). Inorganic polyphosphates in biology: structure, metabolism, and function. *Bact. Rev.* **30**: 772–94.

612   Harris, E.H. (1989). *The Chlamydomonas Source Book*. Academic Press, San Diego.

613   Harris, G.P. (1986). *Phytoplankton Ecology. Structure, Function and Fluctuation*. Chapman & Hall, London.

614   Hartmann, T. & W. Eschrich (1969). Stofftransport in Rotalgen. *Planta* **85**: 303–12.

615   Harvey, W.H. (1851). Nereis Boreali-americana. I. Melanospermeae. *Smithsonian Contribution to Knowledge* **III** (4): 1–150.

616   Hasle, G.R. (1954). More on phototactic migration in marine dinoflagellates. *Nytt Mag. Bot.* **2**: 139–47.

617   Hasle, G.R. (1974). The 'mucilage pore' of pennate diatoms. *Nova Hedwigia, Beih.* **45**: 167–94.

618   Haupt, W. (1982). Movement of chloroplasts under the control of light. In *Progress in Phycological Research*, Vol. 2, ed. F.E. Round & D.J. Chapman, pp. 228–81. Elsevier, Amsterdam.

619   Hausmann, K. (1979). The function of the periplast of the Cryptophyceae during the discharge of ejectisomes. *Arch. Protistenk.* **122**: 222–5.

620   Hausmann, K. & D.J. Patterson (1984). Contractile vacuole complexes in algae. In *Compartments in Algal Cells and their Interaction*, ed. W. Wiessner, D.G. Robinson & R.C. Starr, pp. 139–46. Springer-Verlag, Berlin.

621   Hawkes, M.W. (1978). Sexual reproduction in *Porphyra gardneri* (Smith et Hollenberg) Hawkes (Bangiales, Rhodophyta). *Phycologia* **17**: 329–53.

622   Hawkes, M.W. (1980). Ultrastructure characteristics of monospore formation in *Porphyra gardneri* (Rhodophyta). *J. Phycol.* **16**: 192–96.

623   Hawkes, M.W. (1988). Evidence of sexual reproduction in *Smithora naiadum* (Erythro-

peltidales, Rhodophyta) and its evolutionary significance. *Br. Phycol. J.* **23**: 327–36.

624   Hawkins, A.F. & G.F. Leedale (1971). Zoospore structure and colony formation in *Pediastrum* spp. and *Hydrodictyon reticulatum. Ann. Bot.* **35**: 201–11.

625   Hawkins, E.K. (1972). Observations on the developmental morphology and fine structure of pit connections in red algae. *Cytologia* **37**: 759–68.

626   Haxo, F.T. (1985). Photosynthetic action spectrum of the coccolithophorid, *Emiliania huxleyi* (Haptophyceae): 19'hexanoyloxyfucoxanthin as antenna pigment. *J. Phycol.* **21**: 282–87.

627   Haxo, F.T., A. Neori & M. White (1984). Photosynthetic action spectra of chloromonads. *J. Protozool.* **31**: 25a.

628   Hay, C.H. (1979). Nomenclature and taxonomy within the genus *Durvillaea* Bory (Phaeophyceae: Durvillaeales Petrov). *Phycologia* **18**: 191–201.

629   Heaney, S.I., D.V. Chapman & H.R. Morison (1983). The role of the cyst stage in the seasonal growth of the dinoflagellate *Ceratium hirundinella* within a small productive lake. *Br. Phycol. J.* **18**: 47–59.

630   Heath I.B. & W.M. Darley (1972). Observations on the ultrastructure of the male gametes of *Biddulphia levis* Ehr. *J. Phycol.* **8**: 51–9.

631   Hegewald, E. (1982). Taxonomisch morphologische Untersuchungen von *Scenedesmus*-Isolaten aus Stammsammlungen. *Arch. Hydrobiol.,* Suppl. **60.4** (*Algol. Stud.* **29**): 375–406.

632   Heimans, J. (1962). Desmidiaceën in biogeographie en taxonomie. *Dodonaea* **30**: 239–52.

633   Heimke, J.W. & R.C. Starr (1979). The sexual process in several heterogamous *Chlamydomonas* strains in the subgenus *Pleiochloris. Arch. Protistenk.* **122**: 20–42.

634   Heinhorst, S. & J.M. Shively (1983). Encoding of both subunits of ribulose-1,5-biphosphate carboxylase by organelle genome of *Cyanophora paradoxa. Nature* **304**: 373–74.

635   Hellebust, J.A. & J. Lewin (1977). Heterotrophic nutrition. In *The Biology of Diatoms,* ed. D. Werner, pp. 169–97. Blackwell, Oxford.

636   Hendriks, L., C. van Broeckhoven, A. Vandenberghe, Y. van de Peer & R. de Wachter (1988). Primary and secondary structure of the 18 S ribosomal RNA of the bird spider *Eurypelma californica* and evolutionary relationships among eukaryotic phyla. *Eur. J. Biochem.* **177**: 15–20.

637   Henry, E.C. (1984). Syringodermatales ord. nov. and *Syringoderma floridana* sp. nov. (Phaeophyceae). *Phycologia* **23**: 419–26.

638   Henry, E.C. (1987a). The life history of *Phyllariopsis brevipes* (= *Phyllaria reniformis*) (Phyllariaceae, Laminariales, Phaeophyceae), a kelp with dioecious but sexually monomorphic gametophytes. *Phycologia* **26**: 17–22.

639   Henry, E.C. (1987b). Primitive reproductive characters and a photoperiodic response in *Saccorhiza dermatodea* (Laminariales, Phaeophyceae). *Br. Phycol. J.* **22**: 23–31.

640   Henry, E.C. & K.M. Cole (1982a). Ultrastructure of swarmers in the Laminariales (Phaeophyceae). I. Zoospores. *J. Phycol.* **18**: 550–69.

641   Henry, E.C. & K.M. Cole (1982b). Ultrastrucure of swarmers in the Laminariales (Phaeophyceae). II. Sperm. *J. Phycol.* **18**: 570–9.

642   Henry, E.C. & D.G. Müller (1983). Studies on the life history of *Syringoderma phinnei* sp. nov. (Phaeophyceae). *Phycologia* **22**: 387–93.

643   Henssen, A. & H.M. Jahns (1974). *Lichenes. Eine Einführung in die Flechtenkunde.* Thieme, Stuttgart.

644   Herdman, M. (1982). Evolution and genetic properties of cyanobacterial genomes. In *The Biology of Cyanobacteria,* ed. N.G. Carr & B.A. Whitton, pp. 263–305. Blackwell, Oxford.

645   Herdman, M. & R.Y. Stanier (1977). The cyanelle: chloroplast or endosymbiotic prokaryote? *FEMS Letters* **1**: 7–12.

646   Herndon, W. (1958). Studies on chlorosphaeracean algae from soil. *Am. J. Bot.* **45**: 298–308.

647   Herndon, W. (1958). Some new species of chlorococcacean algae. *Am. J. Bot.* **45**: 308–23.

648   Herth, W., B. Heck & H.U. Koop (1981). The flagellar root system in the gamete of *Acetabularia mediterranea. Protoplasma* **109**: 257–69.

649   Herth, W., A. Kuppel & W.W. Francke (1975). Cellulose in *Acetabularia* cyst walls. *J. Ultrastruct. Res.* **50**: 289–92

650   Heywood, P. (1972). Structure and origin of flagellar hairs in *Vacuolaria virescens. J. Ultrastruct. Res.* **39**: 608–23.

651   Heywood, P. (1973). Intracisternal microtubules and flagellar hairs of *Gonyostomum semen* (Ehrenb.) Diesing. *Br. Phycol. J.* **8**: 43–6.

652   Heywood, P. (1974). Mitosis and cytokinesis in the Chloromonadophycean alga *Gonyostomum*

semen. J. Phycol. **10**: 335–58.

653 Heywood, P. (1980). Chloromonads. In *Phytoflagellates,* ed. E.R. Cox, pp. 351–79. Elsevier/North-Holland, Amsterdam.

654 Heywood. P. (1983). The genus *Vacuolaria* (Raphidophyceae). In *Progress in Phycological Research,* Vol. 2, ed. F.E. Round & D.J. Chapman, pp. 53–86. Elsevier, Amsterdam.

655 Heywood, P. (1990). Phylum Raphidophyta. In *Handbook of Protoctista,* ed. L. Margulis, J.O. Corliss, M. Melkonian & D.J. Chapman, pp. 318–25. Jones & Bartlett, Boston.

656 Heywood, P. & M.B.E. Godward (1973). Chromosome number and morphology in *Vacuolaria virescens* (Chloromonadophyceae). *Ann. Bot.* **37**: 423–5.

657 Heywood, P. & G.F. Leedale (1985). Order 6. Raphidomonadida Heywood & Leedale 1983. In *An Illustrated Guide to the Protozoa,* ed. J.J. Lee, S.H. Hutner & E.C. Bovee, pp. 70–4. Society of Protozoologists, Lawrence, Kansas.

658 Hibberd, D.J. (1970). Observations on the cytology and ultrastructure of *Ochromonas tuberculatus* sp. nov. (Chrysophyceae), with special reference to the discobolocysts. *Br. Phycol. J.* **5**: 119–43.

659 Hibberd, D.J. (1974). Observations on the cytology and ultrastructure of *Chlorobotrys regularis* (West) Bohlin with special reference to its position in the Eustigmatophyceae. *Br. Phycol. J.* **9**: 37–46.

660 Hibberd, D.J. (1973). Observations on the ultrastructure of flagellar scales in the genus *Synura* (Chrysophyceae). *Arch. Microbiol.* **89**: 291–304.

661 Hibberd, D.J. (1976). The ultrastructure and taxonomy of the Chrysophyceae and Prymnesiophyceae (Haptophyceae): a survey with some new observations on the ultrastructure of the Chrysophyceae. *Bot. J. Linn. Soc.* **72**: 55–80.

662 Hibberd, D.J. (1977). Observations on the ultrastructure of the cryptomonad endosymbiont of the red-water ciliate *Mesodinium rubrum. J. Mar. Biol. Ass. U.K.* **57**: 45–61.

663 Hibberd, D.J. (1977). Ultrastructure of cyst formation in *Ochromonas tuberculata* (Chrysophyceae). *J. Phycol.* **13**: 309–20.

664 Hibberd, D.J. (1979). The structure and phylogenetic significance of the flagellar transition region in the chlorophyll c-containing algae. *BioSystems* **11**: 243–61.

664a Hibberd, D.J. (1980a). Prymnesiophytes (= Haptophytes). In *Phytoflagellates,* ed. E.R. Cox, pp. 273–317. Elsevier/North Holland, Amsterdam.

665 Hibberd, D.J. (1980b). Eustigmatophytes. In *Phytoflagellates,* ed. E.R. Cox, pp. 319–34. Elsevier/North Holland, Amsterdam.

666 Hibberd, D.J. (1982a). Xanthophyceae. In *Synopsis and Classification of Living Organisms,* ed. S.P. Parker, pp. 91–4. McGraw-Hill, New York.

667 Hibberd, D.J. (1982b). Eustigmatophyceae. In *Synopsis and Classification of Living Organisms,* ed. S.P. Parker, p. 95. McGraw-Hill, New York.

668 Hibberd, D.J. (1986). Ultrastructure of the Chrysophyceae – phylogenetic implications and taxonomy. In *Chrysophytes, Aspects and Problems,* ed. J. Kristiansen & R.A. Andersen, pp. 23–6. Cambridge University Press, Cambridge.

668a Hibberd, D.J. (1990a). Phylum Xanthophyta. In *Handbook of Protoctista,* ed. L. Margulis, J.O. Corliss, M. Melkonian & D.J. Chapman, pp. 686–97. Jones & Bartlett, Boston.

668b Hibberd, D.J. (1990b). Phylum Eustigmatophyta. In *Handbook of Protoctista,* ed. L. Margulis, J.O. Corliss, M. Melkonian & D.J. Chapman, pp. 326–33. Jones & Bartlett, Boston.

669 Hibberd, D.J., A.D. Greenwood & H.B. Griffiths (1971). Observations on the ultrastructure of the flagella and periplast in the Cryptophyceae. *Br. Phycol. J.* **6**: 61–72.

670 Hibberd, D.J. & G.F. Leedale (1970). Eustigmatophyceae – a new algal class with unique organization of the motile cell. *Nature* **225**: 758–60.

671 Hibberd, D.J. & G.F. Leedale (1971). A new algal class – the Eustigmatophyceae. *Taxon* **20**: 523–5.

672 Hibberd, D.J. & G.F. Leedale (1972). Observations on the cytology and ultrastructure of the new algal class Eustigmatophyceae. *Ann. Bot.* **36**: 49–71.

673 Hibberd, D.J. & G.F. Leedale (1985a). Order 4. Chrysomonadida. In *An Illustrated Guide to the Protozoa,* ed. J.J. Lee, S.H. Hutner and E.C. Bovee, pp. 54–70. Society of Protozoologists, Lawrence, Kansas.

674 Hibberd, D.J. & G.F. Leedale (1985b). Order 7. Prymnesiida. In *An Illustrated Guide to the Protozoa,* ed. J.J. Lee, S.H. Hutner and E.C. Bovee, pp. 74–88. Society of Protozoologists, Lawrence, Kansas.

675   Hibberd, D.J. & R.E. Norris (1984). Cytology and ultrastructure of *Chlorarachnion reptans* (Chlorarachniophyta divisio nova, Chlorarachniophyceae classis nova). *J. Phycol.* **20**: 310–30.

676   Hilenski, L.L. & P.L. Walne (1985a). Ultrastructure of the flagella of the colorless phagotroph *Peranema trichophorum* (Euglenophyceae). I. Flagellar mastigonemes. *J. Phycol.* **21**: 114–25.

677   Hilenski, L.L. & P.L. Walne (1985b). Ultrastructure of the flagella of the colorless phagotroph *Peranema trichophorum* (Euglenophyceae). II. Flagellar roots. *J. Phycol.* **21**: 125–34.

678   Hill, D.R.A. & K.S. Rowan (1989). The biliproteins of the Cryptophyceae. *Phycologia* **28**: 455–63.

679   Hill, D.R.A. & R. Wetherbee (1986). *Proteomonas sulcata* gen. et sp. nov. (Cryptophyceae), a cryptomonad with two morphologically distinct and alternating forms. *Phycologia* **25**: 521–43.

680   Hill, D.R.A. & R. Wetherbee (1989). A reappraisal of the genus *Rhodomonas* (Cryptophyceae). *Phycologia* **28**: 143–58.

681   Hill, G.J.C., M.R. Cunningham, M.M. Byrne, T.P. Ferry & J.S. Halvorson (1989). Chemical control of androspore morphogenesis in *Oedogonium donnellii* (Chlorophyta, Oedogoniales). *J. Phycol.* **25**: 368–76.

682   Hill, G.J.C. & L. Machlis (1968). An ultrastructural study of vegetative cell division in *Oedogonium borisianum*. *J. Phycol.* **4**: 261–71.

683   Hillis, L.W. (1959). A revision of the genus *Halimeda* (order Siphonales). *Inst. Mar. Sci.* **6**: 321–403.

684   Hillis-Colinvaux, L. (1980). Ecology and taxonomy of *Halimeda*: primary producer of coral reefs. *Advances in Marine Biology* **17**: 1–327.

685   Hillis-Colinvaux, L. (1984). Systematics of the Siphonales. In *Systematics of the Green Algae*, ed. D.E.G. Irvine & D.M. John, pp. 271–96. Academic Press, London.

686   Hillis-Colinvaux, L. (1986). Distribution patterns of some Bryopsidales in the past: their bearing on present distributions. *Bot. Mar.* **24**: 271–7.

687   Hills, G.J., M. Guerney-Smith & K. Roberts (1973). Structure, composition and morphogenesis of the cell wall of *Chlamydomonas reinhardii* II. Electron microscopy and optical diffraction analysis. *J. Ultrastruct. Res.* **43**: 79–192.

688   Hindák, F. (1963). Systematik der Gattungen *Koliella* gen. nov. und *Raphidonema* Lagerh. *Nova Hedwigia* **6**: 95–125.

689   Hirayama, T. & T. Hori (1984). Flagellar apparatus of the quadriflagellated zoospore of *Chaetomorpha spiralis* Okamura (Cladophorales, Chlorophyta). *Bot. Mar.* **27**: 335–44.

690   Hirn, K.E. (1900). Monographie und Iconographie der Oedogoniaceae. *Acta Sci. Fenn.* **27**: 1–394.

691   Hoek, C. van den (1958). The algal microvegetation in and on barnacle shells, collected along the Dutch and French coasts. *Blumea* **9**: 206–14.

692   Hoek, C. van den (1963). *Revision of the European Species of Cladophora*. Brill, Leiden.

693   Hoek, C. van den (1966). Taxonomic criteria in four chlorophycean genera. *Nova Hedwigia* **10**: 367–86.

694   Hoek, C. van den (1981). Chlorophyta: morphology and classification. In *The Biology of Seaweeds*, ed. C.S. Lobban & M.J. Wynne, pp. 86–132. Blackwell, Oxford.

695   Hoek, C. van den (1982a). A taxonomic revision of the American species of *Cladophora* (Chlorophyceae) in the North Atlantic Ocean and their geographic distribution. *Verh. Kon. Ned. Akad. Wetensch. Afd. Natuurk.* 2e R., **78**: 1–236.

696   Hoek, C. van den (1982b). The distribution of benthic marine algae in relation to the temperature regulation of their life histories. *Biol. J. Linn. Soc.* **18**: 81–144.

697   Hoek, C. van den (1984a). The systematics of the Cladophorales. In *Systematics of the Green Algae*, ed. D.E.G. Irvine & D.M. John, pp. 157–78. Academic Press, London.

698   Hoek, C. van den (1984b). World-wide latitudinal and longitudinal seaweed distribution patterns and their possible causes, as illustrated by the distribution of rhodophytan genera. *Helgol. Meeresunters.* **38**: 227–57.

699   Hoek, C. van den, W. Admiraal, F. Colijn & V.N. de Jonge (1979). The role of algae and seagrasses in the Wadden Sea: a review. In *Flora and Vegetation of the Wadden sea, Final Report of the Section 'Marine Botany' of the Wadden Sea Working Group*, ed. W.J. Wolff, pp. 9–118, 172–206. Stichting Vetn tot Stevn aan Waddenonderzoek, Leiden.

700   Hoek, C. van den, A.M. Cortel-Breeman, H.

Rietema & J.B.W. Wanders (1972). L'interprétation des données obtenues, par des cultures uni-
algales, sur les cycles évolutifs des algues.
Quelques examples tirés des recherches conduites
au laboratoire de Groningue. *Soc. Bot. France,
Mémoires*: 193–242.

701   Hoek, C. van den, A.M. Cortel-Breeman &
J.B.W. Wanders (1975). Algal zonation in the
fringing coral reef of Curacao, Netherlands
Antilles, in relation to zonation of corals and gor-
gonians. *Aquat. Bot.* **1**: 269–308.

702   Hoek, C. van den & C.A. Flinterman (1968).
The life-history of *Sphacelaria furgicera* Kütz.
(Phaeophyceae). *Blumea* **16**: 193–242.

703   Hoek, C. van den & H.M. Jahns (1978). *Algen.
Einführung in die Phykologie*. Thieme, Stuttgart.

704   Hoek, C. van den, W.T. Stam & J.L. Olsen
(1988). The emergence of a new chlorophytan system and Dr. Kornmann's contribution thereto.
Helgol. Meeresunters. **42**: 339–83.

704a   Hoek, C. van den, W.T. Stam & J.L. Olsen
(1992). The Chlorophyta: systematics and phy-
logeny. In *Phylogenetic Changes in Peroxisomes of
Algae; Phylogeny of Plant Peroxisomes*, ed. H.
Stabenau, pp. 330–68. University of Oldenburg,
Germany.

705   Hoeksema, B. W. & C. van den Hoek (1983).
The taxonomy of *Ulva* (Chlorophyceae) from the
coastal region of Roscoff. *Bot. Mar.* **26**: 65–86.

706   Hoffmann, J.P. & L.E. Graham (1984). Effects
of selected physicochemical factors on growth and
zoosporogenesis of *Cladophora glomerata* (Chlorophyta). *J. Phycol.* **20**: 1–7.

707   Hoffman, L.R. (1960). Chemotaxis of *Oedogonium* sperms. *Southwest. Nat.* **5**: 111–16.

708   Hoffman, L.R. (1965). Cytological studies of
Oedogonium I. Oospore germination in *Oedogonium fovealatum. Am. J. Bot.* **52**: 173–181.

709   Hoffman, L.R. (1970). Observations on the fine
structure of *Oedogonium* VI. The striated component of the compound flagellar 'roots' of *O. cardiacum. Can. J. Bot.* **48**: 189–96.

710   Hoffman, L.R. & I. Manton (1963).
Observations on the fine structure of *Oedogonium*
II. The spermatozoid of *O. cardiacum. Am. J. Bot.*
50: 455–63.

711   Hoffman, L.R. (1976). Fine structure of *Cylindrocapsa* zoospores. *Protoplasma* **87**: 191–219.

712   Hoffman, L.R. (1984a). *Atractomorpha porcata*

sp. nov., a new member of the Sphaeropleaceae
(Chlorophyceae) from California. *J. Phycol.* **20**:
225–36.

713   Hoffman, L.R. (1984b). Male gametes of *Atractomorpha echinata* Hoffman (Chlorophyceae). *J.
Phycol.* **20**: 573–84.

714   Hoffman, L.R. & C.S. Hofmann (1975).
Zoospore formation in *Cylindrocapsa. Can. J. Bot.*
53: 439–51.

715   Hoffmann, M.J. (1985). Precambrian carbona-
ceous megafossils. In *Palaeoalgology*, ed. D.F.
Toomey & M.H. Nitecki, pp. 20–33. Springer-
Verlag, Berlin.

716   Hoham, R.W. (1980). Unicellular chlorophytes
– snow algae. In *Phytoflagellates*, ed. E.R. Cox, pp.
61–84. Elsevier/North Holland, Amsterdam.

717   Holdsworth, R.H. (1971). The isolation and partial characterization of the pyrenoid protein of
Eremosphaera viridis. J. Cell. Biol. **51**: 499–512.

718   Holland, A.F., R.G. Zingmark & J.M. Dean
(1974). Quantitative evidence concerning the stabilization of sediments by marine benthic diatoms.
Mar. Biol. **27**: 191–6.

719   Hollande, A. (1952a). Classe de Chloro-
monadines (Chloromonadina Klebs, 1892). In
Traité de Zoologie, Vol. I, part 1, ed. P.P. Grassé,
pp. 227–37. Masson, Paris.

720   Hollande, A. (1952b). Classe des Eugléniens
(Euglenoidina Bütschli, 1884). In *Traité de
Zoologie*, Vol. I, part 1, ed. P.P. Grassé, pp. 238–84.
Masson, Paris.

720a   Hollande, A. (1952c). Classe des Crypto-
monadines (Cryptomonadina Ehrenberg, 1832). In
Traité de Zoologie, Vol. I, part 1, ed. P.P. Grassé,
pp. 285–308. Masson, Paris.

721   Hollande, A. (1952d). Classe des Chryso-
monadines. (Chrysomonadina Stein, 1878). In
Traité de Zoologie, Vol. I, part 1, ed. P.P. Grassé,
pp. 471–570. Masson, Paris.

722   Hollenberg, G.J. (1935). A study of *Halicystis
ovalis*. I. Morphology and reproduction. *Am. J. Bot.*
22: 783–812.

723   Hollenberg, G.J. (1936). A study of *Halicystis
ovalis*. II. Periodicity in the formation of gametes.
Am. J. Bot. **23**: 1–3.

724   Hommersand, M.H. & S. Frederick (1988). An
investigation of cystocarp development in *Gelidium
pteridifolium* with a revised description of the
Gelidiales (Rhodophyta). *Phycologia* **27**: 254–72.

725 Hooks, C.E., R.R. Bidigare, M.D. Keller & R.R.L. Guillard (1988). Coccoid eukaryotic marine ultraplankters with four different HPLC pigment signatures. *J. Phycol.* **24**: 571–80.

726 Hoopen, A. ten (1983). Effects of daylength and irradiance on the formation of reproductive organs in two algae: *Acrosymphyton purpuriferum* (J. Ag.) Sjöst. (Rhodophyceae) and *Sphacelaria rigidula* Kütz. (Phaeophyceae). Thesis, Univ. Groningen, Van Genderen, Groningen: 1–87.

727 Hoopen, A. ten, S. Bos & A.M. Breeman (1983). Photoperiodic response in the formation of gametangia of the long-day plant *Sphacelaria rigidula* (Phaeophyceae). *Mar. Ecol. Progr. Ser.* **13**: 285–9.

728 Hoops, H.J. (1984). Somatic cell flagellar apparatuses in two species of *Volvox* (Chlorophyceae). *J. Phycol.* **20**: 20–7.

729 Hoops, H.J. & G.L. Floyd (1983). Ultrastructure and development of the flagellar apparatus and flagellar motion in the colonial green alga *Astrephomene gubernaculifera. J. Cell. Sci.* **63**: 21–41.

730 Hoops, H.J., G.L. Floyd & J.A. Swanson (1982). Ultrastructure of the biflagellate motile cells of *Ulvaria oxysperma* (Kütz.) Bliding and phylogenetic relationships among Ulvaphycean algae. *Am. J. Bot.* **69**: 150–9.

731 Hoops, H.J. & G.B. Witman (1983). Outer doublet heterogeneity reveals structural polarity related to beat direction in *Chlamydomonas* flagella. *J. Cell Biol.* **97**: 902–8.

732 Hopkins, A.W. & G.E. McBride (1976). The life history of *Coleochaete scutata* (Chlorophyceae) studied by a Feulgen microspectrophotometric analysis of the DNA cycle. *J. Phycol.* **12**: 29–35.

733 Hori, H., B.-L. Lim & S. Osawa (1985). Evolution of green plants as deduced from 5S rRNA sequences. *Proc. Natl. Acad. Sci. USA* **82**: 820–3.

734 Hori, H., B.-L. Lim, T. Ohama, T. Kumazaki & S. Osawa (1985). Evolution of organisms deduced from 5S rRNA sequences. In *Population Genetics and Molecular Evolution*, ed. T. Ohta & K. Aoki, pp. 369–84. Japan Scientific Societies Press, Tokyo; Springer-Verlag, Berlin.

735 Hori, H. & S. Osawa (1987). Origin and evolution of organisms as deduced from 5S ribosomal RNA sequences. *Molec. Biol. Evol.* **4**: 445–72.

736 Hori, T. (1974). Electron microscope observations on the fine structure of the chloroplasts of algae. 2. The chloroplasts of *Caulerpa* (Chlorophyceae). *Int. Rev. Gesamt. Hydrobiol.* **59**: 239–45.

737 Hori, T. (1977). Electron microscope observations on the flagellar apparatus of *Bryopsis maxima* (Chlorophyceae). *J. Phycol.* **13**: 238–43.

738 Hori, T. (1979). Ultrastructure of cell division in the eucaryotic algae exclusive of green algae. (In Japanese, English summary.) *Jap. J. Phycol.* **27**: 217–29.

739 Hori, T. (1981). Ultrastructural studies on nuclear division during gametogenesis in *Caulerpa* (Chlorophyceae). *Jap. J. Phycol.* **29**: 163–170.

739a Hori, T. (1988). Ultrastructure of gametes and gametic fusion in *Bryopsis maxima* Okamura (Chlorophyceae). *Jap. J. Phycol.* **36**: 113–26.

740 Hori, T. & S. Enomoto (1978a). Electron microscope observations on the nuclear division in *Valonia ventricosa* (Chlorophyceae, Siphonocladales). *Phycologia* **17**: 133–42.

741 Hori, T. & S. Enomoto (1978b). Developmental cytology of *Dictyosphaeria cavernosa*. I. Light and electron microscope observations on cytoplasmatic cleavage in zooid formation. *Bot. Mar.* **21**: 401–8.

742 Hori, T. & S. Enomoto (1978c). Developmental cytology of *Dictyosphaeria cavernosa*. II. Nuclear division during zooid formation. *Bot. Mar.* **21**: 477–81.

743 Hori, T. & J.C. Green (1985a). An ultrastructural study of mitosis in non-motile coccolith-bearing cells of *Emiliania huxleyi* (Lohm.) Hay & Mohler (Prymnesiophyceae). *Protistologica* **21**: 107–20.

744 Hori, T. & J.C. Green (1985b). The ultrastructural changes during mitosis in *Imantonia rotunda* Reynolds (Prymnesiophyceae). *Bot. Mar.* **27**: 67–78.

745 Hori, T. & J.C. Green (1985c). The ultrastructure of mitosis in *Isochrysis galbana* Parke (Prymnesiophyceae). *Protoplasma* **125**: 140–51.

746 Hori, T., I. Inouye, T. Horiguchi & G.T. Boalch (1985). Observations on the motile stage of *Halosphaera minor* Ostenfeld (Prasinophyceae) with special reference to the cell structure. *Bot. Mar.* **28**: 529–37.

747 Hori, T. & T. Kobara (1982). Ultrastructure of the flagellar apparatus in the stephanokont zoospores of *Pseudobryopsis hainanensis* (Chlorophyceae). *Jap. J. Phycol.* **30**: 31–9.

748 Hori, T., R.E. Norris & M. Chihara (1986).

Studies on the ultrastructure and taxonomy of the genus *Tetraselmis* (Prasinophyceae) III. Subgenus *Parviselmis*. *Bot. Mag. Tokyo* **99**: 123–35.

749   Hori, T. & R. Ueda (1967). Electron microscope studies on the fine structure of plastids in siphonous green algae with special reference to their phylogenetic relationships. *Sci. Rep. Tokyo Daigaku*, Sect. B. **12**: 225–44.

750   Hori, T. & R. Ueda (1975). The fine structure of algal chloroplasts and algal phylogeny. In *Advance of Phycology in Japan*, ed. J. Tokida & H. Hirose, pp. 11–42. VEB Gustav Fischer, Jena.

751   Horne, R.W., D. Davies, K. Norton & M. Gurney-Smith (1971). Electron microscope and optical diffraction studies on isolated cell walls from *Chlamydomonas*. *Nature* **232**: 493–5.

752   Hoshaw, R.W. (1968). Biology of the filamentous conjugating algae. In *Algae, Man and the Environment*, ed. D.F. Jackson, pp. 135–84. Syracuse University Press, Syracuse, New York.

753   Hoshaw, R.W. & R.M. McCourt (1988). The Zygnemataceae (Chlorophyta): a twenty year update of research. *Phycologia* **27**: 511–48.

754   Hotchkiss, A.T. & R.M. Brown (1987). The association of rosette and globule terminal complexes with cellulose microfibril assembly in *Nitella translucens* var. *axillaris* (Charophyceae). *J. Phycol.* **23**: 229–37.

755   Hotchkiss, A.T., M.R. Gretz, K.B. Hicks & R.M. Brown (1989). The composition and phylogenetic significance of the *Mougeotia* (Charophyceae) cell wall. *J. Phycol.* **25**: 646–54.

756   Howard, R.J., K.R. Gayler & B.R. Grant (1975). Products of photosynthesis in *Caulerpa simpliciuscula* (Chlorophyceae). *J. Phycol.* **11**: 463–71.

757   Howard, R.J. & B.R. Grant (1977). Storage and structural products formed during photosynthesis in the siphonous alga *Caulerpa simpliciuscula* (Chlorophyceae). *J. Phycol.* **13**: 340–5.

758   Huber-Pestalozzi, G. (1961). *Das Phytoplankton des Süßwassers. Systematik und Biologie, part 5: Chlorophyceae, Ordnung Volvocales*. Schweitzerbart, Stuttgart.

759   Huber-Pestalozzi, G. (1968). *Das Phytoplankton des Süßwassers*, 2nd Ed., part 3: *Cryptophyceae, Chloromonadophyceae, Dinophyceae*. Schweitzerbart, Stuttgart.

760   Hudson, M.L. (1974). *Field, culture and ultrastructural studies on the marine green alga Acrosiphonia in the Puget Sound Region*. Thesis, University of Washington.

761   Hudson, M.L. & J.R. Waaland (1974). Ultrastructure of mitosis and cytokinesis in the multinucleate green alga *Acrosiphonia*. *J. Cell Biol.* **62**: 274–94.

762   Huizing, H.J. & H. Rietema (1975). Xylan and mannan as cell wall contituents of different stages in the life-histories of some siphoneous green algae. *Br. Phycol. J.* **10**: 13–16.

763   Huizing, H.J., H. Rietema & J.H. Sietsma (1979). Cell wall constituents of several siphonous green algae in relation to morphology and taxonomy. *Br. Phycol. J.* **14**: 25–32.

764   Hunt, L.T., D.G. George & W.C. Barker (1985). The prokaryote-eukaryote interface. *BioSystems* **18**: 223–40.

765   Hurdelbrink, L. & H.O. Schwantes (1972). Sur le cycle de développement de *Batrachospermum*. *Soc. Bot. France, Mémoires*: 269–74.

766   Huss, V.A.R., R. Dörr, U. Grossmann & E. Kessler (1986). Deoxyribonucleic acid reassociation in the taxonomy of the genus *Chlorella* I. *Chlorella sorokiniana*. *Arch. Mikrobiol.* **145**: 329–33.

767   Huss, V.A.R., A. Hehenberger & E. Kessler (1987). Deoxyribonucleic acid reassociation in the taxonomy of the genus *Chlorella*. III. *Chlorella fusca* and *Chlorella kessleri*. *Arch. Mikrobiol.* **149**: 1–3.

768   Huss, V.A.R., G. Huss & E. Kessler (1989). Deoxyribonucleic acid reassociation and interspecific relationships of the genus *Chlorella* (Chlorophyceae). *Pl. Syst. Evol.* **168**: 71–82.

769   Huss, V.A.R., E. Schwarzwälder & E. Kessler (1987). Deoxyribonucleic acid reassociation in the taxonomy of *Chlorella*. II. *Chlorella saccharophila*. *Arch. Mikrobiol.* **147**: 221–4.

770   Hustede, H. (1960). Über den Generationswechsel zwischen *Derbesia neglecta* Berth. und *Bryopsis halymeniae* Berth. *Naturwissenschaften* **47**: 19.

771   Hustede, H. (1964). Entwicklungsphysiologische Untersuchungen über den Generationswechsel zwischen *Derbesia neglecta* Berth. und *Bryopsis halymeniae* Berth. *Bot. Mar.* **6**: 134–42.

772   Hustedt, F. (1956). *Kieselalgen*. Kosmos-Verlag, Stuttgart.

773   Hyams, J.S. & G.G. Borisy (1978). Isolated

flagellar apparatus of *Chlamydomonas*. Characterisation of forward swimming and alteration of wave form and reversal of motion by calcium ions in vitro. *J. Cell Sci.* **33**: 235–53.

774 Hyams, J.S. & D. Chasey (1974). Aspects of the flagellar apparatus and associated microtubules in a marine alga. *Exp. Cell Res.* **84**: 381–7.

775 Ichimura, T. & F. Kasai (1984). Time lapse analyses of sexual reproduction in *Closterium ehrenbergii* (Conjugatophyceae). *J. Phycol.* **20**: 258–65.

776 Ikemori, M. & S. Arasaki (1977). Photosynthetic pigments in marine algae. I. Two dimensional paper chromatographic separation of chlorophylls and carotenoids from green algae and sea grasses. *Bull. Jap. Soc. Phycol.* **25**: 54–65.

777 Imai, I. & K. Itoh (1987). Annual life cycle of *Chattonella* spp., causative flagellates of noxious red tides in the Inland Sea of Japan. *Mar. Biol.* **94**: 287–92.

778 Ingham, H.R., J. Mason & P.C. Wood (1968). Distribution of toxin in molluscan shellfish following the occurrence of mussel toxicity in North-East England. *Nature* **220**: 25–7.

779 Inouye, I., T. Hori & M. Chihara (1983). Ultrastructure and taxonomy of *Pyramimonas lunata*, a new marine species of the class Prasinophyceae. *Jap. J. Phycol.* **31**: 238–49.

780 Inouye, I., T. Hori & M. Chihara (1985). Ultrastructural characters of *Pyramimonas* and their possible relevance in taxonomy. In *Origin and Evolution of Diversity in Plants and Plant Communities*, ed. H. Hara, pp. 314–27. Academia Scientific Book Inc., Tokyo.

781 Inouye, I., M. Kawachi & M. Chihara (1988). Uniformity and diversity of the flagellar apparatus and transition region in the Prymnesiophyceae. *Third International Phycological Congress, Monash University, Melbourne, Abstracts:* 19.

782 Inouye, I. & R.N. Pienaar (1984). New observations on the coccolithophorid *Umbilicosphaera sibogae* var. *foliosa* (Prymnesiophyceae) with special reference to cell covering, cell structure and flagellar apparatus. *Br. Phycol. J.* **19**: 357–69.

783 Inouye, I. & R.N. Pienaar (1985). Ultrastructure of the flagellar apparatus in *Pleurochrysis* (class Prymnesiophyceae). *Protoplasma* **125**: 24–35.

784 Inouye, I. & R.N. Pienaar (1988). Light and electron microscope observations on the type species of *Syracosphaera, S. pulchra* (Prymnesiophyceae). *Br. Phycol. J.* **23**: 205–17.

784a Itoh, T. & R.M. Brown (1984). The assembly of cellulose microfibrils in *Valonia macrophysa* Kütz. *Planta* **160**: 372–381.

785 Iversen, E.S. (1968). *Farming the Edge of the Sea*. Fishing News (Books), London.

786 Iyengar, M.O.P. & K.R. Ramanathan (1940). On the reproduction of *Anadyomene stellata* (Wulf). Ag. *New Phytol.* **19**: 175–6.

786a Iyengar, M.O.P. & K.R. Ramanathan (1941). On the life-history and cytology of *Microdictyon tenuis* (Ag.) Decsne. *New Phytol.* **20**: 157–9.

787 Jacobson, D.M. & D.M. Anderson (1986). Thecate heterotrophic dinoflagellates: feeding behavior and mechanisms. *J. Phycol.* **22**: 249–58.

788 Jaenicke, L. (1977). Sex hormones of brown algae. *Naturwissenschaften* **64**: 69–75.

789 Jahn, T.L. & E.C. Bovee (1968). Locomotive and motile response in *Euglena*. In *The Biology of Euglena*, Vol. 1, ed. D.E. Buetow, pp. 45–108. Academic Press, New York.

790 Janet, C. (1912). Le *Volvox*. Ducourtieux & Gout, Limoges.

791 Jarosch, R. (1962). Gliding. In *Physiology and Biochemistry of Algae*, ed. R.A. Lewin, pp. 573–81. Academic Press, New York.

792 Jeffrey, C. (1971). Thallophytes and kingdoms. *Kew Bull.* **25**: 291–9.

793 Jeffrey, S.W. (1976). The occurrence of chlorophyll c_1 and c_2 in algae. *J. Phycol.* **12**: 349–50.

794 Jeffrey, S.W. (1989). Chlorophyll c pigments and their distribution in the chromophyte algae. In *The Chromophyte Algae*, ed. J.C. Green, B.S.C. Leadbeater & W.L. Diver, pp. 13–36. Clarendon Press, Oxford.

795 Jeffrey, S.W., M. Sielicki & F.T. Haxo (1975). Chloroplast pigment patterns in Dinoflagellates. *J. Phycol.* **11**: 374–84.

796 Jeffrey, S.W. & M. Vesk (1976). Further evidence for a membrane-bound endosymbiont within the dinoflagellate *Peridinium foliaceum*. *J. Phycol.* **12**: 450–5.

797 Jeffrey, S.W. & S.W. Wright (1987). A new spectrally distinct component in preparations of chlorophyll c from the microalga *Emiliania huxleyi* (Prymnesiophyceae). *Biochim. Biophys. Acta* **894**: 180–8.

798 Jesus, M.D. de, F. Tabatabai & D.J. Chapman

(1988). Presence and distribution of Cu/Zn superoxide dismutase in green algae: phylogenetic significance. *J. Phycol.* **24** (suppl.): 15.

799 Jesus, M.D. de, F. Tabatabai & D.J. Chapman (1989). Taxonomic distribution of copper-zinc superoxide dismutase in green algae and its phylogenetic importance. *J. Phycol.* **25**: 767–72.

800 Johansen, H.W. (1981). *Coralline Algae, a First Synthesis.* CRC Press, Boca Raton, Florida: 1–239.

801 John, D.M. (1984). On the systematics of the Chaetophorales. In *Systematics of the Green Algae,* ed. D.E.G. Irvine & D.M. John, pp. 207–32. Academic Press, London.

802 Johnson, P.W. & J.M. Sieburth (1979). Chroococcoid Cyanobacteria in the sea: a ubiquitous and diverse phototrophic biomass. *Limnol. Oceanogr.* **24**: 928–35.

803 Johnson, P.W. & J.M. Sieburth (1982). In situ morphology and occurrence of eucaryotic phototrophs of bacterial size in the picoplankton of estuarine and oceanic waters. *J. Phycol.* **18**: 318–27.

804 Johnson, U.G. & K.R. Porter (1968). Fine structure of cell division in *Chlamydomonas reinhardtii. J. Cell Biol.* **38**: 403–25.

805 Joly, A.B. (1967). *Gêneros de algas marinhas da Costa Atlântica Latino-Americana.* University of Sao Paulo.

806 Jónsson, S. (1962). Recherches sur les Cladophoracées marines. *Ann. Sci. Nat. Bot.,* Sér. 12, **3**: 25–230.

807 Jónsson, S. (1968). Sur le cycle ontogénétique et chromosomique du *Monostroma grevillei* (Thur.) Wittr. de Roscoff. *C.R. Acad. Sci. Paris* **267D**: 402–5.

808 Jónsson, S. (1970). Localisation de la méiose dans le cycle de l'*Acrosiphonia spinescens* (Kütz.) Kjellm. (Acrosiphoniaceae). *C. R. Acad. Sci. Paris* **271D**: 1859–61.

809 Jónsson, S. & L. Chesnoy (1982). Étude du cycle chromosomique de l'*Halosaccion ramentaceum* (Rhodophyta, Palmariales) d'Islande. *Crypt. Algol.* **3**: 273–8.

810 Jónsson, S. & L. Chesnoy (1984). Aspects ultrastructuraux de la fécondation chez l'*Acrosiphonia spinescens* (Kütz.) Kjellm. (Acrosiphoniales, Chlorophyta). *Bull. Soc. Bot. Fr.* **131**: 247–63.

811 Joosten A.M.T. & C. van den Hoek (1986). World-wide relationships between red seaweed floras: a multivariate approach. *Bot. Mar.* **29**: 195–214.

812 Jorde, I. (1933). Untersuchungen über den Lebenszyklus von *Urospora* Aresch. und *Codiolum* A. Braun. *Nytt. Mag. Naturvid.* **73**: 1–19.

813 Joyon, L. (1964). Appareil de Golgi et sécrétion de la gelée chez la chrysomonadine *Hydrurus foetidus* (Villars-Trevisan). In *Electron Microscopy 1964. Proc. 3rd European Reg. Conf., Prague,* ed. M. Titbach, pp. 179–80.

814 Kadlubowska, J.Z. (1984). Conjugatophyceae I. Chlorophyta VIII – Zygnemales. *Süßwasserflora von Mitteleuropa,* Vol. 16, ed. H. Ettl, J. Gerloff, H. Heynig & D. Mollenhauer. VEB Gustav Fisher Verlag, Jena.

815 Kageyama, A. & Y. Yokohama (1977). Pigments and photosynthesis of deep-water green algae. *Bull. Jap. Soc. Phycol.* **25**: 168–75.

816 Kageyama, A., Y. Yokohama, S. Shimura & T. Ikawa (1977). An efficient excitation energy transfer from a carotenoid, siphonoxanthin to chlorophyll a observed in a deep-water species of a chlorophycean seaweed. *Plant & Cell Physiol.* **18**: 477–80.

817 Kalkman, C. (1972). *Mossen en vaatplanten.* Oosthoek, Utrecht.

818 Kantz, T.S. & R.L. Chapman (1990). Pleurastrophyceae and Prasinophyceae: a comparison of molecular and non-molecular data sets. *J. Phycol.* **26** (suppl.): 17.

819 Kantz, T.S., R.L. Chapman & E.A. Zimmer (1989). Phylogenetic analysis of the Micromonadophyceae based on cytoplasmic rRNA analysis. *J. Phycol.* **25** (suppl.): 7.

819a Kantz, T.S., E.C. Theriot, E.A. Zimmer & R.L. Chapman (1990). The Pleurastrophyceae and Micromonadophyceae: a cladistic analysis of nuclear rRNA sequence data. *J. Phycol.* **26**: 711–21.

820 Kappers, F.J. (1973). Giftige blauwwieren en de drinkwatervoorziening. H_2O **6**: 396–400.

821 Kapraun, D.F. & P.W. Boone (1987). Karyological studies of three species of Scytosiphonaceae (Phaeophyta) from coastal North Carolina. *J. Phycol.* **23**: 318–22.

822 Kapraun, D.F., M.G. Gargiulo & G. Tripodi (1988). Nuclear DNA and karyotype variation in species of *Codium* (Codiales, Chlorophyta) from the North Atlantic. *Phycologia* **27**: 273–82.

823 Kapraun, D.F. & D.G. Luster (1980). Field and

culture studies of *Porphyra rosengurtii* Coll et Cox (Rhodophyta, Bangiales) from North Carolina. *Bot. Mar.* **23**: 449–57.

824 Karim, A.G.A. & F.E. Round (1967). Microfibrils in the lorica of the freshwater alga *Dinobryon. New Phytol.* **66**: 409–12.

825 Kasai, F. & T. Ichimura (1983). Zygospore germination and meiosis in *Closterium ehrenbergii* Meneghini (Conjugatophyceae). *Phycologia* **22**: 267–75.

826 Kat, M. (1979). The occurrence of *Prorocentrum* species and coincidental gastrointestinal illness of mussel consumers. In *Toxic Dinoflagellate Blooms*, ed. D.L. Taylor & H.H. Seliger, pp. 215–20. Elsevier/North Holland, Amsterdam.

827 Kates, M. & B.E. Volcani (1968). Studies on the biochemistry and fine structure of silica-shell formation in diatoms. Lipid components of the cell walls. *Z. Pflanzenphysiol.* **60**: 19–29.

828 Katsaros, C. & B. Galatis (1986). Ultrastructural studies on zoosporogenesis of *Halopteris filicina* (Sphacelariales, Phaeophyta). *Phycologia* **25**: 358–70.

829 Katsaros, C., B. Galatis & K. Mitrakos (1983). Fine structural studies on the interphase and dividing apical cells of *Sphacelaria tribuloides* (Phaeophyta). *J. Phycol.* **19**: 16–30.

830 Katz, K.R. & R.J. McLean (1979). Rhizoplast and rootlet system of the flagellar apparatus of *Chlamydomonas moewusii. J. Cell Sci.* **39**: 373–81.

831 Kawai, H. (1988). A flavin-like autofluorescent substance in the posterior flagellum of golden and brown algae. *J. Phycol.* **24**: 114–7.

831a Kawai, H. & I. Inouye (1989). Flagellar autofluorescence in forty four chlorophyll c-containing algae. *Phycologia* **28**: 222–7.

832 Kawano, L.S. & G.B. Bouck (1984). CER, cell surface-flagellum relationship during flagellar development. In *Compartments in Algal Cells and their Interaction*, ed. W. Wiessner, D.G. Robinson & R.C. Starr, pp. 76–87. Springer-Verlag, Berlin.

833 Kermarrec, A. (1980). Sur la place de la méiose dans le cycle de deux Chlorophycées marines: *Bryopsis plumosa* (Huds.) C. Ag. et *Bryopsis hypnoides* Lamouroux (Codiales). *Cah. Biol. Marine* **21**: 443–66.

834 Kessler, E. (1977). Physiological and biochemical contributions to the taxonomy of the genus *Prototheca* I. *Arch. Microbiol.* **113**: 139–41.

835 Kessler, E. (1984). A general review on the contribution of chemotaxonomy to the systematics of green algae. In *Systematics of Green Algae*, ed. D.E.G. Irvine & D.M. John, pp. 391–407. Academic Press, London.

836 Kiermayer, O. & B. Dobberstein (1973). Membrankomplexe dictyosomaler Herkunft als 'Matrizen' für die extraplasmatische Synthese und Orientierung von Mikrofibrillen. *Protoplasma* **77**: 437–51.

837 Kiermayer, O. & L.A. Staehelin (1972). Feinstruktur von Zellwand und Plasmamembran bei *Micrasterias denticulata* Bréb. nach Gefrierätzung. *Protoplasma* **74**: 227–37.

838 Kies, L. (1970a). Elektronenmikroskopische Untersuchungen über Bildung und Struktur der Zygotenwand bei *Micrasterias papillifera* (Desmidiaceae) I. Das Exospor. *Protoplasma* **70**: 21–47.

839 Kies, L. (1970b). Elektronenmikroskopische Untersuchungen über Bildung und Struktur der Zygotenwand bei *Micrasterias papillifera* (Desmidiaceae) II. Die Struktur von Mesospor und Endospor. *Protoplasma* **71**: 139–46.

840 Kies, L. (1974). Elektronenmikroskopische Untersuchungen an *Paulinella chromatophora* Lauterborn, einer Thekamöbe mit blaugrünen Endosymbionten (Cyanellen). *Protoplasma* **80**: 69–89.

841 Kies, L. (1976). Untersuchungen zur Feinstruktur und taxonomischen Einordnung von *Gloeochaete wittrockiana*, einer apoplastidalen capsalen Alge mit blaugrünen Endosymbionten (Cyanellen). *Protoplasma* **87**: 419–46.

842 Kies, L. (1979). Zur systematischen Einordnung von *Cyanophora paradoxa*, *Gloeochaete wittrockiana* und *Glaucocystis nostochinearum. Ber. Dtsch. Bot. Ges.* **92**: 445–54.

843 Kies, L. (1984a). Einzeller mit blaugrünen Endosymbionten (Cyanellen) als Objekte der Symbioseforschung und Modellorganismen für die Evolution der Chloroplasten. *Biol. Rdsch.* **22**: 145–57.

844 Kies, L. (1984b). Cytological aspects of blue-green algal endosymbiosis. In *Compartments in Algal Cells and their Interaction*, ed. W. Wiessner, D. Robinson & R.C. Starr, pp. 191–9. Springer-Verlag, Berlin.

845 Kies, L. (1988). The effect of penicillin on the morphology and ultrastructure of *Cyanophora*, *Gloeochaete* and *Glaucocystis* (Glaucocysto-

phyceae) and their cyanelles. *Endocytobiosis and Cell Res.* **5**: 361–72.

846 Kies, L. & B.P. Kremer (1990). Phylum Glaucocystophyta. In *Handbook of Protoctista*, ed. L. Margulis, J.O. Corliss, M. Melkonian & D.J. Chapman, pp. 152–66. Jones & Bartlett, Boston.

847 Kite, G.C. & J.D. Dodge (1985). Structural organization of plastid DNA in two anomalously pigmented dinoflagellates. *J. Phycol.* **21**: 50–6.

848 Klaveness, D. (1972a). *Coccolithus huxleyi* (Lohmann) Kamptner I. Morphological investigations on the vegetative cell and the process of coccolith formation. *Protistologica* **8**: 335–46.

849 Klaveness, D. (1972b). *Coccolithus huxleyi* (Lohm.) Kamptn. II. The flagellate cell, aberrant cell types, vegetative propagation and life cycles. *Br. Phycol. J.* **7**: 300–18.

850 Klaveness, D. (1973). The microanatomy of *Calyptrosphaera sphaeroidea* with some supplementary observations on the motile stage of *Coccolithus pelagicus*. *Norweg. J. Bot.* **20**: 151–62.

851 Klaveness, D. (1976). *Emiliania huxleyi* (Lohmann) Hay & Mohler. III. Mineral deposition and the origin of the matrix during coccolith formation. *Protistologica* **12**: 217–24.

852 Klaveness, D. (1988). Ecology of the Cryptomonadida: a first review. In *Growth and Reproductive Strategies of Freshwater Phytoplankton*, ed. C.D. Sandgren, pp. 105–33. Cambridge University Press.

853 Klein, B. (1987). The phenology of *Dumontia contorta* (Rhodophyta) studied by following individual plants in situ at Roscoff, Northern Brittany. *Bot. Mar.* **30**: 187–194.

854 Klein, R.M. & A. Cronquist (1967). A consideration of the evolutionary and taxonomic significance of some biochemical, micromorphological, and physiological characters in the Thallophytes. *Quart. Rev. Biol.* **42**: 105–296.

855 Kleinig, H. (1967). Über die Struktur von Siphonaxanthine und Siphoneine. *Phytochem.* **6**: 1681–6.

856 Kleinig, H. (1969). Carotenoids of siphonous green algae: a chemotaxonomic study. *J. Phycol.* **5**: 281–4.

857 Kleinig, H., H. Nitsche & K. Egger (1969). The structure of siphonaxanthine. *Tetrahedron Lett.* **1969**: 5139–42.

858 Kloppstech, K. (1982). *Acetabularia*. In *The Molecular Biology of Plant Development*, ed. H. Smith & D. Grierson, pp. 136–58. Blackwell Scientific Publications, Oxford.

859 Knapp, E. (1933). Über *Geosiphon pyriforme* Fr. Wettst. und intrazelluläre Pilz-Algen Symbiose. *Ber. Dtsch. Bot. Ges.* **51**: 210–16.

860 Kobara, T. & M. Chihara (1978). On the life history of *Pseudobryopsis hainanensis* (Chlorophyceae). *J. Jap. Bot.* **53**: 353–60.

861 Kochert, G. (1982). Sexual processes in Volvocales. In *Progress in Phycological Research*, Vol. 1. ed. F.E. Round & D.J. Chapman, pp. 235–56. Elsevier Biomedical Press, Amsterdam.

862 Koeman, R.P.T. (1985). *The taxonomy of Ulva Linnaeus, 1753, and Enteromorpha Link, 1820, (Chlorophyceae) in the Netherlands*. Thesis, University of Groningen, Netherlands.

863 Koeman, R.P.T. & A.M. Cortel-Breeman (1976). Observations on the life-history of *Elachista fucicola* (Vell.) Aresch. (Phaeophyceae) in culture. *Phycologia* **15**: 107–17.

864 Koeman, R.P.T. & C. van den Hoek (1981). The taxonomy of *Ulva* (Chlorophyceae) in the Netherlands. *Br. Phycol. J.* **16**: 9–53.

865 Koeman, R.P.T. & C. van den Hoek (1982a). The taxonomy of *Enteromorpha* Link, 1820, (Chlorophyceae) in the Netherlands. I. The section *Enteromorpha*. *Arch. Hydrobiol.*, Suppl. **63.3** (*Algol. Stud.* 32): 279–330.

866 Koeman, R.P.T. & C. van den Hoek (1982b). The taxonomy of *Enteromorpha* Link, 1820, (Chlorophyceae) in the Netherlands. II. The section Proliferae. *Crypt. Algol.* **3**: 37–70.

867 Koeman, R.P.T. & C. van den Hoek (1984). The taxonomy of *Enteromorpha* Link, 1820, (Chlorophyceae) in the Netherlands. III. The sections Flexuosae and Clathratae and an addition to the section Proliferae. *Crypt. Algol.* **5**: 21–61.

868 Kolkwitz, R. & H. Krieger (1941). Zygnemales. *Dr L. Rabenhorst's Kryptogamen-Flora von Deutschland, Österreich und der Schweiz*, Vol. XIII, part 2. Akademische Verlagsgesellschaft, Leipzig.

869 Komárek, J. (1976). Taxonomic review of the genera *Synechocystis* Sauv. 1892, *Synechococcus* Näg. 1849, and *Cyanothece* gen. nov. (Cyanophyceae). *Arch. Protistenk.* **118**: 119–79.

870 Komárek, J. (1985). Do all cyanophytes have a cosmopolitan distribution? Survey of the freshwater

cyanophyte flora of Cuba. *Arch. Hydrobiol.*, Suppl. **7.1** (*Algol. Stud.* **38/39**): 359–86.

871 Komárek, J. (1989). Polynuclearity of vegetative cells in coccal green algae from the family Neochloridaceae. *Arch. Protistenk.* **137**: 255–73.

872 Komárek, J. & K. Anagnostidis (1986). Modern approach to the classification system of the cyanophytes. 2 – Chroococcales. *Algol. Stud.* **43**: 157–226.

873 Komárek, J. & K. Anagnostidis (1989). Modern approach to the classification system of the cyanophytes. 4 – Nostocales. *Algol. Stud.* **56**: 247–345.

874 Komárek, J. & B. Fott (1983). Chlorophyceae (Grünalgen). Ordnung: Chlorococcales. In *Das Phytoplankton des Süßwassers*, ed. G. Huber-Pestalozzi, Part 7 (1), pp. 1–1044. E. Schweizerbart'sche Verlagsbuchhandlung, Stuttgart.

875 Koop, H.U. (1975). Über den Ort der Meiose bei *Acetabularia mediterranea*. *Protoplasma* **85**: 109–14.

876 Koop, H.U. (1979). The life cycle of *Acetabularia* (Dasycladales, Chlorophyceae): a compilation of evidence for meiosis in the primary nucleus. *Protoplasma* **100**: 353–66.

877 Koop, H.U. (1981). Protoplasmic streaming in *Acetabularia*. *Protoplasma* **109**: 143–57.

878 Koop, H.U., H.H. Heunert & R. Schmid (1977). Division of primary nucleus of *Acetabularia*. *Protoplasma* **93**: 131–4.

879 Kornmann, P. (1938). Zur Entwicklungsgeschichte von *Derbesia* und *Halicystis*. *Planta* **28**: 464–70.

880 Kornmann, P. (1955). Beobachtungen von *Phaeocystis*-Kulturen. *Helgol. Wiss. Meeresunters.* **5**: 218–33.

881 Kornmann, P. (1961a). Über *Spongomorpha lanosa* und ihre Sporophytenformen. *Helgol. Wiss. Meeresunters.* **7**: 195–205.

882 Kornmann, P. (1961b). Über *Codiolum* und *Urospora*. *Helgol. Wiss. Meeresunters.* **8**: 42–57.

883 Kornmann, P. (1962a). Zur Entwicklung von *Monostroma grevillei* und zur systematischen Stellung von *Gomontia polyrhiza*. *Ber. Dtsch. Bot. Ges.*, N.F. **1**: 37–9.

884 Kornmann, P. (1962b). Die Entwicklung von *Monostroma grevillei*. *Helgol. Wiss. Meeresunters.* **8**: 195–202.

885 Kornmann, P. (1962c). Der Lebenszyklus von

Desmarestia viridis. *Helgol. Wiss. Meeresunters.* **8**: 287–92.

886 Kornmann, P. (1962d). Eine Revision der Gattung *Acrosiphonia*. *Helgol. Wiss. Meeresunters.* **8**: 219–42.

887 Kornmann, P. (1963a). Die Ulotrichales, neu geordnet auf der Grundlage entwicklungsgeschichtlicher Befunde. *Phycologia* **3**: 60–8.

888 Kornmann, P. (1963b). Der Lebenszyklus einer marinen *Ulothrix*-Art. *Helgol. Wiss. Meeresunters.* **8**: 357–60.

889 Kornmann, P. (1964a). Zur Biologie von *Spongomorpha aeruginosa* (Linnaeus) van den Hoek. *Helgol. Wiss. Meeresunters.* **11**: 200–8.

890 Kornmann, P. (1964b). Der Lebenszyklus von *Acrosiphonia arcta*. *Helgol. Wiss. Meeresunters.* **11**: 110–7.

891 Kornmann, P. (1965a). Was ist *Acrosiphonia arcta*? *Helgol. Wiss. Meeresunters.* **12**: 40–51.

892 Kornmann, P. (1965b). Zur Analyse des Wachstums und des Aufbaus von *Acrosiphonia*. *Helgol. Wiss. Meeresunters.* **12**: 219–38.

893 Kornmann, P. (1966). *Hormiscia* neu definiert. *Helgol. Wiss. Meeresunters.* **13**: 408–25.

894 Kornmann, P. (1967). Wachstum und Aufbau von *Spongomorpha aeruginosa* (Chlorophyta, Acrosiphoniales). *Blumea* **15**: 9–16.

895 Kornmann, P. (1969). Gesetzmäßigkeiten des Wachstums und der Entwicklung von *Chaetomorpha darwinii* (Chlorophyta, Cladophorales). *Helgol. Wiss. Meeresunters.* **19**: 335–54.

896 Kornmann, P. (1970a). Der Lebenszyklus von *Acrosiphonia grandis* (Acrosiphoniales, Chlorophyta). *Mar. Biol.* **7**: 324–31.

897 Kornmann, P. (1970b). Phylogenetische Beziehungen in der Grünalgengattung *Acrosiphonia*. *Helgol. Wiss. Meeresunters.* **21**: 292–304.

898 Kornmann, P. (1972). Les sporophytes vivant en endophyte de quelques Acrosiphoniacées et leurs rapports biologiques et taxonomiques. *Soc. Bot. France, Mémoires*: 75–86.

899 Kornmann, P. (1973). Codiolophyceae, a new class of Chlorophyta. *Helgol. Wiss. Meeresunters.* **25**: 1–13.

900 Kornmann, P. (1984). *Erythrotrichopeltis*, eine neue Gattung der Erythropeltidaceae (Bangiophyceae, Rhodophyta). *Helgol. Wiss. Meeresunters.* **38**: 207–24.

901 Kornmann, P. (1987). Der Lebenszyklus von

Porphyrostromium obscurum (Bangiophyceae, Rhodophyta). *Helgol. Wiss. Meeresunters.* **41**: 127–37.

902   Kornmann, P. & P.-H. Sahling (1962). Zur Taxonomie und Entwicklung der *Monostroma*-Arten von Helgoland. *Helgol. Wiss. Meeresunters.* **8**: 302–20.

903   Kornmann, P. & P.-H. Sahling (1974). Prasiolales (Chlorophyta) von Helgoland. *Helgol. Wiss. Meeresunters.* **26**: 99–133.

904   Kornmann, P. & P.-H. Sahling (1983). Meeresalgen von Helgoland: Ergänzung. *Helgol. Wiss. Meeresunters.* **36**: 1–65.

905   Korshikov, O.A. (1953). Pidklas Protokokovi (Protococcinaea). *In: Viznacnik prisnovodnich vodorostej Ukranins'koj RSR.* Vidavnictvo Akademii Nauk Ukrains'koj RSR, Kiiv.

906   Kosinskaja, E.K. (1952). Conjugatae (I). In *Flora Plantarum Cryptogamarum URSS*, Vol. II. Akad. Nauk SSSR, Moscow.

907   Kosinskaja, E.K. (1960). Conjugatae (II). Part I. In *Flora Plantarum Cryptogamarum URSS*, Vol. V. Akad. Nauk SSSR, Moscow.

907a   Kouwets, F. (1994). *The Cell Cycle in Multinucleate Coccoid Green Algae: Ultrastructure and Systematics.* Dissertation, University of Leiden.

908   Kowallik, K.V. (1989). Molecular aspects and phylogenetic implications of plastid genomes of certain chromophytes. In *The Chromophyte Algae*, ed. J.C. Green, B.S.C. Leadbeater & W.L. Diver, pp. 101–24. Clardendon Press, Oxford.

908a   Kowallik, K.V. (1992). Origin and evolution of plastids from chlorophyll a+c-containing algae: suggested ancestral relationship to red and green algal plastids. In *Origins of plastids*, ed. R.A. Lewin. Chapman & Hall, New York.

909   Kraft, G.T. & P.A. Robins (1985). Is the order Cryptonemiales (Rhodophyta) defensible? *Phycologia* **24**: 67–77.

910   Kramer, D. (1970). Fine structure of growing cellulose fibrils of *Ochromonas malhamensis* Pringsheim (syn. *Poteriochromonas stipitata* Scherffel). *Z. Naturforsch.* **6**: 281–9.

911   Kreger, D.R. (1962). Cell walls. In *Physiology and Biochemistry of Algae*, ed. R.A. Lewin, pp. 315–35. Academic Press, New York.

912   Kreger, D.R. & J. van der Veer (1970). Paramylon in a chrysophyte. *Acta Bot. Neerl.* **19**: 401–2.

913   Kremer, B.P. (1977). Rotalgen-Chloroplasten als funktionelle Endosymbionten in einem marinen Opisthobranchier. *Naturwissenschaften* **64**: 147–8.

914   Kremer, B.P. (1983). Carbon economy and nutrition of the alloparasitic red alga *Harveyella mirabilis. Mar. Biol.* **76**: 231–9.

915   Kremer, B.P., R. Schmaljohann & R. Rötger (1980). Features and nutritional significance of photosynthates produced by unicellular algae symbiotic with larger Foraminifera. *Mar. Ecol. Prog. Ser.* **2**: 225–8.

916   Krieger, H. (1933–39). Die Desmidiaceen. In *Dr L. Rabenhorst's Kryptogamen-Flora von Deutschland, Österreich und der Schweiz*, Vol. XIII, section 1, parts 1 and 2. Akademische Verlagsgesellschaft, Leipzig.

917   Krieger, H. (1941–44). In: R. Kolkwitz & H. Krieger: Zygnemales. *Dr L. Rabenhorst's Kryptogamen-Flora von Deutschland, Österreich und der Schweiz*, Vol. XIII, section 2. Akademische Verlagsgesellschaft, Leipzig.

918   Krieger, H. & J. Gerloff (1962, 1965). *Die Gattung Cosmarium.* Parts 1 & 2. Cramer, Weinheim.

919   Kristiansen, A. (1984). Experimental field studies on the ecology of *Scytosiphon lomentaria* (Fucophyceae, Scytosiphonales) in Denmark. *Nord. J. Bot.* **4**: 719–24.

920   Kristiansen, A. & P.M. Pedersen (1979). Studies on life history and seasonal variation of *Scytosiphon lomentaria* (Fucophyceae, Scytosiphonales) in Denmark. *Bot. Tidsskr.* **74**: 31–56.

921   Kristiansen, J. (1982). Chromophycota Chrysophyceae. In *Synopsis and Classification of Living Organisms*, ed. S.P. Parker, pp. 81–6. McGraw-Hill, New York.

922   Kristiansen, J. (1990). Phylum Chrysophyta. In *Handbook of Protoctista*, ed. L. Margulis, J.O. Corliss, M. Melkonian & D.J. Chapman, pp. 438–53. Jones & Bartlett, Boston.

923   Kristiansen, J. & P.L. Walne (1977). Fine structure of photokinetic systems in *Dinobryon cylindricum* var. *alpinum* (Chrysophyceae). *Br. Phycol. J.* **12**: 329–41.

924   Kubai, D.F. & H. Ris (1969). Division in the dinoflagellate *Gyrodinium cohnii* (Schiller). A new type of nuclear reproduction. *J. Cell Biol.* **40**: 508–28.

925   Kuckuck, P. (1899). Beiträge zur Kenntnis der

Meeresalgen. Über den Generationswechsel von *Cutleria multifida* (Engl. Bot.) Grev. *Wiss. Meeresunters.* N.F. Kiel **3**: 95–117.

926 Kuckuck, P. (ed. P. Kornmann) (1960). Ectocarpaceen-Studien. *Spongonema. Helgol. Wiss. Meeresunters.* **6**: 93–113.

927 Kuckuck, P. & W. Nienburg (1929). Fragmente einer Monographie der Phaeosporeen. *Wiss. Meeresunters.*, N.F. Helgol. **17**: 1–93.

928 Kugrens, P. (1980). Electron microsocopic observations on the differentiation and release of spermatia in the marine red alga *Polysiphonia hendryi* (Ceramiales, Rhodomelaceae). *Am. J. Bot.* **67**: 519–28.

929 Kugrens, P. & D.J. Koslowski (1981). Electron microscope studies on a unique cytokinetic structure in tetrasporocytes of the red alga *Harveyella* sp. (Cryptonemiales, Choreocolacaceae). *Protoplasma* **108**: 197–209.

930 Kugrens, P. & R.E. Lee (1987). An ultrastructural survey of cryptomonad periplasts using quick-freezing freeze fracture techniques. *J. Phycol.* **23**: 365–76.

931 Kugrens, P. & R.E. Lee (1988). Ultrastructure of fertilization in a cryptomonad. *J. Phycol.* **24**: 385–93.

932 Kugrens, P., R.E. Lee & R.A. Andersen (1986). Cell form and surface patterns in *Chroomonas* and *Cryptomonas* cells (Cryptophyta) as revealed by scanning electron microscopy. *J. Phycol.* **22**: 512–22.

933 Kugrens, P., R.E. Lee & R.A. Andersen (1987). Ultrastructural variations in cryptomonad flagella. *J. Phycol.* **23**: 511–8.

934 Kugrens, P. & J.A. West (1972a). Ultrastructure of spermatial development in the parasitic red algae *Levringiella gardneriana* and *Erythrocystis saccata. J. Phycol.* **8**: 331–43.

935 Kugrens, P. & J.A. West (1972b). Synaptonemal complexes in red algae. *J. Phycol.* **8**: 187–191.

936 Kuhl, A. (1968). Phosphate metabolism of green algae. In *Algae, Man and the Environment*, ed. D.F. Jackson, pp. 37–52. Syracuse University Press, New York.

937 Kuhlenkamp, R. & D.G. Müller (1985). Culture studies on the life history of *Haplosora globosa* and *Tilopteris mertensii* (Tilopteridales, Phaeophyceae). *Br. Phycol. J.* **20**: 301–12.

938 Kuhsel, M.G. (1988). *Molekulare Character-*

isierung *des Plastidengenoms der Braunalge Dictyota dichotoma (Huds.) Lamour.* Thesis, University of Düsseldorf, Germany.

939 Kuhsel, M.G. & K.V. Kowallik (1987). The plastome of a brown alga, *Dictyota dichotoma.* II. Location of structural genes coding for ribosomal RNAs, the large subunit of ribulose-1,5-biphosphate carboxylase/oxygenase and for polypeptides of photosystem I and II. *Molec. Gen. Genet.* **207**: 361–8.

940 Kumar, H.D. (1985). *Algal Cell Biology.* Affiliated East-West Press Private Limited, Delhi.

941 Kumar, H.D. & K. Ueda (1984). Conjugation in the cyanobacterium *Anacystis nidulans. Molec. Gen. Genet.* **195**: 356–7.

942 Kumke, J. (1973). Beiträge zur Periodicität der Oogon-Entleerung bei *Dictyota dichotoma* (Phaeophyta). *Z. Pflanzenphysiol.* **70**: 191–210.

943 Kurogi, M. (1961). Species of cultivated *Porphyras* and their life-histories (Study of the life-history of *Porphyra* II). *Bull. Tohoku Reg. Fish. Res. Lab.* **18**: 1–115.

944 Kurogi, M. (1963). Seaweeds. Recent laver cultivation in Japan. *Fish. News Int.*, July/Sept. 1963: 3.

945 Kylin, H. (1923). Studien über die Entwicklungsgeschichte der Florideen. *K. Svenska Vetensk. Akad. Handl.* **63**: 1–139.

946 Kylin, H. (1928). Entwicklungsgeschichtliche Florideenstudien. *Lunds Universitets Årsskrift*, N.F. Avd. 2, **24** (4): 1–127.

947 Kylin, H. (1930). Über die Entwicklungsgeschichte der Florideen. *Lunds Universitets Årsskrift*, N.F. Avd. 2, **26** (6): 5–103.

948 Kylin, H. (1956). *Die Gattungen der Rhodophyceen.* Gleerups, Lund.

949 La Claire, J.W. (1981). Occurrence of plasmodesmata during infurrowing in a brown alga. *Biol. Cell* **40**: 139–42.

950 La Claire, J.W. (1982a). Light and electron microscopic studies of growth and reproduction in *Cutleria* (Phaeophyta). III. Nuclear division in the trichothallic meristem of *Cutleria cylindrica. Phycologia* **21**: 273–87.

951 La Claire, J.W. (1982b). Cytomorphological aspects of wound healing in selected Siphonocladales (Chlorophyceae). *J. Phycol.* **18**: 379–84.

952 La Claire, J.W. (1983). Inducement of wound motility in intact giant algal cells. *Exp. Cell Res.* **145**: 63–9.

953   La Claire, J.W. (1984a). Actin is present in a green alga that lacks cytoplasmic streaming. *Protoplasma* **120**: 242–4.

954   La Claire, J.W. (1984b). Cell motility during wound healing in giant algal cells: contraction in detergent-permeabilized cell models of *Ernodesmis. Eur. J. Cell Biol.* **33**: 180–9.

955   La Claire, J.W. (1984c). Mechanical wounding induces the formation of extensive coated membranes in giant algal cells. *Science* **225**: 331–3.

956   La Claire, J.W. (1987). Microtubule cytoskeleton in intact and wounded coenocytic green algae. *Planta* **171**: 30–42.

957   La Claire, J.W. (1989). Actin cytoskeleton in intact and wounded coenocytic green algae. *Planta* **177**: 47–57.

958   La Claire, J.W. & R.H. Goddard (1989). Immunolocalization of pericentriolar material in algal mitotic spindles. *Cell Motility and the Cytoskeleton* **13**: 225–38.

959   La Claire J.W. & J.A. West (1979). Light- and electron-microscopic studies of growth and reproduction in *Cutleria* (Phaeophyta). II. Gametogenesis in the male plant of *C. hancockii. Protoplasma* **101**: 247–67.

960   Lambert, D.H., D.A. Bryant, V.L. Stirewalt, J.M. Dubbs, S.E. Stevens & R.D. Porter (1985). Gene map for the *Cyanophora paradoxa* cyanelle genome. *J. Bacteriol.* **164**: 659–64.

961   Lancelot, C., G. Billen, A. Sournia, T. Weisse, F. Colijn, M.J.W. Veldhuis, A. Davies & P. Wassman (1987). *Phaeocystis* blooms and nutrient enrichment in the continental coastal zones of the North Sea. *Ambio* **16**: 38–46.

962   Lang, N.J. (1963). Electron-microscopic demonstration of plastids in *Polytoma. J. Protozool.* **10**: 333–9.

963   Lang, N.J. (1968). Ultrastructure of the blue-green algae. In *Algae, Man and the Environment*, ed. D.F. Jackson, pp. 235–48. Syracuse University Press, New York.

964   Lang, N.J. & B.A. Whitton (1973). Arrangement and structure of thylakoids. In *The Biology of Blue-green Algae*, ed. N.G. Carr & B.A. Whitton, pp. 66–79. Blackwell, Oxford.

965   Larsen, J. (1988). An ultrastructural study of *Amphidinium poecilochroum* (Dinophyceae), a phagotrophic dinoflagellate feeding on small species of cryptophytes. *Phycologia* **27**: 366–77.

966   Leadbeater, B.S.C. (1970). Preliminary observations on differences of scale morphology at various stages in the life cycle of "*Apistonema-Syracosphaera*" *sensu* von Stosch. *Br. Phycol. J.* **5**: 57–69.

967   Leadbeater, B.S.C. (1986). Scale case construction in *Synura petersenii* Korsch. (Chrysophyceae). In *Chrysophytes: Aspects and Problems*, ed. J. Kristiansen & R.A. Andersen, pp. 121–31. Cambridge University Press.

968   Leadbeater, B.S.C. (1989). The phylogenetic significance of flagellar hairs in the Chromophyta. In *The Chromophyte Algae*, ed. J.C. Green, B.S.C. Leadbeater & W.L. Diver, pp. 145–65. Clarendon Press, Oxford.

968a   Leadbeater, B.S.C. (1990). Ultrastructure and assembly of the scale case in *Synura* (Synurophyceae Andersen). *Br. Phycol. J.* **25**: 117–32.

969   Leadbeater, B.S.C. & J.D. Dodge (1966). The fine structure of *Woloszynskia micra* sp. nov., a new marine dinoflagellate. *Br. Phycol. Bull.* **3**: 1–17.

970   Leadbeater, B.S.C. & J.D. Dodge (1967). An electron microscope study of dinoflagellate flagella. *J. Gen. Microbiol.* **46**: 305–14.

971   Leadbeater, B.S.C. & J.D. Dodge (1967). An electron microscope study of nuclear cell division in a dinoflagellate. *Arch. Mikrobiol.* **57**: 239–54.

972   Leadbeater, B.S.C. & I. Manton (1969). *Chrysochromulina camella* sp. nov. and *cymbium* sp. nov., two new relatives of *C. strobilus* Parke and Manton. *Arch. Mikrobiol.* **68**: 116–32.

973   Lee, J.J. & M.E. McEnery (1983). Symbiosis in foraminifera. In *Algal Symbiosis*, ed. L.J. Goff, pp. 37–68. Cambridge University Press.

974   Lee, J.J., S.H. Hutner & E.C. Bovee (1985). *An Illustrated Guide to the Protozoa*. Society of Protozoologists, Lawrence, Kansas, USA.

975   Lee, R.E. (1977). Saprotrophic and phagocytic isolates of the colourless heterotrophic dinoflagellate *Gyrodinium lebouriae* Herdman. *J. Mar. Biol. Ass. U.K.* **57**: 303–15.

976   Lee, R.E. (1980). *Phycology*. Cambridge University Press.

977   Lee, R.E. (1990). *Phycology*. 2nd Ed. Cambridge University Press.

978   Lee, R.E. & P. Kugrens (1986). The occurrence and structure of flagellar scales in some freshwater cryptophytes. *J. Phycol.* **22**: 549–52.

978a   Lee, Y.P. & M. Kurogi (1978). Sexual reproductive structures and post-fertilization in *Rhodochorton subimmersum* Setchell & Gardner. *Jap. J. Phycol.* **26**: 115–9.

979 Lee, Y.P. & I.K. Lee (1988). Contribution to the generic classification of the Rhodochortaceae (Rhodophyta, Nemaliales). *Bot. Mar.* **31**: 119–31.

980 Leedale, G.F. (1964). Pellicle structure in *Euglena. Br. Phycol. Bull.* **2**: 291–306.

981 Leedale, G.F. (1967). *Euglenoid flagellates.* Prentice-Hall, Englewood Cliffs, New Jersey.

982 Leedale, G.F. (1974). How many are the kingdoms of organisms? *Taxon* **23**: 261–70.

983 Leedale, G.F. (1982). Ultrastructure. In *The Biology of Euglena,* Vol. III: *Physiology,* ed. D.E. Buetow, pp. 1–27. Academic Press, New York.

984 Leedale, G.F. (1985). Order 3. Euglenida Bütschli, 1884. In *An Illustrated Guide to the Protozoa,* ed. J.J. Lee, S.H. Hutner & E.C. Bovee, pp. 41–54. Society of Protozoologists, Lawrence, Kansas.

985 Leedale, G.F. (1985). Order 10. Silicoflagellida Borgert, 1891. In *An Illustrated Guide to the Protozoa,* ed. J.J. Lee, S.H. Hutner & E.C. Bovee, pp. 103–5. Society of Protozoologists, Lawrence, Kansas.

986 Leedale, G.F., B.S.C. Leadbeater & A. Massalski (1970). The intracellular origin of flagellar hairs in the Chrysophyceae and Xanthophyceae. *J. Cell Sci.* **6**: 701–19.

986a Leitsch, C.E.W. & K. Kowallik (1992). Nucleotide sequence and phylogenetic implication of the ATPase subunits β and ε encoded in the chloroplast genome of the brown alga *Dictyota dichotoma. Plant Molec. Biol.* **19**: 289–298.

987 Lembi, C.A. (1975). A rhizoplast in *Carteria radiosa* (Chlorophyceae). *J. Phycol.* **11**: 219–21.

988 Lembi, C.A. (1980). Unicellular chlorophytes. In *Phytoflagellates,* ed. E.R. Cox, pp. 5–59. Elsevier-North Holland, Amsterdam.

989 Lembi, C.A. & N.J. Lang (1965). Electron microscopy of *Carteria* and *Chlamydomonas. Am. J. Bot.* **52**: 464–77.

989a Lembi, C.A. & J.R. Waaland (Eds) (1988). *Algae and Human Affairs.* Cambridge University Press.

990 Lemieux, B., M. Turmel & C. Lemieux (1985). Chloroplast DNA variation in *Chlamydomonas* and its potential application to the systematics of this genus. *BioSystems* **8**: 293–8.

991 Lenaers, G., L. Maroteaux, B. Michot & M. Herzog (1989). Dinoflagellates in evolution. A molecular phylogenetic analysis of large subunit ribosomal RNA. *J. Molec. Evol.* **29**: 40–51.

992 Levandowski, M. & P.J. Kaneta (1987). Behaviour in dinoflagellates. In *Biology of Dinoflagellates,* ed. F.J.R. Taylor, pp. 360–97. Blackwell Scientific Publications, Oxford.

993 Levine, R.P. (1968). Genetic dissection of photosynthesis. *Science* **162**: 768–71.

994 Levine, R.P. & W.T. Ebersold (1960). The genetics and cytology of *Chlamydomonas. Ann. Rev. Microbiol.* **14**: 197–216.

995 Levring, T., H.A. Hoppe & O.J. Schmid (1969). *Marine Algae. A Survey of Research and Utilization.* Cramer, de Gruyter & Co, Hamburg.

996 Lewin, J.C. (1962). Silicification. In *Physiology and Biochemistry of Algae,* ed. R.A. Lewin, pp. 445–55. Academic Press, New York.

997 Lewin, R.A. (Ed.) (1962). *Physiology and Biochemistry of Algae.* Academic Press, New York.

997a Lewin, R.A. (1974). Biochemical taxonomy. In *Algal Physiology and Biochemistry,* ed. W.D.P. Stewart, pp. 1–39. Blackwell, Oxford.

997b Lewin, R.A. (1981). The Prochlorophytes. In *The Prokaryotes,* ed. M.P. Starr, H. Stolp, H.G. Trüper, A. Balows & H.G. Schlegel, pp. 257–66. Springer-Verlag, Berlin.

998 Lewin, R.A. (1989). Group II. Order Prochlorales Lewin 1977. In *Bergey's Manual of Systematic Bacteriology,* Vol. 3, Section 19: *Oxygenic photosynthetic bacteria,* ed. J.T. Staley, M.P. Bryant, N. Pfennig & J.H. Holt, pp. 1799–802. Williams & Wilkins, Baltimore.

999 Lewin, R.A. & L. Cheng (eds) (1989). *Prochloron, a Microbial Enigma.* Chapman & Hall, New York.

1000 Lewin, R.A. & K.W. Lee (1985). Autotomy of algal flagella: electron microscope studies of *Chlamydomonas* (Chlorophyceae) and *Tetraselmis* (Prasinophyceae). *Phycologia* **24**: 311–16.

1001 Lewin, R.A. & N.W. Withers (1975). Extraordinary pigment composition of a prokaryotic alga. *Nature* **256**: 735–7.

1002 Lewis, L.A. (1990). Molecular phylogenetic analysis of *Neochloris* (Chlorophyceae). *J. Phycol.* **26** (suppl.): 4.

1003 Li, C.-W. & B.E. Volcani (1987). Four new apochlorotic diatoms. *Br. Phycol. J.* **22**: 375–82.

1004   Li, N. & R.A. Cattolico (1988). Study of chloroplast genome organization and cp gene arrangement in rhodophyte, *Griffithsia pacifica* and chromophyte, *Ochromonas danica*. *J. Phycol.* **24** (suppl.): 8.

1005   Liaaen-Jensen, S. (1977). Algal carotenoids and chemosystematics. In *Marine Natural Products Chemistry*, ed. D.J. Faulkner & W.H. Fenical, pp. 239–59. Plenum Press, New York.

1006   Lichtlé, C. & G. Giraud (1970). Aspects ultra-structuraux particuliers au plaste du *Batrachospermum virgatum* (Sirdt) Rhodophycée-Nemalionale. *J. Phycol.* **6**: 281–9.

1007   Liddle, L.B. (1982). Morphology and distribution of nuclei during development in *Cymopolia barbata* (Chlorophyta, Dasycladales). *J. Phycol.* **18**: 257–64.

1008   Liddle, L.B., Berger, S. & M.S. Schweiger (1976). Ultrastructure during development of the nucleus of *Batophora oerstedii* (Chlorophyta, Dasycladaceae). *J. Phycol.* **12**: 261–72.

1009   Liddle, L.B. & T. Hori (1983). The use of fluorescence staining to study nucleus development in the multinucleate dasycladalean green algae. *J. Phycol.* **31**: 173–9.

1010   Liere, L. van & A.E. Walsby (1982). Interactions of Cyanobacteria with light. In *The Biology of Cyanobacteria*, ed. N.G. Carr & B.A. Whitton, pp. 9–45. Blackwell Scientific Publications, Oxford.

1011   Lim, B.-L., H. Kawai, H. Hori & S. Osawa (1986). Molecular evolution of 5S ribosomal RNA from red and brown algae. *Jap. J. Genet.* **61**: 169–76.

1012   Lin, Hsiu-ping, M.R. Sommerfeld & J.R. Swafford (1975). Light and electron microscope observations on motile cells of *Porphyridium purpureum* (Rhodophyta). *J. Phycol.* **11**: 452–7.

1013   Lindholm, T. (1985). *Mesodinium rubrum* – a unique photosynthetic ciliate. *Adv. Aquat. Microbiol.* **3**: 1–48.

1014   Lindholm, T., P. Lindroos & A.-C. Mörk (1988). Ultrastructure of the photosynthetic ciliate *Mesodinium rubrum*. *BioSystems* **21**: 141–9.

1015   Linnaeus, C. (1754). *Genera plantarum*. Holmiae.

1016   Linne von Berg, K.-H. & K.V. Kowallik (1988). Structural organization and evolution of the plastid genome of *Vaucheria sessilis* (Xanthophyceae). *BioSystems* **21**: 239–47.

1017   Littlefield, L. & C. Forsberg (1965). Absorption and translocation of Phosphorus 32 by *Chara globularis* Thuill. *Physiol. Plant.* **18**: 291–6.

1018   Littler, M.M. & D.S. Littler (1983). Heteromorphic life history strategies in the brown alga *Scytosiphon lomentaria* (Lyngb.) Link. *J. Phycol.* **19**: 425–31.

1019   Littler, M.M., D.S. Littler, S.M. Blair & J.N. Norris (1985). Deepest known plant life discovered on an uncharted seamount. *Science* **227**: 57–69.

1020   Littler, M.M., D.S. Littler, S.M. Blair & J.N. Norris (1986). Deep-water plant communities from an uncharted seamount off San Salvador Island, Bahamas: distribution, abundance, and primary productivity. *Deep-Sea Res.* **33**: 881–92.

1021   Livingstone, D. & G.H.M. Jaworski (1980). The viability of akinetes of blue-green algae recovered from the sediments of Rostherne Mere. *Br. Phycol. J.* **15**: 357–64.

1022   Lobban, C.S., P.J. Harrison & M.J. Duncan (1985). *The Physiological Ecology of Seaweeds*. Cambridge University Press, Cambridge.

1023   Loeblich, A.R. III (1982). Dinophyceae. In *Synopsis and Classification of Living Organisms*, Vol. 1, ed. S.P. Parker, pp. 101–15. McGraw-Hill, New York.

1024   Loeblich, A.R. III & L.A. Loeblich (1984). Dinoflagellate cysts. In *Dinoflagellates*, ed. D.L. Spector, pp. 443–80. Academic Press, Orlando.

1025   Löffelhardt, W., H. Mucke, I. Janssen, C. Michalowski & H.J. Bohnert (1987). Cyanelle genes: evolutionary relationship between Cyanobacteria, cyanelles and chloroplasts. *14th International Botanical Congress, Berlin, Abstracts:* 155. (Collated and edited by W. Greuter, B. Zimmer & H.D. Behnke; produced with the assistance of M.I. Hakki, H. Sipman and staff members of the Botanical Museum Berlin-Dahlem.)

1026   Logan, B.W., R. Rezak & R.N. Ginsburg (1964). Classification and environmental significance of algal stromatolites. *J. Geol.* **72**: 68–83.

1027   Loiseaux, S. & J.A. West (1970). Brown algal mastigonemes: comparative ultrastructure. *Trans. Am. Microsc. Soc.* **89**: 54.

1027a   Loiseaux-de Goër, S., Y. Markowicz & C.C. Sommerville (1991). Ribosomal RNA genes and pseudogenes of the bi-molecular plastid genome of the brown alga *Pylaiella littoralis*. In *The Translational Apparatus of Photosynthetic Organelles*, ed. R. Mache *et al.*, NATO ASI Series, vol. H 55, pp. 19–29. Springer-Verlag, Berlin.

1028 Lokhorst, G.M. (1974). *Taxonomic studies on the freshwater species of Ulothrix in the Netherlands*. Thesis, Free University of Amsterdam.

1029 Lokhorst, G.M. (1978). Taxonomic studies on the marine and brackish-water species of *Ulothrix* (Ulotrichales, Chlorophyceae) in Western Europe. *Blumea* **24**: 191–299.

1030 Lokhorst, G.M. (1984). Current ideas on classification of the Ulotrichales Borzi. In *Systematics of the Green Algae*, ed. D.E.G. Irvine & D.M. John, pp. 179–206. Academic Press, London.

1031 Lokhorst, G.M. (1985). The concept of the genus *Ulothrix* (Chlorophyta) strengthened by comparative cytology. *BioSystems* **18**: 357–68.

1032 Lokhorst, G.M., P.J. Segaar & W. Star (1989). An ultrastructural reinvestigation of mitosis and cytokinesis in cryofixed sporangia of the coccoid green alga *Friedmannia israelensis*. *Crypt. Bot.* **1**: 275–94.

1033 Lokhorst, G.M., H.J. Sluiman & W. Star (1988). The ultrastructure of mitosis and cytokinesis in the sarcinoid *Chlorokybus atmophyticus* (Chlorophyta, Charophyceae) revealed by rapid freeze fixation and freeze substitution. *J. Phycol.* **24**: 237–48.

1034 Lokhorst, G.M. & W. Star (1980). Pyrenoid ultrastructure in *Ulothrix* (Chlorophyceae). *Acta Bot. Neerl.* **29**: 1–15.

1035 Lokhorst, G.M. & W. Star (1983). Fine structure of mitosis and cytokinesis in *Urospora* (Acrosiphoniales, Chlorophyta). *Protoplasma* **117**: 142–53.

1036 Lokhorst, G. M. & W. Star (1985). Ultrastructure of mitosis and cytokinesis in *Klebsormidium mucosum* nov. comb., formerly *Ulothrix verrucosa* (Chlorophyta). *J. Phycol.* **21**: 466–76.

1037 Lokhorst, G.M. & W. Star (1988). *Prasiola velutina* (Lyngbye) Wille in the Netherlands. Growth habit and ultrastructure of mitosis and cytokinesis. *Algol. Stud.* **48**: 313–27.

1038 Lokhorst, G.M. & B.J. Trask (1981). Taxonomic studies on *Urospora* (Acrosiphoniales, Chlorophyceae) in Western Europe. *Acta Bot. Neerl.* **30**: 353–431.

1039 Lokhorst, G.M. & M. Vroman (1972). Taxonomic study on three freshwater *Ulothrix* species. *Acta Bot. Neerl.* **21**: 449–80.

1040 Lokhorst, G.M. & M. Vroman (1974a). Taxonomic studies on the genus *Ulothrix* (Ulotrichales, Chlorophyceae) II. *Acta Bot. Neerl.* **23**: 369–98.

1041 Lokhorst, G.M. & M. Vroman (1974b). Taxonomic studies on the genus *Ulothrix* (Ulotrichales, Chlorophyceae) III. *Acta Bot. Neerl.* **23**: 561–602.

1042 Lott, J.N.A., G.H. Harris & C.D. Turner (1972). The wall of *Cosmarium botrytis*. *J. Phycol.* **8**: 232–6.

1043 Løvlie, A. & T. Bråten (1968). On the division of cytoplasm and chloroplast in the multicellular green alga *Ulva mutabilis* Føyn. *Exp. Cell Res.* **51**: 211–20.

1044 Løvlie, A. & T. Bråten (1970). On mitosis in the multicellular alga *Ulva mutabilis* Føyn. *J. Cell Sci.* **6**: 109–29.

1045 Lucas, I.A.N. (1970a). Observations on the fine structure of the Cryptophyceae. I. The genus *Cryptomonas*. *J. Phycol.* **6**: 30–8.

1046 Lucas, I.A.N. (1970b). Observations on the ultrastructure of representatives of the genera *Hemiselmis* and *Chroomonas* (Cryptophyceae). *Br. Phycol. J.* **5**: 29–37.

1047 Lucas, I.A.N. (1982). Observations on the fine structure of the Cryptophyceae. II. The eyespot. *Br. Phycol. J.* **17**: 13–19.

1048 Lucas, I.A.N. & M. Vesk (1990). The fine structure of two photosynthetic species of *Dinophysis* (Dinophysiales, Dinophyceae). *J. Phycol.* **26**: 345–57.

1049 Ludwig, M. & S.P. Gibbs (1985). DNA is present in the nucleomorph of cryptomonads: Further evidence that the chloroplast evolved from a eukaryotic endosymbiont. *Protoplasma* **127**: 9–20.

1050 Ludwig, M. & S.P. Gibbs (1989). Evidence that the nucleomorphs of *Chlorarachnion reptans* (Chlorarachniophyceae) are vestigial nuclei: morphology, division and DNA–DAPI fluorescence. *J. Phycol.* **25**: 385–94.

1051 Lüning, K. (1971). Seasonal growth of *Laminaria hyperborea* under recorded underwater light conditions near Helgoland. In *Proceedings 4th European Marine Biology Symposium*, ed. D.J. Crisp, pp. 347–61. Cambridge University Press.

1052 Lüning, K. (1980a). Critical levels of light and temperature regulating the gametogenesis of three *Laminaria* species (Phaeophyceae). *J. Phycol.* **16**: 1–15.

1053 Lüning, K. (1980b). Control of algal life history by daylength and temperature. In *The Shore Environment*, ed. J.H. Price, D.E.G. Irvine & W.F. Farnham, pp. 915–45. Academic Press, New York.

1054   Lüning, K. (1981a). Egg release in gametophytes of *Laminaria saccharina:* induction by darkness and inhibition by blue light and U.V. *Br. Phycol. J.* **16**: 379–93.

1055   Lüning, K. (1981b). Photomorphogenesis of reproduction in marine algae. *Ber. Dtsch. Bot. Ges.* **94**: 401–17.

1056   Lüning, K. (1985). *Meeresbotanik.* Thieme, Stuttgart.

1057   Lüning, K. (1986). New frond formation in *Laminaria hyperborea* (Phaeophyta): a photoperiodic response. *Br. Phycol. J.* **21**: 269–73.

1058   Lüning, K. (1988). Photoperiodic control of sorus formation in the brown alga *Laminaria saccharina. Mar. Biol.* **45**: 137–44.

1058a   Lüning, K. (1990). *Seaweeds, their Environment, Biogeography and Ecophysiology.* John Wiley, New York.

1058b   Lüning, K. (1991). Circannual growth rhythm in a brown alga, *Pterygophora californica. Botanica Acta* **104**: 157–62.

1059   Lüning, K. & M.J. Dring (1975). Reproduction, growth and photosynthesis of gametophytes of *Laminaria saccharina* grown in blue and red light. *Mar. Biol.* **29**: 195–200.

1060   Lüning, K. & D.G. Müller (1978). Chemical interaction in sexual reproduction of several Laminariales: release and attraction of spermatozoids. *Z. Pflanzenphys.* **89**: 33–41.

1061   Lüning, K., K. Schmitz & J. Willenbrink (1973). CO_2-fixation and translocation in benthic marine algae. III. Rates and ecological significance of translocation in *Laminaria hyperborea* and *L. saccharina. Mar. Biol.* **23**: 275–81.

1062   Ma, J. & A. Miura (1984). Observations of the nuclear division in the conchospores and their germlings in *Porphyra yezoensis* Ueda. *Jap. J. Phycol.* **32**: 373–8.

1063   Machlis, L., G.G.C. Hill, K.E. Steinback & W. Reed (1974). Some characteristics of the sperm attractant from *Oedogonium cardiacum. J. Phycol.* **10**: 199–204.

1064   Mackie, W. & R.D. Preston (1974). Cell wall and intercellular polysaccharides. In *Algal Physiology and Biochemistry*, ed. W.D.P. Stewart, pp. 40–85. Blackwell, Oxford.

1065   MacRaild, G.N. & H.B.S. Womersley (1974). The morphology and reproduction of *Derbesia clavaeformis* (J. Agardh) De Toni (Chlorophyta). *Phycologia* **13**: 83–93.

1066   Magathan, E.R. (1985). Devonian reef-associated articulate red algae from Western Canada. In *Palaeoalgologie*, ed. D.F. Toomey & M.H. Nitecki, pp. 170–8. Springer, Berlin.

1067   Maggs, C.A. & C.M. Pueschel (1989). Morphology and development of *Ahnfeltia plicata* (Rhodophyta): Proposal of Ahnfeltiales ord. nov. *J. Phycol.* **25**: 333–51.

1068   Magne, F. (1952). La structure du noyau et le cycle nucléaire chez le *Porphyra linearis* Greville. *C.R. Acad. Sci. Paris* **234**: 986–8.

1069   Magne, F. (1956). Sur la présence de l'*Halicystis ovalis* (Lyngb.) Areschoug et du *Derbesia marina* (Lyngb.) Kjellm. dans la Manche. *Bull. Soc. Bot. France* **103**: 488–90.

1070   Magne, F. (1960). Le *Rhodochaete parvula* Thuret (Bangioidée) et sa reproduction sexuée. *Cah. Biol. Mar.* **1**: 407–20.

1071   Magne, F. (1964). Recherches caryologiques chez les Floridées (Rhodophycées). *Cah. Biol. Mar. Roscoff* **5**: 461–671.

1072   Magne, F. (1967a). Sur l'existence, chez les *Lemanea* (Rhodophycées, Némalionales), d'un type de cycle de développement encore inconnu chez les algues rouges. *C.R. Acad. Sci. Paris* **264**: 2632–3.

1073   Magne, F. (1967b). Sur le déroulement et le lieu de la méiose chez les Lémanéacées (Rhodophycées, Némalionales). *C.R. Acad. Sci. Paris* **265**: 670–3.

1074   Magne, F. (1972). Le cycle de développement des Rhodophycées et son évolution. *Soc. Bot. France, Mémoires*: 247–68.

1075   Magne, F. (1982). On two new types of life history in the Rhodophyta. *Crypt. Algol.* **3**: 265–71.

1076   Magne, F. (1988). On a possible site for meiosis in *Rhodochaete parvula. Third International Phycological Congress, Monash University, Melbourne, Abstracts:* 27.

1077   Magne, F. (1990). Reproduction sexuée chez *Erythrotrichia carnea* (Rhodophyceae, Erythropeltidales). *Crypt. Algol.* **11**: 157–70.

1078   Maier, E.X. (1972). De kranswieren (Charophyta) van Nederland. *Wet. Meded. K.N.N.V.* **93**: 1–43.

1079   Maier, I. (1984). Culture studies of *Chorda*

tomentosa (Phaeophyta, Laminariales). *Br. Phycol. J.* **19**: 95–106.

1080 Maier, I. (1987). Environmental and pheromonal control of sexual reproduction in *Laminaria* (Phaeophyceae). In *Algal Development*, ed. W. Wiessner, D.G. Robinson & R.C. Starr, pp. 66–74. Springer-Verlag, Berlin.

1081 Maier, I. & M.N. Clayton (1989). Oogenesis in *Durvillaea potatorum* (Durvillaeales, Phaeophyta). *Phycologia* **28**: 271–4.

1082 Maier, I. & D.G. Müller (1982). Antheridium fine structure and spermatozoid release in *Laminaria digitata* (Phaeophyceae). *Phycologia* **21**: 1–8.

1083 Maier, I. & D.G. Müller (1986). Sexual pheromones in algae. *Biol. Bull. (Woods Hole)* **170**: 145–75.

1084 Maier, I. & D.G. Müller (1990). Chemotaxis in *Laminaria digitata* (Phaeophyceae). *J. Exp. Bot.* **41**: 869–76.

1085 Maier, I., D.G. Müller, G. Gassmann, W. Boland & L. Jaenicke (1987). Sexual pheromones and related egg secretions in Laminariales (Phaeophyta). *Z. Naturforsch.* **42c**: 948–54.

1086 Maier, I., D.G. Müller, C. Schmid, W. Boland & L. Jaenicke (1988). Pheromone receptor specificity and threshold concentrations for spermatozoid release in *Laminaria digitata*. *Naturwissenschaften* **75**: 260–3.

1087 Mandelli, E. (1968). Carotenoid pigments of the dinoflagellate *Glenodinium foliaceum* Stein. *J. Phycol.* **4**: 347–8.

1088 Manhart, J.R. (1990). Phylogenetic relationships of the green algae and the land plants based on RBCL sequences. *J. Phycol.* **26** (suppl.): 17.

1088a Mann, D.G. (1982). Structure, life history and systematics of *Rhoicosphenia* (Bacillariophyta). II. Auxospore formation and perizonium structure of *Rh. curvata. J. Phycol.* **18**: 264–74.

1088b Mann, D.G. (1984). An ontogenetic approach to diatom systematics. In *Proceedings of the 7th International Diatom Symposium*, ed. D.G. Mann, pp. 113–44. O. Koeltz, Koenigstein.

1088c Mann, D.G. & H.J. Marchant (1989). The origins of the diatom and its life cycle. In *The Chromophyte Algae*, ed. J.C. Green, B.S.C. Leadbeater & W.L. Diver, pp. 307–23. Clarendon Press, Oxford.

1089 Manton, I. (1957). Observations with the electron microscope on the internal structure of the zoospore of a brown alga (*Scytosiphon lomentarius*). *J. Exp. Bot.* **8**: 294–303.

1090 Manton, I. (1959). Observations on the internal structure of the spermatozoids of *Dictyota. J. Exp. Bot.* **10**: 448–61.

1091 Manton, I. (1964a). Observations on the fine structure of the zoospore and the young germling of *Stigeoclonium. J. Exp. Biol.* **15**: 399–411.

1092 Manton, I. (1964b). Further observations on the fine structure of the haptonema in *Prymnesium parvum. Arch. Mikrobiol.* **49**: 315–30.

1093 Manton, I. (1966). Observations on scale production in *Prymnesium parvum. J. Cell Sci.* **1**: 375–80.

1094 Manton, I. (1967). Electron microscopical observations on a clone of *Monomastix scherffelii* in culture. *Nova Hedwigia* **14**: 1–11.

1095 Manton, I. (1968). Further observations on the microanatomy of the haptonema in *Chrysochromulina chiton* and *Prymnesium parvum. Protoplasma* **66**: 35–54.

1096 Manton, I. & B. Clarke (1951). Electron microscope observations on the zoospores of *Pylaiella* and *Laminaria. J. Exp. Bot.* **2**: 242–6.

1097 Manton, I. & B. Clarke (1956). Observations with the electron microscope on the internal structure of the spermatozoid of *Fucus. J. Exp. Bot.* **7**: 416–32.

1098 Manton, I. & H. Ettl (1965). Observations on the fine structure of *Mesostigma viride* Lauterborn. *J. Linn. Soc. Bot.* **59**: 175–84.

1099 Manton, I. & I. Friedmann (1960). Gametes, fertilization and zygote development in *Prasiola stipitata* Suhr. II. *Nova Hedwigia* **1**: 443–62.

1100 Manton, I., K. Kowallik & H.A. von Stosch (1969a). Observations on the fine structure and development of the spindle at mitosis and meiosis in a marine centric diatom (*Lithodesmium undulatum*). I. Preliminary survey of mitosis in spermatogonia. *J. Microsc.* **89**: 295–320.

1101 Manton, I., K. Kowallik & H.A. von Stosch (1969b). Observations on the fine structure and development of the spindle at mitosis and meiosis in a marine centric diatom (*Lithodesmium undulatum*). II. The early meiotic stages in male gametogenesis. *J. Cell Sci.* **5**: 271–98.

1102 Manton. I., K. Kowallik & H.A. von Stosch (1970a). Observations on the fine structure and development of the spindle at mitosis and meiosis in a marine centric diatom (*Lithodesmium undulatum*). III. The later stages of meiosis 1 in male gametogenesis. *J. Cell Sci.* **6**: 131–57.

1103 Manton, I., K. Kowallik, H.A. von Stosch (1970b). Observations on the fine structure and development of the spindle and mitosis and meiosis in a marine centric diatom (*Lithodesmium undulatum*). IV. The second meiotic division and conclusion. *J. Cell Sci.* **7**: 407–44.

1104 Manton, I. & G.F. Leedale (1963a). Observations on the fine structure of *Prymnesium parvum* Carter. *Arch. Mikrobiol.* **45**: 285–303.

1105 Manton, I. & G.F. Leedale (1963b). Observations on the microanatomy of *Crystallolithus hyalinus* Gaarder et Markali. *Arch. Mikrobiol.* **47**: 115–36.

1106 Manton, I. & G.F. Leedale (1969). Observations on the microanatomy of *Coccolithus pelagicus* and *Cricosphaera carterae*, with reference to the origin of coccoliths and scales. *J. Mar. Biol. Ass. U.K.* **49**: 1–16.

1107 Manton, I., K. Oates & G. Gooday (1973). Further observations on the chemical composition of thecae of *Platymonas tetrathele* West (Prasinophyceae) by means of x-ray microanalyser electronmicroscope (EMMA). *J. Exp. Bot.* **24**: 223–9.

1108 Manton, I., K. Oates, M. Parke (1963). Observations on the fine structure of the *Pyramimonas* stage of *Halosphaera* and preliminary observations on the three species of *Pyramimonas*. *J. Mar. Biol. Ass. U.K.* **43**: 225–38.

1109 Manton, I. & M. Parke (1960). Further observations on small green flagellates with special reference to possible relatives of *Chromulina pusilla* Butcher. *J. Mar. Biol. Ass. U.K.* **39**: 275–8.

1110 Manton, I. & M. Parke (1962). Preliminary observations on scales and their mode of origin in *Chrysochromulina polylepis* sp. nov. *J. Mar. Biol. Ass. U.K.* **42**: 565–78.

1111 Manton, I. & M. Parke (1965). Observations on the fine structure of two species of *Platymonas*, with special reference to flagellar scales and the mode of origin of the theca. *J. Mar. Biol. Ass. U.K.* **45**: 743–54.

1112 Manton, I. & L.S. Peterfi (1969). Observations on the fine structure of coccoliths, scales and the protoplast of a freshwater coccolithiphorid, *Hymeno-*

monas roseola Stein, with supplementary observation on the protoplast of *Cricophaera carterae*. *Proc. R. Soc. Lond.* **B172**: 1–15.

1113 Manton, I., D.G. Rayns, H. Ettl & M. Parke (1965). Further observations on green flagellates with scaly flagella; the genus *Heteromastix* Korschikoff. *J. Mar. Biol. Ass. U.K.* **45**: 241–55.

1114 Manton, I. & H.A. von Stosch (1966). Observations on the fine structure of the male gamete of the marine centric diatom *Lithodesmium undulatum*. *J. Roy. Microsc. Soc.* **85**: 119–34.

1115 Marchant, H.J., A.T. Davidson & S.W. Wright (1987). The distribution and abundance of chroococcoid Cyanobacteria in the Southern Ocean. *Proc. NIPR Symp. Polar Biol.* **1**: 1–9.

1116 Marchant, H.J. & A. McEldowney (1986). Nanoplanktonic cysts from Antarctica are algae. *Mar. Biol.* **92**: 53–7.

1117 Marchant, H.J. & J.D. Pickett-Heaps (1970). Ultrastructure and differentiation of *Hydrodictyon reticulatum*. *Austr. J. Biol. Sci.* **23**: 1173–86.

1118 Marchant, H.J. & J.D. Pickett-Heaps (1972). Ultrastructure and differentiation of *Hydrodictyon reticulatum* IV. Conjugation of gametes and the development of zygospores and azygospore. *Austr. J. Biol. Sci.* **25**: 279–91.

1119 Marchant, H.J. & J.D. Pickett-Heaps (1973). Mitosis and cytokinesis in *Coleochaete scutata*. *J. Phycol.* **9**: 461–71.

1120 Marchant, H.J., J.D. Pickett-Heaps & K. Jacobs (1973). An ultrastructural study of zoosporogenesis and the mature zoospore of *Klebsormidium flaccidum*. *Cytobios* **8**: 95–107.

1121 Margulis, L. (1970). *Origin of Eukaryotic Cells*. Yale University Press, New Haven, Connecticut.

1122 Margulis, L. (1971). Symbiosis and evolution. *Sci. Am.* **225**: 48–57.

1123 Margulis, L. (1981). *Symbiosis in Cell Evolution*. Freeman, San Francisco.

1124 Margulis, L., J.O. Corliss, M. Melkonian & D.J. Chapman (Eds) (1990). *Handbook of Protoctista*. Jones & Bartlett, Boston.

1125 Margulis, L. & R. Obar (1985). *Heliobacterium* and origin of chrysoplasts. *BioSystems* **17**: 317–25.

1126 Margulis, L. & K.V. Schwartz (1982). *Five Kingdoms. An Illustrated Guide to the Phyla of Life on Earth*. Freeman, San Francisco.

1127 Markowitz, M. (1978). Fine structure of the zoospore of *Oedocladium carolinianum* (Chlorophyta) with special reference to the flagellar apparatus. *J. Phycol.* **14**: 289–302.

1127a Markowitz, Y. & S. Loiseux-de Goër (1991). Plastid genomes of the Rhodophyta and Chromophyta constitute a distinct lineage which differs from that of the Chlorophyta and have a composite phylogenetic origin, perhaps like that of Euglenophyta. *Current Genetics* **20**: 427–30.

1127b Martin, W., C.C. Somerville & S. Loiseaux-de Goër (1993). Molecular phylogenies of plastid origins and algal evolution. *J. Molec. Evol.* (in press).

1128 Maruyama, K. (1980). A cellular approach to phylogenetic relations in eucaryotic algae. *Jap. J. Phycol.* **28**: 1–18.

1129 Maruyama, I., T. Nakamura, T. Matsubayashi, Y. Ando & T. Maeda (1986). Identification of the alga known as 'marine *Chlorella*' as a member of the Eustigmatophyceae. *Jap. J. Phycol.* **34**: 319–25.

1130 Massalski, A. & G.F. Leedale (1969). Cytology and ultrastructure of the Xanthophyceae I. Comparative morphology of the zoospores of *Bumilleria sicula* Borzi and *Tribonema vulgare* Pascher. *Br. Phycol. J.* **4**: 159–80.

1131 Masuda, M. & M. Kurogi (1981). The life history of *Gigartina ochotensis* (Ruprecht) Ruprecht (Rhodophyta) in culture. *J. Fac. Sci. Hokkaido Univ.*, Ser. V, **12**: 165–71.

1132 Mathieson, A.C., T.A. Norton & M. Neushul (1981). The taxonomic implications of genetic and environmentally induced variations in seaweed morphology. *Bot. Rev.* **47**: 313–47.

1133 Matsuda, Y. (1988). The *Chlamydomonas* cell wall and their degrading enzymes. *Jap. J. Phycol.* **36**: 246–64.

1134 Matsuda, Y., A. Musgrave, H. van den Ende & K. Roberts (1987). Cell walls of algae in the Volvocales: their sensitivity to a cell wall lytic enzyme and labeling with an anti-cell wall glycopeptide of *Chlamydomonas reinhardtii*. *Bot. Mag. Tokyo* **100**: 373–84.

1135 Matthijs, H.C.P., T. Burger-Wiersma & L.R. Mur (1989). Status report on *Prochlorothrix hollandica*, a free-living Prochlorophyte. In *Prochloron, a Microbial Enigma*, ed. R.A. Lewin & L. Cheng, pp. 85–7. Chapman & Hall, New York.

1136 Matthijs, H.C.P. & H.J. Lubberding (1989). Dark respiration in Cyanobacteria. In *Biochemistry of the Algae and Cyanobacteria*, ed. L.J. Rogers & J.R. Gallon, pp. 131–45. Clarendon Press, Oxford.

1137 Mattox, K.R. & K.D. Stewart (1973). Observations on the zoospores of *Pseudendoclonium basiliense* and *Trichosarcina polymorpha* (Chlorophyceae). *Can. J. Bot.* **51**: 1425–30.

1138 Mattox, K.R. & K.D. Stewart (1974). A comparative study of cell divisions in *Trichosarcina polymorpha* and *Pseudendoclonium brasiliense* (Chlorophyceae). *J. Phycol.* **10**: 447–56.

1139 Mattox, K.R. & K.D. Stewart (1977). Cell division in the scaly green flagellate *Heteromastix angulata* and its bearing on the origin of the Chlorophyta. *Am. J. Bot.* **64**: 931–45.

1140 Mattox, K.R. & K.D. Stewart (1984). Classification of the green algae: a concept based on comparative cytology. In *Systematics of the Green Algae*, ed. D.E.G. Irvine & D.M. John, pp. 29–72. Academic Press, London.

1141 Mattox, K.R., K.D. Stewart & G.L. Floyd (1974). The cytology and classification of *Schizomeris leibleinii* (Chlorophyceae) I. The vegetative thallus. *Phycologia* **13**: 63–9.

1142 Mayhoub, H. (1975). Reproduction sexuée et cycle de développement de l'*Anadyomene stellata* (Wulf.) Ag. de la Méditerranée orientale. *C.R. Acad. Sci. Paris* **280D**: 587–90.

1143 McArthur, D.E.M. & B.L. Moss (1978). Ultrastructural studies of vegetative cells, mitosis and cell division in *Enteromorpha intestinalis* (L.) Link. *Br. Phycol. J.* **13**: 255–67.

1144 McAuley, M.A., M.A. Buchheim & R.L. Chapman (1990). Parallel evolution and colonial green flagellates: a preliminary study of 18S and 26S rRNA sequence data. *J. Phycol.* **26** (suppl.): 18.

1145 McBride, G.E. (1967). Cytokinesis in the green alga *Fritschiella tuberosa*. *Nature* **216**: 63–9.

1146 McBride, G.E. (1969). Ultrastructure of the *Coleochaete scutata*-zoospore. *J. Phycol.* **4** (suppl.): 6.

1147 McBride, G.E. (1970). Cytokinesis and ultrastructure in *Fritschiella tuberosa* Iyengar. *Arch. Protistenk.* **112**: 365–75.

1148 McCandless, E.L. (1981). Polysaccharides of seaweeds. In *The Biology of Seaweeds*, ed. C.S. Lobban & M.J. Wynne, pp. 559–88. Blackwell, Oxford.

1149 McCandless, E.L. & J. Craigie (1979). Sulfated polysaccharides in red and brown algae. *Ann. Rev. Plant Physiol.* **30**: 41–53.

1150 McCully, M.E. (1966). Correlated light and electronmicroscope studies on the cell walls of *Fucus. Proc. 5th Int. Seaweed Symp.:* 167.

1151 McCully, M.E. (1966). Histological studies on the genus *Fucus. Protoplasma* **42**: 287–305.

1152 McDonald, K.L. & J.D. Pickett-Heaps (1976). Ultrastructure and differentiation in *Cladophora glomerata*. I. Cell division. *Am. J. Bot.* **63**: 592–601.

1153 McGrory, C.B. & B.S.C. Leadbeater (1981). Ultrastructure and deposition of silica in the Chrysophyceae. In *Silicon and Siliceous Structures in Biological Systems*, ed. T.L. Simpson & B.E. Volcani, pp. 201–30. Springer, New York.

1154 McIntyre, C.D. & W.W. Moore (1977). Marine littoral diatoms: ecological considerations. In *The Biology of Diatoms*, ed. D. Werner, pp. 331–71. Blackwell, Oxford.

1155 McLachlan, J. (1985). Macroalgae (seaweeds): industrial resources and their utilization. *Plant and Soil* **89**: 137–57.

1156 McLachlan, J. & J.M. Parke (1967). *Platymonas impellucida* sp. nov. from Puerto Rico. *J. Mar. Biol. Ass. U.K.* **47**: 723–33.

1157 McLaughlin, J.J.A. & P. Zahl (1966). Endozoic algae. In *Symbiosis*, Vol. I, ed. S.M. Henry, pp. 257–95. Academic Press, New York.

1158 Medlin, L.K., R.M. Crawford & R.A. Andersen (1986). Histochemical and ultrastructural evidence for the function of the labiate process in the movement of centric diatoms. *Br. Phycol. J.* **21**: 297–301.

1159 Meeks, J.C. (1974). Chlorophylls. In *Algal Physiology and Biochemistry*, ed. W.D.P. Stewart, pp. 161–75. Blackwell, Oxford.

1160 Meeuse, B.J.D. (1962). Storage products. In *Physiology and Biochemistry of Algae*, ed. R.A. Lewin, pp. 289–313. Academic Press, New York.

1161 Meinesz, A. (1969). Sur la reproduction sexuée de l'*Udotea petiolata* (Turr.) Boerg. *C.R. Acad Sci. Paris* **269**: 1063–5.

1162 Meinesz, A. (1972a). Sur le cycle de l'*Halimeda tuna* (Ellis et Solander) Lamouroux (Udotéacée, Caulerpale). *C.R. Acad. Sci. Paris* **275**: 1363–5.

1163 Meinesz, A. (1972b). Sur le cycle d'*Udotea petiolata* (Turra) Boergesen (Caulerpale, Udotéacée). *C.R. Acad. Sci. Paris* **275**: 1975–7.

1164 Meinesz, A. (1980). Connaissances actuelles et contribution à l'étude de la reproduction et du cycle des Udotéacées (Caulerpales, Chlorophytes). *Phycologia* **19**: 110–38.

1165 Melkonian, M. (1977). The flagellar root system of zoospores of the green alga *Chlorosarcinopsis* (Chlorosarcinales) as compared with *Chlamydomonas* (Volvocales). *Plant Syst. Evol.* **128**: 79–88.

1166 Melkonian, M. (1978). Structure and significance of cruciate flagellar root systems in green algae: comparative investigations in species of *Chlorosarcinopsis* (Chlorosarcinales). *Plant Syst. Evol.* **130**: 265–92.

1167 Melkonian, M. (1979a). An ultrastructural study of the flagellate *Tetraselmis cordiformis* Stein (Chlorophyceae) with emphasis on the flagellar apparatus. *Protoplasma* **98**: 139–51.

1168 Melkonian, M. (1979b). Structure and significance of cruciate flagellar root systems in green algae: zoospores of *Ulva lactuca* (Ulvales, Chlorophyceae). *Helgol. Wiss. Meeresunters.* **32**: 425–35.

1169 Melkonian, M. (1980a). Flagellar roots, mating structure and gamete fusion in the green alga *Ulva lactuca* (Ulvales). *J. Cell Sci.* **46**: 149–69.

1170 Melkonian, M. (1980b). Fate of eyespot lipid globules after zoospore settlement in the green alga *Pleurastrum terrestre* Fritsch et John. *Br. Phycol. J.* **16**: 247–55.

1171 Melkonian, M. (1981a). The flagellar apparatus of the scaly green flagellate *Pyramimonas obovata*: absolute configuration. *Protoplasma* **108**: 341–55.

1172 Melkonian, M. (1981b). Structure and significance of cruciate flagellar root systems in green algae: female gametes of *Bryopsis lyngbyei* (Bryopsidales). *Helgol. Wiss. Meeresunters.* **34**: 355–69.

1173 Melkonian, M. (1982). Structural and evolutionary aspects of the flagellar apparatus in green algae and land plants. *Taxon* **31**: 255–65.

1174 Melkonian, M. (1983). Functional and phylogenetic aspects of the basal apparatus in algal cells. *J. Submicrosc. Cytol.* **15**: 121–5.

1175 Melkonian, M. (1984). Flagellar apparatus ultrastructure in relation to green algal classification. In *Systematics of the Green Algae*, ed. D.E.G. Irvine & D.M. John, pp. 73–120. Academic Press, London.

1176 Melkonian, M. (1989a). Flagellar apparatus

ultrastructure in *Mesostigma viride* (Prasino-phyceae). *Plant Syst. Evol.* **164**: 93–122.

1177 Melkonian, M. (1989b). Centrin-mediated motility: a novel cell motility mechanism in eukaryotic cells. *Botanica Acta* **102**: 3–4.

1178 Melkonian, M. (1989c). D. Taxonomy. I. Systematics and evolution of the algae. *Progress in Botany* **50**: 214–45.

1178a Melkonian, M. (1990a). Phylum Chlorophyta, Class Prasinophyceae. In *Handbook of Protoctista*, ed. L. Margulis, J.O. Corliss, M. Melkonian & D.J. Chapman, pp. 600–7. Jones & Bartlett, Boston.

1179 Melkonian, M. (1990b). Chlorophyte orders of uncertain affinities. Order Pedinimonadales. In *Handbook of Protoctista*, ed. L. Margulis, J.O. Corliss, M. Melkonian & D.J. Chapman, pp. 649–54. Jones & Bartlett, Boston.

1180 Melkonian, M. & B. Berns (1983). Zoospore ultrastructure in the green alga *Friedmannia israelensis:* an absolute configuration analysis. *Protoplasma* **114**: 67–84.

1181 Melkonian, M. & I. Höhfeld (1988). Amphiesmal ultrastructure in *Noctiluca miliaris* Suriray (Dinophyceae). *Helgol. Meeresunters.* **42**: 601–12.

1182 Melkonian, M. & E. Peveling (1988). Zoospore ultrastructure in species of *Trebouxia* and *Pseudotrebouxia* (Chlorophyta). *Plant Syst. Evol.* **158**: 183–210.

1183 Melkonian, M. & H.R. Preisig (1984). An ultrastructural comparison between *Spermatozopsis* and *Dunaliella* (Chlorophyceae). *Plant Syst. Evol.* **146**: 31–46.

1184 Melkonian, M., I.B. Reize & H.R. Preisig (1987). Maturation of a flagellum/basal body requires more than one cell cycle in algal flagellates: studies on *Nephroselmis olivacea* (Prasino-phyceae). In *Algal Development*, ed. W. Wiessner, D.G. Robinson & R.C. Starr, pp. 102–13. Springer-Verlag, Berlin.

1185 Melkonian, M. & H. Robenek (1980). Eyespot membranes of *Chlamydomonas reinhardii:* a freeze fracture study. *J. Ultrastruct. Res.* **72**: 90–102.

1186 Melkonian, M. & H. Robenek (1984). The eyespot apparatus of flagellated green algae: a critical review. In *Progress in Phycological Research*, Vol. 3, ed. F.E. Round & D.J. Chapman, pp. 193–268. Biopress, Bristol.

1187 Menzel, D. (1980). Plug formation and peroxy-dase accumulation in two orders of siphonous green algae (Caulerpales and Dasycladales) in relation to fertilization and injury. *Phycologia* **19**: 37–48.

1188 Menzel, D. (1985). Fine structure study on the association of the caulerpalean plastid with microtubule bundles in the siphonalean green alga *Chlorodesmis fastigiata* (Ducker, Udoteaceae). *Protoplasma* **125**: 103–10.

1189 Menzel, D. (1986). Visualization of cytoskeletal changes through the life cycle in *Acetabularia*. *Protoplasma* **134**: 30–42.

1190 Menzel, D. (1987). The cytoskeleton of the giant coenocytic green alga *Caulerpa* visualized by immunocytochemistry. *Protoplasma* **139**: 71–6.

1191 Menzel, D. (1988). How do giant plant cells cope with injury? – The wound response in siphonous green algae. *Protoplasma* **144**: 73–91.

1192 Menzel, D. & C. Elsner-Menzel (1989). Maintenance and dynamic changes of cytoplasmic organization controlled by cytoskeletal assemblies in *Acetabularia*. In *Algae as Experimental Systems in Cell Biology*, ed. J. Stein, A.W. Coleman & L.J. Goff, pp. 71–91. Alan R. Liss, New York.

1193 Menzel, D. & M. Schliwa (1986a). Motility in the siphonous green alga *Bryopsis*. I. Spatial organization of the cytoskeleton and organelle movements. *Eur. J. Cell Biol.* **40**: 275–85.

1194 Menzel, D. & M. Schliwa (1986b). Motility in the siphonous green alga *Bryopsis*. II. Chloroplast movement requires organized arrays of both microtubules and actin filaments. *Eur. J. Cell Biol.* **40**: 286–95.

1195 Mereschkowsky, C. (1905). Über Natur und Ursprung der Chromatophoren im Pflanzenreiche. *Biol. Zbl.* **25**: 593–604.

1196 Metting, B. (1981). The systematics and ecology of soil algae. *Bot. Rev.* **47**: 195–312.

1197 Meyen, S.V. (1987). *Fundamentals of Paleobotany*. Chapman and Hall, London.

1198 Michajlow, W. (1972). *Euglenoidina Parasitic in Copepoda*. PWN – Polish Scientific Publisher, Warsaw.

1199 Mignot, J.P. (1965). Etude ultrastructurale de *Cyathomonas truncata* (flagellé cryptomonadine). *J. Microsc.* **4**: 239–52.

1200 Mikami, H. (1965). A systematic study of the Phyllophoraceae and Gigartinaceae from Japan and its vicinity. *Scient. Pap. Inst. Algol. Res. Hokkaido Univ.* **5**: 181–285.

1201   Miller, D.H. (1978). Cell wall chemistry and ultrastructure of *Chlorococcum oleofaciens* (Chlorophyceae). *J. Phycol.* **14**: 189–94.

1202   Millington, W.F. & S.R. Gawlik (1967). Silica in the wall of *Pediastrum*. *Nature* **216**: 68.

1203   Mix, M. (1975). Die Feinstruktur der Zellwände der Conjugaten und ihre systematische Bedeutung. *Nova Hedwigia, Beih.* **42**: 179–94.

1204   Mix, M. & E. Manshard (1977). Über Mikrofibrillen-Aggregate in langsgestreckten Vesikeln und ihre Bedeutung für die Zellwandbildung bei einem Stamm von *Penium* (Desmidiales). *Ber. Dtsch. Bot. Ges.* **90**: 517–26.

1205   Miyaji, K. & T. Hori (1984). The ultrastructure of *Spongomorpha duriuscula* (Acrosiphoniales, Chlorophyta), with special reference to the flagellar apparatus. *Jap. J. Phycol.* **32**: 307–18.

1206   Mizuta, S. (1987). Structure and generation of cell walls in cellulosic algae . II. Microfibril formation and regulation of orientation. *Jap. J. Phycol.* **35**: 130–43.

1207   Mizuta, S. & K. Okuda (1987). A comparative study of cellulose synthesizing complexes in certain Cladophoralean and Siphonocladalean algae. *Bot. Mar.* **30**: 205–15.

1208   Mizuta, S., K. Sawada & K. Okuda (1985). Cell wall regeneration of new spherical cells developed from the protoplasm of a coenocytic green alga, *Boergesenia forbesii. Jap. J. Phycol.* **33**: 32–44.

1209   Moe, R.L. & E.C. Henry (1982). Reproduction and early development of *Ascoseira mirabilis* Skottsberg (Phaeophyta), with notes on Ascoseirales Petrov. *Phycologia* **21**: 55–66.

1210   Moe, R.L. & P.C. Silva (1977). Antarctic marine flora: uniquely devoid of kelps. *Science* **196**: 1206–8.

1211   Moe, R.L. & P.C. Silva (1981). Morphology and taxonomy of *Himanthothallus* (including *Phaeoglossum* and *Phyllogigas*), an Antarctic member of the Desmarestiales. *J. Phycol.* **17**: 15–29.

1212   Moestrup, Ø. (1970a). On the fine structure of the spermatozoids of *Vaucheria sescuplicaria* and on the later stages in spermatogenesis. *J. Mar. Biol. Ass. U.K.* **50**: 513–23.

1213   Moestrup, Ø. (1970b). The fine structure of the mature spermatozoid of *Chara corallina*, with special reference to microtubules and scales. *Planta* **93**: 295–308.

1214   Moestrup, Ø. (1973). New observations on scales in green algae. *Br. Phycol. J.* **8**: 214.

1215   Moestrup, Ø. (1974). Ultrastructure of the scale-covered zoospores of the green alga *Chaetosphaeridium*, a possible ancestor of the higher plants and bryophytes. *Biol. J. Linn. Soc.* **6**: 111–25.

1216   Moestrup, Ø. (1975). Some aspects of sexual reproduction in eukaryotic algae. In *The Biology of the Male Gamete*, ed. J.G. Duckett & P.A. Racey. *Biol. J. Linn. Soc.* **7** (suppl. 1): 23–35.

1217   Moestrup, Ø. (1978). On the phylogenetic validity of the flagellar apparatus in the green algae and other chlorophyll a and b containing plants. *BioSystems* **10**: 117–44.

1218   Moestrup, Ø. (1982). Flagellar structure in algae: a review, with new observations particularly on the Chrysophyceae, Phaeophyceae (Fucophyceae), Euglenophyceae, and *Rickertia*. *Phycologia* **21**: 427–528.

1219   Moestrup, Ø. (1984). Further studies on *Nephroselmis* and its allies (Prasinophyceae). II. *Mamiella* gen. nov., Mamiellales ord. nov. *Nord. J. Bot.* **4**: 109–21.

1220   Moestrup, Ø. (1987). The importance of flagellar apparatus ultrastructure in algal systematics and phylogeny. *14th International Botanical Congress, Berlin, Abstracts:* 259. (Collated and edited by W. Greuter, B. Zimmer & H.D. Behnke; produced with the assistance of M.I. Hakki, H. Sipman and staff members of the Botanical Museum Berlin-Dahlem.)

1220a   Moestrup, Ø. (1991). Further studies of presumedly primitive algae, including the description of Pedinophyceae class. nov., and *Resultor* gen. nov. *J. Phycol.* **27**: 119–33.

1221   Moestrup, Ø. & H. Ettl (1979). A light and electron microscopical study of *Nephroselmis olivacea* (Prasinophyceae). *Opera Botanica* **49**: 1–39.

1222   Moestrup, Ø. & L.R. Hoffman (1975). A study of the spermatozoids of *Dichotomosiphon tuberosus* (Chlorophyceae). *J. Phycol.* **11**: 225–35.

1223   Moestrup, Ø., T. Hori & A. Kristiansen (1987). Fine structure of *Pyramimonas octopus* sp. nov., an octoflagellated benthic species of *Pyramimonas* (Prasinophyceae), with some observations on its ecology. *Nord. J. Bot.* **7**: 339–52.

1224   Moestrup, Ø. & H.A. Thomsen (1974). An ultrastructural study of the flagellate *Pyramimonas orientalis* with particular emphasis on Golgi apparatus activity and the flagellar apparatus. *Protoplasma* **81**: 247–69.

1225 Moestrup, Ø. & H.A. Thomsen (1986). Ultrastructure and reconstruction of the flagellar apparatus in *Chrysochromulina apheles* sp. nov. (Prymnesiophyceae= Haptophyceae). *Can. J. Bot.* **64**: 593–610.

1226 Moestrup, Ø. & H.A. Thomsen (1990). *Dictyocha speculum* (Silicoflagellata, Dictyochophyceae), studies on armoured and unarmoured stages. *Biol. Skr. Kong. Dansk. Vidensk. Selsk.* **37**: 1–24, pl. 1–16.

1227 Moestrup, Ø. & J. Throndsen (1988). Light and electron microscopical studies on *Pseudoscourfieldia marina* (Prasinophyceae) with posterior flagella. *Can. J. Bot.* **66**: 1415–34.

1228 Moestrup. Ø. & P.L. Walne (1979). Studies on scale morphogenesis in the Golgi-apparatus of *Pyramimonas tetrarhynchus* (Prasinophyceae). *J. Cell Sci.* **36**: 437–59.

1229 Molnar, K.E., K.D. Stewart & K.R. Mattox (1975). Cell division in the filamentous *Pleurastrum* and its comparison with the unicellular *Platymonas* (Chlorophyceae). *J. Phycol.* **11**: 287–96.

1230 Moner, J.G. & G.B. Chapman (1963). Cell wall formation in *Pediastrum biradiatum* as revealed by the electron microscope. *Am. J. Bot.* **50**: 992–8.

1231 Monty, C. (1977). Evolving concepts on the nature and the ecological significance of stromatolites. In *Fossil Algae*, ed. E. Flügel, pp. 15–35. Springer-Verlag, Berlin.

1232 Moore, L.B. (1951). Reproduction in *Halopteris* (Sphacelariales). *Ann. Bot.* **15**: 265–78.

1233 Morden, C.W. & S.S. Golden (1989). psbA genes indicate common ancestry of prochlorophytes and chloroplasts. *Nature* **337**: 382–5.

1234 Morrill, L.C. & A.R. Loeblich III (1981). The dinoflagellate pellicular wall layer and its occurrence in the division Pyrrophyta. *J. Phycol.* **17**: 315–23.

1235 Morrill, L.C. & A.R. Loeblich III (1983). Ultrastructure of dinoflagellate amphiesma. *Int. Rev. Cytol.* **82**: 151–80.

1236 Moss, B. (1973a). The influence of environmental factors on the distributon of freshwater algae: an experimental study. II. The role of pH and the carbon-dioxide-bicarbonate system. *J. Ecol.* **61**: 157–77.

1237 Moss, B. (1973b). The influence of environmental factors on the distribution of freshwater algae: an experimental study. III. Effects of temperature, vitamin requirements and inorganic nitrogen compounds on growth. *J. Ecol.* **61**: 179–92.

1238 Moss, B. (1973c). The influence of environmental factors on the distribution of freshwater algae: an experimental study. IV. Growth of test species in natural lake waters, and conclusion. *J. Ecol.* **61**: 193–211.

1239 Motomura, T. (1989). Ultrastructural study of sperm in *Laminaria angustata* (Laminariales, Phaeophyta), especially on the flagellar apparatus. *Jap. J. Phycol.* **37**: 105–16.

1240 Motomura, T., S. Kawaguchi & Y. Sakai (1985). Life history and ultrastructure of *Carpomitra cabrerae* (Clemente) Kuetzing (Phaeophyta, Sporochnales). *Jap. J. Phycol.* **33**: 21–31.

1241 Motomura, T. & Y. Sakai (1985). Ultrastrucural studies on nuclear division in the sporophyte of *Carpomitra cabrerae* (Clemente) Kuetzing (Phaeophyta, Sporochnales). *Jap. J. Phycol.* **33**: 199–209.

1242 Motomura, T. & Y. Sakai (1988). The occurrence of flagellated eggs in *Laminaria angustata* (Phaeophyta, Laminariales). *J. Phycol.* **24**: 282–5.

1243 Mukai, L.S. & J.S. Craigie (1981). Chemical composition and structure of the cell walls of the *Conchocelis* and thallus phases of *Porphyra tenera* (Rhodophyceae). *J. Phycol.* **17**: 192–8.

1244 Müller, D.G. (1966). Untersuchungen zur Entwicklungsgeschichte der Braunalge *Ectocarpus siliculosus* aus Neapel. *Planta* **68**: 57–68.

1245 Müller, D.G. (1967). Generationswechsel, Kernphasenwechsel und Sexualität der Braunalge *Ectocarpus siliculosus* im Kulturversuch. *Planta* **75**: 39–54.

1246 Müller, D.G. (1968). Versuche zur Charakterisierung eines Sexuallockstoffes bei der Braunalge *Ectocarpus siliculosus* I. Methoden, Isolierung und gaschromatografischer Nachweis. *Planta* **81**: 160–8.

1247 Müller, D.G. (1970). Diploide heterozygote Gametophyten bei der Braunalge *Ectocarpus siliculosus*. *Naturwissenschaften* **57**: 357–8.

1248 Müller, D.G. (1972). Studies on reproduction in *Ectocarpus siliculosus*. *Soc. Bot. France, Mémoires*: 87–98.

1249   Müller, D.G. (1974). Detection and identification of sex attractants in three marine brown algae. *8th. Int. Seaweed Symp., Bangor, Wales, Abstracts:* 1.

1250   Müller, D.G. (1962). Über jahres- und lunarperiodische Erscheinungen bei einigen Braunalgen. *Bot. Mar.* **4**: 140–55.

1251   Müller, D.G. (1969). Anisogamy in *Giffordia* (Ectocarpales). *Naturwissenschaften* **56**: 220.

1252   Müller, D.G. (1977). Sexual reproduction in British *Ectocarpus siliculosus* (Phaeopyta). *Br. Phycol. J.* **12**: 131–6.

1253   Müller, D.G. (1979). Genetic affinity of *Ectocarpus siliculosus* (Dillw.) Lyngb. from the Mediterranean, North Atlantic and Australia. *Phycologia* **18**: 312–8.

1254   Müller, D.G. (1981). Culture studies on reproduction of *Spermatochnus paradoxus* (Phaeophyceae, Chordariales). *J. Phycol.* **17**: 384–9.

1255   Müller, D.G. (1984). Culture studies on the life history of *Adenocystis utricularis* (Phaeophyceae, Dictyosiphonales). *Phycologia* **23**: 87–94.

1256   Müller, D.G. (1988). Studies on sexual compatibility between *Ectocarpus siliculosus* (Phaeophyceae) from Chile and the Mediterranean Sea. *Helgol. Meeresunters.* **42**: 469–76.

1257   Müller, D.G., W. Boland, L. Jaenicke & G. Gassmann (1985). Diversification of chemoreceptors in *Ectocarpus, Sphacelaria,* and *Adenocystis. Z. Naturforsch.* **40c**: 457–9.

1258   Müller, D.G., M.N. Clayton, G. Gassman & W. Boland (1985). Cystophorene and hormosirene, sperm attractants in Australian brown algae. *Naturwissenschaften* **72**: 97–8.

1259   Müller, D.G., M.N. Clayton & I. German (1985). Sexual reproduction and life history of *Perithalia caudata* (Sporochnales, Phaeophyta). *Phycologia* **24**: 467–73.

1260   Müller, D.G., M.N. Clayton, M. Meinderts, W. Boland & L. Jaenicke (1986). Sexual pheromone in *Cladostephus* (Sphacelariales, Phaeophyceae). *Naturwissenschaften* **73**: 99.

1261   Müller, D.G. & H. Falk (1973). Flagellar structure of the gametes of *Ectocarpus siliculosus* (Phaeophyta) as revealed by negative staining. *Arch. Mikrobiol.* **91**: 313–22.

1262   Müller, D.G. & G. Gassmann (1978). Identification of the sex attractant in the marine brown alga *Fucus vesiculosus. Naturwissensch.* **65**: 389.

1263   Müller, D.G. & G. Gassmann (1980). Sexual hormone specificity in *Ectocarpus* and *Laminaria* (Phaeophyceae). *Naturwissensch.* **67**: 462.

1264   Müller, D.G. & G. Gassmann (1985). Sexual reproduction and the role of sex attractants in monoecious species of the brown algae order Fucales. *J. Plant Physiol.* **118**: 401–8.

1265   Müller, D.G., G. Gassmann, W. Boland, F. Marner & L. Jaenicke (1981). *Dictyota dichotoma* (Phaeophyceae): identification of the sperm attractant. *Science* **212**: 1040–1.

1265a Müller, D.G. & L. Jaenicke (1973). Fucoserraten, the female sex attractant of *Fucus serratus* L. *FEBS Lett.* **30**: 137–9.

1266   Müller, D.G., L. Jaenicke, M. Donike & T. Akintobi (1971). Sex attractant in a brown alga: chemical structure. *Science* **171**: 815–7.

1267   Müller, D.G. & N.M. Lüthe (1981). Hormonal interaction in sexual reproduction of *Desmarestia aculeata* (Phaeophyceae). *Br. Phycol. J.* **16**: 351–6.

1268   Müller, D.G., I. Maier & G. Gassmann (1985). Survey on sexual pheromone specificity in Laminariales (Phaeophyceae). *Phycologia* **24**: 475–7.

1269   Müller, D.G., I. Maier & H. Müller (1987). Flagellum autofluorescence and photoaccumulation in heterokont algae. *Photochemistry and Photobiology* **46**: 1003–8.

1270   Müller, D.G., A. Peters, G. Gassmann, W. Boland, F.-J. Marner & L. Jaenicke (1982). Identification of a sexual hormone and related substances in the marine brown alga *Desmarestia. Naturwissenschaften* **69**: 290–2.

1271   Müller, D.G. & C.E. Schmidt (1988a). Qualitative and quantitative determination of pheromone secretion in female gametes of *Ectocarpus siliculosus* (Phaeophyceae). *Biol. Chem. Hoppe-Seyler* **369**: 647–53.

1272   Müller, D.G. & U.U. Schmidt (1988b). Culture studies on the life history of *Elachista stellaris* Aresch. (Phaeophyceae, Chordariales). *Br. Phycol. J.* **23**: 153–8.

1273   Müller, D.G. & K. Seferiadis (1977). Specificity of sexual chemotaxis in *Fucus serratus* and *Fucus vesiculosus* (Phaeophyceae). *Z. Pflanzenphysiol.* **84**: 85–94.

1274   Müller, D.G., R. Westermeyer, A. Peters & W. Boland (1990). Sexual reproduction of the Antarctic brown alga *Ascoseira mirabilis* (Ascoseirales, Phaeophyceae). *Bot. Mar.* **33**: 251–5.

1275 Müller, E. & W. Loeffler (1971). *Mykologie.* 2nd Ed. Thieme, Stuttgart.

1276 Müller, J. (1981). Fossil pollen records of extant angiosperms. *Bot. Rev.* **47**: 1–142.

1276a Mumford, T.F. & K. Cole (1977). Chromosome numbers for fifteen species in the genus *Porphyra* (Bangiales, Rhodophyta) from the west coast of North America. *Phycologia* **16**: 373–7.

1276b Muscatine, L. (1973). Nutrition of corals. In *Biology and Geology of Coral Reefs*, Vol. 2, ed. O.A. Jones & R. Endean, pp. 77–115. Academic Press, New York.

1277 Nakamura, Y. & M. Tatewaki (1975). The life-history of some species of the Scytosiphonales. *Scient. Pap. Inst. Algol. Res. Hokkaido Univ.* **6**: 57–93.

1278 Nei, M. (1987). *Molecular Evolutionary Genetics.* Columbia University Press, New York.

1279 Neumann, K. (1969a). Protonema mit Riesenkern bei der siphonalen Grünalge *Bryopsis hypnoides* und weitere cytologische Befunde. *Helgol. Wiss. Meeresunters.* **19**: 45–57.

1280 Neumann, K. (1969b). Beitrag zur Cytologie und Entwicklung der siphonalen Grünalge *Derbesia marina. Helgol. Wiss. Meeresunters.* **19**: 355–75.

1281 Neumann, K. (1970). Einkerniges Protonema bei *Bryopsis* und *Pseudobryopsis myura. Helgol. Wiss. Meeresunters.* **20**: 213–5.

1282 Neville, A.C. (1988). The helicoidal arrangement of microfibrils in some algal cell walls. In *Progress in Phycological Research*, Vol. 6, ed. F.E. Round & D.J. Chapman, pp. 1–21. Biopress, Bristol.

1283 Newton, L. (1931). *A Handbook of the British Seaweeds.* British Museum, London.

1284 Nichols, B.W. (1973). Lipid composition and metabolism. In *The Biology of Blue-green Algae*, ed. N.G. Carr & B.A. Whitton, pp. 144–61. Blackwell, Oxford.

1285 Nielsen, R. (1972). A study of the shell-boring marine algae around the Danish island Laesø. *Bot. Tidsskr.* **67**: 245–69.

1286 Nielsen, R. (1977). Culture studies on *Ulvella lens* and *Ulvella setchelii. Br. Phycol. J.* **12**: 1–5.

1287 Nielsen, R. (1978). Variation in *Ochlochaete hystrix* (Chaetophorales, Chlorophyceae) in culture. *J. Phycol.* **14**: 127–31.

1288 Nielsen, R. (1979). Culture studies on the type species of *Acrochaete, Bolbocoleon* and *Entocladia* (Chaetophoraceae, Chlorophyceae). *Bot. Notiser* **132**: 441–9.

1289 Nielsen, R. (1980). A comparative study of five marine Chaetophoraceae. *Br. Phycol. J.* **15**: 131–8.

1290 Nielsen, R. (1983). Culture studies of *Acrochaete leptochaete* comb. nov. and *A. wittrockii* comb. nov. (Chaetophoraceae, Chlorophyceae). *Nord. J. Bot.* **3**: 689–94.

1291 Nielsen, R. (1984). *Epicladia flustrae, E. phillipsii* stat. nov., and *Pseudendoclonium dynamenae* sp. nov. living in bryozoans and a hydroid. *Br. Phycol. J.* **19**: 371–9.

1292 Nielsen, R. & P.M. Pedersen (1977). Separation of *Syncoryne reinkii* nov. gen. nov. sp. from *Pringsheimiella scutata* (Chlorophyceae, Chaetophoraceae). *Phycologia* **16**: 411–6.

1293 Nielsen, T.G., T. Kiørboe & P.K. Bjørnsen (1990). Effects of a *Chrysochromulina polylepis* subsurface bloom on the planktonic community. *Mar. Ecol. Prog. Ser.* **62**: 21–35.

1294 Nipkov, F. (1962). Über die Sexual- und Dauerperioden einiger Zygnemales aus schweizerischen Kleingewässern. *Schweiz. Z. Hydrol.* **24**: 1–43.

1295 Nisizawa, K., K. Kuroda, Y. Tomita & H. Shimahara (1974). Main cell wall constituents of the cysts of *Acetabularia. Bot. Mar.* **17**: 16–19.

1296 Nisizawa, K., H. Noda, R. Kikuchi & T. Watanabe (1987). The main seaweed foods in Japan. *Hydrobiologia* **151/152**: 5–29.

1297 Nisizawa, K. & S.F. Sasaki (1975). Cell wall composition of algae from a phylogenetic point of view. In *Advance of Phycology in Japan*, ed. J. Tokida & H. Hirose, pp. 42–5. VEB Gustav Fischer Verlag, Jena.

1298 Noro, T. & K. Nozawa (1981). Ultrastructure of a red tide chloromonadophycean alga, *Chattonella* sp., from Kagoshima Bay, Japan. *Jap. J. Phycol.* **29**: 73–8.

1299 Norris, R.E. (1966). Unarmoured marine dinoflagellates. *Endeavour* **25**: 124–8.

1300 Norris, R.E. (1967). Algal consortisms in marine plankton. In *Proceedings Seminar on Sea, Salt and Plants*, ed. V. Krishnamurthy, pp. 178–89. Central Salt and Marine Chemicals Research Institute, Bhavnagar, India.

1301 Norris, R.E. (1980). Prasinophytes. In

Phytoflagellates, ed. E.R. Cox, pp. 85–145. Elsevier/North-Holland, Amsterdam.

1302   Norris, R.E. (1982a). Prasinophyceae. In *Synopsis and Classification of Living Organisms*, Vol. I, ed. S.P. Parker, pp. 162–4. McGraw-Hill Book Company, New York.

1302a   Norris, R.E. (1982b). Prymnesiophyceae. In *Synopsis and Classification of Living Organisms*, Vol. I, ed. S.P. Parker, pp. 86–91. McGraw-Hill Book Company, New York.

1303   Norris, R.E. & B.R. Pearson (1975). Fine structure of *Pyramimonas parkeae*, sp. nov. (Chlorophyta, Prasinophyceae). *Arch. Protistenk.* **117**: 192–213.

1304   Norris, R.E. & R.N. Pienaar (1978). Comparative fine-structural studies on five marine species of *Pyramimonas* (Chlorophyta, Prasinophyceae). *Phycologia* **17**: 41–51.

1305   Novaczek, I., C.J. Bird & J.L. McLachlan (1986a). Culture and field studies of *Stilophora rhizodes* (Phaeophyceae, Chordariales) from Nova Scotia, Canada. *Br. Phycol. J.* **21**: 407–16.

1306   Novaczek, I., C.J. Bird & J. McLachlan (1986b). The effect of temperature on development and reproduction in *Chorda filum* and *C. tomentosa* (Phaeophyta, Laminariales) from Nova Scotia. *Can. J. Bot.* **64**: 2414–20.

1307   Novaczek, I. & J. McLachlan (1987). Correlation of temperature and daylength response of *Sphaerotrichia divaricata* (Phaeophyta, Chordariales) with field phenology in Nova Scotia and distribution in Eastern North America. *Br. Phycol. J.* **22**: 215–9.

1308   Nultsch, W. (1974). Movements. In *Algal Physiology and Biochemistry*, ed. W.D.P. Stewart, pp. 864–93. Blackwell, Oxford.

1309   Nygaard, C. (1949). Hydrobiological study on some Danish ponds and lakes. *K. Dansk Vidensk. Selsk.* **7**: 1–263.

1310   Oakley, B.R. (1978). Mitotic spindle formation in *Cryptomonas* and *Chroomonas* (Cryptophyceae). *Protoplasma* **95**: 333–46.

1311   Oakley, B.R. & T. Bisalputra (1977). Mitosis and cell division in *Cryptomonas* (Cryptophyceae). *Can. J. Bot.* **55**: 2789–800.

1312   Oakley, B.R. & J.D. Dodge (1973). Mitosis in the Cryptophyceae. *Nature* **244**: 521–2.

1313   Oakley, B.R. & J.D. Dodge (1974). Kinetochores associated with the nuclear envelope in the mitosis of a dinoflagellate. *J. Cell Biol.* **63**: 322–5.

1314   Oakley, B.R. & J.D. Dodge (1979). Evidence for a double-helically coiled toroidal chromonema in the dinoflagellate chromosome. *Chromosoma (Berl.)* **70**: 277–91.

1315   O'Colla, P.S. (1962). Mucilages. In *Physiology and Biochemistry of Algae*, ed. R.A. Lewin, pp. 337–56. Academic Press, New York.

1316   Ogino, C. (1962). Tannins and vacuolar pigments. In *Physiology and Biochemistry of Algae*, ed. R.A. Lewin, pp. 437–43. Academic Press, New York.

1317   Ohme, M., Y. Kunifuji & A. Miura (1986). Cross experiments of the color mutants in *Porphyra yezoensis* Ueda. *Jap. J. Phycol.* **34**: 101–6.

1318   Ohme, M. & A. Miura (1988). Tetrad analysis in conchospore germlings of *Porphyra yezoensis* (Rhodophyta, Bangiales). *Plant Science* **57**: 135–40.

1319   Ohta, M. & M. Kurogi (1979). On the life history of *Rhodochorton purpureum* (Lightf.) Rosenvinge. *Jap. J. Phycol.* **27**: 161–7.

1320   Okaichi, T., D.M. Anderson & T. Nemoto (eds) (1989). *Red Tides, Biology, Environmental Science and Toxicology*. Elsevier, Amsterdam.

1321   Okazaki, M., K. Furuya, K. Tsukayama & K. Nisizawa (1982). Isolation and identification of alginic acid from a calcareous red alga *Serraticardia maxima*. *Bot. Mar.* **25**: 123–31.

1322   O'Kelly, C.J. (1983). Environmental factors and sexual expression in *Chlorococcum echinozygotum* (Chlorophyceae). *J. Phycol.* **19**: 57–64.

1323   O'Kelly, C.J. (1982). Observations on marine Chaetophoraceae (Chlorophyta) III. The structure, reproduction and life history of *Endophyton ramosum*. *Phycologia* **21**: 247–57.

1324   O'Kelly, C.J. (1983). Observations on marine Chaetophoraceae (Chlorophyta) IV. The structure, reproduction, and life history of *Acrochaete geniculata* (Gardner) comb. nov. *Phycologia* **22**: 13–21.

1325   O'Kelly, C.J. (1989). The evolutionary origin of the brown algae; information from studies of motile cell ultrastructure. In *The Chromophyte Algae*, ed. J.C. Green, B.S.C. Leadbeater & W.L. Diver, pp. 255–78. Clarendon Press, Oxford.

1326   O'Kelly, C.J. & G.J. Floyd (1983). The flagellar apparatus of *Entocladia viridis* motile cells, and the taxonomic position of the resurrected family Ulvellaceae (Ulvales, Chlorophyta). *J. Phycol.* **19**: 153–64.

1327   O'Kelly, C.J. & G.L. Floyd (1984a). The

absolute configuration of the flagellar apparatus in zoospores of two species of Laminariales (Phaeophyceae). *Protoplasma* **123**: 18–25.

1328 O'Kelly, C.J. & G.L. Floyd (1984b). Flagellar apparatus absolute orientations and the phylogeny of the green algae. *BioSystems* **16**: 227–51.

1329 O'Kelly, C.J. & G.L. Floyd (1984c). Correlations among patterns of sporangial structure and development, life histories, and ultrastructural features in the Ulvophyceae. In *Systematics of the Green Algae*, ed. D.E.G. Irvine & D.M. John, pp. 121–56. Academic Press, London.

1330 O'Kelly, C.J. & G.L. Floyd (1985). Absolute configuration analysis of the flagellar apparatus in *Giraudiopsis stellifer* (Chrysophyceae, Sarcinochrysidales) zoospores and its significance in the evolution of the Phaeophyceae. *Phycologia* **24**: 263–74.

1331 O'Kelly, C.J., G.L. Floyd & M.A. Dube (1984). The fine structure of motile cells in the genera *Ulvaria* and *Monostroma*, with special reference to the taxonomic positon of *Monostroma oxyspermum* (Ulvophyceae, Chlorophyta). *Pl. Syst. Evol.* **144**: 179–99.

1332 O'Kelly, C.J. & C. Yarish (1981). Observations on marine Chaetophoraceae (Chlorophyta) II. On the circumscription of the genus *Entocladia* Reinke. *Phycologia* **20**: 32–45.

1333 Okuda, K. (1989). Ultrastructure of mitosis and cytokinesis during gametic differentiation in the siphonous green alga *Pseudobryopsis hainanensis* Tseng. *Scient. Pap. Inst. Algol. Res. Hokkaido Univ.* **8**: 119–56.

1334 Okuda, K., S. Enomoto & M. Tatewaki (1979). Life history of *Pseudobryopsis* sp. (Codiales, Chlorophyta). *Jap. J. Phycol.* **27**: 7–16.

1335 Okuda, K. & S. Mizuta (1987). Modification in cell shape unrelated to cellulose microfibril orientation in growing thallus cells of *Chaetomorpha moniligera*. *Plant Cell Physiol.* **28**: 461–73.

1336 Olsen, J.L., W.T. Stam, P.V.M. Bot & C. van den Hoek (1987). scDNA–DNA hybridization studies in Pacific and Caribbean isolates of *Dictyosphaeria cavernosa* (Chlorophyta) indicate a long divergence. *Helgol. Meeresunters.* **41**: 377–83.

1337 Olsen, J.R. (1988). Marine picophytoplankton studied using flow cytometry. *3rd International Phycological Congress, Monash University, Melbourne, Abstracts*, p. 33.

1338 Olsen-Stojkovich, J.L. (1986). *Phylogenetic studies of genera in the Siphonocladales–Cladophorales complex (Chlorophyta)*. Thesis, University of California, Berkeley: 1–183.

1339 Olsen-Stojkovich, J.L., J.A. West & J.M. Lowenstein (1986). Phylogenetics and biogeography in the Cladophorales complex (Chlorophyta): some insights from immunological distance data. *Bot. Mar.* **29**: 239–49.

1340 Oltmanns, F. (1922a). *Morphologie und Biologie der Algen*. Vol. I. 2nd Ed. Fischer, Jena.

1341 Oltmanns, F. (1922b). *Morphologie und Biologie der Algen*. Vol. II. 2nd Ed. Fischer, Jena.

1342 Oltmanns, F. (1923). *Morphologie und Biologie der Algen*. Vol. III. 2nd Ed. Fischer, Jena.

1343 Ott, D.W. & R.M. Brown (1972). Light and electron microscopical observations on mitosis in *Vaucheria litorea* Hofman ex C. Agardh. *Br. Phycol. J.* **7**: 361–74.

1344 Ott, D.W. & R.M. Brown (1974a). Developmental cytology of the genus *Vaucheria* I. Organization of the vegetative filament. *Br. Phycol. J.* **9**: 11–126.

1345 Ott, D.W. & R.M. Brown (1974b). Developmental cytology of the genus *Vaucheria* II. Sporogenesis in *V. fontinalis* (L.) Christensen. *Br. Phycol. J.* **9**: 333–51.

1346 Ott, D.W. & R.M. Brown (1978). Developmental cytology of the genus *Vaucheria* IV. Spermatogenesis. *Br. Phycol. J.* **13**: 69–85.

1347 Owen, H.A., K.R. Mattox & K.D. Stewart (1990a). Fine structure of the flagellar apparatus of *Dinobryon cylindricum* (Chrysophyceae). *J. Phycol.* **26**: 131–41.

1348 Owen, H.A., K.D. Stewart & K.R. Mattox (1990b). Fine structure of the flagellar apparatus of *Uroglena americana*. *J. Phycol.* **26**: 142–9.

1349 Owens, K.J., M.A. Farmer & R.E. Triemer (1988). The flagellar apparatus and reservoir/canal cytoskeleton of *Cryptoglena pigra* (Euglenophyceae). *J. Phycol.* **24**: 520–8.

1350 Owens, T.G., J.C. Gallagher & R.S. Alberte (1987). Photosynthetic light-harvesting function of violaxanthin in *Nannochloropsis* spp. (Eustigmatophyceae). *J. Phycol.* **23**: 79–85.

1351 Packard, T.T., D. Blasco & R.T. Barber (1978). *Mesodinium rubrum* in the Baja California upwelling system. In *Upwelling Ecosystems*, ed. R. Boje & M. Tomczak, pp. 73–89. Springer, Berlin.

1352 Padan, E. & Y. Cohen (1982). Anoxygenic photosynthesis. In *The Biology of Cyanobacteria*, ed. N.G. Carr & B.A. Whitton, pp. 215–35. Blackwell Scientific Publications, Oxford.

1353 Paddock, T.B.B. (1968). A possible aid to survival of the marine coccolithophorid *Cricophaera* and similar organisms. *Br. Phycol. Bull.* **3**: 519–23.

1353a Palenik, B. & R. Haselkorn (1991). Evolutionary divergence of the prochlorophytes. *J. Phycol.* **27** (suppl.): 322.

1353b Palenik, B.P. & R. Haselkorn (1992). Multiple evolutionary origins of prochlorophytes, the chlorophyll *b*-containing prokaryotes. *Nature* **355**: 265–7.

1354 Palmer, J.D. (1985). Comparative organization of chloroplast genomes. *Ann. Rev. Genet.* **19**: 325–54.

1355 Palmer, J.D., L.A. Herbon, B.G. Milligan, S.L. Baldauf, J.N. Hampton & J.P. Calie (1987). Evolution of chloroplast chromosomes in land plants. *14th International Botanical Congress, Berlin, Abstracts:* 155. (Collated and edited by W. Greuter, B. Zimmer & H.D. Behnke; produced with the assistance of M.I. Hakki, H. Sipman and staff members of the Botanical Museum Berlin-Dahlem.)

1356 Pankratz, H.S. & C.C. Bowen (1963). Cytology of blue-green algae. I. The cells of *Symploca muscorum. Am. J. Bot.* **50**: 387–99.

1357 Papenfuss, G. (1951). Phaeophyta. In *Manual of Phycology*, ed. G.M. Smith, pp. 119–66. Blaidell, Waltham, Massachusetts.

1358 Parke, M. (1961). Some remarks concerning the class Chrysophyceae. *Br. Phycol. Bull.* **2**: 47–55.

1359 Parke, M. (1966). The genus *Pachysphaera* (Prasinophyceae). In *Some Contemporary Studies in Marine Science*, ed. H. Barnes, pp. 555–63. Allen & Unwin, London.

1360 Parke, M. (1971). The production of calcareous elements by benthic algae belonging to the class Haptophyceae (Chrysophyta). In *Proceedings of the 2nd Planktonic Conference, Roma 1970*, ed. A. Farinacci, pp. 929–37. Tecnoscienza, Rome.

1361 Parke, M. & I. Adams (1960). The motile (*Crystallolithus hyalinus* Gaarder et Markali) and non-motile phases in the life-history of *Coccolithus pelagicus* (Wallich) Schiller. *J. Mar. Biol. Ass. U.K.* **39**: 263–74.

1362 Parke, M., G.T. Boalch, R. Jowett & D.S. Harbour (1978). The genus *Pterosperma* (Prasinophyceae): species with a single equatorial ala. *J. Mar. Biol. Ass. U.K.* **58**: 239–76.

1363 Parke, M. & P.S. Dixon (1976). Check-list of British marine algae – third revision. *J. Mar. Biol. Ass. U.K.* **56**: 527–94.

1364 Parke, M. & I. den Hartog-Adams (1965). Three species of *Halosphaera. J. Mar. Biol. Ass. U.K.* **45**: 537–57.

1365 Parke, M., J.W.G. Lund & I. Manton (1962). Observations on the biology and fine structure of the type species of *Chrysochromulina (C. parva* Lackey) in the English Lake District. *Arch. Mikrobiol.* **42**: 333–52.

1366 Parke, M. & I. Manton (1962). Studies on marine flagellates VI. *Chrysochromulina pringsheimii* sp. nov. *J. Mar. Biol. Ass. U.K.* **42**: 391–404.

1367 Parke, M. & I. Manton (1965). Preliminary observations on the fine structure of *Prasinocladus marinus. J. Mar. Biol. Ass. U.K.* **45**: 525–36.

1368 Parke, M. & I. Manton (1967). The specific identity of the algal symbiont in *Convoluta roscoffensis. J. Mar. Biol. Ass. U.K.* **47**: 445–64.

1369 Parke, M., I. Manton & B. Clarke (1955). Studies on marine flagellates II. Three new species of *Chrysochromulina. J. Mar. Biol. Ass. U.K.* **34**: 579–609.

1370 Parke, M., I. Manton & B. Clarke (1956). Studies on marine flagellates III. Three further species of *Chrysochromulina. J. Mar. Biol. Ass. U.K.* **35**: 387–414.

1371 Parke, M., I. Manton & B. Clarke (1958). Studies on marine flagellates IV. Morphology and microanatomy of a new species of *Chrysochromulina. J. Mar. Biol. Ass. U.K.* **37**: 209–28.

1372 Parke, M., I. Manton & B. Clarke (1959). Studies on marine flagellates V. Morphology and microanatomy of *Chrysochromulina strobilus* sp. n. *J. Mar. Biol. Ass. U.K.* **38**: 169–88.

1373 Parke, M. & D.G. Rayns (1964). Studies on marine flagellates VII. *Nephroselmis gilva* sp. nov. and some allied forms. *J. Mar. Biol. Ass. U.K.* **44**: 209–17.

1374 Parker, B.C. (1965). Translocation in the giant kelp *Macrocystis* I. Rates, direction, quantity of C^{14}-labelled products and fluorescence. *J. Phycol.* **1**: 42–6.

1375 Parker, B.C. (1966). Translocation in *Macrocystis* III. Composition of the sieve tube exudate and identification of the major C^{14}-labelled products. *J. Phycol.* **2**: 38–46.

1376 Parker, B.C. & E.Y. Dawson (1965). Noncalcareous marine algae from California marine deposits. *Nova Hedwigia* **10**: 273–95.

1377 Parker, B.C. & J. Huber (1965). Translocation in *Macrocystis* II. Fine structure of the sieve tubes. *J. Phycol.* **1**: 172–9.

1378 Parker, S.P. (Ed.) (1982). *Synopsis and Classification of Living Organisms.* Vols 1 & 2. McGraw-Hill, New York.

1379 Parsons, T.R., M. Takahashi & B. Hargrave (1977). *Biological Oceanographic Processes.* 2nd Ed. Pergamon, Oxford.

1380 Pascher, A. (1914). Über Flagellaten und Algen. *Ber. Dtsch. Bot. Ges.* **32**: 136–60.

1381 Pascher, A. (1939). Heterokonten. In *Dr L. Rabenhorst's Kryptogamen-Flora von Deutschland, Österreich und der Schweiz,* Vol. XI. Akademische Verlagsgesellschaft, Leipzig.

1382 Patrick, R. (1977). Ecology of freshwater diatoms and diatom communities. In *The Biology of Diatoms,* ed. D. Werner, pp. 284–322. Blackwell, Oxford.

1383 Patterson, D.J. (1980). Contractile vacuoles and associated structures: their organization and function. *Biol. Rev.* **55**: 1–46.

1384 Patterson, D.J. (1989). Stramenopiles: chromophytes from a protistan perspective. In *The Chromophyte Algae,* ed. J.C. Green, B.S.C. Leadbeater & W.L. Diver, pp. 357–79. Clarendon Press, Oxford.

1385 Patterson, D.J. & K. Hausmann (1981). The behaviour of contractile vacuole complexes of cryptophycean flagellates. *Br. Phycol. J.* **16**: 429–39.

1386 Pearlmutter, N.L. & C.A. Lembi (1980). Structure and composition of *Pithophora oedogonia* (Chlorophyta) cell walls. *J. Phycol.* **16**: 602–16.

1387 Pearson, B.R. & R.E. Norris (1975). Fine structure of cell division in *Pyramimonas parkeae. J. Phycol.* **11**: 113–24.

1388 Pedersen, P.M. (1980). Culture studies on complanate and cylindrical *Scytosiphon* (Fucophyceae, Scytosiphonales) from Greenland. *Br. Phycol. J.* **15**: 391–8.

1389 Pennick, N. (1981). Flagellar scales in *Hemiselmis brunnescens* Butcher and *H. virescens* Droop (Cryptophyceae). *Arch. Protistenk.* **124**: 267–70.

1390 Pennick, N.C. (1982). Studies of the external morphology of *Pyramimonas* 6. *Pyramimonas cirolanae* sp. nov. *Arch. Protistenk.* **125**: 87–94.

1391 Pennick, N.C. (1984). Comparative ultrastructure and occurrence of scales in *Pyramimonas* (Chlorophyta, Prasinophyceae). *Arch. Protistenk.* **128**: 3–11.

1392 Pennick, N.C. & K.J. Clarke (1977). The occurrence of scales in the peridinian dinoflagellate *Heterocapsa triquetra* (Ehrenb.) Stein. *Br. Phycol. J.* **12**: 63–6.

1393 Pérasso, R., A. Baroin & A. Adoutte (1990). The emergence of eukaryotic algae within the protists: a molecular phylogeny based on ribosomal RNA sequencing. In *Experimental Phycology 1. Cell Walls and Surfaces, Reproduction, Photosynthesis,* ed. W. Wiessner, D.G. Robinson & R.C. Starr, pp. 1–19. Springer-Verlag, Berlin.

1394 Pérasso, R., A. Baroin, L.H. Qu, J.P. Bachellerie & A. Adoutte (1989). Origin of the algae. *Nature* **339**: 142–4.

1395 Percival, E. (1979). The polysaccharides of green, red and brown seaweeds: their basic structure, biosynthesis and function. *Br. Phycol. J.* **14**: 103–17.

1396 Percival, E. & R.H. McDowell (1967). *Chemistry and Enzymology of Marine Algal Polysaccharides.* Academic Press, London.

1397 Peschek, G.A. (1987). Respiratory electron transport. In *The Cyanobacteria,* ed. P. Fay & C. Van Baalen, pp. 119–61. Elsevier, Amsterdam.

1398 Peterfi, L.S. & I. Manton (1968). Observations with the electron microscope on *Asteromonas gracilis* Artari emend. (*Stephanoptera gracilis* [Artari] Wisl.). With some comparative observations on *Dunaliella* sp. *Br. Phycol. Bull.* **3**: 423–40.

1399 Peters, A. (1984). Observations on the life history of *Papenfussiella callitricha* (Phaeophyceae, Chordariales) in culture. *J. Phycol.* **20**: 409–14.

1400 Peters, A. (1987). Reproduction and sexuality in the Chordariales (Phaeophyceae). A review of culture studies. In *Progress in Phycological Research, Vol. 5,* ed. F.E. Round & D.J. Chapman, pp. 223–63. Biopress, Bristol.

1401 Peters, A. (1988). Culture studies of a sexual life history in *Myriotrichia clavaeformis* (Phaeophyceae, Dictyosiphonales). *Br. Phycol. J.* **23**: 299–306.

1402   Peters, A. & D.G. Müller (1985). On the sexual reproduction of *Dictyosiphon foeniculaceus* (Phaeophyceae, Dictyosiphonales). *Helgol. Meeresunters.* **39**: 441–7.

1403   Peters, A. & D.G. Müller (1986a). Critical re-examination of sexual reproduction in *Tinocladia crassa*, *Nemacystus decipiens*, and *Sphaerotrichia divaricata* (Phaeophyceae, Chordariales). *Jap. J. Phycol.* **34**: 69–73.

1404   Peters, A. & D.G. Müller (1986b). Culture studies on the life history of *Myriogloea chilensis* (Mont.) Llaña (Phaeophyceae, Chordariales). *Bot. Mar.* **29**: 43–8.

1405   Petersen, J.B. & J.B. Hansen (1956). On the scales of some *Synura* species. *Biol. Medd. Dansk Vidensk. Selsk.* **23**: 3–28.

1406   Pfiester, L.A. (1984). Sexual reproduction. In *Dinoflagellates*, ed. D.L. Spector, pp. 181–99. Academic Press, Orlando.

1407   Pfiester, L.A. & D.M. Anderson (1987). Dinoflagellate reproduction. In *The Biology of Dinoflagellates*, ed. F.J.R. Taylor, pp. 611–48. Blackwell Scientific Publications, Oxford.

1408   Pfiester, L.A. & J.F. Highfill (1990). Culture and sexual reproduction of 'Hemidinium nasutum - Gloeodinium montanum'. *J. Phycol.* **26** (suppl.): 18.

1409   Pfiester, L.A. & J. Popovsky (1979). Parasitic amoeboid dinoflagellates. *Nature* **279**: 421–4.

1410   Phillips, J.A., M.N. Clayton, I. Maier, W. Boland & D.G. Müller (1990). Sexual reproduction in *Dictyota diemensis* (Dictyotales, Phaeophyta). *Phycologia* **29**: 367–79.

1411   Pickett-Heaps, J.D. (1967). Ultrastructure and differentiation in *Chara* sp. II. Mitosis. *Austr. J. Biol. Sci.* **20**: 883–94.

1412   Pickett-Heaps, J.D. (1968). Ultrastructure and differentiation in *Chara* (*fibrosa*) IV. Spermatogenesis. *Austr. J. Biol. Sci.* **21**: 655–90.

1413   Pickett-Heaps, J.D. (1969). The evolution of the mitotic apparatus: an attempt at comparative ultrastructural cytology in dividing plant cells. *Cytobios* **3**: 257–80.

1414   Pickett-Heaps, J.D. (1970). Mitosis and autospore-formation in the green alga *Kirchneriella lunaris*. *Protoplasma* **70**: 325–47.

1415   Pickett-Heaps, J.D. (1971). Reproduction by zoospores in *Oedogonium*. I. Zoosporogenesis.

Protoplasma **72**: 275–314.

1416   Pickett-Heaps, J.D. (1972a). Cell division in *Cosmarium botrytis*. *J. Phycol.* **8**: 343–60.

1417   Pickett-Heaps, J.D. (1972b). Cell division in *Klebsormidium subtilissimum* (formerly *Ulothrix subtilissima*) and its possible phylogenetic significance. *Cytobios* **6**: 167–83.

1418   Pickett-Heaps, J.D. (1974). Cell division in *Stichococcus*. *Br. Phycol. J.* **9**: 63–73.

1419   Pickett-Heaps, J.D. (1975). *Green Algae. Structure, Reproduction and Evolution in Selected Genera*. Sinauer, Sunderland, Massachusetts.

1420   Pickett-Heaps, J.D. (1976). Cell division in *Raphidonema longiseta*. *Arch. Protistenk.* **118**: 209–14.

1421   Pickett-Heaps, J.D. (1987). Diatom mitosis: implications of a model system. In *Algal Development*, ed. W. Wiessner, D.G. Robinson & R.C. Starr, pp. 28–33. Springer-Verlag, Berlin.

1422   Pickett-Heaps, J.D. & L.C. Fowke (1969). Cell division in *Oedogonium* I. Mitosis, cytokinesis, and cell elongation. *Austr. J. Biol. Sci.* **22**: 857–94.

1423   Pickett-Heaps, J.D. & L.C. Fowke (1970a). Mitosis, cytokinesis, and cell elongation in the desmid, *Closterium littorale*. *J. Phycol.* **6**: 189–215.

1424   Pickett-Heaps, J.D. & L.C. Fowke (1970b). Cell division in *Oedogonium* II. Nuclear division in *O. cardiacum*. *Austr. J. Biol. Sci.* **23**: 71–92.

1425   Pickett-Heaps, J.D. & L.C. Fowke (1970c). Cell division in *Oedogonium* III. Golgi bodies, wall structure, and wall formation in *O. cardiacum*. *Austr. J. Biol. Sci.* **23**: 261–71.

1426   Pickett-Heaps, J.D., D.R.A. Hill & R. Wetherbee (1986). Cellular movement in the centric diatom *Odontella sinensis*. *J. Phycol.* **22**: 334–9.

1427   Pickett-Heaps, J.D., A.-M.M. Schmid & L.A. Edgar (1990). The cell biology of diatom valve formation. In *Progress in Phycological Research*, Vol. 7, ed. F.E. Round & D.J. Chapman, pp. 1–80. Biopress, Bristol.

1428   Pickett-Heaps, J.D. & L.A. Staehelin (1975). The ultrastructure of *Scenedesmus* (Chlorophyceae). II. Cell division and colony formation. *J. Phycol.* **11**: 186–202.

1429   Pickett-Heaps, J.D., D.H. Tippitt & R. Leslie (1980). Light and electron microscopic observations on cell division in two large pennate diatoms, *Hantzschia* and *Nitzschia*. II. Ultrastructure. *Eur. J. Cell Biol.* **21**: 12–27.

1430 Pickett-Heaps, J.D. & R. Wetherbee (1987). Spindle function in the green alga *Mougeotia*: absence of anaphase A correlates with postmitotic nuclear migration. *Cell Motility Cytoskeleton* **7**: 68–77.

1431 Pienaar, R.N. (1969a). The fine structure of *Cricosphaera carterae*. I. External morphology. *J. Cell Sci.* **4**: 461–567.

1432 Pienaar, R.N. (1969b). The fine structure of *Hymenomonas* (*Cricosphaera*) *carterae* II. Observations on scale and coccolith production. *J. Phycol.* **5**: 321–31.

1433 Pienaar, R.N. & M.E. Aken (1985). The ultrastructure of *Pyramimonas parkeae* sp. nov. (Prasinophyceae) from South Africa. *J. Phycol.* **21**: 428–47.

1434 Pocock, M.A. (1960). *Hydrodictyon*: a comparative biological study. *J. S. Afr. Bot.* **26**: 167–319.

1435 Polanshek, A.R. & J.A. West (1977). Culture and hybridization studies on *Gigartina papillata* (Rhodophyta). *J. Phycol.* **13**: 141–9.

1436 Porter, D. (1990). Phylum Labyrinthulomycota. In *Handbook of Protoctista*, ed. L. Margulis, J.O. Corliss, M. Melkonian & D.J. Chapman, pp. 388–98. Jones & Bartlett, Boston.

1437 Preisig, H.R. (1989). The flagellar base ultrastructure and phylogeny of chromophytes. In *The Chromophyte Algae*, ed. J.C. Green, B.S.C. Leadbeater & W.L. Diver, pp. 167–87. Clarendon Press, Oxford.

1438 Preisig, H.R. & C. Wilhelm (1989). Ultrastructure, pigments and taxonomy of *Botryochloropsis similis* gen. et sp. nov. (Eustigmatophyceae). *Phycologia* **28**: 61–9.

1439 Prescott, G.W., H.T. Croasdale & W.C. Vinyard (1977). *A synopsis of North American desmids*. Part II. *Desmidiaceae: Placodermae, section 2.* University of Nebraska Press, Lincoln.

1440 Prescott, G.W., H.T. Croasdale, W.C. Vinyard & C.E. Bicudo (1981). *A synopsis of North American desmids*. Part II. *Desmidiaceae: Placodermae, section 3.* University of Nebraska Press, Lincoln.

1441 Preston, R.D. (1974). *The Physical Biology of Plant Cell Walls*. Chapman & Hall, London.

1442 Prézelin, B.B. (1987). Photosynthetic physiology of dinoflagellates. In *The Biology of Dinoflagellates*, ed. F.J.R. Taylor, pp. 174–223. Blackwell Scientific Publications, Oxford.

1443 Price, I.R. (1972). Zygote development in *Caulerpa* (Chlorophyta, Caulerpales). *Phycologia* **11**: 217–8.

1444 Pringsheim, N. (1860). Beiträge zur Morphologie und Systematik der Algen. III. Die Coleochaeteen. *Jahrb. Wiss. Bot.* **2**: 1–38.

1445 Printz, H. (1964). Die Chaetophoralen der Binnengewässer (eine systematische Übersicht). *Hydrobiologia* **24**: 1–376.

1446 Proctor, V.W. (1980). Historical biogeography of *Chara* (Charophyta): an appraisal of the Braun-Wood classification plus a falsifiable alternative for future considerations. *J. Phycol.* **16**: 218–38.

1447 Prud'homme van Reine, W.F. (1982). A taxonomic revision of the European Sphacelariaceae (Sphacelariales, Phaeophyceae). *Leiden Botanical Series* **6**: 1–293.

1448 Prud'homme van Reine, W.F. & W. Star (1981). Transmisson electron microscopy of apical cells of *Sphacelaria* spp. *Blumea* **27**: 523–46.

1449 Pueschel, C.M. (1977). A freeze-etch study of the ultrastructure of red algal pit plugs. *Protoplasma* **91**: 15–30.

1450 Pueschel, C.M. (1979). Ultrastructure of tetrasporogenesis in *Palmaria palmata* (Rhodophyta). *J. Phycol.* **15**: 409–24.

1451 Pueschel, C.M. (1980a). Pit connections and translocation in red algae. *Science* **209**: 422–3.

1452 Pueschel, C.M. (1980b). A reappraisal of the cytochemical properties of rhodophycean pit plugs. *Phycologia* **19**: 210–7.

1453 Pueschel, C.M. (1982). Ultrastructural observations of tetrasporangia and conceptacles in *Hildenbrandia* (Rhodophyta). *Br. Phycol. J.* **17**: 333–41.

1454 Pueschel, C.M. (1987). Absence of cap membranes as a characteristic of pit plugs of some red algal orders. *J. Phycol.* **23**: 150–6.

1455 Pueschel, C.M. (1989). An expanded survey of the ultrastructure of red algal pit plugs. *J. Phycol.* **25**: 625–36.

1456 Pueschel, C.M. & K.M. Cole (1982). Rhodophycean pit plugs: an ultrastructural survey with taxonomic implications. *Am. J. Bot.* **69**: 703–20.

1457 Pueschel, C.M. & F. Magne (1987). Pit plugs and other ultrastructural features of systematic value in *Rhodochaete parvula* (Rhodophyta, Rhodochaetales). *Crypt. Algol.* **8**: 201–9.

1458 Puiseux-Dao, S. (1962). Recherches biologiques et physiologiques sur quelques Dasycladacées, en particulier la *Batophora oerstedii* J. Ag. et l'*Acetabularia mediterranea* Lam. *Rev. Gén. Bot.*: 409–503.

1459   Puiseux-Dao, S. (1963). Les Acétabulaires, matériel de laboratoire. Les résultats obtenus avec ces Chlorophycées. *Ann. Biol.* **2**: 99–154.

1460   Puiseux-Dao, S. (1970) *Acetabularia and Cell Biology.* Logos Press, London.

1461   Puytorac, P. de, J. Grain & J.-P. Mignot (1987). *Précis de Protistologie.* Boubée, Paris.

1462   Quader, H. (1984). Flagella development in *Chlamydomonas reinhardtii*: some regulatory aspects concerning the shortening response of the flagella. In *Compartments in Algal Cells and their Interaction*, ed. W. Wiessner, D.G. Robinson & R.C. Starr, pp. 109–17. Springer-Verlag, Berlin.

1463   Ragan, M.A. (1981). Chemical constituents of seaweeds. In *The Biology of Seaweeds*, ed. C.S. Lobban & M.J. Wynne, pp. 589–626. Blackwell, Oxford.

1464   Ragan, M.A. & D.J. Chapman (1978). *A Biochemical Phylogeny of the Protists.* Academic Press, New York.

1465   Ragan, M.A. & K.W. Glombitza (1986). Phlorotannins, brown algal polyphenols. In *Progress in Phycological Research*, Vol. 4, ed. F.E. Round & D.J. Chapman, pp. 129–241. Biopress, Bristol.

1466   Ramanis, Z. & D.J.L. Luck (1986). Loci affecting flagellar assembly and function map to an unusual linkage group in *Chlamydomonas reinhardtii. Proc. Natl. Acad. Sci. USA* **83**: 423–6.

1467   Ramm-Anderson, S.M. & R. Wetherbee (1982). Structure and development of the carposporophyte of *Nemalion helminthoides* (Nemalionales, Rhodophyta). *J. Phycol.* **18**: 133–41.

1468   Ramus, J. (1969). Pit connection formation in the red alga *Pseudogloiophloea. J. Phycol.* **5**: 57–63.

1469   Ramus, J. (1972). The production of extracellular polysaccharides by the unicellular red alga *Porphyridium aerugineum. J. Phycol.* **8**: 97–111.

1470   Randhawa, M.S. (1959). *Zygnemaceae.* Indian Council of Agricultural Research, New Delhi.

1471   Rausch, H., N. Larsen & R. Schmitt (1989). Phylogenetic relationships of the green alga *Volvox carteri* deduced from small-subunit ribosomal RNA comparisons. *J. Molec. Evol.* **29**: 255–65.

1472   Raven, J.A. (1987). Biochemistry, biophysics and physiology of chlorophyll b-containing algae: implications for taxonomy and phylogeny. In *Progress in Phycological Research*, Vol. 5, ed. F.E. Round & D.J. Chapman, pp. 1–122. Biopress, Bristol.

1473   Raven, P.H. (1970). A multiple origin for plastids and mitochondria. *Science* **169**: 641–5.

1474   Rawitscher-Kunkel, E. & L. Machlis (1962). The hormonal integration of sexual reproduction in *Oedogonium. Am. J. Bot.* **49**: 177–83.

1475   Ray, S.M. & W.B. Wilson (1957). Effects of unialgal and bacteria-free cultures of *Gymnodinium breve* on fish. *Fish Wildl. Serv. 57, Bull.* **123**: 469–96.

1476   Rayns, D.G. (1962). Alternation of generations in a coccolithophorid *Cricosphaera carterae* (Braarud et Fagerl.) Braarud. *J. Mar. Biol. Ass. U.K.* **42**: 481–4.

1477   Reed, R.H., J.C. Collins & G. Russell (1980). The effects of salinity upon galactosyl-glycerol content and concentration of the marine red alga *Porphyra purpurea* (Roth) C. Ag. *J. Exp. Bot.* **31**: 1539–54.

1478   Reed, R.H., I.R. Davison, J.A. Chudek & R. Foster (1985). The osmotic role of mannitol in the Phaeophyta: an appraisal. *Phycologia* **24**: 35–47.

1479   Rees, A.J.J. and G.F. Leedale (1980). The dinoflagellate transverse flagellum: three-dimensional reconstructions from serial sections. *J. Phycol.* **16**: 73–80.

1480   Reháková, H. (1969). Die Variabilität der Arten der Gattung *Oocystis* A. Braun. In *Studies in Phycology*, ed. B. Fott, pp. 145–96. Schweizerbart, Stuttgart.

1481   Reinke, J. (1889). *Atlas Deutscher Meeresalgen I.* Parey, Berlin.

1482   Reinke, J. (1892). *Atlas Deutscher Meeresalgen. II.* Kommission zur wissenschaftlichen Untersuchung der deutschen Meere. Parey, Berlin: T. 36–50.

1483   Reisser, W. (1986). Endosymbiotic associations of freshwater protozoa and algae. In *Progress in Protistology*, Vol. 1, ed. J.O. Corliss & D.J. Patterson, pp. 195–214. Biopress, Bristol.

1484   Reith, M. & R.A. Cattolico (1986). Inverted repeat of *Olisthodiscus luteus* chloroplast DNA contains genes for both subunits of ribulose-1, 5-biphosphate carboxylase and the 23,000-dalton Q_B protein: phylogenetic implications. *Proc. Natl. Acad. Sci. USA* **83**: 8599–603.

1485 Rentschler, H. (1967). Photoperiodische Induktion der Monosporenbildung bei *Porphyra tenera* Kjellm. (Rhodophyta, Bangiophyceae). *Planta* **76**: 65–74.

1486 Reviers, B. de, S. Marbeau & B. Kloareg (1983). Essai d'interprétation de la structure des fucoidanes en liaison avec leur localisation dans la paroi de Phéophycées. *Crypt. Algol.* **4**: 55–62.

1487 Richardson, W.N. & P.S. Dixon (1968). Life-history of *Bangia fuscopurpurea* (Dillw.). Lyngb. in culture. *Nature* **218**: 496–7.

1488 Ricketts, T.R. (1965). Chlorophyll c in some members of the Chrysophyceae. *Phytochemistry* **4**: 725–30.

1489 Rietema, H. (1969). A new type of life-history in *Bryopsis*. *Acta Bot. Neerl.* **18**: 615–19.

1490 Rietema, H. (1970). Life-histories of *Bryopsis plumosa* from European coasts. *Acta Bot. Neerl.* **19**: 859–66.

1491 Rietema, H. (1971). Life-history studies in the genus *Bryopsis* (Chlorophyceae). IV. Life-histories in *Bryopsis hypnoides* Lamx. from different points along the European coasts. *Acta Bot. Neerl.* **20**: 291–8.

1492 Rietema, H. (1972). A morphological, developmental, and caryological study on the life-history of *Bryopsis halymeniae* (Chlorophyceae). *Neth. J. Sea Res.* **5**: 445–57.

1493 Rietema, H. (1973). The influence of daylength on the morphology of the *Halicystis parvula* phase of *Derbesia tenuissima* (De Not.) Crn. (Chlorophyceae, Caulerpales). *Phycologia* **12**: 11–16.

1494 Rietema, H. (1975). *Comparative investigations on the life-histories and reproduction of some species in the siphoneous green algal genera Bryopsis and Derbesia.* Thesis, University of Groningen.

1495 Rietema, H. (1982). Effects of photoperiod and temperature on macrothallus initiation in *Dumontia contorta*. *Mar. Ecol. Prog. Ser.* **8**: 187–96.

1496 Rietema, H. (1984). Development of erect thalli from basal crusts in *Dumontia contorta* (Gmel.) Rupr. (Rhodophyta, Cryptonemiales). *Bot. Mar.* **27**: 29–36.

1497 Rietema, H. & A.M. Breeman (1982). The regulation of the life history of *Dumontia contorta* in comparison to that of several other Dumontiaceae (Rhodophyta). *Bot. Mar.* **25**: 569–76.

1498 Rietema, H. & A.W.O. Klein (1981). Environmental control of the life cycle of *Dumontia contorta* (Rhodophyta) kept in culture. *Mar. Ecol. Progr. Ser.* **4**: 23–9.

1499 Rieth, A. (1972). Über *Chlorokybus atmophyticus* Geitler 1942. *Arch. Protistenk.* **114**: 330–42.

1500 Rieth, A. (1980). Xanthophyceae, Part 2. In *Süßwasserflora von Mitteleuropa*, Vol. 3, ed. H. Ettl, J. Gerloff & H. Heinig. Gustav Fischer, Stuttgart.

1501 Ringo, D.L. (1967). Flagellar motion and fine structure of the flagellar apparatus in *Chlamydomonas*. *J. Cell Biol.* **33**: 543–71.

1501a Rippka, R., J. Deruelles, J.B. Waterbury, M. Herdman & R. Stanier (1979). Generic assignments, strain histories, and properties of pure cultures of Cyanobacteria. *J. Gen. Microbiol.* **111**: 1–61.

1502 Roberts, K. (1974). Crystalline glycoprotein cell walls of algae: their structure, composition and assembly. *Phil. Trans. R. Soc. Lond.* **B268**: 129–46.

1503 Roberts, K., M.R. Gay & G.J. Hills (1980). Cell wall glycoproteins from *Chlamydomonas reinhardtii* are sulfated. *Physiol. Plant.* **49**: 421–4.

1504 Roberts, K., M. Guerney-Smith & G.J. Hills (1972). Structure, composition and morphogenesis of the cell wall of *Chlamydomonas reinhardtii*. *J. Ultrastruct. Res.* **40**: 599–613.

1505 Roberts, K.R. (1984a). Structure and significance of the cryptomonad flagellar apparatus. I. *Cryptomonas ovata* (Cryptophyta). *J. Phycol.* **20**: 590–9.

1506 Roberts, K.R. (1984b). The flagellar apparatus in *Batophora* and *Trentepohlia* and its phylogenetic significance. In *Systematics of the Green Algae*, ed. D.E.G. Irvine & D.M. John, pp. 331–41. Academic Press, London.

1507 Roberts, K.R. (1985). The flagellar apparatus of *Oxyrrhis marina* (Pyrrophyta). *J. Phycol.* **21**: 641–55.

1508 Roberts, K.R. (1986). The flagellar apparatus of *Gymnodinium* sp. (Dinophyceae). *J. Phycol.* **22**: 456–66.

1509 Roberts, K.R. (1987a). Basal body configuration and the evolution of the dinoflagellate flagellar apparatus. *J. Phycol.* **23** (suppl.): 12.

1510 Roberts, K.R. (1987b). The flagellar apparatus of the dinoflagellates: preliminary phylogenetic implications. *14th International Botanical Congress, Berlin, abstracts:* 260. (Collated and edited by W. Greuter, B. Zimmer & H.D. Behnke; produced with the assistance of M.I. Hakki, H. Sipman and staff members of the Botanical Museum Berlin-Dahlem.)

1511 Roberts, K.R. (1989). Comparative analyses of the dinoflagellate flagellar apparatus. II. *Ceratium hirundinella. J. Phycol.* **25**: 270–80.

1512 Roberts, K.R., H.J. Sluiman, K.D. Stewart & K.R. Mattox (1980). Comparative cytology and taxonomy of the Ulvaphyceae. II. Ulvalean characteristics of the stephanokont flagellar apparatus of *Derbesia tenuissima. Protoplasma* **104**: 223–38.

1513 Roberts, K.R., H.J. Sluiman, K.D. Stewart & K.R. Mattox (1981). Comparative cytology and taxonomy of the Ulvaphyceae. III. The flagellar apparatus of the anisogametes of *Derbesia tenuissima* (Chlorophyta). *J. Phycol.* **17**: 330–40.

1514 Roberts, K.R., K.D. Stewart & K.R. Mattox (1981). The flagellar apparatus of *Chilomonas paramecium* (Cryptophyceae) and its comparison with certain zooflagellates. *J. Phycol.* **17**: 159–67.

1515 Roberts, K.R., K.D. Stewart & K.R. Mattox (1982). Structure of the anisogametes of the green siphon *Pseudobryopsis* sp. (Chlorophyta). *J. Phycol.* **18**: 498–508.

1516 Roberts, K.R., K.D. Stewart & K.R. Mattox (1984). Structure and absolute configuration of the flagellar apparatus in the isogametes of *Batophora* (Dasycladales, Chlorophyta). *J. Phycol.* **20**: 183–91.

1517 Robinson, D.G. & K.D. Preston (1971). Studies on the fine structure of *Glaucocystis nostochinearum* Itzigs. Membrane morphology and taxonomy. *Br. Phycol. J.* **6**: 113–28.

1518 Robinson, G.A. (1968). Distribution of *Gonyaulax tamarensis* Lebour in the Western North Sea in April, May and June 1968. *Nature* **220**: 22–3.

1519 Rochais, J.-D. (1987). Molecular genetics of chloroplasts and mitochondria in the unicellular green alga *Chlamydomonas. FEMS Microbiol. Rev.* **46**: 13–34.

1520 Roessler, P.G. (1987). UDP glucose pyrophosphorylase activity in the diatom *Cyclotella cryptica.* Pathway of chrysolaminarin biosynthesis. *J. Phycol.* 23: 494–8.

1521 Rogers, C.E., K.R. Mattox & K.D. Stewart (1980). The zoospore of *Chlorokybus atmophyticus,* a charophyte with sarcinoid growth habit. *Am. J. Bot.* **67**: 774–83.

1522 Rosenberg, R., O. Lindahl & H. Blanck (1988). Silent spring in the sea. *Ambio* **17**: 289–90.

1523 Ross, R. (1982). Bacillariophyceae. In *Synopsis and Classification of Living Organisms,* ed. S.P. Parker, pp. 95–101. McGraw-Hill, New York.

1524 Roth, W.C. & E.I. Friedmann (1987). Ultrastructure of the siphonous green algae *Avrainvillea* and *Cladocephalus. Phycologia* **26**: 70–81.

1525 Rothschild, L.J. & P. Heywood (1987). Protistan phylogeny and chloroplast evolution: conflicts and congruence. In *Progress in Protistology,* Vol. 2, ed. J.O. Corliss & D.J. Patterson, pp. 1–68. Biopress, Bristol.

1526 Round, F.E. (1971). The taxonomy of the Chlorophyta II. *Br. Phycol. J.* **6**: 235–264.

1527 Round, F.E. (1973). *The Biology of the Algae.* 2nd Ed. Arnold, London.

1528 Round, F.E. (1981). *The Ecology of Algae.* Cambridge University Press.

1529 Round, F.E. (1986). The Chrysophyta – a reassessment. In *Chrysophytes: Aspects and Problems,* ed. J. Kristiansen & R.A. Andersen, pp. 3–22. Cambridge University Press.

1530 Round, F.E. & R.M. Crawford (1981). The lines of evolution of the Bacillariophyta. I. Origin. *Proc. R. Soc. Lond.* **B211**: 237–60.

1531 Round, F.E. & R.M. Crawford (1990). Phylum Bacillariophyta. In *Handbook of Protoctista,* ed. L. Margulis, J.O. Corliss, M. Melkonian & D.J. Chapman, pp. 574–96. Jones & Bartlett, Boston.

1532 Round, F.E., R.M. Crawford & D.G. Mann (1990). *The Diatoms. Biology and Morphology of the Genera.* Cambridge University Press.

1533 Royackers, R.M.M. (1986). Development and succession of scale-bearing Chrysophyceae in two shallow freshwater bodies near Nijmegen, The Netherlands. In *Chrysophytes, Aspects and Problems,* ed. J. Kristiansen & R.A. Andersen, pp. 241–58. Cambridge University Press.

1534 Russell, G. (1973). The Phaeophyta: a synopsis of some recent developments. *Oceanogr. Mar. Biol., Ann. Rev.* **11**: 45–88.

1535 Ruzicka, J. (1977). *Die Desmidiaceen Mitteleuropas.* Vol. 1 (1). E. Schweizerbart'sche Verlagsbuchhandlung, Stuttgart.

1536 Ruzicka, J. (1981). *Die Desmidiaceen Mittel-*

europas. Vol. 1 (2). E. Schweizerbart'sche Verlagsbuchhandlung, Stuttgart.

1537 Sagan, L. (1967). On the origin of the mitosing cell. *J. Theoret. Biol.* **14**: 225–74.

1538 Sager, R. (1965). Genes outside the chromosomes. *Sci. Am.,* January: 71–9.

1539 Sager, R. (1974). Nuclear and cytoplasmic inheritance in green algae. In *Algal Physiology and Biochemistry,* ed. W.D.P. Stewart, pp. 314–45. Blackwell, Oxford.

1540 Sager, R. & G.L. Palade (1957). Structure and development of the chloroplast in *Chlamydomonas. J. Biophys. Biochem. Cytol.* **3**: 463–88.

1541 Salisbury, J.L. (1989). Centrin and the algal flagellar apparatus. *J. Phycol.* **25**: 201–6.

1542 Salisbury, J.L. & G.L. Floyd (1978). Calcium-induced contraction of the rhizoplast of a quadriflagellate green alga. *Science* **202**: 975–6.

1543 Salisbury, J.L. & G.L. Floyd (1978b). Molecular, enzymatic and ultrastructural characterization of the pyrenoid of the scaly green monad *Micromonas squamata. J. Phycol.* **14**: 362–8.

1544 Salisbury, J.L., J.A. Swanson, G.L. Floyd & R. Hall (1981). Ultrastructure of the flagellar apparatus of the green alga *Tetraselmis subcordiformis. Protoplasma* **107**: 1–11.

1545 Sandgren, C.D. (1981). Characteristics of sexual and asexual resting cyst (statospore) formation in *Dinobryon cylindricum* Imhof (Chrysophyta). *J. Phycol.* **17**: 199–210.

1546 Sandgren, C.D. (1988). The ecology of chrysophyte flagellates: their growth and perennation strategies as freshwater phytoplankton. In *Growth and Reproductive Strategies of Freshwater Phytoplankton,* ed. C.D. Sandgren, pp. 9–104. Cambridge University Press.

1547 Sandgren, C.D. & J. Flanagin (1986). Heterothallic sexuality and density dependent encystment in the chrysophycean alga *Synura petersenii* Korsh. *J. Phycol.* **22**: 206–12.

1548 Santore , U.J. (1982). Comparative ultrastructure of two members of the Cryptophyceae assigned to the genus *Chroomonas* – with comments on their taxonomy. *Arch. Protistenk.* **125**: 5–29.

1549 Santore, U.J. (1983). Flagellar and body scales in the Cryptophyceae. *Br. Phycol. J.* **18**: 239–48.

1550 Santore, U.J. & G.F. Leedale (1985). Order 1. Cryptomonadida Senn, 1900. In *An Illustrated Guide to the Protozoa,* ed. J.J. Lee, S.H. Hutner & E.C. Bovee, pp. 19–22. Society of Protozoologists, Lawrence, Kansas.

1551 Sarjeant, W.A.S. (1966). The xanthidia. *Endeavour* **25**: 33–9.

1551a Saunders, G.W. & L.D. Druehl (1992). Nucleotide sequences of the small-subunit ribosomal RNA genes from selected Laminariales (Phaeophyta): implications for kelp evolution. *J. Phycol.* **28**: 544–9.

1552 Sauvageau, C. (1927). Sur l'alternance des générations chez le *Nereia filiformis* Zan. *Bull. Stat. Biol. Arcachon* **24**: 357–67.

1553 Sauvageau, C. (1929). Sur le développement de quelques Phéosporées. I. *Dictyosiphon* Grev. *Bull. Stat. Biol. Arcachon* **26**: 253–64.

1554 Scagel, R.F. (1966). The Phaeophyceae in perspective. *Oceanogr. Mar. Biol., Ann. Rev.* **4**: 123–94.

1555 Scagel, R.F., R.J. Bandoni, G.E. Rouse, W.B. Schofield, J.R. Stein & T.M.C. Taylor (1965). *An Evolutionary Survey of the Plant Kingdom.* Wadsworth, Belmont, California.

1556 Scagel, R.F., R.J. Bandoni, J.R. Maze, G.E. Rouse, W.B. Schofield & J.R. Stein (1982). *Nonvascular Plants, an Evolutionary Survey.* Wadsworth, Belmont, California.

1557 Schechner-Fries, M. (1934). Der Phasenwechsel von *Valonia utricularis* (Roth) Ag. *Öst. bot. Z.* **83**: 241–54.

1558 Schiff, J.A. & S.D. Schwartzbach (1982). Photocontrol of chloroplast development in *Euglena.* In *The biology of Euglena,* Vol. III: *Physiology,* ed. D.E. Buetow, pp. 313–52. Academic Press, New York.

1559 Schiller, J. (1930). Coccolithineae. In *Dr L. Rabenhorst's Kryptogamen-Flora von Deutschland, Österreich und der Schweiz,* Vol. X, part 2. Akademische Verlagsgesellschaft, Leipzig.

1560 Schiller, J. (1933). Dinoflagellatae I. In *Dr L. Rabenhorst's Kryptogamen-Flora von Deutschland, Österreich und der Schweiz,* Vol. X, part 3. Akademische Verlagsgesellschaft, Leipzig.

1561 Schiller, J. (1937). Dinoflagellatae II. In *Dr L. Rabenhorst's Kryptogamen-Flora von Deutschland, Österreich und der Schweiz,* Vol. X, part 3. Akademische Verlagsgesellschaft, Leipzig.

1562 Schlegel, H.G. (1981). *Allgemeine Mikrobiologie.* 5th Ed. Thieme Verlag, Stuttgart.

1563 Schlichting, H.E. (1969). The importance of

airborne algae and protozoa. *J. Air Pollut. Cont. Ass.* **19**: 946–51.

1564 Schlösser, U.G. (1976). Entwicklungsstadien und sippenspezifische Zellwand-Autolysine bei der Freisetzung von Fortpflanzungszellen in der Gattung *Chlamydomonas. Ber. Dtsch. Bot. Ges.* **89**: 1–56.

1565 Schlösser, U.G. (1981). Algal wall-degrading enzymes, autolysines. *Encycl. Plant Physiol.*, New Ser. **13 B**: 333–51.

1566 Schlösser, U.G. (1984). Species-specific sporangium autolysins (cell wall-degrading enzymes) in the genus *Chlamydomonas*. In *Systematics of the Green Algae*, ed. D.E.G. Irvine & D.M. John, pp. 409–18. Academic Press, London.

1567 Schlösser, U.G. (1987). Action of cell wall autolysins in sexual reproduction of filamentous green algae: evidence and species specificity. In *Algal Development*, ed. W. Wiessner, D.G. Robinson & R.C. Starr, pp. 75–80. Springer-Verlag, Berlin.

1568 Schmaljohann, R. & R. Roettger (1978). The ultrastructure and taxonomic identity of the symbiotic algae of *Heterostegina depressa* (Foraminifera: Nummulitidae). *J. Mar. Biol. Ass. U.K.* **58**: 227–37.

1568a Schmid, A.-M.M. (1984). Schalenmorphogenese in Diatomeen. *Mitteilungen des Instituts für leichte Flächentragwerke (IL), Nr. 28, Universität Stuttgart:* 300–17.

1569 Schmid, A.-M.M. (1987). Wall morphogenesis in centric diatoms. In *Algal Development*, ed. W. Wiessner, D.G. Robinson & R.C. Starr, pp. 34–41. Springer-Verlag, Berlin.

1570 Schmidt, B., L. Kies & A. Weber (1979). Die Pigmente von *Cyanophora paradoxa, Gloechaete wittrockiana* und *Glaucocystis nostochinearum. Arch. Protistenk.* **122**: 164–70.

1571 Schmitz, K., K. Lüning & J. Willenbrink (1972). CO_2-Fixierung und Stofftransport in benthischen marinen Algen. II. Zum Ferntransport ^{14}C-markierter Assimilate bei *Laminaria hyperborea* und *Laminaria saccharina. Z. Pflanzenphysiol.* **67**: 418–29.

1572 Schnepf, E. (1964). Zur Feinstruktur von *Geosiphon pyriforme. Arch. Mikrobiol.* **49**: 112–31.

1573 Schnepf, E. & G. Deichgräber (1960). Über das Vorkommen und den Bau gestielter 'Hüllen' bei *Ochromonas malhamensis* Pringsheim und *O. sociabilis* nom. prov. Pringsheim. *Arch. Mikrobiol.* **63**: 15–25.

1574 Schnepf, E. & G. Deichgräber (1969). Über die Feinstruktur von *Synura petersenii* unter besonderer Berücksichtigung der Morphogenese ihrer Kieselschuppen. *Protoplasma* **60**: 85–106.

1575 Schnepf, E. & G. Deichgräber (1984). 'Myzocytosis', a kind of endocytosis with implications to compartmentation in endosymbiosis: observations in *Paulsenella* (Dinophyta). *Naturwissenschaften* **71**: 218–9.

1576 Schnepf, E., G. Deichgräber & G. Drebes (1985). Food uptake and the fine structure of the dinophyte *Paulsenella* sp., an ectoparasite of marine diatoms. *Protoplasma* **124**: 188–204.

1577 Schnepf, E. & M. Elbrächter (1988). Cryptophycean-like double membrane-bound chloroplast in the dinoflagellate, *Dinophysis* Ehrenb.: evolutionary, phylogenetic and toxicological implications. *Botanica Acta* **101**: 196–203.

1578 Schnepf, E. & W. Koch (1966). Über die Entstehung der pulsierenden Vacuolen von *Vacuolaria virescens* (Chloromonadophyceae) aus dem Golgi-Apparat. *Arch. Mikrobiol.* **54**: 229–36.

1579 Schnepf, E., W. Koch & G. Deichgräber (1966). Zur Cytologie und taxonomischen Einordnung von *Glaucocystis. Arch. Mikrobiol.* **55**: 149–74.

1580 Schnepf, E., R. Meier & G. Drebes (1988). Stability and deformation of diatom chloroplasts during food uptake of the parasitic dinoflagellate, *Paulsenella* (Dinophyta). *Phycologia* **27**: 283–90.

1581 Schnepf, E., S. Winter & D. Mollenhauer (1989). *Gymnodinium aeruginosum* (Dinophyta): a blue-green dinoflagellate with a vestigial, anucleate, cryptophycean endosymbiont. *Pl. Syst. Evol.* **164**: 75–91.

1582 Schnetter, R., B. Brück, K. Gerke & G. Seibold (1990). Notes on heterokaryotic cycle phases in some Dasycladales and Bryopsidales (Chlorophyta). In *Experimental Phycology 1. Cell Walls and Surfaces, Reproduction, Photosynthesis*, ed. W. Wiessner, D.G. Robinson & R.C. Starr, pp. 124–33. Springer-Verlag, Berlin.

1583 Schnetter, R., R. Eckhardt & G. Seibold (1985). Die Kernphase von Sporophytenfäden der Grünalge *Derbesia tenuissima* (de Not.) Crn. *Beitr. Biol. Pflanzen* **60**: 293–302.

1584 Schnetter, R., B. Mohr, G. Bula-Meyer & G. Seibold (1981). Ecology, life history and nuclear DNA contents of *Derbesia tenuissima* from the

Caribbean coast of Columbia. In *Xth International Seaweed Symposium,* ed. T. Levring, pp. 357–62.

1585 Schopf, J.W. (1978). The evolution of the earliest cells. *Scient. Am.* **239** (3): 84–102.

1586 Schopf, J.W. & M.R. Walter (1982). Origin and early evolution of Cyanobacteria. In *The Biology of Cyanobacteria,* ed. N.G. Carr & B.A. Whitton, pp. 543–64. Blackwell, Oxford.

1587 Schornstein, K.L. & J. Scott (1982). Ultrastructure of cell division in the unicellular red alga *Porphyridium purpureum. Can. J. Bot.* **60**: 85–97.

1588 Schreiber, E. (1932). Über die Entwicklungsgeschichte und die systematische Stellung der Desmarestiaceen. *Z. Bot.* **25**: 561–82.

1589 Schulz-Baldes, M. & R. Lewin (1976). Fine structure of *Synechocystis didemni* (Cyanophyta: Chroococcales). *Phycologia* **15**: 1–6.

1590 Schulze, D., K.-F. Lechtreck, I. Höhfeld. I.B. Reize & M. Melkonian (1988). Cytoskeleton, centrin and phytoflagellate phylogeny. *Third International Phycological Congress, Monash University, Melbourne, abstracts:* 39.

1591 Schulze, D., G.I. McFadden, J. Otten, I. Höhfeld & M. Melkonian (1987). A 20 kD Ca^{2+}-modulated contractile phosphoprotein is associated with algal basal bodies. *14th International Botanical Congress, Berlin, abstracts:* 113. (Collated and edited by W. Greuter, B. Zimmer & H.D. Behnke; produced with the assistance of M.I. Hakki, H. Sipman and staff members of the Botanical Museum Berlin-Dahlem.)

1592 Schulze, D., H. Robenek, G.I. McFadden & M. Melkonian (1987). Immunolocalization of a Ca^{2+}-modulated contractile protein in the flagellar apparatus of green algae : the nucleus-basal body connector. *Eur. J. Cell Biol.* **45**: 51–61.

1593 Schulze, K.L. (1939). Cytologische Untersuchungen an *Acetabularia mediterranea* und *Acetabularia wettsteinii. Arch. Protistenk.* **92**: 179–225.

1594 Schussnig, B. (1930). Der Generations- und Phasenwechsel dei den Chlorophyceen. *Öst. bot. Z.* **79**: 58–77.

1595 Schussnig, B. (1932). Der Generations- und Phasenwechsel bei den Chlorophyceeen. III. *Öst. bot. Z.* **81**: 296–8.

1596 Schussnig, B. (1938). Der Kernphasenwechsel von *Valonia utricularis* (Roth) Ag. *Planta* **28**: 43–59.

1597 Schussnig, B. (1939). Ein Beitrag zur Entwicklungsgeschichte von *Caulerpa prolifera. Bot. Not.* **1939**: 75–96.

1598 Schussnig, B. (1950). Die Gametogenese von *Codium decorticatum* (Woodw.) Howe. *Svensk Bot. Tidskr.* **44**: 55–71.

1599 Schussnig, B. (1953). *Handbuch der Protophytenkunde,* Vol. I. VEB Fischer, Jena.

1600 Schuster, F.L. (1968). The gullet and trichocysts of *Cyathomonas truncata. Exp. Cell Res.* **49**: 277–84.

1601 Schweiger, H.G., H. Bannwarth, S. Berger, E. de Groot, G. Neuhaus & G. Neuhaus-Url (1984). Interactions between compartments in *Acetabularia* during gene expression. In *Compartments in Algal Cells and their Interactions,* ed. W. Wiessner, D. Robinson & R.C. Starr, pp. 28–38. Springer-Verlag, Berlin.

1602 Schweiger, H.G., H. Bannwarth, S. Berger & K. Kloppstech (1975). *Acetabularia,* a cellular model for the study of nucleocytoplasmic interactions. In *Molecular Biology of Nucleocytoplasmic Relationships,* ed. S. Puiseux-Dao, pp. 203–12. Elsevier, Amsterdam.

1603 Schwimmer, M. & D. Schwimmer (1962). *The Role of Algae and Plankton in Medicine.* Grune & Stratton, New York.

1604 Schwimmer, M. & D. Schwimmer (1968). Medical aspects of phycology. In *Algae, Man, and the Environment,* ed. D.F. Jackson, pp. 279–358. Syracuse University Press, New York.

1605 Scott, J. (1983). Mitosis in the freshwater red alga *Batrachospermum ectocarpum. Protoplasma* **118**: 56–70.

1606 Scott, J. (1984). Electronmicroscopic contributions to red algal phylogeny. *J. Phycol.* **20** (suppl.): 6.

1607 Scott, J., C. Bosco, K. Schornstein & J. Thomas (1980). Ultrastructure of cell division and reproductive differentiation of male plants in the Florideophyceae (Rhodophyta): cell division in *Polysiphonia. J. Phycol.* **16**: 507–24.

1608 Scott, J. & P. Gabrielson (1987). Bangiophycidae (Rhodophyta), a polyphyletic taxon. New evidence from ultrastructural studies. *J. Phycol.* **23** (suppl.): 12.

1609 Scott, J., D. Phillips & J. Thomas (1981). Polar rings are persistent organelles in interphase vegetative cells of *Polysiphonia harveyi* Bailey (Rhodophyta, Ceramiales). *Phycologia* **20**: 333–7.

1610 Scott, J., J. Thomas & B. Saunders (1988). Primary pit connections in *Compsopogon coeruleus* (Balbis) Montagne (Compsopogonales, Rhodophyta). *Phycologia* **27**: 327–33.

1611 Scott, J.L. & K.W. Bullock (1976). Ultrastructure of cell division in *Cladophora*. Pregametangial cell division in the haploid generation of *Cladophora flexuosa*. *Can. J. Bot.* **54**: 1546–66.

1612 Segaar, P.J. (1989a). The cytokinetic apparatus of the green alga *Fritschiella tuberosa* (Chaetophorales, Chlorophyta). *Crypt. Bot.* **1**: 3–14.

1613 Segaar, P.J. (1989b). Dynamics of the microtubular cytoskeleton in the green alga *Aphanochaete magna* (Chlorophyta). II. The cortical cytoskeleton, astral microtubules, and spindle during the division cycle. *Can. J. Bot.* **67**: 239–46.

1614 Segaar, P.J. (1990). The flagellar apparatus and temporary centriole-associated microtubule systems at the interphase-mitosis transition in the green alga *Gloeomonas kupfferi*: an example of the spatio-temporal flexibility of microtubule-organizing centres. *Acta Bot. Neerl.* **39**: 29–42.

1615 Segaar, P.J. & A.F. Gerritsen (1989). Flagellar roots as vital instruments in cellular morphogenesis during multiple fission (sporulation) in the unicellular green flagellate *Brachiomonas submarina* (Chlamydomonadales, Chlorophyta). *Crypt. Bot.* **1**: 249–74.

1616 Segaar, P.J., A.F. Gerritsen & M.A.G. de Bakker (1989). The cytokinetic apparatus during sporulation in the unicellular green flagellate *Gloeomonas kupfferi*: the phycoplast as a spatio-temporal differentiation of the cortical microtubule array that organizes cytokinesis. *Nova Hedwigia* **49**: 1–23.

1617 Segaar, P.J. & G.M. Lokhorst (1988). Dynamics of the microtubular cytoskeleton in the green alga *Aphanochaete magna* (Chlorophyta). I. Late mitotic stages and the origin and development of the phycoplast. *Protoplasma* **142**: 176–87.

1618 Seibold, E. & W.H. Berger (1982). *The Sea Floor*. Springer-Verlag, Berlin.

1619 Seliger, H.H. & W.D. McElroy (1965). *Light: Physical and Biological Action*. Academic Press, New York.

1620 Sheath, R.G. (1984). The biology of freshwater red algae. In *Progress in Phycological Research*, Vol. 3, ed. F.E. Round & D.J. Chapman, pp. 89–157. Biopress, Bristol.

1621 Sheath, R.G., K.M. Cole & B.J. Hymes (1987). Ultrastructure of polysporogenesis in *Pleonosporium vancouverianum* (Ceramiaceae, Rhodophyta). *Phycologia* **26**: 1–8.

1622 Sherman, L., T, Bricker, J. Guikema & H. Pakrasi (1987). The protein composition of the photosynthetic complexes from the cyanobacterial thylakoid membrane. In *The Cyanobacteria*, ed. F. Fay & C. Van Baalen, pp. 1–33. Elsevier, Amsterdam.

1623 Shihira-Ishikawa, I. (1987). Cytoskeleton in cell morphogenesis of the coenocytic green alga *Valonia ventricosa* I. Two microtubule systems and their roles in positioning of chloroplasts and nuclei. *Jap. J. Phycol.* **35**: 251–8.

1624 Shihira-Ishikawa, I. & T. Kuroiwa (1984). Morphological transition of the nucleus during the whole life cycle of *Acetabularia calyculus* Quoy et Gaymard. *Jap. J. Phycol.* **32**: 147–57.

1625 Shilo, M. (1967). Formation and mode of action of algal toxins. *Bacteriol. Rev.* **31**: 180–93.

1626 Shimizu, Y. (1987). Dinoflagellate toxins. In *The Biology of Dinoflagellates*, ed. F.J.R. Taylor, pp. 282–315. Blackwell Scientific Publications, Oxford.

1627 Shivji, M. & R.A. Cattolico (1988). Comparative organization of *Porphyra* and *Olisthodiscus* plastid DNA. *J. Phycol.* **24** (suppl.): 24.

1628 Shubert, L.E. (1988). The use of *Spirulina* (Cyanophyceae) and *Chlorella* (Chlorophyceae) as food sources for animals and humans. In *Progress in Phycological Research*, Vol. 6, ed. F.E. Round & D.J. Chapman, pp. 237–54. Biopress, Bristol.

1629 Sieburth, J.M., P.W. Johnson & P.E. Hargraves (1988). Ultrastructure and ecology of *Aureococcus anophagefferens* gen. et sp. nov. (Chrysophyceae): the dominant picoplankter during a bloom in Narragansett Bay, Rhode Island, summer 1985. *J. Phycol.* **24**: 416–25.

1630 Silva, P.C. (1982). Chlorophycota. In *Synopsis and Classification of Living Organisms*, Vol. I, ed. S.P. Parker, pp. 133–61. McGraw-Hill Book Company, New York.

1631 Silva, P.C. & H.W. Johansen (1986). A reappraisal of the order Corallinales (Rhodophyceae). *Br. Phycol. J.* **21**: 245–54.

1632 Simon, R.D. (1987). Inclusion bodies in the Cyanobacteria: cyanophycin, polyphosphate, polyhedral bodies. In *The Cyanobacteria*, ed. P. Fay & C. Van Baalen, pp. 199–225. Elsevier, Amsterdam.

1633 Simon-Bichard-Bréaud, J. (1971). Un appareil cinétique dans les gamétocystes mâles d'une Rhodophycée: *Bonnemaisonia hamifera* Hariot. *C.R. Acad. Sci. Paris* **273**: 1272–5.

1634 Simon-Bichard-Bréaud, J. (1972). Formation de la crypte flagellaire et évolution de son contenu au cours de la gamétogénèse mâle chez *Bonnemaisonia hamifera* Hariot (Rhodophycée). *C.R. Acad. Sci. Paris* **274**: 1796–9.

1635 Simons, J. & A.P. van Beem (1987). Observations on asexual and sexual reproduction in *Stigeoclonium helveticum* Vischer (Chlorophyta) with implications for the life history. *Phycologia* **26**: 356–62.

1636 Sinclair, C. & B.A. Whitton (1977). Influence of nutrient deficiency on hair formation in the Rivulariaceae. *Br. Phycol. J.* **12**: 297–313.

1637 Skoczylas, O. (1958). Über die Mitose von *Ceratium cornutum* und einigen anderen Peridineen. *Arch. Protistenk.* **103**: 193–228.

1638 Skuja, H. (1964). Grundzüge der Algenflora und Algenvegetation der Fjeldgegenden um Abisko in Schwedisch-Lappland. *Nova Acta Regiae Soc. Sci. Upsal.*, Ser. IV, **18**: 465–9.

1639 Slankis, T. & S.P. Gibbs (1972). The fine structure of mitosis and cell division in the chrysophycean alga *Ochromonas danica. J. Phycol.* **8**: 243–56.

1640 Sleigh, M. (1989). *Protozoa and other Protists.* Edward Arnold, London.

1641 Sluiman, H.J. (1983). The flagellar apparatus of the zoospore of the filamentous green alga *Coleochaete pulvinata:* absolute configuration and phylogenetic significance. *Protoplasma* **115**: 160–75.

1642 Sluiman, H.J. (1984). A pathway of plasma membrane biogenesis bypassing the Golgi apparatus during cell division in the green alga *Cylindrocapsa geminella. J. Cell Sci.* **72**: 89–100.

1643 Sluiman, H.J. (1985a). Mitosis and cell division in *Cylindrocapsa geminella* (Chlorophyceae). *J. Phycol.* **21**: 523–32.

1644 Sluiman, H.J. (1985b). *Comparative studies on the ultrastructure, phylogeny and classification of green algae.* Thesis, Free University of Amsterdam.

1645 Sluiman, H.J. (1989). The green algal class Ulvophyceae. *Crypt. Bot.* **1**: 83–94.

1645a Sluiman, H.J. & P.C.J. Blommers (1990). Ultrastructure and taxonomic position of *Chlorosarcina stigmatica* Deason (Chlorophyceae, Chlorophyta). *Arch. Protistenk.* **138**: 181–90.

1646 Sluiman, H.J., F.A.C. Kouwets & C.J. Blommers (1989). Classification and definition of cytokinetic patterns in green algae: sporulation versus (vegetative) cell division. *Arch. Protistenk.* **137**: 277–90.

1647 Sluiman, H.J. & G.M. Lokhorst (1988). The ultrastructure of cellular division (autosporogenesis) in the coccoid green alga, *Trebouxia aggregata*, revealed by rapid freeze fixation and freeze substitution. *Protoplasma* **144**: 149–59.

1648 Sluiman, H.J., K.R. Mattox & K.D. Stewart (1980). Moderne opvattingen over de phylogenie van groenwieren en landplanten. *Vakbl. Biol.* **60**: 204–12.

1649 Sluiman, H.J., K.R. Roberts, K.D. Stewart & K.R. Mattox (1980). Comparative cytology and taxonomy of Ulvaphyceae. I. The zoospore of *Ulothrix zonata* (Chlorophyta). *J. Phycol.* **16**: 537–45.

1650 Sluiman, H.J., K.R. Roberts, K.D. Stewart, K.R. Mattox & G.L. Lokhorst (1982). The flagellar apparatus of the zoospore of *Urospora penicilliformis* (Chlorophyta). *J. Phycol.* **18**: 1–12.

1651 Sluiman, H.J., K.R. Roberts, K.D. Stewart & K.R. Mattox (1983). Comparative cytology and taxonomy of the Ulvophyceae. IV. Mitosis and cytokinesis in *Ulothrix* (Chlorophyta). *Acta Bot. Neerl.* **32**: 257–69.

1652 Smayda, T.J. (1980). Phytoplankton species succession. In *The Physiological Ecology of Phytoplankton*, ed. I. Morris, pp. 493–570. Blackwell Scientific Publications, Oxford.

1653 Smayda, T.J. & B.J. Boleyn (1965). Experimental observations on the flotation of marine diatoms. I. *Limnol. Oceanogr.* **10**: 499–506.

1654 Smetacek, V.S. (1985). Role of sinking in diatom life history cycles: ecological, evolutionary and geological significance. *Mar. Biol.* **84**: 239–51.

1655 Smith, A.J. (1982). Modes of cyanobacterial carbon metabolism. In *The Biology of Cyanobacteria*, ed. N.G. Carr & B.A. Whitton, pp. 47–85. Blackwell Scientific Publications, Oxford.

1656 Smith, D.C. & A.E. Douglas (1987). *The Biology of Symbiosis.* Edward Arnold, London.

1657 Smith, G.M. (1950). *The Fresh-water Algae of the United States.* 2nd Ed. McGraw-Hill, New York.

1658 Smith, G.M. (1955). *Cryptogamic Botany,* Vol. I: *Algae and Fungi.* McGraw-Hill, New York.

1659 Smith, W.O. & R.T. Barber (1979). A carbon budget for the autotrophic ciliate *Mesodinium rubrum. J. Phycol.* **15**: 27–33.

1660 Smyth, R.D., J. Saranak & K.W. Foster (1988). Algal visual systems and their photoreceptor pigments. In *Progress in Phycological Research,* Vol. 6, ed. F.E. Round & D.J. Chapman, pp. 255–86. Biopress, Bristol.

1661 Sogin, M.L., H.J. Elwood & J.H. Gunderson (1986). Evolutionary diversity of eukaryotic small-subunit rRNA genes. *Proc. Natl. Acad. Sci. USA* **83**: 1383–7.

1661a Solomon, J.A., P.L. Walne & P.A. Kivic (1987). *Entosiphon sulcatum* (Euglenophyceae): flagellar roots of the basal body complex and reservoir region. *J. Phycol.* **23**: 85–98.

1662 Sommerfeld, M.R. & H.W. Nichols (1970). Comparative studies in the genus *Porphyridium* Naeg. *J. Phycol.* **6**: 67–78.

1663 Sotsuka, T. & R. Nakano (1971). Some species of *Vaucheria* collected from the South-western part of Japan. *Hikobia* **6**: 131–8.

1664 Soulié-Märsche, I. (1979). Origine et évolution des genres actuels des Characeae. *Bull. Cent. Rech. Explor.-Prod. Elf-Aquitaine* **3**: 821–31.

1664a Sournia, A. (1986). *Atlas du Phytoplankton Marin,* Vol. 1. Centre National de la Recherche Scientifique, Paris.

1665 South, G.R. & A. Whittick (1987). *Introduction to Phycology.* Blackwell, Oxford.

1666 Spear-Bernstein, L. & K.R. Miller (1989). Unique location of the phycobiliprotein light-harvesting pigment in the Cryptophyceae. *J. Phycol.* **25**: 412–9.

1667 Spector, D.L. (1984a). Unusual inclusions. In *Dinoflagellates,* ed. D.L. Spector, pp. 365–90. Academic Press, Orlando.

1668 Spector, D.L. (1984b). Dinoflagellate nuclei. In *Dinoflagellates,* ed. D.L. Spector, pp. 107–47. Academic Press, Orlando.

1669 Spector, D.L. & R.E. Triemer (1981). Chromosome structure and mitosis in the dinoflagellates: an ultrastructural approach to an evolutionary problem. *BioSystems* **14**: 289–98.

1670 Spero, H.J. (1982). Phagotrophy in *Gymnodinium fungiforme* (Pyrrophyta): the peduncle as an organelle of ingestion. *J. Phycol.* **18**: 356–60.

1671 Spero, H.J. (1985). Chemosensory capabilities in the phagotrophic dinoflagellate *Gymnodinium fungiforme. J. Phycol.* **21**: 181–4.

1672 Spero, H.J. (1987). Symbiosis in the planktonic foraminifer, *Orbulina universa,* and the isolation of its symbiotic dinoflagellate, *Gymnodinium béii* sp. nov. *J. Phycol.* **23**: 307–17.

1673 Spero, H.J. & M.D. Morée (1981). Phagotrophic feeding and its importance to the life cycle of the holozoic dinoflagellate, *Gymnodinium fungiforme. J. Phycol.* **17**: 43–51.

1674 Spring, H., D. Grierson, H. Hemleben, M. Stöhr, G. Krohne, J. Stadler & W.W. Franke (1978). DNA contents and numbers of nucleoli and pre-rRNA genes in nuclei in gametes and vegetative cells of *Acetabularia mediterranea. Exp. Cell Res.* **114**: 203–15.

1675 Stacey, V.J. & R.N. Pienaar (1980). Cell division in *Hymenomonas carterae* (Braarud et Fagerland) Braarud (Prymnesiophyceae). *Br. Phycol. J.* **15**: 365–76.

1676 Stackebrandt, E. (1989). Phylogenetic considerations of *Prochloron.* In *Prochloron, a Microbial Enigma,* ed. R.A. Lewin & L. Cheng, pp. 65–9. Chapman & Hall, New York.

1677 Stal, L.J. (1985). *Nitrogen-fixing Cyanobacteria in a marine microbial mat.* Thesis, University of Groningen.

1678 Stal, L.J. & W.E. Krumbein (1985). Nitrogenase activity in the non-heterocystous cyanobacterium *Oscillatoria* sp. grown under alternating light/dark cycles. *Arch. Microbiol.* **143**: 67–71.

1679 Stam, W.T. (1980). Relationships between a number of filamentous blue-green algal strains (Cyanophyceae) revealed by DNA–DNA hybridization. *Arch. Hydrobiol. Suppl.* **56** (*Algol. Stud.* **25**): 351–74.

1680 Stam, W.T., P.V.M. Bot, S.A. Boele-Bos, J.M. van Rooy & C. van den Hoek (1988). Single-copy DNA–DNA hybridizations among five species of *Laminaria* (Phaeophyceae): phylogenetic and biogeographic implications. *Helgol. Meeresunters.* **42**: 251–67.

1681 Stam, W.T. & G. Venema (1977). The use of DNA–DNA hybridization for determination of the relationship between some blue-green algae (Cyanophyceae). *Acta Bot. Neerl.* **26**: 327–42.

1681a Stanier, R.Y. (1977). The position of the

Cyanobacteria in the world of phototrophs. *Carlsberg Res. Comm.* **42**: 77–98.

1681b Stanier, R.Y., R. Kunisawa, M. Mandel & G. Cohen-Bazire (1971). Purification and properties of unicellular blue-green algae (order Chroococcales). *Bacteriol. Rev.* **35**: 171–205.

1682 Stanley, S.M. (1979). *Macroevolution, Pattern and Process.* W.H. Freeman, San Francisco.

1683 Starks, N.L., L.E. Shubert & F.R. Trainor (1981). Ecology of soil algae: a review. *Phycologia* **20**: 65–80.

1684 Starr, R. (1954). Heterothallism in *Cosmarium botrytis* var. *subtumidum. Am. J. Bot.* **41**: 601–7.

1685 Starr, R. (1955a). A comparative study of *Chlorococcum* Meneghini and other spherical, zoospore reproducing genera of the Chlorococcales. *Indiana Univ. Publ. Sci. Ser.* **20**: 1–111.

1686 Starr, R. (1955b). Zygospore germination in *Cosmarium botrytis* var. *subtumidum. Am. J. Bot.* **42**: 577–81.

1687 Starr, R.C. (1963). Homothallism in *Golenkinia minutissima.* In *Studies in Microalgae and Bacteria*, pp. 3–6. Jap. Soc. Plant Physiol.; University of Tokyo Press.

1688 Starr, R. & L. Jaenicke (1974). Purification and characterization of the hormone initiating sexual morphogenesis in *Volvox carteri* f. *nagariensis* Iyengar. *Proc. Natl. Acad. Sci. USA* **71**: 1050–4.

1689 Stauber, J.L. & S.W. Jeffrey (1988). Photosynthetic pigments in fifty-one species of marine diatoms. *J. Phycol.* **24**: 158–72.

1690 Staves, M. & J.W. La Claire II (1985). Nuclear synchrony in *Valonia macrophysa* (Chlorophyta): Light microscopy and flow cytometry. *J. Phycol.* **21**: 68–71.

1691 Stebbings, H. & J.S. Hyams (1979). *Cell Motility.* Longman, London.

1692 Stegenga, H. (1978). The life histories of *Rhodochorton purpureum* and *Rhodochorton floridulum* (Rhodophyta, Nemaliales) in culture. *Br. Phycol. J.* **13**: 279–89.

1693 Stegenga, H. & W.J. Borsje (1977). The morphology and life history of *Acrochaetium dasyae* Collins (Rhodophyta, Nemaliales). *Acta Bot. Neerl.* **26**: 451–70.

1694 Stegenga, H. & N.D. van Erp (1979). Morphological variation in the genus *Acrochaetium* (Rhodophyta, Nemaliales). *Acta Bot. Neerl.* **28**: 425–48.

1695 Stegenga, H. & I. Mol (1983). *Flora van de Nederlandse Zeewieren.* Koninklijke Natuurhistorische Vereniging, Hoogwoud, The Netherlands.

1696 Steidinger, K. & D.G. Baden (1984). Toxic marine dinoflagellates. In *Dinoflagellates*, ed. D.L. Spector, pp. 201–61. Academic Press, Orlando.

1697 Stewart, A.C. (1988). Molecular biology of photosynthetic reaction centres. In *Biochemistry of the Algae and Cyanobacteria*, ed. L.J. Rogers & J.R. Gallon, pp. 105–20. Clarendon Press, Oxford.

1698 Stewart, K.D. & K.R. Mattox (1975a). Comparative cytology, evolution and classification of the green algae with some consideration of the origin of other organisms with chlorophylls a and b. *Bot. Rev.* **41**: 104–35.

1699 Stewart, K.D. & K.R. Mattox (1975b). Some aspects of mitosis in primitive green algae: phylogeny and function. *BioSystems* **7**: 310–15.

1700 Stewart, K.D. & K.R. Mattox (1978). Structural evolution in the flagellated cells of green algae and land plants. *BioSystems* **10**: 145–52.

1701 Stewart, K.D., K.R. Mattox & C.D. Chandler (1974). Mitosis and cytokinesis in *Platymonas subcordiformis*, a scaly green monad. *J. Phycol.* **10**: 65–79.

1702 Stewart, K.D., K.R. Mattox & G.L. Floyd (1973). Mitosis, cytokinesis, the distribution of plasmodesmata, and other cytological characteristics in the Ulotrichales, Ulvales, and Chaetophorales: phylogenetic and taxonomic considerations. *J. Phycol.* **9**: 128–41.

1703 Stewart, K.D., J.R. Stewart & H.C. Bold (1978). The morphology and life history of *Characiosiphon rivularis* Iyengar (Chlorophyta: Characiosiphonaceae): a light and electron microscopic study. *Arch. Protistenk.* **120**: 312–40.

1704 Stewart, W.D.P. (1973). Nitrogen fixation. In *The Biology of Blue-green Algae*, ed. N.G. Carr & B.A. Whitton, pp. 260–78. Blackwell, Oxford.

1705 Stoddart, D.R. (1969). Ecology and morphology of recent coral reefs. *Biol. Rev.* **44**: 433–97.

1706 Stoecker, D.K., A. Taniguchi & A.E. Michaels (1989). Abundance of autotrophic, mixotrophic and heterotrophic planktonic ciliates in shelf and slope waters. *Mar. Ecol. Progr. Ser.* **50**: 241–54.

1707 Stoermer, E.F., H.S. Pankratz & C.C. Bowen (1965). Fine structure of the diatom *Amphipleura pellucida* II. Cytoplasmic fine structure and frustule formation. *Am. J. Bot.* **52**: 1067–78.

1708   Stosch, H.A. von (1950). Oogamy in a centric diatom. *Nature* **165**: 531–3.

1709   Stosch, H.A. von (1951). Entwicklungsgeschichtliche Untersuchungen an zentrischen Diatomeen I. Die Auxosporenbildung von *Melosira varians. Arch. Mikrobiol.* **16**: 101–35.

1710   Stosch, H.A. von (1954). Die Oogamie von *Biddulphia mobiliensis* und die bisher bekannten Auxosporenbildungen bei den Centrales. *VIIIe Congr. Int. Bot. Rapp. Comm. Sect.* **17**: 58–68.

1711   Stosch, H.A. von (1955). Ein morphologischer Phasenwechsel bei einer Coccolithophoride. *Naturwissenschaften* **42**: 423.

1712   Stosch, H.A. von (1956). Entwicklungsgeschichtliche Untersuchungen an zentrischen Diatomeen II. Geschlechtszellenreifung, Befruchtung und Auxosporenbildung einiger grundbewohnender Biddulphiaceen der Nordsee. *Arch. Mikrobiol.* **23**: 327–65.

1713   Stosch, H.A. von (1958a). Der Geißelapparat einer Coccolithophoride. *Naturwissenschaften* **45**: 140–1.

1714   Stosch, H.A. von (1958b). Kann die oogame Araphidee *Rhabdonema adriaticum* als Bindeglied zwischen den beiden großen Diatomeengruppen angesehen werden? *Ber. Dtsch. Bot. Ges.* **71**: 221–49.

1715   Stosch, H.A. von (1958c). Entwicklungsgeschichtliche Untersuchungen an zentrischen Diatomeen III. Die Spermatogenese von *Melosira moniliformis* Agardh. *Arch. Mikrobiol.* **31**: 274–82.

1716   Stosch, H.A. von (1964). Zum Problem der sexuellen Fortpflanzung in der Peridineengattung *Ceratium. Helgol. Wiss. Meeresunters.* **10**: 140–52.

1717   Stosch, H.A. von (1965). Sexualität bei *Ceratium cornutum* (Dinophyta). *Naturwissenschaften* **52**: 112–13.

1718   Stosch, H.A. von (1967). Haptophyceae. In: H. Ettl, D.G. Müller, K. Neumann, H.A. von Stosch & W. Weber. Vegetative Fortpflanzung, Parthenogenese und Apogamie bei Algen. In *Handbuch der Pflanzenphysiologie*, Vol. 18, ed. W. Ruhland, pp. 597–776. Springer-Verlag, Berlin.

1719   Stosch, H.A. von (1972). La signification cytologique de la 'cyclose nucléaire' dans le cycle de vie des Dinoflagellées. *Soc. Bot. France, Mémoires*: 201–12.

1720   Stosch, H.A. von (1973). Observations on vegetative reproduction and sexual life cycles of two freshwater dinoflagellates, *Gymnodinium*

pseudopalustre Schiller and *Woloszynskia apiculata* sp. nov. *Br. Phycol. J.* **8**: 105–34.

1721   Stosch, H.A. von (1980). Structural and histochemical observations on the organic layers of the diatom cell wall. *Nova Hedwigia, Beih.* **33**: 231–48.

1722   Stosch, H.A. von (1982). On auxospore envelopes in diatoms. *Bacillaria* **5**: 127–51.

1723   Stosch, H.A. von & G. Drebes (1964). Entwicklungsgeschichtliche Untersuchungen an zentrischen Diatomeen IV. Die Planktondiatomee *Stephanopyxis turris* – ihre Behandlung und Entwicklungsgeschichte. *Helgol. Wiss. Meeresunters.* **11**: 209–57.

1724   Stosch, H.A. von & G. Theil (1979). A new mode of life history in the freshwater red algal genus *Batrachospermum. Am. J. Bot.* **66**: 105–7.

1725   Stosch, H.A. von, G. Theil & K.V. Kowallik (1973). Entwicklungsgeschichtliche Untersuchungen an zentrischen Diatomeen. V. Bau und Lebenszyklus von *Chaetoceros didymum*, mit Beobachtungen über einige andere Arten der Gattung. *Helgol. Wiss. Meeresunters.* **25**: 384–445.

1726   Stransky, H. & A. Hager (1970). Das Carotinoidmuster und Verbreitung des lichtinduzierten Xanthophyllcyclus in verschiedenen Algenklassen. II. Xanthophyceae. *Arch. Mikrobiol.* **71**: 164–90.

1727   Stuessey, C.L., G.L. Floyd & C.J. O'Kelly (1983). Fine structure of the zoospores of an *Enteromorpha* species (Ulvales, Chlorophyta) collected from fresh water. *Br. Phycol. J.* **18**: 249–57.

1728   Stulp, B.K. & W.T. Stam (1984). Genotypic relationships between strains of *Anabaena* (Cyanophyceae) and their correlation with morphological affinities. *Br. Phycol. J.* **19**: 287–301.

1729   Stulp, B.K. & W.T. Stam (1985). Taxonomy of the genus *Anabaena* (Cyanophyceae) based on morphological and genotypic criteria. *Arch. Hydrobiol., Suppl.* **71** (*Algol. Stud.* **38**): 257–68.

1730   Stutz, E., P.E. Montandon, E. Roux, B. Rutti & B. Schlunegger (1984). Organization and capacity of the chloroplast genome in algae. In *Compartments in Algal Cells and their Interactions*, ed. W. Wiessner, D.G. Robinson & R.C. Starr, pp. 11–22. Springer-Verlag, Berlin.

1731   Suda, S., M.M. Watanabe & I. Inouye (1989). Evidence for sexual reproduction in the primitive green alga *Nephroselmis olivacea* (Prasinophyceae). *J. Phycol.* **25**: 596–600.

1732   Sullivan, C.M., T.J. Entwisle & K.S. Rowan (1990). The identification of chlorophyll c in the Tribophyceae (= Xanthophyceae) using spectrophotofluorometry. *Phycologia* **29**: 285–91.

1733   Suneson, S. (1937). Studien über die Entwicklungsgeschichte der Corallinaceen. *Lunds Univ. Årsskr.* N.F. (Avd. 2) **33**: 1–101.

1734   Suzaki, T. & R.E. Williamson (1986). Ultrastructure and sliding of pellicular structures during euglenoid movement in *Astasia longa* Pringsheim (Sarcomastigophora, Euglenida). *J. Protozool.* **33**: 179–84.

1735   Swale, E.M.F. (1973). A third layer of body scales in *Pyramimonas tetrarhynchus* Schmarda. *Br. Phycol. J.* **8**: 95–9.

1736   Swale, E.M.F. & J.H. Belcher (1963). Morphological observations on wild and cultured material of *Rhodochorton investiens* (Lenormand) nov. comb. (*Balbiania investiens* [Lenorm.] Sirodot). *Ann. Bot.* N.S. **27**: 281–90.

1737   Swale, E.M.F. & J.H. Belcher (1968). The external morphology of the type species of *Pyramimonas* (*P. tetrarhynchus* Schmarda) by electron microscopy. *J. Linn. Soc. Bot.* **79**: 77–81.

1738   Sweeney, B.M. (1976). *Pedinomonas noctilucae* (Prasinophyceae), the flagellate symbiotic in *Noctiluca* in southeast Asia. *J. Phycol.* **12**: 460–4.

1739   Sweeney, B.M. (1978). Ultrastructure of *Noctiluca miliaris* (Pyrrophyta) with green flagellate symbionts. *J. Phycol.* **14**: 116–20.

1740   Sweeney, B.M. (1984). Circadian rhythmicity in dinoflagellates. In *Dinoflagellates*, ed. D.L. Spector, pp. 343–360. Academic Press, Orlando.

1741   Sweeney, B.M. (1987). Bioluminescence and circadian rhythms. In *The Biology of Dinoflagellates*, ed. F.J.R. Taylor, pp. 269–81. Blackwell Scientific Publications, Oxford.

1742   Sweeney, B.M. & J.W. Hastings (1962). Rhythms. In *Physiology and Biochemistry of Algae*, ed. R.A. Lewin, pp. 687–98. Academic Press, New York.

1743   Tait, R.V. (1981). *Elements of Marine Ecology*. Butterworths, London.

1744   Takatori, S. & K. Imahori (1971). Light reactions in the control of oospore germination of *Chara delicatula*. *Phycologia* **10**: 221–8.

1745   Takeda, H., K. Nisizawa & T. Miwa (1967). Histochemical and chemical studies on the cell wall of *Prasiola japonica*. *Bot. Mag. Jap.* **80**: 109–17.

1746   Takeda, H., K. Nisizawa & T. Miwa (1968). A xylomannan from the cell wall of *Prasiola japonica* Yatabe. *Sci. Rep. Tokyo Kyoiku Daigaku* **13**: 183–98.

1747   Tandeau de Marsac, N. & J. Houmard (1987). Advances in cyanobacterial molecular genetics. In *The Cyanobacteria*, ed. P. Fay & C. Van Baalen, pp. 251–302. Elsevier, Amsterdam.

1748   Tangen, K., L.E. Brand, P.L. Blackwelder & R.R.L. Guillard (1982). *Thoracosphaera heimii* (Lohmann) Kamptner is a dinophyte: observations on its morphology and life cycle. *Mar. Micropaleontol.* **7**: 193–212.

1749   Tanner, C.E. (1979). *The taxonomy and morphological variation of distromatic ulvaceous algae (Chlorophyta) from the Northeast Pacific*. Thesis, University of British Columbia.

1750   Tanner, C. (1981). Chlorophyta: life histories. In *The Biology of Seaweeds*, ed. C.S. Lobban & M.J. Wynne, pp. 218–47. Blackwell, Oxford.

1751   Tappan, H. (1980). *The Paleobiology of Plant Protists*. Freeman, San Francisco.

1752   Tatewaki, M. (1969). Culture studies on the life-history of some species of the genus *Monostroma*. *Sci. Pap. Inst. Algol. Res. Hokkaido Univ.* **6**: 1–56.

1753   Tatewaki, M. (1972). Life history and systematics in *Monostroma*. In *Contributions to the Systematics of Benthic Marine Algae of the North Pacific*, ed. I.A. Abbott & M. Kurogi, pp. 1–15. Japanese Society of Phycology, Kobe, Japan.

1754   Taylor, D.L. (1973). The cellular interactions of algae invertebrate symbiosis. *Adv. Mar. Biol.* **11**: 1–56.

1755   Taylor, D.L. (1983). The coral-algal symbiosis. In *Algal Symbiosis*, ed. L.J. Goff, pp. 19–35. Cambridge University Press.

1756   Taylor, F.J.R. (1974). Implications and extensions of the serial endosymbiosis theory of the origin of Eukaryotes. *Taxon* **23**: 229–58.

1757   Taylor, F.J.R. (1975). Non-helical transverse flagella in dinoflagellates. *Phycologia* **14**: 45–7.

1758   Taylor, F.J.R. (1980). On dinoflagellate evolution. *BioSystems* **13**: 65–108.

1759   Taylor, F.J.R. (1987). Dinoflagellate morphology. In *The Biology of Dinoflagellates*, ed. F.J.R. Taylor, pp. 24–91. Blackwell Scientific Publications, Oxford.

1760   Taylor, F.J.R. (1988). *Evolution of marine*

phytoplankton. Plenary lecture presented to the Third International Phycological Congress, Melbourne, August 1988.

1761   Taylor, F.J.R., D.J. Blackbourne & J. Blackbourne (1969). Ultrastructure of the chloroplasts and associated structures within the marine ciliate *Mesodinimum rubrum* (Lohmann). *Nature* **224**: 819–21.

1762   Taylor, F.J.R. & U. Pollingher (1987). Ecology of dinoflagellates. In *The Biology of Dinoflagellates*, ed. F.J.R. Taylor, pp. 398–529. Blackwell Scientific Publications, Oxford.

1763   Taylor, W.R. (1957). *Marine Algae of the Northeastern Coast of North America*. 2nd Ed. University of Michigan Press, Ann Arbor.

1764   Taylor, W.R. (1960). *Marine Algae of the Eastern Tropical and Subtropical Coasts of the Americas*. University of Michigan Press, Ann Arbor.

1765   Taylor, W.R. (1971). Notes on algae from the tropical Atlantic Ocean, V. *Br. Phycol. J.* **6**: 145–56.

1766   Tewari, K.K. (1971). Genetic autonomy of extranuclear organelles. *Ann. Rev. Plant Physiol.* **22**: 141–68.

1767   Thakur, M. & M.B.E. Godward (1965). The cytology of members of the Cryptophyceae. *Br. Phycol. Bull.* **2**: 518.

1768   Thirb, H.H. & K. Benson-Evans (1982). Cytological studies on *Lemanea fluviatilis* L. in the River Usk. *Br. Phycol. J.* **17**: 401–9.

1769   Thomas, B.A. & R.A. Spicer (1986). *The Evolution and Paleobiology of Land Plants*. Croom Helm, Beckenham, Kent.

1770   Thomas, E.A. (1961). *Hydrodictyon reticulatum* und seine Beziehung zur Saprobität im Zürichsee und in der Glatt. *Vjschr. Naturforsch. Ges. Zürich* **106**: 450–6.

1771   Thompson, R.H. (1974). Sexual reproduction in *Chaetosphaeridium globosum* (Nordst.) Klebahn (Chlorophyceae) and description of a species new to science. *J. Phycol.* **5**: 285–90.

1772   Thorpe, J.P. (1982). The molecular clock hypothesis: biochemical evolution, genetic differentiation and systematics. *Ann. Rev. Ecol. Syst.* **13**: 136–68.

1773   Throndsen, J. (1969). Flagellates of Norwegian coastal waters. *Nytt. Mag. Bot.* **16**: 161–216.

1774   Thuret, G. & E. Bornet (1878). *Études Phycologiques*. Paris.

1775   Tiffany, L.H. (1930). *The Oedogoniaceae*. Columbus, Ohio.

1776   Tomas, R.N. & E.R. Cox (1973). Observations on the symbiosis of *Peridinium balticum* and its intracellular alga I. Ultrastructure. *J. Phycol.* **9**: 304–323.

1777   Tomson, A.M. & R. Demets (1989). *Sexual communication in the green alga Chlamydomonas eugametos*. Thesis, University of Amsterdam.

1778   Tosteson, T.R., D.L. Ballantine, C.G. Tosteson, V. Hensley & A.T. Bardales (1989). Associated bacterial flora, growth, and toxicity of cultured benthic dinoflagellates *Ostreopsis lenticularis* and *Gambierdiscus toxicus*. *Appl. Environm. Microbiol.* (Jan. 1989): 137–41.

1779   Toth, R. & D.R. Markey (1973). Synaptonemal complexes in brown algae. *Nature* **243**: 236–7.

1781   Tovey, D.J. & B.L. Moss (1978). Attachment of the haptera of *Laminaria digitata* (Huds.) Lamour. *Phycologia* **17**: 17–22.

1782   Trainor, F.R. (1985). Survival of algae in a desiccated soil: a 25 year study. *Phycologia* **24**: 79–82.

1783   Trainor, F.R. & C.A. Burg (1965). *Scenedesmus obliquus* sexuality. *Science* **148**: 1094–5.

1784   Trainor, F.R. & J.R. Cain (1986). Famous algal genera. I. *Chlamydomonas*. In *Progress in Phycological Research*, Vol. 4, ed. F.E. Round & D.J. Chapman, pp. 81–127. Biopress, Bristol.

1785   Trainor, F.R. & P.F. Egan (1988). The role of bristles in the distribution of a *Scenedesmus*. *Br. Phycol. J.* **23**: 135–41.

1786   Trainor, F.R. & R.J. McLean (1964). A study of a new species of *Spongiochloris* introduced into sterile soil. *Am. J. Bot.* **51**: 57–60.

1787   Transeau, E.N. (1951). *The Zygnemataceae*. Ohio State University Press, Columbus, Ohio.

1788   Trench, R.K. (1987). Dinoflagellates in non-parasitic symbioses. In *The Biology of Dinoflagellates*, ed. F.J.R. Taylor, pp. 530–70. Blackwell Scientific Publications, Oxford.

1789   Trench, R.K. & R.J. Blank (1987). *Symbiodinium microadriaticum* Freudenthal, *S. goreauii* sp. nov., *S. kawagutii* sp. nov. and *S. pilosum* sp. nov.: gymnodinioid dinoflagellate symbionts of marine invertebrates. *J. Phycol.* **23**: 469–81.

1790   Triemer, R.E. (1980). Role of Golgi apparatus in mucilage production and cyst formation in *Euglena gracilis* (Euglenophyceae). *J. Phycol.* **16**: 46–52.

1791 Triemer, R.E. & R.M. Brown (1974). Cell division in *Chlamydomonas moewusii. J. Phycol.* **10**: 419–43.

1792 Triemer, R.E. & R.M. Brown (1977). Ultrastructure of meiosis in *Chlamydomonas reinhardtii. Br. Phycol. J.* **123**: 23–44.

1793 Triemer, R.E. & L. Fritz (1984). Cell cycle and mitosis. In *Dinoflagellates*, ed. D.L. Spector, pp. 149–79. Academic Press, Orlando.

1794 Triemer, R.E. & L. Fritz (1988). Ultrastructural features of mitosis in *Phloeotia costata* (Heteronematales, Euglenophyta). *J. Phycol.* **24**: 514–19.

1795 Tripodi, G., G.M. Gargiulo & F. de Masi (1986). Electron microscopy of membranous bodies and genophore in chloroplasts of *Botryocladia botryoides* (Rhodymeniales, Rhodophyta). *J. Phycol.* **22**: 560–3.

1796 Tschermak-Woess, E. (1978). *Myrmecia reticulata* as a phycobiont and free-living *Trebouxia* – the problem of *Stenocybe septata. Lichenologist* **10**: 69–79.

1797 Tschermak-Woess, E. (1989a). The algal partner. In *CRC Handbook of Lichenology*, Vol. I, ed. M. Galun, pp. 39–92. CRC Press, Boca Raton, Florida.

1798 Tschermak-Woess, E. (1989b). Developmental studies in trebouxioid algae and taxonomical consequences. *Plant Syst. Evol.* **164**: 161–95.

1798a Tschermak-Woess, E. & A. Schöller (1982). Verteilung und Aufteilung der DNS bei einigen Cyanophyceen, festgestellt durch ihre DAPI-Fluoreszenz. *Plant Syst. Evol.* **140**: 207–23.

1799 Tsekos, I. (1981). Growth and differentiation of the Golgi apparatus and wall formation during carposporogenesis in the red alga, *Gigartina teedii* (Roth) Lamour. *J. Cell Sci.* **52**: 71–84.

1800 Tsekos, I. (1983). The ultrastructure of carposporogenesis in *Gigartina teedii* (Roth) Lamour. (Gigartinales, Rhodophyceae): gonimoblast cells and carpospores. *Flora* **174**: 191–211.

1801 Tsekos, I. (1985). The endomembrane system of differentiating carposporangia in the red alga *Chondria tenuissima:* occurrence and participation in secretion of polysaccharidic and proteinaceous substances. *Protoplasma* **129**: 127–36.

1802 Tsekos, I. & E. Schnepf (1985). Ultrastructure of the early stages of carposporophyte development in the red alga *Chondria tenuisssima* (Rhodomelaceae, Ceramiales). *Pl. Syst. Evol.* **151**: 1–18.

1803 Tseng, C.K. (1981). Commercial cultivation. In *The Biology of Seaweeds*, ed. C.S. Lobban & M.J. Wynne, pp. 680–725. Blackwell, Oxford.

1803a Turmel, M., B. Lemieux & C. Lemieux (1988). The chloroplast genome of the green alga *Chlamydomonas moewusii:* localisation of protein coding genes and transcriptionally active regions. *Molec. Gen. Genet.* **214**: 412–9.

1804 Turner, C.H.C. & L.H. Evans (1978). Translocation of photoassimilated ^{14}C in the red alga *Polysiphonia lanosa. Br. Phycol. J.* **13**: 51–5.

1805 Turner, F.R. (1968). An ultrastructural study of plant spermatogenesis. Spermatogenesis in *Nitella. J. Cell Biol.* **37**: 370–93.

1806 Turner, S., T. Burger-Wiersma, S.J. Giovannoni, L.R. Mur & N.R. Pace (1989). The relationships of a prochlorophyte *Prochlorothrix hollandica* to green chloroplasts. *Nature* **337**: 380–5.

1807 Uherkovich, G. (1966). *Die Scenedesmus-Arten Ungarns.* Ungarische Akademie der Wissenschaften, Budapest.

1808 Umezaki, I. (1967). The tetrasporophyte of *Nemalion vermiculare* Suringar. *Rev. Algol.* N.S. **9**: 19–24.

1808a Urbach, E., D. Robertson & S.W. Chisholm (1992). Multiple evolutionary origins of prochlorophytes within the cyanobacterial radiation. *Nature* **355**: 267–9.

1809 Valkanov, A. (1962). Über die Entwicklung von *Hymenomonas coccolithophora* Conrad. *Rev. Algol.*, N.S. **6**: 220–6.

1809a Van Baalen, C. (1987). Nitrogen fixation. In *The Cyanobacteria*, ed. P. Fay & C. Van Baalen, pp. 187–98. Elsevier, Amsterdam.

1810 Van der Meer, J.P. (1981). The life history of *Halosaccion ramentaceum. Can. J. Bot.* **59**: 433–6.

1811 Van der Meer, J.P. & E.R. Todd (1980). The life history of *Palmaria palmata* in culture. A new type for the Rhodophyta. *Can. J. Bot.* **58**: 1250–6.

1812 Van Valkenburg, S.D. (1971a). Observations on the fine structure of *Dictyocha fibula* Ehrenberg. I. The skeleton. *J. Phycol.* **7**: 113–8.

1813 Van Valkenburg, S.D. (1971b). Observations on the fine structure of *Dictyocha fibula.* II. The protoplast. *J. Phycol.* **7**: 118–32.

1814 Van Valkenburg, S.D. (1980). Silicoflagellates. In *Phytoflagellates*, ed. E.R. Cox, pp. 335–50. Elsevier/North-Holland, Amsterdam.

604   References

1815   Van Valkenburg, S.D. & R.E. Norris (1970). The growth and morphology of the silicoflagellate *Dictyocha fibula* Ehrenberg in culture. *J. Phycol.* **6**: 48–54.

1816   Veer, J. van der (1970). *Ankylonoton luteum* (Chrysophyta), a new species from the Tamar estuary, Cornwall. *Acta Bot. Neerl.* **19**: 616–36.

1817   Veer, J. van der (1969). *Pavlova mesolychnon* (Chrysophyta), a new species from the Tamar Estuary, Cornwall. *Acta Bot. Neerl.* **18**: 496–510.

1818   Veer, J. van der (1972). *Pavlova helicata*, a new species from the Frisian Island Schiermonnikoog, the Netherlands. *Nova Hedwigia* **23**: 131–59.

1819   Veer, J. van der (1979). *Pavlova and the taxonomy of flagellates especially the chrysomonads.* Thesis, University of Groningen.

1820   Veldhuis, M.J.W. (1987). *The ecophysiology of the colonial alga Phaeocystis pouchetii.* Thesis, University of Groningen.

1821   Veldhuis, M.J.W. & W. Admiraal (1985). Transfer of photosynthetic products in gelatinous colonies of *Phaeocystis pouchetii* (Haptophyceae) and its effect on the measurement of excretion rate. *Mar. Ecol. Progr. Ser.* **26**: 301–4.

1822   Veldhuis, M.J.W., F. Colijn & L.A.H. Venekamp (1986). The spring bloom of *Phaeocystis pouchetii* (Haptophyceae) in Dutch coastal waters. *Neth. J. Sea Res.* **20**: 37–48.

1822a Veldhuis, M.J.W. & G.W. Kraay (1990). Vertical distribution and pigment composition of a picoplanktonic prochlorophyte in the subtropical North Atlantic: a combined study of HPLC-analysis of pigments and flow cytometry. *Mar. Ecol. Prog. Ser.* **68**: 121–7.

1823   Vermeglio, A., J. Ravenel & G. Peltier (1990). Chlororespiration: a respiratory activity in the thylakoid membrane of microalgae and higher plants. In *Experimental Phycology 1. Cell Walls and Surfaces, Reproduction, Photosynthesis*, ed. W. Wiessner, D.G. Robinson & R.C. Starr, pp. 188–205. Springer-Verlag, Berlin.

1824   Vesk, M., L.R. Hoffman & J.D. Pickett-Heaps (1984). Mitosis and cell division in *Hydrurus foetidus* (Chrysophyceae). *J. Phycol.* **20**: 461–70.

1825   Vesk, M. & S.W. Jeffrey (1987). Ultrastructure and pigments of two strains of the picoplanktonic alga *Pelagococcus subviridis* (Chrysophyceae). *J. Phycol.* **23**: 322–36.

1826   Vickers, A. & M.H. Shaw (1908). *Phycologia Barbadensis.* Paris.

1827   Vidal, G. (1984). The oldest eukaryotic cells. *Scient. Amer.* **250** (2): 32–41.

1828   Vielhaben, V. (1963). Zur Deutung des semilunaren Fortpflanzungszyklus von *Dictyota dichotoma. Z. Bot.* **51**: 156–73.

1829   Vinogradova, K.L. (1969). K sistematike poriadka Ulvales (Chlorophyta). *Bot. Zhurn.* **54**: 1347–55.

1830   Vinogradova, K.L. (1974). *Ul'vovye vodorosli (Chlorophyta) mor'ej SSSR.* Izdatel'stvo 'Nauka', Leningrad, USSR: 1–167.

1831   Vischer, W. (1953). Über primitivste Landpflanzen. *Ber. Schweiz. Bot. Ges.* **63**: 169–93.

1832   Vogel, K. & B.J.D. Meeuse (1968). Characterization of the reserve granules from the dinoflagellate *Thecadinium inclinatum* Balech. *J. Phycol.* **4**: 317–8.

1833   Volcani, B.E. (1981). Cell wall formation in diatoms: morphogenesis and biochemistry. In *Silicon and Siliceous Structures in Biological Systems*, ed. T.L. Simpson & B.E. Volcani, pp. 157–200. Springer, New York.

1834   Vrind, de-de Jong, E.W., A.H. Borman, R. Thierry, P. Westbroek, M. Gruter & J.P. Kamerling (1986). Calcification in the coccolithophorids *Emiliania huxleyi* and *Pleurochrysis carterae*. In *Biomineralization in Lower Plants and Animals*, ed. B.S.C. Leadbeater & R. Riding, pp. 205–17. Clarendon Press, Oxford.

1835   Waaland, J.R. (1981). Commercial utilization. In *The Biology of Seaweeds*, ed. C.S. Lobban & M.J. Wynne, pp. 726–41. Blackwell, Oxford.

1836   Waaland, J.R. & D. Branton (1969). Gas vacuole development in a blue-green alga. *Science* **163**: 1339–41.

1837   Waaland, J.R., L.G. Dickson & J.E. Carrier (1987). *Conchocelis* growth and photoperiodic control of conchospore release in *Porphyra torta* (Rhodophyta). *J. Phycol.* **23**: 399–406.

1838   Waffenschmidt, S. & L. Jaenicke (1990). Autolysins in *Chlamydomonas*. In *Experimental Phycology 1, Cell Walls and Surfaces, Reproduction, Photosynthesis*, ed. W. Wiessner, D.G. Robinson & R.C. Starr, pp. 69–80. Springer-Verlag, Berlin.

1839   Wal, P. van der (1984). *Calcification in two species of coccolithophorid algae.* GUA papers of geology ser. 1 no 20; Thesis, University of Leiden, the Netherlands. Drukkerij Kanters, Alblasserdam.

1840 Wal, P. van der, E.W. de Jong, P. Westbroek, W.C. de Bruyn & A.A. Mulder-Stapel (1983). Polysaccharide localization, coccolith formation, and Golgi dynamics in the coccolithophorid *Hymenomonas carterae. J. Ultrastruct. Res.* **85**: 139–58.

1841 Wal, P. van der, L. de Jong, P. Westbroek & W.C. de Bruyn (1983). Calcification in the coccolithophorid alga *Hymenomonas carterae. Environmental Biogeochemistry Ecol. Bull. (Stockholm)* **35**: 251–8.

1842 Wal, P. van der, E.W. de Jong, P. Westbroek, W.C. de Bruyn & A.A. Mulder-Stapel (1983). Ultrastructural polysaccharide localization in calcifying and naked cells of the coccolithophorid *Emiliania huxleyi. Protoplasma* **118**: 157–68.

1843 Wall, D. & B. Dale (1969). The 'hystrichosphaeroid' resting spore of the dinoflagellate *Pyrodinium bahamense*, Plate, 1906. *J. Phycol.* **5**: 140–9.

1844 Wall, D., R.R.L. Guillard & B. Dale (1967). Marine dinoflagellate cultures from resting spores. *Phycologia* **6**: 83–6.

1845 Wallentinus, I. (1988). Questionnaire about the bloom of *Chrysochromulina polylepis*. (Sent to colleagues by Prof. Inger Wallentinus, Dept of Marine Botany, University of Göteborg, Carl Skottsbergsgata 22, S–413 19 Göteborg, Sweden.)

1846 Walne, P.L. (1980). Euglenoid flagellates. In *Phytoflagellates*, ed. E.R. Cox, pp. 165–212. Elsevier/North Holland, Amsterdam.

1847 Walne, P.L. & H.J. Arnott (1967). The comparative ultrastructure and possible function of eyespots: *Euglena granulata* and *Chlamydomonas eugametos. Planta* **77**: 325–53.

1848 Walne, P.L. & P.A. Kivic (1990). Phylum Euglenida. In *Handbook of Protoctista*, ed. L. Margulis, J.O. Corliss, M. Melkonian & D.J. Chapman, pp. 270–87. Jones & Bartlett, Boston.

1848a Walne, P.L., Ø. Moestrup, R.E. Norris & H. Ettl (1986). Light and electron microscopical studies of *Eutreptiella eupharyngea* sp. nov. (Euglenophyceae) from Danish and American waters. *Phycologia* **25**: 109–26.

1849 Walsby, A.E. (1973). Gas vacuoles. In *The Biology of Blue-green Algae*, ed. N.G. Carr & B.A. Whitton, pp. 340–52. Blackwell, Oxford.

1850 Walsby, A.E. (1987). Mechanisms of buoyancy regulation by planktonic Cyanobacteria with gas vacuoles. In *The Cyanobacteria*, ed. P. Fay & C. Van Baalen, pp. 377–92. Elsevier, Amsterdam.

1851 Walsby, A.E. & C.S. Reynolds (1980). Sinking and floating. In *The Physiological Ecology of Phytoplankton*, ed. I. Morris, pp. 371–412. Blackwell, Oxford.

1852 Walsby, A.E. & A. Xylopyta (1977). The form resistance of chitan fibres attached to the cells of *Thalassiosira fluviatilis* Hustedt. *Br. Phycol. J.* **12**: 215–23.

1853 Wanders, J.B.W., C. van den Hoek & E.N. Schillern-Van Nes (1972). Observations on the life-history of *Elachista stellaris* (Phaeophyceae) in culture. *Neth. J. Sea Res.* **5**: 458–91.

1854 Wasmann, C.C., W. Loeffelhardt & H.J. Bohnert (1987). Cyanelles: organization and molecular biology. In *The Cyanobacteria*, ed. P. Fay & C. Van Baalen, pp. 303–24. Elsevier, Amsterdam.

1855 Watanabe, M.M., Y. Takeda, T. Sasa, I. Inouye, S. Suda, T. Sawaguchi & M. Chihara (1987). A green dinoflagellate with chlorophylls a and b: morphology, fine structure of the choroplast and chlorophyll composition. *J. Phycol.* **23**: 382–9.

1856 Watanabe, S. & G.L. Floyd (1989). Ultrastructure of the zoospores of the coenocytic algae *Ascochloris* and *Urnella* (Chlorophyceae), with emphasis on the flagellar apparatus. *Br. Phycol. J.* **24**: 143–52.

1857 Watanabe, S., G.L. Floyd & L.W. Wilcox (1988). Ultrastructure of the zoospores and vegetative cells of *Tetraedron* and *Chlorotetraedron* (Chlorophyceae). *J. Phycol.* **24**: 490–95.

1858 Waterbury, J.B. (1989). Subsection II. Order Pleurocapsales Geitler 1925, emend. Waterbury and Stanier 1978. In *Bergey's Manual of Systematic Bacteriology*, Vol. 3. Section 19: *Oxygenic photosynthetic bacteria*, ed. J.T. Staley, M.P. Bryant, N. Pfennig & J.H. Holt, pp. 1746–70. Williams & Wilkins, Baltimore.

1859 Waterbury, J.B. & R. Rippka (1989). Subsection 1. Order Chroococcales Wettstein 1924, emend. Rippka *et al.*, 1979. In *Bergey's Manual of Systematic Bacteriology*, Vol. 3. Section 19: *Oxygenic photosynthetic bacteria*, ed. J.T. Staley, M.P. Bryant, N. Pfennig & J.H. Holt, pp. 1728–46. Williams & Wilkins, Baltimore.

1860 Watson, M.W. (1975). Flagellar apparatus, eyespot and behaviour of *Microthamnion kuetzin-*

gianum (Chlorophyceae) zoospores. *J. Phycol.* **11**: 439–48.

1861 Weber, A. (1973). Über die Chlorophylle und Carotenoide einiger Ulotrichales. *Mitt. Staatsinst. Allg. Bot. Hamburg* **14**: 25–9.

1862 Webster, J. (1980). *Introduction to Fungi.* 2nd Ed. Cambridge University Press.

1863 Wehrmeyer, W. (1970). Struktur, Entwicklung und Abbau von Trichocysten in *Cryptomonas* und *Hemiselmis* (Cryptophyceae). *Protoplasma* **70**: 295–315.

1864 Wehrmeyer, W. (1990). Phycobilisomes: structure and function. In *Experimental Phycology 1. Cell Walls and Surfaces, Reproduction, Photosynthesis,* ed. W. Wiessner, D.G. Robinson & R.C. Starr, pp. 158–72. Springer-Verlag, Berlin.

1865 Weiler, S.C. & D.M. Karl (1979). Diel changes in phased-dividing cultures of *Ceratium furca* (Dinophyceae): nucleotide triphosphatases, adenylate energy charge, cell carbon, and patterns of vertical migration. *J. Phycol.* **15**: 384–91.

1866 Wenzl, S. & M. Sumper (1987). Pheromone-inducible glycoproteins of the extracellular matrix of *Volvox* and their possible role in sexual induction. In *Algal Development,* ed. W. Wiessner, D.G. Robinson & R.C. Starr, pp. 58–65. Springer-Verlag, Berlin.

1867 Werff, A. van der & H. Huls (1957–74). *Diatomeeën-Flora van Nederland.* Abcoude, the Netherlands.

1868 Werner, D. (1977). Introduction with a note on taxonomy. In *The Biology of Diatoms,* ed. D. Werner, pp. 1–17. Blackwell, Oxford.

1869 Werz, G. & H. Clauss (1970). Über die chemische Natur der Reserve-Polysaccharide in *Acetabularia*-Chloroplasten. *Planta* **95**: 165–8.

1870 Werz, M. & K. Zetsche (1970). Biochemische Aspekte des heteromorphen Generationswechsels von *Halicystis-Derbesia. Ber. Dtsch. Bot. Ges.* **83**: 229–30.

1871 West, J.A. (1969). The life-histories of *Rhodochorton purpureum* and *Rh. tenue* in culture. *J. Phycol.* **5**: 12–21.

1872 West, J.A. (1972). The life history of *Petrocelis franciscana. Br. Phycol. J.* **7**: 299–308.

1873 West, J.A., A.R. Polanshek & M.D. Guiry (1977). The life history in culture of *Petrocelis cruenta* J. Agardh (Rhodophyta) from Ireland. *Br. Phycol. J.* **12**: 45–53.

1874 West, J.A., A.R. Polanshek & D.E. Shevlin (1978). Field and culture studies on *Gigartina agardhii* (Rhodophyta). *J. Phycol.* **14**: 416–26.

1875 West, W. & G.S. West (1904–1912). *A Monograph of the British Desmidiaceae,* Vols I–IV. Ray Society, London.

1876 West, W., G.S. West & N. Carter (1923). *A Monograph of the British Desmidiaceae,* Vol. V. Ray Society, London.

1877 Westbroek, P. (1989). Lynn, Gaia en geologie. *Biovisie* **69**(1): 4–5.

1878 Wetherbee, R. (1979). 'Transfer connections': specialized pathways for nutrient translocation in a red alga? *Science* **204**: 858–9.

1878a Wever, R. (1988). Ozone destruction by algae in the Arctic atmosphere. *Nature* **335**: 501.

1878b Wever, B, & B.E. Krenn (1990). Vanadium haloperoxidases. In *Vanadium in Biological Systems,* ed. N.D. Chasteen, pp. 81–97. Kluwer, Dordrecht, The Netherlands.

1879 Whatley, F.R. & R.S. Alberte (1989). Biochemical features of *Prochloron.* In *Prochloron, a Microbial Enigma,* ed. R.A. Lewin & L. Cheng, pp. 53–64. Chapman & Hall, New York.

1880 Whatley, J.M. & F.R. Whatley (1981). Chloroplast evolution. *New Phytol.* **87**: 233–47.

1881 White, H.H. (1979). Dinoflagellate luminescence and ingestion rates of herbivorous zooplankton. *J. Exp. Mar. Biol. Ecol.* **36**: 217–24.

1882 Whittle, S.J. (1976). The major chloroplast pigments of *Chlorobotrys regularis* (West) Bohlin (Eustigmatophyceae) and *Ophiocytium majus* Naegeli (Xanthophyceae). *Br. Phycol. J.* **11**: 111–14.

1883 Whittle, S.J. & P.J. Casselton (1969). The chloroplast pigments of some green and yellow-green algae. *Br. Phycol. J.* **4**: 55–64.

1884 Whittle, S.J. & P.J. Casselton (1975a). The chloroplast pigments of the algal classes Eustigmatophyceae and Xanthophyceae. I. Eustigmatophyceae. *Br. Phycol. J.* **10**: 179–91.

1885 Whittle, S.J. & P.J. Casselton (1975b). The chloroplast pigments of the algal classes Eustigmatophyceae and Xanthophyceae. II. Xanthophyceae. *Br. Phycol. J.* **10**: 192–204.

1886 Whitton, B.A. (1987). Survival and dormancy of blue-green algae. In *Survival and Dormancy of Microorganisms,* ed. Y. Hennis, pp. 109–67. John Wiley, New York.

1887 Whitton, B.A. & N.G. Carr (1982). Cyanobacteria: current perspectives. In *The Biology of Cyanobacteria*, ed. N.G. Carr & B.A. Whitton, pp. 1–8. Blackwell Scientific Publications, Oxford.

1888 Whitton, B.A., N.G. Carr & I.W. Craig (1971). A comparison of the fine structure and nucleic acid biochemistry of chloroplasts and blue-green algae. *Protoplasma* **72**: 325–57.

1889 Whitton, B.A. & J.P.C. Harding (1978). Influence of nutrient deficiency on hair formation in *Stigeoclonium*. *Br. Phycol. J.* **13**: 65–8.

1890 Wiencke, C. & M.N. Clayton (1990). Sexual reproduction, life history, and early development in culture of the Antarctic brown alga *Himantothallus grandifolius* (Desmarestiales, Phaeophyceae). *Phycologia* **29**: 9–18.

1891 Wiese, L. (1965). On sexual agglutination and mating type substances (gamones) in isogamous heterothallic *Chlamydomonas* I. Evidence of the identity of the gamones with the surface components responsible for sexual flagellar contact. *J. Phycol.* **1**: 46–54.

1892 Wik-Sjöstedt, A. (1970). Cytogenetic investigations in *Cladophora*. *Hereditas* **66**: 233–62.

1893 Wilce, R.T. & A.N. Davis (1984). Development of *Dumontia contorta* (Dumontiaceae, Cryptonemiales) compared with other higher red algae. *J. Phycol.* **20**: 336–51.

1894 Wilcox, L.W. & G.L. Floyd (1988). Ultrastructure of the gamete of *Pediastrum duplex* (Chlorophyceae). *J. Phycol.* **24**: 140–6.

1895 Wilcox, L.W. & G.J. Wedemeyer (1984). *Gymnodinium acidotum* Nygaard (Pyrrophyta), a dinoflagellate with an endosymbiotic cryptomonad. *J. Phycol.* **20**: 236–42.

1896 Wilcox, L.W. & G.J. Wedemeyer (1985). Dinoflagellate with blue-green chloroplasts derived from an endosymbiotic eukaryote. *Science* **227**: 192–4.

1896a Wilcox, L.W., G.J. Wedemeyer & L.E. Graham (1982). *Amphidinium cryophilum* sp. nov. (Dinophyceae) a new freshwater dinoflagellate. II. Ultrastructure. *J. Phycol.* **18**: 18–30.

1897 Wilhelm, C. (1987). The existence of chlorophyll c in the chlorophyll b-containing, light-harvesting complex of the green alga *Mantoniella squamata* (Prasinophyceae). *Botanica Acta* **101**: 14–17.

1898 Wilhelm, C., I. Wiedemann, P. Krämer, I. Lenartz-Weiler & C. Büchel (1990). The molecular architecture of the thylakoid membrane from various classes of eukaryotic algae. In *Experimental Phycology 1. Cell Walls and Surfaces, Reproduction, Photosynthesis*, ed. W. Wiessner, D.G. Robinson & R.C. Starr, pp. 173–87. Springer-Verlag, Berlin.

1899 Willey, R.L. & R.G. Wibel (1987). Flagellar roots and the reservoir cytoskeleton of *Colacium libellae* (Euglenophyceae). *J. Phycol.* **23**: 283–8.

1900 Williams, M.M. (1925). Cytology of the gametangia of *Codium tomentosum* (Stackh.). *Proc. Linn. Soc. New S. Wales* **50**: 98–111.

1901 Williamson, R.E. (1980). Actin in motile and other processes in plant cells. *Can. J. Bot.* **58**: 766–72.

1902 Williamson, R.E. & C.C. Ashley (1982). Free Ca^{2+} and cytoplasmic streaming in the alga *Chara*. *Nature* **296**: 647–51.

1903 Wit, R. de (1989). *Interactions between phototrophic bacteria in marine sediments*. Thesis, University of Groningen.

1904 Wit, R. de, W.H.M. van Boekel & H. van Gemerden (1988). Growth of the cyanobacterium *Microcoleus chthonoplastes* on sulfide. *FEMS Microbiol. Ecol.* **53**: 203–9.

1905 Wit, R. de & H. van Gemerden (1989). Growth responses of the cyanobacterium *Microcoleus chthonoplastes* with sulfide as electron donor. In *Microbial Mats, Ecological Physiology of Benthic Microbial Communities*, ed. Y. Cohen & E. Rosenberg, pp. 320–5. American Society for Microbiology, Washington.

1906 Wit, R. de & H. van Gemerden (1987). Oxidation of sulfide to thiosulfate by *Microcoleus chthonoplastes. FEMS Microbiol. Ecol.* **45**: 7–13.

1907 Withers, N.W., E.R. Cox, R. Tomas & F.T. Haxo (1977). Pigments of the dinoflagellate *Peridinium balticum* and its photosynthetic endosymbiont. *J. Phycol.* **13**: 354–8.

1908 Withers, N.W., A. Fiskdahl, R.C. Tuttle, and S. Liaaen-Jensen (1981). Carotenoids of the Chrysophyceae. *Comp. Biochem. Physiol.* **68B**: 345–9.

1909 Witman, G.B., K. Carlson, J. Berliner & J.L. Rosenbaum (1972). *Chlamydomonas* flagella. I. Isolation and electrophoretic analysis of microtubules, matrix, membranes and mastigonemes. *J. Cell Biol.* **54**: 507–39.

1910 Witt, D. & E. Stackebrandt (1988). Disproving the hypothesis of a common ancestry for the *Ochromonas danica* chrysoplast and *Heliobacterium chlorum*. *Arch. Microbiol.* **150**: 244–8.

1911 Woelkerling, W.J. (1983). The *Audouinella* (*Acrochaetium-Rhodochorton*) complex (Rhodophyta): present perspectives. *Phycologia* **22**: 59–92.

1912 Woelkerling, W.J. (1988). *The Coralline Red Algae: an Analysis of the Genera and Subfamilies of Nongeniculate Corallinaceae*. British Museum (Natural History), Oxford University Press, London and Oxford.

1913 Woese, C.R. (1981). Archaebacteria. *Scient. Am.* **244** (6): 94–106.

1914 Woese, C.R. (1987). Bacterial evolution. *Microbiol. Rev.* **51**: 221–71.

1915 Wolfe, K.H., M. Gouy, Y.-W. Yang, P.M. Sharp & W.-H. Li (1989). Date of monocot-dicot divergence estimated from chloroplast DNA sequence data. *Proc. Natl. Acad. Sci. USA* **86**: 6201–5.

1916 Wood, P.S. (1968). Dinoflagellate crop in the North Sea. Introduction. *Nature* **220**: 21.

1917 Wood, R.D. & K. Imahori (1964–65). *A Revision of the Characeae*. 2 Vols. Cramer, Weinheim.

1918 Woodcock, C.L.F. (Ed.) (1977). *Progress in Acetabularia Research*. Academic Press, London.

1919 Woods, J.K. & R.E. Triemer (1981). Mitosis in the octoflagellate prasinophyte, *Pyramimonas amylifera* (Chlorophyta). *J. Phycol.* **17**: 81–90.

1920 Wright, S.W. & S.W. Jeffrey (1987). Fucoxanthin pigment markers in marine phytoplankton analysed by HPLC and HPTLC. *Mar. Ecol. Prog. Ser.* **38**: 259–66.

1921 Wutz, M. & K. Zetsche (1976). Zur Biochemie und Regulation des heteromorphen Generationswechsel der Grünalge *Derbesia-Halicystis*. *Planta* **129**: 211–6.

1922 Wynne, M.J. (1969). Life-history and systematic studies of some Pacific North American Phaeophyceae (Brown Algae). *Univ. Calif. Publ. Bot.* **50**: 1–88.

1923 Wynne, M.J. (1972). Culture studies of Pacific coast Phaeophyceae. *Soc. Bot. France, Mémoires*: 129–44.

1924 Wynne, M.J. (1982). Phaeophyceae. In *Synopsis and Classification of Living Organisms*, ed. S.P. Parker, pp. 115–27. McGraw-Hill, New York.

1925 Yabu, H. (1964). Early development of several species of Laminariales in Hokkaido. *Mem. Fac. Fish. Hokkaido Univ.* **12**: 1–72.

1926 Yamanouchi, S. (1906). The life-history of *Polysiphonia violacea*. *Bot. Gaz.* **42**: 401–49.

1927 Yamanouchi, S. (1909). Cytology of *Cutleria* and *Aglaozonia*. *Bot. Gaz.* **48**: 380.

1928 Yentsch, C.S. (1962). Marine Plankton. In *Physiology and Biochemistry of Algae*, ed. R.A. Lewin, pp. 771–97. Academic Press, New York.

1929 Yokohama, Y. (1981). Green light-absorbing pigments in marine green algae, their ecological and systematic significance. *Jap. J. Phycol.* **29**: 209–22.

1930 Yokohama, Y. (1982). Distribution of lutein and derivatives in marine green algae. *Jap. J. Phycol.* **30**: 311–7.

1931 Yokohama, Y., A. Kageyama, T. Ikawa & S. Shimura (1977). A carotenoid characteristic of chlorophycean seaweeds living in deep coastal waters. *Bot. Mar.* **20**: 433–6.

1932 Zajic, J.E. (1970). *Properties and Products of Algae*. Plenum Press, New York.

1933 Zechmann, F.W., E.C. Theriot, E.A. Zimmer & R.L. Chapman (1990). Phylogeny of the Ulvophyceae (Chlorophyta): cladistic analysis of nuclear-encoded rRNA sequence data. *J. Phycol.* **26**: 700–10.

1934 Ziegler, J.R. & J.M. Kingsbury (1964). Cultural studies on the marine green alga *Halicystis parvula - Derbesia tenuissima* I. Normal and abnormal sexual and asexual reproduction. *Phycologia* **4**: 105–16.

1935 Zingmark, R.G. (1970). Sexual reproduction in the dinoflagellate *Noctiluca miliaris* Suriray. *J. Phycol.* **6**: 122–6.

1936 Zinnecker, E. (1935). Reduktionsteilung, Kernphasenwechsel und Geschlechtsbestimmung bei *Bryopsis plumosa* (Huds.) Ag. *Öst. bot. Z.* **84**: 53–72.

1937 Zuccarello, G. & L.J. Goff (1988). Host-infection and the development of the adelphoparasite *Gracilariophila oryzoides*. *J. Phycol.* (suppl.) **24**: 10.

Species index

General index

Lightning Source UK Ltd.
Milton Keynes UK
UKOW07f2346240715

255791UK00006B/193/P